OXFORD WORLD'S CLASSICS

THE KARAMAZOV BROTHERS

FYODOR MIKHAILOVICH DOSTOEVSKY was born in Moscow in 1821, the second in a family of seven children. His mother died of consumption in 1837 and his father, a generally disliked army physician, was murdered on his estate two years later. In 1844 he left the College of Military Engineering in St Petersburg and devoted himself to writing. *Poor Folk* (1846) met with great success from the literary critics of the day. In 1849 he was imprisoned and sentenced to death on account of his involvement with a group of utopian socialists, the Petrashevsky circle. The sentence was commuted at the last moment to penal servitude and exile, but the experience radically altered his political and personal ideology and led directly to *Memoirs from the House of the Dead* (1861–2). In 1857, whilst still in exile, he married his first wife, Maria Dmitrievna Isaeva, returning to St Petersburg in 1859. In the early 1860s he founded two new literary journals, *Vremia* and *Epokha*, and proved himself to be a brilliant journalist. He travelled in Europe, which served to strengthen his anti-European sentiment. During this period abroad he had an affair with Polina Suslova, the model for many of his literary heroines, including Polina in *The Gambler*. Central to their relationship was their mutual passion for gambling—an obsession which brought financial chaos to his affairs. Both his wife and his much-loved brother, Mikhail, died in 1864, the same year in which *Notes from the Underground* was published; *Crime and Punishment* and *The Gambler* followed in 1866 and in 1867 he married his stenographer, Anna Snitkina, who managed to bring an element of stability into his frenetic life. His other major novels, *The Idiot* (1868), *Demons* (1871), and *The Karamazov Brothers* (1880), met with varying degrees of success. In 1880 he was hailed as a saint, prophet, and genius by the audience to whom he delivered an address at the unveiling of the Pushkin memorial. He died six months later in 1881; at the funeral thirty thousand people accompanied his coffin and his death was mourned throughout Russia.

IGNAT AVSEY was a freelance translator, critic, and lecturer. He lectured in a number of British universities and in the States, and wrote on Gogol, Dostoevsky, and Dmitry Merezhkovsky. His other translations include Dostoevsky's *The Village of Stepanchikovo* (1983) and *Humiliated and Injured* (2007). He died in 2013.

OXFORD WORLD'S CLASSICS

*For over 100 years Oxford World's Classics have brought
readers closer to the world's great literature. Now with over 700
titles—from the 4,000-year-old myths of Mesopotamia to the
twentieth century's greatest novels—the series makes available
lesser-known as well as celebrated writing.*

*The pocket-sized hardbacks of the early years contained
introductions by Virginia Woolf, T. S. Eliot, Graham Greene,
and other literary figures which enriched the experience of reading.
Today the series is recognized for its fine scholarship and
reliability in texts that span world literature, drama and poetry,
religion, philosophy and politics. Each edition includes perceptive
commentary and essential background information to meet the
changing needs of readers.*

OXFORD WORLD'S CLASSICS

———

FYODOR DOSTOEVSKY

The Karamazov Brothers

———

Translated with an Introduction and Notes by
IGNAT AVSEY

OXFORD
UNIVERSITY PRESS

OXFORD

UNIVERSITY PRESS

Great Clarendon Street, Oxford OX2 6DP

Oxford University Press is a department of the University of Oxford.
It furthers the University's objective of excellence in research, scholarship,
and education by publishing worldwide in

Oxford New York

Auckland Bangkok Buenos Aires Cape Town Chennai
Dar es Salaam Delhi Hong Kong Istanbul Karachi Kolkata
Kuala Lumpur Madrid Melbourne Mexico City Mumbai Nairobi
São Paulo Shanghai Taipei Tokyo Toronto

Oxford is a registered trade mark of Oxford University Press
in the UK and in certain other countries

Published in the United States
by Oxford University Press Inc., New York

© Ignat Avsey 1994

First published as a World's Classics paperback 1994
Reissued as an Oxford World's Classics paperback 1998
Reissued 2008

British Library Cataloguing in Publication Data

Data available

Library of Congress Cataloging in Publication Data

Data available

ISBN 978-0-19-953637-5

18

Printed and bound in Great Britain by Clays Ltd, Elcograf S.p.A.

ACKNOWLEDGEMENTS

I WISH to express my gratitude first of all to Antony Wood, in particular for his editorial input into my translation of the early Books, and also for his generous help and expert advice at all stages of this enterprise. I also wish to thank the Revd. Dr Gerald Bray for advice on ecclesiastical matters, and Daphne Percival, John Moloney, Ian Millard, Roger Heathcott, Guy Churchill, John T. Smith, John L. Smith, Simon Wilde, and Callum Wright for fruitful and always useful discussions covering a wide variety of pertinent topics. I am most grateful to Alex Poole for technical help in the production of the Time Chart.

Second impression, 1995: My grateful thanks to Neville Collins, Adolf Czech, and above all my sister Ina for a number of helpful comments and suggestions.

Eleventh impression, 2007: My gratitude to Peter Khoroche for his painstaking and perceptive reading of the text, leading to a number of important amendments and improvements.

For Irène

CONTENTS

PART TWO

BOOK FOUR   CRISES

BOOK FIVE   PROS AND CONS

BOOK SIX   A RUSSIAN MONK

PART THREE

BOOK SEVEN   ALYOSHA

BOOK EIGHT   MITYA

BOOK NINE   JUDICIAL INVESTIGATION

PART FOUR

BOOK TEN   SCHOOLBOYS

INTRODUCTION

IT is a commonly held view that Dostoevsky is an excessively pessimistic, even dour writer, obsessed with analysing the criminal tendencies of human nature, 'heavy' and difficult to read. But Dostoevsky stands out first and foremost as a reader's writer, who always seeks to present his themes in a palatable form as an integral part of an absorbing plot in which humour is often a key element. He was never sure, however, of being able to win the critics over to his side, and to the very end of his life he remained decidedly on the defensive. In his correspondence with the Procurator of the Holy Synod, the formidable Konstantin Pobedonostsev, tutor to Aleksander III and to the future Tsar Nicholas II, Dostoevsky wrote: 'I am coming to the end of *The Karamazovs*. This last part, I can see and feel this, is so unusual and different from what other people are writing that I definitely do not expect any plaudits from the critics.'[1]

Dostoevsky's strong urge to shock the 'genteel' readership may provide a clue to his entire creative approach, may even be the principal factor in determining his choice of subject. Sigmund Freud argued that Dostoevsky's preoccupation with the nether side of human nature stemmed from criminal tendencies in his own soul.[2] This, surely, is to misjudge the tree by its fruit. An alternative explanation is that Dostoevsky acted on the principle of 'why should the devil have all the best tunes?', and, being a true artist with an eye for what is popular, he served his readers such fare as was calculated to satisfy their appetites. The price he had to pay was that Turgenev proclaimed him to be a latter-day de Sade, his fictional heroes became bywords for depravity and degeneration, and the Russian language was 'enriched' by such cult terms as *Karamazovshchina* and even *Dostoevshchina*, which are associated with sexual profligacy, violence, psychological deviation, and the breakdown of conventional

---

[1] To K. Pobedonostsev, 16 Aug. 1880, *Collected Works*, 30/pt 2, 209, (henceforth *CW*—see 'Texts used' for full citation).

[2] Sigmund Freud, 'Dostoievski and Parricide', trans. by D. F. Tait, *The Realist*, 1/2 (1929), 19.

morality. One of the eminent critics of his time, Nikolai Mikhailovsky, characterized him as a 'cruel talent'. For Mikhailovsky,
Dostoevsky's heroes were mentally sick people, essentially clinical cases, whose experience could not further the understanding
of the human condition. After his death, so powerful was the
opposition ranged against Dostoevsky that he was virtually
eliminated from his country's cultural consciousness. In the
tense and unstable political atmosphere marked by five unsuccessful attempts on the life of Aleksander II (assassinated at the
sixth attempt, 1 March 1881), nothing was more calculated to go
against the grain of the then politically correct thinking than the
way in which Dostoevsky undermined the pillars of society in his
mature novels. With the student-terrorist Dmitry Karakozov's
shot at the Tsar in 1866—the first of the five assassination
attempts—still ringing in people's ears, even the choice of the
name 'Karamazov' seemed provocative. It was only twenty years
after his death that Dostoevsky was finally culturally rehabilitated
by the Russian Symbolists at the turn of the century, notably by
V. Rozanov and Dmitry Merezhkovsky, thus paving the way for
his popularity abroad.

Although a novelist, the mature Dostoevsky had less in
common with Dickens, Balzac, Tolstoy, and Hugo than with the
dramatists of earlier ages. The range and depth of the nineteenth-century novel was in the main limited to the analysis of
external phenomena; man was seen as a social animal harmonious within himself, whatever his relationship with the outside
world might be; he was free from the internal disharmony that
afflicted Hamlet; free from the latent self-destructive forces that
were unleashed in Othello; free from the irrational senile
extravagance of Lear and the delayed, conceptualized carnality
of Faust. Dostoevsky changed all that. He turned man in upon
himself, dragged each man back into his own private universe
'bounded by a nutshell'. For him, in the beginning was the
thought. Dostoevsky's heroes 'feel deeply because they think
deeply; they suffer endlessly because they were endlessly delib-
erative; they dare to will because they have dared to think'.[3]

---

[3] Dmitry Merezhkovsky, *Tolstoi as Man and Artist with an Essay on Dostoïevski* (1902),
251.

Following on from the dramatists of the past, and basically using the tools of the dramatist, he demonstrated 'how abstract thought may be passionate, how metaphysical theories and deductions are rooted not only in cold reason, but in the heart, emotions and will.'[4] In this his art is of the future, a challenge and an invitation to the reader to enter the arena of debate and participate in the unfolding drama of ideas. 'Faust and Hamlet think more but feel less than all others, act less because they think more',[5] their tragedy lies in the eternal contradiction which they cannot resolve 'between the passionate heart and passionless thought'.[6] The two great tragic heroes in *The Karamazov Brothers*, Ivan and Dmitry, are both very much in the Hamlet mould. Ivan, the reformer *manqué*, cannot resolve the contradictions of the external world and he conjures up his own personal ghosts, first in the shape of the Grand Inquisitor, in the legend he composes and relates to Alyosha. Faced with Christ's unexpected reappearance on earth, the Grand Inquisitor of sixteenth-century Seville can find no place for Him. Humanity's supposed hope and refuge is made to listen in silence as the riot act is read out to Him and He is shown the door and humiliatingly told never to return and never to aspire to the glory of a sacrificial death—a verdict against the Son of God which for Ivan is a stab in the side; he, like Dostoevsky himself, loved Christ deeply, but only a suffering, crucified Christ.[7] Man has firmly decided to become master of his own destiny. But it is in fact the small, select band of professional administrators who have been invested with the authority 'to bind and to loose', who will now take responsibility for the entire human race, rule the world according to their own laws, impose their own interpretation of good and evil, and countenance no interference from the Deity. For the sane person who has understood that this is the rule of the Devil, the only refuge is madness. The Devil himself is Ivan's second personal ghost. He appears at night as a down-at-heel impecunious gentleman-lodger from upstairs, wearing a pair of no longer fashionable check trousers instead of 'in a red radiance amid thunder and lightning and with blazing wings', and sets his

---

[4] Ibid. 250.   [5] Ibid. 251.   [6] Ibid.
[7] V. Petersen (1881), quoted in *CW* 15. 506.

romantic *Weltschmerz* to naught, disorientates Ivan and casts him adrift in a sea of despair. He undermines Ivan's analytical concern for humanity, its suffering, and even the suffering of children. In the face of cosmic upheavals to which he refers, and which themselves are inconsequential, what merit is there in agonizing over the atrocities perpetrated by man? Man will never cease revelling in cruelty and attempting to drown his conscience in a sea of cynicism.

In contrast to the rational Ivan stands the confused, delinquent figure of Dmitry Fyodorovich, also Hamlet-like, contradictory, universal, and at the same time quintessentially Russian. 'Dangerous, emotional, irresponsible, yet conscience-haunted; soft, dreamy, cruel, yet fundamentally childlike. He is assassin and judge, ruffian and tenderest soul, the complete egotist and the most self-sacrificing hero ... he fears nothing and everything, does nothing and everything. He is primeval matter, he is monstrous and soulful.'[8] *In extremis* he matches Hamlet's ruthlessness in every particular.

Even before events turned against him, Dmitry had already taken refuge in something akin to madness. In every conflict he resorts to the irrational, the confrontational, the violent solution. If thou canst nat undo the knotte, cut hym.[9] By nature trusting and honourable (above all, honourable), he is congenitally incapable of 'give and take'. He forever gets hopelessly entangled in one web or another: he cannot extricate himself but has to panic, he cannot panic but has to be violent, he cannot love but has to rage, *excandescentia furibunda*, everything pointing to a deep-seated personality defect and perhaps ultimately to sexual inadequacy.

His passion for the voluptuous Grushenka bears all the marks of madness, and he is an easy prey to her whims and caprices. Full of impotent rage, and with the desperate threat to kill his father, whom he perceives to be his sexual—and financial—rival and arch-enemy, still fresh on his lips, it is inevitable that Dmitry should contemplate suicide. But, as with Hamlet, it is only

---

[8] Herman Hesse, *In Sight of Chaos* (Zurich, 1923), 17–18, 20.
[9] William Horman, *Vulgaria* (1519), 289.

speculation. He lives to continue his crazed pursuit of Grushenka.

To compound his tragedy, he becomes the innocent victim of a plot by his putative half-brother, the scheming bastard Smerdyakov, and from then on his fate is sealed. When Dmitry, full of desires he cannot satisfy and emotions he cannot express, tries to articulate his feelings using the coachman Andrei as a sounding-board, his words tumble forth in an incoherent torrent, voicing what Dr Johnson would have called his 'confused noise within'. He is full of irrepressible inner turmoil. And yet, 'though he is a physical and ungovernable man, he has the vision of some harmony and beauty which he may attain through his body. He cannot deny the body, neither can he find rest in it, and he gropes blindly after the secret and mystery of repose.'[10] His philosophy is instinctive. He continually needs to reassure himself that he is not a thief; a scoundrel—yes, but he is not a thief! Perhaps in this lies the clue to his whole character. While ready to admit to one defect, he hastens to point out that it is not the ultimate on the scale of debasement, that there is another, lower level, and come what may he would never sink to that. And this is reassuring. There is something solid in him, there is a principle he would never betray. Robin Hood for example would never admit to being a scoundrel. A thief—yes, but never a scoundrel! And that is equally reassuring. Neither Dmitry nor Robin Hood would say: 'I'm a scoundrel *and* a thief!' That would put them both on a lower level of humanity. We may conjecture, however, that the careerist seminarian Rakitin *could* say such a thing. Rakitin is an instance of evil-in-the-making, waiting in the wings, desperately eager to stand in the limelight but almost certain to be doomed to remain life's perpetual understudy.

The third son Alyosha, the declared principal hero, is perhaps the least convincing and interesting of all the characters in the novel. But then his turn was due to come later in the major novel to which Dostoevsky alludes in his prologue 'From the author', but which never saw the light of day, for Dostoevsky died three months after completing *The Karamazov Brothers*.

[10] John Middleton Murry, *Fyodor Dostoevsky* (London, 1923), 213.

In 'From the author' Dostoevsky refers to Alyosha as being 'odd and eccentric'. Odd and eccentric, because when dealing with essential matters of faith, unlike the vast majority of mankind, he is incapable of compromise and accommodation, no half measures for him, he has to act on the principle of all or nothing:

> Alyosha did not see how he could possibly continue to live as before. It is written, 'If thou wilt be perfect, give away all that thou hast and come and follow me.' Alyosha said to himself, 'I cannot give two roubles instead of "all", or substitute "go to church" for "follow me".' (Bk. 1, Ch. 5, 'Startsy')

Dmitry Merezhkovsky quotes a popular Indian Buddhist legend in his discussion of *The Karamazov Brothers*.

> Once to tempt Buddha, the Evil Spirit, in the guise of a vulture, pursued a dove; the dove hid in the Buddha's bosom, and he wished to protect it, but the Spirit said, 'By what right do you take away my prey? One of us must die, either it by my talons or I of hunger. Why are you sorry for him and not for me? If you are merciful and wish none to perish cut me a piece of flesh from your own body of the same size as the dove.' Then he showed him two scales of a balance. The dove settled on one. Buddha cut a piece of flesh from his own body and laid it on the other scale. But it remained motionless. He threw in another piece, and another one, and hacked his whole body, so that the blood poured out and the bones showed, but the scale still did not sink. Then with a final effort he went to it and threw himself into it, and it sank, and the scale with the dove rose. We can only save others by giving, not a part of ourselves, but the whole.[11]

Whether it is Alyosha in the service of God and the people, or Dmitry and his father in bondage to their own sensuality, or Ivan to his intellectuality, they are all 'odd and eccentric', they all in their different ways demonstrate the congenital Karamazov inability of doing things by halves, a trait which by his own admission belonged to Dostoevsky himself.

From November 1878, when Dostoevsky began to submit his novel in instalments, mostly book by book, to the periodical *Russky vestnik*, he referred to at least three books in turn as being 'the most important'. The first to be singled out was Book Five,

---

[11] Merezhkovsky, *Tolstoi as Man and Artist*, 232.

'Pros and Cons', containing the chapters 'Rebellion' and 'The Grand Inquisitor'; the next was Book Six, 'A Russian Monk'; in Book Seven 'Cana of Galilee' was 'the most significant chapter in the whole book, perhaps in the novel';[12] in a letter to his editor of 8 December 1879, he referred to Book Nine, 'Judicial Investigation', as being *one* of the most important ones.[13] One can only surmise what his final classification might have been on completion of the whole, but it is possible to imagine that the palm would have gone to 'A Russian Monk'. This extended interpolation is on the whole an oasis of peace and calm, a welcome antidote to the piling up of horror upon horror of such a chapter as 'Rebellion', or the crescendo of ideological onslaught in 'The Grand Inquisitor'. A strong narrative line is maintained with quite significant dramatic climaxes, but the characters are not presented as militant, rather as suppliant and suffering. Whereas in the rest of the novel everything is 'agitated, feverish, intense, screwed up above the normal pitch . . . always trembling on the verge of insanity and sometimes, indeed, [ready] to plunge over into the very middle of it',[14] 'A Russian Monk' is pervaded by optimism and serene faith in the goodness of people and their ability to reach harmony not only amongst themselves, but with the whole of nature. In the futuristically entitled subsection (g), 'Concerning prayer, love and contact with other worlds', we are told:

love man even in his state of sin, for this is already a likeness of divine love and is the highest love on this earth. Love all of God's creation, love the whole, and love each grain of sand. Love every leaf, every ray of God's light. Love animals, love plants, love every kind of thing. If you love every kind of thing, then everywhere God's mystery will reveal itself to you. (Bk. 6, Ch. 3)

This is the enigmatic Starets Zosima, speaking in his most pantheistic vein. For him too there are no half measures, and his commitment to the service of God and man is total. His love and care for mankind is born of a deep insight and understanding of

---

[12] Letter to his editor Nikolai Lyubimov, 16 Sept. 1879, *CW* 30/1. 126.
[13] Ibid. 132.
[14] Quoted in Helen Muchnic's *Dostoevsky's English Reputation*, 67 (henceforth *DER*—see Select Bibliography for full citation).

human nature. Dostoevsky identifies with Zosima's teachings, conceding merely that, had he been speaking in his own name, he would have differed only in 'form and language' rather than substance.[15] But in his forgiving, tolerant, understanding attitudes Zosima sails dangerously close to the humanist point of view, 'heretically' betraying a liberal philosophy of someone who would be prepared to consider relaxing the canon law and compromising on doctrinal principles, eventually even tending towards the 'crucified philanthropist' view of Christ.

From the start, Zosima is established as an authoritative, highly individualistic, and yet tolerant arbiter, a case in point being his compassionate treatment of the peasant woman who has confessed to murdering her husband. It is surely this episode that may serve to illustrate the view that 'Dostoevsky's sympathy for the criminal was boundless',[16] rather than the episode cited by Freud in which Zosima prostrates himself at Dmitry's feet during the meeting at the monastery, for it is Dmitry-the-martyr-to-be, not Dmitry-the-murderer-to-be whom Zosima goes out of his way to venerate. Zosima's spirit continues to pervade the novel to the very end, asserting itself not only in the substance of Alyosha's concluding speech but in the very choice of venue for its delivery, an unconsecrated stone, a traditional symbol of paganism, rather than in the precincts of a church.

It is illuminating to discover to what extent the author's personal experience has been used and recreated in fictional narrative. There is something overpowering and elemental when he speaks of his abject poverty, let alone when he details the gruesome circumstances of his near execution—the Tsar's calculatedly eleventh hour reprieve, when the 28-year-old Dostoevsky, together with two other prisoners, were already before the firing squad. But by the time Dostoevsky's personal experiences have reached the pages of his creative compositions they are transformed and refashioned, and more often than not, presented in a tongue-in-cheek, farcical mode, every line breathing with authenticity. Only someone who had himself been driven to writing begging letters in deadly earnest could have

[15] Letter to Lyubimov, 7 Aug. 1879, *CW* 30/1. 102.
[16] Freud, 'Dostoievski and Parricide', 18.

been responsible for the creation of those two unforgettable Polish charlatans, the caricature officer and his jobbing tooth-pulling companion, who in a state of dire financial embarrassment hit upon the idea of writing jointly to Grushenka, starting with a request for a loan of two thousand roubles 'for the shortest possible time', and ending up by asking for just one rouble. Let us turn to one of Dostoevsky's letters (to his friend Apollon Maykov). 'I know that you have no money *to spare* [Dostoevsky's italics]. I should never apply to you for help, only I am sinking—have almost completely gone under. In two or three weeks' time I shall be without a farthing, and a drowning man will clutch at a straw. Apart from you I have *no one*, and if you do not help me, I shall perish wholly! My dear fellow, save me. I will repay you for ever with friendship and attachment. If you have nothing, borrow from someone for me. Forgive me for writing thus. I am slowly but surely going under.'[17]

All the most sacred cows of Dostoevsky's religious and political philosophy, as expressed in his polemical writings, become, in the hands of Dostoevsky the novelist, objects of ridicule and irreverent fun. The dissolute and grotesque landowner Fyodor Pavlovich Karamazov, father of three sons born in wedlock and of the putative bastard son Smerdyakov, indulges in mock-philosophical discussions that range from the physical nature of hell to the state that Russia is in at the moment:

Russia's a pigsty. My boy, if only you knew how I hate Russia . . . not Russia, mind, but all these vices . . . come to think of it, Russia too. *Tout cela c'est de la cochonnerie.* (Bk. 3, Ch. 8, 'Over a Glass of Brandy')

Dostoevsky was able to reach a far wider audience for the plight of his country by such oblique, apparently provocative statements from the pages of a novel than he could ever have done by 'straight' journalistic commentaries. To be able to love deeply one must be prepared to hate. However much of a Slavophile Dostoevsky was, it never clouded his artistic objectivity, and he remained alive to every social malaise and castigated mercilessly every endemic national and social ill. Dostoevsky's achievement is that he is able to put words of hate into the mouths of basically

[17] Letter to Maykov, 16 Aug. 1867, *CW* 28/2. 216.

hateful people without destroying the reader's sympathy for them. The master's touch is always evident in the choice of topic, the pace of the dialogue, the high degree of dramatic tension, with the result that the reader's interest and attention never flags. One of the first reviewers of *The Karamazov Brothers* was quick to identify this: 'Despite all the weirdness and incongruousness of the situations in which his characters are placed, despite the oddness of their behaviour and reasoning, [Dostoevsky's characters] never cease to be living human beings. The reader may sometimes feel he has strayed into a lunatic asylum, but never into a museum of waxworks. No note ever rang false in Dostoevsky's novels.'[18] But then regarding the 'oddness' of Dostoevsky's characters, it has been pointed out that perhaps they only *seem* 'pathological', whereas in reality they are 'only visualized more clearly than any figures in imaginative literature'. Every man 'seen distinctly enough is abnormal, for the normal is only a name for the undifferentiated, for a failure to see the inescapable nuance.'[19] By this token the old reprobate Fyodor Pavlovich Karamazov, casually referred to as Aesop (see explanatory note to p. 176), is perhaps not as outlandish as first supposed, perhaps it is only that he has been subjected to greater scrutiny, his 'warts' exposed and magnified. And yet if he is merely 'ordinary', *man seen at close quarters*, there is something universally symbolic in his timeless ordinariness—the yellow leaf of decrepitude and the sticky bud of fecundity all on the same stalk.

Past and future fused into an eternal present. The . . . blind force of life, which arose we know not how. It brooded over the face of the waters. Taking the forms of life, high and low, birds of the air and creeping things obscene, terrible and beautiful, it rose through slime and lust and agony to man. Old Karamazov is life under the old Dispensation. He is a force and no more; he does not know himself for what he is. He contains within himself the germ of all potentialities, for he is chaos unresolved. He is loathsome and terrible and stormy for he is life itself.[20]

[18] *Voice*, 156 (7 June 1879), quoted in *CW* 15. 490.
[19] Edwin Muir, quoted in *DER* 99.
[20] Middleton Murry, *Fyodor Dostoevsky*, 249.

Old Karamazov reflects on the past and projects into the future, aware of having transgressed and apprehensive of being called to account. He is chaotic, yet yearns for primary order, yearns for truth and justice. And when, almost halfway through the book, he finally departs the scene, it is as though the life and soul of the party has left the room, so that were it not for the never-ceasing flow of events from the author's 'horn of plenty', the whole proceedings would be in danger of shuddering to a halt.

But the narrative flow continues effortlessly, the whole attention now being focused on the drama enacted between the brothers. Dmitry—ex-army, hard-drinking, hard-playing womanizer and spendthrift, hopelessly in love with the local Jezebel, Grushenka—gets caught up in events which he cannot control or, even less, understand; Ivan—an embittered intellectual, unwittingly infects Smerdyakov with his ideas, who exploits them so successfully and ingeniously that, when it comes to the crunch, the all too clever Ivan is left totally outsmarted, bewildered, and horrified. The confrontational scenes between the two when Smerdyakov, having committed the perfect murder, but by now sick and disillusioned, reveals to his disbelieving listener the full devilish intricacy of his plot, are all variations on the *alter ego* theme. What guarantee is there that they have any other reality except as recurring nightmares in Ivan's febrile imagination? Smerdyakov, like the Grand Inquisitor, and the shabby Devil in the check trousers, readily lends himself to interpretation as an embodied projection of Ivan's own tortured personality, the very worst part of it, which seeks and gains the upper hand in a ruthless, one-to-one psychological combat.

Like all great works of literature *The Karamazov Brothers* can be read in a variety of ways: for sheer enjoyment of the intricacies of its plot, the comedy, tragedy, the folly and wisdom of men's ways, the train of human conflicts, intrigues, passions, joys, and disappointments on the one hand; and for the abstract debates, the philosophical speculations, the demonstration of the author's skill and virtuosity in describing specialist fields (the church and the law in this case), on the other. It is probably Dostoevsky the psychologist (though he vigorously denied being one) rather than Dostoevsky the master story-teller, who has aroused the greater interest beyond his native Russia, though his commentators have often been frustrated by their inability to categorize and compartmentalize him neatly.

More than any other novelist ... Dostoevsky helped to weaken the formal restraints of imaginative literature and to break down the conventional discipline of fiction.[21]

In Dostoevsky's works there are peculiar passages as to which it is difficult to decide (cf. some of Goethe's poems and Leonardo da Vinci's drawings) whether they are Art or Science. At any rate they are neither pure Art nor pure Science. Here accuracy of knowledge and the instinct of genius are mingled.[22]

Dmitry Merezhkovsky, himself an outstanding novelist and poet, was the first to identify the peculiarly 'scientific' element in Dostoevsky's art.

What is called Dostoevsky's psychology is ... a huge laboratory of the most delicate and exact apparatus and contrivances for measuring, testing and weighing humanity. It is easy to imagine that to the uninitiated such a laboratory must seem something of a devil's smithy.[23]

Merezhkovsky has graphically analysed Dostoevsky's special method of creating ideal laboratory conditions in which to observe the behaviour of characters, who conjure up their own *alter egos* and seek to identify themselves with ghosts and devils, which themselves turn out to be as neurotic as their hosts.

In making scientific researches he surrounds in his machines and contrivances the phenomena of Nature with artificial and exceptional conditions. He observes how, under the influence of those conditions, the phenomenon undergoes changes. We might say that the essence of all scientific research consists precisely in deliberately 'artificialising' the surrounding conditions. Thus the chemist, increasing the pressure of atmospheres to a degree impossible under natural conditions, gradually compresses the air and changes it from gaseous to liquid. May we not call unreal, unnatural, supernatural, nay miraculous, that transparent liquid, dark blue as the clearest sky, evaporating, boiling and yet cold, inconceivably colder than ice? There is no such thing as liquid air at

---

[21] Anon., 'Dostoevsky and the Novel', *Times Literary Supplement* (5 June 1930), 465.
[22] Merezhkovsky, *Tolstoi as Man and Artist*, 256.
[23] Ibid. 255.

least in terrestrial nature as it comes within our scrutiny. It seems a miracle. We do not find it; yet it exists.[24]

The motif of the duality of man's nature and the alternation of good and evil has particularly influenced English writers. Robert Louis Stevenson (whose story *Markheim* is a version of *Crime and Punishment*) adopted the idea of the enemy within in his *Dr Jekyll and Mr Hyde*. The influence of Dostoevsky (and other Russian authors too) on writers such as Stevenson, Joseph Conrad, and D. H. Lawrence has been commented upon. The eminent contemporary Dostoevsky scholar W. J. Leatherbarrow includes George Orwell amongst their number;[25] '. . . without the translations of Dostoevsky and Tolstoy, even without translations of Turgenev and Chekhov, it is difficult to believe that the contemporary English novel could have become the thing it is.'[26]

The Karamazov Brothers is a panorama of Dostoevsky's most passionately held beliefs and ideas. The existence of God, the immortality of the soul, the freedom of man, the collective nature of guilt, the disastrous situation of a world operating without God, on rational principles alone (then 'anything goes') . . . These external questions are not only debated as propositions by Dostoevsky's characters, they also underpin the action at a philosophical level. *The Karamazov Brothers* ranges over an immensely wide spectrum of human concerns: family ties, the upbringing of children, the relationship between Church and State, and above all everyone's responsibility to others. Zosima preaches collective expiation through the awareness of collective guilt; Dmitry, in the traditional Christian sense, preaches collective expiation through the suffering of the innocent individual. The atheist Ivan is ready to see the disordered civic state subsumed under the authority of the Church; the saintly Alyosha is ready to leave the certainty of the Church for the turmoil of the world at large. In the discussions and debates the protagonists are aware of and deeply concerned with the cultural environment of the past and present; writers, philosophers, and

---

[24] Ibid. 234.
[25] W. J. Leatherbarrow, *The Brothers Karamazov* (Cambridge, 1992), 106–7.
[26] 'Dostoevsky and the Novel', 465.

poets are mentioned (Hugo, Proudhon, Diderot, Heine), indeed quoted at length (Schiller). Children, on whom a great deal of attention is lavished in the novel, are portrayed as enquiring, assertive individuals with a strong desire for an understanding of the world about them. In a characteristically immature manner they involve themselves amusingly in discussions such as 'who founded Troy?', the meaning of socialism, and the role of the doctor in society. The spirit of enquiry is ever present.

Dostoevsky was passionately interested in the functioning of Russia's legal system, and he was the first author to exploit to the full the dramatic potential of the police inquiry, the detailed interrogation of the suspect, and the procedure of the actual trial itself, laying the foundations for what is now widely enjoyed and popularly known as courtroom drama. He does not attempt to disguise his complete and utter lack of confidence in the workings of the recently reformed judicial system (see explanatory note to p. 723). The author, of course, does not speak in his own name; there is the anonymous, shadowy figure of the narrator, who every now and again, somewhat disconcertingly, addresses the reader in the first person; but since the narrator is positive, wise, and just, it is reasonable to suppose that the author concurs with him. The narrator is particularly mistrustful of the adversarial system of justice, in which the object is not to establish the truth, but to score a point, to win the case whatever the means. The defence counsel who acts for the innocent Dmitry does not believe in his innocence, but, in order to secure his acquittal, he is prepared to commit the worst form of verbal mugging, prepared deliberately to misquote the Scriptures, prepared to see 'truth perverted', prepared to act as the perfect example of a 'hired conscience'. Ironically, had his casuistry succeeded, justice would have been done; in the event, he fails, and an innocent man is convicted. True, the prosecutor expresses his desire to discover the truth *per se*, and to that end he is willing 'to defend' the accused, but then since his brief is to secure a guilty verdict, his words in this respect are verging at best on meaningless rhetoric, at worst on hypocrisy. One look at the rest of the judicial mechanism, as represented by the jury—an ignorant bunch of peasants—and the probability of the defendant receiving a fair trial becomes vanishingly small. Neither

does the public escape the severest censure for its readiness to
view the whole clinical exposure of a man's most intimate details
as pure spectacle. It stands condemned for its supreme smug-
ness, for the air of approving good humour with which it is
unthinkingly prepared to perpetuate the view of the innate
shrewdness of the Russian peasantry. 'Our lads have outsmarted
the sophisticated lawyer from the capital! Who would have
thought it! Jolly well done! "Trust the peasants!"' (never mind
the fact that in the process they had just convicted an innocent
man!). These are the comments heard among the anonymous,
and amorphous, members of the public after the trial. Some
fifteen years after Dostoevsky's death Pobedonostsev wrote: 'In
Russia there is a motley crew of jurors drawn either in a
haphazard way or artificially selected from the masses, who have
neither an understanding of the duties of a judge, nor the ability
to survey masses of facts requiring analysis and logical discrimi-
nation. Is there any wonder that, in such an environment, the
jurors blindly follow one or the other counsel who has succeeded
in making the strongest impression?'[27]

The Karamazov Brothers is the Rome to which all the roads
lead that he trod as a writer. It is the book in which '...
Dostoevsky gathered together all the thought, the doubt, and the
faith of a lifetime, into one timeless survey of life itself.'[28] It
incorporates themes and ideas that go back to his earliest years
as an author. In his second novel *The Double* (1846), he had dealt
with the subject of the split personality (the hero's *alter ego*
distorted as in a fairground mirror), treating the phenomenon as
a psychological, indeed clinical, reality. 'As far as I am concerned
the story was a complete failure, but the idea behind it was quite
sound, and the most significant one I ever tackled in the whole
of my literary career,' he wrote in 1877, a year before he began
The Karamazov Brothers. One is tempted to speculate whether
the original impetus might not have come from the German
Romantics: from Chamisso's Peter Schlemihl. Schlemihl loses
his shadow, Faust, in the legend, his soul. Both are still operating
in the religious, Christian domain, though Chamisso is already

---

[27] Quoted in M. Olgin, *The Soul of the Russian Revolution*, New York (1917), 63.
[28] John Middleton Murry, *Between Two Worlds*, London (1935), 464.

tending towards a psychological perception. The shadow that Chamisso's devil rolls up neatly and pockets triumphantly, leaving the hero deprived and vulnerable, is no mere soul whose perdition will make existence unbearable in the eternal future, he is deprived of something more immediate which will make his existence in the present a living hell. Ivan Fyodorovich Karamazov's dilemma, by contrast, is precisely the reverse; he is tormented not by the *absence*, but by the highly unwelcome *presence* of another identity within himself; with him the quantum leap from a religious to a psychological, clinical discernment, is complete.

The second critically important work after *The Double* in the genesis of *The Karamazov Brothers* is *The Village of Stepanchikovo*. The incongruous Colonel Rostanev (a holy fool if ever there was one) is the direct progenitor of *The Idiot*, and anticipates Alyosha. Yezhevikin, Vidoplyasov, and Foma Fomich Opiskin from *The Village* all reappear in *The Karamazov Brothers*, to a greater or lesser degree recognizable as Snegiryov, Smerdyakov, and Fyodor Pavlovich Karamazov respectively. Gogolian in spirit, Dickensian in structure, Molièrean in concept, this is the work in which the latent dramatist in Dostoevsky first asserts itself. The predominance of dialogue, deftly controlled confrontational *skandal* scenes, dramatically effective entries and exits with which Dostoevsky enlivens *The Village* reach their full potential in *The Karamazov Brothers*. Dostoevsky's last novel is rooted firmly in the spoken word. Dostoevsky's is an infinitely subtle and express-ive use of language which is essentially dramatic. Dialogue is real speech, with all its hesitations, self-corrections, repetitions, emphases, gestures, and passional moments. Each character speaks vigorously in his or her own voice, not in any narrow, type-cast sense, but in a convincingly living way. Each of the Karamazov brothers has his own distinct style of expression, Dmitry and Ivan displaying contrasted emotional and intellectual eloquence. The sorrows of peasants pour out in unchecked flow, in the speech of Staff Captain Snegiryov we hear the desperate accent of insulted self-esteem, in that of the sinister Smerdyakov the deft mimicry of his social superiors. The earthy, ebullient clown Fyodor Pavlovich Karamazov puts on performances that take the art of discordance and vulgarity to preposterous extremes. All these characters speak loudly and insistently at the reader's very ear. Even the narrative of this novel—the utterance, as we have seen, of a rather shadowy but still distinctly present narrator figure—is saturated, in its liberal measure of reported speech, with speech rhythms.

Dostoevsky was always drawn by the idea of comprehensively encapsulating the spirit of the times, of making a definitive creative assessment of his epoch and, by his own admission, attempting it on no less ambitious a scale than Dante's *Divine Comedy*.[29] In a structural sense the world he presents is an intricate collage of conflicting views in different perspectives. It is above all a microcosm, devoid of any historical panorama. The location is a farcically obscure, monumentally insignificant 'one-horse' town rejoicing in the odd name of Skotoprigonyevsk (see explanatory note to p. 719). This ridiculously unlikely name, mentioned once only, is immediately followed, to heightened comic effect, by the narrator's apology for being obliged to reveal it at all. There is a disconcerting momentary suggestion that everything is just a big joke, the author's face dissolving in a clownish grin, and the materializing of the reader's worst fears that he has just been strung along all the time. But this is a story-teller's trick: to relax the grip, only to tighten it again abruptly a split second later.

In its action *The Karamazov Brothers* is compacted beyond measure. The whole of the main action is squeezed into the space of four days (see the Time Chart on p. xxxvi). Event follows event in rapid succession, each chapter terminating in a cliff-hanger ending. To cover the simultaneous progression of different plotlines, real time is often suspended to allow the narrator to backtrack, producing a feverish and at first glance disordered succession of incidents. There is no slow and steady evolution; everything happens in rapid succession, hastening irresistibly and passionately to a conclusion. There is every justification for considering *The Karamazov Brothers* as being outside any time-frame, as being beyond the limitation of night and day, the mere incidentals of the rising or setting of the sun.

As for glimpses of Dostoevsky the man himself, his state of

[29] See *CW* 15. 399.

spiritual and physical health, his mode of working, his personal proclivities as well as the events that moulded his character, there is the vivid testimony of his correspondence. In his novels and short fiction the themes of poverty, hardship, bereavement, imminent fear of death, epilepsy, gambling, and others are rooted in personal experience. Dostoevsky's fiction in the eyes of the critic K. Mochulsky is an attempt to resolve the dilemma of his personal life in the form of a continuous confession. Significant though this confession is in terms of the profundity of the philosophical debate that it engenders, it is the qualities of Dostoevsky's creative writing that have ensured its leading place in world literature.

TRANSLATOR'S NOTE

IT has been said that if a translation is faithful it cannot be elegant, and that if it is elegant it cannot be faithful. And George Steiner reminds us of a point that should be obvious but tends to be forgotten in often heated debate about translation: 'There can be no exhaustive transfer from language A to language B', 'no meshing of nets so precise' that every aspect of sense and association can survive the transfer. In this translation I have taken *style* as the all-important element by which an author is known to his readers, and I have spared no effort to be as faithful as possible to Dostoevsky's style.

The word 'elegant' certainly is not applicable to Dostoevsky's style. He breaks every rule of grammar, syntax, and punctuation; his vocabulary is full of unusual words, to which he even adds one that he introduced into the language, *stushevatsya* (gently to drop out of existence); in short he stretches his own language to its uttermost limits, exploiting its potential to the full, like a good floor gymnast leaving no corner of the floorspace unused. He can throw in here and there an apparently innocuous word which will baffle experts and make native speakers scratch their heads in puzzlement when pressed for a precise meaning. An instance of this is the word *Lyagavy* (applied as a nickname), which may be interpreted in either an equine or a canine context. I have opted for the canine interpretation—Lurcher (see Bk.8, Ch.2). Other translators, including David Magarshack, have opted for an equine interpretation—a horse that kicks.

In trying to follow Dostoevsky's linguistic twists and turns, the translator constantly has to guard against being wrongfooted, being mesmerized by the original, and in the process violating the norms of his target language. It would hardly be helpful to the non-Russian-speaking reader to try to illustrate my point with one of his marathon sentences. One need go no further than the title, the standard English rendering of which is *The Brothers Karamazov*. This follows the original word order, the only one possible in Russian in this context. Had past translators been expressing themselves freely in natural English, without being hamstrung by that original Russian word order, they would no more have dreamt of saying The Brothers Karamazov than they would The Brothers Warner or The Brothers Marx.

TEXTS USED

Collected Works of Dostoevsky in 30 volumes ('Nauka', Leningrad, 1976). *Polnoye sobraniye sochineniy v tridtsati tomakh* Abbreviation *CW*.

Polnoye sobraniye sochineniy, 6 (Tipografiya A. S. Suvorina, St Petersburg, 1885–6).

Polnoye sobraniye sochineniy, 12/1–2 (A. F. Marks, St Petersburg, 1895), a free supplement to the magazine *Niva* for 1895.

SELECT BIBLIOGRAPHY

Anderson, Roger B., *Dostoevsky: Myths of Duality* (Gainesville, Fla., 1986).

Fanger, Donald, *Dostoevsky and Romantic Realism* (Chicago and London, 1967).

Gibson, Boyce A., *The Religion of Dostoevsky* (London, 1973).

Gide, André, *Dostoevsky* (1923; repr. Penguin books, in association with Secker & Warburg, 1949).

Jones, John, *Dostoevsky* (Oxford, 1985).

Jones, Malcolm, *Dostoyevsky: The Novel of Discord* (London, 1976).

Leatherbarrow, W. J., *The Brothers Karamazov* (Cambridge, 1992).

Linnér, Sven, *Starets Zosima in the Brothers Karamazov* (Stockholm, 1975).

Merezhkovsky, Dmitry, *Tolstoi as Man and Artist with an Essay on Dostoïevski* (London, 1902).

Mochulsky, K., *Dostoevsky: His Life and Work*, trans. Michael Minihan (Princeton, NJ, 1967).

Muchnic, Helen, *Dostoevsky's English Reputation* (Smith College Studies in Modern Languages, Northampton, Mass., 1939).

Murry, John Middleton, *Fyodor Dostoevsky* (London, 1923).

Peace, Richard, *Dostoyevsky: An Examination of the Major Novels* (Cambridge, 1971).

Shestov, Lev, *Dostoevsky, Tolstoy and Nietzsche*, trans. Spencer Roberts (Athens, Oh., 1969).

Thompson, Diane Oenning, *The Brothers Karamazov and the Poetics of Memory* (Cambridge, 1991).

Zweig, Stefan, *Three Masters: Balzac, Dickens, Dostoeffsky*, trans. Eden and Cedar Paul (London, 1930).

CHRONOLOGY OF
FYODOR DOSTOEVSKY

Italicized items are works by Dostoevsky listed by year of first publication. Dates are Old Style, which means that they lag behind those used in nineteenth-century Western Europe by twelve days.

1821	Fyodor Mikhailovich Dostoevsky is born in Moscow, the son of an army doctor (30 October).
1837	His mother dies.
1838	Enters the Engineering Academy in St Petersburg as an army cadet.
1839	His father dies, probably murdered by his serfs.
1842	Is promoted to Second Lieutenant.
1843	Translates Balzac's *Eugénie Grandet*.
1844	Resigns his army commission.
1846	*Poor Folk*
	The Double
1849	*Netochka Nezvanova*
	Is led out for execution in the Semenovsky Square in St Petersburg (22 December); his sentence is commuted at the last moment to penal servitude, to be followed by army service and exile, in Siberia; he is deprived of his army commission.
1850–4	Serves four years at the prison at Omsk in western Siberia.
1854	Is released from prison (March), but is immediately posted as a private soldier to an infantry battalion stationed at Semipalatinsk, in western Siberia.
1855	Is promoted to Corporal.
	Death of Nicholas I; accession of Alexander II.
1856	Is promoted to Ensign.
1857	Marries Maria Dmitrievna Isaeva (6 February).
1859	Resigns his army commission with the rank of Second Lieutenant (March), and receives permission to return to European Russia.
	Resides in Tver (August–December).
	Moves to St Petersburg (December).
	Uncle's Dream
	The Village of Stepanchikovo
1861	Begins publication of a new literary monthly, *Vremia*, founded by himself and his brother Mikhail (January).

The Emancipation of the Serfs.
The Insulted and the Injured
A Series of Essays on Literature

1861–2   *Memoirs from the House of the Dead*

1862   His first visit to Western Europe, including England and France.

1863   *Winter Notes on Summer Impressions*
          Vremia is banned for political reasons but through a misunderstanding, by the authorities.

1864   Launches a second journal, *Epokha* (March).
          His first wife dies (15 April).
          His brother Mikhail dies (10 July).
          Notes from the Underground

1865   *Epokha* collapses for financial reasons (June).

1866   Attempted assassination of Alexander II by Dmitry Karakozov (April).
          Crime and Punishment
          The Gambler

1867   Marries Anna Grigorevna Snitkina, his stenographer, as his second wife (15 February).
          Dostoevsky and his bride leave for Western Europe (April).

1867–71   The Dostoevskys reside abroad, chiefly in Dresden, but also in Geneva, Vevey, Florence, and elsewhere.

1868   *The Idiot*

1870   *The Eternal Husband*

1871   The Dostoevskys return to St Petersburg.

1871–2   *Devils* (also called *The Possessed*)

1873–4   Edits the weekly journal *Grazhdanin*.

1873–81   *Diary of a Writer*

1875   *An Accidental Family* (also called *A Raw Youth*)

1878   Death of Dostoevsky's beloved three-year-old son Alesha (16 May).

1879–80   *The Karamazov Brothers*

1880   His speech at lavish celebrations held in Moscow in honour of Pushkin is received with frenetic enthusiasm on 8 June, and marks the peak point attained by his reputation during his lifetime.

1881   Dostoevsky dies in St Petersburg (28 January).
          Alexander II is assassinated (1 March).

PRINCIPAL CHARACTERS

Names in capitals denote the character's most common
appellation in the text.

FYODOR PAVLOVICH Karamazov, landowner
Adelaida Ivanovna, née Miusova, his first wife
DMITRY Fyodorovich Karamazov (also Mitya, Mitenka, Mitka and
Mitry), his son by his first marriage
Sofya Ivanovna, his second wife
IVAN Fyodorovich Karamazov (Vanya, Vanechka), his elder son by his
second marriage
Aleksei Fyodorovich Karamazov (ALYOSHA, Alyoshenka, Alyoshka,
Alyoshechka, Lyoshechka), his younger son by his second marriage
Pyotr Aleksandrovich MIUSOV
Pyotr Fomich KALGANOV
GRIGORY Vasiliyevich Kutuzov
Marfa Ignatyevna, his wife
LIZAVETA Smerdyashchaya
Pavel Fyodorovich SMERDYAKOV
KATERINA IVANOVNA Verkhovtseva (Katya, Katenka, Katka)
Agrafena (Agrippina) Aleksandrovna Svetlova, GRUSHENKA (Grusha,
Grushka)
MATRENA, her cook
Katerina Osipovna KHOKHLAKOVA
LISE, her daughter
HERZENSTUBE, doctor
Starets ZOSIMA
Father THERAPON
Mikhail (Misha) Osipovich RAKITIN (Rakitka, Rakitushka), seminarian
MAKSIMOV (Maksimushka), a landowner
Nikolai Ilyich SNEGIRYOV, STAFF CAPTAIN
MIKHAIL MAKAROVICH (Makarych*) Makarov, Chief of Police
NIKOLAI PARFENOVICH, Investigative Magistrate
IPPOLIT KYRILLOVICH, Prosecutor
MAVRIKY MAVRIKYEVICH (Mavrikych*), District Police Officer
FETYUKOVICH, Counsel for the Defence

* more colloquial form

TIME CHART

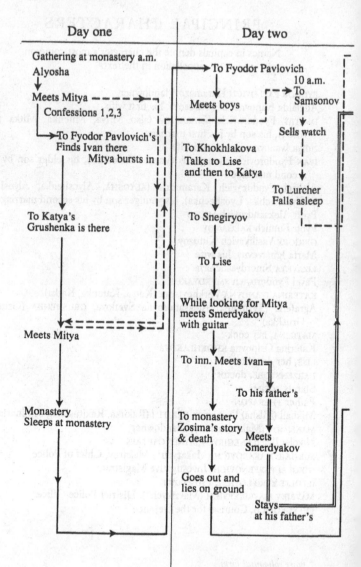

Day one

Gathering at monastery a.m.
Alyosha

Meets Mitya
    Confessions 1, 2, 3

        To Fyodor Pavlovich's
        Finds Ivan there
        Mitya bursts in

To Katya's
Grushenka is there

Meets Mitya

Monastery
Sleeps at monastery

Day two

To Fyodor Pavlovich
                                        10 a.m.
    Meets boys   To
                                        Samsonov

                                        Sells watch
    To Khokhlakova
    Talks to Lise
    and then to Katya
                                        To Lurcher
                                        Falls asleep
    To Snegiryov

    To Lise

While looking for Mitya
meets Smerdyakov
with guitar

To inn. Meets Ivan
                        To his father's

To monastery
Zosima's story
& death   Meets
                        Smerdyakov

Goes out and
lies on ground
                        Stays
                        at his father's

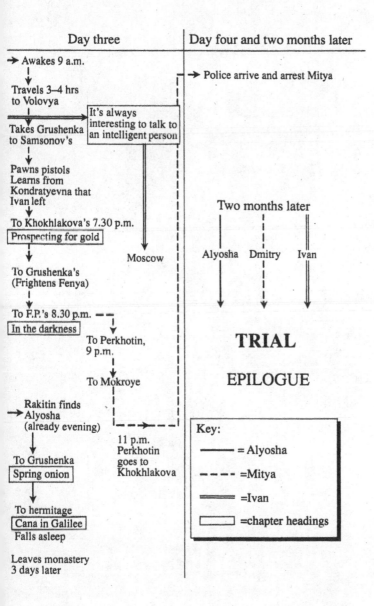

Day three	Day four and two months later

Day three

Awakes 9 a.m.

Travels 3–4 hrs to Volovya

Takes Grushenka to Samsonov's — It's always interesting to talk to an intelligent person

Pawns pistols
Learns from Kondratyevna that Ivan left

To Khokhlakova's 7.30 p.m.
Prospecting for gold

Moscow

To Grushenka's (Frightens Fenya)

To F.P.'s 8.30 p.m.
In the darkness

To Perkhotin, 9 p.m.

To Mokroye

Rakitin finds Alyosha (already evening)

11 p.m. Perkhotin goes to Khokhlakova

To Grushenka
Spring onion

To hermitage
Cana in Galilee
Falls asleep

Leaves monastery 3 days later

Day four and two months later

Police arrive and arrest Mitya

Two months later

Alyosha   Dmitry   Ivan

TRIAL

EPILOGUE

Key:
——— = Alyosha
- - - - = Mitya
═══ = Ivan
▭ = chapter headings

The Karamazov Brothers

For Anna Grigoryevna Dostoevskaya*

Verily, verily, I say unto you, except a corn of wheat fall into the ground and die, it abideth alone: but if it die, it bringeth forth much fruit.

John 12: 24

FROM THE AUTHOR

EVEN as I begin to relate the life story of my hero, Aleksei Fyodorovich Karamazov, I feel somewhat perplexed. The reason is this: although I refer to Aleksei Fyodorovich as my hero, I know very well that he is by no means a great man, and I foresee inevitable questions such as: What makes this Aleksei Fyodorovich so special; why have you chosen him as your hero? What exactly has he done? Who has heard of him, and in what connection? Why should I, the reader, spend my time studying the history of his life?

This last question is the most important, and all I can say is: perhaps you'll find out for yourself from the novel. But what if my readers should read the novel and fail to find out, fail to agree that there is anything remarkable about my Aleksei Fyodorovich? I say this because, sadly, that is precisely what I foresee. To me he is remarkable, but I very much doubt whether I can convince the reader of this. The point is that, in a sense, he is a man of action, but one of indeterminate character, whose mission is undefined. Still, it would be strange in times like ours to expect to find clarity in anyone. One thing, however, is indisputable: he is an odd, not to say eccentric, figure. But oddity and eccentricity, far from commanding attention, are calculated to undermine reputations, especially at a time when everybody is striving to unify what is disparate and to find some kind of common meaning in our universal chaos. And in most cases the eccentric is the very essence of individuality and isolation, is he not?

Should you not agree with this last thesis, however, and reply, 'It is not so', or 'not always so', then I might perhaps take heart over the significance of my hero, Aleksei Fyodorovich. For not only is an eccentric 'not always' a man apart and isolated, but, on the contrary, it may be he in particular who sometimes represents the very essence of his epoch, while others of his generation, for whatever reason, will drift aimlessly in the wind.

Now, I would not have indulged in these tedious and obscure explanations, I would simply have got on with my story, without any preamble—if they like it, they'll read it—but the trouble is, I have one life story and two novels. The second novel* is the main one; this concerns my hero's actions right up to the present time. But the action of the first novel takes place as long as thirteen years ago, and is not so much a novel as a single episode in my hero's early youth. I cannot dispense with this first novel, for that would render much of the second novel incomprehensible. This only compounds my original difficulty: for if I, the biographer, find one novel excessive for such an unassuming, ill-defined hero, how can I possibly produce two, and justify such presumption on my part?

As I am unable to find a solution to these problems, I shall venture to leave them unresolved. Of course, the perceptive reader will have discovered long ago that that was just what I had in mind from the very beginning, and he will only be annoyed with me for wasting so much precious time on so many irrelevancies. To this, I can reply very precisely: I wasted all that precious time on those irrelevancies, firstly, out of politeness, and, secondly, out of canniness—at least people cannot now turn round and say: He didn't even warn us! Anyway, given the essential unity of the whole, I am glad my novel has fallen naturally into two stories: having acquainted himself with the first story, the reader will decide for himself whether it is worth tackling the second. Of course, nobody is under any obligation; anyone is free to close the book after two pages of the first story and never to open it again. But there are readers who are so conscientious that they will undoubtedly want to read to the very end so as not to commit any error of judgement: all our Russian critics, for instance, are of such ilk. There now, I already feel relieved in my own mind with regard to these fastidious and conscientious readers, for I have provided them with the most legitimate excuse for abandoning my story after the first episode of the novel. So much, then, for the introduction. I quite agree it is superfluous, but since it has already been written, let it stand.

And now to business.

PART ONE

BOOK ONE

The Story of a Family

1

FYODOR* PAVLOVICH KARAMAZOV

ALEKSEI* FYODOROVICH KARAMAZOV was the third son of Fyodor Pavlovich Karamazov, a landowner of our district, extremely well known in his time (and to this day still remembered in these parts) on account of his violent and mysterious death exactly thirteen years ago, the circumstances of which I shall relate in due course. All I shall say now about this landowner (as we used to call him, even though he scarcely ever lived on his estate) is that he was an eccentric, a type not uncommon however, not only worthless and depraved but muddle-headed as well, yet one of those whose muddle-headedness never stops them from making an excellent job of their business affairs. Fyodor Pavlovich, for instance, started with next to nothing at all; the smallest of landowners, he used to do the rounds and cadge a meal off other people, was content to be a hanger-on, but at the time of his death it turned out that he was worth a round hundred thousand roubles* in cash. And yet all his life he had been one of the craziest crackpots in the whole of our district. Let me repeat yet again: this was not a case of stupidity—most of these crackpots are shrewd and cunning enough—but of muddle-headedness, and of a special, typically Russian kind.

He had been married twice and had three sons: the eldest, Dmitry* Fyodorovich, from the first marriage, and the other two, Ivan* and Aleksei, from the second. Fyodor Pavlovich's first wife came from the comparatively wealthy and eminent Miusov family, who were landowners in our district. Precisely how it happened that a young girl possessed of a dowry, and a beauty into the bargain, as well as being quick-witted and clever, of a breed encountered frequently enough in our generation though found in the past too, had married such a 'simpleton', as everybody then called him, I shall not attempt to explain at any great length. Now, I did know a certain young lady of the 'romantic' generation of not so long ago who, after being mysteriously in love for several years with a certain gentleman whom she could have married at any time without the least difficulty, suddenly broke off their relationship, inventing for herself all manner of insurmountable obstacles, and one stormy night plunged from a high, precipitous cliff into a fairly deep and fast-flowing river, where she perished from her own caprice solely through her attempt to imitate Shakespeare's Ophelia, for, had the precipice, which she had long before singled out and been compulsively drawn to, been less picturesque, and had there been only a prosaically flat bank in its stead, perhaps there would have been no suicide at all. This is a true story, and it would be fair to assume that other such cases have occurred not infrequently in Russian life over the past two or three generations.

Likewise, Adelaida Ivanovna Miusova's act was doubtless both a response to foreign influences and an act of defiance of an enslaved soul. Perhaps she had set out to assert her feminine independence, to rebel against the social conventions of her time, against the despotism of her kith and kin, and her fertile imagination had convinced her, let us suppose only for an instant, that Fyodor Pavlovich, despite his notoriety as a ne'er-do-well, was nevertheless one of the boldest and most sharp-witted men of that transitional period before the age of enlightenment, whereas in actual fact he was nothing but a nasty little clown. Piquancy was added to the whole affair by its ending in an elopement, which greatly appealed to Adelaida Ivanovna. As for Fyodor Pavlovich, he was at that time only too ready for any such exploit, his inadequate social standing alone acting as the principal spur to the pursuit of advancement by whatever means, and nothing in the world could have been more alluring to him than the prospect of worming his way into a good family and laying his hands on a dowry. As for mutual desire, it seems not to have existed at all, either on the bride's part or, despite Adelaida Ivanovna's beauty, on her fiancé's. This situation seems to have been unique in the life of Fyodor Pavlovich, a life-long sensualist, ready at the drop of a hat to pursue any petticoat that gave him the least encouragement. His wife, however, happened to be the only woman in his life who failed totally to arouse any passion in him whatsoever.

No sooner had Adelaida Ivanovna eloped than she realized that she quite simply despised her husband. Hence the consequences of their union manifested themselves in no time at all. Even though her family quickly became reconciled to events and granted the runaway a dowry, the newly-weds entered upon a life of complete disorder and constant disharmony. It was said that, during this time, the young wife displayed immeasurably more honour and rectitude than Fyodor Pavlovich, who, as we now know, pocketed her twenty-five thousand roubles at one stroke as soon as she received it, so that, as far as she was concerned, her few thousand vanished into thin air. He made numerous and strenuous attempts to have transferred to his own name the title to the hamlet and the rather fine town house that had come with the dowry, and such was the feeling of disgust and revulsion aroused in his wife by his constant and shameless begging and wheedling, and so exasperated was she and so anxious to be left in peace, that he would in all probability have succeeded, had not her family intervened, fortunately, to stop the blackguard in his tracks. There is firm evidence of frequent fights between husband and wife, but rumour has it that, curiously, the blows were meted out not by Fyodor Pavlovich, but by Adelaida Ivanovna, a fiery, bold, quick-tempered lady of dark complexion and endowed with remarkable physical strength. She finally left home to run off with a practically destitute student teacher from a seminary, leaving Fyodor Pavlovich with the three-year-old Mitya on his hands. In a trice Fyodor Pavlovich set up a veritable harem in his house and plunged into a life of wildest carousing, setting off at intervals on trips around the district, tearfully complaining to all and sundry of having been abandoned by Adelaida Ivanovna and disclosing details of their married life that no husband ought to have revealed. Above all, he seemed to enjoy and even to be flattered by the comic role of cuckolded husband, and he savoured every opportunity to enlarge upon and embellish the details of his grievance. 'Well now, Fyodor Pavlovich,' people teased him, 'anyone would think you'd been decorated, you seem so pleased in spite of all your grievances.' Many said that he was happy to appear in his new-found role of clown, and that for extra comic effect he deliberately pretended not to notice how ludicrous his situation was. And yet, who knows, perhaps he was simply naïve. He finally succeeded in tracking down the runaway wife. It turned out that the poor woman had gone to St Petersburg with her student, and there entered wholeheartedly into a state of total emancipation. Fyodor Pavlovich immediately began to fuss and make preparations to go to St Petersburg—for what, he had not the slightest idea. He would probably have gone, but as soon as he had taken the decision to do so, he considered that he had a perfect right to cheer himself up for the journey by indulging in another of his unrestrained binges. It was just at this time that his wife's family received news of her death in St Petersburg. She had died suddenly in a garret somewhere, some say from typhus, others say most likely from starvation. Fyodor Pavlovich learned of his wife's death when he was drunk; it was said that he ran out into the street with his hands raised to heaven in joy, shouting: 'Lord, now lettest thou thy servant...';* others say he wept convulsively like a child, so much so that, despite all the revulsion he aroused, he was pitiful to behold. Very probably, both accounts are true—that is, he rejoiced in his liberation and shed tears for his liberator at one and the same time. In most cases, people, even evil-doers, are much simpler and more naïve than we generally suppose. And the same is true of you and me.

2

THE ELDEST SON IS PACKED OFF

OF course, one can imagine the sort of parent that such a man would turn out to be, and what sort of upbringing he would give his offspring. As a father, his behaviour was quite in character— that is, he completely and utterly neglected the child of that marriage, not out of malice, nor out of any feelings of ill-will towards his former spouse; he simply forgot about the child's existence. While he was wearying everyone with his tantrums and complaints and turning his house into a den of iniquity, the faithful house-servant Grigory took the three-year-old Mitya into his care, otherwise the child would never have had a change of shirt. Furthermore, Mitya's relatives on his mother's side also appeared to forget all about him at first. His grandfather, that is old Mr Miusov, Adelaida Ivanovna's father, had died by this time; his widowed wife, Mitya's grandmother, had moved to Moscow, where she had fallen ill, and Adelaida's sisters were all married—so that Mitya spent the best part of a year with Grigory, living with him in his quarters across the yard. However, even if his father had remembered him (after all, he could hardly have been totally unaware of his existence), he would have banished him to Grigory's just the same, in order to have the child out of the way during his bouts of debauchery. It so happened that at about this time the late Adelaida Ivanovna's first cousin, Pyotr Aleksandrovich Miusov, returned from Paris; he subsequently lived abroad for many years, but he was at this time still a very young man; he was unusual among the Miusovs in being educated, sophisticated, and cosmopolitan, a true European throughout his life, ending his days a liberal of the 'forties and 'fifties. In the course of his career he maintained relations with many of the most liberal people of his era, both in Russia and abroad, was personally acquainted with Proudhon* and Bakunin,* and towards the end of his peregrinations was particularly fond of recalling the three days of the Paris revolution of February 1848,* hinting that he had very nearly been on the barricades himself. This was one of the most cherished memories of his younger days. His independent means derived from a holding of about a thousand serfs,* according to the old reckoning. His splendid estate was situated just outside our town, bordering the lands of our famous monastery, with which Pyotr Aleksandrovich was engaged in an interminable lawsuit initiated in his young days just after he had come into his inheritance, over certain fishing-rights on the river, or was it timber-felling rights—I really do not know which—anyway, he considered it a matter of civic duty, indeed of enlightened obligation, to instigate proceedings against 'the clericals'. On hearing all about Adelaida Ivanovna, whom he of course remem-

bered and, indeed, had once even seen, and learning about
Mitya, he intervened on the latter's behalf, despite all his
youthful indignation and contempt for Fyodor Pavlovich. Thus
he got to know Fyodor Pavlovich personally for the first time.
He came straight to the point by declaring that he would like to
be personally responsible for the child's upbringing. Many years
later he would often recount, as an example of Fyodor Pavlovich's character, how, when he had first spoken to him about
Mitya, Fyodor Pavlovich had stared at him for some time as if in
utter bewilderment as to the identity of the child, at the very idea
that somewhere in the house there could be a little son of his.
Even if this story of Pyotr Aleksandrovich's was exaggerated,
there was surely a good deal in it that could pass for truth. Now
the fact is that, throughout his life, Fyodor Pavlovich liked to
play-act and would suddenly start acting out, as it were, some
unexpected role, often without any apparent reason, even, as on
this particular occasion, directly against his own interests. But
such a trait is characteristic of very many people more intelligent
than Fyodor Pavlovich. Pyotr Aleksandrovich pursued the matter
enthusiastically and was even appointed, jointly with Fyodor
Pavlovich, the child's guardian, for after all there was the matter
of the mother's estate—the house and the hamlet. And Mitya
actually went to live with this uncle of his, but as the latter had
no family of his own, as soon as he had settled and secured the
income from his estates he immediately hurried back to Paris to
spend another long period abroad, leaving the child with one of
his distant aunts, an old lady who lived alone in Moscow. It
turned out that, having settled permanently in Paris, he too
forgot about the child, especially with the outbreak of the
February revolution, which captured his imagination vividly and
remained in his memory all his life. Then the old lady in Moscow
died, and Mitya was taken in by one of her married daughters. I
seem to remember that he had a fourth change of home. But I
shall not dwell upon that just now, especially since I shall have a
great deal to say later about this first-born son of Fyodor
Pavlovich's—for the moment I shall confine myself to the
essential information about him without which I cannot even
begin my novel.

In the first place, this Dmitry Fyodorovich was the only one of

Fyodor Pavlovich's three sons who grew up in the conviction that he would one day inherit an estate and that, when he came of age, he would be independent. He spent a desultory boyhood and youth, leaving school without finishing his studies; he entered a military college, served in the Caucasus, was promoted, fought in a duel, was demoted, regained his rank, and spent a small fortune on wine, women, and song. He did not begin to receive any money from Fyodor Pavlovich until his majority, by which time he was deeply in debt. He first saw and got to know his father only after his majority, when he came to our neighbourhood with the object of settling the matter of his inheritance with him. By all accounts he disliked his father even then, and departed after a short time with only a meagre sum in his pocket and some sort of agreement regarding the receipt of further income from the estate, without (and this is significant) managing to extract from Fyodor Pavlovich on this occasion any idea either of its value or of the income from it. From the very first (and this is worth bearing in mind), Fyodor Pavlovich perceived that Mitya had an exaggerated and mistaken idea of his own wealth. Fyodor Pavlovich was well satisfied with this, in view of his own personal calculations. He simply concluded that the young man was thoughtless, unruly, passionate, impatient, and dissipated, and that, provided he was given something from time to time, he would be immediately, if temporarily, satisfied. Fyodor Pavlovich began to exploit this by sending him small remittances from time to time, so that when some four years later Mitya, having lost all patience, again arrived in our town for a final showdown with his father, it turned out to his utter amazement that nothing remained to him, that, though exact figures were difficult to obtain, over the years he had already received monies to the full value of his property from Fyodor Pavlovich, that he might even be in debt to his father, and that, in consequence of such-and-such agreements which he had chosen to enter into at such-and-such times in the past, he had no further claim to anything, and so on and so forth. The young man was flabbergasted; he suspected dishonesty and fraud, was beside himself, and was almost like one demented. Such were the circumstances which led to the catastrophe that will be the subject of my first, introductory novel, or, more precisely, its external aspect. But before I proceed with this novel I must also say something about Fyodor Pavlovich's other two sons, Mitya's brothers, and where they fit into the story.

3

SECOND MARRIAGE, SECOND BROOD

HAVING got the four-year-old Mitya off his hands, Fyodor Pavlovich married again very shortly thereafter. This second marriage lasted about eight years. Fyodor Pavlovich took his second wife, Sofya Ivanovna, also a very young girl, from another district to which he had gone on one occasion to conduct some minor business in partnership with a Jew. Though Fyodor Pavlovich was given to revelry, drinking, and getting into scrapes, he was assiduous in the management of his capital, and he always settled his affairs successfully, though almost invariably dishonestly. Sofya Ivanovna, an orphan bereft of family from early childhood and the daughter of an obscure deacon, had been brought up in the wealthy household of her benefactor, guardian, and tormentor, an aristocratic lady, the widow of one General Vorokhov. The details are unknown to me, but I did hear that the meek, inoffensive, and uncomplaining ward of this widow once had to be taken down from a noose which she had slung from a nail in the storeroom; she had been unable to endure any longer the wilfulness and constant nagging of the old woman, who, though not exactly unkind by nature, had through sheer boredom turned into the most insufferable despot. Fyodor Pavlovich offered his hand, enquiries were made about him, and he was shown the door—and there he was again, as with the previous marriage, proposing to elope. It is highly likely that Sofya would have had nothing to do with him had she known more about him beforehand. But she was from a different province, and anyway, what else was a sixteen-year-old girl, who would rather have thrown herself into the river than remain with her benefactress, to do? And so the poor creature exchanged a benefactress for a benefactor. This time Fyodor Pavlovich did not get a kopeck, because the General's widow, in her fury, refused to give them anything, and laid a curse on them both into the bargain; but then, he was not counting on getting anything on this occasion, being attracted solely by the remarkable beauty of this innocent girl, especially by her innocent demeanour, which had fairly captivated him, the corrupt sensualist, who up to that moment had always admired only the coarser kind of female beauty. 'Those innocent eyes of hers slashed me like a razor,' he would repeat later, with one of his vile chuckles. For a debaucher like him, this could not fail to be a sensual attraction. Not having received any dowry, Fyodor Pavlovich was quite unceremonious with his wife and, under the pretext that she was, as it were, 'guilty' before him and that he had virtually 'cut her down from the noose', and also taking advantage of her exceptional meekness and timidity, he even began to defile all the normal marital decencies. He would invite loose women to the house in his wife's presence, when licentiousness would commence. As an indication of how things were, I will relate that the servant Grigory, a gloomy, slow-witted, and stubborn stickler for morals who had detested his former mistress, Adelaida Ivanovna, this time sided with his new mistress, defending her and quarrelling over her with Fyodor Pavlovich in a manner almost unwarrantable for a servant; on one occasion he even broke up one of these gatherings, forcibly ejecting all the unseemly visitors. Subsequently, the unfortunate young woman, who had been frightened out of her wits from early childhood, succumbed to a kind of female nervous disorder more commonly encountered amongst simple peasant women, the sufferers being known, after the symptoms of the disorder, as *klikushi*.* As a result of this illness, which was accompanied by terrible bouts of hysteria, the sufferer would at times even lose her reason. She did, however, bear Fyodor Pavlovich two sons, Ivan and Aleksei, the former in the first year of marriage, and the latter three years later. When she died Aleksei had just turned four, and, though this may appear strange, I do know that he remembered his mother all his life—as in a dream, of course. After her death exactly the same thing happened to the two boys as had happened to Mitya, the first-born: they too were totally ignored and neglected by their father, and they too eventually lived with Grigory in his hut. And it was in this hut that the old

General's despotic widow, their mother's benefactress and guardian, discovered them. She was still alive, and for eight years had been unable to forget the offence committed against her. Throughout those eight years she had kept herself minutely informed of her Sofya's doings and circumstances, and on hearing of her sickness and the depravity surrounding her, had exclaimed two or three times to her cronies: 'It serves her right, God is punishing her for her ingratitude.'

Exactly three months after Sofya Ivanovna's death, the General's widow suddenly appeared in our town in person and went straight to Fyodor Pavlovich's house; she spent no more than half an hour in the town, but accomplished much in that time. It was evening. Fyodor Pavlovich, whom she had not seen for eight years, came out to meet her rather the worse for drink. It is reported that, as soon as she saw him, she dealt him two resounding great slaps on the face without any explanation, pulled him up and down three times by a tuft of his hair, and then, without a word, proceeded straight to the two boys in the hut. Noticing at a glance that they had not been washed and that their clothes were dirty, she immediately dealt Grigory a similar slap and announced to him that she was taking both boys away with her; she led them out just as they were, wrapped them in a rug, bundled them into her carriage, and drove off back to her home town. Grigory accepted the slap without a word of complaint, like a devoted slave; he escorted the old lady to her carriage, bowed from the waist, and pronounced gravely that God would repay her for taking the orphans. 'You're an ass all the same!' cried the General's widow as she drove off. Fyodor Pavlovich, after some reflection, concluded that it was all for the good, and in his formal agreement that the General's widow take over the boys' upbringing did not impose a single condition. As to the slaps on the face that he had received, he himself went all round the town recounting the story to everyone.

It so happened that the General's widow also died soon afterwards, and in her will she left a thousand roubles to each of the young boys 'for their education', stipulating that all the money should be spent on them without fail and that it ought to suffice until they came of age, as even a sum such as this was more than sufficient for such children, but that, should anyone wish to contribute financially, by all means let him do so, etc., etc. I did not read the will myself, but heard that it contained something strange to this effect, expressed in rather odd terms. The old lady's principal beneficiary, however, turned out to be an honest man, one Yefim Petrovich Polyonov, the district Marshal of Nobility.* After writing several times to Fyodor Pavlovich and soon realizing that no money would be forthcoming from him for his children's upbringing (though there was never a direct refusal, merely perpetual procrastination and, from time to time, sentimental outpourings), Polyonov took a personal interest in the orphans and became particularly fond of the younger one, Aleksei, to the extent that the boy spent much of his childhood as one of his family. I ask the reader to note this fact at the outset. If there was any one person to whom these young people were indebted throughout their lives for their upbringing and education, it was certainly this Yefim Petrovich, as noble and humane a person as can ever have been encountered. He preserved untouched the thousand roubles left to each of the boys by the General's widow, so that by the time they came of age both sums had accumulated with interest to two thousand roubles, and, moreover, he spent his own money on their upbringing, which of course amounted to considerably more than a thousand for each. Again, I shall not enter into a detailed account of their childhood and early youth now; I shall merely record the principal events. Of the elder, Ivan, I shall say only that he was a rather morose and introverted young man, far from shy, but acutely aware from the age of ten that he and his brother were growing up in a strange family, dependent on the charity of others, and that their father was the kind of man it was too shameful even to mention, and so on. Very soon, almost from infancy—or so it is said, anyway—this boy began to show an extraordinary and brilliant aptitude for learning. I do not know the details, but he left Yefim Petrovich's family before he was quite thirteen years old, and entered one of the grammar schools in Moscow, lodging as a boarder with an experienced and famous pedagogue, a friend of Yefim Petrovich's from childhood. Ivan himself subsequently recounted that it had all come about from 'a passion for good deeds', as it were, in Yefim Petrovich, who had been carried away by the idea that a brilliant boy ought to be educated by a brilliant tutor. However, by the time the young man left school and entered university, both the brilliant tutor and Yefim Petrovich were dead. Since Yefim Petrovich had not managed to settle everything, and the money left to the boys by the General's widow (its value having doubled with accrued interest) was not immediately available, owing to various formalities and delays of a kind inevitable in our country, the young man found his first two years at the university hard going indeed, having to feed and maintain himself throughout this period while keeping up with his studies. It is worth noting that he made no attempt at this time to enter into correspondence with his father—whether from pride, contempt, or perhaps simply from cool rational deliberation, which told him that it was no good whatsoever expecting serious assistance of any kind from his father. Be that as it may, the young man was not to be dispirited, but went out and found work for himself, first giving lessons at twenty kopecks an hour and later peddling ten-line reports of street incidents to newspaper editors under the byline 'Eyewitness'. It is said that these pieces were always so fascinating that they were soon in great demand, and in this alone the young man demonstrated his practical as well as his mental superiority over that multitudinous, eternally indigent, and miserable band of students of both sexes which is to be seen in our capital cities hanging around from dawn to dusk in the doorways of newspaper and magazine publishers, with no other thought in their heads than the endless search for translations from the French or for copywork. Having made himself known to the editors, Ivan Fyodorovich kept in touch with them and in his final years at university began to publish well-received book reviews on various specialist subjects, so that he even became known in literary circles. However, it was only quite recently that he had suddenly succeeded in attracting the attention of a much wider circle of readers, so that many immediately took note of him and remembered him. It was a rather curious case. Ivan Fyodorovich had already left university and was planning a trip abroad on his two thousand roubles, when one of the leading newspapers published a very unusual article of his which attracted the attention of even the general reader, and, what is more, on a subject with which he was presumably quite unfamiliar, his degree being in the natural sciences. The article was on ecclesiastical courts,* the subject of much debate at the time. After analysing some current opinions, he put forward his own personal view. The most important thing, however, was the tone and the unexpected nature of his conclusion. As a matter of fact, many of the clergy took the author for one of their own. And suddenly, along with them, not only the secularists but the atheists too began to applaud. Finally, some perceptive minds concluded that the article was simply a brazen attempt at mockery. I mention this matter particularly because in due course the article reached the famous monastery outside our town, where the whole question of ecclesiastical courts was arousing intense interest, and, having appeared there, it created general consternation. As soon as the author's name was discovered, further interest was aroused by the fact that he was a native of our town and the son of 'that Fyodor Pavlovich'. And then, just at that very moment, who should appear in the town but the author himself.

Why should Ivan Fyodorovich have come to us at that time? I remember asking myself that question even then with a feeling bordering on anxiety. That fateful visit of his, which was to have so many repercussions, remained, and perhaps always shall remain, an enigma to me. For was it not strange that such a scholarly, proud, and apparently discreet young man should suddenly appear at such a disreputable house to visit a father who had ignored him all his life, who neither knew nor remembered him, and who, though he would never under any circumstances have parted with any money in his possession if his son had ever asked him to, had nevertheless always been afraid that his other sons Ivan and Aleksei might one day come and ask him for money. And now here was the young man suddenly turning up at the house of such a father, staying with him for a month or two, and the two of them getting on famously. This last fact was cause for astonishment not only to myself but to many others. Pyotr Aleksandrovich Miusov, a relative of Fyodor Pavlovich's by his first marriage and of whom I spoke earlier, again happened to be back on his estate near our town on a visit from Paris, where he had now settled for good. I remember it was he who showed the most surprise of all on making the acquaintance of the young man, whom he found fascinating and whom he would, not without an inner disquiet, engage in intellectual debate. 'He's full of pride,' he would say of him. 'He'll never be short of a kopeck—now that he's got money to go abroad, what's keeping him here? Everyone knows he hasn't come to ask his father for money, because he certainly won't get any. He's not one for drinking or debauchery, and yet the old man seems totally dependent on him.' This was perfectly true; Ivan Fyodorovich had a marked hold over the old man, who on occasion, despite his wilful and at times malicious disposition, even appeared to be dominated by his son; he sometimes even began to behave less outrageously...

It was discovered only later that Ivan Fyodorovich had come partly at the request of his elder brother, Dmitry Fyodorovich, whom he got to know—and indeed virtually set eyes on for the first time in his life—during this visit, but with whom he had already entered into correspondence over an important matter which mainly concerned Dmitry Fyodorovich alone. What this matter was the reader will learn in full detail in due course. Nevertheless, even after I found out about this extraordinary business, Ivan Fyodorovich was still a mystery to me, and his visit defied all explanation.

I should add that at this time Ivan Fyodorovich gave the impression of being a go-between and peacemaker between his father and elder brother, Dmitry Fyodorovich, who was having a bitter quarrel with his father and had even instigated legal proceedings against him.

This little family, let me say again, had assembled for the very first time in its history, and some of its members only now met one another for the first time ever. The youngest son, Aleksei Fyodorovich, had been living in our town for about a year and had thus become known to us before his brothers. And I find Aleksei the most difficult of all to speak about in this story, which precedes his arrival on the stage of the novel itself. But I realize that he too needs an introduction, at least in order to explain one very strange point: namely, that I am obliged to present my future hero to the reader in the very first scene of his story wearing a novice's cassock. He had already been living in

the monastery near our town for about a year, and it looked as
though he was preparing to spend the rest of his life there.

4

THE THIRD SON, ALYOSHA

HE was just twenty years old at this time (his brother Ivan was
twenty-three, and his eldest brother Dmitry twenty-seven). I
should explain at the outset that this youth, Alyosha, was no
fanatic and, at least in my opinion, no mystic either. Let me
make myself clear: he was simply a youthful philanthropist, and
if he had chosen the monastic way of life, this was only because
at the time that alone had captured his imagination and, as it
were, offered his parched soul the true path from the darkness
of worldly evil to the radiance of love. And the reason that this
path had so enthralled him was because on it he had met
someone he considered to be an extraordinary being—our
monastery's famous *starets*,* Zosima, to whom he became
attached with all the fervent first love of which his generous
heart was capable. Now, I will not deny that even then he was
very strange and, indeed, had been so from the cradle. By the
way, I have already mentioned that, having lost his mother at the
age of four, he remembered her all his life, her face, her
caresses, 'just as though she were alive and standing in front of
me'. It is possible, as everybody knows, to have such memories
from an even earlier age, from say two, which will continue
erupting throughout one's life like points of light in the darkness,
like a fragment torn out of a vast canvas which, except for this
one tiny corner, has faded and disappeared. And so it was with
him: he recalled one still summer evening an open window, the
slanting rays of the setting sun (he remembered the slanting rays
most of all), an icon with a lamp burning before it in the corner
of the room and, in front of the icon, his mother on her knees,
sobbing hysterically, shrieking and wailing, clutching him with
both hands, clasping him in a painful embrace, praying to the
Mother of God for him, holding him out with both arms

outstretched towards the icon as though placing him under the
protection of the Mother of God... and suddenly the nanny
bursting in and snatching him from her in terror. That was the
picture! Alyosha remembered his mother's face as it had been at
that moment; he would describe it as frenzied but beautiful, as
far as he could recall. But he rarely confided this memory to
anyone. In his childhood and during his youth he was not very
outgoing or talkative, not from mistrust or shyness or sullen
unsociability, but rather because of something quite different,
some kind of inner preoccupation altogether private which was
of no concern to others, but which was important enough to him
to make him appear oblivious of others. Yet he loved people: it
seems that he lived his whole life with an absolute faith in
people, though no one ever thought of him as simple or naïve.
There was something in him that said, and made you believe
(and this was so throughout his life), that he did not wish to sit
in judgement on others and would never take it upon himself to
censure anyone. He seemed willing to tolerate licence in everything without any kind of opprobrium, though he would often be
overcome by bitter sadness. And such was his capacity for
tolerance that, from his very earliest youth, nothing seemed able
either to scandalize or frighten him. Entering his father's
household at the age of twenty, chaste and innocent, and then
finding himself in a den of iniquity, he would, when he could no
longer bear to look, merely retreat in silence, but without the
least indication of contempt or reproach towards anyone. His
father, on the other hand, who had once lived on charity and was
consequently irritable and quick to take offence, initially received
him grudgingly and mistrustfully ('doesn't say much and keeps
his thoughts to himself', he would say), but within two weeks he
was hugging and embracing him at every turn—with drunken
tears and maudlin sentimentality, it is true, but nevertheless with
a deep and genuine affection such as he had never shown
towards anyone before.

But then everybody loved this young man, wherever he went,
from his earliest childhood. When he went to live with his
benefactor and guardian, Yefim Petrovich Polyonov, the whole
family grew so attached to him that he was treated without
reservation as one of the family. And moreover, he entered the

household at such a tender age that there could be no question of deliberate cunning, subterfuge, or artful sycophancy, or of trying to win affection. The gift of engendering love was innate, therefore, stemming from his very nature, as it were, without artifice or stratagem. This was also how it had been at school, and yet he was just the type of child, it would seem, to provoke mistrust, ridicule, or even hatred in his schoolfellows. For instance, he would sometimes become so lost in thought as to seem detached from all those around him. Even as a young boy he loved to go off into a corner and read books, and yet his classmates loved him so much that throughout his school-days he was undoubtedly the most popular boy at school. He was seldom boisterous and seldom even happy, but just one look at him was enough to see that this was not on account of any sullen streak in his nature, and that, on the contrary, he was even-tempered and serene. He never sought to assert himself amongst his peers. Perhaps this was why he was never afraid of anyone, and yet the other boys understood immediately that he took no pride in his courage, but seemed completely unaware of his own bravery and fearlessness. He never bore a grudge. Within an hour of receiving some slight, he would be replying to a question from the perpetrator, or striking up a conversation with him so openly and trustfully that it seemed as though nothing had happened at all. Nor was it that he had forgotten or forgiven the slight; he simply did not look upon it as such, which appealed to the other boys enormously and completely won them over to him. He possessed only one characteristic which, in every class from the lowest to the highest, produced in all his schoolfellows a desire to tease him, not for the sake of malice or ridicule, but purely for fun. This was his excessive, compulsive shyness and modesty. He could not bear certain words and certain conversations about women. These 'certain words' are, unfortunately, endemic in schools. Young boys, although pure in heart and soul and still children, very often like to whisper amongst themselves in class and even to talk out loud about things, pictures and fantasies, of a kind seldom spoken of even by troopers; for even soldiers are in fact ignorant of much that is perfectly well known to the young offspring of the educated and higher circles of our society. Admittedly, there is no moral corruption here as yet, no real, depraved, inner cynicism, but there is the outward appearance of it, and this is frequently regarded by schoolboys as something sophisticated, subtle, smart, and certainly to be emulated. Seeing that Alyoshka Karamazov would clasp his hands over his ears as soon as they started talking about 'it', his schoolfellows would sometimes deliberately crowd around him, force his hands away from his head, and shout obscenities into both his ears, while he struggled and sank to the floor, lay down and shielded his face, without a word, without protest, bearing the insult in silence. In the end, however, they would leave him in peace and not mock him as a 'cissy', but rather pity him for what he had endured. Incidentally, he was always near the top of his class academically, but never actually top.

After Yefim Petrovich died, Alyosha stayed on at school for two more years. Almost immediately after her husband's death, the inconsolable widow set off on an extended visit to Italy together with all her family, which consisted entirely of women, while Alyosha went to live in the house of two ladies whom he had never seen before, distant relatives of Yefim Petrovich, but under what conditions he had not the slightest idea. Another very distinctive characteristic of his was that he never showed the slightest concern about who was supporting him financially. In this respect he was the complete opposite of his elder brother, Ivan Fyodorovich, who had been in a state of poverty during his first two years at university, earning his keep by his own efforts, and who from early childhood had been painfully aware of living on his benefactor's charity. But it seems that this strange trait in Aleksei's character ought not to be judged too severely, because anybody who became in the least acquainted with him was convinced the moment this question arose that Aleksei was clearly one of those young men with an aura of the holy fool* about him, and that, were he suddenly to come into possession of a fortune, he would not hesitate to give it away at the first request, either to a good cause or to any plausible confidence trickster. And on the whole he appeared not to know the value of money, figuratively speaking of course. When he was given pocket money, which he himself never asked for, he would either spend weeks on end not knowing what to do with it, or was terribly careless with it, so that it vanished instantly. Pyotr

Aleksandrovich Miusov, who was extremely punctilious where money and bourgeois honesty were concerned, once offered the following character sketch after close observation of Aleksei: 'Here we have perhaps the only person in the world who, if he were to be suddenly abandoned without a kopeck in the central square of a strange city of a million people, would never come to grief, never die of hunger or cold, because somebody would immediately feed him, immediately take him under their wing, or, failing that, he would survive by his own wits, which would be no hardship or humiliation for him, while anyone who helped him would not find it a chore at all, but perhaps, on the contrary, would even look upon it as a pleasure.'

He did not finish school; he still had one year left when he suddenly announced to the ladies in whose household he was living that he was going to see his father about a matter that had suddenly occurred to him. They were very protective of him and did not want to let him go. The fare was no great expense, and the ladies would not let him pawn his watch, a present from his benefactor's family before their departure abroad, but provided him handsomely with money and even with a new set of clothes and underwear. However, he returned half the money to them, insisting that he would travel third class. Arriving in our town and being at once questioned by his father as to why he had come without completing his studies, he gave no direct reply, but was, it is said, unusually pensive. It soon transpired that he was looking for his mother's grave. He told himself at the time that that was why he had come. But it was unlikely to have been the sole reason for his visit. It was more probable that, at the time, he himself neither knew nor could have explained what it was that had welled up in his soul and begun to draw him relentlessly along a new, unexplored but inevitable path. Fyodor Pavlovich could not tell him where he had buried his second wife; he had never once visited her grave after her interment, and over the course of the years had completely forgotten where she was buried.

And now a word about Fyodor Pavlovich. For a long time before this, he had not been living in our town. Three or four years after the death of his second wife, he had gone to the south of Russia and eventually landed up in Odessa, where he spent several years. There he began by getting to know, as he put it, 'lots of yids, moishes, and shifty back-wheel skids'; eventually, however, he not only found himself dealing with yids, but 'even came to be accepted by respectable Jews'. It is to be assumed that at this period in his life he acquired the knack of making money by fair means or foul. He had returned to our little town, this time for good, only about three years before Alyosha's arrival. His former acquaintances found him terribly aged, although he was by no means an old man. It was not so much that he behaved with more circumspection, but rather that he was simply more arrogant. The former clown had a malicious impulse, for example, to make fools of other people. He still continued to womanize, if anything in an even more flagrantly despicable manner than before. He very soon opened a number of new taverns all round the district. It was apparent that he could be worth as much as a hundred thousand roubles, or not far short of it. Many of the townspeople and many others from all over the district immediately borrowed money from him, on very good security of course. Of late he had become somewhat flaccid in appearance, had begun to lose his composure and self-control, and had fallen into a desultory way of life, flitting from one thing to another, becoming quite scatterbrained, and all the while drinking more and more heavily, so that, were it not for the aforementioned servant Grigory, who by this time had also aged considerably and was looking after him almost like a nurse, Fyodor Pavlovich would very probably have been unable to avoid a great deal of unnecessary trouble. Alyosha's arrival seemed to have a beneficial ameliorating effect on him; it was as if something had awakened in this prematurely aged man that had long lain stifled in his soul. 'You know,' he would often say to Alyosha, looking at him closely, 'you look just like her—like the *klikusha*.' That is what he called his deceased wife, Alyosha's mother. It was Grigory who eventually pointed out the *klikusha*'s grave to Alyosha. He took him to the town cemetery and there, in a distant corner, showed him a cheap but respectable cast-iron memorial plate bearing her name, social status,* age, and year of death; inscribed below these details was an old-fashioned quatrain of the sort that used to be common on the tombstones of the middle classes. Surprisingly, this gravestone was the result of Grigory's initiative. It was he who, at his own expense, had erected it over the grave of the poor *klikusha* after Fyodor Pavlovich, whom he frequently confronted with reminders about the grave, had finally left for Odessa, abandoning not only the grave but all memories of the past. Alyosha betrayed no particular emotion at his mother's grave; he merely listened to Grigory's dignified and rational account of the erection of the memorial, lingered awhile with bowed head, and departed without a word. After that, he probably did not even visit the cemetery for the rest of the year. But this minor incident also had its effect on Fyodor Pavlovich, and a very strange effect indeed. He suddenly produced a thousand roubles and donated it to the monastery for the remembrance of his wife's soul—not the second wife, Alyosha's mother, the *klikusha*, but the first wife, Adelaida Ivanovna, the one who used to beat him. The very same night he got drunk and ridiculed the monks in front of Alyosha. He was far from being religious, and probably never so much as lit a five-kopeck candle in front of an icon in his life. But strange and unpredictable indeed are the thoughts and emotional excesses to which such individuals are sometimes prone.

I have already mentioned that he had become very flaccid in appearance. His face bore ample witness to the manner and nature of the life he was leading. Besides the drooping, fleshy bags under his small eyes, always arrogant, suspicious, and mocking, and besides the multitude of deep wrinkles on his puffy little face, he had a large, fleshy, elongated Adam's apple which dangled like a pouch under his pointed chin and gave his face an aspect of repulsive sensuality; in addition, his wide, carnivorous, thick-lipped mouth revealed small, black stumps of badly decayed teeth. Every time he began to speak, he spattered saliva. Although he enjoyed poking fun at his own face, he seemed well satisfied with it. He particularly liked to draw attention to his nose, which, though not large, was very fine and distinctly aquiline: 'A truly Roman nose,' he would say. 'What with that and my Adam's apple, this face has got decline and fall written all over it!' He appeared to be proud of it indeed.

Shortly after discovering his mother's grave, Alyosha told his father that he wished to enter the monastery and that the monks were willing to accept him as a novice. He explained that this was a very special wish and that he was appealing to him in all seriousness for his consent as a father. The old man already knew that Starets Zosima, who was leading a holy life in a hermitage at the monastery outside our town, had made a deep impression on his 'quiet boy'.

'Of course, this starets is the most honest monk of the lot of them,' he said, after listening in pensive silence to what Alyosha had to say and showing hardly any surprise at his request. 'Hm, so that's what you want to be, my quiet boy!' He was half drunk, and suddenly grinned a wide, drunken grin, full of cunning and inebriated guile. 'Hm, do you know, I had the feeling you'd end up as something like that, can you imagine? That's just what you were heading for. Well now, you've got your two thousand, that'll get you in, and I'll never leave you in the lurch, my dear boy; I'll stump up whatever else is owing now, if they ask. But if they don't ask, why insist, wouldn't you agree? After all, you don't cost more to feed than a canary, two grains a week... Hm. And how about that monastery that runs a little village near by, everyone knows it's where their "apostolic wives" live, that's what they call them, isn't it? There's about thirty of them altogether, I think... I've been there and, my word, it's fascinating, in its own way, of course—and different, you know. The only snag is, it's all so awfully Russian, not a single Frenchwoman in sight, and they could have done with some, it's not as though they couldn't afford it. Still, once the word gets around they'll come flocking in. This place is all right though, no apostolic wives here, just monks, about two hundred of them, and no mistake. Ascetics to a man, that's for sure... Hm, so you want to join the monks, do you? My heart bleeds for you, Alyosha, really it does; if only you knew how I've grown to love you... Still, it's an ill wind... you can pray for us sinners, we've certainly done some sinning. I've always wondered who was going to do my praying for me, and indeed if there was such a person in this world. My dear boy, if you only knew how terribly stupid I am in these matters, you wouldn't believe me. Terribly unknowledgeable. See here: I may be unknowledgeable, but I think about these matters, not too often, of course, but still... Surely, when I'm dead, there's no chance the devils will fail to drag me down with their hooks. So that gets me thinking: hooks? Where do they get them from? What are they made of? Iron? And where do they forge them? Have they got their own works down there, or what? The monks in your monastery probably suppose that hell comes with a roof, for instance. Now I'm ready to believe in hell, but it shouldn't have a roof: it's in better taste without one, more enlightened, Lutheran-like,* if you see what I mean. But really and truly, what does it matter, roof or no roof? But then, that's what the whole damned question is all about! For if there's no roof, it follows there can't be any hooks either. And if there aren't any hooks, then it's all a sham, and it's even harder to swallow: who's going to drag me down with hooks then, because if I'm not going to be dragged down with hooks, what'll happen next, what will become of truth and justice on earth? *Il faudrait les inventer,* these hooks, just for me, for me and me alone, because if only you knew, Alyosha, how low I've sunk!'

'There aren't any hooks there!' said Alyosha softly and seriously, gazing at his father.

'Well, well, only shadows of hooks. I know, I know. Didn't some Frenchman say about hell: *J'ai vu l'ombre d'un cocher, qui avec l'ombre d'une brosse frottait l'ombre d'un carrosse*?* How do you know, my boy, that there aren't any hooks? You'll sing a different tune after you've been with the monks for a while. Anyway, I give you my blessing; see if you can get at the truth, and come back and tell me: after all, it'll be easier to make the trip to the next world once you know for sure what's there. And besides, you'll have a more respectable life with the monks, rather than with an old drunkard like me and those girls of mine... Still, nothing could tarnish an angel like you. But then, perhaps all that holiness won't rub off on you either; that's why I'm letting you go, because deep down that's what I'm hoping will happen. You've got your head screwed on all right. The fire is burning in you now, but it'll die down; you'll get it out of your system and you'll come back here. And I'll be waiting for you, because I feel you're the only person on earth who hasn't condemned me, my dear boy, I really feel this, how can I fail to feel it!...'

And he began to snivel. He was maudlin. He was wicked and maudlin.

5

STARTSY

SOME readers may think of my young man as an immature
individual, prone to spiritual excess, a vapid dreamer, a weak,
hapless creature. On the contrary, Alyosha was at that time a
well-built, ruddy-cheeked, bright-eyed nineteen-year-old, glowing with health. He was very handsome too; slender, of medium
height, with dark-brown hair and a regular if slightly elongated,
oval face, with sparkling, wide-set, deep-grey eyes, very thoughtful and to all appearances very much at peace with himself.
People will say perhaps that rosy cheeks do not preclude either
fanaticism or mysticism; however, to me Alyosha seemed more
of a realist than anything. Of course, in the monastery he
believed absolutely in miracles, but in my opinion miracles never
bother a realist. It is not miracles that incline a realist towards
faith. A true realist, if he is a non-believer, will always find
within himself the strength and the ability not to believe in
miracles, and if he is faced with a miracle as an incontrovertible
fact he will sooner disbelieve his own senses than accept the fact.
And if he does accept the fact, then he will accept it as a natural
occurrence hitherto unknown to him. For the realist, faith is not
born of miracles, but miracles of faith. Once a realist believes,
then, precisely because of his own realism, he must of necessity
believe in miracles. The Apostle Thomas declared that he would
not believe what he could not see with his own eyes, but when
he saw, he said, 'My Lord and my God!'* Was it a miracle that
made him believe? Most probably not; he believed because, quite
simply, he wanted to believe, and perhaps, in the secret depths
of his being already fully believed even as he proclaimed, 'Except
I shall see... I will not believe.'

It will be said, perhaps, that Alyosha was slow-witted, backward, had not completed his studies, and so on. That he had not
completed his studies is true, but to say that he was slow-witted
or stupid would be a great injustice. I shall simply repeat what I
have said already: he took this path because at that time it was
the only one that captured his imagination and offered the ideal
release for his soul, which was striving to escape from darkness

into light. To this I must add that he was already to some extent a youth of our times—in other words, naturally honest, insisting on truth, seeking it and believing in it, and, once believing, demanding instant commitment to it with all the strength of his soul and wanting to rush off and perform great deeds, sacrificing all, if necessary even life itself. Although unfortunately these youths do not understand that the sacrifice of life is in most cases perhaps the easiest of all sacrifices, and that to dedicate, for example, five or six years of their exuberant youth to hard, painstaking study and the acquisition of knowledge for the sole purpose of enhancing tenfold their inherent capacity to serve just that cherished truth, that great work which they are committed to accomplish—such a sacrifice as this remains almost completely beyond the capabilities of many of them. Alyosha simply chose the opposite path to that taken by all the others, but with just the same commitment to the speedy accomplishment of great deeds. Scarcely had he been struck by the conviction, after serious thought, that God and immortality existed, than he at once said to himself, 'I want to live for immortality, and I will accept no compromise.' In just the same way, had he decided that there was no God and no immortality, he would at once have joined the atheists and socialists (for socialism is not only a question of the conditions of labour or of the so-called fourth estate,* but rather, for the most part, a question of atheism, a question of today's particular form of atheism; it is a Tower of Babel* built specifically without God, not in order to ascend to heaven from earth, but in order to bring heaven down to earth). Alyosha did not see how he could possibly continue to live as before. It is written, 'If thou wilt be perfect, give away all that thou hast and come and follow me.'* Alyosha said to himself, 'I cannot give two roubles instead of "all", or substitute "go to church" for "follow me".' Perhaps he retained some childhood memory of the monastery on the outskirts of our town, where his mother might have taken him to church. Perhaps, too, he had been affected by the slanting rays of the setting sun striking the icon as his mother, the *klikusha*, held him up to it. He was thoughtful when he arrived, so perhaps he came to us just to have a look, to see whether it was to be all or only two roubles—and at the monastery he met the starets...

This starets, as I have explained above, was Starets Zosima, but here I should say something about the *startsy* in Russian monasteries, though I am afraid I feel neither sufficiently competent nor confident to do this. However, I will attempt to give a brief and superficial account of the subject. In the first place, experts and competent authorities maintain that the cult of *startsy* appeared in our Russian monasteries only very recently, scarcely a hundred years ago, whereas throughout Eastern Orthodoxy, especially in Sinai and on Mount Athos,* it had already existed for more than a thousand years. We are told that it existed in Russia, too, in ancient times, or that it certainly must have existed, but that, owing to the disasters that befell Russia— the Tatar yoke,* the Troubles,* the severance of our previous relations with Eastern Christendom after the fall of Constantinople*—this cult was forgotten and the tradition fell into abeyance. It was revived again at the end of the last century by one of the great zealots (as they were called), Païsy Velichkovsky* and his followers, but even to this day, a hundred years later, it so far exists in only a very few monasteries and has sometimes been discouraged almost to the point of persecution as an unheard-of innovation in Russia. It flourished especially in Optina Pustyn,* the famous monastery of Kozelsk. Who introduced the cult to our monastery and when, I cannot say, but there had already been three successive generations of startsy, and Zosima was the last of these, but now he too was old, feeble, and close to death, and no one knew who was to succeed him. This was an important question for our monastery, which was not as yet particularly famous for anything; it had no relics of saints or authenticated miracle-working icons, no glorious legends connected with its history, no historic achievements or services to the motherland to its name. It had flourished and become famous all over Russia solely because of its startsy, who attracted crowds of worshippers from thousands of versts around—indeed, from all over Russia—to come and listen to them. And so, what is a starets? A starets is one who subsumes your soul, your will, into his soul and into his will. When a starets accepts you, you renounce your own will and surrender to him in total obedience, total self-abnegation.* He who submits himself to this discipline voluntarily accepts an awesome apprenticeship in the hope that, after a long ordeal, he will achieve self-mastery, subjugate the self to such an extent as to attain at last, through lifelong obedience, perfect freedom, that is, freedom from the self, and escape the fate of those who have lived their whole lives without finding their true selves. This institution—that is, the cult of startsy—does not arise from any theory, but is a practical tradition which evolved in Byzantium and is now already a thousand years old. The obligations due to a starets are not the same as the normal 'obedience' that has always been practised in our Russian monasteries. They involve constant confession to the starets by his pupils, and constitute an indissoluble link between master and disciple. There is a story, for example, of how in the very early days of Christianity one such disciple, having failed to perform some requirement of his starets, departed from his monastery in Syria and went to another country, Egypt. There, after harsh and prolonged ordeals, he was deemed worthy of enduring torture and of meeting a martyr's death. When the church was interring his body, already considered holy, suddenly, as the deacon was intoning the words 'Catechumens, depart!'*, the coffin in which the martyr's body was lying flew from its resting-place and out of the church, and this occurred three times. It was finally discovered that this saintly martyr had broken his vow of obedience and had left his starets, and therefore, in spite of his great spiritual attainments, could not be absolved without the permission of his starets. Only when the starets was summoned and released him from his vow could he be interred. Of course, all this is only ancient legend, but here is something that happened not so long ago. A Russian monk was in retreat on Mount Athos, when his starets commanded him to leave Mount Athos, which he loved from the bottom of his heart as a sacred place and a haven of peace, to go first to Jerusalem to worship at the holy places and then to return to Russia, to Siberia in the north: 'Your place is there, not here.' Overwhelmed with grief, the monk petitioned the Ecumenical Patriarch in Constantinople to be released from his vow, but the Patriarch replied that not only could he (the Ecumenical Patriarch) not do so, but that there was and could be no power on earth that could release him from his obligation once it had been imposed upon him by a starets, except the starets who had imposed it. Thus the startsy are in certain instances endowed with limitless and unimaginable power. That is why, in many of our monasteries, the cult initially encountered what amounted almost to persecution. On the other hand, the laity at large held the startsy in high regard from the very beginning. For instance, both the common people and the noblest in the land flocked to our monastery to prostrate themselves before the startsy, to confess their doubts, their sins, their sorrows, and to seek counsel and instruction. Seeing this, the opponents of the startsy protested and, amongst other things, maintained that the sacrament of confession was being arbitrarily and frivolously debased, since continual confession to a starets by a monk or layman is entirely non-sacramental. In the end, though, the cult survived and gradually became established in Russian monasteries. It is perhaps true, however, that this proven, thousand-year-old instrument for the moral regeneration of mankind, elevating him from slavery to freedom and moral perfection, could become a double-edged sword, and that some could be led not to humility and ultimate self-mastery, but, on the contrary, to utterly satanic pride—that is, not to freedom, but to enslavement.

Starets Zosima was about sixty-five, came from a land-owning family, and in his far-off youth had been a soldier and served as an officer in the Caucasus. No doubt it was some special quality of his soul that impressed Alyosha. The starets grew very fond of Alyosha and actually allowed him to share his cell. It should be noted that while Alyosha was living in the monastery, he was as yet in no way committed, could come and go as he wished, even be absent for a whole day, and though he wore a cassock, it was a voluntary act in order not to be different from others in the monastery. But he was happy to do so, of course. Perhaps the strength of his starets and the aura of holiness that continually surrounded him had a profound effect on Alyosha's youthful imagination. It was often said of Starets Zosima that, because he had received all who came to him to pour out their hearts, anxious for his advice and healing words, for so many years, because he had absorbed so many revelations and confessions, so much grief into his soul, he had acquired a sensitivity so finely tuned that, from one glance at a stranger's face, he could tell why he had come, what his needs were, and even what kind of

suffering tormented his soul, and he astonished, confused, and
sometimes almost terrified the supplicant by a recognition of his
innermost secret even before a word had been uttered. But
Alyosha noticed that many, nearly all, who came to see the
starets in private arrived in a state of fear and anxiety, but nearly
always left radiant with joy, that the gloomiest face became
happy. What astonished Alyosha in particular was that the starets
was not at all severe; on the contrary, his manner was almost
always jovial. The monks said of him that he was particularly
drawn to the worst sinners, that the more sinful a person was,
the more he loved him. Nevertheless, the starets had bitter
enemies and rivals among the monks even to the very end of his
life, but their numbers dwindled and they held their peace,
though they included several extremely prominent and important
figures in the monastery, such as one very venerable monk who
was a great recluse and an extraordinary zealot. Nevertheless,
the great majority were undoubtedly on the side of Starets
Zosima, and, of these, many were passionately and sincerely
devoted to him, even to the point of fanaticism. They were quick
to assert, though not out loud, that he was a saint, that already
there could be no doubt about this, and, foreseeing his approaching demise, they expected that miracles would soon occur and
that the deceased would bring great glory upon the monastery in
the near future. Alyosha too believed implicitly in the miraculous
powers of the starets, just as he believed in the story of the coffin
flying out of the church. He saw that many of those who came
with their sick children or adult relatives, begging the starets to
lay his hands on them and say a prayer over them, would soon
return, some even the next day, to prostrate themselves in tears
before him and thank him for healing their sick ones. The
question of whether such healing was really a cure or merely a
natural remission in the course of the illness did not arise for
Alyosha, for he already believed firmly in the spiritual powers of
his teacher, whose glory he felt as his own. His heart leapt and
his eyes shone, especially when Starets Zosima appeared before
the common people who were waiting in a crowd at the
hermitage gate, having come on pilgrimages from all over Russia
to see the starets and receive his blessing. They would prostrate
themselves before him, weep, kiss his feet, kiss the earth on

which he stood, and wail; women would hold out their children
to him and usher forward their sick *klikushi*. The starets would
talk to them, say a short prayer over them, bless them, and send
them away. Recently, since the onset of his illness, he had
sometimes been so weak that he barely had the strength to leave
his cell, and the pilgrims sometimes waited several days at the
monastery for him to appear. For Alyosha, there was no question
about why they loved him so much, why they prostrated themselves before him and wept with emotion at the mere sight of his
face. Oh, he understood perfectly that for the downtrodden soul
of the Russian man, afflicted by hardship and sorrow and, above
all, by perpetual injustice and perpetual sin, his own and the
world's, there was no more crying need nor greater comfort than
to find some shrine or saint and prostrate themselves in veneration: 'Although we have sinned, lied, and fallen into temptation,
somewhere on earth there is still one who is high and holy, who
comprehends the truth and who knows the truth; and this means
that the truth will not die on earth, but shall one day be given to
us too, and shall reign over all the earth, as it was promised.'
Alyosha knew and understood that that was what the people felt
and how they thought; and in common with those weeping
peasants and their sick wives, holding aloft their children to the
starets, he had not the slightest doubt that the starets was actually
that saint, that guardian of God's truth. And the conviction that
the monastery would gain extraordinary glory when the starets
died persisted in Alyosha's heart, perhaps even more strongly
than in anyone else's at the monastery. Of late, a kind of deep,
incandescent inner ecstasy had been burning more and more
strongly in his heart. The fact that this starets stood before him
as a lone individual did not trouble him in the least. 'It doesn't
matter, he is holy; in his heart he holds the secret of renewal for
all, that power which will finally establish truth upon earth, when
all shall be holy, and shall love one another, and there shall be
neither rich nor poor, neither exalted nor downtrodden, and all
shall be as children of God, and Christ's Kingdom shall truly
have come.' Such was the dream of Alyosha's heart.

The arrival of his two brothers, whom he had not known at all
before then, seemed to make a very strong impression on
Alyosha. He got to know his half-brother, Dmitry Fyodorovich,

more quickly and more closely, despite the fact that he arrived after his full brother, Ivan Fyodorovich. He very much wished to get to know Ivan, but although the latter had already been living in his father's house for two months and they had met quite frequently, they had not been drawn to each other in any way; Alyosha himself was uncommunicative and seemed to be waiting for something, as if he were embarrassed, while Ivan, although initially casting long and curious looks at Alyosha, soon ceased to give him any thought at all. This somewhat confused Alyosha. He attributed Ivan's aloofness to the difference in their ages and especially in their education. But Alyosha also thought of another interpretation: perhaps Ivan's lack of interest in him was due to something quite unknown to him. It seemed to him that Ivan was preoccupied with something profound within himself, that he was striving towards some goal, perhaps one very difficult to attain, so that he had no time for Alyosha, and that this was the sole reason why he was so abstracted in his presence. Alyosha also wondered whether the learned atheist might not feel disdain for him, a foolish novice. He knew for certain that his brother was an atheist. He could not take offence at this disdain, if disdain it was, but waited in a state of anxious confusion, which he himself did not quite understand, for his brother to approach him. Dmitry Fyodorovich spoke of his brother Ivan with the deepest respect and sympathy. It was from him that Alyosha learned all the details of the important matter that had recently forged such a remarkably close bond between the two elder brothers. Dmitry's ecstatic references to his brother Ivan were all the more natural in Alyosha's eyes since, compared with Ivan, Dmitry was almost uneducated, and indeed, seen together, they presented such a striking contrast of personality and character that it would have been almost impossible to imagine two men more dissimilar.

It was just at this time that a meeting, or rather gathering, of all the members of this discordant family was held in the starets's cell, which was to have an enormous influence on Alyosha. This gathering actually took place under a false pretext. By this time the disagreement between Dmitry Fyodorovich and his father Fyodor Pavlovich over the matter of the inheritance and the estate had reached an impossible pitch. Relations between them had become strained to breaking point. It would seem to have been Fyodor Pavlovich who, apparently in jest, had first proposed that they all meet in Starets Zosima's cell, if not to seek his direct mediation, then at least to come to some sort of reasonable understanding, to which the starets's dignity and standing might contribute something by way of inspiration and reconciliation. Dmitry Fyodorovich, who had never visited the starets or even seen him, naturally thought that his father wanted to embarrass him, but as he secretly reproached himself for having recently behaved reprehensibly in the course of the dispute with his father, he accepted the invitation. We must note, incidentally, that he lived not in his father's house, like Ivan Fyodorovich, but by himself on the other side of town. Pyotr Aleksandrovich Miusov, who at that time happened to be living in our neighbourhood, was especially taken with Fyodor Pavlovich's suggestion. A liberal of the 'forties and 'fifties, a freethinker and atheist, he took a very great interest in this matter, out of ennui perhaps, or a taste for levity. He had a sudden urge to take a look at the monastery and the 'holy man'. Since his old quarrel with the monastery was still unresolved, and the legal wrangles about boundaries, claims to the standing timber, fishing-rights on the river, and so forth were still dragging on, he hastened to avail himself of this opportunity, under the pretext of wishing to try to reach an agreement with the Abbot to see whether they could somehow settle their dispute amicably. Of course, a petitioner with such genuine motives would be received at the monastery with more consideration and courtesy than someone who visited merely out of curiosity. The combination of all these considerations may have influenced the monks to prevail upon the ailing starets to grant an audience, since of late he had hardly left his cell because of his illness, refusing to meet even his regular visitors. In the end the starets gave his consent to the meeting, and a day was appointed. With a smile to Alyosha, he said only, 'Who made me a judge over them?'*

Alyosha was very disconcerted when he heard about the meeting. Undoubtedly, the only person from the litigant and contending parties who could regard this conference seriously was Dmitry; the others would all be there for frivolous reasons, which could well be offensive to the starets. Alyosha understood this. Ivan and Miusov would come out of curiosity, possibly of the worst possible kind, and his father perhaps to engage in some kind of buffoonery and histrionics. Indeed, although he kept his silence, Alyosha knew his father through and through. I repeat, this boy was not as ingenuous as everyone considered him to be. He awaited the appointed day with a heavy heart. Undoubtedly, he very much wished that all this family feuding would come to an end. All the same, he was worried most of all about the starets. He was fearful for him, for his reputation; he feared he would be insulted, especially by Miusov's subtle, polite mockery and the supercilious innuendos of the learned Ivan; that is how he pictured the situation. It even occurred to him to forewarn the starets, to say something about these expected visitors, but he thought better of it and held his tongue. He simply let Dmitry know, through an acquaintance, on the eve of the appointed day that he loved him very much and expected him to keep his promise. Dmitry, puzzled because he could in no way recall that he had promised anything, simply replied by letter that he would do his very best to control himself 'in the face of baseness', and that though he deeply respected both the starets and his brother Ivan, he was convinced that there was either some kind of trap for him or some unseemly comedy in prospect. 'All the same, I would rather cut off my tongue than show lack of respect towards the holy man whom you revere so much,' Dmitry ended his note. It gave little cheer to Alyosha.

BOOK TWO

An Unseemly Encounter

1

THEY ARRIVE AT THE MONASTERY

THE day turned out to be wonderfully warm and bright. It was
the end of August. The meeting with the starets had been
arranged for just after the late morning service, at about half past
eleven. Our visitors, however, did not arrive for the service, but
shortly after it had ended. They drove up in two separate
carriages; Pyotr Aleksandrovich Miusov with a distant relative of
his, Pyotr Fomich Kalganov, a young man of about twenty,
arrived in the first, an elegant calash drawn by a fine pair of
horses. This young man was planning to go to university; Miusov,
however, with whom he was staying for some reason at the time,
was trying to persuade him to accompany him on a visit abroad,
to Zurich or Jena, and to study at a university there. The young
man was still undecided. He was of a reflective disposition and
somewhat absent-minded. He had a pleasant face, was well built
and rather tall. His gaze was apt to lapse into a strange
immobility; like all absent-minded people, he would sometimes
stare at you long and hard without seeing you at all. He was
taciturn and a little clumsy, though there were times—but only
if he was alone with someone—when he would become
extremely talkative, excitable, and jocular, sometimes laughing at
God only knows what. But his elation would dry up as quickly
and suddenly as it had erupted. He was always well, even
exquisitely, dressed; he already enjoyed a certain private income
and was expecting a far greater one. He was a friend of Alyosha's.

Fyodor Pavlovich and his son Ivan Fyodorovich rolled up in
an ancient, rickety, but large hackney cab drawn by a pair of old
reddish-grey horses, trailing a long way behind Miusov's calash.
Dmitry Fyodorovich, although he had been informed of the time

and date the day before, was late. The visitors left their carriages outside the monastery at an inn, and passed through the entrance gate on foot. Apart from Fyodor Pavlovich, it is possible that none of them had ever been in a monastery in their lives before, and as for Miusov, he had perhaps not been to church for nigh on thirty years. He kept looking around with a curiosity not devoid of a certain affected jauntiness. But all that met his questing gaze within the monastery's precincts were some non-descript monastic and domestic buildings, nothing out of the ordinary. The last of the congregation were leaving the church, doffing their caps and crossing themselves. Among the common folk could be seen some members of the upper classes, two or three ladies, and a very aged general, all of whom were staying at the inn. The visitors were immediately surrounded by beggars, but nobody gave them anything. Only young Kalganov, in embarrassment and haste, heaven only knows why, took from his purse a ten-kopeck coin and hurriedly thrust it into the hands of a peasant woman, adding quickly, 'To be divided equally.' None of his companions passed any comment, so there was really no need for him to be embarrassed; noticing this, he became even more embarrassed.

It was, however, rather strange; by rights, they should have been met and perhaps even accorded a certain respect, since one of them had recently made a donation of a thousand roubles, and the other was one of the wealthiest and most highly educated landowners, a man in whose hands, one might say, the monastery's future to some extent rested, in view of the pending lawsuit regarding fishing-rights on the river. And yet no dignitary came out to meet them. Miusov distractedly regarded the gravestones around the church and was about to remark that the right to bury their dead in such a 'holy' place must have cost the relatives a pretty penny, but he refrained. His usual liberal irony was brewing into something like anger.

'Confound it, isn't there anybody in this madhouse we could ask?... We should find out what's happening, because time's getting on,' he burst out, as though speaking to himself.

Suddenly they were approached by an elderly, balding gentle-man with ingratiating eyes, wearing a capacious summer coat. Raising his hat and speaking in a honeyed lisp, he introduced himself to the company at large as Maksimov, a landowner from Tula. He immediately concerned himself with our visitors' problem.

'Starets Zosima lives all alone in the hermitage, not quite half a verst from the monastery, through the wood, you go through the wood—'

'I know it's through the wood,' Fyodor Pavlovich replied, 'but we can't quite remember the way, it's a long time since we've been here.'

'Out through this gate and just keep on through the wood... straight through the wood. Come along. If you don't mind... I too... I myself... follow me, follow me...'

They went through the gate and set off through the wood. The landowner Maksimov, a man of about sixty, did not so much walk as run alongside the others, scrutinizing them all with eager, almost insatiable curiosity. He was quite wide-eyed.

'We've come to see the starets on a private matter,' Miusov remarked sternly. 'We have been granted, you might say, an audience with "his holiness", and so, thank you all the same for showing us the way, but we can't invite you to come with us.'

'I've been to see him, I've been, I've already been to see him... *Un chevalier parfait!*'* and the landowner snapped his fingers in the air.

'What *chevalier*?' Miusov enquired.

'Why, the starets, the illustrious starets, the starets... the pride and glory of the monastery. Zosima. There's a holy man for you...'

But his confused explanation was interrupted by a cowled monk, short of stature, very pale and hollow-cheeked, who had caught up with the visitors. Fyodor Pavlovich and Miusov stopped. Bowing from the waist in extreme deference, the monk addressed them.

'The reverend abbot extends his humble invitation to all you gentlemen to have luncheon with him after your visit to the hermitage. One o'clock sharp... And you too,' he said, turning to Maksimov.

'I shall be delighted,' exclaimed Fyodor Pavlovich, overjoyed at the invitation, 'one o'clock without fail. And I'd like you to know, we've all given our word to be on our best behaviour here... and what about you, Pyotr Aleksandrovich, are you coming?'

'Why ever not! What do you think I came for, if not to see what they get up to here? The only fly in the ointment as far as I'm concerned is that you're going to be there, Fyodor Pavlovich...'

'No sign of Dmitry Fyodorovich yet.'

'I wish he weren't coming. Do you think I care for all this ridiculous nonsense of yours, with you as company into the bargain? We'll be there,' he said, turning to the little monk, 'please thank the reverend abbot.'

'I wish I could, but I've been told to take you directly to the starets himself,' replied the monk.

'In that case, I'll go to the reverend abbot, I'll go straight to him,' burbled the landowner Maksimov.

'The reverend abbot is occupied at present, but, as you please...', the monk said uncertainly.

'What a tiresome old fellow,' Miusov remarked out loud after Maksimov had hurried off back to the monastery.

'Reminds me of von Sohn,'* Fyodor Pavlovich exclaimed suddenly.

'Not von Sohn again!... What's he got to do with it? Have you ever seen von Sohn?'

'I've seen his picture. It's not so much what he looks like, it's something else, but I can't quite put my finger on it. The spitting image of von Sohn, though. I can always tell a face.'

'Well, you're the expert. Only one thing, Fyodor Pavlovich, you said yourself just now that we promised to behave ourselves, remember? So there, control yourself. If you start acting the clown, I've no intention of being dragged into it... You see what he's like,' he turned to the monk, 'I'm afraid to visit decent people in his company.'

The subtle ghost of a smile, not devoid of a certain cunning, flitted across the pale, bloodless lips of the little monk, but he said nothing and it was only too evident that his silence stemmed from a sense of his own dignity. Miusov's frown deepened.

'To hell with the lot of them! It's all a façade, this, in fact it's all sham and nonsense,' the thought flashed through his mind.

'Here's the hermitage, we're here!' Fyodor Pavlovich called out. 'Here's the wall, but the gate's locked.'

And he started to make sweeping signs of the cross before the images of saints painted above and on either side of the gate.

'Rule of the house,' he remarked. 'A total of twenty-five holy men saving their souls in this monastery sitting opposite one another and munching pickled cabbage. And not a single woman comes through these gates, that's the most remarkable thing of all. It's a fact. But,' he turned suddenly to the monk, 'what's this I hear about the starets seeing ladies now?'

'Yes, there are peasant women here now, resting over there by the veranda, waiting. And for ladies, two rooms have been built over the veranda, but on the outer side of the wall—you can see the windows—and the starets, when his health permits, reaches them through an internal passageway; oh yes, they're well outside the wall. There's a lady there now from Kharkov, a Mrs Khokhlakova, she's waiting with her sick daughter to see him. He must have promised to talk to them, though he's been very poorly lately and has hardly even been able to go out to see the peasants.'

'So there's a tiny exit from the hermitage to the ladies, after all. Don't think, reverend father, that I'm suggesting anything; I was just observing. But I don't know if you're aware that on Mount Athos no women visitors or any women at all are allowed, nor any female creatures of any kind, such as hens, turkey-hens, heifers...'

'Fyodor Pavlovich, if you're not careful, I'll leave you here, and then you'll be politely asked to leave, so be warned!'

'Have I said anything to upset you, Pyotr Aleksandrovich? I say,' he exclaimed suddenly, stepping through the hermitage gate, 'what a vale of roses they live in!'

It was true; although there were no longer any roses, a large variety of rare and exotic autumn flowers grew wherever there was room to plant them. They were clearly tended by expert hands. The flower-beds were laid out around the walls of the monastic buildings and between the graves. Zosima's cell was in a small, single-storey wooden house which had a veranda in front of the entrance and was also surrounded by flowers.

'I wonder if it was like this in Varsonophy's time? They say he wasn't known for his delicacy of approach, and when he was the starets here he'd jump up and hit people with his stick, women and all,' remarked Fyodor Pavlovich, mounting the steps.

'The starets Varsonophy did sometimes seem like a holy fool, but people do say some foolish things,' the monk replied. 'He never used to hit anybody with a stick, though. Now, gentlemen, please wait here a moment and I'll let him know you're here.'

'Fyodor Pavlovich, for the last time, do you hear me? Remember your promise,' Miusov spluttered once more. 'Behave yourself, or there'll be trouble.'

'I really don't know why you're so upset,' Fyodor Pavlovich observed mockingly. 'Is it your sins that are troubling you? They say he can tell by your eyes what you've been up to. But I'm surprised that a progressive man like you, a Parisian, should value his opinion so highly, really I am!'

But Miusov had no time to reply to this sarcasm; they were bidden to enter. He experienced a sense of irritation as he went in...

'Well, I know what's going to happen,' the thought flashed through his mind, 'I'm annoyed, I'll start an argument... I'll get excited—and disgrace myself and everything I stand for.'

2

THE OLD BUFFOON

They entered the room at almost the same time as Starets Zosima, who emerged from his tiny bedroom as soon as they made their appearance. Two hieromonks* attached to the hermitage were already waiting in the cell for the starets: one was the father librarian and the other was Father Païsy, a sick man, though not old, who was said to be a great scholar. Besides these two, there stood in a corner, where he remained throughout, a youth of about twenty-two wearing a layman's frock-coat, a seminarian and student theologian, who for some reason enjoyed the patronage of the monastery and the monks. He was rather tall, with a fresh complexion, high cheek-bones, and intelligent, alert, narrow, light-brown eyes. His expression was one of total deference, but dignified and unobsequious; being *in statu pupil-*

lari* and socially inferior to the visitors, he did not even presume to bow as they entered.

Starets Zosima entered accompanied by a novice and Alyosha. The two hieromonks rose and greeted him with a deep bow, their fingers touching the floor, and then, after being blessed, kissed his hand. After blessing them, the starets responded to each in turn with an equally deep bow, also touching the floor with his fingers, and asking for a blessing from each of them. The whole ceremony was conducted with the utmost solemnity, sincerity even, and not at all in a perfunctory manner, like a commonplace rite. To Miusov, however, it all appeared to be done for sheer effect. On entering, he found himself standing at the head of the visiting party. Strictly speaking, he should, out of common courtesy—never mind all his ideas—have approached the starets, as was the custom there, and received his blessing, even if he did not kiss his hand (as a matter of fact, he had pondered the matter the night before and was of a mind to do just that). But on seeing the two hieromonks perform all this bowing and kissing of hands, he reversed his decision instantly, made a dignified, restrained bow, as was customary in society, and withdrew to a chair. Fyodor Pavlovich did exactly the same, imitating Miusov like a monkey. Ivan Fyodorovich, though also keeping his arms at his sides, bowed in a very polite and dignified manner, whereas Kalganov was so embarrassed that he did not even bow at all. The starets made as if to deliver his blessing, but lowered his arm prematurely and, bowing to them all once more, bade them be seated. Blood rushed to Alyosha's cheeks; he was ashamed. His worst premonitions were coming true.

The starets sat on a very old-fashioned leather-covered mahogany settee, and motioned all four visitors, except the two hieromonks, to a row of four mahogany chairs with extremely worn black leather seats, ranged along the wall opposite. The hieromonks sat on either side of the guests, one by the door, the other by the window. The seminarian, Alyosha, and the novice remained standing. The cell was not very spacious and was of a drab appearance. The furniture and everything in it was of coarse workmanship and poor quality, and limited to bare essentials. There were two flower-pots on the window-sill and a number of icons in one corner, including a very large one of the

Mother of God, probably painted long before the Schism.* In front of it burned an icon-lamp; nearby were two other icons in shining *rizas*,* and carved cherubim, porcelain eggs, an ivory Catholic crucifix in the embrace of a *Mater Dolorosa*, and some foreign engravings of the great Italian masters of the past. In addition to these exquisite and expensive engravings there were several of the most popular kind of Russian lithographs of saints, martyrs, and holy men, such as can be bought for a few kopecks at any fair. On the walls were some lithographs of contemporary and former patriarchs. Miusov glanced quickly at all this ecclesiastical bric-à-brac and fixed his gaze on the starets. He prided himself on his ability to judge by appearances, a pardonable weakness in one who was already fifty—an age when an intelligent, well-to-do man of the world always starts to take himself seriously, sometimes even against his better judgement.

He took an instant dislike to the starets. And indeed, there was something about the face of the starets that could have aroused dislike in others besides Miusov. He was a short, bent-backed little man, very unsteady on his legs, and although no more than sixty-five years of age seemed at least ten years older because of illness. His whole face was wizened and creased with wrinkles, especially around the eyes. Those eyes were small, pale-coloured, darting and shining, like two shining points of light. Grey wisps around the temples were all that was left of his hair, his tiny, wedge-shaped beard was thin and sparse, and his lips, which often puckered into a smile, were as thin as two pieces of string. His nose was not so much long as sharp and beak-like.

'By all appearances, a nasty, petty, stuck-up little man,' was the thought that flashed through Miusov's mind. He was altogether in a very querulous mood.

The small, cheap, pendulum wall-clock struck twelve in rapid succession, which served to break the ice. 'Dead on the appointed hour,' exclaimed Fyodor Pavlovich, 'but still no sign of my son Dmitry Fyodorovich. I apologize for him, blessed starets!' (Alyosha shuddered from head to toe at 'blessed starets'.) 'Myself, I'm always punctual to the minute, seeing that punctuality is the politeness of kings...'*

'But then, you're no king, are you?' muttered Miusov, already unable to contain himself at the very start of proceedings.

'No, exactly, I'm not a king. And for your information, Pyotr Aleksandrovich, I'm quite well aware of that myself, God's truth. There I go, saying the wrong thing again! Your Reverence!' he exclaimed with a sudden flight of fancy, 'You see before you a clown, a veritable clown! Thus I present myself to you. An old habit, alas! And if I say the wrong thing and speak untruths occasionally, it's all done deliberately, in order to raise a smile, to be nice to people. You've got to be nice, haven't you? About seven years ago I found myself in some God-forsaken hole of a town, on some petty matter or other—setting up a company with a bunch of merchants. Off we went to see the chief of police, the local *ispravnik*,* to make some enquiries and to invite him to have dinner with us. Out comes the *ispravnik*, a tall, fat, fair-haired, morose fellow—they're the most dangerous type in my opinion, it's their livers that let them down. Straight up to him I went, with all the confidence of a man of the world. "Mister Ispravnik," I said to him, "you wouldn't care, as it were, to be our Napravnik,* would you?" "What do you mean, 'Napravnik'?" he says. I could see from the very first instant that our business had got off on the wrong foot; he stood there, all serious and stubborn. "No hard feelings, I was only trying to make a joke, just to amuse the company. I was only thinking of Mr Napravnik, our famous Russian conductor, and seeing as we need, so to speak, a conductor to ensure the harmony of our undertaking..." You'd say that was a reasonable explanation and a suitable metaphor, wouldn't you? "I beg your pardon," he says, "I'm the *ispravnik* here and I don't care much for people who make puns on my profession." And he turned round and stalked off. I went after him, calling out, "Yes, of course, you're the *ispravnik*, and not Napravnik!" "No," he says, "seeing as you've called me that, there's nothing for it, I am Napravnik." And would you believe it, our deal never got off the ground! I'm always getting up to things like that, always. I'm my own worst enemy, what with my gentlemanly approach! For instance, many years ago I said to a rather influential person, "Your wife's a ticklish woman." I was referring to his wife's sense of honour, her high moral qualities, you understand, but he immediately retorted, "Have you been tickling her?" I couldn't stop myself; I suddenly thought: why not be gentlemanly? "Yes sir, I have!" My word, what a tickling he gave me...! The only reason I'm not ashamed to tell the story now is that it all happened so damn long ago; I'm my own worst enemy.'

'You don't say,' Miusov muttered in disgust.

The starets scrutinized each in turn without a word.

'Quite so!' said Fyodor Pavlovich. 'As a matter of fact, that didn't escape me either, Pyotr Aleksandrovich, and, you know, I realized beforehand from the moment I started to speak that that's what would happen, and, think of it, I even anticipated that you'd be the first to point it out to me. During those first moments when I realize that my joke is going to fall flat, my tongue, Your Reverence, begins to stick to my cheek as though I was having a blockage; it goes back to my young days, when I lived with the gentry and learnt to survive by scrounging off them. I'm an out-and-out clown, have been since birth, a buffoon if ever there was one, Your Reverence; quite likely I've got the devil in me too,* one of those small-calibre ones, you know, a more important one would have picked a different abode—not you though, Pyotr Aleksandrovich, you're certainly not much of an abode. But then, I'm a believer, I believe in God. Never had any doubts except recently, but now I'm ready to imbibe your great words of wisdom. I'm like the philosopher Diderot,* Your Reverence. Do you know, Reverend Father, what happened when Diderot, the philosopher, paid a visit to Archbishop Platon* during the time of the Empress Catherine? He went up to him and blurted out, "There is no God!" Whereupon the great patriarch raised his finger and replied, "The fool hath said in his heart, There is no God."* Diderot at once fell to the ground at his feet. "I believe," he cried out, "and let me be baptized."* He was baptized on the spot. Princess Dashkova* was godmother and Field Marshal Potemkin* godfather.'

'Fyodor Pavlovich, this is beyond a joke!' said Miusov in a quivering voice, totally unable to control himself. 'Why do you go on so? You know very well you're lying and that silly story isn't true.'

'Funny thing, that's just what I suspected all my life!'

exclaimed Fyodor Pavlovich with elation. 'But now, gentlemen, let me tell you the whole truth. Reverend starets, forgive that last bit about Diderot's baptism, I made it up myself just now, even as I was telling it to you, it had never entered my head before. I made it up just to please you. I carry on like that, Pyotr Aleksandrovich, so that people'll like me all the more. But then sometimes I don't know myself why I do it. As for Diderot, I must have heard those words "The fool hath said in his heart" scores of times from the landowners of these parts when I was a youngster rubbing shoulders with them, and, incidentally, Pyotr Aleksandrovich, I heard it from your aunt too, from your aunt, Mavra Fominishna. They're all convinced to this day that the infidel Diderot went to the Metropolitan Platon to argue about God...'

Miusov rose to his feet; he was beside himself, his patience completely exhausted. He was in a fury and realized that he too appeared ridiculous. And in fact, what was unfolding in the cell was quite unbelievable. Visitors had assembled in this cell for the past forty, perhaps fifty years in the times of previous startsy, but always in a spirit of deepest reverence, never otherwise. Almost all who were admitted to the cell were conscious of being accorded a great privilege. Many would go down on their knees and not stand up again for the duration of the entire audience. Even the highest in the land, many of the most learned, even some freethinkers, who came either out of curiosity or for some other reason, on entering the cell either in a group or for a private audience, all to a man felt an overriding obligation to show the most profound respect and tact during their entire visit, and all the more so since money had no place here, but only love and kindness on the one hand, or repentance and a longing to resolve some profound spiritual problem or come to terms with a critical moment in the life of the soul on the other hand. Hence the buffoonery suddenly exhibited by Fyodor Pavlovich, in total disrespect of his surroundings, provoked consternation and dismay in those who witnessed it, or at least in some of them. The two hieromonks, their features quite impassive, regarded the starets with rapt attention as they awaited his response, though they, too, must have been on the point of rising to their feet as Miusov had just done. Alyosha was on the verge of tears

and stood with bowed head. What astounded him most of all was
that his brother Ivan Fyodorovich, the only person on whom he
felt able to rely and who alone had sufficient influence over their
father to be able to restrain him, remained seated, quite motionless, on his chair, his eyes lowered, apparently waiting with a
kind of eager curiosity to see how it would all end, as though he
himself were a mere spectator here. Neither could Alyosha look
at Rakitin, the seminarian, whom he knew well and with whom
he was on almost intimate terms; Alyosha knew Rakitin's
thoughts, and he was the only one in the whole monastery who
did.

'Forgive me...', Miusov began, turning to the starets, 'if I too
appear to be participating in this disgraceful charade. My mistake
lay in believing that even a man like Fyodor Pavlovich would
realize his obligations when visiting so revered a person... I never
imagined that I should have to make an apology just for coming
with him...'

Pyotr Aleksandrovich broke off and, in acute embarrassment,
was on the point of leaving the room.

'Please do not distress yourself.' The starets stood up shakily
on his feeble legs and, taking Pyotr Aleksandrovich by both
hands, led him back to his seat. 'Please be at peace. You are my
guest here,' and with a bow he turned and sat down again on his
settee.

'Noble starets, tell me, are my high spirits offensive to you or
not?' Fyodor Pavlovich suddenly exclaimed, gripping the arms of
his chair with both hands and appearing ready to leap out of it,
depending upon the reply.

'I sincerely beg you too not to be distressed and not to be
embarrassed,' the starets replied reassuringly. 'You must feel
completely at ease. Above all, do not be so ashamed of yourself,
because that is the root of your trouble.'

'Feel completely at ease! You mean, be my natural self! Oh,
that's too much, that's too much to expect, but—I accept, deeply
touched! You know, holy father, I'd rather you didn't ask me to
be my natural self, you shouldn't take such a risk... I wouldn't go
so far myself. I'm saying this for your own protection, to warn
you. Well, sir, as to what's going to happen, that's all still
shrouded in mystery, though there are some who would dearly

like to see me discredited. That's right, Pyotr Aleksandrovich,
you're the one I mean, but as for you, holiest of beings—to you
I will pour out my heart in ecstasy.' He rose to his feet and,
lifting up his arms, pronounced: 'Blessed is the womb that bare
thee, and the paps which gave thee suck*—especially the paps!
You said just now, "Don't be so ashamed of yourself, because
that's the root of your trouble"—with those words, you seem to
have reached right into my innermost soul. What I mean is,
when I visit people, I always feel that I'm really the lowest of the
low, that everybody takes me for a buffoon, so I say to myself,
why shouldn't I act the fool, I'm not afraid of what any of you
might think, because every single one of you is even worse than
me. That's why I'm a buffoon, I'm a buffoon born of shame,
great starets, of shame. It's anxiety pure and simple that makes
me so unruly. Now, if only I could be sure when I'm in company
that everyone would immediately take me for the kindest and
cleverest of men—Lord, what a good man I would then turn out
to be! Master!,' and he suddenly fell to his knees, 'what shall I
do that I may inherit eternal life?'* Even now it was difficult to
tell whether he was speaking in jest or whether he really was
moved.

The starets looked up and said with a smile, 'You yourself
have long known what to do, you are intelligent enough; do not
indulge in drunkenness and verbal intemperance, do not indulge
in sensual excess, beware especially of worshipping money, and
close your taverns—if not all of them, then at least two or three.
But, first and foremost—do not lie.'

'You mean, what I said about Diderot?'

'No, I do not. The important thing is not to lie to yourself. He
who lies to himself and listens to his own lies reaches a state in
which he no longer recognizes truth either in himself or in
others, and so he ceases to respect both himself and others.
Having ceased to respect everyone, he stops loving, and then, in
the absence of love, in order to occupy and divert himself, he
abandons himself to passions and the gratification of coarse
pleasures until his vices bring him down to the level of bestiality,
and all on account of his being constantly false both to himself
and to others. He who is false to himself is also the most likely
to feel offended. After all, it is sometimes very gratifying to feel

offended, is it not? A man may be perfectly well aware that no one has offended him, that he has imagined it all and put about a lie just for the sake of it, blown it out of all proportion so as to attract attention, deliberately picked on a word and made a mountain out of a molehill—he may very well realize all this, and yet be the very first to take offence, to the point of deriving enjoyment and pleasure from it, and so fall into a state of real animosity... Please get up off your knees and sit down, I beg you, these are all such false gestures...'

'Blessed father! Let me kiss your hand.' Fyodor Pavlovich rapidly approached the starets and planted a brief kiss on his emaciated hand. 'Exactly, just so, it is gratifying to take offence. You've expressed it better than I ever heard it before. Exactly, all my life I've been taking offence and enjoying it, taking aesthetic pleasure from it, because it isn't only gratifying, at times it can be sheer joy to be offended—that's what you've forgotten, Most Reverend Father, sheer joy! I'll write that down! And I have been lying, I've been lying all my life long, every day, every hour. Verily, I am a liar, the father of lies!* No, perhaps it isn't "father" of lies—I'm getting my texts muddled—perhaps just the son of lies, that'll have to do... Only... merciful one... surely it's all right to mention Diderot from time to time? Diderot can't do any harm, unlike some other stories. Gracious father, now we're talking about it, and before I forget, seeing as I've meant to ask about it these past three years, yes, to come here specially to ask and find out, only for heaven's sake don't let Pyotr Aleksandrovich interrupt me. Well, this is what I wanted to ask: is it true, great father, what is recounted in the *Chety-Miney** about a holy miracle-worker* who was tortured for his faith, and when in the end they struck off his head, he rose, picked up his own head and, "kissing it lovingly", kept on walking for a good while, carrying it in his hands and "kissing it lovingly"? Is that true or not, Reverend Father?'

'No, it is not true,' the starets replied.

'There's nothing of the kind anywhere in the Saints' Calendar,' said one of the hieromonks, the librarian. 'Of which saint did you say this was written?'

'I don't know which one it was. Don't know, haven't any idea. I've been deceived by what somebody said. I just happened to hear it, and do you know who from? Pyotr Aleksandrovich Miusov, who got so upset by Diderot just now, he's the one who told me the story.'

'I never told you anything of the kind. I don't even speak to you.'

'It's true it wasn't me you told it to; but you told it in company where I happened to be present, three or four years ago it must have been. The reason I've mentioned it is because you undermined my faith with that funny story, Pyotr Aleksandrovich. You didn't know, you didn't realize it at the time, but I went home with my faith severely undermined, and it's gone from bad to worse ever since. Yes, Pyotr Aleksandrovich, what a loss of faith there was, and you were the cause of it! Never mind Diderot, sir!'

Fyodor Pavlovich was thoroughly worked up, although it was quite obvious to everyone that he was play-acting again. Miusov, however, was stung to the quick.

'What stuff and nonsense, it's ridiculous,' he muttered. 'Perhaps I did say something some time ago... but not to you. I was told the story myself. I heard it from a Frenchman in Paris who said that it was in our Saints' Calendar and is read at the midday service... He's a great scholar, he's made a special study of Russian statistics... lived for years in Russia... I've never read the Saints' Calendar myself... and I don't intend to either... The things you hear at dinner—we were having dinner at the time.'

'Ah yes, you had dinner and I lost my faith!' Fyodor Pavlovich mocked.

'What has your faith got to do with me!' Miusov began shouting, but he suddenly bit his tongue and said contemptuously, 'You literally defile everything you touch.'

The starets suddenly got up from his seat.

'Excuse me, gentlemen, I have to leave you for a few minutes,' he said, speaking to all the visitors. 'People who arrived here before you are waiting for me. And as for you, stop telling lies!' he added, turning with good humour towards Fyodor Pavlovich.

As he got up to leave the cell, Alyosha and the novice rushed over to help him down the steps. Alyosha was breathless; he was glad to get away, but glad, too, that the starets had not been offended and was in good spirits. The starets was making for the

veranda to give his blessing to those who were waiting for him.
Fyodor Pavlovich, however, stopped him at the door of the cell.

'Most blessed of men!' he exclaimed with feeling. 'Allow me
just once more to kiss your hand. Yes, one can talk to you, one
has such a rapport with you! Do you think I'm always such a liar
and that I never stop clowning? You see, I was deliberately play-
acting all the time just to test you. I've been probing you all the
time to see if we could get along with each other. To see if there
was room enough for my humility alongside your pride. I award
you a certificate of merit: we could indeed get along with each
other! But now I'll keep quiet, I won't say a thing. I'll sit down
in this chair and not say a word. Pyotr Aleksandrovich, it's your
turn to have the floor. You're the principal person here now...
for the next ten minutes.'

3

DEVOUT PEASANT WOMEN

THE crowd waiting down beside the wooden veranda built on
the outer side of the hermitage wall was on this occasion
composed entirely of women, some twenty in all. They had been
informed that the starets would eventually appear, and had
gathered there in expectation. Mrs Khokhlakova, the landowner's
widow, and her daughter had also come out onto the veranda;
they too had been waiting for the starets, but in the separate
quarters allocated for visiting gentlewomen. Mrs Khokhlakova, a
wealthy lady, always dressed with taste, was still quite young and
very comely in appearance, somewhat pale-skinned, with very
lively, almost completely black eyes. She could not have been
more than thirty-three years old and had been a widow for about
five years. Her fourteen-year-old daughter suffered from para-
lysis of the legs. The poor girl had been unable to walk for about
six months, and had to be wheeled around in a long Bath-chair
on rubber-rimmed wheels. She had a charming little face,
somewhat thin from sickness, but cheerful. There was a mischievous sparkle in her large dark eyes with their long lashes.
Her mother had been planning since the spring to take her

abroad, but they had been delayed the whole summer by estate business. They had been staying in our town for about a week, more for business than devotional reasons, but three days previously had paid the starets a visit. Now they had suddenly come again, and even though they knew that the starets could receive hardly anyone, had fervently sought 'the happiness of beholding the great healer once more'.

While waiting for the starets to appear, the mother sat on a chair next to her daughter's invalid chair, and within two paces of her stood an old monk, not from our monastery, but a visitor from a remote and little-known northern settlement. He too wished to be blessed by the starets. But when the starets appeared on the veranda, he went straight to the peasant women. The crowd began to press towards the little porch with its three steps leading from the low veranda to the open ground below. The starets positioned himself on the upper step, put on his stole, and began to bless the women crowding around him. A *klikusha* was dragged up to him by both hands. As soon as she caught sight of the starets, she began to utter absurd squeals, to hiccup and to tremble all over, as though she were in labour. Laying his stole on her head, the starets said a short prayer over her, and she immediately fell silent and became calm. I do not know how it is nowadays, but in my childhood I often saw and heard these *klikushi* in villages and monasteries. They would be brought to the midday service, yelping and barking like bitches, fit to bring the roof down, but when the Host was brought out and they were led up to it, their 'devilry' would immediately cease, and for a time the sufferers would remain calm. As a child, I was greatly surprised and intrigued by all this. But in answer to my enquiries at the time, I was told by other landowners, and especially by my teachers in the town, that this was all a sham to avoid work and that it could be eradicated by suitably strict measures, and various anecdotes were quoted in support of this. But, to my surprise, I later discovered from medical specialists that this was not a case of shamming at all, but an unfortunate women's complaint to be found mostly, it appeared, here in Russia, testifying to the unhappy lot of our village women, an illness caused by debilitating work undertaken too soon after difficult, complicated, and medically unsupervised labour, and further aggravated by hopeless misery, beatings, and so on, which apparently some female constitutions lacked the strength to endure. The strange instantaneous recovery of the raving and flailing woman as soon as she was led up to the Host, which was represented to me as pretence, even trickery, instigated perhaps by the 'clergy' themselves, may in fact have occurred perfectly naturally, and the women ushering her into the presence of the Host, and, more to the point, the sick woman herself, may have sincerely believed that the evil spirits that possessed her would be driven out once she was in the presence of the Host and made to bow before it. And in that case the distraught and, of course, mentally disturbed woman was bound to experience (could not but experience) a shock to her whole system on bowing before the Host, a shock caused by anticipation of the promised miracle and complete faith in its occurrence. And it would occur, if only for a brief moment. Precisely the same thing happened on this occasion too, as soon as the starets laid his stole on the sick woman.

Many of the women crowding around him were moved at this moment to tears of exultation; some pressed forward to kiss the hem of his garment, others began to wail. He blessed all of them and spoke to some. He already knew the *klikusha*, who came from near by, from a village only six versts from the monastery, and had been brought to him on previous occasions.

'And here's one from far away.' The starets pointed to a woman who, while not old, was very emaciated and hollow-cheeked, not so much sunburnt as blackened all over her face. She was on her knees, staring motionless at the starets. There was something akin to frenzy in her gaze.

'Yes, from far away, father, from far away, three hundred versts from here. From far away, father, from far away.' The woman spoke in a singsong voice, continuing to move her head from side to side in a rocking motion, with one cheek resting in the palm of her hand. She spoke as though she were keening. There is a kind of grief among the common people that is mute and long-suffering, that turns inwards and is silent. But there is also a convulsive grief which will sometimes break out into tears and turn to keening. This is found particularly in women. It is no easier to bear than the silent grief. For keening soothes only in that it inflames and wears out the heart. Such grief seeks no consolation; it feeds on its own unassuageable despair. Keening is only a compulsion to keep reopening the wound.

'You're a tradeswoman by the look of you, isn't that so?' the starets asked, studying her with curiosity.

'Yes, we're townsfolk, father, townsfolk. We're peasants, but townsfolk, we're settled in the town now. It's to see you I've come, father. We've heard about you, father, we've heard about you. Buried my baby, my little boy, and set off to pray to God. I've been to three monasteries and they said, "Go there too, Nastasyushka",* meaning here, love, to see you, that is. So I've come, stayed for the midnight service, and come here today to see you.'

'Why are you weeping?'

'My little boy,* father, just short of three, another three months and he'd have turned three. It's my little boy that's tormenting me, father, my little boy. He was the last one that Nikitushka* and I had left out of four, but the little ones just won't stay with us, dear, they won't. I buried the first three and didn't grieve over them too much at all, but I buried this last one and I just can't forget him. It's just as if he's standing before me now and won't go away. I've cried my heart out for him. One look at his little clothes, his little shirt and shoes, and it sets me off. I spread out everything that's left of his, every little thing, I look at it all, and I just howl. I said to Nikitushka, my husband that is, "Husband, let me go on a pilgrimage." He's a coachman, we're not poor, father, we're not poor at all, we run our own cab, it's all our own, the horses and the cab. But what's the good of it all to us now? He's taken to drinking when I'm not at home, my Nikitushka has, he's always been a bit that way; the minute my back's turned, he's at it again. But now I don't even think about him. I've been away from home over two months. I've forgotten he exists, I've forgotten everything, and I'm past caring. What do I need him for any more? I've finished with him, finished with him, finished with everybody. And I don't even want to see my house again or anything I own, I've turned my back on everything!'

'Now listen, mother,' said the starets, 'a long time ago a great saint once saw a mother like you in church, weeping for her infant, her one and only, whom the Lord had claimed too. "Do you not know", the saint said to her, "how indignant these little ones are before the throne of God? There is no one more indignant than them in the Kingdom of Heaven: 'You granted us life, Lord,' they say to God, 'and no sooner did we see it than You took it away from us.' And so fearlessly do they clamour and demand an answer that the Lord at once grants them the rank of angels. And hence", said the saint, "you too must rejoice, woman, and weep not, for your little one also is now amongst God's host of angels." That's what the saint said to the weeping woman in those far-off times. And he was a great saint and could not have told her an untruth. Know, therefore, mother, that your little one too now stands before the throne of Almighty God, happy and rejoicing, and is praying to God for you. Weep therefore, but rejoice too.'

The woman, resting her cheek on her hand, listened to him with downcast eyes. She gave a deep sigh.

'That's just how Nikitushka used to comfort me too, word for word he said the same thing as you. "You foolish woman," he said, "why are you crying? Our little son is surely now with the Lord God, singing with the angels." And he said this to me and he was weeping himself, I could see he was weeping just like me. "I know that, Nikitushka," I said. "Where else could he possibly be if not with the Lord God, but he isn't here, he isn't with us now, Nikitushka, he isn't sitting here beside us as he used to." Oh, if only I could have a peep at him just once, if only I could look at him just one more time, I wouldn't go up to him, wouldn't say a word, I'd stay quiet in a corner, if only I could see him just for one little minute, hear him playing in the yard and running in as he used to and calling out in his little voice, "Mamma, where are you?" If only I could hear him running through the room just once more, only once more, his little feet going pitter-patter, ever so fast, I remember how he used to run up to me shouting and laughing, if only I could hear his little feet again, his little feet, I'd recognize him at once! But he's gone, father, he's gone, and I'll never hear him again! This is his belt, but he's gone and I'll never see him again, or hear him...!'

She drew from her bosom her boy's little woven belt and, after one glance at it, was immediately convulsed by weeping, the tears streaming through her fingers which she held pressed to her eyes.

'And this is as it was of old,' said the starets, "Rachel weeping for her children, and would not be comforted, because they are not",* such is the appointed lot of you mothers here on earth. And be not comforted, for there is no need to be comforted, so be not comforted and weep, only each time that you weep, be sure to remember that your little son is among the angels of God, that he looks down on you from on high and sees you, rejoices in your tears and points them out to the Lord God. And long will you continue to weep the great mourning of mothers, but in the end it will turn to quiet joy,* and your bitter tears will be but tears of quiet tenderness, purifying the soul and absolving it from sin. I shall remember your little one in my prayers for the souls of the departed—what was his name?'

'Aleksei, father.'

'A good name. After Aleksei, the man of God?'*

'Yes, man of God, father, man of God, Aleksei, the man of God.'

'A saint indeed! I shall remember him, mother, I shall remember him and your sorrow in my prayers, and I shall pray for your husband. Only it is wrong for you to abandon him. Go back to your husband and care for him. If your little boy should see from above that you have left his father, he will weep for both of you; why should you disrupt his bliss? For indeed he lives, verily he lives, for the soul lives eternally; he is not in the house, and yet he is at your side, unseen. How can he enter your home if, as you say, you have grown to detest it? To whom will he come if he doesn't find you, his mother and his father, together? Now he appears to you in your dreams and you are tormenting yourself, but if you return home, he will send you pleasant dreams. Go back to your husband, mother, go back to him this very day.'

'I will, dear love, I'll go back just as you say. You've comforted me no end. Nikitushka, my Nikitushka, you're expecting me, my love, I'm sure you are!' The woman started keening, but the starets had already turned to a very old woman who was not dressed as a pilgrim, but like a townswoman. It was evident from her eyes that she had come to the starets about some specific matter. She introduced herself as the widow of a non-commissioned officer from near by, in fact from our town. Her son Vasenka had served somewhere in the Army Commissariat and then gone to Siberia, to Irkutsk. He had written twice from there, but it was a year since he had last written. She had been making enquiries about him, but didn't know the correct person to approach.

'So the other day Stepanida Ilyinishna Bedryagina says to me—she's a merchant's wife, by the way, and she's rich—she says to me, Prokhorovna, why don't you ask at your church, she says, for your son to be remembered with the souls of the departed. Then his soul, she says, will feel the hurt and he'll write you a letter. It's true, says Stepanida Ilyinishna, it's absolutely true, it's been tried many times. Only I'm not quite sure about it myself... Is it true or not, father, will it be all right to do it?'

'You mustn't think of such a thing! Shame on you for asking. How can anyone, and especially a mother, pray for the repose of a living soul! This is a great sin, it's like sorcery, to be forgiven only on account of your ignorance. The best thing you can do is to pray to the Mother of God, our unfailing helper and mediatrix, for your son's well-being, and pray, too, that she should forgive you your erroneous thinking. And here's another thing I will tell you, Prokhorovna: either your son himself will come back to you soon, or, if not, he'll certainly send you a letter. You can be sure of that. Go now without fear. Your dear son is alive, I can tell you.'

'Our dear father, may God reward you, you who are our benefactor, who prays for us all and for our sins...'

But the starets had already caught the blazing eyes of an emaciated, consumptive-looking, but still young peasant woman staring at him from the crowd. She gazed at him mutely, with imploring eyes, but seemed afraid to approach.

'What brings you here, my child?'

'Give my soul absolution, dear father,' she said softly and unhurriedly and, dropping to her knees, bowed down at his feet. 'I've sinned, my dear father, and my sin terrifies me.'

The starets sat down on the lowest step, and the woman drew near without getting off her knees.

'I've been widowed more than two years now,' she began in a

half-whisper, and a shudder seemed to shake her whole body. 'It was a hard life with my husband, he was an old man and he beat me black and blue. He was lying sick, and I thought as I looked at him: what if he recovers and gets up again, what then? And then the idea came to me...'

'Wait,' said the starets and brought his ear to her lips. The woman continued in a soft, barely audible whisper. She soon finished speaking.

'Over two years ago?' asked the starets.

'Yes. Didn't think about it much at first, but I'm poorly now, and it's tormenting me.'

'Have you come from far away?'

'Over five hundred versts from here.'

'Have you confessed?'

'I have, twice.'

'Have you been allowed to receive communion?'

'Yes. I'm frightened, I'm frightened of dying.'

'Don't be afraid of anything, never be afraid, and don't torment yourself. Only be steadfast in your repentance, and God will forgive you everything. There is no sin, nor can there be any sin in the whole world, that God would not forgive the truly penitent. It is altogether beyond any man to commit a sin so great that it would exhaust God's infinite love. For can there be such a sin as would exceed God's love? Keep your thoughts on repentance alone—continually—and cast out fear from your mind. Do not forget that God loves you beyond your imagining, for he loves you sinful as you are and despite your sin. There is more joy in heaven over one that repents of his sins than there is over ten righteous ones;* this was spoken long ago. Go then, and do not be afraid. Do not be distressed by people, nor harbour anger if they have offended you. Forgive the deceased in your heart, however he might have offended you, and be truly reconciled to him. If you repent, you must love. And if you love, you are of God... Love gains everything, redeems everything. And if even I, a sinful being just as you are, have been moved and have pity for you, how much more so will God. Love is such a priceless treasure that you can purchase the whole world with it, and redeem not only your own but other people's sins too. Go now, and have no fear.'

The starets made the sign of the cross over her three times, took a little icon from his own neck, and put it around hers. She bowed down to the ground before him in silence. He half rose and looked cheerfully across at a healthy country wench holding a suckling babe in her arms.

'From Vyshegorye, father.'

'That's six versts you've been struggling with that child. What brings you here?'

'Came to have a look at you. I've been to see you before, have you forgotten? You can't have much of a memory if you've forgotten me already. They said in our village you were sick, so I said to myself, well, I'll go and see for myself: now I can see you, and there's nothing the matter with you at all. You'll last another twenty years, you will, God bless you! Anyway, it's not as though you hadn't enough people praying for you, why should you go and get sick?'

'Thank you for everything, my dear.'

'By the way, there was a little favour I wanted to ask you; here's sixty kopecks, give them, father, to someone that's poorer than me. On my way here, I was thinking to myself: it'd be best to give it to him, he'll know who to give it to.'

'Thank you, my dear, thank you, kind heart. I love you. It will be done without fail. Is that a little girl you're holding?'

'Yes, father, Lizaveta.'

'God bless you both, you and your baby daughter Lizaveta. You've gladdened my heart, mother. Farewell, my dear ones, farewell, my kind, my beloved ones.'

He blessed everybody and bowed deeply to all.

4

LADY OF LITTLE FAITH

THE landowner's widow, who had been following the starets's conversation with the peasant women and watching him give his blessing, was shedding silent tears and dabbing her eyes with her handkerchief. She was a sensitive, socially refined lady, inclined in most matters towards sincerity and goodness. When the starets at last went up to her, she greeted him with rapture.

'I was so, so moved observing the whole of that touching scene...' She broke off in sheer emotion. 'Oh, I understand why the people love you, I too love the people, I have a great desire to love them, one can't help but love the people, our wonderful, simple-hearted, magnificent Russian people!'

'How's your daughter's health? Would you like to talk to me again?'

'Oh, I was imploring and beseeching everyone, I was ready to kneel at your window for three days, waiting for you to see me. We've come to you, great healer, to convey our boundless gratitude. You have cured my Lise, you have cured her completely—and how did you do it? By praying over her last Thursday and laying your hands on her. We rushed here to kiss those hands, to express our sentiments and our veneration.'

'What do you mean, cured? Isn't she still in her invalid chair?'

'But her nocturnal fevers have completely stopped, it's been two nights in a row now, ever since Thursday,' the woman continued, full of nervous energy. 'What's more, her legs have become stronger. This morning she woke up feeling a lot better, she slept all through the night, just look at her rosy cheeks and her sparkling eyes! She was always crying before, but now she's laughing, she's happy and cheerful. Today she insisted we should let her stand on her own feet, and she stood up for a whole minute with no support whatsoever. She's laid a wager with me that in two weeks' time she'll be dancing the quadrille. I consulted our local doctor, Herzenstube, and he just shrugged his shoulders; he was surprised and baffled. Would you really rather we hadn't disturbed you, are you wishing we hadn't hurried here to thank you? Lise, thank Father Zosima, go on, thank him!'

Lise's sweet, laughing little face suddenly became serious. She sat up in her chair as far as she could and, looking at the starets, clasped her hands in front of her face, but, unable to restrain herself, burst out laughing.

'It's him, it's him!' she said, pointing to Alyosha, childishly annoyed with herself for being unable to restrain her laughter.

Anyone looking at Alyosha, who was standing one pace behind the starets, would have noticed a quick flush suffusing his face, a sudden reddening of his cheeks. His eyes sparkled and he looked down at his feet.

'She has a message for you, Aleksei Fyodorovich... How are you?' the mother continued, turning suddenly to Alyosha and stretching out a beautifully gloved hand towards him. The starets turned and looked closely at Alyosha. The latter approached Lise and, with a strange and awkward smile, put out his hand. Lise assumed a serious expression.

'Katerina Ivanovna has asked me to give you this,' and she handed him a small envelope. 'She especially asks you to go and see her, the sooner the better, and mind you don't let me down, you must go without fail.'

'She wants me to go and see her? Me? Whatever for?' Alyosha murmured in great surprise. His face suddenly took on an expression of extreme concern.

'Oh, it's all about Dmitry Fyodorovich and... all those recent goings-on,' the mother hurried to explain. 'Katerina Ivanovna has made up her mind... but she really needs to see you... What for? That, of course, I don't know, but she wants you to go as soon as possible. And you will go, you will definitely go, won't you? It's a matter of Christian duty.'

'I've only ever seen her once,' said Alyosha, still baffled.

'Oh, she's such a noble creature, unfathomable! Her sufferings alone... just imagine what she's had to endure, what she's going through now, just imagine what the future holds for her... it's all so terrible, terrible!'

'All right, I'll go,' Alyosha decided, after reading the short, mysterious note, which contained no explanation, apart from the insistent request that he should go and see her.

'Oh, how kind and splendid of you,' Lise exclaimed with sudden elation. 'And I told mother: nothing will make him go; after all, he's a monk. Aren't you just wonderful! You know, I always thought you were wonderful, I don't mind telling you!'

'Lise,' her mother said firmly, and at once broke into a smile.

'You've neglected us too, Aleksei Fyodorovich, you never even come to see us any more: but Lise has told me several times that she feels well only in your company.' Alyosha raised his eyes, suddenly blushed once more, and smiled again, but he did not know why. The starets, however, was no longer observing him. He had entered into conversation with the visiting monk who, as we have already said, was standing by Lise's chair, waiting. He was to all appearances a monk of the most unassuming kind, that is, of humble birth, with a narrow, restricted view of the world, but devout and, in his own way, stubborn. He announced that he was from somewhere in the far north, from Obdorsk, from St Silvester's, a poor monastery with only nine monks. The starets blessed him and invited him to come to see him in his cell whenever he wished.

'How can you take it upon yourself to do such things?' the monk suddenly asked, with a meaningful glance at Lise. He was referring to her 'cure'.

'Of course, it's too early to talk about that. Improvement is not the same as total cure, which could be due to other causes. But even if there were something of the kind, it would be due to no other power than the will of God. Everything is from God. By all means come and see me, father,' he added to the monk, 'although I've had to restrict the number of visitors. I am ill and I know my days are numbered.'

'Oh no, no, God will not take you away from us, you will live a long time yet,' the mother cried out. 'There's nothing wrong with you! You look so healthy, cheerful, and happy.'

'Today I feel very much better, but I know that this is only temporary. There is no mistaking my illness now. If, however, I seem so cheerful to you, there could be no greater joy for me than to hear you mention that. For the fact is, man has been created for happiness, and he who is wholly happy has a perfect right to say to himself: I have performed God's will on earth. All the righteous, all the saints, all the holy martyrs have been happy.'

'Oh, what wonderful things you say, how courageous and evocative your words are,' exclaimed the mother. 'When you speak, you touch me to the quick. And yet happiness, happiness—where is it? Who can claim that he is happy? Oh, since you've been kind enough to let us see you again today, do listen to what I kept back from you last time, what I didn't dare reveal to you, all that has been causing me so much suffering for so long, for so long! I am suffering, forgive me, I am suffering...', and, moved by some sudden strong emotion, she folded her hands before him in supplication.

'What is it in particular?'

'I am suffering... because of lack of faith...'

'Lack of faith in God?'

'Oh no, no, I wouldn't even dare to contemplate anything like that—it's simply the matter of the life to come, it's such a mystery! And nobody, you see, nobody knows the answer to it! Look, you are a healer, you have knowledge of men's souls; of course, I daren't presume that you should believe everything I say, but I assure you most emphatically that I'm not being trivial; the thought of life after death drives me to distraction, it terrifies me... and I don't know who to turn to, I've lacked the courage all my life... And now I've plucked up the courage to turn to you... Oh God! What will you think of me now?' She held up her hands in an outburst of emotion.

'Do not worry about my opinion,' replied the starets. 'I truly can believe your anguish is genuine.'

'Oh, how grateful I am to you! You see, I often shut my eyes and think: if everybody has faith, where do they all get it from? And yet at the same time we are told that, originally, it all came from fear in the face of the threatening forces of nature, and that really there's nothing at all after death! Well, the thought that occurs to me is this: here I am, a lifelong believer, but I'll die, and suddenly there'll be nothing, just "burdock on my grave", as one author* put it. How terrible! How can one buttress one's faith—how? Anyway, I only really believed when I was a small child, automatically, without thinking about it... What proof is there—what? I've come to prostrate myself before you, to ask you for your answer to my question. If I miss this opportunity, nobody will ever give me an answer. What proof is there, how can I dispel my doubts? Oh, I'm so unhappy! And when I look around, I see that no one's concerned about it at all, or practically no one, no one cares about it now, and that it's only me who's worrying herself to death about it all. It's unbearable—simply unbearable!'

'Quite so, quite so. But it's not so much a matter of obtaining proof, as of dispelling doubt.'

'But how?'

'By the practice of active love. Try to love your neighbours actively and steadfastly. The more you practise love, the more you will be convinced of the existence of God and the immortality of your soul. Should you attain total renunciation of self in your love for your neighbour, then your faith will be absolute, and no doubt will ever assail your soul. This has been tried, this has been tested.'

'Active love? That's the problem, and what a problem, what a problem it is! You see, I love mankind so much that, believe me, I sometimes dream of giving up everything, giving up everything I have, leaving Lise and becoming a sister of mercy. I shut my eyes, I think and I dream, and in those moments I feel an insuperable strength within me. No wounds, no festering sores could hold any terrors for me. I would dress them and wash them with my own hands, I would nurse those poor sufferers, I am ready to kiss their sores...'

'That is more than enough, and it's good that your mind is on such thoughts and no others. Who knows, one day you may succeed in accomplishing something good.'

'Yes, but how long could I endure such a life?' the lady continued passionately, almost in a frenzy. 'That's the most important question. That's the most painful of all my questions! I shut my eyes and keep asking myself: how long could I endure that way of life? If the patient whose sores you were tending should fail to respond with immediate gratitude, were on the contrary to start tormenting you with his caprices, neither valuing nor acknowledging your humanitarian services, start shouting at you, making rude demands, even complaining to the authorities (as often happens with the very sick)—what then? Would you continue to love, or not? And—imagine, to my disgust, I already know the answer: if there were anything that could immediately dampen my "active" love for humanity, it would be ingratitude. In other words, I work for payment, I demand instant payment, that is, to be praised and paid with love for my love. I am incapable of loving on any other terms!'

She was in the throes of the most fervent self-castigation, and, having finished, gave the starets a look full of challenge and resolve.

'That's exactly what a doctor said to me once, a long time ago though,' observed the starets. 'He was already elderly and unquestionably a wise man. He spoke just as frankly as you have done, but with humour, bitter humour. I love mankind, he said, but I'm surprised at myself; the more I love mankind in general, the less I love men in particular, that is, separately, as individuals. In my thoughts, he said to me, I've often had a passionate desire to serve humanity, and would perhaps have actually gone to the cross for mankind if I had ever been required to do so, and yet at the same time, as I well know from my personal experience, I'm incapable of enduring two days in the same room with any other person. The moment anybody comes close to me, his personality begins to overpower my self-esteem and intrude upon my freedom. Within one day I can end up hating the very best of men, some because they take too long over their dinner, others because they've caught a cold and keep blowing their noses. I become a misanthrope, he said, the minute I come into contact with people. And it has always been the same with me; the more I have detested people individually, the more passionately I have loved humanity in general.'

'But what can one do? What is one to do in such cases? Must one be driven to despair?'

'No, for it is enough that you should agonize over it. Do what you can and it will be rendered to your account. You have accomplished much already, for you have come to know your own self deeply and sincerely. If, however, you are speaking as frankly as you are doing now merely in order to be praised for your truthfulness, then of course you will never attain active love, you won't progress beyond the contemplative stage, and your whole life will flash past like a shadow. Naturally enough, you'll forget all about life in the hereafter, though ultimately you may well find contentment of some sort or other.'

'You have crushed me utterly! Even as you were talking, I was conscious that when I was telling you about my inability to tolerate ingratitude, I was really hoping you would praise my sincerity. You have fathomed me, you have seen into my very being, and you've explained to me so much about myself!'

'Are you being sincere? Well, after such an admission, I believe you are honest and of good heart. Even if you do not attain happiness, always remember that you are on the right path, and try not to deviate from it. The main thing is to abhor dishonesty, any kind of dishonesty, but above all, dishonesty with regard to your own self. Be aware of your dishonesty and ponder it every hour, every minute of the day. Never be squeamish, both with regard to yourself and others; what appears to you disgusting in yourself is cleansed by the very fact that you have acknowledged it within yourself. Avoid giving in to fear too, since all fear is only the consequence of falsity. Never be afraid of your own faint-heartedness in the endeavour to love, nor even too fearful of any bad actions that you may commit in the course of that endeavour. I am sorry I cannot say anything more comforting to you, for active love compared with contemplative love is a hard and awesome business. Contemplative love seeks a heroic deed that can be accomplished without delay and in full view of everyone. Indeed, some people are even ready to lay down their lives as long as the process is not long drawn out but takes place quickly, as though it were being staged for everybody to watch and applaud. Active love, on the other hand, is unremitting hard work and tenacity, and for some it is a veritable science. But let me tell you in advance: even as you may realize with horror that, in spite of your best efforts, not only have you not come any nearer to your goal, but you may even have receded from it, it is precisely at that moment, I tell you, that you will suddenly reach your goal and clearly behold the wondrous power of God, who has at all times loved you, at all times mysteriously guided you. I am sorry, I cannot stay any longer with you; people are waiting for me. Goodbye.'

The lady was weeping.

'Please bless my Lise, please bless her!' she said with a start.

'She doesn't deserve to be loved. I saw her playing the fool all the while I was speaking,' the starets said teasingly. 'Why have you been giggling at Aleksei all the time?'

Lise really had been giggling at him. She had been aware ever since their last meeting that Alyosha was embarrassed by her and was trying not to look at her, and this had begun to amuse her no end. She had been trying hard to catch his eye. Unable to withstand her steadfast gaze, which attracted him like an irresistible force, Alyosha would suddenly weaken and look up at her, and encounter her beaming, triumphant smile. This would embarrass and irritate him even more. At last he turned away from her completely and hid himself behind the starets. After a few minutes, drawn by the same irresistible force, he again turned round to see if she was still looking at him, and caught sight of her leaning almost completely out of her invalid chair as she peered round at him, willing him with all her might to look at her. When she caught his eye, she burst into such a fit of laughter that even the starets could not resist remarking:

'Why are you embarrassing him so, you naughty young lady?'

Quite unexpectedly, Lise suddenly blushed, her eyes flashed, her face became deadly serious, and, her voice quivering with indignation and recrimination, she exclaimed:

'Why has he forgotten everything? He used to carry me in his arms when I was small, we used to play together. He used to give me reading lessons, do you realize that? Two years ago, when he was saying goodbye to me, he said he'd never forget that we'd be friends for ever and ever! And now he's suddenly afraid of me, as though I was going to eat him or something! Why doesn't he ever come near me, why doesn't he talk to me? Why doesn't he ever come to see us? Surely you don't stop him, do you? We know very well he goes everywhere. It wouldn't be proper for me to invite him; he ought to act on his own initiative, unless he just doesn't want to know. Oh, I suppose he's a monk now! Why have you dressed him in that flapping cassock?... If he runs he'll trip over it...'

And suddenly, unable to bear it any longer, she covered her face with her hands and was convulsed with laughter, terrible, uncontrollable, protracted, hysterical, silent laughter that made her shake all over. The starets listened to her with a smile and then blessed her tenderly. But when she started to kiss his hand, she suddenly pressed it to her eyes and burst out crying.

'Don't be angry with me, I'm such a fool, I'm worthless... and perhaps Alyosha is right after all, quite right not to want to come and see someone who's so ridiculous.'

'I shall make sure he visits you,' the starets promised.

5

AMEN, AMEN!

THE starets was absent from the cell for about twenty-five minutes. It had already gone half past twelve, but still there was no sign of Dmitry Fyodorovich, on whose account everybody had assembled. It looked almost as though they had forgotten about him, and when the starets returned to the cell, he found his guests engaged in the liveliest of conversations. Ivan Fyodorovich and the two hieromonks dominated the conversation. Miusov kept on trying to join in, clearly very agitated, but once again he was out of luck; he was obviously being ignored, and the others hardly even bothered to reply to him, which only served to exacerbate his increasing irritation. He had in fact crossed swords with Ivan Fyodorovich before on learned matters, and had found his supercilious attitude intolerable. 'At least I've kept abreast of all the latest developments in Europe up to now, but this new generation completely ignores us,' he thought to himself. Fyodor Pavlovich, who had promised to remain seated and keep quiet, did indeed stay silent for some time, although he went on looking at Pyotr Aleksandrovich with a derisive smile, and appeared to be enjoying the spectacle of his discomfiture. He had been intending to settle old scores with him for some time and did not want to miss the opportunity now. Finally, unable to resist, he leaned towards his neighbour and, in a low voice, had another go at him:

'Why didn't you leave just now, after I said "kissing it lovingly"? Why did you agree to stay in such disreputable company? I'll tell you why, you felt insulted and hurt to the quick, so you stayed behind to get your own back by showing off your intelligence. Now you're definitely not going to leave until you've demonstrated your intelligence to them.'

'Don't you start again! You're quite wrong, I'm leaving now.'

'You'll be the last, the very last to leave!' Fyodor Pavlovich goaded him. Just at that moment the starets returned.

The argument subsided briefly, but the starets, having resumed his seat, looked round at his visitors amicably as though inviting them to continue. Alyosha, who was familiar with every expression on the starets's face, could see plainly that he was desperately tired but was trying not to show it. Lately during his sickness he had been suffering from fainting fits due to exhaustion. A pallor such as usually preceded a fainting fit now spread over his face and his lips turned white. But he evidently did not wish to break up the gathering, probably for some special reason—but what? Alyosha watched him intently.

'We are discussing this gentleman's very interesting article,' said Father Yosif, the librarian, turning to the starets and motioning to Ivan Fyodorovich. 'It contains many new ideas, but I think the main idea could be interpreted in two ways. It's an article on the question of ecclesiastical courts and the limits of their jurisdiction, written in reply to a member of the clergy who wrote a whole book on the subject...'

'Unfortunately I've not read your article, but I've heard about it,' the starets interrupted, looking at Ivan Fyodorovich with a sharp, penetrating gaze.

'It is written from a very interesting standpoint,' continued the librarian. 'It would seem that he completely rejects the separation of Church and state as far as the ecclesiastical courts are concerned.'

'That is very interesting, but in what sense do you mean?' the starets asked Ivan Fyodorovich.

After a brief pause the latter replied, not with an air of supercilious politeness as Alyosha had previously feared, but modestly and discreetly, with an obviously obliging air and clearly without any ulterior motive.

'I start from the proposition that this mingling of elements, that is, of the essence of Church and state, taken separately, may very well go on for ever, in spite of the fact that it's impossible and cannot be brought into any normal, let alone reconcilable relationship, because it's based on a fallacy. To my mind a compromise between Church and state in such matters as, for instance, administration of the law is, in the very essence and nature of things, quite impossible. The churchman with whom I took issue maintains that the Church occupies a precisely defined position within the state. However, I argued that, on the contrary, the Church should incorporate the whole of the state within itself rather than occupy a mere niche within it, and that if this is not possible at present for some reason, it should undoubtedly be made the principal and most urgent task throughout the future development of Christian society.'

'Quite correct!' the taciturn and learned Father Païsy remarked with terse authority.

'That's purest ultramontanism!' exclaimed Miusov, impatiently crossing one leg over the other.

'But we haven't got any mountains here!' retorted Father Yosif, and, turning to the starets, continued: 'Anyway, the gentleman replies as follows to the "basic and essential" tenets of his opponent, a churchman, mark you: firstly, that no social institution can or should assume the power to administer the civil or political rights of its members; secondly, that the power of the criminal and civil law should not be vested in the Church, for such power is incompatible with the very nature of the Church, both as a divine institution and as a community of people pursuing religious goals; and thirdly and finally, that the Church is a kingdom not of this world...'

'Playing with words,' Father Païsy again interrupted, unable to contain himself. 'Most unworthy of a member of the clergy. I have read the book with which you take issue,' he said, turning to Ivan Fyodorovich, 'and am astounded that a churchman could claim that "the Church is a kingdom not of this world". If it is not of this world,* then it follows that there is no room for it on earth at all. In the Holy Scriptures the words "not of this world" are used in a different sense. One ought not to juggle with such words. Our Lord Jesus Christ came specifically to establish the Church on earth. The Kingdom of Heaven is, of course, not on earth, but in heaven, which cannot be entered except through the Church which has been founded and established on earth. Therefore, worldly play on words here is inadmissible and unworthy. The Church truly is a kingdom, and is destined to reign, and in the end will without doubt be established upon the whole earth as a kingdom, for so it has been promised...'*

He suddenly checked himself and stopped dead. Ivan Fyodorovich, having respectfully and attentively heard him out, continued to address the starets with extreme composure but as eagerly and ingenuously as before.

'The main argument of my article is that in ancient times,

during the first three centuries of the Christian era, Christianity on earth was the Church and nothing but the Church. When, however, the pagan Roman state chose to embrace Christianity,* it inevitably happened that, on becoming Christian, it merely absorbed the Church into itself, while remaining in very many respects a pagan state. Indeed, that is the only thing that could have happened. But too much of the pagan civilization and wisdom had been retained in the state of Rome, such as, for instance, the very aims and foundations of the state. The Church of Christ, having joined with the state, obviously could not relinquish any of its principles however, or any of the rocks on which it stood, nor could it pursue any other goals except its own, which had been firmly established and revealed by Our Lord Himself, namely, the transformation of the whole world, including the whole of the ancient pagan state, into the Church. Thus (looking ahead to the future) it is not the Church that must seek a well-defined place within the state, just like "any other social institution" or "association of people pursuing religious aims" (as the Church is described by the author with whom I am in dispute), but, on the contrary, all states on earth must eventually transform themselves wholly into the Church and nothing but the Church, having first renounced all aims that are incompatible with those of the Church. This would in no way demean the state, in no way detract from its honour or glory as a great power, nor from the glory of its leaders, but would merely lead it from its false, pagan, and erroneous path to the correct and true path, which alone leads to eternal goals. This is why the author of *The Principles of the Ecclesiastical Court* would have judged correctly if, while investigating and putting forward these principles, he had regarded them as a temporary and unavoidable compromise necessary in our sinful and imperfect times, and nothing more. But the moment the author of these principles presumes to declare that the theses he is now advancing, some of which Father Yosif has just enumerated, are immutable, elemental, and eternal, then he is in direct conflict with the Church and its holy, eternal, and immutable destiny. There you have my article in a nutshell.'

'In short,' said Father Païsy, stressing every word, 'according to some theories which have gained altogether too much currency in this nineteenth century of ours, the Church must be transformed into the state, from a lower into a higher order, as it were, be subsumed into it, making way for science, the spirit of the age, and civilization. Should it be unwilling to do this however, should it resist, it will become a mere appendage of the state, and, what's more, under its supervision—and this is how it is nowadays in all modern European countries. According to the Russian way of thinking,* however, it is not for the Church to be transformed into the state, as from a lower to a higher order, but, on the contrary, the state must eventually make itself worthy of becoming the Church and nothing but the Church. Amen, amen!'

'Well, sir, I must admit you have rather gladdened my heart,' Miusov said with a smile, recrossing his legs. 'As I understand it, it is a question of realizing some kind of ideal in the infinitely distant future, at the Second Coming perhaps. I suppose you know best. A splendid utopian dream of no more wars, diplomats, banks, and so forth. Sounds remarkably like socialism. And there was I thinking that you were in earnest and that the Church would *now*, for instance, sit in judgement on criminals and sentence them to the birch and hard labour, and, come to that, to death.'

'Well, even if there were only ecclesiastical courts nowadays,' said Ivan Fyodorovich calmly and without batting an eyelid, 'even then the Church would not be sentencing people to hard labour or death. Crime and people's attitudes to it would undoubtedly have had time to change by then, little by little, of course—not suddenly and immediately—but soon enough...'

'Are you serious?' Miusov looked hard at him.

'If the Church were to take over everything, then, rather than strike off their heads, it would excommunicate the guilty and the disobedient,' continued Ivan Fyodorovich. 'Where would the excommunicated criminal go, I ask you? Just think, he would have to leave not only his people, as now, but he would have to leave Christ. By his crime, he would have rebelled not only against men, but against Christ's Church. Strictly speaking, of course, this is how it is now, too, though it is not spelled out, and the modern criminal is very often able to come to an accommodation with his own conscience: "All right, so I've committed theft, but I'm not attacking the Church. I'm not an enemy of Christ." That's what the present-day criminal keeps saying to himself, but were the Church to take the place of the state, he'd find it difficult to say that without defying the whole Church throughout the world. "Everybody is mistaken," he would then have to say, "everybody is in error, the whole Church is false. I alone, murderer and thief, am the true Christian Church." That would be very difficult for anyone to say to himself; it would require extraordinary conditions and circumstances which seldom obtain. Now, conversely, take the attitude of the Church itself to crime: would it not have to change its present, almost pagan attitude, and rather than technically sever the diseased limb, as is done nowadays for the protection of society, transform itself totally and truly in order to strive for the regeneration of man, for his resurrection and salvation...?'

'What's all this? You've lost me again,' interrupted Miusov. 'Is this another of your dreams? It doesn't make sense, I don't follow you. What do you mean—excommunication? What excommunication? I suspect you're just making fun of us, Ivan Fyodorovich.'

'As a matter of fact, that's just how it is nowadays.' The starets suddenly spoke, and everyone turned to him. 'If the Church of Christ did not exist now, there would be nothing to deter the criminal from evil, nor would there even be any punishment later, genuine punishment, that is, as opposed to the technical kind that has just been mentioned, and which in the majority of cases only embitters the heart, whereas real punishment, the only kind that is effective, the only kind that deters and reconciles, is that which is conveyed through the awareness of conscience.'

'Well, I never, please explain!' said Miusov, full of the most lively curiosity.

'It is like this,' the starets began. 'All this sentencing to hard labour, and in the past flogging too, has reformed no one, and, what's more, it has done little to deter the criminal, and the number of crimes has not only not decreased, but with the passage of time even continues to increase. Surely you must agree with this. Hence it turns out that society is not protected at all, for even though the criminal element may be technically outlawed and exiled somewhere far out of sight, his place is immediately filled by another criminal, perhaps even two. If there is anything, even in our time, that can protect society and reform the criminal, make a new person of him, then it is Christ's law alone, operating through his own conscience. Only by recognizing his own guilt as a son of Christ's society, that is, of the Church, can the criminal recognize his guilt before society itself, that is, before the Church. Thus it is only before the Church, rather than the state, that the modern criminal can recognize his guilt. Now, if passing judgement were the prerogative of society acting as the Church, society would know whom to pardon and restore to the fold. As things stand, however, the Church, not having any actual judicial power and being capable only of passing moral censure, seeks to refrain from actually imposing punishment upon the criminal. It does not excommunicate him, but nor does it withhold wise counsel. Furthermore, the Church even attempts to preserve its full pastoral role with respect to the criminal; it allows him to attend Church services, to receive Holy Communion, gives him alms, and treats him more as a victim than an offender. And now, what would happen to the criminal if, God forbid, Christian society too, that is, the Church, were to reject him as the law of the state rejects him and cuts him off? What would happen if, after punishment by the law of the state, the Church were immediately to inflict its own punishment of excommunication? There could be no greater despair, at least for the Russian criminal, because Russian criminals are still believers. Who knows, perhaps something terrible would then ensue—perhaps the despairing criminal would suffer a loss of faith. What then? But the Church, like a gentle and loving mother, shrinks from actual punishment, believing that the wrongdoer is sufficiently chastised by the law of the state alone, and that someone at least ought to take pity on him. The main reason that it shrinks from actual punishment, however, is that the judgement of the Church is the only one to incorporate truth, and therefore it cannot in substance or in spirit coexist with any other judgement, even as a temporary expedient. There can be no question of striking any bargains here. The foreign criminal, they say, seldom repents, because all the most modern teachings confirm him in the belief that his crime is not a crime, but merely a rebellion against the injustice

of an oppressive force. Society cuts him off from itself in a
triumph of temporal power over him, and compounds the
severance with hatred (at least, that is what they proclaim in
Europe)—with hatred, being totally indifferent to and oblivious
of his subsequent fate as a fellow human being. Thus everything
takes place without the slightest sympathy from the Church,
because in many places now there is no Church at all, only
churchmen and splendid church buildings, the Church itself
having long striven to make the transition from the lower
ecclesiastical order to the higher temporal order, in order to be
absorbed completely into the state. This would appear to be the
case in the Lutheran countries, anyway. As for Rome, it was
pronounced a state* instead of a Church a thousand years ago.
Therefore the criminal no longer considers himself a member of
the Church, and when he is excommunicated he falls into despair.
Should he return to society, however, then he is often so bitter
that he cuts himself off from it. What the outcome of this will
be, you may judge for yourselves. In many respects it would
seem that the same applies to our country too, but the point is
that, besides the established civil courts, we also have above all
the Church, which never loses touch with the criminal, who is
still a dear and precious son, and the important thing is that the
judgement of the Church exists and is maintained, if only in
thought; the Church does not actually punish at present, but it
reserves its judgement as a vision for the future, and the criminal
instinctively recognizes this. What was said here a moment ago
is perfectly true; if the judgement of the Church really were to
be established in all its power, that is, if the whole of society
were to become the Church, then not only would the judgement
of the Church have a more reforming effect on the criminal than
ever before, but indeed crime itself would perhaps be drastically
reduced. And in many instances the Church of the future would
have a quite different attitude to the criminal and to crime; it
would be in a position to return the outcast to the fold, to warn
the prospective transgressor and to succour the fallen. Granted,'
the starets smiled, 'Christian society itself is not yet ready for
this, and rests merely on seven righteous men;* but, as they are
always sufficient, it stands fast and awaits its total transformation
from a more or less pagan society into the one universal and

omnipotent Church. And this shall be, this shall be, though it may take to the end of time before it shall come to pass, for this, and only this, is ordained! It is not for you to know the times or the seasons,* for the mystery of the times and the seasons is in the wisdom of God, in His providence and in His love. And what by man's reckoning may yet be very distant, by God's preordaining may already be on the eve of its manifestation, even at the doors.* Amen!'

'Amen! Amen!' Father Païsy affirmed reverently and gravely.

'Strange, most uncommonly strange!' said Miusov, in pent-up indignation rather than anger.

'What is it you find strange?' Father Yosif enquired cautiously.

'What are we supposed to make of all this?' Miusov exploded. 'The state is to be done away with on earth, and the Church is to be elevated to the level of the state! That isn't just ultramontanism, that's arch-ultramontanism! Not even Pope Gregory VII* could have thought of anything like that!'

'You've completely misunderstood the position!' said Father Païsy severely. 'It's not the Church that becomes the state, don't you see? That would be Rome's way. That is Satan's third temptation.* On the contrary, it is the state that transforms itself into the Church, elevates itself to the Church and *becomes* the Church over all the earth, which of course is the complete opposite of any ultramontanism and Rome and all your talk, and is nothing less than the preordained task of Orthodoxy upon earth. The star will shine forth from the East.'*

Miusov remained demonstratively silent. His whole bearing expressed immense dignity. A supercilious and condescending smile appeared on his lips. Alyosha had followed the whole scene with a pounding heart. The conversation had disturbed him profoundly. He happened to glance at Rakitin, standing motionless by the door where he had stood throughout, looking and listening intently even though his eyes remained lowered. Seeing his flushed face, Alyosha guessed that Rakitin too was disturbed, probably no less than he; Alyosha knew why he was disturbed.

'Gentlemen, allow me to tell you a little story,' Miusov said suddenly, with an especially imposing air. 'Some years ago in Paris, soon after the December Revolution,* I happened to be visiting an acquaintance of mine, an extremely important person, a member of the government at the time, and at his house I met a very interesting man. This person was not actually a secret agent himself, but was in charge of a whole department of secret agents—a fairly influential post in its way. Taking advantage of the opportunity, I struck up a conversation with him out of sheer curiosity, and since he had not been invited there as a social acquaintance but in an official capacity to deliver some sort of report, and seeing for himself how I was received by his chief, he did me the honour of speaking to me with some frankness—up to a point of course, that is to say he was polite rather than candid, that French kind of politeness, especially as he saw he was addressing a foreigner. But I understood him very well. The subject was the socialist revolutionaries, who were being pursued at the time. To cut a long story short, I'll just quote a most interesting remark that this fellow came out with. "To tell you the truth," he said, "we're not worried about every last one of these socialists—anarchists, atheists, revolutionaries, and the like. We keep an eye on them and their movements are known to us, but amongst them there are a few, though not many, of a special kind: they believe in God, they're Christians, but they are socialists at the same time. They're the ones we fear most of all; they're terrible people! A Christian socialist is more formidable than an atheist socialist." I was struck by these words at the time, and listening to you just now, gentlemen, happened to remind me of them—'

'So you think they apply to us, you take us for socialists?' Father Païsy asked straight out, without mincing his words. But before Pyotr Aleksandrovich had time to reply the door opened and in came the long-awaited Dmitry Fyodorovich. By this time everyone had given up expecting him, and his sudden appearance was greeted with astonishment.

6

A MAN LIKE HIM DOESN'T DESERVE TO LIVE!

DMITRY FYODOROVICH, a young man of twenty-eight, of medium height and pleasing aspect, looked, however, much older than his years. He was muscular and, by all appearances, physically very strong; nevertheless, there was something sickly about his face. It was gaunt, with sunken, unhealthy-looking sallow cheeks. For all the resolute intensity of his protruding, rather large dark eyes, there was a certain indecision in them. Even when he was agitated and spoke in anger, the look in his eyes seemed to be at variance with his mood and to be expressing something quite different, something quite unrelated to the present moment. 'Difficult to tell what he's thinking,' those who talked to him would sometimes remark. Others, seeing something melancholy and pensive in his eyes, would occasionally be astonished at his sudden laughter, indicative of the cheerful and playful nature of his thoughts at the very moment when he appeared to be so gloomy. There was a possible explanation, however, for his sickly-looking appearance at that time: everyone knew of the extremely wild and dissolute life to which he had abandoned himself since his arrival, and everyone was equally well aware of the extreme state of exasperation to which he had been driven by the squabbles with his father over the disputed money. This had already become a topic of conversation in the town. It is true that he was irritable by nature, 'erratic and unstable', as our justice of the peace, Semyon Ivanovich Kachalnikov, had aptly described him at a gathering in our town. He entered the cell impeccably dressed, in a buttoned-up frock-coat and black gloves, holding a top hat in his hand. As a military man who had recently resigned his commission, he still sported a moustache, but was otherwise clean-shaven. His dark-brown hair was trimmed short and brushed forward at the temples. He walked with long, resolute, soldierly strides. He stopped briefly in the doorway, glanced round the room, and made straight for the starets, whom he surmised to be the host. He bowed deeply and asked for his blessing; the starets half rose and blessed him.

Dmitry Fyodorovich kissed his hand respectfully and said in extreme agitation, almost in vexation:

'Will you be so kind as to excuse me for keeping you waiting so long, but my father's servant, Smerdyakov, when I asked him specially about the time of the meeting, assured me twice most definitely that it was at one o'clock. And now I discover...'

'Don't worry,' the starets interrupted. 'You're a little late, but it doesn't matter, it's no great misfortune.'

'I'm very grateful to you, and I couldn't have expected any less from your kindness.' Having snapped out these words, Dmitry Fyodorovich bowed once more and then, turning towards his father, gave an equally deep and respectful bow to him. It was clear that he had thought about this bow beforehand and that he intended it sincerely, considering it his duty to convey his humble respect and good intentions. Fyodor Pavlovich, although taken by surprise, made a prompt and fitting gesture; in response to Dmitry Fyodorovich's bow, he jumped to his feet and reciprocated with an equally deep bow. His face suddenly took on a grave expression, which, however, lent it an air of extreme malice. Then, without saying another word, Dmitry Fyodorovich made a general bow to the rest of the company, strode to the window with his long decisive steps, sat down on the only available chair close to Father Païsy, and leaned forward with his whole body in immediate readiness to concentrate on the conversation that he had interrupted.

Dmitry Fyodorovich's entry could not have taken more than about two minutes, and the conversation resumed immediately. By now, however, Pyotr Aleksandrovich did not deem it necessary to reply to Father Païsy's determined and almost peeved question.

'With your permission, I should like to drop this subject,' he said with a nonchalant air. 'It's a pretty complicated one, anyway. There, Ivan Fyodorovich is smiling at us: no doubt he too has something interesting to say about this. Ask him!'

'I've nothing much to say, except for one small point,' Ivan Fyodorovich replied immediately, 'and that is that European liberals in general, and even our Russian liberal dilettanti, frequently confuse the end results of socialism with those of Christianity, and have done so for a long time. This outlandish conclusion is, of course, very typical. As a matter of fact, it seems that it's not only the liberals and dilettanti who confuse socialism with Christianity,* but in many cases the forces of law and order do so too—foreign ones, of course. Your Parisian story is quite typical, Pyotr Aleksandrovich.'

'Once and for all, I would ask permission to drop the subject,' Pyotr Aleksandrovich repeated. 'Instead, gentlemen, let me tell you another story about Ivan Fyodorovich himself, a most interesting and characteristic one. Only five days ago, in the course of an argument in local company consisting mostly of ladies, he solemnly observed that there was absolutely nothing in the whole world to induce men to love their fellow men, that there was absolutely no law of nature to make man love humanity, and that if love did exist and had existed at all in the world up to now, then it was not by virtue of the natural law, but entirely because man believed in his own immortality. He added as an aside that it was precisely that which constituted the natural law, namely, that once man's faith in his own immortality was destroyed, not only would his capacity for love be exhausted, but so would the vital forces that sustained life on this earth. And furthermore, nothing would be immoral then, everything would be permitted, even anthropophagy. And finally, as though all this were not enough, he declared that for every individual, such as you and me, for example, who does not believe either in God or in his own immortality,* the natural moral law is bound immediately to become the complete opposite of the religion-based law that preceded it, and that egoism, even extending to the perpetration of crime, would not only be permissible but would be recognized as the essential, the most rational, and even the noblest *raison d'être* of the human condition. By this paradox, gentlemen, you may judge for yourselves what other weird ideas our beloved eccentric and paradoxist Ivan Fyodorovich may entertain, and may perhaps yet have in store for us.'

'Just a moment,' Dmitry Fyodorovich burst out suddenly and unexpectedly. 'If I heard you correctly: "Crime must not only be permitted, it must be recognized as the most necessary and most intelligent way out of the situation in which every non-believer finds himself." Is that what you actually said?'

'Quite right,' said Father Païsy.

'I'll remember that.'

With these words, Dmitry Fyodorovich fell silent just as abruptly as he had interrupted the conversation. Everyone looked at him with curiosity.

'Is that really what you think the consequence would be if man were to lose faith in the immortality of the soul?' the starets suddenly asked Ivan Fyodorovich.

'Yes, that is what I argued. There can be no virtue without immortality.'

'You are blessed if that is what you believe, or else you must be very unhappy!'

'Why unhappy?' Ivan Fyodorovich smiled.

'Because in all likelihood you believe neither in the immortality of your soul nor even in what you wrote about the Church and its role in society.'

'You may be right!... Still, I wasn't just joking either...', Ivan Fyodorovich confessed suddenly and unexpectedly, and immediately blushed.

'You were not just joking, that is very true. You have not yet come to terms with this idea in your heart, and you are tormented by it. But the martyr too may sometimes trivialize his despair, out of desperation you understand. As things stand, your magazine articles and discussions at social gatherings are no more than trivialized pursuits born of desperation; having lost faith in your own dialectics, you have turned at heart into a bitter cynic... The problem remains unresolved in your mind, and until it is, you shall remain profoundly unhappy...'

'But can I resolve it? Can I resolve it in a positive sense?' Ivan Fyodorovich continued his strange questioning, still looking at the starets with the same enigmatic smile.

'If the question cannot be resolved in a positive sense, it will never be resolved in a negative one either; you yourself know this attribute of your soul, and therein lies the whole reason for your torment. But give thanks to the Creator for endowing you with such a noble soul, capable of undergoing such torment: "Set your affections on things above, for our conversation is in heaven."* Pray God that the question may be resolved in your soul while you are still on earth, and may God sanctify your path!'

The starets, remaining seated, raised his hand and was about to bless Ivan Fyodorovich, when the latter suddenly rose from his chair, went up to him, accepted his blessing, and, kissing his hand, returned in silence to his seat. His expression was resolute and serious. This action, like the whole of the preceding conversation with the starets, so unexpected from Ivan Fyodorovich, impressed everyone with its mystery and even gravitas, so that the whole room fell silent for a moment, and an expression close to apprehension appeared on Alyosha's face. But suddenly Miusov shrugged his shoulders, and at the same moment Fyodor Pavlovich sprang to his feet.

'Most divine and holy starets!' he cried, pointing at Ivan Fyodorovich, 'that is my son, flesh of my flesh, my most beloved flesh! He is, so to speak, my most respectful Karl Moor, while this son who has just come in, Dmitry Fyodorovich, and against whom I am seeking justice from you, he is the most disrespectful Franz Moor—both from Schiller's *The Robbers,** and so it follows that I must be the *Regierender Graf von Moor*! Be our judge and save us! Not only do we want you to pray for us, we also want you to enlighten us.'

'Stop acting the fool, and do not start by insulting your family,' said the starets in a feeble, exhausted voice. He was clearly becoming more and more tired, and his strength was visibly ebbing.

'This is a most unworthy farce, which I foresaw on my way here!' Dmitry Fyodorovich exclaimed indignantly, also leaping to his feet. 'I'm sorry, Reverend Father,' he turned to the starets, 'I am an uneducated man and I don't even know how to address you, but you've been deceived, and you were much too kind to allow us to meet here. My father only wants a scandal—he's got his own reasons—he's always got his own reasons. This time, however, I think I know what he's up to...'

'Everybody accuses me, everybody!' Fyodor Pavlovich shouted back. 'Pyotr Aleksandrovich over there, he also accuses me!' He suddenly turned towards Miusov, though the latter had no intention of interrupting him.

'They accuse me of pocketing my children's money and not giving a damn, but, if I'm not mistaken, don't courts of law exist? You'll get what's due to you, Dmitry Fyodorovich; your own receipts, letters, and agreements will show how much you've already received, how much you've squandered, and how much you've still got left! Why doesn't Pyotr Aleksandrovich say something? He knows about Dmitry Fyodorovich. It's because everybody's against me, and when all's said and done it's Dmitry Fyodorovich who owes me money, and not just kopecks but several thousand roubles, I've got all the documentation! Hasn't he been causing havoc right across the town, what with all his goings-on? And in the town where he was garrisoned, he'd think nothing of spending a thousand or two just to seduce some decent young girl; we know all the sordid details, Dmitry Fyodorovich, and I'm going to prove it... Most Reverend Father, would you believe it? He persuaded a most respectable young lady to fall in love with him, one from a good family, well off, the daughter of his former commander, a brave colonel who was awarded the order of St Anne with crossed swords,* compromised her by offering marriage, now she's here all alone, his fiancée, while he goes and deserts her for one of the town's floozies. But even though this floozie has been living, so to say, in common-law wedlock with a certain respectable gentleman, she's an independent type, an impregnable fortress, just like a lawful wedded wife, because she's virtuous—yes, holy fathers, she is virtuous! But Dmitry Fyodorovich wants to unlock this fortress with a golden key, which is why he's here now, trying to bully me into giving him more money when he's already squandered thousands on her; that's why he borrows money all the time, and by the way, can you guess who from? Shall I tell them, Mitya?'

'Don't you dare!' yelled Dmitry Fyodorovich. 'Wait till I've gone. Don't you dare besmirch the name of a most honourable woman in front of me... That you should have the audacity to refer to her is an insult to her... I won't have it!'

He was choking.

'Mitya! Mitya!' Fyodor Pavlovich mocked, his voice quavering as he attempted to shed a few tears. 'What about my parental blessing? What if I put a curse on you, what then?'

'Brazen humbug!' Dmitry Fyodorovich shouted, beside himself.

'His own father, his own father! Think how he must treat others then! Gentlemen, imagine this: there is in this town of ours a poor but respectable man, a retired captain, burdened

with a large family, who had got into trouble and been cashiered—but not publicly, no court martial, his reputation still
intact. Three weeks ago our Dmitry Fyodorovich grabbed him
by his beard in a tavern, dragged him by his beard out into the
street, and beat him up in full view of everyone—and all because
this man happened to be on a small confidential errand of mine.'

'That's a complete lie! On the face of it, it's true, but when
you examine it in more detail, it's a lie!' Dmitry Fyodorovich's
whole body was shaking with rage. 'Father! I'm not trying to
justify my actions. Yes, I openly admit, I behaved like a wild
beast towards the captain, and I now despise myself for my
uncontrollable rage, but that captain, that messenger of yours,
went to the lady whom you referred to as a floozie, and told her
on your instructions that if I persisted in demanding an account
of my property from you, she should take my promissory notes,
which are now in your possession, and sue me to have me
convicted and put behind bars. And now you're reproaching me
for fancying that lady, whereas it was you yourself who instructed
her how to trap me! Didn't you know she owned up and told me
everything, and she just laughed at you! But the real reason you
want to see me in gaol is that you're jealous, because you've
begun to make advances to her yourself, and I know all about it,
she was killing herself with laughter—do you hear me?—killing
herself with laughter as she told me the story. So there you have
the man himself, reverend sirs, the father, reproaching his
depraved son! You gentlemen who are my witnesses, pardon my
rage, but I knew this wily old devil would get us all together just
to create a scandal. I came to forgive and forget if only he'd
offered me his hand! But seeing that he has just insulted not
only me, but also the most honourable of ladies, whose very
name I refuse to mention out of respect for her, I've decided to
expose his whole game in public, father or no father!...'

He was unable to continue. His eyes were blazing and his
breathing was laboured. And everyone else in the cell was
agitated too. All except the starets rose to their feet in alarm.
The hieromonks looked on sternly, but waited to see how the
starets would respond. The latter, however, remained seated,
still looking extremely pale, not from agitation but rather from
the exhaustion of illness. A suppliant smile flickered over his

lips; now and again he would raise his hand as though to restrain the demented visitors, and of course a single gesture of his would have sufficed to terminate the proceedings; but it appeared that he too was waiting for something, and he watched intently, as if trying to fathom something, as though there were something he had not yet grasped. Finally, Pyotr Aleksandrovich Miusov announced that he felt he had been utterly demeaned and disgraced.

'We're all to blame for the scandalous scene we've just witnessed!' he said heatedly. 'Believe me, on my way here I never anticipated it would come to this, even though I knew who I was dealing with... We must put a stop to this at once! Your Reverence, believe me, I really did not have any detailed knowledge of all the goings-on that have just come to light, I didn't want to believe them, and it's the first time I've heard of such a thing... a father jealous of his own son over a disreputable woman and conspiring with the creature herself to put his son behind bars... And this is the company in which I've been obliged to appear here... I've been deceived; I say to all of you that I have been deceived just as much as everybody else has been...'

'Dmitry Fyodorovich!' Fyodor Pavlovich suddenly shouted in an unrecognizable voice. 'If you were not my son, I'd challenge you to a duel this instant... with pistols, at three paces... across a pocket handkerchief!* Across a handkerchief!' he yelled, stamping both his feet.

There are occasions on which old liars, who have spent their whole lives dissembling, get so carried away that they really do tremble and weep with emotion, despite the fact that at that very moment (or only a split second later) they could well admit to themselves, 'You're lying, you old reprobate, you're play-acting even now, never mind all that "sacred" anger of yours, it's all a sham.'

Dmitry Fyodorovich scowled viciously and looked at his father with indescribable contempt.

'I imagined... I imagined', he spoke quietly and with self-control, 'that I would come home to my father with the angel of my heart, my fiancée, and that I would cherish him in his old age, but all I see before me is a depraved old roué and the vilest of buffoons!'

'To a duel!' the old reprobate shrieked again, panting for breath and spluttering saliva with every word. 'As for you, Pyotr Aleksandrovich Miusov, know you this, my good sir, that in the whole of your lineage there isn't and probably never has been a single woman more high-minded and more honest—more honest, do you hear?—than this "creature", as you had the audacity to call her just now! And as for you, Dmitry Fyodorovich, you've exchanged your fiancée for this "creature", and so it follows, in your own estimation, that your fiancée isn't fit to touch the hem of her dress—that's the sort of "creature" she is.'

'For shame!' Father Yosif could not contain himself.

'Shame and disgrace indeed,' Kalganov, who had been silent until now, shouted suddenly, blushing to the roots of his hair, his adolescent voice quivering with emotion.

'A man like him doesn't deserve to live!' Dmitry Fyodorovich growled, beside himself with rage, his awkwardly raised shoulders lending him a hunched appearance. 'Tell me, is he to be allowed to continue to contaminate the earth with his existence?' He looked at everyone in turn, pointing at the old man with his finger. He spoke slowly and deliberately.

'Did you hear him, holy fathers, did you hear the murderer?' Fyodor Pavlovich turned on Father Yosif. 'Here's the answer to your "for shame"! What shame? This "creature", this "disreputable woman", is holier, perhaps, than any of you monks seeking salvation here! Maybe her fall goes back to her youth, to her repressive background, but she "loved much",* and Christ forgave her that loved much...'

'It wasn't for that kind of love that Christ forgave...', the meek Father Yosif objected querulously.

'Wrong, it *was* for that kind, precisely for that kind, holy monks, for just that kind! Here you are, saving your souls on pickled cabbage, and you imagine yourselves to be righteous! You eat gudgeon, one gudgeon a day, and you think you can buy God with gudgeon!'

'Intolerable, quite intolerable!' The words resounded all round the cell.

But this whole disgraceful scene came to an abrupt end. The starets suddenly stood up. Alyosha, overcome by fear and embarrassment, nevertheless managed to reach out and support him by the arm. The starets walked towards Dmitry Fyodorovich and, when he was right next to him, went down on his knees before him. For a brief second Alyosha thought he had stumbled from exhaustion, but this was not so. As he went down on his knees, the starets made an obeisance, a full, unmistakable and conscious obeisance, even touching the floor with his forehead at Dmitry Fyodorovich's feet. Alyosha was so astonished that he even failed to assist him when he was rising to his feet. A faint smile played around the starets's lips.

'Forgive me! Forgive me, all!' he said, bowing in all directions to his guests.

For a few moments Dmitry Fyodorovich stood thunderstruck: the starets kneeling at his feet—what could it mean? At last he cried out, 'Oh God!' and, covering his face with his hands, rushed out of the room. The other guests followed him in a crowd, forgetting in their confusion to take leave of their host. Only the hieromonks went up to him again for his blessing.

'Why did he kneel before him—was it some kind of symbolism again, or something?' muttered Fyodor Pavlovich in an attempt to strike up a conversation, but not daring to address anyone in particular and visibly cowed for some reason. At that moment the whole company was leaving through the hermitage gates.

'I cannot be responsible for a madhouse or the madmen inside it,' Miusov immediately retorted angrily, 'but I shall rid myself of your company once and for all, Fyodor Pavlovich. Where's that monk now?...'

That monk, the one who had invited them to dine with the abbot, did not keep them waiting. He met the guests at the bottom of the steps leading down from the starets's cell, as though he had been waiting for them there all the time.

'Honourable father,' Pyotr Aleksandrovich said to the monk irritably, 'would you be kind enough to convey my profound respects to the reverend abbot, with my personal apologies to his eminence, and say that, owing to sudden and unforeseen circumstances, it will be quite impossible for me, despite my most heartfelt wishes, to have the honour of partaking of the repast.'

'My word, unforeseen circumstances—he means me!' Fyodor Pavlovich immediately joined in. 'Did you hear that, father?

Pyotr Aleksandrovich objects to my company, otherwise he'd
have accepted immediately. You must go, Pyotr Aleksandrovich,
you must accept the reverend abbot's invitation and—*bon appétit!*
Remember, though, I'm the one who's declining the invitation,
not you! I'm going straight home, I shall eat at home. I find it
impossible to eat here, Pyotr Aleksandrovich, my very dear
cousin.'

'I'm not your cousin and never have been, you despicable
wretch!'

'I said it on purpose to annoy you, because you insist on
denying that you're a relative of mine; you're my kinsman though,
however much you may try to deny it. I can prove it to you from
church records. You can stay here if you want, Ivan Fyodorovich.
I'll send the horses to fetch you when it's time. As for you, Pyotr
Aleksandrovich, it's only common politeness that you should go
to the reverend abbot to apologize for what we both got up to
just now...'

'Are you really going home then? Or is it just one of your
tricks?'

'Pyotr Aleksandrovich, after what's happened I simply
wouldn't dare to show my face there! I got carried away; I'm
sorry, gentlemen, I got completely carried away! I'm deeply
shocked! And, what's more, ashamed! My dear sirs, one man
will have a heart like Alexander the Great's, another like a little
lap-dog's; mine's like the little lap-dog's. I've lost my nerve!
After a scene like that, how could I possibly stay for lunch and
tuck into the monastic delicacies? I'd be too ashamed, I couldn't,
I'm sorry!'

'God only knows, he's up to something!' Miusov paused to
reflect, following the retreating buffoon with a mistrustful eye.
The latter turned round and, noticing that Pyotr Aleksandrovich
was watching him, blew him a kiss.

'What about you, are you going to go?' Miusov asked Ivan
Fyodorovich curtly.

'Why not? After all, I did have a special invitation from the
abbot yesterday.'

'Unfortunately, I really do feel I have an obligation to go to
this wretched lunch,' Miusov continued with the same bitter
irritability, paying not the slightest attention to the presence of

the little monk. 'At least we should apologize for the scene we created and explain that it wasn't our fault. What do you think?'

'Yes, we must explain it wasn't our fault. Besides, father isn't going to be there,' Ivan Fyodorovich added.

'Your father would be the last straw! This damned lunch!'

At last they all set off. The monk kept quiet and listened. On the way through the wood he commented only that the reverend abbot had already been waiting a long time and that they were over half an hour late. No one replied. Miusov glanced at Ivan Fyodorovich with loathing.

'Off he goes to lunch as if nothing had happened!' he said to himself. 'A brazen face and a Karamazov's conscience.'

7

THE CAREERIST SEMINARIAN

ALYOSHA took the starets into the bedroom, and helped him to sit down on his bed. It was a very small room containing only essential furniture; instead of a mattress, the narrow iron bed had just a strip of felt on. In a corner of the room, by the icons, stood a lectern on which lay a crucifix and a copy of the New Testament. The starets lowered himself on to the bed, exhausted; his eyes were staring and he breathed with difficulty. Having settled on the bed, he gave Alyosha a penetrating look, as though he were deliberating about something.

'Off you go now, my dear boy, off you go! Porfiry will see to me, you hurry along. You should go to the abbot's and serve at table.'

'I'd rather stay here, with your blessing,' Alyosha said imploringly.

'You're of greater need there. There is no peace between them. You will help them at table and make yourself useful. Should devilry rear its head, say a prayer. You must know, my son (the starets liked to address him thus), this will not be the place for you in the future. Remember that, my boy. As soon as God sees fit that I should pass away—leave the monastery. Leave it for ever.'

Alyosha shuddered.

'What is wrong? This is not the place for you. I give you my blessing to go out into the world in humility and obedience. You still have a long pilgrimage before you. And you must marry, you must. You will have to endure all things before you return. There is much to accomplish. But I have confidence in you, which is why I am sending you forth. Christ be with you. Do not forsake Him, and He will not forsake you. You will experience much grief, and in grief you will find happiness. Here is my commandment to you: seek happiness in grief! Toil, toil unceasingly. Remember my words henceforth, for even though I shall talk with you again, not only my days but my hours too are numbered.'

Alyosha's face crumpled. The corners of his mouth trembled.

'What is it now?' the starets smiled gently. 'Let the lay people bid farewell to their departed ones in tears, here we rejoice when a father departs. We rejoice and we pray for him. Leave me now. I must pray. Go, you must make haste. Stay close to your brothers. Not just to one, but to both.'

The starets raised his hand in blessing. Although Alyosha would dearly have liked to stay behind, there was no room for argument. On the tip of his tongue was a question he was dying to ask—what had been the significance of that obeisance before his brother Dmitry—but he did not have the courage. He knew that the starets would have explained it to him of his own accord if that were possible. But it seemed that that was not his wish. That obeisance had made an extraordinary impression on Alyosha; he believed blindly that it had a mysterious purpose. Mysterious, and perhaps even terrible. As he hurried through the gates of the hermitage on the way to the monastery for the abbot's dinner (merely to serve at table, of course), his heart suddenly contracted with pain and he stopped dead: it was as if he heard the words of the starets once more, foretelling his impending death. What the starets foretold, especially with such exactitude, would undoubtedly come about, that was a sacred article of faith for Alyosha. But how was he to survive without him, what would it be like not to see him or hear him any more? And where would he go? 'He commands me not to weep and to leave the monastery. Oh Lord!' It was a long time since Alyosha

had experienced such deep anguish. He quickened his pace
through the wood which separated the cloister from the monastery and, unable to endure the thoughts weighing so heavily upon
him, looked up at the ancient pines growing on either side of the
forest track. The walk was not long, about five hundred paces,
no more; at this hour he was unlikely to meet anyone. But
suddenly, on the first bend, he noticed Rakitin. He was waiting
for someone.

'You're not waiting for me, are you?' asked Alyosha as he drew
level with him.

'Yes, I am,' Rakitin smiled. 'You're hurrying to the abbot's,
aren't you? I know. He's giving a lunch. There hasn't been a
lunch like it since he entertained the archbishop and General
Pakhatov, do you remember? I shan't be there, but you go along,
and serve the garnished meats. Tell me one thing, Aleksei: what
was that performance all about? That's what I wanted to ask
you.'

'What performance?'

'Well, that obeisance he made to your brother Dmitry Fyodorovich. He put his head right down to the floor!'

'Are you talking about Father Zosima?'

'Yes, Father Zosima.'

'His head?'

'Oh, I'm being disrespectful! Well, too bad if I am. So, what
was that performance supposed to mean?'

'I don't know, Misha.'

'Ah, I knew he wouldn't explain it to you. Of course, there
was nothing out of the ordinary, it seemed to be just the usual
holy nonsense. Still, the gesture was quite deliberate. It will get
all the sanctimonious hypocrites in town talking, and soon the
whole province will want to know: "What was all that performance about?" I think the old man's really pretty shrewd: he's
smelt a crime in the air. Your family reeks of it.'

'What crime?'

Rakitin was evidently anxious to have his say.

'Someone's going to get hurt in your family. It will be
something between your brothers and your wealthy father. So,
in anticipation of what might happen, Zosima struck the ground
with his forehead. Next thing it'll be: "After all, the holy man

predicted it, his prophecy has come true"—some prophecy, just because he struck the ground with his forehead! They'll say it was a sign, a portent, and heaven knows what else! He'll be celebrated, he'll be remembered: he'll have predicted a crime, they'll say, identified the criminal. That's always the way with these holy fools: they insist on making the sign of the cross in front of a tavern and will hurl stones at a church. Just the same with your starets: he drives the righteous away with a stick, and grovels at the feet of a murderer.'

'What crime? What murderer? What are you talking about?' Both Alyosha and Rakitin stopped dead in their tracks.

'What murderer? As though you didn't know! I bet it had already occurred to you too. Come to think of it, I'm intrigued: listen, Alyosha, you're forever telling the truth, even though you always end up sitting on the fence: had it occurred to you, or not? Come now.'

'Yes, it had,' Alyosha replied softly. Even Rakitin was taken aback.

'What was that? You mean, it really had occurred to you too?' he exclaimed.

'I... I hadn't exactly thought about it,' Alyosha mumbled, 'but when you began to talk about it so strangely just now, it seemed to me that it had already occurred to me.'

'You see, I couldn't have put it clearer myself, you see? Today you looked at your father and your brother Mitya, and you thought, there's going to be a crime. So I'm not mistaken after all?'

'Wait, just a minute!' Alyosha interrupted him in alarm. 'What makes you say all that?... And anyway, why should you be so concerned, that's the first thing?'

'Two separate but quite understandable questions. I'll deal with them in turn. What makes me say all that? I wouldn't have spoken if I hadn't suddenly understood your brother Dmitry Fyodorovich today, the way he really is, all of him, through and through. Just one single thing told me immediately all there is to know about him. These wholly honest but all too passionate people have a limit which they mustn't overstep. If they do... they're liable to stick a knife in someone, even their own father. And if the father's a drunken, intemperate libertine who never had the sense to set a limit to anything, neither will know where to draw the line, both will end up rolling headlong into the ditch...'

'No, Misha, no, if it's only that, you've reassured me. It won't come to that.'

'And why are you shaking all over? Do you know something? He might be an honest man—Mitya, I mean (he's stupid, but honest)—but he's a sensualist. That defines the man, that's him in a nutshell. He's inherited his debased sensuality from his father. But Alyosha, it's you who surprise me: how is it you're still a virgin, you—a Karamazov? You must admit, in your family sensuality is a disease. So there you have the three sensualists stalking one another... knives at the ready. All three of them have bashed their heads together, you might turn out to be the fourth.'

'You're wrong about that woman. Dmitry... despises her,' Alyosha exclaimed with a shudder.

'You mean Grushenka? No, my friend, he doesn't despise her. Seeing as he's openly swapped his fiancée for her, he doesn't despise her. Here... here's something that's way beyond your understanding at the moment, my friend. Here we have a man who's fallen in love with beauty, with a woman's body, or even with just one part of a woman's body (a sensualist would understand that), and for her sake he's ready to desert his children, sell his father and mother, sell Russia, sell his motherland down the river: for all his honesty, he'll go and steal; for all his meekness, he'll kill; for all his loyalty, he'll betray. Pushkin, the bard of women's feet,* glorified feet in poetry; others don't glorify, but they go weak at the knees at the mere sight of them. But it's not just feet... Despising doesn't apply in this case, my dear fellow, even assuming that he did despise Grushenka. He might well despise her and still be unable to tear himself away from her.'

'I understand that,' Alyosha suddenly blurted out.

'Really? Yes, I suppose you do understand, if you can admit to it so readily,' Rakitin said with malevolence. 'You couldn't help admitting it, it simply tripped off the tongue, isn't that it? That makes the admission more valuable: that means the subject's already familiar to you, you've thought about it, about the sins of the flesh, I mean. Oh, you virgin! Butter wouldn't melt in your mouth... you're a saint, I agree, but, docile as you are, the devil only knows what you haven't thought about already, what goes on inside that head of yours! A virgin, yet the depths you've already plumbed! You know, I've been observing you for a long time. You're a Karamazov, you're a Karamazov through and through—so there must be something in the idea of breeding and natural selection. On your father's side, you're a sensualist; on your mother's, a holy fool. Why are you shaking? Am I not telling the truth? Do you know—Grushenka kept telling me: "Bring him to me (meaning you), I'll tear that cassock off him." You should have heard her pleading: "Bring him to me, bring him to me!" Fancy her getting so worked up about you? You know, women are strange, but she takes the biscuit.'

'Give her my regards, tell her I shan't come,' Alyosha said with a wry smile. 'Finish what you were going to say Mikhail, I'll tell you what I think later.'

'What more is there? Everything's pretty clear. It's the same old story, my dear fellow. But if there's a sensualist in you too, then what about your brother Ivan? He's a Karamazov. The whole of the Karamazov family problem boils down to this: you're sensualists, money-grubbers, and holy fools! For some unknown stupid reason your brother Ivan, never mind being an atheist, keeps publishing theological articles as a practical joke, and he's not at all embarrassed about his shamelessness—that's your brother Ivan for you. Besides, he's after his brother Mitya's fiancée, and he'll probably get what he wants. And can you imagine, with Mitya's willingness too, because Mitya's ready to hand over his fiancée on a plate to Ivan just to be shot of her and run off to Grushenka as quickly as possible. And this without sacrificing any of his honour and integrity—you understand? What do you do with people like that? The devil only knows what to make of you all—the man's aware of his own depravity, and just wallows in it! And that's not all: his own father is even now trying to queer his pitch. The old man has gone mad over Grushenka, he slobbers every time he looks at her. Do you know, it was all because of her that he started that row in the cell, all because Miusov dared to call her a dissolute creature. He's worse than a lovesick tom-cat. She used to be in his pay, helped him in his shady business deals and in his drinking-dens, but now that she's really caught his eye he's head over heels about her and keeps running to her with all sorts of propositions, none of them honourable of course. So father and son are going to collide on that slippery path. And Grushenka won't choose one or the other; she keeps playing hard to get and teasing both of them, trying to make up her mind which is the better deal, for though there's lots of money to be extracted from the father, he's not the marrying kind and in the end he'll probably turn Jew and become tight-fisted. In that case, Mitenka's value goes up; he hasn't any money, but he's available. Capable, that is, of abandoning his fiancée, that peerless beauty Katerina Ivanovna, wealthy, noble, a colonel's daughter, and marrying Grushenka, the former mistress of the head of the town council—old Samsonov, that trumped-up petty merchant and debauched muzhik. All this could easily lead to a clash and end in a crime. And that's just what your brother Ivan is waiting for, he'll be over the moon: he'll have Katerina Ivanovna, whom he's pining for, and he'll lay his hands on a dowry of sixty thousand roubles. Just what a little runt like him needs in order to get his foot on the ladder. And, what's more, not only will he not offend Mitya, he'll be doing him a lifelong favour. I happen to know that last week, when he was drunk in a tavern with some gypsy girls, Mitya was shouting that he wasn't worthy of his fiancée Katerina, but that his brother Ivan was. And as for Katerina Ivanovna—of course in the end she's not going to turn down such a charmer as Ivan Fyodorovich, but for the time being she doesn't know which one to go for. I just wonder what it is about Ivan that's made you all worship him so? He's laughing at you: "I'm sitting pretty," he's saying to himself, "what a time I'm having at your expense!"'

'How do you know all this? What makes you so sure?' Alyosha enquired sharply, frowning.

'Why are you asking me that, and why are you so scared of what my answer will be? It can only mean that you admit I'm telling the truth.'

'You don't like Ivan. Ivan will never be tempted by money.'

'Really? And what about Katerina Ivanovna's beauty? It's not just a question of money, though sixty thousand is not to be scoffed at.'

'No, Ivan has set his sights higher. Even thousands of roubles wouldn't tempt him. It's not money he's after, nor peace of mind. Perhaps it's suffering he's seeking.'

'Pull the other leg! You make me laugh... you gentlefolk!'

'Misha, he has a restless soul. His mind's trapped. He has great, unresolved thoughts. It isn't millions he needs—his need is to resolve his own ideas.'

'That's plagiarism, Alyosha. You've just paraphrased your starets. What a riddle Ivan has set you all!' Rakitin exclaimed in unconcealed anger. His whole expression changed and his lips contorted. 'And a pretty stupid riddle too, not difficult to unravel. Use your common sense and you'll see what I mean. His newspaper article was ridiculous and grotesque. And did you hear that stupid theory of his: "Immortality of the soul does not exist, therefore there is no virtue, therefore everything is permitted." (By the way, you remember your brother Mitya shouting out: "I'll remember that!") Scoundrels would be attracted by a theory like that!... I'm being abusive, that's stupid of me... no, not scoundrels, but schoolboy show-offs, for all their "profound, unfathomable ideas". He's all talk, all he's saying is: "On the one hand, one can't deny... and on the other, one must admit!" His whole theory's a sham! Mankind can find the strength within itself to live virtuously without believing in the immortality of the soul! Mankind will find the strength in love of freedom, equality, and fraternity...'

Rakitin had worked himself up into such a passion that he was scarcely able to control himself. But suddenly he stopped, as though remembering something.

'Well, that'll do,' he said, smiling even more wryly than before. 'Why are you laughing? Do you think I'm a vulgar idiot?'

'No, the thought never crossed my mind. You're clever, but... let it pass, it was silly of me to laugh! I know why you've got so heated, Misha. From your attitude I take it you're not indifferent to Katerina Ivanovna yourself; I've suspected as much for a long time, my friend, and that's the reason you don't like my brother Ivan. Are you jealous of him?'

'And jealous of her money? Go on, say it!'

'No, I'm not going to say anything about money, I've no wish to insult you.'

'I believe that, because you say so, but to hell with you and your brother Ivan! None of you seems to realize that he's an extremely disagreeable person *per se*, and that Katerina Ivanovna has nothing to do with it. And why ever should I like him, damn him! He hasn't hesitated to revile me! Why should I hesitate to revile him?'

'I've never heard him say anything at all about you, either good or bad; he doesn't mention you at all.'

'And yet I heard that a couple of days ago he was running me down at Katerina Ivanovna's for all he was worth—that's how disinterested he is in yours truly. Now, my friend, after that, who's jealous of whom—you tell me! He went so far as to suggest that if I didn't settle for a career as an archimandrite and didn't decide to become a monk soon, then without a doubt I would go to St Petersburg and join the staff of an intellectual journal, where I would almost certainly work for the literary section, write for about ten years, and finally run the journal myself. I'd continue to publish it, certainly with a liberal and atheist tendency, with a hint of socialism, just a tinge of socialism, but all the time keeping my ear close to the ground and being all things to all men, and leading fools by the nose. The high point of my career, according to your brother, would be reached when, in spite of my socialist tendencies, I'd start diverting the subscription money into my current account, letting it work for me profitably on the investment market under the management of some little Jew, till I was able to afford to build a grand house in St Petersburg to which I'd transfer the editorial office and cram the remaining floors with lodgers. He even selected the site for the house: next to the new stone bridge which they say is being planned in St Petersburg across the Neva, to link up the Liteiny with the Vyborg...'

'Oh Misha, it'll probably all come true, down to the last word!' Alyosha cried out, unable to contain himself and beaming joyfully.

'So, you're trying to be sarcastic too, Aleksei Fyodorovich?'

'No, no, I was only joking, forgive me. I've got something else on my mind. Just a moment, though: who could have told you all that—where could you have heard it? After all, you couldn't have been at Katerina Ivanovna's yourself when he was talking about you, could you?'

'I wasn't, but Dmitry Fyodorovich was, I heard it all with my own ears from Dmitry Fyodorovich—that is, he didn't exactly tell me, I happened to overhear—unintentionally, of course—because I was at Grushenka's at the time, closeted in her bedroom, and couldn't very well leave while Dmitry Fyodorovich was in the next room.'

'Oh yes, I quite forgot, she's a relative of yours, isn't she?...'

'A relative? Grushenka, a relative of mine?' Rakitin exclaimed, going red in the face. 'Are you out of your mind, or what? You're crazy.'

'Well? Isn't she? That's what I heard...'

'Where could you have heard that? I know you Karamazovs like to make out that you're from some illustrious and ancient noble line, whereas in fact your father used to run from table to table as a jester, and used to be allowed into the kitchen out of kindness. Granted, I'm just the son of a village priest and am nothing compared to you gentlefolk, but don't insult me quite so freely and gratuitously. I too have a sense of honour, Aleksei Fyodorovich. Grushenka couldn't be a relative of mine—she's a loose woman, I'll have you know!'

Rakitin was beside himself with fury.

'Forgive me, for pity's sake, I had no idea, and anyway, what do you mean, "loose woman"? Surely she isn't... that sort?' Alyosha suddenly blushed. 'I repeat, I heard she was a relative of yours. You often go to see her, and you told me yourself there's nothing between you two... Well, I'd never have thought that you of all people despised her so much! Does she really deserve it?'

'If I do go to see her, that's my business, and that should be good enough for you. As for kinship, it's your brother or even your father you have to watch, otherwise before you know where you are it'll be you who'll end up as one of her in-laws. Well, here we are. You'd better make for the kitchen now. Good heavens! What's going on, what's all that? We can't be late, surely? They can't have finished eating so soon! Or have you Karamazovs been up to some tricks again? It looks like it.

There's your father with Ivan Fyodorovich hot on his tail—look, they've just come running out of the abbot's quarters. There's Father Isidore calling out something to them from the porch. And your father's shouting and waving his arms about too, he's probably swearing. There's Miusov in his carriage, off he goes, there, see? Maksimov's taken to his heels too—there's been a scene; so, no lunch! I wonder if they've given the abbot a bloody nose? Or perhaps he's given them one? That'd serve them right!...'

Rakitin's surmise proved to be correct. There really had been a scene, unexpected and unprecedented. Everything had occurred 'spontaneously'.

8

A SCANDALOUS SCENE

As Miusov and Ivan Fyodorovich were entering the abbot's quarters, Pyotr Aleksandrovich, being the truly decent and sensitive person he was, immediately experienced a feeling of regret—he felt ashamed of himself for losing his temper. He considered the worthless Fyodor Pavlovich to be so far beneath contempt that he regretted having been provoked by him into losing his composure and self-control in the starets's cell. 'At least it's not the monks' fault,' he suddenly concluded, as he stood in the abbot's porch, 'and if the people here are decent (and this Father Nikolai, the abbot, appears to belong to the gentry), why shouldn't one be pleasant, considerate, and polite to them?... I shan't argue, I'll agree with everything they say, I'll win them over with politeness, and... and... I'll show them I've nothing in common with that Aesop, that buffoon, that Pierrot, and that I've simply been deceived along with the rest of them...'

As for the disputed tree-felling and fishing-rights (he did not even know where the areas in question were located), he decided to drop the matter once and for all that very day, especially as the sums involved were paltry, and to end all litigation against the monastery.

All these charitable intentions were strengthened as they

entered the abbot's dining-room. Actually, the abbot did not have a dining-room; he had only two rooms, though admittedly they were much more spacious and comfortable than those of the starets. Not that the rooms were particularly smart or comfortable: the leather and mahogany furniture was in an old-fashioned style dating back to the 'twenties, and the floorboards were bare; but everything was spotlessly clean, with a large number of exotic flowers arranged on the window-sills; the most luxurious feature (relatively speaking, of course) was the sump-tuously laid table; the tablecloth was spotless, the china gleamed; there were three different kinds of beautifully baked bread, two bottles of wine, two bottles of excellent monastery mead, and a large glass jug of monastery kvass, which was renowned through-out the neighbourhood. There was no vodka at all. Rakitin later recounted that this dinner consisted of five courses: sterlet soup with fish *pirozhki;** then boiled fish exquisitely prepared in a special way; this was followed by salmon rissoles, ice cream and fruit *compote*, and, finally, a delicate blancmange. Rakitin had sniffed all this out, unable to resist having a peep into the abbot's kitchen, where he had his connections. He had connections, eyes and ears everywhere. He was not content with his lot and was consumed with envy. He was well aware of his considerable abilities, but exaggerated them in his excessive self-esteem. He knew for certain that he would become an influential figure of some sort, but Alyosha, who was very attached to him, was tortured by the fact that his friend was dishonourable—and that not only was he totally unaware of this, but just because he knew he would not steal money lying on a table he considered himself unquestionably to be a man of the highest integrity. No one, not even Alyosha, could convince him otherwise.

Rakitin, being a person of no social standing, could not be invited to the lunch party, but Father Yosif, Father Païsy, and one of the hieromonks were. They were already in the dining-room waiting for the abbot when Pyotr Aleksandrovich, Kalga-nov, and Ivan Fyodorovich entered. The landowner Maksimov was there too, inconspicuous in a corner. The abbot strode into the middle of the room to welcome his guests. He was a tall, lean old man, still vigorous, with dark, greying hair and a long, pious, grave face. He bowed silently to everyone, and they all came forward to receive his blessing. Miusov even went so far as to try to kiss his hand, but the abbot withdrew it just in time, thwarting the attempt. Ivan Fyodorovich and Kalganov, on the other hand, each received a full blessing, which they reciprocated with an open-hearted, smacking kiss on the hand, in peasant style.

'We must offer you our most sincere apologies, Your Reverence,' Pyotr Aleksandrovich began with a broad grin, but maintaining a dignified and respectful tone, 'that we have come without our companion Fyodor Pavlovich, whom you also invited; he has been obliged to decline your kind invitation to dine, and not without good reason. In the Reverend Father Zosima's cell he got carried away somewhat by the unfortunate family feud with his son, and said one or two highly inappropriate things... to be honest, his comments were downright indecent... of which matter,' he stole a glance at the two hieromonks, 'Your Reverence, I think, may already have been informed. And so, deeply conscious of his own guilt and full of sincere remorse, he was unable to overcome his shame, and asked us, myself and his son Ivan Fyodorovich, to convey to you his sincere regrets, his remorse, and contrition... In a word, he hopes and expects to make amends for everything later, but for the moment he seeks your blessing and begs you to forget what has happened...'

Miusov fell silent. As he uttered the closing words of his speech, he experienced a feeling of complete self-satisfaction, so that not a trace of his earlier vexation remained in his heart. He was again full of sincere love for humanity. The abbot, having listened to him gravely, inclined his head slightly and said in reply:

'I very much regret that our guest is unable to be here. Perhaps at our table he would have grown to like us, as we would have grown to like him. Please accept our hospitality, gentlemen.'

He stood in front of the icon and began to say grace. All bowed their heads reverently, and the landowner Maksimov even leaned forward perceptibly, with his hands together in an attitude of extreme devotion.

It was at this moment that Fyodor Pavlovich played his last trick. It should be noted that he really had intended to leave, and had indeed felt unable, after his disgraceful behaviour in the starets's cell, to lunch at the abbot's as though nothing had happened. Not that he was particularly ashamed or self-reproachful— perhaps, in fact, quite the reverse— nevertheless, he felt that to dine there would be somehow inappropriate. But just as he was about to get into his rickety calash which had drawn up at the entrance to the inn to take him away, he suddenly hesitated. He recalled his own words in the starets's cell: 'When I meet people, I always feel I'm the lowest of the low and everyone takes me for a buffoon, so I say to myself, why shouldn't I act the fool, seeing that you're all more stupid and vile than I am.' He wanted to take revenge on everyone for his own tricks. He remembered too how he had once been asked long ago: 'Why do you hate so-and-so so much?' And he had replied in a fit of clownish impudence: 'How shall I put it to you? It's true he hasn't done me any harm, whereas I played one of the dirtiest tricks imaginable on him, and the moment I had done so, I suddenly couldn't stand the sight of him.' Recalling this, he smiled to himself maliciously in a moment of reflection. His eyes gleamed and his lips even began to quiver. 'Now I've started, I won't stop,' he decided suddenly. His innermost feeling at this moment could perhaps have been expressed as follows: 'I can't hope to rehabilitate myself now, so I'll spit in their faces and be damned! I'll not be ashamed of myself in front of them and that's that!' He told his driver to wait, retraced his steps quickly to the monastery, and went straight to the abbot's quarters. He still had no clear idea what he was going to do, but he knew he no longer had any control over himself—just one tiny pretext, and he would commit the ultimate outrage—but simply an outrage, mark you, and by no means any sort of crime or act for which he could be punished in law. When it came to the crunch, he was always able to restrain himself, and on occasion he marvelled at this capacity in himself. He appeared in the abbot's dining-room just when grace had finished and everyone was moving to the dining-table. He stopped in the doorway, cast his eyes around the room, and burst into prolonged, insolent, wicked laughter, brazenly staring everyone in the face.

'They thought I'd left, but here I am!' he shouted at the top of his voice.

For a moment the whole company stared at him in dead

silence, and suddenly everyone realized that something indecent and abominable was going to happen, that there was undoubtedly going to be a scandalous scene. Pyotr Aleksandrovich immediately passed from a mood of extreme good humour to one of utter fury. Everything that had died down and grown calm in his heart immediately revived and rose up again.

'No, this is too much!' he exclaimed, 'I won't... No, I won't tolerate this!'

Blood rushed to his face. His speech became confused, but this was not the moment for concern over decorum, and he grabbed his hat.

'What is it he won't tolerate?' exclaimed Fyodor Pavlovich. ' "This is too much, I won't tolerate this?" What's he talking about? Your Reverence, can I come in or not? Will you let me join you at your table?'

'I welcome you with all my heart,' replied the abbot. 'Gentlemen,' he added suddenly, 'let me beseech you in all sincerity to set aside all your incidental quarrels and to come together in kindred love and harmony and in prayer to God at our humble repast...'

'No, no, impossible,' shouted Pyotr Aleksandrovich, who was quite beside himself.

'And if it's impossible for Pyotr Aleksandrovich, it's impossible for me, and I shan't stay either. That's why I came. From now on, I'll always be with Pyotr Aleksandrovich: if Pyotr Aleksandrovich goes, I go, if he stays, I stay. But you really annoyed him with that kindred love of yours, Your Reverence: he doesn't accept me as a relation! Isn't that so, von Sohn?* Look at von Sohn standing there. How do you do, von Sohn?'

'You... mean me, sir?' mumbled the astonished landowner Maksimov.

'Yes, you, of course,' cried Fyodor Pavlovich. 'Who else? You don't imagine that the abbot is von Sohn, do you!'

'Well I'm not von Sohn either, I'm Maksimov.'

'Oh no you're not, you're von Sohn. Your Reverence, do you know who von Sohn was? There was a murder case: he was murdered in a whore-house—that's what those places are called here, am I right?—they murdered and robbed him and, in spite of the fact that he was an old man, boxed him up and dispatched him from St Petersburg to Moscow in a freight wagon with a label attached. And as they were nailing him in, the dancing whores sang songs and played the psaltery, the pianoforte, I mean. And he really is that same von Sohn. You've risen from the dead, haven't you, von Sohn?'

'What's all this? What's he talking about!' the hieromonks were heard to say.

'Let's go!' cried Pyotr Aleksandrovich to Kalganov.

'No sir, permit me!' Fyodor Pavlovich interrupted shrilly, taking another step into the room. 'Allow me to have my say. In the starets's cell I was criticized for behaving disrespectfully, because I shouted about gudgeon. Pyotr Aleksandrovich Miusov, a relative of mine, likes to speak with *plus de noblesse que de sincérité*,* but I'm just the reverse, I like *plus de sincérité que de noblesse*—and damn your *noblesse*! Isn't that right, von Sohn? Begging your pardon, Your Reverence, I may be a clown and I may act the clown, but I'm a "veray parfit gentil knight",* and I will have my say. Yes sir, a "parfit gentil knight", whereas Pyotr Aleksandrovich is a man with a chip on his shoulder and that's all there is to it. I came here today, perhaps, to try and find out what was what and to express my opinion. My son Aleksei is seeking salvation here; I'm his father, I care for his fate, and so I should. All the while I've been here I've been listening and acting dumb, keeping my eyes open and not saying a word, but now I want to present the final act of the performance to you. What usually happens in this town? In this town, once you're down, you're down. You trip once, and you stay down for good. How else could it be! But I want to get up. Holy fathers, you infuriate me. Confession is a great sacrament, which I too venerate, and I'm prepared to bow down myself, but in that cell they're all suddenly down on their knees, confessing out loud. Now, is it proper to confess out loud? The Church fathers instituted auricular confession,* which goes back to ancient times, and only in that form is confession a sacrament. Otherwise how could I, for instance, explain to him (he glanced at one of the monks) in front of everybody that I did such and such... I mean, such and such... you understand? Sometimes it might even be downright improper to mention certain things. Scandalous, in fact! No, holy fathers, you lot are enough to drive anyone to self-flagellation...* I'm going to write to the Synod at the first opportunity and I'm taking my son Aleksei home...'

Nota bene: Fyodor Pavlovich was *au fait* with the situation. Malicious rumours had circulated at one time (not only in our monastery but in others too, where the cult of startsy had become established), and had even reached the bishop, that the startsy were being held in excessive reverence, to the detriment of the abbatial office, and that, among other things, the startsy were abusing the sacrament of confession, and so on and so forth. Absurd accusations, which eventually died without trace, of their own accord, both in our monastery and elsewhere. But the demon of stupidity, which had taken possession of Fyodor Pavlovich and was driving him further and further into the depths of irrationality, had reminded him of these past accusations, though he did not understand the first thing about them. He was quite unable to be specific on the matter, not least because on this occasion no one had knelt in the starets's cell or confessed out loud, so that Fyodor Pavlovich could not have seen anything of the sort himself and was merely repeating old rumours and gossip which he had somehow remembered. But, having uttered such nonsense, he realized that he had blurted out an absurdity and was immediately anxious to convince his listeners, but most of all himself, that what he had said was not nonsense at all. And though he knew perfectly well that with each successive word he would only be adding more and more to the nonsense that he had already uttered, he was no longer able to restrain himself and gave full vent to his emotions.

'Despicable!' exclaimed Pyotr Aleksandrovich.

'If you will allow me,' the abbot said suddenly. 'It was said of old:* "And they began talking about me much, even saying such things as gave offence. On hearing it all I said to myself: It is a remedy sent to me by Jesus to cure my soul of vanity." And therefore we thank you in all humility, dear guest!'

And he bowed from the waist to Fyodor Pavlovich.

'Bah-bah-bah! Humbug and antiquated phrases! Antiquated phrases and antiquated gestures! Antiquated lies and the empty formality of all this bowing to the ground! We know all about this bowing! "A kiss on the lips and a dagger through the heart," as in Schiller's *The Robbers*. I don't like falsehood, Reverend Fathers, I want the truth! But truth will not be revealed in eating gudgeon—take my word for it! Reverend Fathers, why do you fast? Why do you expect a reward for it in heaven? I too would fast for a reward like that! No, holy monk, be thou virtuous in this life, make a contribution to society, that would be more of a challenge, rather than shut yourself up in a monastery on full board in expectation of reward in heaven. You see, Your Reverence, I've a way of putting things too. So, what have we here?' He approached the table. 'Vintage Factory Port, Médoc bottled by Yeliseyev Bros.,* you've done yourselves proud, holy fathers! Not a gudgeon in sight. Just look at the bottles the fathers have displayed, he-he-he! And who has provided you with all this? The Russian peasant, the worker, who has deprived his family and disregarded the pressing needs of the state to hand over to you the few kopecks he earned with his calloused hands! Holy fathers, you suck the blood of the people!'

'That is quite unworthy of you,' said Father Yosif. Father Païsy maintained a stubborn silence. Miusov made a dash for the door, followed by Kalganov.

'Well, holy fathers, I'll follow Pyotr Aleksandrovich! I'll never come here again, you can implore me on your knees, I won't come! I sent you a thousand roubles, so now your greedy eyes are popping out for more, he-he-he! No, I'm not going to give you another kopeck. I'm taking vengeance for my lost youth, for all my humiliation!' And he slammed his fist on the table in a fit of false indignation. 'This monastery has meant a lot in my life! I've shed many bitter tears over it! You turned my wife, the *klikusha*, against me. You've damned me at all the seven Councils,* you've slandered me all over the district! Enough, fathers, today we live in the age of liberalism, the age of ocean liners and railways. Not a thousand, not a hundred roubles, not even a hundred kopecks, you'll get nothing from me!'

Once again, *nota bene*: our monastery had never meant anything at all in his life, nor had he ever shed any bitter tears over it. But he had got so carried away by his crocodile tears that for a brief moment he was on the point of believing in them himself; he was so touched that indeed he very nearly did burst into tears, but at the same instant he felt it was time to restrain himself. In response to his malicious lies, the abbot inclined his head and once more spoke solemnly:

'And again it is written:* "Suffer with joy the dishonour that befalleth thee, and be not confounded, and bear no hatred against him who dishonoureth thee." And we shall do likewise.'

'Tut-tut-tut, confounded nonsense! You confound yourselves, fathers, I'm off. As for my son Aleksei, I'm taking him away from here for good, on my authority as his father. Ivan Fyodorovich, my most obedient son, kindly follow me, and that's an order! Von Sohn, why should you stay here? Come home with me now. We'll enjoy ourselves. It's only a verst from here. Instead of lenten pies, I'll serve you a suckling-pig with stuffing. We'll have a feast; I'll serve you cognac, with liqueur to follow; there'll be raspberry brandy... Now, von Sohn, don't miss this opportunity!'

He left, waving his arms and shouting. This was the moment at which Rakitin caught sight of him and pointed him out to Alyosha.

'Aleksei!' his father called out, catching sight of him in the distance. 'You're coming home with me today for good, and bring your pillow and mattress—the lot, all your personal possessions.'

Alyosha stood perfectly still; he surveyed the scene in silent concentration. In the meantime Fyodor Pavlovich had settled himself in the calash, followed by the grim-faced Ivan Fyodorovich, who sat down beside him without exchanging a single word and not even turning to say goodbye to Alyosha. But then there followed another farcical and almost incredible scene to crown the proceedings. The landowner Maksimov suddenly appeared alongside the tread-board of the calash. He ran up panting, anxious not to be left behind. Rakitin and Alyosha watched him approach. In his haste, he had already placed one foot on the tread-board, where Ivan Fyodorovich's left foot was still resting, and, clutching hold of the frame of the calash, he prepared to jump in.

'Me too, I'm coming with you!' he cried, bobbing up and down, laughing his happy little laugh, his face beaming, and eager to the point of recklessness. 'Take me with you!'

'Well, what did I say,' Fyodor Pavlovich cried triumphantly. 'It *is* von Sohn! It's the real von Sohn risen from the dead! But how did you get away? What sort of von-Sohnish tricks did you get up to in there, and how did you manage to leave the lunch? Talk about being brazen! I'm pretty brazen myself, but you, my friend, you take the biscuit! Hop in, hop in quick! Let him get in, Vanya, it'll be fun. He can sit down at our feet somewhere. Will you sit down, von Sohn? Or shall we put you up on the box with the driver?... Hop up on the box, von Sohn!...'

But Ivan Fyodorovich, who was already seated, without saying a word struck Maksimov a heavy blow in the chest which sent him flying back two or three paces. He was lucky that he did not fall.

'Drive on!' Ivan yelled angrily to the driver.

'What was that for? What's the matter with you? Why did you have to do that to him?' Fyodor Pavlovich remonstrated, but the calash had already gathered speed. Ivan Fyodorovich gave no reply.

'Well, I never!' Fyodor Pavlovich said again, after a couple of minutes' silence, eyeing his son disapprovingly. 'This monastery visit was all your idea, you encouraged me and talked me into it, so why are you so angry?'

'I wish you'd stop ranting, can't we have some peace for a change!' Ivan Fyodorovich cut him short.

Fyodor Pavlovich fell silent again for a couple of minutes.

'Could do with a tot of brandy now,' he remarked gravely. But Ivan Fyodorovich did not reply.

'You'll have some too when we get home, won't you?'

Ivan Fyodorovich continued to maintain his silence.

Fyodor Pavlovich waited another couple of minutes or so.

'I'm taking Alyosha away from the monastery all the same, however disagreeable that may be to you, my esteemed Karl von Moor.'

Ivan Fyodorovich shrugged his shoulders disdainfully, turned his head away, and fixed his eyes on the road. No one spoke for the rest of the journey.

BOOK THREE
Sensualists

1

IN THE SERVANTS' QUARTERS

FYODOR PAVLOVICH KARAMAZOV'S house, though by no means in the centre of the town, was not exactly on the outskirts either. It was a single-storey building with a mezzanine, painted grey, with a red metal roof. The exterior was pleasing, if somewhat dilapidated. However, it would stand for a long time yet, and was spacious and comfortable. It had many odd little rooms, glory-holes, and unexpected staircases. It was overrun with rats, but Fyodor Pavlovich was not unduly bothered. 'Well, they help to relieve the boredom when you're here by yourself of an evening.' For it was actually his habit to send the servants to the outhouse to sleep, and to lock himself alone inside the main house for the night. The outhouse stood, spacious and solid, in the yard; Fyodor Pavlovich had had a kitchen installed there, although there was a kitchen in the main house too; he disliked the smell of cooking, and food was brought across the yard in winter and summer alike. The house had been built for a large family and could have accommodated five times as many occupants and servants. But at the time of our story only Fyodor Pavlovich and Ivan Fyodorovich lived in the house, while there were only three servants, old Grigory, his wife Marfa, and a young man called Smerdyakov, in the outhouse. It is necessary to say a little more about these three servants. Of Grigory Vasilyevich Kutuzov we have already said enough. He was a steadfast, unyielding, stubborn man, who always went straight to the point so long as it seemed to him, for some (often quite illogical) reason, to be indisputably on the side of truth. In short, he was honest and incorruptible. For example, just after the emancipation of the serfs, his wife Marfa Ignatyevna, despite her lifelong unquestioning obedience to her husband, had pestered him incessantly to leave Fyodor Pavlovich, go to Moscow, and set himself up there in some kind of small business (they had a little money put by); but Grigory decided once and for all that the woman was talking rubbish, as all women do, and that to leave their old master, no matter what he was like, would not be right, because 'it is our duty to stick by him'.

'If you understand what duty is!' he remarked to Marfa Ignatyevna.

'I understand about duty, Grigory Vasilyevich, but what duty do we have to make us stay here? That I don't understand at all,' Marfa Ignatyevna answered obstinately.

'All right, you don't understand, but that's how it's going to be. From now on you can keep quiet.'

And so it was; they didn't leave, and Fyodor Pavlovich agreed to pay them a small wage, which he did. Grigory also knew that he had an undoubted influence on his master. He felt this, and it was true. Fyodor Pavlovich, that cunning and obstinate buffoon, resolute 'in certain matters' as he himself said, was to his own astonishment utterly weak-willed in some other 'matters'. He himself knew what these matters were, and admitted he was certainly afraid of many things. There are certain situations in this life in which you have to have your wits about you, and in such situations it is difficult to survive without someone who is loyal, and Grigory was loyal in the extreme. There were many times throughout his life when Fyodor Pavlovich could have had his nose thoroughly bloodied, but Grigory always came to his rescue, although every time he would lecture his master afterwards. But it was not only the prospect of a bloody nose that frightened Fyodor Pavlovich: there were more important situations, of great delicacy and complexity, when Fyodor Pavlovich himself would probably have been quite unable to express that indefinable need for someone close and faithful which he inexplicably began to perceive in himself at unexpected moments. These were almost painful occasions; debauched in the extreme and, in his sensuousness, often as cruel as some evil insect, Fyodor Pavlovich would from time to time, in moments of drunkenness, experience a spiritual terror and a moral torment which had an almost physical effect upon him. 'My soul simply trembles in my throat at such times,' he would say. At these moments he loved to have at his side, nearby—not necessarily in the same room, but in the outhouse—someone who was loyal and steadfast, quite unlike himself, not debauched, but who nevertheless witnessed all these acts of debauchery and knew all his secrets, but who out of loyalty would tolerate everything and, most important, would neither reproach him nor ever scold him, then or in the future, and if the need arose would protect him—from whom? From someone unknown, but terrible and dangerous. The essential thing was that it had to be *another* person, someone familiar and friendly, who could be summoned at the painful moment to look him straight in the eyes and perhaps exchange a word or two, even on some quite unconnected matter, and if that person was not angry, all well and good, one's heart would feel somehow lighter, and if he was angry, then one was sadder. It even happened—though extremely rarely—that Fyodor Pavlovich would wake Grigory at night and summon him to the house at once. And he would come, and Fyodor Pavlovich would start to talk about the most trivial everyday matters and would soon dismiss him, sometimes even with gibes and mockery, then shrug his shoulders, retire to bed, and sleep the sleep of the just. Something of this sort happened when Alyosha arrived. Alyosha's attitude, 'seeing everything and judging nothing', affected him profoundly. He brought in addition something quite unprecedented—a complete absence of contempt towards him, the old man, but on the contrary an endless capacity for affection and an absolutely natural and straightforward attachment to him, however little he might deserve it. For the old profligate, the man without a family, all this came as a great surprise; to him who had hitherto loved only 'filth', it was totally unexpected. After Alyosha's departure, he admitted to himself that he had come to understand something which until then he had not wished to understand.

I have already mentioned at the beginning of my story that Grigory hated Adelaida Ivanovna, Fyodor Pavlovich's first wife and the mother of his eldest son, Dmitry Fyodorovich, but that on the other hand he would defend the second wife, the *klikusha* Sofya Ivanovna, against her own husband and against all who might be inclined to say anything nasty or disrespectful about her. His sympathy for this unhappy woman had reached such a pitch of religious fervour that even twenty years later he could not bear the slightest hint of a slur upon her name and would immediately take the offender to task. Outwardly, Grigory was cold, dignified, and reserved, inclined to make weighty and considered pronouncements. It would also have been impossible to tell at first sight whether he loved his meek, submissive wife, whereas, truth to tell, he did love her, and she of course understood this. Not only was Marfa Ignatyevna not stupid, but she was perhaps cleverer than her husband—more sensible in worldly matters, at any rate—and yet she submitted meekly and uncomplainingly to him from the very beginning of their marriage and unquestioningly respected him for his spiritual superiority. Remarkably, throughout their life together they talked very little to each other about anything, except perhaps the most necessary daily matters. The imposing and dignified Grigory kept his affairs to himself and brooded over his worries alone, and Marfa Ignatyevna had long since understood once and for all that he had absolutely no need of her advice. She felt that her husband valued her silence and thus recognized that she had a brain. He never beat her, except on one occasion, and then only lightly. In the first year of the marriage of Adelaida Ivanovna and Fyodor Pavlovich, all the girls and women of the village had assembled (this was still in the time of serfdom) in the courtyard of the manor to sing and dance. 'In the Meadows' had just started when Marfa Ignatyevna, then still a young girl, leapt in front of the singers and flung herself into a 'Russian' dance, flaunting herself, dancing not like the peasant women but like she had danced when she had been a domestic servant with the wealthy Miusovs, in their private theatre, where actors were trained by a dancing-master from Moscow. Grigory saw his wife dancing, and an hour later, in their hut, taught her a lesson by pulling her around a little by the hair. And that was the one and only beating, and Marfa Ignatyevna was never beaten again for the rest of her life—and never danced again.

God had not blessed them with children; there had been one child, but it died. Grigory loved children—he did not hide the fact, and indeed was not afraid to show it. When Adelaida Ivanovna ran off, he led the three-year-old Dmitry Fyodorovich

by the hand to his own house, where he spent nearly a year
looking after him, combing his hair himself and even washing
him in the washtub. Then he took charge of Ivan Fyodorovich
and Alyosha until the day he got his face slapped, but I have
already related all this. His own child gladdened him with hope
only while Marfa Ignatyevna was pregnant. When it was born,
he was overcome by grief and horror. The fact was, the boy was
born with six fingers on one hand. Seeing this, Grigory was so
horrified that he not only fell silent right up to the day of the
christening, but deliberately went out into the garden to brood.
It was spring, and he spent three whole days digging beds in the
kitchen garden. The third day was the day of the christening;
Grigory by this time had pondered what to do. Coming into the
hut where the clergy and guests had congregated, the last being
Fyodor Pavlovich, who was acting as godfather, he suddenly
announced that the child 'shouldn't be christened at all'; he
uttered this quietly, without elaboration, just let the words slip
out, and stared dully at the priest.

'Why ever not?' enquired the priest in good-humoured
amazement.

'Because it's... a monster,' muttered Grigory.

'What do you mean—a monster, what kind of a monster?'

Grigory remained silent for a while.

'It's an abomination of nature...', he muttered indistinctly but
very firmly, obviously not wishing to elaborate further.

They all laughed, and of course the poor child was christened.
Grigory prayed conscientiously at the font, but did not change
his opinion about the infant. However, he did not interfere, but
for the whole two weeks that the sickly infant lived he almost
never glanced at him, refused to look at him, and most of the
time kept away from the hut. But when after two weeks the child
died of thrush, he laid him in the coffin himself, gazed at him in
deep sorrow, and when they had filled in his shallow little grave,
stayed kneeling before it, his head bowed to the ground. From
that time and for many years afterwards, he never once referred
to his child, and Marfa Ignatyevna never mentioned their child
in his presence, and if she had occasion to talk of her 'little one'
with others, she did so in a whisper even when Grigory
Vasilyevich was not there. Marfa Ignatyevna noticed that, from

the time of the burial, he began to immerse himself most of the time in 'religious matters', took to reading the *Lives of the Saints*, for the most part in silence and when he was alone, and for this purpose always put on his big, round, silver-framed spectacles. He rarely read aloud, except perhaps at Lent. He loved the Book of Job and, having obtained from somewhere a collection of the sayings and sermons of 'our blessed Father Isaac the Syrian',* read them painstakingly for many years, understood practically nothing in them, and yet perhaps precisely for that reason valued and cherished the book all the more. Recently he had begun to listen with great interest to the doctrines of the flagellants, having an opportunity to do so locally, and had clearly been greatly influenced by them, but he had not seen fit to change his faith. Being so steeped in 'religious matters', of course, lent his face even greater gravity.

He had, perhaps, a natural leaning towards mysticism. And then, as though by destiny, the appearance on this earth of his six-fingered infant and his subsequent death coincided exactly with another extremely strange, unexpected, and peculiar event which was 'imprinted', as he later expressed it, on his very soul. It happened that on the very day the six-fingered child was buried, Marfa Ignatyevna had been woken in the night by what sounded like the crying of a newborn infant. She was frightened and woke her husband. He listened and concluded that it was more like someone groaning, 'probably a woman'. He got up and dressed; it was quite a warm May night. Going out to the porch, he could clearly hear that the groans were coming from the garden. But the gate between the garden and the yard was locked at night, and there was no other entrance, for a stout, high fence ran all round the garden. Grigory retraced his steps, lit a lantern, took the key to the garden gate, and, ignoring the hysterical terror of his wife, who remained convinced that she was hearing a child's voice and that it was probably her own son crying and calling for her, entered the garden without a word. There he clearly perceived that the groans were coming from their bath-house in the garden, not far from the gate, and that it was indeed a woman groaning. Opening the bathhouse door, he beheld a sight that held him rooted to the spot: the idiot girl who wandered the streets and was known to the whole town as

'Lizaveta Smerdyashchaya'* had got into the bathhouse and had just given birth to a child. The child was lying at her side, and she was dying beside it. She said nothing, for she could not speak anyway. But all this will require its own explanation.

2

LIZAVETA SMERDYASHCHAYA

THERE was one particular circumstance that deeply shocked Grigory, finally confirming an earlier disquieting and quite sickening suspicion that he had been harbouring. This Lizaveta was extremely short in stature, 'two *arshins** and a bit', as many of the pious old women of the town affectionately recalled after her death. At the age of twenty her face was healthy, full, and ruddy, but clearly that of an idiot; the expression in her eyes, though submissive, was fixed and unpleasant. All her life, summer and winter alike, she went barefoot and wore the same hempen shirt. Her almost black hair, extremely thick and as frizzy as sheep's wool, covered her head like an enormous cap. Besides, it was always spattered with earth and dirt and matted with leaves, splinters, and wood-shavings, for she always slept on the ground, in the mud. Her father, a homeless townsman named Ilya, ailing and ruined by drink, had eked out a living for many years by doing odd jobs for a certain well-to-do family, also living in our town. Lizaveta's mother had long since died. Ilya, always ill and evil-tempered, beat Lizaveta mercilessly whenever she came home. But she rarely came home, because she was regarded all over the town as a holy simpleton and lived on alms. Ilya's masters and even Ilya himself, as well as many sympathetic townspeople, mainly merchants and their wives, had tried more than once to dress Lizaveta more decently than just in a shirt, and in winter they clothed her in a sheepskin coat and shod her feet in boots; but invariably, having obediently submitted to being dressed, she went off somewhere, generally into a church porch, and quickly took off all that she had been given— be it kerchief, skirt, sheepskin, or boots—left everything there, and went off barefoot and wearing just a shirt as before. Once it happened that the new governor of our province, on a visit of inspection to our little town, felt his finer feelings sorely offended on seeing Lizaveta, and although he understood, as had been explained to him, that she was a 'holy simpleton', nevertheless insisted that for a young girl to wander the streets in nothing but a shirt was an offence against decency, and that a stop should be put to it. But the governor left and Lizaveta stayed as she was. Eventually her father died, and as an orphan she became even dearer to the devout amongst the townspeople. In fact, everyone seemed to love her, even the boys did not tease or insult her, and the boys in our town, especially the schoolboys, are a mischievous lot. She went into strangers' houses and no one drove her out; on the contrary, everyone made a fuss of her and gave her coins. Whenever someone handed her a coin she would take it and immediately deposit it in some collection-box at the church or the prison. If someone in the market gave her a bagel or a bun, she would invariably go and give it to the first child she met, or else she would stop one of our wealthiest ladies and offer it to her; and the lady would accept it with delight. She herself ate only dark rye bread and water. She would go and sit down in a smart shop with expensive goods on display, and money lying about, and the proprietors never worried about her, knowing that even if they left thousands of roubles lying around and forgot about her, she would not touch a kopeck. She rarely entered a church, but slept either in church porches or, having climbed over a wattle fence—we still have many wattle rather than wooden fences to this day—in someone's kitchen garden. At home, that is to say at the house of the people with whom her deceased father had lived, she would turn up about once a week, and in winter she would come back every day, but only for the night, which she would spend either in the porch or in the cowshed. People marvelled at her, wondering how she could endure such a life, but she was used to it; although small, she had extraordinary strength and resilience. Some of the gentry even suggested that she did all this from pride, but somehow this did not appear likely; she could not pronounce a single word, the best she could do was to move her tongue to utter an inarticulate sound—what pride was there in that? Now it so happened (quite a while ago, it was) that one bright warm September night by the light of a full moon, at a very late hour for our town, a drunken gang of young bucks, five or six in all, were making their way home by the backs of the houses. On either side of the path were wattle fences and behind them kitchen gardens belonging to the houses. The way led across a bridge over the large, stinking pond that we sometimes dignified with the name of 'river'. Beside the wattle fence, our gang saw Lizaveta sleeping among the nettles and burdock. The tipsy gentlemen stood over her roaring with laughter and began to mock her in a most indecent fashion. One lordling suddenly took it into his head to ask an utterly stupid question on an impossible theme. 'Could anyone— anyone at all—regard such an animal as a woman—now for instance?...' They all declared with disdainful loathing that it was impossible. But Fyodor Pavlovich happened to be among the group, and he immediately came forward and declared that it was indeed possible to regard her as a woman, very much so, that in fact one could even consider her a particularly tasty morsel, and so on and so forth. It is true that at this time he tended to overplay his clownish role, he loved to show off and amuse the gentlemen, aspiring to be their equal, but in fact appearing to them utterly crude. He had also just received from St Petersburg the news of the death of his first wife, Adelaida Ivanovna, and while still in mourning was drinking and rampaging so much that some in the town, even the most dissolute, were revolted by the mere sight of him. The gang, of course, laughed at this unexpected point of view; one of them even began to egg Fyodor Pavlovich on, but the rest just spat more and more profusely, although still finding it all highly amusing, and finally they all went their separate ways. Fyodor Pavlovich swore afterwards that he had left with them, and perhaps he had, no one will ever know for sure, but five or six months later the whole town began to talk with extreme and unfeigned revulsion about the fact that Lizaveta was pregnant, and to rack their brains as to whose was the sin, who was the sinner. And just then the curious rumour suddenly spread through the town that the culprit was in fact Fyodor Pavlovich. Where did this rumour come from? By this time only one member of that merry gang was still in the town, and he was by now a middle-aged, respectable state councillor, with a family of grown-up daughters, who was certainly not going to start gossiping, even if there was anything in it; the other members of the gang, about five of them, had all gone to other parts of the country by now. But the finger pointed straight at Fyodor Pavlovich and continued to do so. Of course, he did not exactly admit to anything, but neither did he deny the accusations: after all, he was not going to start trading words with shopkeepers and parvenus. At the time, he was haughty and conversed only with his own set, the civil servants and gentry who found him so amusing. And Grigory stood by his master with all his strength and might, and not only defended him against all this slander but also argued and remonstrated on his behalf and persuaded many people to change their minds. 'She's the guilty one, she's just a slut,' he would say with conviction; the culprit, he suggested, was none other than 'Karp the Screw' (a fearsome convict who, as was well known locally, had escaped from the provincial gaol at about that time and gone to earth in our town). This surmise seemed plausible; people remembered Karp, and recollected in particular that on those very nights in the early autumn he had indeed been roaming about the town and had robbed three people. Not only did this whole incident and all the conjecture not diminish the sympathy felt generally for the poor simpleton, but people began increasingly to take her under their wing. Kondratyeva, the widow of a prosperous merchant, even went so far as to take Lizaveta into her own home at the end of April to shelter her until she gave birth. She was guarded closely, but it turned out that on the evening of the last day, despite all vigilance, Lizaveta managed to creep out of Kondratyeva's house and turned up in Fyodor Pavlovich's garden. How she had managed to climb the high, stout garden fence in her condition remains something of a mystery. Some maintained that she had been carried over, others that she had been 'spirited' over. Most probably, though, it had all happened in some contrived but perfectly natural manner, and Lizaveta, skilled as she was at climbing wattle fences to sleep in other people's gardens, had somehow managed to scale Fyodor Pavlovich's fence and then, in spite of her condition, jump down into the garden, hurting herself as she did so. Grigory rushed in to Marfa Ignatyevna and urged her to go and help Lizaveta, while he himself ran for the old midwife, a townswoman who lived nearby. The child was saved, but Lizaveta died towards dawn. Grigory carried the newborn infant into the house, sat his wife down, and put it in her arms so that she could hold it to her breast. 'A child of God, an orphan, is everyone's kin, but especially ours. Our dead little one has sent him, and he is born of the devil's son and a righteous woman. Attend to him and stop crying.' So Marfa Ignatyevna reared the child. He was christened Pavel, and everyone, including themselves, began spontaneously to call him by the patronymic Fyodorovich. Fyodor Pavlovich raised no objection and even found it all highly amusing, although he continued strenuously to deny any involvement on his part. In the town, people were pleased that he had taken in the foundling. Later Fyodor Pavlovich even devised a surname for the foundling: he called him Smerdyakov,* after his mother's nickname, Lizaveta Smerdyashchaya. Thus this Smerdyakov became Fyodor Pavlovich's second servant and, until the beginning of our story, lived in the outhouse together with the old couple Grigory and Marfa. He was assigned the duties of a cook. I should really have said more about him in particular, but I am ashamed to have engaged the reader's attention for so long in describing such nondescript servants, and so I shall now return to my tale, in the hope that further information about Smerdyakov will somehow or other be revealed naturally as my story unfolds.

3

CONFESSIONS OF A PASSIONATE HEART. IN VERSE

ALYOSHA, hearing his father's order shouted from the coach as he left the monastery, stopped dead in his tracks for a moment in astonishment. But he did not hesitate for long, that was not his way. Instead, troubled as he was, he went straight to the abbot's kitchen to find out what his father had been doing upstairs. Then he set off for the town, hoping that on the way he would somehow manage to solve the problem that was tormenting him. I must make it clear from the beginning that he was not in the least alarmed by his father's shouting or by his order to return home 'with his pillow and mattress'. He knew very well that the order to go home, shouted so publicly and demonstratively, had been delivered in a fit of pique, as a flamboyant gesture, one might say—as in the case of one of our local townsmen, who not long ago, after celebrating rather too well, lost his temper in his own home and in front of his guests, because no one would give him more vodka, suddenly began to smash his own crockery, tear his own and his wife's clothes, break up the furniture, and, finally, smash the windows of his house, and all simply for effect; his father's behaviour now, of course, was in much the same vein. Naturally, the following day, when he had sobered up, the overenthusiastic reveller regretted breaking the cups and plates. Alyosha knew that his father would probably let him go back to the monastery the next day or even, perhaps, that same day. What is more, he was quite sure that his father, whatever he might do to others, meant him no harm. Alyosha was certain that no one in the whole world would ever want to harm him, and not only would not want to, but could not. This was axiomatic for him, established once and for all, to be accepted without question, and in this spirit he faced the world without faltering.

But at this moment fear of a quite different kind was stirring within him. It was all the more troubling because he could not define it—it was in fact a fear of women, and in particular of Katerina Ivanovna, who, in the note that Mrs Khokhlakova had passed to him, had so urgently implored him to see her for some reason. Her urgent request that he see her without fail had induced a sudden torment in his heart, and this sensation had been growing more and more acute all morning, despite the subsequent scenes in the monastery and then with the abbot, and so on and so forth. His fear was not occasioned by ignorance of what she wanted to talk to him about, nor of what he should say to her. And it was not womankind in general that he feared in her. He knew little of women, even though he had lived exclusively with them all his life, from infancy until he entered the monastery. It was this particular woman that he feared, this Katerina Ivanovna, and he had been afraid of her from the moment he had first set eyes on her. He had seen her only once or twice, perhaps three times in all, and had only once had

occasion to exchange a few words with her. He remembered her
as a beautiful girl, proud and imperious. But it was not her
beauty that troubled him, it was something else. The very
inexplicability of his fear increased that fear within him now.
That the girl's intentions were of the noblest kind, he accepted;
she was trying to save his brother Dmitry, who had behaved
badly to her, and she was trying to do so out of sheer magnanimity. And yet, in spite of his awareness of these noble and
generous intentions and the legitimacy that he had to accord
them, a chill ran down his spine the closer he drew to her house.

He reasoned that his brother Ivan Fyodorovich, who was on
such friendly terms with her, would not be there: Ivan was sure
to be with their father now. It was even less likely that Dmitry
would be with her, for reasons that Alyosha could guess. So the
conversation would be just between the two of them. Before that
fateful conversation he very much wanted to see his brother
Dmitry and perhaps have a word with him, without showing him
the letter. But Dmitry lived quite a distance away and was
probably not at home now. He stood for a moment, and then
made his decision. Crossing himself quickly, as was his habit, he
smiled momentarily about something, and then set off with a
firm step to meet the woman who instilled such fear in him.

He knew her house, but if he went along the High Street,
then crossed the square and continued on, it was quite a long
way. Ours is a small, straggling town with some outlying houses
separated by quite considerable distances. Besides, his father
might not yet have forgotten the order he had shouted to him to
leave the monastery and might start being difficult, therefore he
would have to hurry to reach both places. Having considered all
these factors, he decided to take a short cut round the back
lanes, for he knew all the town's byways like the back of his
hand. Taking this route meant going over deserted ground,
skirting fences where there were no proper roads, sometimes
clambering over other people's wattle fences and passing their
yards, but where everyone knew him and would greet him. By
this route he could get to the High Street in half the time. In
one place he had to pass very near to his father's house, next to
his father's neighbour's garden, which belonged to a ramshackle
little house with four windows. Alyosha knew that the owner of

this house was a crippled old townswoman living with her daughter, who until recently had been a lady's maid in the residences of various generals in the capital, but who had been at home for a year now because of her mother's illness, and who liked to parade around in her sumptuous dresses. Now, however, the old woman and her daughter had been reduced to abject poverty and even resorted to daily visits next door to Fyodor Pavlovich's kitchen for soup and bread. Marfa Ignatyevna gave it willingly, but the daughter who came for the soup never sold a single one of her dresses, one of which even had an extremely long train. Alyosha had heard about this quite by chance from his friend Rakitin, who knew all there was to know in our little town, and having found out, needless to say promptly forgot it. But now, as he reached the old woman's garden, he suddenly remembered about that train, snapped out of his reverie, raised his head, and... stumbled into a most unexpected meeting.

Behind the wattle fence of the next garden his brother Dmitry, perched on something, was leaning over the fence, gesticulating wildly and beckoning to him, obviously afraid of shouting or even speaking aloud for fear of being overheard. Alyosha at once ran up to the fence.

'It's a good thing you looked up, otherwise I'd have had to call out,' Dmitry Fyodorovich whispered quickly and excitedly. 'Quick. Climb over here. It's wonderful to see you. I was just thinking about you...'

Alyosha too was glad, only he could not fathom how to get over the fence. But Mitya, with his strong arm, supported his elbow and helped him to jump over. Hitching up his cassock, Alyosha leapt across with the agility of a barefoot street urchin.

'Well done, now come here!' said Mitya in an excited whisper.

'Where?' whispered Alyosha, peering around on all sides and finding himself in a garden completely empty except for the two of them. The garden was small, but the house to which it belonged was at least fifty paces from them. 'There's nobody here. What are you whispering for?'

'What for?' Dmitry Fyodorovich suddenly shouted aloud. 'Hanged if I know! Well, you see for yourself how ridiculous one can be. I'm here in secret, and I've come to spy on a secret.

I'll explain later, but since it was a secret I started to talk secretively, and was whispering like an idiot when there was no need. Come on! This way! And don't say a word. But let me give you a hug!

> Glory on earth to the Highest,*
> Glory to the Highest in me!...

That's what I was saying to myself, sitting here just now, before you arrived...'

The garden was about a *desyatina** or a little more, planted with trees around the edges only—apple trees, maples, limes, and birches. The middle of the garden was empty and formed a small clearing where in summer several *poods** of hay were harvested. From spring the owner let the garden for a few roubles. Near the perimeter fence there were also rows of raspberry-canes and gooseberry and currant bushes, and near the house vegetable-beds had recently been dug. Dmitry Fyodorovich led Alyosha to the remotest corner of the garden. There, among a clump of lime trees and elders, old currant bushes, guelder rose, and lilac, they came upon the ruin of some kind of old green summer-house, blackened and crooked, with trellised walls, but with a roof sufficient to keep out the rain. God only knows when the summer-house had been built; according to rumour some fifty years before by the then owner of the house, a retired lieutenant-colonel by the name of Alexander Karlovich von Schmidt. But it was already falling apart, the floor was sagging, the floorboards were loose, and all the timbers smelt of damp. In the summer-house there stood a green wooden table, its legs inserted into the ground, and around it there were benches, also painted green, on which one could still sit. Alyosha immediately noticed his brother's state of elation, and now, on entering the summer-house, he saw on the table half a bottle of brandy and a glass.

'It's brandy,' said Mitya with a laugh, 'and I can tell what you're thinking: "He's drinking again." But don't jump to conclusions.

> Do not believe the false and shallow crowd,
> And doubts dismiss...*

I'm not getting drunk, I'm just "treating myself", as that swine Rakitin would say and will still be saying when he's a state councillor. Sit down, Alyosha. I want to hug you, yes, that's right, a real bear-hug, because in the whole wide world... dee-eep down (listen! listen to me!), you're the only person I love!'

He uttered these last words almost in a kind of frenzy.

'Only you, and a little slut that I've fallen in love with, to my undoing. But to fall in love is not the same as to love. You can be in love even while hating someone. Remember that! But just now I'm cheerful and I feel like talking. Sit down here at the table and I'll sit near you, where I can see you, and I'll tell you everything. Just listen, and I'll do the talking, because now's the time. And by the way, I think we ought to keep our voices down, because here... here... the grass can have long ears. I'll explain everything, as I said, the rest will follow. Why have I been dying to talk to you—just now, these past few days, and particularly just now? (It's already five days since I've been hanging around here.) Why all this time? Because you're the only one to whom I can tell the whole truth, because I have to, because I need you, because tomorrow I'm going to dive out of the clouds, because tomorrow, for me, life ends and life begins. Have you ever had the feeling, have you ever dreamt that you were falling over a precipice into a deep pit? Well, that's how I feel now, but I'm not dreaming. And I'm not afraid, and you mustn't be afraid. Actually, I am afraid, but I'm at ease with myself, no, not at ease, in ecstasy... Oh hell, it's all the same, what do I care! Strong in spirit, weak in spirit, fickle in spirit—doesn't matter a jot! Let's celebrate nature: look, everything's drenched in sunlight, the sky, it's so clear, the leaves are all green, it's still high summer, four o'clock in the afternoon and it's so peaceful everywhere! Where are you off to?'

'I was going to father's, but first I wanted to call on Katerina Ivanovna.'

'You're going to her and then to father! Splendid! What a coincidence! That's just why I called you, why I was longing to see you with every sinew of my heart, with every fibre of my body! I wanted you to go to father on my behalf, and then to her, to Katerina Ivanovna, and so kill two birds with one stone. I wanted to send an angel. I could have sent anyone, but I needed to send an angel. And there you were, going to her and to father of your own accord.'

'Surely you didn't really want me to go on your behalf?' Alyosha burst out, his expression pained and sorrowful.

'Go on, you knew it. I can see by your face that you understood at once. But hush, don't make a fuss now! Don't be sorry for me, and no tears!'

Dmitry Fyodorovich stood up looking thoughtful, and put his finger to his forehead:

'She sent for you herself, she wrote you a letter or something, otherwise you wouldn't be going to her!'

'Here's her note,' said Alyosha, taking it from his pocket. Mitya read it quickly.

'And you were taking a short cut round the back lanes! Ye gods—may you be thanked for sending him this way into my arms, like the golden fish to the silly old fisherman in the fairy tale.* Listen, Alyosha, listen, my young brother. Now I'm going to tell you everything. I must get it off my chest. I've already told an angel in heaven, now I have to tell an angel on earth, too. You're my angel on earth. You'll listen to me, judge me, and forgive me... What I need is—for someone higher than myself to forgive me. Listen: if two beings were suddenly to escape from all that is earthly and go floating off into the unknown, or one of them did anyway, and if that one, before flying away or perishing, were to go to the other and say: do this or that for me, do for me what you can never ask of anyone, what you can only ask on your deathbed—surely he would do it... if he were a friend, if he were a brother?'

'I'll do what you ask, only tell me what it is, and make it quick,' Alyosha said.

'Quick... Hm. Don't be impatient, Alyosha: you're getting impatient and flustered. There's no need to hurry. Now the world is entering a new era. Ah, Alyosha, what a pity you've never discovered ecstasy! But what am I saying to you? It's I who've never discovered ecstasy! So, like a fool, I say:

Be noble, O Man!*

Who wrote that?'

Alyosha decided to wait. He realized that at this moment his duty was to be here and, perhaps, nowhere else but here. Mitya was lost in thought, with his elbow propped on the table and his chin resting in the palm of his hand. They both fell silent for a while.

'Alyosha,' said Mitya, 'you're the only one who won't laugh at me! I'd like to start my... confession... with Schiller's *Ode to Joy*. *An die Freude*.* But I don't know any German; all I know is 'An die Freude'. And don't think it's the brandy talking. I'm not in the least drunk. Brandy is brandy, but it takes two bottles to get me drunk—

> And ruddy-faced Silenus*
> On his stumbling donkey—

but I haven't even drunk a quarter of a bottle, and I'm no Silenus. Not Silenus, but Hercules, because I've made a heroic decision. Forgive the analogy, you'll have a lot to forgive me today besides analogies. Don't worry, I'm not rambling. I'm talking seriously and I'll get to the point in a moment. I'm going to be brief. Just a minute, how does it go?...'

He raised his head, thought for a moment, and then began excitedly:

> 'Timidly in rocks concealed*
> Naked Troglodyte lies low;
> Nomad races let the field
> Perish, as they errant go.
> Armed with deadly bow and spear,
> Strides the hunter through the land.
> Woe to strangers who appear
> On that unforgiving strand!
>
> 'When, in her sad wandering lost,
> Seeking traces of her child;
> Ceres hailed the dreary coast,
> Ah, no verdant plain then smiled;
> Not a roof its refuge gave
> Where the guest unwelcome trod,
> And no temple's architrave
> Testified a worshipped god.
>
> 'No refreshing grain or fruit
> Offer her their nourishment;

> Human bones the fanes pollute
> And the altar's sacrament.
> Wheresoe'er her footsteps turned,
> Sorrow only could she scan,
> And her lofty spirit burned,
> Grieving for the fall of man.

Suddenly, Mitya broke down and sobbed. He seized Alyosha by the hand.

'My boy, my dear boy, the fall of man, the fall of man—he is still fallen. It is man's lot on earth to endure terrible suffering, terrible calamities! Don't imagine I'm only a brute of an officer who drinks brandy and leads a life of debauchery. That's all I think about, my brother, the fall of man, I'm being completely honest with you. God forbid that I should be lying or boasting. I think about man in his fallen state because I myself am in that state.

> Would man rise from degradation*
> He must join his mother earth,
> Join in everlasting union
> With the source that gave him birth.

But that's the whole trouble—how am I to join the earth for ever? I can't kiss the earth or cut open her bosom—should I become a ploughman or a shepherd? I walk without knowing where I'm going—towards the stench of ignominy or towards radiance and joy. That's the trouble, everything on earth is such a riddle. And whenever I have sunk to the most abject, the most appalling degradation (and this has always happened to me), I've always read this poem about Ceres* and man's degradation. And has it made me any better? Never! Because I am a Karamazov. Because if I fall into the abyss, I go head first and even take pleasure in the extent of my own degradation, even find beauty in it. And from those depths of degradation, I begin to sing a hymn. I may be damned, I may be base and despicable, but I kiss the hem of the robe that envelops my God; I may be serving the devil at that same moment, but I'm still your son, O Lord, and I love you and feel that joy without which the world could not exist.

'Joy in Nature's wide dominion,*
Mightiest cause of all is found;
And 'tis Joy that moves the pinion,
When the wheel of time goes round;
From the bud she lures the flower—
Suns from out their orbs of light;
Distant spheres obey her power,
Far beyond all mortal sight.
'From the breasts of kindly Nature
All of Joy imbibe the dew;
Good and bad alike, each creature
Would her roseate path pursue.
'Tis through *her* the wine-cup maddens,
Love and friends to man she gives!
Lust the meanest insect gladdens—
Near God's throne the Cherub lives!

But that's enough of poetry! I've shed tears, let me carry on weeping. This may be just foolishness that everyone will laugh at, but not you. Your eyes are glistening too. No more poetry. Now I want to tell you about the "insects", those that God's endowed with lust:

Lust the meanest insect gladdens!

I'm that very insect, it's me that's meant. And none of us Karamazovs is any different; even in you, angel that you are, this insect lives and whips up a fever in the blood. Yes—a fever: for lust is febrile, it's more than a fever! Beauty's an awesome, terrible thing! It's awesome because it's indefinable; as indefinable and mysterious as everything in God's creation. It's where opposites converge, where contradictions rule! I'm not an educated man, Alyosha, but I've thought about it a lot. There are so many mysteries! Man is beset by too many mysteries on this earth. Fathom them as best you can, and survive unscathed. Beauty! Sometimes it's just too much to bear, to see a man of noble heart and high intellect begin with the ideal of the Madonna and finish with that of Sodom.* And what's even worse, his heart can be aglow with the perfection of the Madonna as it was in the innocence of his youth—and still he won't renounce Sodom. Yes, man's prodigious, much too prodigious, I'd cut him down to size. The devil only knows what to make of all this, that's my opinion! What the intellect finds shameful strikes the heart as sheer beauty! Is there beauty in Sodom? Take it from me, that's just where it lurks for the vast majority of people—you didn't know that, did you? The awesome mystery of beauty! God and the devil are locked in battle over this, and the battlefield is the heart of man. But I'm getting on my hobby-horse. Let's get to the point now.'

4

CONFESSIONS OF A PASSIONATE HEART.
IN ANECDOTES

'I LED a life of debauchery there. Father has been accusing me recently of spending thousands of roubles on seducing young girls. It's a dirty lie, it was never true, the fact is that I've never had to pay for it. To me, money is just an accessory, it fuels the passions and provides the wherewithal. Today my love is a lady, tomorrow a street-walker. And I entertain them both, I spend money like water—on music, fun, gypsies. And if need be I give them money, because, one has to admit, they're more than willing to accept it, they're only too happy to take it and are grateful. I've been loved by young ladies—not always, but it has been known to happen—but I've always frequented back alleys and dark, secluded corners, away from the public square—there you'll find adventure, surprises, gold in the mire. I'm speaking metaphorically, Alyosha. In that little town of ours there weren't really any back alleys like that, but metaphorically speaking they existed all right. If you were like me, you'd understand what I mean. I loved debauchery, I loved the stench of debauchery too. I loved cruelty: am I not a louse, an evil insect? I'm a Karamazov, don't forget that! On one occasion the whole town went on an outing in seven troikas; it was winter, it was dark, and in the sledge I began to squeeze the hand of the girl next to me, a civil servant's daughter, a shy, sweet, poor defenceless little thing. I forced my kisses upon her. In the darkness, she permitted me liberties, many liberties. She thought, bless her, that I'd come the next morning and ask for her hand (I was considered very eligible); but I never said a word to her afterwards, five months and not a word. Often at dances (we were always having dances in our town), I saw her gaze following me from a corner of the hall, her eyes glowing with gentle indignation. This game served to satisfy the insect lust that I nourished inside me. Five months later she married a civil servant and left the town... still angry and perhaps still in love with me. Now they live happily together. Mind you, I didn't tell anyone, I didn't compromise her; in spite of my vile desires and my love of baseness, I'm not dishonourable. You're blushing, your eyes are flashing. You've had enough of this filth. Yet this was only the beginning, a few Paul de Kock* blossoms, and all the while the cruel insect was already maturing, already flourishing in my soul. I've a whole album of memories, Alyosha. But God bless them, the little dears. When the time came to part, I preferred not to quarrel. And I never betrayed or compromised a single one of them. But enough of that. Surely you didn't think I brought you here just to make you listen to all this rubbish? No, I've got something more interesting to tell you; but don't be surprised that I'm not ashamed in front of you; in fact, I'm positively glad.'

'You mean, because I'm blushing?' Alyosha interrupted suddenly. 'But that's not because of what *you've* been saying or what *you've* done. It's because I'm just the same as you.'

'You? That's going a bit far.'

'No, it isn't,' Alyosha said excitedly. (Evidently this thought had already been on his mind for a long time.) 'The ladder's the same for all of us. I'm on the bottom rung and you're a long way up, somewhere near the thirteenth. As I see it, there's absolutely no difference between us. Once one steps on to the first rung, one is bound to go right to the top.'

'So the best thing is not to step on it in the first place?'

'Not if you can help it.'

'Can you?'

'I don't think I can.'

'Hush, Alyosha—hush, my dear brother. I want to kiss your hand, I'm so touched. That vixen Grushenka knows all about men. She told me once that, sooner or later, she'd eat you up. All right, all right, I'll stop! Let's leave all that filth, that fly-ridden dung-heap and talk about my tragedy, also a foul, fly-ridden dung-heap that's teeming with all kinds of vileness. The fact is, although that silly old man was lying about my seducing innocent girls, still, there was in fact one occasion in my tragedy, only one, mind, but nothing actually happened. When he was accusing me of things he'd dreamt up, he didn't know the half of it: I've never told anyone about this, you're the first I've ever told, except Ivan of course, Ivan knows all about it. He's known for ages. But he's as silent as the grave.'

'Ivan—as silent as the grave?'

'Yes.'

Alyosha listened very attentively.

'You see, even though I was an ensign in that Siberian battalion in the back of beyond, I was constantly under surveillance, like a convict. But in the little garrison town they welcomed me with open arms. I spent money like water and people thought I was rich, and I believed it myself. But they must have liked me for some other reason too. Although they shook their heads over me, they were really fond of me. But my commanding officer, a Lieutenant-Colonel, who was already an old man, took a sudden dislike to me. He started to pick on me; still, I was able to pull a few strings and all the town was on my side, so he couldn't actually get at me. I'm not saying I was altogether blameless. I was proud and deliberately refused him the respect that was his due. The old boy, who wasn't a bad sort really, and was extremely kind and hospitable too but stubborn with it, had been married twice, and both his wives had died. His first wife, who was of peasant stock, had left him a daughter. She took after her mother, and when I first knew her she was a young woman of twenty-four, living with her father and her aunt, the sister of her dead mother. The aunt was a quiet, unassuming woman, and her niece, the Lieutenant-Colonel's elder daughter, was a lively and open-hearted girl. Looking back, my dear Alyosha, I'll say this: I've never known a girl of such delightful character. Her name was Agafya, Agafya Ivanovna. She was really not at all bad-looking in a Russian way—tall, buxom, with a good figure and lovely eyes, but unfortunately rather a coarse face. Although she'd had two offers of marriage, she'd stayed single and had kept her vivaciousness. I got to know her very well—not in that way, it was quite innocent, we were just good friends. You know, I've had plenty of quite innocent friendships with women. I could say the most outrageous things to her—and she'd just laugh. Many women love indiscretions, remember that, and what with her being a virgin, I found it most intriguing. She wasn't a prude, that's for sure. She and her aunt lived with her father in a kind of self-imposed subservience, and made no claims to be on the same level as the rest of society. She was well loved and valued for her dressmaking skills; she had a real talent, but didn't charge for her services, helping out from the goodness of her heart, though she didn't refuse payment if it was offered. As for the Lieutenant-Colonel, he was every inch an officer! He was one of the most notable figures in our society. He wasn't mean with his money, and would entertain the whole town at dinners and balls. When I arrived in the town and enlisted in the battalion, the whole place was buzzing in expectation of the imminent arrival from the capital of the Lieutenant-Colonel's second daughter, a renowned beauty, said to have just finished at a high-class finishing-school in the capital. This second daughter—Katerina Ivanovna—was from the Lieutenant-Colonel's second marriage. And the second wife, now dead, had been from a well-known, important military family, although I have it on good authority that she brought the Lieutenant-Colonel no dowry. She had the background, and there must have been some expectations, but in the event—nothing. However, when the young lady arrived (just for a visit, not for good), our whole town seemed to take on a new lease of life, our foremost ladies—two of them titled, one a colonel's wife—took the lead, and everyone else followed them. She was fêted everywhere, she was the queen of balls and picnic outings, events were arranged in aid of distressed governesses. I bided my time, I was living it up, I'd just pulled off some stunt that had got the whole town buzzing. I saw her looking me up and down, it was at the battery commander's house; well, I didn't go over to her then, you could say I declined to make her acquaintance. I approached her some time later, again at a party. I spoke to her but she hardly glanced at me, she curled her lips disdainfully, and I thought, "You wait, I'll get my revenge!" At that time I was generally behaving like a frightful cad, and was well aware of this myself. And I was even more aware that "Katenka" was no innocent little schoolgirl, she had character, she was proud and indeed virtuous, moreover she was intelligent and educated, while I was none of these things. You think I had designs on her? Not at all, I simply wanted to get my revenge on her for not recognizing what a fine fellow I was. Meanwhile, I continued to paint the town red. Finally, the Lieutenant-Colonel put me on a charge for three days. It was just at that time that father sent me six thousand roubles in exchange for my formally renouncing all my rights and agreeing that we were quits and that I wouldn't make any further demands on him. At that time I didn't understand a thing: I understood absolutely nothing about those financial wrangles with father, and that's still the case, old chap, right up to the last few days even, perhaps till today. But to hell with all that now, I'll come to that later. But then, when I had just received that six thousand, a friend sent me a letter containing an item of reliable information which I personally found most interesting, namely, that our Lieutenant-Colonel was under a cloud, that he was suspected of some irregularity—in short, his enemies were plotting to do the dirty on him. And indeed, the divisional commander arrived and gave him a piece of his mind. A short while later he was obliged to resign his commission. I won't bore you with all the details of how this came about; he had some real enemies. Suddenly he and all his family were cold-shouldered in the town, everyone gave them a wide berth. That was when I played my first trick. I met Agafya Ivanovna, with whom I'd always kept up a friendship, and I said: "So, four thousand five hundred roubles are missing from the battalion funds." "What on earth do you mean? The General was here not long ago and it was all there..." "It was there then, but it isn't now." She was terrified. "Don't frighten me, please. Where did you hear that from?" "Don't worry," I said, "I won't tell anyone; you know that in matters like this I'm as silent as the grave, but while we're on the subject, may I add one thing, just in case something happens: when they ask your papa for that four thousand five hundred that he hasn't got, rather than let him be court-martialled and reduced to the ranks in his old age, why don't you send your schoolgirl sister along to me on the quiet, I've just come into some money and, you know, I could probably see my way to helping her out with the four thousand odd, and no one need be any the wiser." "How could you!" she said, "You scoundrel!" (Her very words!) "You wicked scoundrel, you! You haven't got an ounce of shame in you!" She went away in high dudgeon, and I called after her once more that her secret would be safe and inviolate with me. I have to admit that both those simple women, Agafya and her aunt, behaved like perfect angels throughout the affair, they sincerely worshipped Katya, their proud sister, they humbled themselves before her, they were her maidservants... But Agafya repeated everything to her, our conversation, that is. I found this out afterwards, and I'm not telling you a lie. She made no secret of it, and that of course played right into my hands.

'Suddenly, a new Major arrived to take over the battalion. He assumed command. The old Lieutenant-Colonel fell ill suddenly, and couldn't move; he stayed indoors for two days and didn't hand over the battalion funds. Our Doctor Kravchenko informed everybody that he was really ill. But here's what I knew for a fact, and had known for some time: after each annual audit, the money would disappear for a while, and this had happened four years running. The Lieutenant-Colonel lent it to a most trustworthy man, a local merchant by the name of Trifonov, an elderly widower with a beard and gold-rimmed spectacles. He'd go to the fair, use the money for his own purposes, and would then return the whole sum to the Lieutenant-Colonel with interest, and also give him some presents. Only this time (I heard this quite by chance from Trifonov's slobbering son, his heir, a depraved youngster if ever there was one), this time Trifonov came back from the fair and returned nothing. The Lieutenant-Colonel rushed round to see him. "I've received nothing from you and couldn't possibly have done so," was the answer he got. Well, our Lieutenant-Colonel sat at home with his head wrapped in a towel while all three women applied ice to his brow; suddenly an orderly arrived with the accounts book and an order to "Hand over the battalion funds at once, promptly, within two hours." He signed the book (later I saw this signature), stood up, said he was going to put on his uniform, rushed into his bedroom, took down his double-barrelled shotgun, loaded it with a live cartridge, took off his right boot, put the weapon to his chest, and tried to pull the trigger with his toe. But Agafya, remembering my words, suspected something and followed him: she rushed in, grabbed him from behind and clasped her arms around him, the gun went off and the shot hit the ceiling, harming no one; the others ran in and seized him, took the weapon away, and held him by his arms... I learned all these details later. I was at home, it was dusk and I had just decided to go out; I put on my coat, combed my hair, put some perfume on my handkerchief, and picked up my fur hat, when the door suddenly opened—and there before me stood Katerina Ivanovna.

'Strange things happen: no one had noticed her in the street on her way to me, no one in the town knew of her visit. I rented the rooms from two civil service widows, two very old women, who also looked after me. They were very respectful towards me, trusted me implicitly and would have taken a secret to the grave if I'd asked them. Of course, I realized the situation at once. She entered and looked straight at me with an expression of determination, even harshness in her dark eyes, but in her lips and the set of her mouth I could detect uncertainty.

'"My sister told me you'd lend me four thousand five hundred roubles if I came for it... if I came myself. Here I am... give me the money...!" She broke down, gasping, terrified, her voice broke, and her lips and her whole mouth began to tremble. Alyosha, are you listening or are you asleep?'

'Mitya, I know you're going to tell me the whole truth,' said Alyosha apprehensively.

'Certainly I am. If it's the whole truth you want, then this is how it happened, I won't conceal a thing. My first thought was— a Karamazov one. Once, Alyosha, I was bitten by a scorpion, and for two weeks I was confined to bed with fever; and that's what I felt then—the sudden sting of a scorpion in my heart, an evil insect, you know? I eyed her up and down. You've seen her! She's beautiful, isn't she? But it wasn't just her beauty then. What made her particularly attractive at that moment was that she was pure and I was a scoundrel, she was magnificent in her generosity and in her sacrifice for her father, and I was just a louse. And she was now *utterly* dependent on me, louse and scoundrel that I was, she was at my mercy, body and soul. I had

her cornered. I don't mind telling you that that thought, the
insect's thought, was the sweetest thing I ever experienced. It
seemed as if there could be no question of any struggle: why
stop now, why not just go ahead like the louse, like the evil
tarantula that I am, without the slightest compunction... I
couldn't breathe. Listen: of course, it goes without saying that
the next day I'd have asked for her hand in marriage, to bring
the matter to an honourable conclusion, so to speak, so that no
one would ever have known anything about this business.
Because, all my base desires apart, I still claim to be a man of
honour. And then suddenly at that very moment it was as though
someone whispered in my ear, "But she's the sort who wouldn't
have anything to do with you if you went to her tomorrow with a
proposal of marriage, and what's more, she'd get her coachman
to throw you out on your ear. 'You can drag my name in the
mud through the whole town,' she'd say, 'I'm not afraid of you!'"
I looked at the girl, the voice was not lying; that was certainly
how it would be. Her face said it all; I'd be out on my neck. I
was suddenly in a rage. I felt I wanted to play the lowest, most
swinish trick on her, some tradesman's trick: give her a look of
derision and then, as she stood there before me, humiliate her,
saying in the tone of voice only market traders use:
    '"Four thousand! You didn't really fall for that little joke of
mine, did you, ma'am? You're too credulous, my dear lady, to
believe in a thing like that. I could let you have a couple of
hundred, perhaps, the pleasure would be all mine, but four
thousand—that, madam, is not the sort of money that one
splashes about. You've come on a fool's errand."
    'Of course, you can see, I'd have lost everything, she'd have
run away, but that sweet moment of vengeance would have been
worth it. Afterwards I know I'd have wept with remorse all my
life, but I still wish I'd gone through with it. You may not believe
it, but in all my life nothing of the sort had ever happened to me
before, not with any woman, I had never looked at any woman
with such hatred—I swear by all that's holy, I looked at her then
for two or three seconds with a terrible hatred—a hatred that's
only a hair's breadth away from love, from the most desperate
love! I walked over to the window, pressed my forehead against
the frosted pane of glass, and I remember that the ice burned

my skin like fire. I didn't keep her waiting long, don't worry; I turned round, went to my desk, pulled out a drawer and produced a five-thousand-rouble, five-per-cent promissory note *au porteur* (it was there, between the pages of my French dictionary). I showed it to her, didn't say a word, folded it and gave it to her. Then I opened the door for her, took a step back and bowed, respectfully and correctly, I can assure you! She stared at me for a second, trembling all over and as white as a sheet, and then all of a sudden, also without a word, softly, gently, quietly, went down on her knees at my feet, her forehead touching the ground, not like a schoolgirl, but in the traditional Russian way! Then she jumped up and fled. When she ran out I had my sword on me; I unsheathed it and was going to run myself through with it there and then; why—I don't know. Of course it was utter stupidity, but it must have been from sheer ecstasy. Do you realize, there are times when one can kill oneself from ecstasy? But I didn't kill myself, I just kissed the sword and replaced it in its scabbard—anyway, I shouldn't have told you that. It seems to me now that in describing all these struggles of mine, I've laid it on a bit thick to present myself in the best light. But never mind, what will be will be, and to hell with all who pry into the human heart! So there, that was the "incident" between Katerina Ivanovna and myself. Only Ivan knows about it, and now you—no one else.'

Overcome by emotion, Dmitry Fyodorovich got up, took one step and then another, pulled out his handkerchief, wiped the sweat from his brow, and then sat down again, not where he had just been sitting but on a bench against the opposite wall, so that Alyosha had to turn right round to face him.

5
CONFESSIONS OF A PASSIONATE HEART.
'IN FREE FALL'

'FAIR enough,' said Alyosha, 'now I've got some idea of what all this is about.'

'That's good. The first part's a drama and it happened in

another town. The second part's a tragedy and it will take place here.'

'I can't say I understand anything of the second part,' Alyosha said.

'What about me? Do you think I can?'

'Wait a moment, Dmitry, there's one thing that's really important. Tell me, are you still engaged? You are, aren't you?'

'We didn't get engaged immediately, but three months later. The day after it all happened, I told myself that the whole thing was over and done with and that was the end of it. To propose to her then would have seemed to me a vile thing to do. And for the whole of the six weeks that she lived in the town after that, I never heard a word from her, except, however, on one occasion. The day after her visit, their maid turned up at my lodgings and, without saying a word, handed me an envelope. It was addressed to me. I opened it and found the change from the five thousand roubles. Only four and a half thousand had been needed, but it cost over two hundred roubles to cash the promissory note. She returned two hundred and sixty roubles in all, I think, I don't remember the exact amount—no message, no explanation, not a word. I examined the envelope for any pencil marks—nothing! So I went on a spree with the rest of my roubles, so much so that the new major eventually felt obliged to reprimand me. As for the Lieutenant-Colonel, he duly paid over the outstanding money, much to everyone's surprise, as no one believed he still had it. As soon as he had handed it over, he fell ill, took to his bed and stayed there for about three weeks, after which softening of the brain set in and he died five days later. He was buried with full military honours, as he hadn't actually retired yet. Within ten days of their father's funeral, Katerina Ivanovna and her sister moved with their aunt to Moscow. And just before they left, on the very day of their departure (I hadn't seen them at all in the meantime and hadn't gone to say goodbye), I received a little note, a small blue sheet of fancy paper, with one line written in pencil: "I'll write to you. Be Patient. K." That was all.

'Now I'll explain everything to you briefly. In Moscow their situation changed with the speed of lightning and the unexpectedness of an Arabian tale. Her nearest relative, a General's widow, suddenly lost both her heirs, her two nieces—they both died the same week of smallpox. The grief-stricken old woman greeted Katya's arrival with as much joy as if she were her own daughter, and turned to her as to a star of salvation. She changed her will in her favour—that was for the future; but in the meantime she gave her eighty thousand roubles in cash, saying, "Here, this is for you, it's your dowry, do what you like with it." A highly eccentric lady, as I had occasion to discover for myself later in Moscow. Well, next thing I knew, I received out of the blue by post four thousand five hundred roubles: of course, I was dumbfounded. Three days later the promised letter arrived. I've got it now, I keep it on me all the time, I shall take it to the grave with me—shall I show it to you? You must read it: she offers to marry me, offers herself to me: "I love you hopelessly," she says, "it doesn't matter that you don't love me, just be my husband. Don't worry, I shan't be an embarrassment to you in any way, I'll be like a piece of furniture, I'll be the carpet under your feet... I want to love you for ever and ever, I want to save you from yourself..." Alyosha, I'm not worthy even to repeat these lines in my own shameless words, in my own disgraceful tone of voice, that shameless tone of voice that I always use, that I've never been able to rid myself of! That letter pierced me to the quick, and do you think I've got over it yet, to this day? I sent my reply at once (I couldn't possibly go to Moscow in person). I wrote it with my tears; there's one shameful thing that still haunts me though, I mentioned in the letter that she was rich now and had a dowry, while I was nothing but a penniless humbug—I mentioned the money! I should never have done that, but it slipped from my pen. Then I wrote at once to Ivan in Moscow and explained everything to him, everything I could put in a letter, six pages of it, and asked him to go and see her. Why are you looking at me like that? Well, Ivan fell in love with her, he's still in love with her. I know that in your eyes and in the eyes of the world I did a foolish thing, but perhaps it's just that foolish thing that will save us all now. Surely you can see why she looks up to him and respects him? Surely, when she compares the two of us, she can't love someone like me, especially after all that's happened?'

'I'm sure it is someone like you she loves, and not someone like him.'

'It's her own virtue she loves, not me,' Dmitry Fyodorovich suddenly burst out almost with bitterness, in spite of himself. He laughed, but a moment later his eyes glinted, he flushed and struck the table hard with his fist.

'I swear, Alyosha,' he exclaimed with a rush of unfeigned anger at himself, 'believe it or not, but as God is holy and Christ is Our Lord, I swear that although I was mocking her noble sentiments just now, I know that my soul is a million times inferior to hers, and that those elevated sentiments of hers are as sincere as those of an angel in heaven! The tragedy is that I know it perfectly well. What harm is there in a bit of melodrama? Am I not being melodramatic? And yet I'm sincere—really sincere. As for Ivan, I understand perfectly how he must be cursing the whole of creation, especially with his intelligence! Who is it who's been shown preference? A swine like me, who's engaged to be married and when all eyes are upon him still refuses to cease his debauchery—and in front of his fiancée, his fiancée no less! It's monstrous for someone like me to be preferred while he's rejected. And all because a young girl wants to ruin her life and her future out of gratitude! It's absurd! I've never said anything about this to Ivan, naturally, and Ivan hasn't said a word to me, not the slightest hint; but fate will run its course, he who is worthy will have his day and the unworthy one will slink away and hide himself in a back alley for ever—in his own dirty little back alley, in his beloved back alley, his home, and there in the filth and the stench he will perish of his own free will and with the greatest delight. I'm getting carried away, I've run out of words, I'm ranting, but it'll be as I've said. I'll perish in my iniquity and she will marry Ivan.'

'Listen, Mitya,' interrupted Alyosha once more in extreme agitation. 'You know there's one thing you still haven't explained. You're engaged, you are still engaged to her, aren't you? How can you break it off if your fiancée doesn't want to?'

'I am her fiancé, our engagement has been blessed, it all happened in Moscow after I arrived there—we had a ceremony with icons, in the grandest style. The General's widow gave us her blessing and—can you believe it—even congratulated Katya: "You've made a good choice," she said, "I can see he's a fine man." And, can you imagine, she took a dislike to Ivan and treated him with disdain. While I was in Moscow I talked a lot to Katya and told her everything about myself, honestly, in all sincerity, omitting nothing. She listened to all I had to say:

> And there was sweet confusion,
> There were tender words...*

Well, there were defiant words too. She made me promise solemnly to mend my ways. I promised. And now...'

'Well?'

'Now I've stopped you, now we're here, this day of the week, this month—mark it well!—in order here and now to ask you to go this very day and see Katerina Ivanovna for me, and...'

'Well?'

'Tell her that I shall never see her again and tell her that I send her my regards.'

'You can't do that!'

'No, *I* can't. That's why I'm sending you in my stead. I couldn't possibly do it myself.'

'And where will you go?'

'Back to the gutter.'

'To Grushenka, you mean!' Alyosha exclaimed sadly, holding up his hands. 'Was Rakitin telling the truth after all? And I thought she was just a passing infatuation and that it was all over.'

'Can a husband-to-be have passing infatuations? Is it possible with such a fiancée and so openly? After all, I do still have some sense of honour. From the moment I started seeing Grushenka that was the end of my engagement and I ceased to be a man of honour, that much I understand. Don't look at me like that! You see, at first I only wanted to give her a good hiding. I had found out, and now I know for sure, that the Staff Captain,* who was father's go-between, had taken a promissory note of mine to Grushenka with the idea that she should demand payment from me in order to put me down and shut me up. They just wanted to frighten me. So I went straight to Grushenka to give her a beating. I had seen her around before. She isn't stunning to look at. I knew about that elderly merchant of hers, who was ill and senile by then and was going to leave her a nice little nest egg. I knew also that she liked to make money, that she lent at an exorbitant rate of interest, and that she was a cheat and a merciless bitch. I went to her place to give her a hiding, but instead I stayed with her. The thunder crashed, the fever struck, I caught it and it's still in my blood; I knew straight away that my fate was sealed, and that that was the end of the matter. The wheel had turned full circle. So there I was. And then suddenly, out of the blue, this miserable wretch had managed to come by three thousand roubles. The two of us went straight to Mokroye, that's about twenty-five versts from here, I invited some gypsies along, together with all the peasants, their wives and daughters, brought bottles of champagne and ended up drunk; I got through thousands of roubles. In three days I was cleaned out but undaunted. And do you think it got me anywhere? Not a bit of it. She never let me get near her. I tell you—that figure of hers! The body of that hell-cat of a woman is nothing but curves from top to bottom, right down to the little toe on her left foot... I saw that toe and I kissed it, but that's all, I swear. She said, "If you want, I'll marry you, pauper as you are. Just say you won't beat me and you'll let me do what I like, and then perhaps I will marry you." She laughed—and she's still laughing!'

Dmitry Fyodorovich stood up almost in a frenzy, he seemed as though he were drunk all of a sudden. His eyes had suddenly become bloodshot.

'Do you really want to marry her?'

'If she'll let me, I'll marry her at once, and if she doesn't, I'll stay with her anyway; I'll be her odd-job man. Alyosha, do you... do you...', he faltered, seizing him by the shoulders and shaking him, 'do you realize, you innocent child, that all this is delirium, sheer delirium, because this is a tragedy! You know, Alyosha, I may be a base creature, a lost soul, prey to base passions, but a thief, a pickpocket, a common thief, Dmitry Karamazov could never be. Well now, you can see I'm a thief, a pickpocket, a common thief! Just as I was going to Grushenka's to give her a hiding, that very morning Katerina Ivanovna sent for me in great secrecy so that no one would know (I don't know why, she must have had her reasons), and asked me to go to the provincial capital and post three thousand roubles to Agafya Ivanovna in Moscow—I was to post it from there so that no one in our town would know. I arrived at Grushenka's with that three thousand roubles in my pocket, and that was the money we went to Mokroye with. Afterwards I pretended I'd been to the town, but I never gave her the postal receipt: I told her I'd sent the money and would bring the receipt, but I still haven't done it, because I conveniently "keep forgetting". Now, what do you think, suppose you went to her today and said, "He sends his regards," and she said, "And what about the money?" Then you could reply: "He's a despicable debauchee, a vile creature, uncontrollable in his urges. He never posted your money, he spent it, because, just like an animal, he couldn't control himself," and you could have added for good measure: "However, he's not a thief, here's your three thousand, he's returning it, you can post it to Agafya Ivanovna yourself, and by the way he sends his regards." But as it is, all she'll be able to say is, "Well, where's the money?"

'Mitya, you're unhappy, that's obvious. But things are not as bad as you think. Don't let despair get the better of you, for heaven's sake!'

'What do you imagine I'm going to do? Shoot myself if I don't get the three thousand to pay her back? Well, I shan't shoot myself. I haven't got the courage at present, later perhaps, now I'm going to see Grushenka... And let the world go to blazes!'

'And when you get there?'

'I'll be her husband, I'll prove my worth, and if a lover comes I'll go into another room. I'll clean the muddy boots of her admirers, I'll fan the embers under the samovar, I'll run errands...'

'Katerina Ivanovna will understand,' said Alyosha solemnly. 'She'll understand the depth of your sorrow and she'll forgive you. She's a very understanding person, she'll see for herself that no one could be more miserable than you.'

'She won't forgive everything,' Mitya grinned. 'There are some things, my young brother, that no woman can forgive. But you know what would be the best thing to do?'

'What?'

'Return the three thousand.'

'Where would you get hold of such a sum? Listen, I've got two thousand, Ivan will give you another thousand, that makes three. Take it and give it to her.'

'But when could I have it, your three thousand? You're still a minor, and it's absolutely essential that you go today and break off the engagement on my behalf, money or no money, because things have come to such a pitch that I can't put it off any longer. Tomorrow would be too late. Go to father for me.'

'To father?'

'Yes, go to father before you go to her, and ask him for three thousand.'

'But Mitya, you know he won't give it to me.'

'Of course, I know only too well he won't give it to you. Aleksei, do you know what despair is?'

'Indeed I do.'

'Listen, legally he owes me nothing. I've had it all, I know that. But morally he owes me something, doesn't he? After all, he made a hundred thousand from my mother's twenty-eight thousand roubles. Let him give me three thousand out of the twenty-eight, only three, and he'll save my soul from damnation; that will atone for a lot of his sins! As for me, I shall be content with the three thousand, I give you my solemn word on that, and I shan't bother him ever again. I'm giving him one last chance to be a father. Tell him that God himself has sent him this chance.'

'Mitya, he won't give it to you whatever I say.'

'I know he won't, I know that perfectly well. Especially now. What's more, I also know that very recently, perhaps only yesterday, he recognized for the first time *seriously* (notice I say "seriously") that Grushenka may not actually be joking and that she might rush into marriage with me. He knows what a minx she is. So, how on earth could he give me the money to enable that to happen when he's crazy about her himself? But that's not all, I've got something else to tell you: I know that five days ago he got three thousand roubles in one-hundred-rouble notes from the bank and put the money in a large envelope sealed with five seals and tied both ways with a red ribbon. You see, I know all the exact details! On the envelope it says: "To my angel Grushenka, if she will come to me." He wrote that himself in the utmost secrecy, and no one knows he has all that money in his house, except his servant Smerdyakov, who's scrupulously honest as far as he's concerned. And he's been waiting for Grushenka for the last three or four days, hoping she'd come for the envelope, because he told her about it and she sent a message in reply saying that she "might come". So, if she goes to the old man, I can't marry her, can I? Now do you understand why I'm hiding here and keeping watch?'

'For her?'

'Yes, for her. Foma rents a little room here from the old women who own the house. He's from these parts, he's an old soldier. At night he works as a watchman for them, and by day he shoots blackcock. That's how he earns his living. I'm staying at his place for the moment: neither he nor the owners know the secret—that is, that I'm keeping watch.'

'Only Smerdyakov knows?'

'Yes. He'll let me know if she goes to father.'

'Did he tell you about the envelope?'

'Yes. It's a big secret. Even Ivan doesn't know about the money or anything. Father wants him to go on a trip to Chermashnya for two or three days. A buyer has turned up who'll pay eight thousand roubles for the timber and fell it, so father keeps asking Ivan to help him out and go there for two or three days. But it's just to get him out of the way when Grushenka comes!'

'So he's expecting Grushenka today?'

'No, she won't come today, at least I don't think so. In fact I'm sure she won't!' Mitya cried suddenly. 'That's what Smerdyakov thinks too. Father's getting drunk now, sitting at the table with Ivan. Listen, Alyosha, go and ask him for the three thousand...'

'Mitya, my dear fellow, what's the matter with you?' exclaimed Alyosha, jumping up and staring at Dmitry Fyodorovich's frenzied expression. For a moment Alyosha thought he had lost his reason.

'Don't worry! I haven't gone mad,' said Dmitry Fyodorovich, fixing him with a penetrating, solemn gaze. 'Don't be afraid; I want you to go to father and I know what I'm doing: I believe in miracles.'

'Miracles?'

'The miracles of divine providence. God knows my heart, He sees all my despair. He sees this whole scene. Surely He won't allow anything bad to happen? Alyosha, I believe in miracles. Off you go!'

'I'll go. Will you wait here?'

'Yes. I realize it'll take time, that you can't ask him straight out as soon as you get there. He's getting drunk now. I'll wait three, four, five, six, seven hours even—but just remember that today, even if it's at midnight, you must go to Katerina Ivanovna *with or without the money* and give her my regards.'

'But Mitya! Suppose Grushenka were to come today... or if not today, then tomorrow or the day after?'

'Grushenka? I'll be watching for her, I'll burst into the house and stop her...'

'But if...'

'In that case, someone's going to get killed. I won't stand for it.'

'Who's going to get killed?'

'Father. I wouldn't kill her.'

'Mitya, do you realize what you're saying!'

'I don't suppose I do, I'm not sure... Perhaps I wouldn't kill him, perhaps I would. I'm afraid that the moment I set eyes on him, his face will become loathsome to me... I hate his bulging gizzard, his nose, his eyes, his shameless mockery. I feel a physical revulsion. That's what I'm afraid of, that I wouldn't be able to control myself...'

'I'll go, Mitya. I believe that God will ensure that everything's for the best and won't allow anything bad to happen.'

'And I'll stay here and wait for a miracle. But if there isn't one, then...'

Alyosha set off for his father's house deep in thought.

6

SMERDYAKOV

AND, indeed, he found his father still eating—in the sitting-room as usual, even though there was a perfectly adequate dining-room in the house. The sitting-room was the largest room in the house, furnished with outmoded stylishness. The furniture was extremely old, of white-wood and upholstered in faded red satin. Pier-mirrors between the windows were mounted in elaborately carved, old-fashioned frames, painted white and gilt. On the walls, on which the white wallpaper was already torn in several places, hung two large portraits—one of a certain prince who, about thirty years before, had been the local governor-general, the other of an archbishop, also long since deceased. In the corner nearest the entrance were several icons, in front of which a lamp was lit at night—not so much in devotion as to provide a source of light in the room. Fyodor Pavlovich went to bed very late, at two, three or four o'clock in the morning, and until then he would pace up and down the room or sit in an armchair and think. Such was his habit. He quite often spent the night completely alone, having sent the servants to the outhouse, though Smerdyakov would generally stay with him at night and sleep on a chest in the entrance hall. When Alyosha arrived, dinner was over and coffee and preserves were being served. Fyodor Pavlovich loved to have something sweet with his brandy after dinner. Ivan Fyodorovich was also at the table, drinking coffee. The servants Grigory and Smerdyakov were standing nearby. Both master and servants were in a state of unusual jollity. Fyodor Pavlovich was roaring with laughter; Alyosha could hear that shrill voice which was so familiar to him from the porch, and he concluded that his father was still far from drunk, and merely in a convivial mood.

'Here he is, here he is!' yelled Fyodor Pavlovich, delighted at the sight of Alyosha. 'Come and join us. Sit down and have some coffee—don't worry, look, it's black, piping hot, it's just been made! Won't offer you brandy—you're fasting, but you'd like some, wouldn't you? No, I'd better give you a drop of liqueur instead, it's very nice! Smerdyakov, go to the cupboard; it's on the second shelf on the right—here are the keys, stir yourself!'

Alyosha refused the liqueur.

'We'll pour it anyway, if not for you, then for us,' Fyodor Pavlovich beamed. 'By the way, have you had dinner?'

'Yes, I have,' said Alyosha, who, truth to tell, had eaten only a crust of bread and a glass of kvass in the abbot's kitchen. 'But I'll gladly have a cup of coffee.'

'Excellent, my dear boy! He'll have a cup of coffee. Should we heat it up? No need, it's still hot. It's excellent coffee, Smerdyakov made it. When it comes to coffee or fish pie Smerdyakov's an artist and no mistake, the same goes for his fish soup. You must come one day and have some fish soup, but let me know beforehand... Wait a minute though, didn't I tell you to bring your mattress and pillow and come home this very day? Have you brought your mattress? He-he-he...'

'No, I haven't,' Alyosha smiled.

'But you were frightened this morning? You were, weren't you? Ah, my dear boy, I wouldn't hurt you for the world. Look, Ivan, look at the way he fixes you with his eyes and smiles, it's just too much. It really is. All my insides turn to jelly. I really do love him! Alyosha, let me give you my paternal blessing.'

Alyosha stood up, but Fyodor Pavlovich had already thought better of it.

'No, no, I'll just make the sign of the cross over you for now, there you are, sit down. And now, you're going to enjoy this—it'll make you laugh. Our Balaam's ass* has spoken—and on a subject close to your heart. And can he talk, my word, can he talk!'

'Balaam's ass' turned out to be Smerdyakov. Still a young man, only twenty-four years old, he was thoroughly surly and unsociable. It was not that he was shy or in any way embarrassed; on the contrary, he was arrogant by nature and seemed to despise everyone. But at this point it is impossible to avoid saying something about him. Marfa Ignatyevna and Grigory Vasilyevich had brought him up, but, as Grigory put it, the boy had grown up "without the slightest gratitude", and had turned into a wild, unsociable youth who regarded the world as if trapped in a corner. As a child he had loved to string up cats and then bury them with full ceremony. He would dress up in a sheet, to represent a chasuble, and chant while swinging some imagined censer over the dead cat. He would do this very secretly and surreptitiously. Grigory caught him at it one day and gave him a good birching. The boy slunk off into a corner and remained there for a week, glaring sullenly at everyone. 'He doesn't love us, the monster,' Grigory would say to Marfa Ignatyevna. 'In fact, he doesn't love anyone... You can't be human,' he once addressed Smerdyakov outright, 'You're not human, you're the spawn of bathhouse slime, that's what you are...' Smerdyakov, it turned out later, never forgave him for these remarks. Grigory taught him to read and write, and when he was twelve started to teach him the Scriptures. But it soon proved to be a wasted effort. One day, during only his second or third lesson, the boy suddenly burst out laughing.

'What's the matter with you?' asked Grigory with a thunderous look from under his glasses.

'Nothing, sir. God created light* on the first day, and the sun, the moon, and the stars on the fourth day. So where did the light come from on the first day?'

Grigory was dumbfounded. The boy looked mockingly at his teacher. There was even something arrogant in his look. Grigory could not contain himself. 'This'll teach you where from!' he shouted in a fury, and slapped his pupil across the cheek. The boy suffered the slap without a word, but retreated to his corner again for several days. A week later he suffered the first of the epileptic fits which afflicted him for the rest of his life. Hearing of this, Fyodor Pavlovich suddenly seemed to change his attitude to the boy. Previously he had been fairly indifferent to him, although he never scolded him and always gave him a kopeck when he saw him. When he was in a good mood, he sometimes sent the boy sweetmeats from the table. But now, on hearing of his illness, he began to show a genuine concern and sent for the doctor to treat him, but the illness turned out to be incurable. On average, the attacks occurred about once a month at irregular intervals. They also varied in severity—some were slight, while others were extremely violent. Fyodor Pavlovich absolutely forbade Grigory to inflict any corporal punishment, and gave the boy permission to come up to the house. He also stopped all lessons for the time being. But one day, when the boy was about fifteen, Fyodor Pavlovich noticed him lurking near the bookcase and reading the titles of the books through the glass. Fyodor Pavlovich had a large collection of books, over a hundred, but no one ever saw him open one. He promptly gave Smerdyakov the key to the bookcase. 'Well, if you want to read, go ahead, you can be my librarian. Rather than loiter about in the yard, it's better that you sit down and read. Here, have a look at this one,' and Fyodor Pavlovich took down *Evenings on a Farm near Dikanka.**

The boy read it, but remained unimpressed; it did not so

much as produce a smile on his face, on the contrary, after finishing it he scowled.

'Well? Didn't you find it funny?' asked Fyodor Pavlovich.

Smerdyakov said nothing.

'Answer me, you fool.'

'None of it's true,' muttered Smerdyakov with a smirk.

'Well, go to hell! This is just the sort of thing a lackey would say. Wait, here's Smaragdov's *Universal History*;* that's true enough for you. Read that.'

But Smerdyakov did not even read ten pages of Smaragdov; it bored him stiff. So the bookcase was locked up again. Soon Marfa and Grigory informed Fyodor Pavlovich that Smerdyakov was gradually becoming terribly fastidious; he would sit at the table, take a spoon and, with head bent, would stir his soup intently, as if searching for something, then lift a spoonful and hold it to the light.

'What is it, a cockroach?' Grigory would ask.

'A fly perhaps,' Marfa would comment.

The fussy youth never replied, but did exactly the same thing with bread, meat, and all kinds of food; he would take a morsel on his fork, hold it up to the light and subject it to microscopic scrutiny, taking a long time to make up his mind, before at last venturing to put it into his mouth. 'Look at that,' Grigory would mutter, watching him, 'thinks he's a proper little gentleman.' Fyodor Pavlovich, on hearing of Smerdyakov's new habit, promptly decided that he should be a cook and sent him to be trained in Moscow. He spent several years in training, and returned quite changed in appearance. He had somehow suddenly aged extraordinarily; his skin was wrinkled and yellow quite beyond his years, and he had the appearance of a eunuch. Emotionally, there was almost no change; he returned much as he had left, just as unsociable and not demonstrating the slightest desire for company. It turned out that in Moscow too he had kept himself to himself all the time; Moscow as such had interested him hardly at all, so that while he did not exactly ignore everything about it, he certainly did not manifest much interest in the city. He did go to the theatre on one occasion, but came home morose and disgruntled. To do him justice, however, he returned from his stay in Moscow well dressed, wearing a clean frock-coat and a spotless white shirt; he brushed his clothes carefully, as often as twice a day, and, using a special English wax, took great delight in polishing his elegant calfskin boots to a deep shine. He turned out to be an excellent cook. Fyodor Pavlovich paid him a salary, nearly all of which he spent on clothes, pomade, perfume, and the like. But he seemed to despise women as much as men, and was very reserved with them—indeed almost unapproachable. Gradually, Fyodor Pavlovich began to revise his opinion about him. The fact was, his epileptic fits were getting worse, and on those occasions the food had to be prepared by Marfa Ignatyevna, which did not suit Fyodor Pavlovich one little bit.

'Why is it your fits are becoming more frequent these days?' he would ask him from time to time, peering into his face. 'What about getting married? Would you like me to find you a wife...?'

But Smerdyakov paled with resentment at these remarks, and refused to answer. Fyodor Pavlovich would walk away, shrugging his shoulders. The most important thing was that he was convinced of his honesty; without a shadow of doubt he knew that he would never take anything, never steal. Once Fyodor Pavlovich, when somewhat drunk, dropped three hundred-rouble notes that he had just got in the dust in his own courtyard, and did not realize his loss till the following day. Hardly had he begun to turn out his pockets when suddenly there they were, all three of them, lying on the table. Where had they come from? Smerdyakov had picked them up and placed them there the night before. 'Well, old chap, I've never met anyone else like you,' he said, and gave him ten roubles. It must be added here that not only did he have complete trust in him, but also, for some reason, was fond of him, even though the youth looked askance at him just as he did at everyone else, and maintained a stubborn silence. He rarely spoke. Had anyone thought to wonder at that time what he was interested in and what he really had on his mind, it would have been impossible to say by looking at him. Nevertheless, he would sometimes stop dead in the house or the courtyard or the street and stand there, as if lost in thought, for ten minutes at a time. A physiognomist, seeing him thus, would have said that he had no thoughts or ideas in his head at such times, but that he was simply deep in contemplation.

There is a remarkable picture by the painter Kramskoy* entitled *Contemplative*: it depicts a forest in winter, and in the forest, on a track, stands the lone, diminutive figure of a peasant dressed in a ragged kaftan and bast sandals. Standing there in utter solitude, he seems lost in thought, but in reality he is not thinking at all but merely 'contemplating'. If you were to nudge him, he would start and look at you as if he had just woken up, oblivious of his surroundings. True, he would soon snap out of his reverie, but if you were to ask him what he had been thinking about as he stood there, he would probably remember nothing, although that would not stop him from locking away, deep inside him, a memory of the sensations that he had experienced during his contemplation. Those sensations are dear to him, and he probably stores them away instinctively and without conscious thought—why and for what purpose, of course, he does not know: perhaps, after many years of hoarding them, he might unexpectedly throw up everything and go off to Jerusalem as a wandering pilgrim, or perhaps he might suddenly set fire to his native village, or perhaps both. There are any number of contemplatives among the peasantry. Very likely Smerdyakov was one such, and he too, no doubt, was avidly accumulating his impressions, scarcely knowing what for.

7

CONTROVERSY

BUT then, suddenly, Balaam's ass started to speak. And the subject was a strange one: that morning, while shopping at the stall of the merchant Lukyanov, Grigory had heard from him about a Russian soldier* who had been captured in some far-off place by Asiatics, who threatened him with a slow and agonizing death unless he renounced Christianity and adopted Islam. He refused to abandon his faith and accepted martyrdom, submitted to being flayed alive, and died praising and glorifying Christ— which heroic sacrifice was announced in the newspaper that had arrived that very day. Grigory had begun to talk about this at table. After dinner, after the dessert, Fyodor Pavlovich always loved to have a laugh and a chat, even with Grigory. On this occasion he was in an amiable and expansive mood. Having listened to this piece of news as he sipped his brandy, he commented that the soldier should be promptly canonized and his flayed skin sent to a monastery: 'That'd bring in people and money.' Grigory frowned, seeing that Fyodor Pavlovich was not only unmoved, but, as was his wont, was beginning to mock. Smerdyakov, who was standing by the door, suddenly grinned. He had often before been allowed to come and stand near the table, though not till dinner was nearly over. Since Ivan Fyodorovich's arrival in the town, he had appeared at dinner nearly every night.

'What's so funny?' asked Fyodor Pavlovich, immediately noticing the grin, and fully aware, of course, that it was aimed at Grigory.

'Well, sir, I was just thinking,' began Smerdyakov loudly and unexpectedly, 'commendable though the sacrifice of this good soldier was, sir, it would on the other hand have been no sin in my opinion, if, under the circumstances, he had for instance renounced Christ's holy name and his own baptism to boot in order to save his life so as to be able to perform such good deeds as would in the course of years have atoned for his cowardice.'

'What do you mean, it would have been no sin? What damn cheek; you'll go straight to hell for that, where you'll be roasted like a piece of mutton,' rejoined Fyodor Pavlovich.

It was at this moment that Alyosha entered. As we have seen, Fyodor Pavlovich was delighted to see him.

'Come and join us, this'll interest you!' he chuckled delightedly, gesturing to Alyosha to sit down and listen.

'As for the mutton, sir, there wouldn't be anything like that, no, not if there's any justice left, there wouldn't,' Smerdyakov announced with dignity.

'Any justice left? Well, I never!' cried Fyodor Pavlovich, even more delighted, and nudged Alyosha with his knee.

'A scoundrel, that's what he is!' Grigory could not contain himself. He glared angrily at Smerdyakov.

'As for scoundrels, you needn't be so hasty, Grigory Vasilyevich,' said Smerdyakov coolly and calmly. 'What I want to put to you is this: if I was captured by enemies of Christendom who demanded that I curse the name of God and abjure holy baptism, I think I'd be fully authorized by my own reason to submit, for really there'd be no sin attached to it whatsoever.'

'Well, you've already said that. Don't elaborate, prove it!' cried Fyodor Pavlovich.

'Soup-stirrer!' muttered Grigory under his breath.

'Begging your pardon sir, that's you being too hasty again with your "soup-stirrer". Let's be reasonable about it, Grigory Vasilyevich, let's not resort to insults. You see, the instant I'd have said to my torturers, "No, I am not a Christian and I curse my true God," I should promptly have been declared anathema by God's supreme judgement and excommunicated from the Holy Church; I would have been exactly the same as any heathen, not only from the moment that I'd said the words, but from the moment that I'd even thought of saying them, so that not a quarter of a second would have passed but I'd have been excommunicated; isn't that so, Grigory Vasilyevich?'

He was addressing Grigory with obvious relish, actually answering only Fyodor Pavlovich's questions, while being perfectly aware of this, but deliberately giving the impression that it was Grigory who was putting the questions.

'Ivan!' said Fyodor Pavlovich suddenly, 'a word in your ear. He's dreamt all this up for your benefit, to win your admiration. Say something nice to him.'

Ivan Fyodorovich listened with the utmost seriousness to his father's enthusiastic remark.

'Smerdyakov, be quiet for a moment,' Fyodor Pavlovich exclaimed. 'Ivan, another word in your ear.'

Ivan Fyodorovich again leaned towards him with a perfectly serious air.

'I love you every bit as much as Alyosha. Don't you ever forget that. Some brandy?'

'Please...', said Ivan. 'You've already had one too many, old boy,' thought Ivan, darting a quizzical glance at his father. As for Smerdyakov, Ivan continued to regard him with the utmost fascination.

'You're already damned as it is, confound you,' burst out Grigory, 'how dare you even speak after that, if...!'

'Don't be abusive, Grigory. No need to be abusive!' interrupted Fyodor Pavlovich.

'Bear with me, Grigory Vasilyevich, don't charge like a bull at a gate, and hear me out, because I haven't finished yet. You see, as soon as I am damned by God, at that very moment, sir, at that supreme moment, I would become the same as a heathen, and my baptism would be expunged and become null and void—are you with me, sir?'

'Get to the point, old chap. Hurry up and get to the point,' Fyodor Pavlovich egged him on, slurping his brandy with relish.

'And if I'm no longer a Christian, then that means I haven't lied to the torturers when they asked me: "Are you a Christian or not?" for I've already been deprived of my Christianity by God Himself by reason of the thought alone, before I could even say a word to my torturers. And if I've already been stripped of my faith, then how, and according to what justice, could I be held responsible in the other world as a Christian for having renounced Christ, when just because of the thought alone, before the renunciation, my baptism had already been revoked? If I am no longer a Christian I cannot renounce Christ, because I have nothing to renounce. Who, Grigory Vasilyevich, would hold a heathen Tatar responsible, even in heaven, for not having been born a Christian, and who would punish him for this, since as the saying goes one doesn't take two hides from one ox? And if God the Almighty himself holds the Tatar responsible when he dies (admittedly he couldn't be let off scot-free altogether), then He'll inflict only the very slightest of punishments on the grounds that, after all, it's not his fault that he came into this world a heathen, born of heathen parents. One couldn't very well expect the Lord God to grab hold of a Tatar and say to him that he too was a Christian? Well, that would mean that God Almighty was telling a downright lie. And surely the Almighty Ruler of heaven and earth couldn't very well utter a lie, even if it was only contained in just one little word, sir.'

Grigory was struck dumb and stared open-mouthed at the orator. Even though he had not properly understood what had been said, he had nevertheless managed to extract something from all that drivel, and he stood stock-still, with the expression of someone who has suddenly hit his head against a wall. Fyodor Pavlovich emptied his glass and let out a shrill laugh.

'Alyosha, Alyosha, what about that! Oh, the casuist! He must have been mixing with some Jesuits somewhere, Ivan. Oh, you stinking Jesuit, you! Whoever taught you all that? But you realize you're talking absolute rubbish, you casuist, rubbish, rubbish, and yet more rubbish. Don't cry, Grigory; we'll knock him into a cocked hat in a moment. You just tell me this, you ass: you may be right in the eyes of your tormentors, but all the same, in your heart of hearts you had renounced your faith, and didn't you yourself say that from the moment you became anathema and had been pronounced anathema, as a result you'd immediately be accursed and damned? Don't tell me that when you get to hell you're going to get patted on your head for that anathema! So, what do you say to that, my fine Jesuit?'

'There's no doubt, sir, that in my heart I'd have renounced my faith, but there's no particular sin in that, sir, or if there is, then it's a very small venial sin, sir.'

'What do you mean—venial?'

'That's not true, d-damn you!' spluttered Grigory.

'Judge for yourself, Grigory Vasilyevich,' Smerdyakov continued calmly and steadily, sensing his victory, but as if wanting to show generosity to his defeated adversary. 'Judge for yourself, Grigory Vasilyevich: it is written in the Scriptures* that if you have but the smallest grain of faith, and you command a mountain to move into the sea, it will do so without hesitation at your first command. Well, Grigory Vasilyevich, if I'm an unbeliever and you're such a believer that you can keep on abusing me, why don't you command that mountain to move not to the sea (because the sea is a long way from here, sir), but even just down to our smelly little river, the one that flows past our garden, and you'll see at once that nothing will budge, and that everything will remain just as it was, sir, no matter how much you might shout, sir. And that means that you too, Grigory Vasilyevich, do not believe in the proper manner, and that you abuse others just because of your own lack of faith. And then again, considering that no one in our times, not just you, sir, but absolutely no one, from the highest in the land to the lowliest peasant, sir, can move mountains into the sea, except perhaps one man on all the earth, or at most two, and they're probably saving their souls in secret somewhere out in the Egyptian desert, so that you'd never find them—so, if that is the case, sir, if all the others turn out to be unbelievers too, is it possible that all those others, that is the whole population of the earth, sir, except the two desert-dwellers, would be damned by God and that, in spite of His bountiful mercy, none of them would be forgiven? That's why I trust that, if I'm assailed by doubt, I shall be forgiven when I shed tears of repentance.'

'Just a moment!' squealed Fyodor Pavlovich in excitement. 'So you really think they exist, those two who can move mountains—you think they actually exist? Ivan, remember that one, make a note of it: that's the real voice of Russia for you.'

'You're absolutely right that it's a characteristic expression of popular faith,' agreed Ivan Fyodorovich with an approving smile.

'You agree, do you? That means I'm right if you agree! Alyosha, what do you say? That is the real faith of Russia, am I right or am I right?'

'No, Smerdyakov's faith is not at all the Russian faith,' said Alyosha firmly and seriously.

'I'm not talking about his faith; I mean that point about those two desert-dwellers, just that little point; that really smacks of Russia, doesn't it?'

'Yes, I suppose it does,' Alyosha replied with a smile.

'Your words deserve a gold coin, you ass, you, and I'll let you have it before the day's out, but as for the rest of what you said, it's rubbish—rubbish, rubbish, and again rubbish; remember this, you fool, in Russia we've lost our faith purely on account of our own frivolity, and because we simply don't have enough time; to begin with, we're overloaded with work, and, secondly, God's given us so little time, just twenty-four hours in a day, which is hardly enough to have a good sleep, let alone make a confession. But you, with nothing else to do but concentrate on your faith, went and renounced it in front of your tormentors, and precisely when you were most expected to demonstrate that faith! That's the situation, my friend, isn't it? I think it is.'

'It may very well be the situation, but just work it out for yourself, Grigory Vasilyevich, that's where the rub is. After all, if I really had believed as one should believe at that time, then, true enough, it would have been sinful to go over to the heathen religion of Muhammad rather than accept martyrdom for my faith. But the point is that there wouldn't have been any martyrdom in that case because, sir, all I'd have needed to do at that moment would have been to say to the mountain: "Move and crush my persecutors," and at that instant it would have moved and crushed them like cockroaches, and I'd have gone off as if nothing had happened, chanting and glorifying God. But then again, what if at that very moment I had put all this to the test and deliberately cried out to the mountain, "Crush these torturers!" and it hadn't crushed them? Well then, tell me, how could I have stopped myself being assailed by doubt, especially with me being in such a state of mortal terror? And so, knowing full well that I wouldn't enter the Kingdom of Heaven (for the mountain hadn't moved at my command, which means they've precious little confidence in my faith up there and that no great reward awaits me in the next world), why should I then, on top of everything, have let them flay me alive for no useful purpose? For even if they had torn half the skin off my back, even then, neither my command nor my screaming would have made the mountain budge. At a moment like that not only might one have been assailed by doubt, but one might easily have become petrified from sheer terror and taken leave of one's senses to the point where one wouldn't have been able to reason at all. And so, why should I have been deemed at all guilty if, seeing as there was no benefit or reward for me either down here or up there, I'd at least saved my skin? That's why, sir, in the expectation of God's eternal mercy, I go on harbouring the hope that I'd have been granted complete forgiveness...'

8

OVER A GLASS OF BRANDY

THE argument was over, but, strangely enough, Fyodor Pavlovich, who had been in such high spirits, suddenly became sullen towards the end. He scowled and downed another brandy, and this was certainly one too many.

'Clear out, you Jesuits! Out!' he yelled at the servants. 'Get out, Smerdyakov! I'll see you get the ten roubles I promised today, now go! Cheer up, Grigory, go to Marfa, she'll comfort you and put you to bed. The scoundrels won't even let one sit in peace after dinner,' he snapped irritably as soon as he had dismissed the servants. 'Smerdyakov worms his way in every time we have dinner. It's you he's so curious about—what have you done to charm him?' he asked Ivan Fyodorovich.

'Nothing at all,' replied Ivan. 'He's decided to show me respect, he's a lackey and a scoundrel. But when the time comes, he'll be top dog.'

'Top dog?'

'There'll be others—even worse than him, but there'll be his sort too. First his sort, and then the really bad ones.'

'And when will that be?'

'The rocket will go up and fizzle out perhaps. Just now, people don't particularly want to listen to these soup-stirrers.'

'True, my boy, but this Balaam's ass won't stop thinking and, left to his own devices, heaven only knows what he might come up with in the end.'

'He's collecting his thoughts,' Ivan smiled.

'That's as may be, but I know he can't abide me, or anybody else for that matter, including you, even though you might think he's decided to "look up to you". As for Alyosha, it goes without saying he despises him. It's true he doesn't steal or gossip, he keeps his mouth shut, never washes dirty linen in public, makes an excellent *koulibiaca*,* but when all's said and done—to hell with him! Surely he's not worth talking about?'

'Of course he's not.'

'As to what he may think up, if you ask me, the Russian peasant ought to be flogged. I've always maintained as much. Our peasant's a rogue, he doesn't deserve pity, and it's a good job he's still birched. Russia's strength is in its birches. Once they do away with the forests—that'll be the end of Russia. I'm all for clever people. But we were too clever by half when we stopped flogging the peasants, they carry on flogging one another just the same though. And a good thing too. With what measure ye mete, it shall yourself be measured,* or words to that effect... In short, it shall be measured. But Russia's a pigsty. My boy, if only you knew how I hate Russia... not Russia, mind, but all these vices... come to think of it, Russia too. *Tout cela c'est de la cochonnerie.** You know what I really like? I like a sense of humour.'

'You've already had another brandy, haven't you? That's enough for now, isn't it?'

'I'm just going to have another one, and then one more after that, and that'll be it. No, wait a minute, you interrupted me. When we passed through Mokroye, I talked to an old peasant and he said: "What we enjoy most of all", he said, "is sentencing the girls to a thrashing and letting the lads get on with it. The one the lad thrashes today, he'll marry tomorrow, so it works out well for the girls too," he says. Can you imagine such Marquises de Sade,* eh? Still, say what you like, you must admit it's clever... Why don't we go there and see for ourselves, eh? Alyosha, you're blushing? No need to be bashful, my child. Pity I didn't stay for lunch at the abbot's, I could have told the monks about the girls at Mokroye. Alyosha, don't be angry with me for offending your abbot. It infuriates me, my boy. If there is a God, if He exists— well then of course I'm guilty and I'll be answerable, but if He doesn't, those fathers of yours should get what's coming to them! Chopping off their heads would be too good for them, they stand in the way of progress. This question torments me, do you believe me, Ivan? No, you don't believe me, I see it in your eyes. You believe those who say I'm just a buffoon. Alyosha, do you believe that I'm not just a buffoon?'

'Of course.'

'And I believe that you believe that, and that you're being sincere. You look sincere, and you speak sincerely. But not you Ivan. You're arrogant... Still, if I were you Alyosha, I'd leave that monastery of yours. It would be nice to sweep all this mystical mumbo-jumbo clean out of Russia and bring all fools to their senses once and for all. Think how much gold and silver that would bring the Exchequer!'

'Why sweep it away?' Ivan asked.

'So that truth should triumph all the sooner, that's why.'

'Once truth triumphed, you'd be the first to get fleeced and then... thrown on the scrap heap.'

'Ah! Come to think of it, you may be right. Oh, what an ass I am,' Fyodor Pavlovich suddenly cried out, lightly striking his forehead. 'Well then, let your monastery stay, Alyosha, if that's the case. We smart ones will carry on sitting pretty, enjoying our brandy. You know, Ivan, God must have arranged things like this on purpose, mustn't He? Tell me, Ivan: does God exist or not? Wait, be serious, tell me the truth! Why are you laughing again?'

'I'm laughing at your witty comment on Smerdyakov's belief in the two hermits who can move mountains.'

'What's that got to do with it?'

'A lot.'

'Well, that means I'm a true Russian, I too have that Russian streak in me, and you, you philosopher, I can catch you out by your Russian streak. Do you want me to catch you out? It's a bet, tomorrow I'll do it. But I still want you to tell me: does God exist or not? Seriously now! I insist you be serious.'

'No, there is no God.'

'Alyosha, does God exist?'

'Yes.'

'And what about immortality, Ivan, any sort of immortality, just a tiny bit, just a teeny bit of immortality?'

'There's no immortality either.'

'None at all?'

'None.'

'You mean absolutely none, or just a little something after all? Perhaps a smidgen of something? Surely not complete nothingness!'

'Complete nothingness.'

'Alyosha, is the soul immortal?'

'Yes.'

'So there is God and immortality?'

'Yes, both God and immortality of the soul. Immortality is in God.'

'Hm, I'd say Ivan's right. Oh Lord, to think how much faith, how much energy man has wasted on this forlorn hope for thousands of years! Who is it who's been mocking mankind so cruelly, Ivan? For the last time, yes or no: does God exist or not? For the last time!'

'And for the last time, no.'

'Who is it, then, who's been mocking mankind, Ivan?'

'The devil, perhaps,' Ivan Fyodorovich smiled.

'Does the devil exist?'

'No, there's no devil either.'

'Pity. Dammit, I'd like to lay my hands on whoever first invented God! Stringing him up from an aspen tree would be too good for him.'

'There wouldn't have been any civilization at all if God hadn't been invented.'

'There wouldn't, would there? You mean without God?'

'That's right. And no brandy either. I think I'd better take that bottle from you now.'

'Wait, wait, wait, my dear chap, just one more glass. I've offended Alyosha. Are you angry with me, Aleksei? My dear, dear Aleksei!'

'No, I'm not angry. I know your thoughts. Your heart is better than your head.'

'"My heart is better than my head"?... Good Lord, and it's you who says so? Ivan, do you love Alyosha?'

'Yes, I do.'

'You should.' (Fyodor Pavlovich was getting very drunk.) 'Listen, Alyosha, I was awfully rude to your starets. But I was distraught. But that starets is a clever one, don't you think, Ivan?'

'I'd say he is.'

'He is, he is, *il y a du Piron là-dedans.** He's a Jesuit, a Russian one, that is. As befits a noble soul, he's tortured by repressed indignation at the need to dissemble... to put on a sanctimonious act.'

'But surely he believes in God.'

'Not a bit of it. Didn't you know? He's quite frank about it to everyone, well, not everyone, but to all the intelligent people that come to him. He came straight out with it to Governor Schulz: "*Credo,** but what in, I don't know."'

'Really?'

'That's what he said. Word for word. But I respect him. There's something mephisophelean about the man, or rather, something of *A Hero of Our Time...* Arbenin* or someone... in a word, you see, he's a sensualist, he's such a sensualist that even now I'd be afraid if my daughter or wife were to go to confession to him. Once he starts telling stories... About three years ago he invited us to a tea party, liqueur was passed round (the ladies keep him stocked up with liqueur), and you should have heard him go on about the olden days, we nearly split our sides... Especially how he came to cure a palsied woman. "If it wasn't for my bad leg," he said, "I'd dance for you." Fancy that! "The unholy things I got up to in my time," he says. He got sixty thousand off the merchant Demidov.'

'What, he stole it?'

'Yes, the man brought the money to him in all good faith: "Look after it for me, my friend, I'm expecting a police raid tomorrow." And he did look after it for him. "You donated it to the Church," he said to him. "You're a rogue," he said. "No," he says, "I'm not a rogue—I'm just broad-minded..." On second thoughts, it wasn't him... It was someone else. I'm getting him mixed up with someone else... Don't know what I'm talking about. Well, one more glass and that'll be it; take the bottle away, Ivan. I was talking out of the back of my head, why didn't you stop me, Ivan?... Why didn't you tell me I was talking out of the back of my head?'

'I knew you'd stop of your own accord.'

'Liar, it was out of spite, out of sheer spite! You despise me. You come to my house and you despise me in my own house.'

'In that case I'll go now; the brandy's gone to your head.'

'I've been asking you for the love of Christ to go to Chermash-nya for a day or two, but you won't.'

'I'll go tomorrow, if you insist.'

'You won't. You want to spy on me here, that's what you want, you're evil, that's why you don't want to go!'

The old man refused to calm down. He had reached that point of inebriation when some drunkards suddenly switch from a sociable to an aggressive and histrionic state.

'What are you staring at me for? Just look at your eyes! Your eyes are staring at me and they're saying: "You drunken sot." They're suspicious, your eyes, there's contempt in those eyes... You've come here for a purpose. Look, Alyosha's looking at me, but his eyes are shining. Alyosha doesn't despise me. Aleksei, you shouldn't love Ivan...'

'Don't be angry with my brother! Stop insulting him,' Alyosha said suddenly in a firm voice.

'All right then. Oh, my head. Take the brandy away, Ivan, I'm telling you for the third time.' He mused a while, and suddenly an expansive, cunning smile spread over his features. 'Ivan, don't be angry with a foolish old man. I know you don't like me, but still, there's no need to be angry. I know there's not much to love in me. If you go to Chermashnya, I'll come to visit you myself and bring you a present. There's a girl I want to show you, I've had an eye on her for a long time. She still runs around barefoot. Don't shy away from the barefooted ones, don't turn your nose up at them—they're pearls!...'

And he blew an enthusiastic kiss of appreciation.

'For me,' he said animatedly, as though he had sobered up for an instant as soon as he had touched upon his favourite topic, 'for me... oh, my children! You innocent little puppies of mine, for me... in my whole life, there's never been such a thing as an ugly woman, that's my motto! Do you know what I mean? But how can you: you've still got milk in your veins instead of blood; you're not weaned yet! By my rule, dammit, in every woman you can find something extraordinarily interesting that you won't find in any other—only you must know how to look for it, that's the secret! It's an art! For me, there's no such thing as an ugly woman: the very fact that she's a woman means I'm halfway there already... but how can you understand! Even in an old maid you can sometimes uncover things that'd make you wonder why the stupid punters had left her on the shelf and allowed her to grow old! The barefoot, ugly little one must first and foremost be taken by surprise—that's how you deal with her. You didn't know? You have to surprise her, sweep her off her feet, spellbind her, even make her ashamed that such a gentleman has fallen for such a common little trollop. It's truly wonderful, there always have been and always will be gentlemen and scoundrels in this world, and every little skivvy will always have her very own lord and master—what more does one need for happiness in life! Wait... listen, Alyosha, I was always full of surprises for your dear departed mother, but in a different way. I'd ignore her for days on end, and then suddenly, without warning, I'd be kneeling, grovelling in front of her, kissing her feet, till in the end she'd always burst out laughing—I can still remember it as if she were here now—that queer, soft, nervous, fragile, tinkling laughter of hers. She always laughed like that. I'd take it as a sign she was going to be ill again, that come the next day she'd be shrieking her head off once more; I knew that that soft laughter of hers had no joy in it, but pretence too can bring ecstasy with it. Now that's what I call getting to the heart of things! One day Belyavsky—a local fellow, handsome and rich too—who'd taken a fancy to her and started dropping in on us, suddenly dealt me a slap across the face, in my own house and in front of her. Normally she wouldn't say boo to a goose, but I thought she was going to kill me because he'd slapped my face— how she set about me! "You've been thrashed now, utterly thrashed," she says. "He slapped your face!" she says. "You've prostituted my honour... How dare he strike you in my presence! Don't you dare come near me ever again, ever! Go at once and challenge him to a duel..." That's when I had to take her to the monastery for the holy fathers to say prayers over her and calm her down. But as God is my witness, Alyosha, I never wronged my little *klikusha*! Except perhaps once only, in our first year: she was always praying then, especially on any feastdays of the Holy Virgin,* and then she'd banish me from her sight to the study. So I thought, let's knock that holy nonsense out of her! "Look," I said, "look, here's your icon, here it is, I'm going to take it down. Watch this. You think it can work miracles, but I'm going to spit on it now, in front of you, and nothing will happen to me!..." When she saw me do that, Good Lord, I almost thought she was really going to kill me, but she merely jumped up, held up her hands, then suddenly buried her face in them, began to shake all over, and fell to the floor... collapsed, just like that... Alyosha, Alyosha! What's the matter, what's the matter with you?'

The old man leapt to his feet in terror. Alyosha's expression had begun to change the moment his father had started to talk about his mother. His face reddened, his eyes glared, his lips quivered... The tipsy old man was spluttering saliva and had noticed nothing until the moment when something very strange happened to Alyosha, exactly as it had happened to his mother. Alyosha suddenly jumped to his feet, held up his hands, covered his face and slumped into a chair, shaking violently in a sudden fit of hysterical, silent weeping. The uncanny resemblance to his mother astounded the old man.

'Ivan, Ivan! Quick, some water. It's just like her, just like his mother that time! Take a mouthful of water and spit it in his face, that's what I did to her... He's only doing this to me because of his mother, because of his mother,' he mumbled to Ivan.

'Doesn't it occur to you that his mother was my mother too?' Ivan suddenly burst out with uncontrollable rage and contempt. The glint in his eyes sent a shudder down the old man's spine. But at this point something very strange happened, though only for a brief instant: it actually appeared to have slipped the old man's memory that Alyosha's mother was Ivan's mother too...

'What do you mean, your mother?' he mumbled in bewilderment. 'You're not suggesting...? What mother are you talking about...? Was she really...? Goddammit! Of course, she was yours too! Goddammit! Well, my boy, never had such a lapse of memory before, I'm sorry, I really thought, Ivan... He-he-he!' He stopped. A broad, drunken, half-witted leer spread over his face. But at that very moment a terrible commotion erupted in the hall, wild shouts were heard, the door burst open, and Dmitry Fyodorovich rushed into the room. The old man ran towards Ivan in terror:

'He's going to kill me, he's going to kill me! Stop him, stop him!' he shouted, holding on to Ivan Fyodorovich's coat-tails.

9

SENSUALISTS

GRIGORY and Smerdyakov ran into the drawing-room hard on Dmitry Fyodorovich's heels. They had struggled with him in the porch to prevent him entering (as instructed by Fyodor Pavlovich himself a few days earlier). Taking advantage of the fact that he had managed to enter the room, Dmitry Fyodorovich stopped momentarily to get his bearings, Grigory ran around the table to the far end of the room, bolted the double doors that led to the inner rooms, and stood before the closed doors with his arms akimbo, ready as it were to defend the entrance to the last drop of his blood. Seeing this, Dmitry hurled himself at Grigory with a shout that was more like a shriek.

'So she's there! They've hidden her in there! Out of the way, you wretch!' He tried to pull Grigory away, but the latter pushed him off. Beside himself with rage, Dmitry lashed out and struck Grigory with all his strength. The old man fell as if poleaxed, and Dmitry leapt over him and flung open the door. Smerdyakov, pale and trembling, remained at the other end of the room, clinging to Fyodor Pavlovich.

'She's here,' Dmitry Fyodorovich yelled, 'I saw her myself just now, going towards the house, only I couldn't catch up with her. Where is she? Where is she?'

The cry: 'She's here!' had an electrifying effect upon Fyodor Pavlovich. All fear left him.

'Stop him, stop him!' he howled, and dashed after Dmitry Fyodorovich. In the meantime Grigory had got up from the floor, still somewhat dazed. Ivan Fyodorovich and Alyosha rushed after their father. From the third room came a resounding crash of something falling to the floor and shattering: it was a tall glass vase (not a particularly valuable one), which Dmitry Fyodorovich had knocked off its marble pedestal as he ran past.

'After him!' yelled the old man. 'Help!'

Ivan and Alyosha caught up with the old man and forcibly dragged him back to the drawing-room.

'Why are you running after him!' Ivan Fyodorovich shouted angrily at his father. 'He'll end up by killing you.'

'Vanechka, Lyoshechka, she's here, she must be, Grushenka's here, he said so himself—he saw her hurrying here?'

He was choking. He had not been expecting Grushenka on this occasion, and the unexpected news that she was there had immediately driven him out of his mind. He was shaking all over, as if demented.

'Surely you can see for yourself she isn't here!' yelled Ivan.

'Maybe she came through that door?'

'That door is locked and you've got the key...'

Suddenly, Dmitry reappeared in the drawing-room. He had

found the rear door locked, of course, and, true enough, the key to it was in Fyodor Pavlovich's pocket. All the windows in the rooms were also locked; thus there was no way that Grushenka could have entered the house and no way that she could have escaped.

'Grab him!' Fyodor Pavlovich screamed as soon as he saw Dmitry again. 'He's stolen some money from my bedroom.' And, tearing himself loose from Ivan's grip, he once again rushed at Dmitry. But the latter, with both hands, grabbed the old man by the last remaining tufts of hair sprouting from his temples, jerked him up, and brought him violently to the floor. As he lay there he managed to kick him two or three times in the face with the heel of his shoe. The old man moaned loudly. Though Ivan Fyodorovich was not as strong as Dmitry, he seized him and exerted all his strength to pull him off the old man. Alyosha too helped as best he could by grabbing his brother from the front.

'You're mad, you've killed him!' Ivan shouted.

'Serves him right!' cried Dmitry, out of breath. 'And if I haven't, I'll come back and finish him off. You won't stop me!'

'Dmitry, get out of here at once!' commanded Alyosha.

'Aleksei! You tell me, you're the only one I trust: has she been here or hasn't she? I saw her myself going past the fence and turning into here from the lane. I called to her, but she ran off...'

'I swear to you she hasn't been here, and what's more, no one was expecting her!'

'But I saw her... That means she's... I'll soon find out where she is now... Goodbye, Aleksei! Remember, not a word to Aesop* about the money, but off you go to Katerina Ivanovna immediately and make sure you say: "He sends his regards, his regards!" Those very words, "He sends his sincere regards!" Explain the situation to her.'

In the meantime Ivan and Grigory had helped the old man up and sat him in an armchair. His face was covered in blood, but he was fully conscious and was listening attentively to Dmitry's shouting. He was still under the impression that Grushenka really was somewhere in the house. Dmitry Fyodorovich gave him a parting look of hatred.

'I'm not sorry that I made you bleed!' he shouted. 'Watch out, old man, watch out for your dream, because I too have a dream! I curse you and dissociate myself from you for ever...'

He rushed out of the room.

'She's here, she must be here! Smerdyakov, Smerdyakov,' the old man croaked, scarcely audibly, beckoning with his finger for Smerdyakov to approach.

'She's not here, she's not, you're out of your mind,' Ivan shouted in anger. 'He's going to faint! Get some water and a towel! Move yourself, Smerdyakov!'

Smerdyakov rushed off for some water. Finally, they undressed the old man, carried him into the bedroom, and put him to bed with a wet towel round his head. Exhausted by the brandy, the unexpected excitement, and the beating, no sooner had his head touched the pillow than he closed his eyes and fell asleep. Ivan Fyodorovich and Alyosha returned to the drawing-room. Smerdyakov was clearing up the pieces of the broken vase, while Grigory stood by the table, his head hanging despondently.

'You ought to put something wet on your head and lie down, too,' Alyosha said, turning to Grigory. 'We'll take care of him; my brother gave you a nasty blow... on the head.'

'He dared to hit me!' Grigory said sombrely, pausing after each word.

'You're not the only one, he "dared" to hit his own father!' said Ivan Fyodorovich with a wry grin.

'I used to bath him in a tub... and he dared to hit me!' Grigory repeated.

'Dammit, if I hadn't pulled him away, he'd have probably killed him. It wouldn't take much to finish Aesop off!' Ivan Fyodorovich whispered to Alyosha.

'God forbid!' exclaimed Alyosha.

'Why "God forbid"?' continued Ivan in a whisper as before, his lips contorted in malice. 'Let dog eat dog, and to hell with them both!'

Alyosha shuddered.

'I prevented a murder just now, and you can be sure I'd do the same again. You stay here, Alyosha, I'm going for a walk in the yard; I've got a headache coming on.'

Alyosha went to his father's bedroom and sat at his bedside, behind the screen, for about an hour. The old man suddenly opened his eyes and stared at Alyosha in silence, apparently attempting to gather his thoughts. Suddenly, his face contorted with alarm.

'Alyosha,' he whispered warily, 'where's Ivan?'

'Out in the yard, he's got a headache. He's keeping a lookout.'

'Give me the little mirror, it's over there, let me have it!'

Alyosha passed him a small, round, folding mirror which stood on the dresser. The old man took a look at himself: his nose had swollen badly and on his forehead, just above the left eyebrow, was a prominent red bruise.

'What was Ivan saying? Alyosha, my dear Alyosha, my one and only child, Ivan scares me. Ivan frightens me more than the other one does. You're the only one who doesn't frighten me...'

'Don't be afraid of Ivan either, Ivan's angry, but he'll defend you.'

'Alyosha, what about the other one? He's run off to find Grushenka! Dear boy, tell me the truth: was Grushenka here just now or not?'

'Nobody saw her. It's all in your imagination, she hasn't been here!'

'Do you realize, Mitka wants to marry her—to marry her!'

'She won't have him.'

'She won't, she won't, she won't, she won't, not for all the tea in China, she won't!...' The old man worked himself up into a fit of joy, as though this was the most gratifying thing that anybody could have said to him. In his rapture he grabbed Alyosha's hand and pressed it tightly to his heart. There were even tears in his eyes. 'Take the little icon, the one of the Mother of God I was telling you about, and look after it. And I'll let you go back to the monastery... I was only joking before, don't be angry. My head's aching, Alyosha... Put my mind at rest, my boy, tell me the truth!'

'Are you still worrying about the same thing, whether or not she was here?' Alyosha said with sadness.

'No, no, no, I believe you, there's something else though: go to Grushenka yourself, or try to see her somehow; ask her straight out, as soon as possible, try to find out who she wants, me or him. Now, can you do that or not?'

'If I see her, I'll ask,' Alyosha mumbled in embarrassment.

'No, she won't tell you,' the old man interrupted, 'she's not to be trusted. She'll start kissing you, and she'll say that she wants to marry you. She's devious, she's shameless, no, you mustn't go to her after all, you mustn't!'

'I agree, father, it wouldn't be a good idea at all.'

'Where was it he wanted you to go when he called out to you just before he ran out?'

'He wanted me to go to Katerina Ivanovna.'

'For money? To ask for money?'

'No, not money.'

'He's got no money, not a kopeck. Listen, Alyosha, I'll sleep on it tonight, but you can go now. Maybe you'll run into her... Only make sure you come and see me in the morning, without fail. I'll tell you something tomorrow; will you come?'

'Yes, I will.'

'When you do, pretend you've come of your own accord, to see how I am. Don't tell anyone I asked you. Don't say a word to Ivan.'

'All right.'

'Goodbye, my dear boy, you stood up for me, I'll never forget that. I'll tell you something special tomorrow... but I must think it over first...'

'And how do you feel now?'

'Come tomorrow, I'll be up and about tomorrow, I'm all right, I'm perfectly all right, I really am all right!...'

As he was crossing the yard, Alyosha caught sight of Ivan, who was sitting on a bench by the gate; he was pencilling something in his notebook. Alyosha informed Ivan that the old man was awake and conscious, and had given him permission to spend the night at the monastery.

'Alyosha, I'd really love to see you tomorrow morning,' Ivan said affably, rising; his good humour came as a complete surprise to Alyosha.

'I shall be at the Khokhlakovas' tomorrow,' replied Alyosha. 'I may call on Katerina Ivanovna too, tomorrow, if I don't find her in today...'

'So you're going to Katerina Ivanovna now after all! To convey his respects, is that it?' Ivan said suddenly with a smile. Alyosha was embarrassed.

'All the shouting, on top of everything else, has given me a pretty shrewd idea of what's going on. Dmitry has probably asked you to go along and... well... well, in short, say that he's washing his hands of the whole affair, hasn't he?'

'Ivan!' exclaimed Alyosha, 'how will all this terrible business between father and Dmitry end?'

'It's impossible to know for sure. Probably, nothing at all will happen: the whole affair will just peter out. That woman's a dangerous animal. In any case, father ought to be kept indoors, and Dmitry mustn't be allowed in the house.'

'Let me ask you something else: does any man really have the right to decide who of the people around him deserves to live, and who doesn't?'

'Why complicate the issue with the idea of who deserves to live? For the most part, this question is decided in men's hearts not on the basis of who deserves to live, but according to quite different, much more obvious, criteria. As regards the "right", doesn't everyone have the right to wish?'

'Surely not for someone else's death?'

'Well, why not? Why deceive oneself, seeing that that's how all people live, and can't live in any other way. Are you referring to what I said earlier, "let dog eat dog"? In that case, allow me to ask you something else: do you consider that I too, like Dmitry, am capable of spilling Aesop's blood, well, of killing him, eh?'

'Ivan, what do you mean! Nothing of the sort ever occurred to me! And I don't think even Dmitry...'

'I'm grateful for that at least,' Ivan said with a smile. 'Remember one thing, I shall always stand up for him. But as for my wishes in this case, I reserve the right to do exactly what I want. Au revoir till tomorrow. Don't judge me and don't look upon me as a murderer,' he added with a smile.

They shook hands warmly, as never before. Alyosha felt that his brother had made a move towards reconciliation with him, and that he had done so for a reason, for some particular purpose.

10

BOTH TOGETHER

NEVERTHELESS, Alyosha left his father's house even more distraught and depressed than when he had entered it. His thoughts were in disarray, and he was afraid to collect them and form a general conclusion from all the painful contradictions that he had experienced that day. It was as if he were verging on despair, and this had never happened to Alyosha before. The overriding, insoluble, and fateful question loomed over everything like a mountain: what would be the outcome of his father's and Dmitry's relationship with that terrible woman? On this occasion he himself had been a witness. He had been present and had seen them confront each other. Still, it was Dmitry who was likely to end up unhappy, totally and terribly unhappy: a calamity was undoubtedly awaiting him. As it happened, there were other people who felt that all this concerned them too, and to a far greater extent than Alyosha might previously have imagined. What emerged was mysterious. His brother Ivan had made the step towards reconciliation which Alyosha had desired for so long, and now for some reason he felt intimidated by this move towards a greater intimacy. And those women? It was very strange: earlier, he had felt acutely embarrassed about going to Katerina Ivanovna; now, however, he did not feel so at all; quite the contrary, he was hurrying to get there, as though expecting to obtain some guidance from her. However, it certainly appeared to be more difficult to pass the message to her now than had previously been the case: the matter of the three thousand roubles had been resolved once and for all, and his brother Dmitry, now feeling himself to be completely without honour and hope, would stop at nothing, no matter what humiliation he might suffer. Besides, he had instructed him to describe to Katerina Ivanovna the whole scene that had just taken place at their father's.

It was already seven o'clock and getting dark when Alyosha set off to visit Katerina Ivanovna, who lived in a very spacious and comfortable house on the main street. Alyosha knew that she lived with two aunts. In actual fact, one of them was an aunt only to her sister Agafya Ivanovna; she was the taciturn woman in her father's house who, together with her sister, had looked after her when she came back from boarding-school. The other aunt, although from a humble background, was a rather grand Muscovite lady. It was said that they both deferred to Katerina Ivanovna in everything and continued to live with her only for the sake of appearances. Katerina Ivanovna, on the other hand, deferred only to her benefactress, the General's wife, who was too sick to leave Moscow and to whom she had to write two letters a week with all the news about herself.

When Alyosha stepped into the entrance hall and asked the maid who opened the door to announce him, it seemed that they were already aware in the drawing-room of his arrival (perhaps he had been spotted from the window), and then suddenly he heard a noise, the sound of women scurrying and the rustling of dresses; it could have been two or three women running out of the room. It seemed strange to Alyosha that his arrival could have caused such a disturbance. He was, however, immediately shown into the drawing-room. It was a large room, elegantly and sumptuously furnished, with no trace of provincial taste about it. There were many sofas, couches, and divans, large and small tables; there were pictures on the walls, lamps and vases on the tables, flowers were very much in evidence, and there was even an aquarium by the window. It was dusk, and it had become somewhat dark in the room. Alyosha noticed a silk mantilla lying on the sofa, which had evidently just recently been vacated, and on the table in front of the sofa stood two unfinished cups of chocolate, some biscuits, and a crystal plate with dark raisins and another one with sweets. Someone was being entertained. Alyosha realized that he had intruded upon visitors and frowned. But at that very instant the curtain hanging over the door was raised, and Katerina Ivanovna entered the room with hurried steps and, beaming with delight and joy, held out both hands towards Alyosha. At the same time a maid brought in two lighted candles and placed them on the table.

'Thank God, you're here at last! You're the very person I've been praying to see all day long! Do sit down.'

Katerina Ivanovna's beauty had made a great impression on Alyosha ever since his brother Dmitry had first taken him to her house to meet her, at her own express request, about three weeks before. However, they had not said much on that occasion. Sensing that Alyosha was very embarrassed, Katerina Ivanovna had done her best to spare his feelings and spent the whole time talking to Dmitry Fyodorovich. Alyosha had remained silent, but succeeded in observing a great deal. He was astonished at the air of authority, ease, and self-confidence that this proud young woman displayed. All this was beyond doubt. Alyosha felt that his impressions were not exaggerated. He was captivated by her large, dark, burning eyes, which perfectly complemented her pale, even somewhat olive-hued, oval face. But although there was indeed something in those eyes, as well as in the shape of her wonderful lips, with which his brother might fall terribly in love, there was maybe something about them that one could not love for long. He had made little attempt to disguise his thoughts from Dmitry when, after the visit, the latter began to press him for an opinion of his bride-to-be, imploring him to hide nothing.

'You will be happy with her, but perhaps... it will be a troubled happiness.'

'You're right, my boy, some people will never change, they won't submit to their fate. So, you don't think my love for her will last for ever?'

'Well, perhaps you'll love her for ever, but perhaps you won't be happy with her for ever...'

Alyosha had given his opinion on that occasion, blushing and rebuking himself for giving in to his brother's importuning and for expressing such 'silly' thoughts. He himself had been struck by the naïvety of his opinion as soon as he had expressed it. And besides, he felt ashamed to have passed such a definite opinion about a woman. His surprise was all the greater when he realized, on catching sight of Katerina Ivanovna as she entered the room to greet him, that perhaps he had been terribly mistaken on that previous occasion. This time her face shone with genuine, simple-hearted kindness, open and passionate sincerity. All that remained of her former 'pride and disdain', which had so struck Alyosha previously, was a bold and noble vitality and a powerful, evident faith in her own self. From his first glance at her, from her very first words, Alyosha realized that the whole tragedy of her situation with regard to the man whom she loved so deeply was no secret to her, that perhaps she already knew everything, absolutely everything. And yet in spite of that, there was so much radiance in her face, so much faith in the future. Alyosha suddenly felt that he had gravely and deliberately maligned her. He was at one and the same time vanquished and attracted by her. On top of everything else, he noticed from the first words she spoke that she was in a state of great excitement, perhaps quite unprecedented for her—an excitement bordering on ecstasy.

'I've been so wanting to see you, because now you're the only person who can tell me the whole truth —you and no one else!'

'I've come...', mumbled Alyosha in confusion, 'I... he sent me...'

'Oh, he sent you,' exclaimed Katerina Ivanovna with a sudden glint in her eyes, 'well, that's just what I expected. Now I know everything, all there is to know. Wait, Aleksei Fyodorovich, I'll tell you first why I've been so anxious to see you. You see, maybe I know much more than you do yourself; it's not information I need from you. You must give me your very own personal and honest opinion about him, you must be absolutely direct and frank, even cruel (be as cruel as you wish!), about what you think of him and of his attitude now, after your meeting with him today. This would be better, perhaps, than if I myself, whom he no longer wishes to see, were to seek an explanation from him personally. Do you understand what it is I want from you? So why has he sent you to me now? (I was sure he would send you to me!) Be frank, tell me the truth!'

'He bade me convey to you... his regards, and tell you that he'll never see you again... he sends his regards.'

'His regards? Is that what he said, his very words?'

'Yes.'

'Perhaps he said it on the spur of the moment, spontaneously, came out with the wrong word without meaning to?'

'No, that is the precise word he asked me to convey to you: "regards". He told me about three times not to forget it.'

Katerina Ivanovna flushed.

'Help me now, Aleksei Fyodorovich, I really need your help now: I'll tell you what's on my mind, and all I'm asking you to do is to say whether I'm right or not. Listen, had he sent me his regards on the spur of the moment, without insisting on the precise word, without emphasizing the particular word, then that would have been the end... That would have been the end of everything! But as he kept insisting on that word, as he specifically asked you not to forget to convey to me that *form of words*— then it follows that he was agitated, that he was beside himself, perhaps? He had made a decision and taken fright! Instead of walking boldly away from me, he jumped headlong into the abyss. Emphasizing this word can only be a sign of bravado...'

'That's right!' Alyosha agreed eagerly, 'that's how it seems to me too.'

'In that case, there's hope for him yet! He's only in a state of despair, but I can still save him. Wait: he didn't mention anything to you about money, a sum of three thousand roubles, did he?'

'Not only did he mention it, but that's probably what's been weighing upon him most of all. He said he had lost his honour and that nothing mattered any more,' Alyosha replied eagerly, sensing with every fibre that hope was flowing back into his heart, and that perhaps there was a way out and a chance of saving his brother. 'But how is it... you know about this money?' he added, and suddenly cut himself short.

'I've known about it for a long time, and I know for sure. I telegraphed Moscow and I've known for some time that the money hasn't arrived. He didn't send it, but I didn't say anything. During the past week I've found out that he's desperate for even more... My only aim in all this was that he should know who to turn to and who his most loyal friend is. But he doesn't want to believe that I'm his most loyal friend, he doesn't want to recognize me for what I am, he sees me only as a woman. All week long I've been racking my brains, trying to think how to stop him feeling shamed before me for having squandered those three thousand roubles. I mean, let him be shamed before everybody, himself included, but not before me. After all, he tells God everything without feeling ashamed. Then why is it he still doesn't know how much I can endure for his sake! Why, why doesn't he know me, how dare he not know me, after all that's passed between us? I want to save him for ever. He should forget that I'm his fiancée! And now he fears his honour is besmirched in my sight! Look, Aleksei Fyodorovich, he wasn't afraid to confide in you, was he? Why is it I still haven't earned the same confidence?'

She spoke the last words in tears; tears were streaming from her eyes.

'I must tell you', Alyosha said, his voice trembling too, 'what has just passed between him and father.' And he described the whole scene; he told her how Dmitry had sent him to get some money, how he had then burst in, assaulted his father, and made a point of insisting that he, Alyosha, should go and convey his, Dmitry's, regards... 'He went to that woman...', Alyosha added softly.

'And do you think I shan't be able to reconcile myself to that woman? Does he think that too? But he's not going to marry her,' she said suddenly, with a nervous laugh, 'surely even a Karamazov can't burn with a passion of that sort for ever? It's lust, not love... He's not going to marry her, because she won't have him...', Katerina Ivanovna added with another of her strange smiles.

'Perhaps he will marry her,' Alyosha said sadly, his gaze lowered.

'He won't marry her, I tell you. That girl', Katerina Ivanovna suddenly exclaimed with unusual fervour, 'is an angel, do you realize that? Do you? She's the most fantastic of all fantastic beings! I know how seductive she is, but I also know how good, how trustworthy and how noble she is. Why do you look at me like that, Aleksei Fyodorovich? Perhaps you're surprised at my words, perhaps you don't believe me. Agrafena Aleksandrovna, my angel!' she called out suddenly to someone in the next room, 'come and join us, it's a good kind person, it's Alyosha, he knows all about us, come and show yourself to him!'

'I was just waiting behind the curtain for you to call,' said a gentle, sugary, woman's voice.

The curtain over the door was pulled aside and... Grushenka herself, all sweetness and smiles, approached the table. Alyosha gaped in disbelief. His eyes were riveted on her and he could not tear them away. Here she was, that terrible woman—that 'dangerous animal', as Ivan had called her barely half an hour before. And yet there stood before him, it would seem, a very simple and ordinary woman, kind and pleasant—beautiful, certainly, yet very much like all other beautiful but 'ordinary' women! Certainly, she was extremely attractive—with that kind of Russian beauty that is so passionately adored by many men. She was tall, though somewhat shorter than Katerina Ivanovna (the latter was very tall), plump, and her movements were soft and silent, refined, it would seem, like her voice, to an excess of sensuality. She did not approach as Katerina Ivanovna had done, with a confident, brisk stride, but inaudibly. Her feet made not the slightest sound on the floor. With a soft rustling of her luxurious black silk dress, she gently lowered herself into an armchair, ostentatiously wrapping an expensive black woollen shawl round her full, milky-white neck and plump shoulders. She was twenty-two years old, and her face precisely reflected that age. Her complexion was very pale, with just a hint of rosiness in her cheeks. Her face was almost too broad, and her lower jaw even protruded a little. Her upper lip was thin, and the slightly prominent lower one, twice as thick, appeared a little pouting. But her magnificent, luxuriant dark-brown hair, her dark sable eyebrows, and her delightful greyish-blue eyes with their long lashes would have made even the most casual and inattentive passer-by, walking in the hustle and bustle of a crowd, stop dead in his tracks and remember that face long afterwards. What astounded Alyosha most of all was her child-like, simple-hearted expression. Her gaze was that of a child, joyful and radiant like a child's as she now approached the table, as though expecting something, full of the most child-like impatience and trusting curiosity. The look in her eyes gladdened the heart, Alyosha felt. There was something else about her which he could not define, but of which he was instinctively aware; once again, it was the softness and suppleness of her movements, the feline stealth of those movements. And yet she had a strong, generously built body. Under her shawl one could discern broad, rounded shoulders and the firm breasts of a young girl. This body promised to take on the shape of a Venus de Milo, although inevitably in somewhat exaggerated proportions—one could not help but feel this even now. Connoisseurs of Russian female beauty, looking at Grushenka, could unfailingly have predicted that, by the age of thirty, this still fresh, youthful beauty would lose its harmony, become obese, her face would sag, lines would quickly appear on her forehead and round her eyes, her complexion would perhaps turn coarse and redden—in a word, it was an ephemeral, fleeting beauty, of a kind so often encountered in Russian women. It goes without saying that Alyosha did not dwell on this, but though he was charmed, he kept asking himself with an unpleasant feeling of regret why she spoke with a drawl instead of naturally. Evidently, she found this drawling delivery and cloying emphasis of sounds and syllables attractive. Of course, this might simply have been a bad habit in bad taste, indicative of an unrefined background and of a misconception from childhood of what was proper. Certainly, Alyosha felt this pronunciation and intonation to be a gross incongruity alongside the childishly guileless, joyful expression of her face, the soft, happy, youthful radiance of her eyes! In a trice, Katerina Ivanovna had seated her in an armchair facing Alyosha and rapturously kissed her several times on her smiling lips. It was as though she were in love with her.

'This is the first time we have seen each other, Aleksei Fyodorovich,' she said in transports of delight, 'I wanted to get to know her, to meet her, I've been wanting to go and visit her, but as soon as I expressed my wish to see her, she came to see me herself. I knew very well that together we would resolve everything, everything! My heart told me that... Everyone tried to dissuade me from taking this step, but I knew it would work and I wasn't mistaken. Grushenka has explained everything to me, all her intentions; she has descended like a ministering angel, bringing peace and joy...'

'You didn't shun me, my sweet, kind lady,' Grushenka drawled in her singsong voice, still with that same sweet, radiant smile.

'Don't you dare say such words, you delightful, enchanting creature! Shun you? There, I'll kiss that lower lip of yours again. It looks as if it's a little swollen, so let's make it swell a little more, and more, and again some more... Look at her laughing, Aleksei Fyodorovich. It makes one's heart glad to look at this angel...' Alyosha kept blushing, seized by a barely perceptible trembling.

'You're spoiling me, sweet lady, why, I'm quite unworthy of your affection.'

'Unworthy! She thinks she's unworthy!' Katerina Ivanovna exclaimed with the same fervour. 'Listen, Aleksei Fyodorovich, we've a unique little mind, but we've a wilful and proud, ever such a proud little heart! We're noble, Aleksei Fyodorovich, we're magnanimous, do you realize that? We were just unfortunate! We were too ready to make any kind of sacrifice for the sake of an unworthy or, you might say, frivolous person. There was this officer, we fell in love with him, we laid everything at his feet, this was a long time ago, five years in fact, but he abandoned us and went off and got married. Now he's a widower and has written to say he's coming—and don't forget, he's the only man we've ever loved and will continue to love all our life! He'll come, and Grushenka will be happy again after five years of unhappiness. But who will reproach her, who can boast of her favours? No one except that crippled old merchant—and he has been more of a father to us, a friend, a protector. He found us in desperate straits then, in torment, abandoned by the man we loved so much... Do you know, she was going to drown herself, and it was that old gentleman who saved her, he actually saved her!'

'You're being too protective towards me, dear lady,' Grushenka drawled again, 'you do rather exaggerate everything.'

'Me, too protective? It's not for me to protect you; in any case, what right have I to offer protection? Grushenka, my angel, let me have your hand, just look at this wonderful, plump little hand of hers, Aleksei Fyodorovich; can you see it, it has brought me happiness and helped me to be reborn, and I'm going to kiss it now, first on one side and then on the little palm, there, there, and there!' And, as though in ecstasy, she went on to kiss Grushenka's truly delightful, but perhaps slightly over-plump hand three times. The latter held it out with a nervous, deliciously ringing laugh as she watched, with obvious enjoyment, the 'dear lady' kissing her hand in this way. 'This rapture is perhaps rather overdone,' the thought flashed through Alyosha's mind. He blushed. All the time he had been feeling, for some reason, particularly uneasy at heart.

'You shouldn't embarrass me, dear lady, kissing my hand so, in front of Aleksei Fyodorovich.'

'But I had no intention of embarrassing you!' Katerina Ivanovna said, somewhat surprised. 'Oh, how you misunderstand me, my dear!'

'Ah, but perhaps you too, dear lady, have not quite understood me either, perhaps I'm much worse than I appear to you. I'm wicked and wilful. When I broke poor Dmitry Fyodorovich's heart that time, I did it just for fun.'

'But now you're going to save him. You've given your word. You'll make him understand, you'll make it clear to him that you've been in love with someone else for a long time, and that now he's coming to offer you his hand...'

'Oh no, I never gave you any such word. It was you who kept saying this to me, but I never made any promises.'

'Then I must have misunderstood you,' Katerina Ivanovna said quietly, blanching a little. 'You did promise...'

'Oh no, my sweet angel-lady, I never promised you anything,' interrupted Grushenka softly but firmly, maintaining the same innocent and blithe demeanour. 'It must be quite clear to you now, worthy lady, how nasty and headstrong I am compared to you. I do just as I please. Perhaps I did make you a promise earlier, but only just now I was saying to myself: "Supposing Mitya takes my fancy again—after all, he did once... for nearly an hour. So perhaps I'll go to him and tell him that from now on he must stay with me... See how unpredictable I am?...'

'That's not...', Katerina Ivanovna gasped, 'what you said before.'

'Oh, before! But you know how silly and spoilt I am. Just think how much he had to suffer because of me! And supposing I went home and took pity on him—what then?'

'I didn't expect this...'

'Oh, my lady, how good and noble you are compared to someone like me. And now you probably won't love me any more because of my character, silly me... Give me your sweet hand, my darling lady,' she said softly, taking hold of Katerina Ivanovna's hand with apparent deference. 'There, my darling lady, I'll take your hand and kiss it, just like you did mine. You kissed it three times, I ought to kiss yours three hundred times to repay you. So be it, the rest is in God's hands: perhaps I'll be your slave and carry out all your wishes slavishly. As God has willed, so let it be, whatever we may have agreed or promised to each other. Your hand, your hand, what a sweet little hand you have! My darling lady, how impossibly lovely you are!'

She began slowly to draw the hand to her lips, for all the world as though proposing to go ahead with her bizarre intention of 'repaying' those kisses. Katerina Ivanovna did not withdraw her hand; grasping at straws, she listened to Grushenka's bizarre promise to carry out all her wishes 'slavishly'; she kept looking intently into her eyes, and still saw in them the same expression of simple-hearted trust, the same bright cheerfulness... 'Perhaps she's just too naïve!' Katerina Ivanovna thought, a glimmer of hope fluttering in her breast. Meanwhile, as though in raptures at the 'sweet little hand', Grushenka continued to draw it slowly to her lips. But just when they were nearly touching it, she hesitated, as though pausing for reflection.

'You know, my darling lady,' she drawled in the gentlest, sweetest little voice imaginable, 'you know, I think I'd rather not kiss your hand after all.' And she broke into a cheerful little giggle.

'As you please... What's the matter with you?' Katerina Ivanovna suddenly shuddered.

'I want you always to remember that you kissed my hand, but I refused to kiss yours.' There was a sudden glint in her eyes. She stared into Katerina Ivanovna's eyes with a terrible intensity.

'Impudent hussy!' Katerina Ivanovna yelled out, as though she had suddenly understood something, and leapt to her feet. Grushenka stood up, too, but in her own time.

'That's just what I'll tell Mitya; you kissed my hand, but I didn't kiss yours. Won't it make him laugh!'

'Out, you trollop!'

'For shame, lady, for shame, that you should be using such unbecoming language, dear lady.'

'Get out, you money-grubbing trollop!' yelled Katerina Ivanovna. Her whole face was contorted and quivering.

'Money-grubbing too, my, my. Who was it, my young lady, that went to her gentlemen friends when it was dark to ask for money, offering her beauty for sale? Yes, I know all about it.'

Katerina Ivanovna shrieked and was about to pounce on Grushenka, but Alyosha restrained her with all his strength.

'Calm down, let her be! Don't say anything, don't answer her, she's going, she's going now!'

At this moment both of Katerina Ivanovna's aunts, hearing the shriek, ran into the room followed by the maid. They all rushed towards her.

'Yes, I'm going now,' Grushenka said, picking up her mantilla from the sofa. 'Alyosha darling, take me home!'

'Leave now, immediately!' Alyosha begged her, his hands pressed together in supplication.

'Darling Alyoshenka, take me home! I've got something really nice to tell you on the way! I made that little scene all for you, Alyoshenka. Do see me home, sweetheart, you'll be so pleased afterwards.'

Alyosha turned away, wringing his hands. Grushenka ran out of the house, her voice ringing with laughter.

Katerina Ivanovna was having hysterics. She sobbed convulsively, gasping for breath. Everyone was fussing round her.

'I warned you,' the elder aunt said to her, 'I tried to stop you doing this... you would have your own way... what possessed you to do such a thing! You've no idea what these creatures are like, and as for this one, they say she's the worst of the lot... You're too headstrong!'

'She's a vixen!' Katerina Ivanovna screamed. 'Why on earth did you stop me, Aleksei Fyodorovich, I'd have beaten her to a pulp!'

She was unable to restrain herself in front of Alyosha, nor did she wish to do so.

'She ought to be flogged on the scaffold by a hangman, publicly!...'

Alyosha started backing towards the door.

'Good God!' Katerina Ivanovna suddenly yelled out, clasping her hands. 'As for him! How could he have been so despicable, so cruel! He told that creature what happened on that fateful, accursed, for ever accursed day! "You went to offer your beauty for sale, my darling lady!" She knows everything! Your brother's a scoundrel, Aleksei Fyodorovich!'

Alyosha wanted to say something, but he could find no words. His heart was convulsed with pain.

'Go away, Aleksei Fyodorovich! I'm so ashamed, I feel

dreadful! Tomorrow... I implore you on my knees, come tomorrow. Don't judge me, please forgive me, I still don't know what I might do to myself!'

Alyosha went out reeling into the street. He felt a strong urge to weep, like her. Suddenly the maid caught up with him.

'The mistress forgot to give you this letter from Miss Khokhlakova, she's had it since lunch-time.'

Alyosha automatically took the small pink envelope and, not giving it another thought, thrust it into his pocket.

11

ONE MORE RUINED REPUTATION

IT was just over a verst from the town to the monastery. Alyosha hurried along the road, which was deserted at this hour. It was almost night and at thirty paces objects were difficult to distinguish. Halfway along there was a crossroads. There, under a solitary willow tree, he caught sight of a figure. Alyosha had hardly reached the crossroads when the figure suddenly emerged from the shadows and pounced on him with a furious yell.

'Your money or your life!'

'It's you, Mitya!' Alyosha exclaimed in surprise, nearly jumping out of his skin.

'Ha-ha-ha! I caught you by surprise. I thought to myself: where shall I wait for him? Near her house? There are three roads leading from there, and I might have missed you. In the end I thought I'd better wait here; you were bound to pass by here because there's no other way to the monastery. Well, let's have the truth, come straight out with it, even if it kills me... But what's the matter?'

'Nothing, Mitya... you frightened me. Oh, Dmitry! You really hurt father, you drew blood...' Alyosha burst into tears; he had wanted to cry for a long time, and now it was as if something had snapped inside him. 'You nearly killed him... you cursed him... and now... you're playing practical jokes... "Your money or your life!"'

'So what? Is it bad form or something? Inappropriate in the circumstances?'

'No, it's not that... only I—'

'Listen. Just look at the sky: see what a foul night it is, all those clouds, and the wind has picked up! I was hiding under this willow lying in wait for you, and a thought struck me, as God is my witness: why carry on struggling, why wait any longer? Here's a tree, I've got my scarf and my shirt that could be twisted into a noose, my braces too, and... I won't be a burden on this earth any longer, I won't continue to degrade it with my despicable presence! Then I heard you coming—Lord, I thought in a flash, there's someone even I can love, after all: and here he is, here's that someone, my dear brother, whom I love more than anyone on earth and who is the only person I love! And I loved you at that moment, I loved you so much that I said to myself: I must give him a hug! And then this stupid thought came to me: let me play a joke on him, give him a fright. So I called out like an idiot: "Your money!" Forgive my foolishness... it's all such nonsense, but deep down... it isn't inappropriate at all really... But to hell with all that! Tell me, what happened? What did she say? Don't spare my feelings, don't spare me! Did she fly into a rage?'

'No, it wasn't like that... It wasn't like that at all, Mitya. In her house... I found them both in her house just now.'

'What do you mean, both?'

'Grushenka was there with Katerina Ivanovna.'

Dmitry Fyodorovich was thunderstruck.

'Impossible!' he exclaimed. 'You must have been mistaken! Grushenka, in her house?'

Alyosha told him everything that had happened from the moment he had entered Katerina Ivanovna's house. He spoke for about ten minutes, giving, if not a coherent and fluent account, at least a clear one, emphasizing the most important words, the most significant gestures, and vividly indicating, often with just the barest suggestion, what his own feelings were at the time. Dmitry listened in silence, staring with a dreadful intensity, but it was obvious to Alyosha that he understood everything and had the measure of the whole situation. As the story progressed, however, his expression grew not so much dejected as menacing. He frowned and ground his teeth, the look in his eyes became ever more fixed, implacable, and terrible... It was all the more unexpected when, with incredible rapidity, his wild and angry demeanour suddenly changed, the tightly pressed lips relaxed, and Dmitry Fyodorovich burst into the most uncontrollable, spontaneous laughter. He literally roared with laughter and for a good while was even unable to speak.

'So she never kissed her hand! Never kissed it, and ran off just like that!' he cried, almost doubling up with delight. Had his outburst not been so spontaneous, one could almost have said that he was gloating. 'So she called her a vixen? She is a vixen! She must be flogged publicly, must she? Yes indeed she must, I quite agree. It should have been done a long time ago. Let her be flogged but you see, Alyosha, I've got to sort myself out first. I know her, she's the queen of insolence, that refusal is absolutely typical of her. What an infernal hussy! She's the queen of all the infernal hussies you can imagine in this world! You've got to admire her in a way! So she ran off home, did she? Wait... oh... I'll join her! Alyosha, don't be too harsh on me, I quite agree, strangling would be too good for her...'

'What about Katerina Ivanovna?' Alyosha asked sadly.

'I can see through that one, too, right through her, as never before! This is like discovering all four, I mean five continents in one go! What a woman! And this is that same Katenka, the sweet little schoolgirl who didn't hesitate to approach a grotesque, uncouth army officer in a noble attempt to save her father, at the risk of being severely humiliated! What pride, though, what recklessness, what a leap into the unknown! If that's not tempting fate, I don't know what is! You say that aunt of hers tried to restrain her? That aunt, you know, is pretty wilful herself, she's the sister of that General's widow in Moscow and used to put on even more airs than the girl, but when her husband was caught embezzling government funds and lost his property and everything he had, the proud woman quietened down and she's never been the same since. So she was trying to restrain Katya, and Katya would have none of it? "I can triumph over everything," she must have said to herself, "nothing's impossible for me; if I want to, I'll cast a spell on Grushenka too", and she must have believed it all and made a fool of herself, so who's to blame? You think she had deliberately planned to kiss Grushenka's hand with some kind of ulterior motive? Not at all; she really had, she well and truly had fallen in love with Grushenka, I don't mean with Grushenka as such, but with her own image, her own fantasy of Grushenka—because it's *my* image, *my* fantasy! Poor Alyosha, how ever did you manage to get away from those two? Just picked up your cassock and ran for your life, did you? Ha-ha-ha!'

'I don't suppose you realize how much you've hurt Katerina Ivanovna by telling Grushenka what happened that time—she didn't hesitate to fling it in her face that she "visited gentlemen on the sly, offering her beauty for sale"! Mitya, what could be more insulting?' Alyosha was tortured by the thought that his brother might be pleased at Katerina Ivanovna's humiliation, though of course such a thing was impossible.

'Ah!' Dmitry Fyodorovich suddenly exclaimed, knitting his brows and striking his forehead with the flat of his hand. Only now did he fully realize what he had done, though Alyosha had told him the whole story, including the insult and Katerina Ivanovna's exclamation: 'Your brother is a scoundrel!'

'Yes, I may well have told Grushenka about that "fateful day", as Katya likes to call it. Yes, that's right, I did tell her, I remember now! It was that time we were in Mokroye, I was drunk, the gypsy girls were singing... But I was weeping, I was on my knees, I was worshipping Katya's image, and Grushenka knew this. She understood, I remember it clearly now, she was in tears herself... Oh, to hell with it all! It was bound to end like this! That time she wept, but now... a dagger through the heart! That's women for you.'

He lowered his gaze and was lost in thought.

'Yes,' he said suddenly, in a gloomy voice, 'I'm a scoundrel! No doubt about it, a scoundrel. What does it matter if I wept or not, I'm still a scoundrel! Tell her I accept her verdict, if that's any consolation. Well, that'll do, goodbye, enough of this talk! Not a very cheerful topic. You go your way, I'll go mine. Can't say I want to see you again, except perhaps when it's all up with me. Goodbye, Aleksei!' He shook Alyosha's hand vigorously and, without raising his eyes or head, turned abruptly and set off swiftly towards the town. Alyosha followed him with his eyes, in disbelief that he could depart just like that.

'Just a moment, Aleksei,' Dmitry Fyodorovich turned and said suddenly, after he had taken only a few steps, 'one more confession, only to you! Look at me, look hard. Do you see, here, just here—there's something dreadfully shameful being hatched here.' (Saying 'just here', Dmitry Fyodorovich struck his chest with his closed fist in a strange manner, as though this shameful 'something' were indeed there, in that spot, in a pocket perhaps, or sewn into something and hanging round his neck.) 'You know me, a scoundrel, a self-confessed scoundrel! But remember, whatever I may have done in the past, am doing now, or will do in the future—nothing, nothing can be as despicable as the villainy that I'm harbouring here now, that I carry in my heart this very minute, here, just here, this villainy—active and developing—which I'm fully capable of stopping, which I can stop or let it take its course, be sure of that! Well, you might as well know, I shan't stop it, I shall let it take its course. When we talked earlier I told you everything, but not this, because even I didn't have the gall for that! I can still stop myself; and if I do, tomorrow I'll recover half of my lost honour, but I'm not going to stop myself, I'm going to carry out my terrible intention, and you can be my witness that I've said so deliberately in advance! Iniquity and hell let loose! No need to explain, you'll find out when the time comes. The stinking alley-way and the infernal hussy! Goodbye. Don't pray for me, I'm not worth it, there's no need, no need at all... I don't need your prayers! Let me be!'

And he walked off abruptly, this time for good. Alyosha turned towards the monastery. 'How can I... how can I possibly not see him again?' he wondered in desperation. 'What does he mean? I'll certainly see him again. Tomorrow! I'll go and look for him, I'll go specially, just to find out what he means!...'

He walked round the outside of the monastery, straight through the pine copse and into the hermitage. The door was opened for him, although no one was normally admitted at this hour. His heart was beating fast as he entered the starets's cell. Why, oh why had he gone out today, why was the starets sending him 'out into the world'? Here was peace and sanctity, whereas out there—confusion and darkness, in which one wandered and lost one's way.

In the cell he found the novice Porfiry and Father Païsy, who had been dropping in every hour throughout the day to enquire about Starets Zosima, whose condition, Alyosha was shocked to learn, was deteriorating rapidly. Even the customary evening assembly of the monks could not take place on this occasion. Usually, every evening after the liturgy, the monks would gather in the starets's cell before retiring for the night, and each of them would confess to him his wrongdoings, his sinful thoughts and desires, his temptations, and even the quarrels he may have had with his brother monks. Some confessed on their knees. The starets made his pronouncements, conciliated, counselled, imposed penance, gave his blessing, and dismissed them. It was these communal 'confessions' that the opponents of the cult of startsy objected to, denouncing them as violations of the sacrament of confession and nothing short of sacrilege (they were wrong of course). It was even suggested to the diocesan authorities that such confessions, far from being of any benefit, actually led directly to temptation and sin. Many, it was said, were reluctant to go to the starets, and went only because others did so and to avoid being accused of the sin of pride and spiritual defiance. There were stories of some monks going to the evening confession having previously agreed amongst themselves: 'I'll say I lost my temper with you this morning and you confirm it,' merely in order to have something to say and be done with it. Alyosha knew that this did actually occur sometimes. He was also aware that there were some amongst the brethren who took great exception to the custom whereby even the letters which the monks at the hermitage received from their relatives were first brought to the starets to be opened and read, before being handed over to the addressee. The intention was, of course, that all this should be done openly and sincerely, from the heart, in the name of voluntary humility and spiritual edification; in practice however much insincerity—indeed, contrivance and hypocrisy—would result. The older and more experienced monks stood their ground nevertheless, arguing that 'whosoever has sincerely entered these walls in order to attain salvation will undoubtedly find all these acts of obedience and sacrifice salutary and beneficial; on the other hand, he who finds them burdensome and who complains ought not even to be considered a monk and has no business in the monastery, his proper place being in the world outside. And since no one can be safe from temptation or the devil in the Church any more than in the world at large, it follows therefore that the guard against sin must never be relaxed.'

'He's become weaker and sleeps most of the time,' Father Païsy whispered to Alyosha after he had blessed him. 'It's even difficult to wake him. But there's no need to. He woke up for about five minutes and asked that his blessing be sent to the monks and that they remember him in their evening prayers. He intends to receive Holy Communion once more in the morning. He asked after you, Aleksei, whether you had gone away, and we told him you were in the town. "He has gone there with my blessing; that is where he ought to be just now, rather than here"—that is what he said about you. He spoke of you with kindness and concern—you realize what an honour that is? Only, why did he instruct you to go out into the world for a while? It surely means he has foreseen something in your life! Remember this, Aleksei, that even if you do return to the world, it will be in obedience to your starets's will, and not to indulge in vain pursuits and worldly pleasures...'

Father Païsy left the cell. That the starets was failing, Alyosha was in no doubt, although he might live for another day or two. Overcome with emotion, Alyosha definitely decided—in spite of his promise to go and see his father, the Khokhlakovas, his brother, and Katerina Ivanovna—not to leave the monastery at all the next day, but to remain with his starets until he died. His heart was overflowing with love, and he reproached himself bitterly that while he was in the town he could have forgotten, even for a moment, this man whom he revered more than anyone else in the world, and could have left him lying on his deathbed in the monastery. He went into the starets's tiny bedroom, knelt down, and bowed to the ground in front of the sleeping figure. The starets was lying silent and motionless, breathing regularly and almost imperceptibly. His face was peaceful.

Alyosha went back to the room in which the starets had received his visitors that morning and, taking off his boots and hardly undressing any further, lay down on the hard, narrow, leather-covered settee on which he had for so long been accustomed to sleeping with only a pillow under his head. He had already quite some time ago given up using the mattress that his father had referred to. He simply used to take off his cassock and cover himself with it in place of a blanket. But before falling asleep, he went down on his knees and prayed for a long time. In his ardent prayer he did not ask God to resolve his confusion, but yearned only for inner joy, the joy that he always experienced in his soul after praising and glorifying God, which was usually the sole content of his prayers before going to sleep. This joy, which filled his soul, would invariably induce a deep and peaceful sleep. While praying, he suddenly felt in his pocket the little pink envelope that Katerina Ivanovna's maid had handed to him as she caught up with him on the road. He felt uneasy, but finished his prayer. Then, after some hesitation, he opened the envelope. It contained a letter to him, signed 'Lise', that same young daughter of Mrs Khokhlakova's who had teased him in front of the starets that morning.

'Dear Aleksei Fyodorovich,' she wrote. 'No one knows that I'm writing to you, not even my mother, and I know how deceitful that is. But I couldn't possibly survive unless I told you what is going on in my heart, though only we two should know about it for now. But how am I to tell you what I so much long to tell you? They say that paper does not blush, but I assure you that this is not true and that it is blushing just as much as I am now, all over. My dear Alyosha, I love you, I've loved you since childhood, since our Moscow days, when you were quite different from now, and I'll love you for life. I have chosen you with all my heart, chosen to be united with you, and to live all our days together—of course, on condition that you leave the monastery. As for our ages, we'll wait as long as the law prescribes. By then, I'm sure to be cured, I shall be able to walk and dance. There can be no doubt of that.

'You see, I've thought of everything; however, one thing worries me: what will you think of me after you've read this? I'm always laughing and misbehaving, and earlier today I made you angry, but I assure you that before I put pen to paper just now I prayed before the icon of the Holy Virgin, and I am still praying, almost in tears.

'There, my secret is in your hands now; when you come to see us tomorrow, I don't know how I'll be able to look you in the eye. Oh, Aleksei Fyodorovich, what if I can't control myself again and start laughing like a silly fool, as I did when I looked at you today? You'll probably take me for a wicked tease and won't take my letter seriously. And therefore I beg you, my dear Alyosha, if you have any compassion for me, when you come tomorrow don't look me straight in the eyes, because if I catch your eye I might suddenly burst out laughing, and what with you in your long cassock... Even now I go cold all over when I think about it, so when you come, don't look at me at all for a time, look at my mother, or at the window...

'There, I've written you a love-letter, my God, what have I done! Alyosha, don't despise me, and if I've done something wicked and have hurt you, forgive me. The secret that could ruin my reputation for ever is in your hands.

'I will certainly cry today. Au revoir. I simply *dread* the thought of meeting you. Lise.

'PS. Alyosha, you must, you must come, you must come whatever happens! Lise.'

Alyosha read the letter with surprise, he read it twice, thought to himself a little, and then suddenly began to laugh softly and contentedly. He shuddered; his laughter struck him as sinful. But a second later he was laughing again just as softly and joyfully. He slowly returned the letter to its envelope, crossed himself, and lay down. The turmoil in his soul had passed. 'Lord have mercy on them all,' he murmured, 'the unhappy and the tempestuous ones, protect them and give them Your guidance. You know the true path and will lead them all to salvation. You, who are love, will bring joy to them all!' Alyosha crossed himself as he drifted off into a tranquil sleep.

PART TWO

PART TWO

BOOK FOUR
Crises

1
FATHER THERAPON*

ALYOSHA awoke early, before sunrise. The starets was already up; he was feeling very weak, but nevertheless had decided to move from his bed to his chair. He was in full possession of his faculties. Though he looked very tired, the expression on his face was bright, almost joyful, and the look in his eyes was cheerful, kindly, and welcoming. 'Perhaps I shall not live to see the end of this day,' he said to Alyosha; then he expressed a desire to make his confession and take Holy Communion immediately. His confessor was always Father Païsy. Following these two sacraments, Extreme Unction was administered. The hieromonks gathered in the cell, which then gradually began to fill with other monks. It was now past daybreak. Monks from the monastery also began to arrive. After the service was over, the starets expressed a desire to bid farewell to all, and he kissed everyone. Because of the cramped conditions in the cell, those who had come first left to make room for the others. Alyosha stood next to the starets, who by now had returned to his chair. Then he began to speak and to preach as best he could in a voice which, though weak, was still quite firm. 'I've been teaching you for so many years, and consequently have spoken out loud so much, that speaking—and in speaking, my dear brethren, teaching you—has almost become a habit with me, so much so that even now, weak as I am, to remain silent would be more difficult than to speak,' he joked, looking benignly at those who were crowding around him. Alyosha was later to recall some of the things the starets said on that occasion. But though he spoke clearly and his voice was firm enough, his discourse was quite disjointed. He spoke about many things, evidently wishing before the moment of death to say everything once more, all that there was to say, all that he had left unsaid during his life, and this not merely for the sake of preaching, but as though yearning to share his happiness and exultation with all and sundry, and to pour out his heart once more before he died...

'Love one another, my brothers,' the starets exhorted (as far as Alyosha could recall later). 'Love God's people. Just because we have shut ourselves within these walls, it does not make us any holier than the laity; on the contrary, anyone who has come here has by that very act acknowledged to himself that he is worse than any lay person and all that is on this earth... And the longer a monk lives within the walls of his monastery, the more deeply he will realize this. If this were not the case, there would be no need for him to come here at all. When, however, he realizes that not only is he worse than any layman, but that he is guilty before all, for everything and before everyone, for the sins of all men, individually as well as collectively, only then will the goal of our seclusion be attained. For know you this, my dearly beloved brethren: each one of us is unquestionably answerable for all men and all things on earth, not cnly by virtue of the collective guilt of the world, but also individually, for all men and everyone on earth. This realization is the crowning glory not only of the monastic way of life, but of every human being on earth. For monks are just like other people, except that they are as all men on earth ought to be. It is only through this realization that our hearts will be moved to boundless, universal, all-consuming love. Thus will each one of us be able to redeem the world and with his tears wash away its sins... Each should attend to his own heart, each should ceaselessly render account unto himself. As long as you are repentant, do not be alarmed at your own sin even in the full knowledge of it, and do not attempt to strike bargains with God. Again I say unto you—be humble. Be humble with the weak, be humble with the mighty. Bear no ill will against those who reject, defame, malign, and slander you. Bear no ill will against atheists, false prophets, materialists, even the evil ones, for there are many good ones among them too, especially in our time. Remember them in your prayer: save, O Lord, all those who have no one to pray for them, save also those who do not want to pray to You. And add forthwith: it is not out of pride that I beseech you, for I myself am the vilest of the vile... Love God's people, do not let strangers take possession of your flock, for if you are indolent and full of false pride—or, worse still, avaricious—they will come from all the corners of the earth and lure your flock away. Explain the Gospels to the people ceaselessly... Do not practise usury... Do not worship gold and silver, or hoard it... Be true to your faith and hold up the banner. Raise it on high...'

The starets, it must be said, spoke less coherently than Alyosha recorded later. Sometimes he would stop speaking altogether, as though pausing to gather his strength, gasping for breath but appearing to be in a state of exultation. His listeners were deeply moved, although many wondered at his words, for they saw no light in them... Subsequently, everyone recalled these words. When Alyosha happened to leave the cell briefly, he was astounded at the general excitement and sense of expectation among the monks crowding both inside and outside the cell. Some waited almost fearfully, others solemnly. Everyone expected something significant to happen immediately the starets died. To some extent this was an idle expectation, although even the most solemn of the clergy were not immune to it. Father Païsy looked the most solemn of all. Alyosha left the cell only because he had been mysteriously summoned by a monk at the behest of Rakitin, who had arrived from the town with a strange letter for Alyosha from Mrs Khokhlakova. The latter informed Alyosha of a very curious piece of news, which turned out to be extremely pertinent. It related to the fact that, amongst the God-fearing peasant women who had come the previous day to pay their respects to the starets and seek his blessing, had been an old townswoman by the name of Prokhorovna, the widow of a non-commissioned officer. She had asked the starets if, in the prayers for the dead at her church, she could include her son Vasya, who had gone to a distant part of Siberia, to Irkutsk, on business, and whom she had not heard from for a year. The starets had responded severely to her request, forbidding such a practice and likening it to sorcery. But then, having pardoned her for her ignorance, he had offered, 'as though reading from a book of prophecy' (as Mrs Khokhlakova wrote in her letter), the following consolation, namely that her son Vasya was undoubtedly alive, and that he would either return or write to her soon, and that she should go home and wait. 'And would you believe it?' Mrs Khokhlakova continued excitedly, 'The prophecy's been fulfilled, word for word, and there's more to it!' No sooner had the old woman returned home than she was handed a letter that had arrived earlier from Siberia. But that was not the end of the story: in this letter, written from Yekaterinburg on his return journey, Vasya informed his mother that he was travelling back to Russia in the company of a certain official, and that he 'looked forward to embracing his mother in about three weeks'. Mrs Khokhlakova fervently begged Alyosha to pass on immediately the news of this new 'miracle of prophecy' to the abbot and to the whole of the community. 'Everybody must know about this!' she stressed at the end of her letter. The letter had been dashed off in great haste, every line reflecting the writer's agitation. But there was nothing for Alyosha to inform the brethren about, because everyone already knew all about it; Rakitin, having sent the monk to fetch Alyosha, had instructed the former respectfully to inform his eminence, Father Païsy, that he, Rakitin, had a matter of such urgency to communicate to him that it could not be delayed for a moment, and that he humbly begged his pardon for his impertinence. Since the monk had passed Rakitin's request to Father Païsy before he communicated it to Alyosha, all that the latter could do on returning to his cell and reading the letter was simply to hand it to Father Païsy as documentary confirmation. And even that stern and mistrustful man, on reading the report of the 'miracle' with furrowed brow, could not wholly restrain his feelings. His eyes flashed and his lips curled in a smile of grave premonition.

'We have not yet seen the end of this!' he said with involuntary urgency.

'Indeed not, indeed not!' the monks responded from all sides. But Father Païsy, frowning again, enjoined everyone not to mention the matter to anyone, for the time being at least, 'until we have further confirmation, because there's bound to be a lot of idle gossip... And in any case,' he added cautiously, as though to salve his conscience, 'there could equally well be a natural explanation.' However, he hardly seemed convinced by his own reservations, which his listeners did not fail to notice. Of course, news of the 'miracle' spread through the monastery, and within the hour it had also reached the ears of the many visitors who had come to the monastery to attend the liturgy. But the person who showed the most surprise at the miracle was the little monk who had come the day before from St Silvester's, the small monastery in Obdorsk in the far north. The previous day, while standing next to Mrs Khokhlakova, he had bowed to the starets and, pointing to the lady's daughter who had been 'cured', said to him indignantly: 'How dare you do such things?'

The truth of the matter was that he now found himself somewhat perplexed, and hardly knew what to believe. The previous evening he had paid Father Therapon a visit in his cell behind the apiary, and this meeting had made an extraordinary and terrifying impression on him. Father Therapon was that same elderly monk, the great adherent of the vow of fasting and silence, whom we have already mentioned as an adversary of Starets Zosima, and especially of the cult of startsy, which he considered to be a harmful and mindless practice. As an adversary he was extremely dangerous, even though, because of his vow of silence, he hardly exchanged a word with anyone. The danger lay chiefly in the fact that a great number of the monks shared his views, and many of the visiting worshippers revered him as a man of God and a zealot, although they undoubtedly considered him to be a holy fool and an oddity. But his oddness was the very thing that appealed to people. Father Therapon never visited Starets Zosima. Though he lived in the hermitage, little attempt was made to impose its discipline upon him, again because his manner was so distinctly eccentric. He was about seventy-five years old, if not more, and lived behind the apiary in the corner of the wall in an old, ramshackle timber cabin, erected on this spot way back in the previous century for another outstanding adherent of the vow of fasting and silence, Father Jonah, who had lived to the age of a hundred and five and of whose accomplishments many very strange tales continue to circulate in the monastery and its surrounding neighbourhood to this day. On his own insistence, Father Therapon had eventually been moved about seven years previously to this small, isolated cabin, in truth a shack, but which greatly resembled a small chapel on account of the numerous votive icons and the perpetually burning lamps arrayed in front of them, for the care and maintenance of which Father Therapon had in fact ostensibly been installed there. He ate, it was said (and this was true), two pounds of bread in three days, no more; the bread was brought to him every three days by the bee-keeper, who also lived next to the apiary, but Father Therapon rarely spoke even to this bee-keeper who attended to his needs. These four pounds of bread, together with the consecrated Sabbath wafer which the recluse received regularly from the abbot after late morning service, comprised his whole weekly sustenance. As for the water in his jug, it was changed every day. He seldom attended liturgy. The followers who came to visit him saw him kneeling in prayer, sometimes for the whole day, without rising or looking up. Even if he deigned to enter into conversation with them, he was always curt, abrupt, odd, and almost invariably rude. There were, however, very rare occasions when he would engage in conversation with his visitors, though for the most part he would merely utter some incongruous word which would cause the visitor much consternation, after which, despite all pleading, he would say nothing by way of explanation. He had never been ordained to the priesthood, but was just an ordinary monk. There was a very strange rumour, circulating, it is true, only amongst the less educated people, that Father Therapon communed with heavenly spirits and conversed only with them, which was why he did not enter into conversation with ordinary mortals. The little monk from Obdorsk, having been directed to the apiary by the bee-keeper, also a very taciturn and morose monk, made for the corner where Father Therapon's cabin stood. 'Perhaps he'll speak to you, seeing as you're a stranger, but there again, you may get nothing out of him,' the bee-keeper warned. The little monk, as he himself subsequently recounted, approached with the greatest trepidation. It was already getting quite late. On this occasion Father Therapon was sitting on a bench by the door of the cabin. Above him rustled the leaves of an enormous old elm tree. There was an evening chill in the air. The little monk from Obdorsk prostrated himself on the ground before the zealot and asked for his blessing.

'Dost thou expect me too to fall flat on my face before thee, monk?' said Father Therapon. 'Arise!'

The little monk got up.

'Blessed be he who blesseth, sit thee down beside me. Whence comest thou?'

What astounded the little monk most of all was the fact that Father Therapon, despite his undeniably strict fasting and very advanced years, was still apparently a strong man, tall, erect, with a spare, fresh, and healthy-looking face. He undoubtedly still retained considerable physical strength. He had the body of an athlete. In spite of his great age, he was not even particularly grey, and still had a thick growth of hair and a beard, which had formerly been completely black. His eyes were large, grey, shining, and noticeably protruding. When he spoke, he strongly accented the letter *o*.* He was dressed in a long, reddish peasant's coat made of that coarse material formerly known as prison cloth and tied round the waist with a length of thick rope. His neck and chest were bare. An almost black, extremely thick sackcloth shirt, which had not been changed for months, extended beneath his coat. On his chest, under his coat, he was said to wear thirty-pound iron chains. On his bare feet he wore a pair of old shoes which were nearly falling apart.

'I come from our small monastery in Obdorsk, from St Sylvester's,' replied the little visiting monk humbly, surveying the recluse with keen, curious, though slightly apprehensive eyes.

'I know thy Sylvester. I have sojourned there. How fareth thy Sylvester?'

The little monk hesitated.

'You are devoid of sense, you people! How keep you your fasts?'

'Our fare accords with the ancient traditions of the hermitage: during Lent, no provender on Mondays, Wednesdays, or Fridays. On Tuesdays and Thursdays the monks take white bread, an infusion with honey, cloudberries or pickled cabbage with soaked oatmeal. On Saturdays skimmed cabbage soup, gruel, and noodle soup with peas—all with hemp-seed oil. In Passion Week, from Monday right up to Saturday night, only bread and water and uncooked vegetables for six days, and this too in moderation; on some days we take no food at all, as is ordained for the first week of Lent. No food on Good Friday, and total fasting on Holy Saturday too, till three o'clock, and then we can take a little bread with water and one cup of wine. On Maundy Thursday we eat food cooked without oil, but take wine, and for the rest—dry provender only. For in the Laodicean Council* it was thus said of Maundy Thursday: "Whosoever fails to keep the fast on the last Thursday of Lent, he has dishonoured the whole of Lent." That is our way... But,' said the little monk, summoning up courage, 'what is that compared to you, hallowed father, for the whole year, even including Holy Easter, you eat nothing, save bread and water, and the bread we eat in two days lasts you a week. Verily, such remarkable abstinence is to be marvelled at.'

'And mushrooms?' Father Therapon suddenly asked, pronouncing it as they do in the south.

'Mushrooms?' the little monk repeated in astonishment.

'Thus it is. I spurn their bread, I have no need of it, even if I go to the forest and eat mushrooms and berries, they will not forgo their bread, nay, never, thus they deliver themselves unto Satan. Now do the heretics declare it is not needful to keep the fasts. Foul and arrogant is this notion.'

'That's true,' the little monk sighed.

'Didst thou see devils amongst them?'

'Amongst whom do you mean?' asked the little monk shyly.

'I betook myself to the abbot's on Holy Whitsuntide past, and never since returned thither. Verily, did I see them. A devil sat upon the chest of one, it lurked beneath his cassock, and naught save the horns did show; and one peeped from the pocket of another one, and its eyes were busy for very fear of me; one monk there was with a devil in the unclean pit of his belly, and a devil hung around the neck of another, who knew it not.'

'You... saw them?' the little monk enquired.

'Thus have I spoken—I see all things. Even as I departed from the abbot, I beheld one that did lurk behind the door, big, about an *arshin* and a half high it stood, nay more, and it had a long, thick, brownish tail, which it waved by the doorpost, and thereon did I slam the door and lo, the tail was made fast, for verily I am no fool. Then it screeched and flailed, and then I made over it the sign of the cross—thrice. It expired like a squashed spider. Verily must it be rotten in the corner now and powerful must be the stench thereof, yet neither can they see it nor can they smell it. A year have I not set foot there. To thee alone I reveal this, for thou art come from afar.'

'These are frightening words! I say, holy and blessed father,' the little monk was growing more and more confident, 'is it true—you know, your fame is so great, even in the remotest parts of the land—is it true that you are in constant communion with the Holy Ghost?'

'He doth fly down. Sometimes.'

'Fly down? In what shape?'

'As a bird.'

'The Holy Ghost in the shape of a dove?'

'There is the Holy Ghost, and then there is the Paraclete. The Paraclete is another matter, he cometh not only as a dove, but as other birds; sometimes he cometh as a swallow, sometimes as a goldfinch, and sometimes as a tomtit.'

'How can you tell him from a tomtit?'

'He speaketh.'

'How does he speak, in what tongue?'

'In the human tongue.'

'And what does he say to you?'

'This day he pronounced that a fool would come unto me asking all manner of rascally questions. Thou seekest to know too much, monk.'

'Your words are frightening, blessed and holy father,' said the little monk, shaking his head. There was now a glint of distrust in his restless eyes.

'Seest thou yon tree?' asked Father Therapon after a brief silence.

'I do, holy father.'

'To thee it is an elm tree, but to me it is something quite different.'

'What?' the little monk said, after waiting vainly for some elucidation.

'It happeneth in the night. Seest thou those two branches? In the night it is Christ, who reacheth out His arms and seeketh me with His arms, I behold it clearly and I tremble with fear. Fearful, oh fearful!'

'Why fearful, if it is Christ Himself?'

'What if he seize me and bear me aloft?'

'What, alive as you are?'

'In the spirit and glory of Elias,* hast thou not heard? I shall be gathered into his arms and borne away...'

Though the little monk from Obdorsk returned extremely perplexed to the cell he had been allocated to share with one of the monks, he was nevertheless undoubtedly more sympathetic to Father Therapon than to Starets Zosima. To begin with, the little monk from Obdorsk was all for fasting, and it did not seem at all surprising to him that such a famous advocate of fasting as Father Therapon should have 'witnessed the miraculous'. True, his words were somewhat incongruous, but the Lord would surely know what they signified; after all, the words and deeds of a holy fool when the spirit is upon him could well be a good deal more absurd. As for the devil's tail being jammed in the door, he was quite ready to believe it not only figuratively, but literally too. Moreover, even before his arrival at the monastery he had been deeply prejudiced against the cult of startsy, which he knew only from hearsay, but which, along with many other people, he regarded as a harmful innovation. Even before the day was out, he had happened to overhear at the monastery the surreptitious mutterings of some of the more outspoken monks opposed to the cult of the startsy. Being a tireless busybody, he was by nature insatiably curious about everything. That is why the news of the new 'miracle' performed by Starets Zosima plunged him into profound confusion. Alyosha subsequently remembered seeing among the monks crowding round the entrance to the cell and striving for a view of the starets, the diminutive figure of the visitor from Obdorsk inquisitively scurrying from one group to another, listening to everything and gleaning and gathering every scrap of available information. But he paid little attention to him at the time, and only subsequently did it all come back to him... Anyway, his mind was then on other things: Starets Zosima, who was again feeling tired and had gone to bed, had suddenly, just as he was closing his eyes, remembered Alyosha and summoned him. Alyosha immediately hurried to him. The starets was alone except for Father Païsy, Father Yosif, and the novice Porfiry. He opened his weary eyes, looked hard at Alyosha and said suddenly:

'Is your family expecting you, my son?'

Alyosha hesitated.

'Do they need you? Did you tell anyone yesterday that you would see them today?'

'Yes... my father... my brothers... and others too...'

'You see, you must go without fail. Do not be sad. Do not be afraid, I shall not die before I have said my final words to you on this earth. Those words will be for you and you alone, they will be my bequest to you. To you, my precious one, because you are the one who loves me. And now, my son, go to whoever is waiting for you.'

Alyosha obeyed immediately, though he departed with a heavy heart. But the promise that he would hear the starets's final utterance on earth and, above all, that it would be bequeathed to him and to him alone, filled Alyosha's soul with ecstasy. He began to hurry so as to complete all his business in town and return all the sooner. Just then, Father Païsy also addressed some parting words which had a most profound and unexpected effect on him. This occurred after they had both left the starets's cell.

'Always remember, young man,' Father Païsy began without any preamble, 'that secular science, having become a powerful force, has examined in detail, especially in this last century, everything divine bequeathed to us in the Holy Scriptures, but having subjected all that is holy to such a rigorous analysis the scientists of the world have ended up empty-handed. For in looking at the component parts in isolation they have quite overlooked the whole, and with a truly astounding lack of vision. But the whole stands inviolate before their eyes, as it always has done, and the gates of hell shall not prevail against it.* For has it not survived for nineteen centuries, and does it not still continue to live in the souls of individuals, amidst the decline and fall of nations? It lives on, immutable as ever, even in the souls of those very atheists who have destroyed everything. For those who have renounced Christianity and are in revolt against it, they too still retain the image and likeness of Christ, and to this day neither in their wisdom nor in the passion of their hearts have they been able to offer mankind a more exalted and dignifying image than that which was revealed in the beginning by Christ. And where attempts have been made, they have produced only abomination. Remember this especially, my son, for you are being sent forth into the world by your dying starets. Perhaps when you look back upon this fateful day you will also recall my words given to you in heartfelt farewell, for you are young, and the temptations of this world are great and more than a match for your strength. Well, off you go now, my orphan.'

Thus saying, Father Païsy blessed him. On leaving the monastery and reflecting on these unexpected words Alyosha suddenly realized that in this monk, who had hitherto been strict and severe towards him, he had discovered a new and wonderful friend and a deeply sympathetic mentor, appointed, it would seem, by Starets Zosima himself on his deathbed. 'Perhaps that really did take place between the two of them,' Alyosha mused. As for the unexpected and learned discourse which Father Païsy had just delivered, it was that and that alone which amply testified to the goodness of his heart; he felt he had to arm the immature mind as soon as possible for the struggle against temptation, and shield the young soul entrusted to his care with the most impregnable defence imaginable.

2

AT HIS FATHER'S

ALYOSHA first of all went to see his father. As he approached the house he remembered his father insisting the day before that he should arrive without Ivan noticing him. 'I wonder why?' it suddenly occurred to Alyosha. 'If father wants to tell me something in confidence, why should I have to enter the house unobserved? He probably meant to say something else yesterday, but he was so upset it completely slipped his mind,' he concluded. Nevertheless, he was much relieved when Marfa Ignatyevna, on opening the gate (Grigory, it transpired, had fallen ill and was confined to bed in his quarters), informed him in answer to his question that Ivan Fyodorovich had already left two hours before.

'How is father?'

'He's already up, having coffee,' Marfa Ignatyevna replied somewhat dryly.

Alyosha went in. The old man, seated at the table and wearing a pair of slippers and a shabby old coat, was going through some accounts in a rather desultory fashion. He was completely on his own in the house (Smerdyakov had gone to town to buy some food for the midday meal). But it was not the accounts that preoccupied him. Even though he had got up quite early that morning and was trying to keep his spirits up, he nevertheless looked tired and weak. A red kerchief was tied round his forehead, on which extensive purple bruising had developed overnight. His nose had swollen appreciably in the night and it too was slightly bruised, which made him appear particularly angry and bad-tempered. The old man was aware of this himself, and he glared at Alyosha as he entered the room.

'Coffee's cold,' he said brusquely. 'Shan't offer you any. All I'm having today is plain fish soup, and I'm not entertaining anybody. Why've you come?'

'To find out how you are,' Alyosha said.

'Yes. I know I told you yesterday to come and see me. It was all a big mistake. You needn't have bothered. But I knew you'd turn up soon enough...'

His tone was exceptionally hostile. He rose from his seat and (for perhaps the umpteenth time that morning) looked at his nose with concern in the mirror. He also began to adjust the kerchief on his head for appearance's sake.

'Prefer the red. White would have smacked too much of the infirmary,' he remarked thoughtfully. 'Well, what's up? How's your starets?'

'He's very ill. He may die today,' Alyosha replied, but his father ignored the answer and even forgot that he had asked the question.

'Ivan's left,' he said suddenly. 'He's doing his damnedest to steal Mitya's bride-to-be... That's why he's staying here,' he added angrily, and glanced at Alyosha with a grimace.

'Did he tell you that himself?' asked Alyosha.

'Yes, quite a while ago too; about three weeks ago in fact. He didn't come here to cut my throat, did he? He must have come for some reason!'

'Stop it! You shouldn't say things like that!' Alyosha felt dreadfully confused.

'He hasn't asked for money, that's true, though he's not going to get a kopeck from me anyway. Let me inform you, my dear Aleksei Fyodorovich, that I intend to live upon this earth as long as possible and shall therefore need every kopeck I can get, and the longer I live, the greater will be my need,' he continued, pacing up and down the room, his hands thrust into the pockets of his loose-fitting, grimy, lightweight, yellow calamanco coat. 'I'm still a man, remember, only fifty-five, and I've got another twenty years or so of manhood left in me, because surely they won't want to come to me of their own volition when I'm old and decrepit, and that's just when I'll really need the money. That's why I'm saving as much as I possibly can purely for myself, my dear Aleksei Fyodorovich, and let me tell you this too, my son, I intend to continue to have women right up to the end, I'll have you know. Up with fornication! They all condemn it, yet they all enjoy it, but they do it on the sly, whereas I'm open about it. And because I'm not a hypocrite, all the scoundrels take me to task. As for your paradise, Aleksei Fyodorovich, you can keep it, thank you very much: in fact, any honest person would feel positively uncomfortable entering that paradise of yours, even if it did exist. As far as I'm concerned, once you're dead, that's the end of it, but if you want to commemorate me, that's fine by me, if not, to hell with you! That's my philosophy. Ivan talked a lot of sense yesterday, even though we were all drunk. Ivan's a braggart, and he's certainly no intellectual... he's not even particularly well educated, he just smiles at you and doesn't say a word—that's how he gets away with it.'

Alyosha listened to him in silence.

'Why won't he talk to me? And when he does condescend to, it's all a sham. Your Ivan's a scoundrel! I can marry Grushka any time I choose. Because if you've got money, you only have to snap your fingers and it's done, Aleksei Fyodorovich. That's precisely what Ivan's afraid of, so he's keeping a close watch on me and encouraging Dmitry to marry Grushka so as to prevent me from marrying her (as though I'd leave him any money even if I didn't marry her!); if, furthermore, Dmitry did marry her,

Ivan would pick up his wealthy bride, that's his little game! He's a scoundrel, that Ivan of yours!'

'You're in such a bad mood. It must be because of what happened yesterday; why don't you go and lie down?' Alyosha said.

'Coming from you,' the old man suddenly remarked, as though the thought had struck him for the first time ever, 'coming from you it doesn't make me angry at all, but if Ivan had said that to me, I'd have taken offence. It's only with you that I have moments of goodness, because on the whole I'm a wicked person.'

'You're not wicked, just a little muddled,' Alyosha smiled.

'Listen, I wanted to get that criminal Mitka put behind bars today, and I might still do so, I haven't decided yet. Of course, in these enlightened times it's customary to regard your parents as a damned nuisance, but I put it to you that even these days you're not allowed to grab your father by the hair, or kick him in the face while he's on the floor in his own house, and then brag that you'll be back later to finish him off—and all in front of witnesses. I could destroy him if I wanted to, I could have him put behind bars immediately for what he did yesterday.'

'So you're not going to lodge a complaint then?'

'Ivan's talked me out of it. Not that I care a damn about Ivan, but there's one thing I do know...'

And, leaning across to Alyosha, he continued in a confidential whisper:

'If I have the scoundrel locked up she'll get to hear of it and will immediately go running to him. But if she finds out that he beat the living daylights out of a helpless old man, she might leave him and come to me... That's her nature all over—as contrary as they come. I know her through and through! Fancy some brandy? The coffee's cold, but I'll add a drop of brandy—that should improve it no end.'

'No thank you. I'll have this piece of bread though, if I may,' Alyosha said, and picked up a three-kopeck French roll, which he put in his cassock pocket.

'And you shouldn't have any brandy either,' he added, cautiously peering into the old man's face.

'You're right, it gets you worked up but doesn't give you any peace of mind. Just one more glass though. I'll just get it from the cupboard...'

And with that he unlocked a small cupboard, poured himself a glass, downed it, then locked the cupboard and put the key back in his pocket.

'And that's enough. One glass won't kill me.'

'Well, you're already more sociable,' Alyosha smiled.

'Hm! I love you anyway, brandy or no brandy, but when it comes to scoundrels, I give as good as I get. Ivan hasn't gone to Chermashnya—I wonder why? He wants to spy on me: he wants to find out how much I'll give Grushenka if she comes. Everybody's a scoundrel! I've no time for Ivan at all. Where did he come from? He's not one of us. You think I'm going to leave him anything? For your information, I shan't even make a will. As for Mitka, I'll crush him like a cockroach. They make a crunching noise under my feet when I tread on them in the night. Your Dmitry will end up the same way. *Your* Dmitry, because you love him. You do love him, don't you? But I couldn't care less even if you do. But if Ivan were to love him, I'd be scared. The fact is, Ivan doesn't love anyone. Ivan isn't one of us; people like Ivan, my boy, are strangers in our midst, they're like chaff in the wind...* A puff of wind, and it's gone... It was a stupid idea of mine yesterday to ask you to come here today: I wanted you to find out for me from Mitya—if I were to give him a thousand or two, would he agree, beggar and scoundrel that he is, to clear out for say five years, or better still thirty-five, and give up Grushka altogether?'

'I... I'll ask him...', Alyosha mumbled. 'If it were a whole three thousand, he just might...'

'Rubbish! No need to ask now, no need for anything! I've changed my mind. It was just a stupid idea I got into my head yesterday. I shan't give him anything, not one kopeck, I need all the money myself,' the old man waved his hands. 'I'll crush him like a cockroach anyway. Don't tell him anything, otherwise you'll raise his hopes. And there's nothing for you to do here either, so off you go. What about that fiancée of his, Katerina Ivanovna, that he's been hiding from me so jealously—is she going to marry him or not? You went to see her yesterday, didn't you?'

'She won't give him up under any circumstances.'

'That's the sort those refined ladies go for, libertines and scoundrels! They're rubbish, those lily-faced ladies; not like... Well! If I had his youth and the looks I used to have (because, at twenty-eight, I was better looking than him), I could make as many conquests as him. He's a villain! He's not going to get Grushenka, he's not!... I'll grind him into dust!'

His rage boiled up again as he pronounced these last words.

'You be off too, there's nothing here for you today,' he said sharply.

Alyosha went up to him and kissed him on the shoulder in parting.

'What was that for?' the old man asked in some surprise. 'We're going to see each other again, aren't we? Or don't you think so?'

'Of course we are, don't take any notice of me, I didn't mean anything special.'

'Well, neither did I, I didn't mean it...', the old man watched him go. 'I say, listen,' he called after him, 'come again sometime, don't leave it too long, come and join me for a bowl of fish soup, I'll have it made specially, a really good one, not like today's, make sure you come! Yes, tomorrow, do you hear me, come tomorrow!'

And as soon as Alyosha had gone, he went back to the small cupboard and downed another tot of brandy.

'Shan't have any more!' he mumbled with a croak, then he locked the cupboard again, put the key back in his pocket and withdrew to his bedroom, where he slumped exhausted on to his bed and immediately fell asleep.

3

AN ENCOUNTER WITH SOME SCHOOLBOYS

'THANK God he didn't ask me about Grushenka,' Alyosha
thought as he was leaving his father to set off for Mrs Khokhlakova's, 'otherwise I'd probably have had to tell him about meeting
her yesterday.' Alyosha reflected with sadness that the adversaries had replenished their strength overnight and had steeled
their hearts for another day's confrontation. 'Father's upset and
angry, he's got hold of some idea and won't budge; and what
about Dmitry? He too must have become more entrenched
overnight, and what's more is probably angry and upset and will
have hatched some plan... Oh, I must definitely find him today,
whatever happens...'

But Alyosha had no opportunity to spend much time in
thought: an incident happened on the way which, though not
very significant in itself, nevertheless left a strong impression on
him. As soon as he had crossed the square and turned into a
side-alley in order to reach Mikhailovskaya Street, which runs
parallel to the High Street and is separated from it only by a
ditch (the whole of our town is criss-crossed with ditches), he
spotted a small group of schoolboys, all young lads between the
ages of nine and twelve, no more, down by the bridge. They
were heading for home with their satchels on their backs or with
leather bags on straps across their shoulders, some in short
jackets, others in little overcoats, and there were some who wore
high boots with folded-over tops, such as spoilt children, darlings
of well-to-do fathers, are particularly fond of wearing. The
whole group was involved in animated discussion, apparently
conferring about something or other. Alyosha could never pass
children without a sense of curiosity, it had been the same in
Moscow, and although he was fond of children of three or
thereabouts, he also liked to stop to talk to ten- or eleven-year-
olds too. Therefore, although he was preoccupied at that
moment, he suddenly felt an urge to approach them and strike
up a conversation. On coming closer, he studied their rosy,
excited faces, and suddenly noticed that every boy had a stone in
his hand, and some even two. On the other side of the small

ditch, at a distance of about thirty paces from the group, beside a fence, stood another lad, a schoolboy too, with a small bag over his shoulder, about ten years of age to judge by his height, not more, perhaps even less—pale, sickly-looking, and with brilliant black eyes. He was keenly and attentively watching the six boys in the group, seemingly his friends, with whom he had just left the school building but was now apparently at loggerheads. Alyosha approached and, turning to one fair, curly-haired, rosy-cheeked lad in a black jacket, looked at him closely and said:

'When I had a bag like yours, we used to carry them over our left shoulder so we could get at them easily with the right hand; but you've got it over your right shoulder, which makes it awkward to get at.'

Alyosha began straight away with this matter-of-fact remark, without any premeditated guile, which indeed is the only way for an adult to begin if he wants to win the confidence of a child, more especially of a whole group of children. One should begin in perfect seriousness and come to the point, so as to be entirely on an equal footing; Alyosha understood this intuitively.

'But he's left-handed,' promptly replied another healthy-looking, cocky boy of about eleven. The remaining five turned their eyes on Alyosha and stared hard at him.

'He throws stones with his left arm, too,' a third boy remarked. Just at that moment a stone landed among the group, slightly grazing the left-handed boy but missing everybody else, although it had been projected accurately and with force. It had been thrown by the boy on the far side of the ditch.

'Hit him, get him, Smurov!' everybody shouted. Smurov (the left-handed boy) did not need prompting, and immediately responded by throwing a stone at the boy across the ditch, but missed; the stone hit the ground. The boy across the ditch threw another stone at the group, this time straight at Alyosha, and hit him rather painfully on the shoulder. The boy had his pockets full of stones in readiness, as was evident at thirty paces by the way his coat pockets bulged.

'He was trying to get you, you know, he was deliberately aiming at you. You're Karamazov, aren't you?' the boys shouted, roaring with laughter. 'All together now, take aim, fire!'

And six stones soared into the air from the group. One caught the boy on the head and he fell, but he was up again in a trice and began to retaliate with more stones. A continuous barrage of stones ensued from both sides; it turned out that most of the group had stones in their pockets too.

'What are you doing, boys! You should be ashamed of yourselves! Six against one, you'll kill him!' Alyosha shouted.

He dashed out to face the hail of stones so as to shield the boy across the ditch. Three or four of the boys paused for a moment.

'He started it!' shouted a boy in a red shirt in a shrill, childish voice. 'He's a rat; in the classroom today he stabbed Krasotkin with a penknife, there was blood all over. Krasotkin didn't want to report him, but we're going to beat him up...'

'Why? You've probably been teasing him, haven't you?'

'There goes another of his stones, straight at your back. He knows you,' the boys shouted. 'Now it's you he's aiming at, not us. Well, all together now, let's get him, don't miss, Smurov!'

This time the stone-throwing recommenced in all its viciousness. The boy on the far side of the ditch was hit on the chest; he cried out, burst into tears, and ran up the hill towards Mikhailovskaya Street. Some of the boys yelled out: 'Aha, coward, running away! Loofah, loofah!'

'You've no idea, Karamazov, what a rat he is, it'd serve him right if we killed him,' repeated the boy in the jacket, his eyes gleaming. He seemed to be the eldest.

'Why, what's he done?' Alyosha asked. 'Has he been telling tales or something?'

The boys exchanged knowing grins.

'You're going his way, to Mikhailovskaya, aren't you?' continued the same boy. 'Well then, why don't you catch him up... Look, he's stopped again, he's waiting and looking at you.'

'He's looking at you, he's looking at you!' the boys echoed.

'You want to ask him if he likes a wispy bath-tub loofah. Go on, ask him that.'

There was a general burst of laughter. Alyosha looked at the boys and they looked at him.

'Don't!' Smurov warned. 'He'll knock you down.'

'Boys, I shan't ask him about the loofah, that's obviously something you've been teasing him about, but I'll find out from him why it is you hate him so...'

'Go ahead and find out,' the boys laughed.

Alyosha crossed the bridge and went up the hill by the side of the fence, straight towards the ostracized boy.

'Watch out,' the boys shouted after him, 'he's not afraid of you, he'll stab you without warning when you're not looking... just like he did Krasotkin.'

The boy was waiting for him, rooted to the spot. As he approached, Alyosha saw before him a child of not more than nine, slightly built and short of stature, with a pale, thin, elongated little face and large dark eyes that looked at him full of hatred. He was awkwardly dressed in a very old coat which was much too small for him. His bare hands protruded from the sleeves. There was a large patch on the right knee of his trousers, and a large hole in his right boot over his big toe, which was liberally stained with ink. Both his coat pockets were bulging with stones. Alyosha stopped a couple of paces in front of him and regarded him inquiringly. The boy, who guessed at once from the look in Alyosha's eyes that he was not going to hit him, also lowered his guard and was even the first to speak.

'There's only one of me, but six of them...', he said suddenly, his eyes flashing, 'I'll beat them all single-handed.'

'One stone must have hit you pretty hard,' observed Alyosha.

'But I got Smurov in the head!' the boy exclaimed.

'They said that you know me. Do you?' Alyosha asked. 'And did you throw a stone at me for some reason?'

The boy looked at him darkly.

'I don't know you. Do you really know me?' persisted Alyosha.

'Leave me alone!' the boy suddenly burst out irritably, but went on standing there as though waiting for something to happen, and his eyes again flashed angrily.

'All right, I'll go,' said Alyosha, 'only I don't know you and I haven't been teasing you. They told me they'd been teasing you, but I've no desire to tease you, goodbye!'

'Monk in a funny skirt,' the boy cried out, continuing to look at Alyosha menacingly and defiantly, at the same time adopting a posture which left no doubt that this time he fully expected Alyosha to pounce on him, but Alyosha merely turned, glanced at him, and began to walk away. He had hardly taken three steps when a piece of rock, the biggest that the boy had in his pocket, hit him painfully in the back.

'From behind, eh? They were right after all when they said that you steal up on people.' Alyosha turned to face him, and this time the stone that the boy threw at him in evident rage was aimed straight at his head, though Alyosha managed to deflect it and it struck his elbow.

'Shame on you!' he cried out. 'What have I done to you?'

The boy maintained his attitude of sullen defiance, fully expecting that Alyosha was bound to attack him this time; when he realized, however, that Alyosha was still not going to do so, the boy went completely wild with rage: with his head bent low, he hurled himself forward, grabbed Alyosha's left hand in both his hands, and before the latter had time to react, bit him painfully in his middle finger. He sank his teeth into it and would not let go for about ten seconds. Alyosha yelled with pain, desperately trying to free his finger. At last the boy released it and withdrew to his previous position. The bite had penetrated to the bone, just behind the nail; blood was pouring out of it. Alyosha produced a handkerchief and wound it tightly round the injured finger, taking his time. All the while the boy stood and waited. Finally, Alyosha raised his gentle eyes and looked at the boy.

'Well,' he said, 'you see, you've hurt me pretty badly, that should be enough, shouldn't it? Now tell me, what have I done to deserve that?'

The boy looked at him with surprise.

'Even though I don't know you', Alyosha continued in the same quiet tone, 'and have never seen you before, I can't imagine that I've done nothing, otherwise you wouldn't have hurt me so much. So, what have I done? Tell me what you've got against me.'

Instead of replying, the boy burst out crying and ran off. Alyosha followed him in silence in the direction of Mikhailovskaya Street, and for quite a considerable while he could see the boy running ahead in the distance, without slowing down, without looking around, and, probably, still crying at the top of his voice. Alyosha decided that as soon as he had some spare time he would definitely seek him out and clear up this most puzzling incident. But just now he had other things on his mind.

4

AT THE KHOKHLAKOVAS'

HE soon reached Mrs Khokhlakova's imposing two-storey stone house, one of the best in our town. Even though Mrs Khokhlakova lived for the most part in another province, where she had a country house, or in her town house in Moscow, she also kept this house in our town, which she had inherited from her family. Her estate in our district was the largest of the three that she owned, yet until now she had very seldom come to stay in our province. She rushed out into the entrance hall to meet Alyosha.

'Did you... did you get my letter about the new miracle?' she said quickly, her voice full of agitation.

'I did.'

'Have you shown it to everybody, have you spread the news? Thanks to him, a son's returned to his mother!'

'He is going to die today,' said Alyosha.

'I've heard, I know; oh, I want to talk to you so badly! To you or anybody else about all this. No, to you, to you! And what a pity I can't see him! The whole town's in a state of excitement, full of expectation. But right now... would you believe it, Katerina Ivanovna's come to see us!'

'Ah, how fortunate!' exclaimed Alyosha. 'I'll be able to see her now—yesterday she was very insistent that I should call on her today.'

'I know all about it, I know. I've heard all the details of what happened at her place yesterday... including that dreadful business with that... creature. *C'est tragique.** If I'd been in her place—I don't know what I'd have done, I really don't! And then there's that brother of yours—Dmitry Fyodorovich—my God, he's a fine one! Aleksei Fyodorovich, I'm so confused, imagine: your brother's here now, no, not the one who was so horrible yesterday, but the other one, Ivan Fyodorovich, he's in there talking to her; they're having a very serious conversation... You wouldn't believe what's going on between them now—it's dreadful, it's a disaster, I tell you, it's a nightmare, the mind boggles: they're both aware that they're ruining each other for no reason at all, and they're both actually enjoying it. I was so hoping to see you! I simply had to see you! This is really all too much for me. I'll tell you all about it, but right now there's something else, which is really the most important thing of all—there, I've gone and forgotten what it was. Tell me, why is Lise hysterical? The moment she heard you were coming she became hysterical!'

'Mama, it's you who's hysterical, not me,' Lise's voice suddenly chimed in from the next room, through a chink in the door. It was the narrowest of chinks, and her voice was strained with excitement as if she were on the point of bursting into laughter which she was desperately trying to hold back. Alyosha noticed this chink at once and imagined, though he could not see, that Lise was peering at him from her invalid chair.

'Hardly surprising, Lise, hardly surprising... it's your capricious behaviour that drives me to hysteria. But she's so sick, Aleksei Fyodorovich, she was ill all night, groaning and feverish! I could hardly wait for the morning until Herzenstube arrived. He said he can't make anything out at all, and that we should wait and see. That Herzenstube always comes and says he can't make anything out at all. As soon as you approached the house she let out a cry and became hysterical, demanding to be taken back to the room where she was before...'

'Mama, I had no idea he was coming, it wasn't at all because of him that I wanted to move to this room.'

'Now that's not true, Lise; Yulia rushed in to tell you that Aleksei Fyodorovich was coming—you'd asked her to be your lookout.'

'Mother dear, that's not very clever of you. But if you want to make up for it and say something very astute, dear mama, why don't you tell our kind Mr Aleksei Fyodorovich, who's just come, that his visit here today, after all that happened yesterday and in spite of everybody laughing at him, just goes to show how obtuse he is.'

'Lise, you're being impertinent, and I warn you, I shall be

obliged to resort to disciplinary measures. Nobody's laughing at him, I'm so glad he came, I need him, I can't do without him. Oh, Aleksei Fyodorovich, I'm so miserable!'

'What's wrong with you, mama darling?'

'Oh, Lise, this capriciousness of yours, this instability, your illness, your nocturnal fever, that awful, everlasting Herzenstube, he's such a bore, such a crashing bore! It's just everything... And then, on top of it all—that miracle! I must admit, I was astonished and shaken by that miracle, my dear Aleksei Fyodorovich! And what about the tragedy that's taking place in my sitting-room now—I might as well tell you, I can't bear it any more, I just can't. Perhaps it's only a comedy, and not a tragedy. Tell me, will Starets Zosima last till the morning, will he? Oh God! What's happening to me, every time I shut my eyes I realize that everything's so pointless, so utterly pointless.'

'I wonder', Alyosha suddenly interrupted, 'if I could ask you for something clean to put round my finger. I've injured it rather badly, and the pain is getting quite intense now.'

Alyosha unwrapped the finger which the boy had bitten. The handkerchief was covered in blood. Mrs Khokhlakova let out a cry and shut her eyes.

'My God, it looks dreadful!'

But no sooner had Lise caught sight of Alyosha's finger through the chink than she flung the door wide open.

'Come in, come in,' she cried out urgently and authoritatively, 'and this time there'll be no nonsense! Oh God, how could you stand there and not say a word all this time! He could have bled to death, mama! How on earth did you manage to do it, where did it happen? The first thing to do is to get some water! We must wash the wound, just hold it in cold water and keep it there till the pain goes... Quick, quick, mama, get some water in a bowl. Hurry up!' she finished on a note of distress. She was terribly agitated; Alyosha's wound had horrified and alarmed her.

'Shouldn't we perhaps send for Herzenstube?' asked Mrs Khokhlakova, and stopped.

'Mama, you'll be the end of me. Your Herzenstube will come and say he can't make anything out at all! Water, water! Mama, for goodness' sake, go and tell Yulia to hurry up, she's obviously doing something else as usual, and it'll be ages before she finishes what she's doing. Come on mama, hurry up, or I'll die...'

'It's nothing,' Alyosha interjected, frightened to see them in such a panic.

Yulia came running in with a bowl of water. Alyosha immersed his finger in it.

'Mama, for goodness sake, bring some lint; some lint and that dark-coloured, stinging stuff you put on cuts, what's it called? We have some, I know we have... Mama, you know where that bottle is, it's in your bedroom, in the little cupboard on the right, there's a large bottle and the lint...'

'I'll bring everything in a moment, Lise, only don't shout and don't panic. Look how brave Aleksei Fyodorovich is in spite of his accident. How did you manage to hurt yourself so badly, Aleksei Fyodorovich?'

Mrs Khokhlakova hurried out of the room. That was just what Lise had been waiting for.

'First I want to know', she said quickly, turning to Alyosha, 'where on earth did this happen? After that I want to talk to you about something else. Well?'

Realizing instinctively that time was short and that her mother might return at any moment, Alyosha hurriedly gave her a condensed yet clear and precise summary of his strange encounter with the schoolboys.

When he had finished speaking, she clasped her hands in bewilderment.

'But how could you, how could you have got involved with those schoolboys, especially dressed as you are,' she exclaimed angrily, as though she had some authority over him. 'It just goes to show you're nothing but a little boy yourself, the silliest little boy you can imagine! Still, somehow you really must find out about that disgusting child and tell me everything, because there's something strange going on. Now the next question— but first, Aleksei Fyodorovich, in spite of your finger, are you able to talk about something absolutely trivial, and talk sensibly?'

'Of course I am, and the pain's nearly gone.'

'That's because you've got your finger in the water. We should change the water straight away, because otherwise very soon it won't be cold enough. Yulia, quickly, fetch a lump of ice from the cellar and another bowl of water. So. Now she's gone, we can get down to business: my dear Aleksei Fyodorovich, would you kindly give me back the letter I sent you yesterday—immediately, because mama may come back at any moment, and I don't want...'

'I haven't got it on me.'

'That's not true, you have got it. I knew you'd say that. It's in your pocket. I've been regretting that stupid joke all night. Let me have the letter, I want it back!'

'I've left it behind.'

'You shouldn't treat me like a child, like a little girl, just because I wrote you a letter as a silly joke! I apologize to you for the silly joke, but you must return the letter to me—if you really haven't got it on you, make sure you bring it later today!'

'I won't be able to bring it today, because I'm going back to the monastery and I shan't see you for two, three, perhaps four days, because Starets Zosima...'

'Four days, what nonsense! Listen, did you laugh a lot at what I said?'

'Not at all.'

'Why not?'

'Because I took everything perfectly seriously.'

'You're insulting me.'

'Not a bit. As soon as I read it, I realized that that was just how everything would turn out, because as soon as Starets Zosima dies I shall have to leave the monastery straight away. I shall then continue my studies and take an exam, and when you come of age, we'll get married. I shall love you. Though I haven't had a chance to think about it, it seems to me I'm not going to find a better wife than you, and the starets has instructed me to get married...'

'But I'm a freak!' Lise laughed, and her cheeks flushed pink. 'I've got to be wheeled around in an invalid chair!'

'I'll wheel you around, but I'm sure you'll get better by then.'

'You're mad', Lise exclaimed excitedly, 'to take such a silly joke so seriously!... Ah, here's mama, very opportune, I'm sure. Mama, you're always so slow, why did you take so long! Here's Yulia too with the ice!'

'Oh, Lise, stop shouting, for heaven's sake—do stop shouting. It's giving me a headache. What could I do if you've hidden the lint in another place... I looked everywhere for it... I suspect you did it deliberately.'

'How was I to know he'd turn up with his finger half bitten off—if I'd known, then perhaps I might really have gone and hidden the lint deliberately. Mama darling, now you're trying to be too clever.'

'Too clever! Have it your own way, but why all this fuss, Lise, just because Aleksei Fyodorovich has hurt his finger and all the rest of it! Oh, my dear Aleksei Fyodorovich, it's not things in isolation that upset me, not Herzenstube or the likes of him, but it's when it all comes at once, everything together, that's what I find unbearable.'

'That'll do, mama, forget about poor Herzenstube,' Lise said, laughing joyfully. 'Let's have the lint quickly, mama, and that stuff. I've remembered the name, Aleksei Fyodorovich, it's Goulard's extract,* it's very good. Mama, just imagine, he got into a fight with some boys on the way here and one of them bit him in the finger, well, isn't that just childish, he's nothing but a child himself, and how after all this, mama, can he be allowed to get married, can you imagine, mama, he wants to get married! Can you picture him married, it's simply ridiculous, it doesn't bear thinking about!'

And Lise continued giggling nervously to herself as she eyed Alyosha slyly.

'What do you mean, getting married, Lise; why on earth should he, you really shouldn't...! Besides, that boy could have had rabies.'

'Really, mama! Can boys really have rabies?'

'Why not, Lise, you'd think that I'd said something stupid. Supposing that boy had been bitten by a rabid dog, and then he in turn became rabid and went and bit somebody else. Hasn't she applied that dressing well, Aleksei Fyodorovich, I'd never have been able to do it as well as that. Do you still feel any pain?'

'Hardly any.'

'You don't feel frightened of water by any chance?' asked Lise.

'That'll do, Lise; perhaps I went too far, saying the boy could have had rabies, but there's no need for you to laugh. As soon as

Katerina Ivanovna found out that you were here, Aleksei Fyodorovich, she wouldn't give me any peace; she wants to see you,
she really wants to see you.'

'Oh, mama! Why don't you talk to her yourself, he can't see
her now, he's in too much pain.'

'No, I'm not,' said Alyosha, 'I can easily talk to her...'

'What! You're going to leave me? How can you?'

'Why not? As soon as I've seen her, I'll come back and we can
continue chatting as long as you like. But I really would like to
see Katerina Ivanovna without delay because, whatever happens,
I'd like to get back to the monastery as soon as possible this very
day.'

'Mama, get rid of him at once! Aleksei Fyodorovich, don't
bother to come back after you've seen Katerina Ivanovna, go
straight to your monastery, and good riddance! I want to sleep, I
haven't slept all night.'

'Oh Lise,' exclaimed Mrs Khokhlakova, 'is this another one
of your jokes? Unless, perhaps, you really should go and have a
good sleep!'

'I don't know that I...', Alyosha mumbled. 'I'll stay another
three minutes, even five, if you wish.'

'Even five! Show him the door at once, mama, he's a monster!'

'Are you out of your mind, Lise? Let's go, Aleksei Fyodorovich, she's so capricious today, I don't want to excite her too
much. A temperamental woman can be so trying, Aleksei
Fyodorovich! Come to think of it, she really may want to sleep.
It must have been something you did that made her feel so
sleepy while you were here, well done!'

'Oh mama, you say such kind things, I want to kiss you for it,
dear mama.'

'Me too, Lise. Listen, Aleksei Fyodorovich,' Mrs Khokhlakova
began in a rapid conspiratorial whisper as she left the room with
Alyosha, 'I don't want to influence you or deliberately reveal
what's going on, but see for yourself what the situation is, it's
simply awful, it's the most incredible comedy. Even though she
loves your brother Ivan Fyodorovich, she's trying to convince
herself that she loves your brother Dmitry Fyodorovich instead.
It's awful! I'll accompany you, and if I'm not thrown out I'll stay
and see how it all ends.'

5

CRISIS IN THE DRAWING-ROOM

THE conversation in the drawing-room was already coming to an end, however; although Katerina Ivanovna appeared resolute, she was extremely agitated. As Alyosha and Mrs Khokhlakova came into the room, Ivan Fyodorovich had already got up, ready to leave. His face was rather pale, and Alyosha glanced at him apprehensively. The fact was that an uncertainty, an enigma which had been worrying Alyosha for some time was about to be cleared up. For about a month now various people had been telling him that his brother Ivan was in love with Katerina Ivanovna and, what is more, was prepared to 'steal' her from Mitya. Until very recently this had seemed monstrous to Alyosha, and had caused him a great deal of anxiety. He loved both his brothers and was horrified by the thought of such rivalry between them. The day before, however, Dmitry Fyodorovich had suddenly announced to him that he himself was even glad of Ivan's rivalry, and that it could be of considerable help to him. But in what way? To marry Grushenka? Alyosha regarded this as a desperate last measure. Quite apart from all this, until the previous night Alyosha had been firmly convinced that Katerina Ivanovna herself was deeply and passionately in love with Dmitry—but this belief had lasted only until the previous evening. On top of everything, he could not help feeling that she was incapable of loving someone like Ivan, but that she loved his brother Dmitry deeply and passionately just as he was, however preposterous that might seem. The previous night, however, after the scene with Grushenka, another idea had occurred to him. The word 'disaster' which Mrs Khokhlakova had just used almost made him shudder, because he had woken at dawn that very morning and, while still half asleep and probably in response to a dream, had suddenly burst out, 'Disaster, disaster!' All night long he had in fact been dreaming of this scene at Katerina Ivanovna's. And now, when Alyosha considered Mrs Khokhlakova's direct and insistent assertion that Katerina Ivanovna loved Ivan but that, as a result of a deep emotional crisis and a peculiar sense of gratitude, she continued in some kind of bizarre game perversely to delude and torture herself with a fanciful love for Dmitry, he was completely taken aback: 'Yes, perhaps that really is the truth of the matter! So where does that leave Ivan?' Alyosha instinctively felt that a woman such as Katerina Ivanovna had an overwhelming need to dominate, but that she could only dominate someone like Dmitry and never someone like Ivan. For although Dmitry might in the long run submit himself to her, for his own happiness of course (which Alyosha could even have wished for), Ivan would never submit to her, nor could such a submission possibly bring him happiness. Alyosha somehow could not help thinking this way about Ivan. All these doubts and considerations flashed through his mind now, as he entered the drawing-room. There was also another thought that went through his mind suddenly and irresistibly: what if she didn't love either of them? I must point out that Alyosha blamed himself for such thoughts, and had been ashamed whenever he had entertained them during the past month. 'What do I know of love and of women,' he reproached himself every time he thought or surmised in that way, 'and how can I draw such conclusions?' And yet he could not rid himself of such thoughts. He instinctively understood that now, for instance, this question of rivalry was of profound importance in the life of his brothers, and that much would depend on it. 'Let dog eat dog' his brother Ivan had said angrily yesterday, speaking of their brother Dmitry and their father. So, in Ivan's eyes, Dmitry was that proverbial dog, and perhaps had been so for a long time. Ever since, perhaps, Ivan had got to know Katerina Ivanovna? Of course, Ivan had let slip the words involuntarily, but that made them all the more significant. If that was so, how could there be talk of peace? On the contrary, did this not provide new grounds for enmity and hatred within their family? But above all, which one of them should he, Alyosha, pity? What words of encouragement could he offer either of them? He loved them both, but what could he say to them in the face of such contradictions? It was easy to become totally lost in all this confusion, but Alyosha's heart could not tolerate uncertainty, because his love was always of an active kind. He could not love passively; once he began to love he immediately had to offer help. But to do this he had to set a goal, he had to establish firmly what would be in the best interests of each and what exactly they both needed, and then, having assured himself of the validity of this goal, he would have to help each of them individually. But instead of a definite goal there was only confusion and uncertainty at every turn. The word 'disaster' had been spoken! But what could he possibly understand of this disaster? Right from the word go, everything he came across in this confusion defied his understanding!

When Katerina Ivanovna caught sight of Alyosha she turned joyfully to Ivan Fyodorovich, who had already got to his feet and was about to leave.

'Don't go straightaway,' she said, 'stay just one more moment. I want to hear the opinion of this gentleman, whom I trust with all my heart. Katerina Osipovna,' she added, turning to Mrs Khokhlakova, 'why don't you stay too.' She bade Alyosha sit down next to her, while Mrs Khokhlakova took the seat opposite, next to Ivan Fyodorovich.

'You are my friends, the only ones I have in the whole world, my dear friends,' she began in a voice shaking with emotion. She was on the verge of tears, which made Alyosha's heart go out to her again in sympathy. 'Yesterday, Aleksei Fyodorovich, you witnessed that... scene, and you saw the state I was in. Ivan Fyodorovich, you didn't see it; he did. What he must have thought of me yesterday, I don't know, but I do know that if the same thing happened today, at this very moment, I would say exactly the same as I did yesterday—the same sentiments, the same words, the same gestures. You remember, Aleksei Fyodorovich, what I did, because you yourself restrained me at one point...' As she said this, blood rushed to her face and her eyes flashed. 'You might as well know, Aleksei Fyodorovich, that I cannot reconcile myself to anything. Listen, Aleksei Fyodorovich, I don't even know whether I love *him* now. To me, he's just *pathetic*, and that's no basis for love. If I loved him, if I continued to love him, I probably wouldn't pity him, I'd hate him instead...'

Her voice faltered, and tear-drops glistened on her eyelashes. Alyosha shuddered inwardly: 'This young woman', he thought, 'is sincere and she is telling the truth, and... and she no longer loves Dmitry!'

'Yes! That's right!' exclaimed Mrs Khokhlakova.

'Wait, my dear Katerina Osipovna, I haven't come to my main point yet, I haven't told you what I finally decided during the night. I appreciate that my decision will perhaps spell disaster for me, but I know that as long as I live I'll never, never alter it, I shan't change my mind. My kind, my good, my ever-constant and noble counsellor and great diviner of human hearts, the only friend I have in the world, Ivan Fyodorovich, supports me in everything and agrees with my decision... He knows what it is.'

'Yes,' said Ivan Fyodorovich quietly but firmly, 'I agree with it.'

'But I wish that Alyosha too (oh, Aleksei Fyodorovich, forgive me for calling you simply Alyosha), I wish that Aleksei Fyodorovich would also tell me, in front of my two friends, whether I am right or not? I feel instinctively that you, Alyosha, dear brother (because you are a dear brother to me),' she repeated rapturously, clasping his cold hand in her warm fingers, 'I feel that your decision, your approval, will bring me peace in spite of all my suffering, because after you have spoken I shall not say another word and shall accept my fate—I feel sure of this!'

'I don't know what it is you're going to ask me,' Alyosha said, blushing, 'I only know that I love you and wish you more happiness now than I could possibly wish for myself!... But I really don't know anything at all about these matters...', he added, for some reason hurriedly.

'In these matters, Aleksei Fyodorovich,' she began solemnly, 'in these matters, the most important thing now is honour and duty, and I don't know what else, perhaps something higher, higher even than duty itself. In my heart of hearts I feel there is an even higher sentiment which urges me on relentlessly. To put it very simply, in a couple of words, I've already made up my mind, even if he does marry that... creature, whom I shall never be able to forgive, *I shall never leave him!* From now on I shall never, never leave him!' she said, her voice quivering in barely concealed anguish. 'What I mean to say is that I'm not going to chase after him, or irritate him constantly by my presence, or be a burden to him—oh no, I shall go and live in another town, no matter where, but all my life long I shall keep track of him whatever happens. And when he becomes unhappy with her, which he is bound to, then let him come to me, and he will find a friend, a sister... Only a sister, of course, and nothing more, but he will discover at long last that there is someone who really is a true sister to him, who loves him and has sacrificed her whole life for him. I shall not relent, I shall persist until finally he begins to understand me and learns to confide in me without any inhibition!' She spoke in a kind of frenzy. 'I'll be the god to whom he will pray—and that is the least he can do for having betrayed me, and for what I had to go through for his sake yesterday. And let him see, as long as he lives, that I shall remain faithful to him till I die, and shall remain true to my word in spite of his infidelity and betrayal. I'll... I'll simply be the means by which he attains his happiness, or, how shall I put it, the instrument, the vehicle for his happiness, and this I shall be for life, his whole life, and he should not lose sight of this as long as he lives! That's my decision! Ivan Fyodorovich supports me completely.'

She was gasping for breath. She may have wished to express her thoughts in a far more dignified, more accomplished and natural way, but she sounded far too uncompromising and far too agitated and blatant. There was much youthful insouciance, much that merely harked back to the previous day's aggravation, a desire to show off, which she herself was only too well aware of. Her expression suddenly became overcast, and distress showed in her eyes. Alyosha noticed all this immediately, and compassion for her stirred in his heart. Just then Ivan saw fit to interject.

'I was only expressing an opinion,' he said. 'Coming from any other woman all that would have sounded contrived and stilted, but not from you. Any other woman would have been in the wrong, but you are in the right. I don't know how to account for it, but I can see that you are absolutely sincere, and that's why you are quite right...'

'Yes, but only at this particular moment... And what is this moment? Nothing but a direct consequence of yesterday's insult!' Mrs Khokhlakova, reluctant to get involved but unable to restrain herself, observed perceptively.

'Quite so, quite so,' Ivan broke in somewhat impatiently, evidently resentful at being interrupted, 'quite so, but in any other woman that moment would have been confined to the previous day's insult, a fleeting instant, whereas for someone of Katerina Ivanovna's character that moment will persist throughout her life. What for some would be just a promise, will be for her an unending, exhausting, relentlessly onerous burden. And she'll be forever sustained by the awareness that she's fulfilling her duty! Your life, Katerina Ivanovna, will pass in painful contemplation of your personal feelings, your personal act of valour and your personal grief, but eventually this pain will ease, and then your life will turn into blissful contemplation of that firm and noble commitment to which you have pledged yourself once and for all, a decidedly noble commitment in its way, even if reckless, but one you will have come to terms with, and the awareness of it will give you the most perfect contentment and reconcile you to everything else in the world...'

He said this adamantly and with some acrimony, clearly fully aware of the effect this would have, and making no attempt at all to conceal his derision.

'Oh God, this is so utterly misconceived!' exclaimed Mrs Khokhlakova.

'Aleksei Fyodorovich, why don't you say something! I'm dying to know what you have to say to me!' exclaimed Katerina Ivanovna, and suddenly burst into tears. Alyosha got up from the sofa.

'It's all right, it's all right!' she continued through tears. 'It's only nerves. I've been so upset since last night, but now, being with such friends as you and your brother, I feel strong... because I know... neither of you will ever abandon me...'

'Unfortunately, I may have to go to Moscow tomorrow and leave you for a long time... And what's more my plans can't be changed,' Ivan Fyodorovich said suddenly.

'To Moscow, tomorrow!' Katerina Ivanovna's whole face was suddenly contorted. 'But, my God, isn't that fortunate!' she exclaimed, her voice completely altered, all tears banished without trace. It was the suddenness of the transformation that so amazed Alyosha: in place of the poor insulted girl, weeping in heartbroken misery, here suddenly was a woman in full control of herself, even delighted somehow, as though she had just heard some good news.

'What is fortunate is not that we're parting, certainly not that,' she said with a gracious smile, as though to correct herself. 'A friend like you could not possibly think that; quite the contrary, I'm most unhappy to lose you.' She suddenly dashed forward and, taking hold of Ivan's hands, shook them warmly. 'I'm so happy you'll be able to tell Agasha and my aunt yourself, honestly, without hurting my dear aunt's feelings, what a dreadful situation I'm in, and I'm sure you'll find a way to do it. You cannot imagine how unhappy I was yesterday, and this morning I was racking my brains trying to think how to write this dreadful letter to them... because something like this just can't be conveyed in a letter at all... Now, however, it'll be easy for me to write it, because you'll be there in person and will explain everything. Oh, how glad I am! But believe me, that's the only thing I'm glad about. To me, of course, you are irreplaceable... I'll go and write the letter at once,' she concluded suddenly, and even took a step towards the door.

'But what about Alyosha?' exclaimed Mrs Khokhlakova. 'What about Alyosha's opinion that you were so anxious to hear?' There was a sharp, angry edge to her words.

'I've not forgotten him.' Katerina Ivanovna stopped momentarily. 'And why are you so hostile to me at such a time as this, Katerina Osipovna?' she said, bitterly reproachful. 'I stand by what I said; it's vital for me to have his opinion; I'll go further, I need him to decide for me! Whatever he says, I'll abide by— that's how badly I need to hear what you have to say, Aleksei Fyodorovich... But what's wrong?'

'I'd never have imagined this!' Alyosha exclaimed suddenly, in sorrow.

'Imagined what—what?'

'He's going to Moscow and you cried out that you were glad— you said that deliberately. Then you went on to explain that you weren't really glad about it, but that, on the contrary, you were sorry... to be losing a friend—and that too was just deliberate play-acting... everything was play-acting, just as they do in the theatre!...'

'The theatre? What?... What did you say?' Katerina Ivanovna exclaimed, looking flushed, and frowned in utter amazement.

'However much you insist that you'd miss him as a friend,'

Alyosha said, his voice almost breaking, 'you nevertheless declared to his face that it was fortunate he was leaving...' He remained standing by the table and did not sit down.

'What are you talking about, I don't understand...'

'Nor do I... It's as though I'd just had a revelation...', Alyosha continued in the same shaking, faltering voice. 'I know I'm not expressing myself clearly, but I'll tell you everything anyway. This revelation means that you were never in love with my brother Dmitry at all... from the very beginning... And perhaps Dmitry has never loved you either... from the very beginning... only respected you... I really don't know that I have the right, but someone must tell the truth... because nobody here wants to tell the truth...'

'What truth?' cried Katerina Ivanovna, her voice verging on the hysterical.

'If you want to know,' mumbled Alyosha, as though about to fall off a precipice, 'send for Dmitry now—I'll find him—and let him come here and take you and Ivan by the hand and let him join your hands. You are torturing Ivan only because you love him... and you're torturing him because your love for Dmitry is an obsession... your love is a lie... you have simply persuaded yourself of it...'

Alyosha broke off and was silent.

'You... you...', Katerina Ivanovna snapped, her face blanching, her lips contorted with anger, 'you're a miserable, hair-shirted little fool, that's what you are!' Ivan Fyodorovich burst out laughing and stood up. He was holding his hat in his hands.

'You're wrong, my dear Alyosha,' he said, with an expression on his face that Alyosha had never seen before—an expression of youthful candour and strong, irrepressible, undisguised emotion. 'Katerina Ivanovna has never loved me! She knew all along that I loved her, even though I never said a word to her about my love—she knew it, but she didn't love me. Nor have I been her friend, not even for one single day: she's a proud woman who has no need of my friendship. She needed me only in order to satisfy her continual craving for vengeance. She was constantly taking revenge on me for all the insults she suffered at the hands of Dmitry, insults going back to their first meeting... Because, in her heart, she has come to regard their very first meeting as an insult. That's what her heart is like! All I ever did was listen to her ranting on about her love for him. I'm leaving now, but understand this, Katerina Ivanovna: he's the only man you really love. And the more he insults you, the more you love him. That's your undoing. You love him precisely as he is, insulting you as he does. Were he to reform, you'd discard him immediately and stop loving him altogether. But you need him in order to glory continually in your feat of loyalty and to reproach him for his disloyalty. And it's all because of your pride. Oh, I know there's a lot of self-deprecation and humiliation in this, but it all stems from your pride... I'm too young and I've loved you too much. I realize I shouldn't be telling you this, and that it would be more dignified for me simply to leave you now; also, it would be less insulting for you. But I'm going far away and I shall never return. This is for ever, you know... I've no wish to be witness to a pantomime. Besides, there's nothing more I can say, I've said everything... Goodbye, Katerina Ivanovna, you mustn't be angry with me, I've been punished a hundred times more than you have—punished, if only because I shall never see you again. Goodbye. No, don't give me your hand. You've tortured me too deliberately for me to forgive you at this moment. Later I'll forgive you, but I shan't shake your hand now.

Den Dank, Dame, begehr ich nicht,'*

he added with a wry smile, thereby demonstrating quite unexpectedly that he too had read Schiller and had gone to the trouble of memorizing him by heart, something which Alyosha would not previously have imagined him doing. He left the room without even taking leave of Mrs Khokhlakova, his hostess. Alyosha was desperate.

'Ivan,' he shouted after him, distraught, 'come back, Ivan! No, no, now he'll never come back!' he exclaimed with bitter realization. 'I am to blame, it was my fault, I started it all! Ivan spoke in anger and bitterness. He's been spiteful and malicious...' Alyosha was ranting like one demented.

Katerina Ivanovna suddenly left the room.

'You've done nothing wrong,' whispered Mrs Khokhlakova excitedly to the dejected Alyosha, 'you've acted wonderfully, like an angel. I shall make every effort to persuade Ivan Fyodorovich not to go away...'

To Alyosha's great chagrin, her face shone with happiness; but then Katerina Ivanovna returned. In her hands were two hundred-rouble notes.

'I've a great favour to ask of you, Aleksei Fyodorovich,' she began, addressing Alyosha directly in an apparently calm and even voice, just as though nothing had happened the moment before. 'A week—yes, it must have been a week ago—Dmitry Fyodorovich did something stupid and unjust, something very disgraceful. There's a rather disreputable place, a tavern, where he met that retired Staff Captain who used to run errands for your father. For some reason Dmitry Fyodorovich quarrelled with this Captain, grabbed him by his beard, and humiliated him in front of everybody by dragging him out of the tavern and pulling him along the street, and, what's more, they say that the Captain's son, a little boy, a mere child who goes to the local school, saw it all and ran alongside, crying loudly, pleading on behalf of his father and appealing for help, but everyone just laughed. Forgive me, Aleksei Fyodorovich, I cannot recall this shameful behaviour of his without feeling indignant... it's the sort of thing that only Dmitry Fyodorovich would be capable of, such is his anger... and his passion! I can't describe it properly, I just can't... words fail me. I've been making enquiries about this poor man and have found out that he's living in poverty. His name's Snegiryov. He got into trouble in the army and was cashiered. I can't tell you more than that. Now he and his family are absolutely destitute, his wife, by all accounts, is mentally deranged, and his children are ill. He's been living in the town quite a long time now, getting the occasional job; he was working as a copy-clerk somewhere, but hasn't been earning anything recently. I thought of you because... that is, I thought—I don't know, I'm rather confused—you see, I wanted to ask you, Aleksei Fyodorovich, my dear Aleksei Fyodorovich, to go to him, to find an excuse to visit them, the Staff Captain, that is—Oh God! I'm so confused—and discreetly, tactfully, as only you would be able to do it (Alyosha blushed suddenly), give him this small contribution, these two hundred roubles. He'll probably accept it... that is, you must persuade him to accept it... No, that's not what I meant! You see, it's not really a bribe to appease him, to stop him lodging a complaint—it seems he was thinking of doing precisely that—but just a token of sympathy, a desire on my part to offer some assistance, purely from me as Dmitry Fyodorovich's fiancée, and not in any way from him... that's it in a word... you can do it... I'd have gone myself, but you'll be able to handle it much better than I could. He lives in Ozernaya Street, in the house of a Mrs Kalmykova... I beg you, Aleksei Fyodorovich, do this for me... But now... I'm rather tired, so goodbye...'

She turned suddenly, and disappeared behind the door-curtain so quickly that Alyosha could not even utter a word—and he certainly wanted to say something to her. He wanted to ask her forgiveness, to reproach himself, to say anything at all, because his heart was full to overflowing, and he did not under any circumstances wish to leave the room without saying something. But Mrs Khokhlakova grabbed him by the arm and led him out herself. In the entrance hall she stopped him again.

'She's proud, she's struggling against something deep down,' said Mrs Khokhlakova in a half-whisper, 'but she's kind and charming and magnanimous! Oh, how I love her, sometimes beyond all reason, and how glad, how delighted I am once more about everything! You, of course, my dear Aleksei Fyodorovich, know nothing of this: but let me assure you that all of us, I, both her aunts—well, everyone, even Lise—have been hoping and praying for a whole month for only one thing, that she should give up your precious Dmitry Fyodorovich, who doesn't love her and doesn't want to have anything to do with her at all, and marry Ivan Fyodorovich, that nice, educated young man, who loves her more than anything in the world. We've all conspired in this, and perhaps that's the only thing that's preventing my leaving...'

'But she was weeping, she's still feeling hurt!' Alyosha exclaimed.

'Never believe a woman's tears, Aleksei Fyodorovich—in such cases I'm always against the women and side with the men.'

'Mama, you're misleading him and not helping him at all,' Lise's thin voice came from the adjacent room.

'No, I'm to blame for everything, it's all my fault!' repeated

Alyosha inconsolably; he was deeply ashamed of his outburst, and even buried his face in his hands.

'On the contrary, you acted like an angel, just like an angel, I don't mind repeating it.'

'Mama, what do you mean, like an angel?' Lise's faint voice was heard again.

'When I saw what was going on,' Alyosha continued as though he had not even heard Lise, 'for some reason I suddenly imagined that she loved Ivan, and I said a very stupid thing... and now what will happen?'

'Happen to whom?' Lise called out. 'Mama, you'll surely be the end of me. I keep asking you—and you don't want to answer.'

At that moment the maid ran in.

'Katerina Ivanovna's poorly... She's crying... she's having a fit, she'll do herself an injury.'

'What's going on?' Lise cried out with a note of alarm in her voice. 'It's me who'll be having a fit, mama, not her!'

'For God's sake, Lise, stop shouting, have some consideration for me. You're still too young to be told everything that concerns grown-ups; I'll come back and tell you everything I can. Oh, my God! I'm coming, I'm coming... Hysteria—that's a good sign, Aleksei Fyodorovich, it's excellent that she's hysterical. It'll do her good. When things get to this stage, I always take a stand against women, what with all their hysterical fits and tantrums. Yulia, run along and say that I'll be with them just as soon as I can. And it's her own fault that Ivan Fyodorovich left as he did. But he's not going to go away. Lise, for goodness sake, stop yelling! Oh, it's not you who's yelling, it's me; forgive your loving mother, but I'm so excited, oh dear, I'm so excited, so excited! And did you notice, Aleksei Fyodorovich, how splendid young Ivan Fyodorovich looked as he went out of the room. He had his say and just left! I mistakenly took him to be merely a scholar, just a dull academic, but he turned out to be so delightfully passionate, so sincere and virile, spontaneous and manly, and it was all such a delight to watch, so fascinating, just as though... and the way he came out with that line of German verse too, precisely as I expect you'd have done! But I must fly, I must fly.

Aleksei Fyodorovich, do hurry up with that errand of yours and
come back quickly. Lise, can I get you anything? For goodness
sake, don't hold up Aleksei Fyodorovich a second longer, he'll
come back to you straight away...'

At last Mrs Khokhlakova hurried off. Before Alyosha too left,
he thought he would try to open the door and have a look at
Lise.

'Not on your life!' Lise yelled out. 'Now it's come to this, stay
where you are! Say what you have to say through the door. What
I'd like to know is how you came to be known as an angel?'

'By doing a terribly stupid thing, Lise! Goodbye.'

'Don't you dare go away just like that!' cried Lise.

'Lise, I must! I can't tell you how desperate I am! I'm worried
out of my mind, but I'll be back as soon as I can!'

And he dashed out of the room.

6

CRISIS IN THE TENEMENT

HE was indeed desperately worried, as he had seldom ever been
before. In his eagerness he had blundered—and where had he
gone wrong? In matters of the heart! 'I'm absolutely ignorant
about such things, I don't know the first thing about them!' he
repeated to himself for the hundredth time, blushing. 'Embarrassment wouldn't matter so much, embarrassment would be a
fitting punishment for me—the trouble is that now I'm going to
be the cause of further misfortunes... But the starets sent me
forth to reconcile and to unite. Is this the right way to unite?'
Here he suddenly recalled again just how he had 'joined their
hands', and once again he was overcome with embarrassment.
'Though I've been acting in all sincerity, I ought to be wiser in
future,' he concluded suddenly, without even the ghost of a smile
at his own reasoning.

Katerina Ivanovna had asked him to go to Ozernaya Street;
his brother Dmitry's place was on the way to it, in a side-street
which was close to Ozernaya Street. Even though he did not
expect to find his brother in, Alyosha decided to call on him

anyway, before continuing on to the Staff Captain's. He suspected that the former might even now be attempting to hide from him but, come what may, he had to find him. Time was running out, moreover, and the thought of the starets's life slowly ebbing away had been preying on his mind constantly ever since he left the monastery.

In Katerina Ivanovna's account there was one detail that had aroused his curiosity: when she mentioned the young schoolboy, the Staff Captain's son, who had run crying at his father's side, it had occurred to Alyosha even then that this boy was very probably the same schoolboy who had bitten his finger while he was questioning him as to how he might have offended him. Now he was almost convinced of this, though he did not quite know why. Having become absorbed in other matters, he stopped brooding and decided not to think about the 'calamity' he had just caused, nor to torture himself with remorse, but to be positive and to tackle each situation as it arose. This decision finally restored all his good humour. Feeling hungry as he turned into the side-street on his way to Dmitry's, he reached into his pocket and took out the bread roll he had taken at his father's and ate it. He felt better.

Dmitry was not in. The occupants of the little house—an old carpenter, his aged wife, and their son—looked at him with suspicion. 'He's not slept here the last three nights,' replied the old man in answer to Alyosha's persistent questioning, 'maybe he's gone away.' Alyosha realized that the old man had been told what to say. In response to his question as to whether Dmitry might be at Grushenka's or perhaps hiding again at Foma's (Alyosha mentioned these details intentionally), the whole family looked at him with apprehension. 'It seems that they want to protect him,' Alyosha thought, 'they're on his side—that's a good sign.'

At last he found Mrs Kalmykova's house on Ozernaya Street, a decrepit and lopsided building with only three windows looking on to the street, and with a dirty yard in the middle of which stood a solitary cow. The entrance from the yard led into a hall; to the left lived the landlady and her daughter, both aged and both apparently deaf. In reply to his question, repeated several times, regarding the Staff Captain, one of them, realizing at last that it was the tenants who were being sought, pointed across the hall to a door in a separate wing of the house. The Staff Captain's accommodation consisted of a single room. Alyosha was just about to grasp the iron latch to open the door when he was struck by the odd silence which reigned on the other side. And yet he knew from what Katerina Ivanovna had told him that the retired Staff Captain had a family: 'They're either asleep, or perhaps they've heard me coming and are waiting for me to open the door; I'd better knock first,' which he did. There was a reply, not immediately, but about ten seconds later.

'Who's there?' enquired a loud, overtly aggressive voice.

Alyosha opened the door and stepped over the threshold. He found himself in a fairly spacious room full of people and cluttered with all kinds of household belongings. To the left was a large Russian stove. A line with various rags hanging on it had been strung across the room from the stove to the window on the left. Two beds with knitted counterpanes stood to the left and right, one along each wall of the room. On the left-hand bed was a stack of four chintz-covered pillows, arranged in decreasing order of size. Only one very small pillow lay on the other bed on the right. In the corner nearest the door was a small area screened off with a curtain or a bed-sheet, also slung over a line suspended between the two abutting walls. Behind this curtain was another bed, made up on a bench extended by a chair. A plain, rectangular, rustic table had been moved from the corner nearest the door to the middle window. The three windows, each containing four small, discoloured, and greenish panes, were shut tight, making it rather stuffy and dark in the room. On the table stood a frying-pan containing the remains of fried eggs, a half-eaten piece of bread, and a bottle of vodka with a few dregs left in the bottom. A woman of refined appearance, wearing a print dress, was sitting on a chair by the bed on the left. Her face was very emaciated and sallow; her deeply sunken cheeks told one at a glance how very ill she was. But what struck Alyosha most of all was the look in the poor woman's eyes—intensely enquiring, but at the same time terribly disdainful. Up to the moment that she opened her mouth to speak, and all the time that Alyosha was in conversation with the head of the household, she kept turning her large brown eyes from one speaker to the other with the same degree of enquiry and disdain. Next to the woman, by the left-hand window, stood a young, rather plain-faced girl with thin, reddish hair, dressed cheaply but neatly. She inspected Alyosha with disapproval as he entered. Beside the bed on the right sat another wretched female. She was a very pathetic creature, also young—about twenty—but hunchbacked, her legs, as Alyosha learned later, completely wasted and useless. Her crutches rested close by, against the corner between the bed and the wall. The wretched girl looked at Alyosha; her exquisitely beautiful and kind eyes were full of meek resignation. At the table, finishing off the fried eggs, sat a man of about forty-five, short of stature, gaunt, frail, with reddish hair and a thin, reddish beard which looked for all the world like a loofah (this comparison, especially the word 'loofah', immediately flashed through his mind the moment he set eyes on him, Alyosha later recalled). It was evidently he who had called out, 'Who's there?' because there was no other man in the room. But as Alyosha entered he literally shot up from the bench on which he was sitting at the table and, hastily wiping his mouth on a ragged napkin, darted up to Alyosha.

'A monk come to ask for alms for the monastery,' the girl who was standing in the left-hand corner said in a loud voice. 'He knew who to come to!' But the man who had rushed up to Alyosha instantly swung round on his heels towards her and replied in an agitated, strained voice:

'Not so, Varvara Nikolavna, not true, you're mistaken!' And then, suddenly turning towards Alyosha, he asked: 'May I be so bold as to ask, sir, what induced you to visit this... hovel?'

Alyosha regarded the man attentively, for he had never seen him before. There was something awkward, impatient, and irascible about him. Although it was obvious that he had just been drinking, he was by no means drunk. The expression on his face was arrogant in the extreme, but at the same time—and this was strange—unmistakably timid. He seemed like a man who had been tyrannized for a long time and had suffered a great deal, but who had suddenly decided that enough was enough, and wished to give vent to his feelings; or, better still, a man who was simply itching to deal you a blow, but was terribly afraid of being struck first. His manner of speaking and the intonation of his rather shrill voice revealed a warped sense of humour, now vicious, now submissive, sporadic, and faltering. When he uttered the word 'hovel' he appeared to shake all over, his eyes bulged, and he approached Alyosha so closely that the latter instinctively took a step back. The man was wearing a very poor-quality dark, patched, and stained nankeen coat. His very light-coloured check trousers, of a style no longer in fashion, were of a very thin material, rumpled at the bottom and consequently seeming too short for him, as though he had outgrown them.

'I'm... Aleksei Karamazov...', said Alyosha in response.

'I'm perfectly well aware of that,' the man immediately snapped back, making it clear that he knew only too well who Alyosha was. 'Staff Captain Snegiryov, at your service; all the same, I'd still like to know what exactly induced you to...'

'I just thought I'd call on you. As a matter of fact, there was something I wanted to tell you... If only you'd allow me...'

'In that case here's a chair sir, pray be seated. That's what they used to say in the old-time comedies: "Pray be seated...",' and with a sudden gesture the Staff Captain grabbed an empty chair (a plain, rustic, hard chair) and placed it almost in the middle of the room; then, pulling up a similar chair for himself, he sat down opposite Alyosha, face to face, so that their knees almost touched.

'Staff Captain Nikolai Ilyich Snegiryov, sir, retired from one of the Russian army's finest regiments of the line, fallen upon hard times, but Staff Captain notwithstanding. Or should I say perhaps, Staff Captain "Three bags full, sir", rather than Snegiryov, the "Three bags full, sir" having come at quite the wrong time of life. One is obliged to eat humble pie in deprivation.'

'Quite so, quite so,' Alyosha smiled. 'But, does this sort of thing happen more by design or by accident?'

'As God is my witness, quite by accident. All my life I resisted, never once was I known to kowtow to anyone. Then disaster struck, and before I could say Jack Robinson, I was "Three bags full, sir". It's all a matter of divine providence. I see you take a keen interest in what's going on in the world about you. Still, I wonder how I could have excited your curiosity, unable as I am in my circumstances to offer any hospitality.'

'I came... about that incident...'

'What incident?' the Staff Captain interrupted impatiently.

'That encounter of yours with my brother Dmitry Fyodorovich,' Alyosha replied awkwardly.

'Now I wonder what encounter would that have been, sir? You don't mean to say...? So you've come about that loofah, that bathhouse loofah business?' He thrust himself forward so violently that their knees actually touched. He pursed his lips tightly.

'What loofah?' mumbled Alyosha.

'He's come to complain to you about me, papa,' cried a familiar child's voice from the corner behind the curtain. 'I bit his finger earlier today!'

The curtain parted, and in the corner under the icons Alyosha saw his former adversary lying on the makeshift bedding arranged on the bench and chair. The boy was covered with his little coat and an old quilt. It was obvious that he was not well and, judging by his burning eyes, was feverish. Now he regarded Alyosha without any fear, as if to say: 'I'm in my own home, you can't touch me.'

'What's all this about your finger being bitten?' the Staff Captain began to rise from his chair. 'Did he bite your finger?'

'Yes. He and some boys were throwing stones at one another in the street; it was six against one. I went up to him, and he threw a stone at me too, then another one hit me on the head. I asked him what I'd done to deserve that. Then he rushed at me and bit my finger very painfully, I can't think why.'

'I'll give him a hiding this minute, sir! I'll whip him straight away, sir.' The Staff Captain had now risen fully from his chair.

'But I'm not complaining at all, I'm simply telling you what happened... I certainly don't want you to punish him. Besides, he looks ill to me...'

'And did you really think I was going to give him a hiding? That I'd take my little Ilyushechka and whip him in front of you just to satisfy you? Would you like me to do it right away?' the Captain asked, turning on Alyosha as though intending to attack him. 'I'm very sorry about your delicate little finger, sir, but before I whip my Ilyushechka, you wouldn't like me to hack off four of my fingers with this knife before your very eyes for your righteous satisfaction, would you? Four should be enough I think to gratify your desire for revenge, sir, you wouldn't ask for the fifth one too, would you?...' He stopped suddenly, as though choking. Every line on his face was twitching, and there was an extraordinary challenge in his eyes. He seemed frantic.

'Now I think I understand everything,' Alyosha said softly and sorrowfully, without getting up from his seat. 'So, your boy, your good little boy, loves his father and attacked me, the brother of the man who humiliated you... Now I understand,' he repeated thoughtfully. 'But my brother Dmitry Fyodorovich is sorry for what he did, I know that, and if only he could come to you, or, better still, meet you where it all occurred, he would ask your forgiveness in front of everyone... should you want him to do so.'

'So, first he pulls my beard and then he asks to be forgiven... All over and done with, is that it?'

'Oh no, on the contrary, he'll do anything you want, you only have to say!'

'So, were I to ask His Highness to kneel in front of me in the *Stolichny Gorod** or on the square, he'd do it?'

'Yes, indeed he would.'

'You touch me deeply, sir. I'm almost in tears and, I have to admit, deeply moved. It's almost more than I can bear. Allow me to complete the introductions: my family, my two daughters, and my son—my brood. If I die, who's going to love them? And while I'm alive, who, other than they, would love a miserable wretch like me? It's a wonderful thing the Lord has done for the likes of me. For it needs be that even a beggar such as me should be vouchsafed someone to love him...'

'Oh, that's perfectly true!' exclaimed Alyosha.

'Enough of this nonsense!' the girl by the window exclaimed, unexpectedly turning to her father with an expression of contempt and disgust. 'Just because some idiot's turned up, you don't have to demean yourself.'

'Now, now, Varvara Nikolavna, there's no need for that,' her father observed, and though his voice was authoritative he continued to look at her approvingly. 'It's in her character, bless her,' he said, turning to Alyosha again.

And nothing in the whole of Nature
Did he deign to bless.*

It ought to be in the feminine: did *she* deign to bless. But allow me to introduce you to my wife. This is Arina Petrovna, a lady with no legs you might say, about forty-three, got some movement in the legs still, but not much. She's from a humble background. Arina Petrovna, cheer up: this is Aleksei Fyodorovich Karamazov. Stand up, Aleksei Fyodorovich.' He took him by the arm and quickly helped him up, with a strength that belied his apparent frailty. 'You're being introduced to a lady, you must stand up, sir. It's a different Karamazov, mother, not the one who... hm, you know what I mean, but his brother, who's kindness itself. Permit me, Arina Petrovna, permit me, mother, to kiss your hand first.'

And he kissed his wife's hand respectfully, even tenderly. The girl by the window indignantly turned her back on the scene; his wife's disdainful, questioning expression suddenly relaxed into one of total friendliness.

'How do you do, please sit down, Mr Chernomazov,'* she said.

'Karamazov, mother, Karamazov,' he repeated in a whisper. 'We're only simple people, sir.'

'Well, Karamazov or what have you, but for me it's Chernomazov... Do sit down, and why ever did he make you stand up? "Lady with no legs", he says—well, I do have legs, but they're swollen like tree-trunks, while the rest of me is withered. I used to be nice and plump, but now I'm as thin as a rake...'

'We're just simple people, sir, just simple people,' the Captain reiterated.

'Papa, oh papa!' said the hunchbacked girl, who had kept silent until then, and suddenly buried her face in her handkerchief.

'Buffoon!' the girl by the window blurted out.

'Now you understand the situation?' the woman said, spreading out her arms and pointing towards her daughters. 'It's like clouds; the clouds will drift past and we'll have music again. When we belonged to the military, we used to have lots of visitors like him. No, bless you, I shan't make an issue of this.

Whoever loves, let him go on loving. Along comes the deacon's wife and says: "Aleksander Aleksandrovich is an excellent man, but Nastasya Petrovna", she says, "is a fiend out of hell." "Well," I reply, "each to his own, but as for you, small though you are, you stink to high heaven." "And you," she says, "you must be kept under." "You swarthy hag," say I to her, "you haven't come to teach me how to suck eggs, have you?" "I'm letting in some fresh air," she says, "but you're fouling it." "Well," I replied, "ask any of the gentlemen officers if my breath smells or what." And this has been preying on my mind ever so much since then; I was sitting here the other day, just as I am now, and in comes that very same General, large as life, who was here at Easter. "Your highness," I say to him, "may a lady of breeding be permitted to let in a breath of fresh air?" "Yes," he replies, "you ought to open a window or the door a little, it's awfully stuffy in here." It's always the same! And what's wrong with my breath? Corpses smell even worse. "I'll not foul your air," I say, "I'll order me a pair of boots and leave you, so there." My dears, my beloved ones, don't blame your poor old mother! Nikolai Ilyich, my dear, haven't I looked after you well, all I've got left is Ilyushechka, who comes home after school full of love for me. He brought me an apple the other day. Forgive your poor old mother, my dears, forgive me, my beloved ones, forgive me, alone that I am... and how come, suddenly, none of you can stand the smell of my breath?'

And the poor creature began to weep, tears streaming down her face. The Staff Captain was at her side in a trice.

'Mother, mother darling, that'll do, that'll do! You're not alone. Everyone loves you, everyone adores you!' and he again began to kiss both her hands and gently stroke her face with the palms of his hands; picking up a napkin, he started dabbing her face. Alyosha felt tears beginning to prick in his own eyes. 'Well, sir, you've seen it all, you've heard everything, haven't you?' He suddenly turned to Alyosha with some vehemence, pointing with his hand at the hapless, crazed woman.

'I have, I have indeed,' Alyosha muttered.

'Papa, papa! You're not going with him... Don't go, papa!' the little boy cried out, raising himself up in bed slightly, his burning eyes fixed upon his father.

'It's about time you stopped making an exhibition of yourself and ceased your stupid antics that never lead to anything!...' Varvara Nikolavna called out from her corner, stamping her foot and utterly beside herself with anger.

'Your outburst on this occasion, Varvara Nikolavna, is totally justified, and I shall accede to your request forthwith. Be so kind as to don your cap, Aleksei Fyodorovich, and I'll take mine too— and off we go. I've something important to say to you, only not within these four walls. The young lady seated here is my daughter, Nina Nikolavna, I forgot to introduce her... one of God's angels in the flesh... descended from heaven... if you could but see what I mean...'

'He's shaking all over, as though he's got the ague,' Varvara Nikolavna continued, full of indignation.

'And as for her, who's been stamping her foot at me and denounced me as a buffoon just now, she's also one of God's angels in the flesh, sir, and is quite within her rights to call me names. Let's go, Aleksei Fyodorovich, we need to settle this matter...'

And grabbing Alyosha by the arm, he led him from the room straight out into the street.

7

AND IN THE FRESH AIR

'IT's nice and fresh outside—not like in that palace of mine, where it's pretty stuffy in every sense of the word. Let's take a short walk, sir. I'd really like to discuss something with you.'

'I too have come on a rather extraordinary errand...', remarked Alyosha, 'only I don't know how to begin.'

'It's quite obvious you've come on business. You were hardly likely to pay me a social call. Unless perhaps you came to complain about my young son? But that's impossible. Talking about my boy, I couldn't explain the situation when we were indoors, but now I can describe the whole incident to you. Look—only a week ago this loofah of mine used to be much thicker—I'm talking about my beard; it's mainly the schoolboys who call it a loofah. So, there was your brother Dmitry Fyodorovich dragging me along by this beard of mine, right out of the tavern and into the square, and just then the schoolboys, Ilyusha amongst them, came out of school. As soon as he saw my predicament he rushed towards me, crying: "Papa, papa!" He kept reaching out, trying to put his arms around me to drag me free, and shouting at my attacker: "Let go, let go, it's my papa, my papa, forgive him"—that's just what he said, "forgive him". He flung his arms around him too and was kissing his hand, the same hand which... I can remember him at that instant, the expression on his face, I haven't forgotten it, nor ever will!...'

'I swear', Alyosha vowed, 'my brother will demonstrate to you the most sincere, the most heartfelt repentance... on his knees, if you wish, on that same square... I'll make him do it, or I'll disown him as my brother!'

'Ah, so this is still all talk. And you haven't actually come on his behalf, but simply out of the goodness of your heart. You should have said so. Well, in that case, let me tell you more about the sense of honour and chivalry displayed on that occasion by your officer brother. He stopped pulling me by the beard and let me go: "You're an officer," he said, "so am I. If you can find a decent second, tell him to come—I'll give you full satisfaction, even though you're a proper scoundrel!" That's what he said. Now wasn't that truly chivalrous! Ilyusha and I left, but that picture of our family honour will for ever be imprinted in Ilyusha's memory. How can we still call ourselves honourable after that? Judge for yourself, you've just come from my home—what did you see there? Three ladies, one completely lame and mentally deranged, the other also lame and hunchbacked, and the third, though able to walk, too clever by half, a student,* what's more, aching to get back to St Petersburg again to seek justice for Russian women on the banks of the Neva.* That's not to mention Ilyusha, who's only nine years old, my only son. What if I died—what would become of our hovel, I ask you? And if I challenged him to a duel and he killed me on the spot, what then? What would become of them all? Even worse, if instead of killing me he merely injured me, then I'd be out of work, but there'd still be an extra mouth to feed, my mouth, and who'd be there to look after the rest of them? Unless I sent

Ilyusha out each day to beg. That's what would happen if I were to challenge him to a duel, it's a stupid idea, doesn't bear thinking about.'

'He shall ask your forgiveness, he shall kneel before you in the middle of the square,' Alyosha exclaimed again, his eyes blazing.

'I thought of taking him to court,' the Staff Captain continued, 'but you only have to look at our legal system to see how much compensation I'd be likely to get from my assailant. And then there's Agrafena Aleksandrovna, who summoned me and shouted: "Don't you dare! If you take him to court, I'll make it look for all the world as if he beat you for your misdeeds, then you'll end up in the dock yourself." And the Lord above knows who's responsible for all this villainy and who I was acting for, small fry that I am—was it not for her and for Fyodor Pavlovich, too? "And what's more," she went on, "I'll give you the push for good, and you'll not get any more work from me in future. And I'll tell my friend the merchant," that's what she calls the old man, "my friend the merchant". "He'll also give you the push." So I thought to myself: if the merchant gives me the push, what then, who else is going to employ me? They're the only two who still give me any work, because not only has your father Fyodor Pavlovich stopped trusting me, due to some matter between us, but he's even thinking of taking me to court on account of some IOUs. As a result of all this I'm having to lie low, and you've seen the hovel I live in. And now let me ask you: did he hurt that finger of yours very badly, my Ilyusha? When we were in the house I didn't dare to enquire too deeply.'

'Yes, it hurt a lot, and he was most upset. He picked on me as a Karamazov to avenge you, I can see that now. But you should have seen him and his schoolmates throwing stones at one another. That's very dangerous, he could get killed, they're just children, they don't realize a stone can crack a skull.'

'They've already hit him with a stone, not in the head but in the chest, just above the heart, there's a bruise there now. He came home crying and groaning with pain, now he's fallen ill.'

'And do you know, he's always the first one to attack, he's so upset on your account that they say he stabbed a boy called Krasotkin in the side with his penknife...'

'I heard about that too, it's dangerous, his father's a local civil servant, it could lead to repercussions...'

'My advice to you', Alyosha said animatedly, 'would be to keep him at home for some time until he calms down... and his anger subsides...'

'Anger!' the Staff Captain quickly retorted. 'That's right, anger. He may be small, but he's got a lot of pent-up anger. You don't know the half of it. Let me tell you the full story. The point is that after this incident, all his schoolmates started calling him loofah. Schoolchildren are a cruel lot: individually they're God's little angels, but as a group, especially at school, they're very often completely merciless. So, the more they teased him, the more his noble spirit rebelled within him. Any other less spirited boy would have given in, would have felt embarrassed for his father, but this one turned on them and stood up for his father— for his father and for justice and truth. God only knows what he suffered when he was kissing your brother's hands and imploring him: "Forgive my papa, forgive my papa." Yes, that's how our children—not yours, mark you, but ours, the children of despised but honourable paupers—learn to understand the world by the time they're nine. It's all right for the rich: they probably never have to plumb such depths in their lives, but that occasion on the square when my Ilyusha was kissing his hands, at that instant he fathomed the truth in its entirety. He was confronted by the truth, and it dealt him a mortifying blow,' the Staff Captain continued in a state of feverish excitement, hitting the palm of his left hand with the clenched fist of his right, as though to demonstrate the blow that 'the truth' had dealt his Ilyusha. 'He was in a state of delirium during the day and was raving the whole night. He hardly spoke to me the whole day, wouldn't say a word, but I noticed him peering at me from the corner of the room. He sat near the window for most of the time, pretending he was doing his lessons, though I could see his mind wasn't on his lessons. Next day, overcome with sorrow, I went and got drunk, sinner that I am, and couldn't quite follow what was going on. My good lady wife was in one of her crying moods just then—I do love her ever so much—so, in sorrow, I blew my last kopeck on drink. Don't despise me for that, sir: the best people in Russia are the ones who drink the most. So, while I lay drunk that day, my mind was not wholly on Ilyusha, and it was that very morning that the schoolboys started taunting him. "Loofah," they shouted at him, "your father was dragged out of the tavern by his beard and you ran alongside asking for forgiveness." On the third day he came home from school looking pale, like death warmed up. "What's the matter?" I asked. Not a peep out of him. Couldn't talk indoors, else my good lady and the girls would have wanted to join in. Varvara Nikolavna was already muttering: "Clowns, buffoons, can't you ever do anything right?" "That's just the point, Varvara Nikolavna," I said. "Can we ever do anything right?" And that was that, for the time being. Come evening, I went for a walk with the boy. I should tell you, we used to go out for a walk together every night, along exactly the same route that we're taking now, from our front gate as far as that huge, solitary stone by the wattle fence, where the common pasture land begins: a desolate, wonderful place. So there we were, both of us walking along, his hand in mine as usual; he's got a tiny hand and thin cold fingers—it's his chest, you know. "Papa," he said to me, "papa!" "What?" I replied. I could see his eyes were burning. "Papa, the way he treated you that time, papa!" "What's to be done, Ilyusha?" I said. "Don't make it up with him, papa, don't. The boys at school are saying he offered you ten roubles for that." "No, Ilyusha," I said, "I wouldn't take money from him under any circumstances." His whole body began to shake, he took my hand in both of his and started kissing it. "Papa," he said, "papa, why don't you challenge him to a duel, they're teasing me at school that you're a coward and won't challenge him, they say you'll accept the ten roubles instead." "Ilyusha," I replied, "I can't challenge him to a duel," and I explained to him briefly what I've just said to you about that matter. He listened. "Papa," he said, "papa, don't make it up with him all the same: I'll grow up I'll challenge him myself and I'll kill him!" His eyes were glinting and burning. Well, I am his father after all, and it was up to me to tell him the truth. "It's a sin to kill," I said to him, "even in a duel." "Papa," he said, "papa, when I'm grown up I'll throw him to the ground, I'll knock his sword out of his hand with my sword, I'll attack him, I'll knock him down, I'll raise my sword and say to him: 'I could kill you now, but I forgive you, so there!' " Do you see what

must have been going on in his mind in those two days, he must
have been thinking day and night about this revenge with the
sword, and probably raving about it at night too. He started
coming home from school badly bruised; the other day I found
out everything, and you're right, I shan't send him to that school
any more. I discovered that he tries to fight the whole class and
provokes everybody; he's angry, his heart is seething with hatred.
I was frightened for him. We continued walking. "Papa," he
asked me, "papa, the rich are the most powerful people in the
world, aren't they?" "Yes, Ilyusha," I said, "there's no one in the
world more powerful than a rich man." "Papa," he said, "I'll be
a rich man and become an officer, and I'll defeat everybody, the
Tsar will reward me, I'll come along and nobody will dare to..."
He stopped for a while and said, his lips still trembling as
before: "Papa, isn't our town a nasty, horrible place, papa!"
"Yes, Ilyushechka," I said, "it's really not a nice place at all."
"Papa," he said, "let's move to another town, to a nice town
where nobody knows about us." "So we shall, Ilyusha," I said,
"so we shall; just let me save some money." I was glad of the
opportunity to take his mind off the depressing subject, and we
started day-dreaming about how we'd move to another town,
buy our own horse and cart. We'd settle mother and the girls
on the cart, tuck them in, and the two of us would walk alongside, though occasionally I'd lift him on to the cart, but I'd walk
to spare the horse, it wouldn't do for us all to ride, and so we'd
be on our way. He was over the moon about it, especially the
fact that we'd have a horse of our own and he himself would ride
on it. There's nothing a Russian boy is more fond of than a
horse, that's for sure. We went on chatting for a long time.
"Thank God," I thought, "I've managed to cheer him up, I've
consoled him." This was the evening of the day before yesterday,
but last night everything changed. In the morning he went to
school again, and returned all depressed and gloomy. In the
evening I took him by the hand and we went for a walk, but we
walked in silence, not saying a word. The wind picked up, the
sun went in, there was a hint of autumn and, besides, it was
getting dark; we kept on walking, both of us dejected. "Well, my
boy," I said, "how shall you and I get ready for the move?" The
intention was to return to the conversation of the day before.

Not a word. All I felt were his fingers tightening in my hand. We reached that same stone, I sat down on it; there were kites flying in the sky, flapping and rustling, I could see about thirty. It's the kite season. "Look here, Ilyusha," I said, "it's about time we flew that kite we made last year. I'll mend it, where have you hidden it?" Not a word from my little boy, he just kept gazing into the distance, refusing to look at me and standing with his back to me. Just then the wind began to howl and raise the dust... He rushed towards me suddenly, flung his arms round my neck, and held me tightly. You know how children who are proud and reserved and have been fighting back their tears for a long time will suddenly be unable to contain them any longer, if the grief is bad enough, and the tears won't just flow, but will gush forth in torrents. A veritable flood of warm tears poured down my face. He was convulsed with sobs, trembling all over, pressing himself tightly against me as I sat on the stone. "Papa," he exclaimed, "papa, dear papa, the way he humiliated you!" That's when I began to cry too; we just sat and cried, hugging each other. "Papa," he said, "papa!" "Ilyusha," I said to him, "Ilyushechka!" No one saw us then, only God, perhaps He'll make a note of it in my record. Thank your brother for me, Aleksei Fyodorovich. No, I shan't give my boy a thrashing just to please you!'

As he finished this speech, he reverted to his former abrupt manner. Alyosha sensed, however, that he trusted him, and that had he been anyone else he would not have talked so freely and would not have confided in him as he had just done. This heartened Alyosha and moved him to tears.

'Oh, how I wish I could be friends with your little boy!' he exclaimed. 'If only you could do something...'

'Certainly,' the Staff Captain mumbled.

'But that's not the important thing now, not at all, listen,' Alyosha continued with passion, 'listen. I've come on an errand: that same brother of mine, Dmitry, insulted his fiancée too, a most honourable girl whom you've probably heard of. I feel justified in telling you that she was insulted, in fact I must, because when she found out about the way you had been mistreated and all the other details of your unfortunate circumstances, she instructed me now... today... to give you some money

as a small token of help... it's just from her, you know, not from
Dmitry, he abandoned her, it's certainly not from him, nor from
me, his brother, nor from anyone else, but just from her and her
alone! She begs you to accept an offer of help from her... you've
both been wronged at the hands of one and the same person...
As it happens, she thought of you only after she herself had been
insulted by him every bit as badly as you were! In other words, a
sister coming to her brother's assistance... She specifically asked
me to try and persuade you to accept these two hundred roubles
from her as if she were your sister. Nobody shall know of this,
there's no danger of any malicious gossip... here's the two
hundred roubles, I do urge you to accept it, or else... or else that
would mean the world was peopled with enemies! There must
be brothers too in this world... You have a noble soul... you must
understand this, you really must!...'

Whereupon Alyosha offered him two brand-new hundred-
rouble notes. They were both standing by that very same large
stone by the fence, and there was no one around. The banknotes
seemed to have an electrifying effect upon the Staff Captain: he
shuddered, at first apparently in sheer surprise; he could never
have imagined or anticipated such a development. Not in his
wildest dreams could he have expected help from anyone,
especially help on such a generous scale. He took the notes and,
for about a minute, was almost speechless, then something
altogether new flitted across his face.

'Is it all for me? All this money? Two hundred roubles! My
word! It must be four years since I've seen so much money, my
God! And she said she's my sister, did she?... Can that be true,
can that really be true!'

'I swear all I've told you is the truth!' Alyosha exclaimed. The
Staff Captain's face flushed.

'Listen, my friend, listen to me. If I were to accept this money,
surely I'd be a scoundrel. In your eyes, Aleksei Fyodorovich,
wouldn't I be a scoundrel? No, Aleksei Fyodorovich, hear what I
have to say, hear me out,' the Staff Captain continued excitedly,
every now and again touching Alyosha with both hands, 'you are
trying to talk me into taking this money because it comes from
my "sister", but deep down, in your heart of hearts, wouldn't
you despise me if I took it, eh?'

'No, not at all! I swear to you on my life I wouldn't! And no one would ever find out, it's strictly between the three of us: you, me, and her—and one other lady, a great friend of hers...'

'Oh, never mind the lady! Listen, Aleksei Fyodorovich, just listen to me, it's about time you heard what I've got to say, because you can't even imagine what these two hundred roubles could do for me,' continued the poor man, gradually succumbing to a kind of grotesque, almost frantic elation. He appeared thoroughly disoriented, and went on talking in great haste and passion, as though afraid that he would not be allowed to have his say. 'Not only has this money been honestly acquired from an esteemed and revered "sister", sir, but do you realize that now I'll be able to get medical treatment for my lady wife and for Ninochka, my humpbacked angel, my daughter? Doctor Herzenstube came to us out of the goodness of his heart and spent a whole hour examining them both: "Can't make anything out at all," he said. Nevertheless, the mineral water at our chemist's should certainly do some good (he prescribed some of that); he also prescribed medicinal foot-baths. But mineral water costs thirty kopecks, and she has to drink perhaps forty jugs of it. So I just put the prescription on the shelf, under an icon, and haven't touched it since. As for Ninochka, he instructed us to bathe her in some kind of solution, and make sure that she took hot baths every morning and evening, but how can we arrange such treatment for her where we live, in our mansion, with no maids, no help, no facilities, not even any water? What's more, Ninochka's crippled with rheumatism—I hadn't told you that, had I?—she suffers at night, the whole of her right side hurts, but would you believe it, the darling angel puts on a brave face so as not to disturb us, she doesn't even groan, so as not to wake us. We eat whatever's available, anything we can lay our hands on, and yet she always takes the last of the leftovers, which are only fit for a dog: "I don't deserve it," she seems to say, "I'm depriving you of your last morsel, I'm a burden to you." That's what her angel eyes are trying to say. We look after her, but it embarrasses her: "I'm not worthy, I'm not, I'm a worthless cripple, I'm useless." How can she be useless if in her angelic humility she's been praying to God for all of us, for without her, without her gentle supplication, it would have been sheer hell at

home—even Varya's heart has softened. And please don't blame
Varvara Nikolavna either, she too is an angel, but she's been
hard done by. She came home this summer with sixteen roubles
in her pocket which she'd saved giving lessons and had put by
for when she returned to St Petersburg in September, which will
be soon. But we took her money and lived off it, and now she
can't return because she's got nothing left, that's what's happened. She can't possibly go back because she works for us like
a slave—we've harnessed and saddled her like a workhorse, she
looks after everybody, darns, washes, scrubs the floor, puts her
mother to bed, and, don't forget, mother's capricious, mother's
tearful, mother's not all there!... Now, with these two hundred
roubles I can employ a housemaid you understand, Aleksei
Fyodorovich, I can start getting treatment for my dear ones, I'll
send the girl back to St Petersburg, I'll buy some beef, we'll have
proper meals at last. My God, it's all a dream!'

Alyosha was overjoyed that the money had brought so much
happiness and that the poor devil had agreed to accept it.

'Wait, Aleksei Fyodorovich, wait,' the Staff Captain suddenly
latched on to a new idea which had presented itself to him and
again, in his enthusiasm, he rattled on nineteen to the dozen,
'you know, Ilyusha and I shall really be able to make our dream
come true now: we'll buy ourselves a horse and cart, the horse'll
be black, he specially asked for it to be black, and off we'll go,
just as we planned the day before yesterday. In the province of
K* there's a lawyer I've been friends with since childhood, and
I'm reliably informed that if I went there he'd probably give me
a secretarial job in his office; who knows, perhaps he would... So
then, my good lady will go in the cart, so will Ninochka,
Ilyushechka will be the driver, and I'll lead the way on foot...
God, if only I could recover a small local debt, I might really just
be able to afford all that!'

'Of course you will!' Alyosha exclaimed. 'Katerina Ivanovna
will send you some more, as much as you want, and do you know
what, I too have some money, take all you need, as from a
brother or a friend, you can repay me later... You'll grow rich,
I'm sure you will! What's more, this move to another province is
the best thing you've ever thought of! It'll be your salvation,
especially for your little boy—and you know, you ought to hurry

before the winter sets in, before it gets too cold, you must write to us from there, and we'll always stay brothers... No, this is not a dream!'

Alyosha was so pleased that he made as if to embrace him. But when he glanced at him, he stopped abruptly: the man stood there, with his neck outstretched, his countenance pale and agitated, his lips protruding and moving as though trying to articulate something; no sound emerged, yet his lips continued to twitch strangely.

'What's the matter?' asked Alyosha with a sudden shudder.

'Aleksei Fyodorovich... I... you...', the Staff Captain mumbled haltingly, staring at him strangely and wildly, like someone who has resolved to jump off a cliff, yet at the same time retaining a semblance of a smile about his lips, 'I... you... you wouldn't like me to show you a trick, would you?' he said suddenly, in a rapid, resolute whisper, without stumbling over his words this time.

'What trick?'

'A trick, a hocus-pocus,' the Staff Captain went on in a whisper, his mouth twisted over to the left, his left eye half shut, and staring at Alyosha as if transfixed.

'I don't understand, what's the matter, what on earth do you mean?' Alyosha cried out, utterly bewildered by now.

'Just this, look!' the Staff Captain shrieked.

He held up the two banknotes, both of which he had been holding by their corners between the thumb and forefinger of his right hand all the while they had been talking, then brandished them in the air, and suddenly crumpled them furiously in his fist.

'Did you see that!' he shrieked at Alyosha, pale and distraught, and suddenly, raising his fist, he flung the crumpled notes to the ground. 'Did you see that?' he shrieked again, pointing at them. 'There you are!...'

All of a sudden, wild with anger, he raised his right foot and began to trample the notes with his heel, exclaiming and gasping each time he brought his foot down.

'There's your money! There's your money! There's your money! There's your money!' Suddenly he jumped back and stood up straight, watching Alyosha. His whole appearance was one of indescribable pride.

'Tell whoever sent you', he exclaimed, raising his arm in the air, 'that loofah's honour is not for sale!' Then he swung round and began to run, but he had barely covered five paces when, turning right round again, he waved his arm at Alyosha. He took five more paces and turned for the last time; no warped smile distorted his face this time, just the opposite, tears were streaming down his face. He fairly shouted, the words tumbling forth, his voice breaking and choking as he fought to contain his sobs.

'What could I have said to my little boy if I had accepted money for the shame we suffered?' Having said this, he continued running, but this time he did not look back. Alyosha gazed after him, his eyes full of indescribable sadness. He understood only too well that the Staff Captain himself had not known until the very last moment that he would crumple the banknotes and throw them to the ground. The fleeing man did not look back, and Alyosha knew that he would not. Nor did he want to go after him or call him back. However, after he had vanished from view, Alyosha picked up both the notes. They were badly creased and had been ground into the sandy earth, but otherwise they were quite undamaged; indeed, they even sounded crisp and new when Alyosha straightened them and smoothed them out. Having straightened them out, he folded them, put them in his pocket, and returned to Katerina Ivanovna to report on the completion of his mission.

BOOK FIVE

Pros and Cons

1

BETROTHAL

MRS KHOKHLAKOVA was again the first person whom Alyosha encountered. She was completely flustered. Something serious had happened; Katerina Ivanovna's hysterics had turned into a fainting fit, followed by a terrible, frightening debilitation; she had become delirious and lay senseless. By now she was feverish, and both Herzenstube and her aunts had been sent for. Her aunts were there, but Herzenstube had still not arrived. While everyone sat in the room and waited to see what would happen, Katerina Ivanovna lay unconscious. If only her temperature did not rise too high!

Mrs Khokhlakova's face as she relayed this news was troubled and anxious: 'This is serious, serious!' she added after every few words, as though everything that had happened to her before was less than serious. Alyosha heard her out with a troubled heart; he was about to start describing his own adventures, but no sooner had he uttered a few words than she interrupted him; she had no time, she begged him to keep Lise company and to wait with her.

'Lise, my dear Aleksei Fyodorovich,' she whispered, practically in his ear, 'Lise has exasperated me recently, but she's been so sweet that I couldn't help but forgive her everything. Imagine, hardly had you left than she began to feel really sorry that she had, it appears, laughed at you yesterday and today. But it turns out she wasn't really mocking you, she was only teasing. But she was so truly sorry, almost in tears, that I was amazed. Whenever she's made fun of me she's never been really sorry, always used to turn it into a joke. And you know, she's always making fun of me. But now she's taking it all seriously, everything has become important. She has an extremely high regard for your opinion, Aleksei Fyodorovich, so if you can, do try to be nice to her, don't hold it against her. I'm trying to do the same myself, to treat her gently. She's such an intelligent little thing. Would you believe it, you were her childhood friend—"the most steadfast friend of my childhood"—"the most steadfast", imagine that! What does that make me? She has very deep feelings about this, and even memories, but most of all phrases and expressions like that, they're so unexpected these expressions, one is quite unprepared, and she suddenly comes out with them. Recently, for example, there was one about a pine tree: when she was very little there was a pine tree in our garden, maybe it's still there. Perhaps I shouldn't use the past tense, Aleksei Fyodorovich; pine trees are not people, they remain unchanged for a long time. "Mama," she said, "I dreamt I repined under a pine tree"—"repined under a pine tree"! just imagine, that's what she said—well, perhaps not quite, perhaps she was just out to confuse me; "repined", I ask you! But she just chatted on about it, which left me quite speechless, but it's all gone right out of my head anyway, so I couldn't possibly repeat any of it. Well, I must leave you now. I'm all upset and probably going slowly mad. Ah, Aleksei Fyodorovich, I've suffered two lots of mental illness in my life, and I had to have treatment. Go and see Lise. Cheer her up, as you always manage to do in your own inimitable way. Lise,' she called, going to her door. 'There's Aleksei Fyodorovich to see you; you were so beastly to him, but he's not in the least bit upset, I assure you; on the contrary, he's most surprised that you could have thought he would be!'

'*Merci maman.* Come in, Aleksei Fyodorovich.'

Alyosha went in. Lise looked at him somewhat shyly, and suddenly blushed. She was obviously embarrassed about something and, as always when this was the case, she started to chatter non-stop about a quite different matter, as if that was all that interested her at that moment.

'Mama's just told me the whole story of the two hundred roubles and of your errand... to that poor officer... she told me the whole dreadful story about the offence perpetrated against him, and even though mama rambles on when she tells a story... you know the way she jumps from one thing to another... I listened and I wept. Well then, have you given him the money, and how are things with the poor man now?...'

'That's just the point, I haven't, and thereby hangs a story,' answered Alyosha, as if it were simply the fact of not having handed over the money that troubled him, while Lise saw perfectly well that he was avoiding her eyes and was also trying to avoid the real subject. Alyosha sat down at the table and began to tell his story, but as soon as he began to speak he lost his shyness and captured Lise's attention. Although he was in such an emotional state and still very upset by his recent encounter, he managed to give her a clear and detailed account. Even before, in Moscow, when Lise was still a child, he had loved to visit her and tell her what had been happening in his life, what he had read or what he remembered of his childhood. Sometimes they would dream up whole stories together, mostly cheerful and amusing. Now it seemed as if they had both suddenly been transported back to those times in Moscow two or so years ago. Lise was profoundly moved by his story. Alyosha, seething with emotion, painted such a picture of 'Ilyushechka' that Lise could almost visualize him. When he had finished describing in detail how the poor man had stamped on the money, Lise clasped her hands and cried out with emotion:

'So, you didn't give him the money after all, you let him walk off! My God, surely you could at least have run after him yourself and caught up with him...'

'No, Lise, it was better not to run after him,' said Alyosha, getting up from his chair and walking distractedly about the room.

'Better? How could it be better? Now they've no bread and they'll starve!'

'They won't starve, because those two hundred roubles will get to them just the same. He'll accept them tomorrow, you'll see. He's bound to take the money then,' Alyosha said, pacing up and down deep in thought. 'Do you see, Lise,' he went on, suddenly coming to a stop in front of her, 'I made a mistake there, but even that mistake has turned out to be for the best.'

'What mistake, and why is it for the best?'

'Because he's a weak and timorous man. He's at the end of his tether, and he's very good-natured, you know. Now I keep thinking about the reason for the sudden outburst that caused him to stamp on the money, and I assure you that it was because until the very last moment he didn't know that he would reject it. It seems to me that he was angry about a lot of things... in his situation he couldn't help but be angry. Firstly, he resented appearing to be too pleased about the money and letting me see this. If he had been pleased but not too pleased, if he hadn't made it so obvious but had dissimulated, as others do when accepting money, then he could still have accepted it, but he was too openly delighted, and he resented that. Oh, Lise, he's a sincere man—a good man, that's the root of the problem! All the time he was talking his voice was so weak, so feeble, and he talked so fast and with such a funny kind of tremor, or perhaps he was already crying... really, he was crying, he was so delighted... and he talked about his daughters... and about the job he was going to get in another town... And then, no sooner had he poured out his heart than he was suddenly stricken with shame for having bared his soul so completely to me. So he immediately began to hate me. He's poor and terribly ashamed of his poverty. Most of all, he was angry that he had accepted me as his friend too quickly and had made himself vulnerable; one minute he was lunging at me, trying to frighten me, and then suddenly, as soon as he saw the money, he was all over me. He kept hugging me. He must have felt so humiliated in this situation, and then right at that moment I made an awful mistake: I said that if the money was not enough for him to move to the other town, he could have more; I would even give him whatever he needed out of my own money. The thought then suddenly struck him: why was I too rushing to his aid? You know, Lise, after a man has been wronged it's very hard for him to accept that everyone's regarding him with the eyes of a benefactor... I've heard that, my starets told me. I don't know how to express it, but I myself have often seen it. Besides, I would feel exactly the same. But the important thing is that although he himself didn't realize till the last moment that he'd stamp on the notes, nevertheless he had some inkling of what he'd do, I'm sure of it. It was just because he was so absolutely delighted that he anticipated it... And so, unpleasant as all this is, it's still all for the best. For the very best even, I think, it couldn't be better...'

'Why, why couldn't it be better?' cried Lise, looking at Alyosha in astonishment.

'Because, Lise, if he hadn't stamped on the money but had picked it up, then, when he came home after an hour or so he'd have wept from humiliation—I'm sure that's what would have happened. He'd have wept and, very probably, would have come to me first thing tomorrow and would perhaps have thrown down the notes and trampled on them then, as he did just now. But now he's gone off proud and victorious, even though he knows that but for his pride he could have saved the situation. And so, nothing could be easier now than to make him accept these two hundred roubles tomorrow at the latest, because he has demonstrated his honour, rejected the money, trampled on it... He wasn't to know when he was trampling on it that I'd return with it tomorrow. Besides, he needs this money desperately. Although he's feeling proud of himself now, still, even today he'll be thinking what a chance he's thrown away. In the night he'll think about it even more, he'll dream about it, and, come the morning, he'll be ready to run to me and beg forgiveness. And that's just when I'll turn up and say: "You're a proud man, you've proved it. Now take the money and forgive us." And he'll take it, you'll see!'

Alyosha pronounced these last words in a kind of ecstasy. Lise clapped her hands.

'Oh, that's true. Now I understand! Oh, Alyosha, how do you know all that? So young, and yet you know what goes on in the soul... I'd never have thought it possible...'

'The important thing now is to convince him that even though he has accepted money from us, he has not demeaned himself,' continued Alyosha, still ecstatic, 'not only that he has not demeaned himself, but even that one could look up to him...'

'Look up to him? Lovely, Aleksei Fyodorovich, but go on, do go on!'

'I expressed myself badly... about looking up to him, that is... but it doesn't matter, because...'

'Oh, it doesn't matter, of course it doesn't matter! Forgive me, my dear Alyosha... You know, up to now I wasn't sure I really respected you... that is, I respected you, but as an equal, and now I shall respect you and look up to you. Dear Alyosha, don't be angry with me for joking,' she added at once, passionately.

'I'm young and silly, but you, you... Listen, Aleksei Fyodorovich, isn't there in all our reasoning, that is to say, your... no, it's better to say "our" reasoning... isn't there some kind of condescension towards him, towards this unfortunate man... in the patronizing way we bare his soul? In the way we're so certain he'll take the money?'

'No, Lise, not condescension,' Alyosha answered firmly, as if he had been prepared for this question. 'I already thought about that on my way here. Think about it. What condescension can there be when we ourselves are like him, when everyone's like him. Because, after all, we're all like him, we're no better. And even if we were better, we'd be just the same in his situation... I don't know about you, Lise, but in my own case I think I have in many ways a shallow soul. But his isn't shallow, rather it's sensitive... No, Lise, there's no condescension towards him in this! You know, Lise, my starets once said: "Mostly you have to look after people like you do children, and some you have to look after like patients in hospital"...'

'Oh, Aleksei Fyodorovich, oh, my dear Alyosha, let's look after people like patients!'

'Yes, Lise, let's do that. I think I'm ready, but I'm not really ready; sometimes I'm very impatient, and at other times I don't see what's staring me in the face. You're quite different.'

'Oh, I don't believe it! Aleksei Fyodorovich, I'm so happy!'

'I'm so happy that you say that, Lise.'

'Aleksei Fyodorovich, you're unbelievably good, but sometimes you're a bit of a pedant... and yet, when one looks closer, you're not pedantic at all. Go to the door and have a look, open it quietly and see if mama's listening,' Lise's voice suddenly dropped to a sort of nervous, hurried whisper.

Alyosha went to the door, opened it a crack, and reported that there was no one there.

'Come here, Aleksei Fyodorovich,' Lise continued, blushing, 'give me your hand, that's right. Listen, I have to make a big confession to you. When I wrote that letter yesterday I wasn't joking, I was serious...', and she covered her eyes with her hand. It was obvious that confessing this embarrassed her greatly. Suddenly she seized his hand and hurriedly planted three kisses on it.

'Oh, Lise, that's marvellous,' exclaimed Alyosha delightedly, 'and you know, I was quite certain you were serious.'

'"Certain", well imagine that!' she suddenly pushed his hand away but did not release it, blushed crimson, and gave a happy little laugh. 'I kiss his hand, and all he says is "That's marvellous."' But her reproach was unfair; Alyosha too was deeply embarrassed.

'I would like to please you always, Lise, but I don't know how to do it,' he muttered, also blushing.

'Alyosha, my dear, you're cold and presumptuous. How shall I put it? He condescends to choose me for his spouse and thinks nothing of it! Fancy being certain I was serious when I wrote that! If that's not presumptuous, what is!'

'Surely it wasn't wrong of me to be certain, was it?' Alyosha began to laugh.

'Oh, Alyosha, on the contrary, you were absolutely right,' Lise said, casting him a look of tenderness and happiness. Alyosha stood there, still keeping his hand in hers. Suddenly he bent over and kissed her right on the lips.

'Whatever next? What's come over you?' exclaimed Lise. Alyosha was overcome with confusion.

'Forgive me if I shouldn't have... Perhaps I'm terribly stupid... You said I was cold, so I kissed you... only now I see that it misfired...'

Lise collapsed into laughter and hid her face in her hands.

'And in that dress!' she burst out between peals of laughter, but suddenly checked herself and became quite serious, almost severe.

'Now, Alyosha, the kissing can wait, because neither of us knows how, and we'll have a long time to wait,' she concluded suddenly. 'It'd be better if you told me why you want to marry me, such a silly little fool, such a silly little invalid, and you so clever, so thoughtful, so observant. Oh, Alyosha, I'm terribly happy, but I'm not worthy of you!'

'Yes, you are, Lise. In a few days I'll be leaving the monastery for good. Once I'm back in the world I'll have to marry, I know that. *He* told me that. Who could I find better than you... and who but you would have me? I've already thought about it. In the first place, you've known me since childhood, and then, secondly,

you have many qualities that I totally lack. You have a happier
nature than I have and, most importantly, you're more innocent
than me; I've already experienced so much in my life, so much...
Oh, you don't know the half of it; after all, I too am a Karamazov!
What if you do laugh and make fun, even of me; I don't mind,
on the contrary I'm happy... But you laugh like a little girl, while
inside you have the thoughts of one who has suffered...'

' "One who has suffered"? What do you mean?'

'Yes, Lise; for example, the question you posed a little while
ago—wasn't there something condescending about the way we
were dissecting the soul of that poor unfortunate man?—only
someone who's suffered would ask such a question... you see, I
don't know how to express it, but someone who thinks of
questions like that is someone who's capable of suffering. Sitting
in your invalid chair, you must have thought about a lot of
things...'

'Alyosha, give me your hand, why have you taken it away?'
said Lise feebly, her voice overcome with happiness. 'Listen,
Alyosha, what will you wear when you leave the monastery, what
clothes? Don't laugh and don't be angry, it's very important to
me.'

'As to clothes, Lise, I haven't thought about that yet, but I'll
wear whatever you want me to.'

'I want you to wear a dark-blue velvet jacket, a white piqué
waistcoat, and a soft, fluffy, grey felt hat... Tell me, when I
denied what I said in my letter yesterday, did you think I didn't
love you?'

'No, I didn't think that.'

'Oh, you unbearable man, you're incorrigible!'

'You see, I knew you loved me... well, I thought you did, but I
pretended to believe you, to believe that you didn't, to... make
things easier for you...'

'That's even worse! Both worse and best of all. Alyosha, I love
you terribly. Just now, when I was waiting for you, I said to
myself, "I'll ask him for the letter I sent yesterday, and if he
calmly takes it out and gives it to me (as one might expect him
to), that will mean that he doesn't love me at all, that he feels
nothing for me, that he's just a foolish, unworthy youth, and I
shall die." But you left the letter in your cell, and that reassured

me. It's true, isn't it, that you left the letter in your cell because you guessed that I would ask for it back. You wanted to avoid giving it back, didn't you? It's true, isn't it?'

'Oh, Lise, it wasn't like that at all. I've got the letter with me now, and I had it all along; here it is in this pocket, here you are.'

Laughing, Alyosha took out the letter and showed it to her from a distance.

'Only I'm not going to give it back to you. You can look from there.'

'So you were lying before—a monk, and you lied?'

'Well, I suppose I was lying,' laughed Alyosha. 'I lied so as not to give you the letter. It's very dear to me,' he added, suddenly blushing again with emotion. 'It's mine for ever now, and I'll never give it to anyone!'

Lise gazed at him in admiration.

'Alyosha,' she murmured suddenly, 'have a look and see if mama's listening.'

'All right, Lise, I'll have a look, but wouldn't it be better not to look? Why do you suspect your mother of such shameful behaviour?'

'Shameful? How is it shameful? To eavesdrop on her daughter is her right; it isn't shameful,' Lise retorted. 'Rest assured, Aleksei Fyodorovich, that when I'm a mother and I have such a daughter, I shall certainly eavesdrop on her.'

'Surely not, Lise. That's not nice.'

'Oh, my God, where's the harm in it? If it were some ordinary sort of conversation and I eavesdropped, that would be shameful, but here's my own daughter closeted with a young man... Listen, Alyosha, you may as well know that I shall eavesdrop on you too as soon as we are married and, what's more, I shall open all your letters and read everything... So, you have been warned...'

'Yes, of course, in that case...', muttered Alyosha. 'Still, it isn't nice...'

'Oh, don't be silly! Alyosha, dear, let's not quarrel right from the start. It's better that I tell you the truth; of course, it's very bad to listen at doors—I'm wrong and you're right—but all the same I shall listen.'

'Do! You won't be able to catch me out in anything,' laughed Alyosha.

'And, Alyosha, will you do what I tell you? We have to decide that beforehand as well.'

'Willingly, Lise, of course, only not when it comes to essentials. In that case, even if you don't agree with me, I shall still do what my duty dictates.'

'That's as it should be. I, on the other hand, am ready to obey you not only in essentials but in everything, I'll do as you tell me in all things, and I give you my word on that now—in all things and for my whole life,' Lise cried passionately, 'and I shall do so happily! What's more, I swear to you that I shall never eavesdrop on you, never, not once, not one letter of yours will I open, because you're right and I'm wrong. And although I shall be terribly tempted to listen at doors I shall not do so, because you consider it dishonourable. You are now my guiding light... Listen, Aleksei Fyodorovich, why have you been so sad the last few days, yesterday and today? I know you have troubles, that you have problems, but I can see that you have some other, special sadness, a secret grief perhaps?'

'Yes, Lise, I have a secret grief,' Alyosha said sadly. 'I can see you love me, since you guessed that.'

'What is it? What are you sad about? Can't you tell me?' Lise pleaded timidly.

'I'll tell you later, Lise... later...', Alyosha said, troubled. 'Just now I don't think you'd be able to understand. Perhaps I wouldn't even know how to explain it to you.'

'I know too that you're worried to death about your brothers and your father.'

'Brothers, yes, that too,' said Alyosha thoughtfully.

'I don't like your brother Ivan Fyodorovich,' Lise remarked suddenly.

Alyosha noted this remark with some surprise, but let it pass.

'My brothers are destroying themselves, and so is my father. And they're destroying others along with themselves. It's a kind of elemental force in the Karamazovs, as Father Païsy put it, elemental and frenzied, primitive... I wonder even whether there is a divine spirit watching over that force. I only know that I too am a Karamazov. I'm a monk—a monk? Am I a monk, Lise? You said a moment ago that I was a monk, didn't you?'

'Yes, I did.'

'And yet perhaps I don't even believe in God.'

'You don't believe! What's the matter with you?' Lise said quietly and cautiously. But Alyosha did not answer. There was in this spontaneous statement of his something too mysterious, too subjective, something not clear, perhaps, even to himself, but which was undoubtedly tormenting him.

'And now, on top of all that, my dearest friend is leaving us; the greatest man on earth is leaving this world. If you only knew, Lise, if you only knew how I am bound, indissolubly linked in spirit to that man! And now I shall be alone in the world... I shall come to you, Lise... From now on we'll be together...'

'Yes, together, together! From now on, always together for the rest of our lives. Listen, kiss me, I give you permission.'

Alyosha kissed her.

'Now go. Christ be with you!' And she made the sign of the cross over him. 'Quickly, go to him while he's still alive. I can see that it's cruel to keep you. I'll pray for him and for you today. Alyosha, we will be happy! We will be happy, won't we?'

'I think we will, Lise.'

When he left Lise, Alyosha saw no need to say goodbye to Mrs Khokhlakova, and he was about to set off for home without taking leave of her. But scarcely had he opened the door and stepped out on to the landing than there appeared before him, from he knew not where, Mrs Khokhlakova in person. Alyosha guessed straight away that she had deliberately been lying in wait for him there.

'Aleksei Fyodorovich, this is dreadful. This is juvenile nonsense and quite ridiculous. I hope you're not seriously presuming... It's so utterly silly, it really is,' she said, rushing up to him.

'Don't say that to her, whatever you do,' said Alyosha, 'or she'll get upset, which is bad for her at present.'

'Sensible words from a sensible young man. Am I to understand that you went along with her only out of consideration for her delicate state of health, not wanting to make her angry by contradicting her?'

'No, certainly not. I was absolutely serious in what I said to her,' said Alyosha firmly.

'It is unthinkable that you should be serious. In the first place, I shall not invite you again, and in the second place, you'd better know that I'm leaving and taking her with me.'

'But why?' said Alyosha, 'after all, it's still a long way off, we'll have to wait perhaps a year and a half.'

'Ah, Aleksei Fyodorovich, of course that's true, and in a year and a half you will have a thousand chances to quarrel and separate. But I'm so miserable, so miserable! All this may well be just childish nonsense, but it has crushed me. Now I'm like Famusov* in his last scene, you're Chatsky, she's Sofia, and... imagine, I deliberately ran out here on to the stairs to intercept you, and in the play too all the significant events take place on the staircase. I heard everything and could hardly contain myself. So that's the explanation of all last night's horrors and all the recent tantrums! To the daughter, love; and to the mother, death. Lay her in her grave. Now we come to the second and the most important thing! What's all this about a letter she wrote you? Show it to me now, at once, straight away!'

'No, it's none of your business. Tell me, how is Katerina Ivanovna? I really must know.'

'She's still delirious, she hasn't regained consciousness; her aunts are here, and they just tut-tut and give themselves airs in front of me, and Herzenstube came and got into such a state that I didn't know how to help him or what to do; I even thought about getting him a doctor. They took him away in my carriage. And now suddenly on top of everything, you turn up with this letter. Admittedly, none of this will be for a year and a half yet. In the name of all that's great and holy, in the name of your dying starets, show me the letter, Aleksei Fyodorovich; show it to me, I'm her mother! Don't let it out of your hands if you like, and I'll read it while you hold it.'

'No, I shall not show it to you, Katerina Osipovna, even if she'd let me, I wouldn't show it to you. I'll come tomorrow and, if you wish, I'll have a long talk with you then, but for now—goodbye!'

And Alyosha ran out of the hallway into the street.

2

SMERDYAKOV WITH A GUITAR

BESIDES, he did not have time. An idea had suddenly occurred to him even while he was saying goodbye to Lise, an idea as to the best way of catching Dmitry, who was clearly avoiding him. It was already quite late, about three in the afternoon. Every fibre of Alyosha's being urged him towards the monastery, towards his dying 'idol', but the urgent need to see Dmitry overcame everything else; in Alyosha's mind the conviction that a terrible, inescapable catastrophe was imminent was growing with every passing hour. Exactly what form the catastrophe would take, or what he wanted to say to his brother at this moment, was perhaps not clear even to himself. 'Let my mentor die without me, but at least I shan't reproach myself all my life that I could have saved someone and didn't, that I passed by on the other side and hurried home. In doing this, I'm carrying out his great command...'

His plan was to catch Dmitry unawares: he would climb over the wattle fence into the garden, as he had done the day before, and sit in the summer-house. 'If he isn't there,' thought Alyosha, 'I'll hide there without saying anything to Foma or to the owners, and I'll wait there till evening if need be. If he's still watching for Grushenka to arrive, then he'll most probably come to the summer-house...' Alyosha had not actually considered his plan in much detail, but he decided to carry it out, although it would mean that he would be unable to go to the monastery that day...

Everything went without a hitch; he climbed over the fence at almost exactly the same place as before and slipped into the summer-house unobserved. He did not want to be seen; both the owner's wife and Foma (if he was there) might take his brother's side, accede to his request, and then might not let Alyosha into the garden or, alternatively, they might warn Dmitry that Alyosha was asking questions and looking for him. There was no one in the summer-house. Alyosha sat down on the same seat as the day before and began to wait. He looked around inside the summer-house. It seemed, for some reason, much shabbier than before; today it seemed to him really dilapidated. The day, however, was just as bright. The green table bore a circular stain that could have been from yesterday's spilt brandy. As always during tedious periods of waiting, empty and inappropriate thoughts crept into his mind; why, for example, on entering, had he sat in exactly the same spot as the day before, and not in any other? In the end he began to feel downcast, with a sadness that stemmed from a worrying uncertainty. But he had not been sitting there a quarter of an hour when he heard, from somewhere very close by, the sound of chords being played on a guitar. Someone was sitting, or had just sat down, among the bushes, about twenty paces from him at the most. Alyosha suddenly remembered that the previous day, as he was leaving his brother, he had glimpsed a small green bench among the bushes, not more than twenty paces to his left. Probably there were people sitting there now. But who? A man's voice began to sing in a sweet falsetto to the accompaniment of a guitar:

> I am joined to my love
> By an invincible force.
> God have mercy,
> On her, on me!
> On her, on me!
> On her, on me!

The singing stopped. It was a cloying, affected tenor voice. Suddenly, another voice, a woman's, spoke caressingly and somewhat timidly, but also with much affectation.

'Why haven't you been to see us all this time, Pavel Fyodorovich, why do you neglect us?'

'Nothing of the kind,' replied the man's voice firmly and with dignity, but politely. Clearly, the man was the dominant person, and the woman was playing up to him. 'Surely that's Smerdyakov,' thought Alyosha, 'it sounds like his voice, and I suppose the woman's the daughter of the house, the one who's just arrived from Moscow, wears a dress with a train, and goes to Marfa Ignatyevna for soup...'

'I adore poetry when it all fits nicely together,' continued the woman's voice. 'Why don't you go on?'

The man began singing again:

> Provided my dear one's well—
> What's one Tsar's crown to me?
> Lord have mercy,
> On her, on me!
> On her, on me!
> On her, on me!

'Last time it sounded even better,' remarked the woman's voice. 'In the bit about the crown you sang: "if my little darling's well". That sounded more tender, you probably forgot today.'

'Poetry's rubbish,' cut in Smerdyakov.

'Oh no, I really love the poetry bits.'

'When it comes to poetry, it's a lot of rubbish. Just think about it: who in the world speaks in rhyme? And if we all began to speak in rhyme, even if it was by order of the authorities, would we really say anything much? Poetry's irrelevant, Marya Kondratyevna.'

'How do you come to be so intelligent? Where does it all come from?' The woman's voice sounded more and more caressing.

'You don't know the half of it; given the chance I'd have shown you a thing or two, but it wasn't to be, right from the day I was born. I'd have shot dead with a pistol in a duel any man who called me a scoundrel because I was Smerdyashchaya's bastard; I used to get taunted about that even in Moscow, where they knew all about it thanks to Grigory Vasilyevich. Grigory Vasilyevich reproaches me that I resent having being born: "You", he says, "tore her guts out."* That's all very well, but I'd rather they'd killed me in my mother's womb and not let me come into the world at all. They used to say in the market—and even your mother, crude that she is, couldn't resist telling me—that she went around with filthy, matted hair and that she was scarcely two *arshins* and a *bit*. Why "a bit", why not say "just over", like everyone else does? Deep down, all this folksy talk is nothing but peasant sentimentality. I ask you, is a Russian peasant worthy of holding a candle to an educated person? Being the yokel that he is, he's not fit for anything. Ever since I was little, whenever I heard that "a bit", it used to drive me up the wall. I hate the whole of Russia, Marya Kondratyevna.'

'If you were an army cadet or a dashing young hussar, you

wouldn't talk like that, you'd seize your sabre and defend all of
Russia.'

'Not only would I not want to be a dashing hussar, Marya
Kondratyevna, but on the contrary I'd gladly do away with all
soldiers.'

'And when the enemy came, who'd defend us?'

'There'd be absolutely no need. In 1812 Russia was invaded
by Emperor Napoleon 1, the father* of the present one, and it
would have been an excellent thing if we'd have been conquered
by the French; an intelligent nation would have overpowered a
thoroughly stupid one and annexed it. Everything would have
been different.'

'As though, where they come from, they were any better than
our own lot! There are some of our young blades I wouldn't
swap for three young Englishmen,' said Marya Kondratyevna
tenderly, no doubt accompanying these words with a most
languid gaze.

'Each to his own, in a manner of speaking.'

'You yourself are just like a foreigner to us, a most distinguished foreigner, I don't mind telling you.'

'If you want to know, when it comes to depravity there's
nothing to choose between them and us. They're all blackguards,
but there they walk about in patent leather boots while our
scoundrels go around like stinking beggars and don't see anything wrong in it. The Russian people need thrashing, as Fyodor
Pavlovich quite rightly said yesterday, even if he is mad, and all
his offspring to boot.'

'You said yourself, you respect Ivan Fyodorovich.'

'And he treats me like a stinking lackey. He thinks I may
rebel, but he's wrong. If I had money in my pocket, I'd have
upped and left long ago. Dmitry Fyodorovich is worse than any
lackey in his behaviour, his way of thinking, and his poverty; he's
a good-for-nothing—but that doesn't stop him being respected
by everyone. As for me, you could say I'm no more than a soup-
stirrer, and yet given half a chance I could open a restaurant in
Moscow on Petrovka,* because I can do *haute cuisine*, which
none of them in Moscow can do, except foreigners. Dmitry
Fyodorovich is a guttersnipe, yet he could challenge the noblest
count's son and he would agree to fight a duel with him, but how

is he any better than me? He's far stupider than me. Look how much money he's squandered without having anything to show for it.'

'I think a duel must be ever so exciting,' remarked Marya Kondratyevna suddenly.

'What do you mean exactly?'

'It's so frightening and so brave of them, especially when young officers with drawn pistols fire at each other over a girl. You can just picture it. If only they'd let girls watch; I'd just love to watch.'

'It's fine if you're the one who's pointing the pistol, but if someone else is aiming at you smack between the eyes, you feel pretty stupid. You'd run a mile, Maria Kondratyevna.'

'Surely *you* wouldn't run away?'

Smerdyakov did not deign to reply. After a moment's silence another chord sounded and the falsetto voice began the last verse:

> No matter what you do,
> Off I shall go,
> And enjo-oy life so.
> In the capital I shall live!
> I shall not grieve,
> Not at all shall I grieve,
> Not the least bit shall I grieve.

All of a sudden there was an unexpected interruption; Alyosha suddenly sneezed. The two people on the bench fell silent. Alyosha stood up and walked over to them. It was indeed Smerdyakov, all dressed up, wearing patent leather boots and with his hair pomaded and looking almost as if it had been curled. His guitar lay on the bench. The woman was indeed Marya Kondratyevna, the daughter of the owner of the house; she was wearing a pale-blue dress with a two-*arshin* train; she was still quite a young girl, and would have been not bad-looking had it not been for her very round face and unsightly freckles.

'Will my brother Dmitry be back soon?' asked Alyosha as calmly as he could.

Smerdyakov got up slowly from the bench; Marya Kondratyevna also stood up.

'Why should I know anything about Dmitry Fyodorovich? It would be a different matter if I'd been meant to keep guard over him,' replied Smerdyakov softly, distinctly, and with disdain.

'I merely asked if you knew,' explained Alyosha.

'I know nothing of his whereabouts and, what's more, I don't wish to know.'

'But my brother specifically told me that it was you who kept him informed about everything that went on in the house, and that you'd promised to let him know when Agrafena Aleksandrovna came.'

Slowly and imperturbably Smerdyakov raised his eyes and looked at Alyosha.

'And how did you manage to get in this time, seeing that the gate here has already been locked for an hour?' he asked, gazing fixedly at Alyosha.

'I went along the alley, climbed over the fence, and went straight into the summer-house. I hope you will forgive me for this,' he addressed Marya Kondratyevna. 'I had to catch my brother as soon as possible.'

'Oh, how can we be offended by you?' drawled Marya Kondratyevna, flattered by Alyosha's apology. 'After all, Dmitry Fyodorovich gets into the summer-house the same way; sometimes we don't even realize that he's already there, sitting in the summer-house.'

'It's very urgent that I find him. I really need to see him or to find out from you where he is now. Believe me, it's about something of the utmost importance to him.'

'He doesn't keep us in the picture,' prattled Marya Kondratyevna.

'I've been coming here purely on social visits,' Smerdyakov continued, 'but even here he keeps on pestering me with endless questions about the master; how things are there, who's coming and going, and can't I tell him this or that. Twice he's threatened to kill me.'

'What do you mean, kill you?' cried Alyosha, astonished.

'He wouldn't think twice about it, what with his character, which you had the pleasure of observing for yourself yesterday. "If", he says to me, "you let Agrafena Aleksandrovna slip past and she spends the night here, you're as good as dead." I'm scared to death of him, and by rights I should have gone to the local authorities to warn them about him, only that scares me even more. God knows what he might do.'

'The other day he said to him, "I'll grind you in a mortar",' added Marya Kondratyevna.

'Well, if he said that, perhaps it's just talk...', remarked Alyosha. 'If I could only see him for a second I could tackle him about it...'

'There's only one thing I can tell you,' said Smerdyakov, as if he had suddenly come to a decision. 'I come here out of normal neighbourly friendliness; after all, why shouldn't I? On the other hand, Ivan Fyodorovich sent me before daybreak today to Dmitry Fyodorovich at his rooms in Ozernaya Street, no letter or anything, to tell him myself to be sure to come to this inn on the square to have lunch with him. I went, but I didn't find Dmitry Fyodorovich at home, and it was only eight o'clock. "He was here," they said, "but he's gone out"—those were the exact words the landlord and his wife used. It looks as if there's some sort of plot between your two brothers. Perhaps right now, at this very minute, he's sitting in that inn with Ivan Fyodorovich, since Ivan Fyodorovich hasn't been home for lunch, and Fyodor Pavlovich lunched alone an hour ago and is now taking a nap. But I beg you, don't say anything to him about me or about what I've told you; don't say anything, otherwise he's sure to kill me.'

'Ivan invited Dmitry to come to the inn?' Alyosha queried quickly.

'Exactly.'

'To *The Stolichny Gorod*, the inn on the square?'

'That's the one.'

'That's quite possible,' exclaimed Alyosha in great excitement. 'Thank you, Smerdyakov, you've been very helpful. I'll go there straight away.'

'Don't let on I told you,' Smerdyakov called after him.

'Oh no, I'll turn up at the inn as if by chance, don't worry.'

'Where are you going? I'll open the gate for you,' cried Marya Kondratyevna.

'No, it's quicker this way; I'll go over the fence again.'

The news had really shaken Alyosha. He hurried to the inn. It would be unseemly for him to enter the inn in his cassock, but he could enquire at the entrance and get someone to fetch them. However, no sooner had he reached the inn than a window opened and Ivan himself called down to him.

'Alyosha, can you come up or not? I'd be really grateful.'

'Of course I can, but what about my cassock?'

'I'm in a private room, go round to the front and I'll come down and meet you...'

A minute later, Alyosha was sitting with his brother. Ivan was alone, eating his lunch.

3

THE BROTHERS GET TO KNOW EACH OTHER

IVAN was not in a private room, however. It was merely an alcove by the window, partitioned off by a screen, but all the same anyone sitting behind the screen could not be seen from the room. This was the first room one encountered on entering the inn, and it had a dresser against the side wall. Waiters dashed through it every minute or so. As for the customers, there was only one old man, a retired soldier, drinking tea in a corner. But in the other rooms there was all the normal bustle of an inn; one could hear orders being shouted, beer bottles being opened, the click of billiard balls, and the droning of a harmonium. Alyosha knew that Ivan hardly ever came to this inn and that he did not normally frequent inns. Therefore he was here, it seemed to him, for a prearranged meeting with Dmitry. Only Dmitry was not there.

'Shall I order you some fish soup or something? You can't live by tea alone,' said Ivan, evidently extremely pleased to have enticed Alyosha to enter the inn. He himself had already finished his lunch and was drinking tea.

'I'll have some fish soup and then some tea; I'm starving,' said Alyosha cheerfully.

'And some cherry preserve? It's on the menu here. Do you remember how you used to love cherry preserve at Polyonov's when you were little?'

'Fancy you remembering that! Yes, let's have some preserve, I'm still partial to it.'

Ivan rang for the waiter and ordered fish soup, tea, and preserve.

'I remember everything, Alyosha, I remember you up to the age of eleven, I was nearly fifteen then. Fifteen and eleven, that's such a big difference that brothers are never friends at that age. I don't even know if I liked you. When I went away to Moscow I didn't even think about you for the first few years. Then when you came to Moscow we met only once, I think, somewhere. And now I've been living here for over three months and we haven't exchanged a word. I'm leaving tomorrow and I was just thinking, sitting here, "When can I see him to say goodbye?" and just at that moment you happened to turn up.'

'And did you really want to see me?'

'Very much. I want to get to know you at last, and you to get to know me. And then, adieu. In my opinion the best time to get to know someone is before a farewell. I've seen how you looked at me these last three months; there was a kind of perpetual anticipation in your eyes, and that's what I couldn't bear; that's why I avoided you. But in the end I learned to respect you; "The boy's got guts," I said to myself. Mind you, I may laugh at it now, but I'm talking seriously. Well, you have got guts, haven't you? I like people who stand by their beliefs, whatever they are, even if they're little scallywags like you. In the end your expectant gaze no longer irritated me; on the contrary, in the end I even got to like your expectant gaze... I think for some reason you're fond of me, Alyosha, aren't you?'

'Yes, I am, Ivan. Dmitry says about you, "Ivan is the soul of discretion." I always say, "Ivan's an enigma." You're still an enigma to me, but there's one thing about you that I've worked out, but only since this morning!'

'What's that?' laughed Ivan.

'You won't be angry?' Alyosha laughed too.

'No, go on.'

'That you're just the same as any other young man of twenty-three, just as young and impressionable, just as wholesome and splendid, just a fledgling! Well, have I offended you very much?'

'On the contrary, I'm struck by the coincidence,' exclaimed Ivan warmly and cheerfully. 'Would you believe it, ever since we saw Katerina Ivanovna this morning, I haven't stopped thinking about it, about the way I behaved just like a naïve twenty-three-year-old, and suddenly, as if you'd guessed it, you came straight out with it. I was just sitting here, and you know what I was thinking to myself? "Take away my belief in life, my trust in a good woman, destroy my faith in the order of things, convince me that, on the contrary, everything is just chaos, disordered, damned, and perhaps diabolical, drive me to despair at the thought of losing all earthly hope—I shall still want to go on living; having put this goblet to my lips, I shall not tear them away until I have drained it! Or rather, when I'm getting on for thirty, I shall probably throw the goblet away even if I haven't emptied it, and leave for good... I don't know where. But until I'm thirty, of one thing I'm sure, my youth will triumph over everything—all disillusion, all revulsion against life, everything. I've asked myself many times whether there's a despair on earth that's powerful enough to extinguish this frenzied, perhaps even indecent, thirst for life in me, and I decided that apparently there was not, at least not before the age of thirty, and then I'll no longer want it, or so it seems to me. Some feeble, snivelling moralists, especially poets, condemn this thirst for life as vile. This trait, this thirst for life, is in one sense, it's true, a typical Karamazov trait—in spite of everything you have it too—but why should it be vile? A very strong centripetal force exists on our planet, Alyosha. I want to live, and I do live, although it's against all logic. I may not believe in an ordered world, but the tiny, sticky leaf-buds of spring are dear to me, the blue sky is dear to me, one or two people are dear to me—though for the life of me I sometimes really wonder why—and so is the occasional human achievement, which perhaps I long ago ceased to believe in, but nevertheless still can't help respecting from sheer nostalgia. Here's your soup, tuck in. The fish soup's excellent, the food's good here. I want to take a trip to Europe, Alyosha, and I shall leave straight from here. I know I shall be going to a graveyard, but to the dearest, most beloved graveyard! The beloved departed lie there, each gravestone testifying to such splendid past lives, to such passionate, fervent belief in their achievements, in their truth, in their struggles and in their learning, that I know already that I shall fall to my knees and kiss those stones and weep over them—and all the time knowing in my heart that it has long been a graveyard and nothing more. And I shall weep, not from despair, but simply out of happiness that I'm shedding tears. I shall be intoxicated by my own emotions. I love the tiny, sticky spring leaves, the blue sky, so there it is! There's no sense in it, no logic, it's instinct, it's a gut feeling; one loves one's first youthful impulses... Do you understand anything of my nonsense, Alyosha, or not?' Ivan laughed suddenly.

'Only too well, Ivan,' exclaimed Alyosha, 'a longing to love instinctively from the depth of one's being—you put that beautifully, and I'm so happy you have such an urge to live. I think that everyone should, above all else on this earth, love life.'

'Love life rather than the meaning of it?'

'Certainly, it must come before logic, as you said, it must certainly come before logic, for only then can one come to understand the meaning. I've thought that for a long time already. You're half-way there, Ivan, half your task is accomplished; you love life. Now you have to tackle the next half, and then you're saved.'

'You're saving me already, though perhaps I was never in danger of perishing! But what is this second half of yours?'

'You have to resurrect your dead, who maybe never died anyway. Come on, let's have some tea. I'm glad we're talking, Ivan.'

'I can see you're feeling optimistic. I love, I really love, these *professions de foi** from such... novices. You're a resolute fellow, Aleksei. Is it true you want to leave the monastery?'

'Yes, it is. My starets is sending me out into the world.'

'So, we'll meet again out in the world, we'll meet before that thirtieth year when I begin to tear the cup from my lips. Father, you know, doesn't want to tear himself from his cup before he's seventy, he even dreams of keeping it up till he's eighty, he says so himself; he's quite serious about it, even if he is an old buffoon. He's used his sensuality as a rock to cling to, except that... perhaps after thirty there isn't much else to hold on to... But to persevere till seventy is obscene, it'd be better to give up at thirty; that way one can preserve a modicum of decency while deceiving oneself. You haven't seen Dmitry today, have you?'

'No, I haven't, but I saw Smerdyakov,' and Alyosha gave his brother a rapid but detailed account of his meeting with Smerdyakov. Ivan suddenly began to listen attentively, and even asked him to repeat certain details.

'But he asked me not to tell Dmitry that he'd discussed him,' added Alyosha.

Ivan frowned and became pensive.

'Is it because of Smerdyakov that you're frowning?' asked Alyosha.

'Yes. To hell with him! It's Dmitry I really wanted to see, but now it's no use...', grunted Ivan.

'Are you really going away so soon, Ivan?'

'Yes.'

'And what about Dmitry and father? How is it all going to end between them?' said Alyosha anxiously.

'You're still harping on about that! What's it got to do with me? Am I my brother Dmitry's keeper?' snapped Ivan irritably, but then he suddenly smiled somewhat bitterly. 'Cain's answer to God about his murdered brother, eh? Perhaps that's what you're thinking at this moment? But dammit, I really can't be expected to stay here to watch over them, can I? I've finished my business and I'm going. Surely you don't think I'm jealous of Dmitry, or that for the last three months I've been trying to steal his beautiful Katerina Ivanovna from him, do you? For heaven's sake I've had other fish to fry. I've completed my business and I'm off. It's all over now; you saw what happened.'

'This morning at Katerina Ivanovna's?'

'Yes, I made a clean break. And so what? Why drag Dmitry into this? Dmitry's got nothing to do with it. I had business of my own with Katerina Ivanovna. You know yourself that in fact Dmitry made it look as if he was in cahoots with me. I never asked him for anything; it was he himself who solemnly handed her to me on a plate. You have to laugh at it all. Listen, Alyosha, if only you knew what relief I feel now! I've been sitting here having lunch and, believe me, I wanted to order some champagne to celebrate my first hour of freedom. Phew, six months nearly— and suddenly at one go I'm shot of the whole thing. Little did I think yesterday that if you wanted to finish a relationship, it could all be over and done with just like that!'

'Are you talking about your love, Ivan?'

'Yes, if you like, you can call it love. I fell in love with a young girl, a schoolgirl. We made life hell for each other. I was obsessed with her... and suddenly it was all over. This morning when I was talking to her I was inspired, but when I left, I burst out laughing—believe me. I'm telling the truth.'

'You're still cheerful now,' remarked Alyosha, glancing at his face, which had indeed suddenly lit up.

'Well, how was I to know that I didn't love her at all? Ha-ha, and it turns out that I didn't. And yet I was so fond of her! You won't believe how fond of her I was, even when I was holding forth this morning. Would you believe it, I still like her terribly, and yet how easy it is to break with her! Do you think I'm exaggerating?'

'No. Only perhaps that wasn't true love.'

'Alyosha,' laughed Ivan, 'don't start philosophizing about love! It doesn't become you. Oh, how you let fly this morning! I should have hugged you for that... But she was tormenting me so! I was really sitting on a volcano. Oh, she knew that I loved her! It was me she loved, and not Dmitry,' Ivan continued cheerfully. 'Dmitry was just an excuse for emotional self-indulgence. Everything I said to her this morning was the absolute truth. Only, what you have to understand is that it will take her perhaps fifteen or twenty years to realize that she doesn't love Dmitry at all, that she loves only me, whom she torments. Or maybe she'll never realize it, in spite of today's lesson. Well, it's all for the best; I've made a stand and left her for good. Incidentally, how is she now? What happened after I left?'

Alyosha told him of her hysterical outburst and that she was now delirious.

'That Khokhlakova woman could be lying?'

'Apparently not.'

'We'll have to find out. Anyway, nobody has ever died of hysterics. Hysterics, huh! God, in his love for them, gave women hysterics. I shan't go to her place. What's the use of getting involved again?'

'All the same, you did say to her this morning that she'd never loved you.'

'I said it deliberately. Alyosha, I'm going to order some champagne and we'll drink to my freedom. Oh, if only you knew how happy I am!'

'No, Ivan, we'd better not drink,' said Alyosha suddenly. 'And anyway, I'm sad in a way.'

'Yes, you've been sad for a long time; I've noticed it for a while.'

'So you're definitely leaving tomorrow morning?'

'In the morning? No, I didn't say I was going in the morning... But perhaps I will after all. You know, I had lunch here today purely so as not to have to eat with the old man, he's begun to disgust me so much. If it were only him, I'd have gone long ago. But why are you so worried about my leaving? Lord knows how much time we have before I leave. Ages and ages, a whole eternity!'

'If you leave tomorrow, how can it be an eternity?'

'Well, what's that to us?' laughed Ivan. 'Surely we'll find time to discuss what interests us, what we came here to talk about, won't we? Why are you looking so surprised? Answer me. What did we come here for? To talk about my love for Katerina Ivanovna, about the old man and Dmitry? About foreign parts? About the disastrous situation in Russia? About the Emperor Napoleon? Is that what we came here for?'

'No, not for that.'

'That means you do understand what we came for. Others have their own problems to discuss, but for us young fledglings the main thing is to resolve the eternal questions, that's our concern. All the youth of Russia now talks of nothing but the eternal questions. Especially now, when all the old ones are suddenly getting together to concern themselves with practical matters. Why have you been looking at me so expectantly for the past three months? To ask me, "Do you believe or don't you believe at all?"* That's what your glances of these three months have been leading up to, Aleksei Fyodorovich, haven't they?'

'Perhaps that's it,' smiled Alyosha. 'You're not laughing at me now, are you?'

'Me, laughing? I wouldn't want to distress my little brother, who's been staring at me in such expectation for three months. Alyosha, take a good look at me. I'm just a little boy, exactly like you, except that I'm not a novice. After all, how have Russian boys always behaved? Some of them, anyway. Here, for example, in this stinking little inn, they come and sit in a corner. All their previous lives they haven't got to know each other, they walk out of the inn and, forty years later, they still won't know each other, so what are they going to discuss when they snatch a minute at the inn? The universal questions, what else! Does God exist? Is there such a thing as immortality? And those that don't believe in God will start to talk about socialism and anarchism, about refashioning mankind according to some new system. Well, they'll all end up in a hell of a mess, the same damned questions just looked at from opposite points of view. And on the whole, the most original of our young Russians in this day and age spend all their time talking about eternal questions. Isn't that so?'

'Yes; for true Russians, of course, the questions that arise first and foremost are whether God exists, whether there is such a thing as immortality, or, as you say, it's a matter of looking at the issue from opposite points of view, and that's only right and proper,' said Alyosha, looking at his brother all the while with that same quiet, searching smile.

'Sometimes, Alyosha, to be Russian is not to be at all clever, but all the same one can't imagine anything more absurd than the questions that interest the Russian youth today. But there's one Russian youth—you, Alyoshka—whom I love very dearly.'

'How cleverly you led up to that,' laughed Alyosha.

'Well now, where shall we start? You tell me—with God? Does God exist or not?'

'Start wherever you like, from "the opposite point of view", if you prefer. After all, yesterday, at father's, you said that there was no God.' Alyosha glanced probingly at his brother.

'Yesterday at dinner at the old man's I said that deliberately to provoke you, and I could see your eyes flashing. But now I feel like discussing it with you, and I'm being perfectly serious. I want to get closer to you, Alyosha, because I have no friends, so I'd like to try. Now, try to imagine that I too, perhaps, accept God,' laughed Ivan. 'You didn't expect that, did you, eh?'

'Of course I didn't; that is, provided you're really being serious now.'

'Serious? Yesterday at the starets's they said I wasn't serious. Look, my dear brother, in the eighteenth century there was one old sinner who claimed that if there were no God, it would be necessary to invent him: *s'il n'existait pas Dieu il faudrait l'inventer.** And man really has invented God. But that's not what's strange—what's amazing is not that God actually exists; what's amazing is that such an idea—the idea of the necessity of God—could enter the head of such a savage and evil creature as man, an idea so holy, so moving, so wise, and which does so much honour to man. As for me, I've long since given up wondering whether man created God, or God man. It goes without saying that I'm not going to start wading through all the latest axioms spouted by Russian youth on this subject, all of them without exception drawn from European hypotheses; because what constitutes a hypothesis in Europe immediately becomes an axiom to Russian youth—and not only to the young, but perhaps to their professors too, because Russian professors themselves are very often just like those same Russian youngsters. So, I shall avoid all hypotheses. Well then, what is the question that concerns us now, you and me? It is this: I have to explain to you as quickly as possible what is the essential me, that is, what sort of person I am, what I believe in and what I hope for, that's it, isn't it? And so I declare that I accept God purely and simply. Here, however, we have to accept the fact that if God exists and if He really did create the world, He created it, as we know full well, according to Euclidean geometry, and gave man a mind that can understand only three dimensions of space. However, there have been, and are even now, even amongst the most eminent mathematicians and philosophers, some who question whether the whole universe or, to take it even further, the whole of existence, was created purely according to Euclidean theory; they even venture to suggest that two parallel lines, which according to Euclid cannot meet on earth under any circumstances, will perhaps meet somewhere at infinity.* I decided, my dear fellow, that if I couldn't even understand that, then how could I presume to understand God? I humbly admit that I don't have the ability to decide such questions. I have a Euclidean mind, a terrestrial mind, and so I maintain that we cannot decide questions that are not of this world. And I advise you too, Alyosha, my friend, never to think about such things, especially about God and whether He exists or not. These questions are most definitely unsuited to a mind created with an understanding of only three dimensions. And so, I accept God, and not only do I wholeheartedly accept Him, but, what's more, I accept his wisdom and his unfathomable plan, I believe in order, in the meaning of life, I believe in the eternal harmony into which, so it is said, we shall all melt, I believe in the Word* towards which the universe is moving, which is "in God" and which is God, and so on and so forth, *ad infinitum.* A lot has been written and said on that subject. I seem to be on the right path, don't I? Well then, consider this: in the final analysis I reject this God-created universe, and although I know it exists, I reject it out of hand. It is not God that I don't accept—understand that—it's His creation, His world that I reject and that I cannot agree to accept. Let me put it another way: even though I'm convinced, with a childlike faith, that suffering will be relieved and eliminated, that all the obscene comedy of human contradictions will vanish like a pitiful mirage, like a sordid invention of the Euclidean mind of man, feeble and puny, minuscule as an atom, and that at last on the day of reckoning, at the moment of eternal harmony, something so precious will occur and come to pass that, in every heart, it will suffice to assuage every indignity, expiate every evil committed by men, all the blood spilt by men, that it will suffice not only for the forgiveness but also for the justification of everything that has happened on earth—let it, let it all be so and let it all come to pass, but I still do not accept it and have no wish to accept it! Let parallel lines meet and let me see it with my own eyes: I will see it and I will say that they have met, and yet at the same time I will not accept it. There, Alyosha, there you have my thesis, the essence of my being. This time I have spoken in all seriousness. I purposely began our conversation as absurdly as I could, but I have led up to my confession, because that's all you need. You didn't want to hear me talk about God; you only want to find out what makes your favourite brother tick. There, now you know.'

Ivan concluded his long exposition suddenly and with unaccustomed and unexpected emotion.

'But why did you begin "as absurdly as you could"?' asked Alyosha, looking at him thoughtfully.

'Well, in the first place, simply to keep it in the Russian tradition; in Russia all conversations about such matters are always conducted in the most absurd manner possible. And secondly, because the more absurd the approach, the closer one gets to the crux of the matter. Clarity in absurdity. Absurdity is direct and guileless, whereas the intellect is evasive and illusive. The intellect is a blackguard, but absurdity is undeviating and honourable. I have steered the argument towards what fills me with despair, and the more absurdly I've presented it, the closer I've got to the truth.'

'Are you going to explain to me why you "do not accept the world"?' asked Alyosha.

'But of course; it's no secret. That's what I was leading up to. My little brother, I don't want to corrupt you or undermine your faith; perhaps I want to redeem myself through you,' Ivan smiled suddenly, just like a shy little boy. Alyosha had never seen him smile like that before.

4

REBELLION

'THERE'S one thing I have to confess to you,' began Ivan, 'I could never understand how one could love one's neighbour. In my opinion it's precisely those who are near to us that it is impossible to love, and one can love only those who are distant from us. I read something somewhere about a saint called "John the Merciful";* how on one occasion when a traveller, hungry and frozen, came to him and asked for warmth, he lay down with him in his bed, embraced him, and began to breathe into his mouth, which was purulent and stinking from some dreadful disease. I'm sure that he did so with a certain degree of hypocrisy, in response to a dutiful love, as a self-imposed penance. One can love a man only when he's out of sight; as soon as he shows his face, that's the end of love.'

'Starets Zosima said that more than once,' said Alyosha. 'He also said that in the case of many who were inexperienced in the art of loving, a man's face was often a hindrance to love. And yet, you know, there's a lot of love in mankind, even Christlike love; I know this personally, Ivan...'

'Well, I wouldn't know anything about that, and frankly it's beyond me, like it is too for countless other people. The question is: does this result from man's evil qualities, or is it simply in his nature? In my opinion the love of Christ for man is a kind of miracle that's impossible on earth. True, He was God. But we are not gods. Let us suppose that I, for example, suffer deeply; now, another person cannot know how deeply I suffer, because he is another person and not me, and then on top of that it is rare for one person to recognize the suffering of another—as if it were a question of rank. Why won't he agree to recognize it; what do you think? Because, perhaps, I smell, I have a stupid face, or because I once trod on his foot. What's more, there is suffering and suffering: my benefactor will accept that I may suffer from a degrading kind of suffering that humiliates me— hunger, for example—but that I may suffer from a rather nobler kind of suffering—suffer for an idea, for example—no, he'll rarely accept that, because he, for instance, will look at me and suddenly realize that, according to his preconceptions, my face is not the face of someone who suffers for an idea. So he immediately deprives me of his charity, but not at all from ill will. Beggars, especially well-born beggars, should never disclose their identity openly, but rather should appeal for charity in the newspapers. One can love one's neighbour in the abstract and sometimes even at a distance, but close up almost never. If only it were as it is on the stage, in the ballet, where beggars appear dressed in silk rags and torn lace and dance gracefully as they beg for alms, then one might be able to admire them. Admire, but still not love. But enough of that. I just had to give you my point of view. I wanted to start by talking about the suffering of mankind in general, but instead we'd better stick to the suffering of children. That will reduce the scale of my argument tenfold, so it will be better to stick to children. It's less favourable to my argument, of course. Well, first, one can love children even close up, even dirty or ugly children—although it seems to me that children can never be ugly. Secondly, if I don't speak of adults, it's also because, besides being repugnant and undeserving of love, they have retribution to make: they have eaten of the apple and know good and evil, and they have become "as gods".* And still they continue to eat of it. But children have eaten nothing and are still completely innocent. Do you love children, Alyosha? I know you do, and you'll understand why I just want to talk only about children now. If they also suffer terribly on this earth, then naturally they suffer for their fathers; they are punished for their fathers, who have eaten of the apple—but you know, that way of reasoning belongs to another world and is quite incomprehensible to the human mind on earth. The innocent—above all such innocents as these—should not have to suffer for others! You'll be surprised to hear, Alyosha, that I too love children very much. And note well that cruel, passionate people, with unbridled desires, like the Karamazovs, often have a great love of children. Children, while they're still children, say up to the age of seven, differ greatly from adults, as if they were a totally different species with a totally different nature. I knew a robber who was sent to prison; in the course of his life of crime he had massacred whole families in their homes while robbing them, and what's more he had cut the throats of several children on those occasions. But while he was in prison he showed an uncommon love for them. He would spend all his time looking out of the window of his cell, watching the children playing in the prison yard. He trained one little boy to come to his window, and they became great friends... You don't know, Alyosha, why I'm telling you all this, do you? I have a headache, and I feel sad.'

'You're talking strangely,' remarked Alyosha anxiously, 'as if you were in the grip of some madness.'

'Incidentally,' continued Ivan Fyodorovich, as if he had not heard his brother, 'not long ago a Bulgarian I met in Moscow was telling me about the atrocities being committed all over Bulgaria by the Turks and the Circassians,* who fear a mass uprising by the Slavs—it appears they set fire to homes and property, they cut people's throats, they rape women and children, they nail prisoners to the palisades by their ears and leave them there till the morning and then hang them, and so on; it really defies imagination. We often talk of man's "bestial" cruelty, but this is terribly unjust and insulting to beasts: a wild animal can never be as cruel as man, as artistic, as refined in his cruelty. The tiger mauls and tears its prey because that is all it knows. It would never enter its head to leave people all night nailed by their ears, even if it could do it. These Turks, incidentally, took a sadistic pleasure in torturing children, starting with cutting them out of their mothers' wombs with a dagger, and going so far as to throw babes-in-arms into the air and impale them on the points of their bayonets before their mothers' very eyes. Doing it before the mothers' eyes was what gave it particular piquancy. But here is one example that I find quite fascinating. Picture the scene: an infant in the arms of its trembling mother, surrounded by Turks. They have thought up an amusing game: they caress the child, laugh to make it laugh; they succeed, the child laughs. At just that moment a Turk aims his pistol at the child, six inches from its face.* The child chuckles gleefully, holds out its little hands to grab the pistol, and suddenly the evil joker discharges the pistol full in its face and blows its little head to pieces... Artistic, isn't it? By the way, they say Turks have a very sweet tooth.'

'Ivan, what's the point of all this?'

'I think that if the devil didn't exist and if man has created him, then he has created him in his own image and likeness.'

'You mean, the way he created God?'

'It's amazing how you manage "to crack the wind of the poor phrase",* as Polonius says in *Hamlet*,' laughed Ivan. 'You've caught me out, fair enough, I don't mind admitting it. He's fine, your God, if man has made him in his own image and likeness. You want to know what point I'm making, do you? You see, I'm a collector of certain little facts that appeal to me, and, would you believe it, I note down and save anecdotes of a particular kind from newspapers and stories, wherever I find them, and I already have a good collection. The Turks of course feature in the collection, but they're all foreigners. I have some stories from this part of the world too, and they're even better than the

Turkish ones. You know, with us it's more likely to be birching, flogging, and whipping,* it's a question of national characteristics. For us it would be unthinkable to nail someone up by the ears, after all, we're Europeans, but the birch, the whip—that's our speciality, and no one can take it away from us. Abroad, apparently, they don't allow flogging at all now, either because of a better social awareness or because the laws are such that a man daren't even lay a finger on another person, but then they've compensated for it in another way, as unique to them as our way is to us, so much so in fact that it would probably be impossible in Russia, although, incidentally, it seems it's beginning to catch on here, especially since the start of the religious movement among our upper classes. I have one delightful pamphlet translated from French, which describes the execution in Geneva, as recently as five years ago, of a criminal, a murderer, a youth of twenty-three called Richard, who it seems repented and was converted to Christianity when he was actually on the scaffold. This Richard was somebody's natural son and had been *given away* by his parents at the tender age of six to some shepherds in the Swiss mountains, who treated him like a slave. He had grown up with them like a young wild animal: the shepherds didn't teach him anything; on the contrary, when he was seven they sent him to graze the flocks in the wet and the cold, with hardly any clothes on and almost without any food. And, of course, they saw nothing wrong in this and felt no remorse for the way they treated him; indeed, they even considered themselves quite within their rights, as Richard had been given to them as one might donate an object, and they didn't even feel obliged to feed him. Richard himself testified that during those years, like the prodigal son in the Bible, he desperately wanted to eat the swill that they fed to the pigs they were fattening for sale, but they wouldn't even give him that and they beat him when he stole from the pigs, and that's how his whole childhood and youth were spent, until he grew big enough and strong enough to go stealing. This savage began to earn money as a day labourer in Geneva, drank all his wages, lived like an animal, and ended up by robbing and killing some old man. He was caught, tried, and sentenced to death. They're not sentimental in those parts. And there he was in prison, where he was at once surrounded by preachers and members of various Christian fraternities, philanthropic ladies, and so on. In prison they taught him to read and write, they expounded the Bible to him, appealed to his conscience, they exhorted him, nagged, admonished and pressured him until, in the end, he solemnly confessed to his crime. He was converted, and he himself wrote to the tribunal that he was a monster but that he had been privileged to see the light, and God had blessed him with His grace. The whole of Geneva was moved, all the pious and philanthropic people of Geneva. All the most high-born and well-brought-up people rushed to visit him in prison; they embraced and kissed Richard, saying, "You are our brother, you have been touched by the grace of God!" And Richard himself just wept from emotion: "Yes, I have been touched by the grace of God! All through my childhood and youth I was grateful for pigswill, but now I have been blessed and will die in a state of grace!" "Yes, yes, you will die in the Lord, you have shed blood and you must die in the Lord. Granted, you are innocent, you knew nothing of the Lord when you envied the pigs their food and when you were beaten for stealing it (though you did wrong because it is forbidden to steal)—nevertheless, you still shed blood and you must die." Then his last day dawned. Richard, weakened, did nothing but weep, and kept repeating, "This is the best day of my life, I am going to my God!" "Yes," cried the pastors, the judges, and the philanthropic ladies, "this is your happiest day, for you are going to the Lord!" They all wended their way in their carriages or on foot behind the tumbril in which Richard was being transported to the scaffold. "Die, dear brother," they called to Richard when they reached the scaffold, "die in the Lord, for you have been touched by the grace of God." And so, smothered with the kisses of his brothers, brother Richard was dragged on to the scaffold, his head was placed under the guillotine and fraternally chopped off for having been touched by the grace of God. Isn't that just typical! That pamphlet was translated into Russian by some aristocratic Russian Lutheran philanthropists and was distributed free with newspapers and other publications for the edification of the Russian people. The interesting thing about Richard's case is that it's typical of that country. Here it is considered mad to cut off your brother's head simply because he's become your brother and has been touched by the grace of God, but, as I've already said, we have a custom of our own that would almost match it. Historically, the infliction of pain by beating has been our favourite national pastime. Nekrasov* wrote a poem about a peasant who lashes a horse across its eyes, its "gentle eyes". Who hasn't seen such things; it's the Russian way. He describes a feeble old nag, overburdened, getting stuck with her load and unable to drag it. The peasant beats her and beats her until, intoxicated by his own cruelty, he no longer knows what he's doing and is raining countless, painful blows on her. "Even if you haven't the strength, pull; even if it kills you, go on, pull!" The defenceless old horse strains at the harness, and he begins to beat her on her weeping "gentle eyes". Beside herself with terror, she makes a supreme effort and, trembling all over, scarcely breathing, starts to stagger with a kind of stumbling, crab-like motion, somehow unnatural and shameful—Nekrasov portrays the full horror of it. But after all, it's only a horse, and God Himself created horses to be beaten. The Tatars taught us that and left us the knout as a memento. But you know, one can thrash human beings too. An educated, cultured couple beat their own daughter with a birch, a little girl of seven*—I took detailed notes of this. Her father was glad they had left the switches with butts on them—"that'll hurt more", he says—and begins to lay about his own daughter. I know there are people who certainly take a sadistic pleasure in thrashing, enjoying every stroke literally to the point of ecstasy, becoming progressively more frenzied with every stroke. They start off by thrashing for a minute, and finish by thrashing for five minutes, ten minutes, even longer, and harder and quicker. The child screams and then at last can't scream any more and sobs, "Papa, papa!" By some devilish twist of fate the matter comes to court. A lawyer is engaged. The Russian people have long called a lawyer a "hired conscience". The lawyer protests in defence of his client, "It's just a simple ordinary domestic matter, a father chastising his daughter, and that's all there is to it—it's a shameful sign of our times that the case was ever brought to court!" The jury are convinced, they retire and bring in a verdict of "not guilty". The public whoops with delight to see the torturer acquitted. Alas, I wasn't there, otherwise I'd have shouted out that a foundation should be set up in honour of the torturer!... A pretty picture, isn't it?... But I have even better ones of children, I've lots more of Russian children, Alyosha. A little girl of five* was abused by her parents, "decent and most respectable people, well educated and cultured". You see, once more I firmly maintain that in many people there's a particular trait, and that's a delight in torturing children, but only children. Towards the rest of humanity these same torturers are considerate, even gentle, as befits educated and humanitarian Europeans, but they love to torture children; in a sense, that's their way of loving children. It's precisely the defencelessness and the angelic trust of children that seduces these cruel people; the children have nowhere to run and no one to turn to—that's what inflames the vile instincts of the torturer. Of course, in every person there lurks a beast, a demon of fury, whose passions are inflamed by the cries of the victim, an unrestrained wild beast loosed from his chains, a beast riddled with disease contracted through debauchery—gout, liver disorder, and so on. Those educated parents subjected that poor little five-year-old to every conceivable torture. They beat her, whipped her, kicked her till she was black and blue, all for no reason. Finally, they thought of the ultimate punishment; they shut her up all night in the outside privy, in the cold and the frost, because she wet herself at night (as if a five-year-old, sleeping soundly like an angel, could excuse herself in time)— for this, they smeared her face with her excrement and forced her to eat it, and it was her mother, her mother who did this to her! And that mother slept unconcernedly at night, oblivious to the sobs of the poor child shut up in that foul place! Can you understand such a thing: that small child, unable even to comprehend what is being done to her, in the dark and the cold of that foul place, beating her little panting breast with her tiny fists, sobbing, weeping humble tears of bloodstained innocence, praying to "Dear Father God" to protect her—do you understand this obscenity, my friend, my brother, my holy and meek monk, do you understand why such an obscenity should be so necessary, and what is the point of it? They say that without it man could not live on this earth, for he would not understand the difference between good and evil. Why should one under-

stand that damned difference between good and evil if that's the
price to be paid? All the knowledge in the world is not worth that
child's tearful prayers to "Dear Father God". I'm not talking
about the suffering of adults, they have eaten of the apple, they
can go to the devil and suffer all the fires of hell, but the little
ones, the children! I'm making you suffer, Alyosha, you seem
distressed. I'll stop if you like.'

'It's all right. I'm happy to suffer too,' muttered Alyosha.

'Just one more example, just for curiosity's sake. It's very
typical. I just read about it in some antiquarian collection, *The
Archive* or *Ancient Times*, I forget which; I'll have to check. It was
during the very darkest period of feudal times, at the beginning
of the century—thank God for our Tsar Liberator!* At that
time, at the beginning of the century, there lived a certain
General, a fabulously rich landowner* with connections in high
places. He was one of those individuals (even then it seems
they were very few in number) who, having retired from active
service, were almost convinced that they had earned the right of
life and death over their serfs. Such people existed then. Well,
this General lived on his estates with two thousand serfs. He
considered himself very high and mighty, and treated his poorer
neighbours as spongers and made them the butt of his jokes. He
had kennels with hundreds of dogs, and close on a hundred
huntsmen, all in uniform and all on horseback. Well, a little serf
boy, not more than eight years old, threw a stone while playing
and hit the paw of the General's favourite hound. "Why's my
favourite dog limping?" They explained to him that apparently
this child had thrown a stone at it and hurt its paw. "Aha, it was
you, was it?" said the General, taking a good look at him. "Seize
him!" They seized him, dragged him away from his mother, and
locked him up all night in a closet. At dawn the General emerged
all ready for the hunt; he sat on his horse, surrounded by his
retainers, his dogs, his servants, and his huntsmen on horseback.
All the domestic staff were assembled for their edification, and
in front of them all was the mother of the guilty boy. The boy
was brought out of the lock-up. It was a dark, cold, foggy autumn
day, splendid for hunting. The General ordered that the child
be undressed, and he stood there stark naked, shivering and
petrified with fear, not daring to make a sound... "Make him

run!" ordered the General. "Run, run!" the huntsmen shouted at him, and the boy ran... "After him!" roared the General, and set his whole pack of borzoi hounds on him. Before his mother's very eyes, the child was hunted down and torn to pieces by the dogs!... The General had his estates put into trusteeship, I believe. Well... what should they have done with him? Shot him? Should he have been shot to gratify moral outrage? Tell me, Alyosha!'

'Yes, shot him!' muttered Alyosha, looking at his brother with a kind of weak, twisted smile.

'Bravo!' whooped Ivan, delighted. 'If you say that, it means... What a fine monk you are! So there's a proper little demon residing in your heart after all, Alyoshka Karamazov!'

'What I said was absurd, but...'

'Ah, but that "but" is all important... You know, novice, absurdity is all too necessary on this earth. The world rests on absurdity, and without it perhaps nothing would be accomplished. We know what we know.'

'What do you know?'

'I understand nothing, and now', Ivan went on as if delirious, 'I don't want to understand anything. I want to stick to facts. I gave up trying to understand long ago. As soon as I feel I want to understand something I immediately have to renounce facts, whereas I have decided to stay true to facts...'

'Why are you testing me?' Alyosha burst out in bitter desperation. 'Are you going to tell me in the end?'

'Of course I'm going to tell you, I was leading up to that. You're very dear to me, and I don't want to lose you and I shall not let your Zosima take possession of you.'

Ivan paused for a moment, and his expression suddenly became very sad.

'Listen: I've confined myself to children to make it clearer. I've said nothing about all the other human tears in which the world is drowning; I've deliberately limited my thesis. I'm a flea on the face of the earth, and I admit in all humility that I cannot understand in the least why things are the way they are. It must be men themselves who are to blame; they were offered paradise, but they wanted freedom and stole fire from heaven knowing that they would be unhappy, so there's no need to pity them.

Oh, in my poor, earthly, Euclidean mind I know only that suffering exists, that no one is to blame, that one thing leads to another just like that, that life goes on and things find their own equilibrium in the end—but then, that is just Euclidean nonsense, I know that, and when it comes down to it I can't agree to live by it! What difference does it make to me that no one is to blame and that I accept it—I must have retribution, otherwise I'll do away with myself. And that retribution must not be at some unspecified place and some unspecified time, but here and now on earth, where I myself can witness it. I have believed, so I want to witness it for myself, and if by then I'm already dead, may I be resurrected, for it would be too awful if it were all to come to pass without me. It was not for that that I suffered, that I, evil sinner that I am with my agonies and misdeeds, might be exploited for the benefit of someone else's future harmony. I want to see the lion lying down with the lamb with my own eyes, and the murdered rising up and embracing their murderers. I want to be here when everyone suddenly finds out the why and the wherefore of everything. This is the desire on which all religions on earth are based, and I am a believer. But then, what about the children, what shall I do about them? That's the question I cannot answer. For the hundredth time I repeat—the questions are endless, but I am only considering the children because in their case what I have to say is incontrovertibly clear. Listen: if everyone has to suffer in order to bring about eternal harmony through that suffering, tell me, please, what have children to do with this? It's quite incomprehensible that they too should have to suffer, that they too should have to pay for harmony by their suffering. Why should they be the grist to someone else's mill, the means of ensuring someone's future harmony? I understand the universality of sin, I understand the universality of retribution, but children have no part in this universal sin, and if it's true that they are stained with the sins of their fathers, then, of course, that's a truth not of this world, and I don't understand it. Some cynic may say that the children will grow up and will in time sin themselves, but he didn't grow up, that eight-year-old torn apart by the dogs. Oh, Alyosha, I'm not blaspheming! I understand how the universe will shake when heaven and earth shall unite in a single paean of praise, and all that lives and has lived will cry out, "You are just, O Lord, for your ways are revealed to us!" When the mother embraces the murderer whose dogs tore her son apart, and all three shall cry out weeping, "You are just, O Lord"—that, of course, will be the summit of all knowledge, and all will be explained. But here's the snag; that's just what I can't accept. And while I'm still on this earth I resort to my own methods. You see, Alyosha, perhaps it really will happen like that, and I shall live to see it or be resurrected, and then perhaps I too, seeing the mother embracing her child's torturer, will cry out in unison with them, "You are just, O Lord", but it will be against my will. While there's still time I want to guard myself against this, and therefore I absolutely reject that higher harmony. It's not worth one little tear from one single little tortured child, beating its breast with its little fists in its foul-smelling lock-up, and praying with its unexpiated tears to its "Dear Father God!" No, it's not worth this, because those tears have remained unexpiated. And they have to be expiated, otherwise there can be no harmony. But how, how can they be expiated? Surely it isn't possible? Or is it going to be done by avenging them? But what's the good of avenging them, what's the good of consigning their murderers to hell, what good can hell do when the children have already been tortured to death? And how can harmony exist if hell exists too? I want forgiveness, I want to embrace everyone, I want an end to suffering. And if the suffering of children is required to make up the total suffering necessary to attain the truth, then I say here and now that no truth is worth such a price. And above all, I don't want the mother to embrace the torturer whose dogs tore her son apart! She has no right to forgive him! Let her, if she will, forgive him her own suffering, her own extreme anguish as a mother, but she has no right to forgive the suffering of her mutilated child; even if the child himself forgives, she has no right! And if that is so, if the right to forgive does not exist, then where is harmony? Is there in all the world a single being who could forgive and has the right to do so? I don't want harmony; for the love of humankind, I don't want it. I would rather that suffering were not avenged. I would prefer to keep my suffering unavenged and my abhorrence unplacated, *even at the risk of being wrong*. Besides, the price of harmony has been set too high, we can't afford the entrance fee. And that's why I hasten to return my entry ticket. If I ever want to call myself an honest man, I have to hand it back as soon as possible. And that's exactly what I'm doing. It's not that I don't accept God, Alyosha; I'm just, with the utmost respect, handing Him back my ticket.'

'That's rebellion,' Alyosha said quietly, without looking up.

'"Rebellion"? I wouldn't have expected to hear such a word from you,' said Ivan thoughtfully. 'Can one live in a state of rebellion? For I want to live. Tell me honestly, I challenge you—answer me: imagine that you are charged with building the edifice of human destiny, whose ultimate aim is to bring people happiness, to give them peace and contentment at last, but that in order to achieve this it is essential and unavoidable to torture just one little speck of creation, that same little child beating her breast with her little fists, and imagine that this edifice has to be erected on her unexpiated tears. Would you agree to be the architect under those conditions? Tell me honestly!'

'No, I wouldn't agree,' said Alyosha quietly.

'And could you accept the idea that the people for whom you are building the edifice have agreed to buy their own happiness with the price of the unexpiated blood of a little tortured child, and that, having accepted this, they could remain happy for ever?'

'No, I couldn't accept that. Ivan,' Alyosha said suddenly, his eyes flashing, 'you asked just now: "is there in all the world any single being who could forgive and who has the right to do so?" But there is such a being, and He can forgive everything, He can forgive everyone *for everything*, because He Himself shed His innocent blood for everyone and for everything. You forgot about Him; it is He who is the cornerstone of the building, and it is to Him that people will cry out, "You are just, O Lord, for your ways are revealed to us."'

'Ah, this "only one without sin", who has shed his blood! No, I haven't forgotten about Him; on the contrary, I've been wondering all this time why you hadn't brought Him up for so long, for your lot usually play that card first in any argument. You know, Alyosha, don't laugh, but I wrote a kind of a poem about a year ago. If you can bear with me for a little longer, I'll let you hear it.'

'You've written a poem?'

'Oh no, I didn't write it,' Ivan laughed, 'and in all my life I've never written so much as two verses. But I dreamed up this tale and I can still remember it. I dreamed it up in a moment of inspiration. You'll be my first reader, that is, my first listener. Why indeed should an author neglect a single listener?' laughed Ivan. 'Do you want to hear it or not?'

'I'd like very much to hear it,' said Alyosha.

'My tale is called "The Grand Inquisitor", an absurd title, but I'd like you to hear it.'

5

THE GRAND INQUISITOR

'WELL, first of all there has to be an introduction, a literary introduction, that is.' Ivan laughed. 'God knows, I'm no author! You see, the action takes place in the sixteenth century, and at that time, as you will remember from school, at that time it was the custom to introduce celestial beings in poetical works. I'm not talking about Dante. In France juristic clerks and even the monks in the monasteries used to perform plays where Our Lady, angels, saints, Christ, and God Himself appeared on stage. These pieces were all very naïve. In Victor Hugo's *Notre Dame de Paris*, to celebrate the birth of the French Dauphin in the reign of Louis XI, the public is regaled in the Paris town hall with an edifying free performance entitled *Le Bon Jugement de la très sainte et gracieuse Vierge Marie*,* in which the Virgin appeared in person and pronounced her own *bon jugement*. In Moscow before the time of Peter the Great we also occasionally used to have somewhat similar dramatic performances, mostly based on the Old Testament; but in addition to dramatic performances, many poems and stories circulated throughout the whole world at that time, in which saints, angels, and all the heavenly hosts appeared as appropriate. In our monasteries too such works

were translated, copied, even written—and all this while under
the Tatar yoke. There is for example one minor monastic poem
(translated from the Greek, of course), *The Virgin among the
Damned*, which in its descriptive power and daring can be
compared with Dante. The Mother of God visits hell and the
Archangel Michael acts as her guide. She sees the sinners and
their torments. There is by the way one particularly curious
category of sinners in a burning lake; some of these have been
plunged into this lake and can never escape from it, even God
has forgotten these—a conception of remarkable depth and
power. The Virgin, devastated and weeping, falls to her knees
before the throne of God and begs mercy for all in hell, for all
those she has seen there, without favour. Her conversation with
God is interesting in the extreme. She begs, she insists, and
when God shows her the marks of the nails on the hands and
feet of her son and asks, "How can I forgive his torturers?" she
calls upon all the saints, all the martyrs, all the angels and
archangels to kneel with her and to plead for mercy for all,
without distinction. It ends with her winning from God an annual
cessation of tortures from Good Friday to Pentecost, and the
sinners from hell thank Him there and then, crying out to Him,
"You are just, O Lord, in your judgement of us." Well, my little
tale would have been something along those lines had it been
written in those times. In my piece He appears on the scene;
true, He doesn't say anything in the poem, but just appears and
passes by. Some fifteen centuries have elapsed since He promised to come into His kingdom, fifteen centuries since His
prophet wrote, "Behold, I come quickly".* "But of that day and
hour knoweth no man, no, not the angels of heaven, but my
Father only,"* as He himself said when He was still on this earth.
And the human race awaits Him with all its former faith and
emotion, or rather with even greater faith, for fifteen centuries
have elapsed since heaven ceased to give pledges to man:

> Believe what your heart says,
> Heaven makes no pledges.*

'So there was faith only in what the heart had decreed! True,
many miracles also occurred then. There were saints who
performed miraculous cures; certain righteous men, so it is

written in the hagiographies, were visited by the Queen of Heaven herself. But the devil doesn't sleep, and mankind began to doubt the authenticity of these miracles. Just at that time a terrible new heresy* erupted in the north, in Germany. A great star* "like a flaming torch" (that is, the Church) "fell upon the sources of the waters and turned them bitter". This heresy began blasphemously to deny the miracles. But the faithful believed all the more ardently. The tears of humanity ascend to Him as before, they await Him, love Him, place their hopes in Him as before, long, as before, to suffer and die for Him... And thus for so many centuries has mankind fervently and devoutly implored, "Lord appear unto us",* for so many centuries have they cried to Him that in his infinite mercy He finally vouchsafed to come down to his supplicants. He had already come down on occasion and revealed Himself to certain just men, martyrs, and saintly anchorites on earth, as has been recorded in their "lives". Our Tyutchev, a poet of great sincerity wrote:

> In slave's guise and laden with the Cross,
> Over you, my native land,
> Passed heaven's Lord
> And blessed you as he passed.*

That this was truly so, I can promise you. And He wanted to appear, if only for a moment, to his tortured, suffering, wickedly sinful people, who nevertheless loved Him with the innocent love of childhood. The action of my poem takes place in Spain, in Seville, at the most terrible time of the Inquisition, when to the glory of God pyres were lit daily in the country and

> In magnificent *autos-da-fé*
> They burned the evil heretics.*

O, of course, it was not that coming when, according to His promise, He will return at the end of time in all His celestial glory, suddenly, "as the lightning cometh out of the east and shineth even unto the west".* No, He simply wanted to appear, if only for a moment, to visit his children at the very place where the heretics' fires crackled. In his infinite mercy He walks once more among the people in that human form in which, for three years, he went among men fifteen centuries previously. He

descends into the scorching streets of a southern city, where
only the night before, on the order of the Grand Inquisitor and
in the presence of the King, the court, knights, cardinals, and the
most beautiful ladies of the court, and watched by the thronging
populace of Seville, nearly a hundred heretics had been burned
in a "magnificent *auto-da-fé*" *ad majorem gloriam Dei.** He arrives
quietly, surreptitiously, and everyone—strange to say—recognizes Him. That could well be one of the most intriguing ideas
in the tale, namely, precisely why they recognize Him. The
people, drawn by an irresistible force, stream towards Him,
surround Him, and the crowd grows and follows Him. He walks
silently among them with a serene smile of infinite compassion.
The flame of love burns in his heart, rays of light, wisdom, and
omnipotence flow from his eyes over the people, lighting upon
them and causing their hearts to throb with a reciprocal love. He
stretches out His arms to them, blesses them, and healing flows
from His touch, even from the touch of His garments. Then,
from the crowd, an old man, blind from childhood, cries out,
"Lord, heal me, that I too may see You," and, as if the scales
had fallen from his eyes, the blind man sees Him. The crowd
weeps and kisses the ground where He walks. Children throw
flowers before his feet, sing and cry "Hosanna!" "It is He, it is
really He," they all keep repeating, "It must be He, it can be no
one but He." He stops on the steps of Seville Cathedral, just as
weeping relatives are carrying in the little white open coffin of a
child, a seven-year-old girl, the only daughter of a prominent
citizen. The dead child lies bestrewn with flowers. "He will
resurrect your child," the crowd cries to the weeping mother.
The prebendary who comes out to receive the coffin stares in
amazement and frowns. But the wailing of the bereaved mother
rings out. She throws herself at His feet. "If it is You, raise my
child from the dead," she cries, reaching out her hands to Him.
The cortège comes to a halt, and the coffin is lowered on to the
steps at His feet. He looks at the child with compassion, and
gently His lips pronounce once more, "Talitha cumi"—"and
straightway the damsel arose".* The little girl sits up in the
coffin and looks around her, smiling, her eyes wide open and
astonished. In her hands she has a posy of white roses which had
been placed in the coffin with her. There is confusion in the

crowd, cries, sobbing, and then, just at that very moment, through the square in front of the cathedral, suddenly comes the Cardinal, the Grand Inquisitor himself. He is an old man of nearly ninety, tall and erect, with a withered face and sunken eyes, which, however, still glint with a fiery gleam. No, he isn't wearing his magnificent cardinal's vestments in which he paraded before the people the previous night, when the enemies of the Roman faith were burned—no, now he wears only an old, coarse, monk's cassock. Behind him, at a respectful distance, follow his sombre aides, his servants, and the Guardians of the Holy Office. He stops and observes the crowd from afar. He has seen everything, seen them lay the coffin at His feet, seen the child raised from the dead—and his face darkens. His thick, grey brows contract, and his eyes gleam with a sinister fire. He points a finger and orders his guards to seize Him. And such is his power, and so accustomed to it, so cowed and so tremulously obedient are the people, that the crowd promptly parts before the guards and, in the deathly silence that has suddenly fallen, they lay hands on Him and lead Him away. The crowd, as one man, immediately bows down to the ground before the old Inquisitor, who silently blesses them and passes on. The guards take the prisoner to a cramped and dark vaulted prison in the ancient building of the Holy Office, and lock Him up. The day passes and night falls, a dark, hot, airless Seville night. The air is heavy with the scent of laurel and lemon. In the dark depths the iron door of the prison suddenly opens and the Grand Inquisitor himself slowly enters with a flaming brand in his hand. He is alone; the door is immediately locked behind him. He stops on the threshold and gazes for a long time, a minute or two, into His face. At last he quietly advances, places the brand on the table, and says to Him, "Is it You? You?" There being no answer, he adds quickly, "Don't answer, remain silent. After all, what could You say? I know only too well what You would say. And You have no right to add anything to what You have already said. So why have You come to disturb us? For You really have come to disturb us, and You know it. But do You know what is going to happen tomorrow? I don't know who You are and I don't want to know—whether You are He or whether You are just a semblance of Him—but tomorrow I shall judge You and burn You at the stake, like the vilest of the heretics, and that same crowd which today kissed Your feet, tomorrow, at a sign from me, will rush to stoke up the fire, do You know that? Yes, perhaps You do know it," he added thoughtfully, never taking his gaze from his prisoner for a moment.'

'I don't quite understand what this means, Ivan,' smiled Alyosha, who had been listening quietly all this time. 'Is it sheer unrestrained fantasy or some sort of mistake by the old man, a kind of impossible confusion?'

'Accept the latter proposition, if you like,' laughed Ivan, 'if modern realism has rendered you incapable of accepting anything supernatural—if you want confusion, so be it. It's true', he laughed again, 'that the old man is ninety and his Idea* could long ago have driven him mad. Alternatively, he could just have been struck by the appearance of the prisoner. It could turn out to be nothing but delirium, the hallucination of a ninety-year-old man nearing his death, over-excited as he was by the *auto-da-fé* of a hundred heretics the night before. But what does it matter to us whether it's confusion or unrestrained fantasy? What matters is that the old man has to speak out, that in his ninetieth year he at last says out loud what he has refrained from saying all his ninety years.'

'And the prisoner is also silent? He looks at him and doesn't say a word?'

'Yes, that's how it has to be and will always have to be,' Ivan laughed again. 'As the old man himself says to Him, He doesn't have the right to add anything to what He has already said. You could say this is the fundamental principle of Roman Catholicism, in my opinion at least: "You've delegated everything to the Pope, now the Pope's responsible for everything, so there's no need for You to return at all, don't disturb us, at least not until the appointed hour." They not only talk like that, they write like that too, at least the Jesuits do. I've read their theologians myself. "Have You the right to reveal to us one single mystery of that world from which You came?" the old man asks Him, and answers himself. "No, You have not, so as not to add to what has already been said, and so as not to take away from mankind that liberty that You valued so highly when You were on earth. Anything further that You might say would endanger men's freedom of faith, for it would appear as a miracle, and freedom of faith was dearer than everything else to You then, fifteen hundred years ago. And didn't You Yourself say so often, 'I want to make you free'?* Well, now You've seen them, these 'free' men," adds the old man suddenly, with a knowing grin. "Yes, that business cost us dearly," he continues, looking at Him sternly, "but in the end we dealt with it in Your name. For fifteen centuries we suffered from that freedom, but now it's all finished, settled once and for all. Don't You believe it's settled? You look at me so humbly, won't You even honour me with Your indignation? But let me tell You that now, at this very time, these people are more than ever convinced of their absolute freedom, and yet they themselves have brought their freedom to us and laid it submissively at our feet. But it is we who have brought this about, and is that what You wanted, that kind of freedom?"'

'Again, I don't understand,' Alyosha broke in. 'Is he being sarcastic, is he mocking Him?'

'Not in the least. He's claiming credit for himself and those like him for having done away with freedom and for having done so in order to make mankind happy. "For only now"—he is speaking of the Inquisition, of course—"has it become possible to contemplate human happiness for the first time. Man was created a rebel; surely rebels cannot be happy, can they? You were warned," he says to Him, "there was no lack of warnings and signs, but You didn't listen to the warnings, You rejected the only means of making people happy, but fortunately when You departed You left the task in our hands. You promised, You gave Your word, You gave us the right to bind and to loose,* and, of course, You cannot think of taking away that right now. Why then have You come to disturb us?"'

'And what does that mean: "there was no lack of warnings and signs"?' asked Alyosha.

'That's the essence of what the old man said.'

'"The terrible and clever spirit, the spirit of self-destruction and annihilation," the old man continues, "the great spirit spoke to You in the wilderness, and it has been written in the books that he is said to have tempted You.* Isn't that so? And could anything more truthful have been said than that which he revealed to You in the three offers, that which You rejected, and which in the books are called the 'temptations'? And if there ever really was a truly awesome miracle on earth, then it was on that day, on the day of those three temptations. For truly the miracle was contained in the conception of those three temptations. If it were possible, for the sake of argument, to suppose that those three temptations devised by the terrible spirit had been erased from the books and that it were necessary to rediscover them, to reinvent them, to imagine them anew so as to restore them to the books, and to this end all the wise men of the world were gathered together—rulers, high priests, sages, philosophers, poets—and were given this task: to conceive and devise three temptations which would not only correspond to the enormity of the event, but above and beyond that would also, in three words, in three human phrases, express the whole future history of the world and of mankind—do You think that all the wise men of the world together could imagine anything approaching the power and the depth of those three temptations which were in fact put to You at that time in the desert by that mighty and cunning spirit? By those temptations alone, by the sheer audacity of their conception, we can see that we are not dealing with a temporal human mind, but with an eternal and absolute one. For those three temptations combine and predict, as it were, the whole future history of mankind, and manifest three images in which all the insoluble historical contradictions of human nature the world over will come together. At that time this could not have been so evident, because the future was unknown, but now that fifteen centuries have passed we see that everything in those three temptations has been foreseen and predicted, and proven true to such an extent that nothing more can be added to or subtracted from them.

'"Decide for Yourself: who was right, You or he who tempted You? Remember the first temptation: perhaps not literally, but the sense of it was, 'You want to enter the world, and You go with empty hands, with some vague promise of freedom which they, in their simplicity and innate stupidity, could not even comprehend and which frightens and overawes them—for nothing has ever been so intolerable to man and to human society as freedom! And do You see these stones in this barren white-hot desert? Turn them into bread, and mankind will come running after You, a grateful and obedient flock, although they will always tremble in fear that You may withdraw Your hand and stop their supply of bread.' But You did not want to deprive man of his freedom, so You rejected the suggestion, for what sort of freedom would it be, You judged, if obedience were bought with bread? You replied that man does not live by bread alone. But do You know that it will be in the name of just that terrestrial bread that the spirit of the earth will rise against You, will do battle with You and defeat You, and all men will follow that spirit, exclaiming, 'Who is like unto the beast? He maketh fire come down from heaven.'* Do You know that ages will pass and mankind will proclaim with its voice of wisdom and science that there is no crime and consequently no sin, but only starving people. 'Feed them, and then ask for virtue!' That's what they'll write on their banner which they will raise against You and with which they will destroy Your temple. A new edifice will arise in place of Your temple, the terrible Tower of Babel will arise anew, and although this, like the other one, will remain uncompleted, nevertheless You could have avoided the erection of that new tower and cut short men's suffering by a thousand years, for it is to us that they will turn after they have suffered with their tower for a thousand years! And they will seek us out when we are underground once more, hiding in the catacombs (because we shall be tortured and persecuted again), they will find us and cry out to us, 'Feed us, for those who promised us heavenly fire did not give it to us.' And then we shall complete their tower, for he who feeds them will complete it, and we alone shall feed them in Your name, and when we say that it is in Your name, we shall be lying. Oh, never, never will they be able to feed themselves without us! So long as they remain free no science will ever give them bread, and in the end they will bring their freedom and lay it at our feet, saying, 'Enslave us, but feed us!' And they will come to understand that freedom together with an abundance of earthly bread for all is inconceivable, for they will never, never learn to share among themselves! They will become convinced, too, that they can never be free because they are weak, depraved, worthless, and rebellious. You promised them the bread of heaven, but, I repeat again, can that, in the eyes of the weak, eternally depraved and eternally ignoble human tribe, compare with earthly bread? And if, in the name of the bread of heaven, thousands and tens of thousands follow You, what will become of the millions and tens of thousands of millions who will not have the strength to forgo earthly bread for the bread of heaven? Or are only the tens of thousands of the great and the strong dear to You, while the remaining millions, the weak, who are as numerous as grains of sand on the shore, but who love You, must serve only as chattels for the great and the strong? However, the weak too are dear to us. They are depraved and rebellious, but in the end it is they who will become obedient. They will wonder at us and take us for gods because, placing ourselves at their head, we shall have agreed to take away their freedom and rule over them—so terrible will they find it in the end to be free! But we shall tell them that we obey You and rule in Your name. We shall be deceiving them again, because we shall no longer let You near us. This deception will bring us suffering too, for we shall have to lie. That was the meaning of that first temptation in the desert, and that is what You rejected in the name of freedom, which You elevated above everything else. But in that temptation lay the great mystery of this world. In accepting the 'loaves', You would have responded to the universal and eternal dilemma of man as an individual and of humanity as a whole: whom to worship? When man finds himself free, there is no concern more pressing and more tormenting to him than the desire immediately to seek out someone to worship. But man seeks to worship only what is indisputable, so indisputable that all men will agree unanimously to worship it universally. For these pitiful creatures yearn to find not only that which I or someone else could worship, but something in which we all believed and before which all bowed down, and indeed necessarily *together*. It is this demand for a *universality* of worship that has been the chief torment of each and every man individually and of the whole of humankind from the beginning of time. For this universality of worship, men have put one another to the sword. They have created gods and appealed to one another, 'Leave your gods and come and worship ours, otherwise death to you and to your gods!' And thus it will be till the end of the world, and even when the gods have vanished from the face of the earth they will still prostrate themselves before idols. You knew, You could not but know, this fundamental secret of human nature, but You rejected the one absolute banner that was offered to You to make all men worship You uniquely—the banner of earthly bread—and You rejected it in the name of freedom and the bread of heaven. Look what You have done since then. And again, all in the name of freedom! I tell You, man has no more pressing need than to find someone to whom he can give up that gift of freedom with which he, unhappy being that he is, was endowed at birth. But only he who appeases men's consciences can relieve them of their freedom. In bread, You were offered an incontrovertible banner: give man bread and he will worship You, for nothing is more incontrovertible than bread, but if at the same time someone other than You relieves him of his conscience—oh, then he will even throw away Your bread and follow him who seduces his conscience. You were right about this. For the secret of human existence lies not only in living, but in knowing what to live for. Without a firm conviction of the purpose of living, man will not consent to live and will destroy himself rather than remain on earth, though he be surrounded by bread. This is so, and yet what happened? Instead of relieving men of their freedom, You increased it even more! Had You forgotten that peace and even death are dearer to man than freedom of choice in the knowledge of good and evil? Indeed, nothing is more beguiling to man than freedom of conscience, but nothing is more tormenting either. But, instead of tangible grounds for the appeasement of the human conscience once and for all, You took all that was most extraordinary, most hypothetical, and most vague, all that was beyond the understanding of the people, and thus You acted as though You did not love them at all—and who was this? The one who had come to give His life for them! Instead of taking control of human freedom, You intensified it and burdened man's spiritual domain with its torments for ever. You desired man to have freedom of choice in love so that he would follow You freely, lured and captivated by You. Instead of the old immutable law, man should henceforth decide with a free heart what is good and what is evil, having only Your image before him as a guide— but didn't it occur to You that in the end men would reject and dispute even Your image and Your truth if they were saddled

with such a terrible burden as freedom of choice? They will cry
out in the end that truth is not in You, for they could not have
been left in worse confusion and torment than that in which You
left them, bequeathing them so many problems and unresolved
questions. So You Yourself sowed the seed of the destruction of
Your own kingdom; blame no one else for this. But was that in
fact what You were offered? There are three forces, only three
forces on earth that can subdue and imprison the conscience of
these weak-willed rebels for ever for their own good—these
forces are miracle, mystery, and authority. You rejected all three,
and thus You Yourself set the example. When the terrible and
clever spirit set You on a pinnacle of the temple and said to
You, 'If You would know whether you are the Son of God, cast
Yourself down: for it is written, the angels will take charge of
Him and bear Him up lest He fall and be hurt, and you will
know then if You are the Son of God, and have proved what
faith You have in your Father,'* You, having listened, rejected
the temptation, did not submit and did not cast Yourself down.
Oh, of course, You acted proudly and magnificently, like God,
but men, that weak and rebellious tribe—are they gods? Oh, You
understood then that had You taken a single step, made a single
move to cast Yourself down, You would immediately have
tempted the Lord, would have lost all Your faith in Him, and
would have been dashed to pieces on the earth that You had come
to redeem, and the cunning spirit that had tempted You would
have rejoiced. But, I repeat, are there many like You? Surely You
can't suggest, even for a moment, that men too would be able to
resist such a temptation? Is human nature fashioned in such a
way as to refuse a miracle and, at such terrible moments,
moments beset with the most profound and terrible spiritual
problems, to hold on only to a free decision of the heart? Oh,
You knew that Your glorious deed would be recorded in the
Scriptures, would reach to the depths of time and to the furthest
limits of the earth, and You hoped that, in following You, man
too would remain with God without need of miracles. But You
didn't know that as soon as man rejected miracles he would also
reject God, for man seeks not so much God as miracles.* And
since man cannot manage without miracles he will create new
miracles for himself, his own this time, and he will worship false

miracles of sorcery and witches, though he be a hundred times rebel, heretic, and atheist. You did not come down from the cross when they shouted at You, mocking You and ridiculing You, 'Come down from the cross, and we shall believe that it is you.'* You did not come down because once again You did not want to enslave man by a miracle, and You thirsted for a faith that was free and not inspired by miracles. You thirsted for love freely given, and not the slavish gratitude of the captive before the mighty power that has terrified him for all time. But there too You judged men too highly, because of course they are slaves even though they have been created rebels. Look around and decide, now that fifteen centuries have passed, take a look at them: whom have You raised up to Yourself? I swear to You, man was created weaker and baser than You thought! Can he, can he do what You did? You respected him so much that You acted as if You had ceased to feel compassion for him, because You demanded too much of him—and who was this? He who loved mankind more than Himself! Had You respected him less You would have demanded less of him, and that would have been closer to love because the burden would have been lighter. He is weak and base. Does it matter if at present he is in revolt everywhere against our authority and is proud of his rebellion? This is the pride of a child, of a schoolboy. They are little children who have rebelled in class and driven their teacher out. But there comes an end to children's triumphs, and it costs them dearly. They will tear down the temples and drench the earth with blood. But at last the foolish children will realize that, rebels though they may be, they are feeble rebels, unable to sustain their own revolt. Weeping their foolish tears, they will finally admit that He who created them rebels undoubtedly wished to make fools of them. They will say this in despair, and what they say will be blasphemy and that will render them even more unhappy, for human nature cannot endure blasphemy and in the end always avenges it. And so, restlessness, confusion, and unhappiness—that is the present lot of men after You suffered so much for their liberty! In a vision and an allegory Your great prophet tells how he saw all the participants in the first resurrection, and that there were twelve thousand from each of the twelve tribes of Israel.* But, to be so numerous, they would have to be not men but gods. They endured Your crucifixion, they endured decades in the arid and barren desert, living on locusts and roots*—so of course You can point with pride to these children of freedom, of love freely given, of free and magnificent sacrifice made in Your name. But remember that they were only several thousand, and gods at that, and what of the others? What are they guilty of, the others, the weak, who cannot endure what the strong endure? How is the weak spirit guilty for not being able to cope with such terrible gifts? Can it really be that You came only to the chosen ones and on behalf of the chosen ones? But if so, then there is a mystery here which we shall not be able to understand. And if there is a mystery, then we too were right to preach mystery and to teach them that what is important is not the free choice of the heart, nor love, but mystery, to which they must submit blindly, even against the dictates of their conscience. That is what we have done. We have improved upon Your creation and founded it instead on *miracle, mystery,* and *authority*. And men were delighted that once more they were led like sheep, and that that terrible gift which had brought them so much suffering was lifted from their hearts at last. Tell us, were we right to teach thus and to act thus? Have we not really loved man when we have so humbly recognized his weakness, have lightened his burden out of love, and out of consideration for his feeble nature have even allowed him to sin, so long as it is with our permission? So why then have You come to interfere now? And why do You look at me so silently with your humble, piercing eyes? Why are You not angry? I do not want Your love, because I do not love You. Why should I conceal anything from You? I know who I am talking to, don't I? Everything I have to tell You, You already know, I can read it in Your eyes. How can I keep our secret from You? Perhaps that is precisely what You want, to hear it from my lips—listen then: we are not with You but with *him*—that is our secret! We ceased to be with You and went over to *him* a long time ago, already eight centuries ago.* Exactly eight centuries ago we accepted from *him* what You had rejected with indignation, that last gift that he offered You, showing You all the kingdoms of the earth: we accepted Rome and the sword of Caesar from *him*, and we proclaimed ourselves the only kings on earth, the only true kings, although we have not yet been able to complete our work. But who is to blame? Oh, this work is still in its infancy, but it has begun. We shall have to wait a long time for its completion, and the world will have to endure much suffering, but we shall achieve it and we shall be the Caesars, and then we shall think about universal human happiness. And meanwhile, You could still have accepted the sword of Caesar. Why did You refuse that last gift? Had You accepted that third suggestion of the mighty spirit, You could have provided all that man seeks on earth—that is to say, someone to worship, someone to take charge of his conscience, and finally, a way to be united unequivocally in a communal and harmonious antheap, for the need for universal unity is mankind's third and last torment. Mankind as a whole has always striven towards universal organization above all. There have been many great peoples, each with an illustrious history, but the more elevated the nations the unhappier they were, because they were more conscious than others of the need for universal unity of mankind. The great conquerors, the Tamerlanes and the Genghis Khans, rampaged over the earth like whirlwinds, seeking to conquer the world, but they too, even if unconsciously, were giving expression to that selfsame overriding need of mankind for a universal and general unity. By accepting the world and Caesar's purple, You would have founded a universal kingdom and brought universal peace. For to whom is it given to rule over men, if not to those who rule over their conscience and in whose hands is their bread? And so we took Caesar's sword and, having taken it, of course we renounced You and followed *him*. Oh, there are still centuries of excess to come, excess of spiritual freedom, of science and anthropophagy, because having started to erect their Tower of Babel without us they will end in anthropophagy. But that is when the beast will come crawling to us, lick our feet, and spatter us with bloody tears from its eyes. And we shall mount the beast and raise up the cup, and on it will be written 'Mystery'.* And only then will the kingdom of peace and happiness for mankind begin. You pride Yourself on Your chosen ones, but You have only the chosen ones, whereas we shall bring peace to all. Besides, that's not all: how many of those chosen ones, of those mighty ones who could have become the chosen ones, have grown weary of waiting for You and have taken and will continue to take their strength of spirit and their passionate hearts to another altar, and will end by raising their banner of *freedom* against You Yourself? But it is You Yourself who will have raised the banner. With us, on the other hand, everyone will be happy and will not rebel any more or exterminate one another, as they did everywhere under Your freedom. Oh, we shall convince them that only in surrendering their freedom to us and submitting to us can they be free. Well, shall we be right or shall we be lying? They will see for themselves that we are right, for they will remember to what horrors of slavery and confusion Your freedom led them. Freedom, science, and independence of spirit will lead them into such a labyrinth and confront them with such miracles and such insoluble mysteries that some of them, intractable and savage, will destroy themselves, while others, intractable but less strong, will destroy one another; and those who remain, feeble and unhappy, will crawl up to our feet and will cry out to us, 'Yes, you were right, you alone held his secret, and we are returning to you: save us from ourselves.' When they receive bread from us they will understand, of course, that we take their own bread from them, made by their own hands, in order to redistribute it without any miracle; they will see that we have not turned stones into bread, and they will truly rejoice not so much over the bread itself, but over the fact that they receive it from our hands! Because they will remember only too well that without us the very bread that they made turned to stones in their hands, but that when they returned to us the very stones turned to bread in their hands. They will appreciate, they will appreciate only too well what it means to subjugate themselves for ever! And as long as men do not understand this, they will be unhappy. Who has contributed most of all to this incomprehension, tell me? Who divided the flock and dispersed the sheep into unknown ways? But the flock will reassemble and will submit again once and for all. Then we shall endow them with a quiet, humble happiness, a happiness suited to feeble creatures such as they were created. Oh, we shall persuade them in the end not to be proud, for You elevated them and taught them pride; we shall show them that they are feeble, that they are only pitiful children, but that childish happiness is the sweetest of all. They will become scared and will begin to look to us and to huddle up to us in fear, as chickens huddle up to the broody hen. They will wonder at us and fear us, and be proud that we are powerful and clever enough to subdue such a turbulent flock, a thousand million strong. They will tremble mightily before our anger, their spirit will be rendered submissive, their eyes tearful like those of children and women, but at a sign from us they will readily give themselves to gaiety and laughter, shining joy and happy, childlike singing. Yes, we shall require them to work, but in their free time we shall devise for them a life such as a child's game, with children's songs in chorus and innocent dances. Oh, we shall even allow them to sin, for they are weak and feeble, and for having been allowed to sin they will love us in the way that children do. We shall tell them that every sin will be expiated if it is committed with our permission; we shall allow them to sin because we love them, and the punishment for those sins—so be it, we shall take that upon ourselves. We shall take it upon ourselves, and they will worship us as benefactors who have taken on the burden of their sins before God. And they shall have no secrets from us. We shall permit or forbid them to live with their wives and mistresses, to have children or not to have them—subject to their obedience—and they will submit to us cheerfully and willingly. They will bring us their most tormenting problems of conscience—everything, they will bring everything to us and we shall resolve everything, and they will accept our judgement with joy, because it will spare them the great burden and terrible torment of personal and free choice that they suffer today. And everyone will be happy, all the millions of beings, except the hundred thousand who govern them. For only we, we who guard the mystery, only we shall be unhappy. There will be thousands of millions of happy children, and a hundred thousand martyrs who have taken upon themselves the curse of the knowledge of good and evil. They will die in peace, depart peacefully in Your name, and beyond the grave will encounter only death. But we shall withhold the secret and, to keep them happy, we shall opiate them with promises of eternal reward in heaven. Because even if there really were anything in the hereafter, it certainly would not be for such as them. It is said and prophesied* that You will return triumphant, that You will come with Your chosen ones, Your proud and mighty ones, but we shall tell them that they saved only themselves, whereas we have saved everyone. It is said that the whore* riding the beast and holding her *mystery* in her hands shall be disgraced, that the weak shall rise up again, that they shall tear her finery and lay bare her impure body. But then I shall arise and show You thousands of millions of happy children who have not known sin. And we who have, for their own happiness, taken upon ourselves their sins, we shall stand before You and say, 'Judge us if You can and if You dare.' Know that I do not fear You. Know that I too was in the desert, that I too fed upon locusts and roots, that I too have blessed the freedom with which You have blessed mankind, and that I was ready to join Your chosen ones, to unite with the strong and the mighty ones who yearn 'to make up their number'. But I came to my senses and did not wish to serve insanity. I have turned back and joined the legions of those who *have improved upon Your creation*. I have left the proud and have turned back to the humble, for the sake of the happiness of those humble ones. What I have said shall be, and our kingdom will be created. I tell you again, tomorrow You shall see that obedient flock, at a sign from me, rush to stoke with hot coals the pyre on which I shall burn You for having come to interfere with us. For if anyone deserves our pyre more than all others, it is You. Tomorrow I shall burn You. *Dixi.*'*

Ivan stopped. While speaking, his speech had become more and more impassioned; when he finished, he smiled suddenly.

Alyosha, who had listened in silence, but towards the end had many times in extreme agitation wanted to interrupt his brother but had clearly been restraining himself, suddenly began to speak as if electrified.

'But... this is absurd!' he exclaimed, reddening. 'Your story is in praise of Jesus, not in disparagement... as you claim. And who will believe what you say about freedom? Is that really how freedom should be understood? Is that how the Orthodox Church understands it?... It is Rome, but not all of Rome, it isn't true—it is the worst of the Catholics, the inquisitors, the Jesuits!... And then, such a fantastic character as your Inquisitor couldn't exist. What are these sins of men that they have taken upon themselves? Who are these guardians of a mystery who have taken upon themselves some curse for the good of mankind? When have they been seen? We all know about the Jesuits, who are greatly maligned, but are they like your characters? They are nothing of the sort, absolutely not... They are simply the Roman Church's army for a future world state, with an emperor—the Roman pontiff—at its head... that's their goal, but with no mystery and no false sentimentality... Just normal desire for power, for sordid worldly gain, for the enslavement of others... a kind of future serfdom where they'll become the landowners... that's all it is they want. Perhaps they don't even believe in God. Your suffering Inquisitor is just a fantasy...'

'Just a minute, just a minute,' laughed Ivan, 'you're getting so worked up. Fantasy—you say—all right! Of course it's fantasy. But admit this nevertheless: surely you don't really think that all this Catholic activity of recent centuries has sprung from nothing but a desire for power and sordid worldly gain? That can't be what Father Païsy teaches you?'

'No, no, on the contrary, Father Païsy once said much the same as you... but, of course, not the same, definitely not the same,' Alyosha promptly collected himself.

'Nevertheless, it's a valuable pointer, in spite of your "definitely not the same". I would very much like to know: why have your Jesuits and inquisitors united only for sordid material gain? Why doesn't a single martyr exist among them, afflicted with a great sorrow and loving humanity? You see, suppose among all those who seek only sordid material gain there were to be found even just one such as my old Inquisitor, who has himself lived on roots in the desert, mortifying his flesh in order to be free and perfect, but who, nevertheless, has loved humanity all his life, and suddenly the scales drop from his eyes and he sees that it is a poor kind of moral bliss to reach perfection of self-control only to become convinced that millions of the rest of God's creatures remain beings created in mockery, and that they will never have the strength to come to terms with their freedom, that the giants who will raise the tower will never emerge from petty rebels, that it was not for such simpletons as these that the great idealist dreamt of harmony. Realizing all this, he turns back and joins forces with... the intelligent ones. Surely all this could have happened?'

'Who does he join forces with, what intelligent ones?' exclaimed Alyosha, almost beside himself. 'None of them has such intelligence and no such mysteries or secrets... except perhaps godlessness, that's all their secret consists of. Your Inquisitor doesn't believe in God, that's all there is to his secret!'

'That's as may be! You've guessed at last. And that really is it, that's really the whole secret, but surely that represents suffering, for such a man as he anyway, who has sacrificed his whole life to self-denial in the desert and has still not cured himself of his love for humanity? In the twilight of his days he comes to see clearly that only the advice of the great and fearful spirit could bring about any kind of order endurable by the feeble rebels, "those experimental, unfinished creatures, created in a spirit of mockery". And so, having become convinced of this, he sees that he must proceed in the direction indicated by the clever spirit, the fearful spirit of death and destruction, and thus accept falsehood and deception and knowingly lead men to death and destruction, deceiving them the whole way so that they don't notice where they are being led at all, and so that, at least during the journey, these poor blind ones will believe themselves to be happy. And note well, this deception is in the name of Him in whose ideal the old man has believed so passionately all his life! Is this not misfortune? And if only one such appeared at the head of the whole of this army "thirsting for power, for nothing but sordid material gain", then wouldn't just that one be sufficient to bring about tragedy? Moreover, it would take just one man at the head to realize ultimately the guiding Idea of the whole business of the papacy, with all its armies and Jesuits, which is the supreme Idea of this system. I'm telling you truly, it's my strong belief that there has always been such a unique man standing at the head of the movement. Who knows, perhaps there may even have been such singular men among the Roman pontiffs. Who knows, perhaps that damned old man, who in his own way loves humanity so stubbornly, exists even now in the form of a whole legion of such singular old men, and not fortuitously either, but as a conspiracy, as a secret society, established long ago for the preservation of mystery, for its preservation from unhappy and weak men, so as to render them happy. This is undoubtedly so, and has to be. I imagine that even Freemasonry is based on some mystery of this kind, and that that is why the Catholics so hate the Masons, because they see them as rivals, as a fragmentation of the unity of their Idea, whereas there must be a single flock and a single shepherd... However, in defending my theory I seem to be an author who cannot stand up to your criticism. Enough of this!'

'Perhaps you're a Mason yourself!' Alyosha burst out suddenly. 'You don't believe in God,' he added, this time with extreme sadness. Besides, it seemed to him that his brother was regarding him mockingly. 'So how does your tale end,' he asked quickly, looking at the ground, 'or is that it?'

'I wanted to finish it like this. When the Inquisitor stops speaking, he waits a little while for the prisoner to answer him. He finds His silence disconcerting. He has seen the captive listening all the while quietly and attentively, looking him straight in the eye, and apparently not wishing to respond. The old man wants Him to say something, no matter how unpleasant and terrible. But He suddenly approaches the old man in silence and calmly kisses him on his bloodless ninety-year-old lips. That is His only response. The old man shudders. His lips quiver; he goes to the door of the cell, opens it, and says, "Go and don't come back any more... never... never, never!" And he releases Him into the dark backstreets of the city. The prisoner walks away.'

'And the old man?'

'The kiss sears his heart, but he doesn't let go of his Idea.'

'And you are with him, you too?' Alyosha said sorrowfully. Ivan laughed.

'But it's all nonsense, Alyosha; it's just a muddle-headed poem by a muddle-headed student who has never written so much as two verses. Why do you take it so seriously? Do you really think I shall go straight there now, to the Jesuits, to join the legions who are improving upon His creation? O Lord, what's it got to do with me? I've told you. All I want is to spin it out to thirty years, and then—I shall dash the cup to the ground!'

'And the tiny, sticky leaf-buds, the dear graves, the blue sky, the beloved woman? How will you live, how will you love them?' Alyosha said sadly. 'How is it possible with such a hell in your heart and in your head? Yes, you are leaving now precisely in order to join them... or if not, then you will surely kill yourself, you won't be able to endure it!'

'There is a kind of strength that can endure anything,' said Ivan with a cold smile.

'What strength?'

'The Karamazov strength... the strength of Karamazov depravity.'

'Drown in debauchery, bludgeon your soul with degradation, is that it?'

'Yes, probably... only perhaps I can avoid it till I'm thirty, and then...'

'How? How can you avoid it? It's impossible, thinking as you do.'

'Once again, in the Karamazov way.'

'You mean, "everything is permitted"? It's all permitted; that's it, is it?'

Ivan frowned and suddenly went strangely pale.

'Aha, you've seized on that expression which so offended Miusov... and which our brother Dmitry latched on to so naïvely,' he said with a crooked smile. 'Yes, all right, since it's been said, "everything is permitted". I won't retract my words. Anyway, Mitya's interpretation was quite good.'

Alyosha regarded him in silence.

'You know, Alyosha,' said Ivan suddenly and with unaccustomed emotion, 'I thought I was leaving with one friend in the world—you—but now I see that even in your heart, my dear recluse, there is no room for me. I will not reject the maxim that "everything is permitted"; so, well then, for that you will reject me, won't you?'

Alyosha stood up, went over to him and, without speaking, kissed him on the lips.

'Plagiarism!' cried Ivan, in a transport of delight. 'You stole that from my tale! But thank you all the same. Come on, Alyosha, let's go. It's time for us to leave.'

They went out, but on the steps of the inn they stopped.

'I'll tell you what, Alyosha,' said Ivan in a firm voice, 'if ever I bring myself to love those tiny, sticky leaf-buds, I'll do so only in memory of you. It will be enough for me that you are somewhere here, and I shall not lose the desire to live. Are you satisfied with

that? If you like, you can take that as a declaration of love. But
for now, you'll go to the right and I'll go to the left—and enough,
you hear me, enough. That's to say, even if I don't go tomorrow
(though I think I probably shall go), and if we do meet again
somehow, don't raise any of these matters, not a word. I ask you
this in all seriousness. And also, on the subject of Dmitry, I ask
you especially,' he added, suddenly angry, 'don't even mention
him to me again; we've exhausted the subject, said all there is to
say, haven't we? And as for me, I'll promise you one more thing:
when I'm approaching thirty and I start to feel I want to "dash
the cup to the ground", then, wherever you are, even if you are
in America, I'll come to you once more and... talk it over, be
sure of that. I'll come especially to do that. Besides, it'll be very
interesting to have a look at you then, to see what you'll be like.
That's quite a solemn promise. But we may well be saying
goodbye for about seven or ten years. Well, off you go now to
your Pater Seraphicus,* after all, he's dying; if he dies without
you, you might be angry with me for keeping you from him.
Goodbye, kiss me once more, that's right, now off you go...'

Ivan turned suddenly and walked away, without looking back.
It was how Dmitry had walked away from Alyosha the day before,
although that had been very different. This strange observation
flashed through Alyosha's grief-stricken mind like an arrow. He
waited a while, his gaze following his brother. For some reason,
he suddenly noticed that Ivan was walking somewhat unsteadily
and that his right shoulder, seen from behind, seemed lower
than his left. He had never noticed this before. Now he too
turned, and practically ran all the way to the monastery. It was
already getting dark, and he was almost afraid. Something new
that he could not define was welling up inside him. As he entered
the little wood surrounding the monastery the wind began to
rise, just as it had the day before, and the ancient pines groaned
around him. He was almost running. ' "Pater Seraphicus"—he
had got that name from somewhere—but where?' Alyosha
thought suddenly. 'Ivan, poor Ivan, when shall I see you again?...
Here's the hermitage. Lord! Yes, yes, Pater Seraphicus, he'll
save me... from him and for ever!'

Several times later in his life he was to wonder perplexedly
how, on leaving Ivan, he could so totally have forgotten about

Dmitry, when only that very morning, just a few hours before, he had intended to seek him out immediately and not to rest without having done so, even if it meant that he could not return to the monastery that night.

6

STILL VERY UNCLEAR

AFTER Ivan Fyodorovich left Alyosha he went straight home to Fyodor Pavlovich's. It was strange, but he felt a sudden anguish that was unbearable and above all increased with every step as he neared the house. It was not the anguish itself that was strange, but the fact that Ivan Fyodorovich could in no way account for it. He had experienced anguish often before, and he was not surprised that it should afflict him at such a moment, when he was preparing to tear himself away tomorrow from all that had drawn him here, and to change course abruptly once more and set off on a new and unknown path, again completely alone as before, hoping for much, but for quite what he did not know, expecting a lot, too much, from life, but totally unable to define either his expectations or even his desires. Nevertheless, at this moment, although he was indeed disturbed by the thought of a new and unknown chapter in his life, it was not this that tormented him. 'Could it be revulsion at the thought of my father's house?' he mused. 'It could be, I am indeed revolted by it, and even today, crossing that hated threshold for the last time, I'm still revolted... But no, it's not that either. Could it be my parting from Alyosha, and the conversation we had? I've kept my silence for so many years, declining to talk to anyone, and now suddenly I come out with such nonsense.' In fact, it could have been the juvenile anger of immaturity, lack of experience and juvenile vanity, anger at his failure to express himself, especially to someone like Alyosha, from whom in his heart he had expected so much. Of course there was that too, that anger, there had to be, but that was not it either, it was inexplicable.

'I'm so unhappy that I feel ill, yet I can't define what I want. Perhaps I'd better not think...'

Ivan Fyodorovich tried 'not to think', but that too failed to assuage his grief. What was most infuriating about this grief, what angered him most, was that it had a sort of fortuitous quality quite external to himself; he could sense this. Someone or something was worrying him, getting in the way, in the way that something can intrude upon one's vision sometimes, and, if one is busy or engrossed in conversation, may remain unnoticed for a long time; nevertheless one is certainly irritated, almost tormented, until finally one realizes and removes the intruding object, often something quite trivial and silly, something mis-placed, perhaps a kerchief dropped on the floor or a book not replaced in the bookcase, and so on and so forth. At last Ivan Fyodorovich reached his father's house in a thoroughly foul and irritable mood and suddenly, about fifteen paces from the gate, looked up and realized what it was that had been so tormenting and worrying him.

The servant Smerdyakov was sitting on the bench by the gate, cooling himself in the evening breeze, and from the moment that Ivan Fyodorovich set eyes on him he understood that this same Smerdyakov was also occupying his thoughts and that it was precisely this man that he could not rid himself of. At once confusion was dispelled and everything became clear. When he had heard earlier from Alyosha about his meeting with Smer-dyakov, a gloomy and unpleasant feeling had suddenly pierced his heart, eliciting in him a responding malice. Then afterwards, in the course of the conversation, he had forgotten about Smerdyakov for a while, but he still remained in his thoughts however, and no sooner had Ivan left Alyosha and returned alone to the house than the forgotten feeling suddenly resurfaced. 'Surely,' he thought with intolerable fury, 'such a good-for-nothing scoundrel can't upset me to this extent!'

The fact was that Ivan Fyodorovich had recently come to dislike the man very much, especially in the last few days. He himself had even begun to notice this growing feeling of near-hatred for the creature. Perhaps the hatred was intensified precisely because at first, when Ivan Fyodorovich had just arrived among us, things had been quite different. Then Ivan Fyodorov-ich had started to take a particular interest in Smerdyakov, and even considered him a unique individual. He had encouraged him to enter into discussion with him, although he was always surprised at a certain incoherence, or rather a certain uneasiness of mind, and wondered what it was that disturbed that 'contemplative' so constantly and incessantly. They talked about philosophical matters and even about why there had been light on the first day, since the sun, the moon, and the stars had been created only on the fourth day, and about how one should interpret this; but Ivan Fyodorovich had soon become convinced that it was not a question of the sun, the moon, and the stars, and that, however strange the subject of the sun, the moon, and the stars might be, it was nevertheless of altogether minor importance to Smerdyakov, and that he was concerned about something completely different. Whatever the truth of that, he had in any case begun to exhibit an overweening self-esteem and, what is more, an injured self-esteem. Ivan Fyodorovich took great exception to this. That was how his aversion had begun. After that, the squabbling had started in the house, Grushenka had appeared on the scene, the trouble with Dmitry had begun, the domestic routine had been disturbed—this too they had discussed, but although Smerdyakov talked about it most excitedly it had nevertheless been impossible to discover exactly what he himself wanted. There was even a surprising illogicality and confusion about some of his desires, which as a rule surfaced involuntarily and invariably remained vague. Smerdyakov was always enquiring, asking indirect, obviously spurious questions, though he never explained why, and usually at the culmination of his interrogation he would suddenly fall silent or change the subject entirely. But what had above all finally exasperated Ivan Fyodorovich, and given rise to such an aversion, was the loathsome and strange familiarity with which Smerdyakov increasingly treated him. Not that he ever allowed himself to be impolite, on the contrary, he always spoke with the utmost respect, but somehow, God knows why, he had begun to adopt an attitude of familiarity with Ivan Fyodorovich; he always spoke as if some secret complicity existed between them, something which had at some time been agreed by both sides, to which only they were privy and which was even incomprehensible to the other mortals bustling around them. Yet again, it was some time before Ivan Fyodorovich understood the real reason for his growing aversion, and it was only at this very last moment that it finally dawned upon him what it was all about. Now, disgusted and irritated, he was going to walk through the gate in silence, without looking at Smerdyakov, but the latter got up from the bench, and from that movement Ivan Fyodorovich guessed immediately that he wanted to talk to him about something in particular. Ivan Fyodorovich glanced at him and stopped, and the fact that he had stopped so suddenly, instead of walking past as he had intended a moment before, made him seethe with anger. With fury and revulsion he looked at Smerdyakov's emaciated eunuch's face, with his hair combed over his temples and fluffed up into a topknot. His left eye, slightly screwed up, winked and smiled as if to say, 'Where are you going? You won't fail to stop; you know that we, we the intelligent ones, have something to discuss.' Ivan Fyodorovich began to shake.

'Go away, you scoundrel, I've nothing in common with you, you fool!' he meant to say, but to his great surprise the words that escaped his lips were quite different.

'Is my father sleeping or is he awake?' he asked softly and meekly, surprising even himself, and suddenly, also quite unexpectedly, he sat down on the bench. For a moment, as he recalled later, he was almost afraid. Smerdyakov stood facing him with his hands behind his back, and looked at him confidently, almost severely.

'Still sleeping, sir,' he replied without hurry. ('You were the first to speak, not me.') 'I'm surprised at you, sir,' he added after a pause, lowering his eyes in a kind of affectation, extending his right foot and wriggling the toe of his patent leather boot.

'Why are you surprised at me?' asked Ivan Fyodorovich abruptly and drily, desperately repressing his feelings and suddenly realizing with revulsion that he was intensely curious and that not for anything would he leave without satisfying his curiosity.

'Why don't you go to Chermashnya, sir?' Smerdyakov suddenly raised his eyes and smiled familiarly. 'And the reason I'm smiling,' his winking left eye seemed to say, 'he can work out for himself if he's at all clever.'

'Why would I go to Chermashnya?' asked Ivan Fyodorovich, astonished.

Smerdyakov again remained silent a while.

'Fyodor Pavlovich himself implored you to go, sir,' he said at last, unhurriedly, as if implying that his reply was of no consequence, an insignificant remark, just for something to say.

'Oh, damn you, come straight out with it, what do you want?' shouted Ivan Fyodorovich at last, furiously, his meekness turning to rudeness.

Smerdyakov pulled his right foot back until it was level with his left and straightened up, but he seemed just as calm, and still had that same little smile.

'Nothing important, sir... it's nothing, sir... just by the way...'

Silence fell again. They said nothing for nearly a minute. Ivan Fyodorovich knew that he must stand up now and show his anger, but there was Smerdyakov standing in front of him as if waiting. 'Well, I'm watching, are you going to get angry or not?' At least, that is how it seemed to Ivan Fyodorovich. Finally he made a move to rise. Smerdyakov seized upon the moment.

'My situation is dreadful, Ivan Fyodorovich, sir; I simply don't know what to do about it,' he said suddenly, in a resolute and measured tone, and on the last word he sighed. Ivan Fyodorovich sat down again.

'Both of them are so odd, sir, and they're both behaving just like children, sir,' Smerdyakov continued. 'I'm talking about your father, sir, and your brother Dmitry Fyodorovich. He'll get up soon, Fyodor Pavlovich will, and straight away he'll be nagging me every minute. "Hasn't she come? Why hasn't she come?" and so on, right up to midnight or even later. And if Agrafena Aleksandrovna doesn't come (because, sir, perhaps she's no intention of coming), he'll pounce on me again in the morning, "Why didn't she come? Why not? When is she coming?" just as if I'm somehow to blame. And then on the other hand, sir, it's the same story; as soon as it begins to get dark, or even earlier, your brother will turn up in the neighbourhood with some weapon in his hand. "Look here, you scoundrel, you soup-stirrer, if you miss her and don't let me know she's here—I'll kill you if it's the last thing I do." The night will pass, and in the morning he too, like Fyodor Pavlovich, will start to torment me, "Why didn't she come? Will she turn up soon?" just as if it's my fault again that his fancy lady hasn't appeared. All the time, sir, day after day, hour after hour, they get so angry with me that sometimes I think I'll kill myself from fear. I can't trust them, sir.'

'So why did you get involved? Why did you start telling Dmitry Fyodorovich about everything?' asked Ivan Fyodorovich, irritated.

'How could I help getting involved, sir? If you really want to know the truth, sir, I didn't involve myself at all. Right from the start I kept quiet all the time, not daring to answer, it was he who made me into his servant Lichard to do his bidding.* Since then he's only had one thing in mind: "I'll kill you, you scoundrel, if you miss her!" I think, sir, that tomorrow I'm probably going to have a bad attack.'

'What do you mean, "a bad attack"?'

'A bad attack, sir, a very bad attack. Several hours perhaps; could last for a day or so, sir. Once I had an attack that lasted for about three days; I fell from the attic that time. The shaking stopped and then started again, and for three whole days I didn't come round. Fyodor Pavlovich sent for Herzenstube, the local doctor, he applied ice to my forehead and used some remedy or other... I could have died, sir.'

'Yes, but they say it's impossible to predict an epileptic fit, that it will occur at such and such a time. So how can you say you'll have one tomorrow?' Ivan Fyodorovich enquired with a certain irritated curiosity.

'It's true enough that one can't predict it, sir.'

'Besides, that time you fell from the attic.'

'I climb up to the attic every day, sir, I could fall from it tomorrow. And if I don't fall from the attic, sir, I shall fall down the cellar; I also go into the cellar every day in the course of my duties.'

Ivan Fyodorovich looked at him long and hard.

'You're inventing things, I can tell, and there's something I don't quite understand,' he said quietly and somehow threateningly. 'You're intending to fake an attack tomorrow for three days, aren't you, eh?'

Smerdyakov, looking at the ground and again wriggling the end of his right boot, brought his right foot back and stretched out the left one instead, raised his head, and said with a smirk:

'Even if I could pull off such a trick, sir, that is, if I could fake it, and it wouldn't be too difficult for someone experienced like me, I'd be quite within my rights to save my life; after all, if Agrafena Aleksandrovna came to his father while I was lying ill, he couldn't ask a sick man, "Why didn't you tell me?" Even he'd be ashamed to do that.'

'Oh damn!' exploded Ivan Fyodorovich with an angry grimace. 'Why do you have to make such a fuss about your life being endangered! All those threats of Dmitry's are nothing but empty words, that's all. He won't kill you; he'll kill somebody, but not you!'

'He'll kill me like swatting a fly, sir, me first of all. But I'm more afraid of something else: that I'll be implicated if he does something really dreadful to your father.'

'Why should you be implicated?'

'I'll be implicated because I told him in the utmost confidence about the signals.'

'What signals? Told whom? Say what you mean, damn you!'

'I have to confess', Smerdyakov drawled calmly and pedantically, 'that Fyodor Pavlovich and I share a certain secret. As you well know (and I'm sure you do), for several days now, as soon as it's night or even evening, he locks himself in. You've taken to going up to your own room early, and yesterday, sir, you went up and didn't come down at all, so perhaps you don't know how religiously he's begun to lock himself in at night. And even if Grigory Vasilyevich himself came, he wouldn't open the door—unless, perhaps, he recognized his voice, sir. But Grigory Vasilyevich doesn't come any more, because it's only me that serves him in his rooms now, sir—he arranged that himself as soon as he got involved with that Agrafena Aleksandrovna—and at night I have to go back to the outhouse, but I mustn't go to sleep till midnight, I have to keep watch, get up and do a round of the yard and watch for Agrafena Aleksandrovna, because he's been waiting for her like a maniac for several days already. He reckons like this, sir: she's afraid, he reckons, of Dmitry Fyodorovich ("Mitka" he calls him), "so she'll come to me at night by the back ways; and you", he says, "keep a look out for her till midnight or later. And if she comes, you come and knock on my door, or go to the garden and knock on the window twice, at first softly, like this, one, two, and then three times quickly, tap-tap-tap. Then", he says, "I'll know at once that she's come, and I'll open the door quietly." The other signal was if something unusual cropped up: first, two quick raps, tap-tap, and then, after a pause, again two raps, but much louder. Then he'd understand that something unexpected had happened and that I really needed to see him, and he'd open up and I'd go in and let him know. That was if Agrafena Aleksandrovna couldn't come herself but sent a message about something or other; besides, Dmitry Fyodorovich might come too, and I'd have to tell the master that he was around. He's very afraid of Dmitry Fyodorovich, so much so that even if Agrafena Aleksandrovna has already come and he's locked himself in with her and then Dmitry Fyodorovich turns up, I have to let him know without fail by giving three knocks; so, the first signal of five knocks means "Agrafena Aleksandrovna has come", the second signal of three knocks means "I must speak to you, it's urgent"—that's how he explained it, and he even showed me himself several times. And so, sir, since only he and I in the whole universe know about these signals, he'll open up without hesitation and without asking who it is (he's too frightened to ask out loud). Well, Dmitry Fyodorovich has found out about these signals.'

'How does he know about them? Did you tell him? What did you do that for?'

'It was just because I was afraid, sir. How could I have dared to keep it from him, sir? Every day Dmitry Fyodorovich demanded, "You're not deceiving me, are you? You're not hiding anything from me? If you do, I'll break both your legs!" So I told him about those secret signals to prove my loyalty and show him that I wasn't deceiving him and would tell him everything.'

'If you think he'll try to use those signals to get in, you mustn't let him.'

'And if I'm lying unconscious with an attack, sir, how can I stop him, even supposing I would dare to refuse him, sir, knowing him to be so desperate.'

'Oh, for heaven's sake! Why the devil are you so sure you're going to have an attack? Are you having me on, or something?'

'How would I dare to make fun of you, even to laugh, when I'm so terrified? I feel that I'm going to have an attack, I do get such premonitions, fear alone can bring it on, sir.'

'For heaven's sake! If you're going to be unconscious, Grigory will have to keep watch instead. Warn Grigory not to let him in, and make sure he doesn't.'

'I daren't for the life of me tell Grigory about the signals, sir, without orders from the master. And as for Grigory Vasilyevich hearing him and not letting him in, he's been ill since yesterday, and Marfa Ignatyevna is planning to give him his medicine tomorrow. That's what's been agreed. And this treatment of hers is really strange, sir: Marfa Ignatyevna knows how to prepare a concoction, something really strong, from some sort of herb, it's a sort of secret she has, and she always keeps some by her. And she doses Grigory Vasilyevich about three times a year with this secret concoction, sir, when he gets his lumbago and he's half paralysed, about three times a year, sir. And then she takes a towel, sir, dips it in this infusion, and rubs all his back with it for half an hour, till it's dry, it even goes all red and swollen, sir, and then what's left, what's in the glass, she gives it to him to drink and says a sort of prayer, but he doesn't get it all because she takes advantage of the situation and keeps a bit back and drinks it herself. And both of them, I tell you, like people who're not used to drinking, are quite knocked out and sleep for ages, sound asleep, sir; and when Grigory Vasilyevich wakes up, sir, he's nearly always cured, but Marfa Ignatyevna always wakes up with a headache. So if Marfa Ignatyevna carries out her plan tomorrow, it's unlikely that they'll hear Dmitry Fyodorovich either and not let him in, sir. They'll be asleep.'

'What nonsense!' exclaimed Ivan Fyodorovich. 'And all those coincidences as if on purpose: you having your fit and both of them stoned out of their minds!' Suddenly he frowned menacingly. 'And I suppose you haven't thought of arranging for all this to coincide?' he burst out.

'How could I arrange it, sir... and why should I arrange it, when it all depends only on Dmitry Fyodorovich and what his plans are... If he wants to do something, he'll do it, sir, and if not, I'm not going to go looking for him and force him to see his father.'

'But why should he go to father, and in secret too, if, as you yourself say, Agrafena Aleksandrovna is certain not to come?' continued Ivan Fyodorovich, blanching with anger. 'You said it yourself and for the whole month I've been here I too was sure the old man was fantasizing and that that creature wouldn't come to him. Why should Dmitry Fyodorovich burst in on the old man if she isn't coming? Tell me: I want to know what you think.'

'You know why he'll come, what does it matter what I think? He'll come just because he's angry or because he suspects something—if for example I'm ill, he'll have doubts and he'll get impatient and come storming in like he did yesterday, to see if she hasn't got in somehow without him knowing. He's bound to know that Fyodor Pavlovich has put three thousand roubles in a large envelope sealed with three seals and tied with a ribbon, and that he wrote on it in his own hand, "For my angel, Grushenka, if she comes to me," and that two or three days later he added, "my little chicky-bird". That's what's interesting.'

'Rubbish!' exclaimed Ivan Fyodorovich, almost in a frenzy. 'Dmitry won't try to steal the money or kill Father while he's about it. Yesterday he could easily have killed him in his stupid, frenzied anger over Grushenka, but he won't come to rob him!'

'Right now he needs money, he needs it desperately, Ivan Fyodorovich. You don't know how desperately,' Smerdyakov explained very calmly and painstakingly. 'Those three thousand roubles—he regards them as his rightful share and said as much to me himself. "My father", he said to me, "still owes me exactly three thousand roubles." And besides, consider, Ivan Fyodorovich, sir, there's a kind of poetic justice here; after all, it's pretty certain, it must be said, that Agrafena Aleksandrovna, if she wanted to, could undoubtedly force him to marry her—my master, that is, Fyodor Pavlovich, if she wanted to—and perhaps she'll start wanting to. I only mean, you know, that she won't come—well, perhaps she'll want more than that, perhaps she'll want to become the real mistress of the house. I know that her merchant friend Samsonov used to tell her quite frankly that it wouldn't be at all a bad thing, and he'd laugh about it. What's more, she's not stupid. She's not going to marry a pauper like Dmitry Fyodorovich. So when you take that into account, Ivan Fyodorovich, you'll see that in that case when your father dies nothing will be left for Dmitry Fyodorovich, nor, for that matter, for yourself or your brother Aleksei Fyodorovich, not a rouble, sir, because Agrafena Aleksandrovna will marry him precisely so that he'll put everything in her name and assign any capital he may have to her. But if your father dies now, sir, before anything happens, then each of you is sure to get forty thousand roubles straight away, even Dmitry Fyodorovich, whom he hates so much, because he hasn't made a will, has he?... Dmitry Fyodorovich knows this perfectly well...'

Ivan Fyodorovich made a kind of shaky grimace. He flushed suddenly.

'So why, after all that,' he abruptly interrupted Smerdyakov, 'are you advising me to go to Chermashnya? What are you up to? I'd go there, and look what would happen here.' Ivan Fyodorovich was breathing heavily.

'Quite so, sir,' said Smerdyakov quietly and reasonably, but nevertheless watching Ivan Fyodorovich intently.

'What do you mean, "quite so"?' repeated Ivan Fyodorovich, controlling himself with difficulty, his eyes flashing angrily.

'I said it for your own good. If I were in your shoes, if it was only me, I'd clear out of here... rather than get mixed up in such an affair...', answered Smerdyakov, looking into Ivan Fyodorovich's flashing eyes with an expression of utmost innocence. They were both silent for a moment.

'You are, I think, a stupid fool and, of course... an out-and-out scoundrel!' Ivan Fyodorovich got up abruptly from the bench. Then, just as he was on the point of going straight to the gate, he stopped suddenly and turned to Smerdyakov. Something strange occurred: Ivan Fyodorovich suddenly bit his lip as if in a spasm, clenched his fists, and the next moment would certainly have attacked Smerdyakov. The latter at least thought so, and immediately shuddered and gave a start. But the moment passed, Ivan Fyodorovich did not hit Smerdyakov, and without a word, apparently somewhat bewildered, he turned to the gate.

'I'm leaving for Moscow tomorrow, if you must know, tomorrow morning, early—and that's that!' he said angrily, loudly, and clearly. Later he would be surprised that he felt the need to say this just then to Smerdyakov.

'That'd be best, sir,' said the latter, just as if he'd been expecting this response, 'but of course they'll reach you by telegraph in Moscow if anything of that sort happens.'

Ivan Fyodorovich stopped again, and once more turned quickly towards Smerdyakov. But the latter was equally affected. All his familiarity and nonchalance had abruptly left him, his expression was totally attentive and expectant, and yet timid and obsequious. 'Aren't you going to say anything else, haven't you got anything to add?' was the question in his gaze, directed so firmly, straight into Ivan Fyodorovich's eyes.

'And wouldn't they reach me in Chermashnya as well... if anything like that happened?' exclaimed Ivan Fyodorovich, for some reason unknown to himself suddenly raising his voice alarmingly.

'In Chermashnya as well, sir, yes... they'd reach you...', muttered Smerdyakov almost in a whisper, as though groping for words, but continuing to stare straight into Ivan Fyodorovich's eyes.

'Moscow's further away and Chermashnya's closer, that's all; are you suggesting Chermashnya because you're worried about the cost of the round trip, or are you bothered that I've got to make a detour?'

'Quite so, sir,' muttered Smerdyakov, his voice breaking; he was leering at Ivan Fyodorovich, and ready to step back if need be. But to Smerdyakov's amazement, Ivan Fyodorovich simply laughed and, still laughing, walked quickly through the gate. Anyone catching sight of his face would probably have concluded that his laughter was not prompted by joyfulness. And he himself would have been at a loss to explain what he felt at that moment. His movements as he walked were erratic.

7

'IT'S ALWAYS INTERESTING TO TALK TO AN INTELLIGENT PERSON'

AND that was how he talked, too. Meeting Fyodor Pavlovich, who had just entered, in the hall, he waved his arms and shouted at him, 'I'm going up to my room, I don't want to see you, goodbye,' and brushed past, trying to avoid looking at his father. Just at that moment he very probably hated the old devil, but even Fyodor Pavlovich did not expect such a blatant exhibition of hostile feeling. Apparently the old man had in fact wanted to tell him something urgently, and to that end had purposely come out into the hall to meet him, but on receiving such a greeting, he said nothing and stood gazing in amusement after his son as he went up the stairs to the mezzanine and disappeared from view.

'What's got into him?' he asked Smerdyakov, who had followed Ivan Fyodorovich in.

'Something's annoyed him, you never know with him,' muttered Smerdyakov evasively.

'Well, to hell with him! So what if he's angry! Bring the samovar and clear off, and be quick about it. Is there any news?'

There now commenced the sort of interrogation about which Smerdyakov had complained to Ivan Fyodorovich, that is, about the expected visitor, but we shall omit those questions here. Half an hour later the house was locked up and the crazy old man was pacing alone from room to room, waiting in a fever of expectation for the prearranged five knocks, glancing from time to time through the dark windows, and seeing nothing there but the night.

It was already very late, but Ivan Fyodorovich still could not sleep and kept turning things over in his mind. He had gone to bed late that night, at about two o'clock. But we shall not stop to retrace the whole train of his thoughts, nor is it time yet for us to consider his soul; that will come in due course. And even if we were to try to reproduce his thoughts it would be a very complicated task, for they were not thoughts but something inchoate and, above all, very disturbed. He felt that he had lost all his points of reference. He was also tortured by various strange and almost totally unexpected desires: for instance, just after midnight he suddenly felt a persistent and unbearable urge to go downstairs, unlock the door, go into the outhouse, and beat up Smerdyakov, but had anyone asked him why, he certainly could not have advanced a single specific reason, except perhaps that he had come to hate that servant as deeply as one might hate the most detested of enemies one could possibly encounter in this world. On the other hand, more than once that night his soul was seized by an inexplicable and humiliating timidity, which he felt even deprived him of his physical strength. His head ached and was spinning. Something hateful oppressed his heart, as if he were about to exact vengeance on someone. Every time he recalled their earlier conversation he hated even Alyosha, and there were moments when he hated himself greatly, too. He even almost forgot all about Katerina Ivanovna, which later surprised him greatly, especially as he remembered quite clearly that yesterday morning, at her place, boasting with bravado that he would leave for Moscow the next morning, he had whispered to himself in his heart: 'Rubbish, you won't go, and you won't get out of this as easily as you're bragging now.' Much later, remembering this night, Ivan Fyodorovich would recall with particular disgust how he had suddenly got up from the divan several times, and quietly, as if very frightened that someone might be watching him, opened the door, gone out on to the landing, and listened to Fyodor Pavlovich moving about and pacing up and down in his rooms downstairs—he listened for a long time, about five minutes each time, with a sort of strange curiosity; why he did this, what he was listening for, of course he did not know. For the rest of his life he thought of this act as 'disgusting', and for the rest of his life, in his innermost depths, in his most secret soul, he considered it to be the basest act he had ever committed. He felt not the slightest hatred for Fyodor Pavlovich at these moments, only a lively curiosity for some reason. He wondered what he must be doing down there now, imagined him pacing about, peering out of the dark windows, and suddenly stopping in the middle of the room to wait, wait—in case someone knocked. Ivan Fyodorovich went out on to the stairs a few times to indulge his curiosity. When, at about two o'clock, Fyodor Pavlovich went to bed and all grew quiet, Ivan Fyodorovich also went to bed with the firm intention of going straight to sleep, as he felt thoroughly exhausted. And indeed he fell at once into a deep and dreamless sleep, but he awoke early, about seven o'clock. Dawn had already broken. Opening his eyes, he felt to his amazement a sudden inrush of unusual energy; he jumped up and dressed quickly, then pulled out his suitcase and, without wasting any time, began hurriedly to pack it. The laundress had sent back all his linen just the previous morning. Ivan Fyodorovich smiled at the thought that everything had transpired in such a way that there was nothing to prevent him from making a sudden departure. And his departure was indeed sudden. Although he had said the day before (to Katerina Ivanovna, to Alyosha, and then to Smerdyakov) that he would leave today, still, he remembered perfectly well that when he went to bed he had not at that moment been thinking about his departure, at least he certainly had not dreamt that, on waking in the morning, he would immediately rush to pack his case. At last his case and bag were ready: it was already nine o'clock when Marfa Ignatyevna came into his room with her usual daily question, 'Where would you like your tea: here, or are you coming down?' Ivan Fyodorovich went downstairs; his expression was almost cheerful, although there was a hint of impulsiveness and of haste in his words and gestures. Having greeted his father amiably and even asked particularly after his health, he informed him abruptly, without incidentally waiting for his father to finish answering his question, that he was leaving for Moscow for good in an hour, and asked him to send for the horses. The old man listened to this news without the least surprise and pointedly failed to exhibit any sign of chagrin at the departure of his 'dear' son; instead, he suddenly became extremely agitated as he remembered at that precise moment a matter of great urgency and personal importance.

'Oh, if that isn't just like you! You didn't say anything about it yesterday... but never mind, we'll sort something out somehow. Do me a great favour, my dear boy, go by way of Chermashnya, you only need to turn left at Volovya staging post, just twelve little versts and there it is, Chermashnya.'

'I'm sorry, I can't: it's eighty versts to the railway, and the Moscow train leaves at seven in the evening—I'll only just have time to catch it.'

'You'll get there tomorrow or the day after, but pop over to Chermashnya today. What would it cost you to set your old father's mind at rest! If I didn't have business to attend to, I'd go myself, because the matter there is urgent and important, but I can't, because here, just now... Look, I've got two lots of standing

timber there, in Begichevo and Dyachkino, on some uncultivated
land. The merchants Maslov senior and his son will give me
eight thousand for the timber, but only last year a buyer turned
up who was more than willing to pay me twelve, but the snag
was he wasn't a local. The locals aren't interested in buying
timber at the present time; old Maslov and his son are taking
advantage of this situation, they're loaded with money: they can
afford to drive a hard bargain. None of the locals dares to take
them on. But last Thursday, out of the blue, I got a letter from
the priest at Ilyinskoye telling me that Gorstkin had arrived—
he's also a merchant of sorts, I know him, only the good thing
about him is that he's not from around here, but from Pogrebovo,
that means he's not afraid of the Maslovs because he's not local.
He says he'll give me eleven thousand for the timber, do you
hear that? And the priest writes that he'll only be there for one
more week. So couldn't you go over there and fix it with him?...'
  'Why don't you write to the priest yourself, and he'll handle it.'
  'He can't, it's not that simple. The priest wouldn't know how
to go about it. He's pure gold, I'd ask him to look after twenty
thousand without a receipt, but he doesn't have the least idea,
he's a babe in arms, a crow could outwit him. And yet, you know,
he's an educated man. This Gorstkin looks like any other
peasant, what with his blue tunic, but he's an out-and-out rogue,
and that's the problem: he's an inveterate liar. Sometimes he
tells such lies that one wonders why. Three years ago he said his
wife had died and that he'd already married another, and, can
you believe it, not a word of it was true: his wife never died,
she's alive, and, what's more, she beats him every third day. So
that's what we need to find out: is he lying or not when he says
he'll buy it for eleven thousand?'
  'Well, what can I do about it? I don't know what he's up to
either!'
  'Hold on, wait a minute. You'll manage fine, because I'll tell
you everything to look out for with him, Gorstkin, that is; I've
had dealings with him for ages. Look, you have to watch his
beard; he's got a nasty reddish wisp of a beard. If his beard
shakes and he gets angry when he speaks—that means everything's fine, he's telling the truth, he wants to do a deal; but if
he strokes his beard with his left hand and chuckles—well, that

means he wants to swindle you, he's up to something. Never look him in the eye, you won't learn anything from his eyes, he's a deep one, a swindler—watch his beard. I'll give you a note for him; just show it to him. He's Gorstkin, only he's not Gorstkin, he's called Lurcher, but don't call him that, otherwise he'll go berserk. If you do a deal with him and everything looks fine, write to me at once. Just a couple of words, "he's not lying". Hold out for eleven thousand, though you can come down one thousand, no more. Just think: eight and eleven—three thousand difference. Three thousand's better than a kick in the shins; besides, it could be ages before I found another purchaser, and I really need the money. Let him know I'm serious, and I'll dash up there myself and settle the deal, I'll find time somehow. But right now, what do I want to go rushing out there for if this priest fellow has made it all up? Well, are you going or not?'

'I haven't got time. Let me off this once.'

'Oh go on, do your old father a favour, I won't forget it! You're all heartless, all of you, that's what you are! What's a day or two to you? Where are you going now, to Venice? Your Venice won't fall down in a couple of days. I'd send Alyosha, but what does Alyosha know about such matters? I only ask you because you're an intelligent person, as anyone can see. You don't know the timber trade, but you've got your wits about you. You just have to find out whether the man's talking seriously or not. I'm telling you, watch his beard; if it shakes, he's serious.'

'You're twisting my arm to go to that damn Chermashnya, aren't you?' exclaimed Ivan Fyodorovich with a nasty grin.

Fyodor Pavlovich either did not notice the nastiness or chose to ignore it, but he picked up on the grin.

'So you'll go then, will you? I'll scribble a note at once.'

'I don't know if I'm going or not, I'll decide on the way.'

'Why "on the way"; decide now. My dear boy, decide now! When you've done the deal, write me a couple of lines, hand them to the priest, and he'll send them to me before you can say Jack Robinson. And then I won't hold you up any more, you can go to Venice. The priest will take you back to Volovya staging post himself...'

The old man was simply delighted; he scribbled the note, sent for the horses, and gave Ivan the note and some brandy. Usually, when he was happy, the old man would become effusive, but this time he seemed to be holding himself in check. For instance, he did not say a single word about Dmitry Fyodorovich. He was not in the least moved by their parting. He did not even seem to be able to find anything to talk about, which fact was not lost on Ivan Fyodorovich. 'He's had enough of me,' he thought to himself. It was only as he accompanied his son down the steps that the old man began to get excited and made to kiss him. But Ivan Fyodorovich quickly held out his hand, obviously to foil the attempt. The old man understood at once, and checked himself.

'Well, God be with you, God be with you!' he called from the steps. 'You'll be back sometime, won't you? I mean it, do come, I'll always be glad to see you. Well, Christ be with you.'

Ivan Fyodorovich climbed into the tarantass.

'Goodbye Ivan. Don't be too hard on me!' shouted his father for the last time.

All the servants had come to see him off: Smerdyakov, Marfa, and Grigory. Ivan Fyodorovich gave them all ten roubles each. When he had settled himself into the tarantass, Smerdyakov rushed to adjust the mat under his feet.

'You see... I'm going to Chermashnya after all,' Ivan Fyodorovich somehow burst out. As on the previous day, this was a spontaneous exclamation and was even accompanied by a nervous little laugh. He was to remember this for a long time.

'So it's true what people say, that it's always interesting to talk to an intelligent person,' observed Smerdyakov weightily, with a penetrating glance at Ivan Fyodorovich.

The tarantass started up and gathered speed. The traveller's soul was troubled, but he looked around eagerly at the fields, at the hills, at the villages, at a flock of wild geese flying past him high in the clear sky. And suddenly he began to have a feeling of well-being. He attempted to strike up a conversation with the driver, and something the peasant said interested him enormously, but a minute later he realized that it had all gone in one ear and out the other, and that, in truth, he had understood nothing of what the man had said. He fell silent, and that was fine, too; the air was clean, fresh, chilly, the sky was clear. The faces of Katerina Ivanovna and Alyosha flashed across his mind's eye, but he smiled to himself, blew gently on the dear ghosts, and they flew away. 'Their time will come,' he thought. They reached the staging post quickly, changed horses, and rushed on to Volovya. ' "Interesting to talk to an intelligent man", what did he mean by that?' he held his breath suddenly. 'And why did I tell him I was going to Chermashnya?' They reached Volovya. Ivan Fyodorovich got out of the tarantass and was immediately surrounded by drivers plying for hire. They were competing to take him to Chermashnya, twelve versts by country tracks. He gave orders to harness the horses. He entered the staging-post house, looked around, glanced at the caretaker's wife, and walked quickly out again on to the steps.

'No need to go to Chermashnya. Can you get me to the station in good time for the seven o'clock train, boys?'

'We'll just make it. Shall we harness the horses?'

'Yes, as quick as you can. Will any of you be going into town tomorrow?'

'Why yes, Mitry's going.'

'Mitry, could you do me a favour? Call on my father, Fyodor Pavlovich Karamazov, and tell him I didn't go to Chermashnya after all. Can you do that?'

'Of course, I'll drop in; I've known Fyodor Pavlovich for ages.'

'And here's a tip for you, because I doubt he'll give you one...', Ivan Fyodorovich laughed cheerfully.

'That's for sure, he won't,' Mitry laughed too. 'Thank you, sir, I'll be sure to do it...'

At seven o'clock that evening Ivan Fyodorovich boarded the train and sped off to Moscow. 'That's the end of that chapter of my life, I've done with my old world for ever, and it's all in the past now, the lot; I'm off to a new world, new places, and I shan't look back!' But instead of exultation darkness enveloped his soul, and sadness such as he had never felt before in his whole life overwhelmed his heart. He spent the night thinking; the train flew along, and it was only at dawn, as it drew into Moscow, that he came to himself.

'I'm a scoundrel!' he whispered to himself.

As for Fyodor Pavlovich, having seen off his 'dear' son, he was quite satisfied. For a whole two hours he felt almost happy and partook of a little brandy; but suddenly an incident occurred in the house that was annoying and upsetting for everyone and, in the twinkling of an eye, plunged Fyodor Pavlovich into great confusion: Smerdyakov went to fetch something from the cellar and fell from the top step. It was a good thing that Marfa Ignatyevna happened to be in the yard just then and heard him in time. She did not see him fall, but she heard the shriek—that special shriek, strange, but already long familiar to her—the shriek of an epileptic having a fit. Whether the fit began as he started down the stairs, in which case, of course, he would have fallen unconscious to the bottom, or whether, on the contrary— Smerdyakov being a known epileptic—the fall and the shock had brought on the fit, it was impossible to tell, but they found him at the bottom of the cellar steps, foaming at the mouth, and his body twisting and thrashing about in convulsions. They thought at first that he had probably injured himself, broken something, an arm or a leg, but 'God protected him', as Marfa Ignatyevna said; nothing of that sort had happened, only it was difficult to lift him and carry him up from the cellar into the daylight. However, they asked the neighbours to help, and somehow they managed it. Fyodor Pavlovich was present throughout this incident and, obviously scared and somewhat dazed, personally lent a hand. The patient, however, did not come round: the fit ceased for a while, but then recommenced, and everyone concluded that it would go on as it had the year before, when he had accidentally fallen from the attic. They remembered that on that occasion they had applied ice to his temples. There was still some ice in the cellar, and Marfa Ignatyevna saw to that, while in the afternoon Fyodor Pavlovich sent for Herzenstube, who came promptly. Having examined the patient carefully (he was one of the most conscientious and attentive doctors in the whole province, an elderly and respectable little man), he concluded that it was an extremely serious fit and 'could have serious complications' which he, Herzenstube, did not yet fully understand, but that the next morning, if the initial treatment had not proved effective, he would consider alternative treatment. They installed the patient in the outhouse, in the little room next to Grigory and Marfa Ignatyevna's. From then on, the whole day was nothing but a succession of misfortunes for Fyodor Pavlovich: Marfa Ignatyevna prepared the dinner, the soup was dishwater compared to Smerdyakov's soup, and the chicken was so dried up that he simply could not chew it. To the bitter but nevertheless justified reproaches of her master, Marfa Ignatyevna retorted that she had never studied *haute cuisine* and that the chicken had been very old in any case. By the evening another problem had arisen: Fyodor Pavlovich was informed that Grigory, who had been ailing for three days, was finally about to take to his bed completely, with lumbago. Fyodor Pavlovich finished his tea as quickly as possible and locked himself alone in the house. He waited in a terrible state of trepidation. The fact was that he was expecting Grushenka almost for sure that very evening; at least, Smerdyakov had practically assured him earlier that morning that 'she promised to come, sir, without fail'. The irrepressible old man's heart was beating violently, and he paced up and down the empty rooms, listening attentively. He had to keep a sharp look-out: Dmitry Fyodorovich might be lying in wait somewhere or other, and when she knocked on the window (Smerdyakov had already assured Fyodor Pavlovich three days before that he had told her where and when to knock), he would have to open the door as quickly as possible and not keep her waiting on the doorstep even for a second, in case, God forbid, she took fright and ran away. This made Fyodor Pavlovich restless, but never before had his heart seethed with sweeter hope: it was almost certain that this time she would come!...

BOOK SIX

A Russian Monk

1

STARETS ZOSIMA AND HIS VISITORS

WHEN Alyosha, with a heavy heart and in a state of panic, entered the starets's cell, he stopped short in astonishment: instead of the dying man, sick and unconscious, that he had feared he would find, the first thing he saw was the starets sitting in his chair, exhausted by weakness, yet with a cheerful and alert expression and surrounded by visitors, with whom he was conducting a calm and enlightened conversation. As a matter of fact he had left his bed not more than a quarter of an hour before Alyosha's arrival; the visitors had already congregated in his cell, waiting for him to awake, Father Païsy having firmly assured them that the teacher, as he himself had promised that same morning, would definitely get up once more to talk to those who were dear to his heart. Father Païsy firmly believed this promise as he believed the failing starets's every word in fact, to the extent that were he to see him completely unconscious and not even breathing, as long as he had his promise to rise once more and say farewell he would probably refuse to believe even in death itself, and would fully expect the dying man to regain consciousness and keep his promise. And that very morning Starets Zosima had clearly said to him before falling asleep: 'I shall not die until I have had the pleasure of talking once more to you, dearly beloved friends of my heart, until I have seen your kind faces and opened my heart to you all again.' Those who had gathered for this, in all probability, last conversation with the starets were his most devoted friends, whom he had known for many years. There were four of them; three of them were hieromonks—Father Yosif, Father Païsy, and Father Mikhail, the Father Superior of the hermitage, still not very old, not nearly as learned as the others, of humble birth but resolute in spirit, artless and unshakeable in his faith, endowed in spite of his stern appearance with a profound kindness of heart, yet concealing that kindness even to the point of being ashamed of it. The fourth visitor, Brother Anfim, was a very old and unprepossessing little monk from the poorest peasant stock, almost illiterate, taciturn and reticent, hardly ever entering into conversation with anyone, the humblest of the humble, with the appearance of having been permanently frightened by some prodigious and awesome event quite beyond his powers of comprehension. Starets Zosima loved this apparently intimidated monk dearly, and throughout his life had treated him with the utmost respect, although there was probably no one with whom he had exchanged fewer words, despite the fact that in the past the two of them had spent many years wandering together throughout the length and breadth of Holy Russia. This was a very long time ago, maybe forty years or so, when Starets Zosima had first taken up his vocation as a monk in a poor, obscure Kostromsk monastery and, soon afterwards, had set out to accompany Father Anfim on his wanderings to beg for offerings for that poor little monastery. The host and his visitors had settled in the starets's bedroom, which, as previously mentioned, was rather cramped, so that there was barely enough space for all four of them (the novice Porfiry remained standing) to sit round the starets's armchair on chairs that had been brought in from the other room. Dusk was falling, and the room was lit by night-lamps and wax candles in front of the icons. Catching sight of Alyosha, who had stopped in the doorway in some confusion, the starets gave him a joyful smile and extended his hand.

'Welcome, my quiet one, welcome, my kind one, so here you are. I knew you'd come.'

Alyosha approached him, bowed to the ground before him, and burst into tears. Something was striving to tear itself free from his breast, his soul was in turmoil, he wanted to cry his heart out.

'Come, come, it's too soon to shed tears over me,' the starets smiled, placing his right hand on Alyosha's head. 'You see, I'm sitting here talking, perhaps I'll go on living for the next twenty years, as that good, kind woman wished me yesterday, the one from Vyshegorye with her daughter Lizaveta in her arms. Lord, remember the mother and her little Lizaveta!' He crossed himself. 'Porfiry, have you delivered her gift as I told you?'

He had remembered the sixty kopecks which his jolly, good-humoured follower had left the day before to be given to 'someone that's poorer than me'. Such offerings are made as a penance which people voluntarily impose upon themselves for some reason, and which invariably consist of money earned by their own labour. Before the day was out the starets had dispatched Porfiry to a townswoman of ours whose house had recently burned down, a widow with two children, who had to go begging for alms after the fire. Porfiry hastened to inform him that the matter had been accomplished and that, as instructed, he had handed over the gift 'from an unknown benefactress'.

'Stand up, my boy,' the starets continued, addressing Alyosha, 'let me have a look at you. Did you visit your family and see your brother?'

It seemed strange to Alyosha that he should be enquiring so deliberately and specifically about only one of his brothers—which one though? Whichever one it was, it seemed probable he had sent him away yesterday as well as today for the sake of this brother.

'I saw one of my brothers,' Alyosha replied.

'I'm talking about the elder one, the one I bowed to.'

'I've not seen him since yesterday; I couldn't find him at all today,' Alyosha said.

'Hurry up and find him, try again tomorrow, and hurry, leave everything, don't waste any time. Perhaps you'll still be able to prevent something terrible happening. I bowed down yesterday in recognition of the great suffering that he is to endure.'

Suddenly he fell silent and appeared to be lost in thought. What he had said was strange. Father Yosif, who had witnessed the starets bowing down, exchanged glances with Father Païsy. Alyosha was unable to contain himself any longer.

'Father and teacher,' he said with extraordinary agitation, 'I don't understand what you're saying... What suffering is he going to endure?'

'Don't be puzzled. I sensed something terrible yesterday... it was as though the look in his eyes had revealed his whole destiny. He looked like that just for an instant... so that my soul shuddered momentarily at what the man was laying in store for himself. I have seen that kind of expression on people's faces once or twice before in my life... as though it revealed the whole of their destiny, and their destiny, alas, came to pass. I sent you to him, Aleksei, because I thought that the sight of a brother's face would help him. But everything comes from the Lord, and so too our destinies. "Verily, verily, I say unto you, except a corn of wheat fall into the ground and die, it abideth alone: but if it die, it bringeth forth much fruit." Remember this. And besides, Aleksei, you should know, many's the time I've blessed you in my mind because of your face,' said the starets with a gentle smile. 'I think of you thus: you will leave these walls and will live in the world as a monk. You'll have many enemies, but even your very enemies will love you. Life will bring you much misfortune, but therein will be your very happiness, you will rejoice in life and convince others to rejoice in it too, which is the most important thing of all. That is your nature. My teachers and fathers,' he said with a benign smile, turning to his visitors, 'never till this day have I spoken about why the face of this youth is so dear to my soul—not even to him. Now I shall explain: for me, his face was like a reminder and a prophecy. At the dawn of my days, when I was still a child, I had an elder brother who died in his youth, before my very eyes, only seventeen years of age. And later, as I went through life, I gradually realized that in my destiny this brother was like a sign and a portent from above, for if he had not come into my life, if he had never been born, I don't think I would ever have become a monk and entered upon this precious path. He belonged to my childhood days, and now, at the end of my journey, I have as it were encountered before my very eyes a reincarnation of him. It is wonderful, my fathers and teachers, how without being much like him facially well, perhaps a little, Aleksei appeared to me to be so like him spiritually that many's the time I have thought of him as if he were actually that same young man, my brother, come to me mysteriously at the end of my journey to make me think back and delve into the past, so that even I was surprised at the strangeness of my own thoughts. Did you hear that, Porfiry?' he turned to the novice who was attending him. 'I have often seen in your face something akin to resentment that I loved Aleksei more than you. Now you know why this has been so, but I love you too, I want you to know that, and I have often been saddened at the thought that you were resentful. I do though, beloved visitors, want to tell you about that youth, my brother, for in all my life there has been nothing more precious, more prophetic, and touching. My heart has mellowed, and at this moment I look back over my whole life as though I were reliving it...'

Here I ought to point out that this final conversation of the starets with his visitors on the last day of his life has been only partially recorded. Aleksei Fyodorovich Karamazov wrote it down from memory some time after the starets's death. But whether it was only that conversation, or whether he added to it from his notes of previous conversations with his teacher, that I can no longer decide; besides, the whole of the starets's story runs on in the notes without interruption, as though he had described the whole of his life to his friends as one continuous tale, whereas according to later accounts what undoubtedly happened was somewhat different in fact, for the discussion that night was of a general nature, and although the visitors seldom interrupted their host, they themselves nevertheless had something to say for themselves, perhaps even interspersing his account with stories of their own; moreover, no such continuous flow of the story could have been maintained, because the starets was often out of breath, lost his voice, and would even lie down on his bed to rest, although he did not fall asleep, nor did his visitors leave their seats. Once or twice the conversation was interrupted by Father Païsy reading from the Gospels. What is also remarkable is that none of them thought that he would actually die that night, the more so since on this, the last night of his life, after sleeping soundly during the day he appeared suddenly to have gained a new strength which sustained him throughout the whole of this long conversation with his friends. This was his last tender communion with his friends and it lifted his spirits enormously, but only for a short while, for suddenly his life was ended... but of this, later. As for now, I wish it to be known that I have preferred not to elaborate on all the details of the conversation, but have confined myself to the starets's story as recorded in Aleksei Fyodorovich Karamazov's manuscript. That way it will be shorter and not so tedious, although of course, I repeat, Alyosha took many things from previous conversations and interwove them.

2

FROM THE LIFE OF THE SCHEMAHIEROMONK* FATHER ZOSIMA, RESTING IN THE LORD, IN HIS OWN WORDS, AS RECORDED BY ALEKSEI FYODOROVICH KARAMAZOV

Biographical information

(a) Starets Zosima's elder brother

MY beloved fathers and teachers, I was born in a distant northern province in the town of V, the son of a nobleman, but of modest, even insignificant lineage. He died when I was only two years of age, and I do not remember him at all. He left my mother a medium-sized wooden house and some capital, not very much, but sufficient to keep her and the children from want. There were two of us, my elder brother Markel and myself, Zinovy. Markel was about eight years older than me, very fiery and quick-tempered, but kind and never sarcastic, strangely quiet, especially when at home with me, his mother, and the servants. He studied well at school but did not mix with the other boys, though neither did he quarrel with them; that at any rate is how our mother remembered him. Six months before his death, when he had already turned seventeen, he began to visit a certain political exile in our town, a very solitary man who had been banished from Moscow on account of his unconventional views. This exile was no mean scholar and had formerly been a well-known philosopher at the university. For some reason he grew to like Markel and invited him to his home. The youth spent evening after evening with him, and this went on throughout the winter until, at his own request, the exile was transferred to a government post in St Petersburg, where he had patrons.

Lent began, but Markel would not fast, he kept mocking and ridiculing the fast: 'This is all such nonsense,' he said, 'and there isn't any God either,' which horrified our mother and the servants, and also myself, the youngest in the family, for even though I was only nine years of age I was extremely frightened on hearing these words. We had four servants, all serfs, bought in the name of a landowner with whom we were acquainted. I still remember my mother selling one of them, the cook Afimya, an elderly woman with a limp, for sixty roubles in cash, and taking on an enfranchised servant. In the sixth week of Lent my brother, who had always had a weak constitution and was sickly, chesty, and consumptive, suddenly took a turn for the worse; although quite tall and with a very comely face, he was thin and weak. He must have caught a chill or something, for the doctor arrived and soon whispered to my mother that it was a case of galloping consumption and that he wouldn't last out the spring. My mother began to cry and suggested to my brother (casually, so as not to frighten him) that he should observe the fast and receive the Holy Sacrament, for he was still up and about then. On hearing this he flew into a rage and poured all manner of scorn on the Church, but then he started to think: he had realized at once that he was dangerously ill, and that that was why mother had wanted him to fast and to receive the Sacrament while he still had the strength. To be sure, he himself had known for a long time that he was ill, and even the year before he had once somewhat nonchalantly remarked to mother and me at table: 'I wasn't meant to live in this world amongst you, I probably shan't last the year,' which proved prophetic. Some three days passed, and Passiontide began. Starting on Tuesday morning, my brother began to fast. 'To tell you the truth,' he said to mother, 'I'm doing it for you, to cheer you up and to put your mind at rest.' She began to cry from joy and grief: 'His end must surely be near, if such a change has come over him.' But soon he was no longer able to get to church; he took to his bed, and made his confession and received Holy Communion at home. The days were beginning to get lighter and brighter, and spring was in the air, for Easter was late. I remember how he'd cough all through the night and sleep badly, but when morning came he'd always get dressed and try to sit up in a soft chair. I can remember it exactly, his sitting there, quiet, meek, smiling, and, though he was sick, his face shining with happiness and joy. He was completely changed spiritually—such was the wonderful metamorphosis he had suddenly undergone! Our old nanny would enter his room: 'Let me light the night-lamp by the icon, my precious.' Formerly he'd never let her, and would even blow out the light. 'Go on, nanny, light it, it was horrid of me to stop you doing so before. You pray to God as you light the lamp, and I pray out of joy for you. That means we're both praying to the same God.' These words seemed strange to us, and mother would go off to her own room, have a good cry, and then come back into his room, wiping her eyes and trying to look cheerful. 'Darling mother, don't cry,' he used to say, 'I'll live a long time yet and share much joy with you, and life, you know, life is so full of joy and happiness.' 'Oh, my precious, what joy can there be for you when you are burning with fever all night and coughing your heart out.' 'Mother,' he'd say, 'don't cry, life is paradise, and we're all in paradise, though we don't want to acknowledge it; but if only we acknowledged it, there'd be paradise on earth tomorrow.' And we all wondered at his words, for he spoke so strangely and with such certitude; our hearts were full of tenderness, and we wept. Our neighbours used to come to see us. 'My dear kind friends,' he'd say to them, 'what have I done to deserve your love, why should you love someone like me, and how is it I didn't recognize, didn't appreciate that love before?' To the servants who attended to his needs, he would say over and over again: 'My dear kind souls, why should you attend to me, do I really deserve to be waited upon? If God were to have mercy on me and allow me to live, I would serve you myself, for we must all serve one another.' Mother would shake her head when she heard this. 'My darling boy, it's your illness making you talk like that.' 'Mother,' he'd say, 'joy of my heart, it is not possible for there to be no masters and no servants, but let me be a servant to my servants, just as they are to me. And there is something else I will tell you, mother: each one of us is guilty of the other's sin, and I most of all.' Hearing this, mother could not help smiling, she would just smile and weep. 'And why should you be more guilty than anyone else?

There are murderers and thieves out there, and what sins could you possibly have committed to blame yourself more than anyone else?' 'Mother dear, my sweet, my lovely,' he'd say (he had begun to use such words of endearment, such unexpected words), 'my sweetly beloved, joy of my heart, I tell you this: truly, each one of us is guilty of the sins of all other men. I don't know how to explain this to you, but I feel the truth of it so deeply that it torments me. How could we have lived together, quarrelled with one another, and not realized this?' He used to speak thus when he woke from his sleep, and with each day he became more and more tender-hearted, full of joy, and brimming over with love. Occasionally Eisenschmidt, the old German doctor, would arrive: 'Well, doctor,' he would joke, 'am I going to live another day in this world?' 'Not just a day, you'll live many days', the doctor would reply, 'and months and years.' 'Years and months, well now!' he'd exclaim. 'Why count the days, when one day is sufficient for man to experience all the happiness there is? My dearly beloved, why do we quarrel, why do we show off to one another, why do we bear grudges? Let us go straight into the garden, let us stroll and enjoy ourselves, let us love and exalt one another, let us kiss and rejoice in our life.' 'He's not long for this world, that son of yours,' the doctor said to mother as she was seeing him to the door. 'His illness is affecting his mind.' The windows of his room looked out on to the garden. Ours was a shady garden with ancient trees, which had come into bud with the spring, and the early birds flew up to their branches, chirping and singing at his window. And as he looked at them, and admired them he suddenly began to ask their forgiveness too. 'Little birds of God, little birds of joy, forgive me, you too, because I have sinned against you as well.' This was something none of us could understand at the time, but he would continue, weeping for joy: 'Yes,' he'd say, 'I was surrounded by such divine glory—birds, trees, meadows, skies, I alone lived an abject life, I alone desecrated everything and did not even notice the beauty and the glory.' 'You take too many sins upon yourself,' mother would say, weeping. 'My darling mother, my joy, I am crying from happiness, not from grief; I want to declare my guilt before them, but I cannot explain to you how to love them, for I do not

even know myself. Although I have sinned against everyone, I
too shall be forgiven, and that's paradise. Am I not in paradise
now?'

And there was much more that cannot be recalled or recorded.
I remember once I went to his room alone, when there was no
one else there. It was a bright evening, the sun was setting, and
the whole room was lit by a slanting shaft of light. He beckoned
me to him and, seeing this, I approached him, whereupon he
placed both hands on my shoulders and gazed into my face
tenderly and lovingly; for about a minute he said nothing, just
looked at me: 'Well,' he said, 'off you go now, go and play and
live for me!' I left his room and went out to play. And later in
life I recalled many times, in tears, how he had urged me to
live on his behalf. He spoke many more such amazing and
wonderful words, which, however, were incomprehensible to us
at the time. He died in the third week after Easter, fully
conscious, and although he had stopped speaking he did not
change right up to his last hour: he kept looking around joyfully,
his eyes full of gaiety as they sought out each of us, smiling and
beckoning us towards him. Even in the town his death was much
talked about. None of this affected me too much at the time,
even though I did cry profusely when he was buried. I was
young, still a child, but it was all indelibly imprinted on my heart,
and the feeling stayed with me. It was all bound to come to the
surface some time and manifest itself. And thàt, in fact, is what
happened.

(b) The Holy Scriptures in the life of Father Zosima

My mother and I were now all by ourselves. Our neighbours soon
started to advise her. 'Look,' they said, 'you've only one son left
and you're not poor either, you've got some capital, so why don't
you do what other people do and send your son to St Petersburg;
if he stays here you might be stopping him from getting on in
life.' And they advised my mother to enrol me in the cadet corps
in St Petersburg so that I could join the Imperial Guards later.
My mother hesitated for a long time; how could she part with
her remaining son? Finally, however, hoping to improve my
future prospects, she did make up her mind, although not
without a good many tears. She took me to St Petersburg and

enrolled me, and I never saw her again because three years later she died, having spent the whole of those three years grieving and worrying about us both. Of my parental home, I have only memories of the most precious kind, for there can be no memories more precious than those of early childhood in the parental home, and this is almost always the case even if there is very little love and harmony in the family. One can retain precious memories of even the worst families provided one's soul is capable of seeking out what is precious. Amongst my recollections of home I include memories of the Holy Scriptures, which even as a child I studied with great enthusiasm. I had a book on the Holy Scriptures with wonderful pictures, it was called *One Hundred and Four Holy Stories from The Old and New Testaments*, and I even learned to read from it. And I still keep it as a treasured memento, lying there on the shelf. But even before I learned to read, I remember how a certain spiritual revelation came to me for the first time when I was just eight years of age. My mother had taken me to church on my own (I can't remember where my brother was at the time), to the midday service on Passiontide Monday. It was a bright day, and when I recall it now I see anew the incense rising from the thurible and floating silently up, with God's rays pouring down upon us through the narrow window in the cupola above, the incense ascending in waves to meet them and appearing to dissolve into them. I watched with emotion, and for the first time in my life the seed of the meaning of God's word entered my soul. A youth came out into the nave of the church, holding a book so large that it seemed to me he could hardly carry it; he placed it upon the lectern, opened it, and began to read, and suddenly I understood something for the first time, for the first time in my life I understood what it was that they read in the house of God. There was a man in the land of Uz,* upright and devout, and he had considerable riches, a number of camels, sheep, and asses, and his children made merry and he loved them very much; he prayed to God for them, lest perchance they sinned whilst making merry. And there came a day when Satan ascended together with the sons of God, and presented himself before the Lord and said to the Lord that he had walked the world over and through the nether regions too. 'And hast thou seen my servant Job?' the Lord asked him. And the Lord boasted to Satan, pointing to His great and holy servant. And Satan smiled at the Lord's words: 'Surrender him to me and Thou shalt see that Thy servant will cry out and curse Thy name.'* And the Lord surrendered to Satan His righteous servant, whom He loved so much, and all at once, like a thunderbolt from the clouds, Satan smote Job's children and his cattle, and scattered his riches, and Job rent his mantle and fell down upon the ground and cried out: 'Naked came I out of my mother's womb, and naked shall I return in the earth: the Lord gave, and the Lord hath taken away. Blessed be the name of the Lord now and forever!'* Fathers and teachers, forgive me my tears now— the whole of my childhood seems to appear before me, and my chest heaves as it did at the tender age of eight, and as then I feel surprise, confusion, and joy. And the camels captured my imagination so much, and Satan who talked to God in this manner, and God who had abandoned His servant to perdition, and His servant calling out: 'Blessed be Thy name, even though Thou art punishing me,' and then the soft and sweet singing in the church: 'Let my prayer be answered,' and again incense from the priest's thurible, genuflection and prayer! From that time on—only yesterday I took the book down again—I have not been able to read this holiest of stories without tears. That there should be in it so much grandeur, so much mystery, so much that is inconceivable! Later I heard the words of cynics and detractors, words full of false pride: how could the Lord have abandoned His favourite servant to Satan's pleasure, taking away his children, plaguing him with disease, and covering him with sores so that he had to use a potsherd to clean the pus from his wounds, and for what? Merely in order to boast before Satan: 'Behold what My servant will endure for My sake!' But the greatness of the story lies precisely in its mystery, in eternal truth being demonstrated in transient earthly terms. Eternal truth has been established in the face of earthly truth. Here the Creator, looking down upon Job, exults once again in His work, as He did at the end of each day in the first days of creation, saying: 'That which I have created is good.' And Job, praising the Lord, not only serves Him but will serve the whole of His creation, from generation unto generation and so on through all eternity, for he was ordained for this. Lord, what a book it is and what lessons it contains! What a book—the Holy Scriptures! And with it what miracles and what power have been given to man! It is just like a sculpture of the world, of man and of human nature, and in it everything is named and set out for all eternity. And how many mysteries are revealed and resolved? God raises Job up again, and gives him wealth; many years elapse and, behold, he has new children, different ones, and he loves them. 'But how, oh Lord,' one might ask, 'could he have loved those new children, when all the others were no more, when they had been taken from him? Remembering them, could he ever have been truly happy as before, with the new children, however dear they might be to him?' Indeed he could, indeed he could: through the great mystery of human life, old sorrow is gradually transformed into peaceful and benign joy; impetuous youth is succeeded by humble, reflective old age. I bless the daily sunrise, and my heart sings in praise of it as before, but already I love the sunset more, its long, slanting rays and with them the quiet, modest, soothing recollections, the gentle images of a long and blessed life—and, over and above all, God's truth, healing, reconciling, and all-forgiving! My life is approaching its end, I know that, I can sense it, but I feel that with each remaining day my earthly life is drawing ever closer to the new, the infinite, the unknown one that is already lying close at hand, and in anticipation my soul leaps with ecstasy, my mind becomes lucid, and my heart weeps for joy... Friends and teachers, I have often heard, recently more frequently than ever, that our priests, particularly the rural ones, complain bitterly everywhere about their meagre subsistence and humble position; they openly assert, even in print—I have read it myself—that apparently, due to their low stipend, they are no longer able to interpret the Holy Scriptures to the people, and if heretics and Lutherans come to lure away their flock they say, 'So be it, because our stipend is so low.' Lord, I think, let them have more of that subsistence which is so precious to them (for their complaint is justified indeed), but verily I say unto you: if any blame has to be apportioned for this, half of it is ours! Let us suppose that they have no time, that they are right in claiming that they are weighed down all the time with work and official church duties, but surely not all the time, for even they must have at least one hour out of a whole week when they can think of God. Nor can they be working all the year round either. So, one evening a week, to begin with, let them gather the children round them—and the fathers will hear of it and they too will start coming. And there is no need to build a mansion for this either, simply invite them into your hut; don't worry, they won't make a mess of your hut, they'll only be with you for an hour. Open this book and start reading to them in simple language and without conceit, but warmly and humbly, without elevating yourself above them, just enjoy reading them a well-beloved text and take pleasure in their listening to you and understanding you, pause once in a while to explain the odd word which may be beyond the grasp of simple folk, but don't worry, they'll understand it all, the truly believing heart will understand everything! Read to them of Abraham and Sarah,* of Isaac and Rebecca,* of how Jacob* went to Laban and, in his sleep, wrestled with the Lord* and said: 'How dreadful is this place',* and you will astound the pious minds of the simple folk. Read to them, and to the little ones especially, of how the brethren sold their own brother, the lovable youth, the dreamer and great prophet Joseph* into slavery, and of how they said unto his father, showing him the bloodstained clothes, that an evil beast had rent him in pieces. Read how his brethren later came to Egypt to buy corn and did not recognize him, and how Joseph, by now a great governor, tormented them, accused them of theft, and detained his brother Benjamin, and all for love of them: 'I torment you, for I love you.' For throughout his life he had never ceased to remember how he had been sold to merchants somewhere by a well in the scorching desert, and how, wringing his hands, he had implored his brothers not to sell him into slavery in a foreign land; and now, seeing them after so many years, he loved them again unreservedly, but, though he loved them, he punished and tormented them. Finally, unable to bear the pain in his heart, he left them and threw himself on his couch and wept; later, he dried his eyes and returned, radiant and joyful, and announced to them: 'Brethren, I am Joseph, your brother!' Read further about how the old man Jacob rejoiced on learning that his beloved son was still alive, how he even abandoned the land of his birth, made his way to

Egypt, and died in a foreign land, proclaiming for all eternity the greatest of messages in his testament, which had lain mysteriously in his humble, timid heart throughout his life: that from his tribe of Judah would come forth the greatest hope of the world, its peacemaker and its saviour! Fathers and teachers, forgive me, and do not take offence that I talk like a small child about something which you have known for a long time already, and which, indeed, you can teach me a hundred times more skilfully and eloquently. I am talking merely out of happiness and excitement; forgive my tears, for I do so love this book! Let him, God's priest, also weep, and he will see how his listeners' hearts will tremble when they hear his words. All that is needed is a small, a tiny seed: if he sows it in the heart of the common man, it will not die, but will live in his soul all his life; it will hide there in the darkness, in the stench of his sins, as a glimmer of light, a sublime reminder. And there is no need, no need to explain or to teach much, he will understand everything simply. Do you think the common man will not understand? Then try reading him the touching and moving story of the fair Esther and the haughty Vashti,* or the wondrous tale of Jonah in the belly of the whale.* Don't forget the Lord's parables either, particularly from the Gospel according to St Luke (that is how I did it), and then the conversion of Saul, from the Acts of the Apostles (you must tell them that one, you really must!), and finally tell them something from the *Chety-Miney*, be it only the story of Aleksei the man of God,* and also of the greatest of all the joyous sufferers, the mother, Mary of Egypt,* who beheld God and bore Christ—you will pierce his heart with these simple tales, and all it takes is just one hour a week, however meagre your subsistence, just one hour. And the priest will see for himself that our ordinary people are gracious and grateful and will reward him a hundredfold; remembering their priest's zeal and his kindly words, they will willingly help him in his pastoral work and in his home too, and they will also accord him more respect than before—hence there will be an immediate improvement in his circumstances. It is so obvious that at times we are afraid to mention it lest people laugh at us, and yet it is so true! He who does not believe in God will not believe in God's people. Yet he who believes in God's people will behold the holiness of God, even if he has previously not believed at all. Nothing but the people and their innate spiritual power will convert our atheists who have broken away from the land of their birth. And what is Christ's word without example? Without the word of God the people will perish, for their souls yearn for the Word and for all kinds of beautiful visions. In my youth, a long time ago, nearly forty years, Father Anfim and I wandered all over Russia collecting alms for the monastery, and once we stopped for the night with fishermen on the bank of a large navigable river, where we were joined by a fine-looking peasant youth about eighteen years of age, who was in a hurry to get to work towing a merchant's barge the next day. I noticed in his eyes a look of warmth and openness. It was a bright July night, quiet and warm, the river was wide, mist was rising from its surface to cool us, a fish splashed gently every now and again, the birds had fallen silent, everything was still, serene, in prayer to God. Only the two of us were still awake, this youth and I, and we began to talk of the beauty of God's creation and its great mystery. Every blade of grass, every tiny insect, ant, honey-bee, all unthinking, astonishingly fulfil their purpose, thereby testifying to and continually perpetuating God's mystery, and I sensed the gentle youth's heart swell with emotion. He informed me that he loved the forest and its wild birds; he was a bird-catcher who recognized every sound that the birds made and could lure them all. 'I know nothing better', he said, 'than to be in a forest, everything there is so good.' 'True,' I replied, 'everything is good and magnificent, because everything is truth. Take the horse,' I said to him, 'a great animal that stands at man's side, or the ox that provides his food and works for him, its head bowed and submissive: just consider the faces of these animals—what humility, what devotion to man, who often beats them mercilessly, what meekness, what trust, and what beauty in those faces. It is indeed moving to know that they are completely without sin, for everything is perfect; everything except man is completely without sin, and Christ was with the animals even before He was with us.' 'Is it really possible', asked the youth, 'that Christ is with them, too?' 'How could it be otherwise,' I replied, 'since the Word is for all? All the world and all that lives on it yearns for the Word, every tiny leaf yearns for the Word, sings in praise of God, weeps for Christ without knowing it, and it does so through the mystery of its own guiltless existence. Out there,' I said to him, 'the fearsome bear prowls through the forest, terrible and ferocious, completely free of guilt.' And I told him how a bear once came to a great saint who was seeking salvation in a little cabin in the forest, and the great saint felt compassion for the bear and went out to it fearlessly and gave it a piece of bread: 'Go,' he said, 'Christ be with you,' and the ferocious beast went away obediently and quietly, without doing any harm. The youth was moved by the thought that the beast went away without doing any harm, and that Christ was with it too. 'Oh, how good it is,' he said, 'how good and wonderful is everything that comes from God!' He sat there quietly, absorbed in gentle thoughts. I could see that he had understood. And as he sat next to me, he fell into a light, innocent sleep. Lord, blessed be youth! And as I was dropping off to sleep, I prayed for him myself. Lord, send peace and light to all Thy people!

(c) Recollections from Starets Zosima's youth, before he became a monk. The duel

I spent a long time, nearly eight years, in the cadet corps in St Petersburg, and the different kind of education I received there dulled many of my childhood impressions, although I forgot nothing. In exchange, I adopted so many new habits and even opinions that I was transformed into an almost wild being, uncouth and cruel. Along with French, I also acquired a superficial politeness and a veneer of social graces, and we all, myself included, regarded the soldiers who served under us in the corps as complete animals—I perhaps more than anyone else, because of all of us I was the most impressionable. After graduating as officers we were ready to shed our blood in defence of our regimental honour, and as for true honour, hardly any one of us knew what that was, and even if anyone had discovered what it was he himself would have been the first to ridicule it. Drunkenness, rowdiness, and bravado were almost something to be proud of. I can't say that we were wicked; all those young people were good, but they behaved badly, and I was the worst of all. The worst of it was that I came into some money and was therefore able to indulge all my desires without restraint, with the full ardour of youth, six sails to the wind. But the surprising thing was that although I also read books at that time, with much enjoyment even, the one book I hardly ever opened was the Bible, but I never discarded it either, and I carried it with me everywhere; without being aware of it, I was really keeping that book 'for the day and the hour, for the month and the year'.* After serving thus for about four years, I finally found myself in the town of K, where our regiment was stationed at the time. Social life in the town was hectic, varied and extravagant, cheerful and hospitable, and being by nature of a cheerful disposition I was made welcome everywhere; added to which, it was known that I was not poor, which counts for a great deal in society. Thus it was that an incident occurred which was to form the basis of everything. I began to pay court to a young and beautiful girl, intelligent and worthy, of honourable character, the daughter of respectable parents. They were people of considerable standing, who could boast of wealth, influence, and power, and they received me in their house with kindness and warmth. It seemed to me that the girl was favourably disposed towards me, and my heart glowed at the prospect. I came to the conclusion later that perhaps I wasn't all that much in love with her, that I merely looked up to her because of her kind and noble character, which was as it should be. However, self-indulgence prevented me from asking for her hand at the time; it seemed rash and even perverse to say goodbye at such a tender age to the temptations of a debauched and free and easy bachelor life, especially as I was not without money. I did drop a few hints, though. Anyway, for the time being I put off taking any decisive step. And then, all of a sudden, we happened to be posted to another part of the country for two months. To my surprise, when I came back two months later I found the girl already married to a wealthy neighbouring landowner, a man of great charm, a little older than myself, but still young, with connections in the capital, better placed socially than myself, and, on top of everything, educated—education being something that I totally lacked. I was so astounded by this unexpected development that my mind went blank with anger. The most maddening part about it was that, as I found out at the time, this young landowner had been her fiancé for ages and I myself had met him many times at their house, but, blinded by my personal sense of superiority, I had noticed nothing. By and large, that was what offended me most deeply: how was it that nearly everybody else knew, and I was the only one who knew nothing at all? I was overcome with uncontrollable rage. Blushing furiously, I began to recall one by one how I had been on the point of declaring my love for her on numerous occasions and, since she had not stopped me, given me no warning, I naturally deduced that she had been laughing at me. Later, of course, I realized that she hadn't been laughing at me at all, quite the contrary, for she herself had jokingly interrupted such conversations and changed the subject— at the time, however, I was quite unable to grasp this and began to seethe with vengeful rage. I remember with astonishment that this anger and desire for revenge was extremely tiresome and objectionable to me personally, because, being affable by nature, I could not bear a grudge against anyone for long and had therefore, as it were, to provoke myself artificially, and in the end I became vulgar and stupid. I waited for an opportune moment and then, at an important social gathering, I suddenly contrived to insult my 'rival' regarding an apparently totally unconnected matter, ridiculing his opinion about a prominent event at the time*—this was back in '26—and, what's more, it was said that I did it rather cleverly and wittily. Then I forced him to explain himself, and was so rude in the process that he accepted my challenge in spite of the huge gulf between us, for not only was I younger than he, but I was altogether insignificant and of low rank. Later I learned for certain that he had also accepted my challenge out of some kind of feeling of jealousy towards me; he had been a little jealous of me before, when his wife was still his fiancée; if she were to find out now, he thought, that he had suffered an insult from me and had been afraid to challenge me to a duel, she might not be able to stop herself despising him and her love for him would be shaken. I soon found myself a second, a friend of mine, a Lieutenant in our regiment. Even though duelling was prohibited on pain of severe punishment, it had become fashionable amongst the military at the time—so wild are the fashions that at times tend to proliferate and become established. It was the end of June and our duel was set for the following day, at seven in the morning, outside the town—and then something truly fateful happened to me. On returning home on the eve of the duel in a savage and ugly mood, I flew into a rage at my batman Afanasy and struck him twice in the face with all my might, so that blood poured from his face. He hadn't been in my service long, and although I had occasionally struck him before, I had never done so with such vicious cruelty. And, would you believe it, my friends, forty years have passed since then and I still remember it with shame and remorse. I lay down and slept for about three hours, and when I awoke day was breaking. Not being able to sleep any longer, I suddenly got up, went to the window, opened it—my room faced the orchard—and saw that the sun was rising, it was warm, wonderful, and the dawn chorus was starting. 'But what's wrong?' I asked myself, and I was overcome by a feeling of shame and disgust. Was it because I was going to shed blood? No, apparently not, I thought. Was it because I was afraid of death, afraid of being killed? No, not at all—in fact, anything but that... And suddenly I realized what it was: it was because I had hit Afanasy the night before! And suddenly I saw it all before my eyes again, as though everything was being repeated: there he was, standing in front of me, and I was hitting him straight in the face with all my might, while he remained standing to attention, his hands at his sides, his head erect, eyes front, rocked by each blow, not even daring to raise an arm to protect himself—could a human being be reduced to this, could one man be hitting his fellow being thus! What a crime! It was as though a sharp needle had pierced my heart. I stood there as though demented, but the sun still shone, the tiny leaves shimmered with joy, and the birds, the little birds, kept singing in praise of God... I put both hands over my eyes, fell on my bed, and burst into tears. And I remembered my brother Markel and his words to the servants before his death: 'My beloved ones, my dear ones, why should you serve me, why should you love me, and do I really deserve to be waited upon?' 'Well, do I deserve it?' the thought suddenly struck me. Truly, why should I deserve that another man, created like me in the image and likeness of God, should serve me? This question struck me for the first time in my life. 'Mother dear, joy of my heart, each of us is truly guilty of the other's sin, only people don't want to acknowledge it, but if they were to acknowledge it—there'd be paradise on earth immediately!' 'Lord!' I thought, and wept, 'surely that can't be untrue? Truly, I am perhaps the guiltiest of the guilty, and the worst of men upon this earth!' And the whole truth suddenly dawned upon me in all its significance: what was I about to do? I was going to kill a good, clever, noble man who was in no way guilty of wronging me, and thereby I would be depriving his wife of happiness for ever, causing her suffering and death. I lay there, stretched out on my bed with my face buried in the pillow, and lost all track of time. Suddenly, my friend the Lieutenant came in with the pistols. 'Ah,' he said, 'I'm glad to see you're up already, it's time to go.' I was confused and did not know what I was doing; however, we went out of the house to get into the calash: 'Wait a second,' I said to him, 'I'll just run back quickly, I've forgotten my wallet.' And I rushed back into the building by myself, straight into Afanasy's cubby-hole. 'Afanasy,' I said to him, 'yesterday I struck you twice in the face, forgive me.' He just shuddered, as though in fright, and stared at me—and I could see that this was not enough, not nearly enough, and suddenly, just as I was, in my full dress uniform with epaulettes, I threw myself down at his feet and touched the floor with my forehead. 'Forgive me,' I said. Now he was completely nonplussed. 'Your Honour, my kind sir, whatever for... I don't deserve it...', and suddenly he burst into tears just as I had done a short while before, covered his face with his hands, and turned to the window, shaking all over and sobbing; I rushed out to my friend and jumped into the calash. 'Drive on,' I yelled. 'Do you see the victor?' I shouted, 'here he is, sitting opposite you!' Throughout the drive I was on top of the world, laughing and talking incessantly, though I can't remember now what it was that I said. He kept looking at me: 'Well, my friend, you're a splendid fellow, I can see you'll uphold the honour of the regiment.' So we arrived at the appointed place, and they were already there, waiting for us. We were instructed to stand twelve paces apart, and my opponent was to shoot first—there I was, facing him, happy as could be, not blinking an eyelid, looking at him with love in my heart, knowing what I was about to do. He fired, the bullet merely grazed my cheek slightly and caught my ear. 'Thank God,' I shouted out, 'you haven't killed your fellow man!' and I grabbed my pistol, turned round, and hurled it high into the trees of the forest. 'There,' I shouted, 'that's where you belong.' I turned to my adversary: 'Sir,' I said to him, 'forgive me for being a stupid young man, for offending you so deeply, and for forcing you to shoot at me. I'm ten times worse than you are, perhaps even more. Please convey this to that lady for whom you have the highest regard in the world.' Hardly had I said this than all three of them began to protest. 'I beg your pardon,' said my adversary almost angrily, 'if you didn't want to fight, why did you cause all this trouble?' 'Yesterday I was foolish, but today I'm wiser,' I replied joyfully. 'As regards yesterday, I believe you,' he said, 'but it's difficult to come to the same conclusion about today's behaviour.' 'Bravo,' I shouted, and clapped my hands, 'I agree with you on that; it serves me right!' 'Are you going to fire, my dear sir, or not?' 'No,' I said, 'but if you want to, you may fire a second time, only it would be better if you didn't.' The seconds began to shout too, especially mine: 'It's a disgrace to the regiment to ask for pardon right at the firing-line... If only I'd known!' I turned to them all, but I was no longer laughing: 'My dear gentlemen,' I said, 'is it really so surprising nowadays to find a person who'll repent of his own stupidity and admit his guilt in public?' 'But surely not at the firing-line!' my second yelled again. 'That's the whole point,' I replied, 'that's the crux of the matter, because I should have asked for forgiveness as soon as we arrived here, even before he fired, and not let him commit a serious and mortal sin, but we've arranged things so disgracefully in this world that it would have been almost impossible to do that, because only after I had allowed myself to be shot at at twelve paces could my words have any meaning for him, whereas if I'd done it when I arrived and before being fired at, everyone would have simply said: "He's a coward, afraid of a pistol, there's no point in listening to him." Gentlemen,' I cried suddenly from the depths of my heart, 'look around you at God's gifts: the bright sky, the fresh air, the tender grass, the birds, all nature is wonderful and without sin, and only we, we alone are godless and foolish and do not understand that life is a paradise, but all that is necessary is for us to want to understand this, and paradise would immediately come about in all its beauty, and we would hug one another and weep for joy...' I wanted to continue, but I couldn't. I couldn't catch my breath; I felt such joy, such sweetness, my heart was so full of happiness, a happiness such as I had never known before in my life. 'That's all very commendable and pious,' my adversary said to me, 'and, I must say, you're an unusual man.' 'You may laugh!' I said, laughing at him in turn, 'but you will praise me for it later.' 'Yes,' he said, 'I'm prepared to give you credit for it even now; allow me to offer you my hand, because, it would seem, you really are genuine.' 'No,' I said to him, 'not now, later, when I am a better man and have earned your respect—if you'll offer me your hand then, you'll be doing a good thing.' We returned home, my second railed at me all the way, but I just kept hugging him. All my friends got to hear of what had happened and met the same day to pass judgement upon me: 'He's brought disgrace on the uniform,' they said, 'he should resign.' There were also those who came to my defence: 'Let's face it,' they said, 'he didn't flinch from being shot at.' 'No, but he was afraid to continue, and asked for pardon at the firing-line.' 'But if he was afraid of being shot at,' retorted my defenders, 'he'd have fired his own pistol first, before asking for pardon, but instead he threw it into the trees while it was still loaded; no, there's more to it than that, there's something very strange here.' I kept listening, and it was a joy to behold them. 'My dearest friends,' I said to them, 'my friends and comrades, don't concern yourselves about my resignation, because I've already resigned, I handed in my resignation this very morning to my commanding officer, and when it's accepted I'll enter a monastery straight away, that was the whole purpose of my resignation.' The moment I said that, they all, to a man, roared with laughter. 'You should have said so at the very outset, now everything's clear, a monk can't be sentenced.' They couldn't stop laughing, but they were not jeering at me, their laughter was affectionate and cheerful, and suddenly they all loved me, even those who had condemned me most vehemently, and then, for the rest of the month, while my resignation was being processed, they were almost ready to carry me shoulder-high. 'Fancy you, a monk!' they said. And everyone had a kind word for me, they tried to talk me out of it, they were even sorry for me: 'Do you really know what you're doing?' 'Yes,' they said, 'he's brave all right, he allowed himself to be shot at, and could have fired his own pistol if he'd wanted to, but the night before he dreamt he should become a monk, that's what it was.' Almost exactly the same thing happened in local society. Formerly, though I was welcome enough, no one had paid any particular attention to me, but now they vied with one another to make my acquaintance and to invite me to their homes. They couldn't help laughing at me, but they loved me all the same, and I should add that, though everyone discussed the duel openly at the time, the authorities did not pursue the matter because my adversary was a close relative of our general; and in fact, since it had ended without bloodshed and almost farcically, and because, to cap it all, I had tendered my resignation, the whole affair was regarded as a joke. And so, in spite of their laughter, I began to talk about it openly and without embarrassment, for after all their laughter was not malicious but good-natured. For the most part all these conversations took place at soirées, in the company of ladies, as it was the women who most loved to listen to me then, and they obliged their menfolk to do likewise. Anyone who caught my eye would laugh and say, 'How can I possibly be guilty of the sins of all other men? How can I, for instance, be guilty of what you have done?' 'How can I', I said to them, 'expect you to understand that, when the whole world has gone down another path, when we regard a blatant lie as a truth, and when we expect others to perpetuate that same lie? For once in my life I did something genuine,' I said to them, 'and what happened? I became a kind of holy fool in all your eyes, and even though you've taken a liking to me, you still go on making fun of me.' 'Well, is it any wonder we love you?' my hostess suddenly laughed out loud; this exchange happened at a large party with lots of guests present. Then suddenly, among the ladies, there stood up the same young woman on whose account I had thrown down the gauntlet, and whom until just recently I had been wooing; I had completely failed to notice her arrival at the party. She stood up, approached me, and extended her hand: 'Allow me', she said, 'to declare that I for one am not making fun of you; on the contrary, I'm grateful to you from the bottom of my heart, and confirm my admiration for what you did.' Her husband too came up, then everyone crowded round to shake my hand, all but kissing me. I was brimming with joy. I particularly noticed among those who had gathered round me a certain gentleman, a middle-aged man with whom I was not acquainted, though I had known him by name for some time, and with whom, until that night, I had not even exchanged a single word.

(d) The mysterious visitor

He had been working in our town for a long time, occupied an important position in the civil service, and was respected by everyone. He was wealthy and renowned for his charity, had donated a considerable sum of money towards an almshouse and an orphanage, and moreover, as was revealed later after his death, had performed many anonymous acts of charity. He was about fifty, almost severe in appearance, and a man of few words; he had been married for not more than ten years to a young wife by whom he had three small children. There I was, sitting at home the next evening, when all of a sudden the door opened and this very same gentleman entered.

I should point out that I was by this time no longer living at my former lodgings, for immediately after submitting my resignation I moved to other rooms, which I rented from an old woman—the widow of a clerk—who lived there herself with her maid. The move to these rooms took place only because, when I returned from the duel, I sent Afanasy back to the regiment the very same day, being too ashamed to look him in the eye after what had occurred between us, such is the embarrassment of an unprepared, worldly man concerning even his most noble deed.

'I have been listening to you', said the gentleman, 'with great curiosity for several days in various people's homes, and at last I decided to get to know you personally and to have a more detailed conversation with you. Would you be so good as to do me a really great service, my dear sir?' 'Certainly,' I replied, 'with the greatest of pleasure; I'd consider it a particular honour.' That's what I said, but such was my initial surprise on meeting him that I nearly took fright. For although people had listened to me and expressed curiosity, until then no one had approached me with such a serious and solemn appeal. And he had actually come to my rooms. He sat down. 'I see a great strength of character in you,' he went on, 'for you were not afraid to bear witness to the truth in a matter in which, for doing what you thought was right, you risked bringing universal scorn upon yourself.' 'You are too generous, perhaps, in your praise of me,' I said. 'No, not at all,' he replied, 'believe me, to do such a thing is far more difficult than you think. As a matter of fact,' he continued, 'that was precisely what astonished me, and why I have come to see you. Would you, if my curiosity is not too unseemly, describe to me precisely what you felt as you forced yourself to ask forgiveness at the duel—if you still remember, that is. Do not regard my question as an idle one; it is anything but, and in posing it I have my own secret motive, which I shall probably reveal to you in good time if it be God's will to bring us closer together.'

All the time he was saying this I had been looking him straight in the face, and suddenly I was overcome by a feeling of great trust towards him, and I too began to experience an extraordinary curiosity, because I felt that he was indeed harbouring a particular secret in his heart.

'You ask me', I replied, 'exactly what I felt when I asked my adversary for forgiveness, but it would be better if I told you what happened from the very beginning, which is something I haven't told anyone yet,' and I related to him everything that had happened with Afanasy, right down to how I had bowed down to the ground in front of him. 'From this, you can see for yourself', I concluded, 'that it was easier for me at the duel, because I had already taken the first step before I left the house, and once having taken that course everything else followed not only easily, but almost cheerfully and joyfully.'

Having heard me out, he regarded me warmly: 'All this is extremely curious and I shall certainly call on you again.' And from then on he began to visit me nearly every night. And we would have become great friends if he had only told me something about himself. However, he hardly said a word about himself, but instead questioned me incessantly about myself. In spite of this I became very fond of him and soon confided all my feelings in him, for it occurred to me: why do I need to know his secrets; I can see plainly that he's a righteous man. Besides, he's such a serious person and so much older than I, and yet he visits me, a mere youth, and does not spurn my company. And I learned a great deal that was useful from him, because he was a man of great wisdom. 'That life is paradise', he said suddenly, 'is something I've thought about for a long time,' and then he added immediately: 'That's all I think about.' He looked at me and smiled. 'I'm more convinced of it than you are,' he said, 'and you'll find out why later.' I listened to him, thinking to myself: 'This is probably because he wants to reveal something to me.' 'Paradise', he said, 'is concealed within each one of us, it is hidden in me too at this moment, and I need only to wish it, and it will come about the very next day and remain with me for the rest of my life.' I gazed at him. He spoke with feeling and looked at me mysteriously, as though he were probing me. 'As to every man being guilty for everyone and everything, quite apart from his own sins,' he continued, 'you did indeed judge correctly, and it is surprising how you managed to get so completely to the heart of the matter straight away. Indeed, it is true that as soon as people start to understand this concept it will be the beginning of the kingdom of heaven for them, not merely in their dreams but in reality too.' 'And when', I exclaimed with bitterness, 'is this likely to come about, if at all? Is it not just a dream?' 'Well,' he said, 'you're still a sceptic, you preach, and yet you yourself don't believe. Don't forget though that this dream, as you put it, will come to pass—you must believe, but it will not happen yet, for there is an appointed time for everything. It is a spiritual and a psychological matter. In order to refashion the world, it is necessary for people themselves to adopt a different mental attitude. Until man becomes brother unto man, there shall be no brotherhood of men. No kind of science or material advantage will ever induce people to share their property or their rights equitably. No one will ever have enough, people will always grumble, they will always envy and destroy one another. You ask when will all this come about. It will come about, but first there must be an end to the habit of self-imposed *isolation* of man.' 'What isolation?' I asked him. 'The kind that is prevalent everywhere now, especially in our age, and which has not yet come to an end, has not yet run its course. For everyone nowadays strives to dissociate himself as much as possible from others, everyone wants to savour the fullness of life for himself, but all his best efforts lead not to fullness of life but to total self-destruction, and instead of ending with a comprehensive evaluation of his being, he rushes headlong into complete isolation. For everyone has dissociated himself from everyone else in our age, everyone has disappeared into his own burrow, distanced himself from the next man, hidden himself and his possessions, the result being that he has abandoned people and has, in his turn, been abandoned. He piles up riches in solitude and thinks: 'How powerful I am now, and how secure,' and it never occurs to the poor devil that the more he accumulates, the further he sinks into suicidal impotence. For man has become used to relying on himself alone, and has dissociated himself from the whole; he has accustomed his soul to believe neither in human aid, nor in people, nor in humanity; he trembles only at the thought of losing his money* and the privileges he has acquired. Everywhere the human mind is beginning arrogantly to ignore the fact that man's true security is to be attained not through the isolated efforts of the individual, but in a corporate human identity. But it is certain that this terrible isolation will come to an end, and everyone will realize at a stroke how unnatural it is for one man to cut himself off from another. This will indeed be the spirit of the times, and people will be surprised how long they have remained in darkness and not seen the light. It is then that the sign of the Son of man will appear in heaven...* But, nevertheless, until then man should hold the banner aloft and should from time to time, quite alone if necessary, set an example and rescue his soul from isolation in order to champion the bond of fraternal love, though he be taken for a holy fool. And he should do this in order that the great Idea should not die...'

Thus, evening after evening was spent in heated and exhilarating discussions. I even gave up socializing and visited friends far less often, and anyway I was becoming less of a novelty in people's eyes. I say this without reproach, because they continued to be fond of me and to treat me with kindness; all the same, it must be admitted that the appeal of novelty is a force to be reckoned with in this world. As regards my mysterious visitor, I finally began to regard him with admiration, for apart from the enjoyment I derived from his wisdom I began to sense that he was nurturing some kind of a plan and was perhaps preparing himself for some great deed. Maybe what also appealed to him was that, on the face of it, I did not appear to be unduly interested in his secret and did not, either directly or indirectly, attempt to prise it out of him. But in the end I noticed that he himself was beginning desperately to want to tell me something. This became especially apparent about a month after he started visiting me. 'Do you know', he once asked me, 'that people in the town are very curious about us and are surprised that I come to see you so often; but let them, because *everything will soon be revealed.*' Occasionally he would suddenly become extremely agitated and at such times would almost invariably get up and leave. At other times he would fix me with a long, penetrating gaze which made me think: 'Now, surely, he's going to say something,' but instead he'd break off and begin to talk of something ordinary and commonplace. He also began to complain frequently of headaches. And then on one occasion, quite unexpectedly, after a long and impassioned discourse, I noticed that he suddenly grew pale, his face twisted, and he just stared at me blankly.

'What's the matter with you,' I asked, 'are you ill?'

He had just been complaining of a headache.

'I... you know... I... killed someone.'

Saying this, he smiled, white as a sheet. 'Why is he smiling?' the thought suddenly struck me like a blow, even before I had taken in what he said. I too went pale.

'What did you say?' I exclaimed.

'You see', he replied with the same wan smile, 'how dearly it cost me to utter those first words. Now that I've said them, I'm sure I've done the thing. I can go on.'

For a long time I could not believe him, and I finally did so only after he had been coming to me for three days and had told me everything in detail. At first I took him for a madman, but in the end, to my great chagrin and surprise, I had to admit that he was telling the truth. Fourteen years previously he had committed a serious and terrible crime, the victim being a beautiful and wealthy young widow who owned land and had a *pied-à-terre* in our town. He had fallen passionately in love with her, had declared his feelings for her, and had tried to persuade her to

marry him. But she had already given her heart to someone else,
a distinguished high-ranking army officer, who was on active
service at the time but was expected to return soon. She rejected
his offer and asked him not to call on her any more. He stopped
calling on her, but, being familiar with the layout of her house,
with extraordinary recklessness and with a good chance of being
discovered, he broke in one night over the roof from the garden.
But, as is very often the case, it is the audacious crime that
succeeds where others fail. Having got into the attic through the
skylight, he descended the staircase into the living-quarters,
knowing that the servants sometimes carelessly left the door at
the foot of the stairs unlocked. He was relying on this careless-
ness and, sure enough, he found it unlocked. On entering the
living-quarters, he made his way in the dark into her bedroom,
where a night-light was burning. As luck would have it, both her
chambermaids had secretly gone without permission to a name-
day party in a neighbouring house in the same street. The rest
of the servants were asleep in their quarters and in the kitchen
on the ground floor. Seeing her sleeping there, his passion
exploded, his heart was gripped by a vengeful and jealous anger,
and, as though in a drunken frenzy, he went up to her and
plunged a knife straight into her heart, so that she did not even
utter a cry. With heinous and criminal intent he then made it
look as if the servants had been responsible: without compunction he stole her purse, withdrew the keys from under her pillow,
unlocked her chest of drawers, and took a few items from it, just
as a common servant would have done, leaving all the valuable
documents but taking the money; he also took a few of the more
weighty pieces of gold jewellery, worth ten times the value of the
money, and ignored the small knick-knacks. One or two items
he took as keepsakes, but of this later. Having committed this
terrible deed, he left by the same route. Neither the following
day, when the alarm was raised, nor ever again did it enter
anyone's head to suspect the real culprit! Nor did anyone know
of his love for her, because he had always been of a taciturn and
incommunicative nature and did not have a friend in whom he
could confide. Since he had not been to see her at all during the
previous two weeks, he was regarded simply as an acquaintance
of the deceased, and not a very close one at that. Instead,

suspicion immediately fell on her manservant Peter, a serf, and all the circumstances appeared to confirm this suspicion, for this servant knew that the lady intended—she made no secret of it—to send him to the army as part of the quota of conscripts that she was obliged to supply from her peasants, he being single and of unruly behaviour to boot. It was said that once, in a tavern, when he was drunk and wild with anger, he had threatened to kill her. Two days before her death he had run away and was living somewhere in the town, no one knew where. The very next day after the murder he was found lying blind drunk on the road leading out of town, with a knife in his pocket, and, to make matters worse, the palm of his right hand was for some reason stained with blood. He maintained that this was from a nosebleed, but no one believed him. The maids admitted that they had been to a party and had left the front door of the porch unlocked until their return. There was a lot more circumstantial evidence, on the strength of which the innocent servant was apprehended. He was arrested and the trial began, but precisely a week later the defendant fell ill with fever and died unconscious in hospital. That was the end of the matter, it was deemed to be God's will, and everyone, the judges, the authorities, and the public at large, remained convinced that the murder had been committed by none other than the deceased servant. Then followed the punishment.

The mysterious visitor, now my friend, told me that to begin with he had felt no pangs of conscience whatsoever. He suffered for a long time, not because of that, but only out of regret that he had killed a beloved woman, that she was no longer living, and that in killing her he had killed his love while the flames of passion were still raging in his heart. As for the spilling of innocent blood, the murder of another human being, he hardly gave that a thought at the time. The idea that his victim could become someone else's wife seemed inconceivable to him, and for a long time therefore he was convinced in his own mind that there was nothing else he could have done. At first he was slightly troubled by the servant's arrest, but the latter's sudden illness and then death put his mind at rest, for, to all appearances (that is how he argued, anyway), the servant had died not from the arrest and the shock of it, but from catching cold while absconding and lying all night blind drunk on the wet ground. The stolen goods and money did not worry him unduly, for (he continued to argue in the same vein) the theft had been committed not for the sake of greed but to allay suspicion. Besides, the sum was quite insignificant, and anyway, shortly afterwards he donated all the money, in fact even more, to an almshouse that had been founded in our town. He had done it specifically to salve his conscience regarding the theft and, strangely enough, for a time (quite a considerable time in fact) he enjoyed peace of mind—he said so himself. He immersed himself in intensive administrative activity, deliberately sought out a most difficult and awkward assignment which took him about two years to accomplish, and, being of a strong character, he almost managed to forget what had happened; whenever the event did return to haunt him, however, he tried to dismiss it from his mind altogether. He threw himself into charitable work, accomplished a great deal, and made numerous donations to worthy causes in the town; he also became known in the big cities, and was elected on to the committees of charitable societies in Moscow and St Petersburg. Nevertheless, he began to be tortured beyond all endurance by his thoughts. At this point he became attracted to a beautiful, sensible young woman, and he married her soon afterwards, thinking that marriage would dispel his morbid introspection and that, by entering upon a new path and zealously performing his duties with respect to his wife and children, he would be able to distance himself completely from his old memories. But what happened was exactly the reverse. Even in the first year of their marriage he began to be tortured by the nagging thought: 'My wife loves me, but what if she were to find out?' When she became pregnant with their first child and told him about it, he was in a quandary: 'I'm giving life, though I myself have taken life.' Then he had children. 'How will I dare to love them, to teach them and bring them up, how will I speak to them of virtue? I have spilt blood.' They grew up to be delightful children and he wanted to caress them: 'But I cannot look at their innocent, bright faces; I am unworthy.' Finally he began to be painfully and menacingly haunted by the blood of the murdered victim, her lost young life, her blood crying out for vengeance. He began to have terrible dreams. But, being stoical, he bore the anguish for a long time: 'I will atone for everything by this secret suffering of mine.' But this too proved to be a vain hope; the more time passed, the greater the suffering became. Although he was generally disliked because of his severe and morose nature, he began to be respected in society for his charitable works, but the more respect he was accorded, the more unbearable his life became. He admitted to me that he had thought of killing himself. But instead, he began to be haunted by another idea—an idea which he took to be crazy and impossible at first, but which finally weighed upon his heart to such an extent that he could no longer escape it. The idea was simply this: to stand up and announce in public that he had murdered someone. For about three years he carried this idea around with him, which haunted him in various guises. Finally he became convinced with all his heart that by confessing his crime he would without doubt cleanse his soul and find peace once and for all. But having reached this conclusion, he panicked: how could he do this? And then unexpectedly the incident at the duel occurred. 'Observing you, I finally made up my mind.' I stared at him.

'Can it really be true', I exclaimed, throwing up my hands in surprise, 'that such a small incident could fill you with such resolution?'

'My resolve took three years to mature,' he replied, 'but this incident of yours was the final spur. Seeing your example, I reproached myself and was full of envy,' he added, almost with severity.

'But no one will ever believe you,' I remarked. 'Fourteen years have passed.'

'I've got indisputable evidence. I'll submit it.'

I burst into tears at this and hugged him closely.

'However, you must decide one thing for me, just one thing!' he said (as though everything depended on me now). 'What about my wife and children! My wife may die of grief, perhaps, and though my children will not lose their titles or their estates, they'll still have a convict for a father, and that will stay with them for ever. And what a legacy, what a legacy I'll have left them in their hearts!'

I said nothing.

'And to part with them, to leave them for ever? It will be for ever, won't it?'

I just sat there, saying nothing and muttering a prayer to myself. Finally I got up. I was terrified.

'Well?' he said, looking at me.

'Go,' I said, 'announce it publicly. Everything will pass, truth alone will remain. When they grow up, your children will understand how outstandingly noble your decision was.'

On that occasion he left me, seemingly fully resolved. But he came back to see me every night after that for a full two weeks, screwing up his courage, unable to take the plunge. It almost broke my heart to see him. There'd be times when he'd turn up determined and say, deeply moved:

'I know that as soon as I've confessed, it'll really be paradise. I've had fourteen years of hell. I want to suffer. I will accept suffering, and I will begin to live. The more one becomes entangled in a tissue of lies, the harder it is to extricate oneself. Now, not only am I unable to love my fellow man, I dare not even love my own children. Lord, surely my children will understand what my suffering has cost me, and perhaps they won't judge me! God is to be found in truth, not in power.'

'Everyone will understand your act of courage,' I'd say to him, 'if not now, then later, because you will have served truth, the highest of truths, which is not of this world...'

And he would depart seemingly comforted, but the next day he'd be back again, angry and pale, and say sarcastically:

'Every time I come to see you, you have such a curious look on your face, it's as if you were saying: "So you still haven't confessed, eh?" Wait, don't be too eager to despise me. It's not as easy as you may imagine. In fact, I may never do it at all. You won't denounce me, will you?'

But, as it happened, not only was I not looking at him with any kind of idle curiosity, but I could not bear to look at him at all. I was exhausted to the point of collapse, and kept wanting to burst into tears. I could not even sleep at night.

'I've just come from my wife,' he continued. 'Do you know what it's like to have a wife? As I was leaving, my children called out to me: "Goodbye, papa, don't be long, hurry back and read us *Children's Stories*." No, you don't understand that! No one can really understand another man's sorrow.'

His eyes smouldered, his lips began to tremble. Suddenly he slammed his fist on the table so violently that things leapt into the air—such a gentle man, he had never done such a thing before.

'Why should I do it?' he exclaimed, 'Why? No one's been convicted, have they? No one's been sent to penal servitude because of me; the servant died of an illness. As for the blood I spilt, haven't I been punished enough by my suffering? Besides, no one at all will believe me, none of my evidence will convince anyone. Is there any need to make a public confession; is there? I'm ready to suffer all my life for the blood I've spilt, if only my wife and children may be spared. Would it be fair to destroy them along with myself? Are we not making a mistake? What is truth? And anyway, will people recognize the truth, will they know it for what it is, will they respect it?'

'Lord!' I thought to myself, 'he's thinking of people's respect at a time like this!' And I began to feel so sorry for him that I was ready to share his fate, if it would do any good. I could see that he was almost demented. I was horrified, realizing not just in my mind but in the very core of my soul what this resolve would cost him.

'You decide my fate!' he exclaimed again.

'Go and make your confession,' I whispered to him. My voice was failing, but I managed to whisper firmly enough. I took the Gospels from the table, the Russian version,* and showed him St John, chapter 12, verse 24:

'Verily, verily, I say unto you, Except a corn of wheat fall into the ground and die, it abideth alone: but if it die, it bringeth forth much fruit.' I had been reading this verse just before he arrived.

He read it.

'Correct,' he said, but smiled bitterly. 'Yes,' he added after a short silence, 'it's frightening what one comes across in this book. It's easy enough to shove it under someone's nose. And who was it that wrote it, was it really people?'

'The Holy Ghost wrote it,' I said.

'It's easy enough for you to prattle on,' he smiled again, but now almost malevolently. I took the book again and opened it at another place, Hebrews, chapter 10, verse 31. He read: '*It* is a fearful thing to fall into the hands of the living God.'

He read it and thrust the book aside. He even began to shake all over.

'A terrible passage,' he said, 'I must say, you picked a good one.' He rose from his chair. 'Well,' he said, 'farewell, perhaps I shall not see you again... We shall meet in paradise. So, it's been fourteen years since I've "fallen into the hands of the living God", now I know what those fourteen years were all about. Tomorrow I will be asking those hands to set me free...'

I was on the point of hugging and kissing him, but I dared not—his face was so contorted and bore such a grim expression. He left. 'Lord,' I thought, 'where is the man going?' I fell on my knees in front of the icon, and wept as I prayed for him to the Holy Mother of God, our ever-present mediatrix and friend in need. Half an hour passed as I knelt weeping in prayer—it was already late at night, about twelve o'clock. Suddenly, I looked up and saw the door opening, and there he was again. I was astonished.

'Where have you been?' I asked him.

'I,' he said, 'I, I think I've forgotten something... my handkerchief, I think... Well, perhaps I haven't forgotten anything after all, let me sit down...'

He sat down on a chair. I stood beside him. 'Won't you sit down too?' he said. I sat down. We sat there for about two minutes; he gazed at me, and suddenly he smiled—I shall never forget that smile—then he got up, hugged me closely, and kissed me...

'Be sure, my friend,' he said, 'be sure to remember that I came back to see you a second time. Do you hear me, Zinovy, I want you to remember that!'

It was the first time he had called me by my name. And then he left. 'Tomorrow,' I thought to myself.

And so it came about. I did not know that evening that it was his birthday the next day. I had not been out anywhere recently, and consequently couldn't have found out from anyone. On that day every year he used to hold a large reception, which the whole town would attend. And so it was this time. When dinner was over, he walked to the middle of the room with a document in his hand—a formal denunciation of himself, addressed to his superiors. And as his superiors were in fact present, he proceeded there and then to read out the document to the assembled company. It contained a full and detailed description of his crime: 'I cast myself out as a monster from the community of men, I have seen the light,' he concluded, 'I want to suffer!' Whereupon he produced and laid on the table everything that he imagined would testify to his crime and that he had been keeping for fourteen years: the deceased's gold jewellery, which he had appropriated in order to deflect suspicion from himself, her locket and crucifix, taken from her neck—the locket contained a portrait of her bridegroom—her notebook and finally two letters: a letter from the bridegroom informing her of his imminent arrival, and her reply, which she had started and had left unfinished on the table, intending to post it the following day. He had taken both those letters—why? And why had he kept them for the next fourteen years, instead of destroying them as evidence? And this is what happened: everyone was shocked and astonished, and no one wanted to believe him; they listened to him with extreme curiosity, as to one deranged, and a few days later it was universally accepted that the poor devil had gone out of his mind. His superiors and the judiciary had to pursue the matter, but then they suspended proceedings; although the personal belongings and letters which had been produced aroused suspicion, it was nevertheless decided that, however genuine they proved to be, it would still not be possible to secure a safe conviction on the strength of this evidence alone. As for her belongings, since he was an acquaintance of hers she could have given them to him to be held in trust. Indeed, I heard that, with the help of many of the deceased's relatives and acquaintances, the true ownership of the items was subsequently confirmed beyond all shadow of a doubt. But again, the case was not destined to be concluded. About five days later it was learned that the unfortunate man had fallen ill and that there were fears for his life. What illness it was, I cannot say; some said it was heart trouble, and then it became known that, on his wife's insistence, medical opinion had been sought and he had been diagnosed mentally disturbed. Although people were eager to question me I disclosed nothing, but when I wanted to visit him I was prevented from doing so for a long time, mainly by his wife. 'It was you', she said, 'who upset him; he had always been melancholic, and in the last year everyone had noticed he was becoming unusually neurotic and was behaving strangely, and then you came along and destroyed him completely; all that reading was just too much for him, he hadn't left your place for a whole month.' And it wasn't just his wife—I was attacked and accused by everybody in the town. 'It's all your fault,' they said. I held my peace, but there was joy in my heart, for I could see the undoubted mercy of God towards the man who had triumphed over himself and brought about his own punishment. As for his mental illness, I doubted it. At last, wishing to bid me farewell, he insisted that I should be allowed to see him. As soon as I entered his room I saw that not only his days, but indeed his hours were numbered. He was weak, breathless, his complexion sallow, his hands shaking, but his eyes were full of serenity and joy.

'I did it!' he said. 'I've been wanting to see you for a long time, why didn't you come?'

I did not tell him that I had not been allowed to see him.

'God has taken pity on me and is calling me to Him. I know I am dying, but I feel happiness and peace for the first time after so many years. As soon as I had done what I had to, I immediately felt heaven fill my soul. I now have the courage to love and kiss my children. People don't believe me, no one believed me then, neither my wife nor my judges; and my children will never believe me. In this, I see God's mercy towards my children. I shall die and my name will remain honourable in their memory. And now I sense the presence of God, and my heart overflows with joy as if I were in paradise... I have done my duty...'

He stopped, short of breath, squeezed my hand warmly, and looked at me with burning eyes. But our conversation did not last long, for his wife was constantly coming in and out and looking in on us. He managed to whisper to me, however:

'Do you remember that occasion when I came to see you the second time, at midnight? I even asked you specially not to forget it. Do you know why I came back? I came back to kill you!'

I shuddered.

'I walked out that time into the darkness and wandered through the streets, struggling with my inner self. And suddenly I felt such hatred for you that my heart could hardly bear it. "He's the only one", I thought, "who has me in his clutches and can judge me; now I can no longer escape tomorrow's punishment, because he knows everything." And it wasn't that I was afraid that you'd report me (the idea never occurred to me), but I thought: "How am I going to look him in the eye if I don't denounce myself?" And even if you were on the other side of the world, but alive, I would still not be able to abide the thought that you were alive, that you knew everything and were judging me. And I began to hate you, as though you were responsible for everything. I returned to you that time, remembering that there was a knife lying on your table. I sat down and asked you to sit down too, and I spent a whole minute thinking. If I'd killed you, I'd have certainly perished for that murder, even if I hadn't reported the previous crime. But I wasn't thinking about that at all, nor did I want to just then. I simply hated you, and wanted to avenge myself upon you with all my strength. But the Lord overcame the devil in my heart. I tell you, though, you had never been closer to death.'

A week later he was dead. The whole town followed his coffin to the grave. The archpriest delivered a moving oration. People wept over the terrible illness that had ended his days. But after he was buried the whole town ostracized me and stopped inviting me to their homes. True, some people—very few at first, but in increasing numbers as time went by—began to believe that his testimony had been true, and they began to visit me frequently and to question me excitedly and curiously, for men love to see the downfall of the righteous and their humiliation. But I maintained my silence and soon left the town for good, and five months later the Good Lord set me on a firm and righteous path, and I give thanks for His invisible hand, which has been guiding me so surely ever since. As for God's servant Mikhail, I remember him constantly in my prayers, even unto this day.

3

CONCERNING THE DISCOURSES AND TEACHINGS OF STARETS ZOSIMA

(e) Some thoughts on the Russian monk and his likely significance

FATHERS and teachers, what is a monk? In our enlightened world this word nowadays is used ironically by some, and by others even as a term of abuse. And things are going from bad to worse. It is true, oh yes, it is true that amongst the monks too there are many parasites, sensualists, pleasure-seekers, and impudent rogues. This has been noted by educated laymen: 'You', they say, 'are sluggards and useless members of society, living off other people's labour, shameless beggars all of you.' And yet there are many monks who are meek and humble, who long only to pray fervently in peace and solitude. But they are seldom mentioned, they are passed over in silence, and what surprise it would cause if I were to say that from these meek souls, yearning for solitary prayer, Russia's salvation might perhaps spring once again! For in silence they have indeed been preparing 'for that day and that hour, for that month and that year'. In their solitude they have been preserving Christ's image unspoiled and magnificent in the purity of divine truth, as handed down from the earliest fathers, apostles, and martyrs, and when it becomes necessary they will bring it forth to confront the sullied truth of the world. This is a profound thought. It is from the East that the star will shine forth.

That is what I think about monks, but am I wrong, am I being presumptuous? Just look at the world and at the laity, who consider that they are superior to God's people: have they not distorted the image of God and his truth? They have science, but a science wholly subservient to the senses. As for the spiritual world, the highest pinnacle of man's existence, that has been rejected completely, banished with a degree of triumphalism, not to say hatred. The world has celebrated liberty, especially in recent times, and what is it that we see in this liberty of theirs? Nothing but slavery and suicide! For the world says: 'You have needs, therefore satisfy them, for you have the same rights as the most illustrious and the richest amongst you. Do not be afraid to satisfy them, nay multiply them,' such is the present-day teaching of the world. It is in this that they see freedom. And so, what comes of this right to multiply one's needs? *Isolation* and spiritual suicide for the rich, envy and murder for the poor, for though rights have been granted, the means of material gratification have not yet been prescribed. We are assured that the longer time goes on, the closer the world draws towards fraternal communion, when distances will be bridged and thoughts transmitted through the air. Oh, do not believe in such a union of men. By interpreting freedom as the propagation and immediate gratification of needs, people distort their own nature, for they engender in themselves a multitude of pointless and foolish desires, habits, and incongruous stratagems. Their lives are motivated only by mutual envy, sensuality, and ostentation. To give dinner-parties, to travel, to have carriages, titles, and slavishly devoted servants is considered such a necessity that, in order to satisfy this need, people will even sacrifice their lives, honour, and sense of humanity, and if they cannot satisfy it, they will even commit suicide. The same thing is true for those who are not rich, but in the case of the poor the inability to satisfy their needs and feelings of envy are for the present drowned in drink. But instead of wine, they will soon quench their thirst with blood, for that is what they are being led to. I ask you: are such men free? I once knew 'a fighter for a cause' who told me himself that when he was deprived of tobacco in prison he was in such agony that he nearly betrayed his 'cause' just to get some tobacco. And people like him say: 'I shall go and fight for mankind.' But where will he go and what is he capable of? A short burst of activity, perhaps—but he will not be able to sustain it for long. And so it is not surprising that instead of being free, people have become enslaved, and instead of serving the cause of brotherly love and human harmony, they have, as my mysterious visitor and teacher once told me in my youth, fallen into *disharmony* and isolation. So the idea of service to mankind, of brotherhood and human solidarity, grows ever weaker in the world, and truly it is now treated almost with derision, for how is one to shed one's habits, whither can the bondsman turn, if he has grown so accustomed to gratifying the multifarious needs which are of his own devising? He is isolated, and the world at large means nothing to him. We have reached a stage at which we have surrounded ourselves with more things, but have less joy.

The monastic way is altogether different. Obedience, fasting, and prayer are now almost objects of ridicule, but it is precisely in them that the path to real and genuine freedom is to be found: I sever myself from needs which are superfluous and unnecessary, I humble my selfish and proud will and punish it with obedience, and so, with God's help, I attain spiritual freedom and with it spiritual joy! Who is the more capable of conceiving a great idea and of renouncing the world to serve it—the rich man in his isolation or the man *liberated* from the tyranny of material things and habits? People take the monk to task for having isolated himself: 'You have cut yourself off in order to seek salvation behind monastery walls, but you have forgotten about brotherly service to mankind.' We shall see though who will do more for the cause of brotherly love. For it is they who are isolated, not us, except that they do not see it. Even in times of old, it was from amongst our brethren that national figures arose, so why should they not arise now too? These same meek, humble, and abstemious recluses will rise up and champion a great cause. Russia's salvation is in its people. Russian monasticism has, from ancient times, been at one with the people. If the people are isolated, we too are isolated. The people share our faith, and a non-believing politician will achieve nothing in Russia, even if he is sincere at heart and a man of genius. Remember this. The people will confront the atheist and overcome him, and there will emerge a Russia united in the Orthodox faith. Cherish the people and let them not be disheartened. Nurture them in silence. That will be your monastic challenge, for this nation is the bearer of the word of God.

(f) Concerning masters and servants and whether it is possible for masters and servants to be brothers in spirit

Good Lord, who would deny that even the common people are plagued by sin. And, by the very hour, the flame of corruption is spreading downwards from above, even for all to see. Isolation has afflicted the people, too, we already have kulaks and bloodsuckers; the merchant is getting greedier and greedier for honours, and although he has no schooling whatsoever, he nevertheless strives to pass for an educated man; full of scandalous disregard for ancient custom, he is even ashamed of the faith of his fathers. He consorts with princes, and yet he himself is no more than a depraved muzhik. The people are debauched by drink, which they can no longer forgo. And how much cruelty there is towards the family, the wife, and even the children; and all because of drink. I have seen even ten-year-old children in factories, weak, sickly, worn out, and already degenerate. Airless sweatshops, noisy machinery, working all hours of the day, obscene language, and drink, nothing but drink—is that what the soul of a little child needs? He needs sunlight, children's games, and to be set a good example in everything, as well as some love, be it ever so little. Monks, this must not go on, there must be no abuse of children. Go forth and proclaim this as a matter of urgency. But God will save Russia, for though the common man may be degenerate and incapable of resisting the stench of sin, he nevertheless knows that his sin is accursed by God and that, in committing it, he is behaving badly. Hence our people continue to believe steadfastly in the truth, to accept God, and to shed tears of compassion. The upper classes are quite another matter. Drawn by science, they want to create a just world by means of the intellect alone, but, unlike former times, without Christ, and they have already pronounced that there is no crime, no sin. From their point of view this is quite correct: for if there is no God, how can there be any crime? In Europe the people are already in violent revolt against the wealthy, and their leaders everywhere are inciting them to bloody confrontation and preaching that their anger is justified. But 'cursed be their anger, for it was fierce'.* Yet God will save Russia, as He has saved it many times before. Salvation will come from the people, from their faith and humility. Nurture the faith of the people, fathers and teachers, it is not a dream: all my life I have been astounded by the noble and genuine dignity of our great people, I have experienced it myself, I can vouch for it, I have seen it and marvelled; yes, I have seen it, in spite of the stench of sin and the wretched state of our people. They are not servile, in spite of two centuries of slavery.* They are free in manner and deed, and bear no rancour whatsoever. Nor are they vindictive or jealous. 'You are famous, you are rich, you are clever and talented—good luck to you, and God bless you. I respect you, but remember that I'm a human being, too. The fact that I respect you without envy is an expression of my human dignity.' Indeed, even if they don't actually say this (for they do not know how to say it yet), that is how they *behave*, I myself have seen it, I myself have experienced it; and, would you believe it, the poorer and humbler our common Russian man, the more he embodies this noble truth, for the rich kulaks and bloodsuckers amongst them have already been corrupted in many ways, and much, much of this is due to our negligence and inattention! But God will save his people, for Russia's greatness lies in its humility. I dream about the future, and I seem to see it clearly already: for it will come about that even the most corrupt man among our wealthy will become ashamed of his riches when confronted by the poor man, and the latter, on seeing this humility, will understand and yield to him with joy, and will respond with tenderness to his noble shame. Believe me, that is how it will end: that's the way everything is going. Equality is only to be found in the spiritual dignity of man, and nowhere save in Russia will this be understood. If there are brothers, there will be brotherhood, and there will be no sharing save in brotherhood. We stand guard over the image of Christ, which will shine forth to the whole world like a precious diamond... It shall be, it shall be!

Fathers and teachers, something happened to me once which moved me deeply. In my travels, when I was in the provincial capital K, I met my former batman Afanasy eight years after he had left my service. He happened to notice me by chance in the market-place, recognized me, rushed up to me and, my goodness, how glad he was, he was so overjoyed that he practically threw himself at me. 'My God, sir, is it really you? Can it really be you I see?' He took me back to his house. He had already left the army and was now married and had two infant children. He scratched a living from petty trading at a market stall. His room was poorly furnished, but clean and cheerful. He offered me a seat, put the samovar on, and sent word to fetch his wife, just as though my visit to his home had transformed the day into a festive occasion. He brought his children to me. 'Bless them, father.' 'Who am I to bless them,' I replied. 'I'm just a simple and humble monk, I'll pray to God for them, but as for you, Afanasy Pavlovich, I've always prayed for you every day, ever since that day,' I said, 'because it was with you that everything began.' And I explained it to him as best I could. Poor man, he looked at me in disbelief, he could not believe that I, his former master, an officer, was sitting there before him now, looking like that, dressed as a monk, and he even burst out crying. 'Why are you crying?' I said to him. 'You, whom I can never forget, should be rejoicing for me with your whole being, my dear fellow, for my path ahead is bright and happy.' He didn't say much, just ooh'ed and ah'ed and kept shaking his head with compassion. 'Where', he asked me, 'has all your wealth gone?' I replied: 'I gave it to the monastery, and we now all live as a community.' After tea, I was starting to make my farewells, when he suddenly produced fifty kopecks as an offering for the monastery, and I realized that he was trying to slip another fifty into my hand. 'That's for you,' he said, 'for a very unusual pilgrim, it may come in useful perhaps, father.' I accepted his fifty kopecks, bowed to him and to his wife, and left in joy, thinking along the way: 'Here we are, the two of us, he in his own home, I on the road, and both probably marvelling and beaming with joy, with our hearts full of happiness, and musing over how God brought about this chance meeting.' I have never seen him again. I was his master, and he was my servant, but after we had embraced each other in love and spiritual tenderness a great human bond was forged between us. I have thought about this a great deal, and here is what I think now: is it so beyond the bounds of imagination that this great and simple-hearted bond could be forged between our Russian people everywhere and in its own good time? I believe that this will come about, and that the time is nigh.

As for servants, I shall add the following: formerly, in my youth, I used to be very impatient with my servants: 'The cook has served up the meal too hot, the batman hasn't cleaned my coat.' But I was suddenly enlightened by the observation that I had heard my brother make in my youth: 'Is it fitting that another man should wait upon me, and that I should abuse him because of his poverty and ignorance?' It amazed me that the simplest, the most obvious thoughts should be so slow in coming to us.

One cannot survive without servants in this world, but you should arrange things in such a way that your servant is freer in spirit than if he were not a servant. For why should I not be a servant to my servant, and why, for that matter, should he not be aware of it, and without any self-righteousness on my part or mistrust on his? Why should I not treat my servant as a relative and accept him finally into my family, and do so with joy? Even now, this could still come about and serve as the basis for the future, glorious union of people, when man will not, as now, be looking for servants and will not, as now, be making servants of his own kind, but on the contrary will himself wish, from the bottom of his heart to become a servant to everyone, as is laid down in the Gospels.* And can it really be just a dream that man will ultimately seek his joy only in acts of enlightenment and compassion, and not, as now, in brutal satisfactions—in gluttony, fornication, pride, in boasting and in envious rivalry between one man and another? I firmly believe that it is not a dream, and that the time is nigh. People laugh and ask when this time will come, and is it likely even that it ever will come. I believe, however, that with Christ we shall accomplish this. And how many ideas have there been on this earth, in the history of mankind, which, seemingly unthinkable even ten years previously, nevertheless when their mysterious time was ripe suddenly emerged and swept over the whole earth? Thus will it be with us too, and our people will shine forth in the world, and all will say: 'The stone which the builders refused is become the head of the corner.'* One could well ask our very detractors: 'If our idea is only a dream, when are you going to erect your edifice and establish a just way of life by reason alone, without Christ?' And even if they maintain that, on the contrary, it is they who strive for unity, then surely it is only the most naïve amongst them who believe this, and one can only marvel at their naïvety. Truly, they are more given to dreamlike fantasies than we are. They hope to establish a just way of life, but, having rejected Christ, they will end by engulfing the world in blood because blood calls for blood, and he who lives by the sword, shall perish by the sword.* And if it had not been for Christ's promise, they would have annihilated one another, even down to the last two persons on earth. And even those last two, in their pride, would not have been able to restrain themselves, so the one would have destroyed the other and then himself too. And had it not been for Christ's covenant, which He made for the sake of the humble and the meek, that is indeed what would have come to pass.* I was still in my officer's uniform, after the duel, when I began to talk about servants in public, and, I remember, everyone was surprised. 'Do you', they said, 'want to seat your servant on the sofa and serve him tea?' And I replied: 'Why ever not, even if only once in a while.' Everybody laughed then. Their question was frivolous, and my answer vague, but I think it did contain a certain amount of truth.

(g) Concerning prayer, love, and contact with other worlds

Young man, do not neglect prayer. Each time you say your prayers, provided you are sincere, there will be a new spark of emotion and, along with it, a new idea, previously unknown to you, which will raise your spirits anew, and you will understand that prayer is education. Remember, too, every day and, whenever you can, keep repeating in your mind: 'Lord, have mercy on all who have now come before Thee.' For, each hour, each instant, thousands of people leave this earthly life, and their souls stand before God—and many of them will have departed this earth unbeknown to anyone, utterly alone, sad and anguished, with no one to pity them or know that they even existed. And behold, even though you may not know them nor they you, perhaps your prayer for the repose of their souls will rise up from the far side of the world and reach the Lord. How comforting it will be for their souls to feel, at that instant, standing in fear before the Lord, that there is someone who prays even for them, that there is still a human being on earth who loves them. God too will look upon you all with more kindness, for if you have shown such mercy to them, how much more mercy will He show to you, He who is infinitely more merciful than you. And He will forgive them for your sake.

Brothers, be not afraid of human sin, love man even in his state of sin, for this is already a likeness of divine love and is the highest love on this earth. Love all of God's creation, love the whole, and love each grain of sand. Love every leaf, every ray of God's light. Love animals, love plants, love every kind of thing.

If you love every kind of thing, then everywhere God's mystery will reveal itself to you. Once this has been revealed to you, you will begin to understand it ever more deeply with each passing day. And finally you will be able to love the whole world with an all-encompassing universal love. Love animals. God gave them the beginnings of thought and a sense of untroubled joy. Do not disturb this, do not torment them, do not take away their joy, do not oppose God's intent. Man, set not thyself up above the animals. They are without sin, it is you in your grandeur who is fouling the earth by your presence on it and leaving your foul mark behind you—alas, this goes for nearly every one of us! Love children in particular,* for they too are without sin, like angels, and they live to be a balm upon our lives and to cleanse our hearts and show us the way ahead. Woe unto him who abuses the infant. It was Father Anfim who taught me to love children. Always so kind and silent, as we journeyed around, he used to spend the few kopecks collected along the way on cakes and sweets and distribute them. He could never pass children without being deeply affected by them spiritually; such was the man's nature.

Some thoughts are bewildering, especially when one is confronted by the sins of people, and one asks oneself: 'Is it better to resort to force or to rely on humility and love?' Always say to yourself: 'I shall conquer by humility and love.' Having made such a decision once and for all, you'll be able to conquer the whole world. Humility in love is an overpowering force, the strongest there is, and there is no other like it. Every day and every hour, every minute even, watch over yourself to ensure that you have not sullied this precept. You have walked past a small child, you have walked past in anger, foul-mouthed, ill-tempered; perhaps you may not even have noticed the child, but he has seen you, and the vision of your unsightly and profane aspect has maybe lodged in his defenceless little heart. You did not know him, but you may have sown a bad seed in him which will probably grow, and all because you have behaved badly in front of the small child, because you have not nurtured a watchful, active love within yourself. Brothers, love is a teacher, but you must know how to go about acquiring love, for it does not come easily, one achieves it through relentless and protracted effort, because one must love not casually, just for an instant, but to the very end. Anyone at all is capable of casual love, even a felon. My brother, young though he was, asked the little birds for pardon: that might seem senseless, but he was right, because everything is like an ocean, everything flows and intermingles, you have only to touch it in one place and it will reverberate in another part of the world. Granted, it may seem mad to ask birds for pardon, but how much better it would be for the birds and the child and every other creature around you now, if you yourself preserved your human dignity, even a little. Everything is like the ocean, I tell you. Then, in a kind of ecstasy, driven by an all-encompassing love, you would start to pray to the birds, and you would pray that they too should forgive your sins. Cherish that ecstasy, however absurd it may seem to people.

My friends, ask God for joy. Be as joyful as children, as the little birds in the sky. Do not let human sin confuse you in your mission, do not be afraid that it will stifle your endeavour and prevent it coming to fruition, do not say: 'Sin is powerful, sacrilege is powerful, the foul world is powerful, and we are lonely and helpless, we will be overwhelmed by this foul world, and it will not allow us to accomplish our virtuous endeavour.' My children, shun such despondency! There is but one salvation for you. Take yourself in hand, and be answerable for the sins of all men. My friend, this is actually true: you need only make yourself sincerely answerable for everything and everyone, and you will see immediately that it really is so, and that it is you who are actually guilty of the sins committed by each and every man. Whereas, if you blame one another for your own sloth and weakness, you will end up by becoming imbued with satanic pride and will turn against God. This is what I think of satanic pride: it is difficult for us on earth even to comprehend it, and therefore it is easy to fall into error and to accept it, thinking at the same time that we are doing something grand and wonderful. In fact, while we are still here on earth many of the strongest feelings and emotions of our nature are beyond our comprehension, but do not be misled by this and do not think that it may serve as justification for your actions, for the eternal judge will hold you to account only for that which you could comprehend, and not for that which you could not. You only need to make sure of this yourself to see things as they really are and from then on stop raising objections. Indeed, on earth we wander as if lost, and had we not the precious image of Christ before us, we would lose our way completely and perish, as mankind did before the flood. There is much on earth that is hidden from us, but in exchange we have been blessed with a secret sense of a vital, mysterious bond linking us to another world, a celestial, exalted world, and in any case the roots of our thoughts and feelings are to be found not here, but in other worlds. This is why philosophers say that the essence of things cannot be understood on earth. God took seeds from other worlds and sowed them on this earth, where He cultivated His garden and all that could grow sprouted, yet all that grows owes its life only to its sense of the mysterious intermingling with other worlds; should this sense within you either wither or be destroyed, that which grows within you will also die. Then you will become indifferent to life, and even come to detest it. Such are my thoughts.

(h) Can one sit in judgement over one's fellow men? On keeping the faith to the end

Remember especially that you may not sit in judgement over anyone.* No man on this earth can sit in judgement over other men until he realizes that he too is just such a criminal as the man standing before him, and that it is precisely he, more than anyone, who is guilty of that man's crime. When he does become aware of this, then he may be a judge. However mad this may appear, it is the truth. For if I had been righteous myself, there might not be a criminal in the dock before me. If you are able to take upon yourself the crimes of the criminal standing before you, whom you`are condemning in your heart, then do so immediately and endure the suffering for him, allowing the man himself to go free and unrebuked. And even if the law itself has appointed you to be his judge, act as much as possible in this spirit, for he will go away and pass a judgement upon himself that is far more severe than yours. However, if after you have shown him your good will he remains unmoved and even laughs at you, don't be deterred by this either; it means that his time has not yet come, but it will come by and by, and if it doesn't, never mind; if it is not to be him, someone else will come along who will show greater understanding than him, and will give himself up to suffering and pass judgement upon himself, and truth will have been served. Believe this, believe this implicitly, because therein is contained all the hope and all the faith of the saints.

Be forever active. If you remember at night, as you fall asleep: 'I have not finished that which I should have done,' arise immediately and finish it. If you are surrounded by bad-tempered and insensitive people who do not want to listen to you, fall down before them and ask their forgiveness, for, verily, you too are to blame that they do not want to listen to you. And if you can no longer talk to the embittered, carry on serving them in silence and in humility, never losing hope. And if everyone abandons you, and even if they cast you out by force, then, alone as you are, fall down upon the ground, kiss it and soak it with your tears, and the earth will bear fruit from your tears, even though nobody has seen or heard of you in your solitude. Believe to the end, even if it should come to pass that everyone on earth falls into error and that you alone remain true, make your sacrifice even then and praise the Lord, you who are the lone survivor. And if you come together with one other person like yourself, there you have a whole world, a world of vibrant love; embrace each other in tenderness and praise the Lord, for His truth will have been accomplished, if only in just the two of you.

If you yourself sin and repent of your sins even unto death, even of just one accidental sin, rejoice for another, rejoice for the righteous man, rejoice that even though you have sinned, he has remained righteous and has not sinned.

If men's evil should arouse your indignation and cause you unbearable distress, even to the point of making you feel vindictive towards the malefactors, fear this feeling more than anything; go at once and seek torments for yourself such as you ought to suffer were you yourself guilty of the crime. Take these torments upon yourself and endure them, and your heart will be appeased and you will understand that you too are guilty, for you could have been the one without sin and the guiding light unto the malefactors, and you were not. If your light had shone forth it would have illumined the path for others, too, and the one who committed the crime might not perhaps have transgressed by your light. And even if your light shines forth and you observe that people are not seeking salvation by the light which you are casting, you should remain steadfast and not doubt the power of heavenly light; know ye that though they have not yet sought salvation, they will be saved later. And if they are not saved, their sons will be, for your light will not die, even though you yourself may then be dead. The just man will pass away, but his light will live on. Salvation is always found through the death of the saviour. The human race is loath to accept its prophets, and chastizes them, but people love their martyrs and will venerate those whom they have tortured to death. You, however, are working for all mankind; what you do is for the future. Be sure never to seek reward, for even as it is, your reward upon this earth is great enough—the spiritual happiness which only the righteous can attain. Fear neither the rich nor the powerful, but be wise and always preserve your dignity. Know the limits, know the times, learn to observe them. When you are left on your own, pray. Be ready to throw yourself on the ground and smother it with kisses. Kiss the ground, love insatiably, ceaselessly, love everyone, love everything, seek this exaltation, this ecstasy. Flood the earth with tears of joy, and love those tears. Do not, however, be ashamed of this ecstasy, cherish it, because it is a gift from God, a great one, vouchsafed to the few, the chosen ones.

(i) On hell and the fire of hell: a mystical discourse

Fathers and teachers, I ask myself: 'What is hell?'* I argue thus: 'It is the suffering caused by not being able to love any more.' Once, in the infinity of existence which cannot be measured either by time or space, a certain spiritual entity, appearing on earth, was granted the possibility of saying: 'I am and I love.' Once, and once only, was it vouchsafed an instant of actual, *living* love, and for that purpose it was granted earthly life and, with it, its times and its seasons—and what happened: this fortunate creation rejected this priceless gift as something of no value; it did not love, it cast a contemptuous look and remained unmoved. Such a one, having departed from this world, sees the bosom of Abraham and converses with Abraham, as revealed to us in the parable of the rich man and Lazarus,* and he contemplates paradise and is able to ascend to the Lord, but that is precisely the reason for his suffering, for if he ascends to the Lord as one who has not loved, he will encounter those who have loved and whose love he has scorned. For he sees things clearly now, and says unto himself: 'Now at last I have know-ledge, and though I have been yearning to love, there will be no merit in my love, nor will there be sacrifice, for my earthly life is at an end and Abraham will not come with even a drop of the water of life (that is, bringing the gift of earthly life again, real life as before) to quench the flames of thirst for spiritual love, that love which I spurned once upon earth and for which I now long; there is no more life, and time is at an end! Though I might be glad to give up my life for others, this is no longer possible, for the life which could have been sacrificed for the sake of love is no more, and now a great gulf has appeared between it and this existence.' People speak of the physical flames of hell: I am not going to delve into this mystery, and I fear it, but I think that even if there were physical flames people would be truly glad of them, for I think that in physical torment they might, if only for an instant, forget the far worse spiritual torment. Nor can they be delivered from this spiritual torment, for they are tormented not from outside but from within. And even if they could be delivered from it, then, I think, they would become even more unhappy. For though the righteous in paradise, seeing their agony, might pardon them and in their infinite love even call to them to come and join them, this would cause them even more suffering, for it would only exacerbate the intense yearning to reciprocate with an active and grateful love, which is now no longer possible. In the humility of my heart I think that the very realization of this impossibility would serve them finally as an assuagement, for, by recognizing the love of the righteous and the impossibility of responding to it, they would by this very submission and act of humility at last gain some idea of that practical love which they spurned on earth, and, as it were, by a kindred effect... My friends and brothers, I regret that I cannot express this clearly. But woe to those who destroy themselves on this earth, woe to those who commit suicide! I think there can be no one more miserable than they. We are told that it is a sin to pray to God for them, and outwardly the Church appears to reject them, but in the depth of my soul I think that one could say a prayer for them too. After all, Christ will not be offended by love. I have prayed inwardly for such ones all my life, I confess this to you, fathers and teachers, and I pray for them still each day.

Oh, even in hell there are those who remain proud and defiant in spite of indisputable knowledge and the contemplation of irrefutable truth; there are terrible creatures who are in complete communion with Satan and his proud spirit. They have chosen hell voluntarily, and they are never sated with it; they indeed are willing martyrs. For in cursing life and God, they have damned themselves. They feed upon their own evil pride, just as if a hungry man in a desert were to suck blood from his own body.* They are unfulfilled for ever and ever, but they reject forgiveness and deny the God who beckons them. They are unable to contemplate the living God save with hatred, and they demand that there be no God of life, that God destroy Himself and all His creation. And they shall burn everlastingly in the flames of their own hatred, and long for death and for non-being. But death shall not be granted them...

Thus ends Aleksei Fydorovich Karamazov's manuscript. I repeat: it is incomplete and fragmentary. For instance, the biographical information covers only the starets's early youth. As regards his teachings and opinions, they have been collected together as if to form a unified whole, although in actual fact they were spoken at different times and prompted by a variety of circumstances. However, not everything that the starets said in those final hours of his life has been reproduced word for word, only a general idea of the spirit and substance of the discourse is presented here, unlike other entries in Aleksei Fyodorovich's manuscript, which relate to the starets's former teachings. The starets's end actually came very unexpectedly. For although everyone who had gathered to see him that final night understood full well that his end was nigh, it was nevertheless impossible to imagine that it would come so suddenly; on the contrary, his friends, as I have already remarked above, seeing how alert and talkative he seemed to be, were even convinced that there had been a marked improvement in his condition, even if only temporarily. Even five minutes before his death, as they subsequently related with surprise, it was still not possible to foresee anything. He suddenly felt the most acute pain in his chest, became pale, and clasped his hands tightly to his heart. Thereupon everyone rose from their seats and rushed towards him; but he, continuing to smile at everyone through his pain, gently slumped from his chair and fell to his knees, turned his face to the ground, spread out his arms and, as though in a transport of joy, kissing the ground and praying (as he himself had taught), gave up his soul to God peacefully and gladly. The news of his demise immediately spread through the hermitage and reached the monastery. Those who were closest to the deceased and those selected by order of seniority began to prepare the body in accordance with ancient ritual, and all the monks assembled in the monastery chapel. Before dawn, as rumour later had it, news of his death had reached the town. By morning, nearly the whole town was talking about the event, and many of its citizens had flocked to the monastery. But we shall speak of this later, in the next book; for the present, we shall merely add that even before the day was out something had happened which was so unexpected and, judging by the effect both within the monastic community and in the town, so strange, alarming, and perplexing that even now, all these years later, our town still preserves the most vivid memories of that day, which left so many of its inhabitants filled with alarm...

PART THREE

BOOK SEVEN
Alyosha

1

ODOUR OF PUTREFACTION

THE body of the deceased schemahieromonk, Father Zosima, was prepared for burial according to the prescribed rites. As is well known, ablutions are not performed on the bodies of deceased monks. 'If a monk departs in the Lord (so it is written in the Great Book of Prayers), the designated monk (that is, the one appointed to the task), after making the sign of the cross with a Greek sponge on the forehead, fingers, hands, feet, and knees, merely sponges the body with warm water, and nothing else.' Father Païsy himself performed these rites on the deceased. After sponging him down he clothed him in a monk's robe and laid him in a shroud, in which, as stipulated in the rules, he cut a slit so as to be able to wind it round the body in a cruciform manner. Over his head he drew a cowl on which was embroidered a Slavonic cross, leaving his face exposed, but covered with a thin black veil. An icon of Our Saviour was placed in his hands. In the early morning the body, thus vested, was placed in a coffin which had been prepared long before. The intention was to leave the coffin in the cell (in the ante-room, the room where before his death the starets used to receive his fellow monks and lay visitors) for the whole day. Since by title the deceased was a schemahieromonk, it was a requirement that the hieromonks and hierodeacons read the Gospels, rather than the Psalter, over his body. Father Yosif began reading straight after the liturgy for the dead; Father Païsy, who wanted to take over and continue the reading himself all through the following day and night, was temporarily distracted and preoccupied by something else; he and the prior of the hermitage had noticed with concern that the monastic community, as well as the visiting clergy and the laity who had been flocking to the monastery from the town, had begun to manifest an uncommonly strange, nay unbecoming, agitation and impatient expectation which, as time passed, began to intensify rapidly. Both Father Païsy and the prior did their best to try to quell this restlessness and agitation. By daybreak more people began to arrive from the town, some even bringing their sick ones with them, especially children, as though they had been waiting specifically for this event, apparently putting their trust in the healing power which, they believed, would manifest itself soon. It was this that finally demonstrated how much our local people had come to revere the deceased starets as a great and undoubted saint, even in his lifetime. And those who came were by no means only the simple, uneducated folk. This eager expectation on the part of the faithful, expressed in such an urgent, blatant, even impatient and almost demanding manner, struck Father Païsy as scandalous, and though he had foreseen it long ago, in the event it exceeded even his worst fears. On encountering the more restless of the monks, Father Païsy even began to admonish them: 'Such an anxious wish for something momentous to happen is a mark of shallowness befitting only the laity, but for us it is unbecoming.' But no one paid much heed to him, and Father Païsy noted with anxiety that even he himself (if the whole truth be known), while professing indignation at the excessive expectancy and regarding it as something shallow and vain, secretly, deep down in his heart of hearts, longed for almost the very same thing, and could not help but admit this to himself. Nevertheless, there were some people whose company he found particularly unpleasant and in whose presence he had a strange premonition that caused him serious misgivings. In the crowded cell of the deceased he noticed with deep loathing (for which he immediately reproached himself) the presence of Rakitin, for instance, as well as the guest from afar—the monk from Obdorsk, who was still staying in the monastery. For some reason Father Païsy immediately began to regard them both with suspicion—even though they were not the only ones who could be said to arouse such suspicion. Among the expectant multitude the most excited was the monk from Obdorsk; he was to be seen everywhere, in every corner, questioning everyone, listening everywhere, and whispering in a particularly mysterious manner. His face wore the most impatient expression, as though resentful that the awaited event was taking so long to materialize. As for Rakitin, he, it later transpired, had come to the hermitage at this early hour on the express orders of Mrs Khokhlakova, who could not be admitted to the hermitage in person. As soon as she woke and learned what had happened, that kind but weak-willed lady had been overcome by such irrepressible curiosity that she had immediately dispatched Rakitin to the hermitage to make copious notes and report immediately to her in writing, at approximately half hourly intervals, *everything that was going on.* She regarded Rakitin as one of the most pious and religious young men—so clever was he at handling people and ingratiating himself with everyone if he saw even the slightest personal gain therein. The day was sunny and bright, and many of the devout visitors crowded round the hermitage graves, which were particularly numerous near the church, others being scattered throughout the grounds. While going round the hermitage, Father Païsy suddenly remembered about Alyosha and the fact that he had not seen him for some time, to be precise since the previous night. And no sooner had he remembered about him than he caught sight of him in the furthest corner of the hermitage, by the fence, sitting on the gravestone of a spiritually valiant and long-deceased monk. He sat with his back to the hermitage, facing the fence, and appeared to be hiding behind the gravestone. Going up to him, Father Païsy saw that he had buried his face in his hands and was crying bitterly, though without a sound, his whole body convulsed with every sob. Father Païsy stood beside him for a while.

'That will do, my son, that will do, my friend,' he said at last, with compassion, 'there's no need for this! You should rejoice, not weep. Don't you know that this is *his* greatest day? Just think where he is now, at this moment, just think of that!'

Alyosha half glanced at him, revealing his swollen, tear-stained face, like a small child's, and immediately without a word turned away and buried his face in his hands again.

'Perhaps it's just as well,' Father Païsy said thoughtfully, 'weep, if you must. Christ has sent you these tears.' And as he left Alyosha, he thought affectionately: 'Your sweet tears are a respite for your soul and will contribute to the joy of your dear heart.' With that, he departed quickly, because he realized that if he looked at Alyosha any longer he himself might burst into tears. Meanwhile, time was passing, and the monastic services and prayers appointed for the dead were being said. Father Païsy relieved Father Yosif at the coffin and continued the reading of the Gospels. But it was not yet three o'clock in the afternoon when something took place to which I have referred at the end of my previous book, something so unforeseen and so contrary to general expectation that, even to this day, a detailed but confused version of the story is still vividly recalled in our town and throughout the district. Here I shall add a personal observation: I can hardly bear to recall that disturbing and scandalous event, in reality quite insignificant and natural, and of course I would have omitted it from my story altogether had it not had a most important and pronounced influence on the heart and soul of the principal, *albeit future*, hero of my story, Alyosha, producing a kind of crisis in him, an upheaval that shook him profoundly, but at the same time finally and irrevocably confirmed him in his beliefs and determined his future direction.

And so, let us proceed with the story. Before daybreak, when the starets's body had been robed, placed in the coffin in readiness for burial and transferred to the ante-room, formerly the reception room, the question arose amongst the people assembled round the coffin as to whether or not to open the windows. However, this question, raised casually and in passing by someone, was left unanswered, almost unnoticed—and even if anyone present did notice it, he kept it to himself, since the very idea of putrefaction or an odour of putrefaction from the body of such a man was utterly absurd, worthy even of pity (if not ridicule), and would indicate a lack of faith and a shallowness in whoever had raised the question in the first place. For everyone was expecting precisely the opposite. And so, shortly after midday, something occurred that at first was observed in silence and without comment by those present—they were evidently afraid of communicating their nagging doubts to anyone else—but which by three in the afternoon had manifested itself so clearly and unmistakably that news of it spread in a flash throughout the whole hermitage and amongst all the mourners

and visitors, then immediately throughout the monastery, causing
consternation among the community, and finally, in no time at
all, reached the town too and affected everyone in it, both
believers and non-believers. The non-believers were triumphant,
and as for the believers, there were some amongst them who
gloated even more than the non-believers, for 'people do love
the downfall of a righteous man and his degradation', as the late
starets himself had once said in one of his homilies. The fact
was that, little by little and then ever more noticeably, an odour
of putrefaction began to emanate from the coffin which, by three
o'clock in the afternoon, was already only too evident and was
becoming even worse. It was a long time since such a scandal
had occurred; indeed, never in the whole living memory of the
monastery had there been so blatant and crude an example,
simply unimaginable under any other circumstances, as the
scandal that took place amongst the monks themselves immediately after this event. Much later, even after the passage of many
years, some of the more intelligent of our brethren, recalling this
day in all its detail, were astonished, indeed aghast, that the
scandal could have reached such proportions. For in the past,
too, it happened at times that very pious, God-fearing monks,
whose piety was apparent to all, would die, and from their
humble coffins, naturally, as from all corpses, would emanate an
odour of putrefaction, but this in no way affected people's faith
or caused the least disquiet. Of course, there were also long-
since departed brethren who were still remembered in the
monastery and whose remains, so legend had it, had not
undergone decay, producing instead a soothing and mysterious
effect upon the whole community and surviving in people's
memories as an example of something magnificent and holy and
as a pledge of even greater glory to come from their sepulchres
in the future if, God willing, the time for this should come to
pass. A particularly vivid memory had been preserved of one
such starets, Job, a famous ascetic and observer of the vows
of silence and fasting, who, having lived to the age of one
hundred and five, died long ago, in the first decade of our
century, and whose grave used to be pointed out with inordinate
reverence to all visiting worshippers, accompanied by mysterious
references to some future great events. (It was by this very grave

that Father Païsy had found Alyosha seated that morning.)
Besides this long-deceased starets, there was the similarly
remembered and fairly recently deceased famous schemahieromonk, Starets Varsophony—whom Father Zosima had succeeded, and who, in his lifetime, had been regarded simply as a
holy fool by all the worshippers who came to the monastery.
Both of them, it was said, lay in their coffins as though still alive
and were buried with no signs of putrefaction, and their faces
even appeared to glow. Some even claimed to remember that
these bodies had exuded a distinctly sweet odour of sanctity.
But, despite these striking reminiscences, it was still difficult to
explain the real reason why such a senseless, grotesque, and
unholy phenomenon should have occurred around the coffin of
Starets Zosima. Personally, I think that many other factors
coincided here, that there were many different reasons which all
conspired together. One such, for instance, was the aforementioned long-running enmity, still deeply buried in the memory of
many of the monastery monks, towards the cult of startsy as a
pernicious innovation. But, of course, the main reason was
envy of the deceased's sanctity, a sanctity which had been
established so firmly during his lifetime that it seemed unseemly
to dispute it. For even though the deceased starets had attracted
many people, more through love than through miracles, and
had gathered around him a whole circle of disciples, yet in
spite of this, indeed because of it, he had engendered much
envy, which in turn had created bitter enemies, overt as well as
covert, and not only in the monastic community but also beyond
it. For instance, he had not done anyone any harm, and yet:
'Why is he considered so holy?' And this question alone, repeated
as it was over a period of time, eventually led to a veritable
outburst of the most vicious hatred. It is for this reason I think
that many, having detected the smell of putrefaction from his
body, and so soon after the event—for not even a day had
elapsed since his death—were inordinately glad; even amongst
the followers who up to that day had venerated him there were
those who immediately interpreted the event as a personal insult
and affront. Subsequent events unfolded in the following
manner.

As soon as the putrefaction began to be noticeable, one could tell just by looking at the monks who entered the cell of the deceased what had brought them there. They would come in, stay for a while, and then hurry out to confirm the news to the others waiting in a crowd outside. Some of those who were waiting shook their heads sadly, while others made no attempt at all to conceal the pleasure that was clearly evident in their hate-filled eyes. And no one reproached them, no one spoke in praise of the starets, which was most strange, as his supporters in the monastery were after all in the majority; apparently it was the Lord Himself who had decreed that, on this occasion, the minority should be triumphant. Soon the lay people too, mainly the more educated ones, started coming to the cell to discover the situation for themselves; of the common people, few actually entered the cell, although many had gathered at the gates of the hermitage. It remains beyond dispute that just after three o'clock, purely as a result of the scandalous news, the number of lay visitors increased appreciably. Those who might not have come at all that day, perhaps, and had had no intention of coming, now made a point of coming; amongst these were some person-ages of considerable standing. It must be said that at that stage a semblance of decorum was still being observed, and Father Païsy continued to read the Gospels with a stern face and in a firm and clear voice, as if unaware anything was amiss, although it was some time now since he had noticed that something unusual was happening. Soon, however, he too began to hear the voices, low at first, but gradually becoming more strident and insistent. Suddenly he heard someone say, 'God's judgement is not man's judgement!' It was a layman who was the first to say this, the town clerk, a man well advanced in years and, as far as was known, very pious, but in saying this out loud he was only repeating what the monks had already been whispering to one another for a long time anyway. They had already uttered this ominous pronouncement, and what made matters worse was the fact that, with every passing minute, this seemed to heighten the atmosphere of gloating. Soon even the last vestiges of decorum began to evaporate, and there came a point when no one felt constrained any longer. 'And why should *this* have happened,' some of the monks said, initially with a note of regret, 'after all, his body was only small, shrivelled, nothing but skin and bones, where could the smell have come from?' 'In that case, it is a deliberate sign from God,' others were quick to add, and their opinion was accepted immediately and unquestioningly, for again they pointed out that even if the odour had been natural, as from any deceased sinner, it would have been emitted somewhat later rather than so soon after the event—at least a whole day would have elapsed. As things stood, however, 'this one had transgressed the laws of nature', and it follows, therefore, that this is a deliberate sign from God, verily it is His finger.* A portent from on high. Such judgement was irrefutable. The gentle hieromonk Father Yosif, the librarian, of whom the deceased had been particularly fond, was about to remonstrate with some of the detractors, saying that 'it is not like that everywhere', and that, in any case, the requirement that the body of the righteous should not suffer decomposition was not a matter of Church dogma, but merely an opinion, and that even in the most Orthodox communities, Mount Athos for instance, no one was unduly concerned about the odour of putrefaction, and that it was not the incorruptibility of the flesh which was to be regarded as the main sign of glorification of the hallowed, but the colour of their bones after their bodies had lain in the ground for several years and had even decayed, for 'if the bones are found to be yellow as wax, then that is the main indication that the Lord has hallowed the righteous deceased; but if they are not yellow, but appear black, it means that the Lord has not vouchsafed him glory—so it is on Mount Athos, a renowned place where, from antiquity, the Orthodox faith has been preserved intact in all its purity,' concluded Father Yosif. But the words of the humble Father Yosif remained unheeded, and even provoked a derisive rebuttal. 'This is all unseemly, newfangled speculation,' the monks concluded among themselves. 'We observe the old traditions; there are too many new ideas about for us to keep up with,' added others. 'If it comes to it,' joined in those who were the most scornful, 'we've had at least as many holy fathers as they have. They've been sat under the Turks for so long down there, they've forgotten everything. Their very Orthodoxy has been corrupted, why, they've even given up church bells!' Father Yosif insisted with bitterness, the more so as he himself had not been entirely convinced of the veracity of his own opinion, as though he were more than a little dubious himself. He noted with alarm that something very unseemly was about to happen, and that outright disobedience was beginning to rear its head. Following Father Yosif's example, all the other prudent voices fell silent one by one. And so it came about that all those who had loved the deceased starets and had hitherto accepted the cult of startsy in obedient humility, suddenly appeared to take fright and, on meeting one another, would simply exchange diffident glances. On the other hand, those who opposed the cult of startsy, regarding it as an innovation, were emboldened. 'Not only was there no odour of putrefaction from the late Starets Varsophony,' they remarked sarcastically, 'but he exuded the sweet odour of sanctity, not by virtue of his being a starets, but because he was righteous.' Soon not only reproaches but even accusations began to be heaped upon the recently deceased starets. 'His teaching was false; he taught that life was not a vale of tears, but a garden of joy,' said some of the least intelligent. 'He practised his faith the modern way, he wouldn't accept there was real fire in hell,' joined in those who were even more stupid. 'He was not strict in his fasting, and he loved to indulge himself in sweet things, to sip tea with cherry preserve and the like; ladies kept him stocked up with it. A recluse drinking tea, whoever heard such a thing?' said those who were consumed with envy. 'He was puffed up with pride,' asserted the most malevolent of his denigrators, 'he considered himself to be a saint, people knelt in front of him, and he took it as his due.' 'He abused the sacrament of confession,' added in a malicious whisper the most inveterate opponents of the cult of startsy, amongst whom numbered the most senior monks, those strictly dedicated to worship, true observers of the vows of silence and of fasting, who had not spoken out during the lifetime of the deceased but who now suddenly gave vent to their jealousy, which was all the more shocking as their words had a strong effect on the minds of the young and still impressionable monks. The little monk who had come from St Silvester's in Obdorsk listened avidly to all this, sighing deeply and nodding his head in agreement. 'No, it seems Father Therapon was quite right in his judgement yesterday,' he thought to himself, and just at that moment who should appear, as though to add fuel to the flames, but Father Therapon himself.

As I already mentioned earlier, he seldom used to leave his timber cabin in the apiary, missing even church services for long periods of time, which meant that he did not observe a ruling which was applicable to all but from which he was exempt by virtue of being regarded as one of God's holy fools. However, if the truth be known, he was excused out of sheer necessity. It would have been almost pointless to impose general monastic rules on one who observed the laws of fasting and silence as rigidly as he did (he spent days and nights in prayer and would even fall asleep on his knees), if he himself did not wish to abide by them. 'By rights,' said some of the monks, 'he's holier than any of us and is more conscientious than the rules require anyway, and as for not attending services, he himself knows best whether to go or not, for he's got his own set of rules.' It was to avoid these likely rumblings of discontent and scandal that Father Therapon was left in peace. As was common knowledge, he disliked Starets Zosima intensely; and now, suddenly, the news reached him in his little cabin that 'God's judgement is different from that of people, and the law of nature has been transgressed.' One must assume that one of the first to rush to him with the news was the visitor from Obdorsk, who had been to see him the day before and had come away in terror. I have also mentioned that though Father Païsy, who had been keeping a strict, constant vigil over the coffin, was not aware of events outside the cell, he had in his heart, knowing his community through and through as he did, unerringly predicted the main course of events. He remained calm, however, and fearlessly awaited whatever was still to come, prophetically considering the future outcome of the unrest as it already presented itself to his mind's eye. And then, from the ante-room, his ears were suddenly assailed by a strange noise that rudely disturbed the sanctity of the surroundings. The door burst open and Father Therapon appeared on the threshold. Behind him, crowding around the porch and clearly visible from within the cell, were many monks who had accompanied him, amongst them some laity. His followers did not enter however, nor did they mount

the steps, but instead stood waiting to see what Father Therapon
would say and do next, for they anticipated and, despite all their
boldness, feared that it was not for nothing that he had come.
Pausing on the threshold, Father Therapon raised his arms—
and from under his right arm there peered the sharp, curious
little eyes of the visitor from Obdorsk, who alone had been
unable to contain his curiosity and had dashed up the steps
behind Father Therapon. The others, on the other hand, as
soon as the door was flung open, were overcome with sudden
fear and even backed away slightly. His arms uplifted menacingly, Father Therapon thundered:

'In the name of God, I cast thee out!' whereupon, turning
successively to all four directions, he began to make the sign of
the cross on the walls and four corners of the room. Father
Therapon's followers immediately understood the significance
of this behaviour, for they knew that he always did this wherever
he entered, and that he would not sit down or say a word before
he had expelled the powers of darkness.

'Get thee gone, Satan! Get thee gone, Satan!' he repeated
with each sign of the cross. 'In the name of God, I cast thee out!'
he declaimed again. He was wearing his coarse cassock with a
rope round his waist. The open sackcloth shirt revealed his bare,
grey, hairy chest. He was barefoot. As soon as he started to wave
his arms about, the chains he wore under his cassock began to
clink and rattle. Father Païsy interrupted his reading, stepped
forward, and stood facing him expectantly. Finally, looking at
him sternly, he spoke.

'Wherefore hast thou come, worshipful father? Why disturbest
thou the peace? Why seekest thou to disturb a peaceful flock?'

'Wherefore have I come? Wherefore? What thinkest thou?'
shouted Father Therapon, defiantly. 'I am come to cast out thy
house guests, the foul devils. I can see thou hast gathered a
goodly number of them in my absence; I shall sweep this place
clean with a birch besom.'

'Thou art casting out the devil, but perchance it is him thou
servest,' Father Païsy continued fearlessly, 'and who can say of
himself: "I am holy"? Canst thou, father?'

'Not holy, but foul and sinful am I. I shall not sit upon my
chair and desire that people bow down to me as to an idol!'

thundered Father Therapon. 'Today, people are destroying the holy faith. Your deceased saint', he turned towards the crowd, pointing his finger at the coffin, 'denied the existence of devils. He prescribed purges to exorcise devils. Therefore have ye so many of them now, like unto spiders in every corner. Now has he himself begun to reek. Therein we see a glorious sign from the Lord.'

And such a thing really had happened in Father Zosima's lifetime. One of the monks had begun to dream of devils, and later they began to appear to him in his waking hours. When, in utter terror, he revealed this to the starets, the latter had recommended unremitting prayer and constant fasting. When this too had no effect, he advised him to take a certain medicine while continuing to pray and fast. Many were scandalized by this, shaking their heads when they talked about it—and the most vociferous was Father Therapon, who had immediately been informed by certain detractors of the starets that it was he who had advocated this 'unusual' remedy for such a peculiar case.

'Get thee hence, father!' said Father Païsy authoritatively. 'It is for God, not for man, to judge. Well may we see a "sign" here beyond our understanding—thine or mine or any man's. Get thee hence, father, and cease disturbing the peaceful flock!' he repeated firmly.

'He did not observe the days of fasting as befits a monk of his monastic title, hence this sign from on high. It is there for all to see, and to deny it is a sin!' The zealot could restrain himself no longer and, in his fervour, overstepped all bounds of reason. 'He was tempted by sweets brought to him by ladies in their pockets, he sipped tea for pleasure, he indulged his stomach with sweet things, and his mind with arrogant notions... Therefore hath this ignominy befallen him...'

'Thou speakest empty words, father!' Father Païsy, too, raised his voice. 'I can only marvel at thy abstinence and at the zeal of thy devotion, but thy words are empty, like unto the utterings of a worldly youth, ephemeral and asinine. So get thee hence, father, I adjure thee!' Father Païsy again thundered in conclusion.

'I shall depart!' said Father Therapon, a little nonplussed, but still as furious as ever. 'Ye are the learned ones! With your

superior science, ye have exalted yourselves above an insignificant wretch such as I. I came here lacking instruction, and here *I
forgot* the little I knew, for it is the good Lord Himself who hath
guarded me, insignificant as I am, from your excess of wisdom...'

Father Païsy stood his ground firmly, and waited. Father
Therapon paused a moment and then, in a sudden access of
melancholy as he regarded the coffin of the deceased starets,
pressed the palm of his right hand against his cheek and said in
a singsong voice:

'Tomorrow they will sing "Succour and Guardian" over him,
a glorious hymn, and when I shall give up my ghost it will only
be "What Earthly Bliss", an insignificant little canticle,'[1] he said
plaintively with tears in his eyes. 'Ye have elevated and exalted
yourselves. Cursed be this place!' he wailed suddenly, as though
demented, and, shaking his fist, turned abruptly and quickly
descended the steps of the porch. The crowd below hesitated;
some followed him immediately, while others stayed behind, for
the door of the cell was still open and Father Païsy, who had
followed Father Therapon to the porch, was standing there
expectantly. But the enraged old man had not finished: having
walked about twenty paces he suddenly turned towards the
setting sun, raised both his arms, and fell to the ground as if
struck dead, shouting loudly.

'My Lord hath vanquished! Christ hath vanquished the setting
sun!' he cried, beside himself with woe, and, raising his arms
towards the sun and then falling flat on his face, he began to
weep like a small child, his whole body convulsed with sobs and
his arms outstretched on the ground. This time everyone rushed
towards him immediately, some shouted, some sobbed in sympathy... Everyone was seized with ecstasy.

'There's a holy man for you! There's a righteous man!' came
voices from all sides, fearlessly this time. 'It is he who should be
a starets,' others added angrily.

'He'll not agree to be a starets... He is certain to refuse... He'll
not follow the accursed modern ways... He won't be beguiled by

---

[1] When the body of a monk or a schemamonk is borne from the cell to the church
and, after the service for the dead, to the graveyard, the canticle 'What Earthly Bliss...'
is sung. If, however, the deceased is a schemahieromonk, the hymn 'Succour and
Guardian...' is sung. (*Author's note*)

their foolishness,' echoed voices from everywhere, and it is difficult to imagine how it would all have ended had not the bell sounded, summoning the faithful to prayer. Everybody suddenly started crossing themselves. Father Therapon too rose from the ground and, making the sign of the cross, headed for his cell, not looking back and continuing to hold forth, but now quite incoherently. Some people, only a few, made as if to follow him, but the majority began to disperse, hurrying off to attend the service. Father Païsy let Father Yosif continue the reading, and came down the steps. He refused to be swayed by the frantic cries of the fanatics, but for some reason he suddenly felt his heart gripped by a peculiar sorrow and remorse. He stopped suddenly, asking himself: 'Where does this sorrow come from, to crush my spirit like this?' and to his surprise he realized immediately that the most trivial and peculiar reason apparently lay at the root of this sudden sorrow, for amongst the frenzied crowd round the entrance to the cell he had noticed Alyosha, and he recalled that as soon as he spotted him he immediately felt a stab of pain in his heart. 'Is it really true that this youth is now so dear to my heart?' he asked himself with astonishment. Just then Alyosha happened to approach, apparently hurrying somewhere, though not in the direction of the church. Their eyes met. Alyosha quickly averted his eyes and lowered his gaze to the ground, and just by looking at the youth Father Païsy understood what an enormous struggle was raging in his heart.

'Have you too been led astray?' Father Païsy exclaimed. 'Are you too with those of little faith?' he added sorrowfully.

Alyosha stopped and looked at Father Païsy somewhat vaguely, but again averted his eyes and once more lowered his gaze. He stood half facing away, and refused to turn to look at his interlocutor. Father Païsy observed him closely.

'Where are you hurrying to? The bell is summoning us to prayer,' he continued, but Alyosha did not respond.

'Or is it that you are leaving the hermitage? Just like that, without leave, without a blessing?'

Suddenly Alyosha smiled wryly, glanced strangely, very strangely at this priest, to whom he had been entrusted by his former mentor, the custodian of his heart and mind, his beloved starets, on his deathbed; then suddenly, and still without replying, he made a gesture of resignation and, as though neglecting to observe even common courtesy, walked with quick strides towards the gate and out of the hermitage.

'You will return!' Father Païsy whispered, gazing after him in sad wonderment.

2

HERE'S AN OPPORTUNITY

FATHER PAÏSY, of course, was not mistaken in concluding that his 'young friend' would return again, and he had even (perhaps not fully, but shrewdly for all that) discerned Alyosha's true state of mind. Nevertheless, I admit candidly that I myself would find it difficult to convey clearly the precise significance of such a strange and indefinable moment in the life of my all too young, but dearly beloved hero. In reply to Father Païsy's pained question to Alyosha: 'Are you too with those of little faith?', I could of course reply firmly on Alyosha's behalf: 'No, I am not.' Rather, quite the reverse was true; his whole confusion was precisely the result of too much faith. All the same, he was confused, and the events were so distressing that even later, after much time had elapsed, Alyosha was to recall this sad day as one of the most painful and fateful in his whole life. If, however, I were asked outright: 'Could his anguish and alarm have arisen merely because the starets's body, instead of immediately manifesting healing powers, had started to putrefy prematurely?' I would reply without hesitation: 'Yes, this was indeed so.' However, I would merely beg the reader not to be too hasty in ridiculing unduly my young hero's purity of heart. As for myself, not only am I not prepared, for example, to ask forgiveness on his behalf, to make excuses for him, or to justify his naïve faith on account of either his tender age or his hitherto scant progress in his studies, and so on and so forth, but on the contrary I will declare unhesitatingly that I have the utmost respect for the nature of his soul. No doubt some other young man, cautious in his response to spiritual influences, lukewarm and detached in his affections, and possessing an astute but, for his years, altogether too calculating and therefore meretricious mind, such a young man, I maintain, would have avoided the situation that confronted my hero, but in certain cases it is truly nobler to succumb to one's emotions, even imprudent ones, than not to give in to them at all. This is especially true in our youth, for the young man who is too dispassionate cannot be relied upon with certainty, and in my opinion is pretty worthless. 'But,' level-headed people would probably exclaim, 'surely not every youth can be expected to believe so uncritically, and your young friend ought not to be held up as an example to others.' To this I shall again reply: 'Yes, my young friend believed, he believed fervently and unquestioningly; all the same, I am not going to make excuses on his behalf.'

You see, even though I stated earlier (all too hastily, perhaps) that I would not offer any explanations, excuses, or justifications on behalf of my hero, nevertheless I realize that some clarification is called for in order to understand properly the story that is to follow. Let me put it this way: it was not just a question of miracles. It was by no means a case of frivolous expectation of the miraculous. Alyosha needed miracles neither to confirm any particular convictions of his (that least of all) nor to bolster the triumph of any deep-seated, preconceived theory over other theories—not that either; in his case it was first and foremost a question of love and veneration for one individual person, that and nothing else—the person of his beloved starets, his mentor. The point to bear in mind is that at that particular time and throughout the whole of the preceding year, all the love that he had borne in his pure young heart towards 'all and sundry' had appeared on occasion and particularly at times of spiritual crisis to be concentrated, however mistakenly, on one single individual, that is on his beloved starets, who was now dead. In fact, this being had been an unquestionable paragon for him for so long that all his youthful energy and all his aspirations were chan-nelled perforce towards that same paragon, on occasion even to the exclusion of 'all and sundry'. He later recalled how, on this trying day, he had totally forgotten about his brother Dmitry, about whom he had been so concerned and worried the previous day; also, he had forgotten to take the two hundred roubles to

Ilyushechka's father, something that he had also been very anxious to do the previous day. But again it was not miracles he needed; rather, some 'supreme justice' that he believed had been violated, and as a consequence of which violation his heart had been so cruelly and unexpectedly wounded. Is it any wonder, therefore, that by the very nature of things Alyosha should expect this 'justice' to take the form of the instant miracle expected from the bodily remains of his beloved erstwhile teacher? After all, this was just what everyone at the monastery thought and expected, even those whose intellect Alyosha venerated—Father Païsy, for instance—and hence Alyosha, untroubled by the least doubt, had begun to nurture the same dreams. He had long since accepted this in his heart, a year's life at the monastery had accustomed him to such expectations. But it was justice he yearned for, justice, and not just miracles! And now the one who, by rights, ought to have been elevated above everyone else in the whole world—that one, instead of being glorified as was his due, was suddenly cast down and disgraced! For what? By whose judgement? By whose decree? These were the questions which at once began to torment his immature and innocent heart. His heart was offended—indeed, incensed beyond endurance—that the most righteous amongst men had been subjected to such ignominious and vituperative scorn at the hands of such an ignorant and vulgar crowd. Well then, so what if there was no miracle at all, so what if there were to be no miraculous manifestations, if the imminently awaited event had not occurred; but why this ignominy instead, why this scandal, why this premature putrefaction which 'violated nature', as the vindictive monks had expressed it? Why this 'sign' over which they were now gloating together with Father Therapon, and why did they imagine that they were entitled to gloat? Where was providence and where was its hand? Why, thought Alyosha, had it withdrawn its hand at 'the most vital moment', as though wishing to submit to the blind, insensate, and pitiless laws of nature?

That is why Alyosha's heart bled, and, of course, as I said before, this was above all the one person whom he cherished more than anyone in the world, and this person was now 'disgraced', was now 'defiled'! It may well be that this resentment on the part of my young hero was frivolous and wrong-headed, but, on the other hand, let me repeat for the third time (and I admit in advance that this also may be frivolous) that I am glad my young hero did not turn out to be too rational at such a moment, since there will always be plenty of opportunity for an intelligent person to employ his intellect, but if love did not hold sway in his heart at such an exceptional moment, would it ever do so? Nor, incidentally, would I wish to pass over something rather odd which, however fleetingly, nevertheless made Alyosha stop and think at this fateful and confusing moment in his life. This new and unexpected *something* consisted of a certain agonizing impression which had been left by yesterday's discussion with his brother Ivan, and which now haunted his mind incessantly. Especially now. Oh, it was not that any of his basic, as it were elemental beliefs had been undermined; despite his momentary rebellion, he continued to love his God and to believe in Him implicitly. Nevertheless, some vague though painful and sinister impression evoked by the memory of yesterday's discussion with his brother Ivan began to stir again in his soul now, trying ever more insistently to assert itself.

It was already well after dusk when Rakitin, walking through the pine wood on his way from the hermitage to the monastery, suddenly spotted Alyosha lying under a tree, his face to the ground, motionless and seemingly asleep. He approached and called out to him.

'What are you doing here, Aleksei? Has it...', he said in surprise, but did not finish and stopped. He had meant to say: 'Has it really *come to this*?' Alyosha did not look up at him, but Rakitin realized by some movement of his body that he had heard and understood him.

'What's the matter with you?' he continued in surprise, though the surprise on his face was beginning to give way to a derisive smile.

'Listen, I've been looking for you for over two hours already. You suddenly vanished. What are you doing here? What sanctimonious foolery is this? Look at me...'

Alyosha raised his head, sat up, and leant back against the tree. He was not crying, but there was suffering on his face and annoyance in his eyes. He did not look directly at Rakitin, but beyond him, to one side.

'You know, your face has changed completely. You don't look your usual meek and mild self. Are you angry with somebody, or what? Has someone upset you?'

'Go away!' Alyosha said suddenly, with a weary gesture, still refusing to look at Rakitin.

'My word! So we're capable of raising our voice just like any other mortal. An angel, eh? Well, Alyosha, to be quite frank with you, you know, you really astonish me. I've long ceased to be surprised at anything that goes on here. Still, I always considered you to be an educated fellow...'

Alyosha looked at him at last, but absent-mindedly somehow, as though still unable to follow his meaning.

'Is it really just because your old boy has started to stink?' Rakitin asked again, in tones of the most genuine amazement. 'Did you really seriously expect him to start working miracles?'

'I did believe, I do believe, and I want to believe and I shall believe, so what else do you want!' Alyosha shouted in annoyance.

'Nothing whatsoever, my dear fellow. Dammit, not even a twelve-year-old schoolboy would believe any of this now. But what the hell... So you've fallen out with your God, you've rebelled against Him: it appears the old man's been done out of an honour, he's not had his decoration on the big occasion! You're pathetic!'

Alyosha fixed Rakitin with a long look through half-closed eyelids, and something flashed in his eyes... but it was not anger at Rakitin.

'I'm not rebelling against my God, I merely "refuse to accept His world"', Alyosha suddenly said with a wry smile.

Rakitin thought for a moment before replying. 'What do you mean, "you refuse to accept His world"? What rubbish!'

Alyosha did not reply.

'Well, enough of these trifles, let's get down to business... have you eaten today?'

'I don't remember... I probably have.'

'You look hungry, you need something to keep body and soul together. You're a sorry sight. It's obvious you haven't slept all night, either. I hear you've had a powwow back there. And then there was all that carry-on... I bet all you've had is a bit of consecrated bread. I've got some smoked sausage in my pocket. I grabbed some just in case, when I was on my way from town, only I don't suppose you'll eat sausage...'

'Let me have some of your sausage.'

'Aha! So that's how it is! So we've got an out-and-out rebellion on our hands. To the barricades! Well, my good fellow, I wouldn't miss this for anything. Let's go to my place... I wouldn't mind a glass of vodka right now, I'm dog-tired. Now I don't suppose you'd join me in a glass of vodka, would you... or would you?'

'I wouldn't mind.'

'I don't believe it! You're joking, my good fellow!' Rakitin looked at him aghast. 'Well, one way or another, sausage or vodka, the world's gone mad. Splendid! I wouldn't miss this for the world. Let's go!'

Alyosha got up from the ground in silence and followed Rakitin.

'If your brother Vanechka was to see this, it'd give him a turn! Your dear brother Ivan Fyodorovich, by the way, left for Moscow this morning, did you know that?'

'Yes,' said Alyosha listlessly, and suddenly a vision of his brother Dmitry flashed through his mind, but only momentarily, and even though it reminded him of something, of some urgent matter which ought not to be put off for an instant, of some duty, some terrible obligation, this recollection did not make any impression on him either, it failed to move his heart, and was gone and forgotten in a trice. And yet the memory of it kept haunting him for a long while afterwards.

'Your dear brother Vanechka once categorized me as a "tiresome liberal clot". There was one occasion when you too didn't refrain from informing me that I was "dishonourable"... Fair enough! Now I'm going to see how sensible and honourable you both are,' Rakitin concluded to himself in a whisper. 'Listen!' he continued in a normal voice, 'let's give the monastery a miss and take this footpath straight to the town... Hm, by the way, I wouldn't mind dropping in on Khokhlakova. Imagine! I informed her about all that had happened and, would you believe it, she replied immediately with a pencil-written note (that lady will write a note at the drop of a hat), saying that "she never expected

such a venerable starets as Father Zosima *to behave in this way!*"
That's exactly what she wrote, "behave in this way"! She was
really angry too; honestly, what a lot you all are! Wait!' he
suddenly exclaimed again, stopped dead, and, putting his hand
on Alyosha's shoulder, made him stop too.

'Do you know, Alyoshka,' he looked him straight in the eyes,
completely taken by the new idea which had suddenly struck
him; though aware of the funny side of it, he was reluctant to
spell out this new idea which had come to him out of the blue,
such was his wonderment at the unexpected mood in which he
now found Alyosha. 'Alyoshka, do you know where the best place
to go would be?' he said finally, tentatively feeling his way.

'Doesn't matter... wherever you wish.'

'Let's go to Grushenka, eh? Will you come?' Rakitin said
finally after a pause, quivering with nervous expectation.

'Yes, let's go to Grushenka,' replied Alyosha calmly and
without hesitation. That Alyosha could agree so calmly and
readily came as such a surprise to Rakitin that he nearly fell over
backwards.

'W-well!... Yes!' he exclaimed in surprise, and suddenly
seizing Alyosha by the elbow, he quickly led him along the
footpath, still fearful lest the latter's resolve might evaporate.
They walked in silence, Rakitin not daring even to start a
conversation.

'She'll be delighted, really delighted...', he started to mumble,
but cut himself short. And it was certainly not to please
Grushenka that he was taking Alyosha to her; he was a calculating person, and would not undertake anything that was not in his
own interest. His intentions on this occasion, however, were
twofold: firstly, a spiteful one, namely, to witness 'the shame of
the righteous man' and the probable 'fall' of Alyosha 'from saint
to sinner', something that he had been relishing in advance; and,
secondly, he also had in mind a certain material advantage, of
which I shall speak later.

'Well now, here's an opportunity and no mistake,' he thought
cheerfully and maliciously, 'I must take the bull by the horns—
it'll suit my purpose right down to the ground.'

3

A SPRING ONION

GRUSHENKA lived in the busiest quarter of the town, near
Cathedral Square, in the house of one Mrs Morozova, a
merchant's widow, from whom she rented a small timber annexe
facing the courtyard. Morozova's house was large, stone-built,
two-storeyed, old, and most unprepossessing; it was occupied by
the owner, an elderly woman who led a solitary existence, and
her two nieces, both of them confirmed old maids. There was
no necessity for her to rent out the annexe, and everyone knew
that she had taken on Grushenka as a tenant (about four years
ago) solely as a favour to the merchant Samsonov, who was a
relative of hers and, as was an open secret in the town,
Grushenka's lover. It was said that the jealous old man had
initially installed his 'pet' at Morozova's so that the old woman
would be able to keep a watchful eye on her. But the watchful
eye had soon become unnecessary and, in the end, Morozova
rarely encountered Grushenka and made no attempt to spy on
her at all. True, four years had passed since the old man had
installed the eighteen-year-old girl from the county town, meek,
shy, thin, skinny, pensive, and sad, in the house, and a lot of
water had passed under the bridge since then. However, the
people of our town knew little of her past, and what they did
know was fragmentary and contradictory; even now that Agrafena
Aleksandrovna had blossomed into a beauty and aroused the
interest of many, they were still none the wiser. It was rumoured
that she had been seduced at the age of seventeen by some army
officer or other, and immediately abandoned. The officer, it was
said, then went away and got married somewhere, leaving
Grushenka in disgrace and poverty. It was also said, however,
that though Grushenka had indeed been rescued from poverty
by the old man, she came from a decent family with a clerical
background, the daughter of a supernumerary deacon or something of that sort. And so, in the space of four years she had
changed from a sensitive, deprived, pitiful orphan into a rosy-
cheeked, shapely, Russian beauty, a woman of firm, decisive
character, proud and impudent, acquisitive, knowing how to

handle money, mean and calculating, who had already managed by hook or by crook, as people said, to put by a nice little pile for herself. On one thing, however, everyone was agreed: it was not easy to gain access to Grushenka, and apart from the old man, her benefactor, no man could boast of enjoying her favours during those four years. This fact was beyond dispute because, in the last two years especially, there had been many eager bidders for her favours. But all their attempts had come to nought, and because of the firm and scornful rejection they received from that spirited young lady, some of the suitors had been obliged to withdraw in comical and bizarre circumstances. People also knew that the young lady had taken to what is known as 'speculating', especially during the last year, and that she had demonstrated extraordinary talent in this respect, so much so that in the end she had come to be called a veritable Jewess by many. It was not that she lent money on interest, but it was known, for instance, that for some time, together with Fyodor Pavlovich, she used to buy up bills of exchange for a song, ten kopecks for a rouble, and on some of them later make a rouble for every ten kopecks. Although he was a tight-fisted millionaire and a tyrant to his grown-up sons, the ailing widower Samsonov, who for a year now had lost the use of his badly swollen legs, had nevertheless fallen under the spell of his protégée, whom, as some used to remark with a snigger, he had previously kept in complete subjugation and under his heel. But Grushenka had managed to emancipate herself, at the same time inspiring in him unlimited trust as regards her loyalty. This old man, a highly successful merchant (now long deceased), was also a remarkable character, an out-and-out miser and hard as flint, and though Grushenka had captivated him to the extent that he could hardly survive without her (that was how it had been for the past two years for example), he nevertheless would not hand over to her any significant sum of money, and even had she threatened to leave him altogether, he would still have remained adamant. Nevertheless, he did give her a small amount of capital, and when this became known it too astonished everyone. 'You've got your head screwed on, young lady,' he said to her, as he parted with about eight thousand, 'make the most of it, and remember this, apart from your usual annual maintenance you won't get any more from me, and I'm not going to leave you anything in my will, either.' And he was true to his word: on his death he left everything to his sons, whom, together with their wives and children, he had treated no better than his servants throughout his life, and as for Grushenka, she was not even mentioned in the will. All this came to light subsequently. But advice was another matter—when it came to managing her own private capital he helped Grushenka a great deal and guided her in business. When Fyodor Pavlovich made his initial contact with Grushenka in connection with a routine business deal and, to his own astonishment, finished by falling head over heels in love with her, almost to the point of losing his sanity, old Samsonov, who by that time was already knocking on death's door, had chuckled derisively. It is remarkable that throughout her acquaintance with the old man she was totally and, one could say, obsessively frank with him, and he was probably the only person in the world with whom she was so frank. Just recently, when Dmitry Fyodorovich turned up and declared his love for her, the old man had stopped laughing. In fact, on one occasion he had turned to Grushenka with a piece of blunt and serious advice: 'If you have to choose between the two, father or son, go for the old man, but whatever you do, see to it that the old rogue marries you and settles at least some capital on you beforehand, and mind you get it in writing. And steer clear of the Captain, there's no future with him.' These were the very words of Grushenka's old lecher, who was already anticipating his own impending demise and who did indeed die five months after giving this advice. I shall just add in passing that, although many people in the town knew of the bizarre and grotesque rivalry between old Karamazov and his son for Grushenka's favours, very few at the time fully understood her true attitude towards the two of them. Even Grushenka's two servants testified in court (after the events of which we shall speak later) that Agrafena Aleksandrovna had admitted Dmitry Fyodorovich only out of fear, since it would appear he had 'threatened murder'. She had two servants, one, a very old woman, the cook, who originally came from her parents' household and was in poor health and wellnigh deaf, and her granddaughter, a young energetic girl of about twenty, who was Grushenka's maid. Grushenka herself lived very frugally, in unostentatious surroundings. The annexe that she occupied comprised only three rooms, furnished by her landlady with mahogany furniture in the style of the 1820s. When Rakitin and Alyosha entered it was well after dusk, but the rooms were still not lit. Grushenka herself was in her drawing-room, reclining on her large, hard, ugly sofa with its mahogany-veneered backrest and badly worn leather seat full of holes. Under her head were two white, down pillows taken from her bed. She was lying motionless on her back, with her arms behind her head. She was dressed to the nines as though expecting someone, in a black silk frock and a fine lace head-dress which suited her admirably, and draped over her shoulders was a lace shawl fastened with a massive gold brooch. She was indeed expecting someone, and as she lay there she seemed tense and impatient, her face rather pale, her eyes and lips glowing, and her right foot restlessly tapping on the armrest of the sofa. A certain commotion ensued following Rakitin and Alyosha's admittance: from the hall they heard Grushenka call out in alarm as she jumped up from the sofa, 'Who's there?' But the servant girl greeted the visitors and immediately called back to her mistress.

'It's not him, it's someone else, these two are all right.'

'I wonder what's going on here?' mumbled Rakitin, as he led Alyosha by the elbow into the drawing-room. Grushenka was standing by the sofa, still seemingly frightened. A thick lock of flaxen hair had slipped out from beneath her head-dress and fallen over her right shoulder, but she paid no attention and did not adjust it until she had surveyed her visitors and established who they were.

'Ah, it's you, Rakitka? You gave me such a fright. Who's that with you? Who is it? Lord, look who he's brought!' she exclaimed, recognizing Alyosha.

'Fine, we could do with some candles here!' Rakitin said in the offhand manner of a close friend and acquaintance who was even entitled to issue orders in the house.

'Candles... of course, candles... Fenya, get him a candle... Well, you really have picked a time to bring him here!' she exclaimed again, motioning with her head towards Alyosha, and, turning towards the mirror, she quickly began to tuck back her plait with both hands. She seemed annoyed.

'So I've picked the wrong time, have I?' asked Rakitin, briefly appearing offended.

'You gave me a fright, Rakitin, if you must know,' Grushenka turned towards Alyosha with a smile. 'Don't be frightened of me, my darling Alyosha, I'm so frightfully glad to see you, you're an unexpected visitor. But you really gave me quite a turn, Rakitka; I thought it was Mitya trying to break in. You see, I deceived him a while ago and he swore he believed me, but I was lying. I told him I was going to spend the evening doing the accounts with Kuzma Kuzmich, he's an old crony of mine, and that I wouldn't be back until late. You see, I go to his place once a week for the whole evening to balance the accounts. We lock the door, and he gets the abacus and I sit down and enter the figures in the books—I'm the only one he trusts. Mitya believed me, so he thinks I'm there, but instead I'm at home with the door locked, waiting for this message. How come Fenya let you in? Fenya, Fenya! Go and open the gate and see if you can see the Captain anywhere! Maybe he's hiding and watching us, I'm frightened to death!'

'There's no one there, Agrafena Aleksandrovna, I've just had a good scout around and I've been checking through the crack in the door every minute, I'm scared out of my wits myself.'

'Are the shutters closed, Fenya? We ought to draw the curtains—there we are!' She herself drew the heavy curtains. 'Otherwise he'll notice the light. Today, Alyosha, I'm frightened of your brother Mitya.' Grushenka spoke loudly, with alarm in her voice, but also with a kind of elation.

'Why should you be so scared of Mitenka today?' Rakitin enquired. 'You're not normally afraid of him, he dances to your tune.'

'I told you, I'm waiting for some news, a sweet little message, Mitenka's the last person I need at this moment. Frankly, I have a feeling he didn't believe me when I said I was going to stay at Kuzma Kuzmich's. I suppose he's still lying in wait for me at the bottom of Fyodor Pavlovich's garden. And if he's hiding there it means he won't come here, thank goodness! But actually I did

pop down to Kuzma Kuzmich's, Mitya came with me; I said I'd
stay till midnight and that he should come at midnight without
fail to take me home. He left, and after ten minutes at the old
man's I came back home again, God, I was so scared—I ran all
the way in case I met him.'

'Where are you off to in all that finery? That's a curious little
bonnet you've got there!'

'It's you that's curious, Rakitin! I told you, I'm waiting for a
message. As soon as it comes I'll be off like a shot and you'll not
see me for dust. That's why I'm all dressed up, ready to go.'

'So where are you off to?'

'Curiosity killed the cat.'

'Just look at you. Beaming with joy... I've never seen you like
that—dressed up as if for a ball.' Rakitin was looking her up and
down.

'A lot you know about such things.'

'More than can be said for you.'

'At least I've been to a ball. Kuzma Kuzmich was marrying off
one of his sons three years ago, and I watched from the gallery.
But why am I talking to you, Rakitka, when there's such a prince
standing near by. Now there's a welcome sight! Alyosha, darling,
I can hardly believe my eyes; Good Lord, that you should have
come to me! To tell you the truth, I never expected, never
dreamt, never even believed you'd come. It may not be the most
convenient time, but you've made me so terribly happy! Sit on
the sofa, over here, that's right, let me have a look at you, you're
a fine looking lad! Really, I'm still in a daze... As for you,
Rakitka, if only you'd brought him yesterday or three days ago!...
Never mind, though, I'm delighted all the same. Maybe it's even
better that it's now, at a time like this, than three days ago...'

She sat down coquettishly next to Alyosha on the sofa, and
looked at him boldly, full of admiration. And she really was glad,
she was telling the truth. Her eyes were shining and her lips
were laughing, but with a happy, good-natured laughter. Alyosha
had hardly expected to see such a kind expression on her face...
Until the day before he had hardly seen her, and had then
formed a formidable impression of her; moreover, he had been
shocked by her mean and vicious treatment of Katerina Ivanovna
yesterday, and was now very surprised to see her suddenly in an

altogether different light. And, however much he was burdened
with his own grief, his gaze was involuntarily drawn to her. All
her gestures appeared to have undergone a transformation since
yesterday; gone was yesterday's affectation in her voice, as well
as those effete and mannered movements... now everything about
her was simple and artless; she moved briskly, boldly, and
uninhibitedly, altogether she was very excited.

'Good Lord, the things that have happened today, really,' she
prattled on. 'And why I'm so happy to see you, Alyosha, I
honestly don't know. If you asked me, I really couldn't tell you.'

'You don't know why you're so happy, that's a good one!'
sniggered Rakitin. 'Why did you nag at me then: "Bring him,
bring him along." You must have had a reason.'

'I did have a reason earlier on, but it's gone now, things have
changed. Well now, can I offer you anything? I'm a nicer person
now, Rakitka. Go on, sit down, Rakitka, what are you standing
for? Oh, so you've already decided to sit down, have you? Trust
my little Rakitushka to make himself at home. Look at him,
Alyosha, sitting over there sulking, wondering why I didn't invite
him to sit down first. He's so sensitive is my Rakitka, ever so
sensitive!' laughed Grushenka. 'Stop sulking, Rakitka, today I'm
in a generous mood. Why are you sitting there, looking so sad
my dear Alyoshechka, you're not frightened of me, are you?' she
peered into his eyes with a coquettish smile.

'He's very upset. The starets didn't get his promotion,' Rakitin
said lugubriously.

'What promotion?'

'His starets has started to stink.'

'What do you mean, "stink"? You're talking some kind of
rubbish, you've got something filthy on your mind again. Shut
up, you silly fool. Will you let me sit on your knees, Alyosha—
like this!' And in a flash she suddenly leapt up and, laughing,
plumped herself down on his lap, cuddly as a kitten, her right
arm coiled tenderly around his neck. 'Let me cheer you up, my
darling little altar boy! No, seriously, please let me sit on your
lap for a bit, you won't be angry, will you? I'll get off if you want
me to.'

Alyosha said nothing. He sat still, afraid to move; he heard the
words 'I'll get off if you want me to,' but he did not reply, he

seemed stunned. But the reason for this was not what Rakitin, who was eyeing them rapaciously from his seat, might have imagined or expected. The profound grief afflicting his soul had smothered all the other sensations that might have welled up in his heart, and if he had only been able to reason rationally at that moment he would have realized that he was thoroughly shielded against all possible temptation and seduction. Nevertheless, in spite of his clouded and confused spiritual state and notwithstanding all the grief which oppressed him, he could not help marvelling at the new and strange sensation which was stirring in his heart. This woman, this 'frightful' woman, not only no longer failed to generate any of his former fear of her, the fear which used to paralyse him at the very thought of a woman, but, on the contrary, though he had feared her above all other women, the woman who was now sitting on his knees and was cuddling up to him evoked in him a completely different, unexpected, and peculiar sensation, a sensation of some huge, unprecedented, and open-hearted curiosity, and all without a trace of fear, without any of his former terror—this was the most significant and astonishing thing of all.

'You've talked enough nonsense,' exclaimed Rakitin, 'let's have the champagne, you owe it to me, you know you do!'

'Yes, I do. You know, Alyosha, on top of everything else, I promised him a bottle of champagne if he brought you along. Let's have the champagne, I'll have some too! Fenya, Fenya, fetch the champagne, the bottle that Mitya left, hurry up. Even though I'm mean I'll stand you a bottle, but not for you, Rakitin, you're a wet blanket, but he's a prince! I'm not really in the mood, but never mind, I'll drink with you, let's be reckless!'

'What's come over you, and what's this "message", may I ask, if it's not a secret?' probed Rakitin again, full of curiosity, but deliberately pretending that he did not notice the gibes that were continually being directed at him.

'Oh, it's no secret, as you well know yourself,' Grushenka said suddenly with a preoccupied air, turning her head towards Rakitin and leaning slightly away from Alyosha, although continuing to sit on his lap with her arm around his neck. 'My officer friend's coming, Rakitin, my officer's on his way!'

'I heard he was coming, but is he really in the neighbourhood already?'

'He's in Mokroye now, he's going to send a dispatch-rider from there, that's what he wrote, I had a letter from him not long ago. Now I'm waiting for the messenger to arrive.'

'Really! Why in Mokroye?'

'It's a long story, but I've told you enough.'

'Well, where does that leave Mitenka now? My goodness! Does he know?'

'Know what? He knows nothing! If he found out, he'd kill me. But I'm not afraid of that at all now, I'm not scared he'll knife me. Be quiet, Rakitka, don't mention Dmitry Fyodorovich to me: I've had more than my fill of him. But I don't even want to think about that at the moment. Now I can think about Alyoshechka instead, that's different, let me look at you Alyoshechka... Give me a smile, my darling, cheer up, laugh at my joy and my silliness... There, he's smiling, he's smiling! Look at his sweet expression! You know, Alyosha, I really thought you were angry with me about what happened the day before yesterday, about that young lady. I was a bitch, I really was... Only perhaps it's just as well it turned out the way it did. There was a good and a bad side to it,' Grushenka suddenly smiled thoughtfully, and a streak of malice glinted through her smile. 'Mitya told me she shouted: "She ought to be whipped!" Oh, I insulted her all right. But it was she who invited me, just to make me feel small, to bribe me with her chocolate... No, it's as well it turned out the way it did,' she smiled again. 'Only it worries me that you're angry...'

'Now I see,' Rakitin suddenly interjected in genuine astonishment. 'You know, she really is scared of you, Alyosha, you little mouse you.'

'He's only a mouse to you... because you don't know what you're saying! You see, I love him with all my soul! Do you believe me, Alyosha, that I love you with all my soul?'

'You shameless hussy! Just listen to her, she's declaring her love for you, Aleksei!'

'So what if I do love him?'

'And what about the officer? What about the precious message from Mokroye?'

'That's one thing, this is another.'

'There's female logic for you!'

'Don't annoy me, Rakitka,' Grushenka snapped back, 'that's one thing, this is another. My love for Alyosha is different. True, Alyosha, I did harbour some wicked thoughts about you. Let's face it, I'm mean, I'm violent, but there are times, Alyosha, when I look upon you as my own conscience. I keep thinking: "Someone like him must surely despise anyone as bad as me." I was thinking about it the other day too, when I was hurrying back from the young lady's. You know, I've had my eye on you a long time now, Alyosha; Mitya knows too, I told him. Mitya understands everything. You know, Alyosha, really, I keep looking at you, and there are times I feel ashamed, so thoroughly ashamed of myself... I wonder, how did I start thinking about you? And when did it all start? I don't know and I can't remember...'

Fenya came in and placed a tray on the table with an open bottle of champagne and three glasses already poured.

'Champagne's here!' exclaimed Rakitin. 'You're excited, Agrafena Aleksandrovna, you're a different person. After one glass you'll be dancing. Ugh! You can't trust them to do anything,' he added, eyeing the champagne. 'The old woman poured it out in the kitchen and has brought the bottle without the cork... and it's warm. Well, never mind.'

He went up to the table, raised a glass, drained it in one gulp, and poured himself another one.

'One doesn't get champagne that often,' he said, licking his lips. 'Well, Alyosha, take a glass, show us what you're made of. What shall we drink to? The gates of paradise? Raise your glass, Grusha, you must drink to the gates of paradise too.'

'What gates of paradise?'

She took a glass. Alyosha picked his up, took a sip, and put it down.

'No, better not!' he smiled gently.

'It was all talk, wasn't it!' exclaimed Rakitin.

'In that case, I shan't either,' Grushenka joined in, 'I don't really feel like it anyway. Rakitin, you carry on, drink the whole bottle yourself. I'll drink only if Alyosha does.'

'What a touching little scene!' jeered Rakitin. 'Are you quite comfortable, sitting on his knees? Let's face it, he's grieving, but what's your excuse? He's rebelled against his God, he was going to tuck into my sausage...'

'What?'

'His starets has died, Starets Zosima, the saint.'

'Starets Zosima has died!' exclaimed Grushenka. 'God, I didn't know!' She crossed herself devoutly. 'My God, and here am I sitting on his knees!' she started as though in panic, jumped up, and sat down on the sofa. Alyosha fixed her with a long look full of wonderment, and something appeared to light up in his face.

'Rakitin,' he suddenly pronounced in a loud and firm voice, 'don't mock me for rebelling against my God. I don't want to bear a grudge against you, so try and understand how I feel. I've lost a treasure such as you've never had, so you've no right to judge me now. Look at her! Did you notice how she spared my feelings? When I came here I expected to find a wicked person— I was attracted to her because I am mean and wicked myself, but instead I found a true sister, a treasure—a loving soul... She spared me... I'm talking about you, Agrafena Aleksandrovna. You've uplifted my soul.'

Alyosha's lips began to tremble, his chest constricted. He stopped talking.

'"Uplifted your soul", my foot!' said Rakitin with a malicious laugh. 'And she was ready to gobble you up, did you know that?'

'Don't, Rakitka!' Grushenka suddenly leapt to her feet. 'Shut up, both of you. Now I'll tell you everything. You, Alyosha, keep quiet, because your words fill me with shame, because I'm evil, I'm no good—that's the way I am. And you, Rakitka, hold your tongue, because you're a liar. I did have this wicked thought of wanting to seduce him, but now you're wrong, now everything has changed... and I don't want another sound out of you, Rakitka!' Grushenka said all this in a state of great agitation.

'Look at the two of them, they're completely out of their minds!' hissed Rakitin, eyeing them both in astonishment. 'You're mad! Have I wandered into an asylum or something? You've gone soft in the head, both of you, all we need is for the pair of you to burst into tears!'

'And I'm going to cry, I am!' Grushenka continued. 'He called me his sister just now, and I'll never forget that as long as I live! Only remember this, Rakitka, I may be evil, but I did offer to give someone a spring onion once.'

'What are you talking about—an onion? Hell, they really have gone batty!'

Rakitin was surprised to see them so elated and continued to sulk, although he should have realized that for both of them everything that could shake them to the core spiritually had coalesced, which is something that occurs only rarely in life. But Rakitin, though highly sensitive as regards everything relating to himself, was most unobservant when it came to gauging the feelings and sentiments of those close to him—this was partly due to his youth and inexperience, but mostly to his colossal egoism.

'You see, Alyoshechka,' Grushenka turned to him with a sudden burst of nervous laughter, 'I was boasting when I told Rakitka that I'd offered someone an onion, but I'll tell you about it for a different reason. It's only a fable,* but a good one; I heard it when I was still a child from Matrena, who now works for me as a cook. How does it go? Once upon a time there lived a horrid woman who was as wicked as could be, and she died. And she hadn't done a good deed in her life. The devils grabbed her and threw her into a burning lake. Her guardian angel was looking on and thought to himself: "What good deed can I possibly recall to tell God about?" He remembered one, and said to God: "She once", he said, "picked a spring onion from her garden and gave it to a beggar woman." And God answered him: "Why don't you", he said, "take this same onion, hold it out to her in the lake, and let her grab it and hold tight, and if you manage to pull her out of the lake, may she go to heaven, but if the onion breaks, may the old woman remain there." The angel ran off to the woman and held out the onion to her: "There you are, old woman," he said, "grab this and hold tight." And he began to pull her out ever so carefully, and he had almost pulled her out when the other sinners in the lake, seeing that she was being rescued, began to cling to her so that they too might be pulled out. But the woman was as wicked as can be, and she began to lash out with her feet: "He's pulling me out, not you, it's my onion, not yours." No sooner had she said this, than the onion snapped. And the woman fell back into the lake, where she's burning to this very day. And the angel burst into tears and left. There's the fable for you, I've remembered every word of it, because that wicked woman is me. I boasted to Rakitka that I'd offered someone an onion, but to you I'll put it another way: an onion is *all* I've ever given anyone in my life, that's all the charity there is in me. So don't think too highly of me because of it, Alyosha, don't think I'm good, I'm evil and wicked as can be, and if you go on praising me you'll only make me more ashamed. Well then, I'd better make a clean breast of it. Listen, Alyosha, I was so eager to entice you here, and I pestered Rakitka so much, that I promised him twenty-five roubles if he brought you to me. Stay there, Rakitka, wait!' She walked quickly over to the table, pulled out a drawer, took out a wallet, and produced a twenty-five-rouble note.

'What nonsense! What utter nonsense!' Rakitin repeated, squirming with embarrassment.

'Take it, Rakitka, my debt, I don't suppose you'll refuse it, it was you who asked for it.' And she flung the banknote at him.

'Why refuse it?' grunted Rakitin, visibly embarrassed, but putting a brave face on it. 'This'll come in very handy, that's what fools are for, to profit the wise.'

'And now just keep quiet, Rakitka; the rest of what I'm going to say is not for your ears. Sit down there in the corner and keep quiet. You don't like us, so just shut up.'

'There's not much to like about you!' Rakitin snapped back, no longer making any attempt to conceal his anger. He put the twenty-five-rouble note in his pocket, but he was thoroughly embarrassed in front of Alyosha. He had expected to be paid later, so that the latter would not find out, and now his shame made him furious. Up to this moment he had found it expedient not to contradict Grushenka too much, however much she taunted him; she obviously had some kind of power over him. But now he was really incensed.

'One likes people for what they've done, but what have you two ever done for me?'

'You shouldn't need reasons for liking people; Alyosha doesn't.'

'You think Alyosha likes you! And what's he got that sends you into raptures?'

'Hold your tongue, Rakitka!' Grushenka was standing in the middle of the room, speaking animatedly, with a note of hysteria in her voice. 'You don't know a thing about us! Don't you dare be so familiar! Show a bit of respect! What makes you think you can speak to me like that! Go into the corner, sit still, and don't say a word, you should know your place. And now, Alyosha, I'll tell you the whole gospel truth, to you alone, so that you will see the sort of creature I am! It's for your ears alone, not for Rakitka. I was going to seduce you, Alyosha, that's the honest truth, I was fully determined to. I wanted to do it so much that I bribed Rakitka to bring you here. And why should I have wanted to do it so much? You didn't suspect a thing, Alyosha, you kept turning away from me, you used to lower your eyes when you passed by, but I had looked at you a hundred times before I started questioning everyone about you. Your face haunted me: "He hates me," I thought, "he doesn't even want to look at me." In the end I was surprised at the state I had got myself into: why should I be scared of such a boy? I could eat two of him for dinner. I was really furious. Don't forget, no man here would dare to say or even imagine that he could just drop in on Agrafena Aleksandrovna for his pleasure; the old man's another matter, I'm tied body and soul to him; it was a marriage made in hell—Satan himself gave us his blessing. So looking at you, I said to myself: "I'll devour him. I'll gobble him up and lick my lips." You see what a wicked bitch I am, and you called me your sister! But my seducer's arrived, and I have to sit and wait for his message. You've no idea what that rat meant to me! It was five years ago that Kuzma brought me here—there I was, sitting alone, hiding from people, just wanting to slink into a corner and stay there; I was skinny, silly, crying my eyes out, couldn't sleep for nights on end, thinking: "Where's that rat now, where is he? Probably laughing about me with some other woman. Just let me get my hands on him..." and I'd think: "If only I could see him, meet him, I'd get my own back, I would!" I used to cry into my pillow all night long, turning things over in my mind, deliberately torturing myself and trying to console myself in my rage. "I'll get my own back, I will." There'd be times I'd suddenly scream in the dark. But then it would suddenly hit me that I wouldn't really do anything to him, and he was probably laughing at me at that very moment, or perhaps he'd even forgotten me altogether, and I'd fall out of bed on to the floor, crying my heart out with helpless tears, and sobbing till daybreak. In the morning I'd get up like a mad bitch, ready to tear the world apart. Then, you know what, I started saving money. I became ruthless, grew fat—you'd think I would have become wiser, wouldn't you? Not so... no one, no one in the whole universe knew that in the darkness of the night I'd lie on the sofa, grinding my teeth, as I used to five years before when I was still a girl: "I'll show him, I'll show him," I thought. Do you hear what I say? So, what do you think of me now? Then suddenly, a month ago, this letter arrived: he's coming, he's a widower now, he wants to see me. Oh God! I nearly choked, and the thought occurred to me: "He'll come and whistle, he'll beckon me, and I'll creep back to him like a beaten cur, with my tail between my legs!" That's what I thought, but I could hardly believe it: "This'll show what I'm made of, will I run to him or not?" And I've been so angry with myself for the whole of this past month that it's been even worse than five years ago. Now do you see, Alyosha, how vicious, how violent I am, I've told you the whole truth! I'm only playing around with Mitya so as to stop myself running to that one. Shut up, Rakitka, you've no right to judge me, I'm not talking to you. I was lying here before you arrived, waiting, thinking, my whole fate in the balance, and you'll never know what went on in my mind. Look, Alyosha, tell that young lady of yours not to be angry about what happened the other day!... Nobody in the whole world knows how I feel now, and how can they?... Because I might even take a knife with me when I go there... I still haven't made up my mind...'

And as she uttered these words of anguish, Grushenka suddenly could bear it no longer; she stopped, buried her face in her hands, threw herself on to the pillows on the sofa, and burst into tears like a small child. Alyosha got up and approached Rakitin.

'Misha,' he said, 'don't be angry. She has offended you, but don't be angry. You heard what she said. We shouldn't ask too much from a human soul, we should have more compassion...'

Alyosha spoke in a torrent of uncontrollable emotions. He needed to pour his heart out, and he turned to Rakitin. If Rakitin had not been there, he would have continued to expostulate anyway. But Rakitin was looking at him derisively, and Alyosha did not finish.

'You're so full of that starets of yours, you want to try his medicine out on me, Alyoshechka, your holiness,' Rakitin said with a malicious grin.

'Don't laugh, Rakitin, don't snigger, don't even mention his name—he was holier than anyone on this earth!' Alyosha was on the verge of tears. 'I'm not setting myself up as a judge over you, I'm speaking as the lowliest of defendants. Who am I compared to her? I came here to lose my soul, and I kept saying: "Well, why not?" and all because of my moral cowardice; but she, after five years of suffering, as soon as the first person came along and spoke a sincere word to her, forgave and forgot everything and now she's weeping! Her seducer has returned, he's calling her, and she's ready to forgive him everything and eagerly rush back to him, and she won't take a knife with her, she won't! Well, I'm not like that. I don't know if you are, Misha, but I'm not! Today was a lesson for me... She's nobler than us in her love... Have you ever heard her tell anyone what she has just told us? No, you haven't; if you had, you'd have forgiven her everything long ago... And as for that woman she offended the other day, she should forgive her, too! And, you know, she'll forgive if she finds out... and she will find out... Grushenka's soul is not yet at peace, she should be pitied... there may still be treasure in that soul...'

Alyosha stopped, completely overcome. In spite of his anger, Rakitin looked at him in astonishment. He would never have expected such a tirade from the placid Alyosha.

'What an advocate we have here! Have you fallen in love with her, or something? Agrafena Aleksandrovna, our recluse, has really fallen in love with you, you've won!' he exclaimed with impudent laughter.

Grushenka raised her head from the pillow, and looked at

Alyosha with a tender smile that suddenly lit up her swollen, tear-stained face.

'Leave him alone; Alyosha, my cherub, you see what he's like, there's no use talking to him. Mikhail Osipovich,' she turned to Rakitin, 'I was about to apologize for having been nasty to you, but I don't feel inclined to now. Alyosha, come to me, come and sit here,' she beckoned to him with a happy smile, 'that's right, sit here; tell me,' she took his hand and peered into his face, smiling, 'you tell me, do I love that man or not? The man who seduced me, I mean, do I love him or not? I was lying here in the dark before you came, searching my heart: do I love that man or not? You decide for me, Alyosha, the time has come; whatever you say shall be. Am I to forgive him or not?'

'But you've already forgiven him,' Alyosha said with a smile.

'I suppose I have,' Grushenka said pensively. 'There's a cowardly heart for you! To my cowardly heart!' She suddenly snatched a glass from the table, drained it in one gulp, raised it up, and smashed it on the floor. The glass shattered. There was a suggestion of cruelty in her smile.

'But perhaps I haven't forgiven him after all,' she said menacingly, staring at the floor, as though talking to herself. 'Perhaps I'm just beginning to feel forgiveness in my heart. I'll still have to get the better of my feelings, though. You see, Alyosha, I've grown awfully fond of my tears in the last five years... Maybe it's my unhappiness I've fallen in love with, not him!'

'Well, I'd hate to be in his shoes!' Rakitin hissed.

'Nor will you, Rakitka, you'll never be in his shoes. I'll turn you into my cobbler instead, Rakitka. There's a job for you, and you'll never find anyone else like me... Nor will he, I dare say...'

'Oh, yes? And why are you dressed up to the nines?' Rakitin jeered maliciously.

'And you needn't be spiteful about my getting dressed up, Rakitka, you don't know how I feel! I could discard all this finery right now if I wanted to,' she cried out sharply. 'You don't know what this finery's for, Rakitka! Maybe I'll go up to him and say: "Have you ever seen me like this?" Do you realize that I was a thin, consumptive, seventeen-year-old cry-baby when he left me. What if I snuggle up to him, excite him, inflame him: "See what

I'm like now," I'll say to him, "and that's as far as you'll get, my dear sir, and no further... put that in your pipe and smoke it!" Perhaps that's what this finery's for, Rakitka,' Grushenka ended with a malicious little laugh. 'I'm violent, Alyosha, I'm vicious. I'll rip off this finery, I'll mutilate myself, destroy my beauty, I'll burn my face with acid, I'll slash it with a knife, and go begging for alms. If I don't want to, I won't go anywhere, to anyone; but if I choose—I'll give Kuzma back everything he gave me, all his money, tomorrow, and I'll go out to work for the rest of my life!... You think I won't do it, Rakitka, that I wouldn't dare? I will, I will, I can do it right now, don't you provoke me... and as for him, I'll send him packing with a flea in his ear, and not so much as a glimpse of me!'

She shouted these last words hysterically and broke down again, hid her face in her hands, and collapsed on to the pillow again, convulsed with sobs. Rakitin stood up.

'Time to go,' he said, 'it's getting late, they won't let us into the monastery.'

Grushenka leapt to her feet.

'You're not going too, Alyosha, are you!' she exclaimed in desperate alarm. 'You can't do that to me now, not after the excitement and pain you've caused me, you can't let me face another night on my own again!'

'You don't expect him to spend the night here with you, do you? But if that's what he wants—let him! I'll find my own way back!' Rakitin said sarcastically.

'Shut up, you foul little man,' Grushenka flared up, 'you could never say what he's said to me.'

'What did he say to you?' grunted Rakitin irritably.

'I don't know. I've no idea. I've no idea at all what he said to me. He spoke to my heart. He pierced my heart... He was the first to pity me, the one and only, that's what! Why didn't you come to me before, my cherub? She fell on her knees before Alyosha, like someone in a frenzy. 'All my life I've been waiting for someone like you, I knew someone like you would come along and forgive me. I held on to the belief that, despite the fact that I'm a slut, someone would love me, and not just want me for my body!...'

'What have I done for you?' replied Alyosha, bending over her with a tender smile and gently holding her hands. 'I offered you an onion, one tiny little onion, that and no more!...'

And having said this, he burst into tears himself. At this moment they were startled by a noise outside; someone had come into the entrance hall. Fenya burst into the room, shouting loudly.

'Madam, my dearest madam, the courier has arrived!' she cried joyfully and breathlessly. 'There's a tarantass from Mokroye come to fetch you, it's Timofei with his troika, they'll have changed the horses in a moment... The letter, the letter, madam, here's the letter!'

The letter was in her hand, and she kept waving it about and shouting all the time. Grushenka snatched the letter from her and brought it near a candle. It was just a small note, a few lines, and she read them instantly.

'He's clicked his fingers at me!' she exclaimed, her pale face contorted by a sickly smile. 'He's whistled for me! Crawl, you little bitch!'

But, just for one second, she stood still as though undecided; in an instant blood rushed to her face and her cheeks flushed scarlet.

'I'm going!' she exclaimed suddenly. 'Five years of my life! Goodbye! Goodbye, Alyosha, my fate is sealed... Go away, clear off, all of you, I don't want to see any of you!... Grushenka's flying off to a new life... Even you mustn't think ill of me, Rakitka. I may be going to my death! Oh dear! I think I'm drunk!'

Suddenly she left them and ran into her bedroom.

'Well, she's got more important things than us on her mind now!' grunted Rakitin. 'Let's go, otherwise there'll be more of that female screeching, I'm fed up with all that weeping and screaming...'

Alyosha let himself be led out like a puppet. A tarantass was standing in the courtyard, horses were being unharnessed, someone was walking around with a lantern, there was a lot of bustle. A freshly harnessed troika was being led in through the gates. But scarcely had Alyosha and Rakitin descended the steps of the porch than Grushenka's bedroom window opened and she called out after Alyosha in a clear voice.

'Alyoshechka, give my love to your brother Mitenka, and tell him not to think ill of his wicked Grushenka. And tell him I said: "It's a scoundrel who'll win Grushenka, and not a nice person like him!" And one more thing, say that Grushenka loved him for just one hour, one single hour is all she loved him for—so let him remember this hour for the rest of his life, and tell him that's all Grushenka asks of him!...'

She broke off, sobbing. The window slammed shut.

'Hm, hm!' observed Rakitin, laughing. 'First she sticks a knife in your brother Mitenka, then she asks him to remember her all his life. What a bitch!'

Alyosha did not respond, he seemed not to have heard; he walked very fast alongside Rakitin, as if in a dreadful hurry, and seemed to be in a kind of trance, walking almost mechanically. Suddenly Rakitin started, as though someone had touched an open wound. This was not at all what he had expected earlier, on the way to Grushenka's with Alyosha; something quite different had happened, and not at all what he would have wished.

'He's a Pole, that officer of hers,' he began again, trying to control himself, 'he's not even an officer now, he used to be a customs official in Siberia—somewhere on the Chinese border I suppose—he's just an insignificant little Pole. They say he lost his job. Then he heard that Grushenka was in the money, so he came back—that's all there is to it.'

Again Alyosha appeared not to hear. Rakitin could stand it no longer.

'So, you've saved a sinner, have you?' he laughed maliciously at Alyosha. 'You've set the fallen woman on the path of virtue, is that it? You've cast seven devils out of her,* eh? So the miracle everyone's been expecting has happened!'

'Stop it, Rakitin,' responded Alyosha with a heavy heart.

'Is it the twenty-five roubles you despise me for? I suppose you think I've betrayed a true friend. But you're not Christ, nor am I Judas.'

'Honestly, Rakitin, I assure you, I'd stopped thinking about the money altogether,' exclaimed Alyosha, 'it's you who brought it up just now...'

But Rakitin was completely incensed by now.

'You can all go to hell, every single one of you!' he burst out suddenly. 'Why the devil did I ever have anything to do with you! You can drop dead as far as I'm concerned! Go on, clear off!'

He turned around abruptly and went off along another road, leaving Alyosha alone in the dusk. Alyosha left the town and set off across the field, towards the monastery.

4

CANA OF GALILEE*

IT was already quite late in the monastery day when Alyosha returned to the hermitage, and the gatekeeper let him in through a special entrance. The clock struck nine—it was time for rest and peace after a day that had been so disquieting for all. Alyosha timidly opened the door and entered the starets's cell, where the coffin was now standing. The cell was empty apart from Father Païsy, solitarily reading the Gospels over the coffin, and the novice Porfiry, who, exhausted by the previous night's discussion and the day's excitement and events, was now sound asleep on the floor in the neighbouring room. Although Father Païsy heard Alyosha come in, he did not even turn around to glance at him. As he came through the door Alyosha turned right, went to the corner, and knelt down to pray. His soul was full to overflowing, but in a state of confusion in which no single feeling predominated, for as soon as one feeling welled up it was overtaken by another, in a steady, unending stream. His heart felt at ease but, strangely, he was not surprised at this. Once again he saw the coffin before him and the shrouded corpse which was so precious to him, but he no longer felt any of that harrowing, distressing, agonizing regret that he had felt in the morning. On entering the cell he fell to his knees in front of the coffin, as if before a shrine, but it was joy, sheer joy which filled his heart and mind. One window of the cell was open and the air was fresh and cool—'the odour must have got even stronger, if they had to open the window', thought Alyosha. But even the thought of the odour of putrefaction, which had appeared so repulsive and degrading to him earlier on, did not now arouse that former anguish and revulsion. He began to pray in an undertone, but he soon realized that he was unable to concentrate. Fragmented thoughts kept flashing through his mind and flaring up, like shooting stars, in quick succession, but he himself was well aware of something whole, steadfast, and comforting in his soul. Every now and again he would begin a fervent prayer; he so much wanted to offer thanks and to love... But having started a prayer he would suddenly be distracted, become lost in thought, and forget not only the prayer but also what had distracted him. He started listening to what Father Païsy was reading but, overcome by exhaustion, gradually fell asleep...

'*And the third day there was a marriage in Cana of Galilee,*' read Father Païsy, '*and the mother of Jesus was there: And both Jesus was called, and his disciples, to the marriage.*'

'Marriage? What's that... marriage...', the words hurtled through Alyosha's mind, 'she too is fortunate... she's gone to the feast... No, she hasn't taken a knife with her, she hasn't... that was just a cry of anguish. Well... cries of anguish must be forgiven, certainly. Cries of anguish are a comfort to the soul... Without them, grief would be unbearable. Rakitin went off into a side-street. All the while Rakitin keeps thinking about his grudges, he'll always be slinking off into side-streets... And the road... the road is wide, straight and bright, crystalline, and the sun is at the bottom of it... Ah?... What's he reading?'

'*And when they wanted wine, the mother of Jesus saith unto him, They have no wine...*', Alyosha heard.

'Oh yes, I've missed something, and I didn't want to miss it, I like this bit: it's Cana of Galilee, the first miracle... Oh, that miracle, oh, that sweet miracle! It was not people's grief, it was their joy that Christ was sharing when He performed the first miracle; He was helping to celebrate their joy... "Whosoever loves the people, loves their joy too...", the starets used to repeat this constantly, it was one of his main teachings... Without joy, one cannot live, says Mitya... Ah yes—Mitya... All that's true and wonderful is always full of forgiveness—he said that too...'

'*Jesus saith unto her, Woman, what have I to do with thee? mine hour is not yet come.*

'*His mother saith unto the servants, Whatsoever he saith unto you, do it.*'

'"Do it"!... Joy, the joy of some poor people, some very poor people... They must have been poor, of course, if they didn't even have enough wine for a wedding... Historians* tell us that some of the poorest people imaginable were scattered around Lake Genezareth and its surroundings at the time... And another superior being, His Mother, also with a great heart, was there with Him, and she knew that He had become incarnate not merely to accomplish his awesome mission, but also to show that His heart was open to the innocent, artless joys of any simple and guileless people who might kindly invite Him to their humble marriage feast. "Mine hour is not yet come," He had said to her with a gentle smile (He could not but give her a gentle smile)... Really, would He have come down to earth merely to provide more wine at the marriage feasts of the poor? And yet, at her behest He did just that... Oh, he's reading again.'

'Jesus saith unto them, Fill the waterpots with water. And they filled them up to the brim.

And he saith unto them, Draw out now, and bear unto the governor of the feast. And they bare it.

When the ruler of the feast had tasted the water that was made wine, and knew not whence it was: (but the servants which drew the water knew;) the governor of the feast called the bridegroom,

And saith unto him, Every man at the beginning doth set forth good wine; and when men have well drunk, then that which is worse: but thou hast kept the good wine until now.'

'But what's this, what's this? Why is the room expanding?... Oh yes... it's the wedding, the marriage... yes, of course. Here are the guests, here's the young couple sitting down, and the merry crowd, and... where could the wise governor be? But who's this? Who? The walls have moved again... Who's that getting up at the top table? What... he's here too? But surely he's in his coffin... But he's here too... He's got up, he's seen me, he's coming here... Lord!...'

Yes, he was coming straight to him: the small, wizened old man, his face covered in tiny wrinkles, was coming up to him, full of joy and laughing gently. His coffin had gone, and he was dressed as he had been when he sat with them yesterday and his guests had assembled to see him. His expression was unclouded, his eyes shining. 'It's him all right, so it appears he too is at the feast, he too has been called to the marriage in Cana of Galilee...'

'I was, my friend, I was indeed called and invited,' he heard a soft voice sigh over him. 'Why are you hiding from us here?... Come and join us.'

'That's his voice, Starets Zosima's voice... Yes, who else could it be, calling?' The starets put out his hand to help Alyosha to his feet.

'Let us make merry,' continued the wizened little old man, 'let us drink the new wine, the wine of new happiness, of great happiness; see how many guests there are! There's the bride and bridegroom, there's the wise governor, he's tasting the new wine. Why are you surprised to see me? I offered an onion and that's why I'm here too. And many people here have offered just one onion, just one little onion each... What do all our works amount to? And you too, my gentle, my humble child, today you too managed to offer an onion to a hungry woman. Begin, my kind, my humble child, begin your task!... And do you see our light, do you see Him?'

'I'm afraid... I daren't look...', whispered Alyosha.

'Don't be afraid of Him. He is terrible in his grandeur, awesome in His majesty, but He is infinitely merciful, He has taken on our likeness through his love for us and has joined in our merrymaking, He has turned water into wine that the guests' joy should not be interrupted, He is expecting new guests to arrive, always inviting new ones, and for all eternity this time. There, they're bringing in the new wine, do you see them carrying the pitchers?...'

Something burned in Alyosha's heart, something swelled in it till it hurt, tears of ecstasy welled up within him... He put out his arms, cried out, and woke up...

There was the coffin again, the open window, and the soft, solemn, steady voice reading the Gospels. But Alyosha was no longer listening to what was being read. Strange, he had fallen asleep on his knees and now he was on his feet—and suddenly, with three resolute, rapid steps, he went right up to the coffin. He even brushed Father Païsy with his shoulder without noticing it. The latter momentarily raised his eyes from the book to look at him, but averted them immediately, realizing that something strange had come over the young man. For about half a minute Alyosha kept looking at the coffin with the shrouded, still figure stretched out in it, an icon on his chest, and a barred cross on his cowl. He had just heard that voice, and it was still ringing in his ears. He was still listening, still expecting to hear more... but suddenly, turning abruptly, he went out of the cell.

He did not even stop in the porch, but descended the steps quickly. His soul, brimming with ecstasy, was yearning for freedom, for wide-open spaces. Overhead, stretching into infinity, was the heavenly dome, full of silent, shimmering stars. From the zenith to the horizon stretched the forked outlines of the faintly visible Milky Way. A cool, silent, motionless night had enveloped the earth. The white towers and gilded cupolas of the monastery church gleamed in the sapphire night. The splendid autumn flowers in the beds around the house were dormant for the night. The silence of the earth seemed to merge with the silence of the heavens, the mystery of the earth appeared to reach out to the stars... Alyosha stood gazing; suddenly he fell to the ground, as though stunned.

He did not know why he was embracing the earth, he could not explain to himself why it was that he wanted to kiss it with such abandon, to kiss the whole of it, and yet he kept kissing it as he wept and sobbed, drenching it with his tears, and passionately swearing to love it, to love it for ever and ever. 'Drench the earth with the tears of thy joy and love these thy tears...', these words echoed in his soul. What was he weeping about? Oh, in his ecstasy he was weeping even for those stars which shone upon him from infinity, and 'he was not ashamed of his passion'. It was as though threads from all of God's countless worlds had converged in his soul, and it quivered 'on contact with these distant worlds'. He wished to forgive everyone for everything and to ask forgiveness—oh, not for himself, but for others! 'They would then ask forgiveness for me,' were the words that echoed in his mind. But with each passing moment he became distinctly, almost palpably aware that something as firm and immutable as the vault of heaven was entering his soul. An idea seemed to be taking possession of his mind—and it would be for his whole life and for eternity. He fell to the ground a weak adolescent, but when he rose to his feet he was a hardened warrior for life, and he felt and recognized this in a flash of ecstasy. And never, never in his whole life would Alyosha be able to forget this moment. 'Someone visited my soul on that occasion,' he would repeat later, firmly believing his own words...

Three days later he left the monastery, in accordance with the instruction of his deceased starets to 'go out into the world'.

BOOK EIGHT
Mitya

1
KUZMA SAMSONOV

Now, while Grushenka, rushing to embrace her new life, was bidding farewell to Dmitry Fyodorovich, enjoining him to remember for ever the one hour during which she had loved him, Dmitry Fyodorovich himself, knowing nothing of what had befallen her, was burdened with cares and in a terrible state of confusion. His mental state had been so extreme during these past two days that he really could have developed inflammation of the brain, as he himself said later. Alyosha had not been able to find him the previous morning, nor had his brother Ivan been able to arrange a meeting with him in the tavern. The couple who owned the rooms where he was lodging had, on his orders, refused to reveal his whereabouts. He himself had been nothing short of frantic for the last few days, 'struggling with my soul and trying to find my own salvation', as he himself admitted later, and despite the fact that he was afraid to go away even for a minute in case he missed Grushenka, he had actually left town for a few hours on an urgent matter. All this subsequently came to light in the most detailed and official manner, but we shall now record only the main events of the two dreadful days preceding the frightful catastrophe which was to engulf him so unexpectedly.

Although it was true that Grushenka had loved him genuinely and sincerely for that one hour, she had also managed to torture him cruelly and mercilessly at the same time. The fact of the matter was that he could not fathom any of her intentions—there was no possibility of coaxing them out of her with kindness, nor of forcing her to reveal them—she would never have given in, but would have rounded on him and rejected him altogether; that he fully realized. At the time he had reason to suspect that she too was experiencing an inner struggle, that she was torn by some kind of extreme indecision, was trying to decide on a course of action but was incapable of coming to a decision, and he therefore, not surprisingly, assumed with a sinking heart that at times she must positively detest him and his passionate advances. Perhaps that was precisely how things had been, but he still could not understand what it was that troubled Grushenka. In truth, the whole question resolved itself in two ways for him: 'Either it'll be me, or it'll be Fyodor Pavlovich.' Here, by the way, it is necessary to be quite clear about one thing: he was quite sure that Fyodor Pavlovich would (if he had not done so already) certainly offer to marry Grushenka, and he did not think for a moment that the old lecher believed he could get away with just paying three thousand roubles. Mitya surmised this from his knowledge of Grushenka and her character. And so it could have appeared to him at times that all Grushenka's troubles and all her indecisiveness stemmed merely from the fact that she did not know which of the two to choose and which choice would turn out to be the more advantageous. As for the 'officer', that fateful figure in Grushenka's life, whose imminent arrival she was expecting with such fear and anxiety, strangely enough it did not even occur to Mitya to think about him during these days. True, Grushenka had kept very quiet about this just recently. However, he knew from Grushenka herself all about the letter she had received a month ago from her one-time seducer, and to some extent he also knew its contents. Once, in a spiteful moment, she had shown it to him, but to her surprise he had attached almost no significance to it whatsoever. And it would have been very difficult to explain why—perhaps simply because, weighed down as he was by all the embarrassment and frustration of his struggle with his father over this woman, he could not imagine facing something even more frightening and dangerous, at least not then. And as for the suitor suddenly appearing out of the blue after a five-year absence, this he simply refused to believe, especially the possibility of his arriving so soon. It was also true that in that very first letter from the 'officer', which Mitya had been shown, the officer's return was mentioned only very vaguely; the letter was very vague, very flowery, and full of sentimental outpourings. It should be noted that, on that occasion, Grushenka had managed to conceal the last few lines from him, in which his return was mentioned rather more specifically. Moreover, Mitya recalled later that, at that moment, he had seemed to detect in Grushenka's face a certain involuntary and proud contempt for that communication from Siberia. Following this, Grushenka had given no hint of any further contact she might have had with this new rival of Mitya's. Thus, little by little, he had even managed to forget about the officer. All he thought about was the fact that whatever happened and however things turned out, the impending final confrontation between himself and Fyodor Pavlovich was nigh, and was bound to occur before anything else. He had been awaiting Grushenka's imminent decision with bated breath, which he believed she would make on the spur of the moment, on impulse as it were. She might suddenly say to him: 'Take me, I'm yours for ever,' and that would be the end of the matter: he would seize her and carry her off to the other end of the world straight away. Oh, he'd take her far away at once, as far away as possible, if not to the other end of the world then at least to the other end of Russia, where he would marry her and they would settle down incognito, so that no one at all, anywhere, should know who they were. Then, oh then, would begin a totally new life! He dreamed unceasingly and obsessively of this fresh, rejuvenated, and from now on 'virtuous' life, 'virtuous, at all costs virtuous'. He yearned for this resurrection and rejuvenation. The foul morass into which he had sunk of his own volition was too unbearable for him, and like very many other people in his situation he based his hopes most of all on a change of scene: if only it were not for these people, if only it were not for these circumstances, if only one could flee from this place—everything would be reborn and begin anew! That is what he believed and longed for.

But that was only in the event of a *happy* resolution of the problem. He could also imagine a different decision, with another and truly dreadful outcome. Supposing she were suddenly to say to him: 'I don't want to see you again. I've decided to throw in my lot with Fyodor Pavlovich and marry him, so I don't need you any more.' Then... but then... In truth, Mitya was not sure what would happen then, right up to the last he did not know; this much must be said in his defence. He had no definite intentions and was not planning to commit any crime. He merely watched, spied, and suffered, but all his plans hinged upon that first, happy outcome. He refused even to consider any other possibility. But therein he encountered yet another cause for anguish, for he found a quite new, additional, but at the same time fateful and insurmountable obstacle.

It was this: if she were to say to him, 'I'm yours, take me away,' how exactly would he do it? Where would he find the means for this, where would he find the money? It so happened that just at that time his entire income, which had consisted of a regular allowance from Fyodor Pavlovich throughout all the preceding years, had now dried up completely. Grushenka of course had money, but in this respect Mitya suddenly became inordinately proud: he wanted to take her away himself and begin a new life with her at his own expense, not at hers; he could not even imagine taking her money, the very thought disgusted him. I am not going to expatiate upon this fact or analyse it, I shall merely say: such was his frame of mind at that particular moment. Quite likely, it was all indirectly and perhaps even unconsciously the result of his secret pangs of conscience for having appropriated Katerina Ivanovna's money: he himself subsequently admitted that at the time he thought: 'One woman thinks I'm a scoundrel, and I'd immediately look like a scoundrel to the other one; if Grushenka finds out later, she won't want such a scoundrel.' And so, where was he to obtain the means, where was he to obtain that damned money? He had to get it, otherwise everything would be lost and it would all come to nought, 'and just because I couldn't lay my hands on some money! What a fiasco!'

But let me anticipate a little: the whole point was that maybe he did know where to find the money, perhaps he even knew where it was kept. I shall not go into any more detail on this score, because everything will become clear later; I shall merely describe, however inadequately, his main dilemma at the time. In order to be able to take the money which was secreted somewhere, in order to *have the right* to take it, he would first have to return the three thousand owing to Katerina Ivanovna— 'otherwise I'd be a petty thief, I'd be a scoundrel, and I don't want to begin my new life as a scoundrel,' concluded Mitya, and with this in mind he decided to turn the whole world upside down if necessary, but, come what may, to return the three thousand to Katerina Ivanovna *before doing anything else*. He arrived at this decision during the hours following his last meeting with Alyosha that evening two days before, on the highway, after Grushenka had insulted Katerina Ivanovna; Mitya, on hearing the full story from Alyosha, had confessed to being a scoundrel and had asked that this be communicated to Katerina Ivanovna, 'if it is any consolation to her'. That very same night, after seeing his brother, he had felt, desperate as he was, that it would even be better 'to rob and kill someone than not to repay the debt to Katya'. 'I'd rather stand before my victim and everyone else as a robber and a murderer and go to Siberia, than give Katya cause to say that I betrayed her, stole her money, and used it to run away with Grushenka to begin a new life of virtue! That I could never do!' Thus said Mitya, gritting his teeth, and sometimes he really felt he would end up with inflammation of the brain. But for the time being he battled on...

It was very strange. One would have thought that having made such a decision, there would be nothing left for him but despair; where was a pauper like him suddenly to lay his hands on so much money? Nevertheless, he continued to hope till the very last that he would get hold of that three thousand, that the money would somehow materialize of its own accord, perhaps even fall out of the sky. But that is usually the way with those who, like Dmitry Fyodorovich, know no better than to spend and squander the money that they have inherited without having the least idea of how it was earned. Immediately following his meeting with Alyosha two days previously, his head reeling with the most unlikely schemes which left him totally confused, he had come up with the craziest idea of all. Maybe, in just such circumstances, people like him do in fact consider the most impossible and outlandish schemes to be the most feasible. He had suddenly decided to go to the merchant Samsonov, Grushenka's patron, and propose a certain 'plan' to him, on the strength of which the latter would give him the whole of the required sum. He did not doubt the commercial viability of his plan in the least, his only doubt was how Samsonov would react to his proposition if he decided to consider it from anything other than a purely commercial standpoint. Though Mitya knew this merchant by sight, he was not acquainted with him and had never even spoken to him. For some reason he had, as it happens, concluded long ago that this old libertine, who already had one foot in the grave, might not object if Grushenka were to turn over a new leaf and marry someone 'reliable', and that not only would he not object, but, were an opportunity to present itself, would even actively encourage it. Some rumour that he had heard, or something that Grushenka had let slip, had made him think that perhaps the old man might prefer him to Fyodor Pavlovich as a match for Grushenka. Perhaps many readers of our tale may consider it rather naïve and low of Dmitry Fyodorovich to rely on such help, and to be willing to accept his bride straight from the arms of her benefactor. I can only say, however, that to Mitya Grushenka's past appeared to be well and truly over. He regarded this past with infinite compassion, and believed with the full ardour of his soul that were Grushenka to say that she loved him and would marry him, this would immediately mark the beginning of a totally new Grushenka and, for that matter, a totally new Dmitry Fyodorovich, both free from all vices and having only virtues to their credit: they would forgive each other and start a completely new life together. As for Kuzma Samsonov, Mitya regarded that man from Grushenka's vanished past as someone who had played a fateful role in her life, but whom she had never loved and who, most important of all, was now quite 'spent', finished, as though completely irrelevant. Moreover, Mitya could not even look upon him as a man now, for it was known to all and sundry in the town that he was just a pale shadow of a man, whose relationship with Grushenka was, as it were, purely platonic, quite unlike what it had been previously, and that this had been the case for a long time, in fact almost a year. It might be said that this pointed to a considerable naïvety on Mitya's part; in spite of all his vices, he was very naïve. It was this naïvety, incidentally, that led him to believe that old Kuzma, in preparing to depart from this life, would feel genuine repentance for his past association with Grushenka, and that she now had no more devoted friend or benefactor than this harmless old man.

The day following his conversation with Alyosha in the field,

Mitya hardly slept the whole night, and then turned up at Samsonov's house at about ten in the morning and asked to be announced. The house was an old, bleak, very spacious, two-storeyed building with an annexe and some outhouses in the yard. On the lower floor lived Samsonov's two married sons with their families, and also his elderly sister and one unmarried daughter. The annexe was occupied by his two stewards, one of whom had a large family. His children as well as the stewards lived in cramped conditions, whereas the old man occupied the upper floor all by himself and would not even share it with his daughter, who looked after him and who, in spite of suffering from breathlessness, had to dash upstairs not only at regular intervals but also whenever he chose to summon her. This top floor contained many large reception rooms furnished in the old-fashioned merchant style, with long, monotonous rows of ugly mahogany chairs and armchairs ranged along the walls, crystal chandeliers shrouded with dust-covers, and gloomy pier-glasses between the windows. All of these rooms remained empty and unused, because the frail old man had confined himself to only one small room, a tiny, separate bedroom, where he was looked after by an old woman servant, her hair gathered under a kerchief, and a servant boy, who was usually to be found stretched out on a bench in the entrance hall. On account of his swollen legs the old man was hardly able to walk at all, and would only occasionally get up from his leather couch; the old woman, holding him under his arms, would walk him once or twice up and down the room. He was strict and taciturn even with this old woman. When the 'Captain' was announced, he immediately gave orders to refuse admittance. But Mitya persisted and asked to be announced once more. Kuzma Kuzmich questioned the lad closely: 'What does he look like, is he drunk? Is he violent?' And the answer was: 'He's sober, but he insists on seeing you!' The old man still refused to see him. Thereupon Mitya, who had foreseen all this and had purposely taken a piece of paper and a pencil with him, wrote one line, in his clearest handwriting, on the scrap of paper: 'On a very urgent matter closely concerning Agrafena Aleksandrovna,' and requested that it be given to the old man. Having pondered a while, the old man told his lad to admit the visitor into the hall and sent the old woman downstairs to summon his youngest son to come up immediately. This youngest son, a man of enormous height and strength, with a clean-shaven face and dressed in the German fashion (Samsonov himself wore a caftan and sported a beard), appeared forthwith and stood in silence. They were all terrified of their father. The father had summoned the strapping youth not exactly because he was afraid of the Captain (he was not of a particularly timid disposition), but more to have a witness present—just to be on the safe side. Supported on either side by his son and the young lad, he finally shuffled into the hall. It would be correct to assume that he felt a certain degree of curiosity. The hall in which Mitya was waiting was an enormous, bleak, depressing room with a double row of windows, a gallery, imitation marble-panelled walls, and two huge, shrouded crystal chandeliers. Mitya was sitting on a chair by the door, waiting impatiently for his fate to be resolved. When the old man appeared at the opposite entrance, about twenty-five paces from Mitya's chair, the latter immediately sprang to his feet and went forward to meet him with long, firm, military strides. Mitya was dressed for the occasion in a fully buttoned frock-coat, and was holding a top hat in his black-gloved hands, just as he had been about three days before, when visiting the starets in the monastery on the occasion of the family gathering with his brothers and Fyodor Pavlovich. The old man stood stern and imperious, and as Mitya approached he felt he was being scrutinized from head to toe. He was also astonished to see how badly swollen Kuzma Kuzmich's face had become lately: his lower lip, which was thick at the best of times, now resembled a kind of sagging doughnut. After bowing gravely and silently to his guest, he motioned him towards an armchair near the settee and, leaning heavily on his son's arm, began slowly, with painful groans, to lower himself on to the settee facing Mitya, so that the latter, seeing the old man in such pain, immediately felt he wanted to apologize and was even sensitive enough to feel embarrassment at his own insignificance before a person of such dignity.

When he had finally settled himself the old man spoke slowly, distinctly, with gravity, but politely: 'How can I be of help to you, my dear sir?'

Mitya started. He jumped to his feet, but sat down again. Then he at once began to speak loudly, quickly, nervously, waving his arms about in dire distress. It was clear he was at the end of his tether, he knew the situation was hopeless and he was clutching at straws, and that if he did not succeed, he would be sunk. Samsonov had probably realized all this in a trice, but his face remained impassive and cold as a mummy's.

'Esteemed Kuzma Kuzmich, you've probably heard a lot already about my dispute with my father Fyodor Pavlovich Karamazov, who robbed me of my inheritance after the death of my mother... the whole town's talking about it already... because they all gossip here about things that don't concern them... You might have heard about it from Grushenka, too... I beg your pardon—from Agrafena Aleksandrovna... from Agrafena Aleksandrovna, whom I honour and respect so deeply...', thus began Mitya, and broke off in mid-sentence. But we shall not attempt to repeat the whole of his speech word for word, only the gist of it. The fact was that as long ago as three months he, Mitya, had by design (he said 'by design' rather than 'purposely') consulted a lawyer in the county town, 'a famous lawyer, Kuzma Kuzmich, one Pavel Pavlovich Korneplodov—you've probably heard of him? Huge forehead, almost intelligent enough for a statesman... he knows you... spoke very highly of you...' Mitya faltered for a second time. But he was undeterred and, after a moment's hesitation, continued in full spate. This Korneplodov, having questioned Mitya carefully and examined such documents as he could produce (when it came to documents, Mitya became vague and would not dwell on the subject), observed that, as far as the village of Chermashnya was concerned, which he should have inherited from his mother, it would be perfectly possible to file a lawsuit and thereby teach the old reprobate a lesson... 'Not all doors are shut, the law can get round that.' In other words, one could expect another six thousand or so from Fyodor Pavlovich, perhaps even seven, because Chermashnya had to be worth not less than twenty-five thousand, 'that is, probably twenty-eight, thirty, thirty, Kuzma Kuzmich, and yet, would you believe it, I didn't even get seventeen from that old skinflint!... Well, I let the matter drop then because I don't really understand much about the law, but when I came back here I was knocked sideways—

there was a counter-claim waiting for me (here Mitya faltered again, and once more went off on a different tack). So, esteemed Kuzma Kuzmich, how would you like to take over my claim against that villain, and let me have just three thousand in return?... There is not the slightest chance of your losing, I swear to you on my honour, on my honour; quite the reverse, you stand to gain about six or seven thousand for your three thousand... The main thing is, it must be settled before the day's out. I'll go and see the lawyer for you, or whatever... In fact, I'll do anything, I'll give you all the documents, whichever ones you want, I'll sign anything... we could draw up an agreement in no time, and if possible, if at all possible, before the morning's out... If you were to give me the three thousand... I mean, in this wretched tinpot town there's no one who can hold a candle to you as a businessman... and thereby you'd save me from... in a word, you'd save my neck, and then I could do a noble deed, one could even say a sublime one, in fact... because I nourish the noblest of sentiments towards a certain lady whom you know only too well and whose welfare is a matter of disinterested concern to you. Otherwise I wouldn't even have come if it hadn't been disinterested. And you might say that we're involved in a three horse race here, because fate is a frightening thing, Kuzma Kuzmich! No, let's be realistic, Kuzma Kuzmich, realistic! Since you've been out of the running for a long time, only two horses remain, as I've already put it, clumsily perhaps, but then I'm not a man of letters. What I mean is, I'm one of the runners and the other's the villain. And so you must decide: me or the villain? Everything's in your hands now—three destinies and two choices... I'm sorry, I don't know what I'm saying, but you understand... I can see it in those venerable eyes of yours, that you understand... and if you don't, I'll go and drown myself, this very day, there you have it!'

With this 'there you have it', Mitya broke off his absurd speech, jumped to his feet, and waited for a reply to his ridiculous proposal. With his last phrase he had suddenly been over-whelmed by a feeling of hopelessness, that everything was lost and, worst of all, that he had been spouting the most incredible drivel. 'Isn't it funny,' the thought suddenly flashed through his hopelessness, 'when I was on my way here the whole idea seemed all right, but now it sounds utter nonsense!' All the while he was speaking the old man had sat motionless, watching him with an icy stare. Having kept him waiting for about a minute, Kuzma Kuzmich finally said, in a most decisive and uncompromising tone of voice:

'I'm sorry, sir, that is not our kind of business.'

Mitya suddenly felt his knees buckle.

'What am I to do then, Kuzma Kuzmich?' he mumbled with a faint smile. 'I'm done for now, wouldn't you say?'

'I'm sorry...'

Mitya stood and stared straight ahead, and suddenly he noticed a change in the old man's expression. He shuddered.

'You see, my dear sir, we'd rather not get involved in such matters,' the old man said slowly, 'all the litigation, lawyers, there'll be no end of trouble! But if you like, there *is* someone you could approach...'

'My God, who?...' Mitya started to babble. 'You've given me a new lease of life, Kuzma Kuzmich.'

'He's not a local man, he doesn't live in town. He's a peasant, deals in timber, they call him Lurcher. He's been haggling with Fyodor Pavlovich over a stretch of woodland in Chermashnya for more than a year now, but they can't agree on the price, you may have heard about it. As it happens he's back in the district just now, staying with Father Ilyinsky in the village of Ilyinsky, about twelve versts from the Volovya station. He wrote to me as well about the business, that stretch of forest land I mean, and wanted to know what I thought. Fyodor Pavlovich wants to go and see him himself. So if you were to get there first and offer Lurcher the same deal you mentioned to me just now, it might just...'

'A brilliant idea!' Mitya interrupted him enthusiastically. 'That's the very man I need, it'll be just up his street! There he is, haggling over the price, and suddenly he's presented with the deeds to the property itself, ha-ha-ha!' And Mitya suddenly burst out laughing, a dry, forced laugh, which took Samsonov completely by surprise and made him start.

'How can I thank you, Kuzma Kuzmich?' said Mitya effusively.

'Don't mention it,' said Samsonov with a nod.

'But you've no idea, you've saved me, oh, it was a premonition that led me to you... Well then, I'm off to go and see this priest!'

'Glad to have been of service.'

'I'm off, I'm off. Sorry to have disturbed you when you're not well. I'll never forget this, you have the word of a Russian, Kuzma Kuzmich, of a real R-Russian!'

'You don't say.'

Mitya reached out to take his hand in order to shake it, but noticed a sudden, vicious glint in the old man's eyes. Mitya drew his hand back, and immediately reproached himself for being too mistrustful. 'It's because he's tired...', he thought.

'It's for her sake! For her, Kuzma Kuzmich! Do you understand, it's all for her sake!' he yelled suddenly at the top of his voice, and bowed, turned abruptly on his heels and, without looking back, headed for the door with the same brisk, long strides. He was shaking with elation. 'I thought I'd had it, but my guardian angel saved me,' flashed through his mind. 'And if a real businessman like this old man (a truly venerable old gentleman, and what a dignified bearing!) has advised me to take this course, then... then, of course, I've as good as won. Must hurry. Whether I get back before nightfall or during the night, the battle's won. The old man couldn't have been making a fool of me, could he?' This is what Mitya was debating out loud as he approached his lodgings and, of course, it had to be one or the other: either it was sound business advice, coming from such a noted businessman, a man who was familiar with the case, who even knew that fellow Lurcher (what a funny name!), or—or the old man was sending him on a wild-goose chase! Alas, the latter supposition was the correct one. Subsequently, a long time later, after all the dust had settled, old Samsonov himself laughed as he boasted of having made a fool of the 'Captain'. He was malicious, cold, and nasty, characteristics which were exacerbated by his illness. I do not know what provoked the old man— whether it was the Captain's agitated behaviour, or the profligate spendthrift's stupid conviction that he, Samsonov, would fall for such a hare-brained scheme in the first place, or whether it was his jealousy as regards Grushenka, in whose name this good-for-nothing had come to him with his 'plan' for raising money—

save to say when Mitya stood before him, feeling his legs give way under him and repeating inanely that he was lost—at that moment the old man had regarded him with infinite hatred and decided to play a trick on him. After Mitya had left, Kuzma Kuzmich, pale with anger, turned to his son and commanded him to ensure that that ne'er-do-well should never darken his door again, nor even be allowed into the courtyard, or else...

He did not finish his threat, but even his son, who had often seen him angry, shuddered with fear. For a whole hour the old man shook with rage; towards evening he became ill and sent for the doctor.

2

LURCHER

HE would have to hurry of course, but he had no money to pay for horses; that was not quite true, he had two twenty-kopeck pieces left, but that was all—all that was left from so many years of previous prosperity! But he had an old silver watch which had long since stopped working. He fetched it and took it to a little shop run by a Jewish watchmaker on the market-place. He got six roubles for it. 'I didn't even expect to get that much!' exclaimed Mitya in amazement (he was still exhilarated), grabbed his six roubles, and ran home. At home he supplemented this sum by borrowing three roubles from his landlord, who, although it was all he and his wife had, gave it to him willingly—such was their fondness for him. In his state of elation Mitya revealed to them on the spot that his fate was in the balance, and he recounted to them—in great haste, of course—nearly the whole of the 'plan' he had just proposed to Samsonov, then Samsonov's decision, his future prospects, and so on and so forth. His landlords were already privy to many of his secrets and regarded him as one of the family, not at all the standoffish gentleman. Having thus scraped together nine roubles, Mitya sent for post-horses to take him to Volovya staging post. Thus, it subsequently came to light that at midday on the eve of a certain event Mitya did not even have a kopeck to his name, and in order to obtain some money sold his watch and borrowed three roubles from his landlord's family, and all this in front of witnesses.

I am mentioning this in advance, and the reason why will become clear later.

Although, as he raced off in the cab to Volovya, Mitya was beaming in anticipation of finally settling 'all these matters', he was nevertheless also trembling with anxiety; what would Grushenka get up to in his absence? What if she were to go to Fyodor Pavlovich that very day? That is why he had left without letting her know, and had given his landlords strict instructions not to reveal where he had gone if anyone were to enquire. 'Must be back by evening,' he kept repeating as he jolted along in the cart, 'as for this Lurcher, I might even have to drag him back here... to clinch the deal...' Mitya speculated, his heart beating with nervous excitement, but, alas, things were fated not to work out according to his 'plan'.

Firstly, by taking the country road from Volovya, he lost time. It turned out to be eighteen versts instead of twelve. Secondly, the Ilyinsky priest was out; he had gone to the neighbouring village. By the time Mitya found him, having set out for the neighbouring village with the same, exhausted horses, night had already fallen. The priest, to all appearances a meek and kindly man, immediately explained to him that though Lurcher had initially stayed with him, he had left for Sukhoy Posyolok, a little village, to spend the night in the forester's hut, because he was negotiating a timber deal there too. Though the priest was initially reluctant to accede to Mitya's urgent entreaties to take him to Lurcher forthwith and thereby, as it were, save him, he nevertheless agreed, his sense of curiosity having been aroused, to accompany him as far as Sukhoy Posyolok, though, as ill luck would have it, he suggested going on foot since it was only a verst and 'not all that much more' away. Mitya agreed, of course, and set off with giant strides, so that the poor priest almost had to run to keep up. He was a small man, not all that old, and exceedingly reserved. Mitya immediately began to tell him about his plans as well; he kept pressing him with nervous insistence for information about Lurcher, and talked incessantly the whole way. The priest listened attentively, but was unable to give much advice. His replies were evasive: 'I don't know, really I don't. How would I know?' and in a similar vein. When Mitya began to talk of his disputes with his father over the inheritance, the priest became downright frightened, for he happened to be involved with Fyodor Pavlovich in some business transactions. It must be noted that he enquired with surprise why Mitya referred to the peasant trader Gorstkin as Lurcher, when, as he explained at some length, this was actually only a nickname and was grossly offensive to him, and Mitya should definitely call him Gorstkin, 'otherwise,' concluded the priest, 'you'll get nowhere with him, and he won't even listen to you.' Mitya was somewhat nonplussed for a moment, and he explained that that was what Samsonov himself had called him. Hearing this, the priest promptly dropped the subject, though in fact it would have been better to have explained to Dmitry Fyodorovich there and then that, in his opinion, if Samsonov himself had sent him to this peasant and had referred to him as Lurcher, then might this not be a hoax and, if so, might there not be something sinister behind it? However, Mitya would not have had any time for such 'trifles' anyway. He was in a hurry and he strode on, and only when they reached Sukhoy Posyolok did he realize that they had covered not one, or one and a half, but more than three versts. He was annoyed about this, but said nothing. They entered the hut. The forester occupied one part of the hut, while Gorstkin occupied the larger part, by the entrance hall. They entered the latter part and lit a tallow candle. It was stiflingly hot inside. On the pine table stood an extinguished samovar, next to it a tray with some cups, an empty rum bottle, a half-empty bottle of vodka, and a few half-eaten slices of wheat bread. The occupant himself lay stretched out on the bench, his outer garments stuck under his head in place of a pillow, and was snoring loudly. Mitya stood there nonplussed. 'Of course we must wake him up, it's absolutely vital, I hurried to get here, I have to get back tonight.' He was getting worried. But the priest and the forester, who were standing silently nearby, made no response. Mitya approached Gorstkin and tried quite violently to rouse him, but the sleeping man refused to wake up. 'He's drunk,' concluded Mitya, 'what am I to do, for God's sake, what am I to do!' and suddenly, losing his patience, he began pulling the man's arms and legs, tugging his head, raising and propping him up on the bench, but, despite all his efforts, the man merely uttered coarse, incoherent oaths punctuated by oafish groans.

'Wouldn't it be better to wait a little?' the priest said at last, 'he doesn't seem to be in a fit state at all.'

'He's been drinking the whole day,' observed the forester.

'God!' exclaimed Mitya, 'if only you knew how urgent it is that I talk to him, and how desperate I am.'

'Honestly, it really would be best if you waited till the morning,' repeated the priest.

'Till the morning? What are you talking about? That's out of the question!' And, in desperation, he tried once again to wake the drunken man, but he stopped as soon as he realized the total futility of his efforts. The priest remained silent, and the half-asleep forester looked on morosely.

'What terrible tragedies one is confronted with in life!' exclaimed Mitya in complete despair. Sweat was pouring down his face. Sensing an opportune moment, the priest observed sensibly that even though one might eventually succeed in waking the sleeping man, being drunk he would be in no fit state to hold a conversation, 'and as your business is so important, wouldn't it be better to wait till the morning?...' Letting his arms drop in resignation, Mitya agreed.

'I'll stay here and keep the candle, father, to wait for an opportune moment. When he wakes up, I'll try again... I'll pay for the candle', he turned to the forester, 'and the night's lodging, you won't be out of pocket on account of Dmitry Karamazov, rest assured. But what about you, father, where on earth will you sleep?'

'No, I'd rather make tracks for home. His mare will get me there,' he said, glancing at the forester. 'So, goodbye, I wish you every success.'

Thus it was settled. The priest set off on the mare, glad to have extricated himself at last, but still shaking his head in perplexity and debating whether he ought to inform his benefactor Fyodor Pavlovich of this curious event in good time the next day, 'otherwise, who knows, he might get to hear of it from someone else, have a fit and stop my benefits.' The forester, scratching himself, withdrew in silence to his part of the hut, while Mitya sat down on the bench and began, as he had put it, to wait for an opportune moment. Deep melancholy enveloped his soul like a thick fog. Deep, terrible melancholy! He sat and cogitated, but was unable to gather his thoughts. The candle guttered, a cricket began to chirp, it was beginning to feel unbearably stuffy in the overheated room. Suddenly he imagined the garden, the back gate into the garden, the door to the house opening mysteriously, and Grushenka running in through the doorway... He leapt to his feet.

'What a mess!' he muttered, grinding his teeth, and automatically walked over to the sleeping man and began to stare down at him. The man was a muzhik, gaunt, not particularly old, with a very elongated face, light-brown curly hair, and a long, sparse, reddish beard; he wore a cotton shirt and a black waistcoat with a silver watch-chain protruding from its pocket. Mitya surveyed his face with hatred, and for some reason was particularly repelled by the fact that the fellow's hair was curly. What exasperated him above all was that he, Mitya, should now find himself standing here, totally exhausted, having sacrificed and abandoned so much, while this idler, on whom his whole fate now depended, was snoring without a care in the world, as though he had just come from another planet! 'Oh, the fateful irony of it all!' Mitya exclaimed, and suddenly, losing his self-control completely, lunged forward once again to waken the drunken muzhik. He flew into a kind of rage, he tugged, he pushed, he even beat him, but after struggling for about five minutes and again achieving nothing, he sat down again on the bench in helpless desperation.

'How stupid, how utterly stupid!' he exclaimed, 'and... how dishonourable!' he added suddenly, on impulse. His head was beginning to throb terribly: 'Shall I give up? Leave now?' the thought flashed through his mind. 'No, I'll wait till the morning. I'll stay, just to be bloody-minded! Otherwise what was the point in coming? Anyway, there's no way of getting back tonight, how am I to get out of this place, oh, what a mess!'

His headache was getting steadily worse. He sat motionless, and did not notice that he was beginning to doze off, and suddenly he fell asleep sitting up. He must have slept for about two hours or more. He woke up with such a splitting headache that he almost cried out. His temples were pounding, the crown of his head was splitting with pain; for quite a while he was totally unable to collect his thoughts and realize exactly what had happened to him. Finally, it dawned upon him that the over-heated room was full of fumes, and that he could have been asphyxiated. But the drunken muzhik was still lying there snoring; the candle was nearly spent and was about to go out. Mitya let out a cry and, stumbling, rushed across the entrance hall into the forester's part of the hut. The latter did not take long to wake up, but although, on hearing that the next room was full of fumes, he was prepared to attend to the matter, he nevertheless greeted the news with amazing indifference, which surprised and annoyed Mitya.

'But he's dead, he's dead, what shall we do... what now?' Mitya kept shouting in a frenzy.

They flung open the door, and opened the window and the flue. Mitya dragged a bucket of water from the hall, first immersed his own head in it and then, having found some kind of a rag, dipped it in the water and applied it to Lurcher's face. The forester continued to regard the whole procedure almost contemptuously and, having opened the window, said lugub-riously: 'That'll do,' and went back to sleep, leaving the iron lantern with Mitya, who then spent about half an hour repeatedly wetting the head of the asphyxiated drunk in an attempt to revive him. He had already resolved to stay up the whole night, but from sheer exhaustion sat down just for a moment to catch his breath, shut his eyes, quite unconsciously stretched himself out on the bench, and promptly fell asleep.

He woke up terribly late. It was already about nine in the morning. The sun was shining brightly into the hut through the two little windows. The curly-haired muzhik of the previous day was sitting on the bench, with his coat already on. Before him on the table stood a fresh samovar and a fresh bottle of vodka. Yesterday's bottle was finished, and the new one was more than half empty. Mitya sprang to his feet and realized that the damned muzhik was drunk again, completely and utterly drunk. He stared at him for about a minute, his eyes almost bursting out of their sockets. The muzhik kept eyeing him craftily, without a word, insolently indifferent, and almost, it seemed to Mitya, with supercilious contempt. He rushed towards him.

'Excuse me, you see... I... you've probably heard from the forester who lives here, I'm Lieutenant Dmitry Karamazov, son of old man Karamazov with whom you're negotiating about a strip of standing timber...'

'You're lying!' the muzhik pronounced calmly and steadily.

'What do you mean, lying? Surely you know Fyodor Pavlovich?'

'Like hell I know your Fyodor Pavlovich,' drawled the muzhik.

'You're buying some timber, some timber from him; wake up, snap out of it. Father Pavel Ilyinsky brought me here... You wrote to Samsonov, and he sent me to you...' Mitya was breathless.

'You're l-y-ing!' repeated Lurcher slowly and distinctly.

Mitya broke into a cold sweat.

'Merciful heaven, this is no joke! All right, so you've been drinking. All the same, surely you can talk, you can understand... otherwise... otherwise I don't know what's going on!'

'You're that house-painter!'

'Oh, for God's sake!... I'm Karamazov, Dmitry Karamazov, I've got a proposition to make to you... an advantageous one... very advantageous... it's all to do with the timber.'

The muzhik was pompously stroking his beard.

'I remember, you've taken on a contract and done the dirty. You're a nasty piece of work!'

'I assure you, you're mistaken!' Mitya was wringing his hands in despair. The muzhik continued to stroke his beard, and suddenly narrowed his eyes roguishly.

'Look here, you tell me this. You tell me what law lets people play dirty tricks, go on, tell me! You're a nasty piece of work, do you hear?'

Mitya stepped back dejected, and suddenly it seemed as though something hit him on the head. In a flash everything became clear in his mind. As he himself put it later: 'I saw the light, and understood everything.' He stood bewildered, wondering how he—a sensible person after all—could possibly have fallen for such nonsense, could have allowed himself to become involved in such an escapade and persisted in it for so long, fussing over this Lurcher, wetting his face... 'Well, the man's drunk, smashed out of his mind, and he won't stop drinking for another week—what's the point of waiting? And what if Samsonov did send me here deliberately? And what if she... Oh God, what have I done!...'

The muzhik just sat there, looking at him and smirking. In different circumstances Mitya would perhaps have killed the idiot in sheer rage, but now he felt as weak as a child. He went quietly over to the bench, took his coat, put it on, and left the room without saying a word. He did not find the forester in the other part of the hut, there was no one there. He took fifty kopecks in small change out of his pocket and left it on the table for the lodging, the candle, and the trouble. When he walked out of the hut he saw that all around there was nothing but forest. He set off blindly, not even knowing whether to turn right or left; yesterday, when he was hurrying to get here with the priest, he had not bothered to remember which way they came. There was no vengeance against anyone in his heart, not even against Samsonov. He walked aimlessly along the narrow forest track, disoriented, all his hopes shattered, without the slightest idea of where he was going. Any child could have taken advantage of him, so weak had he suddenly become in body and spirit. Somehow or other he managed to find his way out of the forest; bare, harvested fields stretched before him as far as the eye could see. 'Death and despair all round!' he kept repeating to himself as he strode on and on.

He was picked up by some people who happened to be travelling in the same direction; it was a cab-driver, driving along the country road with an old merchant as his fare. When they drew level, Mitya asked the way, and it turned out they too were going to Volovya. After exchanging a few words they agreed to give Mitya a lift. About three hours later they reached their destination. At Volovya staging-post Mitya immediately ordered horses to take him to the town, and then suddenly realized that he was ravenous. While the horses were being harnessed he ordered a plate of fried eggs. He devoured them instantly, ate a large hunk of bread and some sausage that happened to be on the table, and drank three glasses of vodka. Having satisfied his hunger, he felt better, and his spirits rose. The horses galloped full pelt along the road as Mitya urged the driver on, and suddenly he conceived a new and, this time, 'quite foolproof' plan to obtain 'that damned money' before the day was out. 'And to think that a man's life should be ruined because of a mere three thousand roubles!' he exclaimed disgustedly. 'I'll settle the matter today, and no mistake!' Had it not been for Grushenka, whom he could not get out of his mind, and the fear that something might have happened to her, his spirits would perhaps have been completely restored. But every time he thought of her, it was like a sharp stab in his heart. They finally arrived back, and he dashed off to see her.

3

PROSPECTING FOR GOLD

IT was precisely this visit from Mitya that Grushenka had been referring to with such anxiety when she spoke to Rakitin. At the time she had been awaiting her 'message' and had been most relieved that Mitya had not come either that day or the previous day, and she had been hoping against hope that perhaps he would not turn up at all before she left, but then suddenly there he was. The rest we know already: in order to deceive him, she at once persuaded him to take her to Kuzma Samsonov's on the pretence that she was needed there urgently to do the accounts, and when they arrived, as they stood at the gate saying goodbye to each other, she had made him promise to come and collect her towards midnight and take her home. Mitya too was pleased with this arrangement: 'If she's going to be at Kuzma Samsonov's, that means she's not going to go to Fyodor Pavlovich... assuming she's not lying,' he added as an afterthought. As far as he could tell, she was not lying. Such was his jealous nature that whenever he parted from his beloved he was apt to let his imagination run wild and assume that she would be 'unfaithful' to him, but when he came rushing back, bewildered and dejected, convinced beyond all doubt that she had been unfaithful to him, he would regain his spirits instantly the moment he

caught sight of her bright, cheerful, kindly face, immediately
dismiss all suspicion and, overjoyed and ashamed, would
reproach himself for his jealousy. Having taken his leave of
Grushenka, he rushed back home. There was still so much to be
done before the day was out! At least his mind was at rest now.
'Only I must find out from Smerdyakov as soon as possible
whether anything happened there last night, you never know,
she might have gone to see Fyodor Pavlovich!' the thought
flashed through his mind. Thus, before he had even reached his
lodgings, jealousy once again began to gnaw at his restless heart.

Jealousy! 'Othello's not jealous, he's trusting,' Pushkin once
noted, and this observation alone is proof enough of our great
poet's powers of understanding. Othello's soul is shattered and
his view of the world is perverted, because *his ideal has perished*.
But Othello is trusting; he is not going to skulk behind corners,
to snoop, or eavesdrop. On the contrary, he has to be led,
prompted, provoked, before he even begins to suspect infidelity.
That is not the way with the truly jealous. One cannot even
begin to imagine the ignominy and moral degradation to which
the truly jealous can manage to reconcile themselves without the
least pangs of conscience. And it is not that they are all worthless
and depraved souls. On the contrary, one may be noble at heart,
may love with a pure and utterly self-sacrificing love, yet at the
same time hide under tables, offer bribes to the most despicable
of characters, and become inured to the most odious obscenity
of spying and eavesdropping. Othello could under no circumstances have reconciled himself to infidelity—not forgiven, but
reconciled himself to it—even though his soul was as pure and
innocent as a child's. Not so the truly jealous man: it is difficult
to imagine what some jealous men can tolerate, reconcile
themselves to, and indeed forgive! It is they in fact who are the
most likely to forgive, and all women know this. The jealous man
can, after an amazingly short period of time (preceded, naturally,
by a dreadful scene), forgive for example an act of flagrant
infidelity, even if he himself witnessed the embraces and kisses,
provided he can somehow reassure himself there and then that
this is 'for the last time', and that henceforth his rival will vanish,
disappear off the face of the earth, or that he himself can carry
his beloved off to some place where his hated rival will never

venture. Reconciliation, it goes without saying, would be but for an hour, because even if his rival were to vanish he would surely invent another one the very next day, a new one, and become jealous all over again. One may well ask, what is the point of love if it has to be watched so closely, what is love worth if it must be guarded so assiduously? But that is precisely what the truly jealous men will never stop to consider, and yet amongst them may be found some who are truly noble-hearted. What is also remarkable is that those same noble-hearted people, hiding in some closet, eavesdropping and snooping, although in 'their noble hearts' they understand perfectly the depths of shame to which they have sunk, will never, at least while hiding in the closet, feel any pangs of conscience. At the sight of Grushenka, Mitya's jealousy would vanish, and for a brief moment he would become trusting and noble, and would even despise himself for his vile suspicions. But this merely proved that his love for this woman contained something much higher than he himself suspected, more than just sensuality, more than just that 'curvaceous body' of which he had spoken to Alyosha. On the other hand, when Grushenka was out of his sight Mitya would at once begin to suspect her again of all manner of subterfuge and treachery, and moreover without any pangs of conscience whatsoever.

And so he was consumed yet again with jealousy. He knew above all that time was of the essence. First and foremost, he had to scrape together some money to tide him over, at least for the present. The nine roubles from the day before had nearly all been spent on the trip, and without money, of course, there was nothing he could do. But along with his 'new plan', it had suddenly occurred to him, while travelling on the road this morning, where to lay his hands on enough money to tide him over for the present. He owned a brace of fine duelling pistols, together with cartridges, and the only reason he had not already pawned them was that he treasured them more than anything else in his possession. Some time before, in *The Stolichny Gorod*, he had struck up a passing acquaintance with a young clerk and had learned that this clerk, who was a bachelor and was very well off, had a passion for weapons, and collected pistols, revolvers, and daggers, which he would hang on his walls and show off proudly to his friends, and could describe precisely the action of a gun, how to load it, how to fire it, and so on. Without a moment's hesitation Mitya went to see him and offered to pawn the pistols to him for ten roubles. The clerk was happy to oblige and tried to persuade him to sell them outright, but Mitya refused, and the clerk gave him ten roubles, adding that under no circumstances would he charge any interest. They parted great friends. Mitya was in a hurry and, in his anxiety to see Smerdyakov as soon as possible, rushed off to his vantage point in the summer-house beyond the bottom of Fyodor Pavlovich's garden. Therefore, it was possible subsequently to establish that only some three or four hours prior to a certain incident (of which I shall speak later), Mitya did not have a single kopeck to his name and had pawned his favourite possession for ten roubles, whereas suddenly, three hours later, he had thousands in his hands... But I anticipate.

At Marya Kondratyevna's (Fyodor Pavlovich's neighbour), some very surprising and disturbing news awaited him—Smerdyakov was ill. He listened to the story of the fall in the cellar, the epileptic fit, the doctor's arrival, and Fyodor Pavlovich's solicitousness; he was also interested to learn that his brother Ivan Fyodorovich had already departed for Moscow that same morning. 'Must have passed through Volovya before I did,' thought Dmitry Fyodorovich, but Smerdyakov's illness worried him no end. 'What now, who'll keep an eye out for me, who'll be my informant?' He began to question the two women avidly as to whether they had noticed anything the night before. They knew very well what he meant and put his mind at rest: no one had been there, Ivan Fyodorovich had spent the night there, 'nothing had happened'. Mitya had to think hard. There was no doubt about it; from today, he had to mount a watch, but where—here, or at the gate to Samsonov's house? He decided it would have to be in both places—depending on circumstances—whereas right now, right now... The thing was that right now he had in mind that latest, that 'new and quite foolproof' plan that he had devised while travelling on the road, the implementation of which could not be delayed. Mitya decided to devote an hour to this. 'One hour'll be enough to settle the whole thing, I'll find out everything, and then, then, first of all I'll go to Samsonov's

to check if she's still there, then I'll dash back here and wait till
eleven, after which I'll return to Samsonov's to take her back
home. That's what I'll do.'

He flew home, washed, combed his hair, brushed his clothes,
dressed, and set off for Mrs Khokhlakova's. That, alas, was his
'plan'. He had resolved to borrow three thousand roubles from
this lady, for he had suddenly become totally convinced that she
would not refuse him. One might perhaps wonder why, if he was
so sure, he had not gone to her earlier, since she belonged, as it
were, to his social circle, instead of going to Samsonov, a man of
a different ilk with whom he had nothing in common. The fact
was, however, that in the past month he had rather lost contact
with Mrs Khokhlakova, with whom incidentally he had not been
particularly well acquainted before, and moreover he was perfectly well aware that she could not abide him. This lady had
taken a particular dislike to him from the outset, simply because
he was Katerina Ivanovna's fiancé, and for some reason she
wanted Katerina Ivanovna to drop him and marry the 'charming,
chivalrous, well-educated Ivan Fyodorovich, who had such
exquisite manners'. As for Mitya's manners, she abhorred them.
Mitya used to make fun of her, and on one occasion had even
remarked that the lady was 'as lively and uninhibited as she is
uneducated'. And this morning, on his way back to the town, a
brilliant idea had struck him: 'If she's so against my marrying
Katerina Ivanovna, if she's so opposed to it (he knew that she
was hysterically opposed to it), surely she won't refuse me the
three thousand that would enable me to break off with Katya
once and for all and leave the district for ever? Once these spoilt,
society ladies set their capricious minds on something, they'll
stop at nothing to achieve it. Besides, she's so rich,' argued
Mitya. As for the 'plan' itself, it was just the same as his previous
one, namely, he was going to offer to assign to her his rights to
Chermashnya, but not on commercial terms, as he had suggested
to Samsonov the day before, nor by trying to entice her with the
possibility—the way he had approached Samsonov—of doubling
her money to about six or seven thousand roubles, but simply by
offering her a gentleman's security on the loan requested.
Developing this new idea of his, he grew more and more elated,
but that was his way in all undertakings born of sudden decisions.

He always abandoned himself without reservation to any new idea. Nevertheless, when he stepped into the porch of Mrs Khokhlakova's residence he suddenly felt a cold shiver run down his spine: it was only then that he suddenly realized, with total certainty, that this was now his final chance, that if this were to fail there would be nothing else left for him in the world, 'except to cut someone's throat and rob him of three thousand, and that's all...' It was about half past seven when he rang the bell.

At first, fate seemed to smile upon him; as soon as he announced himself he was admitted immediately. 'As though she was expecting me,' the thought flashed through Mitya's mind, and then suddenly, no sooner had he been shown into the drawing-room, than the lady of the house entered the room quickly and confirmed that she had indeed been expecting him...

'I've been expecting you, I really have! You must agree, there was no reason whatsoever for me to suppose that you'd come to see me, and yet I was expecting you; you may marvel at my intuition, Dmitry Fyodorovich, but I was convinced the whole morning that you'd come today.'

'That, my dear lady, really is amazing,' said Mitya, as he awkwardly took a seat, 'but I've come on an extraordinarily important matter... desperately important for me, that is, my lady, for me alone, I haven't much time...'

'I know you've come on an extraordinarily important matter, Dmitry Fyodorovich, that's no longer even intuition, nor even a superstitious hankering after miracles (have you heard about Father Zosima?); it's as clear as two and two make four—after all that happened with Katerina Ivanovna, it was inevitable you'd come, you couldn't help it, it was a foregone conclusion.'

'It was the stark reality of life, my dear lady, that's what it was! Allow me to explain, however...'

'Reality, to be sure, Dmitry Fyodorovich. I'm all for reality, I'm a bit long in the tooth for miracles now. Have you heard that Father Zosima is dead?'

'It's the first I've heard of it,' Mitya sounded a little surprised. Alyosha's image flashed in his mind's eye.

'Last night, and can you imagine...'

'My dear lady,' interrupted Mitya, 'all I know is that I'm in the most desperate plight, and that if you won't help me everything will collapse around my ears. I'm sorry if my words sound a bit dramatic, but I'm frantic, I'm in a real panic...'

'I know, I know, you're in a panic, I know everything, you couldn't possibly be in any other state of mind, and whatever you might say, I know everything in advance. I've long been interested in your situation, Dmitry Fyodorovich, I've been investigating it and studying it... Oh, believe me, I'm an experienced spiritual healer, Dmitry Fyodorovich.'

'My dear lady, if you're an experienced healer, I'm an experienced patient,' Mitya forced himself to be polite, 'and something tells me that if you've been taking such an interest in me, then you'll help me in my hour of dire need and allow me at last to explain to you the plan which I have the temerity to submit to you... and what I'm expecting from you... I have come, my dear lady...'

'Don't explain, there's no need for that at the moment. As for help, you won't be the first one I've helped, Dmitry Fyodorovich. I'm sure you've heard of my cousin Belmesova, her husband was on the verge of ruin, everything collapsing around his ears, as you so vividly put it, Dmitry Fyodorovich, and guess what, I suggested stud-farming to him, and now he's doing fine. Do you know anything at all about stud-farming, Dmitry Fyodorovich?'

'Nothing, my dear lady—oh, my dear lady, nothing at all!' exclaimed Mitya with nervous impatience, ready to rise from his chair. 'I do implore you, my dear lady, hear me out, just let me speak for two minutes so that I can explain everything, all about my project. Besides, I don't have any time, I'm in a dreadful hurry!...' He shouted hysterically, sensing that she was about to start speaking again, and hoping to shout her down. 'I've come to you in desperation... in the final throes of desperation, to ask you to lend me some money, three thousand roubles, a secured loan, you understand, the surest possible guarantee, my dear lady, a really cast-iron guarantee! Only allow me to explain...'

'Later, we can talk about that later!' Mrs Khokhlakova waved aside his explanation. 'In any case, you don't have to explain, I already know all about it, I've said so already. You're asking me for a certain sum of money, three thousand, but I shall give you more, immeasurably more, I shall save you, Dmitry Fyodorovich, but you must do as I tell you!'

Mitya fairly leapt out of his seat.

'My dear lady, how can you be so kind!' he exclaimed, deeply moved. 'God, you've saved me. You're saving a man from violent death, my dear lady, from a bullet... I'll be eternally grateful to you...'

'I shall give you more, infinitely more than three thousand!' cried Mrs Khokhlakova with a beaming smile as she looked at the ecstatic Mitya.

'Infinitely? But I don't need that much. All I need is just this damned three thousand, and in return I'll give you a guarantee for this sum, I'm infinitely grateful, and what's more, I'm proposing to you a plan, which...'

'Enough, Dmitry Fyodorovich, it's a deal,' Mrs Khokhlakova cut him short with the morally triumphant air of a benefactress. 'I promised to save you, and I shall save you. I shall save you as I saved Belmesov. Have you ever thought about prospecting for gold, Dmitry Fyodorovich?'

'Prospecting for gold, my dear lady! I must admit I have never thought about it.'

'Well then, I have, on your behalf! I've thought it over and over! I've had my eye on you for the best part of a month with that in mind. I've watched you going about your business a hundred times if I've watched you once, and I said to myself, "Now there's an energetic young man if ever there was one, he should go prospecting for gold." I even made a point of observing the way you walk, and came to the conclusion, "This man is sure to find many seams of gold."'

'The way I walk, my dear lady?' Mitya smiled.

'And what's wrong with that? You don't mean to deny that one can tell a person's character by the way he walks, do you, Dmitry Fyodorovich? The natural sciences all support this. Oh, I'm a realist now, Dmitry Fyodorovich. As from today, after all those goings-on at the monastery, which have upset me so much, I've become a complete realist and I want to immerse myself in practical activity. I have been cured. "Enough!" as Turgenev* said.'

'But, my dear lady, that three thousand which you so gener-ously promised to advance me...'

'You'll get it, Dmitry Fyodorovich,' interjected Mrs Khokhla-kova immediately, 'that three thousand roubles is as good as in your pocket, not three thousand but three million, Dmitry Fyodorovich, and all in less than no time at all! Let me tell you what I have in mind for you; you will find plenty of gold, you will make millions, you will come back and become a man of affairs, you will be our driving force, leading us towards a common good. Are we to leave it all to the Jews? You will erect buildings and you will establish various enterprises. You will help the poor, and they will all bless you. This is the age of the railway, Dmitry Fyodorovich. You will become famous and indispensable to the Ministry of Finances, which is now in such dire straits. I lose sleep over the way the rouble has fallen, Dmitry Fyodorovich, this is a side of me that is all too little known...'

'My dear lady, my dear lady!' Dmitry Fyodorovich interrupted again, overcome by a distressing presentiment, 'it is highly, highly likely I shall follow your counsel, my dear lady, your very wise counsel, my dear lady, and perhaps I shall go... prospecting for gold... and I'll return and tell you about it... not just once, but many many times... but now, that three thousand which you have so generously... Oh, it would get me out of this mess... and if I could have it today... that is to say, you see, I can't afford to waste any time, not even a single hour...'

'Enough, Dmitry Fyodorovich, that's enough!' Mrs Khokhla-kova interrupted him firmly. 'I'm asking you: will you go prospecting for gold or not, are you fully determined, I need a straight answer, yes or no.'

'I will, my dear lady, later... I'll go wherever you like, my dear lady... but as for now...'

'Wait!' cried out Mrs Khokhlakova, and she jumped to her feet, dashed over to her magnificent bureau with its innumerable drawers, and began to pull them out one by one, frantically looking for something.

'Three thousand!' thought Mitya in astonishment, 'just like that, without any bits of paper, without any formalities... oh, that's really splendid of her! An amazing woman, if only she didn't chatter so much...'

'Here we are!' Mrs Khokhlakova exclaimed joyfully. 'This is what I was looking for!'

It was a tiny silver icon on a ribbon, the kind that is sometimes worn round the neck, together with a crucifix.

'This is from Kiev, Dmitry Fyodorovich,' she said reverently, 'from the relics of the holy martyr Varvara.* Permit me to hang it round your neck and thereby to bless you on the eve of your new life and new endeavours.'

And she proceeded to loop the ribbon over his head and began to tuck the icon under his shirt. Much embarrassed, Mitya leant forward slightly and began to help her, finally tucking the icon under his necktie and shirt-collar so that it lay against his chest.

'Now you may go!' said Mrs Khokhlakova, solemnly resuming her seat.

'My dear lady, I am so touched... I hardly know how to thank you... for such sentiments, but... if only you knew how precious time is for me now!... This sum of money which I was so expecting you'd lend me in your generosity... Oh, dear lady, as you're so kind, so touchingly generous towards me,' exclaimed Mitya with sudden inspiration, 'allow me to reveal something to you... something that you have indeed known for a long time... I'm in love with a certain young woman here... I've been unfaithful to Katya... I mean, to Katerina Ivanovna. Oh, I've been cruel and dishonourable towards her, but I've fallen in love with someone else here... a certain young woman whom you perhaps despise, because you already know everything, my dear lady, but I cannot possibly abandon her, and therefore that three thousand...'

'Abandon everything, Dmitry Fyodorovich!' Mrs Khokhlakova interrupted him in the most decisive of tones. 'Abandon everything, especially women. Your sights should be set on the gold-mines, and that's no place for women. Later, after you return famous and rich, you'll find yourself a sweetheart from the best of circles. She'll be a thoroughly modern girl, knowledgeable and without any prejudices. The feminist question, which is so topical nowadays, will have been resolved by then, and a new type of woman will have emerged...'

'My dear lady, you don't understand, you really don't...', said Dmitry Fyodorovich, his hands folded in supplication.

'Oh, but I do, Dmitry Fyodorovich, I understand just what you need, what you yearn for without being aware of it yourself. I'm not at all indifferent to the present-day feminist point of view. The advancement of women, even a role in politics for women in the very near future, too, to be sure—that is my ideal. That's a side of me that's all too little known, Dmitry Fyodorovich, I've got a daughter myself, you know. I've written to the author Shchedrin* about this matter. He's been such an inspiration to me on the question of women's place in society; I wrote him an anonymous letter last year, just a couple of lines: "I hug you and kiss you, my mentor, here's to the modern woman, carry on with the good work," signed, "A mother". I thought of signing "A modern mother", but hesitated and settled on simply "A mother"—morally more uplifting, you know, Dmitry Fyodorovich, in any case the word "modern" would have reminded him too much of *The Modernist**—a bitter reminder, I'm sure, considering our present-day censorship... Oh, my God, what's the matter with you?'

'My dear lady,' Mitya finally leapt to his feet, his hands folded in helpless supplication, 'you'll make me cry, my dear lady, if you keep putting off what you so generously...'

'Do have a good cry, Dmitry Fyodorovich, do! These are splendid sentiments... you have such a journey before you! Tears will lighten your burden and will give you joy. You will hurry back from Siberia especially to see me, to let me share your happiness...'

'Please let me get a word in,' Mitya implored suddenly, 'I beg you for the last time, tell me, may I have the sum of money you promised me today? If not, when precisely can I receive it?'

'What sum, Dmitry Fyodorovich?'

'The three thousand you promised... which you so magnanimously...'

'Three thousand? You mean roubles? Oh no, I haven't got three thousand,' said Mrs Khokhlakova in understated surprise. Mitya was thunderstruck.

'What... just now... you said... you even said they were as good as in my pocket...'

'Oh no, you misunderstood me, Dmitry Fyodorovich. If you thought that, you really did misunderstand me. I meant prospecting for gold... True, I promised you more, infinitely more than three thousand, I do recall, but I simply meant prospecting for gold.'

'And what about the money? What about the three thousand roubles?' Dmitry Fyodorovich stammered.

'Oh, if it was actually money you had in mind, I haven't got any. I don't have any money at all at the moment, Dmitry Fyodorovich, right now I'm waging a running battle with my business manager, and only the other day I myself had to borrow five hundred roubles from Miusov. No, no, I have no money. And if you want to know, Dmitry Fyodorovich, even if I had, I wouldn't give it to you. Firstly, I never lend to anybody. If you lend, you lose a friend. But I wouldn't lend to you of all people. Because of my love for you I wouldn't lend you anything, because of my wish to save you I wouldn't lend you anything. Take it from me, the only place for you is the gold-mines, the gold-mines, and I'll repeat it again and again...!'

'What the hell...!' roared Mitya, and with his full might he crashed his fist on to the table.

'A-ah!' Mrs Khokhlakova cried out, and ran to the other end of the room.

Mitya spat, turned on his heels, and with quick strides marched out of the room, out of the house, and into the street and the darkness! He walked as though demented, striking his chest in the same place as he had struck it two days ago in front of Alyosha, when they met that dark evening on the road. The significance of striking his chest *in the same* place, and what he wanted to prove thereby—that, for the moment, remained a secret from the whole world, and one which he had not revealed even to Alyosha, but there was more than just ignominy for him in that secret, there was downfall and suicide too, for he had decided that if he could not obtain the three thousand to pay Katerina Ivanovna and thereby expunge from his chest, from *'that place on his chest'*, the ignominy with which he was burdened and which so oppressed his conscience, he would commit suicide. All this will be explained to the reader subsequently, but now that his last hope had failed to materialize, this man, who was possessed of such physical strength, had no sooner covered a few steps from

Mrs Khokhlakova's house than he suddenly burst into tears like a small child. He walked on in a daze, wiping away the tears with his hand. In this state he reached the town square, and there he suddenly bumped straight into someone. An old woman, whom he had nearly sent flying, let out a piercing shriek.

'My God, you nearly killed me! Why don't you look where you're going, you brute!'

'Who is it, is that you?' exclaimed Mitya, staring at the old woman in the darkness. She turned out to be the old servant woman who worked for Kuzma Samsonov and whom Mitya remembered only too clearly from the previous day.

'And who might you be, dearie?' enquired the old woman in a totally different tone of voice. 'Can't quite make you out in the dark.'

'You live at Kuzma Samsonov's, you work for him, don't you?'

'I do indeed, dearie, just nipped over to see Prokhorych... I still can't quite place you, you know.'

'Tell me, granny, is Agrafena Aleksandrovna at your place now?' asked Mitya, bursting with impatience. 'I took her there myself earlier.'

'She was, dearie; she came, stayed for a bit, and then left.'

'What? Left?' exclaimed Mitya. 'When did she leave?'

'Just after she arrived, only stayed a minute, that's all. Told Kuzma Kuzmich a story that made him laugh, and off she went.'

'You're lying, damn you!' yelled Mitya.

'A-ah!' the old woman cried out, but Mitya was already gone, running as fast as his legs would carry him to Morozova's house. It was just at this very moment that Grushenka was setting off for Mokroye, and he reached the house no more than a quarter of an hour after she had left it. Fenya was sitting in the kitchen with her grandmother, the cook Matryona, when the 'Captain' suddenly burst in. At the sight of him, Fenya screamed at the top of her voice.

'Shut up!' yelled Mitya. 'Where is she?' But before Fenya, petrified with terror, had a chance to utter a word, he had fallen at her feet.

'Fenya, for Christ our Lord's sake, tell me where she is!'

'My dearest sir, I don't know anything, dear Dmitry Fyodorovich, I don't know a thing, you can kill me if you want, I don't know anything,' Fenya swore by everything holy, 'she left with you...'

'She came back!...'

'Dearest sir, I never saw her come back, by all that's holy, I never saw her come back!'

'You're lying,' yelled Mitya, 'I can guess where she is from the look in your eyes!...'

He turned towards the door. The frightened Fenya was glad that she had escaped his wrath so lightly, but she was well aware that had he not been in such a tearing hurry, there would have been all hell to pay. But as he dashed out, Mitya astonished both Fenya and Matroyna by doing something completely unexpected: on the table stood a brass mortar containing a pestle, about seven inches long, also made of brass. As he was leaving the room, having already opened the door with one hand, he suddenly reached out with his other hand and, without pausing, snatched the pestle from the mortar, stuck it in his side pocket, and was gone.

'Oh Lord, he's going to kill someone!' Fenya clasped her hands in horror.

4

IN THE DARKNESS

WHERE did he run to? It was quite obvious; where else could she be, if not at Fyodor Pavlovich's? She must have run straight to him from Samsonov's, that was quite clear now. The whole intrigue, the whole deception was now as plain as a pikestaff... All these thoughts were whirling round madly in his head. He did not call at Marya Kondratyevna's, 'No need to go there, no need at all... mustn't give the slightest cause for alarm... they'll only alert her straight away and betray me... There's a plot, and Marya Kondratyevna's probably involved, Smerdyakov too, they're all in it up to their necks!' He had another idea: he ran up a side-street, past Fyodor Pavlovich's house, making a wide detour, then to the bottom of Dmitrovskaya Street, crossed the little bridge, and found himself in a lonely alley behind the houses; it was deserted and devoid of any sign of life, bordered on one side by the wattle fence of the neighbouring kitchen garden and on the other side by the high solid fence enclosing Fyodor Pavlovich's garden. Here he chose a place, probably that same spot where, according to the old local story, Lizaveta Smerdyashchaya had scaled the fence. 'If she could climb over it,' the thought flashed through his mind, God knows why, 'surely I can?' Whereupon he jumped up and immediately managed to grab hold of the top of the fence, then pulled himself up with all his strength, swung one leg across, and ended up astride the fence. Close by, in the garden, there was a little bathhouse; from the top of the fence he could also see the lighted windows of the house. 'Just as I thought, there's a light in the old man's bedroom. She's there!' and he jumped down from the fence into the garden. Even though he knew that Grigory was sick and that perhaps Smerdyakov too really was ill, which meant that no one would hear him, he nevertheless ducked down instinctively and listened, remaining absolutely still. But all around was deathly silence and, to make matters worse, there was not a breath of wind.

'And just the hushed breath of silence,'* the line suddenly came into his head. 'I only hope no one heard me—doesn't look like it.' After standing still for about a minute, he tiptoed for some distance through the garden, silently and stealthily, over the grass, skirting the trees and bushes, straining to listen after each step. It took him about five minutes to reach the lighted window. He knew that, right under the windows, there were several large, tall, thick guelder rose and elder bushes. The garden door on the left of the house was shut, and he noted this particularly as he passed. Finally he reached the bushes and hid himself behind them. He held his breath. 'Now I must wait', he thought, 'until they think there's no one there, in case they heard me coming and are listening... mustn't cough or sneeze.'

He waited a minute or two, but his heart was pounding frantically, and every so often he gasped for breath. 'My heart won't stop thumping,' he thought, 'I can't wait any longer.' He stood in the shadow of the bushes, the far side of which was lit by the light from the window. 'Guelder rose berries, aren't they red!' he whispered for no reason at all. Quietly, a step at a time, he approached the window and raised himself on tiptoe. The whole of Fyodor Pavlovich's bedroom was plainly visible in front of him. It was a smallish room, partitioned by a line of red screens, 'Chinese,' as Fyodor Pavlovich used to say. 'Chinese,' went through Mitya's mind, 'and Grushenka's on the other side.' He began to scrutinize Fyodor Pavlovich. He was wearing his new, striped, silk dressing-gown, which Mitya had not seen him wear before, fastened with a tasselled silk belt. From under the collar protruded a clean, elegant shirt of fine Dutch linen, the sleeves fastened with gold cuff-links. His head was bandaged with the same red kerchief that Alyosha had seen on him. 'Dressed up to the nines,' thought Mitya. Fyodor Pavlovich was standing near the window, apparently immersed in thought; suddenly he started and listened, but, hearing nothing, went over to the table, poured himself half a glass of brandy, and gulped it down. Then he took a deep breath, stood awhile again, absent-mindedly approached a pier-glass, lifted one edge of the kerchief on his head with his right hand, and began to examine his cuts and bruises, which had not yet healed. 'He's on his own,' thought Mitya, 'more than likely on his own.' Fyodor Pavlovich walked away from the mirror and suddenly turned towards the window and peered out. Mitya immediately stepped back into the shadow.

'Perhaps she's behind the screen,' the thought pierced his heart, 'perhaps she's already asleep.' Fyodor Pavlovich moved away from the window. 'Though, if he was looking out of the window for her, it means she's not there: why else would he be peering out into the darkness?... He's dying of impatience...' Mitya crept up to the window again and peered in. The old man was already seated at the table, visibly crestfallen. Finally he leaned on his elbows and rested his cheek in the palm of his right hand. Mitya watched him intently.

'He's alone, quite alone!' he kept repeating. 'If she was there, he'd behave differently.' Strangely enough, a kind of absurd, bitter-sweet anguish welled up in his heart that she was not there. 'It's not because she's not here,' he realized at once, 'but because I've no means of finding out whether she's here or not.' Mitya recalled later that his mind was extraordinarily lucid at that moment, that nothing escaped him, and that he observed everything down to the last detail. He felt his heart quickly consumed with anguish, the anguish of being in a state of ignorance and indecision. 'Is she there, or isn't she, for God's sake?' Anger raged in his heart. And suddenly he made up his mind; he raised his hand and tapped lightly on the window frame. He tapped as agreed between the old man and Smerdyakov: two slow taps, followed by three taps in quick succession: tap-tap-tap—a sign indicating 'Grushenka's here'. The old man started, looked up quickly, sprang to his feet, and rushed over to the window. Mitya jumped back into the shadow. Fyodor Pavlovich opened the window and poked his head out.

'Grushenka, is that you? Who's there?' he uttered in a kind of tremulous whisper. 'Where are you, my pet, my little angel, where are you?' He was terribly agitated and breathless.

'He's on his own!' concluded Mitya.

'Where on earth are you?' the old man called out again, peering right and left and leaning fully out of the window. 'Come here; I've got a little present for you, come along, I'll show it to you!...'

'He means the envelope with the three thousand,' Mitya realized in a flash.

'Where are you then?... At the door? I'll go and open it...'

The old man was half out of the window as he looked to the right, in the direction of the garden door, and peered into the darkness. A second later he would surely have run to unlock the door, without waiting for Grushenka to reply. Mitya looked on from the side, motionless. The whole of the old man's profile which he hated so intensely, the pendulous Adam's apple, the hooked nose, the lips smiling in voluptuous expectation, all this was brightly illuminated from the left by the slanting beam of light from the lamp in the room. A terrible, savage rage suddenly welled up in Mitya's heart: 'Here he is, my rival, the bane of my life!' This was an outburst of that same sudden, vindictive, and savage rage which, as though with foresight, he had told Alyosha about some four days previously in the summer-house, when the latter had asked him, 'How can you say you'll kill father!'

'I really don't know, I don't know,' he had said at the time. 'Perhaps I won't kill him or perhaps I will. I'm afraid that *the moment I set eyes on him, his face* will suddenly become just too loathsome for me... I hate his bulging gizzard, his nose, his eyes, the way he sneers. I feel a physical revulsion. I'm scared stiff I won't be able to control myself...'

This physical revulsion was welling up within him. Mitya, no longer conscious of his actions, suddenly pulled the pestle out of his pocket...

'It was God', Mitya himself said later, 'who saved me then.' Just at that very moment Grigory Vasilyevich woke up on his sickbed. That same evening he had performed the special treatment that Smerdyakov had described to Ivan Fyodorovich—that is, aided by his wife, he had rubbed himself all over with a mixture of vodka and some kind of extra-strong secret infusion, and had then drunk the rest to the accompaniment of 'a certain prayer' whispered by his wife, after which he had lain down to sleep. Marfa Ignatyevna had also drunk some of the mixture and, being teetotal, had fallen into a deep sleep next to her husband. But, quite unexpectedly, when Grigory woke up at that instant, took a moment or two to come to his senses and, although this immediately brought on a searing pain in his back, sat up in bed. Then he thought awhile, got up, and dressed hurriedly. Perhaps he felt a pang of conscience that he had been sleeping and the house had been left unattended 'at such a dangerous time'. Smerdyakov, disabled by his attack of epilepsy, was lying motionless in the next room. Marfa Ignatyevna did not stir. 'The old girl's completely exhausted,' thought Grigory Vasilyevich, glancing at her, and, wheezing, walked out on to the steps of the porch. Of course, he merely wanted to glance round from the porch, since he could hardly walk due to the excruciating pain in his back and his right leg. But just then he suddenly remembered that he had left the garden gate unlocked that evening. Being quite the most careful and meticulous of men, set in his ways and with habits ingrained over many years, he descended the steps and, hobbling and grimacing with pain, made for the garden gate. As he expected, the gate was wide open. Automatically, he stepped into the garden: perhaps he thought he saw something, perhaps he heard some sound, but as he glanced to the left, he noticed his master's window wide open, empty, no one looking out of it. 'Why's it open? It's not summer now!'

thought Grigory, and suddenly, at that very instant, a figure flitted across the garden in front of him. Someone was running away in the darkness, about forty paces away, shadowy, and moving very fast. 'Lord!' said Grigory, and without thinking, oblivious of the pain in his back, he dashed forward to intercept the intruder. He chose a shorter route, for he knew the garden better than the intruder; the latter, however, headed for the bathhouse and, running past it, made a dash for the fence... Grigory followed him without letting him out of his sight, and ran for all he was worth. He reached the fence just as the runaway was about to scale it. Letting out an almighty shout, Grigory hurled himself forward and clung on to the intruder's leg with both hands.

So that was it, his premonition had been correct; he recognized him, it was him all right, 'the monster-patricide'!

'You've killed your father!' the old man shouted at the top of his voice, but that was all he managed to shout out; he fell suddenly, as though struck by lightning. Mitya jumped back down into the garden and bent over the injured man. The brass pestle was still in his hand and, quite unconsciously, he flung it aside towards the grass. In fact, the pestle fell only a couple of paces away from Grigory, not in the grass but on the footpath, the most conspicuous place of all. For a few seconds Mitya scrutinized the man lying in front of him. There was blood all over the old man's face; Mitya ran his hand over his head. Later he recalled clearly that, at that instant, he was terribly anxious 'to find out for certain' whether he had fractured the old man's skull or had merely 'knocked him out' by hitting him on the temple with the pestle. But the blood was pouring, flowing copiously from the wound, and in no time at all a warm stream of it had soaked Mitya's trembling fingers. He remembered later that he pulled a clean white handkerchief, which he had taken with him when going to see Mrs Khokhlakova, out of his pocket and pressed it to the old man's temple. Hardly aware of what he was doing, he tried to wipe the blood away from the old man's face and forehead, but the handkerchief too immediately became soaked with blood. 'Lord, why am I doing all this?' the thought suddenly struck Mitya. 'I might have fractured his skull, but how can I tell?... And what difference does it all make anyway!' he

added suddenly, hopelessly, 'if I've killed him, I've killed him...
that's what comes of interfering, you stupid old man, I can't help
you now!' he said loudly, and ran towards the fence, scaled it,
jumped down into the alley-way, and ran off. Crumpled in his
right fist was the blood-soaked handkerchief, which he thrust
into his back coat-pocket as he ran. He ran flat out, and the few
lone people whom he passed in the dark on the streets of the
town recalled later that, on that night, they had encountered a
man running for all he was worth. He flew back to Morozova's
house. When he had left earlier Fenya had immediately rushed
to the janitor, Nazar Ivanovich, begging him, for the love of
Christ, not to let the Captain in, either that day or the next.
Nazar Ivanovich had listened and agreed but, as ill luck would
have it, he had gone upstairs briefly to attend to the lady of the
house, who had summoned him unexpectedly, and, meeting his
twenty-year-old nephew, newly arrived from the country, he had
told him to stay in the yard but had forgotten to mention about
the Captain. Mitya came rushing up to the gate and banged on
it. The lad recognized him immediately; Mitya had often given
him drinking-money in the past. He opened the gate at once, let
him in and, smiling cheerfully, immediately informed him that
'Agrafena Aleksandrovna, as it happens, isn't in, you know, sir.'

'Where is she then, Prokhor?' Mitya suddenly stopped dead.

'She's gone to Mokroye, must be about two hours ago,
Timofei took her.'

'What for?' cried Mitya.

'That I wouldn't know, sir, she's gone to some officer,
someone sent her a message from there, and sent horses for
her...'

Mitya left the lad and, half out of his mind, ran to Fenya.

5

A SUDDEN DECISION

FENYA and her grandmother were sitting in the kitchen
together, and were about to go to bed. Relying on Nazar
Ivanovich, they had not bothered to lock the door on the inside.

Mitya burst in, ran towards Fenya, and grabbed her tightly by the throat.

'Tell me this instant! Where is she, who's she gone to Mokroye with?' he yelled, quite beside himself.

Both women let out a shriek.

'Oh, I will, oh, Dmitry Fyodorovich dear, I'll tell you everything, I won't keep anything back from you,' spluttered Fenya, in fear for her life. 'She's gone to Mokroye, to the officer.'

'What officer?' yelled Mitya.

'The one she used to know, that same officer of hers she knew five years ago, the one that left her and went away,' Fenya spluttered on.

Dmitry Fyodorovich released his grip on her throat. He stood before her, pale as death, without saying a word, but from his eyes one could tell that he had understood everything in a flash, absolutely everything, down to the last detail; as soon as she opened her mouth, he had guessed everything. Of course, poor Fenya was in no state at that moment to notice whether he had guessed or not. She remained petrified, sitting on the wooden chest, as she had been when he had just burst in, and was trembling all over, both her arms outstretched as if to protect herself. She stared at him motionless, her pupils dilated in terror. To make matters worse, both his hands were covered in blood. And while running, he must have kept touching his forehead and wiping the sweat off his face, with the result that both his forehead and his right cheek were smeared with blood. Fenya was close to hysterics. The old cook had leapt to her feet and was looking at him as though stupefied, almost out of her mind. Dmitry Fyodorovich stood still for about a minute, and then suddenly slumped down into the chair next to Fenya.

He sat, not like one lost in thought, but as though terrified out of his wits. Now everything was as clear as daylight: this officer— he knew about him, he knew absolutely everything, for Grushenka herself had told him that he had sent her a letter a month ago. And so for a month, a whole month, this affair had been conducted completely on the quiet, right up to the arrival of the officer, and he had not even given him a moment's thought! But how, how was it possible that he had not even considered him? Why had he simply disregarded this officer, forgotten him as soon as he had found out about him? This was the question that confronted him now in all its enormity. And, as he contemplated the awesome nature of the question, he grew cold from fear.

But suddenly he addressed Fenya softly, patiently, like a gentle, friendly child, as though he had completely forgotten that he had frightened and insulted her and caused her so much distress just a moment ago. He began to question her with a clarity and precision altogether astounding under the circumstances. And though Fenya kept staring wild-eyed at his blood-stained hands, she answered each of his questions with astonishing readiness and urgency, as though impatient to tell him the whole 'gospel truth'. Little by little, even with a certain eagerness, she began to recount all the details, not at all in order to hurt him but merely because she was anxious, out of the goodness of her heart, to be of assistance. She also gave the most detailed account of the day's events—Rakitin and Alyosha's visit, how she, Fenya, had kept a lookout, how, before driving off, the mistress had shouted out of the window to Alyosha that he should tell him, Mitenka, that 'he must always remember that I loved him for one short hour'. When he heard about the message, Mitya suddenly smiled and his pale cheeks flushed. Just at that moment Fenya remarked, without the least fear of seeming too inquisitive:

'Your hands, Dmitry Fyodorovich, they're covered in blood!'

'Yes,' Mitya replied mechanically, glancing at his hands absent-mindedly, and then immediately forgot about them and about Fenya's remark. He fell silent again. About twenty minutes had elapsed since his arrival. His initial fear had receded, and now he was apparently gripped by a new, resolute determination. Suddenly he got up and smiled pensively.

'What's happened to you, sir?' Fenya asked, again pointing to his hands—she spoke with compassion, as though she were now the closest of all to him in his grief.

Mitya glanced at his hands once more.

'That's blood, Fenya,' he said, looking at her strangely, 'human blood and, my God, why ever should it have been spilt! But... Fenya... there's a fence hereabouts (he was looking at her as though talking riddles), a very high one and rather daunting to look at, but... tomorrow at dawn, when "the sun leaps into the sky", Mitya will jump over that fence... You don't understand, Fenya, which fence I mean... doesn't matter, you'll hear about it tomorrow and then you'll understand everything... and now, goodbye! I won't bother you any more, I'll take my leave, my mind's made up. Never say die... she loved me for an hour, long may she remember Mitenka Karamazov... She always called me Mitenka, you know.'

With these words, he abruptly left the kitchen. However, his departure seemed to strike even more fear into Fenya than when he had run in just before and accosted her.

Precisely ten minutes later Dmitry Fyodorovich called on the young clerk, Pyotr Ilyich Perkhotin, to whom he had previously pawned his pistols. It was already half past eight and Pyotr Ilyich, having drunk several cups of tea, had just put on his coat to go to *The Stolichny Gorod* for a game of billiards. Mitya caught him as he was about to leave. The latter, seeing his bloodstained face, let out a gasp.

'Good Lord! What's happened to you?'

'Here you are,' Mitya said hurriedly, 'I've come to reclaim my pistols and I've brought you the money. I'm ever so grateful to you. I'm in a hurry, Pyotr Ilyich, so please be as quick as you can.'

Pyotr Ilyich was becoming more and more surprised—he had suddenly noticed the wad of banknotes in Mitya's hand and, most surprising of all, the strange way he held this money and the fact that he walked into the room displaying the notes in his outstretched right hand for all to see, which no one in his right mind would ever normally think of doing. The clerk's servant, a young boy who had met Mitya in the entrance hall, testified later that he had come into the entrance hall holding the money in his hand like that, which meant that even as he was walking along the street he must have been holding the money in his outstretched right hand. It was all in hundred-rouble notes, which he grasped tightly in his bloodstained fingers. Subsequently, when questioned by official investigators as to how much money there actually was, Pyotr Ilyich replied that it was difficult to estimate at the time, perhaps two thousand, perhaps three, but that the wad had been a big one, 'pretty thick'. As for Dmitry Fyodorovich himself, Perkhotin also testified later that he was 'not quite himself—not drunk, mind, but sort of excited', he had been very absent-minded, yet at the same time also strangely circumspect, as though he were pondering something deeply but was unable to resolve it. He was in a tearing hurry, and his responses were brusque and very odd. Some of the time, however, he did not seem to be weighed down with grief at all; he even appeared cheerful.

'What's the matter with you, what's happened?' Pyotr Ilyich exclaimed once more, looking at his visitor in bewilderment. 'How did you get so much blood on you? Did you fall or something? Just look at yourself!'

He grabbed him by the elbow and stood him in front of the mirror. Mitya saw his bloodstained face, shuddered, and frowned angrily.

'Oh, hell! That's all I need,' he mumbled furiously, switched the banknotes from his right hand to his left hand, and abruptly pulled his handkerchief out of his pocket. But the handkerchief too was all soaked in blood (he had used it to wipe Grigory's head and face), and there was hardly anywhere clean on it; it was not that it was beginning to dry out, rather it had become stiff and sticky. Mitya threw it down angrily.

'Oh, hell! You wouldn't have a piece of cloth... to wipe myself on...'

'So it's not your blood, you're not hurt? You'd better have a wash,' replied Pyotr Ilyich. 'There's a washstand over there, let me help you.'

'Washstand? Fine... but what am I going to do with this?' he said to Pyotr Ilyich in a very odd tone of voice, pointing to the wad of hundred-rouble notes with a questioning look, as though it were up to the latter to decide what he should do with the money.

'Put it in your pocket or on the table here, no one's going to steal it.'

'In my pocket? Yes, in my pocket. Of course... No, you see, all this is crazy!' he exclaimed, as though suddenly snapping out of his absent-mindedness. 'Look, let's do one thing at a time, you give me the pistols and here's your money... because I need them, I have to have them... I've no time to lose, none at all...'

And, peeling off a hundred-rouble note, he proffered it to the clerk.

'I haven't got any change,' said Perkhotin, 'you wouldn't have something smaller?'

'No,' said Mitya, taking another look at the wad, and, as if lacking confidence in his own words, he checked the top two or three notes with his fingers, 'no, I've only got hundreds,' he added, and again looked quizzically at Pyotr Ilyich.

'How on earth did you get so much money?' he asked. 'Wait, I'll ask my boy to run over to Plotnikov's. They're open quite late—perhaps they can change your money. Hey, Misha!' he called to the boy in the entrance hall.

'Plotnikov's—that's splendid!' concurred Mitya enthusiastically, as though an idea had suddenly struck him. 'Misha,' he turned to the boy who had just entered, 'look, run over to Plotnikov's and tell them Dmitry Fyodorovich sends his regards and will be over himself shortly... But listen: ask them to get some champagne ready before I get there, say about three dozen bottles, and to pack it so I can take it with me, like that time when I went to Mokroye...' He suddenly turned to Pyotr Ilyich, 'I took four dozen that time. Don't worry, Misha,' he turned to the boy again, 'they know already. And one more thing, ask them to include some cheese, some Strasburg pies, smoked salmon, ham, caviar, well, some of everything, all they've got, about a hundred or a hundred and twenty roubles' worth, like last time... Oh, and one more thing: they mustn't forget the dessert—some sweets, pears, two or three melons, four perhaps—well, no, one melon will do, but some chocolate, some boiled sweets, fruit drops, caramels—well, all the stuff they packed for me last time when I went to Mokroye... all together, including the champagne, it came to about three hundred roubles... Well, I want the same again this time. And don't forget anything, Misha... by the way, you are Misha, aren't you?... Is his name Misha?' he turned to Pyotr Ilyich again.

'Wait,' interjected Pyotr Ilyich, gazing anxiously at him as he listened, 'hadn't you better tell them yourself when you're in the shop, he'll only get everything wrong.'

'Yes he will, you're quite right! Oh, Misha, and I was going to give you a hug as your commission... Look here, if you don't get it all muddled up there'll be ten roubles for you at the end, quick, hurry... Champagne, that's the main thing, they've got to get the champagne ready, and brandy too, as well as red and white wine and all the rest of it, just like last time... They'll know, like last time.'

'Why don't you listen!' Pyotr Ilyich interrupted, growing impatient. 'What I'm saying is: why doesn't he just run over to change the money and tell them not to close yet, and then you go and place your order yourself... Let's have that note of yours. Off you go, Misha, left right, left right!' Clearly, Pyotr Ilyich deliberately ushered Misha away because he was rooted to the spot in front of the visitor, staring open-mouthed at the blood-stained face and shaking hands holding the wad of money, just standing there goggle-eyed with astonishment and horror, and probably understanding very little of Mitya's instructions.

'Well now, let's give you a wash,' Pyotr Ilyich said brusquely. 'Put the money on the table or in your pocket. That's right. Come on, take your coat off.'

He began to help him off with his coat, and suddenly exclaimed again:

'Look, there's blood on your coat too!'

'No... not on the coat. Only a little round the sleeve here... It's only here, where the handkerchief was. Must have seeped out of the pocket. At Fenya's I sat on the handkerchief, and the blood must have seeped through,' Mitya immediately explained with extraordinary candour. Pyotr Ilyich listened, frowning.

'What on earth have you been up to? You must have been in a fight,' he muttered.

They set about washing the blood off. Pyotr Ilyich held the jug and poured the water. Mitya was in a tearing hurry and was not soaping his hands properly. (They were shaking, Pyotr Ilyich recalled later.) Pyotr Ilyich immediately told him to use more soap and to scrub harder. It was as though he began to exert more and more authority over Mitya at that stage. It should be noted in passing that he was quite a bossy young man.

'Look, you haven't cleaned under your nails; go on, wash your face now, at the side here, by your ear... Aren't you going to change your shirt before you go? Where are you going, anyway? Look, the cuff of your right sleeve is all covered in blood.'

'Yes, blood,' observed Mitya, scrutinizing the cuff of his shirt.

'Change it.'

'Haven't got time. Look, I know what I'll do...', Mitya continued with the same trusting candour, as he put on his coat, having first wiped his face and hands on the towel, 'I'll roll back the cuff here, no one will see it under the coat... See!'

'Now tell me what you've been doing. Did you have a fight with somebody, or what? Not in the tavern again, like the other time? You haven't been dragging that Captain about and beating him up like you did before, have you?' Pyotr Ilyich recalled with a note of reproach. 'So who did you beat up this time... or kill, perhaps?'

'Rubbish!' said Mitya.

'What do you mean, "rubbish"?'

'Don't go on about it,' said Mitya, and smiled suddenly. 'I knocked down an old woman in the town square.'

'You knocked down an old woman?'

'An old man, actually!' said Mitya loudly, looking Pyotr Ilyich straight in the eye, laughing and shouting as if the latter were deaf.

'An old man, an old woman, what's the difference... Have you killed someone, or what?'

'We've made up. We fell out—and made up. Somewhere or other. We parted friends. An idiot... but he's forgiven me... he has now, that's for sure... If he'd managed to get up, he wouldn't have forgiven me,' Mitya winked suddenly. 'Only, you know, Pyotr Ilyich, he can go to hell, you hear me, he can go to hell, I've had enough! Right now—I've had enough!' Mitya declared categorically.

'What I meant was, you should be more careful who you associate with... like that stupid business that time with the Staff Captain... Now you get into a fight and then you rush off to paint the town red—typical! Three dozen bottles of champagne—why so much?'

'Bravo! Now let's have the pistols. Honestly, I haven't got time. I really wish I could stay behind and talk to you, my dear fellow, but there isn't any time to lose. And anyway, what's the use, it's too late for talking. Hey! Where's the money, where did I put it?' he shrieked, and began to go through his pockets.

'On the table... you put it there yourself. There it is. Have you forgotten? You really do treat money as though it grew on trees. Here are your pistols. It's amazing, you pawned them just after five o'clock for ten roubles, and now look, you've got thousands. Two or three thousand, I wouldn't mind betting.'

'I'd say, three,' Mitya said with a smile, thrusting the money into his left trouser-pocket.

'You'll lose it if you keep it there. Have you acquired a gold-mine or something?'

'A mine? A gold-mine!' Mitya exclaimed at the top of his voice, and rocked with laughter. 'Perkhotin, do you want to go prospecting for gold? There's a lady here who'll pay you three thousand on the nail to go there. She paid me all right, that's how fond she is of gold-mines! Do you know Khokhlakova?'

'Only by sight and what I've heard. Did she really give you three thousand? Just like that?' Pyotr Ilyich looked highly incredulous.

'Tomorrow, when the sun, the eternally youthful Phoebus, praising and glorifying God,* leaps into the sky, go to Khokhlakova and ask her whether or not she gave me three thousand. Do that.'

'I wouldn't know how things stand between you two... but if you say so, then she must have given it to you... And you, of course, having got your hands on the money, instead of going to Siberia you're going on the rampage... But where are you really off to now, eh?'

'To Mokroye.'

'Mokroye? At this time of night?'

'Mastryuk* had aplenty, now his hands are empty!' Mitya said suddenly.

'"Empty"? All those thousands, and you say empty?'

'I don't mean the thousands. To hell with the thousands! I mean women's moods:

> Woman's love is fickle—
> Unreliable, deceitful.*

'I agree with Ulysses, he said it.'

'I don't understand you!'

'Am I drunk?'

'You're worse than drunk.'

'My soul is, Pyotr Ilyich, my soul is drunk, but enough of that, enough...'

'What are you doing?'

'Loading a pistol.'

Mitya had indeed opened the case containing the pistols, undone the powder-horn, carefully poured in the charge and rammed it down. Then, taking a bullet between finger and thumb, he held it up to the candle-flame.

'Why are you looking at the bullet?' Pyotr Ilyich asked anxiously.

'No reason. Just thinking. Listen, if you were planning to blow your brain out with this bullet, wouldn't you like to have a good look at it before inserting it into the barrel?'

'Why look at it?'

'It's going to go through my brains, so I was just curious to see what it looks like... On second thoughts, it's all a lot of nonsense, utter nonsense. There, that's done it,' he added, having inserted the bullet and rammed it tight with hemp. 'My dear Pyotr Ilyich, nothing, but nothing makes sense, if only you knew how desperately true that is! Give me a piece of paper.'

'Here you are.'

'No, a clean piece, not a crumpled one, a piece of writing-paper. Yes, that'll do.' And, grabbing a pen that was lying on the table, Mitya quickly wrote a couple of lines, folded the piece of paper in four, and thrust it into his waistcoat-pocket. He put the pistols in the case, locked it, and picked it up. Then he looked at Pyotr Ilyich and gave him a long, thoughtful smile.

'Now let's go,' he said.

'Go where? No, wait... so you want to blow your brains out with that bullet, do you?...' Pyotr Ilyich asked in alarm.

'Never mind the bullet! I want to live, I love life! Don't ever forget that. I love the golden-haired Phoebus and his warming rays... My dear Pyotr Ilyich, do you know how one makes oneself scarce, do you?'

'What do you mean, "makes oneself scarce"?'

'To clear off. To make way for the beloved one and for the hated one. So that the hated also becomes the beloved. That's what I mean by making oneself scarce! To say to them: God speed, carry on, go right ahead, while I...'

'While you...?'

'Enough, let's go.'

'My God,' Pyotr Ilyich said, looking at him, 'I really will have to tell them to stop you from going there. Why on earth would you want to go to Mokroye now, anyway?'

'There's a woman there, a woman, and that's the end of the matter, Pyotr Ilyich, just forget about it!'

'Listen, you may be a bit of a wild one, but I've always had a soft spot for you somehow... that's why I'm worried.'

'Thank you, my friend. I'm a wild one, you say. The wild ones, the wild ones! That's what I keep saying to myself: the wild ones! Ah, look, here's Misha, I'd forgotten all about him.'

Misha entered breathless, clutching a wad of banknotes, and announced that the Plotnikovs were 'all in a tizzy' and were sorting out the bottles, the cured fish, the tea—it would all be ready soon. Mitya took a ten-rouble note and gave it to Pyotr Ilyich, and threw another ten-rouble note to Misha.

'Don't!' shouted Pyotr Ilyich. 'Not in my house, you shouldn't spoil him so. Put your money away, here, that's right, why squander it? Come the morrow you'll need it, and you'll be back asking for another ten roubles. Why are you putting it in your side pocket? You'll lose it, you know!'

'Listen, my friend, why don't we go to Mokroye together?'

'Why should I go there?'

'Listen, if you want I'll open a bottle now and we'll drink to life! I want to have a drink, especially with you. We've never had a drink before, have we?'

'We can have one at the tavern, I suppose; let's go, I was on my way there myself.'

'No time to go to the tavern, let's go to the back room at Plotnikov's instead. I say, do you want me to set you a riddle?'

'Go on then.'

Mitya produced the piece of paper from his waistcoat-pocket, unfolded it, and showed it to him. On it, in large, bold letters, was written:

'To punish myself for what I have done with my life, with my whole life.'

'I'm really going to go and tell someone, I'm going to go and tell someone straight away,' said Pyotr Ilyich, after he had read the piece of paper.

'You won't have time, my dear fellow, let's go and have a drink, come on!'

Plotnikov's was situated only about a block away, on the corner of the street. It was the principal grocer's in our town, and a very good one it has to be said, owned by a family of rich merchants. It had everything, all kinds of groceries: wines 'bottled by Yeliseyev Bros', fruit, cigars, tea, sugar, coffee, and much else besides. There were always three shop assistants in attendance, and the two delivery boys were kept constantly busy. Although our district had become impoverished, many landowners having left and trade generally having become slack, grocery sales were booming with every passing year, as never before, and there was no lack of customers. Mitya was eagerly awaited at the shop. Everyone remembered only too well that three or four weeks previously he had also bought a few hundred roubles' worth of all kinds of groceries and wines in one go, cash down (no one of course would have advanced him credit), and they also remembered that on that occasion too he had been clutching a whole wad of hundred-rouble notes which he had spent freely, with gay abandon, and without stopping to explain why he needed to buy so much food and wine, and so on. It was the talk of the town afterwards, that having gone to Mokroye with Grushenka he had in the course of just twenty-four hours squandered some three thousand roubles and had returned from his revels utterly cleaned out, without a kopeck to his name. He had invited a whole crowd of gypsies (recently encamped in the neighbourhood), and in just two days they had relieved him, drunk as he was, of a huge sum of money and had consumed vast quantities of expensive wine. People recounted with laughter how Mitya had got the local bumpkins drunk on champagne and had plied the village girls and women with sweets and Strasburg pies. They also laughed, especially in the tavern, at Mitya's own candid and unsolicited admission (no one laughed in his face of course, for that would have been too dangerous) that, in return for the entire escapade, all that Grushenka had granted him was permission to kiss her foot, and that she had not allowed him to go any further.

When Mitya and Pyotr Ilyich approached the shop they found an already harnessed troika outside, caparisoned with bells, a carpet-rug flung across the seat, and the driver Andrei waiting for Mitya. In the shop they had almost finished packing a box with provisions, and were only waiting for Mitya to appear before nailing down the lid and loading it on to the carriage. Pyotr Ilyich was astounded.

'How did you manage to get hold of a troika?' he asked Mitya.

'On my way here I met Andrei and told him to bring it straight to the shop. Why waste time! Last time I came with Timofei, but he's already left, he's gone on ahead with a certain enchantress. Andrei, are we going to be very late?'

'They might only be about an hour ahead of us, perhaps not even that, perhaps not as much as an hour!' Andrei responded enthusiastically. 'It was I who got Timofei ready for the journey, so I know how fast he'll be going. Nowhere near as fast as us, Dmitry Fyodorovich, we'll leave them standing. They won't even get there an hour ahead of us!' Andrei concluded cheerfully; he was a gaunt, red-haired, middle-aged man in a *poddyovka*,* an *armyak** slung over his left arm.

'There's fifty roubles' drinking-money for you if you get there not more than an hour after him!'

'I can guarantee it won't be more than an hour, Dmitry Fyodorovich, not even half an hour, come to that.'

Though Mitya busied himself with giving orders, he spoke and issued instructions in a somewhat strange manner, disjointedly rather than logically. He would start a conversation and forget to finish it. Pyotr Ilyich thought it necessary to intervene and help him.

'Four hundred roubles' worth,' commanded Mitya, 'not less than four hundred roubles' worth, just like last time. Four dozen bottles of champagne, not a bottle less.'

'Why so many, what's it all for? Just a moment!' yelled Pyotr Ilyich. 'What's that box? What's it got in it? You don't mean to tell me there's four hundred roubles' worth of stuff in there, do you?'

The bustling assistants hastened to explain to him, with servile deference, that this first box contained only half a dozen bottles of champagne, together with 'all kinds of emergency items', some *zakuski*, some sweets, fruit drops and the like, but that the main provisions would be packed and dispatched definitely within the hour, just as on the previous occasion, in a special carriage also drawn by a troika, and that it would get there on time, 'an hour at the most after Dmitry Fyodorovich himself arrives'.

'Not more than an hour, make sure it's not more than an hour, and include plenty of fruit drops and caramels—the girls love them,' Mitya insisted enthusiastically.

'Caramels—fair enough. But what do you need four cases of champagne for? One'll be enough,' said Pyotr Ilyich, hardly able to contain his irritation. He began to haggle, demanded to see the bill, and generally made a nuisance of himself. All he managed to save, however, was a hundred roubles. In the end it was agreed that the total cost of the goods to be delivered should not exceed three hundred roubles.

'Oh, to hell with it!' cried Pyotr Ilyich, as though he had suddenly had enough. 'What's it to do with me? By all means chuck your money about if you found it so easy to come by!'

'Come here, my economist, come along, don't be angry,' Mitya dragged him into the room at the rear of the shop. 'They'll bring us a bottle here, and we'll have a few. Eh, Pyotr Ilyich, let's go together, because you're a nice chap, I like your type.'

Mitya settled down in a small wicker chair by a tiny table covered with the grimiest of tablecloths. Pyotr Ilyich took a seat opposite; the champagne arrived instantly. 'Maybe the gentlemen would like some oysters, prime oysters, only just come in.'

'To hell with oysters,' Pyotr Ilyich snapped back angrily, 'I don't eat them, and we don't need anything.'

'We don't have time for oysters,' observed Mitya, 'and we're not hungry either. You know, my friend,' he said suddenly with feeling, 'I've never gone in for this sort of nonsense.'

'Who has! Three cases of champagne for peasants, I ask you! That's enough to send anyone up the wall.'

'That's not what I meant. I'm talking about a higher order of sense, don't misunderstand me. It's that higher order of sense that I lack, that higher level of order... But... all that's finished now, no regrets. Too late, and to hell with everything! All my life's been an absolute mess, it's time I did something about it. Do you find it funny, eh?'

'Anything but. You're mad.'

'Glory to the Highest in the world,
Glory to the Highest in me!

'That little verse was once a cry from the heart, a lament rather than a verse... made it up myself... but not when I was dragging the Staff Captain by the beard, mind...'

'Why suddenly bring him up?'

'Why bring him up? Nonsense! Everything comes to an end, everything falls into place, you come to the bottom line—and that's it.'

'You know, it's your pistols I can't get out of my mind.'

'Pistols don't matter either! Drink up and stop imagining things. I love life, I love it too much, I love it so much it's disgusting. Enough! To life, my dear fellow, let's drink to life, I propose a toast to life! Why am I satisfied with myself? I'm vile, but I'm satisfied with myself. And yet it pains me that though I'm vile, I'm satisfied with myself. I bless all creation, I'm ready this minute to bless God and all His creation, but... first I have to destroy a nasty insect and stop it crawling about and making other people's life a misery... Let's drink to life, my good friend! What can be more precious than life? Nothing, nothing at all! To life, and to a queen among queens!'

'Yes, let's drink to life, and if you like to your queen too.'

They both drained their glasses. Mitya was excited and restless, but sad with it. It was as if an enormous, threatening shadow were looming over him.

'Misha... is that your Misha who's just come in? Misha, be a good boy, come here, take this glass of champagne, drink to the golden-haired Phoebus of tomorrow...'

'You shouldn't give him champagne!' Pyotr Ilyich exclaimed irritably.

'Go on, let him, just for my sake.'

'All right!'

Misha drained the glass, bowed, and ran off.

'He won't forget that in a hurry,' Mitya observed. 'I love a woman, a certain woman! What is a woman? She's the queen of this earth! I'm miserable, absolutely miserable, Pyotr Ilyich. Do you remember Hamlet: "Thou wouldst not think how ill all's here about my heart"*... *"Alas! poor Yorick."** Perhaps that's exactly who I am—Yorick. Yorick now, and then the skull.'

Pyotr Ilyich listened and did not say a word. Mitya too fell silent for a moment.

'What's that little dog you've got there?' he suddenly asked the shop assistant vaguely, having spotted a pretty little poodle with black eyes in the corner.

'That little poodle belongs to Varvara Alekseyevna, our pro-prietress,' replied the assistant. 'She brought it in herself and left it here. I must take it back to her.'

'I saw one just like it... in the regiment...', Mitya said thoughtfully. 'Only that one had a broken hind paw... Pyotr Ilyich, I meant to ask you something, by the way: have you ever stolen anything?'

'What do you mean?'

'What I said. Have you ever reached into someone's pocket and taken something that didn't belong to you? And I'm not talking about government money, everyone pilfers that, including you, of course...'

'Go to hell!'

'I mean something that didn't belong to you: straight from someone's pocket, from someone's wallet, eh?'

'Once, when I was nine, I stole a twenty-kopeck coin of my mother's that was lying on the table. I took it while no one was looking, and clenched it in my fist.'

'And what then?'

'Well, nothing. I kept it for three days, felt ashamed, con-fessed, and gave it back.'

'And what then?'

'Naturally, they gave me a birching. But why do you ask, have you ever stolen anything yourself, or what?'

'Yes, I have,' Mitya said with a sly wink.

'What did you steal?' Pyotr Ilyich asked, full of curiosity.

'A twenty-kopeck coin of my mother's when I was nine... gave it back three days later.' With this, Mitya suddenly rose to his feet.

'Dmitry Fyodorovich, don't you think we should hurry?' Andrei, who was standing in the doorway of the shop, called out suddenly.

'You're ready, are you? Let's go!' said Mitya with a start. 'One last tale I'll tell* and... Give Andrei one for the road, quickly! And a glass of brandy as a chaser! This pistol-case goes under the seat. Goodbye, Pyotr Ilyich, don't think ill of me.'

'But aren't you coming back tomorrow?'

'Most definitely.'

'You wouldn't like to settle your bill now, would you?' asked the assistant, rushing up to him.

'Ah, yes, the bill! But of course!'

He pulled out the wad of banknotes again, peeled off three hundred-rouble notes, threw them down on the counter, and hurried out of the shop. Everyone followed him, bowing and wishing him well. Andrei cleared his throat after the brandy which he had just downed, and leapt on to the driver's box. But, just as Mitya was about to take his own seat, Fenya suddenly and quite unexpectedly appeared in front of him. She arrived completely out of breath, folded her hands, and with a cry collapsed at his feet.

'My kindest, sweetest Dmitry Fyodorovich, spare my good lady! I told you everything!... And don't harm him either, he's from way back, he's hers! Now he'll marry Agrafena Aleksandrovna, that's why he's come back from Siberia... Dear Dmitry Fyodorovich, don't bring ruin and damnation upon others!'

'Well, well, well, so that's what it's all about! I shudder to think what you're going to get up to there!' Pyotr Ilyich muttered to himself. 'I can see it all now, it's as plain as a pikestaff. Dmitry Fyodorovich,' he shouted out loudly to Mitya, 'give the pistols back to me at once, if you want to call yourself a reasonable man. Do you hear me, Dmitry?'

'The pistols? Don't worry, my good fellow, I'll throw them in a ditch on the way,' Mitya replied. 'Fenya, get up, you shouldn't prostrate yourself before me. Mitya's not going to harm anybody, this foolish man is never going to harm anybody ever again. Look here, Fenya,' he called out to her, after he had already taken his seat, 'I hurt you back there, forgive me and take pity, forgive a scoundrel... But it won't matter if you don't, because nothing matters any more now! Come on, Andrei, let's get going!'

Andrei lashed his horses; the harness bells began to tinkle.

'Goodbye Pyotr Ilyich! Chin up!...'

'He's not even drunk, but he doesn't half talk a lot of rubbish!' thought Pyotr Ilyich to himself as Mitya pulled away. Fearing that Mitya would be cheated and given short measure, he intended to stay and keep an eye on the loading of the rest of the provisions and wine into the second carriage (also drawn by a troika), but suddenly losing his temper, he swore and went off to the tavern to play billiards.

'A fool, but a splendid fellow all the same!' he mumbled to himself on the way. 'Now I remember it all, that officer of Grushenka's, I've heard about him. Well, if he's arrived, then... My God! Those pistols! Ah, what the hell, am I his nursemaid or what? Let them get on with it! Nothing will happen. Windbags, that's all they are. They'll get sloshed, knock the daylights out of each other, and then make up. They don't mean business! What was all that about "make oneself scarce", "punish himself"—it'll never come to that! He's shouted things like that dozens of times at the tavern when he's been drunk. He's not drunk now. "My soul is drunk"—these bastards love to wax poetic. What am I, his nursemaid or something? Of course he's been in a fight, all that blood on his damned face. I wonder who with, though? I'll find out at the tavern. Handkerchief soaked in blood, too... Dammit, it must still be on the floor at my place!... What the hell!'

He arrived at the tavern in a very foul temper, and began to play immediately. The game cheered him up. He played another, and mentioned casually to one of the players that Dmitry Fyodorovich appeared to be in the money again, 'saw it myself, he had as much as three thousand on him!' and that he had gone chasing after Grushenka to Mokroye to paint the town red again. This piece of news was received with a great deal of eager curiosity on the part of the listeners. They stopped laughing, and began to talk about it in all seriousness. Even the game came to a halt.

'Three thousand? Where on earth could he have got three thousand from?'

They began to ply him with more questions. The reference to Khokhlakova was received with scepticism.

'Very likely he's gone and robbed his old man.'

'Three thousand, though! There's something that doesn't quite add up here.'

'He did boast out loud that he'd kill his father, everybody here heard him say so. And he specified exactly three thousand...'

Pyotr Ilyich listened, and suddenly became less forthcoming. He did not say a word about Mitya's bloodstained face and hands, although, on his way there, he had fully intended to mention it. They started the third game, and little by little the conversation turned to other topics. But after finishing the third game, Pyotr Ilyich did not want to carry on playing; he laid down his cue and left the tavern without having eaten, though he had originally intended to have supper there. When he reached the town square he stopped in bewilderment and wondered what he was doing. He realized that he had wanted to go to Fyodor Pavlovich's house to find out if anything had happened. 'But if it all turns out to be a false alarm, I'll only wake up the whole house and create a disturbance. Oh hell, I'm not their keeper, am I?'

He headed for home in one of his worst moods ever, and suddenly he remembered Fenya: 'Dammit, I wish I had questioned her,' he thought with regret, 'At least I'd have some idea what was going on.' All of a sudden he felt such an impatient and irresistible urge to talk to her and discover what had happened that, half-way home, he suddenly changed direction and headed for Morozova's house, where Grushenka lived. On reaching the gate he knocked, and the sound echoing through the stillness of the night seemed to sober him up and annoy him. No one answered, everyone was asleep. 'I'll create a disturbance here too!' he thought, with a sinking heart, but instead of going away altogether, he began to beat on the gate again with all his might. The noise filled the whole street. 'I'll make them answer me, I'll keep it up till they do!' he muttered, growing progressively angrier with himself and more determined, which only served to intensify the blows that he rained on the gate.

6

HERE I COME!

MEANWHILE, Dmitry Fyodorovich was speeding along the road. Mokroye was just over twenty versts away, but Andrei's troika was going so fast that they would reach their destination in an hour and a quarter. Travelling at such a pace seemed to clear Mitya's head. The air was fresh and cool, the clear night sky was studded with stars. It was the same night, perhaps even the same hour, that Alyosha, prostrating himself on the ground, was vowing ecstatically to love the earth till the end of time. But Mitya's heart was heavy, very heavy, racked by so much pain, and yet his whole being was straining towards her at this moment, towards his queen, as he now sped to see her for the last time. I must be quite clear about one thing: there was not the least shadow of doubt in his heart. I may not be believed when I say that the normally jealous Mitya did not feel the least bit jealous towards this new individual, this 'officer', this new rival of his, who had simply appeared out of the blue. Had anyone else appeared on the scene like that, his jealousy would have been aroused immediately, and perhaps he would have stained his awful hands with blood once again, but for this man, 'her first one', he felt, racing along in his troika, neither jealous hatred nor even hostility—though, it has to be admitted, he had not seen him yet. 'There's no getting away from it, she has her rights and he has his; he is her first love, whom she still remembers even after five years, and that means she has loved only him all those five years, so why am I interfering? What am I doing here, what's it got to do with me? Step aside, Mitya, and make way! Anyway, what am I now? Officer or no officer, it's all over now; even if he hadn't turned up at all, everything would still have come to an end...'

Thus he might have been able, more or less, to express his feelings, had he been capable of reasoning. But he was no longer capable of rational thought. His present resolve went back to when he was still at Fenya's; the decision had been taken in a flash, without reasoning, immediately after her first words—he had taken it and had accepted all its consequences. And yet, despite all his resolve, his heart was heavy, unbearably heavy, for not even his resolve could give him peace of mind. There was too much oppressing him and tormenting him. At times he was afraid too; after all, he had already written his own death sentence on a piece of paper: I'm punishing myself for... my whole life. And that piece of paper was there, in his pocket, ready and waiting; his pistol too was loaded, the decision had already been taken, he would greet the early warming rays of 'golden-haired Phoebus' and... and yet he was tortured by the knowledge that it was impossible to atone for all that had gone before, for all that he was leaving behind and which tormented him, and at the thought of this his heart was pierced by despair. There was a moment during the journey when he suddenly wanted to stop Andrei, jump down from the carriage, take his loaded pistol and put an end to everything, without even waiting for the dawn. Yet the moment flashed by like a spark. The troika sped on and on, 'eating up the versts', and as they approached their destination the mere thought of her made him pant with excitement, driving all the other, terrifying visions from his mind. Oh, how he wanted to gaze on her, even for an instant, even if only from afar! 'She's *with him* now, so I'll just take a look, to see her with him, her beloved of long ago, that's all I need.' Never before had he felt such love for that woman who was so inextricably bound up with his own destiny, never had he felt so many new emotions, emotions that he had never experienced before, emotions that he had not even expected, such tender emotions verging on adoration, on self-extinction. 'And I shall vanish!' he said suddenly, in a fit of hysterical ecstasy.

They had been driving at a gallop for about an hour. Mitya was silent, and Andrei, though he was a garrulous fellow, had not said a word either, as if afraid to speak; he merely urged on his steeds, three spindle-shanked but lively bays. Suddenly Mitya exclaimed in terrible anxiety:

'Andrei! What if they're asleep?'

This eventuality, which he had not even considered until then, suddenly struck him with devastating force.

'Very likely they've gone to bed, Dmitry Fyodorovich.'

Mitya winced; of course, he'd go dashing in... in such an

emotional state... and they'd be asleep... she'd be asleep, too, perhaps... Rage welled up within him.

'Go faster, Andrei, go on, Andrei, faster!' he yelled, beside himself.

'And then again, perhaps they haven't gone to sleep yet,' argued Andrei after a pause. 'Timofei was saying back there that there's lots of them there...'

'At the coaching station?'

'No, at the Plastunovs', the coaching-inn where the gentry stop.'

'I know the place. So, what do you mean, "lots"? How many? Who?' Mitya erupted, thoroughly alarmed at this unexpected news.

'Timofei said they were all gentlemen: two from the town, but I wouldn't know who, all Timofei said was that there were two local gentlemen and two others who looked like strangers, perhaps there was someone else too, I didn't really ask. They all sat down to play cards, he said.'

'Play cards?'

'So, perhaps they haven't gone to sleep after all, if they've started playing cards. I'd say it was just coming up to eleven now, no later.'

'Faster, Andrei, faster!' Mitya shouted again, frantically.

'There's something I was meaning to ask you, sir,' Andrei began again, after a pause, 'only I wouldn't like to offend you, sir.'

'What is it?'

'Fedosya Markovna was on her knees just a while ago, begging you not to harm her ladyship or anyone else... so you see, sir, now as I'm taking you there... I do beg your pardon, sir, if in all conscience perhaps I've said something silly.'

Mitya suddenly grabbed him from behind by the shoulders.

'Call yourself a coachman, do you?' he began furiously

'Yes...'

'Don't you see, you should give way. Just because you're a coachman doesn't mean you can charge on regardless and run people over, as though to say, watch out, here I come! No, that won't do, my good man! You've no right to trample the poor sods under hoof, you mustn't run people into the ground; and if you ruin someone's life—you must pay the penalty... the minute you trip someone up, the minute you ruin someone's life—take what's coming to you, and never show your face again.'

Mitya was nearly hysterical as the words came tumbling forth. Andrei was puzzled, but he kept up the conversation.

'True enough, Dmitry Fyodorovich, sir, you're so right, it wouldn't do to run people over, nor torture them either, nor any other living creature, because all creatures—are God's creatures. Take the horse for example, there's folk that never know when to stop, even some coachmen... There's no holding the fellows back, they'll just go on and on regardless.'

'All the way to hell?' Mitya interrupted suddenly, and gave vent to a characteristically unexpected burst of laughter. 'Andrei, you honest soul,' he grabbed him firmly by the shoulders again, 'tell me: will Dmitry Fyodorovich Karamazov end up in hell or not, what do you think?'

'I wouldn't know, sir, it depends on you, because you... You see, sir, when the Son of God was crucified on the cross and died, He came down from the cross and went straight to hell* and freed all the sinners who were being tortured there. And hell groaned mightily on account of this, thinking that no one, no more sinners would come there. And then the Lord said unto hell: "Groan not, hell, for henceforth you will be visited by all manner of moguls, rulers, high judges, and rich men, and you will be filled just as plentifully as you have been from time immemorial, until the day of my coming again." Indeed, those very words were spoken...'

'A folk legend. I like it! Give the one on your left a lash, Andrei!'

'So that's who hell is meant for, sir.' Andrei lashed the horse on his left. 'But to us, sir, you are like a small child... that's how we look upon you... Short-tempered you may be, sir, no getting away from that, but the Lord will forgive you on account of your honest heart.'

'And what about you, Andrei, will you forgive me?'

'I've nothing to forgive, you haven't done anything to me.'

'No; on behalf of others I mean, on behalf of everyone, you alone, now this very minute here on the road, would you grant

me forgiveness on behalf of everyone else? Speak up, you honest
soul!'

'Oh, sir! I'm almost too scared to take you any further, you do
say such weird things...'

But Mitya was already oblivious to this. He was praying
ecstatically, muttering wildly to himself.

'Lord, take me in all my transgressions, but judge me not. Let
me pass without being subject to Your judgement... Judge me
not, for I've already passed judgement upon myself; judge me
not, for I love You, Lord! I am vile, but I love You: and should
You send me to hell, I shall continue to love You there too, and
will keep proclaiming that I'll love You for ever and ever... But
let me have my fill of love too... here, let me have my fill of love,
five more hours and then let Your searing ray strike... For I love
the queen of my heart. I love her and cannot help loving her.
You can see for Yourself what I'm like through and through. I'll
rush up to her and prostrate myself at her feet and say: "You
were right to ignore me... goodbye, and forget your victim, never
trouble yourself any more!"'

'Mokroye!' shouted Andrei, pointing ahead with his knout.

Through the pale cover of the night the dark solid shapes of
widely scattered buildings suddenly appeared. The village of
Mokroye contained some two thousand souls, but at this hour
everyone was already fast asleep, and only here and there could
one discern the odd light twinkling through the gloom.

'Faster, faster, Andrei, here I come!' Mitya called out, as
though in delirium.

'They're still up!' Andrei shouted again, pointing with his
knout at the Plastunovs' inn, which stood right at the approach
to the village and where six windows overlooking the street were
brightly lit.

'They're still up!' Mitya echoed cheerfully. 'Let them know
we're coming Andrei, roll up in style, at full pelt, raise the roof!
Let them all know who's here! It's me! Here I come!' Mitya
shouted ecstatically.

Andrei lashed the exhausted horses into a gallop and really
did roll up with a clatter at the lofty porch, where he pulled his
breathless, steaming bays to a dead halt. Mitya jumped off the
carriage just as the innkeeper, who had been on his way to bed,

emerged on the steps, curious to find out who on earth had driven up like that.

'Trifon Borisych, is that you?'

The innkeeper leant down, peered intently, ran down the steps hurriedly and with obsequious joy rushed towards the visitor.

'My dear Dmitry Fyodorovich! Can it really be you again?'

This Trifon Borisych was a well-built, healthy-looking muzhik of medium height, with a somewhat fleshy face and, especially when dealing with the Mokroye peasants, a severe and uncompromising expression, but with the gift of being able to alter his expression instantly to the most obsequious one possible, whenever he felt he could make a quick rouble. He dressed in the Russian style, a shirt buttoned down across the shoulder, worn under a *poddyovka*. He already possessed considerable capital, but strove constantly to acquire even greater wealth. More than half the peasants were in his clutches and up to their necks in debt to him. He used to buy and lease land from the estate owners, and the peasants would till this land for him in order to clear their debts, and would never quite manage to do so. He was a widower with four grown-up daughters; one was already a widow and lived in his house with her two small children, his granddaughters, and worked for him as a hired hand. Another one, although a simple peasant woman, was married to a government clerk, a sort of superior pen-pusher, and on a wall in one of the rooms of the inn one could recognize, among some family photographs, a miniature portrait of this clerk in his uniform with epaulettes. For church festivals the two younger daughters would put on their fashionable green or light-blue dresses, which were tight at the back and had trains a yard long, and call on friends and neighbours, but come the morrow they would be up at the crack of dawn, as on any other day, sweeping the rooms with a birch broom and removing the washing water and rubbish left by the visitors. In spite of having thousands of roubles already stashed away, Trifon Borisych was very fond of fleecing the revelling visitor and, recalling that it was less than a month since he had made over two hundred roubles, if not three, in a single night from Dmitry Fyodorovich on the occasion of the latter's spree with Grushenka, he now rushed up to him and greeted him joyfully and effusively, sensing from the very manner in which Mitya rolled up to the porch that there would be profit in it for him again.

'My dear Dmitry Fyodorovich, can it really be our good fortune to welcome you again?'

'Wait, Trifon Borisych,' Mitya began, 'first things first: where is she?'

'Agrafena Aleksandrovna?' The innkeeper, peering closely into Mitya's face, immediately realized the situation. 'She's here, too... staying...'

'Tell me, who's she with!'

'Some visitors... One's an official, very likely a Pole, judging by the way he speaks; he's the one that dispatched the horses from here to fetch her. The other's his friend, or just another traveller: who can tell? They're not in uniform...'

'Are they having a party? Are they rich?'

'A party? Not really! They're nothing to worry about, Dmitry Fyodorovich.'

'Honestly? Well, what about the others?'

'Two gentlemen from the town... They were on their way from Chernya and stopped here. One's a young man, a relative of Mr Miusov's, I'm told, I can't think of his name for the moment... and you probably know the other one too—the landowner Maksimov—they say he dropped in at your monastery to attend a service, since when he's been travelling about with this young relative of Mr Miusov's...'

'No one else?'

'No one.'

'Hold on a minute, Trifon Borisych, now tell me the most important thing of all: how does she seem? What's she doing?'

'She arrived with them earlier, and she's sitting with them at the moment.'

'Does she seem cheerful? Has she been laughing?'

'Don't know about laughing, not really... Rather sad if anything, she was combing the young man's hair.'

'What, the Polish officer's?'

'He's hardly young, and he's no officer either; no, sir, not him, I meant that young chap, Miusov's nephew... keep forgetting his name.'

'Kalganov?'

'That's the one.'

'Good, leave it to me. Are they playing cards?'

'They were, but not any more; they were drinking tea, now the Pole's asked for some liqueur.'

'That'll do, Trifon Borisych, my friend, that'll do, leave it to me. Now, tell me the most important thing of all: no gypsies?'

'There's no gypsies left in the district at all, Dmitry Fyodorovich, they've been driven out by the authorities; but there's some Jews over at Rozhdestvenskaya, they play the dulcimer and the violin, we could even send for them now if you like. They'll come.'

'Send for them, of course, you must!' Mitya exclaimed. 'Can you wake the girls up, like the other time, especially Marya, Stepanida as well, and Arina. Two hundred roubles for the chorus!'

'I'll get the whole village up for that much, even if they've all gone to bed. But, my dear Dmitry Fyodorovich, are the local peasants worth such favours, or the girls for that matter? To spend such a sum on those scurvy ruffians! Whoever heard of our muzhiks smoking cigars, and that's what you treated them to last time. They stink, the bastards. And all the girls are full of lice, every one of them. Look, I'll wake up my own daughters for you for free, never mind such a sum, even if they've gone to sleep, I'll kick their backsides and they'll sing for you all right. And did you really have to give the muzhiks champagne to drink that time, for heaven's sake!'

It was hypocritical of Trifon Borisych to be solicitous of Mitya: he had kept back half a case of champagne for himself on that occasion, and had picked up a hundred-rouble note from under the table, which he had crumpled in his fist and purloined.

'Trifon Borisych, I blew a good few thousand here that time. Do you remember?'

'You did, my dear sir, how could I forget, you spent not much short of three thousand.'

'Well, I've brought just as much this time, too, see?'

And he pulled out his wad of money and waved it right under the innkeeper's nose.

'Now listen, and listen carefully: in an hour the wine, food, and sweets will arrive—I want the whole lot taken upstairs at once. And that case that Andrei's got over there, take it straight upstairs now, and start pouring the champagne... But the main thing is—the girls, the girls, and make sure Marya's there...'

He turned towards the carriage again, and removed the case with the pistols.

'Let's settle up, Andrei! Here's fifteen roubles for the troika, and fifty for vodka... for your willingness, for your kindness... to remember your master Karamazov by!'

'You shouldn't, sir...', wavered Andrei, 'five roubles will do for a tip, I won't take any more than that. Trifon Borisych is my witness. It's silly of me, I know, but there you are...'

'What are you scared of?' Mitya looked him up and down. 'Well, to hell with you, if that's the way you want it!' he shouted, flinging five roubles at him. 'And now, Trifon Borisych, you'd better take me in unannounced, but first of all let me have a good look at them, but make sure they don't spot me. Are they in the blue room?'

Trifon Borisych looked apprehensively at Mitya, but carried out his request obediently and without hesitation: he led him cautiously into the hallway, went straight ahead into a large room immediately next to the one in which the guests were seated, and brought out a candle. Then he quietly escorted Mitya inside and led him to a dark corner, from where he could easily observe the occupants of the adjoining room while remaining out of sight himself. But Mitya did not observe them for long, he was in no mood to scrutinize the company. He had caught sight of her, and his heart started to thump, everything began to spin in front of him. She was seated beside the table in an armchair, and next to her, on a settee, sat the young and handsome Kalganov; she was holding his hand and appeared to be laughing, whereas he, his eyes averted, was saying something in a loud, somewhat exasperated voice to Maksimov, who was seated across the table from Grushenka. Maksimov was laughing heartily at something. But *he* was sitting on the settee, while on a chair next to the settee sat another stranger. The man on the settee was leaning back and smoking a pipe, and from what Mitya could discern, he was short of stature, stoutish, with a broad face, and appeared to be annoyed about something. The other stranger, his companion, struck Mitya as being enormously tall; but more than that he was unable to make out. The sight of them almost took his breath away. He could not stand still for a second, he placed the case with the pistols on the sideboard and, with bated breath and with cold shivers running down his spine, marched straight into the blue room to join the party.

'Ai-ai!' Grushenka, who was the first to notice him, screeched in terror.

7

THE FORMER AND INDISPUTABLE ONE

MITYA walked quickly, with long strides, right up to the table.

'Gentlemen,' he said in a loud voice, almost shouting, and stuttering over every word, 'I... I don't mean to disturb you! Don't worry. I'm not, you know, I'm not...', he suddenly turned to Grushenka, who had leaned over in her armchair towards Kalganov, and was tightly clasping his hand. 'I... I'm just passing through. Only here till the morning. Gentlemen, would you let a passing traveller... join your company till the morning? Only till the morning, for the last time, here in this room?'

These last few words were addressed to the fat little man sitting on the settee and smoking a pipe. With pompous solemnity, the man removed the pipe from his mouth and said officiously:

'*Panie*,* here is private. Surely, there are other places.'

'Good heavens, Dmitry Fyodorovich! What are you doing here?' Kalganov suddenly interjected. 'Good evening, come and sit down!'

'Good evening, my dear fellow... how very kind of you! I've always had the greatest respect for you...', Mitya responded cheerfully, eagerly extending his hand to him across the table.

'Ouch, that hurt! You nearly broke my fingers,' laughed Kalganov.

'He always shakes hands like that, always!' Grushenka's voice sang out, and she smiled apologetically and seemed suddenly reassured by Mitya's demeanour that he was unlikely to make a scene; she was gazing at him, still anxious, but consumed with terrible curiosity. Something about him astonished her greatly; the last thing she had expected of him was that he would arrive at such a moment and address them like that.

'Good evening,' the unctuous voice of the landowner Maksimov chimed in from the left. Mitya turned to him too.

'Good evening, you're here too, I see, I'm so glad to see you! Gentlemen, gentlemen, I...' He turned again to the man with the pipe, evidently considering him to be the most important person there. 'I hurried... I wanted to spend my last day, my last hour, in this room, in this very room... where I too have adored... my queen!... I beg your pardon, sir!' he gabbled, 'I rushed here, and I swore... Oh, don't worry, this is my last night! Let's drink to friendship, sir! The wine's on its way... I brought this along.' For some reason he suddenly produced his wad of banknotes. 'Allow me, sir! I want music, noise, let's bring the roof down, like the other time... But the worm, the worthless worm will slither along the ground and will be no more! On this, my last night, I want to celebrate my day of happiness!...'

He was fighting to get his breath, and although he wanted to say many, innumerable things, all that emerged were these strange utterances. The Polish gentleman sat perfectly still, looking now at him, now at the wad of notes, now at Grushenka; he was clearly baffled.

'If my *królowa* will allow...' he began.

'"Krulova", my foot, does he mean queen?' Grushenka suddenly interrupted. 'You make me laugh, you lot, the way you talk. Sit down, Mitya, what were you saying? Please don't make a scene. You won't make a scene, will you? You're welcome, but you frighten me...'

'Me, frighten you?' Mitya cried out, raising his arms. 'Oh, don't mind me, take no notice of me, I shan't get in your way!...' And suddenly, to everyone's consternation, his own included, he slumped into a chair and burst into tears; his face was turned towards the opposite wall and he was clutching the backrest of the chair as though hugging it.

'Well now, come on, just look at you!' Grushenka said reproachfully. 'He always used to be like that when he came to see me. He'd start saying something, and I wouldn't have a clue what he was on about. And on one occasion he burst into tears just like now, this is already the second time—how embarrassing! What are you crying for? *As if there was anything to cry about!*' she added mysteriously, stressing her words with a note of irritation in her voice.

'I... I'm not crying... Well, greetings!' he turned abruptly in his chair and started to laugh, but it was not his customary, stiff, jerky laughter, but rather subdued laughter, drawn out, nervous, and tremulous.

'Here we go again... Well, cheer up, cheer up!' Grushenka continued to humour him. 'I'm very glad you came, very glad, Mitya; you know I really am delighted! I want him to sit here with us,' she proclaimed imperiously, apparently addressing the assembled company, though her words were clearly intended for the man on the settee. 'I insist, I insist! And if he leaves, I leave too, so there!' she added, her eyes suddenly flashing.

'My queen's word is law!' said the Polish gentleman, gallantly kissing Grushenka's hand. 'Please join us!' he said courteously, turning to Mitya. Mitya leapt to his feet and seemed about to deliver another oration, but what came out was quite different.

'Let's have a drink, my good sir!' he interjected, instead of launching into a speech. They all burst out laughing.

'Goodness!' exclaimed Grushenka nervously, 'I thought he was going to start spouting again. Now listen, Mitya,' she added assertively, 'don't keep jumping up and down, but as for getting some champagne, that's a splendid idea. I'll have some myself, can't stand these liqueurs. But the best thing of all is that you're here now, it was so boring before... I say, are we going to have a party again? Why don't you put the money back in your pocket! Where did you get all that money from?'

Mitya, who was still clutching the wad of crumpled banknotes, which everyone, especially the two Polish gentlemen, had noticed, quickly thrust them back into his pocket in embarrassment. He blushed. At that very moment the proprietor brought in an opened bottle of champagne on a tray with some glasses. Mitya grabbed the bottle, but was so flustered he did not know what to do with it. It was left to Kalganov to take it from him and pour out the champagne.

'It's not enough, another bottle!' Mitya shouted to the propri-

etor and, having forgotten to touch glasses with the gentleman to
whom he had so solemnly proposed drinking a toast to friendship, suddenly drained his glass without waiting for anyone else.
His whole face had changed suddenly. Instead of the tragic and
solemn expression with which he had entered, there was now
something almost childlike in his behaviour. All at once he
seemed to calm down and become submissive. He regarded
everyone meekly and joyfully, often breaking into a nervous
giggle, and all the while wearing the grateful expression of a
naughty lap-dog that had been pardoned and allowed to come
back into the room again. It seemed as though he had forgotten
everything, and he kept looking around rapturously, a childlike
smile playing on his lips. He kept laughing and looking at
Grushenka, and moved his chair right up to her armchair. Little
by little he managed to scrutinize the two Polish gentlemen,
though he was still puzzled by them. The one on the settee
impressed him by his bearing, his Polish accent and, most of all,
his pipe. 'Well, what of it?' thought Mitya. 'It's nice that he
smokes a pipe.' The slightly sagging features of the man, who
must have been all of forty, his diminutive nose, his pert, finely
trimmed and dyed moustache, did not raise any questions in
Mitya's mind. Even the very poor-quality Siberian toupee, with
its ridiculous little sideboards brushed forward at the temples,
failed to surprise Mitya unduly. 'So what if it's a toupee!' he
mused unconcernedly. On the other hand, the only thing that
struck Mitya about the younger gentleman, sitting by the wall
and surveying the whole company with an arrogant, defiant air
of silent contempt as he listened to the general conversation in
the room, was his extraordinary height, in complete contrast to
the gentleman on the settee. 'If he stands up,' the thought
flashed through Mitya's mind, 'he'll be about seven foot.' The
other thing that flashed through his mind was that this tall fellow
was probably the friend and stooge of the man on the settee, his
'bodyguard' as it were, and that the short gentleman with the
pipe was clearly in command. But all this too struck him as being
perfectly right and proper. All spirit of rivalry had suddenly
evaporated from the lap-dog. Grushenka's attitude and the
ambiguous tone of some of her comments had not sunk in yet;
all he understood, and his heart was ecstatic at the thought, was

that she was being kind to him, that she had 'forgiven' him and had allowed him to sit next to her. He was beside himself with joy to see her take a sip of wine from her glass. The silence of the assembled company suddenly struck him, however, and he began to survey everyone with anxious eyes. 'What are you waiting for, gentlemen,' his smiling gaze appeared to be saying, 'why don't you get on with it?'

'He has been regaling us with a lot of fibs and making us all laugh,' began Kalganov, motioning to Maksimov, as though he had guessed Mitya's thoughts.

Mitya quickly turned his gaze on Kalganov and then immediately on Maksimov.

'Fibs?' he gave a short, staccato laugh, evidently amused.

'Yes. Imagine, he insists that in the 'twenties, apparently, the whole of our cavalry got married to Polish women, but that's absolute nonsense, isn't it?'

'To Polish women?' repeated Mitya, perfectly delighted.

Kalganov understood Mitya's relationship with Grushenka only too well, and he also had a pretty good idea about the Polish gentleman, but none of this was of particular interest to him, perhaps even of no interest whatsoever, for what interested him most of all was Maksimov. He and Maksimov happened to be at the inn quite by chance, and had met the Poles there for the first time. As for Grushenka, he had met her before and had even visited her with somebody once; on that occasion she had found him quite unattractive. But now she kept looking at him very tenderly; before Mitya's arrival she had even been cuddling up to him, but he had remained somewhat unresponsive. He was a young man, not more than twenty, stylishly dressed, with a pleasant pale complexion and a magnificent head of light-brown hair. And set in this pale face was a pair of wonderful light-blue eyes with an intelligent, at times unfathomable expression, surprising in one so young, and yet the young man sometimes talked and looked round as unselfconsciously as a child. On the whole he seemed very unpredictable, even capricious, though obviously kind. Occasionally his face reflected something stubborn and obstinate: he would be looking at you and listening, but all the while he would be preoccupied exclusively with his own thoughts. He could be lethargic and pacific one minute and flare up the next, often for the most trivial of reasons.

'Imagine, I've been travelling with him for the last four days,' he continued in his slightly drawling voice, which seemed perfectly natural, however, without any affectation. 'Ever since your brother pushed him off the calash and sent him flying, remember? He intrigued me a lot on that occasion, and I took him with me to the village, but he tells fibs all the time, and it's becoming embarrassing. We're on our way back...'

'The *pan* saw not Polish lady and is saying things which cannot be,' the gentleman with the pipe observed to Maksimov.

The gentleman with the pipe spoke reasonable Russian, at least far better than he pretended to. If he used Russian words, he distorted them to sound like Polish.

'I was married to a Polish lady myself, you know,' chortled Maksimov.

'So you served in the cavalry, did you?' Kalganov butted in. 'You were talking about the cavalry. So you're a cavalryman?'

'Well, of course he isn't a cavalryman! Ha-ha!' shouted out Mitya, who was listening avidly and kept turning his inquisitive gaze on whomever happened to be talking, as though expecting to hear goodness knows what.

'No, sir,' said Maksimov, facing him, 'what I meant was that in Poland the fillies... the pretty ones... only have to dance a single mazurka with one of our lads... she only has to dance one mazurka with him, and she'll be on his lap, like a kitten... milky-white, yes, sir... and her Polish daddy and her Polish mummy would just look on and allow it to happen... allow it all to happen... and next morning the uhlan would be back, offering his hand... that's right, sir... offering his hand, he-he!' Maksimov ended with a chuckle.

'*Pan* is blackguard!' the tall man on the chair suddenly grunted, and crossed his legs. An enormous greasy boot with a thick, grimy sole caught Mitya's eye. On the whole, the clothes of both gentlemen were rather grubby.

'So it's blackguards now! Does he have to be so insulting!' Grushenka suddenly lost her temper.

'*Pani Agrippina,** pan widział v polskim kraju chłopki, a nie* *szlachetne panie*' (My lady Agrafena, the gentleman saw country wenches in Poland, but not fine ladies), observed the man with the pipe, turning towards Grushenka.

'*Możesz na to rachować*,' (That you can be sure of), the tall man on the chair remarked contemptuously.

'There we go again! Why don't you let him speak! Why interrupt when people are talking? At least they're fun,' Grushenka snapped back.

'I don't bother them, *pani*,' the man with the toupee remarked weightily, fixing Grushenka with a long stare, and, after a pregnant pause, resumed sucking on his pipe.

'I say, our Polish friend is quite right,' Kalganov was getting excited again, as though they were talking about God only knows what. 'After all, he hasn't been to Poland, so how can he talk about the place? You didn't get married in Poland, did you? Or perhaps you did?'

'No, sir, in the Smolensk district. The point is she'd been brought out, my wife-to-be, that is, sir, by this uhlan, together with her lady-mother, her auntie, another female cousin, and a grown-up son, straight out of Poland... he brought them straight out and deposited them on my doorstep, he did, bless him. He was one of our regular Lieutenants, a very nice young man. He intended to marry her himself at first, but he didn't in the end, because she turned out to have a limp...'

'So you married her with a limp?' exclaimed Kalganov.

'Yes, sir. They both rather took advantage of me over that, they concealed it from me. I thought she was just hopping... she kept hopping all the time, and I thought it was just her cheerful nature...'

'Overjoyed at the prospect of getting married to you?' Kalganov burst out in a childishly clarion voice.

'Yes, sir, overjoyed. But the explanation turned out to be quite different. Later, after the wedding, when the ceremony was all over, she confessed to me that very same night, and she was ever so sorry, she said, she'd jumped over a puddle in her younger days and that was how she'd hurt her foot, he-he!'

Kalganov simply doubled up with laughter and nearly fell across the settee. Grushenka began to laugh too. As for Mitya, he was in raptures.

'This time, you know, he's telling the whole truth, this time he isn't fibbing at all!' Kalganov shrieked, turning to Mitya. 'And, you know, he's been married twice—that was his first wife he was telling us about—his second wife, would you believe it, ran off, and she's alive to this day, how about that?'

'Well I never!' Mitya turned abruptly towards Maksimov with an expression of the utmost astonishment on his face.

'Yes, sir, ran off, I did suffer that inconvenience,' Maksimov affirmed modestly. 'With a *monsieur*. And what was worst of all, the first thing she did was to get me to assign my whole estate, village and all, to her. "You're an educated man," was how she saw it, "you'll never be short of a meal." And that's how I got duped. A venerable bishop once observed to me: "One of your wives had a limp, and the other one was unusually fleet of foot." He-he!'

'Listen to that, just listen!' said Kalganov, bursting with excitement. 'Even if he is fibbing—and he does fib a lot—then he only does it to give pleasure to others—surely there's nothing nasty in that, is there? You know, I really love him for that sometimes. He's nasty all right, but he's not malicious with it, if you know what I mean. Wouldn't you say so? Some people might behave nastily for a reason, in order to gain some advantage, but he does it just for the hell of it, without trying... Imagine, he pretends for instance (last night he argued about it for the whole journey) that Gogol wrote his *Dead Souls* with him in mind.* If you remember, one of the characters is a landowner, Maksimov, whom Nozdryov thrashes, and he's subsequently prosecuted "for causing landowner Maksimov a personal affront with birches while in a state of inebriation"—do you remember? Well then, picture the scene—he pretends it was him, and that he was the one who got birched! Can you imagine anything like it? Chichikov was travelling around in the early 'twenties at the very latest, so the dates don't tally at all. He couldn't have been birched then. Obviously he couldn't, could he?'

It is hard to see why Kalganov should have got so worked up, but his excitement was genuine. Mitya was beginning to share his enthusiasm wholeheartedly.

'So what if he was birched!' he shouted out with a burst of laughter.

'It wasn't exactly what you would call a birching,' interjected Maksimov unexpectedly.

'What do you mean? Either you were birched or you weren't!'

'*Która godzina, panie?*' (What time do you make it, sir?) the pipe-smoking gentleman enquired of the tall man on the chair, with a yawn. The latter shrugged his shoulders: neither of them had a watch.

'Why don't you two have a chat and let the others carry on talking. If you're bored, it doesn't mean the others have to keep quiet,' Grushenka retorted angrily again, evidently trying deliberately to provoke them. Something seemed to dawn on Mitya for the first time. This time the Polish gentleman responded with evident annoyance.

'*Pani, ja nic nie mówię przeciw, nic nie powiedziałem*' (Madam, I didn't raise any objections, I didn't say anything).

'Well, all right. And you, carry on with your story,' Grushenka urged Maksimov. 'Why have you all stopped talking?'

'There's nothing much to tell, it's all rather silly,' Maksimov resumed, clearly delighted and play-acting a little. 'Anyway, Gogol portrays it all as an allegory, because all the names he chooses are allegorical. Let's face it, Nozdryov wasn't Nozdryov, he was Nosov; as for Kuvshinnikov—that's quite wrong, because he was Shkvornyov. Whereas Fenardi* really was Fenardi, only he wasn't Italian, he was Russian—Petrov actually—and Mamselle Fenardi really was a pretty little thing, all shapely legs and stockings, the way she twirled round in her little short skirt with spangles, but only for four minutes, mind, not four hours... and she had them all licking their chops...'

'But why were you birched, why did they birch you?' Kalganov howled in exasperation.

'On account of Piron,'* replied Maksimov.

'Who's Piron?' shouted Mitya.

'On account of the famous French writer Piron, sir. We were all drinking wine at the time with the gentry at the tavern, during that fair I told you about. I'd been invited along, and the very first thing I did was to start reciting epigrams: "Is that you, Boileau? What a ridiculous attire!"* And Boileau replies that he's on his way to a masked ball, to the bathhouse that is, he-he, and they all took it personally. Whereupon I recited another one, very well known to all educated people, a really biting one, sir:

> You're Sapho, I'm Phaon, that I will attest,
> But when it comes to getting to the coast,
> You're as clueless as the rest.*

They became even more offended and began to swear at me most indecently, and just at that moment, as bad luck would have it, in order to save the situation I went and recited another very crudite anecdote about Piron, about the way he was not allowed to join the French Academy, and how, to avenge himself, he wrote his own epitaph for his tombstone:

> Ci-gît Piron qui ne fut rien
> Pas même académicien.*

That's when they gave me a birching.'

'But what on earth for?'

'For my erudition. There's all manner of things a man can be birched for,' concluded Maksimov in a subdued, schoolmasterish tone of voice.

'Hey, enough of this, I think it's all quite boring, I don't want to listen, I thought it was going to be fun,' Grushenka cut him short. Mitya looked startled and stopped laughing immediately. The tall Polish gentleman stood up and, hands behind his back, began to pace up and down the room with the bored and supercilious air of a man who has found himself in the wrong company.

'Just look at him pacing up and down!' said Grushenka, giving him a contemptuous look. Mitya began to fret, all the more so as he noticed the gentleman on the settee beginning to eye him with irritation.

'Sir,' Mitya shouted out, 'let's drink, my dear sir! You too, sir—both of you gentlemen!' And he immediately took three glasses and poured champagne into them.

'To Poland, *panowie*, I drink to your Poland, here's to Poland!'

'*Bardzo mi to miło, panie, wypijem*' (I'd be delighted, sir, let's drink), said the man on the settee, with benign gravity, and picked up his glass.

'And the other *pan* too, what's his name, I say, Your High-and-Mightiness, pick up your glass!'

'*Pan* Wrublewski,' prompted the man on the settee.

Mr Wrublewski ambled up to the table, but remained standing as he took the glass.

'To Poland, gentlemen, hurrah!' Mitya proclaimed, raising his glass.

All three of them downed their drinks. Mitya immediately grabbed the bottle and refilled the glasses.

'Now to Russia, gentlemen, and friendship!'

'Pour me one, too,' said Grushenka, 'I want to drink to Russia as well.'

'So do I,' said Kalganov.

'I wouldn't mind either... to old Granny Russia then, the dear old girl,' chortled Maksimov.

'Everyone's having a drink!' Mitya exclaimed. 'Landlord, some more bottles!'

The three remaining bottles that Mitya had brought with him were produced. Mitya filled the glasses.

'To Russia, hurrah!' he proposed again. All except the Polish gentlemen drank up, and Grushenka drained her glass in one gulp. The Polish gentlemen did not even touch their glasses.

'What's the matter, *panowie?*' exclaimed Mitya. 'What's up?'

Mr Wrublewski took his glass, raised it, and said in a booming voice:

'To Russia, inside her pre-1772 borders!'*

'*Oto bardzo pięknie!*' (That's better!) shouted the other Pole, and they both drained their glasses in one gulp.

'You're just a couple of fools, *panowie!*' Mitya blurted out before he could check himself.

'I beg your pardon!' both the Poles shouted menacingly, confronting Mitya like a pair of turkeycocks. Mr Wrublewski was particularly agitated.

'*Ale nie można nie mieć słabości do swojego kraju?*' (Why shouldn't one love one's country?) he vociferated.

'Shut up!' shouted Grushenka imperiously, and stamped her foot on the floor. 'No quarrelling! I won't have any quarrels.' Her face was flushed and her eyes glinted. The wine was beginning to have an effect on her. Mitya became really worried.

'*Panowie*, I'm sorry! It's all my fault, I won't do it again. Wrublewski, *Pan* Wrublewski, really I won't!...'

'I do wish you'd keep quiet,' Grushenka snapped at him in exasperation, 'why don't you sit down, you're so silly!'

They all sat down, fell silent, and looked at one another.

'Gentlemen, it's all my fault!' Mitya began once more, quite missing the sting in Grushenka's remark. 'Aren't you bored just sitting here? Why don't we do something... to cheer us all up, to cheer us all up again.'

'True enough, it is unspeakably boring,' Kalganov drawled.

'A game of cards wouldn't be a bad idea, like the other time...' chortled Maksimov.

'Cards? Splendid!' echoed Mitya, 'provided the *panowie*...'

'*Późno, panie!*' (It is late, sir!) the Polish gentleman on the settee responded reluctantly.

'You right,' agreed Mr Wrublewski.

'"Puzno"? What does "puzno" mean?' asked Grushenka.

'Means late, *pani*, late, late in day,' explained the gentleman on the settee.

'It's always late for them, there's always something the matter!' Grushenka almost shrieked with exasperation. 'They're bored to death themselves, so they want others to be bored too. Before you arrived, Mitya, neither of them would say a word, just put on airs in front of me...'

'Goddess!' cried the gentleman on the settee, '*co mówisz to się stanie* (everything shall be as you say). *Widzę niełaskę, i jestem smutny* (I can see you're displeased, that's why I'm sad). *Jestem gotów, panie*' (I'm ready, sir), he concluded, turning to Mitya.

'You start, *pan*!' replied Mitya, pulling out the banknotes from his pocket, and laying two one-hundred rouble notes on the table. 'I want you to win a lot of money from me, *pan*. Take the cards and deal!'

'Landlord's cards, if you please, *pan*,' said the short gentleman firmly and seriously.

'*To najlepszy sposób*' (That's the best way), said Mr Wrublewski approvingly.

'The landlord's? All right, I understand, the landlord's they shall be! Good idea, *panowie*! Cards!' Mitya commanded the landlord.

The landlord brought a sealed pack of cards and announced to Mitya that the gypsy girls had just arrived, that the Jews with the dulcimer would probably also be there soon, but that the troika with the food and drink had not yet turned up. Mitya jumped to his feet and ran into the next room to issue instructions. But only three girls had arrived so far, and Marya was not among them. Besides, he himself did not know what instructions he should give or why he had rushed out; he merely ordered that the girls be given boiled sweets and toffees from the box. 'And some vodka for Andrei, give him some vodka!' he ordered hastily. 'I offended him!' Suddenly Maksimov, who had followed him, touched him on the shoulder.

'Let me have five roubles,' he whispered to Mitya, 'I'd like to make a little bet too, he-he!'

'Wonderful, splendid! Here you are, have ten!' He pulled out the wad of notes from his pocket again and found ten roubles. 'And if you lose, just ask for more...'

'That I will, sir,' Maksimov gasped with excitement and hurried back. Mitya too returned at once and apologized for having kept everybody waiting. The Polish gentlemen were already seated, and the pack had been opened. Their expressions were now a great deal more good-humoured, almost amiable. The gentleman on the settee lit himself a fresh pipe and made ready to deal; his face took on a look of solemnity.

'*Na miejsca, panowie!*' (Take your seats, gentlemen) called out Mr Wrublewski.

'I don't want to play any more,' Kalganov responded, 'I already lost fifty roubles to them earlier on.'

'*Pan był nieszczęśliwy* (The gentleman was unlucky). *Pan* perhaps have better luck this time,' remarked the gentleman on the settee.

'How much is in the bank? What are the stakes?' Mitya's impatience was beginning to get the better of him.

'Beg pardon, *pan*, hundred or two hundred, what you stake.'

'A million!' Mitya burst out laughing.

'Perhaps the *Pan* Captain heard of *Pan* Podwysocki?'

'What Podwysocki?'

'In Warsaw, bank holds all bets and anyone can make a stake.

Comes Podwysocki, sees thousand zlotys, and bets all. Banker says to him, "*Pan* Podwysocki, you betting with gold or you betting on your word?" "My word of honour, *pan*," says *Pan* Podwysocki. "Is much better, *pan*." Banker deals cards, Podwysocki takes thousand zlotys. "Wait a minute, *pan*," says banker, and he pulls out a drawer and gives him million. "Take this, *panie, oto jest twoj rachunek!*" (here's your winnings). There was million in bank. "I had not idea," says *Pan* Podwysocki. "*Pan* Podwysocki," says banker, "you bet on word of honour, and we bet on word of honour." Podwysocki took million.

'That's not true,' said Kalganov.

'*Panie Kalganov, w szlachetnej kompanii tak móvić nie przystoi*' (Mr Kalganov, you don't contradict someone in polite company).

'I'd like to see a Polish gambler give away a million!' exclaimed Mitya, but stopped dead. 'Sorry, *panie*, I really didn't mean it, he'd pay up, he'd pay up a million, on his honour, on his *polsky* honour he would! How do you like my Polish, ha-ha! Here, ten roubles on the jack.'

'And I'll stick my little rouble on the queenie, the pretty red one, the Polish missy, he-he!' giggled Maksimov, pushing forward his queen. Then, leaning right down to the table, as though attempting to conceal his action from everyone, he crossed himself hastily. Mitya won. So did Maksimov's rouble.

'Same again!' shouted Mitya.

'And I'll bet one more little rouble again, one little, itsy-bitsy roubly-woubly,' mumbled Maksimov blissfully, overjoyed that his little rouble had won.

'Lost!' yelled Mitya. 'Double on seven!'

He lost again.

'Stop!' said Kalganov suddenly.

'Double again, double.' Mitya kept doubling the stakes, and each time he did so, he lost. But the little 'roubly-woubly' went on winning.

'Double!' Mitya yelled in a rage.

'*Dwieście przegrałeś, panie. Jeszce stawisz dwieście?*' (You've lost two hundred, sir. Are you staking another two hundred?) enquired the gentleman on the settee.

'What, I've lost two hundred? So what, here's another two

hundred! The whole two hundred, double or quits!' and, pulling the money out from his pocket, he was about to put it on the queen, when Kalganov suddenly covered it with his hand.

'Enough!' he called out in a ringing voice.

'Why did you do that?' Mitya stared at him.

'That's enough, I don't want you to! You're not to play any more.'

'Why?'

'Just because. Cut your losses and leave, that's what I'm telling you. I won't let you play any more!'

Mitya stared at him in astonishment.

'Don't, Mitya, perhaps he's right; you've already lost a lot as it is,' said Grushenka, with a strange note in her voice. Both Polish gentlemen suddenly rose to their feet, looking very offended.

'*Zartuyesz, panie?*' (You're joking, sir?) said the little gentleman, staring hard at Kalganov.

'*Jak się odważasz to robić, panie!*' (How dare you!) Mr Wrublewski also yelled at Kalganov.

'Stop it, stop shouting!' cried Grushenka. 'Just look at them, the turkeycocks!'

Mitya looked at each of them in turn; suddenly, something about Grushenka's face struck him, and at the same instant an altogether new thought flashed through his mind.

'*Pani Agrippina!*' the little gentleman was about to launch forth, all hot and flustered, when Mitya suddenly came up to him and slapped him on the shoulder.

'Your High-and-Mightiness, a couple of words in your ear.'

'*Czego chcesz, panie?*' (What can I do for you, sir?)

'Let's go to the other room, over there, I want a couple of words with you, something to your advantage, you won't be disappointed.'

The little gentleman was surprised, and he looked apprehensively at Mitya. He agreed immediately, however, on the sole condition that Mr Wrublewski should accompany him.

'Your bodyguard, is that it?' exclaimed Mitya. 'Yes, let him come too if he wants, we need him also! In fact, we can't do without him! Let's go, gentlemen!'

'Where are you off to?' asked Grushenka anxiously.

'We'll be back in just a minute,' replied Mitya. His face

expressed courage, an unexpected vitality; when he made his entry an hour before, he had looked altogether different. He took the Polish gentlemen into the room on the right, not into the large one where the gypsy-girl chorus was assembling and where the table was being laid, but into a bedroom containing trunks and travelling-cases and two large beds with a stack of pillows in chintz pillowcases on each. Here, on a small deal table in the far corner, a candle was burning. The little gentleman and Mitya settled themselves at this table, facing each other, while the huge Mr Wrublewski stood to one side, with his hands folded behind his back. The gentlemen looked stern, but noticeably curious.

'*Czym mogę służyć panu?*' (What can I do for you, sir?) muttered the little gentleman.

'Here's what, *panie*, I'll keep it short: take this money,' he pulled out his banknotes, 'there's three thousand there, just take it and clear off.'

The gentleman looked at him enquiringly; his eyes seemed to bore into Mitya.

'*Trzy tysiące, panie?*' (Three thousand, sir?) He exchanged glances with Wrublewski.

'"*Trzy, panowie, trzy*"! (Three, gentlemen, three!) Listen, *pan*, I can see you're a sensible man. Take the three thousand and get the hell out of here, and take Wrublewski with you—do you hear me? But at once, this very instant, do you understand, *pan*, there's the door. What have you got in there—a coat, a fur coat? I'll bring it out to you. They'll harness a troika for you straight away and—*do widzenia, panie!* (Goodbye!) Well, what do you say?'

Mitya waited confidently for an answer. He was sure of himself. A look of resolution flashed across the Pole's face.

'*A ruble, panie?*' (What about the roubles?)

'Roubles, *pan?*' Mitya enquired. 'Five hundred immediately as a deposit and payment for the coach, and two thousand five hundred tomorrow, in the town—on my honour, you'll get them if I have to dig them out of the ground!'

The Poles glanced at each other again. The little gentleman began to scowl.

'Seven hundred; seven hundred now, not five hundred, cash

in hand!' Mitya raised the offer, sensing something untoward. 'What's up, *pan*? Don't you believe me? You can't expect me to give you the whole three thousand at once! If I give it to you, how do I know you're not going to come back to her the very next day... Anyway, I haven't got the three thousand on me just now, it's at home in the town,' Mitya prattled on with a sinking heart, his hopes ebbing with every word, 'honest to God, it's there, hidden away...'

In a trice, the little gentleman's face began to glow with dignity.

'*Czy nie potrzebujesz jeszcze czego?*' (You haven't got any more requests, have you?) he enquired ironically. 'Pff! Pff! Shame to you!' And he spat in disgust. Mr Wrublewski did likewise.

'Is it that you're not satisfied, *pan*,' said Mitya despairingly, realizing it was all up, 'because you expect to get more out of Grushenka? You're a couple of rogues, that's what you are!'

'*Jestem do żywego dotknięty!*' (I am most grievously offended!) The little gentleman suddenly went as red as a beetroot and, apparently not wishing to hear another word, strutted out of the room in a state of extreme indignation. He was followed by Mr Wrublewski, swaying from side to side, and finally by Mitya, confused and disheartened. He was afraid for Grushenka, and he expected the Pole to start shouting. And that is exactly what happened. The Pole came into the room and adopted a theatrical pose in front of Grushenka.

'*Pani Agrippina, jestem do żywego dotknięty!*' (I'm cut to the quick!) he exploded, but Grushenka suddenly seemed to lose all patience, as though she had been touched on a raw nerve.

'In Russian, speak Russian!' she yelled at him. 'I don't want to hear a word of Polish! Your Russian was good enough then, you couldn't have forgotten it in five years!' Her face was red with rage.

'*Pani Agrippina...*'

'I'm Agrafena, I'm Grushenka; speak Russian, otherwise I'm not going to listen!' The Pole began to puff with pride and, in broken Russian, said quickly and pompously:

'Miss Agrafena, I came forgive and forget past, forgetting what happen before today...'

'What do you mean "forgive"?' Grushenka interrupted him, jumping to her feet. 'You came to forgive me?'

'*Tak jest, pani*' (That's right, my lady), I'm not coward, I am brave man. But I *byłem zdziwiony* (was surprised) when I saw your lovers. *Pan* Mitya offered me *trzy tysiące* (three thousand) in that *pokoju* (room) to bribe me to leave. I spit in the *pan*'s visage.'

'What? He offered you money for me?' Grushenka yelled out hysterically. 'Is that true, Mitya? How could you! Am I to be bought and sold?'

'*Panie*, gentlemen,' protested Mitya, 'she's pure and spotless, and I've never been her lover! It's a lie...'

'Don't you dare defend me before him,' shrieked Grushenka, 'it was not because of virtue that I was pure, nor because I was afraid of Kuzma, but so I could keep my pride in front of *him*, so I could call him a scoundrel when I met him again. Has he really not accepted any money from you?'

'He was going to, of course he was!' exclaimed Mitya. 'Only he wanted the whole three thousand at once, and I was only going to give him seven hundred in advance.'

'Well, it's pretty clear now: he heard I'd got money, that's why he came to offer marriage!'

'*Pani Agrippina*,' cried the Pole, 'I am chevalier, *szlachcic*,* I am not scoundrel! I *przybył* (came) to take you for wife, but I see different *pani*, not like formerly, *uparty i bez wstydu* (wilful and shameless).

'Well then, go back to where you came from! If you're not careful I'll tell them to throw you out, and they will!' shouted Grushenka, at the end of her tether. 'What a fool, what a fool I've been to torture myself for five years! And it wasn't really because of him that I tortured myself, I tortured myself out of spite! No, this can't be him! He wasn't like this at all! You'd think this one was his father! Where did you get that hairpiece from? That one was a hero, this one's just nothing. That one laughed and sang songs to me... And there was I, crying my eyes out for five years, what a damned fool, I'm contemptible, I've made myself look ridiculous!'

She slumped into her chair and buried her face in her hands. At this moment the Mokroye gypsy girls, who had finally assembled, struck up a song in the room on the left—a lively dance-tune.

'This is Sodom!' Mr Wrublewski let out a roar. 'Landlord, get rid of shameless ones!'

The landlord, who had been standing near the door for some time shooting curious glances at them, heard the cries and, realizing that the guests had begun to quarrel, promptly entered the room.

'What are you yelling blue murder for?' he turned on Wrublewski with quite astonishing impoliteness.

'Pig!' yelled Mr Wrublewski.

'Pig? What cards did you use to play with just now? I gave you a pack, but you hid it! You were using marked cards! I could have you sent to Siberia for card-sharping, do you know that, because it's the same as forging money...' And, going up to the settee, he thrust his hand between the backrest and a cushion and retrieved a still-sealed pack of cards.

'Here's my pack, unopened!' He raised it for all to see. 'From where I stood I saw him shove my pack down behind the cushion and substitute his own—you're a cheat, not a gentleman!'

'And I saw him cheat twice,' cried Kalganov.

'Oh, what a disgrace, oh, what a disgrace!' exclaimed Grushenka, clasping her hands and genuinely blushing with shame. 'Lord, how he's changed!'

'I had my suspicions,' cried Mitya. But hardly had he spoken than Mr Wrublewski, embarrassed and enraged, turned to Grushenka and, threatening her with his fist, yelled out:

'Common trollop!'

Scarcely had he uttered the words, than Mitya pounced on him, seized him bodily, lifted him into the air, and, in a trice, carried him into the room on the right, where he had been with the two of them just before.

He came straight back, puffing, and announced, 'I've put him on the floor in there! He struggled, the dirty dog, but he won't bother us again!...' He shut one of the double doors and, holding the other open, called across to the little gentleman:

'You wouldn't like to go in there, too, Your High-and-Mightiness, would you? *Przepraszam*!' (This way, sir, please!)

'My dear Dmitry Fyodorovich,' wailed Trifon Borisych, 'why don't you take the money from them, the money you lost to them! They might just as well have stolen it from you.'

'I don't want to take my fifty roubles,' Kalganov called out.

'I don't want my two hundred either, I don't want it!' exclaimed Mitya. 'I'll never take it back, let him keep it.'

'Well done, Mitya! I love you for that, Mitya!' cried Grushenka, and a terribly vicious note rang through her voice. The little gentleman, red with fury but his composure unruffled, had started moving towards the door, but stopped suddenly and said turning to Grushenka,

'*Pani, jeżeli chcesz iść za mną, idźmy, jeżeli nie—bywaj zdrowa!*' (My lady, if you wish to come with me—let's go, if not—goodbye!)

And, huffing and puffing with indignation and pride, he strutted through the door. He was a man of character; even after all that had happened, he still refused to give up hope that the lady would follow him—such was his arrogance. Mitya shut the door after him.

'Lock them up,' said Kalganov. But the lock clicked on the other side; they had locked themselves in.

'Splendid,' Grushenka again cried out viciously and without pity. 'Splendid! Serves them right!'

8

DELIRIUM

WHAT took place was almost an orgy, a feast of feasts. Grushenka was the first to ask for the wine: 'I want to drink, I want to get completely drunk, like before, do you remember, Mitya, remember, like the last time!' Mitya himself appeared to be in a state of delirium, and was anticipating 'his moment of bliss'. Grushenka, however, kept rebuffing him all the time: 'Go on, enjoy yourself, tell them to dance, let everybody enjoy himself, let's raise the roof, like before, like last time!' she kept exclaiming. She was terribly excited. Mitya rushed around issuing instructions. The chorus had assembled in the adjacent room. The room in which they had been sitting up till now was not big enough; besides, it was partitioned by a chintz curtain, on the other side of which was yet another huge bed, with a thick eiderdown and a pile of matching chintz pillows. There were beds in every one of the four 'reception' rooms of this house. Grushenka settled herself right by the door, where Mitya had put an armchair for her; that was exactly how she had sat 'then', during those first revels, watching the chorus and the dancing. The girls were the same ones; the Jewish musicians had also arrived with their fiddles and zithers, and at last the long-awaited troika, with its consignment of wines and comestibles, pulled up too. Mitya could not stop fussing. The room filled up with locals, peasant men and women who had been sleeping but who had roused themselves, sensing an unexpected treat like the month before. Mitya went around greeting acquaintances, recognizing people's faces, opening bottles, and pouring wine for all and sundry. No one was particularly keen on champagne, except the girls; the menfolk preferred rum and brandy, and especially hot punch. Mitya gave instructions that hot chocolate should be available for the girls all through the night, and that three samovars should be kept on the boil for tea and punch, to cater for any chance visitors: whoever wanted to could help himself to anything. To cut a long story short, this was a prelude to a chaotic and bizarre denouement. Mitya, however, seemed to be in his element, and the more bizarre the proceedings became, the more animated he became. Had a peasant asked him for some money, he would have pulled out the whole wad at once and started doling out money to all and sundry, without bothering to count it. It was probably for that reason, in order to save Mitya from himself, that the innkeeper Trifon Borisych decided it seems not to go to sleep at all that night and kept hovering around him, maintaining a close watch over his interests; Trifon Borisych, incidentally, drank very little—one glass of punch was all he had. At critical moments he would solicitously and unctuously restrain him from treating the peasants to cigars and Rhenish wine, as he had 'the other time', and above all from doling out money; he particularly objected to the girls drinking liqueurs and eating sweets. 'They're full of lice, Mitry Fyodorovich,' he would say, 'I'll give them a kick up their backsides to teach them what an honour it is to be here—that's the sort they are.' Mitya remembered about Andrei again, and ordered some punch to be sent to him. 'I offended him,' he repeated in a maudlin tone. To begin with Kalganov did not want to drink and the chorus of gypsy girls did not appeal to him at all, but after a couple of glasses of champagne he cheered up immensely, started strutting around the rooms, laughing and praising everyone and everything, including the songs and the music. Maksimov, blissfully tipsy, was constantly at his side. Grushenka, who was also getting a little drunk, kept pointing Kalganov out to Mitya: 'Isn't he nice, isn't he a sweet boy!' And Mitya, delighted, would rush to hug Kalganov and Maksimov. Oh, he had great hopes; as yet, she had said nothing significant to him, and in fact she seemed to be deliberately procrastinating, although she would occasionally bestow upon him a caressing, passionate glance. Finally, she grabbed him firmly by the arm and pulled him over to her with all her strength. She was sitting in the armchair by the door at the time.

'Fancy you marching in like that, earlier on, eh? Coming in like that!... you gave me such a fright. Did you really mean to abandon me to him, eh? Is that really what you wanted?'

'I didn't want to spoil your happiness!' muttered Mitya, in a transport of joy. But she was no longer interested in his reply.

'Go along then... enjoy yourself,' she dismissed him yet again, 'and don't cry, I'll call you when I want you.'

And off he went, while she resumed listening to the songs and watching the dancing. She did not let him out of her sight, however, wherever he was, and every quarter of an hour or so she would call him over and he would come rushing to her again.

'Well, sit down next to me and tell me how you found out yesterday that I was coming here; who was it who told you first?'

And Mitya would begin telling the whole story disjointedly, incoherently, passionately, speaking strangely, and frequently wrinkling his brows and coming to an abrupt halt.

'Why are you frowning?' she would ask.

'It's nothing... I left a sick man behind. I only hope he gets better, if I knew he'd get better, I'd give ten years of my life!'

'Well, if he's sick, forget about him. So did you really want to shoot yourself the next day, what a silly man you are, and what on earth for? I love crazy ones like you,' she was beginning to slur her words. 'So you're ready to do anything for me? Ah? And did you really want to shoot yourself the next day, you little fool! No, you must wait a while, tomorrow I might have something to say to you... tomorrow, but not today. You'd like to hear it today, wouldn't you? But I don't want it to be today... Off you go now, run along, enjoy yourself.'

On one occasion, however, she called him over, apparently perplexed and worried.

'Why are you sad? I can see you're sad... Yes, I can,' she added, peering closely into his eyes. 'Even though you're whooping and kissing your peasant friends over there, I can see there's something wrong. Look, I want you to enjoy yourself, I'm having fun and you should be, too... There's someone here I love, guess who?... Oh look! My poppet's fallen asleep, it's the wine, isn't he a darling!'

She was speaking about Kalganov; the wine had really affected him and, for an instant, he had dozed off where he sat on the settee. And it was not just the drink; he had begun to feel rather low for some reason, or rather, as he himself said, 'bored'. In the end, the dancing girls' songs, which as the drinking progressed became rather lewd and vulgar, began to irritate him. It was the same with their dancing: two of the girls dressed up as bears, and Stepanida, a boisterous wench with a cane in her hand, pretended to be their tamer and began 'to parade' them. 'On your toes, Marya,' she cried, 'or you'll feel the touch of my cane!' Finally the bears collapsed on the floor in a most indecent fashion, accompanied by the raucous laughter of the assembled motley crowd of peasants. 'Let them, why shouldn't they,' Grushenka kept saying sententiously, 'if they get a chance to enjoy themselves, why on earth shouldn't they?' Kalganov, on the other hand, looked for all the world as though he had trodden on something nasty. 'All this folksiness makes me sick,' he remarked, turning his back on them, 'these are their rites of spring, when they celebrate the sun the whole night through.' But he took particular exception to a certain 'newfangled' song, with a lively dance rhythm, about a wayfaring gentleman who stopped and propositioned some girls:

To the girls the young man turned,
Will they love him, will they not?

But the girls didn't think that they could love the young man:

He will beat us black and blue
If to him we are not true.

Then it was a passing gypsy who asked:

To the girls the gypsy turned,
Will they love him, will they not?

But the gypsy, too, proved hard to love:

The gypsy will a-stealing go
And will leave me in the lurch.

And there were numerous people who passed by, propositioning the girls; there was even a soldier:

To the girls the soldier turned,
Will they love him, will they not?

But the soldier was rejected out of hand:

The soldier will march to seek his luck,
And leave me dying for a...

There then followed the most indecent verse of all, sung explicitly and producing a furore amongst the audience. Finally, it was the turn of a merchant:

To the girls the merchant turned,
Will they love him, will they not?

And it turned out they would, most willingly, because, ran the song:

To the wealthy merchant I'll be wed,
And a queen I'll lie, all day in bed!

Kalganov was positively enraged.

'That song's probably only just been written,' he remarked out loud, 'I wonder who composes them! All we need is for some railwayman or a Jew to come along: they'd win hands down.' And, thoroughly offended, he announced there and then that he was bored, sat down on the settee, and promptly fell asleep. His pretty boyish face turned even paler, and his head flopped back on the cushion.

'Look, isn't he just lovely,' said Grushenka, calling Mitya over to him, 'I was combing his hair just now; it's like flax and so thick...'

And bending over him full of admiration, she kissed him on his forehead. In a flash Kalganov opened his eyes, looked at her, made an attempt to get up and, with a most preoccupied air, enquired, 'Where's Maksimov?'

'Listen to him, asking for Maksimov,' Grushenka burst out laughing, 'you don't need him, stay here with me for a while. Mitya, run along and find his Maksimov for him.'

It appeared that Maksimov had been with the dancing girls all the time, leaving them only occasionally to pour himself a liqueur; he had already drunk two cups of chocolate. His little face was flushed, his nose had turned scarlet, his moist eyes were oozing with sentimentality. He ran up and announced that he would like to dance the *sabotière** to 'a certain little tune'.

'I was taught all these refined society dances when I was only a child, yes indeed...'

'Go along, go with him, Mitya, I'll watch him dance from here.'

'Yes, me too, I'll go and watch too,' exclaimed Kalganov, naïvely refusing Grushenka's offer to stay with him. Everyone went off to watch. Maksimov did indeed perform his dance, but apart from Mitya no one seemed particularly impressed by it. The whole dance consisted of a series of hops and turns, with the dancer kicking up his heels sideways and striking his soles with the flat of his hand at every hop. Kalganov remained totally unimpressed, but Mitya was delighted and even gave the dancer a hearty hug.

'Well, thank you, you must be tired, what are you looking over there for? You want a sweet, eh? A cigar perhaps, would you like one?'

'A cigarette would be nice.'

'You wouldn't like a drink, would you?'

'Just a small liqueur... You wouldn't happen to have some chocolates by any chance?'

'Look, there's a whole pile on the table, help yourself, my dear chap!'

'No, I'd like one of those... vanilla ones... the ones we old folk go for... he-he!'

'I'm afraid, my friend, there aren't any of that sort.'

'Listen!' the old man suddenly leaned right across to whisper into Mitya's ear, 'that girl Maryushka, he-he, I wonder if I could... er... I don't suppose you could introduce me, seeing as you're so kind?'

'So that's what you're after! No, my friend, I can't.'

'I don't mean anyone any harm,' Maksimov whimpered disconsolately.

'Well, all right, all right. These girls are only here to sing and dance, my friend, but on second thoughts, what the hell! Wait though... Why don't you have a bite to eat, have a drink, enjoy yourself. Do you need money?'

'Perhaps later then...', Maksimov leered.

'All right, all right...'

Mitya's head was throbbing. He went out through the hallway onto the wooden gallery that ran round the inner courtyard. The fresh air cleared his head. Mitya stood alone in a corner in the dark, and suddenly he buried his head in his hands. His fragmented thoughts coalesced, all his emotions fused into a single sensation, and there was light! Awesome, terrible light! 'If I'm going to shoot myself, now's as good a time as any!' the thought flashed through his mind. 'I could fetch the pistol and put an end to it right here and now, in this dark, filthy corner.' He stood undecided for about a minute. Even while he had been hurrying here in the troika, the ignominy, the theft he had committed, was beginning to overwhelm him, and also that blood, all that blood... But then it had been easier, oh, far easier! Everything had been over and done with then: he had lost her, surrendered her—for him, she had ceased to exist—oh, the sentence had been more lenient then, at least it had seemed inevitable, unavoidable, because what would have been the point in staying alive? Whereas now! There could be no comparison between then and now! At least one ghost had been laid now, one phantom dealt with; the ominous spectre of the 'former', the indisputable one, had vanished without trace. That which had inspired such fear had turned out to be something trivial, a figure of fun—to be picked up and shut up in a bedroom. That was a thing of the past now, never to return. She was ashamed, and by the look in her eyes he could clearly tell who it was she really loved now. Yes, now was the time to live... but he couldn't live, he couldn't, oh, what a curse! 'Please God, bring the man by the fence back to life! Let this terrible cup pass from me!* Surely, Lord, You worked Your miracles for precisely such sinners as me! Would that the old man were alive. Oh, then I'd make amends for that other dastardly, shameful deed, I'd return the stolen money, I'd give it back, I'd get it one way or another... No trace of my shame will remain, except for the shame that is in my heart for ever! But no, no, oh what desolate, faint-hearted hopes! Oh cursed fate!'

However, a ray of bright hope seemed to pierce the darkness. He turned and dashed into the room—to her, to her, his queen for evermore! 'Surely an hour, a minute of her love is worth anything, even all the tortures of shame for the rest of one's life.' This wild thought possessed him. 'To her, to be with her alone, to see her, to listen to her, to forget everything and stop thinking altogether, even if only for one night, one hour, one instant!' Before he had even left the gallery, he ran into the innkeeper Trifon Borisych. The latter seemed gloomy and uneasy, and Mitya thought he had come to look for him. 'What's the matter, Borisych, were you looking for me?'

'No, not you,' the innkeeper replied, as though caught off guard, 'why should I be looking for you? And where... where've you been?'

'Why've you got such a long face? You're not angry, are you? It won't be long now, you'll soon be able to go to bed... What time do you make it?'

'I'd say three o'clock. Perhaps later.'

'It'll all be over soon, very soon.'

'It's all right, I don't mind. In fact, carry on for as long as you like...'

'What's wrong with him?' Mitya wondered briefly, and rushed into the room where the girls were dancing. But she was not there. Nor was she in the blue room; Kalganov was alone, snoozing on the settee. Mitya peered behind the curtains—she was there. She was sitting in the corner, on a trunk, her head resting on her arms on the bed, and crying her heart out, making every effort to stifle her sobs so as not to be heard. Catching sight of Mitya, she beckoned to him, whereupon he rushed over to her and she clutched his hand.

'Mitya, Mitya, I loved him, do you realize that!' she began in a whisper, 'I loved him so much, all these five years, all that time! Was it him I loved, or merely my own spite? No, it was him! Yes, him! I'm not being honest when I say it was my spite I loved, rather than him! Mitya, I was only seventeen then, he was so kind to me then, so cheerful, he sang songs to me... Or did I just think he was like that, stupid girl that I was... And Lord, just look at him now, that's not the same man, he's quite different. He doesn't even look like him, it's not him at all. I didn't even recognize him. On the way here with Timofei I was thinking all the time, all along the way: "How am I going to greet him, what am I going to say, how will we look at each other?..." I felt all numb inside, and suddenly he made me feel so filthy. He started talking to me like a schoolmaster; he was so stuffy, so smug, he greeted me so pompously that I didn't know what to say. I felt so tongue-tied. At first I thought he was embarrassed because that tall Polack was there. There I was, sitting looking at them both and thinking: why can't I find anything to talk to him about now? You know, I think it's his wife that ruined him, the one he married when he left me... It's she who's changed him. Mitya, it's awful! Oh, I'm so ashamed, Mitya, so ashamed, oh, my whole life's been a disgrace! Damn them, damn those five years, damn them!' And she burst into tears again, clinging to Mitya's hand even more desperately.

'Mitya, darling, wait, don't go away, I've a little something to tell you,' she whispered, and suddenly raised her face towards him. 'Listen, tell me, who do I love? There's one person here I love. Who is it? That's what I want you to tell me.' A smile began to glimmer on her tear-stained face, her eyes shone in the half-light. 'A falcon entered the room, and my heart leapt with joy. "You fool," my heart whispered to me, "that's the one you love." You entered, and everything was sweetness and light. "Well, what's he afraid of?" I thought to myself. And you were afraid, really afraid, you couldn't say a thing. "Surely," I thought to myself, "it's not those two he's afraid of!" Can you be frightened of anyone? "It's me he's afraid of," I thought, "just me." Fenya must have told you, you silly fool, how I shouted to Alyosha from the window that I'd loved my Mitenka for one short hour, and that I was off to love... someone else. Mitya, Mitya, fool that I was, how could I have imagined I loved someone else after you! Do you forgive me, Mitya? Do you forgive me or not? Do you love me? Do you?'

She leapt to her feet and grabbed him by the shoulders. Mitya, struck dumb with ecstasy, gazed into her eyes, her face, her smile, and suddenly clasped her tightly and began to kiss her.

'Will you forgive me for torturing you? I made you all suffer out of spite. I even drove that pathetic old man out of his mind through sheer spite... Do you recall the time you had a drink in my room and dashed your glass to the ground? Today I remembered it and broke a glass myself, I drank "to my treacherous heart". Mitya, my falcon, why aren't you kissing me? He kisses me once and draws back, just stares at me and listens... Don't just stand there! Kiss me... harder, that's better. Love me, love me more! From now on I'm your slave, your slave for life! It's lovely being a slave!... Kiss me! Hurt me, torture me, do something to me... Oh, I really deserve to be tortured... Don't! Wait, later, I don't want it like that...', she pushed him away suddenly. 'Go away, Mitka, I want plenty of wine, I want to get drunk; I want to get drunk and I want to dance, I do, I do!'

She struggled free and dashed out through the curtains. Mitya followed her as though drunk himself. 'So what, so what, who cares what happens next,' flashed through his head, 'one single minute of this, and the world can go to hell.' Grushenka did gulp down another glass of champagne, in fact, and promptly became very tipsy. She slumped down in the armchair in which she had sat before, smiling beatifically. Her cheeks were glowing, her lips burning, her bright eyes grew languorous, and her glances passionate and seductive. Even Kalganov felt his heart flutter, and he went up to her.

'Did you feel me kiss you just then, when you were asleep?' she whispered to him. 'I'm drunk now, that's what it is... Aren't you drunk? Why isn't Mitya drinking? Why aren't you drinking, Mitya, I'm drinking and you're not...'

'I am drunk! I'm drunk as it is... because of you, and now I want to get even more drunk with wine.' He drank another glass, and—this struck him as being odd—it was this last glass which made him groggy, quite unexpectedly groggy, he was sober one minute and drunk the next, he remembered this clearly. From that moment, everything began to spin, as if in delirium. He walked around, he laughed, he spoke to everyone, and all as if in a trance. But all the time, one stubborn, searing thought recurred relentlessly, 'like a red-hot brand in my soul', as he recalled later. He would approach her, sit down next to her, look at her, listen to her... She herself grew very garrulous and kept beckoning people over; every now and then, a dancer from the troupe would approach her, and she would either kiss the girl and let her go or make the sign of the cross over her. She was liable to burst into tears at any moment. Maksimov, 'the little old chap', as she used to call him, amused her no end. He was constantly rushing up to plant a kiss on her hand, on 'her every little finger', and in the end he even performed a dance to an old ditty which he himself sang. His cavortings grew particularly sprightly when it came to the refrain:

> Little piglet went grunt-grunt-grunt,
> And the calf went moo-moo-moo,
> But the duckling quack-quack-quacked,
> And the gosling pee-pee-peeped.
>
> While the chicken clucked-clucked-clucked
> As it in the farmyard paced,
> As it in the farmyard paced!

'Give him something, Mitya,' said Grushenka, 'let him have a present, he's poor. Woe to the poor, woe to the wretched ones!... You know, Mitya, I'm joining a nunnery. Yes, I really shall one of these days. There was something Alyosha said to me today that I'll never forget as long as I live... Yes... Let's dance today, though. Tomorrow to the nunnery, but today we'll dance our hearts out. I want to be mischievous, my good people, so what, God will forgive. If I were God, I'd pardon all people: "My dear little sinners, from now on, you're all pardoned." But I'm off to seek forgiveness: "Look you kind people, why not forgive a silly woman?" I'm an animal, you know. But I want to pray. I did offer someone an onion once. I'm so evil, but I want to pray! Mitya, let them dance, don't interfere. All people on this earth are good, without exception. It's good on this earth. Even though we're rotten, it's still nice on this earth. We're rotten and we're nice, both rotten and nice... Yes, really, tell me, I want to ask you, come closer all of you, I want to ask you; do tell me this, all of you: why am I so nice? I am nice, I'm very nice... Well then: why am I so nice?' Grushenka prattled on, steadily becoming more and more drunk, and finally announced decisively that she intended to dance herself. She rose from her chair, and swayed. 'Mitya, don't let me have any more wine, even if I ask for it—don't give me any. Wine brings no peace. Everything's spinning, the stove and everything. I want to dance. Let them all watch me dance... let them see how well, how wonderfully well I dance...'

And she really meant to: she pulled out a white cambric kerchief from her pocket and held it by one corner in her right hand, so as to wave it about during the dance. Mitya started fussing about, the girls fell silent, ready to break into a dance-tune as soon as the signal was given. On realizing that Grushenka herself was going to dance, Maksimov squealed with delight and started prancing around her, singing:

> Shapely-legged,
> Slender-waisted,
> Bushy-tailed she goes.

But Grushenka waved her kerchief and shooed him off.

'Sh-shush! Mitya, why don't they come and watch? Let them all see me... let them watch. Get the ones that have been locked up to come too... Why did you lock them up? Tell them I'm going to dance, let them watch me dance and watch too...'

Mitya, unsteady from the wine, staggered over to the locked door and banged on it with his fist.

'Hey, you... Polsky-podvisolsky! Come out, she wants to dance, she wants you to watch her.'

'Blackguard!' cried one of the Poles.

'Same to you! You're a puny, insignificant little blackguard, too, that's what you are.'

'I wish you'd stop mocking Poland,' Kalganov, also the worse for drink, observed irritably.

'Keep quiet, boy! Calling him a blackguard doesn't mean I want to malign the whole of Poland. One blackguard doesn't make up the whole of Poland. So you keep quiet, pretty boy, and carry on sucking your sweets.'

'Just listen to them! You'd think they weren't civilized. Why don't they just kiss and be friends?' Grushenka said, and stepped forward to dance. The chorus broke into song: 'Fly, falcon, fly.' Grushenka threw back her head, parted her lips, smiled, gave one wave of her kerchief, and suddenly swayed helplessly, standing there in the middle of the room, bewildered.

'I don't feel well...', she said in an exhausted voice, 'I'm sorry, I don't feel very well, I can't... It's my fault...'

She bowed to the chorus, and then four more times in all directions, 'It's all my fault... I'm sorry...'

'The young lady's had one too many, she's really had one too many, the pretty young lady,' voices echoed all around.

'She's drunk,' Maksimov giggled, offering his explanation to the girls.

'Mitya, take me away... take me, Mitya,' Grushenka said, utterly exhausted. Mitya rushed towards her, snatched her in his arms, and bundled his precious burden behind the curtains. 'Well, it's time I was off,' thought Kalganov, and, stepping out of the blue room, closed both panels of the double doors behind him. But the party in the big room continued unabated. Mitya laid Grushenka on the bed and pressed his lips to hers in a deep kiss.

'Don't touch me...', she whispered in a suppliant voice, 'don't touch me just yet... I told you I was yours, so don't touch me... have pity... Not with them there, we mustn't while they're still around. And him. It's horrible here...'

'Just as you say! I wouldn't think of it... I adore you...', mumbled Mitya. 'Yes, it's horrible here, oh, it's vile.' And, without releasing his hold on her, he sank down on his knees beside the bed.

'I know you're a wild one, but you're noble with it,' Grushenka said with effort, 'we mustn't spoil it... from now on, everything will be decent... we too must be decent, we too must be good, not like animals, but good... Take me away, take me far away, do you hear me?... I want you to take me away from here, far, far away...'

'Oh yes, of course, of course!' Mitya clutched her in his arms. 'I'll take you away, we'll fly away... Oh, I'd give my whole life for just one year with you, if only I knew what to do about the blood!'

'What blood?' Grushenka echoed in consternation.

'Never mind!' said Mitya through clenched teeth. 'Grusha, you're asking for decency, but I'm a thief. I've stolen money from Katka... I'm so ashamed, so ashamed!'

'From Katka? You mean from the young lady? No, of course you haven't stolen it. Give it back to her, I'll give you the money... What are you on about! All that's mine is yours now. What's money to us? We'd blow it anyway... that's for sure! We can always go and work on the land. I want to work the soil with these bare hands of mine. We must toil away, do you hear me? Those were Alyosha's orders. I shan't just be your mistress, I'll be faithful to you, I'll be your slave, I'll work for you. We'll go to the young lady and we'll both beg forgiveness, and then we'll go away. And if she won't forgive us, we'll go away all the same. So you just return the money to her, and give your love to me... Don't you give it to her. You mustn't love her any more. If you fall in love with her, I'll strangle her... I'll poke both her eyes out with a needle...'

'I love you, no one but you, I'll love you even in Siberia...'

'Why Siberia? All right, in Siberia too if you wish, it makes no difference... we'll work... there's snow in Siberia... I love riding in the snow... and there must be a bell... Listen, can you hear a bell tinkling?... Where's that tinkling coming from? Someone's coming... there, the tinkling's stopped.'

She shut her eyes in exhaustion, and seemed suddenly to drop off to sleep for a second. A bell really did tinkle somewhere in the distance, and then suddenly stopped. Mitya rested his head on her bosom. He did not notice when the sound of the bell stopped, nor did he notice that the singing too had ceased abruptly, and that instead of the drunken shouting a deathly silence had suddenly descended upon the whole house. Grushenka opened her eyes.

'What's going on, I must have fallen asleep? Yes... the bell... I slept and had a dream: I was riding in the snow... the bell kept tinkling, but I was asleep. I was with my beloved, I was with you. And a long way away... I had my arms around you, I was hugging and kissing you, but still I was cold, in the glittering snow... Do you know, when the snow glitters at night, and the moon is shining, and it feels like you're no longer on this earth... I woke up, and there was my beloved close by, how lovely...'

'Close by,' mumbled Mitya, kissing her dress, her bosom, her hands. And suddenly he felt something strange: he had the impression that she was looking straight past him—not at him, not into his face—but over his shoulder, fixedly and with a strange immobility. Her face suddenly registered surprise, almost fear.

'Mitya,' she whispered, 'who's that over there, looking at us?' Mitya turned and saw that someone had indeed pulled the curtains aside and appeared to be staring at them. And there seemed to be others there, too. He leapt to his feet and strode quickly towards the onlooker.

'This way, if you please, over here,' the voice spoke softly, but firmly and insistently.

Mitya stepped out from behind the curtain and stood stock-still. The whole room was full of people, not those who had been there before, but newcomers, people he had not seen there earlier. A momentary shiver ran down his spine, and he shuddered. He recognized them all in a flash. That tall, pale-looking old man in the coat with the cockade on his cap was Mikhail Makarych, the chief of police. And that consumptive-looking, fastidious dandy—'his boots are always polished to a deep shine'—was the assistant public prosecutor. 'He's got a watch worth four hundred roubles, he showed it to me once.' And that young fellow in the spectacles... His name was on the tip of Mitya's tongue, he knew him, he had seen him before: it was the investigative magistrate, just out of law school. That one over there, that was the district police officer, Mavriky Mavrikych, there was no mistaking him, Mitya knew him well. And what about those men with the badges, what were they doing here? And the two strangers, they were just a couple of peasants... And over in the doorway stood Kalganov and Trifon Borisych...

'Gentlemen... What is it, gentlemen?' began Mitya and, beside himself with panic, he suddenly yelled out at the top of his voice: 'I understand!'

The bespectacled young man pressed forward and, stepping up to Mitya, began in a dignified, though not altogether steady voice:

'We are charged... in a word, would you step this way, that's right, to the settee... We must seek an explanation from you urgently.'

'The old man!' yelled Mitya in a frenzy. 'The old man's blood!... I understand!'

And he collapsed, as if poleaxed, on a nearby chair.

'You understand? So he understands!' yelled the old chief of police, confronting Mitya. 'Murderer, fiend, your father's blood cries out against you!' He was beside himself, shaking all over, his face crimson.

'That's out of order!' interjected the short-statured young man. 'Mikhail Makarych, Mikhail Makarych! That's out of order, you shouldn't!... If you don't mind, I'll do the speaking, no one else... You realize this is highly irregular...'

'But gentlemen, this is unbelievable, absolutely unbelievable!' the chief of police persisted, 'just look at him: blind drunk, with a loose woman, in the middle of the night, and all the while his own father's blood is on his hands... Absolutely unbelievable!'

'I insist, my dear Mikhail Makarych, that you control yourself at once,' the assistant prosecutor hissed, 'or I shall be forced to take...'

But the little examining magistrate did not allow him to finish; he turned to Mitya and addressed him in a firm, loud, and grave voice:

'Ex-Lieutenant Karamazov, I must inform you, sir, that you are hereby charged with the murder of your father Fyodor Pavlovich Karamazov, last night...'

He went on to say something else, the prosecutor also appeared to add something, but, though Mitya was listening, he no longer understood anything. He was staring at everyone in wild-eyed consternation...

BOOK NINE

*Judicial Investigation**

1

THE BEGINNING OF CIVIL SERVANT
PERKHOTIN'S CAREER

PYOTR ILYICH PERKHOTIN, whom we left banging with all his might on the stout, firmly locked gate of the house of merchant Morozov's widow was, needless to say, finally admitted. On hearing such frantic banging at the gate, Fenya, who had been so frightened some two hours before and who was still too upset and bewildered to go to bed, found herself scared out of her wits once more, imagining (in spite of the fact that she herself had seen him leave) that it was Dmitry Fyodorovich again, for he alone was capable of raising such a din. She rushed to the janitor, who had now woken up and was already on his way to the gate to investigate the noise, and begged him not to let him in. But the janitor, after questioning the visitor and discovering who he was and that he wished to see Fedosya Markovna on a very urgent matter, finally agreed to open up. On entering Fedosya Markovna's kitchen, Pyotr Ilyich, followed by the janitor, whom Fenya, with Pyotr Ilyich's permission, had requested to be present 'just in case', began to question her and in no time at all established the salient facts, which were that Dmitry Fyodorovich, rushing out to look for Grushenka, had picked up the pestle from the mortar and had returned without it, his hands covered in blood: 'His hands were simply dripping with blood,' Fenya kept exclaiming, 'just dripping!' her disturbed imagination having apparently furnished this horrific detail. Pyotr Ilyich himself had seen those hands, bloodstained though not actually dripping with blood, and had helped to wash them, but the point was not how quickly the blood had dried, but where Dmitry Fyodorovich had rushed off to with the pestle, that is, whether he really had gone to Fyodor Pavlovich's, and why everyone had leapt to that conclusion with such certainty. Pyotr Ilyich kept insisting doggedly on this point, and though he found out nothing definite, he was nevertheless forced to admit that the only place Dmitry Fyodorovich could have run to was his father's house, and that it was precisely there that *something* must surely have occurred. 'And when he came back', Fenya added excitedly, 'he made me tell him everything, and then I asked him: my dear Dmitry Fyodorovich, why are your hands covered in blood?' Apparently he then came straight out with it, that it was blood—human blood—and that he had just killed a man; that's right, he admitted it, he confessed everything to me on the spot, and after that he suddenly ran off, like he was demented. So I sat myself down and I thought, where could he have run off to in that state? He'll go to Mokroye, I thought to myself, and he'll kill my young lady. So I dashed out and went straight to his lodgings to beg him not to kill her, but on my way past Plotnikov's store, I saw him drive off, and there wasn't any blood on his hands then.' (Fenya had noticed this fact and remembered it.) As far as she could, her old grandmother supported her statements. After questioning her a little further, Pyotr Ilyich left the house even more disturbed and puzzled than when he had entered it.

One would have thought that the most obvious thing for Pyotr Ilyich to do now would have been to go to Fyodor Pavlovich's house to find out if anything had happened and, if so, what, and then to go to the chief of police only when he was sure of his facts, which indeed is what he proposed to do. However, the night was dark, Fyodor Pavlovich's gate was very sturdy and he would have to start banging again, and, moreover, as he was only slightly acquainted with Fyodor Pavlovich, what if someone heard him and let him in, and it finally transpired that nothing had happened: would not the sneering Fyodor Pavlovich go round the town the next day, describing how the civil servant Perkhotin, almost a total stranger, had forcibly attempted to enter his house late at night in order to find out if anybody had killed him? That would be a scandal! And there was nothing in the world that Pyotr Ilyich feared more than a scandal. Nevertheless, the feeling that gripped him was so strong that, cursing once more and stamping angrily, he immediately set off again, but for Mrs Khokhlakova's rather than Fyodor Pavlovich's. If, he thought, she denied giving Dmitry Fyodorovich three thousand roubles that evening, at such-and-such a time, he would go to the chief of police immediately, without calling on Fyodor Pavlovich; if, however, she confirmed that she had given him the money, he would put everything off till tomorrow and go home. It is quite clear at this point, of course, that the young man's decision to go, at almost eleven o'clock at night, to the house of a respectable, completely unknown lady, and perhaps get her out of bed merely in order to ask her such a bizarre question was in itself more likely to lead to a scandal than if he had gone to Fyodor Pavlovich's. But this is sometimes the case, particularly in circumstances such as this, with decisions made by even the most calculating and phlegmatic of people. And Pyotr Ilyich was anything but phlegmatic at that moment! All his life he was to remember the persistent anxiety which gradually welled up inside him until, eventually, it reached an unbearable pitch, urging him on even against his will. All the same, he kept cursing himself all the way to the house, but 'I'll get to the bottom of this, I will, I will!' he repeated over and over, grinding his teeth, and he did get to the bottom of it—indeed he did.

It was exactly eleven o'clock when he reached Mrs Khokhlakova's house. He was let into the yard fairly promptly, but when he enquired whether the lady had already retired for the night, the janitor was unable to give a precise answer, only that she usually retired at about that time. 'Go upstairs and announce yourself; if she's prepared to see you, she will, if she's not—she won't.' Pyotr Ilyich went upstairs, but there he encountered an unexpected difficulty. The butler refused to announce him and finally summoned a maid. Pyotr Ilyich firmly but very politely asked her to notify the lady that a local official, Perkhotin, had come about an important matter, and that were the matter not so important he would never have presumed to come—'be sure to use those words exactly,' he instructed the girl. She went away. He waited in the entrance hall. Mrs Khokhlakova herself, although she had not yet retired for the night, was already in her bedroom. Ever since Mitya's visit she had been very upset and she already knew that tonight she would have one of her migraine attacks, which usually occurred on such occasions. She listened in vexed bewilderment to the girl's announcement and instructed her to ask him to leave, although an unexpected visit by a mysterious town clerk at such an hour was highly intriguing to her feminine curiosity. This time, however, Pyotr Ilyich turned out to be as stubborn as a mule; having been told that she would not see him, he demanded to be announced once more, and that the maid should tell her 'in exactly these words' that he had come 'about a very urgent matter, and the lady might regret it later if she doesn't agree to see me'. 'I felt I was being swept along,' he recounted later. The maid looked at him in astonishment, and went to announce him the second time. Mrs Khokhlakova was flabbergasted, she thought awhile, asked what he looked like, and was informed that he was 'very properly dressed, young, and ever so polite'. Let us add here, incidentally, that Pyotr Ilyich was quite a handsome young man and was well aware of this himself. Mrs Khokhlakova decided to see him. She was in her dressing-gown and slippers, but had wrapped a black shawl round her shoulders. The clerk was shown into the same drawing-room in which Mitya had been received earlier that day. The lady of the house came to meet her visitor with an imperious and stern air, and, without offering him a seat, came straight to the point: 'What can I do for you?'

'I have taken the liberty of disturbing you, madam, to ask you about something concerning our mutual acquaintance Dmitry Fyodorovich Karamazov,' began Perkhotin, but no sooner had he uttered that name than the lady's face registered total exasperation. She let out a near shriek and interrupted him angrily.

'How long have I got to put up with being plagued by that awful man?' she yelled furiously. 'How dare you, my dear sir, what right have you to disturb a lady with whom you are not acquainted, in her own house, at such an hour... and to come to speak to her about a person who, on this very spot, in this very room, barely three hours ago, having come to kill me, stamped his feet and departed in a manner that is simply unbecoming in a visitor to a respectable house! You might as well know, sir, that I shall lodge a complaint against you, I shall not let this pass,

please leave at once... I am a mother, I shall, this instant... I...
I...'

'Kill you! So he wanted to kill you, too?'

'Has he killed someone already then?' asked Mrs Khokhlakova
eagerly.

'Have the kindness to hear me out, my lady,' Perkhotin replied
firmly, 'allow me half a minute, and I shall explain everything as
briefly as possible. Today, at five o'clock in the afternoon, Mr
Karamazov borrowed ten roubles from me as a friend, and I
know for a fact that he had no money then, but later, at nine
o'clock, he came to my room clutching a wad of hundred-rouble
notes, two or even three thousand roubles in all. His face and
hands were covered in blood and he seemed quite demented. In
reply to my question as to where he had got so much money, he
replied very distinctly that you had given it to him a short time
before, and that in fact you had loaned him a sum of three
thousand, apparently on condition that he would go prospecting
for gold...'

Mrs Khokhlakova's face suddenly registered the utmost panic.

'God! He's killed his old father!' she exclaimed, clasping her
hands. 'I did not give him any money, none at all! Oh, hurry,
hurry!... Don't say another word! Run and save the old man, run
to his father, quickly!'

'Just a minute, madam. So, you didn't give him any money?
You distinctly remember that you didn't give him any money at
all?'

'I did not, I did not! I refused, because it would have been
wasted on him. He stamped his feet and left in a fit of rage. He
tried to attack me, and I had to take evasive action... And I'll tell
you something else, too, seeing as you're the type of person I
wouldn't want to hide anything from—he even spat at me, can
you imagine? Well, don't just stand there! Oh, do sit down... I
do apologize, I... Better still, hurry, hurry, you must run and save
that unfortunate old man from a terrible death!'

'But what if he's already killed him?'

'Oh my God, of course! So what are we going to do now?
What do you think, what should we do now?'

Having got Pyotr Ilyich to sit down, she herself sat down

opposite him. Pyotr Ilyich gave her a brief but fairly lucid account of the day's events, at least of those events which he himself had witnessed, and he also recounted the story of his visit to Fenya and what she had said about the pestle. All these details unbalanced the impressionable woman completely, who kept crying out and covering her eyes with her hands...

'Imagine, I anticipated it all! I have this gift: whatever I anticipate, inevitably happens. How many, many times have I looked at that abominable man and thought: here's someone who'll end up murdering me. And that's just what happened... If he didn't murder me on this occasion, but merely his father, that's probably because the hand of God is in all this, protecting me; anyway, he'd probably be ashamed to murder me, because I personally, on this very spot, hung around his neck a locket containing a relic of St Varvara, the martyr... And how close I was to death at that moment, I went right up to him, right up close to him, and he stretched his neck right out for me! Do you know, Pyotr Ilyich (I'm sorry, you did say your name was Pyotr Ilyich, didn't you?)... do you know, I don't really believe in miracles, but that little locket and now this undoubted miracle—my miraculous escape—has had a profound effect upon me, and now I'm ready to believe absolutely anything again. Have you heard about Starets Zosima?... Look, I don't really know what I'm talking about... Do you realize, he already had the locket round his neck when he spat at me... only spat, of course, didn't actually kill me, and... so that's where he rushed off to! But what about us, what should we do now, what do you think?'

Pyotr Ilyich stood up and announced that he would go straight to the chief of police and tell him everything; he would know what to do.

'Oh, I know Mikhail Makarovich, such a wonderful, wonderful man! You really must go to him, not to anyone else. You're so resourceful, Pyotr Ilyich, you've really handled the situation so well; you know, if I'd been in your place, I'd never have come up with such a marvellous idea!'

'As a matter of fact, the chief of police is a very good acquaintance of mine too,' observed Pyotr Ilyich, still standing there and obviously quite anxious to escape from this enthusiastic lady who simply would not let him make his farewells and depart.

'And you know,' she rambled on, 'you must come back and tell me what you find out and what's going on... what they decide to do with him and what sentence he'll get. By the way, capital punishment has been abolished, hasn't it? But you must definitely come back, even if it's three o'clock in the morning, or four, even half past four... If I'm not up, tell them to rouse me, shake me if need be... Oh God, I'll never be able to sleep tonight. Look here, perhaps I should go with you?...'

'N-no madam, but if you were to put something down in writing, just in case, saying that you didn't give Dmitry Fyodorovich any money, that might come in handy... you never know...'

'Gladly!' Mrs Khokhlakova rushed to her bureau in excitement. 'You know, I can't stop marvelling at you, you simply astound me with your resourcefulness and your experience in such matters... Do you work locally? How nice it is to hear that you work locally...'

And without so much as a pause for breath, she quickly scribbled the following few lines in a firm hand on half a sheet of writing paper:

I have never in my life loaned three thousand roubles to the unfortunate Dmitry Fyodorovich (he is, despite everything, unfortunate) today, nor any other monies, ever! So help me God.

Khokhlakova

'Here's the note!' she turned quickly towards Pyotr Ilyich. 'See what you can do to help him. It will be an honourable deed on your part.'

And she made the sign of the cross over him three times. She even rushed out into the hall to see him to the door.

'I'm so grateful to you. You won't believe how grateful I am to you for coming to me first. How is it we've never met before? I should be most flattered to welcome you in my house in future. It really is nice to hear that you work locally... such attention to detail, such resourcefulness... You must be in great demand, surely they can't fail to appreciate you, and if I can be of any service to you, believe me... Oh, I love the younger generation so much! I do love the younger generation. The young people—they are the cornerstone of the whole of our long-suffering modern Russia, they are its only hope... Oh, hurry, do hurry!...'

But Pyotr Ilyich was already on his way out, otherwise she might have detained him even longer. On the whole, however, Mrs Khokhlakova had made rather a favourable impression upon him, and this even helped to alleviate his disquiet about his involvement in the wretched business. There is no accounting for tastes; that is well known. 'She really doesn't look all that old,' he thought with gratification, 'on the contrary, I'd have taken her for her daughter.'

As for Mrs Khokhlakova, she was simply charmed by the young man. 'Such aptitude, such scrupulousness, and in one so young, so unexpected nowadays, and all this along with such manners and such a pleasing appearance. Young people nowadays are said to be quite ignorant, but you can't say that about him, can you?' and so on and so forth. As for the 'dreadful incident' itself, she nearly forgot about it, and it was only as she was about to retire that she suddenly remembered how 'close to death' she had been. 'Oh, but this is dreadful!' she said, and immediately fell into a deep and most satisfying sleep. To be sure, I would never have dwelt on such trivial and episodic details had not this bizarre meeting between the meticulous and scrupulous young man and the far from old widow subsequently set the seal on the young man's entire career, a fact that is remembered in our small town to this day, and to which we ourselves may return, perhaps, especially once we have completed our protracted story of the Karamazov brothers.

2

ALARM

OUR chief of police, Mikhail Makarovich Makarov, a retired Lieutenant-Colonel who on retirement had been given an equivalent rank in the police, was a widower and by nature a kindly person. He had arrived in our town only three years before, but had already managed to win universal approbation, mainly because of his 'knack of bringing people together'. He was always entertaining guests, and seemed unable to do without them. As a rule he would always have some people, even if only one or two, to dinner, and would never dine without some guest or other. He also held formal dinner-parties on various, sometimes quite unexpected pretexts. The food served was plentiful, if not particularly choice, though the *koulibiaca*, for example, was excellent, and as for the wine, that too made up in quantity what it lacked in quality. A billiard-table stood in the large entrance hall, which was very well appointed, even down to the prints of English racehorses in dark wooden frames on the walls, an essential accoutrement of any bachelor's games room. They would play cards every evening, even if only at one table. But the smart society of our town, husbands accompanied by their wives and daughters, would frequently gather there to dance the hours away. Although Mikhail Makarych was a widower he nevertheless enjoyed a family life, for his daughter, also long-since widowed and the mother of two girls, his granddaughters, still lived with him. The granddaughters, who were already grown up and had completed their education, were of a cheerful disposition and not unattractive, and although it was common knowledge that they would not receive any dowry, the most eligible of our young men still flocked to their grandfather's house. Mikhail Makarovich was not particularly astute as regards his work, though he performed his duties as conscientiously as the next man. If the truth be known, he was somewhat uneducated and was even rather cavalier in the precise interpretation of the limits of his administrative authority. At times he made some glaring errors in the interpretation of certain reforms introduced by the Tsar, not because he was unable to comprehend them fully, or because of any particular lack of ability, but simply because of his innate irresponsibility, always blaming insufficient time to study them in depth. 'Deep down, gentlemen, I'm more of a military man than a civilian,' he would say about himself. It would appear that he had not even formulated a precise and firm view as regards the fundamental provisions of the peasant reforms, and used to obtain his information, as it were, piecemeal, picking it up involuntarily as he went along, in spite of being a landowner himself. Pyotr Ilyich was sure that he would meet some guests at Mikhail Makarovich's that evening, but he did not know exactly who. Meanwhile, at Mikhail Makarovich's, the public prosecutor and the local doctor, Varvinsky, a young man newly arrived from St Petersburg, one of a number of brilliant graduates from the St Petersburg Medical School, were at that precise moment playing *yeralash*.* Ippolit Kyrillovich, the prosecutor, actually the deputy prosecutor, but referred to as the prosecutor by everyone in the town, was, it must be owned, an unusual character, still relatively young, about thirty-five at most, but consumptive and married to a very fat, childless woman. By nature proud and irritable, he nevertheless had a good mind and a kind heart. It would appear that his basic trouble stemmed from the fact that he thought rather more of himself than his true worth warranted. That is why he always seemed ill at ease. On top of everything, he entertained certain rather lofty and even artistic pretensions, for example in the field of psychology, claiming to possess special insights into the human soul and, in particular, an understanding of the criminal and his actions. In this regard he believed he had been ignored and passed over for promotion, and was quite convinced that he had enemies and that his superiors had failed to recognize his abilities. In moments of deepest despair he had even threatened to change sides and become a defence counsel. The unexpected Karamazov patricide case seemed to shake him to the core: 'The Karamazov case could become a *cause célèbre* throughout Russia!' But I anticipate.

In the neighbouring room with the young ladies sat our young investigative magistrate, Nikolai Parfenovich Nelyudov, who had arrived only two months before from St Petersburg. People subsequently remarked in astonishment that, on the very evening of the crime, so many had gathered at the house of the upholder of law and order, as if by prior arrangement. In actual fact, however, there was a much simpler explanation; everything had occurred perfectly spontaneously: Ippolit Kyrillovich's spouse had been suffering from toothache for two days, and he just had to escape from her groans somewhere; as for the doctor, he was the sort of person who could not spend his evenings any other way than playing cards. For some three days Nikolai Parfenovich Nelyudov had been planning to appear, as if fortuitously, at Mikhail Makarovich's that evening in order 'naughtily' and unexpectedly to astonish the elder granddaughter, Olga Mikhai-lovna, by disclosing that he was privy to her secret and knew it was her birthday, and that she had deliberately concealed this fact so as not to have to invite the whole town to the celebrations. He anticipated a great deal of laughter and allusions to her age, which she was apparently anxious to conceal, and to the fact that he was in possession of her secret now and would tell everyone about it tomorrow, and so on and so forth. This amiable young man was given to practical jokes, and our ladies had actually nicknamed him 'the prankster', which seemed to please him no end. It has to be said that he was from a good family and society, well brought up and of refined sensibility, and even if he was inclined to levity it was all quite innocent and proper. In stature he was short and of small and delicate build. Several unusually large rings always sparkled on his thin, pale fingers. However, when it came to the performance of his duties he would exhibit an extraordinary pomposity and a wellnigh sacred regard for his own importance and duties. During cross-examination he was particularly adept at uncovering murderers and other criminals of the peasant class, and he really did evoke in them if not respect, then at least a certain sense of awe.

When he entered the house of the chief of police, Pyotr Ilyich was simply astounded: he realized immediately that everyone already knew what had happened. And, true enough, no one was playing cards any more, everyone was standing around busily conferring, and even Nikolai Parfenovich had left the ladies in a hurry and looked full of energy and resolve. Pyotr Ilyich was greeted by the astonishing news that the elderly Fyodor Pavlovich really had been murdered that very evening—murdered and robbed. It had all come to light just a little while before and in the following manner.

Marfa Ignatyevna, whose husband Grigory had been struck down by the garden fence, was sleeping soundly in her bed and would have continued thus till morning had not something suddenly woken her up. What had woken her was the terrible epileptic scream emitted by Smerdyakov, who was lying unconscious in the adjacent room—that scream with which Smerdyakov's fits always began and which always wrought such terror in Marfa Ignatyevna and had such a frightening effect upon her. She could never get used to it. Still half asleep, she rushed headlong into Smerdyakov's cubby-hole. But it was dark there, and all she could hear was the sick man thrashing about violently and groaning. Marfa Ignatyevna herself let out a cry and was about to call her husband, but she suddenly realized that when she had stumbled out of bed Grigory had not seemed to be there. She rushed back to the bed and felt all over it, but it was completely empty. He must have gone out, but where? She ran out on to the steps and called him softly. Needless to say there was no reply, but in the silence of the night she heard some groans coming from the depths of the garden. She pricked up her ears; the groans were repeated, and it was clear now that they really were coming from the garden. The thought flashed through her poor head, 'Lord, this is just like the other time with Lizaveta Smerdyashchaya!' She descended the steps gingerly, and discovered that the garden gate was open. 'The poor dear must be there,' she thought. She approached the gate, and suddenly she distinctly heard Grigory calling her: 'Marfa, Marfa!' came his voice, weak, groaning, and terrible. 'Lord, have mercy on us,' whispered Marfa Ignatyevna, and rushed towards the beckoning voice, and that was how she found Grigory. She discovered him not by the fence, not where he had been struck down, but about twenty paces from the fence. Later it transpired that, having regained consciousness, he had begun to crawl and in all probability had crawled for a long time, fainting several times along the way. Noticing immediately that he was covered in blood, she let out an almighty cry. Grigory kept on mumbling softly and incoherently: 'He's killed him... he's killed his father, stop yelling, you stupid woman... hurry, call...' But Marfa Ignatyevna would not calm down and went on shrieking, then suddenly, noticing that her master's window was open and that there was a light in the window, she ran towards it and began to call Fyodor Pavlovich. But when she peered through the window, she beheld a ghastly sight; her master was lying flat on his back, motionless. His light-coloured dressing-gown and shirt-front were stained with blood. The candle on the table shone brightly on the blood and on Fyodor Pavlovich's lifeless face. In a state of absolute panic Marfa Ignatyevna recoiled from the window, dashed through the garden, unbolted the main gate and, like one possessed, ran along the back alleys to her neighbour, Marya Kondratyevna. The two neighbours, mother and daughter, had already retired for the night, but on hearing Marfa

Ignatyevna's cries and her relentless, frenzied banging on the shutters they woke up and rushed to the window. Marfa Ignatyevna, screaming and crying, managed to convey incoherently the gist of what had happened and to ask for help. It so happened that the vagrant Foma was staying with them that very night. They woke him up in a trice, and all three of them dashed back to the scene of the crime. On the way Marya Kondratyevna recalled that earlier on, between eight and nine, she had heard a terrible, ear-splitting shriek coming from their garden, loud enough to wake the dead—that was the howl that Grigory had let out when Dmitry Fyodorovich was already astride the fence and he had clung to his foot and shouted, 'Murderer!' 'Someone yelled out and then it stopped,' recounted Marya Kondratyevna as they hurried along. When they reached the spot where Grigory was lying, the women, with Foma's help, carried him into the outhouse. They struck a light and noticed that Smerdyakov's fit was not yet over, that he was still flailing about in his cubbyhole, his eyes rolling, and foaming at the mouth. They sponged Grigory's head with water and vinegar; this revived him, and he immediately asked: 'Has the master been killed?' The two women and Foma then rushed to the master and, on entering the garden, they now noticed that not only the window, but also the door to the garden was wide open, despite the fact that the master himself had locked it regularly every night for the past week, and that not even Grigory had been allowed to knock on it under any circumstances after that. Seeing the open door, they all, the two women and Foma, were afraid to enter the house, 'just in case there are complications later'. When they returned, Grigory urged them to hurry immediately to the chief of police. That was when Marya Kondratyevna ran to the house of the chief of police and caused general consternation. She arrived only five minutes before Pyotr Ilyich, so the latter came as a corroborative witness, whose account, far from being a mere collection of assumptions and conclusions, confirmed all the more strongly the general opinion as to the identity of the criminal (something that he himself, in his heart of hearts, right up to this very last moment, had steadfastly refused to believe).

It was decided to take prompt action. The assistant chief of the local police was immediately instructed to summon four independent observers.* This he did, and then, in accordance with all the prescribed regulations, which I shall not describe here, they gained access to Fyodor Pavlovich's house and carried out an investigation on the spot. The keen, newly qualified doctor insisted on accompanying the chief of police, the prosecutor, and the investigative magistrate. I shall be brief: Fyodor Pavlovich had been killed outright, his skull had been fractured, but with what? Very likely the same weapon with which Grigory had subsequently been struck down. And it was not long before they found the weapon, for Grigory, who had been given all possible medical treatment, had given a faltering but fairly rational account of how he had been struck down. They went out with a lighted lantern to look for it near the fence, and discovered the brass pestle lying right there, on the garden footpath, for all to see. There were no particular signs of disturbance in the room where Fyodor Pavlovich's body was lying, although behind the curtains, by his bed, they picked up a large, stiff, business envelope with the inscription: 'A little present of three thousand roubles for my angel Grushenka, if she feels inclined to come to me,' and underneath it had been added, probably subsequently by Fyodor Pavlovich himself: 'for my chicky-bird'. The envelope bore three large red seals, but it had been torn open and was empty: the money had gone. They also found on the floor the thin, pink ribbon that had been used to tie the envelope. One thing struck the prosecutor and the investigative magistrate as particularly significant in Pyotr Ilyich's statements, namely that the latter believed Dmitry Fyodorovich would shoot himself before dawn—that he had resolved to do so, had said as much to Pyotr Ilyich himself, had loaded the gun in his presence, had written a note, had stuck it in his pocket, and so on and so forth. And when Pyotr Ilyich, unwilling to believe him, had nevertheless threatened to go and tell someone in order to prevent him committing suicide, Mitya had rounded on him and said: 'You won't have time.' Consequently, it was necessary to hurry to Mokroye to apprehend the criminal before he really did decide to shoot himself. 'It's obvious, it's clear what happened!' the prosecutor reiterated in a pitch of excitement, 'that's just what you'd expect of a hothead like him: I'll kill myself tomorrow, but before I die, I'm going to paint the town red.' The account of how Mitya had stocked up with wine and provisions at the store only reinforced the prosecutor's conviction. 'You remember, gentlemen, that fellow who killed the merchant Olsufyev, robbed him of fifteen hundred roubles, went straight off to have his hair curled and then, not even attempting to conceal the money, holding it almost brazenly in his hands, set off for the brothel.' What delayed them, however, was the search of Fyodor Pavlovich's house, the routine formalities, and so on. All this took time, which is why, about two hours before their own departure for Mokroye, they sent on ahead the district police officer, Mavriky Mavrikyevich Schmerzov, who, as it transpired, had arrived in the town that very morning to collect his salary. Mavriky Mavrikyevich was instructed that when he arrived in Mokroye, he should, without raising any suspicion, keep a constant surveillance on 'the criminal' until the arrival of the appropriate authorities, and also assemble some independent observers, alert the local police, and so on and so forth. Mavriky Mavrikyevich did in fact do just that; he kept the purpose of his arrival secret, and only partially confided in Trifon Borisych, who was an old acquaintance of his. This was shortly before Mitya had encountered the landlord in the dark of the gallery and had immediately noticed a sudden change in his voice and face. Consequently, neither Mitya nor anyone else realized that he was being observed, and as for the case containing the pistols, Trifon Borisych had removed it well before and hidden it in a safe place. It was not until four o'clock in the morning, nearly dawn, that the chief of police, the prosecutor, and the investigative magistrate arrived in two separate carriages pulled by two troikas. The doctor had stayed behind at Fyodor Pavlovich's in order to carry out a post-mortem on the body of the murdered man the next morning; what particularly interested him was the condition of the sick servant Smerdyakov: 'Such severe and prolonged attacks of epilepsy, occurring repeatedly over some forty-eight hours, are seldom encountered and are a clinical rarity,' he said in great excitement to his departing colleagues, who laughed and congratulated him on his findings. The prosecutor and investigative magistrate, incidentally, took note of the fact that the doctor was sure that Smerdyakov would not live to see the morning.

Now, after a long but seemingly necessary explanation, we shall return to that point in our story where we left off at the end of the preceding book.

3

A SOUL'S JOURNEY THROUGH TORMENTS.*
FIRST TORMENT

AND so Mitya sat and stared at them wild-eyed, without comprehending what was being said to him. Suddenly he jumped to his feet, raised his arms, and cried out loudly:

'Not guilty! I'm not guilty of shedding his blood! I didn't kill him... I wanted to, but I didn't! It wasn't me!'

But no sooner had he finished than Grushenka dashed out from behind the curtain and collapsed in a heap at the feet of the chief of police.

'It was me, it was me, miserable wretch that I am, I'm the guilty one!' she cried with a heart-rending wail, tears streaming down her face, her arms outstretched to them all, 'it was because of me he killed him!... I was the one who tortured him and drove him to it! I tormented the poor old man as well, God rest his soul, out of spite. I'm the one who's responsible! I'm the guilty one, I started it, I'm the culprit, I'm to blame!'

'Yes, you are the guilty one!' yelled the chief of police, shaking his fist at her. 'You're the real criminal! You're the evil woman, you're a harlot, you're the principal culprit,' but he was promptly and unceremoniously silenced. The prosecutor even had to restrain him physically.

'This is totally out of order, Mikhail Makarovich,' he shouted, almost out of breath. 'You're deliberately interfering in the investigation... you'll disrupt everything...'

'We must go by the book, we really must, we must stick to the rules!' Nikolai Parfenovich too began to fuss, 'otherwise it's just impossible!...'

'Put us both on trial!' Grushenka continued frantically, still on her knees. 'Sentence us together, I'll go with him even to the scaffold!'

'Grusha, my dear heart, my darling, my precious one!' Mitya fell to his knees beside her, and clasped her tightly in his arms. 'Don't believe her,' he cried, 'she's not guilty of anything, neither of anyone's blood nor of anything at all!'

Later he recalled that several people dragged him forcibly away from her, that she was immediately escorted from the room, and that he then found himself seated at the table. Beside and behind him stood men in uniform with brass badges. The investigative magistrate, Nikolai Parfenovich, was sitting on a divan across the table from him and was trying to persuade him to have a drink of water from a glass that stood on the table. 'It'll refresh you, it'll calm you down, don't be afraid, don't worry,' he kept repeating with the utmost courtesy. Mitya, however, as he himself recalled later, was totally fascinated by his large rings, one of which contained an amethyst, and the other a bright yellow, very clear stone, which sparkled brilliantly. A long time thereafter he remembered with astonishment how irresistibly his gaze had been drawn to these rings throughout the dreadful hours of the interrogation, and that for some reason he had been quite unable to tear his eyes away from them and ignore them, objects which had no connection whatever with his present plight. The prosecutor now sat down on Mitya's left where Maksimov had sat the night before, while the place to Mitya's right, where Grushenka had been sitting then, was occupied by a rosy-cheeked young man wearing a kind of hunter's jacket that had seen better days, and before whom an inkstand and paper had suddenly materialized. It turned out that he was the magistrate's official clerk, whom the latter had brought with him. The chief of police was standing by the window at the far end of the room now, next to Kalganov, who had settled himself down on a chair by the same window.

'Have a drink of water!' repeated the investigator softly, for the umpteenth time.

'I've had some, gentlemen... but... well then, gentlemen, get on with it, sentence me, decide my fate!' burst out Mitya, staring at the magistrate with a blank, eerily immobile gaze.

'So you positively maintain that you are not guilty of your father's, Fyodor Pavlovich's, death?' asked the magistrate softly, but firmly.

'No! I'm guilty of shedding someone else's blood, the blood of another old man, but not my father's. And I'm full of remorse! I killed him, I killed the old man, I struck him down and killed him... But it's unjust that I should have to pay for his blood with someone else's blood, with the dreadful blood I didn't shed... It's a preposterous accusation, gentlemen, like a bolt from the blue! But who on earth could have murdered my father, who did it? Who could have murdered him, if I didn't? It's a mystery, it's preposterous, it's inconceivable!...'

'Yes, I wonder who could have murdered him...', began the magistrate, but the prosecutor, Ippolit Kyrillovich (he was the assistant prosecutor, but for brevity we shall refer to him as the prosecutor), having exchanged glances with the magistrate, observed, turning to Mitya:

'You needn't worry yourself about the old servant Grigory Vasilyev. For your information he's alive and has regained consciousness in spite of the heavy blows which, according to his and your own testimony, you inflicted upon him, and it looks as if he's going to survive, or so the doctor says anyway.'

'He's alive? So he's alive!' Mitya cried out suddenly, clasping his hands. His whole face lit up. 'God, I thank You for this, the greatest of miracles, which You have performed for me, an evil-doer and a sinner, in answer to my prayers!... Yes, yes, in answer to my prayers, I prayed all night!...' and he crossed himself three times. He was quite breathless.

'Well, Grigory has supplied us with evidence about you which is so significant that...', began the prosecutor, but Mitya suddenly leapt up from his chair.

'Just a second, gentlemen, for God's sake, just a second, let me quickly run out and see her...'

'Certainly not! At this present moment it's simply out of the question!' Nikolai Parfenovich, also leaping to his feet, almost shrieked. Mitya was seized by the men wearing the badges, but sat down again of his own accord...

'What a pity, gentlemen! I just wanted to see her for an instant... I wanted to let her know that it's been washed off, the blood that's been tormenting my heart the whole night through has gone, I'm no longer a murderer! Gentlemen, do you realize, she's my fiancée!' he said exultantly and reverentially, looking at everyone in turn. 'Oh, I thank you, gentlemen! You've given me a new lease of life, you've resurrected me just like that!... That old man—do you realize he carried me in his arms, gentlemen, he bathed me in a trough, after everyone had abandoned me at the age of three, he was like a true father to me!...'

'And so you...', the magistrate began.

'Allow me, gentlemen, one more minute,' interrupted Mitya, resting both his elbows on the table and burying his face in his hands, 'let me gather my thoughts, let me get my breath back, gentlemen. All this has come as such a dreadful shock, dreadful; a man isn't a drum that you can beat regardless, gentlemen!'

'Why don't you have another drink of water...?' mumbled Nikolai Parfenovich.

Mitya took his hands away from his face and burst out laughing. There was a gleam in his eyes; suddenly he seemed a changed man. His whole demeanour was different; here was a man who was facing all these people, these former acquaintances of his, as their equal once again, just as if they had all gathered together for an evening of social intercourse and nothing had happened yet. Let me add here, in passing, that when Mitya first arrived in our town the chief of police had welcomed him to his home very warmly, but lately, especially during the last month, Mitya had virtually stopped visiting him, and if they happened to meet in the street, for example, the chief of police would frown angrily and barely acknowledge his greeting, a point which Mitya had been quick to observe. He was even less well acquainted with the prosecutor, but had occasionally paid his wife, a nervous and eccentric woman, the most courteous of visits and, although he could not explain exactly why he went to see her, she had always made him most welcome and for some reason had continued to manifest an interest in him right up to the last. As for the magistrate, he had not been formally introduced to him, but he had run into him and had even spoken to him once or twice, on both occasions on the subject of women.

'You, Nikolai Parfenovich, I can tell, are a very smart investigator,' began Mitya, and burst into a cheerful peel of laughter, 'but I'm going to make it easy for you. Gentlemen, I've been given a new lease of life... and don't hold it against me that I'm addressing you so bluntly and directly. Besides, let me be frank, I'm slightly tipsy. I seem to recall I had the honour... the honour of meeting you, Nikolai Parfenovich, at the house of my relative Miusov... Gentlemen, gentlemen, I know I'm at your mercy, don't imagine I don't understand the position in which I now find myself. I am under... if it was indeed Grigory who made the allegation against me... then I'm under—oh, of course, I'm obviously under suspicion! I understand the enormity of the situation—don't get me wrong! But to business, gentlemen, I'm ready, and we'll settle it in no time at all, because, look here, you see, gentlemen... Let's face it, if I know I'm not guilty, then of course we'll get it over and done with in no time at all! Isn't that so? Isn't it?'

Mitya, nervously voluble, spoke quickly and expansively, treating his listeners as if they were his best friends.

'So, we shall record for the time being that you deny outright the charge that has been laid against you,' said Nikolai Parfenovich weightily and, turning to his secretary, he dictated in a low voice what was to be written.

'Record it? You want to write that down? All right, go ahead, I agree, you have my full agreement, gentlemen... Only, look here... Wait, wait, put it down like this: "He's guilty of violence, of causing grievous bodily harm to the poor old man, that's what he's guilty of." Well, I am guilty deep down, in my heart of hearts, I am guilty—but there's no need to put that down,' he turned suddenly to the clerk, 'that belongs to my personal life, gentlemen, that has nothing to do with you, these profundities of the heart, I mean... But as regards my father's murder—I'm not guilty! It's a preposterous idea! It's absolutely preposterous!... I'll prove it to you, and you'll see it in no time. You'll laugh, gentlemen, you'll be roaring with laughter at your own suspicion!...'

'Calm down, Dmitry Fyodorovich,' exhorted the magistrate, as though attempting by his cool and collected manner to impose his authority upon the distraught man. 'Before we continue with the interrogation, I'd like, provided you agree to reply, of course, to hear you confirm the fact that apparently there was no love lost between you and the deceased, and that you were engaged in some kind of a permanent dispute with him... As a matter of fact, it is alleged that you stated here, just quarter of an hour ago, that you even wished to kill him: "I didn't kill him, but I wanted to," you shouted.'

'Is that what I shouted out? Oh, that may well be so, gentlemen! Yes, unfortunately, I did want to kill him, many times... unfortunately that's true!'

'You did, did you? Would you care to explain what precise grounds you had for hating your father?'

'What is there to explain, gentlemen?' Mitya bowed his head and shrugged his shoulders disconsolately. 'After all, I've never concealed the way I feel, the whole town knows about it—everyone in the tavern knows. I blurted it out only recently at the monastery, in Starets Zosima's cell... That same evening I hit my father and almost killed him, and I swore I'd return and kill him, I said it in front of witnesses... oh, a thousand witnesses! I never stopped shouting about it for a month, everyone's a witness!... The fact is beyond dispute, there's not the slightest doubt, but as for feelings, gentlemen, my feelings are quite another matter. You see, gentlemen,' Mitya frowned, 'it seems to me, you've no right to ask me about my feelings. You have your duty to perform, I understand that, but this is my own affair, a personal matter of no concern to anyone, but... since I did not conceal my feelings before... in the tavern, for instance, and told all and sundry, I... I shan't make a secret of it now, either. You see, gentlemen, I quite understand that the evidence against me in this case is overwhelming: I've been telling everyone I was going to kill him, and now, all of a sudden, someone's gone and killed him: so who else could it be but me? Ha-ha! I don't hold it against you, gentlemen, honestly I don't. I'm absolutely mystified, because who on earth could have killed him if it wasn't me? Isn't that right? If it wasn't me, who was it then, who? Gentlemen,' he exclaimed suddenly, 'I want to know, in fact, I demand to know from you, gentlemen: where was he killed? How was he killed, what with? Tell me,' he asked quickly, turning his gaze from the prosecutor to the magistrate.

'We found him lying on the floor in his study, face up, with a broken skull,' said the prosecutor.

'It's dreadful, gentlemen!' Mitya suddenly shuddered, leaned his elbows on the table, and buried his face in his right hand.

'Let us continue,' interrupted Nikolai Parfenovich. 'What gave rise to your feelings of hatred? You stated publicly, I believe, that it was jealousy?'

'Well, yes, jealousy, but not only jealousy.'

'Disputes over money?'

'Well, yes, over money, too.'

'I believe there was a dispute over three thousand roubles which had allegedly been withheld from your inheritance.'

'Three thousand, my foot! More, much more,' exploded Mitya, 'more than six, perhaps more than ten. I told everybody about it, everybody's heard me going on about it! But I made up my mind to cut my losses and call it three thousand. I desperately needed the three thousand... therefore, the envelope with the three thousand that I knew he kept under his pillow to give to Grushenka—I regarded it as having been virtually stolen from me, that's right, gentlemen, I considered it as belonging to me by right...'

The prosecutor cast a meaningful glance at the magistrate, and gave him a furtive wink.

'We shall return to this point,' said the magistrate promptly, 'with your permission, however, we shall record this specific detail: that you regarded the money in that envelope virtually as yours by right.'

'Go ahead, gentlemen, I fully realize it's just one more piece of evidence against me, but I'm not afraid of evidence or of testifying against myself. You heard me—against myself! You see, gentlemen, it looks as though you're under a misapprehension as to what I'm really like,' he suddenly added dejectedly. 'You're talking to a man of honour, to a man of the highest honour, and above all—don't you ever forget this—to a man who, though he's committed a myriad of misdeeds, is and always has been by nature a most honourable being inside, deep down—well, in a word, I don't know how to put it... That's precisely why I've suffered all my life, because I longed to be honourable; I was, so to speak, a martyr to honour and sought it with a lantern, like Diogenes with his lantern,* and yet at the same time I've done nothing but wallow in filth all my life, like all of us, gentlemen... I beg your pardon, I don't mean everyone—I alone wallowed, only I, it was a slip of the tongue, only I, I alone!... Gentlemen, I've got a splitting headache,' he winced painfully, 'you see, gentlemen, I hated his appearance, there was something underhand about him, his bragging and his disregard for all that's sacred, his mockery and godlessness, it was foul, just foul! But now that he's dead, I think differently.'

'How do you mean "differently"?'

'Not differently, but I regret having detested him so much.'

'You feel remorse?

'No, not quite remorse, don't put that down. I'm no angel myself, gentlemen, I'm not particularly good-looking and therefore I had no right to find him repugnant, that's what it amounts to! You can put that down, if you wish.'

Having said this, Mitya suddenly became very dejected. He had been getting steadily more morose as the magistrate's questioning progressed. And, just at that moment, another unexpected incident occurred. Though Grushenka had been taken away, they had not taken her very far, only to the next room but one from the blue room, where the interrogation was taking place. That other room was small, with only one window, immediately adjacent to the large room where there had been dancing and carousing fit to bring the roof down the night before. She sat there alone except for the devastated Maksimov, who, scared out of his wits, now clung to her as though seeking salvation from her presence. At the door of their room stood a man with a brass badge on his chest. Grushenka was weeping, and suddenly, no longer able to contain the grief which was choking her, she flung out her arms, leapt to her feet with a loud cry of distress: 'Woe is me, woe!' and rushed out of the room to him, to her Mitya, so unexpectedly that no one had time to stop her. Mitya, hearing her scream, simply shuddered, jumped up, let out a cry and, oblivious of everything, rushed headlong towards her. But once again they were prevented from touching one another, even though they were already so close. He was seized firmly by the arms: he fought back and struggled, and it took three or four men to restrain him. She too was seized, and he saw her stretch out her arms towards him, screaming as she was dragged away. When the scene was over he found himself sitting in his former place at the table again, and pleading with them.

'What do you want from her? Why don't you leave her alone? She's innocent, innocent!...'

The magistrate and prosecutor tried to pacify him. This continued for about ten minutes; finally, Mikhail Makarovich hurried back into the room and spoke to the prosecutor in a loud, agitated voice.

'She's out of the way, she's downstairs. Would you mind, gentlemen, if I said just a few words to the unfortunate man? In your presence, gentlemen, of course!'

'You're welcome, Mikhail Makarovich,' the magistrate replied, 'under the circumstances we have no objection.'

'Dmitry Fyodorovich, listen to me, my dear fellow,' Mikhail Makarovich turned to Mitya, the whole of his agitated face expressing a warm, almost fatherly compassion towards the unfortunate man, 'I've taken your Agrafena Aleksandrovna downstairs and left her in the care of the proprietor's daughters, and that old man Maksimov never leaves her side. I've had a word with her—are you listening?—I've spoken to her and calmed her down, I've explained to her that you've got to prove your innocence and that she mustn't make things difficult for you, she mustn't upset you, or you'll get flustered and incriminate yourself, do you see? Anyway, I've spoken to her, and she understands. She's no fool, my friend, and her heart's in the right place, she was pleading for you, and she wanted to kiss my hands, old man that I am. She asked me to tell you not to worry yourself on her behalf, and now, my good friend, I really should go and tell her that you're all right and that you aren't going to worry yourself to death about her. So calm down, you've got to understand how things are. I feel guilty about it, she's a Christian soul, yes, gentlemen, she's a meek soul and quite innocent. So what shall I tell her, Dmitry Fyodorovich, are you going to behave yourself or not?'

The kind old fellow had said more than he need have, but Grushenka's grief, her human grief, had touched his compassionate heart, and there were even tears in his eyes. Mitya sprang to his feet and rushed up to him.

'Pardon me, gentlemen, I beg your pardon, oh, I really do!' he exclaimed. 'You've the soul of a saint, you have, Mikhail Makarovich, I thank you on her behalf! I shan't worry, really I shan't, I shall be cheerful, tell her in your infinite kindness that I'm quite happy, really happy, I'll even start laughing soon, seeing that she's got a guardian angel such as you with her. I'll be done with this in a moment, and as soon as I'm free I'll go straight to her, she can be sure of that, ask her to wait! Gentlemen,' he suddenly turned to the prosecutor and the magistrate, 'now I'm going to bare my soul to you, I'll pour out my heart to you, we'll be done with all this in no time, it'll be fun—we'll laugh about it in the end, won't we? That woman, gentlemen, is the queen of my heart! Oh, I wish you'd listen, I won't hide a thing... Look, I realize I'm amongst gentlemen... She's my guiding light, my holy of holies, if only you knew! You heard her cry: "I'll go with him even to the scaffold!" And what have I given her, I, a pauper, a tramp! Why such love for me; how have I, a clumsy, disgraceful, ugly-faced brute, deserved such love that she'd go to the scaffold with me? Just now she was grovelling at your feet because of me, she who's so proud and guilty of nothing! How could I not help but adore her, how could I not cry out, not try to get to her, as I did just now? Oh gentlemen, forgive me! But now, now I'm all right!'

He collapsed in his chair and, burying his face in his hands, started to cry uncontrollably. But these were tears of happiness now. He immediately recovered his composure. The old chief of police was well pleased, so apparently were the lawyers; they sensed that the interrogation was about to enter a new phase. When the chief of police had departed, Mitya quite cheered up.

'Well, gentlemen, now I'm completely in your hands. And... if it hadn't been for these minor details, we'd have come to an understanding at once. I'm on about trifles again. I'm in your hands, gentlemen, but I swear, the trust must be mutual—you've got to believe me and I've got to believe you—otherwise we'll never see the end of this. I'm saying this for your sakes. To business, gentlemen, let's get down to business, but above all don't go probing into my soul like you were doing, don't torment me with irrelevancies, just stick to the point and to the facts, and

I'll tell you all you need to know. And to hell with all that's irrelevant!'

So said Mitya. The interrogation resumed.

4

SECOND TORMENT

NIKOLAI PARFENOVICH took off his glasses. 'You've no idea how heartened we are, Dmitry Fyodorovich, by your willingness to co-operate...', he began enthusiastically, real pleasure gleaming in his large, protruding, light-grey, and, incidentally, very short-sighted eyes. 'And you're so right about the need for mutual trust, without which it's often quite impossible to proceed, and even in cases of such gravity it's always possible to establish such trust provided that the person under suspicion can prove his innocence and really co-operates. As far as we're concerned, we shall make every effort, and you can see for yourself how we're conducting the hearing... Would you not agree, Ippolit Kyrillovich?' he turned suddenly to the prosecutor.

'Oh, without any doubt,' the prosecutor acquiesced, though compared to Nikolai Parfenovich's exuberance, he sounded less optimistic.

I shall mention here once and for all that Nikolai Parfenovich, who was a newcomer to our town, had from the very moment of his appointment here been unusually respectful towards Ippolit Kyrillovich, our state prosecutor, with whom he felt a deep affinity. He was perhaps the only person who believed unreservedly in the unusual psychological and oratorical skills of our Ippolit Kyrillovich, and was also the only person who really believed that the latter had been, as he felt, 'passed over' in his profession. He had heard about him while he was still in St Petersburg. Moreover, the young Nikolai Parfenovich also turned out to be the only person in the whole world for whom our 'unacknowledged' prosecutor felt a genuine fondness. On their way here they had managed to agree and to see eye to eye on a few points relating to the matter in hand, and now, as they sat at the table, Nikolai Parfenovich's sharp eye caught every movement on the face of his senior colleague, and from a barely uttered word, a look, even the slightest facial movement, understood every nuance.

'Gentlemen, let me tell you everything myself and don't interrupt me with irrelevancies, and I'll give you the whole story,' persisted Mitya.

'Excellent. Much obliged. But before we hear what you've got to say, perhaps you'd allow me to establish one minor detail which is of great interest to us, namely that at about five o'clock yesterday you borrowed ten roubles from your friend Pyotr Ilyich Perkhotin against the security of your pistols.'

'Yes, I did borrow the money, gentlemen, I did, ten roubles, so what? That's all there is to it; I pawned the pistols as soon as I got back from my journey.'

'You came back from a journey? So you were out of town?'

'Yes, gentlemen, forty versts from here, didn't you know?'

The prosecutor and Nikolai Parfenovich exchanged glances.

'Anyway, why not begin your story by describing everything that happened yesterday, starting from early in the morning? For instance, if you could let us know why you had to leave town, and the precise times of your departure and return... and things like that...'

'I wish you'd asked me this right at the start,' Mitya burst into a loud peal of laughter. 'If that's what you want, we must begin not with yesterday but with the day before, in the early morning, then you'll understand where I went, and why, and how. The day before yesterday, gentlemen, in the morning I went to our local moneybags Samsonov to borrow from him, against good security, the sum of three thousand roubles—it was an emergency, gentlemen, a sudden emergency...'

'Allow me to interrupt you,' the prosecutor cut him short politely, 'why did you suddenly need that precise amount of money, that is, three thousand roubles?'

'Ha, gentlemen, I wish you wouldn't go into all these details: how, when, and why, and why was it precisely this much and not that much, and all that kind of nonsense... that way, it'll run to more than three volumes plus an epilogue!'

Mitya said all this with the good-natured though impatient familiarity of a man who wishes to reveal the whole truth and is motivated by the very best of intentions.

'Gentlemen,' he said, as though something had suddenly occurred to him, 'don't think that I'm being difficult, but I'm asking you once again: believe me, I feel the deepest respect for you and I appreciate how things stand. Don't think I'm drunk. I've sobered up now. And even if I were drunk, it wouldn't matter a jot. What I say is:

> Sobered up, gained some sense—was no wiser than before,
> Had a drink, couldn't think—but could argue all the more.

Ha-ha! On reflection though, gentlemen, I see that it's not quite appropriate for me to be cracking jokes with you yet, not till we've got things straightened out, anyway. Let me keep my personal dignity. Of course, I appreciate the present difference between us: let's face it, I'm just a criminal sitting before you now, and most assuredly not your equal, whereas you're charged with keeping an eye on me: I'm sure you're not going to give me a pat on the head on account of Grigory, after all, one can't go around bashing old men's skulls in with impunity; obviously, you're going to bring me to book and lock me up for six months, say, perhaps a year in gaol—who knows what the verdict will be—but without loss of my legal rights... I won't lose my legal rights, will I, Mr Prosecutor? So there, gentlemen, I am aware of the difference between us... But you must agree, too, that you'd be able to trip up the good Lord Himself with questions like: where did you go, how did you go, when did you go, and when did you last blow your nose? If you carry on like that I'll certainly get confused, and you'll immediately put everything down, word for word, and then what will happen? Nothing'll happen! Fair enough, if I've started telling lies, I'll finish, and as for you, gentlemen, educated and magnanimous as you are, you'll pardon me, I'm sure. But I'll end with a plea: stop beating about the bush in your interrogation; you see, your official minds are trained to start with something trivial, with something insignificant, such as: how did you sleep, what did you have to eat, when did you spit, and then, having "lulled the criminal into a false sense of security", to pounce on him with a devastating question: "who did you kill, who did you rob?" Ha-ha! That's your officialdom for you, that's your procedure, that's what all your cunning amounts to! You may be able to catch your yokels out with such tricks, but not me. I wasn't born yesterday, I've served in the army myself, ha-ha-ha! No offence meant, gentlemen, I hope you don't think I'm being impudent?' he exclaimed, looking at them in good-natured astonishment. 'After all, it was Mitka Karamazov who said it, so it goes without saying he can be forgiven, an intelligent person can't be forgiven, but Mitka can! Ha-ha!'

Nikolai Parfenovich listened, and he too laughed. The prosecutor, who did not laugh, watched Mitya closely, scrutinizing him, never taking his eyes off him, as though unwilling to miss a single word, a single gesture, the least movement or change in his features.

'But that's how we started right from the word go,' responded Nikolai Parfenovich, still laughing, 'we didn't try to trip you up with questions about when you got up in the morning and what you had to eat, we went straight to the heart of the matter.'

'I understand, I understood and appreciated that, and I appreciate your kindness towards me even more, unparalleled kindness, worthy of the noblest of souls. Here we are, three decent people gathered together, so why not let's do everything on the basis of mutual trust, as befits educated and unprejudiced people bound by ties of social background and honour. In any case, allow me at this particular moment in my life, at this moment when my honour is impugned, to regard you as my best friends. Surely you won't be offended by this, gentlemen, you won't, will you?'

'Quite the contrary, you expressed it all so eloquently, Dmitry Fyodorovich,' Nikolai Parfenovich acquiesced with a pompous air of approval.

'As for trivialities, gentlemen, let's dispense with all those irrelevant trivialities,' exclaimed Mitya exultantly, 'otherwise we'll end up in one hell of a mess, wouldn't you agree?'

'I'm only too willing to follow your very sensible advice,' the prosecutor suddenly butted in, turning to Mitya, 'but all the same, I'd rather you answered my question. It's absolutely essential for us to know precisely why you needed such a sum, that is, why exactly three thousand roubles?'

'Why indeed? Well, for this and that... well, to settle a debt.'

'What debt—to whom?'

'That I positively decline to disclose, gentlemen! You see, not because I couldn't say, or because I dare not, or because I'm afraid to—it's a pretty insignificant and trivial matter, anyway— but I decline to say, because there's a principle involved here: it's my personal life, and I shan't let anyone intrude in my personal life. That's my principle. Your question has nothing to do with the matter in hand, and anything that has nothing to do with the matter in hand belongs to my personal life! I wanted to repay a debt, I wanted to repay a debt of honour, but to whom— I'm not telling.'

'By your leave, we shall note that down,' said the prosecutor.

'Feel free. Go ahead and put it all down: say that I'll never, ever bring myself to disclose it, never. You can add, too, gentlemen, that I would even consider it dishonourable to disclose the details. You certainly seem to have all the time in the world for note-taking.'

'My dear sir, let me warn you and remind you once more, in case you haven't realized it,' said the prosecutor in a tone of the utmost gravity, 'that you have every right not to answer any of the questions now being put to you, and that we, conversely, have no right to exact any answers from you if you yourself, for whatever reason, don't wish to reply. This has to be a matter for your personal judgement. Nevertheless, in circumstances such as these we feel duty-bound to draw your attention to this fact and to warn you of the full extent of the harm which you may inflict upon yourself by withholding this or that piece of evidence. That said, please continue.'

'Gentlemen, I'm not angry... I...', Mitya mumbled, somewhat disconcerted by the admonition, 'you see, gentlemen, this same Samsonov, to whom I went on that occasion...'

Of course, we shall not go into any great detail regarding what the reader knows already. Mitya was eager to tell everything, down to the minutest detail, but at the same time to get it over and done with as soon as possible. But the evidence was being recorded as it unfolded, and consequently he was continually being asked to stop. Dmitry Fyodorovich objected to this, but complied; he was irritated but, for the time being, he managed to keep his temper. True, from time to time he would call out: 'Gentlemen, this would drive the Lord God Himself to devilry,' or: 'You know, gentlemen, all you're doing is upsetting me for nothing!', but even during such outbursts his affable and expansive mood did not change. Thus he recounted how he had been duped by Samsonov two days previously. (He was quite sure now that he had been duped on that occasion.) The sale of his watch for six roubles to pay for the trip, about which the prosecutor and magistrate had hitherto known nothing, immediately attracted their attention and, to Mitya's extreme annoyance, it was deemed necessary to record all the details as further confirmation of the fact that even two days before he had hardly a kopeck to his name. By now, Mitya was beginning to feel despondent. Then, having described his visit to Lurcher, the night he had spent in the fume-filled hut, and so on, he reached the point in his story at which he returned to the town and then, without any additional prompting, he began of his own accord to recount in great detail his pangs of jealousy about Grushenka. They listened to him in silent concentration, taking particular note of the fact that he had already, some time before, selected a vantage point in the grounds of Marya Kondratyevna's house, behind Fyodor Pavlovich's property, from where he could keep a lookout for Grushenka, and also that he was being kept informed by Smerdyakov: all this was duly noted and recorded. He spoke passionately and at length of his jealousy, and though he was inwardly ashamed of exposing, so to speak, his most intimate feelings to 'general opprobrium', he managed to overcome his shame in the interests of truth. While he talked, the dispassionate severity reflected in the ever-observant eyes of the magistrate, and especially of the prosecutor, finally deeply unnerved him. The thought flashed through his mind: 'This youngster Nikolai Parfenovich, to whom I was talking nonsense about women only a few days ago, and this feeble prosecutor simply don't deserve to be told all this. What humiliation! "Surrender, suffer, and be still",'* he concluded his train of thought with a quote from a poem, then he took a grip upon

himself once more and continued his account. When he got to
the part about Mrs Khokhlakova he even cheered up, and was
on the point of telling a curious but irrelevant little anecdote
about that lady's recent activities, when the magistrate stopped
him and suggested politely that he should concentrate on 'more
pertinent matters'. Describing his despair, he came to the
moment when, leaving Mrs Khokhlakova's, he had thought "I'll
get the three thousand even if I have to knife someone," and
here they stopped him again and recorded 'wanted to knife
someone'. Mitya let them do so, without uttering a word. Finally
he came to the point in the story where he suddenly discovered
that Grushenka had deceived him by leaving Samsonov's
immediately after he had left her there, despite the fact that she
herself had told him she was going to stay with the old man till
midnight. 'The fact that I didn't kill that Fenya there and then
was only because I was in too much of a hurry', he blurted out
suddenly. This, too, was carefully recorded. Mitya waited a little
in grim silence, and was about to recount how he had run to his
father's garden, when the investigator suddenly stopped him
and, opening his large briefcase, which was lying nearby on the
settee, produced the brass pestle from it.

'Do you recognize this object?' he asked, showing it to Mitya.

'Oh yes!' replied Mitya, with a sad smile. 'How could I not?
Let's have a look... To hell with it, no need!'

'You forgot to mention it,' observed the magistrate.

'Blast it! I wouldn't have concealed it from you on purpose,
you'd have found out about it one way or another, don't you
think? It just slipped my memory.'

'Would you oblige us by recounting how you came to acquire
this weapon.'

'Certainly I'll oblige you, gentlemen.'

And Mitya recounted how he had picked up the pestle and
run off.

'Well, what was your intention when you armed yourself with
such a weapon?'

'Intention? There wasn't any! I just grabbed it and ran.'

'Why then, if you had no intention?'

Mitya was seething with annoyance. He looked hard at the
'youngster', and smiled at him with gloomy hostility. The fact

was that he was feeling more and more ashamed of having spoken so openly and emotionally of his jealousy to 'these people'.

'Who cares about the pestle?' he blurted out.

'Even so.'

'All right, I grabbed it to ward off the dogs. Well, it was dark... well, just in case...'

'And on previous occasions when you left the house at night, did you take some kind of a weapon with you, too, if you are so afraid of the dark?'

'Oh, my God! Gentlemen, it's absolutely impossible to talk to you!' exclaimed Mitya at the end of his tether, and turning flushed with anger to the clerk, he shouted with a note of hysteria in his voice: 'Write down immediately... immediately... "I grabbed the pestle and ran off to kill my father... Fyodor Pavlovich... with a blow on the head!" Well, are you satisfied now, gentlemen? Do you feel better?' He stared provocatively at the magistrate and the prosecutor.

'We are only too well aware that you made that declaration in a fit of pique', the prosecutor replied dryly, 'and because you resent the questions we are putting to you, which you consider trivial, but which in fact are very important.'

'Have a heart, gentlemen! All right, I took the pestle... So what, why do people pick things up in such circumstances? I don't know what for. I grabbed it and ran. That's all there is to it. Do me a favour, gentlemen, *passons*,* or I swear you shan't get another word out of me!'

He put his elbow on the table and leant his head on one hand. He was sitting sideways to them, staring at the wall, at odds with himself. In truth, he would dearly have loved to stand up and announce that he would not say another word, 'you can sentence me to death if you wish.'

'You see, gentlemen,' he took a grip on himself with difficulty, 'you see, I keep listening to you, and I get the feeling... you see, I sometimes have this dream... a dream, and I have it often, it keeps recurring, that someone's chasing me, someone I'm dreadfully scared of, he's chasing me in the dark, at night, looking for me, and I'm hiding somewhere, behind a door or a cupboard, in abject fear, but the main thing is that he knows perfectly well where I'm hiding, and he's only pretending not to know where I am so as to torment me that much longer, so as to enjoy my terror... You're doing that to me now! That's what it feels like!'

'You have such dreams?' enquired the prosecutor.

'Yes, I have... You wouldn't like to put it down, would you?' Mitya said with a wry smile.

'No, no need, but all the same, you do have pretty curious dreams.'

'It's no longer a dream now! Reality, gentlemen, just stark reality! I'm the wolf and you're the hunters, let the chase commence.'

'You're making a fatuous comparison...', began Nikolai Parfenovich unctuously.

'Not fatuous at all, gentlemen, not fatuous!' Mitya expostulated again, though his sudden outburst appeared to have eased his inner tension and he was beginning to mellow with every word. 'You can refuse to believe a criminal or a prisoner in the dock whom you're torturing with your questions, but a man of honour, gentlemen, the noblest stirrings of his heart (yes, I dare to proclaim it!)—no! Him you must not disbelieve... you have no right even... but—

> heart, be still,
> Surrender, suffer and be still!

Well, shall I continue?' he broke off gloomily.

'By all means,' replied Nikolai Parfenovich.

5

THIRD TORMENT

ALTHOUGH, when Mitya resumed speaking, his tone was harsh, he was clearly trying even harder not to forget or omit a single detail from his story. He recounted how he had jumped over the fence into his father's garden, how he had approached the window, and, finally, his feelings as he stood by the window.

Speaking clearly and deliberately, he described the fear that had gripped him during those moments in the garden, when he was so anxious to discover whether Grushenka was with his father or not. But the amazing thing was that, on this occasion, both the prosecutor and the magistrate listened to him with the utmost detachment, their faces impassive, and they asked far fewer questions. Mitya could discern nothing from the expression on their faces. 'They've lost their temper and are annoyed with me,' he thought, 'what the hell!' However, he noticed that when he recounted how he had finally plucked up courage to give the signal that would inform his father that Grushenka had come and that he should open the window, the prosecutor and the magistrate ignored the word 'signal' completely, as though they did not even understand its relevance to the matter. Having finally reached the point where, catching sight of his father leaning out of the window, he had flown into a rage and pulled out the pestle from his pocket, Mitya suddenly stopped, apparently intentionally. He sat staring at the wall, knowing full well that their eyes were riveted on him.

'Well,' said the magistrate, 'you pulled out the weapon... and then what happened?'

'Then? Then I killed him... I struck him across the temple and split his skull open... That's what you think, isn't it?' his eyes flashed suddenly. All the rage that had almost subsided suddenly flared up again in his soul with the utmost violence.

'That's our version,' echoed Nikolai Parfenovich, 'what's yours?'

Mitya lowered his eyes, and for a long time did not say a word.

'My version, gentlemen, my version is this,' he began softly, 'whether it was someone's tears, or perhaps my mother interceded with the good Lord, or perhaps the Holy Spirit descended on me at that moment—I do not know—but the devil was vanquished. I turned away from the window and ran towards the fence... My father took fright and, recognizing me for the first time, cried out and jumped back from the window—I remember it very well. I was already making a beeline for the fence... and that's where Grigory caught up with me, when I was already on top of the fence...'

Here he finally looked up at his listeners. They appeared to be eyeing him perfectly calmly and attentively. Mitya was smitten with indignation.

'I'm sure you're laughing at me at this moment, gentlemen, aren't you?' he interjected suddenly.

'What makes you say that?' enquired Nikolai Parfenovich.

'You don't believe a word, that's why! Look, I've reached the crucial point: the old man is lying there now, with a fractured skull, and you're supposed to believe that I—who have just given you a dramatic description of how I wanted to kill him and how I was already holding the pestle in my hand—that I suddenly ran away from the window... A likely tale! The fellow can be taken at his word! Ha-ha! You're a funny lot, gentlemen!'

And he swung right round on his chair, so that it creaked under him.

'Did you, by any chance, notice,' the prosecutor began suddenly, as though he had not even noticed Mitya's agitation, 'did you by any chance notice, as you were running away from the window, whether the garden door at the far end of the house was open or not?'

'No, it wasn't open.'

'It wasn't?'

'On the contrary, it was shut; and anyway, who could have opened it? Hey, just a second, the door!' he seemed suddenly to have been reminded of something, and he almost shuddered. 'Did you say you found the door open?'

'Yes.'

'So who could have opened it, apart from yourselves?' asked Mitya in utter amazement.

'The door was open, and your father's killer undoubtedly entered through that door and, having committed the murder, left by the same door,' said the prosecutor, enunciating every word slowly and deliberately. 'It is perfectly clear to us. The murder was obviously committed inside the room, *not from outside the window*; this is borne out positively by the investigation, by the position of the body and everything else. There can be no doubt whatsoever on this score.'

Mitya was thunderstruck.

'But that's impossible, gentlemen!' he yelled out, utterly at a loss, 'I... I didn't even enter the room... I'm positive, I categorically assure you the door was shut all the time I was in the garden and when I was running away from the window. I was standing just by his window and I saw him through it, and that's all, that's all... I remember it down to the last split second. And even if I didn't remember it, I'd know it all the same, because the only people who knew the signal were Smerdyakov, myself, and my father, and he would never have opened the door to anyone in the world unless the signal had been given!'

' "Signal"? What signal?' The prosecutor spoke with an eager, almost hysterical curiosity, abruptly abandoning his posture of detachment and sidling up to Mitya. He sensed that there was something important that he still did not know, and was immediately gripped by a terrible apprehension in case Mitya refused to reveal it in full.

'So you didn't know!' said Mitya with a wink, flashing him a derisive, angry smile. 'And what if I don't tell you? Who else are you going to turn to? My late father, Smerdyakov, and I were the only ones who knew about the signal, no one else—the heavens knew too, but you're hardly likely to get an answer from there. So there's a certain intriguing little fact which one could make a hell of a lot of, ha-ha! Relax, gentlemen, I shall reveal it. You've got me all wrong, you've no idea who you're dealing with! You're dealing with a defendant who testifies against himself! Yes indeed, you're dealing with a man of honour—but what would you know about that!'

The prosecutor swallowed his pride; he was seething with impatience to learn about this new fact. Accurately and at length, Mitya described everything relating to the signal that Fyodor Pavlovich had devised for Smerdyakov; he explained the significance of each particular tap on the window, and he even tapped out the signal on the table himself; furthermore, in answer to Nikolai Parfenovich's question—whether, when he was tapping on the window, he had in fact used the signal that meant 'Grushenka's here'—Mitya answered in the affirmative, confirming that that was the precise signal he had given: 'Grushenka's here'.

'Go ahead now, and build your fairy-tale castle!' Mitya broke off abruptly and turned away contemptuously.

'So, only your late father, you, and the servant Smerdyakov

knew of the signal? And no one else?' Nikolai Parfenovich enquired once more.

'Yes, the servant Smerdyakov and the heavens. Make sure you write down the heavens; it won't do any harm to bring them in. You too may want to have God on your side one day.'

And, of course, this was recorded, but while the clerk was actually writing it down the prosecutor as though quite by chance happened to hit on a new thought.

'But surely, if Smerdyakov knew about this signal as well—and since you yourself categorically deny any involvement in your father's death—could it not be that it was he who, after tapping out the agreed signal, persuaded your father to open the door for him and then... murdered him?'

Mitya looked at him with utter hatred and derision. He continued to stare hard, without saying a word, till the prosecutor began to blink.

'You've cornered the fox again!' said Mitya at last. 'You've caught the sly one by her tail, ha-ha! I can see right through you, Mr Prosecutor! You really expected me to jump up at once, to clutch at that straw, and to yell out at the top of my voice: "Aha, it's Smerdyakov, he's the murderer!" Admit it, that's what you were thinking, admit it, then I'll continue.'

But the prosecutor would not admit it. He remained silent, and waited.

'You're wrong, I shan't denounce Smerdyakov!' said Mitya.

'And you don't even suspect him?'

'What about you?'

'We did suspect him, too.'

Mitya fixed his eyes on the ground.

'Joking aside,' he said gloomily, 'listen to me. Right at the beginning, almost from when I first encountered you from behind that curtain, the thought occurred to me: "Smerdyakov!" I sat here at this table, shouting that I wasn't guilty of his blood, and I kept thinking: "Smerdyakov!" Smerdyakov haunted me. Just now I thought again, "Smerdyakov", but only for a second—almost straight away I said to myself: "No, not Smerdyakov!" He's not the murderer, gentlemen!'

'In that case, perhaps you suspect some other person?' enquired Nikolai Parfenovich cagily.

'I don't know who it was, some other person, or the hand of heaven or of Satan, but... but it wasn't Smerdyakov!' Mitya said categorically.

'Why are you so adamant, why are you so certain that it wasn't him?'

'I'm absolutely sure. It's the way he behaves—and because Smerdyakov's a coward and the lowest of creatures. He's not just a coward, he's all the cowards that ever trod the earth rolled into one. That's all he is, an absolute coward. He used to shake every time he spoke to me, he begged me not to kill him, when I hadn't even lifted a finger against him. He used to grovel at my feet and literally lick these very boots of mine, begging me "not to frighten him". Did you hear that: "frighten"—what kind of talk is that? And I'd even given him presents. He's a disease-ridden, brainless epileptic whom any eight-year-old would make mincemeat of. He's pathetic. It wasn't Smerdyakov, gentlemen, and he's not after money either, he used to refuse everything I offered him... And why would he want to kill the old devil? He's very likely his son, his illegitimate son, did you know that?'

'We've heard that story. But you're also his son, and it didn't stop you telling everyone you wanted to kill him.'

'I know what you're getting at! And it's reprehensible and despicable of you! But I'm not afraid! Gentlemen, it's a dirty trick of yours to say it to my face now! It's reprehensible, because I told you about it myself. Not only did I want to kill him, but I could have; what's more, I went around telling people that I would kill him! But the fact remains I didn't kill him, I was saved by my guardian angel—that's what you've failed to take into account... And it's that that makes it underhand and downright mean of you! Because I didn't kill him, I didn't, I didn't! Do you hear me, Mr Prosecutor, I didn't kill him!'

He was gasping for breath. At no time during the interrogation had he felt so agitated.

'And so, what did Smerdyakov tell you then, gentlemen,' he enquired after a short pause, 'if you don't mind me asking?'

'You may ask us anything you wish,' the prosecutor replied with cold severity, 'anything you wish as regards the factual details of the case, and we, I repeat, are obliged to answer all your questions. We found the servant Smerdyakov, whom you were enquiring about, lying unconscious on his bed, having recurrent violent epileptic fits, a dozen or so in succession. The doctor who examined him told us that he might not even survive till the morning.

'Well, in that case, it was the devil who killed father,' Mitya suddenly blurted out, as though right up to the very last moment he had been asking himself: was it Smerdyakov or not?

'We'll come back to this point again,' Nikolai Parfenovich decided. 'As for now, perhaps you would kindly continue with your statement.'

Mitya asked if he could have a rest. This was conceded willingly. Having rested, he continued. But he clearly found it difficult. He was exhausted, demeaned, and spiritually shattered. In addition to everything, as though deliberately trying to rattle him, the prosecutor now began to pester him with 'trivialities'. He had barely finished describing how, sitting astride the fence, he had hit Grigory on the head with the pestle while the latter was holding on to his left leg, and how he had then jumped down immediately to attend to the injured man, when the prosecutor stopped him and asked for a more detailed description of his exact position on the fence. Mitya was surprised.

'Well, I sat like this, astride, one leg here, the other there...'

'And the pestle?'

'The pestle was in my hand.'

'Not in your pocket? You remember that clearly? Did you, in fact, take a hard swing?'

'Probably yes, why do you need to know that?'

'Would you mind sitting on the chair precisely as you sat on the fence? Show us clearly, for our information, how you swung your arm and in what direction.'

'Are you trying to be funny?' asked Mitya, with a supercilious glance at the magistrate, who did not even bat an eyelid. Mitya turned abruptly, sat astride the chair, and swung his arm.

'That's how I hit him! That's how I felled him! Is that enough for you?'

'Thank you. Would you mind informing us precisely why you took the trouble to jump down, what your intention was, what in fact you had in mind?'

'Oh, damn you... the man was hurt and I jumped down... I don't know why!'

'When you were in a panic? And trying to get away?'

'Yes, in a panic and trying to get away.'

'You wanted to help him?'

'Help, my foot... Yes, perhaps it was to help, too, I don't remember.'

'You didn't know what you were doing? You were confused?'

'Not at all, I wasn't confused, I remember it all. Everything, down to the minutest detail. I jumped down to have a look, I wiped the blood off with a handkerchief.'

'We saw your handkerchief. Were you hoping to resuscitate your victim?'

'Don't know about hoping. I just wanted to find out for sure if he was alive or not.'

'Ah, so you wanted to find out? And did you?'

'I'm not a doctor, I couldn't be sure. I ran off thinking I'd killed him, but he regained consciousness.'

'Splendid,' the prosecutor concluded. 'Thank you very much. That's all what I wanted to know. Please be so good as to continue.'

Alas, although he remembered it clearly, it did not even occur to Mitya to say that he had jumped down out of pity and that, standing over Grigory, he had even uttered a few compassionate words: 'That's the way it goes, old man, can't be helped.' The prosecutor, however, came to only one conclusion, that he had jumped down 'at such a moment, when he was in such a panic', merely in order to verify for certain whether the *only* witness of his crime was still alive or not, and, therefore, how pitiless, determined, cold-blooded, and calculating he must have been, even at such a moment... and so on and so forth. The prosecutor was well satisfied: 'The nervous fellow is easily rattled, I've confused him with trivialities and caught him off guard.'

Painful though it was for him now, Mitya continued. However, he was immediately interrupted again, this time by Nikolai Parfenovich:

'How on earth could you run to the servant Fedosya Markovna when your hands and face were covered in blood?'

'I didn't even notice at the time that I was covered in blood!' replied Mitya.

'That makes sense, it's not unusual,' the prosecutor and Nikolai Parfenovich exchanged glances.

'That's right, I didn't notice, you're so right, Mr Prosecutor,' Mitya agreed. The interrogation then turned to Mitya's sudden decision to 'step aside' and to 'make way for the lucky ones'. He now found it quite impossible to begin to bare his soul again, as he had done before, and to talk about 'the queen of his heart'. He felt revolted by these cold people, who were 'sucking his blood like bedbugs'. And thus, in reply to repeated questions, he merely answered briefly and curtly.

'Well, I decided to kill myself. What was the point of carrying on—the question was absolutely inevitable and inescapable. Her former and undisputed one had reappeared; he'd wronged her, but he'd rushed back full of love, even after five years, to make up for the injustice by asking her to marry him. I could see at once I didn't stand a chance... And then there was the infamy, the blood, Grigory's blood... What was the point of living? So I decided to redeem my pistols, load them, and put a bullet through my head before dawn...'

'And to have a final fling?'

'Yes, to have a final fling. Dammit, gentlemen, let's get this over. I really did mean to shoot myself, somewhere near here, outside the town, and I planned to do it at about five in the morning—in my pocket I already had the note I'd written at Perkhotin's after I'd loaded the pistol. Here it is, this piece of paper, read it. It's not for your sakes I'm telling you this,' he added contemptuously. He took a piece of paper out of his waistcoat-pocket and flung it on the table before them; his interrogators read it with interest and, as is customary, added it to the file.

'And it still hadn't occurred to you to wash your hands, even when you went to see Mr Perkhotin? So, then, you weren't bothered about being suspected?'

'Suspected of what? No matter what I was going to be suspected of, I'd still have rushed down here and shot myself at five, and you wouldn't have been able to do anything. If it hadn't been for what happened to my father, you wouldn't have found out anything and you'd never have come here. It was the devil, it was the devil who killed my father; it was from the devil you found out everything so quickly! How did you manage to get here so soon? I can't believe it, it's amazing!'

'Mr Perkhotin told us that when you came to him you had money in your hands... in your bloodstained hands... money... a large sum... a wad of hundred-rouble notes, and his servant boy also saw it.'

'That's right, gentlemen, I seem to remember that's how it was.'

'And now we have another small question to put to you,' Nikolai Parfenovich began very softly. 'Would you care to inform us how you suddenly got hold of so much money, because, from what we've ascertained, you couldn't have had time to go home first.'

The prosecutor winced a little at the bluntness of the question, but he did not interrupt Nikolai Parfenovich.

'No, I didn't go home,' replied Mitya with apparent calm, continuing to stare at the ground.

'Let me repeat my question once more, therefore,' continued Nikolai Parfenovich, stalking round him. 'Where could you possibly have got hold of such a sum so quickly, since, according to your own testimony, at five o'clock that day, you still...'

'I needed ten roubles and took my pistols to Perkhotin, then I went to Khokhlakova to get the three thousand, but she wouldn't give it to me, and so on and so on, and all that irrelevant trivia,' Mitya interrupted harshly, 'yes, there you are gentlemen, I was destitute, and suddenly—thousands, how about that? You know, gentlemen, you're both scared now: what if he doesn't tell us where he got it from? You're dead right: I won't, gentlemen, you're right, you won't find out,' Mitya spelled out with extraordinary determination. The interrogators paused for a moment.

'Please understand, Mr Karamazov,' Nikolai Parfenovich said in a soft, conciliatory tone, 'it is vitally important for us to know this.'

'I understand, but I shan't tell you all the same.'

The prosecutor joined in now, too, repeating once more that, of course, the suspect could refuse to answer the questions if he considered it to be in his best interests, and so on, but that in view of the damage his silence could do to his case, and especially in view of the gravity of the questions...

'And so on and so forth, gentlemen! Enough, I've heard this sermon before!' Mitya interrupted again. 'I can see the seriousness of the situation for myself, and that it is the key question, but I won't tell you all the same.'

'It doesn't matter to us, it's your business, not ours, you'll only damage your case.'

'Well, let's stop playing games now,' Mitya's eyes glinted suddenly, and he looked hard at them both. 'I anticipated right from the start that we'd clash over this issue. But at the start, when I first began my statement, all this seemed in the dim and distant future, everything was vague, and I was even naïve enough to suggest that we trust one another. Now I can see for myself that there was never any possibility of such trust, because, one way or another, we'd have come up against this damned hurdle! And we have! I can't tell you, and that is the end of it! Still, I don't blame you, I know you can't take me at my word, either, I'm well aware of that!'

He fell into a sullen silence.

'But what if, without breaking your resolve to remain silent on this crucial point, you were at the same time to give us a clue, be it only the most tenuous clue, as to the motives that could induce you to remain silent at such a critical juncture in this investigation?'

Mitya smiled sadly and thoughtfully.

'I'm a much nicer person than you think, gentlemen; I'll tell you why, and I'll give you the clue you want, even though you don't deserve it. I'm refusing to say anything, gentlemen, because I feel a sense of shame. The question of where I got the money from is such a shameful matter for me that not even the robbery and my father's death could compare with it—even if I had robbed or killed him. That's why I can't say anything. My sense of shame won't let me. You're not going to write that down, gentlemen, are you?'

'Yes, we are,' mumbled Nikolai Parfenovich.

'I wish you wouldn't, at least, not all that about the sense of shame. I only told you about it out of the goodness of my heart, though I needn't have, it was like a present, and you're making such a meal of it. Well, go ahead, put down anything you want,' he concluded with disdain and contempt, 'I'm not afraid of you... I face you with pride.'

'You wouldn't like to tell us what this shame was all about?' said Nikolai Parfenovich.

The prosecutor winced dreadfully.

'Never, *c'est fini*,* don't even bother. It's not worth putting myself out for. I've put myself out enough for you, as it is. You're not worth it, neither you nor anyone... Enough, gentlemen, this is where I draw the line.'

This was said most peremptorily. Nikolai Parfenovich stopped insisting, but from the look in Ippolit Kyrillovich's eyes he concluded that the latter had still not given up hope.

'Could you not at least inform us as to exactly how much money you had in your hands when you arrived at Mr Perkhotin's, that is, precisely how many roubles?'

'No, I can't tell you that either.'

'Did you not tell Mr Perkhotin about the three thousand you were supposed to have received from Mrs Khokhlakova?'

'Maybe I did. That's enough, gentlemen, I shan't tell you how much.'

'In that case, would you mind describing how you got here and all your actions since then.'

'Oh, you can ask anybody here about that. On second thoughts, though, I suppose I could tell you.'

And he did, but we shall not repeat his story. He spoke quickly and drily. Concerning the raptures of his love, he said nothing. He did explain, however, how his determination to shoot himself had passed, 'in view of the changed circumstances'. He spoke without whys or wherefores, without going into details. But his interrogators did not interrupt him unduly at this stage: it was evident that, for them, this was not the main issue now.

'We'll investigate all this, we'll raise the matter when we come to question the witnesses, which will be done in your presence, of course,' said Nikolai Parfenovich, bringing the interrogation to a close. 'Now, would you mind very much putting on the table everything you have on you—most important of all, any money which is now in your possession.'

'Money, gentlemen? Certainly. I quite understand. I'm only

surprised you didn't show any curiosity on this score earlier. Mind you, I wasn't intending to go anywhere, I'm here for all to see. Well, here it is, my money, go ahead, count it, take it, it's all here, I think.'

He took everything, even the small change, out of his pockets, including two twenty-kopeck coins from his waistcoat-pocket. The money was counted and it came to eight hundred and thirty six roubles, forty kopecks.

'And is that all?' asked the magistrate.

'Yes.'

'In your statement just now you mentioned that you spent three hundred roubles in Plotnikov's shop, you gave ten roubles to Perkhotin, twenty to the driver, you lost two hundred roubles here, at cards, then...'

Nikolai Parfenovich counted up everything. Mitya was completely co-operative. Every kopeck was included and accounted for. Nikolai Parfenovich quickly arrived at a total.

'Including the eight hundred here, it would appear you had fifteen hundred in all to start with.'

'It would indeed,' Mitya snapped back.

'But, with respect, everyone maintains there was far more.'

'Let them.'

'And you yourself did, too.'

'I did indeed.'

'We shall verify all this from the statements of people who haven't been questioned yet; don't worry about your money, it'll be kept safe and it'll be returned to you at the conclusion of all... proceedings... provided it transpires or, as it were, is established that you have a rightful claim to it. Well, as for now...'

Nikolai Parfenovich stood up and informed Mitya tersely that he was 'obliged and duty-bound' to make a most detailed and thorough search both of his 'clothes and everything...'

'Here you are, gentlemen, I'll turn out all my pockets, if you wish.'

And he really did start to turn out his pockets.

'You'll have to take your clothes off as well.'

'What? Undress? To hell with you! Why can't you search me as I am! Why not?'

'Certainly not, Dmitry Fyodorovich. You must take your clothes off.'

'As you wish,' Mitya agreed resignedly, 'only, if you don't mind, behind the curtains, not here. Who's going to search me?'

'Of course, behind the curtains,' Nikolai Parfenovich inclined his head in acquiescence. His boyish face had assumed an air of extreme gravity.

6

THE PROSECUTOR CATCHES MITYA OUT

A QUITE astonishing and unexpected ritual then began for Mitya. He could never have believed, even just a minute before, that anyone could have treated him, Mitya Karamazov, quite like that! The worst thing was the degradation, and their arrogance and contempt for him. It was bad enough having to take off his jacket, but Mitya was asked to undress even further. And not so much asked—rather, ordered; he understood the situation perfectly. Glowering with indignation and defiance, he submitted without a word. Both Nikolai Parfenovich and the prosecutor had followed him behind the curtain; there were also a few muzhiks present, 'obviously to apply force if necessary,' thought Mitya, 'or perhaps for some other reason.'

'Surely I don't have to take my shirt off too?' he asked resentfully, but Nikolai Parfenovich did not answer. He and the prosecutor were engrossed in examining his coat, trousers, waistcoat, and cap, and it was evident that the examination was a source of great fascination to them. 'They don't stand on ceremony much,' the thought flashed through Mitya's mind, 'even basic courtesies have gone by the board.'

'For the second time, do I take off my shirt or not?' he asked impatiently and even more resentfully.

'Not to worry, we'll tell you,' Nikolai Parfenovich responded rather peremptorily; at least, that was how it struck Mitya.

All this time, the prosecutor and the magistrate were busily consulting together in a low voice. It turned out there were some large, dry, caked bloodstains on the frock-coat, in particular on the left side at the back. The same on the trousers. Moreover, Nikolai Parfenovich personally, and in the presence of the witnesses, ran his fingers along the collar, the cuffs, and all the seams of the frock-coat and the trousers, evidently looking for something—money, no doubt. The striking thing was that they made not the slightest attempt to hide from Mitya their suspicion that he could have sewn the money into his garments, that he was actually capable of such a thing. 'This is how one would treat a thief, not an officer,' he said to himself. Also, they kept voicing their opinions quite openly to each other in his presence, making no attempt to be discreet. For instance, the secretary, who had also appeared behind the curtain, busy and ready to oblige, drew Nikolai Parfenovich's attention to Mitya's cap, which they also felt all the way round with their fingers. 'Remember', observed the secretary, 'how the copy-clerk Gridenko went one day in the summer to pick up the wages for the whole office and, on returning, announced that he'd lost it all when he was drunk—and where did it turn up in the end? It was here, in the piping of his cap; the hundred-rouble notes were rolled up tightly and sewn into the piping.' Both the magistrate and the prosecutor remembered the Gridenko case only too well, and so they put Mitya's cap aside to be inspected thoroughly later, along with the rest of his clothes.

'Just a moment,' Nikolai Parfenovich suddenly called out, noticing the bloodstained right cuff of Mitya's shirt, which was tucked inside the sleeve, 'just a moment, what's this—blood?'

'Yes,' Mitya snapped back.

'I'd like to know whose... and why the cuff's tucked in like that.'

Mitya described how he had got blood on it when he was busying himself with Grigory, and that he had tucked it in when he was washing his hands at Perkhotin's.

'I'm afraid we'll have to take your shirt, too, it is most important... as material evidence.' Mitya flushed and exploded with anger.

'You want me to appear naked?' he exclaimed.

'Don't worry... We'll deal with that somehow; in the meantime, would you mind taking off your socks?'

'You're joking! Is that really necessary?' Mitya's eyes flashed.

'We haven't come here to joke,' Nikolai Parfenovich retorted sharply.

'Well, if that's what you want... I'm...', mumbled Mitya and, sitting down on the bed, he started pulling off his socks. He felt acutely embarrassed—while everyone else was fully clothed, he was undressed; and, strangely enough, in his state of undress he began to feel vaguely guilty in front of them and, most important of all, was himself almost ready to accept that he really had become inferior to them all of a sudden and that they now had every right to despise him. 'If everybody were undressed,' the thought flashed through his mind again and again, 'I wouldn't mind so much, but I'm the only one who's undressed, while everybody else has his clothes on and is looking at me—it's shameful! It's like a bad dream, I've experienced this kind of shame in a dream.' But it was almost painful for him to take his socks off—they were not very clean, nor was his underwear, and this was now evident to everyone. Moreover, he himself hated his feet; for some reason he had all his life found his big toes unsightly, especially one thick, flat toenail on his right foot that curved down awkwardly like a hook and would now be exposed for all to see. Utterly ashamed, he became even more arrogant and intentionally provocative. He ripped off his shirt.

'You wouldn't like to search somewhere else, too, if you have the nerve?'

'No, that won't be necessary for the time being.'

'What, you want me to stay naked, as I am?' he said viciously.

'Yes, I'm afraid so, for the time being... Would you mind sitting here for a while, you can take the blanket off the bed to wrap yourself in, and I'll... I'll see to everything.'

All his belongings were shown to the independent observers, an inventory was made, and at last Nikolai Parfenovich left the room, and the clothes were then removed too. Ippolit Kyrillovich also went out. Mitya was left alone with just the muzhiks, who watched him in silence without taking their eyes off him. He tucked himself into the blanket, he was beginning to feel cold. His bare feet were sticking out, and the blanket was not long enough to cover them. Nikolai Parfenovich was a long time returning, 'an agonizingly long time'. 'He's treating me just like

a dog,' Mitya ground his teeth. 'That scoundrel of a prosecutor
has gone away too, probably out of contempt, couldn't stand the
sight of my naked body any more.' Mitya nevertheless assumed
that his clothes would be inspected outside the room and then
returned. But imagine his indignation when Nikolai Parfenovich
suddenly returned, followed by a muzhik carrying a totally
different set of clothes.

'Here's some clothes for you,' he said cheerfully, apparently
well pleased with the result of his effort. 'Courtesy of Mr
Kalganov, who's kindly let us have them in view of the peculiar
circumstances, and a clean shirt to boot. Fortunately, he happened to have them all in his suitcase. You may keep your own
underwear and socks.'

Mitya was furious.

'I'm not having other people's clothes!' he shouted angrily.
'Give me back my own!'

'That's out of the question.'

'I said, give me back my own, to hell with Kalganov and his
clothes, to hell with him!'

They reasoned with him for a long time. They finally managed
to pacify him somehow. They persuaded him that his clothes,
stained as they were with blood, had to be treated 'as part and
parcel of the material evidence', and even that they were not
entitled to let him keep them... 'in view of the possible eventual
outcome of the case'. One way or another, they eventually
managed to convince him. He fell sulkily silent and began to
dress hurriedly. While doing so, he noticed that the clothes were
of a better quality than his old ones, and he felt that he did not
want to 'take advantage'. 'They're ridiculously tight,' he added.
'Do you want me to look like a clown in them... for your
amusement!'

They managed to persuade him once more that he was making
a mountain out of a molehill again, that even though Mr
Kalganov was taller than him, he was only slightly so, and that it
was only the trousers which were, perhaps, on the long side.
However, the frock-coat really was too narrow across the
shoulders.

'Dammit, it won't even button up properly,' Mitya growled
again. 'Do me a favour, tell Mr Kalganov forthwith that I never

asked him for his clothes and that I was forced to dress up like a clown.'

'He's well aware of that and is most concerned... not about his clothes, that is, but regarding this whole incident, so to speak...', mumbled Nikolai Parfenovich.

'To hell with his concern! Well, what next? Or am I to go on sitting here?'

They asked him to go back into 'that room'. Mitya obeyed grudgingly, trying to avoid looking people in the eye. Wearing someone else's clothes, he felt himself to be totally disgraced, especially in front of these peasants and Trifon Borisych, whose face had suddenly appeared briefly in the doorway for some reason. 'He couldn't resist having a peep at the fairy prince,' thought Mitya. He sat down on his former chair. His imagination conjured up weird, nightmarish thoughts, and it seemed to him that he was going out of his mind.

'Well, I suppose all it needs now is for you to start birching me,' he growled at the prosecutor. As for Nikolai Parfenovich, Mitya did not turn towards him, as though he could not even bring himself to speak to him. 'Didn't much care for the way he inspected my socks; the bastard even had them turned inside out, just so that everybody could see how dirty they were!'

'Yes, we'll have to start questioning the witnesses now,' said Nikolai Parfenovich, as though reading Dmitry Fyodorovich's thoughts.

'Yes,' the prosecutor observed thoughtfully, as if he too was turning something over in his mind.

'Dmitry Fyodorovich, we've done our best to help you,' continued Nikolai Parfenovich, 'but having met with such a categorical refusal on your part to explain to us the origin of the money which you had in your possession, we are at this moment...'

'What's that ring on your finger?' Mitya interrupted him suddenly, as though snapping out of a reverie, and he pointed at one of the three large rings adorning Nikolai Parfenovich's right hand.

'Ring?' Nikolai Parfenovich repeated, taken aback.

'Yes, that one there... the veiny one on your middle finger, what stone is it?' insisted Mitya like an irritated, stubborn child.

'It's a smoky topaz,' smiled Nikolai Parfenovich, 'do you want to have a look, I'll take it off...'

'No don't, don't take it off!' Mitya cried fiercely, realizing where he was and furious with himself, 'don't take it off, no need... Hell... Gentlemen, you've besmirched my soul! Do you honestly suppose that I would have concealed it from you if I had really killed my father, that I would have been evasive, lied, and equivocated? No, Dmitry Karamazov is not like that, he couldn't have tolerated that, and if I'd been guilty, I swear, I wouldn't have waited for you to arrive here or for the sun to rise, as was my intention earlier, I'd have put an end to myself before that, long before sunrise! I'm convinced of that now. I couldn't have learned in twenty years what I've learned this accursed night!... And I ask you, would I have carried on as I have tonight, as I am now, at this very instant, sitting here in front of you— would I have spoken to you as I did or behaved as I did, wouldn't I have regarded you and the world about me differently if I'd really killed my father, when even the thought that I had accidentally killed Grigory tortured me all night? Not from fear—oh, no!—it wasn't just fear of your punishment, it was the ignominy! And you want me to reveal to such cynics, such purblind moles as you, who see nothing and believe in nothing, yet another infamy of mine, yet more disgrace, even if it would shift the blame from me! I tell you, I'd rather be sent to the salt-mines! Whoever opened the door to my father's room and entered, he was the one who killed him. Who was he? That's what continues to torture me, that's where I'm at a loss, but it wasn't Dmitry Karamazov, that's for sure—and that's all I can tell you. Enough, stop persecuting me... Send me away, execute me, but don't keep on at me any more. I shan't say another word. Call your witnesses!'

Mitya came to the end of his sudden monologue, and appeared determined to hold his peace thenceforth. The prosecutor had been watching him all the while, and, immediately he stopped, added suddenly, with a most relaxed and indifferent expression, as though referring to something quite matter-of-fact:

'Talking about the open door that you mentioned just now, we can as it happens reveal to you an extremely curious and, for both of us, highly significant piece of evidence given by old

Grigory Vasilyev, whom you injured. When he came to, he clearly and positively stated the following in reply to our questions: hearing a noise outside, he went out on to the steps and decided to enter the garden by the wicket-gate, which was wide open; then, on entering the garden and before spotting you running away in the dark from the open window, through which, as you have already told us, you saw your father, he happened to glance to his left and saw that selfsame open window, but he also noticed that the door, which was much nearer to him, was wide open—that same door which you assured us was shut the whole time you were in the garden. You may as well know that Vasilyev is firmly convinced that you must have run out through that door—although, of course, he didn't see you run out with his own eyes—since, when he first spotted you, you were already some distance away from him in the garden and making for the fence...'

At this point, before he had finished speaking, Mitya leapt to his feet.

'Rubbish!' he yelled, beside himself. 'It's a filthy lie! He couldn't have seen the door open, because it was shut at the time... He's lying!...'

'I repeat, it is my duty to tell you that his evidence is unshakeable. He's absolutely convinced about it. He is adamant. We questioned him several times.'

'That's right, it was I who put the question to him several times!' confirmed Nikolai Parfenovich passionately, in his turn.

'It's not true, that's not true!' Mitya kept shouting. 'It's either a fabrication or the ravings of a lunatic, he was simply raving, what with the blood and the wound, he just imagined things when he came to... Not surprising!'

'Yes, but he noticed the open door not after he regained consciousness following the attack, but before, as he was entering the garden from the outhouse.'

'But that's not true, it isn't, it can't be! He's lying to spite me... He couldn't have seen it... I didn't run out through the door,' Mitya was gasping for breath.

The prosecutor turned towards Nikolai Parfenovich and said gravely:

'Show it to him.'

'Are you familiar with this object?' Nikolai Parfenovich placed on the table a large, stiff, business-size envelope, which still bore the remains of three seals. The envelope itself was empty and was torn open on one side. Mitya stared at it in wide-eyed amazement.

'It's... it's father's envelope, I'm sure,' he mumbled, 'the one that contained the three thousand... and where he's written, if you look, "to my chicky-bird"... Here we are: three thousand!' he exclaimed. 'Three thousand, you see?'

'Yes, of course we can see, but we didn't find any money in it, it was empty and lying on the floor, by the bed, behind the screen.'

For a few seconds Mitya stood thunderstruck.

'Gentlemen, it was Smerdyakov!' he yelled out suddenly, at the top of his voice, 'he's the one who killed him, he's the one who robbed him! He was the only one who knew where the old man had hidden the envelope... It was him, now it's clear!'

'But surely you knew about the envelope, too, and that it was under the pillow.'

'I never knew that! I never saw it before, this is the first time I've actually seen it; Smerdyakov mentioned it to me before, but that's all... He was the only one who knew where the old man had hidden it, I didn't...', Mitya shouted breathlessly.

'The fact remains, you told us yourself just now that the envelope was lying under your father's pillow. Those were your very words, "under the pillow", so you must have known where it was kept.'

'That's what we wrote down,' Nikolai Parfenovich confirmed.

'Rubbish, that's absurd! I had no idea it was under the pillow. And who knows, perhaps it wasn't under the pillow at all... I just said "under the pillow" without thinking... What did Smerdyakov tell you? Did you ask him where it was kept? What did he say? That's what matters... As for me, I deliberately made it up against myself... I blurted it out without suspecting it might have been under the pillow, and now you... It was a silly lie, the sort of thing you sometimes say on the spur of the moment. But in fact it was only Smerdyakov who knew, just Smerdyakov and nobody else!... He didn't reveal to me where it was kept either! But it was him, it was him; he killed him, it's all perfectly clear to me now,' Mitya kept shouting more and more frantically, repeating himself incoherently and becoming increasingly distraught and aggressive. 'Don't you understand, you've got to hurry up and arrest him, hurry... He killed him, after I had run away and while Grigory was lying senseless, that's plain now... He gave the signal, and father opened the door for him... Because only he knew the signal, and without the signal father would never have opened the door to anyone...'

'But again you're forgetting,' remarked the prosecutor as calmly as ever, but with a note of triumph in his voice now, 'that there was no need to give any signal, since the door was already open while you were there, while you were still in the garden...'

'The door, the door,' mumbled Mitya, staring at the prosecutor, and slumped helplessly into his chair. No one said a word.

'Yes, the door!... The damned door! God is against me!' he exclaimed, staring blankly ahead.

'You see,' said the prosecutor pompously, 'judge for yourself now, Dmitry Fyodorovich: on the one hand, we have the evidence of the open door through which you ran out into the garden—a highly incriminating piece of evidence, you have to agree—on the other hand, there's your incomprehensible, stubborn, and almost pathological secretiveness regarding the origin of the money which you suddenly had in your hands, despite the fact that, just three hours previously, you had according to your own testimony pledged your pistols in order to obtain a paltry ten roubles! In view of all this, judge for yourself—what are we to believe and what are we to make of it? And don't berate us for being "cold, derisive cynics", incapable of being moved by the noble sentiments of your soul... Try, on the contrary, to see it from our point of view...'

Mitya was in the most extreme state of agitation. He went pale.

'All right!' he exclaimed suddenly. 'I'll reveal my secret, I'll tell you where I got the money from!... I'll reveal my disgrace, so that I won't blame either you or myself later...'

'And rest assured, Dmitry Fyodorovich,' intoned Nikolai Parfenovich in a soft, gleefully unctuous voice, 'that any genuine and full admission on your part, especially if you make it at this juncture, may subsequently count inestimably in mitigation, and may even...'

But the prosecutor nudged him lightly under the table, and he stopped himself just in time. Mitya, in fact, was not even listening.

7

MITYA'S GREAT SECRET. HE IS MADE A LAUGHING-STOCK

'GENTLEMEN,' he began in the same agitated tone of voice, 'that money... I want to make a full confession... that money was *mine.*'

Both the prosecutor and the magistrate stared at him open-mouthed; this was not at all what they had expected to hear.

'What do you mean "yours"?' mumbled Nikolai Parfenovich. 'By your own admission, at five o'clock that same day...'

'To hell with five o'clock that same day and my own admission—that's beside the point! That money was mine, mine I say, that is, mine because I stole it... it wasn't money I already had, I stole it, fifteen hundred roubles, and I had it on me all the time...'

'But where did you get it?'

'From my neck, gentlemen, from my neck, from this here neck of mine... I had it here, round my neck, sewn into a piece of cloth and hanging round my neck for ages, it's been a month now that I've been carrying it round my neck in shame and ignominy.'

'Yes, but from whom did you... appropriate it?'

'You mean who did I steal it from? Stop beating about the bush. Yes, I suppose I might just as well have stolen it, appropriated it, if you wish. But the way I look at it, I stole it. And last night I really stole it.'

'Last night? But didn't you just say you got it... a month ago?'

'Yes, but not from father—oh no, don't worry, I didn't steal it from father—but from her. Let me give you the full story, and don't interrupt. It's not going to be easy for me. You see, a month ago Katerina Ivanovna Verkhovtseva, my former fiancée, asked me to go and see her... You know her, don't you?'

'Yes, of course.'

'I know you do. You couldn't ask for a nobler person, she's gold, pure gold, but she can't stand the sight of me, hasn't been able to do so for a long time now... and rightly, justifiably so!'

'Katerina Ivanovna?' the magistrate asked with surprise. The prosecutor, too, stared wide-eyed.

'Don't bandy her name about! I'm a scoundrel to have dragged her name into it. I could see she hated the sight of me... all along... right from the very beginning, when she first came to my lodgings... But enough, that's enough, you're not fit even to know about it, so let's not discuss the matter. All you need to know is that she saw me over a month ago, gave me three thousand roubles, some of which was to be sent to her sister and the remainder to a relative of hers in Moscow (as though she couldn't have sent it herself!), and I... this coincided exactly with that fateful hour in my life when I... in short, just when I fell in love with the other one, with *her*, my current one, the one you've got downstairs now, Grushenka... I whisked her off to Mokroye then, and in two days blew half of that damned three thousand, fifteen hundred in other words, but I still kept the other half. Well, it was that fifteen hundred which I was carrying around my neck like an amulet, and yesterday I tore it open and blew the rest of the money. What you've got in your hands now, Nikolai Parfenovich, is the eight hundred roubles change, the change from the fifteen hundred I had yesterday.'

'Just a moment, let's get this straight; a month ago you spent three thousand here, not fifteen hundred, everybody knows that, don't they?'

'Who does? Who counted? Did I let anybody count?'

'Look here, it was you yourself who went around telling everybody at the time that you had spent exactly three thousand.'

'True, I did say that, I told the whole town about it, and the whole town buzzed, and everybody believed that it was three thousand, and here in Mokroye they believed it too. Nevertheless, the fact remains that I spent fifteen hundred and not three thousand then—I stitched the remaining fifteen hundred into a makeshift purse; that's how it was, gentlemen, that's where I got the fifteen hundred I had last night...'

'That's almost incredible...', mumbled Nikolai Parfenovich.

'May I ask you', the prosecutor spoke at last, 'if you have revealed this circumstance to anyone else... that is, that you kept that fifteen hundred to yourself?'

'I haven't told anyone.'

'That's strange. You really mean to say you haven't told anyone?'

'No one at all. I said no one, I meant no one.'

'But why such secrecy? What compelled you to make such a mystery of it? Let me put it this way: you have finally forced yourself to reveal your secret to us, a very shameful one according to you, although in effect—that is, speaking purely relatively of course—that action—to be precise the appropriation, no doubt just as a short-term expedient, of someone else's three thousand roubles—that action was—the way I look at it, anyway, and taking into account your character—at worst, one of absolute stupidity rather than of wickedness... Well, granted, it may have been reckless in the extreme, but reckless as distinct from perfidious... That is to say, what I'm getting at is that, quite apart from your admission, many people in the town over this past month already had a shrewd idea about those squandered three thousand roubles of Miss Verkhovtseva's—I heard the story myself... Mikhail Makarovich, for example, heard it too. In the end it wasn't just a story, it had become the talk of the town. Besides, there is the suggestion, if I'm not mistaken, that you yourself admitted to someone that you had got this money from Miss Verkhovtseva... And so I can't help wondering why, until now, until this very last moment, you should have made such a mystery of this fifteen hundred roubles which, you say, you had retained, thus turning this secret of yours into a kind of phobia... It's incredible that such a secret could have caused you so much heartache to reveal... you even shouted just now that you'd rather go to the salt-mines than reveal it...'

The prosecutor stopped. He was agitated. He had not concealed his mortification, his anger almost, and had poured out

all his frustrations disjointedly and almost incoherently, even at
the expense of niceties of style.

'The ignominy consisted not in the fifteen hundred, but in the
fact that I had taken it from the three thousand,' Mitya said
firmly.

'But what', the prosecutor smirked with irritation, 'what's so
ignominious about splitting the three thousand which you'd
recklessly and, if you wish, ignominiously appropriated, into two
parts as you saw fit? Surely, what's more important is that you
appropriated the three thousand, rather than how you chose to
dispose of it. By the way, why in fact did you split it into two
parts? What for, what was the purpose behind it, would you mind
explaining that to us?'

'Gentlemen, the purpose is the whole point!' exclaimed Mitya.
'I split it out of sheer depravity, deliberately, mind you, because
in this case it's the deliberation which is the essence of the
depravity... And I kept it up for a whole month!'

'I don't understand.'

'You amaze me. Come to think of it, though, I will explain;
perhaps it really is difficult to understand. You see—it's like
this—I pocket the three thousand entrusted to me on my
honour; I then go on a spree with it, I blow every last kopeck,
and next morning I go to her and say: "I'm sorry, Katya, I've
spent your three thousand," well, how about that? It won't do,
will it? It's mean and dishonourable, I'm an animal, and, animal-
like, I've been unable to subdue my baser instincts, isn't that so?
Yet I'm not a thief, am I? Not an out-and-out thief, not really,
you must agree! I blew the money, but I didn't steal it! Now a
second, a more exciting version—listen carefully, I'll get all
muddled again if I'm not careful—I feel a bit dizzy—and so,
version number two: I go through only fifteen hundred here out
of the three thousand, half, in other words. Next day I go to her
with the other half: "Katya, take this half of your money from
me, villain and scoundrel that I am, because I've already blown
half and I'm bound to blow the other half too—I won't be able
to resist the temptation!" Well, what's the verdict in this case?
Anything you like—an animal, a scoundrel, but not a thief, not
yet anyway, because, had I been a thief, I'd surely not have

returned the remaining half. I'd have pocketed that too. This way, however, she can see that if the fellow has returned half, he'll come up with the rest too, in other words what he's already spent; he'll go on trying all his life, he'll slave his guts out, but he'll come up with it in the end and pay it back. This way, he's a scoundrel but not a thief—oh no, say what you like, but he's not a thief!'

'Fair enough, let's assume there is a distinction,' the prosecutor smiled coldly. 'What is puzzling, however, is that you should see it as such a fateful distinction.'

'Yes, I see it as a fateful distinction! Anyone can be a scoundrel—and, come to think of it, everyone is—but not anyone can be a thief, it takes an arch-scoundrel to be a thief. All right, let's not split hairs... It's just that a thief is more scurrilous than a scoundrel. Listen: I carry the money about with me for a whole month, any day I can decide to give it back and I'll no longer be a scoundrel, but the trouble is, I can't bring myself to make that decision, no matter how hard I try every day and no matter how much I keep repeating to myself every day: "Do it, go on, do it, you scoundrel," a whole month goes by and I still haven't done it, that's what! Well, is that a good thing in your view, is it?'

'Granted, it's not a good thing, that I can understand very well and I wouldn't argue about it,' the prosecutor replied with restraint. 'However, let us not indulge in any debates about niceties and fine distinctions; if you don't mind, can we please return to the matter in hand. And that is that, despite our requests, you still have not given us an explanation as to why you split the three thousand roubles in the first place, that is, why you frittered away one half and kept the other. Precisely why did you keep it, and exactly how did you intend to spend the fifteen hundred which you had kept? I insist you answer this question, Dmitry Fyodorovich.'

'Oh yes, of course!' exclaimed Mitya, slapping his forehead. 'I do beg your pardon, I've been keeping you on tenterhooks, and I haven't got around to explaining the main thing, otherwise you'd have understood in a flash, because it's in the intent, the depravity lies in the intent of it all! You see, it was all the fault of that old devil, my late father, he kept trying to lure Agrafena

Aleksandrovna away, making me jealous and convincing me that she couldn't make up her mind between me and him; so each day I thought, what if she suddenly came to a decision, what if she got tired of torturing me and suddenly said: "It's you I love, not him, take me to the ends of the earth." And all I had was two twenty-kopeck coins! How was I going to take her away? What was I to do? I'd have been lost. You see, at the time I didn't know what she was like, I thought she was after money and wouldn't put up with my being poor. So that's why I was crafty, counted out half the three thousand and sewed it up in this makeshift purse with a needle, all in cold blood, I sewed it up quite premeditatedly, before I even went on the spree, and only after I'd done that did I set off to paint the town red with the other half! That's a bit thick, isn't it! Do you understand now?'

The prosecutor simply burst out laughing, as did the magistrate.

'In my opinion, it was even prudent and moral of you to restrain yourself and not squander it all,' giggled Nikolai Parfenovich. 'For the life of me, I can't see what's wrong in that.'

'Because I stole it, that's what's wrong! My God, your lack of understanding terrifies me. All the time I had those fifteen hundred roubles sewn up and hanging round my neck, not a day, not an hour went by but I said to myself: "You're a thief, a thief!" That's why I went on the rampage for a whole month, why I picked a fight in the tavern, why I punched and kicked my father, because I felt I was a thief! I couldn't even bring myself to talk about the fifteen hundred to my brother Alyosha, because I felt I was such a cad, such a scoundrel! But I might as well tell you that while I was carrying the money about with me, I also said to myself every day, every hour: "No, Dmitry Fyodorovich, perhaps you're not quite a thief yet. Why not? Because you can still go to Katya tomorrow and give her back the fifteen hundred." And last night, on my way from Fenya to see Perkhotin, I finally resolved to tear the purse from my neck, something which right up to that moment I couldn't bring myself to do, and as soon I had removed it, that very instant I became a complete and unquestionable thief, a thief and a man without honour for the rest of his life. Why? Because, in removing the purse from my neck, I'd destroyed my cherished hope of going to Katya and saying to her: "I'm a scoundrel, but not a thief"! Now do you understand?'

'Just why did you decide to do it last night rather than at any other time?' interjected Nikolai Parfenovich.

'Why? That's a stupid question to ask. Because I had condemned myself to death, to die here at dawn, at five o'clock in the morning. "It makes no difference", I thought to myself, "whether I die an honourable man or a scoundrel!" But I was wrong, it does make a difference! Would you believe, gentlemen, that what tortured me most of the night wasn't the thought that I had killed the old servant and that I was in danger of being sent to Siberia—just when my love had been requited and heaven had opened up to me again. Don't misunderstand me, it did cause me suffering, but not half as much as the awareness that I had torn that accursed money from round my neck and squandered it, and that consequently I was plainly a thief! Oh, gentlemen, I assure you with all my heart, I have learned a lot during this night! I have learned that not only can one not live as a scoundrel, one cannot die a scoundrel either... No, gentlemen, one must die honourably!...'

Mitya was pale. Although he was extremely excited, he looked haggard and exhausted.

'I'm beginning to understand you, Dmitry Fyodorovich,' the prosecutor said with soft deliberation, almost with compassion, 'but I would suggest, with respect, that all this is just your nerves... you're suffering from nervous exhaustion, that's all it is. Why didn't you, for example, save yourself all this agony, which you've suffered for nearly a whole month in fact, by returning the fifteen hundred to the lady who had entrusted it to you, and why, in view of your circumstances—which as you yourself have indicated were dire at the time—didn't you discuss the matter with her and attempt to come to some reasonable understanding; in other words, why didn't you, after first making a clean and honourable breast of it, ask her for the necessary sum to cover your expenses, which she, with her characteristic magnanimity and seeing your distress, would surely not have denied you, especially if the agreement were backed up by a document or, come to that, by some pledge, like the one you offered to the merchant Samsonov and Mrs Khokhlakova? After all, you don't regard that pledge as worthless now, do you?'

Mitya went red in the face.

'Do you really take me for that much of a scoundrel?' he said, looking the prosecutor in the eye, as though in disbelief at what he heard. 'Surely you can't be serious?...'

'I assure you, I am... What makes you think I'm not serious?' the prosecutor, in his turn, looked surprised.

'Oh, it would have been dastardly! Gentlemen, do you realize, you're torturing me! If you'll bear with me, I'll tell you everything; look, I'm now going to confess to you the full extent of my iniquity, so as to shame you, and you'll be surprised when you see for yourselves what base scheming human emotions can lead to. Do you realize that I had already considered that idea, precisely the one you've just outlined, Mr Prosecutor! Yes, gentlemen, that idea had also occurred to me during that confounded month, and I was almost on the point of going to Katya, wretch that I was! But to go to her, to announce my treachery, and in the name of that treachery, to ask her, Katya, to ask for money (to ask, do you hear, to ask!), in order to perpetrate and, what's more, pay for that treachery and then to run off immediately with another woman, with her rival, the rival who detests and insults her—be sensible, you must be out of your mind, Mr Prosecutor!'

'Out of my mind,' smiled the prosecutor, 'that's as may be, but of course, in the heat of the moment I overlooked... the little matter of feminine jealousy... if it was a question of jealousy, as you maintain... yes, perhaps you have got a point there.'

'But that would have been such a dastardly thing to do,' Mitya struck his fist on the table in a frenzy, 'it would have stunk to high heaven! Do you realize that she could in fact have given me the money, and she would have, I'm sure of it, she'd have given it simply out of contempt for me, out of revenge, glorying in revenge, because she too has an evil soul, she's a woman of overpowering wrath! I'd have taken the money—oh, I would, indeed I would have—and then, all my life long... Oh God! I'm sorry, gentlemen, I keep shouting, because that very idea was still in my mind until recently, only the day before yesterday, even when I was going hammer and tongs at Lurcher that night, and then again yesterday, yes, yesterday, the whole day long, I remember it, right up to that incident...'

'What incident?' Nikolai Parfenovich butted in, full of curiosity, but Mitya didn't hear him.

'I've made a dreadful admission to you,' he concluded despondently. 'Recognize it, gentlemen, for what it's worth. But that's not enough, it's not enough just to recognize it, you have to respect it. If that too leaves your souls unmoved, then, I tell you, gentlemen, you really haven't a grain of respect for me, and I'll die of shame that I confessed to the likes of you! I'll shoot myself! No, you don't believe me, I can see you don't believe me! What, are you going to record that too?' he yelled, frightened now.

'Well, what you've just said,' Nikolai Parfenovich regarded him in amazement, 'namely, that right up to the last minute you still intended to go to Miss Verkhovtseva to ask her for that sum... I assure you, that is a very important piece of evidence for us, Dmitry Fyodorovich—I mean, your observations regarding the whole of this incident... and especially for you, it's especially important for you.'

'Have a heart, gentlemen!' Mitya raised his hands in supplication. 'Surely you don't have to write that down; shame on you! After all, you could say I've bared my soul in front of you, and you're taking advantage of the fact and are delving in the shattered remains... Oh God!'

He buried his face in his hands in despair.

'Don't upset yourself so, Dmitry Fyodorovich,' the prosecutor remarked, 'everything that's been written down will be read to you later, and anything you don't agree with we'll alter according to your wishes, but just for now let me put to you one little question for the third time: do you really mean to say that you told no one, absolutely no one, about the money you had sewn into the purse? I must confess I find that almost impossible to believe.'

'No one, absolutely no one! Haven't you understood anything? Don't go on about it.'

'Very well then, there's plenty of time to clear this matter up, but, meanwhile, think about this: we have maybe dozens of statements from witnesses stating that you yourself spread it around, shouted it from the rooftops in fact, that you spent three thousand last time—three thousand, not fifteen hundred—and even after this money turned up yesterday, you've managed to inform plenty of people that you brought three thousand with you this time too...'

'Not just dozens, you've got hundreds of statements,' exclaimed Mitya, 'a couple of hundred statements, a couple of hundred people heard me, a thousand heard me!'

'Well, there you are; everyone, but everyone will testify. Surely the word *everyone* means something?'

'It means nothing; I lied, and the rest of them just repeated what I said.'

'But why on earth should you have "lied", as you put it?'

'Heaven only knows. To show off, perhaps... I don't know... boasting... that I squandered so much money... To forget perhaps about the money round my neck... yes, that's right... hell... how many times are you going to ask me that question? I lied, and that's the end of the matter, I lied and didn't want to retract it. Why does a man lie sometimes?'

'It's rather difficult to determine, Dmitry Fyodorovich, what makes a person lie,' the prosecutor said thoughtfully. 'Tell me, however: was it large, this purse, as you call it, round your neck?'

'Not particularly.'

'Well, how large for example?'

'A hundred-rouble note folded in half—that's all.'

'Wouldn't it help if you showed us the bit of cloth? Surely you must have it on you somewhere.'

'You must be joking... what nonsense... I don't know where it is.'

'Please try to remember: precisely where and when did you take it off? Didn't you tell us yourself that you hadn't been back home?'

'It was after I'd left Fenya and was on my way to Perkhotin's; I tore it from round my neck and took out the money.'

'In the dark?'

'What would I need a lamp for? It only took a second.'

'Without scissors, on the street?'

'On the square, I think; why should I need scissors? It was an old piece of cloth, it tore easily.'

'What did you do with it then?'

'I dropped it there.'

'Where exactly?'

'On the square, of course, somewhere on the square! Heaven only knows, somewhere on the square. Why do you need to know that?'

'It's extremely important, Dmitry Fyodorovich, it's material evidence that can be helpful to you. Why don't you try to understand that? Who helped you sew it up a month ago?'

'Nobody helped me, I did it myself.'

'You can sew?'

'A soldier has to know how to sew; anyway, it's not much of a skill.'

'So where did you get the material from, I mean the piece of cloth you used?'

'Are you being funny?'

'Not at all, nothing could be further from our thoughts, Dmitry Fyodorovich.'

'I can't remember where I got the cloth from, must have got it from somewhere.'

'Not something one would easily forget, I would have thought!'

'Honest to God, I can't remember, maybe I tore up some of my underwear.'

'That's very interesting: we could look for this item at your lodgings tomorrow—perhaps you tore a piece out of a shirt. What kind of fabric was it, cotton or linen?'

'Who the devil knows. Wait... I don't think I tore it off anything. It was calico... I think I used my landlady's night-cap.'

'Your landlady's nightcap?'

'Yes, I pinched it from her.'

'You did what?'

'Yes, I remember, I really did pinch a nightcap once, to use as a rag or perhaps to wipe my pen on. I took it without telling anyone, it wasn't much good, there were bits of it all over my place, and then I suddenly had that fifteen hundred roubles, so I simply sewed it up... I think I sewed it up in a bit of that, a scrap of old calico that'd been washed thousands of times.'

'Are you sure about that?'

'I don't know about sure. I think it was the nightcap. What the hell!'

'In that case, wouldn't your landlady at least remember that this item of hers had disappeared?'

'Not at all, she didn't even miss it. An old piece of cloth, I'm telling you, just an old piece of cloth, not worth a kopeck.'

'And where did you get the needle and cotton from?'

'For heaven's sake! Enough is enough!' Mitya finally lost his temper.

'There again, it seems strange that you should have totally forgotten precisely where on the square you dropped this... er... purse.'

'Why don't you have the square swept tomorrow, perhaps you'll find it,' Mitya suggested sarcastically. 'Enough, gentlemen, that's enough,' he declared in an exhausted voice. 'I can see plainly that you don't believe me, you haven't believed a word I've said! It's my fault, not yours, I wish I hadn't said anything. Why, why did I have to demean myself by disclosing my secret! For you it's just a joke, I can see it by the look in your eyes. It's you, Mr Prosecutor, who has reduced me to this state! You can be proud of your efforts, that's for sure... I hope you burn in hell, you bloodsuckers!'

He lowered his head and covered his face with his hands. Neither the prosecutor nor the magistrate said a word. A minute later he raised his head and cast them a glazed look. His face expressed absolute, irredeemable despair, and he appeared to be sinking into silence and oblivion. However, it was necessary to continue with the proceedings; the questioning of the witnesses couldn't be delayed any longer. It was already about eight o'clock in the morning. The candles had long since been extinguished. Mikhail Makarovich and Kalganov, who had entered and left the room from time to time during the entire interrogation, now both left it again. Both the prosecutor and the magistrate looked extremely tired. The morning was dismal, the sky was clouded over, and it was pouring with rain. Mitya stared blankly at the windows.

'May I look out of the window?' he asked Nikolai Parfenovich suddenly.

'Yes, of course,' the latter replied.

Mitya got up and approached the window. The rain was beating heavily against the small, greenish panes. The muddy road ran right underneath the window, and further away in the distance, through the pall of rain, could be seen rows of black, dilapidated, unsightly huts, appearing even blacker and more dismal because of the rain. Mitya recalled the 'golden-haired Phoebus' in whose very first rays he had intended to shoot himself. 'On a morning like this it would probably have been even better,' he smiled, dropped his arms to his sides, and turned abruptly to face his tormentors.

'Gentlemen!' he exclaimed. 'I can see very well I've had it. But what about her? Tell me about her, I beg you; is she also going to perish along with me? She's innocent, I tell you, she was out of her mind when she shouted yesterday that she was "to blame for everything". She's completely and utterly innocent! I've been worrying about it all night long, ever since you started questioning me... Couldn't you possibly tell me what you intend to do with her now?'

'Have no fears whatsoever on that score, Dmitry Fyodorovich,' the prosecutor replied immediately, with evident haste, 'so far we've no cause to inconvenience in any way the lady for whom you express so much concern. I trust this will remain so... In fact, we'll do everything we possibly can in this regard. You may rest absolutely assured of that.'

'Gentlemen, thank you, I knew all along in spite of everything that you were fair and honest men. That's taken a load off my mind... Well, what shall we do now? I'm ready.'

'Right, well, we'd better get a move on. We must get down to questioning the witnesses without delay. We are duty-bound to do this in your presence, and therefore...'

'How about some tea first?' interrupted Nikolai Parfenovich. 'I think we've earned it!'

It was decided that if there was some tea ready downstairs (Mikhail Makarovich had, in all probability, gone to have some), it wouldn't be a bad idea to have a glass and then continue with the proceedings and postpone a formal break for tea and snacks until there was a more convenient moment. Tea had in fact been made downstairs, and some was soon brought up to them. At first Mitya declined the glass of tea which Nikolai Parfenovich kindly offered him, but later he asked for one himself and drank it eagerly. On the whole, he had a strangely exhausted look about him. One would have thought that, with his enormous physical stamina, he would have taken a night of revelry, even one filled with the most turbulent of emotions, in his stride. But he felt he could hardly sit straight, and at times everything appeared to sway in front of his eyes. 'It won't be long before I start raving,' he thought to himself.

8

THE WITNESSES' EVIDENCE. THE BAIRN

THE interrogation of the witnesses commenced. However, we shall not continue our story in as much detail as hitherto, and we shall therefore omit Nikolai Parfenovich's instructions to each of the witnesses in turn to testify truly and conscientiously, and his warning that they would be required subsequently to repeat their testimony under oath; nor shall we describe how each witness was asked to sign a record of his testimony, and so on and so forth. We shall merely note one thing, namely, that the main point to which the attention of all the witnesses was directed was the matter of the three thousand roubles, that is, whether it was actually three thousand or fifteen hundred, on the first occasion a month ago, and whether it had been three thousand or fifteen hundred during Dmitry Fyodorovich's second bout of revelry, on the night of the murder. Alas, all the statements without exception incriminated Mitya; not one was in his favour, and some even contained new, quite amazing evidence which contradicted his statements. The first person to be questioned was Trifon Borisych. He appeared before the interrogators without any trepidation; on the contrary, he wore an expression of uncompromising and severe indignation against the accused, which undoubtedly created an impression of absolute veracity and personal integrity. He testified in a restrained manner, spoke succinctly, waited until he was asked, and replied precisely and after due deliberation. He declared firmly and without hesitation that not less than three thousand must have been spent a month ago, and what's more anyone present would confirm that he had heard about the three thousand from 'Mitry Fyodorych' himself: 'The money that he squandered just on the gypsies! That alone would have been over a thousand, I shouldn't wonder.'

'Probably not even five hundred,' Mitya retorted gloomily in response, 'wish I'd counted at the time, was too drunk, more's the pity...'

On this occasion Mitya was sitting at the side of the room, his back to the curtains, listening gloomily with a sad, tired air, as if to say: 'Huh, you can testify anything you want, it makes no difference now!'

'More than a thousand went on them, Mitry Fyodorovich,' Trifon Borisych corrected him firmly, 'you threw money around as if there was no tomorrow, and they were only too happy to take it. Don't you realize they're a pack of thieves and swindlers, they're horse-thieves, we've chased them out of town, otherwise they'd probably have testified themselves as to how much they made out of you. I saw the money in your hands myself—didn't get around to counting it, that's true, you wouldn't let me—but from the look of it I'd say it was much more than fifteen hundred... well over fifteen hundred! I know money when I see it, I wasn't born yesterday...'

As to the previous night, Trifon Borisych declared flatly that as soon as Dmitry Fyodorovich had arrived, he himself had announced that he had three thousand roubles on him.

'Come now, Trifon Borisych,' Mitya objected, 'did I really say in so many words that I had three thousand on me?'

'You did, Mitry Fyodorovich. Andrei was there. Here's Andrei now, he hasn't left yet, he can confirm what I say. And inside, when you were treating the gypsy chorus, you shouted out for all to hear that you were into your sixth thousand—I took you to mean that that included what you'd already spent the previous time. Stepan and Semyon heard you, and Pyotr Fomich Kalganov was standing next to you at the time, perhaps he'll confirm it too...'

The reference to the sixth thousand was greeted with the utmost interest by the interrogators. This new version sounded most convincing: three and three make six, hence, three thousand on that occasion, plus three thousand now, and there you are—six, clear as can be.

Stepan and Semyon, the two peasants whom Trifon Borisych had mentioned, were questioned, as were the driver Andrei and Pyotr Fomich Kalganov. The peasants and the driver readily confirmed Trifon Borisych's evidence. Moreover, particular care was taken to record Andrei's account of his conversation with Mitya during the journey: 'Where do you think I, Dmitry Fyodorovich, will end up, in heaven or in hell, and will I be pardoned in the next world or not?' The 'psychologist' Ippolit Kyrillovich listened with an enigmatic smile, and finished by advising that this statement as to where Dmitry Fyodorovich was going to end up should also be 'entered on the record'.

Kalganov, who was called next, entered reluctantly, behaved sullenly and capriciously, and addressed the prosecutor and Nikolai Parfenovich as though he were seeing them for the first time in his life, whereas in fact he had long been a regular acquaintance of theirs. He began by saying, 'I know nothing about this, nor do I wish to know.' It turned out, however, that he had heard Dmitry's remark about the sixth thousand, and he had to admit that he had been standing close by at the time. When questioned as to the amount of money that was in Mitya's hand, his response was 'I don't know how much.' Regarding whether or not the Poles had been cheating at cards, he testified in the affirmative. In answer to repeated questions, he also explained that after the Poles had been ejected, Mitya's situation with regard to Agrafena Aleksandrovna had really improved and that she had told him that she loved him. He spoke of Agrafena Aleksandrovna with reservation and respect, as though she were a lady of the highest standing, and did not allow himself to refer to her as 'Grushenka' even once. In spite of the young man's evident reluctance to testify, Ippolit Kyrillovich questioned him at length, and it was from him that he learned the full details of what amounted to Mitya's 'romance' that night. Mitya did not interrupt Kalganov once. At long last the young man was allowed to go, and he departed with unconcealed indignation.

The Poles too were interrogated. Even though they had shut themselves in their bedroom they had not slept a wink all night, and with the arrival of the authorities they hurriedly got dressed and smartened themselves up, knowing full well that they would definitely be asked to testify. They presented themselves with dignity, although with some trepidation. The short gentleman, the 'boss', turned out to be a retired civil servant of the twelfth grade* who had served as a veterinary surgeon in Siberia and rejoiced in the name of Mr Mussjalowicz. Mr Wrublewski, on the other hand, turned out to be a jobbing toothpuller. At first, in spite of the fact that Nikolai Parfenovich was asking the questions, they both directed their answers to Mikhail Makarovich, who was standing a little apart from the others; they mistakenly took him for the highest-ranking and principal personage present, and addressed him after every second word as 'Pan Colonel'. Only after they had been corrected several times by Mikhail Makarovich himself did they realize that they should direct their answers to Nikolai Parfenovich. It transpired that, apart from the pronunciation of a few words, their command of spoken Russian was very good indeed. Touching upon his relationship, past and present, with Grushenka, Mr Mussjalowicz began to hold forth with pride and passion, so much so that Mitya lost his temper at once, and shouted that he would not allow a 'scoundrel' to talk like that in his presence. Mr Mussjalowicz immediately latched on to the word 'scoundrel' and asked for it to be entered into the record. Mitya boiled with rage.

'Scoundrel, yes, scoundrel! Go on, put it down, I couldn't care less about your record, I still say he's a scoundrel!' he yelled.

Although Nikolai Parfenovich entered it in the record, he nevertheless displayed a most praiseworthy professionalism and command of the situation during these tense exchanges: after strictly reprimanding Mitya, he immediately put an end to all further questions regarding the romantic aspect of the case, and hastened to turn to substantive matters. Among the substantive matters was one piece of evidence given by the Polish gentlemen which aroused extraordinary interest in the interrogators: Mr Mussjalowicz said that when they were in the small room Mitya had attempted to bribe him and had offered him three thousand roubles to clear off, seven hundred there and then, and the remaining two thousand three hundred 'tomorrow morning, first thing, in the town', and that he had sworn to do this on his honour, saying that he didn't have that amount on him here in Mokroye, but that he'd left the money in town. Mitya remonstrated passionately that he had not said he would definitely give him the money in town the next day, but Mr Wrublewski confirmed the evidence, and after a moment's reflection Mitya himself morosely agreed that the facts were probably as the Poles had said; he had been agitated at the time, and could well have said exactly that. The prosecutor immediately pounced on this admission: it appeared quite clear to the investigators (and that is how it was subsequently represented, in fact) that half, or a part, of the three thousand which Mitya had laid his hands on could well still be hidden somewhere in the town, or even somewhere there in Mokroye, which in turn served to clarify what was still an awkward fact from the investigators' point of view, namely that Mitya had been found with only eight hundred roubles in his possession—a point which, though isolated and rather insignificant in itself, nevertheless spoke in Mitya's favour to some extent. Now, however, even this last remaining piece of evidence in his favour was evaporating into thin air. In reply to the prosecutor's question: where was he thinking of getting the other two thousand three hundred roubles to give to the Polish gentleman in the morning, seeing that he himself maintained that, in spite of his promise to the Pole on his word of honour, he only had fifteen hundred on him, Mitya said firmly that he had wanted to offer 'the Polack' not money, but a formal assignment of his title to the estate in Chermashnya, those same rights which he had offered to Samsonov and Khokhlakova. The prosecutor could not resist a smile at 'the naïvety of the scheme'.

'And do you think he'd have agreed to accept that "title" instead of the two thousand three hundred roubles in cash?'

'Certainly he'd have agreed,' Mitya retorted excitedly. 'Just think, he could have made not just two, but four, even six thousand profit out of it! He could have summoned his lawyers immediately, the Poles and the Jews, and they'd have screwed not just three thousand out of the old devil, but the whole of Chermashnya.'

Mr Mussjalowicz's testimony was, of course, entered in the record in the minutest detail, after which the Polish gentlemen were allowed to go. The card-sharping incident was hardly even mentioned; Nikolai Parfenovich was only too satisfied with their evidence as it was, and he did not wish to bother them with trifles, all the more so as it had all been just a stupid drunken quarrel over cards and nothing more, what with all the revelry and riotous behaviour that night... Thus the money, the two hundred roubles, remained safely in the Polish gentlemen's pockets.

After that, the old man Maksimov was called. He was timidity itself, and approached with mincing steps, looking dishevelled and very downcast. He had been downstairs all this time, huddled next to Grushenka, sitting silently beside her and every now and again 'starting to snivel over her, wiping his eyes with his little blue-chequered handkerchief', as Mikhail Makarovich later recalled. In the end, it was she who was comforting and consoling him. The little old fellow immediately admitted, with tears in his eyes, that it was his fault for borrowing ten roubles from Dmitry Fyodorovich 'on account of my impecuniousness', and that he was ready to return the money... Questioned specifically on this point by Nikolai Parfenovich—had he noticed precisely how much money Dmitry Fyodorovich was holding in his hands, since, while he was borrowing the ten roubles he had been ideally placed to observe him holding the money—Maksimov replied most resolutely that the sum in question was 'twenty thousand'.

'And have you ever seen twenty thousand anywhere before?' asked Nikolai Parfenovich with a smile.

'Certainly I have, only it wasn't twenty, it was seven—when my wife mortgaged my little estate. She let me have a glimpse of it, but not close up, ever so proud she was. A very sizeable wad it was, all in hundred-rouble notes. The ones Dmitry Fyodorovich had were all hundreds, too...'

He was soon allowed to go. Finally, it was Grushenka's turn. The investigators seemed to be apprehensive about the effect her presence might have on Dmitry Fyodorovich, and Nikolai Parfenovich even muttered a few cautionary words, to which Mitya inclined his head in silence, indicating that there would be no outbursts. Mikhail Makarovich himself led Grushenka in. She entered with a grave and dejected expression, outwardly almost calm, and, as instructed, sat down silently on a chair opposite Nikolai Parfenovich. She was very pale; she seemed to feel the cold, and clutched her magnificent black shawl tightly around her shoulders. In fact, this was the onset of a fever—the start of a protracted illness which was to set in at the end of that day. Her stern air, direct and serious expression, and calm demeanour produced a very favourable impression upon everyone. Nikolai Parfenovich even found himself somewhat 'captivated'. Later, during various conversations, he would admit freely that not until that moment had he realized how 'magnificent' the woman really was; formerly, although he had seen her occasionally, he had always regarded her as something of a 'local Jezebel'. 'She has the most aristocratic manners,' he once blurted out ecstatically when talking to some ladies. The ladies affected to greet this with the utmost indignation, and he was immediately pronounced a 'wag', which pleased him no end. On entering the room, Grushenka glanced only fleetingly at Mitya; he, for his part, looked at her with apprehension, but her expression reassured him immediately. After the initial obligatory questions and admonitions, Nikolai Parfenovich, faltering slightly, but nevertheless with the utmost courtesy, asked her about her relationship with Ex-Lieutenant Dmitry Fyodorovich Karamazov. To this, Grushenka replied softly and firmly:

'We're acquainted, he's been calling on me for the past month.'

In response to further personal questions, she declared promptly and with all candour that although she had been fond of him 'on and off', she had not really loved him, but had led him on out of 'shameful wickedness', and the 'poor old fellow' too, that she had noticed that Mitya was very jealous of Fyodor Pavlovich, as he was of everyone else, but that this had only amused her. She had never had any intention at all of going to Fyodor Pavlovich, but was just having him on. 'During the last month my mind's been on something quite different; I was expecting another man, one who had wronged me... Only it seems to me', she concluded, 'you ought not to be prying into this, nor should I be answering you, because it's my own private business.'

Accordingly, Nikolai Parfenovich promptly refrained from probing into the 'romantic' aspects of the relationship, and concentrated instead on the crucial question of the three thousand roubles. Grushenka confirmed that the amount spent in Mokroye a month ago had indeed been three thousand, and that though she had not counted the money herself, Dmitry Fyodorovich had said that it was three thousand.

'Did he tell you that in private, in the presence of someone else, or did you merely overhear him telling others?' the prosecutor immediately wanted to know.

Grushenka replied that she had heard him say this to other people, and that he had told her both in the presence of others and when they were alone.

'Did he tell you this privately once or on several occasions?' the prosecutor enquired further, and learned that it had been on several occasions.

Ippolit Kyrillovich was highly satisfied with this testimony. From subsequent answers it also transpired that Grushenka knew where the money had come from, namely, that Dmitry Fyodorovich had got it from Katerina Ivanovna.

'And did you ever hear it mentioned, even if only once, that the sum squandered a month ago was not actually three thousand, but less, and that Dmitry Fyodorovich had kept no less than half of the original sum for himself?'

'No, I never heard that,' testified Grushenka.

In due course it even transpired that over the last month Mitya had told her frequently that he hadn't got a kopeck to his name. 'He was expecting to receive some money from his father,' Grushenka concluded.

'And did he ever say in front of you... accidentally, perhaps, or in a temper,' Nikolai Parfenovich suddenly dropped the bombshell, 'that he intended to make an attempt on the life of his father?'

'Yes, he did!' sighed Grushenka.

'Once or on several occasions?'

'He said it several times, always when he was in a temper.'

'And did you believe that he would carry out his threat?'

'No, never!' she replied firmly. 'I relied on his sense of honour.'

'Allow me, gentlemen,' exclaimed Mitya, 'allow me to say just one word to Agrafena Aleksandrovna in your presence.'

'Go ahead,' acquiesced Nikolai Parfenovich.

'Agrafena Aleksandrovna,' Mitya half rose from his chair, 'as God is my witness, I am not guilty of the blood of my father who was murdered yesterday!'

Having said this, Mitya sat down on his chair again. Grushenka got to her feet and, facing the icon, crossed herself devoutly.

'Thank God!' she said with heartfelt relief, and, still standing but turning now towards Nikolai Parfenovich, she added: 'You must believe what he has just said! I know him: he'll say anything off the top of his head to raise a laugh perhaps, or sometimes just to be awkward, but if it's a matter of conscience he'll never lie, he'll tell the truth straight out, believe me!'

'Thank you, Agrafena Aleksandrovna, you have comforted my soul!' said Mitya in a tremulous voice.

When asked how much money he had had on him the previous day, she replied that she did not know, but that she had heard him say many times that he had brought three thousand roubles with him. As to where he had got the money from, he had told her that he had 'stolen' it from Katerina Ivanovna, and she had replied that he hadn't stolen it at all and that he really ought to return it the next day, without fail. The prosecutor demanded to know which money he had been talking about when he said that he had stolen it from Katerina Ivanovna—the money he had had yesterday, or the three thousand he had squandered a month ago—and Grushenka thought that he had meant the money that he had had a month ago, or that was what she had understood, anyway.

Grushenka was finally dismissed, and Nikolai Parfenovich hastened to assure her that she could return to the town immediately if she so wished, and that if he, for his part, could be of any assistance, for instance in the matter of providing horses or, if she happened for instance to want an escort, then he... for his part...

'You are most kind,' Grushenka bowed to him in acknowledgement, 'but I'll go with that old gentleman, the landowner, I'll take him home, but meanwhile I'll wait downstairs if you'll allow me, to see what you decide about Dmitry Fyodorovich.'

She left. Mitya was calm and even fully alert, but this was short-lived. A strange physical weakness was coming over him more and more with every passing second. His eyes closed from exhaustion. The questioning of the witnesses was finally over. The final drafting of the record was in progress. Mitya got up from his chair and went into the corner by the curtain, stretched himself out on a large household chest covered with a rug, and immediately fell asleep. He had a strange dream, quite unrelated to both the time and the place. He dreamt he was travelling somewhere across the steppe, somewhere where he had once served in the army, in a carriage pulled through slushy snow by a pair of horses driven by a muzhik. Mitya felt the cold, it was the beginning of November, and the snow kept coming down in large, wet flakes which melted as soon as they touched the ground. The driver, however, valiantly urging his horses on, kept up a brisk pace; with his long, reddish beard, he was hardly an old man, only about fifty, and dressed in a shabby grey *zipun*.*
And there, not far ahead, was a village, its huts black as pitch, half of them burned down, with only the charred beams sticking out. And peasant women lined the road into the village, lots of them, all in a row, every one emaciated, haggard, with peculiarly brown faces. Beyond the crowd he noticed one in particular, tall and gaunt, looking about forty but probably no more than twenty; her face was drawn and ashen, and in her arms she held a crying infant, and her breasts seemed to be so shrunken that there could not be a drop of milk in them. And the child cried incessantly, stretching forth its bare little arms, clenching its fists, which were quite blue with the cold.

'Why are they crying? What's wrong?' asked Mitya, dashing past them at a sprightly pace.

'The bairn,' replied the driver, 'the bairn's weeping.' And what amazed Mitya was the fact that he had said it in dialect, the way they said it in the country—'bairn' rather than 'child'. He was glad the muzhik had said 'bairn'; it was as though this was more compassionate.

'But why is it crying?' Mitya kept insisting fatuously. 'Why are its arms bare, why doesn't someone wrap it up?'

'The bairn's frozen, the cold's gone right through its clothes, there's no warmth in them.'

'But why should that be so? Why?' persisted Mitya, like a fool.

'They're poor, there's been a fire, now they've no bread, they're asking for aid for the burned-out village.'

'No, no,' Mitya still appeared not to understand, 'tell me, why are those homeless mothers just standing there, why are the people so poor, why is the bairn so distressed, why are the steppes so bare, why don't they hug one another, why don't they kiss one another, why don't they sing joyful songs, why are they so ashen-faced and laden with so much despair and grief, why don't they feed the bairn?'

And he felt that although his questions were devoid of rhyme or reason, that was precisely how he wanted to pose them, and that was in fact how they should be posed. And he also felt a totally unprecedented wave of emotion well up in his soul which brought him to the verge of tears and made him want to do something for everyone, something that would make the bairn stop crying, that would make its ashen-faced mother stop crying too, something that, from that moment on, would put an end to all tears once and for all, and he wanted to do it then, immediately, without brooking the least delay and with truly Karamazovian impetuosity.

'And I'm with you, I shan't leave you now, I'll stay with you for life,' he heard Grushenka's dear voice, suffused with emotion, ring out beside him. And suddenly his whole heart began to glow and to surge towards some kind of light, and he wanted to live and go on living, to go and to continue on some kind of a journey to a new and beckoning light, and to do it faster and faster, now, at once!

'What? Where?' he exclaimed, opening his eyes and sitting up on the chest as if he had just recovered from a faint, and smiling brightly. Nikolai Parfenovich was standing over him, asking him to hear the record read out and sign it. Mitya realized that he had been asleep for an hour or more, but he did not listen to what Nikolai Parfenovich was saying. His attention was suddenly attracted by the fact that under his head there was a pillow which had not been there when he had slumped down, exhausted, on top of the chest.

'Who brought the pillow and put it under my head?' he exclaimed with gratitude and elation, his voice shaking with emotion, as though some overwhelming kindness had been

performed. It was never established who the kind person was—
probably one of the witnesses, or perhaps it was Nikolai Parfenovich's secretary who had compassionately instructed that a
pillow be placed under his head—but it stirred his soul and
brought tears to his eyes. He went to the table and announced
that he would sign anything that was required.

'I've had a good dream, gentlemen,' he said in a strangely
altered voice, his face radiating with new-found happiness.

9

MITYA IS TAKEN AWAY

AFTER the record had been signed, Nikolai Parfenovich turned
solemnly to the accused and read out the charge, which stated
that 'having, in such-and-such a year and on such-and-such a
day, in the place indicated, examined the suspect (namely Mitya),
accused of such-and-such crimes (all accusations had been
meticulously listed), and taking into consideration the fact that
the accused, having pleaded "not guilty" in respect of the crimes
with which he has been charged, has not advanced anything in
his own defence, whereas the witnesses (names appended) and
evidence (detailed herewith) incriminate him totally, the regional
investigative magistrate has decreed, under such-and-such sec-
tions of the Penal Code etc., that, in order to prevent him evading
investigation and trial, so-and-so (Mitya) be confined in such-
and-such a prison, the accused to be duly informed thereof, and
a copy of this document to be lodged with the assistant prosecutor
etc., etc.' In a word, Mitya was informed that, as from that
moment, he was a prisoner and was about to be taken to the town,
where he would be confined in some very disagreeable quarters.
Mitya listened attentively and merely shrugged his shoulders.

'All right, gentlemen, I don't blame you, I'm ready... I
understand, you've no alternative.'

Nikolai Parfenovich explained to him gently that he would be
taken to his place of confinement immediately by the district
police officer, Mavriky Mavrikyevich, who happened to be
available...

'Wait!' Mitya suddenly interrupted him, and turning to all the occupants of the room he began to speak with an outburst of emotion. 'Gentlemen, we are all cruel, we are all monsters, we all cause suffering to people—to mothers and their infants— but, have it your way, I'm worse than anyone! So be it! Every day of my life, beating my breast, I've promised to mend my ways, and every day I've continued to wallow in the same vileness. I see now that my kind needs to be taught a lesson by fate, to be caught in a trap and made to submit to some brute, external force. Never, never in my life would I have reformed of my own accord! But the thunder has crashed.* I accept the suffering that will result from the charges laid against me and from my public disgrace, I want to suffer and to seek absolution through suffering! Perhaps I will be absolved, gentlemen, eh? But take note: for the last time, I am innocent of my father's blood! I accept my punishment, not because I killed him, but because I wanted to kill him and, perhaps, really would have killed him... All the same, however, I intend to fight and I give you notice of it here and now. I shall fight you to the bitter end, and let God be the judge! Farewell, gentlemen, don't be angry with me for shouting at you during the interrogation, oh, I was still so naïve then... Soon I shall be a convict, and now Dmitry Karamazov proffers you his hand for the last time as a free man. Farewell to you and farewell to everyone!...'

His voice shook and he was just about to offer his hand, but Nikolai Parfenovich, who was nearest to him, quickly withdrew his hand. Seeing this, Mitya shuddered. He immediately let drop the hand which he had already half extended.

'The examination is not over yet,' mumbled Nikolai Parfenovich, somewhat embarrassed, 'we shall continue the proceedings in town, and I for my part of course wish you the best of luck... and hope that things will go your way... As a matter of fact, Dmitry Fyodorovich, I've always been inclined to regard you as a man rather more sinned against, so to speak, than sinning... We are all, if I may be so bold as to speak on behalf of the company here present, only too ready to regard you as a basically honourable young man, though alas rather too prone to certain passions...'

Nikolai Parfenovich's diminutive figure assumed a posture of the utmost dignity. For a moment Mitya thought that this young 'boy' was suddenly going to take him by his elbow, lead him to the far corner of the room, and there resume their recent conversation about 'girls'. It is amazing what incongruous and inappropriate thoughts can sometimes flash through the mind, even of that of a criminal being led to his execution.

'Gentlemen, you're kind, you're humane—could I see *her*, say goodbye to her for the last time?' asked Mitya.

'Certainly, but in view of... in short, we'll also have to be present...'

'Well, I don't mind if you stay!'

Grushenka was brought in, but the farewell that took place was brief, few words were exchanged, and Nikolai Parfenovich was left rather dissatisfied. Grushenka made a deep bow towards Mitya.

'I've told you that I'm yours and always shall be, I'll go with you for ever, wherever they send you. Farewell, you are a poor innocent who's brought ruin upon himself!'

Her lips trembled and tears streamed down her face.

'Forgive me, Grusha, for my love, my love that has brought about your downfall too!'

Mitya was going to say something else, but he suddenly broke off and left the room. He was immediately surrounded by people who would not let him out of their sight. At the bottom of the steps, to which he had driven up with such brio in Andrei's troika only yesterday, two peasant carts stood ready and waiting. Mavriky Mavrikyevich, a short, stocky man with sagging features, was irritated by some unexpected hitch, and stamped about fuming and shouting. The manner in which he motioned Mitya to get into the cart was scarcely polite. 'You'd never think it was the same man I used to buy drinks for at the tavern,' Mitya thought, as he clambered up into the cart. Trifon Borisych also came down the steps. People had gathered at the gate, peasants, women, drivers—all eyes were turned on Mitya.

'Farewell, my good people!' Mitya suddenly called out to them from the cart.

'And to you,' resounded several voices.

'Farewell to you, too, Trifon Borisych!'

But Trifon Borisych did not even turn round, perhaps he was

just very preoccupied. He was shouting for some reason, and busying himself. It turned out that something was not in order with the second cart, which was to follow with two policemen. The peasant who was to drive the second cart was taking his time putting on his coat, a shabby, ragged garment, and arguing for all he was worth that it was not his turn but Akim's. But Akim was nowhere to be seen, and someone ran to look for him; the peasant continued to object, and argued that they should wait.

'These people, Mavriky Mavrikyevich,' Trifon Borisych kept exclaiming, 'haven't got an ounce of shame! You had twenty-five kopecks from Akim the other day and you blew it all on drink, and now you're making all this fuss. You're astonishingly kind to our good-for-nothing peasants, Mavriky Mavrikyevich, that's all I can say.'

'What do you need a second cart for?' Mitya butted in. 'Why don't we take just one, Mavriky Mavrikyevich; I'm not going to cause trouble or try to escape, so what's the escort for?'

'I wish you wouldn't be so familiar, and I wish you'd learn to address me properly, sir,' Mavriky Mavrikyevich snapped back viciously, as though glad of an opportunity to vent his anger, 'and you know what you can do with your advice...'

Mitya flushed and did not reply. The very next moment, he began to feel terribly cold. The rain had stopped, but the murky sky was full of clouds and a sharp wind was blowing straight into his face. 'Am I getting a chill?' thought Mitya, and shuddered. At long last Mavriky Mavrikyevich got up into the cart, sat down heavily, and spread himself out on the seat, as though unaware that he was cramping Mitya. There was no doubt that he was in a very foul mood and that the mission with which he was charged was not at all to his liking.

'Farewell, Trifon Borisych!' Mitya called out again, and he knew that it was not out of the goodness of his heart that he did so, but in anger and belying his true feelings. But Trifon Borisych remained standing haughtily, his hands behind his back, staring straight at Mitya with a cold angry stare, and did not utter a word.

'Farewell, Dmitry Fyodorovich, farewell!' the words rang out, and Kalganov suddenly appeared from nowhere. He ran up to the cart and held out his hand to Mitya. He was bareheaded. Mitya managed to grab hold of his hand and shake it.

'Farewell, you're a good man, I shan't forget your kindness!' he said warmly. But the cart moved off and their hands drew apart. The harness-bell began to tinkle—Mitya was taken away.

Kalganov rushed back into the entrance hall, sat down in a corner, lowered his head, buried his face in his hands, and began to cry; he sat there and cried for a long time, as though he were a small boy, rather than a twenty-year-old man. He was almost convinced of Mitya's guilt! 'That's people for you, that's what people are really like!' he kept repeating to himself in bitter distress, almost in despair. He was quite sick of life at that moment. 'Is it worth it, is it really all worth it?' the young man repeated bitterly.

PART FOUR

PART FOUR

BOOK TEN
Schoolboys

1
KOLYA KRASOTKIN

THE beginning of November; the temperature in our parts dropped to minus eleven degrees, and the roads became icy. A little dry snow fell on the frozen earth in the night, a wind, 'dry and sharp',* picked it up and whirled it in flurries around the mean streets of our little town, and particularly around the market square. A murky morning, but the snow had stopped. Not far from the square, near the Plotnikovs' shop, stands the small house, neat and tidy both inside and out, of the widow of the civil servant Krasotkin. Krasotkin himself, a provincial secretary, had died a long time before, about fourteen years ago, but his widow, thirty years old and still quite an attractive little woman, is still with us, living 'on her capital' in her neat little house. She leads an honest and humble life, and has a gentle but cheerful character. She was only about eighteen when, after barely a year of marriage and just after the birth of their son, her husband died. From that time, from the moment of his death, she had devoted herself to bringing up her beloved little Kolya, and although she had loved him to distraction all his fourteen years, she had nevertheless, of course, experienced far more suffering than joy on his account, trembling and dying of fear almost every day, afraid that he might fall ill, catch cold, do something naughty, climb on a chair and fall off, and so on and so forth. When Kolya started elementary school and then entered our high school, his mother enthusiastically set about studying all the subjects so that she could help him and revise all his lessons with him; she made it her business to get to know the teachers and their wives, she even fussed over Kolya's schoolmates, flattering them, so that they would not pick on Kolya or tease him or hit him. She carried this so far, in fact, that the boys began to make fun of him because of her, and they mocked him, calling him 'mummy's little boy'. But the boy knew how to stand up for himself. He was a brave lad; a rumour that he was 'terribly strong' grew and spread amongst his classmates; he was sharp, determined in character, and daring and enterprising in spirit. He studied well, and it was even said that in arithmetic and world history he was a match for the schoolmaster Dardanelov himself. But although he was aware of his own abilities, he was a good friend and did not show off. He accepted the boys' respect as his due, but behaved in a friendly manner. Most importantly, he knew where to draw the line, showed discretion when the occasion required and, in his dealings with the authorities, never overstepped that final and inviolable limit beyond which it is forbidden to go, for this would lead to disorder, rebellion, and contempt for rules and regulations. Nevertheless, he was not in the least averse to a bit of mischief-making and, whenever a suitable opportunity presented itself, he could be as unruly as the next boy, not so much indulging in pranks, as being good at inventing things, inventing and imparting a touch of spice, adding zest to events, and putting on a bit of an act. Above all, he had considerable self-esteem. He had even managed to manipulate his own mother into an attitude of submission to himself, behaving almost despotically towards her. And she had submitted; indeed she had submitted long ago, and now she just could not bear to think for a moment that her boy 'did not have much love for her'. It always seemed to her that Kolya was aloof towards her, and on occasion she would weep hysterically and begin to reproach him for his aloofness. The boy did not like this, and the more anyone tried to elicit expressions of sentiment from him the more stubborn he became, as if on purpose. However, he behaved thus not deliberately but involuntarily—such was his nature. His mother was mistaken; he loved her dearly, what he hated was 'all this soppiness', as he used to say in his schoolboy language. His father had left a bookcase in which were kept some books; Kolya loved reading, and he had already read several of them. His mother found this incomprehensible, and was sometimes simply astonished to see the boy standing by the bookcase for hours on end, poring over

some book instead of going out to play. And so it was that Kolya
had read some things that he should not have been allowed to
read at his age. Incidentally, although the boy did not like to take
his pranks too far, there had been some escapades recently
which had seriously frightened his mother—true, they were
nothing immoral, but they were daring, even reckless. In July
that very summer, during the school holidays, it happened that
mother and son had set off to spend a week in another district
seventy versts away, staying with a distant relative whose husband
worked at the railway station (that same station, the nearest one
to our town, where a month later Ivan Fyodorovich Karamazov
was to take the train for Moscow). There Kolya began by
exploring the railway line and learning all about trains, expecting
that, when he returned home, his new-found knowledge would
enable him to cut a dash among the boys at school. However,
there happened to be several other boys there at just the same
time—some were living next to the station, the others nearby—
about six or seven youngsters in all, their ages ranging from
twelve to fifteen, and two of these were from our town. The boys
played together, got up to mischief, and on the fourth or fifth
day of their stay those foolhardy boys made a silly bet of two
roubles with one another: Kolya, almost the youngest and,
therefore, rather patronized by the older boys, suggested out of
sheer bravado that that evening, when the eleven o'clock train
was due, he should lie face down between the rails and remain
there, without moving, while the train passed over him at full
speed. It was true that he had carried out a preliminary
investigation, which had demonstrated that it was indeed possible
to lie prostrate between the rails, and that the train would, of
course, pass over and not touch anyone lying thus, but actually
to bring oneself to do it was quite another matter! Kolya insisted
that he would lie there. At first they laughed at him and called
him a liar and a braggart, but this only heightened his resolve.
The point was that those fifteen-year-olds had turned their
noses up at him once too often, and had even refused to let him
join the gang at first, considering him 'too young', which had
been unbearably humiliating. And so it was decided that they
would go that evening to a spot a verst from the station, so that
the train, having pulled out of the station, would have had time

to reach full speed. The boys met. It was a moonless night, not just dark, but almost black. At the appointed hour Kolya lay down between the rails. The other five who had laid bets waited in the bushes under the embankment by the road, with sinking hearts and, in the end, in a state of terror and repentance. At last the train chugged in the distance, pulling out of the station. Two red headlights winked in the dark, the approaching monster began to rumble. 'Run, get off the track!' the boys, dying from terror, shouted to Kolya from the bushes, but it was already too late; the train leapt upon him and tore past. The boys rushed to Kolya; he lay motionless. They started to tug him and tried to lift him. Suddenly he got up and, without a word, walked down the embankment. At the bottom of the embankment he declared that he had deliberately lain there as if unconscious in order to frighten them, but the truth was, as he admitted much later to his mother, that he really had lost consciousness. Thus he acquired for ever a reputation as a 'desperado'. He came back to the station as white as a sheet. The next day he developed a slight nervous rash, but in spirit he was terribly cheerful, happy, and content. News of the incident did not spread at once, and it was only after they returned to our town that it reached the high school and came to the attention of the teachers. But Kolya's mother lost no time in pleading for her son, and the upshot of it was that the respected and influential master Dardanelov interceded on his behalf and the matter was dropped. This Dardanelov, a bachelor and still quite young, had been passionately in love with Mrs Krasotkina for many years, and had already once, the previous year, plucked up courage and, most respectfully and almost dying from terror and shyness, proposed to her, but she had refused point-blank, considering that to accept would have been to betray her son; nevertheless, due to certain mysterious intimations, Dardanelov was maybe justified in believing that he was not altogether unattractive to the charming but all too chaste and vulnerable widow. Kolya's mad escapade seemed to break the ice, and as a result of his intercession Dardanelov saw a glimmer of hope, faint hope, certainly, but being a paragon of chastity and delicacy himself, this was enough for the time being to render him deliriously happy. He loved the boy, although he would have considered it improper to try to ingratiate himself, and in class he treated him strictly and without favouritism. But Kolya too maintained a respectful distance, did his lessons well, was second in the class, showed due deference to Dardanelov, and the whole class firmly believed that Kolya was so good at world history that he could beat Dardanelov himself at it. And, in fact, one day Kolya asked the question: 'Who founded Troy?' in answer to which Dardanelov offered only generalities about peoples, their migration and resettlement, about how long ago it was, and about myths; but as to who had actually founded Troy, exactly which persons, he could not answer, and he even found the question somewhat flippant and irrelevant. The boys remained convinced that Dardanelov did not know who founded Troy. Kolya looked up the founders of Troy in Smaragdov,* a copy of which had been among the books in the bookcase left by his father. In the end, all the boys began to take an interest: who had, in fact, founded Troy? But Krasotkin did not reveal his secret, and his awesome reputation for erudition remained unchallenged.

After the incident on the railway Kolya's relationship with his mother underwent a certain change. When Anna Fyodorovna (the widow Mrs Krasotkina) learned of her son's exploit, she nearly went out of her mind with horror. She fell into such terrible fits of hysteria, lasting on and off for several days, that Kolya, now seriously frightened, gave her his word of honour that he would never engage in similar exploits again. In response to his mother's demands, he knelt before the icon and swore on his father's memory. The 'manly' Kolya burst into tears from emotion, like a six-year-old, and they spent that day embracing each other and sobbing on each other's shoulders. The next day Kolya awoke as 'cold-hearted' as ever, but he was less talkative, more modest, more mature, and more thoughtful. True, about a month and a half later he was again involved in a prank, and his name even came to the attention of our local magistrate, but this prank was of quite a different order—amusing even, and silly— and besides it appeared he was not the instigator, but only a participant. But more of that later, perhaps. His mother continued to have fits of hysteria and to torment herself, while Dardanelov's hopes increased the more she worried. It should be noted that Kolya guessed Dardanelov's feelings, understood

what was going on, and of course despised him for his 'sentimentality'; previously, he would not even have hesitated to show his
contempt in front of his mother, hinting vaguely that he knew
what Dardanelov was up to. But since the incident on the railway
line, his attitude in this respect too had altered, he did not allow
himself to cast even the slightest aspersion, and he began to be
more respectful when talking to his mother about Dardanelov,
which the sensitive Anna Fyodorovna noticed at once with
infinite gratitude; on the other hand, at the slightest, most
inconsequential mention of Dardanelov by some visitor in
Kolya's presence, she would blush like a beetroot with embarrassment. At such moments Kolya would either gaze gloomily
out of the window, look down at his boots as if studying them for
signs of wear, or brusquely call Perezvon, a rather large, mangy,
shaggy-haired dog which he had suddenly acquired from somewhere or other the previous month, enticed into the house, and
for some reason kept hidden indoors, not showing it to any of
his friends. He tyrannized the dog dreadfully, forcing it to do all
kinds of tricks, and reduced the poor animal to such a state that
it howled when he was at school, but when he returned it yelped
with delight, leapt about as if demented, fawned on him, rolled
on the ground, played possum, and so on—in a word, showed
off all the tricks that he had taught it, no longer on command,
but out of the sheer exuberance of its canine emotions and its
grateful heart.

   Incidentally, I forgot to mention that Kolya Krasotkin was that
same boy whom the retired Staff Captain's son, Ilyusha, already
known to the reader, stabbed in the thigh with a penknife in
defence of his father, mockingly nicknamed 'Loofah' by these
very same schoolboys.

2

CHILDREN

THUS it was that on that cold, frosty November morning, Kolya
Krasotkin was at home. It was Sunday and there was no school.
But eleven o'clock had already struck and he had to go out,

without fail, 'on a very important matter'; meanwhile, however, he was alone in the house as if he were solely in charge, because it so happened that, due to some pressing and unusual circumstance, all the older occupants had gone out. Across the hallway from the rooms that the widow Krasotkina herself occupied were two small letting-rooms, the only ones to let in the house, which were rented out by her to a doctor's wife with two young children. This doctor's wife was the same age as Anna Fyodorovna and a great friend of hers. The doctor himself had left nearly a year ago to go first to Orenburg and then to Tashkent, and nothing had been seen or heard of him for six months, so had it not been for her friendship with Mrs Krasotkina, which helped to assuage her grief, his wife would undoubtedly have wept until she had no tears left to shed. And now, to crown it all, that very Saturday night Katerina, the doctor's wife's only servant, had suddenly and, as far as her mistress was concerned, quite out of the blue, announced that she was going to give birth to a baby before morning. That no one had noticed anything earlier was nothing short of a miracle to everyone. Having barely recovered from her astonishment, the doctor's wife had decided to take Katerina while there was still time to a place in our town which handled such matters and where there was a midwife. As she valued this servant of hers very much, she lost no time in making the necessary arrangements, and not only took her there but even stayed with her. Later—the following morning as it happens—Mrs Krasotkina's own friendly help and support were enlisted for she knew several people she could turn to and who would under the circumstances be able to pull a few strings. So, both ladies were out; Mrs Krasotkina's servant Agafya had gone to the market, and Kolya thus found himself temporarily the minder and guardian of the 'small fry'—the small son and daughter of the doctor's wife—who had been left unattended. He was not worried about being left in charge of the house, and besides he had Perezvon, who had been ordered to lie under the bench in the hall and 'stay', and who therefore shook his head and gave two loud, ingratiating thumps on the floor with his tail every time Kolya entered the hall as he went from room to room, but alas, the summoning whistle failed to materialize. Kolya just looked severely at the poor dog, who would once more freeze into obedient immobility. If anything bothered Kolya, it was the 'small fry'. It goes without saying that he looked upon the unexpected drama caused by Katerina with the deepest disdain, but he was very fond of the small fry left in his charge and had already given them a children's book. The little girl Nastya, the elder of the two and already eight years old, could read, and the younger, seven-year-old Kostya, loved to listen while she read to him. Of course, Kolya could have amused them better if he had involved himself with them and played soldiers and hide-and-seek all over the house. He had done this more than once before and did not mind playing such games, with the result that a rumour had even reached his class once that Krasotkin played hobby-horses at home with his little lodgers, prancing like a trace-horse and arching his neck, but Krasotkin had scornfully denied the accusation, saying that for his contemporaries, his thirteen-year-old friends, it would certainly be shameful to play hobby-horses 'in our day and age', but that he did it for the sake of the 'small fry' because he was very fond of them, and he dared anyone to ask him to justify his feelings. And, consequently, both the little ones worshipped him. But on this occasion there was no question of playing. He had a matter of great personal importance to deal with, a matter even bordering on the mysterious. Meanwhile, time was running out and Agafya, with whom he could have left the children, had still not returned from the market. Several times already he had crossed the hallway, merely opened the door to the other flat and cast an anxious glance at the 'small fry', who, on his instructions, were sitting with a book and grinned from ear to ear each time he opened the door, expecting him to come in and do something exciting and amusing. But something was preying on Kolya's mind and he did not enter. At last eleven o'clock struck, and he made a firm and final decision that if that 'damned' Agafya did not return in ten minutes, he would leave without waiting for her, having first assured himself of course that the 'small fry' would not be scared to be left alone, would not misbehave, and would not cry from fear. Thinking along these lines, he put on his quilted winter coat with the sealskin collar, slung his bag over his shoulder, and, in spite of his mother's earlier, repeated admonitions not to go out in 'such cold' without his overshoes, gave these a scornful glance, crossed the hallway, and went out. Perezvon, seeing him in his outdoor clothes, started to beat his tail on the floor louder than ever, his whole body twitching with excitement, and he even let out a plaintive wail, but at the sight of such passionate canine excitement Kolya decided that it was a breach of discipline and made him stay under the bench until the last moment, whistling to him only after he had opened the hall door. The dog bounded forward crazily and rushed ahead of him, leaping about with delight. Kolya crossed the hallway and opened the door to the room where the 'small fry' were. They were both sitting at the table as before, no longer reading but squabbling heatedly over something. These two often quarrelled amongst themselves over various delicate matters concerning everyday life, and Nastya, the elder, always came off best; Kostya, if he did not agree with her, would appeal to Kolya Krasotkin, whose decision was accepted by both parties as final and binding. On this occasion the children's quarrel intrigued Krasotkin and he stopped at the door to listen. The children saw that he was listening and carried on their dispute with increased intensity.

'I don't believe you,' lisped Nastya fervently, 'I'll never believe that midwives find babies in the kitchen garden between the cabbage-beds. It's winter now and there aren't any cabbage-beds and she couldn't have brought Katerina a little daughter.'

'Phew!' Kolya whistled to himself.

'Or it's like this: they bring them from somewhere or other, but only to ladies who are married.'

Kostya stared at Nastya, listening thoughtfully and considering.

'Nastya, you're so silly,' he said at last, firmly and calmly. 'How can Katerina have a baby when she isn't married?'

Nastya really lost her temper.

'You don't understand anything,' she snapped crossly, 'perhaps she had a husband, but he's in prison and she went and had a baby.'

'Is her husband really in prison?' enquired the trustful Kostya gravely.

'Or perhaps it's like this,' Nastya interrupted excitedly, abandoning and forgetting all about her earlier hypothesis, 'she hasn't got a husband, you're right, but she wants to get married, so she started to think about how to get married, and she thought and thought, and she thought about it so hard that in the end she got a baby instead of a husband.'

'Well, I suppose it could be like that,' agreed Kostya, quite flattened, 'only you didn't mention that before, so how was I to know?'

'Well, you two,' said Kolya, stepping into the room, 'I see you're having a little argument!'

'Is Perezvon with you?' asked Kostya with a wide grin, and began to click his fingers and call Perezvon.

'Children, I've got a problem,' Krasotkin began seriously, 'and I need your help: Agafya must have broken her leg or something, since she hasn't come home yet, and I've got to go out. Will you let me go or not?'

The children looked at each other anxiously, and their smiling faces began to look worried. They did not really understand quite what he expected of them.

'You won't get up to anything while I'm away, will you? You won't go climbing on top of cupboards and break your legs. And you won't cry because you're afraid to be alone?'

The children's faces took on an expression of terrible sorrow.

'And for that, I'll show you something, a real brass cannon that can fire with real gunpowder.'

The children's faces lit up instantly.

'Show us the cannon,' said Kostya, beaming.

Krasotkin put his hand in the bag, pulled out a little bronze cannon, and put it on the table.

'You see! Look at its wheels,' he ran the toy along the table, 'and it can fire. You fill it with shot and you fire it.'

'Will it kill?'

'It'll kill anyone, you only have to point it.' And Krasotkin explained where to put the gunpowder, where to load it with shot, showed them the touch-hole, and explained about the recoil. The children listened with intense curiosity. Their imagination was especially fired by the idea of the recoil.

'Have you got any powder?' enquired Nastya.

'Yes.'

'Show us the powder,' she went on with a pleading smile.

Krasotkin dipped his hand into the bag again and pulled out a little phial, in which there really was a sprinkling of gunpowder, and a screwed-up piece of paper containing a few pieces of lead shot. He even opened the phial and poured a little powder into the palm of his hand.

'It's safe as long as there isn't any fire anywhere, otherwise it'd ignite and kill us all,' warned Krasotkin for effect.

The children gazed at the powder with a respectful fear that enhanced their pleasure even more. But Kostya liked the lead shot better.

'But shot doesn't burn, does it?' he enquired.

'No, shot doesn't burn.'

'Give me a little shot,' he said in a pleading little voice.

'All right—here you are, take it—only don't show it to your mama before I return, or she'll think it's powder and will drop dead with fear, and will give you a hiding.'

'Mama would never birch us,' retorted Nastya at once.

'I know, I only said it because it sounded good. But you must never deceive your mama, only just this once—till I get back. So, children, can I go or not? You won't be scared and cry if I'm not here?'

'We will c-cry,' stammered Kostya, already about to do so.

'We will cry, we're sure to cry,' Nastya took up the refrain in a nervous gabble.

'Oh children, my children, how perilous your years!* There's nothing for it, little fledglings, I'll have to stay with you as long as it takes. But time, time's running out!'

'Tell Perezvon to pretend he's dead,' requested Kostya.

'Yes, there's nothing for it, I'll have to include Perezvon in this. Perezvon, here boy!' And Kolya began to give orders to the dog, who started to show off all the tricks he knew. He was a shaggy dog, the size of a common mongrel, with a sort of lilac-grey coat. He had a squint in his right eye, and his left ear was somewhat torn. He yapped and bounced, begged, walked on his hind legs, rolled on his back with all four legs in the air, and lay motionless, as if dead. During this last trick the door opened and Agafya, Mrs Krasotkina's servant, a fat woman of about forty with a pock-marked face, appeared on the threshold, having returned from the market with a bagful of groceries in her hand. She stood there with her left arm sagging from the weight of the bag, and looked at the dog. Kolya, in spite of having waited for

Agafya with such impatience, carried on with the performance and, having made Perezvon play possum for the required time, finally whistled. The dog leaped up and began to jump with joy at having completed his trick.

'Well, just look at that dog!' she said sententiously.

'And why are you late, you old bag?' asked Krasotkin threateningly.

'"Old bag", how dare you, you snotty-nosed brat!'

'"Snotty-nosed brat"?'

'Yes, "brat". What's it got to do with you if I'm late, any objections?' Agafya, busying herself about the stove, muttered by no means discontentedly or angrily, but rather with considerable satisfaction, as though delighted to have the chance of indulging in banter with the cheerful young master.

'Listen, you silly old woman,' began Krasotkin, getting up from the sofa, 'can you swear to me by all that's sacred in the world, and by even more than that, that you'll keep a constant eye on the kids during my absence? I'm going out.'

'Why should I swear to you?' laughed Agafya. 'I'll look after them anyway.'

'No, only if you swear on the eternal salvation of your soul. Otherwise I won't go.'

'So, don't go. What's it to me? It's freezing outside, stay indoors.'

'Children,' Kolya addressed them, 'she'll stay with you until I return or your mama does—she should have come back long ago. Also, she'll give you breakfast. You'll give them something, won't you, Agafya?'

'Possibly.'

'Bye, little fledglings, you'll be all right now, I'm off. And you, old girl,' he said under his breath importantly, as he walked past Agafya, 'I hope you'll spare them your usual old wives' tales about Katerina, remember their tender age. Perezvon, here boy!'

'Go to hell,' retorted Agafya, this time grumpily. 'Cheeky so-and-so! That boy should be thrashed for talking like that, that's what I say.'

3

THE SCHOOLBOY

BUT Kolya was no longer listening. At last he could leave. Going out of the gate, he looked round, shivered, and muttering to himself 'What a frost!' set off straight down the street and then to the right, down the alley towards the market-place. He stopped at the gate of a house before the market-place, pulled a whistle from his pocket, and blew it as loudly as he could, as if giving a prearranged signal. He did not have to wait more than a minute before a rosy-cheeked boy about eleven years old, also wearing a warm, clean, almost smart coat, rushed from the gateway towards him. This boy was Smurov, a pupil from the preparatory class (whereas Kolya Krasotkin was already two classes higher), the son of a well-to-do civil servant. Smurov's parents did not allow him to associate with Krasotkin, who had the reputation of being an incorrigible rascal, so that he gave the impression of having had to rush out of the house on the sly. This Smurov, the reader may remember, had been among the group of boys who two months previously had been throwing stones across the ditch at Ilyusha, and who had then told Alyosha Karamazov about Ilyusha.

'I've been waiting for you for a whole hour, Krasotkin,' said Smurov resentfully, and the two boys started to walk to the square.

'I know I'm late,' answered Krasotkin. 'I couldn't get away earlier. You won't get beaten, will you, for being with me?'

'Oh, really! Who's going to beat me? Have you got Perezvon with you?'

'Yes.'

'You're going to take him there?'

'Yes.'

'Oh, if only it were Zhuchka!'

'We couldn't take Zhuchka. Zhuchka doesn't exist. Zhuchka's vanished off the face of the earth.'

'But supposing...', Smurov stopped suddenly, 'seeing that Ilyusha said Zhuchka was shaggy too, and the same sort of smoky grey as Perezvon—couldn't we say he's Zhuchka? He might just believe it.'

'Boy, abhor falsehood, that's the first thing! Even in a good cause, that's the second thing. But above all, I hope you haven't been saying anything there about my visit.'

'Of course not! I do understand, you know. But you won't console him with Perezvon,' sighed Smurov. 'You know what: his father, the Captain, that Loofah, was telling us that he's going to get him a puppy today, a real mastiff with a black nose; he thinks that'll console Ilyusha, but I doubt it.'

'And how is Ilyusha?'

'Bad, quite bad! I think he's got consumption. He's fully conscious, only he keeps wheezing, he has difficulty breathing. The other day he asked them to help him take a few steps; they put his boots on and he tried to walk, but he collapsed. "Ah," he says, "I told you, papa, that these boots are no good, they're the ones I had before, and even then I found it difficult to walk in them." He thought it was because of his shoes that he couldn't stand up, but it was just because he was so weak. He'll be dead in a week. Herzenstube's coming. They're rich again now, they've got plenty of money.'

'Money-grubbers.'

'Who?'

'Doctors are charlatans—generally speaking and as individuals of course. I reject medical science. It's a useless pursuit. Anyway, I'm going to look into all that. And what's all this sudden interest in sentimental do-goodism? You and all your class seem to spend all your time there.'

'Not all our time, about ten of us go there each day. It's nothing really.'

'What amazes me about all this is Aleksei Karamazov's involvement: tomorrow or the day after his brother's due to be tried for such a crime, and yet he's got time to waste on sentimental fussing over small boys!'

'It's not a question of sentimental fussing at all. You're going there yourself to make it up with Ilyusha.'

'"Make it up"? What gives you that idea? Besides, I don't need anyone to analyse my actions.'

'But Ilyusha'll be awfully glad to see you! He never thought you'd come in the end. Why on earth did you refuse to come for such a long time?' Smurov exclaimed reproachfully.

'Listen, you, that's my business, not yours. I'm going there of my own free will, because that's what I wanted to do, whereas you were all dragged there by Aleksei Karamazov, that's the difference. And for all you know, I may not be going to make it up with him at all. What a stupid idea!'

'It was nothing to do with Karamazov, nothing at all. Our lot just started going there sort of casually—with Karamazov at first, of course. And there was nothing to it, no question of being dragged there, that's silly. First one went, then another. His father was terribly glad to see us. You know, if Ilyusha dies, he'll simply go mad. He can see that Ilyusha's dying. And he was just so happy we've made it up with him. Ilyusha's been asking after you, that's all he thinks about. He just asks and then shuts up. As for his father, he'll go mad or hang himself. Well, he was already acting like a madman. You know, he's an honourable man, and that business the other day was all a mistake. It was all the fault of that murderer who beat him up.'

'All the same, I can't make Karamazov out. I could have got to know him ages ago, but there are situations in which I like to maintain my pride. Also, I've formed a certain opinion of him which I still need to confirm and clarify.'

Kolya, assumed an air of importance and fell silent; Smurov too. Smurov, it goes without saying, venerated Krasotkin and would not even have dared to think of himself as being on the same level. At this moment, he was terribly intrigued by Kolya's explanation that he was going there 'of his own free will'; there was obviously some kind of mystery about why he had suddenly decided to go on this particular day. They were crossing the market square, which at that time was filled with farm carts, game, and poultry brought from the surrounding country. Under their awnings, the townswomen were selling bagels, cotton thread, and so on. These Sunday events were grandiosely called fairs in our little town, and there were many such fairs in the course of a year. Perezvon ran about in the happiest of moods, making continual sorties to right and left in order to sniff out this or that. Whenever he met another dog, they would indulge in unusually enthusiastic mutual sniffing, in accordance with all the rules of canine social etiquette.

'I love to observe reality, Smurov,' began Kolya. 'Have you noticed how dogs sniff each other when they meet? It's some sort of natural law for them.'

'Funny sort of law.'

'There's nothing funny about it, it's just you don't understand it. Nothing in nature's funny, however it may seem to man, with his prejudices. If dogs could reason and criticize, I'm sure they'd find plenty that would seem funny to them, to say the least, in the social relationships between people, their masters—even more than funny, I should say, because I'm firmly convinced that we're by far the more foolish. That's an idea of Rakitin's, a remarkable idea. I'm a socialist, Smurov.'

'What's a socialist?' asked Smurov.

'It's when everyone's equal, all goods are owned in common, there's no marriage, and religion and all the laws are whatever anyone fancies, and so on and so forth. You're still too young for that, you're not old enough. It's cold, though.'

'Yes, twelve below. My father looked at the thermometer a little while back.'

'And have you noticed, Smurov, that in midwinter, when it gets down to fifteen or even eighteen, it doesn't seem as cold as it does now for example at the beginning of winter, when it's suddenly and unexpectedly frosty like today, when it's twelve degrees below and without snow. That means people aren't used to it yet. With people it's all a question of what they're used to, even in the matter of the state and politics. Habit is the prime mover. Look, what a funny muzhik!'

Kolya pointed to a strapping peasant in a sheepskin coat and with a good-natured face who was standing by his cart and clapping his mittened hands to relieve the cold. His long, light-brown beard was tinged with frost.

'The peasant's got a frozen beard!' Kolya shouted loudly and aggressively as they passed him.

'So have plenty of people,' the peasant retorted calmly and gravely in reply.

'Don't antagonize him,' said Smurov.

'Don't worry, he won't be annoyed, he's a good chap. Bye, Matvei.'

'Bye.'

'Is your name Matvei?'

'Yes, didn't you know?'

'No, I just said it by chance.'

'Get away with you. You at school?'

'Yes.'

'So, do you get beaten?'

'Well, yes and no.'

'Does it hurt?'

'I'll say!'

'Such is life!' said the peasant with a deep sigh.

'Bye, Matvei.'

'Bye, you're a good kid, I'll say that.'

The boys went on their way.

'He's a good peasant,' remarked Kolya. 'I like to talk to the common folk, and I'm always ready to make allowances.'

'Why did you lie to him about us being beaten?' asked Smurov.

'He needed reassuring.'

'How's that?'

'Look, Smurov, I don't like people asking questions when they haven't got a clue what I'm talking about. Some things just can't be explained. As a peasant sees it, schoolboys are meant to be beaten, and that's how it should be: how, he thinks, can a schoolboy call himself a schoolboy if he doesn't get beaten? So if I suddenly tell him that we don't get beaten, it'll upset him. And anyway, you don't understand these things. You have to know how to talk to the common folk.'

'Only please don't antagonize them, or there'll be another incident like that business with the goose.'

'Are you scared?'

'Don't laugh, Kolya. I swear to God, I'm frightened. My father will be furious. He's strictly forbidden me to mix with you.'

'Don't worry, nothing'll happen this time. Hello, Natasha,' he cried to one of the market women under an awning.

'Who are you, calling me "Natasha", I'm Marya,' the woman, who was by no means old, replied shrilly.

'That's fine, Marya's all the same to me. Bye.'

'You scamp, you, not knee-high to a grasshopper, and you have to have the last word!'

'No time to talk to you now, we'll have to leave it till next Sunday,' said Kolya, with a dismissive wave of his hand, just as if it were she who was accosting him and not the other way round.

'What have I got to say to you next Sunday? It's you that's bothering me, not me you, you pest,' shouted Marya. 'You need a good thrashing, you're a well-known troublemaker, that's all I have to say to you, so there!'

Laughter rang out from among the stall-holders on the stalls nearest to Marya's, when suddenly, from under the arcade where the shops were situated, there rushed out for no apparent reason an angry fellow who could have been a trader's assistant, not a local but a stranger to the town. He was quite young, with dark-brown curly hair and a long, pale, pock-marked face, and wore a blue caftan and a peaked cap. He appeared extremely agitated, and immediately began to shake his fist at Kolya.

'I know you,' he exclaimed, 'I know you!'

Kolya stared at him. He could not recall having had an altercation with this person. He had had so many skirmishes in the streets that he could not be expected to remember them all.

'You do, do you?' he enquired sarcastically.

'I know you! I know you!' the fellow repeated idiotically.

'Good for you. Well, I'm in a hurry. Goodbye.'

'What are you up to?' shrieked the fellow. 'You're up to something again, aren't you? I know you! You're up to something, aren't you?'

'It's none of your business, my friend, what I'm up to,' said Kolya, standing still and continuing to scrutinize him.

'What do you mean, "not my business"?'

'Just that, it's not your business.'

'Whose business is it then? Whose? Well then, whose is it?'

'It's Trifon Nikitych's business, not yours.'

'Who's Trifon Nikitych?' the young fellow, although still seething, gazed at Kolya in stupefied amazement. Kolya looked him up and down imperiously.

'Did you go to church on Ascension Day?' he demanded suddenly and severely, and with an air of authority.

'What Ascension? Why should I? No, I didn't,' the young fellow seemed somewhat disconcerted.

'Do you know Sabaneyev?' Kolya continued his interrogation even more severely and with an even greater air of authority.

'What Sabaneyev? No, I don't.'

'Well, you can go to hell in that case!' Kolya snapped, and, turning away abruptly to the left, he continued quickly on his way, as if he did not deign even to acknowledge such a blockhead who didn't know Sabaneyev.

'Hey you, stop! What Sabaneyev?' shouted the young fellow, gathering his wits and becoming excited again. 'What on earth was he talking about?' he turned suddenly to the women traders, looking at them stupidly.

The women burst out laughing.

'A smart lad,' commented one.

'What Sabaneyev, what Sabaneyev was he talking about?' the fellow went on repeating, gesticulating frantically.

'Must be that Sabaneyev who used to work for the Kuzmichevs. That's who it must be,' opined one woman suddenly.

The fellow stared at her wildly.

'Kuz-mi-chev?' repeated another woman. 'His name wasn't Trifon! It was Kuzma, not Trifon, and the boy called him Trifon Nikitych, so it couldn't be him.'

'I tell you, it wasn't Trifon, or Sabaneyev either, it was Chizhov,' suddenly interjected a third woman, who had kept quiet until then and was listening intently. 'Aleksei Ivanych is his name. Chizhov, Aleksei Ivanych.'

'That's the one, Chizhov,' repeated a fourth woman convincingly.

The stupefied fellow looked from one to the other.

'Why did he ask, why, ladies?' he cried out almost despairingly. '"Do you know Sabaneyev?" But who the devil knows who this Sabaneyev is!'

'You're a stupid man, can't you understand it wasn't Sabaneyev, but Chizhov, Aleksei Ivanovich Chizhov, that's who!' one tradeswoman shouted at him authoritatively.

'What Chizhov? Who's he? If you know who he is, tell me.'

'The lanky one with the long hair, what ran a stall here in the market in summertime.'

'But what the hell do I need Chizhov for, I ask you, eh?'

'Damned if I know what you need Chizhov for.'

'Who knows what he is to you,' interjected another one, 'you should know yourself what you want with him, it's you that's making all the fuss. After all, it was you he was talking to, not us, you stupid man. Don't you really know him?'

'Who?'

'Chizhov.'

'He can go and hang himself, that Chizhov of yours, together with you into the bargain! I really will give him what for, that's what! He was making fun of me!'

'You'll give Chizhov what for? More likely he'll give you what for! You're a fool, that's what you are!'

'Not Chizhov, I didn't mean Chizhov, you nasty, spiteful old woman, I'll deal with the boy, that's what! Just let me get hold of him, just give me half a chance. Make fun of me, would he?'

The women guffawed. But Kolya was a long way off by now, walking with a triumphant expression on his face. Smurov was beside him, glancing back now and again at the laughing group in the distance. He too was very cheerful, although he was still afraid that he would be dragged into some incident by Kolya.

'What Sabaneyev were you asking him about?' he enquired, foreseeing the answer.

'How should I know what Sabaneyev. They'll be shouting till evening now. I like winding up idiots in all walks of life. And there's another idiot—see, that muzhik over there. You know, they say there's nothing so stupid as a stupid Frenchman, but the Russian physiognomy gives itself away as well. It's written all over his face that he's an idiot, isn't it, eh?'

'Ignore him, Kolya, just walk past.'

'Not on your life. I'm just starting to enjoy myself. Hey, hello there, peasant!'

A well-built peasant with a round, simple face and a greying beard was ambling slowly by, and he had clearly had a drop to drink already; he raised his head and looked at the boy.

'Well, hello, if you're not joking,' he replied unhurriedly.

'And if I am joking?' Kolya laughed.

'If you are joking, then carry on joking, bless you. No harm in that, there's no law against it. A bit of a joke never did anyone any harm.'

'Sorry, old chap, I was joking.'

'Well, God'll forgive you.'

'And you, do you forgive me?'

'Certainly I forgive you. Off you go now.'

'You know, you are maybe quite intelligent for a peasant.'

'More so than you,' the peasant replied unexpectedly and as seriously as ever.

'I wouldn't bet on it,' said Kolya, somewhat put out.

'I'm telling you the truth.'

'On second thoughts, perhaps you're right.'

'That's better, young fellow.'

'Goodbye, peasant.'

'Goodbye.'

'There are peasants and peasants,' remarked Kolya to Smurov after a short silence. 'How was I to know he'd turn out to be an intelligent one. I'm always ready to recognize intelligence in the population.'

In the distance the cathedral clock chimed half past eleven. The boys began to hurry, and covered the remaining, not inconsiderable distance to the Staff Captain's house quickly and almost in silence. At twenty paces from the house Kolya stopped and sent Smurov ahead to ask Karamazov to come out.

'Have to sound him out first,' he remarked.

'Why do you have to ask him to come out?' objected Smurov. 'Just go in, they'll be delighted to see you. What's the good of meeting each other in the freezing cold?'

'It's for me to decide why I have to ask him to come out here in the cold,' Kolya interrupted sharply, and Smurov ran off to carry out his orders. Kolya loved bossing 'the little ones' about.

4

ZHUCHKA

KOLYA, affecting an air of self-importance, leaned against the fence and waited for Alyosha to appear. It was true, he had wanted to meet him for a long time. He had heard a lot about him from the boys, but until now he had maintained an attitude of seemingly disdainful indifference whenever Alyosha's name was mentioned, even 'criticizing' him whenever there was any discussion about him. Privately, however, he very much wanted to get to know him.

Everything he had heard about Alyosha was positive and attractive. So this moment was important: above all, he must not lose face, must try and be grown-up: 'If not, he'll think I'm only thirteen and take me for a kid like the others. And what are those boys to him? I'll ask him when we get to know each other better. Still, it's a pity I'm so short. Tuzikov is younger than me, but he's half a head taller. Anyway, I've got an intelligent face, I'm not good-looking, I know I have a horrible face, but it's an intelligent one. And I mustn't seem too keen; if I'm too friendly straight away, he'll think... Oh, that would be simply dreadful!...'

Thus Kolya fretted, trying with all his might to maintain an air of the utmost insouciance. What troubled him most of all was his small stature, not his 'ugly' face, just his size. At home he had kept a record of his height since the previous year, with a pencil on a wall in the corner, and every two months he went there in a state of expectation and measured himself to see how much he had grown. But alas, he had grown very little, and this threw him into despair at times. As for his face, it was not at all 'ugly'; on the contrary, it was quite nice-looking, pale with freckles. His grey eyes, small but lively, had a courageous look and often lit up with emotion. His cheekbones were fairly wide, his lips small, not very thick, but very red, his nose was small and decidedly upturned. 'Snub nose, snub nose!' Kolya would mutter to himself when he looked in the mirror, and he always turned away from the mirror in disgust. 'Have I really got an intelligent face?' he mused sometimes, doubting even this. However, one must not suppose that worrying about his face and his stature completely occupied his mind. On the contrary, no matter how painful those minutes in front of the mirror, he quickly forgot about them, even for long periods, and devoted himself whole-heartedly to 'ideas and real life', as he himself defined his activities.

Alyosha soon appeared and hurried towards Kolya, who noticed, while Alyosha was still several paces away, that his expression was joyful. 'Can he really be that pleased to see me?' thought Kolya with gratification. Here we should note that Alyosha had changed considerably since we last met him; he had abandoned his cassock and was now wearing a beautifully cut frock-coat and a soft round hat, and his hair was cut short. All this greatly improved his appearance, and he looked quite a dandy. The expression on his pleasant face was cheerful, but this cheerfulness was quiet and reassuring somehow. Kolya was surprised that Alyosha came out to meet him dressed in his indoor clothes and without an overcoat; clearly, he had hurried out. He immediately extended his hand to Kolya.

'Here you are at last, we've all been waiting for you impatiently.'

'Something cropped up, which I'll tell you all about in a moment. Anyway, I'm glad to meet you. I've been waiting for the chance for a long time, and I've heard a lot about you,' stammered Kolya, rather out of breath.

'Yes, we would have met anyway. I too have heard a lot about you, but you certainly took your time coming to see us.'

'Tell me, how are things?'

'Ilyusha's very bad. He certainly can't last much longer.'

'Do you really think so? You have to agree that the medical profession's a disgrace, Karamazov,' exclaimed Kolya angrily.

'Ilyusha often talks about you, very often, even in his sleep you know, when he's delirious. Obviously he thought a great deal of you before... before the incident... with the penknife. And there's another reason... Tell me, is that your dog?'

'Yes. Perezvon.'

'Not Zhuchka?' Alyosha looked at Kolya, meeting his eye sadly. 'Has Zhuchka really disappeared?'

'I know you've all been hoping and praying that Zhuchka

would turn up, I heard all about it,' Kolya smiled enigmatically. 'Listen, Karamazov, I'll explain the whole thing to you—that's the main reason I came and why I got them to ask you to come out here, so that I could explain everything to you before we went in,' he began excitedly. 'You see, Karamazov, in the spring Ilyusha entered the preparatory class. Well, it's no secret what the preparatory class is like: little urchins, they gang up. They started picking on Ilyusha straight away. I'm two classes above him, so I saw it all from a distance of course, from the sidelines as it were. I saw he was a small boy, weak too, but he wouldn't give in, he'd even fight them, he was proud, his eyes flashed. I love kids like that. But they bullied him all the more. The chief problem was that he was shabbily dressed, his trousers hitched up, and the soles coming away from his shoes. They teased him about that too. They humiliated him. No, I didn't like that at all. I stepped in quickly and boxed their ears for them. You know, the more I beat them, the more they adore me, if you see what I mean, Karamazov,' Kolya boasted chattily. 'And, on the whole, I like kids. I'm looking after two little ones right now, at home, they even delayed me today. So they stopped bullying Ilyusha and I took him under my wing. I can see the kid's proud, I'm telling you he's proud, but in the end he became like a slave, carrying out my every wish, listening to me as if I were a god, and trying to imitate me. At break-times at school he'd come straight to me and we'd walk about together. On Sundays too. At the high school they laugh at any senior boy who strikes up such a friendship with a junior, but that's prejudice. If I want to, so what, don't you agree? I teach him, I widen his horizons—tell me, why shouldn't I widen his horizons if I like him? After all, Karamazov, you mix with all those kids, so you want to influence the younger generation, widen their horizons, be useful, don't you? I admit that it was this trait in your character which I'd heard about that interested me most of all. But, to get back to the subject: I noticed that he was developing a kind of sensitivity and becoming sentimental and, as you know, I've always been decidedly against sloppy sentimentality, ever since I was so high. And on top of that there were contradictions: he was proud and yet slavishly devoted to me—slavishly devoted and yet suddenly his eyes would flash and he wouldn't even be reasonable with me, he'd quarrel and get on his high horse. Sometimes I'd put forward various ideas; he was not really against the ideas, I could see quite clearly that he was rebelling against me personally because I had responded coolly to his affection. And so, in order to restrain him as he became increasingly affectionate, I responded increasingly coolly. I acted like that deliberately, out of conviction. I intended to discipline him, to straighten him out and make a man of him... so there you are... I don't have to spell it out, do I? Suddenly I noticed that for a day—two or three days, in fact—he'd been embarrassed, upset, not because of his affection for me this time, but for some other reason, something stronger, deeper. What's got into him, I wondered. I tackled him about it and found out what was up: somehow or other he'd got to know a servant of your father's (he was still alive at that time) by the name of Smerdyakov, and he taught him, little idiot that he was, a stupid trick, that is a mean and beastly trick—to take a piece of bread, not the crust, stick a pin into it and throw it to some stray, one of those that's so hungry it'll swallow anything without chewing it, and then watch what happens. So they got a piece of bread and threw it to that shaggy Zhuchka, and now there's all this fuss about a stray which ran loose in the yard, which they didn't even feed, and which spent all day barking at the wind. (Do you like that stupid barking, Karamazov? I can't stand it.) So the dog rushed up, swallowed the bread, and started to yelp, then it went sort of crazy and ran off, it ran and ran and disappeared—that's how Ilyusha himself described it to me. He confessed to me, cried non-stop and clung to me, trembling. "He ran and ran, he went crazy"—he just kept repeating it, it haunted him. Well, I could see that remorse was gnawing at him. I took it seriously. Above all, I wanted to teach him a lesson for his past behaviour as well, I was devious, I admit, I maybe pretended to be more disgusted than I really was. "You've done a terrible thing," I said, "you're a swine. I shan't tell on you, of course, but for now I'll have nothing more to do with you. I'll think the matter over, and when I've decided whether to resume our former relationship or to finish with you for ever, being the swine that you are, I'll let you know through Smurov" (that's the boy who came with me today, he's always been devoted to me). That really struck home. I admit I felt at the time that perhaps I was being too harsh, but what of it, that was the line I took at the time. The next day I sent word by Smurov that I wouldn't speak to him any more, that's what we say when two friends fall out. I meant to send him to Coventry for only a day or two, and then to make it up with him after he'd repented. That was my firm intention. But guess what: he listened to what Smurov had to say and suddenly his eyes flashed, "Tell Krasotkin from me", he shouted, "that I'll throw bread with pins to all the dogs, all of them!" "Aha," I said to myself, "now there's a whiff of defiance in the air, I'll have to stamp it out," and I began to treat him with the utmost contempt; whenever we met I'd turn my head away or smile quite ironically. And then the incident with his father occurred: you remember Loofah? You can understand from that how inclined he was to lose his temper. Seeing that I had abandoned him, the boys ganged up against him and taunted him with "Loofah, Loofah". That's when their battles began, which I greatly deplored since it seems that they beat him up really badly one time. And then he set upon them in the playground on one occasion, when they came out of their classes, and I was standing just ten paces away and watching. And I swear I don't remember laughing, on the contrary I started to feel extremely sorry for him; another moment and I'd have rushed to his defence. But suddenly he caught my eye. I don't know what was on his mind, but he pulled out his penknife and lunged at me, stabbing me in the thigh, right here, in my right leg. I didn't move; even if I say so myself, Karamazov, I'm quite brave sometimes, I just looked at him scornfully, as if to say, "Wouldn't you like to stab me again for all the friendship I've shown you? If so, I'm all yours." But he didn't stab me again, he broke down instead, took fright, threw the knife away, began to cry out loud, and then ran off. It goes without saying that I didn't split on him, and I made them all keep their mouths shut so that the teachers shouldn't hear about it—I didn't even tell my mother until it had healed; anyway, it was nothing, just a scratch. Later I heard that he'd been throwing stones the same day and had bitten your finger—but you understand what a state he was in! Well, what was I supposed to do? I was stupid; when he fell ill, I didn't come to forgive him, that is, to make it up, and now I regret it. But I had my reasons at the time. Well, that's the story... only, I think I've been stupid..."

'Ah, what a pity', exclaimed Alyosha with regret, 'that I didn't know about your relationship with him earlier, otherwise I'd have asked you long ago to come with me to see him. Believe me, when he was feverish and ill he was talking to you in his delirium. I really didn't know how dear you were to him! And couldn't you really find this Zhuchka? His father and all the boys have been looking for him all over town. Believe me, ill as he was and weeping, he repeated to his father three times in my presence, "That's why I'm ill, papa, because I killed Zhuchka, God is punishing me." It's impossible to get the idea out of his head! And if only someone could find this Zhuchka and prove to him that he didn't die, that he's alive, I think he'd get better from sheer relief. We've all been counting on you.'

'Tell me, why were you hoping that I'd find Zhuchka, why me in particular?' asked Kolya with extreme curiosity. 'Why were you counting on me rather than on anyone else?'

'There was some rumour going round that you were looking for him and that when you found him, you'd bring him here. Smurov was saying something of the sort. Above all, we've been trying to convince him that Zhuchka's alive, that he's been seen somewhere. The boys got hold of a live hare for him from somewhere or other, but he just looked at it, gave a little smile, and asked us to release it in a field. So we did. His father's just come back with a mastiff puppy for him, he got it somewhere, thinking it would comfort him, but it had just the opposite effect...'

'And tell me this, Karamazov: what's his father like? I know him, but what do you make of him: is he a buffoon, a clown?'

'Oh, no, there are people who feel things deeply but who seem defeated somehow. With them, buffoonery is a kind of spiteful irony towards those to whom they daren't tell the truth directly, because they've long felt a humiliating timidity in their presence. Believe me, Krasotkin, such buffoonery is truly tragic sometimes. For him, everything, everything on earth is now centred on Ilyusha, and if Ilyusha dies, he'll either go out of his mind with grief or commit suicide. I'm almost convinced of that when I look at him now!'

'I can see what you mean, Karamazov, you obviously understand people,' added Kolya perceptively.

'But when I saw you with the dog, I thought it was Zhuchka you were bringing.'

'Don't give up hope, Karamazov, perhaps we can still find him, but this—this is Perezvon. I'll let him free in the room, and perhaps he can cheer Ilyusha up a bit more than the mastiff puppy did. Just you wait and see, Karamazov, we'll sort something out soon. Oh, Good Lord, I'm sure you want to go back indoors!' Kolya exclaimed hurriedly. 'It's so cold, and you haven't got your coat on, and here I am keeping you talking; you see what an egoist I am! Oh, we're all egoists, Karamazov!'

'Don't worry, it is cold, but I don't catch cold easily. But let's go in anyway. By the way, what's your name? I know it's Kolya, but Kolya what?'

'Nikolai, Nikolai Ivanov Krasotkin, or as they say officially, "son of Krasotkin",' Kolya started to laugh for some reason, but then suddenly added, 'Of course, I hate the name Nikolai.'

'Why?'

'It's silly, pretentious...'

'Twelve, aren't you?' asked Alyosha.

'Well, thirteen actually. I'll be fourteen very soon, in two weeks. I'll confess to one weakness of mine in advance, Karamazov, I'll admit this to you straight away, so that you can understand my whole character at once: I hate being asked about my age, hate's not a strong enough word... and finally, by the way... there's a malicious rumour going the rounds, that I played highwaymen with the preparatory class last week. It's true that I played with them, but to say that I did so for fun is really slanderous. I've reason to believe that this has reached your ears, but I played not for my own pleasure, but for the kids', because they couldn't think up anything for themselves without me. That's how rumours spread in this town. It's a fine place for gossip, I assure you.'

'And if you had played for fun, what of it?'

'For fun?... Well, you wouldn't start playing with a hobbyhorse, would you?'

'Look here, think of it like this,' smiled Alyosha, 'adults go to the theatre, for example, and in the theatre they portray the adventures of all sorts of heroes, sometimes even with robbers and fighting—so isn't that just the same, in its own way, of course? And children playing at war and highwaymen at playtime is also, you could say, a kind of rudimentary art, the incipient need for art in the young mind, and sometimes these games are organized even more strictly than stage performances, with one difference, namely that theatre-goers go to see actors, whereas the youngsters themselves are the actors. But that's only natural.'

'You think so? Is that your honest opinion?' Kolya was gazing fixedly at him. 'You know, that's quite an interesting idea you've just expressed; I shall go home now and mull it over. I admit that's just what I expected, that I could learn something from you. I came to learn from you, Karamazov,' he said with good-humoured candour.

'And I from you,' smiled Alyosha, and shook hands.

Kolya was delighted with Alyosha. He was struck by the fact that the latter had communicated with him on a totally equal footing and had talked to him as to a 'real grown-up'.

'I'll show you a trick now, Karamazov, and also a theatrical performance,' he laughed nervously. 'That's precisely what I came for.'

'Let's go to the lodgers' rooms on the left first, that's where all your lot leave their coats because it's hot in the room.'

'The fact is, I shan't be staying long, I'll come in and keep my coat on. Perezvon will stay here in the hall and play possum. Perezvon, here boy, lie down and die! You see, he's dead. I'll go in first to size up the situation, and then at the right moment, I'll whistle "Perezvon, here boy!", and you just watch him fly in at once, like crazy. Only, Smurov mustn't forget to open the door at that moment. I'll fix it, and you'll see the trick...'

5

AT ILYUSHA'S BEDSIDE

THE room already familiar to us as that occupied by the family of retired Staff Captain Snegiryov was stuffy and cramped because of the number of people who were gathered there.

Several boys were sitting with Ilyusha at the time, and although they, like Smurov, were ready to deny that it was Alyosha who had brought about their reconciliation with Ilyusha, this was the case nevertheless. He had accomplished this simply by bringing them to see Ilyusha one by one, as if fortuitously and without any 'soppy sentimentality'. This had greatly alleviated Ilyusha's suffering. Seeing the almost tender friendship and sympathy that these boys, his former enemies, showed him, he was very moved. Only one, Krasotkin, was missing, and that weighed heavily upon his heart. If there was one memory that was more bitter than any other for Ilyusha, it was the incident when he had attacked his one and only erstwhile friend and protector with a knife. Smurov, the bright little boy who had been the first to make peace with Ilyusha, knew this. But Krasotkin, when Smurov informed him vaguely that Alyosha wanted to come and see him 'about something', had cut him short, rebuffing Alyosha's approach and instructing Smurov to inform 'Karamazov' straight away that he knew perfectly well what to do, that he did not need advice from anyone, and that if he was going to go to see the sick boy he would decide for himself when to go, because he had his own ideas on the matter. That had been about two weeks before this present Sunday. That was why Alyosha had not gone to Kolya himself, as he had intended. In the meantime, however, he had sent Smurov twice more to see Krasotkin. But Krasotkin had delivered a sharp and impatient response on both occasions, warning that if Alyosha came to see him, he would not go to Ilyusha at all, and that they should stop pestering him. Even up to the last minute, Smurov did not know that Kolya had decided to visit Ilyusha that morning, and it was only the night before that Kolya, on saying goodbye to Smurov, had abruptly informed him that he would expect him at his house in the morning, as they would be going together to the Snegiryovs', but that he should not dare to breathe a word of the impending visit since he wanted his arrival to be unexpected. Smurov had obeyed. The idea of trying to find the lost Zhuchka had come to him from a chance remark of Krasotkin's, that they were 'all asses if they couldn't find the dog, if it was alive'. But when Smurov, choosing an opportune moment, had timidly broached the subject of the dog to Krasotkin, the latter had flown into a rage.

'Why would I be such a fool as to go looking all over the town for someone else's dog, when I've got Perezvon? And do you really imagine that the dog can still be alive after swallowing a pin? That's nothing but wishful thinking!'

Meanwhile, for two weeks already, Ilyusha had hardly left his bed in the corner under the icons. He had not been to school since the day he met Alyosha and bit his finger. His illness had begun from that day, although for a month, on the rare occasions that he got up from his bed, he had still been able to hobble around the room and the hallway somehow. In the end he grew so weak that he could not move except with his father's help. His father could not do enough for him—he even stopped drinking completely—he nearly went out of his mind from fear that his little boy was going to die, and often, especially after supporting him by his arm so that he could walk a few steps and then helping him back to bed, he would suddenly rush out into the hallway and, leaning his head against the wall in a dark corner, break down, convulsed by sobs, which he stifled so that Ilyushechka should not hear.

Usually, on coming back into the room, he would try to comfort and distract his beloved son, telling him fairy stories and amusing anecdotes and taking off various funny people he happened to meet and even imitating the strange howls and cries of animals. But Ilyusha hated to see his father prancing about and making a fool of himself. Although the boy tried to hide the fact that he found this distasteful, he nevertheless realized with an aching heart that his father had been publicly humiliated, and he was obsessed by the memory of 'Loofah' and of that terrible day. Ninochka, Ilyushechka's quiet, meek, crippled sister, also did not like to see her father playing the fool (Varvara Nikolayevna had long since gone back to St Petersburg to continue her studies); on the other hand, their halfwitted mother was highly amused and laughed wholeheartedly whenever her husband began one of his imitations or started to make some kind of funny gestures. This was the only way to comfort her; the rest of the time she wept and grumbled that no one remembered her now, that no one respected her, that people offended her, and so on and so forth. But in the last few days she too seemed to have changed completely. She began looking frequently towards Ilyusha in his corner, and became thoughtful. She grew much quieter, and if she cried, it was quietly, so that no one would hear. The Staff Captain noticed this change in her with bitter astonishment. At first she was put out by the boys' visits, which merely irritated her, but later the children's happy shouts and stories began to amuse her, and in the end she grew so fond of the boys that had they stopped coming she would have missed them sorely. Whenever the children recounted anything or started playing, she would laugh and clap her hands. She would beckon certain boys over to her and kiss them. She was particularly fond of Smurov. As for the Staff Captain, the children's visits to the house to cheer Ilyusha up had from the very first filled his heart with ecstatic joy and even with hope that Ilyusha would stop pining now and thereby might even get better more quickly. In spite of his fears for Ilyusha, he had never for a moment, until just very recently, doubted that his little boy would spontaneously recover. He welcomed the young visitors warmly, fussed over them, got them anything they needed, would have carried them on his back—and, indeed, even started to do so— but Ilyusha did not like these games, and they were abandoned. He began to buy them presents, gingerbread, nuts, and made tea and sandwiches for them. It should be noted that, during all this time, he was not short of money. He had accepted Katerina Ivanovna's two hundred roubles, exactly as Alyosha had predicted. And then, when she found out more about their circum-. stances and about Ilyusha's illness, Katerina Ivanovna herself visited them, met all the family, and even managed to charm the Staff Captain's halfwitted wife. After that her generosity never flagged, and the Staff Captain, stricken with horror at the thought of his child dying, had forgotten his former pride and meekly accepted her charity. All this time Dr Herzenstube had been visiting the sick boy regularly, every other day, at Katerina Ivanovna's request; his visits, however, had little effect, although he dosed him unmercifully with medicines. But on this day, that is to say this Sunday morning, the Staff Captain was awaiting the visit of a new doctor from Moscow, where he was something of a celebrity. Katerina Ivanovna had especially sent for him from Moscow, at great expense—not for Ilyushechka but for

another reason, of which more later at the appropriate time—
and since he was there she had asked him to visit Ilyushechka
and had informed the Staff Captain of this in advance. He had
had absolutely no forewarning of Kolya Krasotkin's arrival,
however, although he had long wished that this boy, about whom
his Ilyushechka tormented himself so, would come. Just as
Krasotkin opened the door and appeared in the room, the Staff
Captain and the boys were crowding round the sick boy's bed
and gazing at a tiny mastiff puppy, born only the previous day,
but already ordered a week before by the Staff Captain to distract
and comfort Ilyushechka, who was still lamenting the disappear-
ance and presumed death of Zhuchka. Ilyusha had known for
three days that he was going to be given a puppy—and no
ordinary puppy, but a real mastiff (this was, of course, terribly
important)—but although he indicated, not wishing to appear
ungrateful, that he was pleased with the present, both his father
and the boys were clearly aware that the new dog only revived
more intensely the memory of the unfortunate Zhuchka that he
had tormented to death. The puppy lay on the bed and nuzzled
up to him, and he, with a forced smile, stroked it with his thin,
white, emaciated hand; it was obvious that he liked the dog,
but... all the same, Zhuchka was not there, all the same, this was
not Zhuchka, and if only Zhuchka and the puppy could be there
together, that would have been absolute bliss!

'Krasotkin!' cried one of the boys, who was the first to notice
that Kolya had entered. Considerable upheaval ensued, the boys
moved aside and stood on either side of the bed, revealing
Ilyushechka as the focus of attention. The Staff Captain rushed
up enthusiastically to greet Kolya.

'Come in, come in... I'm so pleased to see you!' he prattled.
'Ilyushechka, Master Krasotkin has come to see you...'

But Krasotkin quickly shook his hand and promptly demonstrated his perfect command of social niceties. He turned
immediately to the Staff Captain's wife, who was sitting in her
armchair (and who was feeling terribly put out just then, and
grumbling that the boys were obstructing her view of Ilyushechka's bed and preventing her from seeing the new puppy), bowed
to her with the utmost courtesy, clicking his heels at the same

time, and then turned to Ninochka and bowed in the same way to her. This polite gesture made an unusually good impression on the sick woman.

'What a well-brought-up young man,' she proclaimed loudly, with an expansive gesture, 'not like our other guests, who pile in one after the other.'

'Come now, mummikins, "one after the other", that's no way to talk, is it?' the Staff Captain murmured gently, though somewhat nervous about what 'mummikins' might say next.

'That's just what they do. They climb on each other's shoulders in the hallway and come galloping into respectable people's homes on horseback. What sort of guest does that?'

'But who did, mummikins, who came galloping in like that?'

'That boy there galloped in on that one today, and that one there on that one...'

But Kolya was already standing by Ilyusha's bed. The sick boy paled visibly. He half raised himself in the bed and stared intently at Kolya. The latter had not seen his little friend for about two months, and he stood there visibly shocked; he could not have imagined that his face would be so thin and sallow, his eyes so dilated and burning with such fever, his arms so wasted. He stared with astonished sorrow at the sight of Ilyusha's shallow and rapid breathing and his parched lips. He went up to him, gave him his hand, and, almost at a loss, said:

'Well, old boy... how's life?'

But his voice cracked, he lost his composure, his face suddenly crumpled, and his lips quivered. Ilyusha, still too weak to utter a word, gave him a frail smile. Kolya raised his hand and, for some reason, ran it over Ilyusha's hair.

'Ne-e-ver mind!' he murmured, either to comfort him or without even knowing himself why he said it. They were both silent for a minute.

'What's that you've got, a new puppy?' asked Kolya suddenly, in his most impassive voice.

'Ye-e-s,' replied Ilyusha in a wheezing, long-drawn-out whisper.

'His nose is black, that means his parents are fierce guard dogs,' announced Kolya firmly and importantly, as if all that mattered were the puppy and his black nose. But in fact he was struggling with all his might to subdue his feelings and not start crying like a 'kid', and he had not yet managed this. 'He'll get bigger and you'll have to chain him up, I know about these things, you know.'

'He'll be enormous!' exclaimed a boy from the group.

'It's well known that mastiffs are as big as this, as big as a calf,' several voices rang out.

'As big as a calf, a real calf,' the Staff Captain joined in. 'I specially looked for one like that, the fiercest kind, and its parents are enormous and very fierce too, as tall as this from the floor... Do sit down, young man, here on the bed next to Ilyusha, or on the bench if you wish. You're a welcome guest, a long-awaited guest... Did you come with Aleksei Fyodorovich?'

Krasotkin sat down on the bed at Ilyusha's feet. Although, on the way there, he had intended to start the conversation on a casual footing, he had quite lost the thread now.

'No... with Perezvon... Perezvon's this dog I've got now. It's a Slavonic name. He's waiting out there... if I whistle, he'll come flying in. So I've got a dog, too, you see,' he turned suddenly to Ilyusha. 'Do you remember Zhuchka, old chap?' he sprang the question on him suddenly.

Ilyusha's little face twisted. He gave Kolya an agonized look. Alyosha, standing by the door, made a conspiratorial sign to Kolya not to go on about Zhuchka, but he either did not notice or chose not to notice.

'Where... where is Zhuchka?' asked Ilyusha, his voice breaking.

'Well, my friend, your Zhuchka's—puff! He's snuffed it, your Zhuchka has!'

Ilyusha did not answer, but he shot Kolya another very penetrating glance. Alyosha, meeting Kolya's eyes, signalled again desperately, but Kolya averted his eyes and pretended once again not to notice.

'He's run off somewhere and snuffed it. How could he not snuff it, after such a snack,' he went on pitilessly, although he also, for some reason, caught his breath. 'That's why I've brought Perezvon... a Slavonic name... I've brought him to see you...'

'You didn't have to!' said Ilyushechka suddenly.

'Yes, I did. You really must have a look at him... It'll make you feel better. I brought him specially... he's shaggy, just like Zhuchka was... Will you allow me to call my dog in, madam?' he turned suddenly to Mrs Snegiryova, in a quite inexplicable state of turmoil.

'Don't, don't!' cried Ilyusha, his voice breaking in misery. Reproach burned in his eyes.

'It would...', the Staff Captain broke in suddenly from the trunk by the wall, where he had been sitting, 'it would be better another time...', he muttered, but Kolya, obstinately determined and without further ado, suddenly called to Smurov, 'Smurov, open the door!' and as soon as the door opened he blew his whistle. Perezvon flew eagerly into the room.

'Jump, Perezvon, beg! Beg!' called out Kolya, getting up, and the dog stood up on its back legs, right in front of Ilyusha's bed. Then something occurred that no one anticipated: Ilyusha shuddered and suddenly threw himself forward, leaned towards Perezvon and, scarcely breathing, gazed at him.

'It's... it's Zhuchka!' he shouted suddenly, his little voice convulsed by suffering and happiness.

'And who did you think it was?' Krasotkin's voice rang out loudly and happily and, bending down, he picked up the dog and lifted it up to Ilyusha.

'Look, old chap, you see, a squint in one eye and a torn left ear, just exactly as you described it to me. I found him by your description. Found him almost at once. He didn't belong to anyone, you know, no one owned him,' he explained, turning quickly to the Staff Captain, to his wife, to Alyosha and then to Ilyusha again. 'He was a stray from the village, he'd settled in the Fedotovs' backyard, but they didn't feed him... And I found him... You see, old chap, that means he didn't swallow your titbit. If he'd swallowed it, then of course he'd have died, that's for sure! So he must have managed to spit it out, since he's alive. You didn't see him spit it out, but he did; it had pierced his tongue, and that's why he was squealing. He ran out and squealed, and you thought he had really swallowed it. He must have squealed a lot, because the lining of dogs' mouths is very tender... more tender than humans', much more tender!' Kolya babbled on frantically, his face flushed and shining with enthusiasm.

Ilyusha was speechless. He was as white as a sheet and looked at Kolya with his great eyes nearly popping out of their sockets, his mouth wide open. Krasotkin had no idea what a painful and serious effect such an incident would have on the mind of the sick boy, and had he known, he would never have dreamt of playing such a trick. But Alyosha was maybe the only one in the room who understood this. As for the Staff Captain, he seemed to have become the most juvenile of small boys.

'Zhuchka! So that's Zhuchka?' he cried out blissfully. 'Ilyu-shechka, look, it's Zhuchka, your Zhuchka! Mummikins, look, it's Zhuchka!' He was almost crying.

'And I never even guessed it!' exclaimed Smurov sorrowfully. 'Ah, trust Krasotkin, I said he'd find Zhuchka, and he's found him.'

'He's found him!' someone called out happily.

'Good old Krasotkin!' a third voice rang out.

'Well done, well done!' all the boys shouted and began to applaud.

'Wait, wait,' Krasotkin struggled to make himself heard above all their voices, 'I'll tell you how it happened, that's all that matters, how it happened, and nothing else! Well, I found him, took him home, and hid him; I locked and bolted the house and didn't show him to anyone until today. Only Smurov saw him, he found out two weeks ago, but I assured him it was Perezvon, and he didn't guess. And in the meantime I taught Zhuchka all sorts of tricks, you watch, just watch what tricks he knows! I taught him so that I could bring him to you, old chap, well trained and sleek: look what he's like now, your Zhuchka! Have you got a scrap of meat, I'll show you another trick that'll have you rolling with laughter—surely you've got a scrap of meat, haven't you?'

The Staff Captain rushed eagerly across the landing to the landlord's flat, where their family meal was also being prepared. Kolya, not wanting to waste valuable time and in a desperate hurry, shouted to Perezvon, 'Die!' and the latter promptly rolled over and lay on his back, silent and motionless, with all four paws in the air. The boys laughed, Ilyusha watched with the same painful smile, but it was 'mummikins' most of all who liked Perezvon dying. She burst out laughing and started snapping her fingers and calling:

'Perezvon, Perezvon!'

'He won't get up for anything, not for anything,' cried Kolya triumphantly and proudly, 'even if everyone calls him; but if I call, he'll jump up in a flash! Here boy!'

The dog leapt up and began prancing around, squealing with joy. The Staff Captain ran in with a piece of boiled beef.

'It isn't hot, is it?' enquired Kolya quickly and in a businesslike manner, taking the piece of meat, 'no, not hot, because dogs don't like hot things. Look everybody, Ilyushechka, look then, look old chap, why don't you look? I bring him, and you won't look!'

The new trick consisted of the dog standing motionless, with the tempting piece of meat balanced on his nose. The poor dog had to stand—motionless and without dislodging the meat from his nose—for however long his master decreed, even if this should be half an hour. But Perezvon had to keep it up for only a short minute.

'Take!' Kolya commanded, and in a flash the morsel flew from Perezvon's nose to his mouth. The audience expressed delighted surprise, of course.

'And surely, surely it wasn't just because you were teaching the dog those tricks that you never came!' exclaimed Alyosha with involuntary reproach.

'Precisely for that reason,' said Kolya with total ingenuousness. 'I wanted to let him show off in all his brilliance!'

'Perezvon! Perezvon!' Ilyusha suddenly called the dog, clicking his thin little fingers.

'It's all right. Let him jump up on your bed himself. Here boy!' he smacked the palm of his hand on Ilyusha's bed, and Perezvon flew to Ilyusha like an arrow. Ilyusha wrapped both his arms enthusiastically around the dog's head, and Perezvon promptly responded by licking his cheek. Ilyushechka cuddled up to him, stretched himself out on his bed, and hid his face in the dog's shaggy coat.

'Lord, oh Lord!' exclaimed the Staff Captain.

Kolya sat down again on Ilyusha's bed.

'Ilyusha, I can show you one more trick. I've brought you a little cannon. Do you remember, I told you about this little cannon, and you said, "Ah, if only I could see it!" Well, here you are, I've brought it for you.'

And Kolya hurriedly took out the little brass cannon from his bag. He hurried because he himself was very happy; any other time he would have waited until the magic effect of Perezvon's tricks had worn off, but now he lost no time, throwing all restraint to the wind: 'Since you're so happy, here's some more happiness for you!' He was quite carried away himself.

I saw it at Morozov's—you know Morozov, the civil servant—I've had my eye on it just for you, old chap, just for you. He had no use for it, he got it from his brother, I swapped it for a book from my father's library, *Muhammad's Kinsman or Curative Foolery*.* It's a hundred years old, that book, shocking, it appeared in Moscow before there was any censorship, but Morozov loves that sort of thing. He even thanked me...'

Kolya was holding the little cannon in his hand for all to see and admire. Ilyusha partly sat up and, still with his right arm around Perezvon, contemplated the toy admiringly. The excitement reached a peak when Kolya revealed that he also had some gunpowder and that they could fire it now, 'as long as it wouldn't frighten the ladies'. 'Mummikins' immediately asked to have a closer look at the toy, and it was promptly passed to her. The little brass cannon on wheels delighted her, and she started to roll it on her knees. When they asked her permission to fire it she agreed enthusiastically, without understanding what she was being asked, however. Kolya showed them the powder and the shot. The Staff Captain, being an old soldier, took the task of charging it upon himself, inserting only the least possible quantity of powder and suggesting that the shot be kept for another time. The cannon was placed on the floor with its barrel pointing away from them, three grains of powder were inserted into the priming tube, and a lighted match was applied. There was a quite blinding flash. Mummikins jumped, but then immediately began to laugh with joy. The boys watched in silent triumph, but happiest of all was the Staff Captain, who was gazing blissfully at Ilyusha. Kolya picked up the little cannon and handed it, along with the shot and the powder, directly to Ilyusha.

'It's for you, you have it! I've been meaning to bring it for a long time,' he repeated once more, overflowing with happiness.

'Oh, give it to me! Give it to me instead!' Mummikins suddenly began to ask, just like a small child. Her face reflected acute anxiety at the possibility that they would not give it to her. Kolya was embarrassed. The Staff Captain grew alarmed.

'Mummikins, Mummikins!' he rushed over to her. 'The cannon is yours, of course it's yours, but let Ilyusha have it, as it was given to him, and it'll still be yours, Ilyusha will always let you play with it, you can both have it...'

'No, I don't want us both to have it, no, I want it to be only mine and not Ilyusha's,' the mother went on protesting, and prepared to start crying in earnest.

'Take it, mama, take it!' cried Ilyusha. 'Krasotkin, can I give it to mama?' he suddenly turned a pleading gaze on Krasotkin, as if he were afraid the latter would be offended by the fact that his gift was being given to someone else.

'Of course you can!' Krasotkin agreed at once and, taking the cannon from Ilyusha, gave it to the mother himself and bowed to her most politely. She promptly burst into tears of emotion.

'Darling Ilyushechka loves his mummikins!' she exclaimed tenderly and started to roll the little cannon on her knees again.

'Mummikins, let me kiss your little hand,' her husband rushed over to her, and promptly performed his wish.

'And there's the dearest of young men, that kind boy there!' said the grateful woman, pointing at Krasotkin.

'And as for powder, Ilyusha, I'll bring you as much as you want. We make our own powder now. Borovikov found out the composition: twenty-four parts saltpetre, ten of sulphur, and six of birch charcoal, grind it all together, add water, mix to a paste, and pass it through a sieve—and there you have gunpowder.'

'Smurov told me about your powder,' answered Ilyusha, 'only papa says it isn't real gunpowder.'

'What do you mean, not real?' Kolya retorted indignantly. 'It ignites. Anyway, I don't know...'

'No, I didn't mean that,' the Staff Captain jumped up looking guilty. 'It's true I said real gunpowder wasn't made like that, but it doesn't matter, you can make it that way too.'

'I don't know, you know more about it. We lit some in an earthenware pomade jar, it ignited perfectly, everything was consumed, there was nothing left but the tiniest amount of soot. But it was only paste, and if you pass it through a sieve... Anyway, you know more about it than me, I don't know... But Bulkin's father beat him because of our powder, did you hear about it?' he turned suddenly to Ilyusha.

'Yes, I heard,' answered Ilyusha. He was listening to Kolya with keen interest and fascination.

'We'd made a whole bottle of powder, and he'd been keeping it under his bed. His father found it. He said it could have blown them all up. And he beat him on the spot. He wanted to complain to the school about me. They won't let him go around with me now, no one's allowed to go around with me. Smurov isn't allowed to either, I've really made a name for myself: they say I'm "a bad lot",' Kolya laughed scornfully. 'It all started with that railway business.'

'Ah, we heard about that escapade,' chimed in the Staff Captain. 'How did you manage to lie there? And you must have been frightened when you were under the train. Were you afraid?'

The Staff Captain was fawning on Kolya terribly.

'N-not particularly,' Kolya replied casually. 'It was that wretched goose that really damaged my reputation,' he turned back to Ilyusha. But although he affected an air of nonchalance while telling the story, he still found it difficult to control his feelings, and he continued to stammer.

'Oh, I heard about the goose,' Ilyusha laughed radiantly, 'they told me about it, but I didn't quite understand, did you really have to go to court?'

'It was the stupidest, most piffling little affair, and as usual around here they made a mountain out of a molehill,' began Kolya casually. 'I was passing through the square one day and they had just driven in a flock of geese. I stopped and looked at the geese. Suddenly one local chap, Vishnyakov—he's the delivery boy at Plotnikov's now—looks at me and says, "What are you looking at the geese for?" I took a closer look at him—a chap of about twenty, with a stupid round mug—you know I'm never standoffish with people, I love talking to them... We've cut ourselves off from the people—that's the truth... You seem to find that funny, Karamazov.'

'No, God forbid, I'm all ears,' replied Alyosha with an air of the utmost innocence, and the mistrustful Kolya was instantly reassured.

'My theory, Karamazov, is clear and simple,' he quickly continued. 'I believe in the people and I'm always prepared to give them the benefit of the doubt, but without spoiling them in any way, that's a *sine qua non**... Well now, I was telling you about the goose. So I turn to this idiot and I reply, "I was wondering what a goose thinks about." He stares at me like a real idiot, "What a goose thinks about?" "Well," I say, "you see that cart full of oats standing over there. There's a bag with oats spilling out of it, and a goose is sticking its neck right under the wheel to peck at the grain—do you see?" "Yes, so what," he says. "Well now," I say, "if one was to push the cart forward just a smidgen, would the wheel decapitate the goose or not?" "Certainly," he says, "certainly", and he grins a wide toothy grin, fairly beaming. "Come on then, old chap," I say, "let's do it." "All right," he says. And we didn't have to wait long: he stood casually near the bridle, and I went to one side to shoo the goose towards the wheel. But the peasant was paying no attention just then, he was talking to someone, and there was no need for me to shoo it; it stuck out its head of its own accord to get at the oats in front of the cart, right under the wheel. I gave the lad a wink, he jerked the reins, and—crack, the wheel chopped the goose's neck in half! Then, as bad luck would have it, the men saw us just at that moment, and all started shouting at once: "You did that on purpose!" "No, it was an accident." "No, on purpose!" Now they were really bellowing. "Let's take him to the magistrate!" They grabbed me too. "You too," they said, "you were there too, you're an accomplice, everyone in the market knows you!" And for some reason everyone in the market really does know me,' added Kolya smugly. 'We all trooped off to the court-house, and the goose was taken along too. I could see the lad had taken fright and was blubbing, really blubbing, like an old woman. The owner of the goose was shouting. "They could get as many geese as they like that way!" Of course, there were witnesses. The magistrate settled the matter in a flash: the owner should be paid one rouble for the goose, and the lad could take the goose. And he didn't want to hear of any more such antics. But the lad was still blubbing like an old woman. "It wasn't me," he says, "it was him what put me up to it," and he pointed at me. I replied, without batting an eyelid, that I had in no way incited him, that I had merely expressed a basic idea and had been speaking purely in theoretical terms. The magistrate, Nefedov, smiled, then he got mad at himself for smiling. "I shall have a word with your headmaster," he said to me, "to recommend that in future they don't let you go around testing such theories, but instead make you stick to your books and get on with your studies." He was joking, of course, he didn't speak to my headmaster, but the news spread and the staff got to hear of it; they have long ears, our lot! The classics master, Kolbasnikov, was particularly incensed, but Dardanelov stood up for me again. But Kolbasnikov is really out to get us all now, stupid ass! No doubt you've heard, Ilyusha, that he got married and that the Mikhailovs gave him a thousand roubles as dowry, but his wife's got a face like the back of a stagecoach. The third-formers made up an epigram on the spot:

> Third-formers struck all of a heap,
> Dirty old man Kolbasnikov takes the leap.

And there's more of it, very funny, I'll bring it for you. I've nothing to say against Dardanelov; he's a knowledgeable man, definitely knowledgeable. I admire people like him, and not just because he stood up for me...'

'Still, you did score off him as to who founded Troy!' chipped in Smurov, who was in fact bursting with pride on Krasotkin's account. The story of the goose had delighted him.

'Yes, you really had him there, didn't you?' the Staff Captain joined in obsequiously. 'It was about who founded Troy, wasn't it? We heard all about it. Ilyushechka told me all about it at the time...'

'Oh, papa, he knows everything, he knows more than any of us,' Ilyusha took up the refrain. 'He only pretends to be like that, but he's better than any of us in all subjects...'

Ilyusha was looking at Kolya with an expression of utter happiness.

'Oh, all that about Troy is a load of rubbish. I consider the
question pointless myself,' Kolya pronounced with arrogant
modesty. He had managed to regain his composure, though he
was still somewhat worried. He felt that he had become overex-
cited and spoken too frankly—about the goose, for example—as
for Alyosha, the latter had kept silent throughout the story and
was looking so serious that the self-satisfied boy was now
beginning, little by little, to feel a nagging anxiety. 'Is he keeping
quiet because he despises me, does he think I'm trying to
impress him? If so, if he dares to think that, I'll...'

'I consider the question pointless,' he snapped again,
arrogantly.

'I know who founded Troy,' suddenly announced a boy, one
Kartashov, a handsome lad of about eleven, quiet and apparently
shy, who up to that moment had not said a word. He was sitting
right by the door. Kolya looked at him with astonishment, but
maintained his air of importance. The fact was that the question,
'who actually founded Troy?' was undoubtedly regarded in every
class in the school as a secret, the answer to which was to be
found in Smaragdov. But no one but Kolya had a copy of
Smaragdov's book. However, on one occasion while Kolya's
back was turned, this boy Kartashov had stealthily and quickly
opened Smaragdov, which was lying among his books, and had
chanced upon the very place where the founders of Troy were
mentioned. This had occurred quite a while back, but he had
been rather embarrassed and had not brought himself to admit
publicly that he too knew who had founded Troy, being afraid of
the possible outcome, namely that Kolya might make him pay
for it somehow. But now, suddenly, he could withhold the
information no longer, and he spoke up. And he had wanted to
do so for a long time.

'Well, who did found it?' Kolya turned to him with a haughty
and disdainful air, but it was clear from his expression that he
guessed that the boy really did know and was already prepared
to face all the consequences. In the general atmosphere there
ensued what might be called disharmony.

'Troy was founded by Teucer, Dardanus, Ilus, and Tros,' the
boy enunciated in a flash, blushing scarlet, blushing so profusely
that it was pitiful to behold him. But the boys all stared at him,

stared for a whole minute, and then, with one accord, all those staring gazes turned towards Kolya. The latter continued to consider the impertinent boy with scornful composure.

'And just how precisely did they found it?' he at last condescended to ask, 'and what does it mean, anyway, to found a city or a state? Do you mean they came along and laid a brick each, or what?'

Laughter rang out. The guilty boy turned from pink to crimson. He said nothing, he was close to tears. Kolya let him stew for a full minute.

'Before one can discuss such historical events as the founding of nations,' he pontificated sternly, 'one must first understand what this means. I, incidentally, do not take all those fairy tales seriously, in fact, I don't think much of world history in general,' he added suddenly, addressing himself offhandedly to all those present.

'Not think much of world history?' enquired the Staff Captain, suddenly taking fright.

'Yes, world history. It's merely a catalogue of human stupidity—simply that. I respect only mathematics and the natural sciences,' bragged Kolya and flashed a glance at Alyosha; his was the only opinion here that concerned him. But Alyosha still maintained his silence and the same serious air as before. Had Alyosha said anything at that moment, that would have been the end of the matter, but Alyosha said nothing, 'his silence might be a scornful silence', and Kolya was already thoroughly irritated.

'And take the classical languages we have to study now: it's sheer madness, that's what I say... I think you disagree with me on this too, don't you, Karamazov?'

'Yes, I do,' Alyosha smiled gently.

'Classical languages, if you want my opinion, are an instrument of police repression,* that's the only reason they've been introduced,' Kolya was beginning to falter once more. 'They've been introduced because they're boring and because they dull the mind. There was boredom, so how could they make it more boring? It was stupid, so how could they make it more stupid? And then they thought of classical languages. That is my considered opinion on the matter, and I hope I never change it,' he finished abruptly. A red blush suffused both his cheeks.

'That's true,' Smurov, who had been diligently following every word, chimed in with conviction.

'And he comes top in Latin,' shouted a boy in the group.

'Yes, papa, he says that, but he's top of our Latin class,' Ilyusha struck up, too.

'Well, so what?' Kolya judged it necessary to defend himself, although the compliment pleased him enormously. 'I swot up Latin because I have to, and because I promised my mother I'd finish the course, and in my opinion once you've started something you may as well do it well, but deep down I despise classicism, it's just a conspiracy... Don't you agree, Karamazov?'

'Why "conspiracy"?' Alyosha smiled again.

'Oh, come now, all the classics have been translated into every language, they don't need to force Latin on us so we can read the classics, they only use them as a repressive measure and to dull the mind. Given that, how can you say it's not a conspiracy?'

'Whoever told you all that?' exclaimed Alyosha at last, in astonishment.

'Firstly, I can understand it for myself, without being taught, and secondly, let me tell you, everything I have just said about translations of the classics, our master Kolbasnikov himself said openly to the whole of the third form...'

'The doctor's here,' suddenly exclaimed Ninochka, who had not opened her mouth all this time.

True enough, Mrs Khokhlakova's carriage was drawing up at the front gates. The Staff Captain, who had been waiting for the doctor all morning, rushed out to the gate to meet him. His wife pulled herself together and assumed an air of importance. Alyosha went across to Ilyusha and started to plump up his pillow. Ninochka, from her invalid chair, watched him anxiously as he straightened up the bed. The boys began hurriedly to take their leave, some of them promising to look in that evening. Kolya called to Perezvon, and he jumped off the bed.

'It's all right, I'm not going,' Kolya said quickly to Ilyusha. 'I'll wait in the hall and come back when the doctor's gone. I'll bring Perezvon back.'

But the doctor was already entering the room—an imposing figure in a bearskin coat, with long, dark side-whiskers and a clean-shaven chin. He stepped across the threshold and stopped, as if disconcerted; he must have thought that he had come to the wrong address. 'What's this? Where am I?' he muttered, without taking off either his fur coat or his sealskin hat with the sealskin peak. All the people, the poverty of the room, the sheets hanging on a line in the corner, had put him off his stride. The Staff Captain bowed before him, quite overcome with servility.

'You're here, sir, here, sir,' he babbled obsequiously, 'you're here at my place, you've come to see my...'

'Sne-gi-ryov,' the doctor pronounced loudly and pompously. 'Are you Mr Snegiryov?'

'Yes, sir, that's me.'

'Ah!'

The doctor gave another fastidious look around the room and threw off his fur coat. Round his neck, glinting for all to see, was an important-looking medal. The Staff Captain caught the coat in mid-flight, and the doctor took off his hat.

'Right, where's the patient?' he asked loudly and peremptorily.

6

PRECOCIOUSNESS

'WHAT do you think the doctor's going to say to him?' Kolya said at once. 'Hasn't he got a repulsive mug? I can't stand doctors!'

'Ilyusha's going to die. I think that's certain now,' Alyosha replied sadly.

'Scoundrels! All doctors are scoundrels! Still, I'm glad I've met you, Karamazov. I've been wanting to get to know you for ages. It's just a pity we had to meet under such sad circumstances...'

Kolya very much wanted to say something more friendly, less formal, but he felt somehow inhibited. Alyosha noticed this, smiled, and shook his hand.

'I've admired you as a rare being for a long time,' muttered Kolya, embarrassed and confused. 'I hear you're a mystic and that you've been in the monastery. I know you're a mystic, but... that doesn't bother me. Contact with reality will cure you of that... For people like you, it can't be otherwise.'

'What do you mean by a mystic? And what will I be cured of?' Alyosha was a little surprised.

'Well, God and all that.'

'What, you don't believe in God?'

'On the contrary, I've got nothing against God. Of course, God is only a hypothesis... but... I admit that He is necessary to maintain order... for worldwide order and so on... and if He didn't exist, it would be necessary to invent Him,'* Kolya added, beginning to blush. He suddenly imagined that Alyosha would now think that he was trying to show off his erudition and prove how 'grown-up' he was. 'I don't want to show off how erudite I am in front of him at all,' thought Kolya indignantly. And he suddenly felt very angry.

'I must admit, I can't stand getting involved in that kind of argument,' he said quickly. 'When all's said and done, one can love mankind without believing in God, don't you think? After all, Voltaire didn't believe in God, but he loved mankind, didn't he?' ('I'm doing it again!' he thought to himself.)

'Voltaire did believe in God, but not much, and I don't think he loved mankind that much, either,' Alyosha spoke softly, in a restrained and totally natural manner, as though he were talking to someone of his own age or even someone much older. What surprised Kolya most of all was Alyosha's apparent lack of conviction in his own opinion of Voltaire, and it seemed as though Alyosha was leaving it to him, little Kolya, to make up his own mind.

'Have you read Voltaire?' Alyosha concluded.

'No, not exactly... but I did read *Candide*,* in an old, absolutely dreadfully funny translation...' ('There I go again!')

'And did you understand it?'

'Oh yes, everything... that is... why on earth do you think I wouldn't understand it? Of course, it has a lot of dirty bits... Of course, I understand that it's a philosophical novel and that it was written to promote an idea...', Kolya totally lost his train of thought. 'I'm an incorrigible socialist, Karamazov,' he broke off suddenly, for no apparent reason.

'Socialist?' laughed Alyosha. 'At your age? You're only thirteen, aren't you?'

Kolya winced.

'Firstly, I'm fourteen, not thirteen, I'll be fourteen in two weeks,' he spluttered, 'and secondly, I don't see what on earth my age has got to do with it. It's a question of my convictions, isn't it, not my age?'

'When you're older you'll see for yourself what an influence age has on convictions. Also, I notice you're not using your own words,' Alyosha replied discreetly and calmly, but Kolya interrupted him heatedly.

'Forgive me, but you want obedience and mysticism. You must agree, for example, that the Christian faith has only served to allow the rich and powerful to keep the lower classes in serfdom, isn't that so?'

'Ah! I know where you read that,' exclaimed Alyosha, 'and someone must have been indoctrinating you!'

'Excuse me, but why are you so sure I read it? And nobody has been indoctrinating me. I don't need... And anyway, I'm not against Christ. He was a thoroughly humane person, and if He were alive today he would certainly join the revolutionaries and would perhaps have played an important role... In fact, he certainly would.'

'Well—where on earth did you pick all that up from? What idiot have you been associating with?' exclaimed Alyosha.

'Forgive me, but you can't hide the truth. It's true that I have had occasion to talk to Mr Rakitin quite often, but... they say that old Belinsky* said the same thing.'

'Belinsky? I don't remember. He didn't write it anywhere.'

'Even if he didn't write it, they say he used to say it. I heard it from a... anyway, to hell with it...'

'And have you read Belinsky?'

'Look... no, not exactly, but I read the bit about Tatiana—why she didn't go with Onegin.'*

'Why she didn't go with Onegin? Surely you don't... understand that?'

'Pardon me, but you seem to take me for that boy Smurov,' Kolya retorted indignantly. 'Besides, please don't think I'm such a revolutionary. I often don't agree with Mr Rakitin. I may have mentioned Tatiana, but that doesn't mean I'm at all in favour of the emancipation of women. I admit that a woman is an inferior being and must obey. *Les femmes tricottent*,* as Napoleon said,'

Kolya smiled for some reason, 'and, at least on that score, I fully share the conviction of that pseudo-great man. I too for example consider that to leave one's homeland for America is base—worse than base—stupid. Why go to America when here too one can do so much for humanity? Especially now. There's a tremendous amount of productive activity. That's what I replied.'

'My word, who asked you? Surely someone hasn't invited you to America already?'

'I admit it has been suggested, but I refused. Of course, this is just between us, Karamazov, not a word to anyone, you hear me. It's just between you and me. I have absolutely no desire to fall into the clutches of Section Three and be chastized by the Chain Bridge:*

> Next the Chain Bridge stands a house
> That I never shall forget!

Do you remember? Magnificent! What are you laughing at? You don't think I'm having you on, do you?' ('What if he finds out that I've only got that one copy of *The Bell** in my father's bookcase, and that I haven't read anything else on the subject?' Kolya thought momentarily and shuddered.)

'Oh no, I'm not laughing, and I certainly didn't think you were having me on. I don't think that, because, alas, all that is the plain truth! Well now, tell me, have you read Pushkin, *Evgeny Onegin* say?... You know, you were talking about Tatiana just now.'

'No, I haven't read it yet, but I want to. I have no prejudices, Karamazov. I want to listen to both sides. Why do you ask?'

'Oh, no reason.'

'Tell me, Karamazov, do you think I'm being silly?' Kolya broke off suddenly, and drew himself up to his full height in front of Alyosha, full of defiance. 'Do me a favour, don't beat about the bush.'

'Silly?' Alyosha looked at him in astonishment. 'Why should I? I'm just sad that such a fine character as yours, just on the threshold of life, should already be spoilt by all that dreadful rubbish.'

'Don't you worry about my character,' Kolya interjected, not without some self-satisfaction, 'and if I'm sceptical, so be it. I'm downright sceptical, as sceptical as they come. Just now you smiled, and I thought...'

'Ah, I was smiling at something else entirely. Listen, this is what I was smiling about: I read a piece about our modern students by a German emigré who had lived in Russia. "Give a map of the heavens", he wrote, "to a Russian schoolboy who has never heard of such a map before, and he'll return it to you the next day full of corrections." No knowledge and limitless presumptuousness—that's what the German meant to say about Russian schoolboys.'

'Oh yes, that's exactly it!' Kolya suddenly exploded with laughter, 'exactissimo, point for point! Bravo, German! But the teuton didn't see the good side, did he, what do you think? Presumptuousness—that's nothing, it's merely youthful excess, it'll right itself—if it needs righting, that is—but against that you have to set independence of spirit, practically from infancy, courage in thought and in convictions, instead of their Frankfurter mentality, their slavish obedience to received opinion... But all the same, it was good, what he said, that German! Bravo, German! All the same, I say the Germans should be strangled. They may be good at science, but all the same they should be strangled...'

'Why should they be strangled?' smiled Alyosha.

'Well, I admit I was talking nonsense, perhaps. Sometimes I'm terribly childish, and when I'm pleased about something I get carried away and start talking all kinds of nonsense. But listen, you and I are chattering away here about nothing at all, and that doctor seems to be taking longer than expected. Maybe he's examining the "lady of the house" and that crippled Ninochka while he's about it. You know, I like that Ninochka. When I came in, she whispered to me suddenly, "Why didn't you come before?" And her voice was so reproachful! She seems terribly kind and I feel sorry for her.'

'Yes, yes! Now that you'll definitely be coming again, you'll see what sort of person she really is. You need to get to know such people so that you can learn how to appreciate things, and you'll find out a whole lot more just by mixing with them,' Alyosha remarked enthusiastically. 'That's the best way for you to change.'

'Oh, how I regret that I didn't come before, and I curse myself for it!' Kolya exclaimed bitterly.

'Yes, it's a great pity. You saw for yourself how delighted the little one was to see you, and he was so upset when you didn't come!'

'Don't talk about it! You're rubbing salt in the wound. Anyway, it serves me right: it was pride that kept me from coming, egoistical pride and a base delight in power, which I've been unable to rid myself of all my life, no matter how hard I try. I see now that, in many ways, I'm a scoundrel, Karamazov!'

'No, you've got a delightful character,' Alyosha replied warmly, 'but it's been warped, and I understand only too well how you had such an influence on that innocent and terribly impressionable child!'

'Do you really mean that!' cried Kolya. 'And I thought, just imagine, I thought several times since I've been here that you think I'm silly! If only you knew how much I value your opinion!'

'Are you really such a sceptic? You're so young! But you know, I thought so just now, back in the room, when you were talking, I thought you must be very sceptical.'

'You thought so then? How perceptive you are, you really do understand! I bet that was when I was telling the story about the goose. That was just the point at which I imagined you thought I was silly for trying to make out what a fine chap I was, and suddenly I even hated you for it and I started to talk rubbish. And then (this was just now, out here) when I was saying, "If God didn't exist, it would be necessary to invent him," I imagined I was trying too hard to show off my erudition, especially as I'd got the phrase out of a book. But I swear to you that I was showing off not out of vanity, but out of, I don't know, out of joy, it was from joy, as God is my witness,... although I admit it's a deeply shameful thing to be forcing one's joy on others. I know that. But now I'm convinced that you don't despise me, and that I imagined it all. Oh, Karamazov, I'm so deeply unhappy. Sometimes I imagine God knows what, that everyone, everyone in the world is laughing at me, and then I feel like causing havoc.'

'And you torment those around you,' smiled Alyosha.

'Yes, I torment those around me, particularly my mother. Tell me, Karamazov, do I seem very ridiculous now?'

'Look, don't think about that, don't think about it at all!' exclaimed Alyosha. 'And what does it mean, anyway, to be ridiculous? Aren't there plenty of times when anyone is, or at least seems, ridiculous? What's more, all gifted people these days are awfully afraid of looking ridiculous, and it makes them unhappy. I'm only surprised that you've started to feel it so early, although, incidentally, I've noticed it for a long time, and not only in you. These days even those who are hardly more than children have begun to suffer from it. It's almost a madness. The devil has manifested himself in that pride and has infected a whole generation, and I do mean the devil,' added Alyosha, without a trace of the smile that Kolya had thought momentarily he detected. 'You're like all of them,' concluded Alyosha, 'that is, you're like a lot of people, only you don't have to be like them, like everyone, that's all.'

'Even in spite of the fact that everyone's like that?'

'Yes, despite the fact that everyone's like that. You alone won't be like that. In fact, you aren't like everyone: you didn't flinch just now from admitting not only to base actions but also to ridiculous ones. And who admits to such things these days? No one, and people no longer feel the need to judge themselves. Don't be like that, like everyone; even if you have to stand alone and are the only one who's different, nevertheless, don't be like that.'

'Magnificent! I wasn't wrong about you. You have the power to console. Oh, Karamazov, how I was drawn to you, how long I've been dying to meet you! Were you also thinking about me? You did say just now you'd been thinking about me too, didn't you?'

'Yes, I'd heard about you, and I too had been thinking about you... and if you ask that partly out of pride, it doesn't matter.'

'You know, Karamazov, our conversation is a bit like a declaration of love,' said Kolya feebly and shamefacedly. 'Isn't that ridiculous?'

'Not in the least ridiculous, and even if it were ridiculous, it wouldn't matter either, because it's good,' Alyosha smiled brightly.

'But you know, Karamazov, you have to agree that even you

are a bit ashamed in front of me now... I can see it in your eyes,'
Kolya smiled somewhat craftily, but also somehow happily.

'"Ashamed", how?'

'Why are you blushing?'

'It was you who made me blush!' Alyosha laughed, and he
really blushed crimson. 'But yes, I am a little ashamed, God
knows why, I don't know why...', he muttered, almost overcome
by confusion.

'Oh, how I love and esteem you at this moment, precisely
because you too admit to being ashamed of something! Because
you are just like me!' Kolya exclaimed in an excess of enthusiasm.
His cheeks were flushed and his eyes sparkling.

'Listen, Kolya, you know, by the way, you will be very unhappy
in the course of your life,' Alyosha said suddenly, for some
reason.

'I know, I know, you seem to know everything in advance,'
Kolya agreed promptly.

'But on the whole, all the same, you'll bless life.'

'Exactly! Hurrah! You're a prophet! Oh, we shall understand
each other, Karamazov. You know, what delights me most of all
is that you treat me as an equal. But we're not equal, no, we're
not equal, you're higher! But we shall come to understand each
other. You know, all this last month I've been saying to myself,
"Either we'll hit it off straight away and be friends, or we'll hate
each other on sight and be enemies to the grave!"'

'And so saying, of course, you loved me,' Alyosha laughed
merrily.

'Yes, I loved you, I loved you and dreamed about you! And
how do you know all this in advance? Ah, here's the doctor. My
God, I wonder what he's going to say? Look at his face!'

7

ILYUSHA

THE doctor was leaving, having already donned his fur coat and
with his fur hat on his head. He looked irritated and almost
apprehensive, as if he was afraid all the time of being contami-

nated. He cast his eyes around the entrance hallway and glanced sternly at Alyosha and Kolya. Alyosha signalled from the doorway, and the carriage that had brought the doctor drove up to the front door. The Staff Captain rushed out behind the doctor and, bowing almost obsequiously before him, detained him for a final word. The poor man's expression was devastated, his eyes terrified.

'Your Excellency, Your Excellency, isn't it possible?...' he began, but he broke off, wringing his hands in despair and gazing imploringly at the doctor, as if one last word from him now might reprieve the poor child from his death sentence.

'What can I do? I'm not God,' the doctor replied dismissively, but in his usual impressive tone.

'Doctor... Your Excellency... will it be soon, how long?'

'It could be any time,' the doctor enunciated, stressing every syllable, and, lowering his gaze, he prepared to cross the threshold and enter his carriage.

'For Christ's sake, Your Excellency!' the terrified man detained him once more. 'Your Excellency!... Surely... Won't anything, anything at all, save him now?...'

'It's out of my hands now,' said the doctor impatiently, 'but, however, um,' he stopped suddenly, 'if, for example, you could... send... the invalid... immediately, without delay' (so sternly, not to say angrily, did the doctor pronounce the words 'immediately, without delay', that the Staff Captain even shook), 'to Sy-ra-cuse, then... because of the change of climate and conditions... it could, perhaps, produce...'

'To Syracuse!' shrieked the Staff Captain, still completely uncomprehending.

'Syracuse—it's in Sicily,' Kolya interjected loudly, by way of explanation. The doctor glanced at him.

'Send him to Sicily! But, sir, Your Excellency,' the Staff Captain floundered, 'you saw for yourself, didn't you...', he made a sweeping gesture indicating his quarters, 'my dear wife, my family?'

'No, don't send your family to Sicily, send them to the Caucasus instead, early in the spring... send your daughter to the Caucasus... and your wife should take the cure... at a spa... also in the Caucasus, for her rheumatism... and then straight after that send her to Paris, to Dr Le-pel-let-ier's psychiatric clinic, I could give you a referral note, and then... perhaps it would...'

'But doctor, doctor... can't you see!' the Staff Captain suddenly gestured again despairingly, indicating the bare log walls of the hallway.

'Oh, that's not my business,' the doctor smiled coldly, 'I only gave you my pro-fess-ional opinion in answer to your question about what to do as a last resort, but for the rest... unfortunately, I...'

'Don't worry, quack, my dog won't bite you,' Kolya interposed loudly, having noticed the doctor glancing uneasily several times at Perezvon, who was standing on the doorstep. An undertone of anger sounded in Kolya's voice. He had said 'quack' instead of 'doctor' quite deliberately, and, as he himself said later, 'I said it to insult him.'

'What was that?' the doctor jerked his head up, and stared at Kolya in astonishment. 'Who is that?' he turned suddenly to Alyosha, as though asking him for an explanation.

'That's Perezvon's master, quack, there's no need to know who I am,' Kolya rapped out.

'Zvon?' repeated the doctor, not having understood what was meant by 'Perezvon'.

'Gone, gone is Perezvon. Goodbye, quack, see you in Syracuse.'

'Who is that, who, who?' the doctor suddenly spluttered angrily.

'He's a local schoolboy, doctor, a scallywag, don't take any notice,' said Alyosha hurriedly, with a frown. 'Kolya, shut up!' he shouted to Krasotkin. 'You mustn't take any notice, doctor,' he repeated, this time somewhat more impatiently.

'He should be whipped, whipped, that's what,' the doctor stamped his foot in an altogether excessive show of fury.

'But you know, quack, this Perezvon of mine might bite after all!' Kolya had paled, his voice shook, and his eyes flashed. 'Here boy!'

'Kolya, if you say another word, I'll never have anything more to do with you,' shouted Alyosha furiously.

'Quack, there is only one person in the whole world who can

give orders to Nikolai Krasotkin—that gentleman there,' Kolya pointed to Alyosha, 'that's whom I obey, goodbye!'

He turned away, opened the door, and entered the room quickly. Perezvon rushed after him. The doctor stood gazing at Alyosha for about five seconds, as if stunned, then suddenly he spat and walked to his carriage, repeating loudly, 'This, this, this is too much!' The Staff Captain rushed to help him into his carriage. Alyosha followed Kolya into the room. The latter was already standing by Ilyusha's bed. Ilyusha was holding his hand and calling his father. A minute later, the Staff Captain returned as well.

'Papa, papa, come here... we...', Ilyusha, terribly excited but obviously unable to go on, suddenly stretched out his two wasted arms in front of him and hugged both Kolya and his father as tightly as he could, uniting them in a single embrace and pressing himself against them. The Staff Captain was suddenly shaken by silent sobs, and Kolya's lips and chin began to tremble.

'Papa, papa! I'm so sorry for you, papa!' Ilyusha groaned miserably.

'Ilyushechka... my darling...', the Staff Captain faltered, 'the doctor says... you'll get better... we'll be happy... the doctor...'

'Oh, papa! I know what the new doctor told you about me... I could see!' exclaimed Ilyusha, and he clasped them to him again with all his strength and buried his face in his father's shoulder.

'Don't cry, papa... and when I die, get a good little boy, another one... choose him yourself, from all of them, choose a good one, call him Ilyusha, and love him instead of me...'

'Be quiet, old chap, you're going to get better!' snapped Krasotkin suddenly, as if angry.

'But don't forget me, papa, never forget me,' Ilyusha went on. 'Come and visit my grave... yes, that's it, papa, bury me by our big stone, where we used to go for walks, and come and visit me there with Krasotkin, in the evening... Perezvon too. I'll be expecting you... Papa, papa!'

His voice broke, all three remained in a silent embrace. Ninochka was crying quietly too in her chair, and suddenly, seeing everyone else crying, the mother also burst into tears.

'Ilyushechka! Ilyushechka!' she cried.

Krasotkin released himself suddenly from Ilyusha's embrace.

'Goodbye, old chap, my mother's expecting me for lunch,' he said quickly. 'What a pity I didn't warn her! She'll be very worried... But after lunch I'll come straight back and stay the whole afternoon and evening, and I'll tell you such a lot of things, such a lot! And I'll bring Perezvon too, but I'll take him with me now, because without me he'd start howling and would be a nuisance; goodbye!'

He ran out into the hallway. He didn't want to cry, but nevertheless he burst into tears in the hall. Alyosha found him crying his heart out.

'Kolya, you must keep your word and come back, or he'll be terribly upset,' said Alyosha urgently.

'I promise! Oh, how I curse myself for not coming sooner,' Kolya muttered, weeping and no longer embarrassed by his tears. At that moment the Staff Captain practically burst from the room, shutting the door behind him. His face was haggard, his lips trembling. He stood before the two young men and threw up his arms.

'I don't want a good little boy! I don't want another little boy!' he muttered in a desperate whisper, gritting his teeth. 'If I forget thee, Jerusalem, let my tongue cleave...'*

He broke off, as if choking, and fell to his knees helplessly by the wooden bench. Clasping his head with both hands, he began to sob, emitting absurd little cries, but trying desperately not to be heard inside the room. Kolya rushed out on to the street.

'Goodbye, Karamazov! Are you coming back yourself?' he called sharply and angrily to Alyosha.

'I'll be there for certain this evening.'

'What was that about Jerusalem? What did he mean?'

'It's from the Bible: "If I forget thee, O Jerusalem"—that is, if I forget all that I hold most dear, if I abandon it for anything else, may I be struck down...'

'That's enough, I understand! You must come back too! Perezvon, here boy!' he called to the dog, this time really sharply, and strode off homewards.

BOOK ELEVEN
Ivan Fyodorovich

1

AT GRUSHENKA'S

ALYOSHA set out for the house of Mrs Morozova, the merchant's widow, on Cathedral Square to see Grushenka. The latter had already sent Fenya to him that morning, insisting that he come and see her. Alyosha had questioned Fenya and learned that her mistress had been in a considerable state of panic ever since the previous day. Throughout the two months following Mitya's arrest, Alyosha had gone frequently to Morozova's, both of his own accord and at Mitya's behest. About three days after Mitya's arrest Grushenka had become very sick and was ill for about the next five weeks. One week, she had lain unconscious in her bed. Now, although she had been up and about for nearly two weeks, her appearance had changed a great deal, her complexion had become sallow and she had lost weight. But, in Alyosha's eyes, her face had become even more attractive, and every time he came to see her he enjoyed meeting her gaze. There was something hard and determined in her eyes. One sensed that she had undergone a spiritual crisis and had emerged full of a new, tranquil, benevolent, and unwavering resolve. On her forehead, between her eyes, there was now a short vertical line which lent her sweet face an aspect of inward contemplation bordering, at first glance, almost on the severe. Gone completely was her former frivolity. Alyosha found it strange, too, that in spite of all the misfortune which had befallen the poor woman—her sweetheart arrested for a dreadful crime, almost at the very moment of their engagement—and in spite of her subsequent illness and the almost inevitable verdict looming over Mitya, she had nevertheless lost none of her former youthful gaiety. Her formerly challenging gaze was now aglow with something akin to serenity, and yet... and yet a vicious flame would occasionally flare up in those eyes of hers whenever she remembered a former preoccupation—a preoccupation which not only remained unabated but had even intensified in her heart. The object of this preoccupation was as always Katerina Ivanovna, whom Grushenka, even when she lay delirious on her sickbed, had been unable to exorcise from her mind. Alyosha was aware that she was terribly jealous of her because of Mitya, Mitya the convict, despite the fact that Katerina Ivanovna had not visited him in prison even once, and not for any lack of opportunity. All these factors presented a delicate problem for Alyosha, the more so since he was the only person in whom Grushenka confided and since she continually sought his advice; he, on the other hand, was sometimes at a loss for anything to say to her.

When he arrived at the house he was very worried. She was already at home, having returned from visiting Mitya only an hour previously, and from the alacrity with which she leapt from her chair behind the table to greet him, Alyosha immediately concluded that she had been waiting for him with extreme impatience. On the table was a pack of cards, dealt for a game of 'fools'. Beyond the table some bedding had been spread out on a leather sofa, on which Maksimov reclined in a dressing-gown and cotton nightcap, ill and debilitated, but nevertheless smiling sweetly. Ever since he had left Mokroye with her about two months ago, this destitute little old man had never left her side. When they had returned that time in the rain and the mud he had sat down on the sofa, soaked to the skin and terrified, just staring at her in silence, smiling meekly and pleadingly. Grushenka, preoccupied by her terrible grief and already ill from the onset of fever, had, for half an hour or so after their return, almost forgotten about him—all of a sudden, however, she had looked at him intently: he just smiled back at her in pitiful resignation. She called Fenya and told her to give him something to eat. All that day he remained rooted there and hardly stirred; after dark, when the shutters had been closed, Fenya asked her mistress:

'What about him, Miss, is he really going to stay the night?'

'Yes, make up a bed for him on the sofa,' Grushenka replied.

After questioning him closely, Grushenka learned that he really had nowhere to go at all, and that 'my benefactor Mr Kalganov told me to my face he never wanted to see me again, and gave me five roubles.' 'Well, what's to be done; stay here if you like,' Grushenka decided resignedly, smiling at him with compassion. That smile struck a deep chord in him, tears welled up in his eyes, and his lips began to tremble. And the itinerant pickthank* had stayed put at her place ever since. He did not even move out of the house during her illness. Fenya and her mother, Grushenka's cook,* did not try to get rid of him either, but continued to feed him and make up his bed on the sofa. Subsequently, Grushenka had even got used to him, and whenever she came back from visiting Mitya (she began to visit him the moment she felt slightly better, though long before she had fully recovered)—in order to assuage her grief by taking her mind off the whole affair—she would sit down and start talking to 'Maksimushka' about all sorts of trifles. It turned out that the old fellow could tell a good story, so that he even became indispensable to her in the end. Grushenka entertained hardly anyone except Alyosha, and even he did not visit her every day and he did not stay long. Her old merchant friend was seriously ill by this time, 'failing', as they used to say in the town, and in fact he died within a week of Mitya's trial. Three weeks before his death, sensing his imminent end, he finally summoned his sons upstairs, together with their wives and children, and asked them to remain with him. As for Grushenka, he gave his servants strict orders not to admit her henceforth, under any circumstances, and if she were to come, to tell her: 'The master wishes you a long life full of good cheer, but says you should forget about him altogether.' Nearly every day, however, Grushenka would enquire after his health.

'Here you are at last!' she exclaimed, throwing down the cards and welcoming Alyosha. 'And there was Maksimushka trying to frighten me by saying that you'd probably never come. Ah, I'm so pleased to see you! Come and sit by the table! Well, what will you have, coffee?'

'Yes please,' said Alyosha, pulling a chair up to the table, 'I'm starving.'

'Fenya, Fenya, coffee!' Grushenka called. 'It's piping hot, I kept it for you; and bring some *pirozhki*, Fenya; make sure they're hot though. You know, Alyosha, we had an almighty row today because of those *pirozhki*. I took them to the prison for him, and would you believe it, he threw them in my face and wouldn't eat them. He even threw one on the floor and stamped on it. So I said to him, "I'll leave them with the guard. If you haven't eaten them by this evening, you can choke on your own spite!" and I just left him to it. So we've fallen out again, would you believe it. Every time I go to see him we have a row.'

Grushenka rattled all this off in an outburst of agitation. Maksimov, who had quailed at her tone, was smiling nervously, his eyes downcast.

'So what did you quarrel about this time?' asked Alyosha.

'It came as a total surprise! Imagine, he's become jealous of my ex. "Why", he says to me, "are you looking after him? You are looking after him, aren't you?" He's so jealous, it's not true! He's got jealousy coming out of his ears. Last week he even tackled me over Kuzma.'

'But he knew all about your officer, didn't he?'

'Exactly. He's known from the very beginning, but that didn't stop him abusing me all of a sudden today. I'm too ashamed to repeat the things he said. The fool! As I was leaving, Rakitka was just going in to see him. Maybe it's Rakitka who keeps putting him up to it, eh? What do you think?' she added, somewhat absent-mindedly.

'He loves you, that's what, he's very fond of you. But he's upset just now.'

'So would anybody be, the trial's tomorrow. I went to see him especially to reassure him about tomorrow, because, Alyosha, I daren't even think what's going to happen then! You say he's upset, what about me! And all he can think of is that Pole! What a fool! He'll be getting jealous of Maksimushka next.'

'My wife was awfully jealous,' Maksimov joined in the conversation.

'Was she now,' Grushenka could not suppress a chuckle, 'who could she have been jealous of?'

'The chambermaids.'

'Shut up, Maksimushka, this is not the time for jokes, you'll make me lose my temper. And stop ogling those *pirozhki*, you're not going to get any, they're bad for you, and that goes for the drink too. Now I've got him on my hands too; you'd think this was an old people's home or something,' she said, laughing.

'I'm not worthy of your kindness, I'm a nobody,' Maksimov said pathetically. 'You'd do better to shower your bounty on those who are of more use than me.'

'Oh, Maksimushka, everyone's got his own use, and who knows who's more useful than another? That Pole is the last thing I need now, Alyosha, and today he too has gone and fallen ill. I went to see him. Now I've made up my mind, I'm going to send him too some *pirozhki*; I haven't sent him any before, but seeing as Mitya's accused me of having done so, I'm going to send him some now, on purpose, that's right, on purpose! Ah, here's Fenya with a letter! Just as I thought, it's from him, he and the other one, they're after money again!'

Pan Mussjalowicz had as usual sent an extremely rambling letter asking for a loan of three roubles. Attached was a receipt together with a pledge to repay within three months; the receipt was also signed by *Pan* Wrublewski. Grushenka had already received many such letters from her 'former' one, enclosing similar receipts. It had begun about two weeks ago, just as Grushenka began to feel better. She knew, however, that the Poles had called during her illness to ask after her health. The first letter had been a long one, written on a large sheet of writing-paper and sealed with a large family seal; it was terribly vague and verbose, and Grushenka had only bothered to read half of it, and had thrown it away without understanding a thing. Anyway, there were other things on her mind at the time. That first letter had been followed the next day by a second one, in which *Pan* Mussjalowicz asked her for a loan of two thousand roubles over the shortest possible period of time. Grushenka had left this letter unanswered too. There followed a whole series of letters, one a day, each one just as pompous and long-winded, but in which the sum requested grew smaller and smaller, falling to a hundred roubles, then twenty-five, then ten, and finally Grushenka had received a letter in which the two gentlemen asked her for just one rouble; attached was a receipt signed by both of them. At that, Grushenka had been moved to pity, and after dark she had rushed over to see her Pole. She had found them both in dire poverty, almost destitute, without food, without firewood, without tobacco, and owing money to their landlady. The two hundred roubles they had won from Mitya in Mokroye had simply vanished into thin air. What had surprised Grushenka, however, was that both gentlemen greeted her with affected superciliousness and self-confidence, and with a great deal of bombast and inflated speeches. Grushenka had simply laughed and given her 'former one' ten roubles. She had immediately told Mitya about it as a joke, and he had not been jealous in the least. Ever since then, the two Polish gentlemen had plagued Grushenka and bombarded her every day with begging letters, and she had continued to send them a little money every time. And now, lo and behold, today Mitya had decided to become jealous.

'I was a fool for popping in to see him, it was only going to be for a second, on my way to Mitya's, after all he was really ill, my former *pan* that is,' Grushenka resumed again, disjointedly and hurriedly, 'there I was, laughing, telling Mitya all about it: imagine, I told him my Polish friend thought that if he sang me our old songs again and played his guitar, I'd become all sentimental and marry him. And Mitya jumps up and starts swearing... So there, I shall send them some *pirozhki*! Fenya, where's that girl they sent over? Here, give her these three roubles and a dozen *pirozhki*, wrap them in a piece of paper and let her take them, and you, Alyosha, make sure you tell Mitya I sent them some *pirozhki*.'

'Not on your life,' said Alyosha with a smile.

'Ha, you think he cares? He's just acting jealous, he couldn't care less, really,' said Grushenka bitterly.

'What do you mean "acting"?' asked Alyosha.

'You are stupid, Alyoshenka, that's what! You don't understand anything about it, for all your brains! I don't mind him being jealous, I'd have minded if he hadn't been jealous. I'm like that. I don't mind jealousy, I've got a cruel streak myself, I can be jealous too. What I would mind is if he didn't love me at all and is just pretending to be jealous. Does he think I'm blind, that I can't see or something? Suddenly he starts talking about that Katka. "That Katerina," he says, "fancy getting a doctor from Moscow for the trial, to save me, and the top lawyer, the cleverest one of the lot." That means he loves her, if he's started to praise her to my face. He hasn't got an ounce of shame, that man hasn't! He knows he's in the wrong, that's why he keeps getting at me, he's trying to make out that I'm the guilty one and blame me for everything. "You had your Pole before I came along," he reckons, "so my relations with Katka are none of your business." That's the way it is! He wants me to take all the blame. He deliberately started getting at me, on purpose, I tell you, only I...'

Grushenka broke off, she put her handkerchief to her eyes and began to sob violently.

'He doesn't love Katerina Ivanovna,' said Alyosha firmly.

'Well, whether he loves her or not, I shall be able to find out for myself soon,' Grushenka said, with a menacing note in her voice, and took the handkerchief away from her eyes. She was scowling. Alyosha sadly observed how quickly her expression changed—meek and serenely happy one second, sullenly hostile the next.

'Enough of this nonsense!' she pulled herself together. 'This isn't why I asked you to see me at all. Alyosha, darling, what about tomorrow, what's going to happen tomorrow? That's what's preying on my mind! And I seem to be the only one who gives a damn! I look around me, and as far as I can see no one else is giving it a moment's thought, no one cares. I hope you at least are thinking about it! Tomorrow's the trial, for heaven's sake! What do you think they'll do to him? Surely it was the servant who did it, it must have been the servant! God! Is he going to be made a scapegoat, and isn't any one going to stand up for him? They haven't even questioned the servant, have they?'

'Yes, they have. They interrogated him thoroughly,' Alyosha observed thoughtfully, 'but they all concluded it wasn't him. And now he's very ill in bed. He's been ill ever since, ever since the fit. He really is ill,' Alyosha added.

'My God, why don't you go to the lawyer yourself and tell him the whole story face to face? They say he was paid three thousand to come from St Petersburg.'

'We paid the three thousand—I, Ivan and Katerina Ivanovna—and she paid the two thousand for the doctor from Moscow herself. The lawyer Fetyukovich would have asked for more, but the case has become a *cause célèbre* throughout Russia, all the papers are full of it. Fetyukovich agreed to take it on more for the prestige than anything else, because, after all, the case is the talk of the whole country now. I saw him yesterday.'

'Well, what happened? Did you talk to him?' Grushenka demanded eagerly.

'He listened to what I had to say, but he didn't really say anything. All he said was that he's already prepared his defence. But he promised to take my comments into consideration.'

'Consideration, my foot? What a bunch of rogues! He doesn't stand a chance with that lot! What about the doctor, why did she want to engage a doctor?'

'As an expert witness. They want to suggest that Mitya's insane and that he committed the murder while the state of his mind was unbalanced, that he wasn't responsible for his actions,' Alyosha smiled gently, 'only Dmitry is not going to stand for that.'

'Ah, that's true, except that he didn't kill him!' exclaimed Grushenka. 'He was mad, quite mad, and it was me, me, hateful woman that I am, who's to blame for it! Only he didn't kill him, he didn't! Everyone wants to believe he killed him, the whole town. Even Fenya testified against him. And in the shop, and that clerk, and what people heard him say in the tavern! Everybody, everybody's against him, and they're all baying for his blood.'

'Yes, the evidence against him is overwhelming,' Alyosha observed despondently.

'And that Grigory, Grigory Vasilyevich, he won't budge—as far as he's concerned, the door was open, he saw it, that's his story and he's sticking to it. I went over to see him to have a word with him myself. He even swore at me!'

'Yes, that's probably the strongest item of evidence there is against my brother,' said Alyosha.

'And as to Mitya being out of his mind,' Grushenka suddenly began, in an extraordinarily preoccupied and mysterious tone of voice, 'that's just what he is now. You know, Alyoshenka, I've been meaning to talk to you about this for a long time: I've been visiting him every day, and I simply can't make him out. Tell me what you think: what's he going on about now? I mean the way he talks—I can't understand a thing. I tell myself it must be something clever—well, all right, so I'm stupid, perhaps it's way over my head, I say to myself. Now he's suddenly started going on about some child—a bairn. "Why's the bairn poor?" he says. "It's on account of the bairn that I must go to Siberia. I didn't commit the murder, but I will go to Siberia!" What's all that about, what bairn? I couldn't make head nor tail of it. I just started crying while he was speaking, he's got such a way of talking, you know, he was crying himself, and I burst into tears too, and then he suddenly kissed me and made the sign of the cross over me with his hand. What was all that, Alyosha, tell me, what was all that about a "bairn"?'

'Well, Rakitin's been going to see him lately,' smiled Alyosha, 'but, come to think of it, however... that doesn't sound like Rakitin. I didn't go to see him yesterday, but I'm going today.'

'No, it isn't Rakitka, it's Ivan Fyodorovich who's been putting ideas into his head. He's been going to see him, that's what...', said Grushenka, and suddenly stopped dead. Alyosha stared at her in bewilderment.

'What do you mean, going to see him? Has he really been going to see him? Mitya told me that Ivan hadn't been to see him at all.'

'Oh dear... now I've put my foot in it! Why couldn't I keep my mouth shut!' exclaimed Grushenka in embarrassment, blushing all over. 'Look, Alyosha, don't say a word, all right, now that I've let the cat out of the bag I may as well tell you the whole truth: he's been to see him twice. The first time was straight after he got back—you remember how he came rushing back from Moscow at the time, it was even before I went down with my illness—and then he went to see him again a week ago. He told Mitya not to tell you about it, whatever happened, nor anyone else for that matter. It was a secret visit.'

Alyosha sat deep in thought, turning something over in his mind. Clearly, the news had astonished him.

'Ivan doesn't talk to me about Mitya's case,' he said slowly, 'in fact, he's spoken to me very little these past two months, and whenever I've been over to see him he's never been welcoming,

so I've kept away from him altogether for three weeks. Hm... if
he did go to see him a week ago, then... that explains the change
in Mitya this past week.'

'Yes, there has been a change!' Grushenka echoed quickly.
'They've got a secret, there's some secret between them! Mitya
told me himself it was a secret, and, you know, it's such a secret
that Mitya's lost all his peace of mind. And yet he was quite
cheerful before—not that he's not cheerful now—it's just that
when he starts shaking his head like that and pacing up and
down the room, fingering his hair just here, on his temple, I
know there's something troubling him... I knew it straight away!...
Apart from that, he's been cheerful; he was cheerful today too!'

'Didn't you say he was in a bad temper?'

'In a bad temper, but cheerful at the same time. He gets
irritated, but only for a second, then he's cheerful, and a little
later he's irritated again. And you know, Alyosha, he never ceases
to surprise me; he's facing such an ordeal, and yet he laughs at
the least excuse, just like a child.'

'Is it true, though, that he forbade you to mention Ivan's visit
to me? Is that what he said, "Don't mention it to him?"'

'His very words, "Don't mention it to him!" It's you he's afraid
of most of all, Mitya that is. It's all to do with this secret, that's
what he said—it's a secret... Alyosha, my darling, go and try and
find out for yourself what's going on between them, and then
come back and tell me,' Grushenka pleaded anxiously. 'Put me
out of my misery, I want to know what the future holds in store!
That's why I sent for you!'

'Do you think it's something to do with you? But then, surely
he wouldn't have told you if it was meant to be a secret.'

'I don't know. Maybe he does want to tell me, but can't bring
himself to do it. He's warning me. "There's a secret," he says,
but what the secret is—he won't tell me.'

'So what do you think it is?'

'How do I know? I've been ditched, that's what I think. The
three of them have got it in for me, and it's that Katka's doing.
Katka's behind it all, she's the one. "She's a fine woman," he
says—which means that I'm not, thank you very much. It's his
way of telling me, his way of warning me. He's made up his
mind to abandon me, that's all there is to their secret! The three

of them—Mitka, Katka, and Ivan Fyodorovich—are in it together. Alyosha, I've been meaning to ask you for a long time: about a week ago he suddenly told me that Ivan was in love with Katka—because he keeps going to see her so often. Was he telling me the truth or not? Tell me honestly, I won't be upset.'

'I won't lie to you. Ivan's not in love with Katerina Ivanovna, at least I don't think so.'

'Well, that's what I thought at the time! He was pulling the wool over my eyes, the lying hound, that's what! And his jealousy's just an excuse to pin the blame on me later. He's such a fool, you know, he hasn't got an ounce of guile in him, he's so transparently honest... But I'll show him, I really will! "You think I killed him, don't you?" he says to me. He says that to me, to me, he blames me for that now! God have mercy on him! You just wait, I'll teach that Katka a lesson at the trial! I'll know what to say... I'll tell them everything at the trial!'

And she began to cry again bitterly.

'Look here, Grushenka,' said Alyosha, getting up, 'this is what I know for sure: firstly, he loves you, he loves you above all else in the world, and nobody but you, believe me. I know it. Trust me. Secondly, I must tell you that I don't wish to pry into his secret, but if he reveals it to me himself today, I'll tell him frankly that I've promised to tell you. And then I'll come back this very day and let you know. Only... the way I see it... it has nothing whatsoever to do with Katerina Ivanovna, this secret concerns something else entirely. I'm convinced of it. There's much more behind this than Katerina Ivanovna, that's how I see it. Well, goodbye for now!'

Alyosha shook her hand. Grushenka was still crying. He could see that she gave little credence to his words of comfort, but at least she had done herself some good by baring her soul and unburdening herself of her grief. He felt sorry for leaving her in such a state, but he had to hurry. There was still a lot he had to do.

2

PAINFUL FOOT

His first port of call was Mrs Khokhlakova's, and he hurried straight over there to get things sorted out and not be late for Mitya. For three weeks now Mrs Khokhlakova had been indisposed: for some reason her foot had become swollen, and although she had not taken to her bed she had nevertheless spent the days reclining on a *chaise-longue* in her boudoir, in an attractive but perfectly decorous négligé. On a previous occasion Alyosha had already noted with a sense of innocent amusement that in spite of her indisposition, Mrs Khokhlakova had begun to prettify herself: suddenly there was an abundance of fancy hairbands, little ribbons and bows, and loose-fitting blouses, and though he could guess the reason for this, he immediately dismissed his thoughts as speculation. Amongst the guests whom Mrs Khokhlakova had entertained during the past two months was the young and eligible Perkhotin. It was now some four days since Alyosha's last visit, and when he arrived he wanted to see Lise straight away. Just the day before Lise had sent her servant girl to him with an urgent request to call on her without delay about 'a very important matter', which for a variety of reasons had aroused his curiosity; he had therefore come especially to see her, but before the girl had informed Lise of his arrival Mrs Khokhlakova had already found out from someone else that he was there and had immediately requested him to see her 'for just one second'. Alyosha decided that it was probably best to satisfy mama's request first, since otherwise there were bound to be endless interruptions from her while he was with Lise. Mrs Khokhlakova was lying on her *chaise-longue* in particularly seductive attire and in an obvious state of acute agitation. She greeted Alyosha with exclamations of delight.

'It's been ages, simply ages since I've seen you! A whole week, would you believe it, oh, to be sure you were here just four days ago, on Wednesday. You want to see Lise? I'm sure you wanted to tiptoe straight up to her, so that I wouldn't hear. My dear, dear Aleksei Fyodorovich, if only you knew how much I worry about her! But more of that later. Although it's the most important matter, it can wait. My dear Aleksei Fyodorovich, I entrust my Lise to you totally. Ever since Starets Zosima's death—may God rest his soul! (she crossed herself)—ever since his death, I still regard you as a member of the strictest order of monks, even though you look most fetching in that suit of yours. Where on earth did you find such a tailor in these parts? But no, no, that's not the main thing, it can wait till later. Excuse me calling you Alyosha sometimes, but I'm an old woman, I'm allowed to,' she smiled coquettishly, 'but that can wait too. The main thing is, I mustn't forget about the main thing. Look here, don't hesitate to remind me the minute I start rambling on, just say: "And what about the main thing?" Oh, how should I know what the main thing is now? Ever since Lise withdrew her promise—her childish promise, Aleksei Fyodorovich—to marry you—you must of course have realized that it was nothing but the childish, playful fantasy of a sick girl who's spent a long time in an invalid chair—thank God, she's able to walk now. This new doctor that Katya got from Moscow for your poor brother, who tomorrow... Oh dear, yes, tomorrow! Every time I think about tomorrow I just feel like dying! It's my curiosity first and foremost... In a word, that doctor came to see us yesterday and he examined Lise... I paid him fifty roubles for the visit. But that's not what I wanted to talk about either... You see, I'm going off at a tangent. I'm rushing ahead of myself. Why should I be in such a hurry? I don't know. I'm beginning to lose track of things. Everything seems to have got tangled into a knot in my mind. I'm afraid that if I'm not careful I'll bore you to death and you'll run a mile from me, and that'll be the last I'll see of you. Oh, my God! Why are we just sitting here? But first, coffee—Yulia, Glafira, coffee!'

Alyosha hastened to thank her, and informed her that he had just had coffee.

'Who with?'

'Agrafena Aleksandrovna.'

'What?... With that woman! She's the one who's destroyed everybody, but then again I don't know, they say she's turned into a saint, though a bit late, I fear. She should have thought of it earlier, when there was a need for it, but what's the use now? Don't say a word, not a word, Aleksei Fyodorovich, because there's so much I want to say that I'm afraid I'll end up saying nothing at all. This awful trial... I'll definitely go, even if they have to carry me there, my mind's made up, anyway, I can sit and I'll have people to look after me, and you do know, don't you, that I'm a witness? I shall have plenty to say, indeed I shall! No, really, I don't know what I'm going to say. You have to take an oath, don't you.'

'Yes, but I don't think you're in a fit state to attend.'

'I can sit. Oh, you're interrupting me! This trial, that abominable crime, and then everybody going off to Siberia, others getting married in such haste, such haste, and everything changing, till nothing's left in the end and everyone's old, with one foot in the grave. But what do I care? I'm tired. This Katya—*cette charmante personne*,* she's dashed all my hopes; now she's going to Siberia with one of your brothers, and the other one's going to follow her and live in the neighbouring town, and they're all going to torture one another. It's driving me crazy, but the main thing is the publicity; it's been in all the papers in St Petersburg and Moscow a million times. And, just imagine, they described me as your brother's "dear friend"—I can't bring myself to say the actual words, but just imagine it, just imagine it!'

'That's impossible! Where did you read it?'

'Look, I'll show you. It came yesterday and I read it straight away. Here it is, in *The St Petersburg Tattler*. It's new, it only started up this year, there's nothing I love more than gossip, so I subscribed to it and look where it's got me! A fine tittle-tattle, I must say! Take a look, just here, read this.'

And, from under her cushion, she pulled out a page from a newspaper and handed it to Alyosha.

She was not merely upset, she appeared to be completely shattered, and perhaps everything really had got all confused in her mind. The newspaper report was typical and, of course, must have had a rather disconcerting effect upon her, but luckily for her she was unable to concentrate on anything in particular at this point, and at any moment was liable to forget even about the newspaper and to go off at a complete tangent. Alyosha had been aware for a long time that news of the dreadful trial had spread throughout Russia, and, my God, what wild conjectures and reports he had read these last two months (some accurate ones too, of course) concerning his brother, the Karamazovs in general, and even himself. It even said in one newspaper that, frightened to death by his brother's crime, he had taken the tonsure and entered a monastery; this was denied in another, and it was stated that, on the contrary, he and Starets Zosima had forced open the monastery strongbox and had both 'done a flit' from the monastery. The story that he now read in *The St Petersburg Tattler* was entitled 'From Skotoprigonyevsk* (that alas is the name, which I have long hesitated to reveal, of our little town)—the background of the Karamazov case'. It was very short, and there was no direct reference to Mrs Khokhlakova, nor were any other names mentioned. It merely stated that the accused in the sensational trial which was about to begin was a retired army captain, an arrogant type, an idler, and an advocate of serfdom, who had spent all his time womanizing and had exercised a particular influence on some 'ladies of the bored and lonely sort'. One such lady, a 'frustrated widow' still not reconciled to her lost youth, although the mother of an adult daughter, had become so infatuated with him that not two hours before the crime she had offered him three thousand roubles on the spot to go prospecting for gold with her. But the fiend had preferred to murder his father, which he hoped to do with impunity, and steal the said sum rather than traipse all the way to Siberia with his frustrated admirer and her ageing charms of a forty-year-old. This damning article finished, as was to be expected, with righteous indignation about the immorality of patricide and of the now-abolished feudal system. Having read it with interest, Alyosha folded the page and handed it back to Mrs Khokhlakova.

'That's me they're writing about, it's got to be me?' she prattled. 'I did indeed suggest gold-mining to him almost an hour before, and now suddenly it's "ageing charms of a forty-year-old"! I never heard the like of it! It's a plot! May the almighty judge in heaven forgive him for that "charms of a forty-year-old", as I forgive him, but do you realize... do you realize who's behind all this? It's your friend Rakitin.'

'Perhaps,' said Alyosha, 'although I haven't heard anything about that.'

'It was him, it was, no "perhaps" about it! I threw him out...
You do know the whole story, don't you?'

'I know that you asked him not to call on you in future, but
precisely why... that I haven't heard—at least, not from you.'

'You mean, you've heard it from him! Well then, is he furious
with me, is he very furious?'

'Yes, he is, but he's like that with everyone. But why you
turned him away—that he didn't tell me! In any case, I see very
little of him. We're no longer friends.'

'Well, in that case I'll tell you everything—it can't be helped—
I'll make a clean breast of it, because perhaps I myself may have
been guilty of some little indiscretion. Only a tiny, tiny little
indiscretion, so infinitely tiny you could almost say it wasn't
there. You see, my dear Alyosha,' Mrs Khokhlakova suddenly
assumed a very playful air, and a sweet though mysterious smile
began to flutter about her lips, 'you see, I suspect... you will
forgive me, Alyosha, I'm talking to you as a mother... oh no, no,
quite the contrary, as I would talk to my father... because
"mother" is hardly appropriate... Well then, as I would talk to
Starets Zosima in the confessional, and that's the most apt
comparison of all, because I did refer to you just now as a
member of the strictest order of monks—well then, that poor
young man, your friend Rakitin—my God, I just cannot bring
myself to be angry with him! That's to say, I am angry, I'm
furious, but never mind—to cut a long story short, that frivolous
young man, would you believe it, suddenly took it into his head,
it seems, to fall in love with me. It was only subsequently, only
later that I suddenly realized it; to begin with, that is, a month
ago, he just started calling on me rather more frequently, nearly
every day in fact, although we were of course already acquainted.
There I was, quite unsuspecting... and suddenly it hit me, and to
my surprise I began to notice things. You know that some two
months ago I started to receive that nice, cultured, gentlemanly
young man, Pyotr Ilyich Perkhotin, who works for the council.
You've met him hundreds of times yourself. You must agree, he
is worthy and serious-minded, isn't he? He calls on me every
third day, not every day (but even if it were every day, so what?).
And he's always so well turned out, young people are such a
delight, Alyosha, the gifted, the unpretentious, like yourself for

example, and he has an almost statesmanlike mind, he is so well spoken, and I'm definitely, I'm definitely going to put in a word for him. He's a diplomat in the making. On that dreadful day he practically saved my life, coming to me late that evening. As for your friend Rakitin, he always comes in those boots of his and scuffs them on the carpet... to cut a long story short, he began to drop certain hints, and once, when he was leaving, he shook my hand terribly hard. And no sooner had he shaken my hand than I felt a pain in my foot. He'd met Pyotr Ilyich at my place before and, would you believe it, he always used to needle him and provoke him, and always gave him such black looks for some reason. I used to watch the two of them to see how they were getting on and, deep down, I was laughing really. So there I was, sitting alone—or rather, I was already lying down at the time— anyway, you can picture it, I'm lying there alone, and suddenly in comes Mikhail Ivanovich and, would you believe it, he brings me his poem, just a couple of lines—dedicated to my painful foot—he had actually described my painful foot in verse. Wait, how did it go:

> Dainty little foot in pain*
> Yet again, yet again...

or something of the sort—I can never remember poetry—it was here somewhere—well, I'll show it to you later, it's simply divine, simply divine, and do you know there's more to it than just the foot, there's a moral to it, a divine idea, only I've forgotten it; anyway, it's good enough to go straight into a lady's album. Well, I thanked him, of course, and he was clearly flattered. I'd hardly had time to thank him when suddenly in came Pyotr Ilyich, and Mikhail Ivanovich immediately began to sulk. I could see that Mikhail Ivanovich was annoyed about something, because he was just about to say something after the poem—I could feel it—but Pyotr Ilyich had to come in just at that very moment. I showed it to Pyotr Ilyich straight away, but without revealing who the author was. I'm sure, however, I'm absolutely certain that he guessed at once, although to this day he won't admit it and claims he didn't guess; but he does that on purpose. He immediately burst out laughing and began to criticize the poem: "Rubbish," he said, "doggerel, written by some seminarian," and with such conviction, you know, such conviction! At this your friend, instead of laughing, suddenly flew into a rage... Lord, I thought to myself, they're going to start fighting. "I wrote it," he says, "I wrote it as a joke, because I actually consider it rather shabby to write verses... Only there's nothing wrong with my poem. They want to erect a monument to your Pushkin for his 'women's feet',* whereas mine has something to say, and as for you," he says, "you're just a reactionary. You", he says, "haven't got an ounce of humanity in you, you haven't the faintest idea about today's enlightened thinking, progress hasn't even touched you. You", he says, "are a clerk and you take bribes!" That's when I started shouting and begging them to stop. And Pyotr Ilyich, you know, not being the shy type, listened to him with an air of derision and became terribly apologetic. "I didn't realize," he says, suddenly adopting a mock dignified tone of voice. "If I'd known, I wouldn't have said what I did, I'd have praised it... Poets", he says, "are such a short-tempered lot..." In a word, such sarcasm, and all delivered in the most dignified tones. He explained to me later that he was teasing all the time, and I thought he really meant it. So there I was, reclining, just as I am now, and thinking to myself: would it be undignified if I suddenly showed Mikhail Ivanovich the door for shouting so rudely at a guest in my house? And would you believe it: I was lying there with my eyes shut and thinking to myself: would it or wouldn't it be undignified? And I just couldn't decide, it was all too much, such agony, my heart was thumping: should I shout at him, or shouldn't I? One voice was telling me "shout", while another was telling me "no, don't shout"! And no sooner had this other voice spoken than I suddenly shouted, and immediately fainted. Well, naturally, there was commotion all around. Suddenly I stood up and said to Mikhail Ivanovich: "I find it very hard to say this to you, but you are no longer welcome in my house." And I showed him the door, just like that. Oh, Aleksei Fyodorovich! I realize now that I behaved badly, I was deceiving myself all along and I wasn't at all cross with him really, but suddenly, yes, that's the point, it struck me that a scene like that would be quite appropriate... And, would you believe it, the scene turned out to be perfectly genuine, because I even burst into tears and I cried for several days afterwards, and then one fine day, after lunch, I suddenly forgot all about it. Now it's already two weeks since he last called on me, and I was thinking: is he really never going to come back? That was yesterday, and suddenly, in the evening, the *Tattler* arrived. What I read took my breath away—well, who could have written it? He must have written it himself. He must have returned home that night, sat down, and—and written it; then he sent it off—and they printed it. That was two weeks ago, you know. Only, Alyosha, it's terrible what I'm saying, and it's not at all what I should be talking about, is it? The words just seem to come out by themselves!'

'I really must hurry, or I won't be in time to see my brother,' mumbled Alyosha.

'Of course, of course! That reminds me! Listen, what is diminished responsibility?'

'What do you mean, "diminished responsibility"?'

'You know, legal diminished responsibility. The sort that gets you off scot-free. No matter what you've done—you immediately go free.'

'What exactly do you mean?'

'What I mean is that Katya... Oh, she's so sweet, she's such a darling creature, only I can't for the life of me make out exactly who she's in love with. She came to see me the other day, and I simply couldn't get anything out of her. What's more, our conversations are so superficial now, in a word all she wants to talk about is my health and nothing else, she's even putting on that sort of voice... but I said to myself: well, let her get on with it, I couldn't care less... Oh yes, as I was saying—diminished responsibility: so then this doctor arrived... You know, don't you, they've engaged a doctor? I'm sure you do, the one who can tell if someone's mad, the one that you sent for, I mean Katya, not you. That Katya, she's behind it all! Well, you see, suppose we have a person who's perfectly sane, and suddenly he's suffering from diminished responsibility. He knows exactly who he is, what he does, but he's suffering from diminished responsibility all the same. Well, take Dmitry Fyodorovich, more than likely he was suffering from diminished responsibility. It's only since they set up the new courts* that they've suddenly discovered this business about diminished responsibility. It's one of the benefits of the new courts. The doctor came and started questioning me about the circumstances of that night, well, about the gold-mining, wanted to know what he was like that night. What else could it be, if not diminished responsibility—there he was, shouting: "Money, give me the money, three thousand, give me three thousand!" and then off he went and committed the murder. "I don't want to kill him," he says, "I don't want to," and then suddenly he goes and kills him. Well, that's precisely why they'll acquit him, because he tried to stop himself and couldn't.'

'But he didn't do it,' Alyosha interrupted her somewhat sharply. Anxiety and impatience were steadily getting the better of him.

'I know, it was that old man Grigory who did it...'

'What do you mean, "Grigory"?' exclaimed Alyosha.

'Yes, it was him, it was Grigory. After Dmitry Fyodorovich hit him he lay there for a while, staggered to his feet, saw the door was open, went in, and killed Fyodor Pavlovich.'

'But why, what for?'

'Diminished responsibility. When he came round after Dmitry Fyodorovich hit him on the head, he was in a state of diminished responsibility and he went and committed the murder. And if he says he didn't do it, it's probably because he doesn't remember. Only, you see, it'd be better, much better, if the murderer were Dmitry Fyodorovich. Anyway, it was him, even though I said it was Grigory, but it was more than likely Dmitry Fyodorovich, and it's better that way, much better! No, I don't mean to say it's better because a son killed his father—far be it from me to condone that; on the contrary, children must respect their parents—still, it'd be better if it were him, since in that case there wouldn't even be any need for you to shed tears because he'd have killed him without realizing what he was doing, or rather, realizing perfectly well but not knowing exactly what had come over him. Yes, let them acquit him; that'd be so humane, show people how magnanimous the new courts are, I knew nothing about them, and they say it's been like that for a long time now, so as soon as I got to know this yesterday I was so astonished I wanted to send for you straight away; and after-wards, if they acquit him, he must come straight from the courtroom and have dinner with us, I'll invite my friends along and we'll drink to the new courts. I don't think he's likely to be dangerous—in any case, I'll invite lots and lots of guests, so he can always be escorted out if there's any trouble—afterwards, he can settle down in some other town as a justice of the peace or whatever, because those who've suffered misfortune themselves are best able to judge others. And, come to think of it, who doesn't suffer from diminished responsibility these days? Don't you, don't I? We all do. There's no end of examples: take a man sitting comfortably, humming a song, suddenly something infuriates him, he pulls out a pistol and shoots the first person he sees, and afterwards all's forgiven. I read about a case like that not so long ago, and all the doctors came out in support of the defence. There's nothing the doctors won't support these days. Take my Lise now, she's suffering from diminished responsibility too, she had me in tears only yesterday, and the day before, and only today did it suddenly dawn on me that she's simply suffering from diminished responsibility. Oh, Lise is such a disappointment to me! I think she's gone completely mad. Why did she send for you? Did she send for you, or did you come of your own accord?'

'Yes, she sent for me, and I'm going to her now,' and Alyosha got up resolutely.

'Oh, my dear, my kind Aleksei Fyodorovich!' exclaimed Mrs Khokhlakova, bursting into tears. 'Now we've come perhaps to the most important thing of all. God will see that I've entrusted my Lise to you in all good faith, and what does it matter if she sent for you secretly without telling her mother? But when it comes to your brother Ivan Fyodorovich, you must forgive me, but I cannot entrust my daughter to him so readily, although I shall continue to regard him as the most chivalrous young man I know. Just imagine, he suddenly came to see Lise, and I didn't know anything about it.'

'What? What? When?' Alyosha was dumbfounded. He did not sit down again, but stood still and listened.

'I'll tell you all about it, perhaps that's precisely why I sent for you, because I don't really know why I asked for you to come. Well now: Ivan Fyodorovich has been to see me just twice since his return from Moscow, the first time was a courtesy visit, and the second time, this was quite recently, I had Katya with me, and he came because he had discovered that she was here. It goes without saying, there is no reason why I should expect regular visits from him, especially knowing how preoccupied he must be, as it is—*vous comprenez, cette affaire et la mort terrible de votre papa**—and suddenly I learn that he had been again—only not to see me, but to see Lise—it must have been about six days ago, he came, stayed about five minutes, and then left. I only found out about it three days later, from Glafira, so it came as quite a shock. I immediately questioned Lise, but she just laughed: she said he thought I was asleep and he popped into her room to enquire after my health. Of course, that's just how it was. Only Lise, Lise, O God, she does worry me so! Imagine, suddenly one night—this was four days ago, straight after you'd been here last time and you'd gone—suddenly, in the middle of the night, she had a fit of hysterics, yelling, shrieking, a real tantrum! Why do I never have hysterics? Another tantrum the next day, and again two days later, and yet another one yesterday, and now this diminished responsibility. Suddenly she yelled out, "I hate that Ivan Fyodorovich, I demand that you never receive him again, you must ban him from the house!" It was so unexpected I nearly fainted, and I said, "Why on earth should I turn away such a worthy young man who, apart from anything else, is so erudite and has to bear such misfortune!" Because, let's face it, all these stories one hears these days—it's misfortune pure and simple, wouldn't you agree? She burst out laughing at what I said, and you know it was so rude of her. Well, I thought, I'm glad I've made her laugh, that'll be the end of her hysterics; anyway, I myself wanted to stop Ivan Fyodorovich coming to the house and to demand an explanation for his unauthorized mysterious visits. And then suddenly Lise woke up this morning, flew into a rage at Yulia and, can you imagine, slapped her face. That's monstrous, I always say please and thank you to my girls. Then, barely an hour later, she was hugging Yulia and kissing her feet. And she sent me a message saying that she wasn't going to come to my room and that she never wanted to see me again, and then, when I dragged myself over to her room, she threw her arms round me, kissing me and crying, and then just pushed me away without a word, so I was none the wiser. Now, my kind Aleksei Fyodorovich, all my hopes rest on you, and of course my whole fate is in your hands. I'm asking you just to go to Lise, try and prise it all out of her, as only you know how, and then come back and tell me—me, her mother, because, you understand, I shall die, I shall simply die if this continues, or I'll just walk out of the door and won't come back. I can't stand it any longer, I'm a patient woman but there's a limit to my patience, and then... it just doesn't bear thinking about. Oh, thank God, Pyotr Ilyich at last!' Mrs Khokhlakova exclaimed, suddenly brightening up as Pyotr Ilyich Perkhotin entered. 'You're late, you're late! Well now, do sit down, tell me what's going to happen, what did the lawyer have to say? Aleksei Fyodorovich, where are you off to?'

'To see Lise.'

'Oh yes! So you won't forget, will you, what I asked you about? It's my fate, my fate is hanging in the balance!'

'Of course I shan't forget, if I can... but I mustn't keep her waiting any longer,' mumbled Alyosha, beating a hasty retreat.

'Whatever you do, don't forget to see me before you leave, and no ifs or buts about it, or I'll die!' Mrs Khokhlakova shouted after him, but Alyosha had already left the room.

3

LITTLE SHE-DEVIL

WHEN he entered Lise's room, he found her reclining in the invalid chair in which she had been wheeled around while still unable to walk. She made not the slightest attempt to sit up, but her clear, sharp gaze simply bored into him. The look in her eyes was somewhat feverish, her face was wan and sallow. Alyosha was astounded at how much she had changed in three days; she even seemed thinner. She did not offer him her hand. He bent down to touch her long, thin fingers, lying motionless on her dress, then he sat down opposite her.

'I know you're in a hurry to get to the prison,' Lise said sharply, 'and you've been held up by mother for the last couple of hours, she's just been telling you about Yulia and me.'

'How did you know?' asked Alyosha.

'I was eavesdropping. Why are you staring at me? If I want to eavesdrop, I will eavesdrop, there's nothing wrong with that. I don't need to apologize.'

'Are you upset about something?'

'On the contrary, I'm glad. I was saying to myself just now, for the umpteenth time, how fortunate it was that I'd turned you down and that I'm not going to be your wife. You're not fit to be a husband—if I were to marry you, I might hand you a note one day to take to the man I'd subsequently fallen in love with, and you'd take it and deliver it without fail, you'd even return with his reply. And even at the age of forty, you'd still be acting as my errand boy.'

Suddenly she burst out laughing.

'There's something vicious and yet at the same time naïve about you,' said Alyosha, smiling at her.

'The reason you think I'm naïve is that I'm not embarrassed in front of you. And not only am I not embarrassed, but I don't want to be embarrassed either, especially in front of you, you of all people. Alyosha, why have I got no respect for you? I love you very much, but I don't respect you. If I respected you, I wouldn't have spoken like that without feeling embarrassed, would I?'

'Quite.'

'And do you believe that I'm not embarrassed in front of you?'

'No, I don't.'

Lise gave a nervous laugh again, and started to speak in a rush.

'I've sent some sweets to your brother Dmitry Fyodorovich in prison. Alyosha, do you know, you're so lovely! I shall love you terribly for so readily not letting me love you.'

'Why did you want to see me today, Lise?'

'I want to tell you about a craving I have. I want some man to abuse me—marry me and then abuse me, deceive me, go away and desert me. I don't want to be happy!'

'Have you developed a passion for anarchy?'

'Oh, I long for anarchy. I'd love to burn the house down. I can just imagine stealing up and setting fire to it without anyone seeing me, without anyone knowing. Everybody trying to put it out, and the house just burning down. And I'd just stand there and wouldn't breathe a word. Oh, it's silly really! And such a bore, too!'

She waved her hand in disgust.

'You're too well off,' Alyosha said softly.

'Do you suppose it'd be better to be poor?'

'It would.'

'You've been listening too much to what that monk of yours had to say when he was alive. It's not true. If I were rich and everybody else were poor, I'd still keep eating sweets and cream, and I shouldn't give any of it to anyone. Oh, don't, don't say anything,' she made an admonitory gesture, although Alyosha had not even opened his mouth, 'you've already told me all that, I know it all by heart. It's a bore. If I were poor, I'd kill someone—and if I were rich, I might kill someone just the same—why sit and do nothing? You know, I want to work in the fields at harvest time and reap rye. I'll marry you, and you'll become a muzhik, a real muzhik, we'll have a pony, would you like that? Do you know Kalganov?'

'Yes.'

'He just wanders about and daydreams. He says: why live in the real world? It's better to daydream. You can dream up the most exciting things, whereas life's such a bore. And, you know, he'll be getting married soon, he's even declared his love for me. Can you spin a top?'

'Yes.'

'That's how I think of him, a whipping-top that you set spinning and then whip and whip and keep on whipping. I'll marry him and keep him spinning all my life. You're not embarrassed to be here with me, are you?'

'No.'

'You must be terribly annoyed that I'm not talking about holy things. I don't want to be holy. I wonder what they'd do to someone in the next world for committing the worst sin there is? I bet you know exactly.'

'God will judge,' Alyosha looked at her hard.

'That's just how I'd want it. I'd get there, I'd be judged, and suddenly I'd burst out laughing in their faces. I really do want to burn the house down, Alyosha, our house, you still don't believe me, do you?'

'Why shouldn't I? There are even children who, when they're about twelve, can't resist starting a fire, and they go ahead and do it. It's a sort of illness.'

'That's not true, not true, there may be such children, but that's not what I'm talking about.'

'You are confusing good and evil; it's a momentary crisis, perhaps your former illness is to blame for it.'

'You despise me, don't you? I simply don't want to do good, I want to do evil, and it's nothing to do with my illness.'

'Why do evil?'

'So that there shouldn't be anything left anywhere. Oh, wouldn't it be nice if there were nothing left! You know, Alyosha, sometimes I want to do an awful lot of evil and all sorts of nasty things, and keep doing them secretly for a long time, and then suddenly to have everyone find out. They'd all crowd round, pointing at me, while I'd just keep staring back at them. It'd be jolly nice. Why should it be jolly nice, Alyosha?'

'No particular reason. A need to destroy something good or, as you said, to burn something down. That does happen, too.'

'I wasn't just talking, I shall do it.'

'I believe you.'

'Oh, I really love you for saying that. And I know you're not lying, not one little bit. But perhaps you think I'm doing it on purpose, just to tease you?'

'No, I don't think so... although, perhaps, there may be a little of that in you too.'

'Yes, a little. I'll never lie to you,' she said, with a glint in her eyes.

Alyosha was astounded most of all by her seriousness: there was not a trace of levity or frivolity in her expression, although hitherto she never used to lose her cheerfulness and sense of fun, even at her most 'serious' moments.

'There are moments when people love crime,' Alyosha observed thoughtfully.

'Quite, quite! You've read my thoughts, they love it, indeed they do, everyone loves it, they love it all the time, it's not just a question of "moments". You know, it's as though everyone had suddenly conspired to tell lies, and they've been lying ever since.

Everyone says they hate wickedness, but, deep down, they all love it.'

'And you still persist in reading improper books?'

'Yes. Mother reads them and hides them under her pillow, and I sneak them.'

'Aren't you ashamed of destroying yourself?'

'I want to destroy myself. There's a local boy who lay down between the railway tracks and let the train pass over him. Lucky thing! Listen, your brother is being tried now for murdering his father, and everybody loves the fact that he murdered his father.'

'They love him for murdering his father?'

'Yes, they do, everyone does! Everyone says it's terrible, but, deep down, they simply love it. Me especially.'

'There's a grain of truth in what you say about people,' Alyosha said softly.

'Fancy you admitting things like that!' shrieked Lise ecstatically. 'And you a monk! You've no idea how much I respect you, Alyosha, for never ever telling a lie. I'm going to tell you a funny dream I had: I sometimes see devils in my dreams, it's nighttime and I'm in my room with a candle, and suddenly there are devils everywhere, in every corner, under the table, they open the door and there's a whole throng of them outside and they all want to come in and possess me. And they're getting closer to me and are already reaching out for me. And suddenly I make the sign of the cross and they all shrink back, fearful, only they won't leave altogether, but remain standing by the door and in the corners, waiting. And suddenly I get this terrible urge to scold God out loud, and I begin to scold Him, and back they all rush at me, in a crowd, delighted, and they nearly get me in their clutches again, and suddenly I make the sign of the cross once more—and back they all go again. It's great fun, and awfully exciting.'

'I used to have the same dream,' Alyosha said.

'Really?' exclaimed Lise in surprise. 'Listen, Alyosha, don't laugh, this is terribly important: is it really possible for two different people to have the same dream?'

'Yes, apparently.'

'Alyosha, I'm telling you, this really is important,' continued

Lise, still overwhelmed with astonishment. 'It's not the dream that's important, but that you should have had the same dream as me. You never lie to me, don't lie to me now: is it true? You're not making fun of me?'

'It's true.'

Lise's astonishment knew no bounds, and she was momentarily silent.

'Alyosha, don't stop coming to see me, come more often,' she said at last, pleadingly.

'I'll always come to see you, I'll come to see you all my life long,' Alyosha replied firmly.

'You're the only person I can confide in,' Lise began again. 'I can be honest with myself, and with you. With you and with no one else in the whole world. I'm more ready to admit things to you than I am to myself. And I'm not in the least bit embarrassed in front of you. Alyosha, why is it I'm not embarrassed in front of you, not one little bit? Alyosha, is it true the Jews kidnap children at Easter-time and slaughter them?'

'I don't know.'

'I've got a book here, in which I read about a court case somewhere or other; a Jew first cut off all the fingers on both hands of a four-year-old boy, then crucified him against a wall, nailed him down with nails, like on the cross, and he said later, at his trial, that the boy had died a quick death, in four hours. That's meant to be quick! He said the boy kept groaning, groaning all the time, while he just stood back and admired his handiwork. Don't you think that's good!'

'Good?'

'Yes. I sometimes think it was me who crucified the child. He's hanging there, groaning, and I'm sitting opposite enjoying some pineapple *compote*. I simply love pineapple *compote*. What about you?'

Alyosha continued to look at her in silence. Her pale, sallow face suddenly contorted and her eyes flashed.

'You know, after I read about that Jew, I couldn't stop crying all night long. I could just picture the child crying, groaning—four-year-old children understand things, you know—and then there was this pineapple *compote* that I couldn't get out of my mind. In the morning I sent a letter to a certain individual, asking him to call on me *without fail*. He did, and I told him about the boy and the *compote*, I told him *everything, everything*, and I said "that's good". He suddenly burst out laughing and said that it was indeed good. Then he got up and left. He only stayed five minutes. Do you think he despises me, do you? Say something, Alyosha, say something, does he despise me or doesn't he?' She was sitting up in her chair and her eyes were shining.

'Tell me,' said Alyosha, agitated, 'did you send for this man yourself?'

'Yes.'

'You sent him a letter?'

'Yes.'

'To ask him specifically about the child?'

'No, not about that, not at all. But as soon as he walked in, I asked him about it straight away. He answered, burst out laughing, got up, and left.'

'That man was honest with you,' said Alyosha softly.

'He despises me though! He was laughing at me, wasn't he?'

'No, because he himself maybe believes in pineapple *compote*. He, too, is very sick now, Lise.'

'Yes, he believes in it!' Lise's eyes flashed.

'He doesn't despise anyone,' continued Alyosha. 'It's just that he doesn't believe anyone. If he doesn't believe anyone, then it means, of course, he despises everyone.'

'Including me? Me too?'

'Yes, you too.'

'That's good,' said Lise through clenched teeth. 'When he burst out laughing and left, I felt that it was good to be despised. It was good that the little boy had his fingers cut off, and it was good to be despised...'

And looking Alyosha straight in the eyes, she burst out laughing spitefully and hysterically.

'You know, Alyosha, you know, I wish I'd... Alyosha, save me!' She suddenly jumped to her feet, rushed towards him, and flung her arms around his neck. 'Save me,' she wailed. 'Do you suppose I'd have told anyone in the world what I've told you? And I was telling the truth, the truth, I really was telling the truth! I'm going to kill myself, because I'm sick of everything! I don't want to go on living, because everything makes me sick! I'm sick of everything, everything! Alyosha, you don't love me at all, you don't love me in the least!' she finished in a frenzy.

'I do love you!' replied Alyosha passionately.

'And will you cry for me, will you?'

'I will.'

'Not because I don't want to be your wife, but just cry for me, simply for the sake of it?'

'I will.'

'Thank you! All I need is your tears. Let all the rest punish me and crush me underfoot, all of them, every single one, without exception! Because I love no one. Do you hear me, no one at all! In fact, I hate everyone! Go, Alyosha, it's time you went to your brother!' She suddenly tore herself free from him.

'I can't leave you in this state,' said Alyosha, almost in a panic.

'Off you go to your brother, they'll be closing the prison soon, go on, here's your hat! Kiss Mitya for me, go on, off you go!'

And she almost pushed Alyosha out of the door. He looked at her in perplexed dismay. Suddenly he felt a letter being pressed into his right hand, a little note, folded tightly and sealed. He glanced momentarily at the writing and read: To Ivan Fyodorovich Karamazov. He looked at Lise quickly. Her expression had become almost stern.

'Give it to him, make sure you give it to him!' she commanded frantically, shaking all over. 'Today, now! Otherwise I'll poison myself! That was the only reason I sent for you!'

And she slammed the door quickly. The latch snapped shut. Alyosha put the letter in his pocket and went straight downstairs, without talking to Mrs Khokhlakova, whom he had quite forgotten. As soon as Alyosha had departed, Lise lifted up the latch, opened the door slightly, inserted her finger into the gap, and slammed the door shut, pulling on it with all her strength. About ten seconds later she withdrew her hand, returned slowly and without a sound to her chair, and, sitting bolt upright, stared hard at her darkly bruised finger as blood oozed from under the nail. Her lips quivered as she whispered in quick succession:

'Bitch, bitch, bitch, bitch!'

4

THE HYMN AND THE SECRET

NOVEMBER days being short, it was already beginning to get
dark when Alyosha rang the prison bell. He knew that he would
be allowed to see Mitya without any difficulty. Our little town is
no different from anywhere else. At first, of course, after the
preliminary hearing, permission for relatives and a few other
persons to visit Mitya was subject to certain formalities, but
subsequently, although these formalities were not officially
relaxed, nevertheless, at least in the case of certain people, some
relaxation of the rules came to be taken for granted, to such an
extent that meetings with the prisoner in the visiting-room even
took place virtually unsupervised. To be sure, the number of
these persons was small: only Grushenka, Alyosha, and Rakitin.
The chief of police, Mikhail Makarovich, was very favourably
disposed towards Grushenka. The old man had his outburst
against her in Mokroye on his conscience. Having learned all the
facts he had completely changed his opinion of her. And the
strange thing was that although he was firmly convinced of
Mitya's guilt, from the moment he was locked up he began to
regard him with more and more leniency: 'Perhaps the man had
a kind heart, but just went to rack and ruin through drunkenness
and lack of discipline!' His former abhorrence had given way, in
his soul, to a kind of pity. As for Alyosha, the chief of police
liked him very much and had known him for a long time, while
Rakitin, who had taken to visiting the prisoner more and more
often lately, was one of the closest acquaintances of the 'police
chief's young ladies', as he called them, and was always in and
out of their house. Moreover, he used to give private lessons in
the home of the prison governor, a kindly old man, though a
stickler for work. Alyosha had also known the prison governor
quite well for a long time, and the governor enjoyed talking with
him about the 'wisdom' of things in general. As regards Ivan
Fyodorovich, on the other hand, the governor was not merely
respectful, he was positively in awe of him, especially of his
opinions, and claimed to be no mean philosopher himself—of
the amateur variety, naturally. But for Alyosha he had a great

deal of affection. During the past year the old man had suddenly developed a passionate interest in the Apocrypha and he regularly kept his young friend up to date with his opinions and interpretations. He even used to visit the monastery and spend hours on end in discussion with Alyosha and the hieromonks. Consequently, even on those occasions when Alyosha came to the prison late, he had only to go to the governor's quarters and he would be admitted without difficulty. Moreover, the prison guards to a man had become used to Alyosha's presence. And the night-duty staff, of course, gave him no trouble—all they needed was clearance from the authorities. Whenever he had a visitor, Mitya would be called from his cell to a room specially allocated for visitors. When Alyosha arrived this time, he happened to bump straight into Rakitin, who was just taking leave of Mitya. They were both talking loudly. Mitya was laughing uproariously as he ushered Rakitin out, while the latter on the other hand seemed irritated. Rakitin, especially of late, felt awkward in Alyosha's presence; he hardly stopped to talk to him, and would barely even acknowledge his greeting. Realizing that it was Alyosha who had just entered, he frowned deeply and looked the other way, as though completely absorbed in buttoning up his large, fur-collared coat. Then he immediately began to look for his umbrella.

'Mustn't forget any of my things,' he muttered, just for something to say.

'Mind you don't forget anybody else's either!' Mitya quipped, and immediately burst out laughing at his own joke. Rakitin was furious.

'Tell that to the Karamazovs, your miserable lot, but not to me!' he snapped back, simply seething with anger.

'What's the matter with you? I was only joking!' exclaimed Mitya. 'Oh, hell! They're all the same,' he said, turning to Alyosha and motioning with his head towards the departing Rakitin, 'one minute he was sitting there, laughing, happy as a sandboy, and then he suddenly turns nasty! Didn't even acknowledge you. Have you two fallen out completely or something? Why are you so late? I've been dying to see you the whole day. Well, never mind! Let's make up for lost time.'

'Why has he started coming so often? Have you become friends, or what?' asked Alyosha, also motioning with his head towards the door through which Rakitin had just left.

'Friends with Mikhail? No, not really. What a nasty piece of work he is! He reckons I'm a... scoundrel. No sense of humour either—that's the worst thing about people like that. They never see a joke. Their souls are barren, barren and cheerless, like mine was when I was being brought here and saw the prison walls staring back at me. But he's no fool, I can tell you. Well, Aleksei, I've come to the end of the line, haven't I?'

He sat down on the bench and motioned Alyosha to sit next to him.

'Yes, tomorrow's the trial. But you haven't really lost all hope, have you, Mitya?' enquired Alyosha apprehensively.

'What are you talking about?' Mitya glanced at him absent-mindedly. 'Oh, you mean the trial! Hell! You and I have been talking about such trivia all the time, always about the trial, and I never got around to talking about the most important matter of all. Yes, the trial's tomorrow, only when I said I'd come to the end of the line I wasn't referring to the trial. They're not going to chop my head off, it's just that, mentally, I feel I've come to the end of the line. Why are you looking at me with such disapproval written all over your face?'

'What are you talking about, Mitya?'

'Ideas, ideas, that's what! Ethics. What is ethics?'

'Ethics?' enquired Alyosha, surprised.

'Is it a science of some kind, or what?'

'Yes, a science... only... I must admit I couldn't really explain to you what kind of science.'

'Rakitin would know. Rakitin's pretty knowledgeable, you've got to hand it to him! He's not going to be a monk. He's planning to go to St Petersburg. He'll be a newspaper critic with a mission, he reckons. Well, perhaps he'll make good after all, and forge a career for himself. My word, his kind are so good at feathering their own nest! To hell with ethics! I've reached the end of the line, Aleksei, yes I have, you man of God! I love you more than anyone else. When I look at you, my heart leaps. Who the hell was Karl Bernard?'

'Karl Bernard?' Alyosha was startled again.

'No, not Karl, hang on, I got it wrong, Claude Bernard.* Who was he? A chemist, or what?'

'I think he was a scientist of some sort,' replied Alyosha, 'only I have to admit I don't know much about him either. I've heard he was a scientist, but what sort I wouldn't know.'

'Well, in that case, to hell with him, I don't know either,' cursed Mitya. 'A scoundrel of some sort, more than likely, they're all scoundrels. But Rakitin's going to make it, Rakitin'll come out on top, there's another Bernard for you. My word, those Bernards! The world's teeming with them!'

'What's got into you?' asked Alyosha.

'He wants to write about me, he wants to write an article about my case so as to launch himself on a literary career, that's why he keeps visiting me, he explained it all himself. He wants to give it all a certain slant, along the lines of "The fellow couldn't help killing, he was a victim of society," and so on—that's how he explained it to me. It'll have overtones of socialism, he reckons. Well, to hell with him, if it has overtones, so what, who cares! He doesn't like Ivan, hates him in fact, and he isn't fond of you, either. Still, I don't kick him out, because he's intelligent. He does like to put on airs and graces, though. I told him just now: "The Karamazovs aren't scoundrels, they're philosophers, the way all true Russians are philosophers, and you may have had some learning, but you're no philosopher, you're nothing but a yokel." He just laughed nastily. And I said: "*De* opini*bus non est disputandum*,"* not bad, eh? And that's as far as I go in the classics,' Mitya burst out laughing.

'So what's the matter? What did you mean just now?' Alyosha interrupted him.

'What's the matter? Hm! If the truth be known... all things considered—I feel sorry for God, that's what!'

'What are you talking about, "sorry for God"?'

'Just imagine: in the nerves, in the head, I mean there, in the brain, are these nerves (and little devils they are, too!)... you have these wiggly little tails, the nerves have little tail-endings, well, they only have to start thrashing about... in other words, look, I focus my eyes on something, like so, and they begin to thrash about, those little tails... and as soon as they start thrashing about, that's when the image appears, not immediately, mind, but an instant or so later, a second passes, perhaps, and then the moment comes, I don't mean "moment"—to hell with moments—an image, an actual object or happening, dammit it all... so there you have it—first I see, and only then do I think... it's on account of the little tail-endings, and not at all because I've a soul or that I'm some kind of image or likeness, that's all rubbish. Mikhail explained it all to me yesterday, Alyosha, and you could have knocked me down with a feather. Wonderful thing, science, Alyosha! There will come a new kind of man, that much I understand... Still, I feel sorry for God!'

'Well, that's a start, anyway,' said Alyosha.

'That I feel sorry for God, you mean? It's chemistry, my friend, it's a matter of chemistry! Can't be helped, Your Holiness, shove over a little, here comes Chemistry! But if you ask me, Rakitin doesn't love God, my word, he doesn't! That's the one sensitive spot they all have in common! But they won't own up to it. They lie. They pretend. "Are you going to pursue this line of thinking as a critic?" I asked him. "Well, they won't let me do it openly, that's for sure," he said, and laughed. "So where does that leave man then," I asked him, "with no God and no future life? I suppose now that everything is permitted, one can do whatever one likes?" "Didn't you know that?" he said, and he laughed. "A clever person", he said, "can get away with anything, a clever person knows how to play the system, whereas you", he said, "have committed murder, have been caught red-handed, and now you're rotting in prison!" He said that to me! The damn swine! Time was, I used to chuck the likes of him out on their ears, but now I just have to sit and listen. You know, he does talk a lot of sense. And he can put pen to paper, too. About a week ago he started reading me an article of his; I specially copied out two lines from it, wait, here they are.'

Mitya promptly produced a piece of paper from his waistcoat-pocket and read:

'"In order to resolve this question, one first has to align one's personality in opposition to one's actuality." Do you understand that?'

'No, I don't,' said Alyosha.

He was looking at Mitya, and listening with curiosity.

'Neither do I. Obscure and devious, but clever. "They all", he said, "write like that nowadays, because that's what society demands..." He's concerned about society. The scoundrel writes poetry too. He wrote a poem to Khokhlakova's foot, ha-ha-ha!'

'I heard about that,' said Alyosha.

'You did? Have you heard the poem, though?'

'No.'

'I've got it here; listen, I'll read it to you. You've no idea, I haven't told you before, there's more to it than meets the eye. What a rogue! Three weeks ago he decided to poke fun at me: "You, like a fool," he said, "have got yourself into trouble, all for three thousand roubles, whereas I shall get my hands on a hundred and fifty thousand, I shall marry a widow, and buy myself a stone-built house in St Petersburg." And he told me he'd been making advances to Khokhlakova; she's never been particularly bright, but at forty she's totally gaga. "She's so sentimental it's not true," he said, "and that's how I'll get her. I'll marry her, whisk her off to St Petersburg, and start publishing a newspaper there." And you should have seen him licking his lustful chops at the thought—not of Khokhlakova, but of the hundred and fifty thousand. And in the end I believed him, I really did; he's here every day without exception. "She's giving in," he says, slobbering all over. And suddenly he gets the brush-off, with a flea in his ear too. Pyotr Ilyich Perkhotin beat him to it, splendid fellow! You know, I could smother that idiot-woman with kisses for kicking him out! It was on the way to see me that he composed these little verses. "It's the first time", he says, "I've ever soiled my hands this way, writing love poetry, but it's all for a good cause. When I've got my hands on that idiot-woman's money, I can use it for the public good." Some people can make any dirty trick look like the public good! "And if you want to know," he says to me, "I've made a better job of it than Pushkin, because I've managed to express the anguish of the citizen, even in a nonsense verse." The bit about Pushkin—I understand. After all, if he really was a talented man and only got to write about feet!... But that this fellow should be so proud of his poem! They're so full of themselves, these people, so full of themselves! "To the healing of the painful foot of the object

of my devotion." Trust him to come up with a title like that—
strange fellow!

> Dainty foot a little bent,*
> Swollen, twisted, and in pain.
> Doctors came and doctors went,
> But their efforts were in vain.
>
> Still, 'tis not for feet I grieve;
> That to Pushkin I shall leave.
> My concern is for the head
> Whence all sense has fled.
>
> Just when head was on the mend,
> Came the trouble with the foot instead.
> To the painful limb I shall attend
> And restore some sense unto the head.

'A swine, a real swine! But the rogue hasn't made a bad job of
it! He's even got a bit about the "public good" in. I tell you, he
was furious when she kicked him out. He was hell-bent on
revenge!'

'He's already got his own back,' said Alyosha. 'He's written an
article about Khokhlakova.'

And Alyosha told him quickly about the article that had
appeared in *The St Petersburg Tattler*.

'That's him, that's him!' Mitya agreed, frowning. 'Without a
doubt him. Those articles... yes, I know... I mean, all the muck
that was raked up about Grusha for instance!... And about the
other one, too, about Katya... Hm!'

He paced the room, preoccupied.

'Mitya, I can't stay too long,' said Alyosha, after a pause.
'Tomorrow's going to be an awful, momentous day for you.
God's judgement is going to be passed upon you... and I'm
amazed that you just keep walking up and down and talking
about goodness knows what, instead of talking about things that
matter...'

'You needn't be amazed,' Mitya interrupted passionately. 'You
don't want me to talk about that stinking swine, do you? About
the murderer? I've talked about that enough with you already, I
don't want to hear any more about that stinking bastard! God
will strike him down, you'll see. No, don't say anything!'

He approached Alyosha excitedly and kissed him suddenly. His eyes blazed.

'Rakitin'll never understand this,' he began, in a kind of ecstasy, 'but you, you'll understand everything. That's why I was so longing to see you. Look, there's a lot I've been wanting to say to you for a long time, here within these peeling walls, but I kept quiet about the most important thing—the time just didn't seem right. Now I can't wait any longer to pour out my heart to you. Alyosha, for the last two months, I've felt there was a new man in me, a new man has been born within me! He was imprisoned within me, and he'd never have emerged if it hadn't been for this bolt of lightning. It's frightening! What do I care if I have to spend the next twenty years of my life chipping away at a rock-face, I'm not afraid of that at all, I'm much more afraid of something else now: I couldn't bear the thought of this new person leaving me! There, in the mines, underground, standing right next to you, might be just such a convict and murderer as yourself, with whom you could strike up a friendship, because there too one can live, and love, and suffer! One can resurrect that convict's hardened heart, one can succour it for years, and finally drag it out of the depths of iniquity into the light, and forge from it an ennobled soul, a suffering conscience; one can regenerate an angel, resurrect a hero! And there are many of them, there are hundreds, and we're all guilty of their sins! Why did I dream of the "bairn" that time? "Why is the bairn poor?" It came to me at that instant as a revelation! It's for this "bairn" that I shall go to Siberia. Because we're all guilty of one another's sins. For all the "bairns", because there are small children as well as big children. We are all that "bairn". I'll suffer for everyone, because, when all's said and done, there has to be someone who'll suffer on behalf of all. I didn't kill father, but I'll have to suffer. I accept my cross! It all came to me here... within these peeling walls. And there are many of them, hundreds, the underground ones, wielding their picks. Oh yes, we shall be in chains and there will be no freedom, but the time will come when, from the depths of our despair, we shall rise up once again in joy, without which man cannot survive and God cannot exist, for joy comes from God, and is His greatest gift... Lord, let man be sublimated by prayer! How shall I survive there, underground, without God?

Rakitin's got it wrong. If they drive God off the face of the earth, we shall welcome Him down below! It's impossible for a convict to be without God, even more impossible than for someone who is not a convict! And then the time will come to pass when we, the underground people, will join in a solemn hymn to God, who is the source of joy! Praise the Lord and His joy! I love Him!'

Holding forth in this wild and confused way, Mitya was almost gasping for breath. He was pale, his lips trembled, and tears streamed from his eyes.

'I tell you, life is glorious,' he began anew, 'life goes on, even underground! You're not going to believe how desperately I want to live now, Alyosha, what a yearning for existence and awareness has been born in me, right here, within these peeling walls! Rakitin wouldn't understand that, all he thinks about is building himself a house and filling it with tenants; but it's you I've been waiting for. And what is suffering? I wouldn't be afraid of it, even if it were infinite. I'm not afraid of it now—I was before. Do you know, I might not answer any questions at the trial... And I think there is so much strength in me now that I shall overcome everything, all the suffering, just in order to be able to say to myself: I am! Be it death by a thousand cuts—I am! Be it torture beyond endurance—I am! I may sit in a dungeon, but I exist; I see the sun, but if I didn't see the sun, I'd still know it was there. And to know that the sun's there, that's the very stuff of life. Alyosha, you cherub, all these philosophies will be the death of me, to hell with them! Ivan!...'

'What about Ivan?' Alyosha interrupted him, but Mitya went on, oblivious.

'You see, I had none of these doubts before, but they were lurking inside me all the time. Perhaps it's precisely because, unbeknown to me, ideas were raging in me that I drank and fought and raised hell. I was struggling to quench them within me, to tame them, to suppress them. Ivan is not Rakitin, he harbours an idea. Our brother Ivan is a sphinx, he maintains his silence, and guards it well. But I'm being tortured by the idea of God. That's the only thing that does torture me. Supposing He doesn't exist? What if Rakitin is right that the idea is man's invention? For, if He doesn't exist, man is master of the world, of all creation. Splendid! Only how is he going to be virtuous without God? That's the question! I keep coming back to it. Who is he going to love then—man, I mean? To whom is he going to offer his gratitude, to whom is he going to sing his hymn of praise? Rakitin is ridiculous. Rakitin says you don't need God to love mankind. Only a snotty pipsqueak could assert such a thing, it's beyond me how he can say that. It's all right for Rakitin. "You", he said to me today, "should be fighting for the extension of man's civic rights, or at least for the price of meat not to go up; that's the simplest and most direct way of manifesting your love for mankind, rather than by philosophizing." I came straight back at him: "Without God," I said, "you'd be the first to raise the price of meat if the opportunity presented itself and there was a rouble or two to be made." He was furious. But what is virtue? You tell me, Aleksei. I have one sort of virtue, while a Chinaman has another, so—that means the whole thing is relative. Or is it? Perhaps it isn't relative? It's a tricky question, and no mistake! You mustn't laugh if I tell you I lost two nights' sleep over this. The one thing that really surprises me now is how people can carry on living and never think about it. Too busy with trivialities! But Ivan has no God. He has his own ideas. I'm out of my depth here. But he won't say much. I think he's a mason. I asked him about it—he wouldn't say a word. I wanted to hear it from the horse's mouth—nothing doing. Only once did he let drop a hint.'

'What was that?' Alyosha latched on to this immediately.

'I said to him, "If that's the case, then I suppose everything is permitted?" He frowned. "Fyodor Pavlovich," he said, "our papa, was a proper pig, but he had the right idea." I was speechless. And that was all he said. That goes even further than Rakitin.'

'Yes,' Alyosha agreed bitterly. 'When did he come to see you?'

'We'll talk about that later, there's something else I want to tell you now. Up to now I've hardly talked to you about Ivan. I've been putting it off as long as possible. When all this business with me is over, and they've delivered their verdict, I'll tell you a thing or two, in fact I'll tell you everything. It's something that'll make your hair stand on end... And you'll be my judge in this matter. But don't even ask about it for now. You were talking about the trial tomorrow, but would you believe it, I'm completely in the dark.'

'Have you spoken to the lawyer?'

'Ah, the lawyer! I've told him all I know. He's a smooth operator, no flies on him. A Bernard! Didn't believe a word I said. Just imagine, he thinks I did it—I can see he does. "In that case," I asked him, "why have you come to defend me?" To hell with them all! They've even sent for a doctor, they want to make out I'm mad. It won't work! Katerina Ivanovna's determined to do her "duty", come what may. By fair means or foul!' Mitya smiled bitterly. 'Vixen! Cruel as they come! And she knows exactly what I said about her that time in Mokroye, that she's a woman of infinite fury. Someone told her. Yes, the evidence has been accumulating, like the desert sands! Grigory has dug his heels in. Grigory's honest, but stupid. A lot of people are honest because they're stupid. That's one of Rakitin's theories. Grigory's my enemy. There are some people it's better to have as enemies than as friends. I'm talking about Katerina Ivanovna now. One thing frightens me, frightens me to death—that she'll tell them at the trial how she curtsied to me when I gave her the four thousand five hundred roubles! She'll pay me back to the uttermost farthing.* I can do without her sacrifice! They'll humiliate me at the trial! But I'll survive somehow! Go and see her for me, Alyosha, ask her not to mention that at the trial. What, you can't? Never mind, I'll survive! But I'm not sorry for her. She's brought it upon herself. She's got her just deserts. I'll have my say, Aleksei.' Again he smiled bitterly. 'Only... only what of Grusha, what of Grusha? O Lord! Why should she have taken this cross upon herself?' he exclaimed, with tears in his eyes. 'Grusha's killing me, the thought of her is killing me, it's killing me! She was here not long ago...'

'She told me. She was very upset about you today.'

'I know. My temper will be the downfall of me. I got a bit jealous! I took it all back when we were saying goodbye, and I kissed her. But I didn't say I was sorry.'

'Why not?' exclaimed Alyosha.

Mitya laughed almost cheerfully.

'My dear boy, God forbid that you should ever say you're sorry for what you've done to a woman you love! Especially to the one you love, her of all women, however guilty you are! Because a woman, my dear fellow, is something else altogether, take my word, I happen to know a thing or two about them! You just try and confess your guilt and say to her, "I'm guilty, pardon me, forgive me," and you'll never hear the end of it! She'll make such a meal of it, you won't know whether you're coming or going for humiliation, she'll invent things that never existed, she'll fling everything at you, she'll forget nothing, she'll pile it on, and only then will she pardon you. And that's if you're lucky! She'll scrape the barrel and throw it in your face—that, I tell you, is how bloodthirsty they are, every single one of the angels without whom our lives would simply be inconceivable! Look, my dear boy, you can take it from me: every decent man must be under the heel of a woman. That's my conviction; no, not conviction—feeling. A man has to submit magnanimously, and it will never be held against him. It wouldn't even be held against a hero, against even Caesar himself! All the same, never ask forgiveness, never, not for anything. Just remember that rule, taught to you by your brother Mitya, who came to grief himself because of women. No, I'll try winning Grusha's favour some other way than by asking her forgiveness. I worship her, Aleksei, I worship her! It's just that she doesn't see it, no, she can never get enough love. And she tortures me, she tortures me with her love. It's all different now! Before, it was just the infernal voluptuousness of her body that gave me no peace, but now I've absorbed the whole of her soul into my soul and, through her, have turned into a human being myself! Will they let us marry? If they don't, I'll die of bitterness. I can't help it; I keep imagining things all the time... What did she say to you about me?'

Alyosha repeated in full all that Grushenka had said previously. Mitya listened in silence, paying attention to every detail, asked him to go over many points again, and was well satisfied by the end.

'So she's not angry that I'm jealous!' he exclaimed. 'What a woman: "I've a cruel streak myself." I love them when they're cruel like that, even though I can't stand all this jealousy, I really can't! We're bound to fight. But I shall love her—I shall love her for ever. Will they let us get married? They don't let criminals marry, do they? That's the question. But I can't live without her...'

Mitya paced across the room, frowning. It was getting rather dark in the room. Suddenly he became terribly worried.

'So it's a secret, she says, a secret? She thinks there's three of us conspiring against her, and that Katka's in on it, too. No, my dear Grushenka, you're wrong. You've slipped up there, slipped up in your silly, feminine way! Right you are, Alyosha, old chap! I'm going to reveal our secret to you!'

He looked about him in every direction, stepped right up to Alyosha, who was standing in front of him, and began to whisper with an air of mystery, although in actual fact no one could overhear: the old guard was dozing in a corner on a bench, and no sound could possibly reach the soldiers on sentry duty.

'I'll reveal the whole of our secret to you!' whispered Mitya. 'I meant to tell you anyway; do you imagine I can take any kind of decision without you? You're everything to me! Even if I say that Ivan's the boss, you're my cherub. Your decision alone will count. Perhaps it's you, rather than Ivan, who's the boss after all. You see, this is a matter of conscience, a matter of supreme conscience—the secret's so important that I shan't be able to cope myself, and I've decided to postpone any decision until you can deal with it. However, it's still too early to make a decision, because we've got to wait for the verdict; you'll decide my fate when the sentence has been passed. Don't do anything now. I'll tell you all about it; just listen, but don't say whether you agree or not. Just stand still and keep quiet. I shan't tell you everything. I'll only reveal the idea behind it, no details, and don't say a word. No questions, no gestures, agreed? Lord, though, how can I avoid those eyes of yours? I'm afraid I'll be able to tell from your eyes even if you don't say a word. That's what I'm afraid of! Listen, Alyosha, Ivan says I should make a run for it. I shan't go into detail, it's all planned, everything can be arranged. Don't say a word and don't give your verdict now. I'm going to flee to America with Grusha. I can't possibly live without Grusha! Suppose they won't let her go with me, though! Do they let convicts get married? Ivan says they don't. And what can I do underground with a pickaxe and without Grusha? I'd crack my own skull with that pick! But then again, what about conscience? That would be running away from suffering! I'd

have seen the star and refused to follow it; I'd have been shown
the path to redemption and turned away. Ivan says that, "with
the right intentions", one can do more good in America than
underground. Well, and where will our underground hymn be
sung? And America, America means more problems! I'm sure
there's plenty of villainy in America, too. I'd be running away
from crucifixion. The only reason I'm telling you this, Aleksei, is
because you alone, and no one else, can understand; for others,
everything I've told you about the hymn would be a lot of
nonsense, sheer ranting. They'd say I'd gone crazy, or that I was
just an idiot. But I haven't gone crazy and I'm not an idiot. Ivan
understands about the hymn, he really does, only he won't talk
about it, he just keeps quiet. He doesn't believe in the hymn.
Don't say a word, not a word, I can see by the way you look that
you've already formed an opinion! Please don't decide, spare
me, I can't live without Grusha, wait till the trial's over.'

Mitya stopped, staring as though demented. He was holding
Alyosha by his shoulders, and his eager, feverish gaze bored
right through Alyosha's eyes.

'Do they let convicts marry?' he repeated for the third time, in
a pleading voice.

Alyosha, deeply shaken, had been listening with astonishment.

'Tell me one thing,' he said, 'was Ivan very insistent, and
whose idea was it in the first place?'

'His. He thought it up, and he's adamant about it! He'd never
visited me and then suddenly, a week ago, he turned up and
came to the point straight away. He was terribly insistent. He
didn't ask, he just ordered me. He doesn't doubt for a minute
that I'll obey, even though I've bared my whole soul to him, as I
have to you, and I told him about the hymn. He's told me how
he's going to arrange everything, that he's got all the information—but of that later. He desperately wants me to go. The
main thing is money. He said he'd got ten thousand for me for
the escape, and twenty thousand for America, and that we'd
manage to organize a successful escape with ten thousand.'

'And he really told you not to say anything to me?' Alyosha
enquired once more.

'Not to anyone, least of all to you, not under any circumstances! He's probably afraid you'll act as my conscience. Don't let on I've told you, whatever you do!'

'You're right,' decided Alyosha, 'one can't come to a decision before the verdict of the court. After the trial you'll be able to decide for yourself; you'll find a new man in you then, and he'll decide.'

'A new man, or a Bernard who'll come to a Bernard-type decision! Because, if the truth be known, I'm just a miserable Bernard myself!' Mitya smiled bitterly.

'But, Mitya, do you really and truly feel there's no hope of an acquittal?'

Mitya shrugged his shoulders and shook his head.

'Alyosha, my dear fellow, it's time you went!' he started to fuss. 'The warden has just called out in the yard, he'll be here any moment. It's getting late, it's after visiting time. Give me a hug, kiss me, give me your blessing, my dear fellow, give me your blessing before I set off for my Calvary tomorrow...'

They embraced and kissed each other.

'And our Ivan, he's a fine one,' said Mitya suddenly, 'he suggested I should make a run for it, and yet he believes that I'm the murderer!'

A sad, forced smile appeared on his lips.

'Did you ask him if he really believed that?' enquired Alyosha.

'No, I didn't. I wanted to ask, but I couldn't, I didn't have the strength. But what does it matter, I could see it in his eyes. Well, goodbye!'

They kissed each other once more, hastily, and Alyosha was nearly out of the room when Mitya suddenly called him back.

'Stand in front of me, like that.'

And again he grabbed Alyosha firmly by the shoulders. His face suddenly became very pale and seemed to stand out in the semi-gloom. His lips twisted, his gaze bored into Alyosha.

'Alyosha, tell me the whole truth, before God: do you believe that I killed him, or don't you? You, what do you believe, do you believe it or not? The whole truth now, don't lie to me!' he shouted excitedly.

Alyosha seemed to sway on his feet, and he felt a sharp stab of pain in his heart.

'Stop it, what's come over you?...', he mumbled, distraught.

'The whole truth, all of it, don't lie to me!' repeated Mitya.

'I didn't believe for a single second that you were the murderer,' the words burst out in a trembling voice, and he raised his right hand as though calling upon God to be his witness. Mitya's face immediately lit up with exultation.

'Thank you!' he said, drawing out the words as though exhaling after fainting. 'You've given me a new lease of life... Would you believe it: right up till now I've been afraid to ask you, imagine, afraid of you! Well, off you go now, go! You've given me the strength to face tomorrow, God bless you! Be off! You must love Ivan!' These last words burst from Mitya's lips.

Alyosha left in tears. Such guardedness on Mitya's part, such mistrust even towards him—Alyosha—revealed to Alyosha a veritable abyss of grief and despair in his hapless brother's soul such as he could never have suspected previously. Deep, limitless compassion suddenly overwhelmed and exhausted him. His stricken heart ached unbearably. 'Love Ivan!' Mitya's words echoed in him. And now he was on his way to see Ivan. He had been longing to see him since the morning. Ivan worried him no less than Mitya, and now, since his heart-to-heart with the latter, he was even more fearful about Ivan.

5

NOT YOU, NOT YOU!

ON his way to Ivan he had to pass the house where Katerina Ivanovna lived. There was a light in the window. He stopped and decided to go in. He had not seen Katerina Ivanovna for over a week. It occurred to him that Ivan was maybe with her now, especially on the eve of such a day. He rang the bell and went in. By the dim light of the Chinese lantern he noticed someone coming down the stairs and, as he drew nearer he recognized Ivan. He was apparently just leaving.

'Oh, it's only you,' said Ivan Fyodorovich dryly. 'Well, good-bye. You're going to see her?'

'Yes.'

'I wouldn't if I were you. She's upset, and you'll only make matters worse.'

'Not at all!' came a loud voice from upstairs, through a door which had been flung open just that moment. 'Aleksei Fyodorovich, have you come from him?'

'Yes, I've just been to see him.'

'Did he send me any message? Come in, Alyosha, and you too, Ivan Fyodorovich, you must stay just for another second. Do you hear me?'

There was such an imperious note in her voice that Ivan Fyodorovich followed Alyosha up the stairs without a moment's hesitation.

'She was listening at the door!' he muttered irritably under his breath, but Alyosha heard him.

'If it's all right with you, I'll keep my coat on,' said Ivan Fyodorovich, entering the room. 'I'll stand if you don't mind. I'm only staying a minute, that's all.'

'Won't you sit down, Aleksei Fyodorovich?' said Katerina Ivanovna, but she herself remained standing. She had not changed much in the past few days, but there was a vicious glint in her dark eyes. Alyosha was to recall later that she struck him as being extraordinarily beautiful at that moment.

'So what did he ask you to tell me?'

'Only one thing,' said Alyosha, looking her straight in the eye, 'that you should not be too hard on yourself, and not mention anything in court about...', he hesitated slightly, 'what passed between the two of you... when you first met... in that town...'

'Ah,' she interrupted him with a bitter laugh, 'he means when he gave me the money and I curtsied to him! I wonder if he's worried about me or about himself? He asks me not to be too hard—on whom? On him or on myself? Say something, Aleksei Fyodorovich.'

'Both on yourself and on him,' he said softly.

'Well, well,' she pronounced each word with vicious deliberation, and suddenly flushed. 'You don't know me yet, Aleksei Fyodorovich,' she said menacingly. 'Come to that, I don't know myself either... Perhaps you'll want nothing more to do with me after tomorrow's trial.'

'You will tell the truth, won't you?' said Alyosha, 'that's all that matters.'

'A woman often tells untruths,' she said through clenched teeth. 'Only an hour ago, I thought I'd never bring myself to have anything to do with that monster... that abomination... and yet, to me he's still a human being! Did he really do it? Did he?' she exclaimed hysterically, turning quickly towards Ivan Fyodorovich. In a flash Alyosha realized that she had asked Ivan Fyodorovich this very question perhaps only a minute before his arrival, and not just once, but a hundred times, and that they had ended up quarrelling.

'I've been to see Smerdyakov... It was you Ivan, you persuaded me that he killed his father. I only believed it because you said it!' she continued, still addressing Ivan Fyodorovich. The latter forced a smile.

Alyosha flinched at the familiar *Ivan*. He would never have suspected that they were on such intimate terms.

'Well, I think that's quite enough,' Ivan cut her short. 'I'm going. I'll come back tomorrow.' And, turning round, he immediately left the room and went straight out on to the landing. Katerina Ivanovna grabbed hold of both Alyosha's hands.

'Go after him!' she whispered urgently. 'Don't let him run off! Don't leave him on his own, even for a second. He's mad. Don't you know that he's gone mad? He's got a fever, a nervous fever, the doctor told me! Go on, run after him...'

Alyosha jumped up and rushed after Ivan Fyodorovich. The latter had not gone more than fifty paces from the house.

'What do you want?' Realizing that Alyosha was coming up behind him, Ivan threw him a backward glance. 'She told you to run after me because I was mad. I know it all by heart,' he added exasperatedly.

'She's mistaken about that, of course, but she's right about you being sick,' said Alyosha. 'I was looking at your face just now, back at her place; you really do look ill, Ivan!'

Ivan continued walking. Alyosha followed.

'And have you any idea, Aleksei Fyodorovich, how one becomes mad?' Ivan suddenly enquired in a soft voice devoid of all the former exasperation and now expressing the frankest curiosity.

'No, I don't. I imagine there's more than one kind of madness.'

'But do you suppose one can observe oneself becoming mad?'

'I don't think one can really observe that sort of thing very clearly,' Alyosha replied with surprise. Ivan fell silent for a moment or two.

'If you're going to talk to me,' he said suddenly, 'please change the subject.'

'Oh, before I forget, here's a letter for you,' Alyosha said apologetically and, taking Lise's letter from his pocket, he handed it to Ivan. They had just reached a street lamp. Ivan recognized the handwriting immediately.

'Oh, it's from that little she-devil!' he laughed venomously and, without opening the envelope, he suddenly tore it into several pieces and threw them into the wind. The pieces scattered.

'Hasn't turned sixteen yet and is already offering herself!' he said contemptuously and walked on.

'What do you mean "offering herself"?' exclaimed Alyosha.

'Everyone knows how a loose woman offers herself.'

'You don't mean it, Ivan, you can't mean it!' Alyosha, horrified, leapt passionately to Lise's defence. 'She's just a child, you're maligning a child! She's sick, she too is sick, perhaps she's also going out of her mind... I couldn't not give you her letter... Actually, I expected you to say something... something that would save her.'

'I've got nothing to say to you. If she's a child, I'm not her nanny. Shut up, Aleksei. Don't go on. I'm not even thinking about it.'

They fell silent again for a while.

'Now she'll pray all night to the Mother of God', he began again suddenly, in a sharp and angry voice, 'for guidance, what she should say tomorrow in court.'

'You... you mean Katerina Ivanovna?'

'Yes. Whether to come to Mitenka's rescue or to help convict him. She'll be praying for enlightenment. She's undecided, you see, she's not had time to prepare her thoughts yet. She wants me to be her nanny too, and tuck her in!'

'Katerina Ivanovna loves you, Ivan,' Alyosha observed sadly.

'Perhaps. But the trouble is, I'm not interested.'

'She's suffering. So why did you say... sometimes... things that have given her cause for hope?' Alyosha continued with gentle reproach. 'Look, I hope you'll forgive me for saying so, but I know you've been building up her hopes,' he added.

'I just couldn't force myself to do what had to be done, I just couldn't break it off and tell her to her face!' Ivan said, irritated. 'It'll have to wait till the murder trial's over. If I break it off now, she'll go and incriminate that scoundrel in court tomorrow just to spite me, because she hates him, and she knows she does. It's all a tissue of lies, lies, nothing but lies! You see, for the moment, while I still haven't finished with her, she'll go on hoping and she won't destroy that monster, because she knows how badly I want to get him out of the mess he's in. When the hell is this damned trial going to be over!'

The words 'murder' and 'monster' echoed painfully in Alyosha's heart.

'But what can she do to ruin Dmitry?' he asked, weighing up Ivan's words. 'What precisely could she say that would incriminate Mitya?'

'You don't know the whole story. She's got a certain document in her possession, in Mitya's own handwriting, which proves beyond all shadow of doubt that he killed father.'

'That's impossible!' exclaimed Alyosha.

'What do you mean "impossible"? I've read it myself.'

'No such document exists!' Alyosha repeated vigorously. 'It can't exist, because he's not the murderer. He didn't kill father, it wasn't him!'

Ivan Fyodorovich suddenly stood still.

'Who then in your opinion is the murderer?' he asked unemotionally and with a touch of aloofness in his voice.

'You know who,' said Alyosha gently and firmly.

'Who? Are you referring to that cock-and-bull story about that lunatic of an epileptic? You mean Smerdyakov?'

Alyosha suddenly felt that he was shaking all over.

'You know who,' he mouthed feebly. He felt he was choking.

'Who then, who?' cried Ivan, almost in a frenzy. All his composure had suddenly vanished.

'All I know is,' Alyosha continued, still almost whispering, '*it was not you* who killed father.'

'Not me! What do you mean "not me"?' Ivan was thunderstruck.

'It was not you who killed father, not you!' repeated Alyosha firmly.

There was a long pause.

'I know perfectly well it wasn't me! Are you raving mad?' Ivan said with a faint, pale smile. His eyes were riveted on Alyosha. They were both standing under a street lamp again.

'No, I'm not, Ivan; you know, you've told me yourself several times that you're the murderer.'

'When did I say that?...' Ivan mumbled uncomprehendingly. 'I was in Moscow... When did I say it?'

'You've said it to yourself many times when you were alone during these past two terrible months,' Alyosha went on in the same calm, measured tone of voice. But now he spoke as though in a trance, or in thrall to some invincible force. 'You've been accusing yourself and admitting to yourself that no one but you is the murderer. But it was not you who killed him, you're wrong, you are not the murderer, do you hear me, you are not! God sent me to tell you this.'

They both fell silent. That silence continued for a whole long minute. They stood eyeball to eyeball. They were both as white as a sheet. Suddenly Ivan began to shake all over, and he grabbed Alyosha tightly by the shoulder.

'You were there, weren't you?' he hissed through clenched teeth. 'You were in my room that night, when he came... Admit it... you saw him, you did, didn't you?'

'Who are you talking about?... Mitya?' asked Alyosha, bewildered.

'No, not him, to hell with that monster!' Ivan wailed frenziedly. 'How did you know he's been coming to see me? How did you find out? Tell me!'

'Who is *he*? I don't know who you're talking about,' mumbled Alyosha, who was quite frightened by now.

'Yes you do, you know... otherwise, how else could you...? You couldn't not know...'

But suddenly he seemed to check himself. He stood there,

apparently thinking something over. His lips twisted in a strange smile.

'Ivan,' Alyosha resumed in a trembling voice, 'I said that because I know you will believe what I say. I meant those words for the rest of your life—*not you*! Do you hear me—for the rest of your life. It was God who ordained that I should say that to you, even if it meant you'd hate me for ever from now on...'

But Ivan Fyodorovich already seemed to have regained his composure completely.

'Aleksei Fyodorovich,' he said with a cold smile, 'I can't stand prophets and epileptics; God's messengers least of all, you know that better than anyone. From now on, I want nothing more to do with you, and I think that had better be for good. Be so kind as to leave me here at this crossroads—at once. Besides, you go that way anyway. Mind you stay away from my place tonight, whatever happens! Do I make myself clear?'

He turned round and, with firm steps, walked away without looking back.

'Ivan,' Alyosha called after him, 'if anything should happen to you tonight, remember me before you do anything!...'

But Ivan did not reply. Alyosha stood at the crossroads, under the street lamp, until Ivan had vanished completely in the gloom. Then he turned round and set off slowly down the lane towards his lodgings. He and Ivan were living in separate accommodation: neither of them had wanted to stay in Fyodor Pavlovich's empty house. Alyosha had rented a furnished room from a family in the town; Ivan Fyodorovich lived some distance away, in spacious and rather comfortable rooms in a wing of a nice house belonging to the widow of a well-to-do civil servant. To look after the whole of his part of the house he had only one aged, totally deaf woman, who was crippled by rheumatism and who went to bed at six in the evening and rose at six the next morning. Ivan Fyodorovich had become remarkably self-reliant in the past two months, and very much liked to be left completely alone. He even tidied up after himself in the one room that he now occupied, and he had almost stopped using his other rooms. On reaching the front gate of the house, and with his hand already on the bell, he stopped. He felt that he was still shaking with fury. He suddenly withdrew his hand from the bell, spat, wheeled round, and set off quickly for the opposite end of the town, heading for the tiny, ramshackle log cabin, situated about two versts from his house, in which lived Marya Kondratyevna, Fyodor Pavlovich's former neighbour, who used to come to Fyodor Pavlovich's kitchen for soup, and to whom Smerdyakov, at the time, used to sing songs and play his guitar. She had sold her former house and was now living with her mother in a house which was virtually nothing but a hut, where they had been joined by the sick, slowly failing Smerdyakov, who had settled with them ever since Fyodor Pavlovich's death. It was to him that Ivan Fyodorovich, drawn by a sudden and overpowering compulsion, was now heading.

6

FIRST VISIT TO SMERDYAKOV

FOR the third time since his return from Moscow Ivan Fyodorovich was going to talk to Smerdyakov. The first time that he had seen him and spoken to him after the murder was on the very first day after his return, following which he visited him again two weeks later. But he had stopped visiting him after this second time, so it was more than a month now since he had seen him, and he had hardly heard anything of him in the meantime. Ivan Fyodorovich had not returned from Moscow until five days after his father's death, and so had not even seen his coffin: the funeral had taken place just the day before his return. The reason why Ivan Fyodorovich had not returned sooner was that Alyosha, wishing to send him a telegram but not knowing his exact address in Moscow, had approached Katerina Ivanovna and she, also not knowing the exact address, had sent a telegram to her sister and her aunt, reckoning that Ivan Fyodorovich would call on them while he was in Moscow. But he had not called there until the fourth day after his arrival; having read the telegram, he returned with all due haste of course. The first person he met on his return was Alyosha, and he was astonished to discover on talking to him that he refused even to suspect Mitya and was accusing Smerdyakov of the murder, which was quite contrary to general public opinion in our town. Having seen the chief of police and the prosecutor and having found out the details of the evidence and the arrest, he was even more astonished at Alyosha's opinion, and attributed it to excessive brotherly solicitude and to compassion for Mitya, whom Alyosha loved dearly, as Ivan well knew. Incidentally, let us say just a few words here, once and for all, about Ivan Fyodorovich's feelings towards his brother Dmitry Fyodorovich: he certainly did not love him and, much as he pitied him at times, his pity was compounded by a tremendous disdain amounting almost to disgust. He found Mitya and everything about him altogether unsympathetic. Ivan regarded Katerina Ivanovna's love for Mitya with contempt. Nevertheless, the first day after his return he had gone to see Mitya in prison, and this meeting, far from lessening his conviction of the latter's guilt, had reinforced it. He had found his brother upset and extremely agitated. Mitya was voluble but abstracted and inconsistent, speaking abruptly, accusing Smerdyakov, and getting terribly confused. He talked most of all about the three thousand roubles that the deceased had 'stolen' from him. 'It's my money, it was mine,' Mitya had insisted, 'even if I had stolen it, I'd have been entitled to do so.' He hardly contested the charges brought against him, and if he construed facts to his own benefit, he did so ineptly and contradicted himself, as if he did not want to justify himself to Ivan or to anyone else; on the contrary, he lost his temper, poured scorn on the accusations, cursed and fulminated. As regards Grigory's evidence about the open door, he just laughed scornfully and said that it was 'the devil who opened it'. But he could not produce any coherent explanation of this fact. He had even managed to offend Ivan Fyodorovich at this first meeting, telling him flatly that it was not for those who maintained that 'everything is permitted' to suspect and interrogate him. On the whole, he had been very unfriendly to Ivan Fyodorovich on that occasion. It was straight after that meeting with Mitya that Ivan Fyodorovich had gone to see Smerdyakov.

While rushing back from Moscow on the train, he had already been thinking about Smerdyakov and about his last conversation with him, the night before his departure. There were many things that troubled him, many things that appeared suspicious.

But, while making his deposition before the investigative magistrate, Ivan Fyodorovich had for the time being kept quiet about that conversation. He had decided to wait until he had seen Smerdyakov. The latter was now in the town hospital. In answer to Ivan Fyodorovich's insistent questioning, Dr Herzenstube and Dr Varvinsky, whom he met at the hospital, replied that there was no doubt about Smerdyakov's epileptic fit, and they were quite astonished when he asked: 'Couldn't he have been pretending on the day of the murder?' They gave him to understand that the attack had been unusual and had continued, with recurrent relapses, for several days, so much so that the patient's life had been in real danger and only now, after treatment, could it definitely be said that the patient would live, although it was very likely (added Dr Herzenstube) that his mind would remain somewhat disturbed, 'if not for the rest of his life, then for a considerable time'. To Ivan Fyodorovich's peremptory question: 'So he's mad now, is he?' they replied that he was 'not exactly mad', but that 'there were certain signs of abnormality'. Ivan Fyodorovich decided to find out for himself what these abnormalities were. At the hospital he was immediately given permission to visit Smerdyakov, who was lying in a bed in a side-ward. Next to him was another bed, occupied by a local tradesman who was very weak, bloated by dropsy, and obviously going to die in the next day or so: he was in no state to disturb their conversation. On seeing Ivan Fyodorovich, Smerdyakov flinched and grinned mistrustfully. This, at least, was Ivan Fyodorovich's first impression. But it was only for a second, and during the rest of the conversation, on the contrary, he was struck by Smerdyakov's composure. From the moment he saw him Ivan Fyodorovich was totally convinced of the extreme seriousness of his condition; he was very weak, spoke slowly, and seemed to have difficulty moving his tongue; he had grown very thin and looked jaundiced. Throughout the whole twenty minutes or so of the visit he complained of a headache and pains in all his limbs. His dry, eunuch's face seemed to have shrunk, his hair was tousled over his temples, and instead of his quiff, there was only a thin wisp of hair sticking up. But the half-shut left eye, with that insinuating air, betrayed the presence of the old Smerdyakov. 'It's always interesting to talk to an intelligent person,' Ivan Fyodorovich recalled at once. He sat down on a stool at the foot of the bed. Smerdyakov rearranged himself with difficulty in the bed, but he did not speak first, maintaining his silence and not even betraying any curiosity.

'Do you feel well enough to talk to me?' asked Ivan Fyodorovich. 'It won't tire you too much?'

'Not at all,' mumbled Smerdyakov weakly. 'Have you been back long, sir?' he added condescendingly, as if encouraging an embarrassed visitor.

'I came back just today... to sort out this mess here.'

Smerdyakov sighed.

'Why are you sighing, surely you knew about it?' Ivan Fyodorovich asked bluntly.

Smerdyakov paused deferentially.

'How could I not know, sir? It was clear beforehand. Only how could I know, sir, how things would turn out?'

'What do you mean "turn out"? Don't try to avoid the issue! You even predicted you'd have a fit, didn't you, and that it would happen just as you were going down to the cellar? You particularly mentioned the cellar.'

'Have you told them that at the police station?' Smerdyakov enquired with calm curiosity.

Ivan Fyodorovich suddenly lost his temper.

'No, I haven't told them yet, but I most certainly shall. You've got a lot of explaining to do, and let me tell you, my friend, I have no intention of letting you play games with me!'

'Why should I want to play games with you, when you are my only hope, you and the Lord God?' said Smerdyakov with the same absolute calmness, only momentarily closing his eyes.

'In the first place,' began Ivan Fyodorovich, 'I know that a fit cannot be predicted in advance. I've made enquiries, so don't try to fool me. The day and the time can't be predicted. So how come you told me both the day and the time, and even that it would happen on the cellar steps? How could you know in advance that you would have a fit precisely there, and fall down those steps, if you did not deliberately feign the fit?'

'I go down to the cellar anyway, several times a day, sir,' drawled Smerdyakov. 'It was just like when I fell from the attic last year. Certainly one can't predict the day and time of a fit, but one can have a premonition.'

'But you predicted the day and the time!'

'The doctors here will fill you in with all the details of my epilepsy, sir: ask them whether it's genuine or not, and as for me, I have nothing more to say on the subject.'

'And the cellar, how did you know that in advance?'

'Oh, how you keep going on about that cellar! When I went down the cellar that time, I was frightened and had misgivings, I was frightened mostly because I'd lost your protection and had no one in the whole world to turn to. As I was going down into the cellar, I thought, "It's going to happen now, I'm going to have a fit—will I fall down there or not?" And because of those very doubts, sir, I was seized by the fatal spasm... and down I went. I've told them everything, all about our conversation the night before, at the gate, sir, when I told you how frightened I was, and about the cellar, sir—I've told all this in detail to Dr Herzenstube and Nikolai Parfenovich, the magistrate, and they've written it all down in the case record. And the doctor here, Dr Varvinsky, told them he was convinced that that was what caused it—the fear, that is, the worry about whether I was going to fall or not. And that's how it happened. That's what they wrote down, that it was bound to happen just because of my fear, sir.' Smerdyakov gasped, as if utterly exhausted.

'So, you said all that in your deposition?' asked Ivan Fyodorovich, slightly disconcerted. He had particularly wanted to frighten Smerdyakov by threatening to disclose their conversation, but it turned out that the latter had pre-empted him.

'What have I got to fear? Let them write it all down, the absolute truth,' said Smerdyakov uncompromisingly.

'You told them about our conversation at the gate, too, word for word?'

'No, sir, not quite word for word.'

'And that you can feign an epileptic fit, as you boasted to me, did you tell them that, too?'

'No, I didn't say that either.'

'Will you tell me now why you wanted me to go to Chermashnya?'

'I was afraid you'd go to Moscow, sir, and, after all, Chermashnya's nearer.'

'You're lying. You yourself suggested that I should go away. "Go away," you said, "don't get mixed up in any trouble!"'

'I only said that out of friendship for you, out of my sincere devotion, because I had a premonition of a disaster in the house, sir, and I was concerned for you. Only, I was even more concerned for myself than I was for you, sir. That's why I said, "Don't get mixed up in any trouble," so that you'd understand that there was going to be an accident at the house, and you'd stay and protect your father.'

'Well, you could have been more explicit, you fool!' Ivan Fyodorovich flared up suddenly.

'How could I have been more explicit at the time, sir? I only spoke out of fear, and, what's more, you might have got angry. I was afraid that Dmitry Fyodorovich might cause some kind of rumpus, of course, and that he might come and take the money since he considered it to be his in any case, but who could have known that it would end in such a murder? I thought he'd just sneak off with the three thousand that the master had hidden under his mattress, in the envelope, but he went and killed him, sir. How could you even have guessed that, sir?'

'Well then, if you yourself say that it was impossible to guess, how do you expect me to have guessed? Why are you trying to confuse the issue?' said Ivan Fyodorovich thoughtfully.

'You could have guessed, because I was asking you to go to Chermashnya instead of Moscow, sir.'

'How on earth could I have guessed from that?'

Smerdyakov seemed exhausted, and remained silent again for a minute or so.

'You could have guessed from the simple fact that I was trying to get you to go to Chermashnya and not Moscow, which meant I didn't want you to go too far, because Moscow's a long way away and if Dmitry Fyodorovich knew you were near, it'd deter him. And if need be you could have returned quicker to protect me too, because quite apart from anything else I'd told you about Grigory Vasilyevich's illness and that I was afraid I was going to have a fit. Having told you about the signal to get the master to open the door, and that Dmitry Fyodorovich knew about it from me, I thought you'd guess he was sure to do something, and you'd stay here and not even go to Chermashnya.'

'He's talking very coherently,' thought Ivan Fyodorovich, 'even though he does make you sick; so why was Dr Herzenstube talking about him being "disturbed"?'

'You're trying to make a fool of me, damn you!' he exclaimed angrily.

'I must say, I thought at the time that you had guessed everything,' parried Smerdyakov with an air of utter ingenuousness.

'If I'd guessed, I'd have stayed!' shouted Ivan Fyodorovich, flaring up again.

'Well, sir, I...er... I thought that you'd guessed and you were going away just to get away from any trouble, that you were afraid and were running away to save your own skin.'

'So you think everyone is a coward like you, do you?'

'With respect, sir, yes, I thought you were the same as me.'

'I should have guessed, of course,' said Ivan uneasily. 'I did have an idea that you were up to no good... Only you're lying, you're lying again,' he shouted with sudden realization. 'You remember, you came up to the tarantass and said to me, "It's always interesting to talk to an intelligent person." That means you were glad I was going, seeing that you gave me credit for that, doesn't it?'

Smerdyakov sighed several times. Some colour seemed to come to his face.

'If I was glad,' he said, wheezing, 'it was only because you'd agreed to go to Chermashnya and not to Moscow. Because at least it's not so far; only I didn't say those words in approval, sir, I said them as a reproach. But you didn't understand.'

'Reproach for what?'

'For leaving your father when you knew he could be in danger, and for refusing to stay and protect us, because, sir, they could always drag me into it and accuse me of stealing those three thousand roubles.'

'Go to hell!' swore Ivan again. 'One second: did you tell the magistrate and the prosecutor about the signal and the taps?'

'I told them everything, just as it was, sir.'

Ivan Fyodorovich was surprised once more, but he did not show it this time.

'If I did suspect anything,' he began again, 'it was only that you were up to no good. Dmitry might commit murder, but that he would steal—that I didn't believe at the time... But I was quite prepared for any deviousness from you. You told me yourself you could fake a fit... why did you say that?'

'I suppose it was silly of me. Never in my life have I deliberately faked an attack, I only said it to show off in front of you... It was just stupidity, sir. I'd really taken a liking to you at that time, and I was being absolutely honest with you.'

'My brother's accusing you outright of the murder and the theft.'

'He would, wouldn't he?' Smerdyakov smiled bitterly. 'And who's going to believe him, in the face of all the evidence? Grigory Vasilyevich saw the open door, sir, so how can they believe him? Well, anyway, may God forgive him! He's trying to save his own skin...'

He fell silent, and then, as if suddenly realizing something, he added:

'Look, sir, it's the same old story: they want to pin the blame on me, lay the crime at my door—I've heard it all before, sir—for example, take that business of my being able to fake an epileptic fit; well, would I have told you beforehand that I could fake it if I really had intended to do something to your father? If I'd been planning to murder him, would I have been so stupid as to reveal information like that, and to his own son of all people—I ask you, sir? Does that seem at all likely? Absolutely not, sir, quite the contrary, it's completely out of the question. Now, nobody can overhear this conversation we're having, nobody except providence, but if you were to go and report it to the prosecutor and Nikolai Parfenovich, you could actually use it to protect me, sir, for what sort of criminal would be so stupid as to disclose such information? Anyone can see that.'

'Listen,' interrupted Ivan Fyodorovich, struck by Smerdyakov's last point, and standing up, 'I don't suspect you in the least, and in fact I find it ludicrous to accuse you... on the contrary, I'm grateful to you for setting my mind at rest. I'm going now, but I shall come again. Goodbye for now, get better quickly. Do you need anything?'

'Thank you for the offer, sir. Marfa Ignatyevna hasn't forgotten me, sir, and with her usual kindness sees to everything I need. Kind people visit me every day.'

'Well, goodbye. By the way, I shan't say anything about you being able to fake it... and I'd advise you not to mention it,' said Ivan suddenly, for some reason.

'I quite understand, sir. And if you're not going to tell them about that, I shan't say anything about our conversation at the gate that time...'

Ivan Fyodorovich went out quickly, and it was not until he had gone about ten paces down the corridor that he realized there was something insulting in Smerdyakov's last remark. He thought of going back there and then, but only for a moment, and, saying to himself 'that's stupid', he walked briskly out of the hospital. The fact was that he really did feel reassured—and precisely because it was his brother Mitya and not Smerdyakov who was guilty, although he should have felt quite the opposite. Why this was so, he did not wish to ascertain at that moment, being loath, in fact, to start analysing his own emotions. It was as if he wanted quickly to forget something or other. After that, over the course of the next few days as he got to know more about the evidence against Mitya, he totally convinced himself of the latter's guilt. The evidence, albeit from witnesses who were in themselves totally insignificant—Fenya and her mother, for example—was overwhelming, not to mention Perkhotin and all that business about the inn, about the Plotnikovs' shop, about the witnesses in Mokroye!... The details were particularly incriminating. The investigative magistrate and the prosecutor found the story of the secret 'signal' as significant as Grigory's statement about the door being open. In answer to Ivan Fyodorovich's enquiry, Grigory's wife, Marfa Ignatyevna, told him outright that Smerdyakov had lain all night in their room, behind the partition, 'he wasn't three paces from our bed', and that even though she personally had slept soundly, she had nevertheless woken several times and heard him groaning. 'He groaned all the time, didn't stop groaning.' Ivan had a talk with Herzenstube and told him of his doubts, namely, that Smerdyakov did not really seem mad, but only ill. The old man smiled faintly. 'And do you know what he's doing now?' he asked Ivan Fyodorovich. 'Learning French vocabulary by heart. He's got a notebook under his pillow in which someone has written out French words in Russian charades!' he laughed. In the end, Ivan Fyodorovich abandoned all his doubts. He could not even think about his brother Dmitry without disgust. But what was strange was that Alyosha continued to insist stubbornly that the murderer was 'in all probability' not Dmitry but Smerdyakov. Ivan had always had a high regard for Alyosha's opinion, and he was therefore very puzzled by his attitude. What was also strange was that Alyosha did not seem to want to discuss Mitya with him and never broached the subject, but confined himself to answering Ivan's questions. Ivan noticed this particularly. Incidentally, he was greatly distracted at that time by a quite unconnected matter: from the very first days after his return from Moscow, he had been totally and irresistibly consumed by a burning, irrational passion for Katerina Ivanovna. This is not the place to begin describing this new passion, which was to influence the rest of Ivan Fyodorovich's life; that may serve as the basis for a different story, another novel, which I am not sure that I shall ever undertake. But all the same, I cannot refrain from saying now that when Ivan Fyodorovich, as I have recorded, said on the way to Katerina Ivanovna's with Alyosha, 'I'm not interested,' he was lying through his teeth at that moment; he was madly in love with her, although it was true that at times he also hated her enough even to kill her. There were many reasons for this: thoroughly shaken by what had happened with Mitya, Katerina Ivanovna had thrown herself into the arms of Ivan Fyodorovich on his return, as if he were some kind of saviour. She had been insulted, hurt, and humiliated. And lo, there appeared again the man who had been so madly in love with her once—oh, she had known that only too well—and whom she had always looked up to for his qualities of heart and mind. But being a young lady of unbending nature, she did not, in spite of her admirer's unrestrained, typically Karamazovian passion and all his charm, yield to him entirely. At the time, she was continually tormented by remorse for having betrayed Mitya, and at moments of stormy dispute with Ivan (of which there were many), she would tell him this straight out. This was what he had referred to during his conversation with Alyosha as 'a tissue of lies'. Some people were seriously lying of course, and this irritated Ivan Fyodorovich all the more... but all that can wait. Suffice it to say that, for the time being, he almost forgot about Smerdyakov. Two weeks after that first visit, however, he began to be plagued by the same strange thoughts as before. He constantly wondered why, at Fyodor Pavlovich's house that last night before his departure, he had kept creeping out like a thief on to the landing, eavesdropping on what his father was doing below. Why had he recalled this with revulsion later, why, on the road the next day, had he suddenly felt so remorseful, and why, as he arrived in Moscow, had he said to himself, 'I'm a scoundrel'? And it occurred to him now that, perhaps, because of all these tormenting thoughts and the way in which they were taking control over his mind, he was even ready to forget about Katerina Ivanovna. And just then he met Alyosha in the street. He promptly stopped him and asked him:

'Do you remember that time after dinner when Dmitry burst in and attacked father, and afterwards, outside, I told you I reserved "the right to wish"? Tell me, did you think then that I wished father's death, or not?'

'Yes, I did,' Alyosha replied softly.

'Well, you were right, you didn't have to be a genius to guess that. But didn't it also occur to you that what I actually meant was let "dog eat dog", that is, to be precise, for Dmitry to kill father, and as soon as possible... and that I was even willing to aid and abet this myself?'

Alyosha blanched slightly and gazed in silence into his brother's eyes.

'Tell me, for heaven's sake!' Ivan exclaimed. 'I have to know what you thought at the time. I must have the truth, tell me the truth!' He was breathing heavily, looking at Alyosha with a sort of anticipatory hostility.

'Forgive me, yes, I thought that too,' whispered Alyosha, and fell silent, adding not a single 'mitigating circumstance'.

'Thanks!' Ivan said abruptly, and, leaving Alyosha, went on his way. From then on Alyosha noticed that his brother Ivan suddenly began to distance himself from him and even seemed

to have taken a dislike to him, so that he too stopped calling on
him. But Ivan Fyodorovich, immediately after that meeting, once
again went straight to Smerdyakov without going home.

7

SECOND VISIT TO SMERDYAKOV

BY this time Smerdyakov had already discharged himself from
hospital. Ivan Fyodorovich knew his new address—that dilapidated little wooden house consisting of two rooms joined by a
hallway. Marya Kondratyevna and her mother had moved into
one of these rooms; Smerdyakov, on his own, into the other.
God knows on what conditions he had moved in with them,
whether he was paying rent or living there rent-free. People said
later that he had moved in as Marya Kondratyevna's betrothed,
and for the time being was not paying anything. Both mother
and daughter looked up to him and regarded him as superior to
themselves. When the door was answered Ivan Fyodorovich
stepped into the hallway and, following an indication from Marya
Kondratyevna, turned left, straight into the 'best' room, which
Smerdyakov occupied. This room had a tiled stove which gave
out a lot of heat. The walls were decorated with sky-blue
wallpaper, admittedly all torn and peeling, and under it, in the
cracks, cockroaches swarmed in such profusion that they produced a constant rustling noise. There was very little furniture,
and what there was was very basic: two benches along the walls,
and two chairs by the table. The table, although a simple wooden
one, was nevertheless covered with a pink, patterned tablecloth.
On the sills of each of the two small windows stood a pot with
geraniums. In the corner was an icon-case with icons in it. On
the table stood a small, very battered brass samovar and a tray
with two cups. But Smerdyakov had already drunk some tea and
had let the samovar go out... He himself was seated on a bench
at the table and was scribbling something with a pen in an
exercise book. A bottle of ink stood nearby, and also a cast-iron
candlestick with a tallow candle in it. Ivan Fyodorovich concluded at once from Smerdyakov's appearance that he had quite

recovered from his illness. His face was fuller, fresher, his quiff brushed up, and his hair slicked back from his temples. He was wearing a gaudy quilted dressing-gown which, however, was threadbare and somewhat frayed. On his nose rested a pair of spectacles, which Ivan Fyodorovich had never seen him wear before. This insignificant fact exacerbated Ivan's irritation: 'What a wretch, he's even wearing spectacles now!' Smerdyakov looked up slowly and stared at his visitor through his spectacles, then, without a word, he took them off and half rose to his feet, not deferentially somehow, but lazily, as if he were displaying the least degree of deference that he could possibly get away with. All this flashed through Ivan's mind, and he noticed and took in everything—but in particular the look that Smerdyakov gave him, decidedly hostile and unwelcoming, even condescending: 'Oh,' he seemed to say, 'you again! We've said all we have to say to each other, so what are you doing here?' Ivan Fyodorovich could hardly contain himself.

'It's hot in here,' he said, still standing and unbuttoning his coat.

'Why don't you take your coat off, sir?' Smerdyakov suggested.

Ivan Fyodorovich took off his coat and threw it across a bench, grabbed a chair with shaking hands, pulled it quickly up to the table, and sat down. Smerdyakov managed to sit down first, on his bench.

'First of all, are we alone?' asked Ivan Fyodorovich at once, sternly. 'They won't overhear us in there?'

'No one will hear anything, sir. You saw for yourself, there's a hallway.'

'Now look here, my man, what was all that bloody nonsense you told me when I was leaving the hospital, all that about not telling the magistrate everything about our conversation by the gate if I kept quiet about your being able to fake epilepsy? What did you mean by *everything*? What on earth were you alluding to? Were you threatening me? Do you think I'm in cahoots with you, that I'm afraid of you, or something?'

Ivan Fyodorovich said all this in an absolute frenzy, deliberately making it quite obvious that he wished to come straight to the point and was putting all his cards on the table. Smerdyakov's eyes glittered spitefully, and the left one twitched as if to say, 'So you want to put all your cards on the table, well that's all right by me!' He responded immediately, although with his usual reserve and deliberation.

'What I meant and the reason why I said it was that you knew your father might be murdered and yet you left him to his fate, and therefore people would inevitably come to some nasty conclusion about your feelings and maybe incidentally about something else—that's what I promised not to reveal to the authorities.'

Although Smerdyakov spoke unhurriedly and was obviously in control of himself, there was a hint of something hard and insistent in his voice, something malicious and insolently provocative. He stared insolently at Ivan Fyodorovich, and for a moment the latter lost his self-control.

'What do you mean? Are you out of your mind?'

'Certainly not, sir, I'm perfectly sane.'

'Are you suggesting that I *knew* about the murder?' screamed Ivan Fyodorovich and banged his fist violently on the table. 'What do you mean by "about something else"? Talk, you swine!'

Smerdyakov said nothing and continued to stare insolently at Ivan Fyodorovich.

'Tell me, you stinking scoundrel, what is this "something else"?' yelled the latter.

'What I meant by "something else" just now was that at that time you probably very much wanted your father dead.'

Ivan Fyodorovich leapt up and struck Smerdyakov on the shoulder as hard as he could with his fist, so that he fell back against the wall. In a flash tears streamed down his face, and saying, 'You should be ashamed, sir, to hit a weak man!' he suddenly covered his eyes with his filthy, blue-check cotton handkerchief, and was overcome by quiet sobbing. A minute or so elapsed.

'That's enough! Stop it!' said Ivan Fyodorovich imperiously, sitting down again. 'Don't try my patience.'

Smerdyakov took the rag from his eyes. Every line of his wrinkled face reflected the assault he had just suffered.

'So, you wretch, you thought that I, like Dmitry, wanted to kill my father, did you?'

'I didn't know what you were thinking then, sir,' said Smerdyakov sulkily, 'and I stopped you as you came in the gate to sound you out on precisely that point, sir.'

'Sound me out? About what?'

'About precisely that matter, sir: did you or did you not want your father out of the way as soon as possible?'

What aroused Ivan Fyodorovich's indignation most of all was the obstinately insolent tone that Smerdyakov insisted on using.

'It was you who killed him!' he exclaimed suddenly.

Smerdyakov smiled scornfully.

'You, of all people, know perfectly well that it wasn't me that killed him. And I hardly expected an intelligent person even to suggest it.'

'But, for heaven's sake, why then did you suspect me of such a thing then?'

'As you already know, sir, from sheer fear. Because, the way things were then, I was in such a state that I suspected everyone. So I decided to sound you out, too, sir, because if you wanted the same thing as your brother, then, I thought, by the time this whole thing was over I could have got the chop too.'

'The only thing is, you didn't say that two weeks ago.'

'It's what I meant, exactly what I meant, only when I was talking to you in the hospital, sir, I assumed that you yourself, being a very intelligent person, didn't want me to spell it out.'

'Well, I'm damned! But answer me, damn you, I insist that you answer me: how on earth could I have sown such a foul suspicion in your rotten little mind, and why should I have done it?'

'To kill him. You could never have done it yourself, never in a month of Sundays, sir, and you didn't want to, but you might have hoped someone else would kill him, that's what you wanted.'

'How calmly he says it, damn him! Why the hell should I have wanted that, what reason could I have had?'

'What reason? Well, what about your inheritance, sir?' Smerdyakov retorted vehemently and even somewhat vindictively. 'After all, the three of you stood to gain near enough forty thousand each when your father died, or even more, sir, but if Fyodor Pavlovich married that woman, sir, that Agrafena Aleksandrovna, she'd have got all his capital transferred to her name once they were married, because she's no fool, sir, and then you three wouldn't even have got a couple of roubles on your father's death. And the wedding wasn't far off, was it? A mere hair's breadth away: it only needed that madam to crook her little finger at him, like this, and he'd have followed her to the altar with his tongue hanging out.'

Ivan Fyodorovich restrained himself with difficulty.

'All right,' he said at last, 'you can see, I haven't lost my temper, I haven't hit you, I haven't killed you. Go on: so according to you, my brother Dmitry was the stooge for this, I was counting on him?'

'How could you not have been counting on him, sir? After all, if he committed the murder, he'd lose all his hereditary rights,* his rank and estates, and he'd be exiled. So then, when your father died, his share would come to you and your brother Aleksei Fyodorovich, in equal parts, that's not forty thousand, but sixty thousand each, sir. So you must definitely have been counting on Dmitry Fyodorovich!'

'I'm fast losing my patience with you! Listen, you stupid fool; if I'd been counting on anyone it would have been you of course, not Dmitry, and I swear I did feel... at that time... I was expecting some kind of a dirty trick from you... I remember having that impression!'

'And I also felt then, for a minute, that you were counting on me too,' Smerdyakov smiled sarcastically, 'so you relaxed your guard with me even more, because if you suspected me, and yet at the same time you still intended to go away, that means you might just as well have said: you can kill my father, and I won't try to stop you.'

'You scoundrel! So that's what you thought!'

'And all because of that Chermashnya business, sir. I mean, for heaven's sake! You were intent on going to Moscow, and refused all your father's pleas to go to Chermashnya! And then I just had to say the word, and you suddenly agreed! Why did you have to agree to go to Chermashnya just then? If you went to Chermashnya instead of Moscow for no other reason than the fact that I suggested it, it stands to reason you expected I'd do something.'

'No, I swear I didn't!' yelled Ivan through clenched teeth.

'How can you deny it, sir? On the contrary, as your father's son, you should have had me arrested for what I said to you about him, you should have given me a good beating or at least knocked my block off on the spot, but on the contrary you promptly and obligingly took my utterly stupid advice for what it was worth, if you'll forgive me saying so, without showing the slightest sign of anger, and left, which was quite ridiculous, because you should have stayed and prevented your father's murder... How could I conclude otherwise?'

Ivan sat frowning, both fists clenched tightly on his knees.

'Yes, it's a pity I didn't knock your block off,' he smiled bitterly. 'It would have been no good taking you to the police then, who would have believed me, and what could I have accused you of... but a good thumping... Blast! Pity I didn't think of it! So what if it's forbidden to clout someone, I'd still have smashed you to a pulp.'

Smerdyakov was watching him almost with glee.

'In normal circumstances,' he said, in the same smug, opinion-ated tone of voice in which he used to provoke Grigory Vasilyevich and quarrel with him about religion as he stood by Fyodor Pavlovich's table, 'in normal circumstances it is certainly forbidden by law to knock someone's block off these days, and no one does it any more, but, well, sir, in exceptional circum-stances, not only here but also all over the world, even in the most republican of French republics, they still continue to thump each other, just as in Adam and Eve's time, and they'll never stop, sir, but you, even in that particular exceptional circum-stance, you didn't dare, sir.'

'How come you're learning French grammar?' Ivan motioned with his head towards the exercise book lying on the table.

'And why shouldn't I learn it, sir, so as to improve my education, in case even I might get to go to those more fortunate parts of Europe sometime?'

'Listen, you monster,' Ivan's eyes were flashing and he was shaking all over, 'I'm not afraid of your accusations, you can tell them what you like against me, and the only reason I didn't beat you to death just now is that I suspect you of this crime, and I'm going to haul you before the judge. I haven't finished with you yet!'

'In my opinion you'd do better not to say anything, sir. Because, what could you accuse me of, when I'm totally innocent, and who'd believe you? And if you started anything, sir, I'd tell them everything, because I'd have to defend myself, wouldn't I?'

'Do you think I'm frightened of you?'

'They might not believe all I've just said in court, but the general public will believe it, and you'll be shown up.'

'So that means "it's always interesting to talk to an intelligent person" all over again, eh?' Ivan said through clenched teeth.

'That's about the size of it, sir. So don't be a fool.'

Ivan Fyodorovich stood up with a shudder of disgust, put on his coat and, without saying anything further to Smerdyakov and without even glancing at him, left the house. The fresh evening air cleared his head. The moon was shining brightly. A terrifying nightmare of thoughts and sensations was seething in his brain. 'Should I go now and lay charges against Smerdyakov? But what could I accuse him of? He's innocent really. He would immediately accuse me. Why, in fact, did I go to Chermashnya? What for? What for?' Ivan Fyodorovich asked himself. 'Yes, of course I was expecting something, and he's right...' And for the umpteenth time he recalled how, on that last evening at his father's, he had eavesdropped on him on the stairs, but so painful was the recollection that he even stopped dead and stood as if transfixed: 'Yes, that's just what I was expecting then, it's true! That's exactly what I did want, I wanted the murder to happen! Did I want it or didn't I?... I'll have to kill Smerdyakov!... If I don't have the courage to kill Smerdyakov now, it's not worth going on living!...' Without going home, Ivan Fyodorovich went straight to Katerina Ivanovna, who was frightened by his appearance; he was like a madman. He recounted his entire conversation with Smerdyakov to her, down to the smallest detail. No matter how hard she tried to soothe him he was not to be pacified, and kept pacing backwards and forwards and talking in a strange, disjointed fashion. At last he sat down, elbows on the table and his head in his hands, and made the following strange pronouncement:

'If it wasn't Dmitry but Smerdyakov who killed him, then of course I'm implicated, because I incited him. Did I incite him?

I'm still not sure. But if it was him, if he did it and not Dmitry, then surely I too am a murderer.'

Hearing this, Katerina Ivanovna stood up without speaking, went to her writing-desk, unlocked a casket that stood on it, withdrew a piece of paper, and laid it in front of Ivan. This piece of paper was that same document which Ivan Fyodorovich would later say to Alyosha was 'unequivocal proof' of Dmitry's guilt. It was a letter that Mitya had written in a drunken state to Katerina Ivanovna the evening he had encountered Alyosha on his way to the monastery, after the scene at Katerina Ivanovna's when Grushenka had insulted her. When he left Alyosha on that occasion Mitya had rushed off to Grushenka; it is not known whether he saw her or not, but late that evening he turned up at the *Stolichny Gorod* and proceeded to get thoroughly drunk. While drunk, he demanded pen and paper and wrote a document of subsequent importance for himself. It was frantic, rambling, and incoherent—in short, a 'drunken' letter. It resembled the conversation of a drunk who, on arriving home, begins with excessive volubility to recount to his wife or one of the family how he has just been insulted, what a scoundrel his abuser is, what a fine fellow he himself is on the other hand, how he'll teach the scoundrel a lesson—and, while ranting on incoherently and excitably, he thumps his fists on the table and weeps drunken tears. The sheet of paper that they gave him in the inn was a grubby scrap of cheap ordinary writing-paper, on the back of which was written someone's bill. Evidently Mitya in his drunken state had found insufficient space on the sheet, and not only had he written in all the margins, but by the end had written over the words on the back of the sheet. The content of the letter was as follows:

Fateful Katya,

Tomorrow I shall get some money and shall repay your three thousand roubles, and farewell, woman of great wrath, but farewell also to my love. We shall make an end of it! Tomorrow I shall try to raise the money from everyone I know, and if I can't, I give you my word I'll go to my father, I'll smash his head in, and take the money from under his pillow, provided that Ivan has left. I shall go to Siberia, but I shall give you back the three thousand. As for you, farewell! I prostrate myself before you, because I have wronged you. Forgive me! No, it's better not to forgive me; better for you and for me not to! Better the salt-mines than your love, for I love another, and you have found out today, only too well, what she is like, so how can you forgive me? I shall kill him who has defrauded me! I shall go away to the East and cut myself off from everyone. From *her*, also, for you are not my only tormentor, she is too. Farewell!

PS I am writing curses, but I worship you! I hear it in my heart. One string is left and vibrates. It is better to break the heart in twain! I shall kill myself, but all the same I shall kill the dog first. I'll get the three thousand out of him for you. I may be a scoundrel in your eyes, but I am not a thief! Expect the three thousand. Under the dog's mattress there's a pink ribbon. It's not me who is the thief, I shall kill the thief. Katya, don't look scornfully at Dmitry; he is not a thief, but a murderer! He has killed his father and must perish himself, so as not to be subjected to your scorn. And not to love you.

PPS I kiss your feet, farewell!

PPPS Katya, pray to God that I can get the money from someone else. Then I won't be stained with his blood, but if they don't give it, I will. Kill me!

Your slave and enemy,

D. Karamazov

When Ivan read the document, he was convinced. So, his brother was the murderer after all, not Smerdyakov. Not Smerdyakov, and so consequently not him, Ivan. In his eyes this letter suddenly acquired an unequivocal meaning. For him, there could never be any remaining doubt about Mitya's guilt now. At the same time he never suspected that Mitya might have committed the murder together with Smerdyakov; it just did not fit the facts. Ivan was perfectly reassured. The next morning, when he remembered Smerdyakov and his gibes, he felt only scorn. After a few days he was even surprised that he could have been so tormented by his suspicions. He decided that Smerdyakov was beneath contempt and that he would forget him. A month passed in this way. He no longer asked anyone about Smerdyakov, but he heard in passing a couple of times that he was very ill and not in his right mind. 'He'll end up mad,' the young doctor Varvinsky had said about him, and Ivan remembered that. The last week of that month Ivan himself began to feel very ill. He had already been to see the doctor that Katerina Ivanovna had engaged and who had arrived from Moscow before the beginning of the trial. And just at this time his relationship with Katerina Ivanovna came to a head. They were two enemies in love with each other. Katerina Ivanovna's momentary but fervent, relapses, into her passion for Mitya drove Ivan frantic. Strangely enough, for a whole month, until that last scene at Katerina Ivanovna's when, as I have already described, Alyosha came to her house at Mitya's request, Ivan did not hear a word from her of Mitya's guilt, in spite of all those 'relapses' that he hated so much. And it was also remarkable that though he felt that he hated Mitya more and more every day, at the same time he understood that he hated him not because of Katerina Ivanovna's 'relapses', but precisely because *he had killed their father*! He himself was only too aware of this. Nevertheless, about ten days before the trial he had visited Mitya and had proposed the escape plan to him—a plan which, apparently, he had already been contemplating for some time. Over and above the main reason that drove him to take such a step, there was another—the festering sore in his heart resulting from Smerdyakov's insinuation that it would be to his, Ivan's, advantage if Mitya were found guilty, as then he and Alyosha would each stand to gain sixty thousand from their father's estate instead of forty thousand. He had decided to sacrifice thirty thousand of his share to arrange Mitya's escape. Returning from the prison on that occasion, he had been terribly sad and confused; he had suddenly begun to feel that he wanted Mitya to escape not only so that he could heal his wound by sacrificing thirty thousand to that end, but also for some other reason. 'Is it because, at heart, I am the murderer just as much as he is?' he wondered. Something inchoate ravaged his soul. Mostly over this last month his pride had suffered, but more of that later... When, on returning to his rooms after his conversation with Alyosha, his hand already about to ring his front-door bell, he suddenly decided to go and see Smerdyakov, Ivan Fyodorovich was responding to a single, specific revulsion which suddenly erupted in his heart. He had suddenly remembered Katerina Ivanovna snapping at him in front of Alyosha: 'It was you, only you, who assured me that it was he, Mitya, who was the murderer!' Remembering this, Ivan was quite dumbfounded; never for a moment had he assured her that Mitya was the murderer, on the contrary, he had cast suspicion on himself when speaking to her on his return from visiting Smerdyakov. Indeed, it was *she* who had presented him with that 'document' and accused his brother! And now she had suddenly announced: 'I've been to see Smerdyakov myself!' When was she there? Ivan had known nothing of that. That meant that she was by no means so convinced of Mitya's guilt! And what could Smerdyakov have said to her? What, what exactly had he told her? A terrible anger flared up in his heart. He could not understand how he could have let those words pass without protest. He let go of the bell-pull and rushed off to see Smerdyakov. 'This time, perhaps, I'll kill him,' he thought as he hurried on his way.

8

THIRD AND LAST VISIT TO SMERDYAKOV

BY the time he was half-way there, a keen, dry wind, like the wind that had been blowing early that morning, had got up, and it was snowing heavily, a fine, dry snow. It fell to the ground but did not settle, the wind whipped it up, and soon a veritable snowstorm set in. In the part of the town where Smerdyakov lived there were almost no street lights. Ivan Fyodorovich walked in the gloom, not noticing the snowstorm and finding his way by instinct. His head ached and there was a painful throbbing in his temples. He felt cramp in his wrists. As he drew near Marya Kondratyevna's squalid little house, he encountered a solitary drunk, a peasant of small stature, wearing a patched homespun coat; he was walking with a lurching gait, muttering and swearing, then suddenly he stopped swearing and began to sing loudly and drunkenly:

Shan't stop to wait for Vanya,
Vanya's gone to town!

But he repeatedly broke off at this second line, began cursing someone again, and then struck up the same refrain once more. Ivan Fyodorovich felt a mounting hatred towards him even before he was consciously aware of him, then he suddenly realized what it was. He felt a sudden urge to punch the peasant. Just at that moment they drew level, and the peasant, staggering drunkenly, collided violently with Ivan. The latter pushed him away furiously. The peasant staggered back and collapsed like a pack of cards in the mud, gave one moan, 'O-oh!' and was silent. Ivan strode up to him. He lay on his back, totally motionless, unconscious. 'He'll freeze to death,' thought Ivan, and went on his way to Smerdyakov.

Marya Kondratyevna, with a candle in her hand, ran out to meet him in the porch, and whispered that Pavel Fyodorovich (that is to say Smerdyakov) was 'very ill, sir, not in bed, but not in his right mind, sir, even refuses tea, won't drink anything'.

'Being violent, is he?' Ivan Fyodorovich asked brusquely.

'Not a bit, on the contrary, he's very quiet, only don't talk to him for too long...', Marya Kondratyevna requested.

Ivan Fyodorovich opened the door and walked in. It was just as hot as it had been the first time, but he noticed several changes in the room; one of the benches along the side wall had been removed and in its place was an old, imitation-mahogany divan upholstered in leather. On it a bed had been made up, with passably clean white pillows. Smerdyakov, still wearing the same dressing-gown, was sitting on the divan. A table had been placed by the divan, so the room was very cramped. On the table lay a thick book with a yellow cover, but Smerdyakov was not reading it; he seemed to be just sitting there, doing nothing. He greeted Ivan Fyodorovich with a long silent stare, and apparently was not at all surprised by his arrival. There was a great change in him, he was much thinner and looked even more sallow. His eyes were sunken and there were blue rings under them.

'So you really are ill?' Ivan Fyodorovich stopped. 'I shan't keep you long and shan't even take my coat off. Is there anywhere one can sit down here?'

He walked to the other end of the table, pulled up a chair, and sat down.

'Why do you just look at me, aren't you going to say anything? I've got just one question, and I swear I won't go without an answer. Has Miss Katerina Ivanovna been here?'

Smerdyakov remained silent for a long time, staring at Ivan in the same way, then suddenly he made a dismissive gesture and averted his face.

'What's the matter with you?' snapped Ivan.

'Nothing.'

'What do you mean, "nothing"?'

'Well, she was here, but it's none of your business. Leave me alone, sir.'

'No, I won't! Tell me, when was she here?'

'Can't remember a thing about her,' said Smerdyakov with a scornful smile, and, turning to face Ivan, glared at him with that same expression of frenzied rage with which he had looked at him on the occasion of their last meeting a month ago.

'It's you who looks ill, you're a pale shadow of your former self,' he said to Ivan.

'Never mind my health, just answer the question.'

'Why have your eyes gone so yellow, the whites are all yellow. You're tormenting yourself, aren't you, you're really tormenting yourself.'

He smiled scornfully and then suddenly burst out laughing.

'Listen, I told you, I won't go without an answer!' Ivan shouted, utterly incensed.

'Why are you picking on me, sir? What are you tormenting me for?' said Smerdyakov lugubriously.

'Oh, to hell with it. I don't give a damn about you. Just answer my question and I'll go.'

'I've got no answer to give you,' Smerdyakov looked down again.

'I assure you I shall make you answer me!'

'What are you getting so worked up about?' Smerdyakov suddenly fixed his gaze on him, not so much with scorn this time as with almost a kind of disgust. 'It's because the trial starts tomorrow, isn't it? Calm down, nothing's going to happen to you! Go home, go to bed and have a good night's sleep, don't be afraid about anything.'

'I don't understand you... what have I got to fear tomorrow?' said Ivan, astonished, and suddenly an icy fear gripped his soul. Smerdyakov fixed him with his gaze.

'You don't un-der-stand?' he drawled reproachfully. 'I wonder just what pleasure an intelligent man can get from carrying on with such a comedy?'

Ivan looked at him in silence. Quite apart from anything else, it was the tone of voice that was unusual—that quite unprecedentedly arrogant tone in which the erstwhile flunkey was now addressing him. He had certainly not used that tone of voice with him the previous time.

'I tell you, you've got nothing to be afraid of. I shan't give you away, there's no evidence. Why are your hands trembling? Why can't you keep your fingers still? Go home, *it wasn't you who killed him.*'

Ivan shuddered, he remembered Alyosha.

'I know it wasn't me...', he muttered.

'You kno-ow, do you?' Smerdyakov pounced on him again.

Ivan leapt up and seized him by the shoulders.

'Tell me everything, you swine! Tell me everything.'

Smerdyakov was not in the least disconcerted. He just fixed him with a stare of insane hatred.

'You asked for it—it was you who killed him,' he whispered savagely.

Ivan sank down on to his chair, as if he had just understood. He smiled maliciously.

'You're still on about the same thing, aren't you? The same as last time?'

'Yes, and the last time you understood perfectly, and you understand now, too.'

'All I understand is that you're mad.'

'You don't give up, do you! There's only us here between these four walls, so why should we try to pull the wool over each other's eyes and act out this comedy? Or do you still want to lay all the blame on me—and to my face, what's more? You killed him, you're the chief murderer, I was only your stooge, your faithful servant Lichard,* and I did it at your suggestion.'

'You did it? So it was you who killed him?' Ivan felt a chill strike his soul.

Something seemed to explode in his brain, and he began to shake all over in a cold sweat. Smerdyakov looked at him in astonishment this time; probably he was convinced at last by the genuineness of Ivan's fear.

'Surely you must have known?' he muttered incredulously with a wry grin.

Ivan looked at him; it was as if his tongue had been torn out.

> Shan't stop to wait for Vanya,
> Vanya's gone to town—

The words suddenly rang in his head.

'You know what? I'm afraid that it's all a dream, that you're a ghost sitting there in front of me,' he mumbled.

'There's no ghost here, sir, only us two, and a certain third person. No doubt about it, that third person's right here between us.'

'Who is that? Who's here? Who's this third person?' Ivan, terrified, looked around and glanced quickly into every corner to see if anyone was there.

'That third one is God, sir, providence itself, right here beside us, only it's no good looking for it, you won't find it.'

'You're lying when you say you're the murderer,' screamed Ivan frantically. 'Either you're mad or you're tormenting me, like last time!'

As before, Smerdyakov was not in the least disconcerted, but continued to observe him curiously. He still simply could not overcome his mistrust, he still thought that Ivan 'knew everything' and was only pretending in order to 'blame him, and to his face'.

'Wait, sir,' he said at last, weakly, and suddenly he drew his left leg out from under the table and began to roll up his trousers. The leg was clothed in a long white stocking and a slipper. Taking his time, Smerdyakov undid the suspender and inserted his fingers right down inside the stocking. Ivan

Fyodorovich stared at him and was suddenly shaken by a spasm of fear.

'You're mad!' he yelled, and, jumping to his feet, he staggered backwards, hitting his back against the wall with such force that he seemed suspended there like a plumb-line. Transfixed with fear, he looked at Smerdyakov. The latter, quite oblivious to Ivan's terror, went on digging in his stocking, still apparently struggling to get hold of something and pull it out. At last he got hold of it and started to pull. Ivan Fyodorovich saw that it was some papers or a small bundle of papers. Smerdyakov pulled it out and placed it on the table.

'There you are, sir,' he said quietly.

'What?' asked Ivan, trembling.

'Be so good as to take a look, sir,' said Smerdyakov in the same quiet voice.

Ivan went up to the table, picked up the bundle and started to unwrap it, but suddenly he snatched his fingers away as if he had touched some disgusting, frightful reptile.

'Your fingers are still shaking, sir, must be nerves,' remarked Smerdyakov, and he slowly unwrapped the bundle himself. Inside the wrapping there were three wads of hundred-rouble notes.

'It's all here, sir, the whole three thousand, you don't need to count it. Take it,' he said to Ivan, motioning towards the money. Ivan sank down on his chair. He was as white as a sheet.

'You scared me... with that stocking...', he said with a strange smile.

'Surely, surely you must have realized by now, didn't you?' Smerdyakov asked again.

'No, I didn't. All this time I thought it was Dmitry. Dmitry! Dmitry! Oh!' he suddenly buried his head in his hands. 'Listen: did you kill him on your own? Without my brother, or with him?'

'Just with you, sir, I killed him with you, sir; Dmitry Fyodorovich is completely innocent, sir.'

'All right, all right... We'll talk about me later. Why can't I stop shaking?.. I can't get a word out.'

'You used to be so brave, sir, "everything is permitted", you used to say, and now look how frightened you are,' Smerdyakov muttered, astonished. 'Would you like some lemonade, sir? I'll send for some. It can be very refreshing. Only we'd better hide that first, sir.'

And he motioned again in the direction of the wads of money. He made a move to get up and go to the doorway to call Marya Kondratyevna and ask her to make them some lemonade, but, looking for something to cover the money so that she should not see it, he first took his handkerchief, but then, seeing that it was quite filthy, he picked up the book with the yellow cover that was lying on the table and which Ivan had noticed when he came in, and placed it over the money. The book was called *The Sermons of St Isaac the Syrian.** Ivan Fyodorovich had read the title casually, in passing.

'I don't want any lemonade,' he said. 'We'll talk about me later. Sit down and tell me how you did it. Tell me everything...'

'At least, won't you take off your coat, sir, or you'll be too hot.'

As if he had just become aware of it, Ivan Fyodorovich pulled off his coat and, without leaving his seat, threw it on the bench.

'Tell me, then, please, tell me!'

He seemed calm. He felt really sure that Smerdyakov was going to tell him *everything* now.

'About how it was done, sir?' sighed Smerdyakov. 'It was done in the most natural way, sir, just as you said...'

'We'll talk about what I said later,' Ivan Fyodorovich interrupted again, not shouting as before, but enunciating his words clearly, and apparently having fully regained control over himself. 'Just tell me exactly how you did it. Start at the beginning. Don't leave anything out. Tell me the details, that's the important thing—the details. I beg you.'

'You went away and I fell down the cellar steps, sir...'

'In a fit or pretending?'

'Pretending, of course, sir. I was pretending all the time. I went calmly down the steps, sir, right to the bottom, and lay down calmly, and as I lay down, I started to shriek. And I went on shrieking until they carried me out.'

'Just a minute! And all the time, even afterwards and at the hospital, you were still pretending?'

'Not at all, sir. The next morning, even before they took me to the hospital, I had a real fit, terrible, worse than I've had for years. I was really unconscious for two days.'

'All right, all right. Go on.'

'They laid me on that bed, sir, behind the partition, like I knew they would, because whenever I was ill Marfa Ignatyevna used to put me in their room, behind the partition, for the night. They've always been ever so kind to me, sir, ever since I was born. I groaned in the night, but softly. I was still expecting Dmitry Fyodorovich.'

'What do you mean, you expected him to come to you?'

'Why to me? I expected him to come to the house, I was sure he'd come that very night because without me and therefore without any way of finding out what was going on, he'd certainly have to enter the house by climbing over the fence, like he knew how, sir, and do whatever he had a mind to do.'

'And if he hadn't come?'

'Then nothing would have happened, sir. I wouldn't have dared to do it without him.'

'All right, all right... don't mumble so, take your time, the important thing is—don't leave anything out.'

'I expected him to kill Fyodor Pavlovich, sir... I was sure. Because I'd sown the idea in his head... several days before... and especially as he knew the signal. What with the suspicion and rage that had been building up in him recently, he was bound to use the signal to get into the house, sir, bound to. And that's what I expected, sir.'

'One moment,' Ivan interrupted, 'if he'd killed him, he'd have taken the money. You must have realized that. I don't see what you would have got out of it afterwards.'

'But he'd never have found the money, sir. It was I who told him it was under the mattress. Only it wasn't true. It used to be in a casket, you know. Then I told Fyodor Pavlovich—because I was the only one he trusted in the whole world—to place the envelope containing the money in the corner, behind the icons, because absolutely no one would guess it was there, especially if they were in a hurry. So that envelope was hidden in the corner of his room, behind the icons, sir. And it would have been stupid to keep it under the mattress, he'd have put it in the casket, at least, and locked it. And now everyone believes it was under the mattress. Stupid reasoning, sir. So if Dmitry Fyodorovich did commit the murder, then, finding nothing, either he'd run away, afraid of every sound, like it is with murderers, or he'd be arrested, sir. So then I could always have crept in the next day, or even that same night, and taken the money out from behind the icons and blamed it all on Dmitry Fyodorovich. I could always count on that.'

'Well, what if he didn't kill him, but only beat him up?'

'If he didn't kill him, I wouldn't dare take the money, of course, and it would all have been for nothing. But then there was also the possibility that he might beat him unconscious, and I'd have time to slip in and take the money and then tell Fyodor Pavlovich that it was his attacker, Dmitry, who'd taken it.'

'Wait... I'm getting confused. So it was Dmitry who killed him after all, and you only took the money?'

'No, it wasn't him, sir. Well, yes, if I wanted to I could say even now that he was the murderer... but I don't want to lie to you now, because... because if, as is quite obvious, you really didn't understand anything until now and were not trying to fool me so as to make it look as if I were guilty, you're still guilty overall, sir, because you knew there'd be a murder and you commissioned me to do it, and knowing all about it, you left. That's why I want to prove to you this evening, without any doubt, that it's you who's the real murderer in this case and that, although I killed him, I'm only your accomplice. And, legally, it's you who's the murderer!'

'Why, why am I the murderer? Oh God!' Ivan, forgetting that he had intended to avoid all discussion of his own involvement till the end of the conversation, could no longer restrain himself. 'You're still on about that Chermashnya business, aren't you? Hold on, assuming you took Chermashnya as a sign of acquiescence, why did you need my approval? How are you going to explain that now?'

'Once I had your approval, I knew you wouldn't raise a hue and cry about the missing three thousand when you got back, if for some reason the authorities suspected me instead of Dmitry Fyodorovich, or thought I was his accomplice; on the contrary, you would protect me from the others... And, having received your inheritance, you could then repay me for the rest of my life, because after all you'd have got your inheritance because of me, whereas if he'd married Agrafena Aleksandrovna you'd have got damn all.'

'Aha! So you thought you could go on harassing me afterwards, all my life!' growled Ivan. 'But what if I hadn't gone to Chermashnya, if I'd denounced you instead?'

'What could you have denounced me for? That I persuaded you to go to Chermashnya? That's a load of rubbish, sir. Anyway, you could have left after our conversation, or you could have stayed. If you'd stayed, nothing would have happened; I'd have known you didn't want anything to happen and I wouldn't have done anything. But since you left, that meant you were assuring me that you wouldn't dare denounce me and that you'd turn a blind eye if I took the three thousand. Anyway, you couldn't have denounced me afterwards because I would have told them everything, that is, not that I'd stolen the money and killed him—I wouldn't have told them that, sir—but that you were urging me to take it and to kill him, but that I didn't agree to it. I needed your consent so that you wouldn't be able to put me on the spot, because you wouldn't have any evidence, whereas I could always put you on the spot by letting them know how much you wanted your father dead—as I give you my word, I would have done—and public opinion would believe it and you'd be despised all your life.'

'So I did want it, I wanted him dead, did I?' Ivan growled again.

'Undoubtedly you did, sir, and by your tacit agreement you gave me permission to do it,' Smerdyakov gave Ivan an uncompromising look. He was very weak, spoke quietly, and sounded exhausted, but he was fired by some secret within him, he was obviously hatching something. Ivan could sense it.

'Go on,' he said, 'go on about that night.'

'About that night, all right, sir! Well, there I was, lying on the bed, and then I thought I heard the master cry out. But Grigory Vasilyevich had got up before that and gone out, and he suddenly started to scream, and then everything went quiet and it was all dark. I just lay there, waiting, my heart was thumping, I couldn't bear it. In the end, I got up and went out, sir—I saw his window on the left was open, and I walked a few paces towards it, sir, to listen and see if he was alive and sitting there or not, and then I heard the master shuffling about and mumbling, so that meant he was alive. Aha, I thought! I went up to the window and called out to the master. "It's me," I said. And he said, "He was here, right here, he ran off!" That was Dmitry Fyodorovich he meant, sir, he'd been there. "He's killed Grigory." "Where?" I whispered. "Over there, in the corner of the garden," he pointed, also whispering. "Wait," I said. I went over to the corner to have a look, and stumbled on Grigory Vasilyevich lying by the wall, all covered in blood he was, and unconscious. So, obviously Dmitry Fyodorovich had been there, and at that point I made up my mind, I resolved to stop hesitating and do it straight away, because even if Grigory Vasilyevich was still alive he wasn't going to see anything while he was lying there unconscious. There was only one risk, sir—that Marfa Ignatyevna might suddenly wake up. I was aware of that at the time, but I was quite breathless with excitement and couldn't stop myself. I went back to the master's window and said, "She's here, she's here, Agrafena Aleksandrovna has come, she's asking for you." And you know, he shook all over, like a baby: "What do you mean, 'here'? Where?" he was mumbling, he still didn't really believe it. "There she is," I said, "standing over there. Open the door!" He looked at me through the window; he didn't know whether to believe me or not and he was afraid to open it—he was afraid of me too, I think. And it's funny; I suddenly had the idea of knocking in full view on the window, to give the signal that Grushenka had come; he didn't seem to believe me when I told him, but as soon as I knocked on the window he rushed to open the door. He opened it. I was going to enter, but he stood there, blocking my way. "Where is she? Where is she?" He was looking at me and trembling all over. Well, I thought, if he's that frightened of me, that doesn't bode well, that's when my legs turned to jelly at the thought that he might not let me in, or he might call out, or Marfa Ignatyevna might come running over, or something else, I don't remember what I thought then; I must have gone quite pale myself, standing in front of him. I whispered, "There she is, over there by the window, don't you see her?" "Fetch her, you fetch her," he replied. "She's afraid," I said, "your shouting frightened her and she's hidden in the bushes. Go and call her yourself from your study." He ran to the study and put a candle in the window. "Grushenka," he shouts, "Grushenka, are you there?" He's shouting all right, but he won't lean out of the window, he won't leave me, from sheer terror, because he's become very frightened of me, so he daren't leave me. "There she is," I said (I went right up to the window and leaned out), "over there in those bushes, she's laughing at you, can you see her?" Suddenly he believed me and began to tremble, terribly infatuated with her, he was, sir, and leaned right out of the window. I grabbed the cast-iron paperweight he had on the table—you remember the one, it must weigh a good three pounds—I lifted it up, and hit him right on top of his head with the corner of it. He didn't even cry out. He just slumped down, and I hit him again, and then a third time. With the third blow, I felt I'd broken his skull. He fell back suddenly, face up, all covered in blood. I looked to see if I had any blood on me, if it had splashed, I wiped the paperweight, put it back, went behind the icons, took the money out of the envelope, and threw the envelope and the ribbon on the floor. I went out into the garden, shaking all over. Straight to the hollow apple tree—you know the one—I'd earmarked it a long time ago, there was already a piece of cloth and some paper there, prepared ages before; I wrapped it all in the paper and then in the cloth, and pushed it right down the hole. And it stayed there for more than two weeks, that money, sir, and I retrieved it when I came out of hospital. I then went back to bed and lay there, so frightened, thinking, "If Grigory Vasilyevich really is dead, things could turn out very badly, but if he's not dead and he recovers, then that will be perfect, because he'll testify that Dmitry Fyodorovich came here, and that'll point to him having committed the murder and stolen the money." Then I started to groan with doubt and impatience, so as to wake Marfa Ignatyevna as soon as possible. At last she got up and she rushed over to me first, then suddenly realized that Grigory Vasilyevich wasn't there and ran outside, and I heard her start screaming in the garden. And that's how it went on all night, sir, and I felt quite reassured.'

He stopped. Ivan had listened to him the whole time in deathly silence, not moving, not taking his eyes off him. Smerdyakov, on the other hand, had glanced at Ivan only occasionally throughout his account, mostly staring to one side. Finishing his story, he himself was obviously disturbed and was breathing heavily. A sweat broke out on his face. It was impossible to guess, however, whether or not he felt any remorse.

'Wait a second,' said Ivan thoughtfully. 'What about that door? If he only opened it to you, how could Grigory have seen it open before? Because, after all, Grigory must have seen it before you were there.'

It is a remarkable fact that Ivan asked this perfectly calmly, in such an amiable tone of voice even, that had anyone opened the door just then and glanced at them, that person would certainly have concluded that they were sitting there having a peaceful discussion about some mundane but interesting matter.

'As to the door and the fact that Grigory Vasilyevich claims to have seen it open, he just thought he did,' Smerdyakov smiled wryly. 'I tell you, he's not a man, he's a stubborn mule; he didn't see anything, he thinks it was open, and you can't convince him otherwise. It's lucky for us that he got that impression, because that makes it quite certain that they'll find Dmitry Fyodorovich guilty in the end.'

'Listen,' said Ivan Fyodorovich, as if he had lost track again and was trying to understand, 'listen... There's a lot I still want to ask you, but I've forgotten what it was... I keep forgetting and losing track... Ah, yes! Just tell me this one thing: why did you open the envelope and leave it there, on the floor? Why didn't you simply take the whole lot, envelope and all?... When you were telling me about it, I got the impression that you were saying you had to do that with the envelope... but I don't understand what the point was...'

'I did it for a reason, sir. Because if someone in the know, like me for example, someone who had seen the money beforehand and maybe had even put it in the envelope himself and, with his own eyes, had seen it being sealed and addressed—if, for the sake of example, that person had committed the murder, would he have stopped to open the envelope after the murder, sir, being in such a hurry and knowing pretty well for certain that the money was in there? Not on your life! Suppose for example I was the murderer, I'd have simply shoved it in my pocket without even thinking of opening it, and bolted with it, sir. Now, for

Dmitry Fyodorovich the situation was quite different; he knew about the envelope only from hearsay, he'd never seen it himself, so if he had pulled it out, supposedly from under the mattress, he'd have opened it on the spot to check whether the money was there, in fact, wouldn't he? And he'd have thrown away the envelope, not realizing he was leaving incriminating evidence, because he's not a habitual thief, never stole a thing in his life, being gentry by birth, sir, and if he'd decided to steal this time it wouldn't really have been stealing, but just claiming his inheritance, because he'd been telling all and sundry, even boasting about it, that he'd recover what was his by rights from Fyodor Pavlovich. I let that idea slip out during my interview with the prosecutor, a bit vaguely, as if I didn't really realize myself what I was telling him, sir, so he'd think he thought it out for himself. That really had the old prosecutor licking his lips, sir...'

'You really mean to tell me you thought all that up on the spot?' exclaimed Ivan Fyodorovich in utter astonishment. He was once more looking at Smerdyakov with horror.

'Oh, come now, you don't imagine one could improvize all that on the spur of the moment? It was all worked out beforehand.'

'Well... well, that means the devil himself must have helped you!' exclaimed Ivan Fyodorovich. 'No, you're no fool, you're a lot cleverer than I thought...'

He stood up with the evident intention of stretching his legs a bit. He was in a state of utter dejection. But as the table was in the way, and he would practically have had to climb over in order to squeeze between the table and the wall, he just turned round on the spot and sat down again. Perhaps it was not being able to stretch his legs that irritated him, for he suddenly shouted out almost as frenziedly as before:

'Listen, you miserable, despicable specimen! Surely you can understand that if I haven't killed you already, it's only because I'm letting you live so that you can answer for your deeds tomorrow, in court. As God is my witness,' Ivan pointed heavenwards, 'perhaps I too was guilty, perhaps I really did harbour a secret wish for... my father's death, but I swear to you, I wasn't as guilty as you think, and perhaps I didn't encourage you at all. No, no, I didn't encourage you! But all the same, I'll testify against myself tomorrow in court, I've decided! I'll tell them everything, everything. But we'll be in the dock together, you and I! And whatever you may say about me in court, whatever evidence you may give—I'll admit everything and I won't be afraid of you; I'll confirm everything you say! But you too must confess before the court! You must, you must, we'll testify together! That's how it will be!'

Ivan pronounced all this solemnly and forcefully, and it was clear simply from his blazing eyes that such was, indeed, his intention.

'You're ill, I can see you're really ill, sir. Your eyes are all yellow, sir,' said Smerdyakov, but without the least irony, and even with a touch of compassion.

'We'll testify together,' repeated Ivan, 'and if you don't, it doesn't matter, I'll testify alone.'

Smerdyakov was silent for a moment, apparently thinking.

'None of that is going to happen, sir, and you won't testify,' he said at last, in a tone that defied contradiction.

'You don't understand me!' Ivan exclaimed reproachfully.

'You'll be taking too much blame on yourself, sir, if you admit to everything yourself. And, moreover, it would be pointless, completely pointless, sir, because I should promptly deny that I ever said anything of the sort to you, and I'd say that either you were suffering from some sort of affliction (and, really, it does seem to be something like that, sir) or that you were so sorry for your poor brother that you were sacrificing yourself for him and had thought up all these things against me, always having thought of me as a fly rather than a human being. So who's going to believe you, and what proof have you got, what single item of proof?'

'Listen, you obviously brought that money out just now to convince me.'

Smerdyakov picked up *Isaac the Syrian*, which was lying on top of the money, and laid it to one side.

'Take this money with you,' he sighed.

'Of course I'm going to take it! But why are you giving it to me, when you killed him to get it?' Ivan looked at him in pained surprise.

'I don't need it at all, sir,' said Smerdyakov haltingly, with a dismissive gesture. 'At first I thought that if I had some money I could start all over again, either in Moscow or, better still, abroad; I got that idea, sir, mainly from "everything is permitted"—it was you who taught me that, sir, because you used to say it a lot—because, if there is no eternal God, then there is no virtue and, what's more, absolutely no need for it. You really meant it. That's what I reckoned.'

'You worked it out all by yourself?' Ivan smiled wryly.

'With your guidance, sir.'

'And now, I suppose, you believe in God, since you've decided not to keep the money?'

'No, sir, I don't believe,' whispered Smerdyakov.

'So why aren't you keeping it?'

'I've had enough... it's not worth it, sir!' Smerdyakov waved his hand in resignation. 'You always used to say that everything is permitted, so why are you so troubled now, sir? You even want to go and testify against yourself... Only it's not going to happen! You're not going to give evidence!' Smerdyakov repeated firmly and with conviction.

'You'll see,' said Ivan.

'It's impossible. You're too intelligent, sir. You love money, I know that, sir, and you love honour, because you're very proud, and you're very susceptible to feminine charms, and above all you like a quiet, comfortable life and not to have to kowtow to anyone—that more than anything, sir. You don't want to ruin your life for ever by shaming yourself in court like that. You're the most like Fyodor Pavlovich, sir; of all the sons, you turned out most like him, you have the same soul.'

'You're no fool,' said Ivan, as if it had just struck him; he flushed and turned crimson. 'I used to think you were stupid. You're serious now!' he remarked, looking at Smerdyakov in something of a different light.

'It was your pride that made you think I was stupid. Take the money, sir.'

Ivan took all three bundles of notes and stuffed them, unwrapped, into his pocket.

'Tomorrow I shall show them to the court,' he said.

'No one will believe you, seeing that you have plenty of money yourself now—you could have taken it out of your cash box and brought it along, sir.'

Ivan stood up.

'I repeat, the only reason I haven't killed you is that I need you tomorrow; understand that and don't forget it!'

'Go on then, sir, kill me. Kill me now,' said Smerdyakov suddenly in an odd tone, and looking strangely at Ivan. 'You daren't even do that, sir,' he added, smiling bitterly, 'you daren't do anything, you who used to be so bold, sir!'

'Till tomorrow!' shouted Ivan, and moved to go.

'Wait... show it to me once more.'

Ivan pulled out the banknotes and showed them to him. Smerdyakov looked at them for about ten seconds.

'Well, off you go,' he said waving him away. 'Ivan Fyodorovich!' he shouted after him suddenly.

'What do you want?' Ivan, already on his way out, turned round.

'Goodbye, sir!'

'See you tomorrow!' Ivan shouted again, and walked out of the house.

It was still snowing heavily. He walked briskly for the first few steps, but then he suddenly began to sway. 'It's something physical,' he thought, smiling. It was as if a kind of joy had entered his soul. He felt a kind of unbounded determination within himself; it was the end of the indecision that had been tormenting him constantly just lately! The decision was made, 'and nothing can change it', he thought happily. At that moment, he stumbled against something and almost fell. He stopped and, looking down at his feet, made out the shape of the little peasant whom he had knocked down earlier, still lying in the same spot, unconscious and not moving. The snow had nearly covered his face already. Ivan suddenly lifted him up and swung him over his shoulder. Seeing a light in a hut on his right, he walked over to it, knocked on the shutter, and requested the man who answered to help him carry the little peasant to the police station, promising to reward him with three roubles on the spot. The man got ready and came out. I shall not describe in detail how Ivan Fyodorovich managed to carry the peasant to the police station, where he demanded that he should be examined immediately by a doctor, for which he again paid generously 'for expenses'. I shall say only that the matter took nearly a whole hour. But Ivan Fyodorovich was well pleased. His thoughts were racing. 'If I hadn't made up my mind so definitely about tomorrow,' he thought suddenly with delight, 'I wouldn't have wasted a whole hour in helping the chap out, I'd have just walked past and not bothered about whether he froze to death... But I'm quite able to look at myself objectively,' he thought, still with great satisfaction, 'and they think I'm going out of my mind!' Arriving at his lodgings, he stopped suddenly, struck by an idea: 'Shouldn't I go straight to the prosecutor now and tell him everything?' Turning back to the house, he resolved the matter: 'Tomorrow we'll tell it all together!' he whispered to himself, and, strange to say, all his joy, all his contentment, evaporated in a flash. When he stepped into his room, something icily cold brushed his heart, like the memory, or rather the reminder, of something painful and disgusting which was there in that very room now, as it had been in the past. He slumped exhausted on the divan. The old woman brought the samovar, he made the tea but did not touch it; he sent the old woman away till the morning. He sat on the divan, feeling dizzy. He felt ill and weak. He began to fall asleep but, feeling anxious, got up and walked up and down to try and keep awake. There were moments when he felt he was delirious. But it was not illness that concerned him most of all; sitting down again, he began to glance around from time to time, as if looking for something. This continued for some time. At last his gaze settled fixedly on one point. Ivan smiled, but an angry, flushed expression suffused his face. He sat for a long time, his head clasped firmly in his hands, gazing intently out of the corner of his eye at the same spot as before, at the divan standing against the opposite wall. Something there was evidently irritating him, some object was disturbing him, tormenting him.

9

THE DEVIL. IVAN FYODOROVICH'S NIGHTMARE

I AM not a doctor, but nevertheless I feel that the time has come when I must, of necessity, explain something of the nature of Ivan Fyodorovich's illness. To start with, I shall say just one thing: he was at that moment, that evening, on the verge of the raging fever that was later to overwhelm his whole system, which had long been fighting a losing battle against illness. Knowing nothing of medicine, I shall nevertheless take the risk of suggesting that by exerting his tremendous will-power, he maybe really had managed to delay the onset of the illness, hoping, it goes without saying, to overcome it altogether. He knew he was not well, but he desperately wanted to avoid being ill now, during those fateful moments of his life when he had to be alert, had to speak out boldly and firmly, and 'justify himself in his own mind'. Anyway, he had been to the Moscow doctor that Katerina Ivanovna, acting on one of her whims, had engaged, as I have mentioned above. The doctor, having listened to his symptoms and examined him, had concluded that he was suffering from some sort of mental disorder, and had not been in the least surprised when Ivan, albeit reluctantly, admitted certain facts. 'Hallucinations are quite normal in your condition,' the doctor had pronounced, 'although we should examine you... in general, it's absolutely essential to begin treatment straight away; there's not a moment to lose, otherwise the prognosis could be unfavourable.' However, Ivan Fyodorovich, after consulting the doctor, had not followed the latter's sensible advice to go to the hospital. 'I'm still on my feet, I feel strong enough for now, and if I collapse, that's another matter, time enough then for treatment,' he had decided, dismissing the problem. And so now he was sitting on the divan, almost conscious himself of his delirium, and, as I have already described, staring fixedly at something on the divan against the opposite wall. Someone was sitting there, having suddenly appeared from God knows where, since he was not already in the room when Ivan Fyodorovich entered on his return from visiting Smerdyakov. He was some sort of gentleman of a typically Russian type, no longer young,

'qui frisait la cinquantaine',* as the French say, with a good head
of fairly long hair, dark but greying, and with a neat, wedge-
shaped beard. He was wearing a sort of brown jacket, obviously
from a good tailor, but threadbare after two or three years' wear
and already completely out of fashion, the sort of thing that
smart, well-to-do men had given up wearing two years ago. His
collar and cuffs, his long, scarf-like cravat, everything was what
a smart gentleman would wear, but on closer inspection the
collar and cuffs were grubby and the thick cravat was badly
frayed. The visitor's check trousers were an excellent fit, but
again these were of too light a colour and too narrow, and no
longer in fashion, and the soft, white felt hat was quite inappropriate for the time of year. In short, he was a picture of
impecunious respectability. The gentleman seemed to belong to
that class of erstwhile indolent landowners who had flourished
under serfdom; he had evidently moved in the *beau monde* and
high society, had at some time had connections, which he still
cultivated perhaps, but, little by little, with the impoverishment
brought about by youthful excesses and the recent abolition of
serfdom, he had degenerated into a kind of hanger-on *comme il
faut*, flitting from one old acquaintance to another, accepted
because of his easy, amenable nature and also because he was,
after all, a respectable man who could be invited to dine in
whatever the company, although of course seated below the salt.
Such hangers-on, gentlemen of amenable nature who can
recount a good tale, make up a hand at cards, and are loath to
undertake any commission one might entrust them with, are
usually unattached—either bachelors or widowers, perhaps with
children, though their children are invariably raised elsewhere
by some aunt or other, the latter never, but never, being
mentioned in polite society by the gentlemen, who affect to be
somewhat embarrassed by such kinship. They gradually become
distanced from their children, receiving the occasional letter
from them on their name-day or at Christmas, and even replying
sometimes. The face of this unexpected visitor was not exactly
friendly, but it was amenable nevertheless, and, depending on
the circumstances, capable of assuming an amiable expression.
The visitor was not wearing a watch, but had a tortoiseshell
lorgnette on a black ribbon. The middle finger of his right hand

was adorned with a massive gold signet-ring with an inexpensive opal. Ivan Fyodorovich maintained an angry silence and refused to engage in conversation. The visitor waited, sitting there exactly like a hanger-on who had come down from his room to take tea with his host, and was meekly maintaining his silence since his host was preoccupied and frowning thoughtfully; he was, however, prepared to engage in any friendly conversation so long as his host began it. Suddenly his face took on a worried expression.

'Listen,' he began, 'excuse me, I only wanted to remind you; you went to Smerdyakov to ask about Katerina Ivanovna, and then left without finding out anything, so I suppose you forgot...'

'Ah, yes!' Ivan burst out suddenly, and his face clouded over, 'yes, I forgot... Anyway, it doesn't matter now, it can wait till tomorrow,' he muttered under his breath. 'And as for you', he addressed the visitor irritably, 'I didn't need reminding, because that's precisely what was bothering me! Your butting in like that made me think you'd jolted my memory, but I'd have remembered it myself, wouldn't I?'

'So don't take any notice of what I said,' the gentleman smiled amiably. 'What's the good of believing against your will? Anyway, when it comes to believing, no proof is any use, least of all material proof. Thomas believed not because he saw the risen Christ, but because he already wanted to believe. Take spiritualists, for example... I've got nothing against them... they think they're doing a service to religion just because devils show their horns to them from the next world. "That", they say, "is proof, material proof, so to speak, that that world exists." The next world and material proof, oh really! And in the final analysis, even if the existence of the devil can be proved, does that prove the existence of God? I want to become a member of a society of idealists; I shall be the opposition: "I'm a realist," I'll say, "not a materialist," he-he-he!'

'Listen,' Ivan Fyodorovich got up suddenly. 'I seem to be quite delirious now... yes, of course, that's it, I'm delirious... say what you like, it's all the same to me! You won't get me worked up, like you did last time. Only I feel ashamed of something somehow... I want to walk about the room... Sometimes I can't see you and I can't even hear your voice, just like last time, but I can always guess what you're rambling on about, because *it's me*

that's talking, I myself, not you! Only I can't remember whether I
was asleep last time or whether I really saw you. I shall soak a
towel in cold water and wrap it round my head, in the vain hope
that you'll disappear.'

Ivan Fyodorovich went into the corner, took a towel, and
carried out his intention, and then, with the wet towel round his
head, began to pace up and down the room.

'I'm glad we've managed to get on friendly terms straight
away,' remarked the visitor.

'Idiot,' laughed Ivan, 'Why on earth should I stand on
ceremony with you? I feel fine now, except that I've got a
headache... only please, don't start philosophizing like last time.
If you won't clear off, say something cheerful. Tell me some
scandal—after all, you're just a parasite, so tell me the latest
gossip. This awful nightmare is all I need! But I'm not afraid of
you. I shan't let you browbeat me. They're not going to cart me
off to the asylum!'

'I say, "parasite", *c'est charmant*.* Yes, you couldn't have put it
better. What am I on this earth, if not a parasite? Incidentally,
I've been listening to you, and I'm a bit surprised: goodness
gracious, it seems you're beginning, little by little, to take me for
something real instead of a figment of your own imagination, as
you insisted last time...'

'Not for a moment do I accept that you really exist,' cried Ivan
furiously. 'You're a lie, you're my illness, you're a ghost. Only I
don't know how to get rid of you, so I can see I'll have to put up
with you for a while. You're a hallucination. You're the embodi-
ment of myself, but only a part of myself... only the stupidest and
nastiest of my thoughts and feelings. As such, I might even find
you interesting if I could afford to waste time on you...'

'With respect, allow me to point out your mistake: earlier,
under the street light, when you got angry with Alyosha you
shouted at him: "You found out from *him*! How could you know
he comes to me?" It was me you meant, wasn't it? It means
therefore that for a little tiny moment you really believed, you
believed in my existence,' the gentleman laughed softly.

'That was just human frailty... but I can't believe in you. I
don't know if I was asleep or awake last time. Perhaps it was only
a dream that time, not reality...'

'And why were you so hard on him, on Alyosha? He's a nice lad; I owe him an apology about Starets Zosima.'

'Shut up, you filthy lackey! Leave Alyosha out of it!' Ivan laughed again.

'Being abusive and laughing at the same time—that's a good sign. Incidentally, you're much more friendly towards me now than last time, and I know why: that great decision...'

'Shut up about the decision,' shouted Ivan fiercely.

'I understand, I understand perfectly, *c'est noble, c'est charmant*,* you're going to protect your brother tomorrow and offer yourself up in sacrifice, *c'est chevaleresque*.'*

'Shut up, or I'll kick you!'

'In one sense I'd be glad, because I'd have achieved my goal: if you start kicking me it means you believe in my reality, because one doesn't kick a ghost, does one? But joking apart, it's all the same to me; be abusive if you want to, but a little bit of politeness wouldn't come amiss, even to me. "Idiot", "filthy lackey"—I ask you, really, fancy using language like that!'

'When I malign you, I malign myself!' Ivan laughed again. 'You are me, only with a different face. You say precisely what I'm already thinking... and you can't possibly tell me anything that's new!'

'If our thoughts coincide, that simply does me credit,' said the gentleman graciously and with dignity.

'You only choose my nasty thoughts and, what's more, the stupid ones. You are stupid and vulgar. You're terribly stupid. No, I will not put up with you! What on earth can I do?' Ivan groaned through clenched teeth.

'All the same, my friend, I want to be a gentleman and to be regarded as such,' began the visitor, with that air of self-importance typical of the true parasite, eager to be obliging and conciliatory from the start. 'I'm poor, and... I don't claim to be particularly honest, but... it's generally accepted by the public at large that I'm a fallen angel. I can't for the life of me imagine how I could ever have been an angel. And if I ever was one, then it was so long ago I could be forgiven for having forgotten. Now I value only my reputation as a respectable man, and I live as best I can and try to be pleasant. I sincerely love people—oh,

I've been much maligned! And when from time to time I live among you here, my life takes on a semblance of actuality and that's what I like most of all. After all, just like you, I suffer from the illusory, and that's why I love your terrestrial reality. Here everything is delineated, formulae and geometry exist, whereas there we have only indeterminate equations! Here I can walk about and dream. I love dreaming. Incidentally, I become superstitious here on earth. Don't laugh, please; that's precisely what I enjoy most of all—the chance to become superstitious. Here I get into all the same habits as you: I've started to enjoy going to the public baths, can you imagine, and I love sitting in the steam with merchants and priests. My dream is to be reincarnated immutably once and for all as the fat, eighteen-stone wife of a merchant, and to believe everything she believes. Honest to goodness, my ideal is to walk into a church and light a candle in all sincerity. Then all my tribulations would be over. Also, I've come to enjoy your therapies; in the spring, there was an outbreak of chickenpox, and I went along to the children's hospital and got myself vaccinated—you can't imagine how happy I was that day: I donated ten roubles towards our Slav brethren!...* You're not listening. You know, you're really not at all yourself today.' The gentleman fell silent for a while. 'I know you went to see that doctor yesterday... so how are you? What did the doctor tell you?'

'Idiot,' snapped Ivan.

'You, on the other hand, are so intelligent. Are you maligning me again? I was enquiring not so much out of sympathy, as just to make conversation. You don't have to answer. My rheumatism's come on again...'

'Idiot,' Ivan repeated once more.

'There you go again, but last year I had such an almighty bout of rheumatism that I still can't forget it.'

'The devil suffering from rheumatism? That's a good one!'

'Why ever not, seeing as I take on human form sometimes? If I adopt the form, I accept the consequences. *Satanas sum et nihil humani a me alienum puto.*'*

'*Satanas sum et nihil humani*... not bad for the devil!'

'I'm glad I've managed to please you at last.'

'My word, you didn't get that from me!' Ivan stopped suddenly, as if thunderstruck. 'That never entered my head. How odd...'

'*C'est du nouveau, n'est-ce pas?** This time I'll come clean and explain. Listen: sometimes when a man is asleep, especially when he has a nightmare (due to indigestion or the like), he has such vivid, realistic, and complex dreams, he sees such events—or rather a whole sequence of events linked by a plot which includes such bizarre details, ranging from the highest flights of the human spirit down to the last button on a shirt-front—that I swear Leo Tolstoy* himself couldn't invent them. And, incidentally, it's not always writers who have such dreams, but perfectly ordinary people too, scribblers, journalists, priests... and there you have the nub of the problem: a certain minister even admitted to me that all his best ideas came to him while he was asleep. Well, that's how it is now. Although I'm a hallucination, nevertheless, as in a nightmare, I say things which are original, things that have never occurred to you before, which means I'm not merely repeating your thoughts and yet at the same time I'm simply your nightmare and nothing else.'

'You're lying. Your aim is precisely to convince me that you exist independently as yourself and not as my nightmare, and now you yourself are insisting that you're a dream.'

'My friend, today I have selected a particular method, which I shall explain to you later. Now, where was I? Oh yes, I caught a cold, not here at your place, but over there...'

'Where over there? Tell me, are you intending to stay long, why don't you just go away?' exclaimed Ivan, almost in despair. He ceased pacing about, sat down on the divan, and once more put his elbows on the table and clasped his head in his hands. He pulled off the wet towel and threw it aside angrily; it had obviously been of no help.

'Your nerves are on edge,' said the gentleman casually, but quite amiably. 'You even resent my being able to catch a cold, but in fact it happened in the most natural way. I was hurrying to a diplomatic soirée at the house of a certain aristocratic lady in St Petersburg who was determined to obtain a ministerial post for her husband. So there I was, in tails, white tie and gloves, but I was God knows where, and I had to travel through all of outer space before I could reach earth... of course, it only takes a moment, but even the sun's rays take all of eight minutes, and so you can imagine me, in tails, waistcoat open at the front. Spirits don't die of cold, but when you've taken on human form, then... well, in a word, I was rather foolish and set off, and you know, up there, in outer space, in the ether, "in the midst of those waters above the firmament",* what a frost!... what am I saying, "frost"? You can't really call it frost, imagine: a hundred and fifty degrees below! The village girls have a little trick: when it's thirty degrees below, they invite a greenhorn to lick an axe, his tongue immediately freezes to the metal, and when the fool tears it away his tongue is raw and bleeding. And that's at thirty below, but at a hundred and fifty below, I should think you'd only have to touch the axe with your finger and there'd be no finger left—that is, if there could be such a thing as an axe out there...'

'And could an axe exist there?' Ivan interjected distractedly, with an air of distaste. With all his might he was trying not to believe in this manifestation of his delirium and to resist descent into total madness.

'Axe?' queried the visitor in surprise.

'Yes, what would become of an axe out there?' shouted Ivan Fyodorovich with a kind of wild and insistent obstinacy.

'What would become of an axe in space? *Quelle idée!** If it were to go too far out, I think it would go into orbit round the earth, without knowing why itself—like a sort of satellite. Astronomers would calculate the rise and setting of the axe, Gatsouk* would enter it in his calendar, that's all.'

'You're stupid, utterly stupid!' said Ivan contrarily. 'If you're going to tell lies show a bit more intelligence, or I'm not going to listen. You want to defeat me with realism, convince me that you exist, but I don't want to believe that you exist! I won't believe it!'

'I'm not lying, it's all true; unfortunately, truth is nearly always dull. I can see you're determined to believe I'm something grand, nay grandiose. It's a great pity, because I give only what I can...'

'Don't start philosophizing, you ass!'

'Fat lot of philosophizing I can do when I'm paralysed all down my right side and wheezing and groaning. I've been to see all the doctors; they're brilliant at diagnosis, they'll diagnose your illness symptom by symptom, but they can't cure you. There was one student fellow, terribly enthusiastic: "If you die," he said to me, "at least you'll know what you died of!" And they have a passion for referring you to specialists: "We", they say, "can only give a diagnosis, but go to such-and-such a specialist, and he'll cure you." I tell you, the old-style doctor who used to cure one of all manner of diseases has completely, totally disappeared, and now we only have specialists who advertise in the papers. If your nose hurts they'll send you to Paris, where, they tell you, there is a European nose specialist. You go to Paris and he examines your nose. "I can only treat your right nostril," he says, "I don't do left nostrils, it's not my field, but when I've finished with you go to Vienna; there's a specialist in left nostrils there who'll finish off the job for you." What can one do? I resorted to folk remedies, and one German doctor advised me to rub myself with honey and salt in the sauna. Any excuse to go to the public baths, so I went, smothered myself with the stuff, but all to no avail. In despair I wrote to Count Mattei* of Milan; he sent me his book and some drops, but I might as well not have bothered. And guess what, it was Hoff's malt extract that cured me! I bought some by chance, drank a bottle and a half, and I was dancing on air, a miracle cure. I was determined to put a thank-you notice in the papers, I was so grateful, and thereby hangs another tale; not a single paper would accept my notice! "It's not on," they said, "no one would believe it, *le diable n'existe point.** Publish it anonymously." Well, what sort of a thank-you would it be if it was anonymous? I joked with the clerks, "It's unfashionable to believe in God these days," I said, "but I'm the devil, it's quite acceptable to believe in me." "We understand," they said, "who doesn't believe in the devil, but it's impossible all the same, it would lower the tone of the paper. Unless you were to make a joke of it?" Well, I didn't think it would be a very witty joke. So they didn't print it. And believe me, that really cut me to the quick. Because of my social position, they refuse to believe I can have fine feelings such as gratitude.'

'You're back to philosophy,' Ivan growled.

'Heaven forbid! But one can't help complaining sometimes. I'm a much maligned person. You keep telling me I'm stupid.

There speaks youth. My friend, it's not only a matter of intelligence! I'm blessed with a kind and cheerful disposition; "I've turned my hand to vaudeville and that sort of thing".* You seem to be determined to cast me as a grey-haired Khlestakov,* but I'm destined for far greater things. I was singled out by some sort of prehistoric decree, which I've never been able to understand, as epitomizing "negation", but in fact I am genuinely kind and just not suited for negation. But no, I have to go forth and negate; without negation there would be no satire, and what's the good of a magazine without a critics' section? Without criticism there'd be nothing but Hosannas. But man cannot live by Hosannas alone, those Hosannas have to be tempered in the crucible of doubt—and all that sort of stuff. Anyway, I don't get involved with all that, it wasn't my idea to create the world, and I'm not responsible for it. But they made me the scapegoat and forced me to contribute to the critics' section, and life took off. We all know it's a comedy; I, for one, make no bones about it, and I've asked to be annihilated. "No," comes the answer, "you have to exist because without you there'd be nothing. If everything on earth were run according to reason, nothing would ever happen. Without you life would be uneventful and that would never do, things have to happen." And so, against my better nature, I do my best to make things happen, I create disorder to order, as it were. In spite of their undoubted intelligence, people take all this charade seriously. And therein lies their tragedy. Well, they suffer of course, but... all the same, they live, they live real lives, not a fantasy: for suffering is the very stuff of life. Without suffering, what pleasure would there be in life? Everything would turn into an endless *Te Deum*— holy, but rather boring. And what about me? I suffer, but I don't live. I am the *x* in an indeterminate equation. I'm a sort of ghostly reflection of life that's completely lost its bearings and has finished by even forgetting what to call itself. You're laughing... no, you're not laughing, you're getting angry again. You're always getting angry, you always want everything to be so logical. But I repeat what I told you before, that I'd gladly give up all this superstellar life, all my ranks and honours, just to become in flesh and spirit some eighteen-stone merchant's wife and light candles in church.'

'So you don't believe in God either?' Ivan laughed spitefully.

'How shall I put it? If you're serious, that is...'

'Is there a God or not?' Ivan shouted with aggressive impetuosity.

'Ah, so you are serious? My dear fellow, honest to God, I don't know. Now doesn't that make you think?'

'You don't know, but you see God? No, you don't exist as yourself, you are *me*, you are *me* and nothing else! You are a nobody, a figment of my imagination!'

'You could say we have the same philosophy, that would be justice. *Je pense donc je suis*,* that much I am sure of; as for the rest, what's around me, all those worlds, God, and even Satan himself—all that is unproven for me, whether it exists of itself or whether it is only an emanation of myself, a logical development of my *self*, which has its own personal and timeless existence... that is to say, I cut short my discourse because I have the impression that you are about to leap up and strike me.'

'I'd rather you told me a funny story!' said Ivan despondently.

'I do just happen to have a good story apropos of what we were discussing, that is, it's not exactly a story, rather a myth. You reproach me for my lack of faith; you say: "you see, but you don't believe." But, my friend, I am not alone in that, you know, all of us up there are troubled, and all on account of your science. While it was just atoms, the five senses and the four elements, everything was sensible and coherent. There were atoms even in the ancient world. And then we heard that you had discovered the "chemical molecule" and "protoplasm" and devil knows what else—that really put the cat among the pigeons up there. All hell broke loose; what with all the superstition and gossip-mongering (we have as much gossip-mongering as you, and more besides), and then finally there were the denunciations, for don't forget, we too have our department of "classified information". So there you are, it's a wild sort of myth from our middle ages—ours not yours—and no one believes it, even amongst us, except some eighteen-stone wife of a merchant, that is—again, ours not yours. Everything you have down here, we have up there too, that's one of our secrets I'm revealing to you as a friend, although it's strictly forbidden. Now here's a legend about paradise. Once upon a time, so the story goes, there lived here on this earth a certain thinker and philosopher who repudiated everything—laws, conscience, faith, and, most importantly, the afterlife. He died expecting to experience only darkness and death, but instead there stretched before him—the afterlife. He was astonished and indignant: "This", he said, "is contrary to my convictions." For that, he was promptly condemned... that is, you see, forgive me, I'm only telling you what I've heard, it's only a legend... he was condemned, you see, to travel the dark void for a quadrillion kilometres (we've gone metric, you know), and when he'd travelled his quadrillion, they opened the gates of paradise and forgave him everything...'

'And what other torments do you have in your world, apart from that quadrillion?' asked Ivan with a strange kind of excitement.

'What torments? Oh, don't ask; we used to have all sorts, but now we've gone over to moral torments, "pangs of conscience" and all that rubbish. We owe that to you too, to your "relaxation of moral standards". And who has benefited? Only the unscrupulous, because what are pangs of conscience to those who have no conscience? On the other hand decent, respectable people who still have consciences and honour have suffered... That's what comes of trying to implement reforms without preparing the ground first, and, moreover, when those reforms are copied from foreign institutions—it does nothing but harm! Give me old-fashioned fire any day. Well, so this philosopher who'd been condemned to travel a quadrillion kilometres stood and looked around for a moment or two, and then lay down in the road: "I don't wish to go any further; I refuse on principle!" Take the soul of an enlightened Russian atheist and mix it with the soul of the prophet Jonah, who sulked for three days and three nights in the belly of a whale, and there you have that thinker lying on the road.'

'What did he lie on?'

'Well, he must have had something to lie on. You're being perfectly serious, are you?'

'Smart fellow!' cried Ivan, still strangely excited. Now he was listening with a curiosity he hadn't expected. 'Well, go on, is he still lying there?'

'Actually, no. He lay there for nearly a thousand years, then he got up and walked away.'

'Stupid ass!' Ivan exclaimed with a nervous laugh, desperately trying to gather his thoughts. 'It would come to much the same thing, wouldn't it—to lie there for eternity or to walk a quadrillion versts? After all, that's a billion years' walking, isn't it?'

'Much more; I haven't got a pencil and paper handy, or I could work it out. Anyway he got there a long time ago, and that's where the story begins.'

'What do you mean, "he got there"? What about the billion years?'

'The trouble is you keep thinking in terms of our present-day earth! But the earth itself may have been recycled a billion times over, perished, withstood the ice age, fissured, crumbled to dust, been reduced to its elements, to "the waters which were above the firmament", then back to a comet, from the comet the sun again, from the sun back to the earth again—that cycle has been repeated endlessly perhaps, and always exactly the same, down to the last detail. It's a dreadful bore...'

'Well, go on, what happened when he got there?'

'As soon as they opened the gates of paradise for him he entered, and scarcely had two seconds passed—according to his watch, you know (although his watch, I should think, must have disintegrated into its basic elements in his pocket long ago)— scarcely had two seconds passed when he cried out that in those two seconds one could walk not a quadrillion but a quadrillion quadrillions to the power of quadrillion! In short he sang a Hosanna, in fact he went so far over the top that some of the more noble-minded thinkers even refused to shake his hand at first; he had espoused conservatism rather too readily. That's your Russian character. As I say, it's just a legend. I offer it to you for what it's worth. There you have the kind of ideas that are current up there.'

'I've caught you out!' shouted Ivan with almost childlike glee, as if he had suddenly remembered everything. 'I made that quadrillion story up myself! I was seventeen, and at high school in Moscow... I made it up and told it to one of my friends, his name was Korovkin... That story is so unusual that there's nowhere I could have picked it up from. I'd forgotten about it... but I'd remembered it unconsciously... I myself, it wasn't you who reminded me! Like one remembers a thousand things, sometimes unconsciously, even on the way to the scaffold... I remembered it in a dream. You are that dream! You're a dream and you don't exist!'

'Judging by the vehemence with which you reject me,' laughed the gentleman, 'I'm sure, nevertheless, that you believe in me.'

'Not at all! Not a hundredth part!'

'But a thousandth part. Perhaps homoeopathic doses are the strongest. Come on, admit that you believe, well, a ten-thousandth part.'

'Not for one minute!' cried Ivan furiously. 'Still, I would like to believe in you,' he added strangely.

'Aha! There's an admission! But I'm a kind chap, I'll give you a bit of help. Listen, it was I who caught you out, not the other way round! I deliberately told you your own story, which you had forgotten, so that you would finally stop believing in me.'

'You're lying! The reason for your appearance here is to convince me that you exist.'

'Precisely. But uncertainty, worry, the conflict between belief and disbelief—all that is sometimes such torture to a conscientious man like yourself that it could be enough to make you hang yourself. Knowing that you did believe in me a bit, I instilled a good dose of doubt in you with that story. I'm feeding you belief and disbelief alternately, and I have my own reasons for that. It's the latest method; when you really have ceased to believe in me, it'll be you who will try to convince me that I am not a dream, that I actually exist; I know you. Then I shall have achieved my aim. And my aim is a noble one. I shall throw you only a tiny seed of faith, and from it will grow an oak tree—such an oak that you, sitting in that tree, will want to go and join the "anchorite fathers and the women without sin",* for that is what you want secretly in your heart of hearts, to eat locusts and drag yourself off to seek salvation in the desert!'

'So, you good-for-nothing, you are working for the salvation of my soul, are you?'

'One has to do a good deed sometimes. You're getting angry, I can see you are!'

'You clown! Have you ever tempted those who eat locusts, who have spent seventy years praying in the desert and are covered in moss?'

'My dear fellow, I've done nothing else. For just such a soul, one would give up the whole world and all the worlds, because it is a jewel without price; one such soul can be worth a whole constellation sometimes—we have our own kind of arithmetic, you know. Such a victory is valuable. Some of those anchorites, I swear, are your intellectual equal, although you don't believe it; they can contemplate such infinities of belief and doubt at one and the same time that, in truth, it sometimes seems as if they are a hair's breadth away from falling "head first", as the actor Gorbunov* says.'

'And did you go off with your tail between your legs?'

'My friend,' remarked the visitor sententiously, 'it's better to go off with one's tail between one's legs than to be without a tail at all sometimes, as a certain marquis commented, under treatment (must have been specialist treatment), to his Jesuit father confessor. I was there, it was positively delightful. "Give me back my tail!" he says. And he beats his breast. "My son," says the priest, avoiding the issue, "everything will be accomplished according to the inscrutable laws of providence, and visible misfortune can sometimes bring great, though invisible, good fortune in its wake. If harsh fate has deprived you of your tail, your good fortune is that for the rest of your life no one will ever take the liberty of saying you have your tail between your legs." "Holy father, that is no consolation!" exclaims the despairing marquis, "I would be only too happy to go through life with an ass's tail, so long as it was in the proper place!" "My son," sighs the priest, "one can't ask providence for all blessings at once, and you are already grumbling at providence, which even in this matter has not forgotten you; for if you claim, as you did just now, that you would be delighted to go through life with an ass's tail, then your wish has already been fulfilled indirectly, for, having lost your own tail you will always, for that reason alone, be wearing the ass's tail..."'

'Lord, how stupid!' cried Ivan.

'My friend, I only wanted to make you laugh, but I swear that that was true Jesuit casuistry, and I swear also that it all happened exactly as I described it to you. It was a fairly recent case and caused me no end of trouble. When he arrived home, the unfortunate young man promptly shot himself the same night; I was with him all the time, right up to the last moment... As for those Jesuit confessional boxes, they are truly my most enjoyable distraction at the more boring moments of my existence. Here's another example, this one happened just a few days ago. A young blonde, only twenty-two, went to an old priest in Normandy. She was a beauty, what a body, an absolute peach—a stunner. She knelt and whispered her confession to the priest through the grill. "What's this, my daughter, have you fallen again?" exclaimed the priest. "Oh, *Sancta Maria*, that I should hear this! It was with him again, was it? How long is this going to go on, and aren't you ashamed?" "*Ah, mon père*,"* replies the sinner, weeping tears of repentance, "*Ça lui fait tant de plaisir et a moi si peu de peine!*"* Well, imagine giving an answer like that! Even I gave up: it was the cry of nature itself, one might even say it surpassed innocence. I gave her absolution on the spot and turned to leave, but I had to go back almost at once. I could hear the priest through the grill making a rendezvous with her for that evening; the old man's faith was as firm as rock, and yet he succumbed in a flash! Nature, the verity of nature had come into its own. What are you turning up your nose for now? Are you getting angry again? I don't know what to say to please you...'

'Leave me alone, you're assailing my brain like a recurring nightmare,' Ivan groaned miserably, helpless before his own vision. 'I'm tired of you, I can't stand this torment any longer! I'd give anything to be able to shoo you away!'

'I keep telling you, moderate your demands, don't ask me for "everything great and wonderful", and you'll see how well you and I will get on,' said the gentleman persuasively. 'Really, you're angry with me for appearing in such an unassuming guise instead of in a red radiance, "amid thunder and lightning" and with blazing wings. Your feelings are hurt, firstly your aesthetic sense, and secondly your pride; how, you say to yourself, can such a great man be visited by such a shabby devil? Yes, you still have a streak of that romanticism which Belinsky* so ridiculed. What's to be done, young man? When I was getting ready to come to you earlier, I did think of coming, by way of a joke, as a retired state councillor who had served in the Caucasus and had been decorated with the order of the Lion and Sun, but I desisted because I knew you would tell me off for wearing just the Star of the Lion and Sun on my tailcoat instead of, at the very least, the Pole Star or Sirius.* And you rant about my being stupid. But, my God, I make no claim to be as intelligent as you. When Mephistopheles appeared to Faust* he claimed to desire only evil, but he did only good. Well, that's up to him, but I'm quite another matter. I may be the only person in the whole of the natural world who loves truth and genuinely desires good. I was there when the crucified word ascended to heaven, bearing in His arms the soul of the robber who was crucified on His right, and I heard the exultant, soaring voices of the cherubim singing and proclaiming "Hosanna", and the resounding peal of ecstasy from the seraphim, which shook the heavens and all creation. And I swear by all that's holy that I wanted to join in with the choir and cry out "Hosanna!" with the rest. The cry was already on my lips, already torn from my breast... as you know, I'm very sensitive and impressionable when it comes to artistic effects. But common sense—oh, that is really the most unfortunate of my attributes—restrained me and kept me within the proper bounds, and the temptation passed! "For what would have been the outcome?" I reflected at that same moment. "What would my Hosannas have led to?" Everything on earth would have been extinguished at once, and that would have been the end of things. And so, purely out of a sense of duty and because of my social position, I felt bound to repress my virtuous impulse and to stick to nefarious deeds. All the credit for virtue goes to someone else, and I'm left with just a handful of dirty tricks. But I do not seek to steal anyone's thunder, I'm not vainglorious. So why am I, alone of all beings in the world, condemned to be cursed by all decent people and even physically kicked by them, since when I take human form I have to accept such consequences too? There's a mystery there, but nobody will tell me the secret for all the tea in China because then, being in the know, I might perhaps suddenly shout out "Hosanna", and at once the requisite negativity in the universe would disappear and order would break out all over the world, and that, it goes without saying, would be the end of everything, even of newspapers and magazines, and of subscribers too. I know that I shall come to terms with the situation in the end, travel my quadrillion kilometres and unravel the mystery. But meanwhile I put a brave

face on it and get on with my mission: I send millions to perdition
to save just one. For instance, how many souls had to be lost and
how many good reputations destroyed in order to entrap one just
man, Job, with whom they caught me out so nastily in the days
of yore? No, as long as the secret has not been revealed, there
are two truths for me: one up there, their truth, which is quite
beyond me for the time being; and the other, my own. And it
remains to be seen which is the better of the two... Have you
fallen asleep?'

'That's for sure!' Ivan groaned. 'You're dishing up as new to
me all that's most stupid in my own nature, all that I've grown
out of, pondered over in my mind and spat out as junk!'

'Oh dear, I've put my foot in it again! And I had hoped to
please you with a literary allusion: I didn't make a bad job of that
"Hosanna" in the heavens, did I? And now you're trying out that
sarcastic tone à la Heine,* that's right, isn't it?'

'No, I was never such a lackey! How could my mind have
spawned a lackey like you?'

'My friend, I know a certain most delightful and charming
young Russian squireling, a young savant* and a great lover of
literature and of *objets d'art*, author of a promising poem called
"The Grand Inquisitor"... That's the fellow I was thinking of!'

'Don't you dare speak of "The Grand Inquisitor"!' cried Ivan
blushing crimson with embarrassment.

'Well, what about "The Geological Cataclysm"?* Remember?
Now that was a poem!'

'Shut up or I'll kill you!'

'Kill me? No, you must excuse me. I must have my say first. I
came to give myself this treat. Oh, I do love the dreams of my
ardent young friends, all trembling with a thirst for life! "There's
a new consciousness afoot there," you decided as long ago as
last spring when you were about to come here. "They want to
destroy everything and go back to anthropophagy. Imbeciles, why
didn't they consult me? In my opinion it's not necessary to
destroy anything except the idea of God in the minds of men,
that's where they should start! With that, yes, one has to start
with that—O ye blind ones, who understand nothing! Once
humanity has unanimously rejected God (and I believe that age
will come to pass in step with the geological ages) then all former

conceptions of the world and, most importantly, all former morality, will collapse of its own accord, without any need for anthropophagy, and then everything will begin anew. People will unite in order to derive from life all that it has to give, but they will seek purely earthly happiness and joy. Man will extol himself spiritually in godlike, titanic pride, and the man-god will be born. Triumphing repeatedly and totally over nature by his will and his science, man will in consequence experience a pleasure so exalted that it will replace for him all his former expectation of heavenly bliss. Every man will discover that he is mortal and that there is no resurrection, and he will accept death proudly and calmly like a god. Out of pride he will desist from protest, accept the transience of life and love his fellow man, expecting nothing in return. Love will satisfy only a moment of life, but the mere consciousness of its brevity will fuel its flames as strongly as it was once dissipated in the hope of an eternal love beyond the grave...", and so on and so forth, and more of the same stuff. Charming!'

Ivan was holding his hands over his ears, and sat staring at the floor, beginning to tremble all over. The voice continued.

'The question now is,' thought my young philosopher, 'is it or is it not possible that such an epoch should ever begin? If yes, then everything has been settled, and humanity will organize itself once and for all. But since, due to the inveterate stupidity of the human race, this would take more than a thousand years, everyone who already knows the truth is entitled to arrange his own life as he pleases and to lay down his own new rules. From this point of view, "everything is permitted". What's more, even if such an epoch never came to pass, nevertheless, since God and immortality do not exist, it would be permissible for the new man to become a man-god, even if he were the only one on the earth to do so, and of course it goes without saying that, in this new capacity he could—with gay abandon, if he so wished— transgress all the former moral strictures by which the man-slave had lived. For God, there is no such thing as law! Wherever God steps, that's His patch! Wherever I step, that's virgin soil upturned... "anything goes"—end of argument! All fine and good; you see, if one has decided to chuck the rule-book aside, why, one may ask, does one need the sanction of truth? But that's what our modern Russian man is like; he's so enamoured of the truth, he can't even cheat without its sanction...'

The visitor talked on, clearly carried along by his own eloquence, speaking more and more loudly and throwing mocking glances at his host, but he did not manage to finish; Ivan suddenly grabbed a glass from the table and flung it at the speaker.

'*Ah, mais c'est bête enfin!*'* exclaimed the latter, leaping up from the divan and flicking drops of water from his clothes. 'You've remembered Luther's ink-well!* You think I'm an apparition, but throwing glasses at apparitions—that's childish! You know, that's just what I suspected; you were only pretending not to listen, but you were really all along...'

Suddenly there was a firm and insistent knocking at the window. Ivan Fyodorovich leapt up.

'You hear that, you'd better open the door,' said the visitor. 'It's your brother Alyosha, and I can tell you he's bringing you some strange and unexpected news!'

'Shut up, you imposter, I knew before you did that it was Alyosha. I had a feeling he would come, and of course he's brought some news; he wouldn't come for nothing!' cried Ivan ecstatically.

'Well go on, let him in! There's a hell of a snowstorm out there, and after all he is your brother. *Monsieur, sait-il le temps qu'il fait? C'est à ne pas mettre un chien dehors...*'*

The knocking continued. Ivan wanted to rush to the window, but he seemed suddenly to be transfixed. He tried desperately to move, but to no avail. The knocking at the window was getting louder and more insistent. At last he broke free and leapt to his feet. He looked round frantically. Both the candles had practically burnt themselves out, the glass that he had just thrown at his visitor was standing right there on the table, and there was no one sitting on the divan opposite him. The knocking at the window, although still insistent, was quieter than it had seemed in his dream—in fact, it was quite discreet.

'That was no dream! No, I swear it wasn't a dream, it all really happened!' cried Ivan Fyodorovich, and he rushed to the window and opened the fanlight.

'Alyosha, I told you not to come!' exclaimed Ivan angrily.

'Quickly, what the hell do you want? Quickly, I said! Did you hear me?'

'Smerdyakov hanged himself an hour ago,' answered Alyosha from outside.

'Come round to the porch, I'll open the door,' said Ivan, and he went to let Alyosha in.

10

'HE SAID THAT!'

ALYOSHA entered and informed Ivan Fyodorovich that just over an hour before Marya Kondratyevna had come running to him at home to tell him that Smerdyakov had committed suicide. 'I just went in to fetch the samovar, and there he was hanging from a nail.' When Alyosha asked her if she had reported it, she replied that she had done nothing, that she had dashed straight to him first of all and had run 'all the way non-stop'. She seemed distraught, said Alyosha, and was shaking like a leaf. When Alyosha ran with her into the house, he found Smerdyakov hanging there. On the table lay a note: 'I am taking my own life of my own free will, so no one should be accused.' Alyosha had left the note where it was on the table, and had gone straight to the chief of police and reported everything, and 'from there I came straight to you,' concluded Alyosha, watching Ivan attentively. All the time he was speaking he did not take his eyes off him, as if struck by something about his expression.

'Ivan,' he exclaimed suddenly, 'I'm sure you're not well! You're looking at me as if you don't understand what I'm saying.'

'It's a good thing you've come,' Ivan said thoughtfully, seeming not to have heard Alyosha's comment. 'But you know I knew he'd hanged himself.'

'Who told you?'

'I don't know who told me. But I knew. Did I really know? Yes, he told me. He was telling me just now...'

Ivan was standing in the middle of the room, talking in the same preoccupied manner and looking at the floor.

'Who's *he*?' asked Alyosha, glancing around involuntarily.

'He's cleared off.'

Ivan raised his head and smiled gently.

'He was afraid of you—of a dove like you. You're "a cherub pure".* Dmitry calls you a cherub. A cherub... The resounding outburst of joy from the seraphim! What is a seraph? Perhaps it's a whole constellation. And maybe the whole constellation is nothing but some sort of molecule... Did you know there's a constellation called the Lion and the Sun?'

'Ivan, sit down!' said Alyosha, frightened, 'sit down on the divan for heaven's sake. You're delirious, rest your head on this cushion, that's right. Do you want a wet towel for your head? It might help.'

'Yes, give me a towel, there's one on that chair, I left it there a short while ago.'

'It's not there. Don't worry, I know where to find one; here we are,' said Alyosha, who had found a clean, folded and still unused towel on Ivan's washstand. Ivan looked at the towel strangely; his memory seemed to return suddenly.

'Wait,' he half rose from the divan, 'just now, only an hour ago, I took that very towel from there and wetted it. I held it to my head and then threw it down here... how can it be dry? There wasn't another one.'

'You held this towel to your head?' asked Alyosha.

'Yes, and I was walking up and down, an hour ago... Why have the candles burnt down so far? What's the time?'

'Nearly twelve.'

'No, no, no!' Ivan shouted suddenly. 'It wasn't a dream! He was here, he was sitting there on that divan. When you knocked on the window, I threw a glass at him... that one... But, just a minute, I was asleep the time before too, but that dream wasn't a dream. I've had them before. Sometimes, Alyosha, I have dreams... but they're not dreams, they actually happen; I walk, I talk and I see... but I'm asleep. But he was here, he was sitting here on that divan... He's terribly stupid, Alyosha, terribly stupid,' Ivan laughed suddenly and began to walk about the room.

'Who's stupid? Who are you talking about, Ivan?' asked Alyosha anxiously.

'The devil! He's started to visit me. He's been here twice, if not three times. He taunted me, claiming that I resented his being just a devil, instead of Satan coming in thunder and lightning with blazing wings. But he isn't Satan, he's lying. He's an impostor. He's just any old devil, a trumpery, petty devil. He goes to the public baths. If you undressed him, you'd be sure to find a tail, a long, smooth one like a Great Dane's, an *arshin* long, brown... Alyosha, you must be frozen, you've been out in the snow, would you like some tea? What? It's cold? Shall I get them to make some more? *C'est à ne pas mettre un chien dehors...*'

Alyosha ran quickly to the washbasin, wetted the towel, persuaded Ivan to sit down again, placed the wet towel on his head, and sat down beside him.

'What were you telling me about Lise earlier?' Ivan started talking again. (He was becoming very loquacious.) 'I like Lise. I said something nasty about her to you. It wasn't true, I like her... I'm worried about what Katya's going to say tomorrow, that's what I'm most worried about. About the future. She'll ditch me tomorrow and trample on me like dirt. She thinks I'm going to destroy Mitya out of jealousy! Yes, that's just what she would think! But it's not like that. Tomorrow will be a Calvary, not a hanging. No, I shan't hang myself. You know, Alyosha, I could never take my own life! You think I wouldn't have the guts? That I'm a coward? No, I'm not a coward. I just have a thirst for life! How did I know that Smerdyakov had hanged himself? Yes, *he* told me...'

'And you're really convinced that someone was sitting here?' asked Alyosha.

'Over there, on that divan, in the corner. You would have scared him off. In fact, you did scare him off; he disappeared when you arrived. I love your face, Alyosha. Did you know that I love your face? But *he*—he is me, Alyosha, myself. Everything that is base and vile and despicable in me! Yes, I'm a "romantic", he pointed that out... although that's just another filthy lie. He's terribly stupid, but that's his strength. He's cunning, cunning as a fox, he knew just how to make me wild. He kept goading me, saying I believed in him, and he made me listen to him. He made a fool of me, as if I were a silly young boy. Still, I have to admit he did tell me a lot about myself. Things I'd never have admitted to myself. You know, Alyosha, you know,' he added with a profound seriousness and somehow confidingly, 'I would much prefer him to be *himself* and not me!'

'You're utterly exhausted,' said Alyosha, looking at his brother sympathetically.

'He provoked me! And you know, he was so damn clever: "Conscience! What's conscience? I make it myself. So why do I suffer remorse? From habit. From the universal, human habit of seven thousand years. Divest ourselves of the habit and we'd be gods." He said that! It was him!'

'But not you, it wasn't you, was it?' said Alyosha, staring at his brother, unable to restrain himself. 'Well then, let him go, forget him. Let him take away everything you now curse, and may he never return!'

'Yes, but he's evil. He was mocking me. He was insolent, Alyosha,' said Ivan, shaking with remembered indignation. 'But he slandered me, he slandered me in a lot of ways. He lied to me—right to my face—about myself. "Oh, you're going to perform a virtuous act, you're going to declare that you killed your father, that the servant killed your father at your instigation..."'

'Ivan,' interrupted Alyosha, 'get a grip on yourself. You didn't kill him; that's not true!'

'That's what he himself said and he knows: "You're going to perform an act of great virtue, and you don't even believe in virtue—that's what keeps eating away at you and tormenting you, that's why you're so vindictive." That's what he told me about myself, and he knows what he's talking about...'

'That's you talking, not him!' broke in Alyosha sadly, 'and you don't know what you're saying, you're delirious, you're just tormenting yourself!'

'No, he knows what he's talking about. "You'll go there tomorrow out of honour," he says, "you'll stand up in court and you'll say: It was I who killed him, and why do you all pretend to be horrified? You're lying! I despise your attitude, I despise your feigned horror." That's what he says about me, and then he suddenly adds: "You know, you want them to praise you: he's a criminal, they'll say, a murderer, but what noble sentiments—he wanted to save his brother, so he confessed!" That's such a lie, Alyosha!' Ivan shouted suddenly, his eyes flashing. 'I don't want the rabble to praise me! It was another one of his filthy lies, Alyosha, I swear to you! And I threw the glass at him for that, and it smashed against his ugly face.'

'Ivan, calm down, forget it,' Alyosha begged him.

'Yes, he knows how to torture, he's cruel,' Ivan went on, not heeding him. 'I always had a good idea what he came for. "Let's assume you decide to attend the trial out of honour, but you still hope they might find some evidence against Smerdyakov and sentence him to penal servitude, and then Mitya would be acquitted and you would only be condemned *morally* (you hear, he was laughing then!), and others would sing your praises. But Smerdyakov's dead, he's hanged himself, and who's going to believe you in court now, you, on your own testimony? And yet you're still going, you'll go, you're determined. So why do you want to go?" It's frightening, Alyosha, I can't bear such questions. Who dares to put such questions to me?'

'Ivan,' interrupted Alyosha, his blood running cold, but still hoping to bring Ivan to his senses, 'how on earth could he talk to you about Smerdyakov's death before I got here, when no one knew about it and there hadn't even been time for anyone to find out?'

'He talked about it,' said Ivan obstinately, refusing to admit any doubt. 'If you want to know, he talked of nothing else. "It would have been quite another matter if you believed in virtue," he says: "If they don't believe me, that's up to them, I shall still go on principle. But anyway you're a swine like Fyodor Pavlovich, so what's virtue to you? What's the point of making the effort to go if your sacrifice does no good to anyone? And when you yourself don't know why you're going! Oh, you yourself would give a lot to know, why you're going! And it's not as if you've made up your mind yet. You'll sit up all night trying to decide whether to go or not. But you'll go all the same, and you know that you'll go, and you know that whatever you decide the decision doesn't depend on you. You'll go because you daren't not go. As to why you don't dare—find that out for yourself, there's a riddle for you!" And he stood up and left. As he left, you came. He called me a coward, Alyosha! *Le mot de l'énigme** is that I'm a coward! "It's not for eagles such as you to soar above the earth!" That's what he said, too! And Smerdyakov said it. I must kill him. Katya despises me, I've known that for a whole month, and Lise will start to despise me! "You're going to testify so that they'll praise you." That's a wicked lie! And you despise me too, Alyosha. Now I'm beginning to hate you again. And the foul murderer, I hate him too! I don't want to save the fiend. Let him rot in Siberia! Fancy him starting to sing a hymn! Tomorrow I shall go there, and I shall stand up and spit in their faces, all of them!'

He leapt up in a frenzy, threw away the towel and resumed pacing round the room. Alyosha recalled the words that Ivan had spoken earlier, 'as if I dream reality... I walk, I talk and I see, but I'm asleep'. That was precisely what seemed to be happening now. Alyosha stayed with him. It occurred to him to fetch the doctor, but he was afraid to leave his brother alone; there was no one he could leave him with. Ivan finally gradually began to lose consciousness. He still carried on talking, talking non-stop, but quite incoherently now. He even failed to articulate his words properly, and suddenly stood still and began to sway violently. Alyosha caught him before he fell. Ivan allowed himself to be led to his bed. Somehow Alyosha managed to undress him and helped him into bed. He himself sat there with him for another two hours or so. The patient slept soundly, without moving, breathing quietly and evenly. Alyosha took a pillow and lay down on the other divan without undressing. As he fell asleep, he prayed for Mitya and for Ivan. He was beginning to understand Ivan's illness: 'The torments of a proud decision—an active conscience!' God, in whom he did not believe, and truth were overwhelming his soul, which still did not want to submit. 'Yes,' the thought occurred to Alyosha as he rested his head on the pillow, 'yes, since Smerdyakov is dead, no one will believe Ivan's testimony; nevertheless, he'll go and testify!' Alyosha smiled gently: 'God will win!' he thought. 'Either he will arise in the light of truth or... he will perish in hatred, taking revenge on himself and on everyone for having done something he doesn't believe in,' Alyosha added bitterly, and again he prayed for Ivan.

BOOK TWELVE
Judicial Mistake

1
THE FATEFUL DAY

AT ten o'clock in the morning of the day after the events I have just described, our district court convened and the trial of Dmitry Karamazov began.

Let me say at the outset, and without any prevarication, that I by no means consider myself competent to describe all that occurred in the courtroom, either in full detail or even with any certainty as to the order of events. I am still of the opinion that were one to recount everything and explain everything properly, one would need a whole book, and an enormous one at that. Let it not be held against me, therefore, if I record only that which made an impression upon me personally and which has particularly stuck in my memory. I may well have confused the essential with the irrelevant and even totally omitted the most important aspects... Still, I realize it is better not to make any excuses. I shall do my level best, and the readers themselves will understand that that was all I could do.

But first, before we enter the courtroom, I shall mention what particularly astonished me that day. To be sure it astonished not just me but, as it subsequently transpired, everyone. The fact of the matter is this: for the past two months, much had been said, surmised, marvelled at, and anticipated in local society, everyone knew that the case had captured the public imagination, and everyone was eagerly awaiting the start of the trial. Everyone also knew that the case had attracted nationwide publicity, yet it was not until the very day of the trial that they realized to what a feverish, burning pitch of excitement people had been aroused, not only in our town but throughout the country. On that day visitors arrived not only from our regional town, but from other

Russian towns too, and even from Moscow and St Petersburg. They included lawyers as well as a number of eminent people and also ladies. All the entrance passes had been eagerly snapped up. Special seating arrangements had been provided behind the judicial bench for the more distinguished and eminent gentlemen spectators; a whole row of reserved chairs had been arranged there, something which had never been done before. There was a particularly large number of lady visitors; I would say that ladies, local as well as those from other parts, made up at least half the audience. Lawyers, from various regions were so numerous that there was hardly room to seat them all since all the passes had already been distributed, begged or spoken for. With my own eyes I saw a barrier being hastily erected at the end of the hall behind the podium to form a temporary enclosure into which all these visiting lawyers were shepherded; to save space, all the chairs had been removed from this enclosure, and everyone congregated in that space remained standing, packed like sardines, shoulder to shoulder, throughout the whole trial, and even the lawyers considered themselves lucky to have standing-room. Some of the ladies, particularly those from out of town, appeared in the gallery in all their finery, but the majority were in normal attire. Their faces revealed a hysterical, avid, almost pathological curiosity. One thing that must be mentioned as particularly striking about the assembled company is that, as numerous subsequent observations in fact confirmed, nearly all the ladies, the vast majority at least, supported Mitya and wanted him to be acquitted—mainly, perhaps, because of his reputation as a ladies' man. They knew that two rival women would take the stand. Katerina Ivanovna in particular intrigued everyone; many remarkable stories were told about her, and many astonishing anecdotes were related about her passion for Mitya, despite his alleged crime. Particular attention was drawn to her haughtiness (she deigned to visit hardly anyone in the town) and to her 'aristocratic connections'. It was said that she intended to appeal to the authorities for permission to accompany the criminal to the penal settlement and to marry him somewhere in the mines, down below. An equal fever of anticipation built up around the expected appearance in court of Katerina Ivanovna's rival, Grushenka. With morbid curiosity, the ladies awaited the moment when the two rivals would meet in court—the proud, aristocratic young girl and the local Jezebel; they knew more about Grushenka, incidentally, than they did about Katerina Ivanovna. The former, the one who 'had brought down Fyodor Pavlovich and his hapless son', they were already acquainted with, and almost without exception they could not help wondering how both father and son could have fallen so deeply in love with 'a most ordinary Russian wench, not even particularly attractive'. In a word, rumour was rife. I know for sure that in our town alone several serious family rows erupted over Mitya. Many of the ladies had quarrelled fiercely with their spouses for holding contrary views about the whole of this tragic affair, and it was quite natural that, as a result, all those husbands came to the courtroom not only ill-disposed towards the accused, but even downright antagonistic towards him. Anyway, it can safely be said that, in contrast to the distaff side, all the men were clearly prejudiced against the accused. One could discern stern, scowling faces—even some, quite a few in fact, thoroughly hostile ones. It is true too that Mitya had managed to insult many of them personally during his stay in the town. Amongst the spectators there were those of course who were entertained by the whole affair and were totally indifferent to Mitya's fate, but not, it must be stressed, to the case itself; everyone was interested in the outcome, and the majority of the men wanted the accused to be punished—apart, perhaps, from the lawyers, who were preoccupied not with the moral issues involved but only with the relevant legal arguments. Everyone was thrilled that the famous Fetyukovich was appearing. His skill was universally recognized, and this was not the first time that he had come to the provinces as counsel for the defence in sensational criminal cases. And, whenever he appeared for the defence, the case always became notorious throughout the whole of Russia and was remembered long after. There were also several contemporary anecdotes about both our prosecutor and the president of the bench. It was said that our prosecutor quaked at the thought of confronting Fetyukovich, that the two were old adversaries going back to the beginning of their careers in St Petersburg, and that our sensitive Ippolit Kyrillovich, who had been harbouring a resentment since his St Petersburg days because his talents had been insufficiently appreciated, had become excited at the prospect of the Karamazov case, even hoping that it would revive his flagging career, and it was also said that Fetyukovich was the only man whom he feared. In suggesting that the prosecutor was quaking at the thought of Fetyukovich, the rumour was not entirely correct. Our prosecutor was not a man to quail in the face of adversity; on the contrary, he belonged to that type whose resolve is strengthened and reinforced the more difficult the situation. On the whole, it should be observed that our prosecutor was rather impetuous and extremely sensitive. There were some cases he would put his heart and soul into, and which he conducted as if his whole fame and fortune depended upon their outcome. This was regarded with some amusement in legal circles since precisely because of this attribute our prosecutor had acquired a certain notoriety which, though by no means universal, was nevertheless far greater than could have been expected given the modest position he held at court. His passion for psychology was the object of particular ridicule. In my opinion everyone was mistaken: our prosecutor, both in his behaviour and in his way of thinking, was far more serious-minded than people thought. It was just that from the very beginning of his career this man, prone to ill-health, had got off on the wrong foot and throughout the whole of his life had been unable to rectify the situation.

As for the president of the bench, one can only say that he was an educated and humane man who knew his job well and professed the most modern ideas. He was far from being devoid of self-esteem, but he was not particularly ambitious professionally. The main goal of his life was to be at the forefront of ideas. In addition, he had connections and capital. As it later transpired, he regarded the Karamazov case with a fair measure of concern, but only in the general sense. He was interested in the case *per se*, in its implications—viewed as a product of our social environment, as an illustration of the Russian character, and so on and so forth. As regards the tragic details of the case itself, as well as the personalities involved, starting with the accused, his attitude was fairly indifferent and objective, which was perhaps just as well.

The courtroom was filled to capacity long before the appearance of the bench. The courtroom in our town is a spacious hall, with a high ceiling and good acoustics. To the right of the bench, who were seated on the podium, was a table and two rows of chairs for the members of the jury. To the left sat the accused and his counsel. In the centre, not far from where the bench sat, stood a table on which the exhibits were displayed.* These included Fyodor Pavlovich's bloodstained, white silk dressing-gown; the fateful brass pestle with which the crime had allegedly been committed; Mitya's shirt with the bloodstained sleeve; his frock-coat, the back pocket of which was stained with blood where he had thrust his bloodstained handkerchief at the time; the handkerchief itself, all caked with blood and discoloured by now; the pistol which Mitya had loaded at Perkhotin's with the intention of committing suicide and which had stealthily been removed from him in Mokroye by Trifon Borisovich; the envelope addressed to Grushenka which had contained the three thousand roubles for her; the thin, pink-coloured ribbon with which it had been tied; and several other items which I no longer remember. Some distance away, behind a barrier in the main body of the hall, were seats for the general public, and several chairs had been placed immediately in front of the barrier for those witnesses who had already given their evidence but who were required to remain in the courtroom. At ten o'clock the bench, made up of the president, a lay member, and an honorary magistrate, entered the hall. They were immediately followed as was customary by the prosecutor. The president was a sturdy, shorter than average, and thick-set man of about fifty, with a bloodshot face, dark, greying, cropped hair, and a red sash—of which order I cannot recollect. Everyone, myself included, noticed that the prosecutor appeared extremely pale, almost sallow; his face in fact appeared to have grown thinner suddenly, almost overnight, as I had last seen him only a day or so previously, when he had been his normal self. The president began by asking the court usher* whether all the members of the jury were present... I can see, however, that I cannot continue in this vein, if only because there are some things that I did not quite catch, others that I failed to grasp, and yet others that I have forgotten, but principally because, as

I have already said above, even if I could remember all that was said and all that took place, I would literally have neither the time nor the space to record it. All I know is that only a few jurors were rejected by either side, that is by either the defence or the prosecution. However, I do remember the twelve who were chosen: four local civil servants, two merchants, and six peasants and townspeople. Even long before the trial, people in our town, especially the women, had been asking with some amazement: 'Is it really true that the fateful verdict in such an intricate, complicated, and psychologically involved case is going to be left to a bunch of clerks and, indeed, peasants? What does an ordinary run-of-the-mill clerk, let alone a peasant, understand?' And, true enough, those four clerks who now found themselves on the jury were minor, low-ranking officials with grey hair (only one of them was somewhat younger), little known in our community, where they eked out a living, in all probability with ageing wives, whom they could never show in public, and a herd of children, very likely barefoot; they frequently whiled away their free time at cards somewhere, and, it goes without saying, had never read a single book in their whole life. As to the two merchants, although they looked imposing enough, they were strangely taciturn and passive—one of them was clean-shaven and dressed in the German fashion; the other, with a little grey beard, sported some kind of a medal on a red ribbon round his neck. About the townspeople and peasants, there is nothing to be said. Our Skotoprigonyevsk townspeople are peasants in all but name, they even till the land. Two of them also wore German-style dress, and it was probably for that reason that they looked filthier and more slovenly than the other four. So the thought really might occur, as it did to me, for example, as soon as I saw them: 'What can this bunch understand of such a matter?' All the same, their faces, stern and louring, created a strangely impressive effect.

At long last the president declared the court in session for the hearing of the case concerning the murder of ex-titular councillor* Fyodor Pavlovich Karamazov—I cannot remember the exact expression he employed. The order was given to bring in the defendant, and the usher escorted Mitya in. There was a hushed silence in the hall; one could hear a pin drop. I cannot speak for the rest of the people present, but Mitya made the worst possible impression on me. The main thing was that he was dressed like a dreadful dandy, in a brand-new frock-coat. I subsequently learned that he had ordered the frock-coat expressly for the trial, from his erstwhile tailor in Moscow, who still kept his measurements. He was wearing a pair of brand-new, black, patent-leather gloves and an elegant shirt. He walked in with his customary long stride, staring straight ahead, and took his seat with a most casual air. Close on his heels followed the counsel for the defence, the famous Fetyukovich, and a suppressed gasp ran through the hall. He was a tall, gaunt man with long, thin legs, extremely long, pale, thin fingers, clean-shaven, with neatly combed, fairly short hair, and thin lips, which occasionally twitched into something resembling a smile. He looked about forty. His face would have been quite pleasant had it not been for his eyes, which were small, lacklustre, and so unusually close-set that they were only divided by the fine outline of his bony, elongated nose. In a word, that face had a peculiarly avian appearance that was disconcerting. He wore tails and a white tie. I well remember the president's preliminary questions to Mitya—that is, regarding his name, his title, and so on. Mitya replied briskly, but so excessively loudly that the president even shook his head and glanced at him with surprise. Next, a list of people summoned by the court was read out, that is, witnesses and experts. The list was a long one; four of the witnesses were absent—Miusov, who by then was in Paris but who had already made his deposition at the preliminary investigation, Mrs Khokhlakova and the landowner Maksimov, due to illness, and Smerdyakov, on account of his sudden demise, of which event police evidence was submitted. The news of this death sent a great flurry of whispering through the hall. Many of the audience, of course, were still unaware of his sudden suicide. But it was Mitya's reaction which occasioned the greatest astonishment; no sooner was the news about Smerdyakov announced than he shouted from his seat, in a voice that was heard throughout the court:

'Serves the dog right!'

I remember his counsel rushing towards him, and the president threatening to take severe measures if this sort of thing occurred once more. Nodding his head and speaking haltingly, but apparently without any trace of remorse, Mitya repeated several times to his counsel:

'All right, all right! Just a slip of the tongue! It won't happen again!'

Naturally, this brief episode did nothing to enhance his reputation in the eyes of the jury or the public. He was showing himself in his true colours, his real nature was revealing itself. Thus the mood was already set when the clerk of the court read out the indictment.

This document was quite brief, but comprehensive. Only the principal charges against the accused were read out. Nevertheless, it made an immense impression upon me. The clerk read it out in a clear, distinct, sonorous voice. Once more, the whole of this tragedy seemed to be thrown into sharp relief and revealed in a merciless and fateful manner. I remember that, immediately the clerk had finished reading, the president asked Mitya in a loud and imposing voice:

'Prisoner, do you plead guilty?'

Mitya suddenly got up from his seat.

'I plead guilty to drunkenness and debauchery,' he pronounced in his overwrought tone of voice, 'and to sloth and disorderliness. Just when I wanted to turn over a new leaf and be a decent man for ever, precisely at that moment, fate dealt me a crushing blow! However, as to that old devil, my father and enemy—I'm not guilty of his death! Nor am I guilty of robbing him—no, no, I am not guilty, nor can I possibly be guilty. Dmitry Karamazov may be a scoundrel, but he's not a thief!'

He sat down after this outburst, visibly shaking all over. The president turned to him once more with a brief but cautionary remark that he should only reply to the questions and not indulge in irrelevant hysterical outbursts. Then he gave orders for the trial to begin. The witnesses were led in to be sworn. This was when I saw them all together. Incidentally, the defendant's brothers were allowed to give evidence without being sworn. After a priest and the president had exhorted them to testify truthfully, the witnesses were told to stand down and were seated apart from one another, where possible. Then they were called one by one.

2

DANGEROUS WITNESSES

I DO not know whether the witnesses for the prosecution and the defence had been divided into categories somehow by the president of the bench, or in what order they were actually meant to be called. I presume there was a definite order of precedence. All I know is that the witnesses for the prosecution were called first. I repeat, I do not intend to describe all the questioning point by point. Furthermore, any description I might give could well prove to be superfluous, because the counsels for both the prosecution and defence, with characteristic skill, brought the whole sequence and essence of the depositions into clear and sharp focus in their speeches. I have recorded in full at least part of each of these two remarkable speeches, and I shall quote from them at the appropriate point; I shall also describe an extraordinary and totally unexpected incident which took place before the proceedings had progressed very far, and which undoubtedly had an ominous and fateful bearing on the outcome of the trial. I shall merely say that from the very first moments of the trial it was evident to all that a particular feature of this 'affair' was the extraordinary strength of the prosecution's case compared to that of the defence. Everyone realized this, in the tense atmosphere of the courtroom, as soon as the facts began to emerge and fall into place, revealing the whole horror of the bloody deed. One could say that it became clear to everyone right from the outset that the case was hardly in dispute, that there could be no room for doubt, that as a matter of fact there was even no need for any examination of the facts, that any examination would only be for the sake of formality, and that the defendant was guilty, guilty beyond all shadow of a doubt. I even think that all the ladies, who without exception were so eager to see this debonair defendant acquitted, were at the same time firmly convinced of his guilt. I would even go so far as to say that they would have been disappointed had there been any doubt about his guilt, since, were the criminal to be acquitted, that would have detracted from the ensuing furore. And that he would be acquitted—of that, strange though it may seem, all the ladies were firmly convinced almost up to the last moment: 'guilty, but he'll be acquitted because of the new ideas and new attitudes which are accepted now', and so on and so forth. It is for this reason in fact that they had flocked here in such excitement. The menfolk, on the other hand, were more interested in the contest between the prosecutor and the renowned Fetyukovich. Everyone marvelled and asked himself what on earth could even such a genius as Fetyukovich do with this hopeless mess of a case. They therefore followed his line of argument step by step with intense concentration. But Fetyukovich, right to the very end, right up to his closing speech, remained a mystery to everyone. Experienced people suspected that he had a strategy, that he had already devised some plan, that he had a specific aim, but what aim it was, was practically impossible to guess. His confidence and self-assurance, however, were very evident. Furthermore, everyone was immediately delighted to see that, in the short time he had been with us, three days at the most, he had managed to gain such an amazing grasp of the case and to have 'studied it in the minutest detail'. People subsequently recounted with relish how, for example, he had managed when necessary to 'hoodwink' all the prosecution's witnesses, to trip them up wherever possible, and, most important of all, to impugn their moral reputation and thereby cast doubt on their evidence. Admittedly it was believed that he was doing this as a challenge, out of a desire to score a legal point, so to speak, and to use every trick in the book, for everyone was convinced that none of this muck-raking would bring him any significant advantage in the end, and he probably knew this better than anyone, though he continued to hold some kind of a stratagem in reserve, some kind of secret weapon which when the time came would suddenly be brought into play. In the meantime, however, conscious of his power, he played cat and mouse. Thus, for example, when Fyodor Pavlovich's former manservant Grigory Vasilyevich brought up the vital evidence about the 'open garden door', the counsel for the defence pounced on him immediately, as soon as it was his turn to cross-examine. It should be noted that Grigory Vasilyevich presented himself before the court with a calm, almost majestic air, and was neither flustered by its *gravitas* nor embarrassed by the large number of people listening to him. He gave his statements confidently, as though he were talking privately to Marfa Ignatyevna, only perhaps a little more respectfully. It was impossible to trip him up. First the prosecutor questioned him at length and in detail about the Karamazov family. Everyone had a clear picture of that family. One could hear and see that the witness was forthright and unbiased. Notwithstanding his deep respect for his former master's memory, he nevertheless stated, for instance, that he had treated Mitya unfairly and that he had not 'brought up the children properly'. 'If it wasn't for me,' he added, describing Mitya's childhood years, 'the little lad would have been eaten alive by fleas.' Nor was it right for the father to cheat his son out of his mother's estate. However, in reply to the prosecutor's question as to what grounds he had for asserting that Fyodor Pavlovich had cheated his son over the settlement, Grigory Vasilyevich to everyone's surprise did not present any actual facts, but nevertheless insisted that the deal with the son was 'incorrect' and that it really was true that 'several thousand more was owed to him'. I must point out, by the way, that the question of whether Fyodor Pavlovich really had swindled Mitya was subsequently put by the prosecutor with great persistence to all material witnesses, including both Alyosha and Ivan Fyodorovich, but not one of the witnesses could give him any precise information; everyone insisted on the fact, but no one could present the least shred of hard evidence. After Grigory had described the scene at the table when Dmitry Fyodorovich burst in and beat his father, threatening to come back and kill him, a sense of gloomy foreboding permeated the hall, the more so since the old servant spoke calmly, succinctly, in his own distinctive style, and to overwhelming effect. Regarding Mitya's assault on him, when he struck him and knocked him down, he said that he was not bitter and had long since forgiven him. Of the deceased Smerdyakov, he said, crossing himself, that the fellow had ability but that he was stupid and suffered from an illness and that, worst of all, he was godless, and that Fyodor Pavlovich and his middle son were responsible for his godlessness. But he vouched almost passionately for Smerdyakov's honesty, and went on to recount the story of how Smerdyakov, finding some money which his master had dropped, had not taken it but had given it to his master, for which the latter had 'rewarded him with a gold coin' and from then on had begun to trust him in everything. However, he stubbornly insisted that the garden door had been open. As a matter of fact, he was questioned at such length that I can no longer remember all of it. At last the counsel for the defence took over the questioning, and began straight away by asking about the envelope in which Fyodor Pavlovich had 'allegedly' put three thousand roubles for a 'certain person'. 'Did you see it yourself—after all, you'd been very close to your master for very many years?' Grigory replied that he had not seen it, nor had he even heard anyone mention such a sum, 'not until now that is, now they've all started talking about it'. Fetyukovich put this question about the envelope to each witness, with the same persistence as the prosecutor had put his question regarding the division of the estate, and he too received the same answer from everyone—no one had actually seen it, although many of them had heard about it. From the very beginning everyone noticed that the defence counsel was placing particular emphasis on this question.

'And now may I ask you, if you don't mind,' Fetyukovich suddenly and unexpectedly changed tack, 'what did it consist of, this balsam, or was it an embrocation, which, as we've learned from the preliminary investigation, you rubbed on your back to try and relieve the pain that evening, before going to sleep?'

Grigory cast a long glance at his interrogator and muttered after a pause:

'It had some sage in it.'

'Only sage? You don't remember anything else?'

'Some plantain, too.'

'And pepper, perhaps?' enquired Fetyukovich with interest.

'There was some pepper, too.'

'Well, well, well. And all this was in vodka?'

'In pure alcohol.'

There was a slight ripple of laughter through the hall.

'Really, so it was in pure alcohol? And, having rubbed your back, did you not then drink the rest of the bottle, to the accompaniment of a certain devout prayer known only to you and your spouse, isn't that so?'

'I did.'

'Did you drink much? Roughly how much? A tot or two?'

'About a tumblerful.'

'As much as that! Perhaps you had a tumbler and a half?'

Grigory fell silent. Something was beginning to dawn upon him.

'A tumbler and a half of pure alcohol—not so bad, eh? With that inside you, you could see the gates of heaven open, never mind the garden door!'

Grigory remained silent. There was another ripple of laughter through the hall. The president fidgeted.

'You wouldn't happen to know for sure', Fetyukovich probed deeper and deeper, 'whether or not you were asleep at the time you saw the garden door open?'

'I was standing up.'

'That still doesn't prove you weren't asleep.' (More prolonged laughter in the hall.) 'Would you, for instance, have been able to reply at that moment if you had been asked about something— say, for example, if you'd been asked what year it was?'

'I don't know about that.'

'And what year is it now—*Anno Domini*, since the birth of Christ—do you know?'

Grigory stood there looking bewildered, staring straight at his torturer. It seemed strange that, apparently, he really did not know what year it was.

'Perhaps you can tell me, then, how many fingers you have on your hand?'

'I am not a free man,' Grigory said suddenly, loudly and distinctly. 'If the gentleman wishes to make fun of me, I'll have to put up with it.'

Fetyukovich seemed a little taken aback; the president intervened and reprovingly reminded him that he should ask more appropriate questions. The counsel for the defence acquiesced, made a dignified bow, and announced that he had no more questions. Of course a nagging doubt could well have been left in the minds of both the jury and the public as to the trustworthiness of one who, while applying his embrocation, could 'see the gates of heaven', and who in addition did not even know what year it was; the counsel for the defence had thereby achieved his aim anyway. But before Grigory left the stand, another incident occurred. The president, turning to the defendant, asked him if he had anything to say in connection with the evidence just given.

'Apart from the door, everything he said was true,' Mitya said loudly. 'For combing out my fleas—I thank him. For forgiving me for assaulting him—I thank him. The old man has been honest all his life and as loyal to my father as seven hundred poodles.'

'Defendant, choose your words more carefully,' the president said sternly.

'I'm not a poodle,' grunted Grigory.

'So I am the poodle then, what does it matter!' shouted Mitya. 'If it offends him, I accept responsibility, and I ask his forgiveness. I was a wild beast and I was cruel to him! I was cruel to Aesop, too.'

'What Aesop?' the president intervened again sternly.

'Well, to Pierrot... to my father, Fyodor Pavlovich.'

The president repeatedly warned him, in the strictest and most emphatic tone, to choose his words more carefully:

'You're only doing yourself harm thereby in the eyes of your judges.'

The counsel for the defence dealt with the witness Rakitin just as skilfully. I should point out that Rakitin was one of the most important and valuable of the prosecution's witnesses. It turned out that he knew everything, an astonishing amount, he had met everyone, had seen everything, had spoken to everyone, had the most detailed knowledge of Fyodor Pavlovich's life and of all the other Karamazovs. True, as regards the envelope containing the three thousand, he had only heard about it from Mitya himself. On the other hand, he gave a detailed account of Mitya's exploits in the *Stolichny Gorod* tavern, recounted all his compromising words and gestures, and repeated the story of Staff Captain Snegiryov's 'Loofah'. When it came to the particular point of whether Fyodor Pavlovich had swindled Mitya when settling the estate, even Rakitin was unable to contribute anything, and he avoided the issue with a few general remarks of a disparaging nature: how could anyone possibly sort out who had been the guilty party amongst that lot, and establish who owed what to whom in such a Karamazovian mess, where no one could understand anything or decide what was what? He saw the whole tragedy of this crime as a product of the archaic morality of the serf law and of a Russia wallowing in disorder and suffering from a lack of adequate institutions. In a word, he was allowed to have his say. This trial gave Rakitin his first opportunity to shine and make an impression; the prosecutor knew that the witness was preparing an article on the crime in question for a magazine, and he subsequently quoted a few ideas from this article in his speech (as we shall see later), thus showing that he was already familiar with it. The picture drawn by the witness was depressing and damning, and went a long way to substantiate the charge. On the whole, Rakitin's testimony made a favourable impression upon the public because of the independence of thought and the exalted sweep of its ideas. There were even one or two isolated outbursts of applause, especially when he came to talk of serfdom and the disorder afflicting the Russian state. However Rakitin, on account of his youthful inexperience, made one small blunder which the counsel for the defence immediately managed to exploit to the full. While replying to certain questions about Grushenka, seduced by his success, of which he was of course already aware, and also by the position of moral superiority to which he aspired, he allowed himself to refer to Agrafena Aleksandrovna somewhat disparagingly as 'Samsonov's kept woman'. He would have given anything to retract this subsequently, since in his cross-examination Fetyukovich seized upon these words to trap him, and all because Rakitin had not reckoned on his having had time to study the case in such intimate detail.

'Would you be kind enough to confirm', began the counsel for the defence with the most cordial and even deferential smile when it was his turn to ask the questions, 'that you are, of course, the selfsame Mr Rakitin whose pamphlet, "The Life of Starets Father Zosima, resting in the Lord", I read recently with such pleasure—that treatise with its excellent and pious dedication to the bishop, published by the episcopal office, and replete with profound religious sentiment?'

'I didn't write it for publication... that came later,' muttered Rakitin, suddenly nonplussed and almost as though ashamed of something.

'Ah, wonderful! A thinker like yourself can, and indeed should, manifest the most detached response to any social phenomenon. Under the patronage of His Grace, your most valuable pamphlet has received a wide circulation and brought considerable overall benefit... But what I would be most curious to know from you is this: you stated just now, didn't you, that you were very closely acquainted with Miss Svetlova?' (The reader should note that Grushenka's surname happened to be 'Svetlova'. I discovered this only for the first time that day during the trial.)

'I cannot be held responsible for all my acquaintances!' Rakitin simply exploded. 'I'm a young man... anyway, how can anyone be held responsible for all those whom one happens to meet?'

'I understand, of course I understand!' exclaimed Fetyukovich, as though embarrassed himself and apparently anxious to make amends. 'You, like any young man, could well have been interested in a young and beautiful woman who readily entertained in her home the flower of the local youth, but... I merely wished to raise one point: we are informed that, about two months ago, Miss Svetlova was extremely anxious to make the acquaintance of the youngest Karamazov, Aleksei Fyodorovich, and that just for bringing him to her, in his monk's habit—that was most important—she promised to give you twenty-five roubles on the spot. This, as we know, took place on the evening of the day that ended in the tragic event that led up to the present case. You took Aleksei Karamazov to Miss Svetlova and—did you then receive that twenty-five roubles as remuneration from Miss Svetlova? That's what I would like you to tell the court.'

'That was a joke... I don't see why it should interest you. I took the money in jest... fully intending to return it later...'

'So you took the money. And, let's face it, you haven't returned it to this day... or have you?'

'That's ludicrous...,' mumbled Rakitin, 'I can't answer such questions... Of course I shall return it.'

The president intervened, but the counsel for the defence announced that he had no more questions for Mr Rakitin. Rakitin stepped down, his escutcheon slightly blotted. The impression of moral superiority conveyed by his speech had been dented, and Fetyukovich, following him with his gaze, appeared to say to the public: 'Well, if that's the type of prosecution witness you're relying on...!' I remember that the incident did not pass without intervention from Mitya either. Enraged by the tone in which Rakitin referred to Grushenka, he suddenly shouted from his seat: 'Bernard!' And then, after Rakitin's cross-examination had been completed, as the president turned to the accused to see if he wished to make any comments, Mitya called out loudly:

'Even after my arrest he was asking me for money! Bloody Bernard! Careerist! He doesn't even believe in God, he's pulled a fast one on his grace!'

Of course, Mitya was called to order again for his outrageous remarks, but Rakitin was now discredited. Staff Captain Snegiryov fared equally badly, but for quite a different reason in this case. He presented himself in clothes that were filthy and in tatters, his boots were covered in dirt, and despite all precautions and a preparatory 'rehearsal' he was quite tipsy. In response to questions relating to the humiliation he had suffered at the hands of Mitya, he suddenly refused to answer.

'Good luck to him. Ilyushechka told me not to say anything. God will repay me for it.'

'Who told you not to say anything? Who are you referring to?'

'Ilyushechka, my little boy: "Daddy, daddy, he really humiliated you!" He said that by the stone. Now he's dying...'

The Staff Captain suddenly began to sob, and threw himself flat on the floor at the president's feet. He was hastily ushered out, accompanied by laughter from the audience. The impression that the prosecutor had wanted to create had been ruined.

The counsel for the defence continued to use every possible trick and to create ever more surprise by his knowledge of the case, down to the minutest detail. For example, Trifon Borisovich's statement made a very strong impression, and was of course highly prejudicial to Mitya. Trifon Borisovich did a quick calculation on his fingers and pronounced that, on his first visit to Mokroye almost a month before the murder, Mitya could not have spent less than three thousand, or as near as makes no difference. 'The amount he frittered away on gypsy girls alone! He didn't just fling fifty-kopeck coins at our lousy yokels, he was doling out at least twenty-rouble notes to them, nothing less.

And the amount of money that was simply stolen! You see, the thieving rogues never left a trace behind, so how on earth could you catch them, especially the way he chucked his money around! I tell you, our people are nothing short of thieves, what do they care for the salvation of their souls. And the money that went on the girls! God Almighty! They're rolling in it now, they didn't even have two kopecks to rub together before, and that's the truth.' In a word, he remembered every item of expenditure and was able to account for every kopeck. Thus, the proposition that only fifteen hundred roubles had been spent and that the other half had been put away in the makeshift purse was becoming untenable. 'I saw it myself, I saw three thousand roubles if it was a kopeck in his hands, with my own eyes, do you think I don't know money when I see it!' Trifon Borisych continued to vociferate, making every effort to ingratiate himself with the 'authorities'. But the counsel for the defence, when he took over, made hardly any attempt to refute this evidence, and unexpectedly began to talk about the hundred roubles that the driver Timofei and the muzhik Akim had picked up off the floor in the entrance hall in Mokroye during Mitya's first binge there, about a month before his arrest; he had dropped it, in his drunken state, and they had handed it over to Trifon Borisych, who had then given them a rouble each for their honesty. 'Well then, did you return this one hundred roubles to Mr Karamazov or not?' No matter how hard Trifon Borisych tried to evade the issue, he eventually had to admit that he had been handed the hundred-rouble note, adding, however, that he had faithfully returned everything to Dmitry Fyodorovich there and then, 'handed it all back to him, honestly I did, but him being very much under the influence at the time, he can probably hardly remember any of it now.' Nevertheless, since before the muzhiks' testimony he had denied finding the hundred roubles, his claim of having returned the money to the tipsy Mitya was treated with a great deal of scepticism. Hence, one of the most dangerous of the prosecution witnesses left the stand under a cloud of suspicion and with his reputation severely tarnished. The same fate befell the Poles, who strutted in proudly and confidently. They announced at the top of their voices that, firstly, they were both 'servants of the crown', and that, secondly, '*Pan* Mitya' had offered them three thousand roubles to buy their honour, and that they themselves had seen a lot of money in his hands. *Pan* Mussjalowicz began by including a lot of Polish words in his answers, and then, noticing that this only increased his standing in the eyes of the president and the prosecutor, abandoned all restraint and spoke entirely in Polish. But Fetyukovich caught them too in his snares; no matter how much Trifon Borisych, who had been called yet again to give evidence, dissembled, he nevertheless had to admit in the end that *Pan* Wrublewski had substituted his own pack of cards for the pack provided, and that *Pan* Mussjalowicz in dealing from the pack had deliberately withheld a card. Kalganov confirmed this when it was his turn to take the stand, and both Poles left rather shamefacedly, even accompanied by some laughter from the public.

The same thing happened to practically all the most dangerous witnesses. Fetyukovich succeeded in impeaching the morals of every one of them, and they all left with their reputations somewhat in tatters. Habitual trial-goers and the lawyers could not help but marvel, and yet they were at a loss to explain what ultimate grand scheme it could all serve, because, I repeat, everyone sensed the irrefutability of the charge, the tragic nature of which was becoming increasingly apparent. However, everyone could see by the self-assurance of the 'great magician' that he was unperturbed, and they watched and waited; 'such a man' would not have come all the way from St Petersburg for nothing, nor would such a man leave empty-handed.

3

MEDICAL EVIDENCE AND A POUND OF NUTS

THE medical evidence did not help the accused to any great extent either. Fetyukovich himself, it turned out later, did not pin much hope on it. As a matter of fact, it had been gathered solely on the insistence of Katerina Ivanovna, who had summoned a famous doctor from Moscow expressly for the trial. The defence could not be disadvantaged by it, of course, and if anything stood to gain. The final result turned out to be somewhat comical, and all because of a divergence of opinion amongst the doctors. The medical panel consisted of the famous doctor from Moscow, our local doctor Herzenstube, and, lastly, the young physician Varvinsky. The last two also appeared as ordinary witnesses for the prosecution.* The first to be called to give evidence as an expert was Herzenstube. He was a strongly built seventy-year-old man of medium height, grey-haired, and with a bald patch. He was greatly admired and respected in the town. He was a conscientious doctor, an admirable person and very religious—a Herrnhuter* of some kind, or a Moravian Brother—I can no longer remember which. He had been living in our town for a very long time, and behaved with extraordinary dignity. He was kind and humane, he treated the poor and the peasants free, attended to them personally in their hovels and huts, and would give them money to buy medicine, but at the same time he was as stubborn as a mule. Once he had got an idea into his head, it was impossible to shift it. Incidentally, it was already well known in the town that, in the two or three days that he had been with us, the doctor from Moscow had made a number of extremely derogatory remarks regarding Doctor Herzenstube's professional competence. The situation was that, even though the Moscow doctor charged not less than twenty-five roubles for a consultation, some of our townspeople were glad of his visit, did not begrudge the money, and rushed to him for advice. All these patients were, of course, previously being treated by Doctor Herzenstube, and the famous doctor had been going around openly and severely criticizing the latter's methods. In the end, arriving at a patient's house, he would ask outright: 'Well, so who's been at work here? Herzenstube?' Doctor Herzenstube had found out about all this, of course. Well, all three doctors took the stand one after the other. Doctor Herzenstube declared straight away that 'the abnormality of the mental faculties of the accused is self-evident'. Then, having presented his reasons, which I shall omit, he added that not only could this abnormality be demonstrated in much of the previous behaviour of the accused but that it was evident even now, at that very instant, and when he was asked to explain how it manifested itself at that very instant, the old doctor, with the utmost professional integrity, pointed out the peculiar and, under the circumstances, unexpected manner in which the accused had entered the hall, striding in like a soldier and keeping his eyes fixed straight ahead, whereas one might have expected him to look to the left, 'where there are ladies sitting among the public, because he is a great admirer of the fair sex, and has much to consider what the ladies of him now might say,' concluded the old man in his own peculiar style. I must add that he spoke Russian fluently and volubly, but that all his sentences ended up sounding Germanic, which incidentally never perturbed him in the least, since during the whole of his life he had insisted on regarding his Russian as exemplary, 'better even than that of the Russians', and was even very fond of quoting Russian proverbs, maintaining that Russian proverbs were the best and most expressive in the world. I should also mention that in conversation, possibly due to some kind of absent-mindedness, he often forgot the most ordinary words, which he knew perfectly well but which for some reason would suddenly escape him. The same thing would happen, incidentally, when he spoke German; he would gesticulate in front of his face with his hand, as though seeking to take hold of the missing word, and no one would be able to persuade him to continue speaking until he had found it. His remark about having expected the accused, on entering the hall, to glance at the ladies provoked a ripple of whispering and giggling amongst the public. All the ladies in our town were very fond of the dear old doctor, and they knew that, as a confirmed bachelor, he had led a pious and chaste life and that he had an exalted, idealized view of women. Hence his unexpected remark struck everyone as extremely odd.

The Moscow doctor, when his turn came to testify, confirmed brusquely and confidently that he considered the mental condition of the accused to be impaired, 'very much so, in fact'. He spoke at length and very learnedly of 'mental impairment' and 'mania', and argued that, according to all the available information, the accused had undoubtedly been suffering from temporary insanity for several days before his arrest, that even if he had committed the crime it had been almost involuntary, and that even though he had been aware of it, he had been totally incapable of resisting the pathological urge which had overcome him. But apart from temporary insanity, the doctor also detected signs of mania, which, according to him, directly presaged total insanity. (NB. I am retelling this in my own words, whereas the doctor expressed himself very cleverly, using medical terminology.) 'All his actions are contrary to sound sense and logic,' he went on. 'I'm not talking about what I did not see, that is, about the actual crime and this whole tragedy, but even during his conversation with me the day before yesterday he had an inexplicably staring look in his eyes. He kept laughing unexpectedly and totally inappropriately. He manifested a constant and irrational irritation, and he used strange words such as "Bernard", "ethics", and others which were quite inappropriate.' But, in the doctor's view, the chief symptom of this mania was the inability of the accused to talk about the three thousand roubles of which he considered himself to have been cheated, without somehow becoming excessively irritated, whereas he spoke fairly coherently when recalling any of his other grievances and misfortunes. Towards the end, every time the subject of the three thousand roubles was raised during questioning, he would invariably lapse into a kind of frenzy, and yet he was said to be unselfish and generous. 'As regards my learned colleague's opinion', the doctor from Moscow added, in passing, at the end of his speech, 'that the accused, on entering the courtroom, could have been expected to glance at the ladies rather than to look straight ahead, I shall only say that, quite apart from being frivolous, such a conclusion is also fundamentally erroneous, for though I quite agree that, on entering the place where his fate was to be decided, the accused should not have been staring straight ahead, and that this could in fact have been interpreted at that particular moment as a sign of his disturbed mental state, I would maintain with respect that rather than looking to the left at the ladies he might instead have been expected to look in precisely the opposite direction, namely to the right, in an attempt to make eye-contact with his counsel, whose advocacy represents his only hope and on whose skill the whole of his fate now hangs.' The doctor expressed his opinion in a decisive and forthright manner. But it was Doctor Varvinsky, the last to give evidence, who advanced an unexpected deduction that lent a particularly comical element to the divergence of opinion between the two learned experts. In his view the accused had been—and indeed still was—perfectly sane, and the fact that prior to his arrest he had been in a nervous and extremely agitated state could be attributed to a large number of perfectly obvious causes: jealousy, anger, his constant state of inebriation, and so on. Under no circumstances, however, could this nervous state have been symptomatic of any particular 'mental impairment' such as had just been referred to. As to the question of whether the accused should have looked left or right on entering the courtroom, it was his 'humble opinion' that the accused should have looked straight ahead, as in actual fact he did, to where the president and the rest of the bench were sitting, for it was on them that his whole fate now depended, 'hence it was precisely by looking straight ahead that he proved he was perfectly sane at that particular juncture,' concluded the young physician. He had delivered his 'humble' opinion with some fervour.

'Well said, doctor!' Mitya yelled out from where he was sitting. 'You're perfectly right!'

Mitya was not allowed to continue, of course, but the young doctor's views had the most decisive effect on both the bench and the public, because, as it transpired later, everyone was in agreement with him. Incidentally, Doctor Herzenstube, now testifying as an ordinary witness, suddenly and quite unexpectedly did Mitya a good turn. As a long-time resident of our town who had known the Karamazov family for many years, he made a number of comments which were of great interest to the prosecution, and then all of a sudden added, as though he had just realized something:

'And then again, this poor young man could have been dealt an incomparably better fate, because he had a kind heart when he was a child, and afterwards, too, I know he did. But the Russian proverb says: If one man has a good head, that is fine, but if another clever person joins him, it will be even better, because then there will be two heads, and not just one...'

'Two heads are better than one,' prompted the prosecutor, running out of patience. He was only too familiar with the old man's habit of speaking slowly and long-windedly, regardless of the impression he was creating or of the strain he was putting on others' patience; the old man, on the contrary, being inordinately proud of his unsophisticated and ever-cheerfully smug Germanic sense of humour, loved to show off his wit.

'Oh, *ja-ja*, that is what I say, too,' he acquiesced eagerly, 'one head is good, but two is much better. But he did not have the benefit of another head, and he allowed his own to... How was it again, what did he let his head to do? This word—what did he let it to do, I have forgotten,' he continued, gesticulating with his hand in front of his eyes, 'oh, *ja*, *spazieren*.'

'To wander off?'

'That's right, to wander off, that's what I mean. His mind just wandered off and ended up in such a remote place, where it was totally lost. And yet he is a noble and sensitive young man, oh, I remember him very well when he was still just a tot, abandoned in the backyard of his father's house, running around without any shoes, his trousers hanging on by just one button.'

A sensitive and compassionate note had entered his voice. Fetyukovich pricked up his ears, as though expecting something, and began to pay attention.

'Oh yes, I was still a young man then... I... well, yes, I was then forty-five years old and I just arrived here. And I became very sorry for the little lad, and I wondered if I could buy him a pound of... what was it?... a pound of what? I have forgotten, what they are called... a pound of what children are very fond of, what do you call them—well, you know...', the doctor started to gesticulate again, 'they grow on trees, and they are picked and given as presents to everybody...'

'Apples?'

'Oh n-no-o no! A pound, a pound! Apples are sold by the dozen, not by the pound... no, there are many of them and they are all small, you put them in your mouth and cr-rr-ack...!'

'Nuts?'

'Of course, "nuts", that's what I mean,' the doctor confirmed in the most matter-of-fact way, as though he had not had any difficulty at all in finding the right word, 'and I bought him a pound of nuts, because no one had ever bought the boy a pound of nuts before, and I raised my finger and said to him: "My boy! *Gott der Vater*," and he laughed and said: "*Gott der Vater*." "*Gott der Sohn*." He laughed again and babbled: "*Gott der Sohn*." "*Gott der Heilige Geist*." Then he laughed again and repeated, as best he could: "*Gott der Heilige Geist*." And then I left. I was passing by two days later, and there he was, calling out to me of his own accord: "Uncle, *Gott der Vater, Gott der Sohn*," the only thing he forgot was "*Gott der Heilige Geist*"* but I remembered it to him, and again I felt very sorry for him. But he was taken away, and I did not see him any more. And so twenty-three years passed; my head already white, I was sitting in my surgery one morning, and suddenly in comes a young man in full bloom whom I just could not recognize, but he raised his finger and said, laughing: "*Gott der Vater, Gott der Sohn und Gott der Heilige Geist*! I have just arrived and came to thank you for the pound of nuts, because no one had ever bought me a pound of nuts before, and you were the only one who bought me a pound of nuts." And then I remembered my own happy youth and the poor boy without boots in the yard, and my heart was moved, and I said: "You are a grateful young man, for you have remembered all your life that pound of nuts which I bought you in your childhood." And I embraced him and blessed him. And I began to cry. He was laughing, but he also was crying... because a Russian will often laugh where it is necessary to cry. He was crying, I could see it. But now, alas!...'

'And I'm crying now too, my good German, I'm crying now too, you dear old man!' Mitya shouted out suddenly, from where he was sitting.

Be that as it may, the little anecdote produced quite a favourable reaction amongst the public. But the thing that swayed opinion in Mitya's favour most of all was Katerina Ivanovna's statement, to which I shall come in a moment. On the whole, though, after the witnesses *à décharge*—that is, those called by the defence—began to take the stand, fate suddenly seemed to smile upon Mitya, unmistakably and—this was most extraordinary—even against the expectation of the defence. But before Katerina Ivanovna's testimony Alyosha gave his evidence, and he suddenly recalled one more fact which seemed to refute one of the salient points of the prosecution's case.

4

FORTUNE SMILES ON MITYA

THIS came as a total surprise, even to Alyosha himself. He was called as a witness but without having to take the oath,* and I recall that, from the very beginning of his testimony, he was treated extremely kindly and sympathetically. It was evident that he enjoyed a good reputation. Alyosha testified calmly and with restraint, but every now and again an ardent sympathy for his hapless brother surfaced in his testimony. Replying to one particular question, he portrayed his brother as being perhaps impetuous and given to outbursts of passion, but at the same time noble, exalted, and magnanimous, and even prepared to make sacrifices if he were called upon so to do. He admitted, however, that towards the end, because of his passion for Grushenka and his rivalry with his father on this score, Mitya had been in an unbearable situation. Nevertheless, he indignantly rejected even the suggestion that his brother could have committed the murder with robbery in mind, although he had to admit, however, that the three thousand roubles which Mitya considered to be the rightful inheritance of which his father had illegally deprived him had somehow become an obsession in his mind, and that while being in no way avaricious he was quite incapable of even mentioning the three thousand without flying into a rage. Concerning the matter of the rivalry between the two 'ladies', as the prosecutor chose to call them—that is to say, Grushenka and Katya—he replied evasively, and even refused categorically to answer one or two questions.

'Did your brother ever tell you that he intended to kill his father?' asked the prosecutor. 'You don't have to reply, of course,' he added.

'He didn't say it directly,' replied Alyosha.

'How then? Indirectly?'

'He once told me about his personal hatred towards father and that he was afraid that... in desperation... in a fit of revulsion... he could maybe kill him.'

'And when you heard this, did you believe it?'

'I'm afraid I have to say that I did. But I was convinced that his better self would always protect him at the critical moment, as in fact it did, because it was *not he* who killed father,' Alyosha concluded firmly in a loud voice that echoed throughout the hall. The prosecutor shuddered like a horse in battle on hearing a trumpet-call.

'Rest assured that I believe totally in the sincerity of your conviction, without identifying or confusing it in any way with your love for your unfortunate brother. Your personal interpretation of this whole family tragedy is already known to us from the preliminary hearing. To be frank, it is highly unorthodox and runs counter to all other testimony which the prosecution has heard. I therefore find it necessary to urge you to indicate precisely which factors led you finally to conclude that your brother was innocent and that the guilty party was in fact a completely different person, whom you named at the preliminary hearing?'

'I merely answered questions at the preliminary hearing,' Alyosha said calmly and softly, 'and I did not myself set out to accuse Smerdyakov.'

'Nevertheless, you did mention him by name?'

'Only because my brother Dmitry had already done so. I had been told before I was questioned that when he was arrested, Mitya himself had accused Smerdyakov. I believe totally that my brother is innocent. And since it wasn't he who committed the murder, it must have been...'

'Smerdyakov? Why necessarily Smerdyakov? And what makes you so absolutely sure that your brother is innocent?'

'I could not help believing my brother. I know he would not lie to me. I could see by his face that he was telling the truth.'

'Just by his face? Is that all the proof you have?'

'I've no other proof.'

'And as regards your accusation against Smerdyakov, you also have no proof other than your brother's words and the expression on his face?'

'No. I've no other proof.'

The prosecutor had no more questions. Alyosha's replies appeared to have had a most disappointing effect upon the public. Even before the trial began there had already been talk of Smerdyakov in our town: someone had heard something;

someone had hinted at something; it was said that Alyosha had adduced some extraordinary evidence exonerating his brother and incriminating the servant; but when it came to it—nothing, no evidence whatsoever, only some moral conviction which was only natural, given that he was the brother of the accused.

Then Fetyukovich began his cross-examination. When he asked Alyosha precisely when the accused had told him of his hatred for his father and that he might kill him, and whether he, Alyosha, had heard him say this during their last meeting before the tragedy, Alyosha seemed to shudder suddenly, as though he had only just remembered and understood something.

'There's one thing that comes back to me now, I'd nearly forgotten about it, it was so unclear to me at the time, whereas now...'

And Alyosha recalled with elation—for indeed the idea seemed to have occurred to him suddenly, just at that moment —how, during his last meeting with Mitya that evening by the tree on the way to the monastery, Mitya, beating his breast, 'the upper part of the chest', had told him several times that he had the means to regain his honour, that the means were there, lying right there against his chest... 'I thought at the time that the way he struck his chest, he meant his heart,' Alyosha continued, 'and that he could find the strength in his heart to overcome some great ignominy which was threatening him, and which he did not dare to admit even to me. I must say that at the time I thought he was talking about father and about how the mere thought of going to father and assaulting him made him shudder at the sheer infamy of it, and yet at the same time he seemed to be pointing to his upper chest, so that, as I recall, the thought flashed through my mind at that moment that the heart isn't in that part of the chest at all, it's lower down, whereas the place he was indicating was right here, just below his neck, and he kept pointing to that one spot. At the time the idea struck me as being silly, but he may indeed have been pointing to the purse in which he had sewn the fifteen hundred roubles...!'

'That's right!' Mitya suddenly shouted from where he was sitting. 'That's just how it was, Alyosha, you're right, that's just what I was doing!'

Fetyukovich quickly hurried over to him, begging him to stay calm, and immediately inundated Alyosha with questions. Alyosha, heartened by what he had just recalled, gave an impassioned exposition of his theory, namely that in all probability Mitya's shame was due to the fact that, despite having on his person the fifteen hundred roubles which he owed Katerina Ivanovna and which he could have returned to her, he had nevertheless decided not to return it but to use it for another purpose, namely to finance his escape with Grushenka if she agreed to come with him...

'That's it, that's precisely how it was,' exclaimed Alyosha suddenly excited, 'he really did keep on insisting that he could have expiated half his shame just like that (he repeated several times: *half*!), but that he was so miserably weak-willed that he knew he wouldn't do it... he knew all along that he couldn't do it, he simply hadn't got the will-power to do it!'

'And you remember clearly and distinctly that he pointed there, exactly there on his chest?' Fetyukovich probed eagerly.

'I do indeed, because it went through my mind at the time: why is he pointing so high up, when the heart is lower down, but the thought immediately struck me as silly... I remember it striking me as silly... it did flash through my mind. That's precisely why I remembered it now. How on earth could I have forgotten it till this moment! It was definitely the purse that he was pointing to, meaning that he wasn't going to return the fifteen hundred roubles, even though he could! And that's just what he shouted when he was arrested in Mokroye—I know he did, someone told me—he shouted that it was the most shameful thing in his whole life, that is, having the means to repay half (note, half!) his debt to Katerina Ivanovna and thus ceasing to be a thief in her eyes, and yet knowing that he didn't have the courage to return it, and choosing to stay a thief in her eyes rather than return the money! What he must have gone through, the suffering that his debt must have caused him!' exclaimed Alyosha in conclusion.

Naturally, the prosecutor also wanted to have his say. He asked Alyosha to describe how it all happened once more, and insisted on asking several times whether the accused really had been striking his chest to indicate something. Couldn't he, perhaps, have been simply hitting himself on the chest with his fist, and nothing more?

'It wasn't his fist!' Alyosha exclaimed. 'It was definitely his fingers he was pointing with, and he was pointing here, very high up... But how on earth could I have totally forgotten about it right up to this moment!'

The president turned to Mitya to ask him if he had any comments to make on what had just been said. Mitya confirmed that that was precisely how it had been, that he had been pointing precisely to the money, that it had been hanging there round his neck, and that it was, of course, shameful, 'it was shameful, and I don't deny it, the most ignoble act of my whole life!' shouted Mitya. 'I could have given it back, but I kept it instead. Rather than give it back I preferred to remain a thief in her eyes, and the most ignominious part about it was that I knew full well in advance that I wouldn't give it back! Alyosha's right! Thank you, Alyosha!'

That was the end of Alyosha's cross-examination. The important and significant point was that at least one fact, at least one piece of evidence, however small, a mere suggestion of evidence had emerged which went to prove that the purse really had existed, that it had contained fifteen hundred roubles, and that the accused had not been lying at the preliminary hearing in Mokroye when he announced that the fifteen hundred were his. Alyosha was delighted; his cheeks flushed, and he went and sat down as directed. For a long time he kept on repeating to himself: 'How could I have forgotten it? How could it have happened? And how was it that it all came back to me suddenly just now?'

It was now Katerina Ivanovna's turn to be cross-examined. As soon as she appeared, a wave of excitement rippled through the courtroom. The ladies reached for their lorgnettes and opera-glasses, the men began to stir, some stood up to get a better view. Everyone maintained subsequently that, immediately she entered, Mitya went as white as a sheet. Dressed all in black, she approached—diffidently and almost meekly—the seat allocated for the witnesses. One could not have guessed from her face that she was agitated, but there was a glint of determination in her dark, sombre gaze. It should be pointed out that very many people said later that she appeared extraordinarily beautiful at that moment. She spoke softly, but clearly enough to be heard throughout the hall. Her voice was very steady—or, at least, she made every effort to keep it steady. The president began his questioning cautiously and with extreme deference, as though afraid to broach 'certain matters', and sensitive to her great misfortune. But the first thing Katerina Ivanovna herself said when the questioning began was that she had been the fiancée of the accused 'until he himself left me...', she added softly. When asked about the three thousand roubles entrusted to Mitya for posting to her relatives, she said firmly: 'I didn't mean him to go straight to the post office with the money; I had a feeling that he was in financial difficulties then... just at that time... I gave him the three thousand on the understanding that he need not post it for a month if he so wished. There was no need for him to have worried himself so much over the debt afterwards...'

I am not recounting every question in detail, but am merely giving the essential content of her testimony.

'I was always firmly convinced that he would post the three thousand as soon as he received the money from his father,' she continued in reply to the questions. 'I was always convinced of his generosity and honesty... absolute honesty... in financial matters. He was firmly convinced he was going to receive three thousand roubles from his father, and he mentioned it to me several times. I knew that he was in dispute with his father, and I have always been and am still convinced that his father wronged him. I cannot recall any threats he might have made against his father. He never said anything at all about threats—at least not in my presence. Had he come to me at the time, I'd immediately have set his mind at rest about the miserable three thousand that he owed me, but he didn't come to see me any more... and I myself... I was placed in such a position... that I couldn't ask him to come and see me... Anyway,' she added suddenly with a very determined note in her voice, 'I had no right to make any demands on him regarding this debt. He once lent me even more than three thousand roubles, and I accepted it in spite of the fact that at the time I couldn't even foresee that I'd ever be in a position to repay it...'

One could detect a certain note of a challenge in her voice. Now it was Fetyukovich's turn to cross-examine her.

'Would this have been at the start of your relationship, before you moved to this town?' asked Fetyukovich, immediately sensing a possible advantage and treading carefully. (I shall observe in passing that though Katerina Ivanovna herself had summoned him specially from St Petersburg, he nevertheless knew nothing of the five thousand roubles which Mitya had given her at that time, nor of that obeisant curtsy. She had not told him about this secret! That was astonishing. It can safely be assumed that she herself had not known right up to the last moment whether she would mention this episode in court, and had been waiting for some kind of inspiration.)

No, I shall never forget that moment! She described *every-thing*—the whole of the episode that Mitya had recounted to Alyosha, including the curtsy, the reasons for it all, and about her father—she recounted everything about going to see Mitya, but not a word, not the slightest hint, that Mitya himself had suggested that her sister 'send Katerina Ivanovna to him to borrow the money'. She magnanimously concealed this, and fearlessly disclosed the fact that it was she, she herself, who at that time had come running to the young officer of her own volition, hoping for something... to beg him for some money. The effect was quite shattering. Shivers ran down my spine as I listened, one could have heard a pin drop in the courtroom as everyone strained to catch each word. Here was something quite unexpected; even from such a wilful, arrogantly proud young girl, one could hardly have expected such candid testimony, such sacrifice, such total self-immolation. And to what end, for whom? In order to save the man who had betrayed and wronged her, in order to contribute, in however small a way, to his salvation by showing him in a good light! And of course the image of the officer giving away his last five thousand roubles—all his worldly possessions—bowing respectfully before the innocent girl, turned out to be very moving and appealing, but... my heart shuddered painfully! I felt that it could lead to malicious gossip, as indeed it did! The whole town soon began to laugh spitefully and to say that the story was maybe not altogether accurate, especially when the officer had let the young girl go, allegedly with 'just a respectful bow'. It was hinted that something had been 'omitted'. And, even if nothing had been omitted, if everything was true, said the most respectable of our ladies, even then it was far from certain whether it was 'proper for a girl to do such a thing, even to save her father'. And how could Katerina Ivanovna with her intelligence, her sharp acumen, not have foreseen that there would be such gossip? She must have foreseen it, but she had decided to reveal everything all the same! Of course, all these malicious speculations about the truth of the story only arose later, and the initial effect was stupendous. As for the bench, they listened to Katerina Ivanovna in deferential, one might almost say embarrassed, silence. The prosecutor did not permit himself a single further question on this matter. Fetyukovich bowed deeply to her. Oh, he was almost triumphant! A great victory had been won: that a man would give away his last five thousand roubles on a noble impulse, and that the same man would then go, in the night, to kill his father and rob him of three thousand—that was, to say the least, inconsistent. If nothing else, Fetyukovich could now dismiss robbery as a motive. The case suddenly appeared in quite a new light. There was a wave of sympathy for Mitya. It was said that once or twice during Katerina Ivanovna's statement he jumped to his feet and then finally slumped back on the seat and buried his face in his hands. But after she had finished he suddenly cried out in a despairing voice, his hands outstretched towards her:

'Katya, why have you done this to me!' and started to sob loudly. However, he checked himself instantly and again cried out:

'Now there's no hope for me!'

With that, he clenched his teeth, folded his arms, and sat perfectly still. Katerina Ivanovna remained in the hall, sitting on one of the reserved chairs. She was pale and she gazed down. Those who were near her remembered that she was shaking for a long time, as though suffering from a fever. Grushenka now took the stand.

I shall soon be coming to the tragedy which, occurring as unexpectedly as it did, was in all probability responsible for Mitya's downfall. For I, like everyone else, am convinced—and all the lawyers subsequently agreed on this point—that had it not been for a certain incident, the accused would at least have received a lighter sentence. But I am coming to that. Only first, a couple of words about Grushenka.

She too entered the courtroom dressed all in black, her exquisite black shawl draped around her shoulders. Smoothly and noiselessly, with the slightly swaying gait that buxom women sometimes have, she approached the barrier with her eyes firmly fixed on the president and looking neither to the right nor to the left. I thought she looked very beautiful at that moment, and not at all pale, as some ladies subsequently asserted. They said, too, that she wore a hard and malicious expression. What I believe is that she was merely agitated and felt deeply uncomfortable under the contemptuously curious stare of our prurient public. Hers was a proud nature which could not tolerate disdain, one of those natures which, the moment they suspect they are being regarded with contempt, immediately flare up in anger and adopt an aggressive stance. There was at the same time, of course, an element of timidity as well as an inner shame at this timidity, so that it was hardly surprising that her delivery was uneven—now angry, now contemptuous, now deliberately offensive, followed suddenly by a sincere, heartfelt note of self-reproach, self-castigation. Occasionally she spoke as though she were falling headlong into an abyss: 'Come what may, whatever happens, I'll have my say all the same...' As regards her relationship with the late Fyodor Pavlovich, she commented brusquely: 'It's all a load of nonsense. It's hardly my fault if he wouldn't leave me alone!' And a minute later she added: 'I'm to blame for everything, I was leading them both on—the old boy, and him—and it went too far. It was all because of me that it happened.' Samsonov's name cropped up at one stage. 'Why don't people mind their own business?' she immediately snapped back, insolent and vicious. 'He was my benefactor, he took me in when I was running around barefoot, when my own family threw me out.' The president reminded her, albeit very politely, that she should reply to the questions without going into unnecessary detail. Grushenka flushed and her eyes flashed angrily.

No, she had not seen the envelope with the money, she had only heard from 'that evil man' that Fyodor Pavlovich had got some kind of envelope with three thousand roubles in it. 'Only it's all a load of nonsense, I just laughed, I never had any intention of going there...'

'Who did you mean just now by "that evil man"?' enquired the prosecutor.

'The flunkey Smerdyakov, who killed his master and hanged himself yesterday.'

Of course she was immediately asked what grounds she had for such a deliberate accusation, and it transpired that she had no grounds at all.

'That's what Dmitry Fyodorovich himself told me, he's the one you should believe. If you ask me, it's that mischief-maker who's ruined him, she's the cause of it all, that's what,' Grushenka added, practically shaking with hatred and with a note of malice ringing in her voice.

She was asked whom she had in mind.

'The young lady, that Katerina Ivanovna. She invited me to her place that time and gave me chocolate, she's a sly one. She doesn't know the meaning of the word shame, she doesn't...'

At this point the president stopped her and told her strictly to moderate her language. But the jealous woman's rage was such that she was prepared to go to any length, to plunge headlong into an abyss, if necessary...

'During the arrest in the village of Mokroye,' the prosecutor said, 'everyone saw you run out of the other room and heard you shout: "I'm guilty of everything, we'll both go to Siberia together!" Would this not indicate that you too were convinced at that moment that he had killed his father?'

'I can't remember my feelings at the time,' replied Grushenka. 'Everybody was shouting that he had killed his father, and I felt it was my fault and he had killed him because of me. But as soon as he said he was innocent, I believed him straight away, and I still believe him, and will always believe him. He's not the sort of man who would lie.'

She was now cross-examined by Fetyukovich. Incidentally, I remember him asking about Rakitin and about the twenty-five roubles 'for bringing Aleksei Fyodorovich Karamazov to you'.

'What's so surprising about him taking the money?' Grushenka smirked with contemptuous malice. 'He was always coming to me begging for money, sometimes he'd get as much as thirty roubles out of me in a month and, more often than not, he'd just fritter it away; he always had enough to eat and drink, though, without having to come to me.'

'What was the reason for your generosity towards Mr Rakitin?' interjected Fetyukovich, despite the fact that the judge was showing signs of great unease.

'He's my cousin, he is. My mother and his mother are sisters. It's just that he always begged me not to tell anyone around here about that, he was too ashamed of me.'

This new information came as a total surprise to everyone, for up to this time no one in the whole town had known anything about it, not even in the monastery, not even Mitya. It was said that Rakitin, sitting in his place, blushed as red as a beetroot with shame. Even before coming into the courtroom Grushenka had found out somehow that he had testified against Mitya, and that is what had made her angry. The whole of Rakitin's former speech, with all its airs and graces, with all its censure of the serf laws and the lack of civil organization in Russia—all this was, once and for all, reduced to naught in the eyes of the public. Fetyukovich was pleased—another gift from heaven! On the whole Grushenka was not questioned for very long and, in any case, she did not of course have anything to say that was particularly new. The impression she made in the public mind was very unpleasant. Hundreds of opprobrious gazes were directed at her when, having finished testifying, she sat down at a considerable distance from Katerina Ivanovna. Mitya had not said a word throughout her testimony, but had sat as though petrified, his eyes lowered.

The next witness was Ivan Fyodorovich.

5

UNEXPECTED CATASTROPHE

I SHOULD point out that he had been called even before Alyosha. But the usher had informed the president that, due to a sudden illness or incapacity of some kind, the witness was unable to appear immediately, but that as soon as he recovered he would be available to testify when required. This incidentally had passed unnoticed somehow, and it was only later that it came to light. At first his appearance created a stir; the principal witnesses, especially the two rivals, had already been questioned, and curiosity had been adequately satisfied for the time being. There was even a feeling of fatigue among the public. They still had to listen to the testimony of a number of other witnesses who, in view of all that had already been revealed, could in all probability not contribute anything particularly new. Time was passing, however. Ivan Fyodorovich entered the courtroom surprisingly hesitantly, not looking at anyone, his head bowed, and with a sombre and preoccupied air. He was dressed immaculately, but his face made a shocking impression—on me, at any rate; there was something ashen about it, something reminiscent of one about to die. His eyes were dull and lifeless; he raised them and slowly surveyed the entire hall. Alyosha leapt to his feet with a groan. I remember this. But this too passed almost unnoticed.

The president began by telling him that, as an unsworn witness,* he could remain silent, but that of course any statements he did make must be made in good faith, and so on and so forth. Ivan Fyodorovich listened and gazed impassively at him; but suddenly a smile began to spread slowly over his face, and no sooner had the astonished president finished speaking than he burst out laughing.

'Well, and what else?' he enquired at the top of his voice.

A silence fell on the hall, there was tension in the air. The president became uneasy.

'Perhaps... you're still feeling unwell?' he suggested, looking around for the court usher.

'Don't worry, your honour,' Ivan Fyodorovich replied very calmly and courteously, 'I'm well enough, and can tell you something rather interesting.'

'You have something new to communicate?' said the president, still somewhat sceptical.

Ivan Fyodorovich lowered his gaze, hesitated for a few seconds and, looking up again, said haltingly:

'N-no... I haven't. Nothing in particular.'

Questions followed. He replied most reluctantly and very

curtly, even with a kind of ever-increasing resentment, but sensibly all the same. He prevaricated on many points, claiming ignorance. No, he knew nothing of the dealings between his father and Dmitry Fyodorovich. 'They were no concern of mine,' he remarked. He had heard the accused threaten to kill his father. He had heard about the money in the envelope from Smerdyakov...

'It's all the same old story,' he suddenly stopped, looking exhausted. 'There's nothing in particular that I can tell the court.'

'I can see you are ill, and I understand your feelings...', began the president. He was on the point of inviting both the prosecution and defence to state whether they needed to ask any questions, when Ivan Fyodorovich suddenly requested in an exhausted voice:

'Would you please excuse me, your honour, I don't feel at all well.' So saying, and without waiting for permission, he turned and headed for the exit. However, after taking a few steps, he stopped as though he had suddenly reconsidered something, smiled faintly, and returned to his former place. 'I'm like that peasant girl, your honour... how does it go now? "If I want to put it on—I will, if I don't—I won't." They are following her with a *sarafan** or a *panyova*,* or something, and they want to dress her for her wedding, and all she says is: "If I want to put it on—I will, if I don't—I won't..." It's a custom belonging to one of our ethnic groups...'

'What are you driving at?' asked the president sharply.

'Just this,' Ivan Fyodorovich suddenly produced a wad of money, 'here's the money for which my father was murdered.... the same money that was in that envelope,' he nodded at the table on which lay the exhibits. 'Where shall I put it? Mr Usher, sir, would you kindly take it?'

The court usher took the money and handed it to the president.

'How could this money have come to be in your possession?...' the president asked with surprise, and added, 'if indeed it is the same money!'

'I got it from Smerdyakov, the murderer, yesterday. I went to see him before he hanged himself. It was he who killed my father, not my brother. He killed him, and I put him up to it... Who wouldn't like to kill his father?...'

'Are you in your right mind, or not?' the president could not help interjecting.

'That's just it, I am in my right mind. I've got a foul mind, the same sort as you and all these ugly m-mugs!' he suddenly turned towards the public. 'A father has been killed and they pretend to be shocked,' he hissed, seething with contemptuous rage. 'They're just putting on a show in front of one another. Hypocrites! Everyone wants his father dead. Let dog eat dog... If it wasn't a case of patricide, they'd all be disappointed and go home furious... They want a circus! "Bread and circuses!"* Come to think of it, I'm no better! Have you got any water, give me a glass of water, for Christ's sake!' and he suddenly buried his head in his hands.

The usher went over to him immediately. Alyosha suddenly leapt to his feet and cried out: 'He's sick, don't believe him, he's out of his mind!' Katerina Ivanovna got up hurriedly from her chair and stared at Ivan Fyodorovich, petrified with terror. Mitya too was standing up, hanging on his brother's every word, his face contorted in a wild grimace.

'Calm down, I'm not mad, I'm just a murderer!' Ivan began again. 'After all, you can't expect eloquence from a murderer...', he added suddenly, his face crumpled and he burst out laughing.

The prosecutor, visibly bewildered, leant over to the president. The other members of the bench went into an agitated huddle. Fetyukovich pricked up his ears and listened avidly. A hushed, expectant silence pervaded the courtroom. The president suddenly seemed to take a grip on himself.

'Mr Karamazov, what you've said is unclear and inappropriate. Calm down, if you can, and tell us... provided, of course, you really do have something to tell us... how you can substantiate your confession... are you sure you're feeling well?'

'That's just it, I haven't got any witnesses. That dog Smerdyakov won't send you his evidence from the other world... in an envelope. You just can't get enough envelopes, can you? One'll be enough. I haven't got any witnesses... On second thoughts, perhaps just one,' he smiled pensively.

'Who's your witness?'

'One that's sporting a tail, your honour, and not dressed for the occasion! *Le diable n'existe point!* Ignore him, he's just a shabby, small-time devil,' he added in mock confidentiality, his smile fading, 'he's probably around here somewhere—there he is, under that table, material evidence in hand, where else would you expect him to hide? Look, listen to me! I told him I didn't want to keep quiet, and he just went ranting on about some geological cataclysm... What rubbish! Why don't you set the monster free!... Listen, he's started singing hymns, that's because he hasn't got a care in the world! Sounds just like a bloody drunk caterwauling, "Vanya's gone to town", and for just two seconds of happiness I'd be ready to travel a quadrillion quadrillions. You've no idea what I'm like! To hell with all this, it's just too stupid! Go on, why don't you convict me in his stead! I didn't come here for nothing, you know... Why, oh why should everything, everything under the sun be so damn absurd!...' And once more he began slowly and somewhat thoughtfully to survey the courtroom. The whole court was now in uproar. Alyosha leapt to his feet and rushed towards Ivan Fyodorovich, but the court usher had already grabbed Ivan by the arm.

'What do you think you're doing?' yelled Ivan Fyodorovich, staring hard into the usher's face, and suddenly he grabbed him by the shoulders and threw him furiously to the ground. But the guards were already upon him; as he was seized, he let out an almighty cry. He was manhandled out, crying and shouting incoherently.

Turmoil ensued. I cannot recall the exact sequence of events; I was agitated myself, and could not keep track of all that was going on. All I know is that later, when everything had calmed down and everyone realized what had happened, the court usher was severely reprimanded, even though he was at great pains to explain to his superiors that the witness had been behaving perfectly normally right up to his appearance, that he had been seen by the doctor about an hour before, when he had complained of feeling slightly ill, but that before entering the courtroom he had still been quite coherent and no one could have foreseen that anything untoward would happen; in fact, it was the witness himself who had insisted on giving evidence. But before anyone had managed to calm down and take stock, this scene was immediately followed by another; Katerina Ivanovna went into hysterics. She screeched loudly and began to sob, but refused to leave; she was flailing her arms about and begging to be allowed to remain, and all of a sudden she cried out to the president:

'I wish to submit another piece of evidence, immediately... now! Here, take this, it's a letter... take it, read it now, quickly! It's from that swine, that abomination, over there!' she was pointing at Mitya. 'It was he who killed his father, you'll see in a moment, he wrote and told me he was going to kill his father! But the other one's sick, sick, he's got the shakes! I could see for the last three days that he'd got the shakes!'

She went on shrieking frantically. The usher took the letter that she was proffering to the president, after which she slumped on her chair and, burying her face in her hands, began to sob convulsively and silently, her whole body shaking, suppressing every groan for fear that she might be ordered to leave the courtroom. The letter that she had handed over was that same letter which Mitya had written in the *Stolichny Gorod* and to which Ivan had referred, saying it was 'proof beyond all shadow of doubt'. Alas! It was indeed deemed to be such, and had it not been for this letter, the outcome of the case might have been different, perhaps—or, at least, it might not have been so dreadful. I repeat, it was difficult to follow everything in detail. I am still thoroughly confused about it all. The president probably revealed at once the contents of the new document to the bench, the prosecutor, defence counsel, and members of the jury. I do remember, though, that Katerina Ivanovna was questioned again. When she was asked solicitously by the president whether she had recovered sufficiently, Katerina Ivanovna exclaimed eagerly:

'I'm ready, quite ready! I'm quite able to answer all your questions.' She still seemed terribly worried that, for some reason, they might not let her have her say. She was asked to explain in greater detail about the letter and the circumstances in which she had received it.

'I received it just the night before the crime, but he'd written it the day before that, in the tavern, in other words two days before the crime—look at it, he's written it on the back of some kind of bill!' she could hardly get the words out. 'He hated me at the time because he'd behaved despicably, going after that creature... and also because he owed me that three thousand... Oh, that three thousand was devouring him, because he'd sunk so low! About that three thousand... I beg you, I implore you, hear me out. He came to me one morning, three weeks before he murdered his father. I knew he needed money, and I knew what for—I knew, he needed it to seduce that creature and run away with her. I knew then that he'd already been unfaithful to me and wanted to be rid of me, and I, I myself, gave him the money, pretending I expected him to send it to my sister in Moscow—and as I was giving it to him, I looked him in the eye and told him he could send it whenever he wished, "even in a month's time will do". So, how could he possibly have failed to understand what I was trying to convey to him straight to his face: "You need money to be unfaithful to me with that creature of yours, so here's the money, I'm giving it to you myself, take it if you're such a bastard!..." I wanted to expose him—and what happened? He took it, he really took it and walked off with it, and he spent it there with that creature in a single night... But he saw, he saw that I knew everything; I assure you that at the time he also realized that by giving him the money, I was merely putting him to the test: would he really be such a bastard as to take it? We were face to face and he saw, he saw everything, and he took it, he took my money and left!'

'That's right, Katya!' Mitya burst out suddenly. 'I looked you straight in the eyes and I could see that you thought I was a bastard, but I took your money all the same! Go on, despise me for it, I'm a scoundrel, it serves me right!'

'Mr Karamazov,' the president raised his voice, 'one more word—and I shall order you to be escorted from the court!'

'That money was a thorn in his side,' continued Katerina Ivanovna in feverish haste, 'he wanted to return it to me, he wanted to, that's true, but he needed the money for that creature too. So he went and killed his father, but still he didn't give me my money back—instead, he went with her to that village, where he was arrested. He squandered all the money there that he stole from his murdered father. And the day before he killed his father he wrote me that letter; he was drunk, I could see at once that he'd written it out of malice and in the knowledge, in the sure knowledge, that I wouldn't show it to anyone even if he committed the murder. Otherwise he wouldn't have written it. He knew I wouldn't want to take revenge and ruin him! But go on, read it, read it carefully, very carefully please, and you'll see that he described everything in the letter, everything in advance, how he was going to kill his father and where his father kept his money. Read it carefully, don't omit anything, there's a place where he says: "I'll kill him, provided that Ivan has left." That means he had already thought out in advance how he was going to kill him,' Katerina Ivanovna went on maliciously, venomously poisoning the minds of the jury against Mitya. It was clear that she had considered every nuance of that fateful letter and had thought about it in the minutest detail. 'If he hadn't been drunk he wouldn't have written it, but just look, he disclosed everything in advance, exactly the way he went and murdered him afterwards, there you have his whole plan!'

She continued like this, beside herself with fury, and obviously disregarding all the consequences this might have for her, although she must surely have foreseen them, perhaps as much as a month earlier, but even then she probably thought in her state of fury, 'Why don't I read it out in court?' She was getting totally carried away now. If I remember rightly, the letter was read aloud by the clerk of the court at precisely this juncture, and it produced a shattering effect. Mitya was asked whether he admitted writing the letter.

'Yes, I did!' exclaimed Mitya. 'If I hadn't been drunk I wouldn't have written it!... There were lots of things we hated each other for, Katya, but I swear, I swear I loved you even when I hated you, but you didn't love me!'

He slumped on his seat, wringing his hands in despair. The prosecutor and the counsel for the defence both began to question her, the general drift of their questions being: 'What prompted you to conceal such a document till now, and why didn't you disclose all this before?'

'Yes, all right, I lied, I lied about everything, against my conscience and my honour, but I wanted to save him because he hated and despised me so much,' exclaimed Katerina Ivanovna, as though demented. 'Oh yes, he despised me terribly, he's always despised me, and you know what—he's despised me ever since the time I curtsied to him for giving me that money. I realized it... I felt it immediately then, but I didn't want to believe it for a long time. I hate to think how often I read in his eyes: "You came to me of your own accord that time, didn't you?" Oh, he didn't understand, he didn't understand why I came running to him at all, he's only capable of suspecting baseness! He was judging by his own yardstick, he thinks everyone's the same as he is,' snarled Katerina Ivanovna, having lost all self-control. 'And the only reason he wanted to marry me was because I'd come into an inheritance, that's the reason, the only reason! I always suspected that was the reason! Oh, he's worse than an animal! He's been convinced all along that just because I went to him then I wouldn't stop feeling ashamed of myself in front of him for the rest of my life, and he'd therefore be entitled to despise me for ever and be able to lord it over me—that's why he wanted to marry me! That's the truth, the gospel truth! I tried to win him over with my love, with my undying love, I was even ready to put up with his unfaithfulness, but he understood nothing, nothing at all. You'd think he'd be able to understand something at least! He's a monster! I didn't receive that letter until the evening of the following day, someone brought it from the tavern, and only that very morning, the morning of the same day, I'd been on the point of forgiving him everything, everything, even his unfaithfulness!'

Naturally, the president and the prosecutor tried to pacify her. I am convinced that they were both ashamed to take advantage of her hysterical outburst and to listen to such a confession. I remember hearing them say to her: 'We understand how difficult it must be for you, believe us, we're not made of stone,' and so on and so forth. All the same, this did not prevent them from extracting evidence from a demented, hysterical woman. Finally she described—with extraordinary clarity, as often happens momentarily at such times of tension—how Ivan Fyodorovich had nearly gone out of his mind trying to save 'the monster and murderer', his brother.

'He was tormenting himself,' she went on, 'he always wanted to minimize his brother's guilt by admitting to me that he didn't love his father either, and that he himself perhaps wished him dead. Oh, he was so open about it, so frank! He used to reveal everything to me, everything, he used to come and talk to me every day as if I were his only friend. I have the honour of being his only friend!' she exclaimed suddenly, a challenging glint in her eyes. 'He went to see Smerdyakov twice. On one occasion he came to me and said: "If it wasn't my brother who murdered him, but Smerdyakov—after all, everyone here's spreading the rumour that it was Smerdyakov—then perhaps I too am guilty, because Smerdyakov knew that I didn't love my father, and perhaps he thought I wished him dead." Then I took out the letter and showed it to him, and that was when he became totally convinced that his brother was the murderer, and, of course, this destroyed him totally. He couldn't bear the thought that his own brother was guilty of patricide! I could already see a week ago that he was ill. The past few days, at my place, he's been in a state of delirium. I could see he was going mad. He's been wandering around raving, and he's been seen like that on the streets. The doctor who examined him the other day at my request told me that he was on the verge of a breakdown—and all because of him, all because of that monster! And yesterday he discovered that Smerdyakov was dead—this was such a shock to him that he lost his sanity... and all on account of the monster, all because he wanted to save him!'

Of course, such talk, such a confession can be made only once in a lifetime—in the last remaining moments of one's life, for example, when mounting the scaffold. And Katerina Ivanovna was true to her nature and equal to the occasion. This was the same impulsive Katerina Ivanovna who had previously rushed to the young rake in order to save her father; the same chaste and proud Katerina Ivanovna who previously had sacrificed herself and her maidenly sense of modesty in front of all these people, telling them about 'Mitya's act of chivalry' purely in order to make things easier for him, however slightly. And now she was sacrificing herself again in exactly the same way, only this time for a different man, and perhaps it was only now, only at this instant, that she felt and understood fully for the first time how dear this other one was to her! She had sacrificed herself out of concern for him, realizing that he had ruined himself by testifying that it was he and not his brother who was the murderer; she had sacrificed herself in order to save him, his honour and his reputation! And yet, a terrible thought flashed through her mind—had she been lying when she described her former relationship with Mitya? That was the question. No, not at all, she had not intended to malign Mitya when she declared in front of everyone that Mitya despised her for having curtsied low before him! She believed it—in fact, she had been firmly convinced the moment she made that curtsey that, for all his naïvety and adoration of her, he was none the less mocking and despising her. And it was only out of pride that she had pledged her frenzied, hysterical love for him, out of wounded pride, which made her love look more like vengeance. Perhaps this hysterical love would have turned into genuine love; perhaps that was the one thing that Katya wished for, but he had insulted her to the very depths of her being by his betrayal, and she was unable to find it within herself to forgive him. However, the opportunity for revenge had presented itself unexpectedly, and everything that this scorned woman had been harbouring in her breast so painfully and for so long burst forth all at once and quite unexpectedly. She had betrayed Mitya, but she had also betrayed herself! And, naturally, as soon as she poured her heart out the tension broke and she was overwhelmed by remorse. Once more she became hysterical and collapsed, sobbing and shrieking. She was carried out of the courtroom. And, just as she was being carried out, Grushenka leapt to her feet with a wail and, before anyone had time to restrain her, rushed towards Mitya.

'Mitya,' she wailed, 'your bitch has done for you!' Shaking with fury, she turned to the bench and shouted, 'Now you know what she's like!' At a signal from the president she was seized and led towards the courtroom exit. She resisted, fighting and struggling to get back to Mitya. Mitya let out a cry and rushed towards her. He was seized and overpowered.

Yes, I suppose the ladies in the audience were satisfied; the spectacle was certainly an entertaining one. Then, I remember, the doctor from Moscow reappeared. Apparently, the president had instructed the usher to arrange for Ivan Fyodorovich to receive medical attention. The doctor informed the court that the patient was in a serious condition, and that he ought to be admitted to hospital. In response to the questions of the prosecutor and the defence counsel, he confirmed that the patient himself had visited him two days previously and that he had warned him that he was heading for a nervous breakdown, but that he had refused to have medical treatment. 'He was most decidedly not in his right mind, he admitted to me himself that he saw apparitions in broad daylight, that he encountered all manner of deceased people on the street, and that Satan came to visit him every night,' the doctor concluded. Having made his statement, the famous doctor withdrew. The letter handed over by Katerina Ivanovna was added to the material evidence. After due consultation it was decided that the session should continue, and that the two unexpected statements (those of Katerina Ivanovna and Ivan Fyodorovich) be entered in the record.

But I shall not describe the subsequent court proceedings. In any case, the remaining witnesses merely repeated and confirmed what the others had said, albeit each in his own characteristic way. But I repeat, everything will become clear in the prosecutor's speech, which I am coming to now. Everyone was in a state of excitement, everyone was electrified by the most recent revelations and dying with impatience for the outcome, for the speeches of the two counsels and for the verdict. Fetyukovich had been visibly shaken by Katerina Ivanovna's testimony. The prosecutor, on the other hand, was triumphant. When the session was over, the court went into recess for almost an hour. Finally the president announced the opening of the judicial pleadings. I think it was precisely eight o'clock in the evening when Ippolit Kyrillovich, our prosecutor, began the address for the prosecution.

6

PROSECUTOR'S SPEECH. CHARACTER SKETCH

IPPOLIT KYRILLOVICH began his prosecutor's address shaking nervously all over, a cold feverish sweat breaking out on his brow, and hot and cold shivers running up and down his spine. He mentioned this himself later. He regarded this speech as his *chef d'œuvre*, the crowning achievement of his professional career, his swansong. Indeed, nine months later he was dead from galloping consumption, so if he had foreseen his own end he really could have compared himself to a swan, singing its last song. Our poor Ippolit Kyrillovich put his whole heart and soul and every last vestige of his talent into that speech, and demonstrated, quite unexpectedly, that he had both a sense of civic duty and an awareness of the eternal issues, that is, in so far as he was able to grasp them. It is as well to remember that what gave his speech its strength was its sincerity: he did in all sincerity believe in the guilt of the accused; his address was not that of a hired hack going through the motions; in calling for 'retribution' he really was imbued with a desire to 'save society'. Even our ladies in the audience, who by and large were hostile to Ippolit Kyrillovich, had to admit, however, that he created an extraordinary impression. His voice was strained and faltering at first, but he soon got into his stride and for the rest of the speech his voice reverberated throughout the hall. When he came to the peroration, he nearly fainted.

'Gentlemen of the jury,' began the counsel for the prosecution, 'the present case has become notorious throughout the whole of Russia. But what, one may ask, is so surprising about it, what is so horrifying? For us, especially for us. After all, we have become fairly inured to such things! What is horrifying is that such dreadful crimes have ceased to shock us! What should horrify us is not that a certain individual commits this or that atrocity, but that we take these atrocities for granted. Wherein lies the reason for our indifference, for our barely disguised indifference to such matters, to such manifestations of the times, which augurs a most unenviable future for us? Does it lie in our cynicism or in the premature atrophy of mental faculties and imagination in our society, still so immature and yet already so decadent? Does it lie in the total degeneration of our moral principles, or even in the fact that, when it comes down to it, perhaps we don't have any moral principles at all? I cannot resolve these issues, but they are nevertheless agonizing, and every citizen not only should, but in all conscience must, take them to heart. Our press, though still in its formative stages, has already rendered certain services to society; without it, we would never have obtained anything remotely like a complete picture of all the atrocities of unbridled will-power and depraved morality that it constantly proclaims on its pages for the edification of us all—and not only for those who attend the recently reformed public courts with which we have been blessed in the present reign. And what is it that we read almost daily? We constantly read of things compared to which even the present case pales into insignificance and appears as something almost commonplace. But what is really significant is that the majority of our domestic criminal cases reveal something universal, some common malaise which has become endemic and which, being commonplace, is difficult to combat. Take the case of the brilliant young officer from the best circles, on the threshold of his adulthood and career, who, without the least compunction, stealthily and treacherously goes and slits the throat of a petty clerk—in some respects, his erstwhile benefactor—and that of the latter's maidservant, in order to get his hands on a promissory note, not to mention the rest of the victim's money: "It'll come in handy to support the lifestyle my position demands and for my future career." Having knifed them both, he puts a pillow under the head of each body, and leaves. Or take the young hero, decorated for bravery, who murders the mother of his commanding officer and benefactor when he waylays and robs her on the highway, having previously convinced his accomplices that she loved him like a son and would follow his every advice and not be solicitous for her safety. So, he is a monster, but in our day and age I would not go so far as to say that he is an isolated case. Another, while not actually committing murder, may well think about it and imagine it, and in the depths of his soul is just as dishonourable as the other. In moments of privacy and silent reflection he may well ask himself: "What is honour, and is not the condemnation of bloodshed mere prejudice?" Perhaps people will protest and say that I am sick, hysterical, grossly unfair, that I am out of my mind, that I exaggerate. Let them, let them—oh God, I'd be only too happy to be wrong! You don't have to believe me, you may think I'm mad, but nevertheless mark my words: if only a tenth, only a twentieth part of what I say is true, that is still reason enough for horror! Look, gentlemen, look at the number of young people who blow their own brains out—and without any of Hamlet's rhetoric concerning what awaits us in the hereafter, without even a suggestion of such questions, as though this thesis regarding our soul and everything that awaits us beyond the grave has long been cast out from their consciousness and buried beneath the sands. Finally, look at the depravity that surrounds us, look at the libertines in our society. Compared to some of them, Fyodor Pavlovich, the unfortunate victim in this case, is but an innocent babe. And yet we all knew him, "he lived amongst us..."* Yes, the psychology of the Russian criminal will one day, perhaps, be analysed by the foremost minds both in this country and abroad, for the subject is worthy of such study. But this analysis will be made later, in happier times, when all the tragic bedlam of today has become history and it will be possible to make it in a more rational and balanced manner than I, for instance, could ever hope to. Now, however, we are either horrified or we pretend to be horrified, but one way or another, in our quest for easy excitement and cheap thrills, we savour the spectacle that titillates our cynically idle complacency, or again, like small children, we wave our hands to ward off frightening spectres and bury our heads in the pillow while the frightening vision passes, only to forget about it immediately in fun and games. But there will come a time when we too shall have to make a sober and sensible reassessment of our lives, when we too shall have to look at ourselves as a society, for it is incumbent upon us to grapple with certain issues in our public affairs, or at the very least to make a start in that direction. At the end of one of his greatest works, a great writer in earlier times likened Russia to a jaunty troika rushing headlong towards an unknown destination.* "Oh troika, winged troika, who was it that invented you!" he exclaims, and then adds, in ecstatic pride, that all nations should make way respectfully for the troika rushing along on its course. Fine, gentlemen, let them, let them make way, respectfully or otherwise, but in my fallible opinion the great author ended either in a flourish of childishly naïve exaltation or simply in fear of the censor. For if his troika were hitched up to his own heroes, the Sobakeviches, the Nozdryovs, or the Chichikovs,* then you wouldn't get very far at all with that lot , whoever was the driver! And that's with the horses of yesteryear, never mind the present lot, the present lot are really beyond the pale!...'

At this point Ippolit Kyrillovich's speech was interrupted by applause; the liberal light in which the Russian troika was depicted had struck a chord. True, only two or three people clapped, so the president did not even deem it necessary to threaten to clear the courtroom, and merely cast a stern look at the interrupters. But Ippolit Kyrillovich felt heartened; never before in his life had he been applauded! For years no one had wanted to listen to the man, and suddenly here was an opportunity to address the whole of Russia!

'But let's face it,' he continued, 'what is it about the Karamazov family that has led to such notoriety throughout the whole land? Perhaps I exaggerate, but it seems to me that in this neat little family scene, one can detect, as it were, traces of the basic elements of our modern educated society—by no means all the elements, and then only the merest scintilla, "as the sun in a droplet of water",* nevertheless something is reflected, something can be deduced. Let us consider this hapless, dissolute, depraved old man, this paterfamilias who has met with such an unfortunate end. A gentleman by birth, he starts out as an impecunious hanger-on; by virtue of an unexpected and fortuitous marriage he manages to lay his hands on a tidy little sum, which, with his innate acumen—not inconsiderable, I may add—enables him to come into his own as a moneylender; the petty rogue and obsequious buffoon is now well set up. With the passage of years and as he amasses his wealth, he becomes more and more self-assured. Gone are his submissiveness and sycophancy, what remains is a sarcastic and malicious cynic, a libertine. All spiritual values have been expunged, yet the lust for life is undiminished. He comes to a point where nothing is left in life but sensual gratification, and that is the attitude he imparts to his children. As regards parental and spiritual responsibilities, there is not a trace. He ridicules such notions, he leaves the upbringing of his small children to the servants, and is overjoyed when he is no longer responsible for them. He even forgets about them altogether. The whole of his moral code is reduced to *après moi le déluge.** What we see here is everything that is contrary to the concept of a responsible citizen, we see a total, even hostile, alienation from society: "As long as I'm all right, let the whole world go to blazes." And he is all right, he is satisfied, he yearns to carry on like that for another twenty, no, thirty years. He swindles his own son, he refuses to hand his maternal inheritance over to him, and instead uses his son's own money to entice his mistress away. No, I do not want to leave the defence of the accused solely to my illustrious learned colleague from St Petersburg. I shall take it upon myself to tell the truth, I can understand perfectly well all the indignation he engendered in his son's heart. But enough, enough said about that miserable old man, he has got his just deserts. Let us simply remember that here was a father, a thoroughly modern father. Would I be insulting society too much if I were to say that he was, perhaps, only one of many such modern fathers? Alas, the only reason that so many of our modern fathers refrain from expressing themselves as cynically as he did is that they've had a better upbringing, a better education; but in essence they share his philosophy. Granted, I am a pessimist—all right. We have already agreed that you are prepared to forgive me on that score. Let us agree further—don't believe me if you don't want to, don't; I shall speak but you don't have to believe me. But please let me have my say, please bear in mind just some of my points. And so we come to the children of this old man, this paterfamilias: one of them stands before us—I shall have plenty to say about him later—the other two I shall merely touch upon in passing. One of these, the elder, is a thoroughly modern young man, very well educated, with a not inconsiderable intellect, who, however, no longer believes in anything, having like the father rejected and discarded too much, far too much, in his lifetime. We all know his views, and he has been well received in our society. He has never concealed his opinions—just the opposite, in fact—and this emboldens me now to speak of him with some frankness, not, I hasten to say, as a private individual, but simply as a member of the Karamazov family. Yesterday, here in this town, a sickly halfwit killed himself—Smerdyakov, the late Fyodor Pavlovich's servant and, perhaps, his illegitimate son, who is intimately involved in the present case. At the preliminary investigation, weeping hysterically, he told me how the young Karamazov, Ivan Fyodorovich, had shocked him by his lack of moral sense. "Everything's permitted, according to him, everything in the world, and nothing should be prohibited from now

on—that's what he taught me." I suggest that it was this doctrine
to which the halfwit had been exposed that finally caused him to
go mad, although of course his epilepsy and the whole of the
terrible tragedy that occurred in their household must also have
contributed to his mental derangement. But this halfwit happened to make one highly curious observation which would have
been a credit even to a cleverer observer than he, which is
precisely why I have mentioned the point. "If there is", he told
me, "one among Fyodor Pavlovich's sons who most closely
resembles him in character, it is certainly Ivan Fyodorovich!" I
shall end my character sketch with this remark, as I consider it
would be indelicate to pursue it further. I have no wish to draw
further conclusions, like a raven's cry foretelling nothing but
doom for the young man. We saw today in this hall that truth is
still alive in his young heart, and that his feelings of kinship have
not yet been stifled by his moral cynicism and lack of faith,
caused more by parental example than by true mental suffering.
Now, the other son—oh, he's still a youth, devout and humble,
and far from espousing his brother's gloomy, degenerate outlook
on life, he has sought to follow, so to speak, "populist principles"—or that which masquerades under that somewhat pretentious title in certain of the pseudo-intellectual circles of our
intelligentsia. He actually adopted the monastic life; he even
thought of taking the tonsure. Unconsciously and prematurely
he has come, it seems to me, to represent that timid despair with
which so many people in our impoverished society, frightened of
its cynicism and corruption and mistakenly attributing all evil to
European enlightenment, rush towards "the soil of their birth",
into the maternal embrace, as it were, of their native land, like
children frightened by ghosts, their only desire being to slumber
peacefully in the shrivelled bosom of their exhausted mother, or
even perhaps to spend their whole life sleeping there, merely to
escape the sight of the fearsome visions. For my part, I wish this
gentle and gifted young man all the best, hoping that his splendid
youthful idealism and his attempt to identify with the people will
not, as so often happens, become dreary mysticism at the
psychological level, and mindless chauvinism at the civic level—
both ills which represent, perhaps, an even greater danger to our
nation than the premature degradation which, due to misinter-

preted and all too easily acquired European enlightenment, afflicts his elder brother.'

The references to chauvinism and mysticism again drew one or two tentative outbreaks of approval. It goes without saying that Ippolit Kyrillovich had been carried away by his enthusiasm, and that none of his digressions had much to do with the matter in hand—not to mention the fact that they had turned out to be rather lacking in clarity—but the urge to unburden himself, be it only once in a lifetime, had proved altogether too strong for this consumptive, embittered man. They said in the town later that in his description of Ivan Fyodorovich, Ippolit Kyrillovich had been motivated by basically improper considerations; having been worsted once or twice by Ivan Fyodorovich during arguments in public, he was still smarting and wanted to take revenge. But I don't know whether one should draw such conclusions. In any case, all this was merely an introduction; after that his address became more relevant and to the point.

'And now to the third son of our modern paterfamilias,' continued Ippolit Kyrillovich. 'He stands before us in the dock. Before us, too, are his achievements, his life, and his deeds; his hour has struck, and everything is exposed, everything is revealed. In contrast to the "Europeanism" and the "populism" of his brothers, he represents Russia as she really is—admittedly, not the whole of it, not by any means, and God forbid that it should be the whole! And yet, here she is, Mother Russia; no mistaking her voice, her smell. We are an independent-minded lot, we are a curious amalgam of good and evil, we admire enlightenment and Schiller, yet at the same time we can raise merry hell in taverns and pull out the beards of pathetic drunkards, our drinking comrades. We can be kind and noble-natured, but only provided things are going our way. We can be enthused by—yes, that's right, enthused—by the noblest of ideals, but only on condition that we don't have to expend any effort, that we don't have to make any sacrifices, and above all on condition that the ideals can be achieved free, gratis, that we needn't pay anything. Paying is something we really resent; on the other hand, receiving, that's really up our street, and that goes for everything. Let's have every kind of blessing (nothing less will do, it must be every kind) and, whatever happens, let no

one tell us what to do on any score, and then we too shall prove
that we can be all sweetness and light. We're not greedy—no,
not in the least—however, do keep doling out the money, more,
more, the more the better, and you shall see how generously,
with what contempt for this base metal, we fritter it away in a
single night of unrestrained revelry. And if no one will give us
the money, we will soon show that we can get hold of it ourselves
if we want it badly enough. But of this, later—let us now return
to the matter in hand. To begin with, we have before us a poor,
neglected boy, "in the backyard without shoes", as described just
now by our honourable and respected fellow citizen, alas of
foreign extraction! I repeat, I shall not let anyone else undertake
the defence of the accused! I am here both to prosecute and to
defend. Yes, gentlemen, we too are people, we too are human,
we too are capable of assessing what influence the first impressions of childhood and the parental home can exert on character.
Next we see the boy as a youth, he is already a young man, an
officer; for disorderly conduct and for challenging someone to a
duel he is exiled to a far-flung outpost of our bounteous
motherland. There he continues his military service, there he
sows his wild oats and, of course—eventually, the fish gets too
big for the pond. He develops a need for money, gentlemen of
the jury, money above all else, and so, after protracted arguments, he reaches a compromise with his father whereby he is to
receive six thousand roubles, which are then dispatched to him.
Observe that he wrote a receipt for the money, and a letter of his
exists in which he more or less renounces all claim to the rest,
and accepts the six thousand in final settlement of the dispute
over the inheritance. At this point he makes the acquaintance of
a high-minded and deeply cultured young lady. I do not wish to
repeat the details, you heard them just now; we are dealing here
with honour, with personal sacrifice, and I shall say no more.
The picture of a young man, frivolous and dissolute, who
nevertheless bows before true nobility, before a lofty ideal, made
a deep and sympathetic impression on us. But after that,
suddenly and quite unexpectedly, we were afforded in this same
courtroom a glimpse of the reverse side of the coin. Again, I
dare not jump to conclusions and I shall refrain from analysing
the reasons. And yet, there must have been reasons. This same

young lady, with tears of long-suppressed indignation streaming down her face, informed us that it was in fact he who, in the first place, despised her for her impulsive behaviour—rash and impetuous, perhaps—yet undeniably exalted and magnanimous. This man, her fiancé, would from the outset regard her with a mocking smile, which she would have found bearable from anyone else, but not from him. Knowing that he had already deceived her—deceived her in his conviction that she would excuse everything in advance, even his unfaithfulness—knowing all this, she purposely offered him the three thousand roubles nevertheless, making it clear to him at the same time, quite clear, that she was offering him the money to engineer her own betrayal: "Well now," her reproachful, challenging gaze confronted him in silence, "will you accept it, or won't you? Can you really be that cynical?" He looks at her, understands exactly what she is thinking (after all, he himself has admitted to us here that he understood everything), and in the event he goes ahead, pockets the three thousand, and blows it in the space of a couple of days with his new paramour! What are we to believe? The first version—the noble impulse to give up his remaining few resources in homage to virtue—or the opposite, the other side of the coin, the repugnant side? Usually in life, when one is faced with two opposites one must look for the truth somewhere in the middle; in the case at issue this is certainly not so. The most likely explanation is that on the one hand he was genuinely noble, while on the other hand he was—equally genuinely— base. Why? Precisely because those of the Karamazov ilk are possessed of natures with such a broad sweep—this is the point I am trying to make—capable of encompassing all manner of opposites, of contemplating both extremes at one and the same time—that which is above us, the extremity of the loftiest ideals, and that which is below us, the extremity of the most iniquitous degradation. Let me draw your attention to the brilliant observation made just now by Mr Rakitin, our up-and-coming journalist, who has made a deep and detailed study of the whole of the Karamazov clan. "The experience of ultimate degradation is as vital to such unruly, dissolute natures as the experience of sheer goodness," he says, and this is very true; they have a constant, ceaseless need for this unnatural combination. Two extremes, two extremes, gentlemen, at one and the same time—without them, they are unhappy and dissatisfied, their life is incomplete. They are all-encompassing, as all-encompassing as Mother Russia herself, there is nothing they cannot accommodate, nothing to which they cannot reconcile themselves! Incidentally, members of the jury, we have touched upon the matter of the three thousand roubles, and I shall take the liberty now of anticipating somewhat. Just imagine that he, this individual, having obtained the money by such means, enduring such shame, such infamy, having reached the ultimate stages of humiliation—can you imagine him, that same day, being able to divide it and sew one half into a makeshift purse, and then, for a whole month thereafter, having the will-power to carry it round his neck despite all temptations and overwhelming needs! Neither in his besotted state as he caroused from tavern to tavern, nor when he had to rush back from town to seek, from God knows where, the money that he needed so badly in order to rescue his sweetheart from the enticements of his rival, his father—at no time did he touch the purse. If only so as not to abandon his sweetheart to the enticements of the old man, of whom he was so jealous, he should have opened the purse and stayed at home on constant guard over his sweetheart, awaiting the moment when she would say: "I'm yours!", whereupon he could flee with her as far as possible from those dire straits. But no, he didn't even touch his talisman, and why not? The first reason, as I have already pointed out, was that were she to say to him: "I'm yours, take me where you will", he would need to have the means to do this. But this first reason, according to the accused himself, paled into insignificance before the second. "As long as I had that money on me, I was a scoundrel, but not a thief, because I could always go to my fiancée, whom I'd insulted, and, counting out half the money I had acquired from her on false pretences, I could always say to her: You see, I've blown half your money and have thereby proved that I'm a weak and feckless man—a scoundrel, if you like (I'm using the accused's own language)—I may be a scoundrel but I'm not a thief, for if I were a thief, I wouldn't have returned the remaining half of the money, I'd have spent it along with the first half." An amazing feat of reasoning! This man, so violent and yet so weak, who despite the ignominy, could not resist the temptation of three thousand roubles—this same man now manifests such stoical resolve, and continues to carry thousands of roubles around his neck and does not dare to touch them! Is this in any way consistent with the character of the man whom we are considering now? No, and I shall take the liberty of describing how the real Dmitry Karamazov would have behaved, even if he had decided to sew the money into a purse. At the first temptation—if only to impress this new sweetheart of his, with whom he had already spent half the money carousing—he'd have unstitched the purse and taken, say, only a hundred roubles to start with, because why should he necessarily return half, that is fifteen hundred roubles, when fourteen hundred would do—after all, the end result would be the same: "I may be a scoundrel," he'd have argued, "but I'm not a thief; at least I've returned fourteen hundred roubles, whereas a thief would have taken everything and returned nothing." Then, a little later, he'd have unstitched it again, taken another hundred, then a third, then a fourth, and so on, till by the end of the month, he would have removed the last hundred but one. "Even if I only return a hundred the end result will be the same—a scoundrel, but not a thief. I've blown two thousand nine hundred, but I've still managed to return a hundred; a thief wouldn't have returned even that much." And at long last, having spent even the penultimate hundred, he'd have looked at the last remaining hundred and said to himself: "Let's face it, it's not really worth returning one hundred, is it—why don't I blow that too?" That's how the real Dmitry Karamazov, as we know him, would have behaved! The story about the purse, on the other hand, is so removed from reality that it defies credulity. One might suppose anything but that. But we shall return to that later.'

Having outlined, in the correct sequence, everything that the court knew about the property disputes and relations between father and son, and having stressed again and again that, according to all the available evidence there was not the slightest possibility of determining who had defrauded whom in the question of the distribution of the inheritance, Ippolit Kyrillovich came to the three thousand roubles which had become such an obsession with Mitya, and he now referred to the medical opinion.

7

BACKGROUND HISTORY

'THE doctors have tried to prove to us that the accused is not in his right mind, that he has an obsession. I suggest that he is very much in his right mind, which is to his disadvantage; had he not been in his right mind, he would have acted much more deviously perhaps. As regards his being obsessive, I would probably be willing to go along with this, but strictly with regard to one point only—the same point as was indicated by the doctors, namely the defendant's obsession with the three thousand roubles of which his father had allegedly defrauded him. Nevertheless, when considering the defendant's persistent frustration about that money, it would be possible to find a much easier explanation for this, perhaps, than a mental disorder. For my own part I quite agree with the young doctor, in whose opinion the accused was—and is—in possession of all his mental faculties and was merely manifesting anger and frustration. And that is the crux of the matter, not the three thousand; the defendant was obsessed with rage, not because of the money, but for another very specific reason. And that reason was jealousy!'

At this juncture Ippolit Kyrillovich proceeded to unfold the whole picture of the defendant's fateful passion for Grushenka. He started with the occasion when the defendant first set off to pay 'the young lady' a visit and give her 'a thrashing'. 'I'm using the defendant's own words here,' added Ippolit Kyrillovich. 'But, instead of giving her a thrashing, he "fell at her feet"—that was the beginning of his infatuation. Meanwhile, the young lady had attracted the interest of the old man, the defendant's father. This was a remarkable coincidence and a fateful one, because, although they must both surely have met her before, both men now fell prey to an infatuation of the most intractable, essentially

Karamazovian kind. Here we have her own admission. "I", she said, "was leading them both on." Yes, she suddenly felt like having some fun with the pair of them; she hadn't felt like it before, but suddenly it occurred to her to do so—and the end result was that both were smitten by her. The old man, who idolized money, immediately set a bait of three thousand roubles with the deliberate intent of luring her to his abode, but he was soon reduced to such a state that if only she would consent to become his lawful wife he would consider it a privilege to stake his good name and the whole of his estate on her acceptance. We have incontrovertible evidence of this. As for the accused, his tragedy is self-evident, as all of us can recognize. But, to return to the "game" the young lady was playing. The seductress did not even give the young man any hope—and indeed hope— nay, real hope—came only at the very last moment before his arrest, when he knelt in front of his tormentress, stretching out his hands stained with his father's blood, the blood of his rival. When he was arrested, this woman, now genuinely contrite, shouted, "Send me to Siberia with him, I brought this upon him, I'm the really guilty one!" The intelligent young gentleman who took it upon himself to describe the events with which we are concerned—that selfsame Mr Rakitin to whom I have already drawn your attention—has defined the character of this brave lady in just a few characteristically succinct phrases: "Early disillusionment, early betrayal and fall, next abandonment by her perfidious seducer and fiancé, then her poverty, the curse laid on her by a decent family and, finally, the patronage of a certain wealthy old man, whom incidentally she still considers to be her benefactor. There was probably a great deal in her that was good, but her young heart harboured anger from an all too early age. The character which emerged was calculating and acquisitive. She developed a cynical, vengeful attitude towards society." Knowing all this, it is easy to understand how she could have toyed with the pair of them just out of sheer malice. And so, in the course of that month of unrequited love, moral humiliation, unfaithfulness to his fiancée, and dishonest appropriation of another person's money, the accused was finally reduced by unremitting jealousy to a state of frenzied fury—and against whom? Against his own father! And to crown it all, in order to lure the object of his passion, the crazy old man used the very three thousand which his son regarded as rightfully his, properly inherited from his mother, and for which he already bore a grudge against his father. Yes, I agree, it was difficult to accept! This could, in fact, have unbalanced him. It was not the money as such that mattered, but the fact that it was used in such a cynically despicable way to destroy his happiness!'

Then Ippolit Kyrillovich went on to consider how the idea of killing his father had gradually taken hold of the mind of the accused, and he supported his argument by citing certain facts.

'At first we see him merely blurting out his plans in taverns—this goes on for a whole month. Indeed, he obviously enjoys being in the public eye and keeping the public informed about everything, even about his most infernal and dangerous ideas; he likes to share them with other people, and, for some unknown reason, he demands that those people should respond immediately and unreservedly, become involved there and then in all his worries and anxieties, humour him and not thwart him in any way. Failing which, he would lose his temper and cause mayhem.' (There followed the anecdote about Staff Captain Snegiryov.) 'For the whole of that month, those who saw and heard the accused became convinced that his shouting and threats had become so serious that the threats could well turn into deeds.' (Here the prosecutor described the family gathering at the monastery, the discussions with Alyosha, and the unseemly and violent scene when the accused burst into their father's house after the meal.) 'I would not go so far as to imply', continued Ippolit Kyrillovich, 'that before this scene the accused had already made a conscious decision to settle matters with his father by premeditated murder. Nevertheless, the idea had already occurred to him several times and he had consciously considered it—the evidence, witnesses, and his own admission prove this. I admit, gentlemen of the jury,' added Ippolit Kyrillovich, 'that even right up to this very day, I still hesitated to charge the defendant with complete and conscious premeditation of the crime of which he is accused. I was firmly convinced that, in his heart, although he had contemplated the fateful step several times, he had only considered it, imagined it merely as a possibility, and had determined neither the time nor the circumstances in which it would be accomplished. And it was only today, only when I saw the fateful document presented to the court by Miss Verkhovtseva, that I ceased to give him the benefit of the doubt. Gentlemen, you yourselves heard her exclaim: "This is the plan, the scheme for the murder!" That is how she herself defined the unfortunate "drunken" letter of the hapless defendant. And the letter does indeed set out the whole scheme and his intentions. It was written just two days before the crime, and we now know for certain, therefore, that two days before carrying out his dreadful plan the accused had sworn that if he could not lay his hands on the money the next day he would kill his father and take the money, which was in an envelope tied with a pink ribbon lying under his pillow, "provided that Ivan has left". You hear that—"provided that Ivan has left". Here, it would seem, everything has already been thought out, the circumstances weighed up—and, lo and behold!—the whole plan was subsequently executed just as it had been written down! Premeditation and meticulous planning are manifest; the crime was planned with robbery in mind—this was clearly stated, written down, and signed. The accused is not disputing his signature. It may be said that it was written when he was drunk. But that does not lessen its significance; on the contrary, when he was drunk he wrote what he had planned when sober. If he had not planned it when he was sober, he would not have written it when he was drunk. Some may ask perhaps: why did he go around broadcasting his intentions in taverns? Anyone who is steeling himself to carry out *premeditated* murder will not say a word about it and will keep it a secret. True enough, but when he was shouting about it he still had no definite plans or intentions, only the wish, the craving. Subsequently he showed rather more reticence. On the night this letter was written, having got himself drunk in the *Stolichny Gorod*, his behaviour was, rather atypically, very reserved; he refused to play billiards, but sat alone instead and didn't talk to anyone, and merely had a slight altercation with a local merchant's clerk—this was probably an almost involuntary act, aggression having become second nature to him by now, so that he just could not resist picking a quarrel whenever he entered a tavern. True, having made the final decision, it must surely have occurred to the accused that he had blurted out too much in the town and that this could very well lead to his subsequent arrest and conviction. But what was to be done? He had let the cat out of the bag, and there was no way of replacing it; but, come to think of it, he had got out of tight corners before, and he could do so again. He pinned his hopes on his lucky star, gentlemen! I must admit, by the way, that he expended a great deal of effort in trying to avoid bloodshed, to avoid the inevitable. "Tomorrow I shall try to raise the money from everyone," he writes in his own peculiar language, "and if I can't... then blood will be spilt." Written when he was drunk, but carried out to the letter when he was stone cold sober!'

Here Ippolit Kyrillovich gave a detailed description of all Mitya's efforts to avoid committing the crime. He described his visit to Samsonov, his trip to see Lurcher—everything based on documentary evidence. 'Exhausted, ridiculed, hungry, having sold his watch to pay for the trip (yet having on his person the fifteen hundred roubles all the while—or so we are led to believe!), tortured by jealousy on account of his beloved, whom he had left behind in the town, and suspecting that in his absence she would go to Fyodor Pavlovich, he finally returns to the town. Thank God! She hasn't run off to Fyodor Pavlovich. He then goes and accompanies her himself when she goes to visit her benefactor Samsonov. (Strangely enough, he is not at all jealous of Samsonov, a very telling psychological point this!) Then he hurries back to his vantage point behind the houses, and there—there he learns that Smerdyakov has had an epileptic fit, that the other servant is sick—the field is clear and he knows the signal—what a temptation! Nevertheless, he doesn't act yet; he goes to that universally respected lady, temporarily resident in the town, Mrs Khokhlakova. This lady, who has long had a compassionate interest in his fate, offers him the most honourable of solutions—to turn his back on all this debauchery, this shameless love, this carousing in taverns, this squandering of his youthful energy, and to go prospecting for gold in Siberia: "There is the outlet for your tumultuous energies, your romantic nature, this craving for adventure."'

After describing the outcome of that conversation and the moment when the accused was suddenly informed that Grushenka had not actually spent the evening at Samsonov's, as well as the sudden fury of this tragic, spiritually exhausted, and jealous man at the realization that she had deliberately deceived him and was now at Fyodor Pavlovich's, Ippolit Kyrillovich concluded by drawing attention to the fatal role played by chance: 'If only the servant girl had got around to telling him that his sweetheart had gone to Mokroye and was with her "former and indisputable" one, nothing would have happened. But she became paralysed with fear, started to swear by all that's holy, and the only reason the accused did not kill her there and then was that he rushed off in a frenzy to look for the one who had betrayed him. But note: agitated though he may have been, he nevertheless grabbed the brass pestle and took it with him. Why the pestle and not some other implement? Well, if he had been contemplating murder for a whole month, just the mere glimpse of something resembling a weapon would be sufficient reason to cause him to snatch it. And the fact that some implement like that could serve as a weapon—he had been contemplating that for a whole month. That is precisely why he identified it as a weapon immediately and unhesitatingly! And therefore, I put it to you, it was not an unconscious act, he did not snatch up the fateful pestle involuntarily. And now we see him in his father's garden; the field is clear, there are no witnesses, it is the dead of night—darkness and jealousy. The lurking suspicion that she is in there with him, with his rival, in his arms—perhaps they're both laughing at him at this very moment—enrages him. And not merely suspicion—it's no longer just a question of suspicion. The deceit is self-evident and obvious: she's there, in that room, where the light is coming from, she's there with him, behind the screen—and the poor man creeps up to the window, peers in expectantly, accepts the situation with resignation and departs discreetly, all the quicker to avoid any trouble and before anything dangerous or criminal should happen—and we, knowing the defendant's character, knowing the state of mind he was in, and above all that he was aware of the signal by which he could gain immediate access to the house, are expected to believe all this!'

At this point, having mentioned the signal and wishing to dispose completely of the initial suspicion of Smerdyakov's guilt,

so as to dispense with the idea once and for all, Ippolit
Kyrillovich digressed from the main thrust of his argument for a
time, and found it expedient to discuss the situation of Smerdyakov. He proceeded very methodically, and everyone understood that, despite the scorn he poured on this suspicion, he
nevertheless regarded it as being most significant.

8

MORE ABOUT SMERDYAKOV

'FIRST,' began Ippolit Kyrillovich, 'where could such a suspicion possibly have originated? The first person to accuse Smerdyakov was the defendant himself at the time of his arrest, yet
from the moment he made the accusation until now he has not
produced a single shred of evidence to support his accusation—
and not only no evidence, but not even anything that, in terms of
common sense, could remotely be considered as a suggestion of
evidence. Subsequently only three people have supported this
accusation: the defendant's two brothers and Miss Svetlova. But
the elder brother declared his suspicion only today, when he was
taken ill with a fever and was obviously raving, whereas for the
last two months, as we well know, he has been entirely convinced
of his brother's guilt and has acquiesced with the assumption of
his guilt. But we shall deal with this point specifically later on.
Then the younger brother told us that he had no evidence, none
whatsoever, to substantiate his surmise regarding Smerdyakov's
culpability, but that he had reached his conclusion solely on the
basis of the defendant's words and "by the look on his face"—
indeed, this most convincing of proofs was offered twice just
now by his brother. And then Miss Svetlova presented us with
even more convincing proof, perhaps: 'You can believe everything he says; he's not the sort of man to tell a lie." That is all
the factual proof we have against Smerdyakov from these three
persons, all of whom are too deeply involved in the defendant's
fate to be impartial. In spite of this, the belief in Smerdyakov's
guilt has continued to circulate unabated to this day. Is this
credible, is this conceivable?'

Here Ippolit Kyrillovich deemed it necessary briefly to outline the character of the late Smerdyakov, a man who had 'taken his life while the balance of his mind was disturbed'. He represented him as a feeble-minded person with a rudimentary education, who was confused by philosophical ideas beyond his mental capabilities and terrified of certain modern teachings on duty and responsibility, by which he had been all too strongly influenced through the practical example of the dissolute lifestyle of his late master and putative father, Fyodor Pavlovich, and also through various strange philosophical discussions with his master's son, Ivan Fyodorovich, who, probably bored and needing someone to taunt, and finding no better target, had been only too pleased to take advantage of this source of entertainment. 'Smerdyakov himself described to me his state of mind during the final days of his life in his master's house,' explained Ippolit Kyrillovich, 'and others have spoken about it too—the accused, his brother, and even the servant Grigory, all of whom must have known him very closely. Besides his other disadvantages, debilitated by his epilepsy, Smerdyakov was as timid as a chicken. "He would fall at my feet and kiss them," the accused himself informed us, before he had realized that such an admission could be harmful to himself. "He's an epileptic chicken," is how the accused described Smerdyakov, in his own characteristic language. And that is who the accused (as he himself has testified) chose as his confidant and frightened to such an extent that, in the end, he agreed to be his spy and messenger. In this role of household informer he betrays his master, informs the accused of the existence of the envelope with the money and of the signal by which he can gain access to his master—he informs him, and small wonder too! "He'd have killed me, I could see that straight away, he'd have killed me," he said at the investigation, trembling and quaking at the mere thought, despite the fact that his terrifying tormentor was already under arrest and could not have exacted his revenge. "He suspected me each and every minute, and so, being in fear of my life and just to placate his anger, I used to hurry to inform him of every secret—to prove my innocence, sir, so that he would spare my life and give me time to repent my sins." Here are his very words, which I wrote down so as not to forget them: "As soon as he started to shout at me, I'd immediately fall on my knees before him." On a certain occasion in the past, Smerdyakov had found and returned some money which his master had lost and had thus gained the latter's confidence, who had recognized a streak of honesty in him. The unfortunate Smerdyakov, being a highly trustworthy young man by nature, was, it is fair to assume, mortified at having betrayed his master, whom he regarded as his benefactor and revered accordingly. The most eminent psychiatrists tell us that those who suffer seriously from epilepsy are prone to an all-pervading and of course morbid self-recrimination. They are tormented by their sense of guilt and also, often for no reason at all, by pangs of conscience; they exaggerate their own guilt and even accuse themselves of all manner of imaginary crimes. Such an individual, through fear and intimidation, can easily become convinced of his guilt and criminality. Smerdyakov in fact had a nasty premonition that the events unfolding before his eyes could lead to some catastrophe. When, immediately before the tragedy, Fyodor Pavlovich's eldest son Ivan Fyodorovich was leaving for Moscow, Smerdyakov begged him to stay behind, not daring, however, on account of his usual faint-heartedness, to tell him clearly and unequivocally all his reservations. He limited himself to dropping hints, but his hints were not understood. It should be noted that he saw Ivan Fyodorovich as his protector so to speak, as a sort of guarantee that, while he was in the house, there would be no calamity. Cast your minds back to the statement in Dmitry Karamazov's "drunken" letter: "I'll kill the old man—provided that Ivan has left"; this would suggest that Ivan Fyodorovich's presence in the house served to guarantee peace and quiet. He then leaves, whereupon Smerdyakov almost immediately, within an hour of the young master's departure, has an epileptic fit. But that is quite understandable. Here it should be noted that, beset by fear and almost in a state of despair, Smerdyakov had for some days been particularly conscious of the possible recurrence of his epilepsy, which was always brought on by nervous tension and emotional upheaval. The exact day and hour of these fits cannot of course be predicted, but every epileptic has a premonition. That, anyway, is the accepted medical opinion. And so, no sooner did Ivan Fyodorovich leave than Smerdyakov, feeling so to speak abandoned and vulnerable, thought to himself as he descended the cellar steps in the course of his domestic duties: "Am I or am I not going to have a fit, and what if I have one now?" And he did have a fit, precisely because of his feeling of unease and these questions and because of his state of anxiety; his vocal chords went into spasm, as is always the case before an epileptic fit, and he ended up falling unconscious on the cellar floor. And now some people have contrived to doubt this most natural coincidence and to read into it an indication, a suggestion, that he *deliberately* faked his illness! But if he did fake it, then the question immediately arises: what for? What did he stand to gain by it, what was his objective? I am not talking from a medical point of view now; science, they will say, has made a mistake, it has got it wrong, the doctors have failed to distinguish between fact and fiction. That may well be so, but have the goodness, none the less, to answer my question: why on earth should he have faked his fit? Was it that, having decided to commit the murder, he wanted to draw attention to himself beforehand in the quickest and most effective way? You see, gentlemen of the jury, on the night of the crime there were five people present in Fyodor Pavlovich's house: firstly, there was Fyodor Pavlovich himself, but obviously he didn't kill himself; secondly, there was his servant Grigory, but he himself was nearly killed; thirdly, there was Grigory's wife, the servant Marfa Ignatyevna, but one simply cannot bring oneself to imagine that she could have killed her master; hence, there remain only two people to consider, the accused and Smerdyakov. But since the accused assures us that he didn't commit the murder, it follows that the murder was committed by Smerdyakov, there's no other solution, because it's impossible to find anyone else, there's no other person on whom the murder can be pinned. So now you see the origin of this "crafty" and grave accusation against the hapless idiot who took his own life yesterday! There you have it, he's being accused for one reason only—because they can't find anyone else! Had there been even the slightest suggestion of suspicion about anyone else, about some sixth person, I'm convinced that even the accused himself would have been ashamed to accuse Smerdyakov and would have accused that sixth person instead, for to accuse Smerdyakov of this murder is an utter absurdity.

'Gentlemen, let us leave psychology aside, let us leave medicine aside, let us leave even logic itself aside, and let us just consider the facts, simply the facts, and see what they can tell us. Let us say that the murder was committed by Smerdyakov. But how? Alone, or in complicity with the accused? Let us consider the first suggestion, namely, that Smerdyakov committed the murder on his own. Of course, if he did commit it, then there must have been a motive, some benefit to himself. However, being completely devoid of the motives that the accused had—that is to say, hatred, jealousy, and so on and so forth—Smerdyakov could only have committed the murder for money, simply in order to obtain the three thousand roubles which he himself had seen his master place in the envelope. And so, having decided upon the murder, he gives advance notice to another person—incidentally a highly interested party, namely the accused. He tells him all about the money and the signal, where the envelope is to be found, what exactly is written on the envelope, what it's tied with, and, most important, most important of all, he tells him about the signal which will allow him access to the master of the house. Well, is he just trying to get himself caught? Or is he asking for a rival to get in there first and help himself to the envelope? They will say he did it because he was frightened. Just a moment! How can a man who has no scruples about planning such a reckless and bestial deed pass on information which only he in the whole world knows about and which if only he keeps his mouth shut no one else in the world will ever find out? No, however cowardly he was, he would never, once he had planned such a deed, have told anyone—at least not about the envelope or the signal, because that would have been tantamount to incriminating himself. He might have deliberately invented something, he might have lied if someone had demanded information, but he would have kept quiet about other things! On the other hand, I repeat, if he had only kept quiet about the money and then, after killing his master, he had taken it, no one in the whole world could have accused him of the murder, at least not with robbery as a motive, because after all he was the only person who had seen the money or knew that it was in the house. And even if he had been accused, it would definitely have been assumed that he had killed him for some other motive. But since nobody has at any time been able to pin any motive on him—on the contrary, everyone knew that he was well liked by his master, who let him into his confidence—it therefore follows that he would have been the last person to be suspected; suspicion would have fallen first and foremost on someone who had a motive and did not conceal it, who had told everyone of his motive—in a word, suspicion would have fallen on the son of the murdered man, Dmitry Fyodorovich. So Smerdyakov would have committed both the murder and the theft, and the son would have been accused—surely, that would have suited Smerdyakov-the-murderer down to the ground, wouldn't it? But having planned the murder, Smerdyakov goes and reveals beforehand to the son Dmitry details about the money, about the envelope, and about the signal—how logical, how obvious!

'The day comes on which Smerdyakov plans to commit the murder—and he falls down the stairs in a *sham* fit! What for? Well, obviously so that the servant Grigory, who was thinking of applying his medicinal embrocation, would see that there was no one at all to keep watch on the house, and would perhaps delay applying the treatment and stay and keep guard. And obviously also so that the master himself, seeing that no one was on guard and being petrified that his son might arrive, a fear which he made no attempt to conceal, would become even more wary and intensify his vigilance. Finally, and most obviously, so that he, Smerdyakov, assumed to be incapacitated by his fit, would immediately be carried not into the kitchen, where he always slept at night, away from everybody and therefore able to come and go as he pleased, but into Grigory and Marfa's room at the far end of the outhouse, where he would be put behind the partition, not three steps from their bed—his master and the kind-hearted Marfa had always insisted on this arrangement whenever he had a fit. There, lying behind the partition—and in order to feign illness more credibly—he would of course more likely than not begin to groan and then disturb their sleep throughout the night (as Grigory and his wife testified, in fact)— and all this just so that he could suddenly get up and kill his master more easily!

'But, you will say, perhaps that's exactly why he feigned it all, so that in his incapacitated state he would not be suspected, and perhaps he told the accused about the money and the signal precisely so that the latter would be tempted to enter and commit the murder, and having committed the murder the latter would depart, taking the money with him, and would in addition make a lot of noise and commotion, perhaps wake up witnesses, and, you see, that is when Smerdyakov would get up and leave the room and—well, leave the room and do what? Precisely: he'd leave the room to murder his master for the second time, and for the second time take the money which had already been stolen. You may laugh, gentlemen. I myself am embarrassed to suggest such a farrago, and yet, just imagine: that is in fact exactly what the accused is claiming. "After me," he claims, "after I had already left the house, knocked Grigory to the ground and made a lot of commotion, he got up and proceeded to murder and rob his master." I shall not even speculate as to how it was that Smerdyakov could work all this out beforehand and plan everything in sequence; namely, that the angry, enraged son would come and simply glance cautiously through the window and, though he knew the signal, would withdraw, leaving the whole booty to him, Smerdyakov! Gentlemen, this is a serious question: when exactly is Smerdyakov supposed to have committed this crime? Tell me the precise time, otherwise he cannot be held responsible.

'But perhaps the fit was real. The sick man suddenly regained consciousness, heard a cry, and went out of the outhouse. Then what? He had a look and said to himself: "Why don't I go and kill my master?" But how could he have known who was there, what was going on? Surely, he had been lying unconscious until then. Really, gentlemen, let us not let our imagination run away with us.

'"Ah but," some shrewd people will say, "supposing they were in league with each other. Supposing they committed the murder together and split the money between them, what then?"

'Yes, indeed, there are serious grounds for such a suspicion, and we don't have to look far for some substantial evidence to support it: one of them commits the murder and does all the dirty work, while his accomplice lies flat on his back pretending to have an epileptic fit, expressly in order to divert everyone's

suspicion and to alarm his master and Grigory. One may wonder
what could have led the accomplices to devise such a crazy plan.
But perhaps Smerdyakov was not an active participant at all,
merely a passive one who acquiesced; perhaps the terrified
Smerdyakov had merely agreed not to oppose the murder;
foreseeing that he would be blamed for letting someone kill his
master and for not defending him and raising the alarm, he
persuaded Dmitry Karamazov beforehand to allow him to be
confined to bed on the pretext of having an epileptic fit: "You
just go ahead and murder whom you please, it's nothing to do
with me!" But even if this were so, the epileptic fit would have
caused a commotion in the house, and Dmitry Karamazov,
foreseeing this, could never have agreed to such an arrangement.
But let us for argument's sake assume that he did agree; surely
Dmitry Karamazov would still have been the murderer, the real
murderer, the instigator of the crime, and Smerdyakov just a
passive participant—not even a participant but merely an unwilling accomplice who, out of fear, allowed the crime to take place,
a distinction that the court would surely be able to make. And
what did, in fact, happen? No sooner was the accused arrested
than he instantly laid all the blame on Smerdyakov, on him *alone*.
He did not accuse him of complicity, but of being the sole
perpetrator: "He did it alone," he said, "it was he who committed
the murder and the robbery, it's his handiwork!" Well, what sort
of accomplices would immediately begin to lay the blame on
each other? This sort of thing just doesn't happen. And think
how risky it would have been for Karamazov; he's the actual
murderer, not the other one, the other one was not involved and
lay behind the partition all the time, but now he gets blamed for
it all. Surely that would have infuriated the one who had simply
been lying behind the partion, and he could have blurted out the
whole truth in sheer self-preservation: "We were both in on it,
only I didn't commit the murder, I just went along with it
because I was afraid." Surely we would have expected Smerdyakov to understand that the court would establish the degree
of his guilt immediately, and consequently he could also have
surmised that, even if he were to be punished, his punishment
would be incomparably more lenient than that of the principal
perpetrator. And therefore there's not the slighest doubt that he

would have let the cat out of the bag. This did not happen, however. Smerdyakov did not even mention the possibility of complicity, despite the fact that the defendant categorically accused him specifically and all the time referred to him as the sole murderer. Moreover, it was Smerdyakov who revealed to the investigators that he personally had told the accused about the envelope with the money and about the signal, and that if it had not been for him the accused would not have known anything. If he really had been guilty of complicity, would he have informed the investigators of it so readily, that it was he himself who had given all this information to the defendant? Quite the contrary, he would have prevaricated and would certainly have tried to distort the facts and play down their significance. But he did not distort them and did not try to play down their significance. This is obviously the behaviour of an innocent man, not one who is afraid he will be accused of complicity. And so, in a state of severe depression brought on by his epilepsy and by the whole of this tragedy, he hanged himself yesterday. He left a note, written in his own characteristic style: "I'm going to put an end to myself of my own free will and choice, so as not to blame anybody." Well, why couldn't he have added: "I'm the murderer, not Karamazov"? But he didn't; was he driven by his conscience to make the one statement, but not the other?

'But let me continue. One of the witnesses has shown the court three thousand roubles. "The actual money", he told us, "that was contained in that envelope." (You see it before you, gentlemen, on the table where the material exhibits are.) "I got it from Smerdyakov yesterday," he informed us. But you, gentlemen of the jury, will remember the unseemly spectacle that took place here. No need for me to remind you of the details; however, let me draw your attention to just two or three points—choosing from among the more insignificant ones, precisely because they are insignificant and may therefore be overlooked and easily forgotten by most people. Firstly, we come back to the same situation: yesterday, stricken by conscience, Smerdyakov returned the money and hanged himself. (If it had not been for his pangs of conscience he would not have returned the money.) And, of course, it was only last night (on Ivan

Karamazov's own admission) that he first confessed his guilt to Ivan Karamazov, otherwise why would the latter have concealed it all this time? And so he confessed. But why, I repeat why, knowing that an innocent man was to face trial for murder the next day, did he not admit the whole truth to us in his suicide note? After all, the money alone is no proof. For instance, a week ago, quite by chance, I and two other people in this hall found out that Ivan Fyodorovich Karamazov had sent off to the regional capital to redeem two five-thousand rouble five per cent interest bonds, having a total value of ten thousand roubles. I say this only because any of us may happen to keep money somewhere from time to time, and the fact that three thousand roubles are shown to the court does not actually prove that they necessarily came out of this or that box or envelope. And, as though this were not enough, Ivan Karamazov, having obtained such a vital piece of information from the actual murderer, does nothing about it. Why not pass it on immediately? Why did he delay doing anything till the morning? I think I may hazard a guess. The man has been in poor mental health for about a week now; he himself has admitted to the doctor that he sees apparitions, that he meets people who are already dead; being in the preliminary stages of a severe illness—he did in fact succumb to it today—and learning of Smerdyakov's unexpected demise, he suddenly adopts the following line of reasoning: "The fellow's dead, I might as well accuse him and thereby save my brother. I've got some money; why don't I take a wad of notes and say that Smerdyakov gave them to me before he killed himself." I hear you say: this is disgraceful; a man may be dead, but still one should not slander him, even to save one's brother. All well and good, but supposing he thought that he was telling the truth, supposing, having become quite mentally unbalanced by the sudden death of the servant, he himself was convinced that that was how it had happened. After all, you saw the scene that took place here, you saw the state the man was in. He stood on his feet and spoke, but did he know what he was saying? The sick man's statement was followed by the reading of the letter which the accused wrote to Miss Verkhovtseva two days before committing the crime, and in which he gave full details of his intended crime. So why look any further? The crime was

committed exactly as described in that letter, and by none other
than the writer of that letter. Yes, gentlemen of the jury, it was
carried out point by point as he described it! And he most
certainly did not run from his father's window in embarrassment
and trepidation, knowing full well that his sweetheart was in the
room. No, this is incongruous and quite out of the question. I
put it to you that he entered the room and finished off the job.
He probably did it in a fit of temper, flying into a rage the
moment he saw his hated rival, but, having killed him—which
he evidently did with a single blow, a single swipe of the brass
pestle he was clutching—and having made a thorough search
and established that she was not there, he did not forget to put
his hand under the pillow and pull out the envelope with the
money—that same torn envelope which is lying here on the table
among the material evidence. I am recounting this in order to
draw your attention to one—in my view, highly significant—
circumstance. Would an experienced criminal, especially one
whose only motive was robbery, have left the envelope next to
the body on the floor, where it was found later? Well, let us
suppose for example that it was Smerdyakov who killed him,
with robbery in mind; surely he would simply have taken the
whole envelope with him, without bothering to tear it open as he
stood over his victim's body? He knew for certain that it
contained money, because after all he had been present when
the money was placed in the envelope and the latter was sealed.
Now, had he taken the envelope and its contents without tearing
it open, no one would have known a robbery had been committed. I ask you, gentlemen of the jury, would Smerdyakov have
done such a thing? Would he have left the envelope on the floor?
No, that was the act of a desperate man, one whose judgement
was already impaired, a murderer, not a thief, a man who had
not stolen anything before in his life and who, even when he
withdrew the money from under the pillow, was doing so not as
a common thief, but as the rightful owner retrieving his property
from a thief, for that is precisely how Dmitry Karamazov
regarded the three thousand roubles with which he had become
so obsessed. And so, having discovered the envelope, which he
had never seen before, he tears it open to establish whether in
fact there is any money in it. With the money in his pocket he

then runs away without even stopping to think for a moment that he's leaving behind, on the floor, a vital piece of evidence against himself in the shape of the torn envelope. In the heat of the moment Karamazov, not Smerdyakov, does not stop to think, does not realize the consequences! He takes to his heels. He hears a yell as the servant catches up with him, the servant grabs hold of him, stops him in his tracks, and then slumps to the ground, felled by the brass pestle. The accused jumps down out of pity. Imagine, we are expected to believe that he jumped down, just at that moment, out of pity, out of compassion, to see if he could help him. Was that really an appropriate occasion to demonstrate such compassion? No, I put it to you that he jumped down solely to find out whether the only witness to his evil deed was still alive. Any other feeling, any other motive would have been unnatural! Note, he is very solicitous over Grigory, he wipes his head with a handkerchief, and, having established that he is dead, rushes madly, covered in blood, back to the house of his beloved. How could it not occur to him that, in his bloodstained state, he would immediately be apprehended? But the accused assures us that he paid no attention to the fact that he was covered in blood; that may well be true, that is distinctly possible, criminals always behave like that in such circumstances—cunning and calculating in one respect, and totally lacking in common sense in another. He had only one thing on his mind at that moment: where was *she*? He needed to establish her whereabouts as soon as possible, and so he went running into her house, only to receive an unexpected and totally devastating piece of news: she had gone to Mokroye with her "former", her "indisputable one"!'

9

PSYCHOLOGY LET LOOSE. GALLOPING TROIKA. THE PROSECUTOR'S SUMMING-UP

HAVING come to this point in his speech, Ippolit Kyrillovich, who had evidently chosen to describe the events in a strict chronological order, which all highly strung speakers do when

purposely seeking to contain their argument within strictly
defined boundaries and prevent themselves being carried away
by their own enthusiasm, now made a point of expounding upon
'the former and indisputable one', and put forward a number of
rather amusing ideas regarding this subject. 'Karamazov, having
been insanely jealous of everyone, seems suddenly and totally to
have capitulated and accepted the "former and indisputable
one". And this is all the more strange since he had not previously
paid any attention at all to this new danger looming in the shape
of an unexpected rival. But, since a Karamazov always lives just
for the moment, he imagined that this danger was still remote.
Probably he regarded him as a figment of his imagination. But
then his love-torn heart realized that the reason why the woman
had been deceiving him and concealing the existence of this new
rival from him was perhaps that the newly emerged rival was
anything but a fiction or a fantasy, and epitomized everything for
her, all her aspirations in life; no sooner had he understood this
than he accepted the situation. Well, gentlemen of the jury, I
cannot avoid this peculiar trait in the character of the accused,
which is the last thing one would have expected of him. An
insatiable desire for truth had arisen, a need to show respect for
a woman, to recognize her spiritual rights, and precisely at a time
when he had just stained his hands with his father's blood! It is
also true that the spilt blood was already, at that moment, crying
out for retribution; having consigned his soul and the whole of
his earthly fate to perdition, surely he could not avoid asking
himself what he represented, what he could represent for that
woman *now*, that being whom he loved more than his own soul,
in contrast to her "former and indisputable one", the man who
had ruined her once, but who had now repented and returned to
her with renewed love, with an honourable offer, with the
promise of a new and happy life to come. "Whereas I, miserable
wretch that I am, what can I give her *now*, what can I possibly
offer her?" Karamazov understood all this, he understood that
by his crime he had forfeited his whole future, and that, instead
of being a man with a life ahead of him, he was merely a
condemned criminal! This realization crushed and mortified
him. And so Karamazov immediately conceived a desperate plan
which, given his character, must have appeared to him as his

only, his preordained way out of the dreadful situation in which he found himself. This way out was suicide. He ran to the clerk Perkhotin to redeem the pistols he had pawned, pulling out of his pocket as he ran all the money for which he had just stained his hands with his father's blood. Money is what he needed most of all: Karamazov would die, Karamazov would shoot himself, and that would not be forgotten in a hurry! He's not a poet for nothing! That's what comes of living life to the full! "I'll go to her, to her—and there, there I'll throw a party to end all parties, a party that'll be remembered by people for years to come. We'll raise the roof, we'll join the gypsies in their crazy singing and dancing, and raise our glasses to congratulate the adored woman on her new-found happiness, and then I'll blow my brains out in expiation, there at her feet! One day she'll remember Mitya Karamazov, she'll realize how much Mitya loved her, she'll spare a thought for Mitya!" A surfeit of histrionics, melodrama, typically wild Karamazovian abandon and sentimentality—well, and something else besides, gentlemen of the jury, something that cried out from the depths of his soul, that relentlessly assaulted his brain and fatally poisoned his heart; that *something* was his conscience, gentlemen of the jury, his conscience sitting in judgement upon him and meting out its dreadful punishment! But the pistol would reconcile everything, the pistol was the only way out and there was no other, and as for the rest, who knows whether, at that instant, Karamazov thought *"what will be there?"* In any case, is a Karamazov capable of Hamlet-like reflections as to what will be "there"? No, gentlemen of the jury, others have their Hamlets; so far, we Russians have only our Karamazovs!"'

Here Ippolit Kyrillovich painted a detailed picture of Mitya's efforts to deal with all the arrangements—at Perkhotin's, in the shop, and with the drivers. He cited a multitude of words, expressions, and gestures attested by witnesses—and the effect upon the listeners was overwhelming. What made the strongest impression was the totality of the facts. The guilt of this man, careering about frantically without bothering to cover his tracks, seemed ever more incontrovertible. 'He saw no point in being careful,' said Ippolit Kyrillovich, 'on one or two occasions he nearly confessed everything, he hinted at his guilt without

actually admitting it in so many words' (here followed the statements of witnesses). 'He had even shouted to his driver on the
way: "Do you realize, you're talking to a murderer?" All the
same, he could not bring himself to tell everything: he had to get
to Mokroye first, and there put the finishing touches to the poem.
But what awaited the unfortunate man in Mokroye? The fact was
that, almost from his first moments in Mokroye, he finally realized that his "indisputable" rival was perhaps not as indisputable
as all that after all, and that his congratulations on new-found
wealth and his salute with the festive cup were neither appreciated nor welcome. But, gentlemen of the jury, you already know
the facts as established at the judicial investigation. Karamazov's
triumph over his rival turned out to be beyond dispute, and at
that point—yes, at that point, his soul entered a totally new
phase, perhaps the most terrifying of all the phases his soul had
yet gone through or would ever be likely to go through! One can
positively assert, gentlemen of the jury,' said Ippolit Kiryllovich
emphatically, 'that nature defiled and a heart steeped in crime
can, in themselves, exact a greater degree of vengeance than any
human justice! What is more, the sufferings inflicted by the latter
even take the sting out of the punishment imposed by nature, so
that the criminal may even yearn for them as a deliverance from
despair; I cannot begin to imagine Karamazov's torment and
spiritual suffering on discovering that she loved him, that she
was rejecting her "former and indisputable one" for his sake,
and was beckoning him, Mitya, to a new life, a life filled with the
promise of happiness. And what a moment to choose! When
everything was already over for him, when he had reached the
end of the line! By the way, allow me to make one rather
important observation in passing in order to illustrate the true
nature of the position in which the accused found himself at the
time: until the very last moment, even until the very instant of
his arrest, this woman, this beloved woman, remained unattainable for him, passionately desired, yet unattainable. But why, why
did he not shoot himself there and then, why did he abandon the
decision he had made, how could he even have forgotten where
his pistol was? It was precisely his passionate thirst for love and
the hope of being able to satisfy it on the spot that held him back.
In the intoxication of the merrymaking he clung to his beloved

who, more seductive and attractive to him than ever before, was carousing with him there; he stayed at her side, drooled over her, became oblivious to everything else in her presence. For a brief moment this passion could have subdued not only the fear of arrest, but even the pangs of conscience! But only for a moment, only for a fleeting moment! I can well imagine the accused's state of mind at the time, completely in the grip of several conflicting tensions: firstly, there was his state of inebriation, the carousing and the noise, the high jinks of the singers and dancers, and above all she was there, flushed with wine, singing and dancing for him, intoxicated and full of laughter for him! Then there was the faint but comforting hope that the fateful hour of reckoning was still a long way off—or at least not imminent—they wouldn't come for him until the morning at the earliest. That meant that he still had several hours' grace, and that was a long time, a very long time! Several hours should be enough to come to all kinds of solutions. I imagine his state of mind was not unlike that of a condemned criminal being taken to his execution, to the gallows: there is still a very long road ahead, which must be covered at walking pace, past a crowd of thousands, then there will be a turn into the next street, and only at the end of that second street will he reach the dreadful square! I really believe that at the start of the journey the condemned man, sitting in the tumbril, must feel that an infinite life still stretches ahead of him. However, the houses roll by one by one, the tumbril rumbles on—oh, that's nothing, it's still a long way to the turning into the next street, and he continues to look keenly to the left and the right at the thousands of indifferently curious people with their eyes riveted upon him, and he continues vaguely to imagine that, like all of them, he is still a human being. But here's the turning into the next street! Never mind though, never mind, still a whole street to go. And no matter how many houses he passes, he still thinks: "There are still a lot of houses." And so to the very end, right up until they reach the town square. I imagine that is just how Karamazov must have felt. "They haven't found out yet," he would argue. "I can still think of something, there's still time to devise a plan of action, to think up some arguments, but now, right now—isn't she simply delightful!" His heart must have been heavy and full of gloom, but in spite of that he managed to take half the money he had on him and hide it somewhere—otherwise I cannot for the life of me explain how half the three thousand roubles he had just removed from under his father's pillow could have gone missing. It was not his first visit to Mokroye, he had gone on the binge there once before, for two days. That huge old timber house, with all its outhouses and passageways, was familiar to him. I put it to you that part of the money vanished just then, in that very house, not long before his arrest—in some crack or cranny, or under a floorboard, or in some nook under the roof. What for? You want to know what for? Well, the catastrophe was liable to occur at any moment—he had not thought out how he would deal with it, of course, what with that throbbing in his head and the attraction *she* was exerting on him, there had been no time. So what about the money? One always needs money! Money is the very stuff of life. Perhaps such calculated deliberations at such a time may seem unnatural to you? But he assures us, after all, that a month before, at yet another extremely disturbing and critical moment for him, he had taken half the three thousand roubles which he had on him and stitched the money into a makeshift purse, so even if, as I shall soon prove, this was untrue, the idea was nevertheless familiar to Karamazov, for he had contemplated it. And, what is more, when he was subsequently assuring the investigator that he had taken half the three thousand roubles and put it in the purse (which had never even existed), it is quite likely that he invented the idea of the purse there and then, on the spur of the moment, precisely because he had divided the money in half on an impulse two hours previously, and hidden one half somewhere there in Mokroye—just in case, till the morning—simply in order not to keep it on him. Two extremes, gentlemen of the jury, remember that a Karamazov can encompass two extremes, and both at one and the same time! We searched the house, but found nothing. Perhaps the money is still there, or perhaps it disappeared the following day and the accused has it now. In any case, when we arrested him he was on his knees beside her; she was lying on the bed and he was stretching out his arms towards her, and he was so oblivious to everything at that moment that he did not even hear those who came to apprehend him approaching. Nor had he managed to think of anything to say for himself. He was taken totally unawares.

'And now he stands before his judges, the arbiters of his fate. Gentlemen of the jury, there are moments when, in the performance of our duty, we ourselves are overcome by something akin to fear of a man—and fear for him also! These are the moments when one is aware of the visceral fear of the criminal who, seeing that everything is already lost, nevertheless still resists, still intends to put up a fight. That is when all his instincts of self-preservation rise up in him and, desperate to save his skin, he regards you with a penetrating gaze full of questioning and anguish, stalking you mentally and scrutinizing you, your face, your thoughts, waiting to see where you will strike next, and instantly devising thousands of plans in his mind—but nevertheless too afraid to speak, too afraid of betraying himself! These humiliating moments, this road to Calvary, this animal instinct for self-preservation, are dreadful, and sometimes they provoke hatred as well as compassion for the criminal even in the investigators! We all witnessed this at the time. At first he was bemused and, in his state of terror, he let out one exclamation which seriously compromised him: "Blood! It serves me right!" But he soon regained control over himself. What to say, how to reply, he still had not decided; the only words he could utter were a bare denial: "I am not guilty of my father's death!" That was to be his line of defence for the time being; behind it, when the time came, he could erect some other defence, perhaps. Anticipating our questions, he hastened to explain away his initial, compromising exclamation by insisting that he considered himself guilty only of the death of the servant Grigory. "Of that death I am guilty, gentlemen, but who killed my father? Who could have killed him, *if not me?*" You hear that: he was asking us, us, we who had come to ask him that very question! Note those pre-emptive words, "if not me", the animal cunning, the naïvety, and the Karamazov impetuosity! "I didn't kill him, you can put that right out of your heads. I wanted to kill him, gentlemen, I really wanted to kill him," he hastened to admit (oh, he was in such a hurry!), "but I'm innocent, I didn't kill him!" He concedes that he wanted to commit the murder: "Look how truthful I am, so you should believe me when I say that it wasn't me who killed him." It is at such times that a criminal sometimes becomes extraordinarily stupid and naïve. And just then the investigators slipped in the most ingenuous of questions: "It wouldn't be Smerdyakov who killed him, would it?" What happened then was precisely what we expected: he became terribly angry because we had caught him unawares and had forestalled him before he could prepare himself; he wanted to choose the most convenient and advantageous moment to introduce Smerdyakov as plausibly as possible. True to his nature, he immediately went overboard and began to try for all he was worth to convince us that Smerdyakov could not have committed the murder, that he was incapable of killing anyone. But don't believe him, this is merely his cunning; he had no intention whatever of depriving himself of the Smerdyakov option; on the contrary, he would still point the finger at him—there was simply no one else that he could point to—but he would do that in his own good time; for now, his pitch had been queered. He would not accuse him until the next day perhaps, or even for several days; then, having chosen an opportunity, he would shout: "Don't forget, I myself more than anyone refused to believe in Smerdyakov's guilt, but I'm convinced now: he killed him, who else could it have been!" Meanwhile he presented us with a morose and ill-tempered denial; impetuosity and anger induced him to resort to the wildest and unlikeliest story about peering through his father's window and then withdrawing discreetly. He was still not aware of all the circumstances, including the nature of the evidence given by Grigory, who had recovered in the meantime. We come to the examination and inspection of his personal effects. The examination enraged him, but it also made him defiant. Of the three thousand roubles, we accounted for only fifteen hundred. And, of course, it was precisely at that moment of sullen silence and non-cooperation that the idea of the makeshift purse first came into his head. Without a shadow of doubt, he himself sensed the whole implausibility of his fiction and was at great pains to make it as credible as possible, to embellish it to such an extent that it would turn into a really plausible explanation. In such instances, the first and foremost task facing the investigators is to prevent the criminal having time to prepare himself, to take him by surprise, so that he will divulge his innermost thoughts in all their revelatory crudity, unlikelihood, and incongruity. And when it comes to making the criminal talk, the only way is—suddenly and as though by chance—to present him with some new fact, some highly significant aspect of the case, for which he could have made no allowance and which he could in no way have foreseen. We had such a fact ready and waiting, indeed, we had it ready and waiting for some considerable time. It was the servant Grigory's evidence about the open door through which the accused had left. He had forgotten all about that door, and it had not even occurred to him that Grigory could have seen it. The effect was shattering. He leapt to his feet and shouted at us: "Smerdyakov killed him, it was Smerdyakov!" And so he presented his central, his fundamental argument in its most implausible form, because Smerdyakov could only have committed the murder after he had struck Grigory down and had run away. When we informed him, however, that Grigory had noticed that the door was open before he fell, and that as he was leaving his bedroom he had heard Smerdyakov groaning behind the partition, Karamazov was absolutely devastated. My esteemed and talented colleague Nikolai Parfenovich told me afterwards that he was moved to tears with pity for the accused at that moment. And it was precisely then that the accused, to save the situation, came up with the absurd tale about that infamous makeshift purse, as if to say: you want to hear a tall story—here it is! Gentlemen of the jury, I have already told you why I consider the whole of this story about the money sewn up in a purse a month before the crime to be not only an absurdity, but also the most improbable fabrication, such as could only have been devised in a case like this. Even if one were to try, for a wager, to find or imagine anything less plausible, one could not really come up with anything to beat it. The jubilant storyteller can always be confounded and caught out on details, the same details with which reality abounds and which are always ignored as unimportant and trivial by hapless, compulsive fable-mongers, and which in fact never so much as enter their heads. Their minds are otherwise occupied at such moments, their minds are busy constructing a grandiose structure—how dare anyone bother them with such trivia! But that is precisely how they are caught!

The accused is confronted with a question: "So, would you mind telling us where you got the material for the makeshift purse, who made it for you?" "I made it myself." "But where did you get the material, if you please?" The accused is indignant, he regards this as almost an offensive question, and, would you believe it, genuinely so, quite genuinely so! But they are all like that. "I tore it from a shirt." "Splendid. That means that tomorrow we can look forward to finding this shirt with a piece missing from it." And, let us be clear, gentlemen of the jury, if we had found this shirt (and, if it had existed, how could we have failed to find it in a suitcase or a chest of drawers?)—it would have served as evidence, tangible evidence confirming the truth of his statement!" But he is unable to grasp this. "I don't know, perhaps it wasn't from a shirt... I stitched it up in my landlady's nightcap." "What nightcap?" "I took it, it was lying around at her place, a scrap of calico." "And are you quite sure of this?" "No, I wouldn't say I was quite sure..." And he gets flustered, really angry about it, and yet can you imagine anyone forgetting such a thing? In the direst moments of human life, say when a man is on the way to the place of execution, it is precisely this kind of detail which sticks in his memory. He will forget everything: but a green roof which he sees on the way, or a crow perched on a roadside cross—that he will not forget. When he was making the purse, he hid himself from the rest of his household; surely he would not have forgotten how shamefully he cowered there, needle in hand, lest someone should come in and expose him; he would have been jumping up to run behind the partition at the least knock (there is a partition in his lodgings)... But, gentlemen of the jury, why am I telling you all this, all these details, these trivialities!' Ippolit Kyrillovich exclaimed suddenly. 'Well, for the same reason that the accused has, right up to this very minute, stubbornly refused to recognize all this for the nonsense that it is! During the whole of these two months, ever since that fateful night, he has clarified nothing, he has not offered a single realistically coherent detail in addition to his former fanciful evidence: "These are mere details—you must accept my word!" What are we, jackals thirsting for human flesh? Give us one single piece of evidence in favour of the accused, and we shall be overjoyed—but it must be real, factual evidence, not conjectures derived from the expression on the defendant's face by his own brother, or that brother's assertion that, in striking his chest, he was actually indicating the purse, and all this observed in the dark. We would be delighted to obtain such evidence, we would not hesitate to drop the charges. Now, however, justice demands that we persist, we cannot withdraw any charges.' At this stage, Ippolit Kyrillovich began his summing-up. He had worked himself up into a passion, he lamented the shedding of blood, the blood of a father, murdered by his own son, 'with the base intention of committing a theft'. He emphasized the tragic and dreadful nature of this chain of events. 'And no matter what you may hear from our talented—and rightly famous—counsel for the defence,' Ippolit Kyrillovich was unable to resist the comment, 'no matter how colourful and moving the words with which he will assault your sensibilities, try to remember nevertheless that, at this moment, you are in the hallowed temple of justice. Remember that you are the custodians of truth, the custodians of holy Russia, her foundations, her family life, all that she holds sacred! Yes, you are representing contemporary Russia here, and your verdict will reverberate not just in this hall alone, but throughout Russia, and the whole of Russia will stop to listen to her custodians and judges, and she will be either heartened or saddened by your verdict. Do not torment Russia, therefore, or betray her expectations; the fateful troika is galloping at full pelt, maybe to its doom. Many hands have long reached out throughout the whole of Russia in an attempt to stop its wild, lurching course. And even if other nations step aside to make way for its breakneck progress, then, in all likelihood, this is not out of respect, as the poet would have wished, but out of sheer terror—note this well! Out of terror or perhaps out of disgust, and we should thank our lucky stars that they do step aside, for in order to save themselves and their enlightened civilization, they might fail to step aside, and instead form a solid wall across the path of the charging apparition, thus putting an end to our galloping depravity! We have already heard these threatening voices from Europe. Do not tempt them, do not augment their ever-increasing hatred by passing a verdict acquitting a son of murdering his own father...'

In a word, Ippolit Kyrillovich, after an impassioned speech, finished on a deeply emotional note, and it must be owned that the effect on his listeners was overwhelming. He himself left the hall hurriedly as soon as he finished speaking, and, as I have mentioned, nearly fainted in the next room. The audience did not applaud, but the serious-minded amongst them were well satisfied. It was only the ladies who were not particularly impressed, though even they had been fascinated by his eloquence, the more so since they were not really worried about the outcome and put all their trust in Fetyukovich: 'He'll take the floor at last, and of course he's bound to win!' People kept glancing at Mitya; he had sat silent throughout the prosecutor's speech, arms folded, teeth clenched, staring at the floor. Only occasionally, mostly when Grushenka was mentioned, had he raised his head to catch what was being said. When the prosecutor came to speak of Rakitin's comments about her, an angry, contemptuous smile had appeared on his face and he had said audibly: 'Bernards, the lot of you!' When Ippolit Kyrillovich described how he had interrogated and grilled him in Mokroye, he had raised his head and listened avidly. At one point in the speech he had seemed on the point of jumping to his feet and shouting something, but he had managed to control himself and merely shrugged his shoulders contemptuously. The closing stages of this speech, in particular that part which dealt with the methods employed by the prosecutor during the interrogation of the accused in Mokroye, were later the subject of some debate and amusement locally at the expense of Ippolit Kyrillovich: 'The man couldn't resist bragging about his talents.' The session was adjourned, but only for a very short period—a quarter of an hour, twenty minutes at the most. Snatches of conversation were heard from the spectators. I remember a few of them.

'A solid performance!' one gentlemen, standing with a group, said with a frown.

'Too much psychology for my taste,' came another voice.

'But it was all perfectly true, you have to agree!'

'Summed it all up pretty neatly, didn't he?'

'Summed us up pretty well, too,' a third voice joined in. 'Do you remember the bit at the beginning of the speech about us all being like Fyodor Pavlovich?'

'And that bit at the end. Only he went rather over the top.'

'Pretty obscure in places too.'

'He got carried away a little.'

'It wasn't fair, it wasn't fair, I tell you.'

'Skilful, though. The man had been dying to say all that for a long time, he-he!'

'I wonder what the defence will say?'

From another group:

'He needn't have insulted that chap from St Petersburg, though, with all that stuff about assaulting sensibilities: do you remember?'

'Yes, that wasn't too clever.'

'He was too eager.'

'Excitable sort of chap.'

'It's all right for us to laugh, but what about the defendant?'

'Yes, poor old Mitya.'

'Yes, I wonder what the defence counsel's going to say?'

From a third group:

'Who's that woman with the lorgnette, the fat one sitting at the end of the row?'

'She's the wife of a general, divorced now, though. I know her.'

'Fancies herself, doesn't she? Lorgnette indeed!'

'The old bag.'

'No, she's quite sexy really.'

'That little blonde two seats away from her... she's more like it.'

'That was good, how they nabbed him at Mokroye, wasn't it?'

'Not bad. He had to tell us all over again. You'd think he'd bragged enough about it already all over the town.'

'Couldn't resist one more time. Sheer vanity.'

'He's got a chip on his shoulder, he-he!'

'And he's touchy. Full of rhetoric, too. Did you notice the length of his sentences?'

'And he was scaremongering, you know, scaremongering. Remember about the troika? "Others have their Hamlets; so far we Russians only have our Karamazovs!" Not bad.'

'He was having a dig at the Liberals. He's scared.'

'He's scared of the other lawyer, too.'

'Yes, I wonder what old Fetyukovich will say.'

'Well, whatever he says, he won't be able to pull the wool over the eyes of our peasants.'

'You think not?'

And from a fourth group:

'And that was a good point he made about the troika, and that bit about other nations.'

'Well, it's true, what he said about people not waiting.'

'What was that?'

'Yes, in the British parliament* last week, one member stood up and put a question to the minister about the nihilists, saying wasn't it time we took on that barbarian country and taught them a lesson? That's what Ippolit was talking about, I know it was. He was talking about it only last week.'

'They haven't got a snowball's...'

'What do you mean, "a snowball's"?'

'We'll just close Kronstadt to them and cut off their supply of grain.* Where will they get it from?'

'From America. They'll get it from America.'

'Rubbish.'

The bell rang and everyone rushed back to their seats. Fetyukovich stood up to speak.

10

DEFENCE COUNSEL'S SPEECH.
ALL THINGS TO ALL MEN

A DEATHLY hush fell as the famous advocate's initial words rang out in the hall. Everyone's eyes were riveted upon him. He began very directly, simply, and with conviction, without a trace of arrogance, and with no attempt at eloquence, pathos, or false sentimentality. This was a man speaking to an intimate circle of well-disposed people. His voice was pleasant, sonorous, and persuasive; he sounded sincere and genuine. Nevertheless, everyone was aware from the outset that the orator might, at any moment, rise to real passion and 'strike the hearts with unsuspected power'.* He spoke less formally than Ippolit Kyrillovich perhaps, avoiding long sentences and keeping more to the point. There was one thing about him that the ladies did not like much: he kept arching his back, especially at the beginning of his speech—not bowing, but as though preparing to launch himself upon his audience, seeming as it were to contort the upper half of his long, narrow torso, which appeared to be articulated in the middle, thereby enabling him to bend it almost at right angles. To start with he spoke desultorily, apparently without any fixed plan, choosing facts at random, but it all merged into a unified whole in the end. His speech could be divided into two halves: the first half—refuting the accusation and challenging the case for the prosecution—was vicious and sarcastic by turn. But he suddenly appeared to change his tone, even his approach, in the second half, and to soar to elevated emotional heights, which was just what the audience seemed to have been waiting for, and a wave of expectation swept through the hall. He went straight to the heart of the matter, and began by saying that, though his practice was in St Petersburg, this was not the first time he had travelled elsewhere in Russia as defence counsel, but that he did so only in cases where he was at least reasonably convinced of the innocence of the accused. 'This is just such a case,' he explained. 'Even in the initial newspaper reports one thing caught my attention and swayed me decidedly in favour of the defendant. In a word, I was attracted first and foremost by a certain point of law which, though it occurs often enough in legal practice, has in my previous experience never appeared quite so starkly or with such typical characteristics as in the present instance. By rights, I should deal with the matter only at the culmination of my speech, during my summing-up. However, because of my—people might say—disconcerting tendency to come straight to the point and not to be economical with the truth, I shall outline my argument at the very beginning. This may not be altogether politic of me, but it is sincere for all that. My point, my premise, is as follows: the evidence as a whole is not in favour of the defendant, yet at the same time there is not a single fact which, taken in isolation and on its own merits, could stand up to scrutiny! I became increasingly convinced of this as I followed the case through hearsay and newspaper reports, and then I suddenly received an invitation from the relatives of the defendant to act for the defence. I immediately hurried here and, since my arrival, have become totally convinced of his innocence. It is precisely in order to demolish the apparently overwhelming incriminating evidence and to prove the untenability of each accusation individually that I have agreed to take on this case.'

Thus the counsel for the defence launched into his speech:

'Gentlemen of the jury, I am new here. I have gained all my impressions impartially. The defendant, who is by nature unruly and dissolute, has never offended me personally, as he has offended perhaps a hundred or so people in this town, with the result that many are now prejudiced against him. Of course, I would readily admit that the moral outrage felt by local society is justified: the defendant has been violent and intractable. He was received in local society, however, and welcomed with open arms even by the family of my learned friend, the prosecutor.' (I would add that these words caused one or two hurriedly suppressed outbursts of laughter in the audience, which no one failed to notice. It was common knowledge that the prosecutor, against his better judgement, had entertained Mitya solely because his wife for some reason found Mitya interesting—though a most charitable and respectable lady, she was at the same time wilful and unpredictable, and inclined at times to oppose her husband on certain matters, mostly of a trifling nature. Mitya, it must be owned, visited them rather infrequently.) 'Nevertheless, I shall venture to suppose', continued the counsel for the defence, 'that even such a fair-minded and independent person as my learned friend could well not be entirely devoid of a certain unjustified prejudice against my unfortunate client. That of course is only to be expected; the unfortunate man certainly has no one but himself to blame if he encounters prejudice. Offended moral sensibilities and, even more so, aesthetic sensibilities can sometimes be implacable. Of course, in my learned friend's brilliant speech we have all heard an uncompromising analysis of the defendant's character and behaviour, we have observed his strictly impartial approach to the case—in particular his probing of such psychological depths, which he would never have undertaken had his attitude towards the defendant been in any way intentionally and inimically prejudiced. But, in such cases, some things are even worse, even more destructive than the most hostile and biased attitude to the case in question—for instance, if we get carried away by the exercise, by the need to find an outlet for our imagination and, so to speak, to create a fiction of our own, especially if God has generously endowed us with a gift for psychological insight. Before I left St Petersburg to come here I was warned—though I knew it myself, anyway—that I would do battle here with one of the subtlest and most gifted of psychologists, who had long ago earned for himself a certain, quite distinctive notoriety in that capacity in our still fledgling legal world. But psychology, gentlemen, remarkable science though it may be, can nevertheless be all things to all men' (laughter in the audience). 'I trust you will of course forgive my flippant observation—I have no aptitude for eloquence, but I shall give you an example all the same, the first that comes to mind from the prosecutor's speech. Climbing over a fence while escaping from the garden at night, the defendant fells, with a brass pestle, the servant who has grabbed hold of his leg. Then he immediately jumps down into the garden again and, for a full five minutes, fusses over the injured man, trying to establish whether he has killed him or not. And the prosecutor refuses point-blank to believe that the defendant, as he claims, jumped down to attend to the old man Grigory out of compassion. "No," we are told, "such compassion is not possible at such a moment. It is unnatural," he tells us. "He jumped down solely in order to establish whether the only witness to his foul deed was still alive or not, and in doing so he proved that it was he who had committed the foul deed, because he could have had no other motive for jumping down into the garden, he could not have been prompted by any feelings of compassion." That's psychology for you; but if we take this psychology and apply it to the same case but from a diametrically opposite point of view, the result will be no less convincing. The murderer jumps down just as a precaution, to establish whether the witness is alive or dead, and yet, according to the prosecutor's own words, he has just left behind him, in the room where he killed his father, a most damning piece of evidence in the shape of a torn envelope on which it was written that it contained three thousand roubles. "For if only he had taken the envelope with him, no one else in the whole world would have known that such an envelope existed, that there had been money in it, and, consequently, that this money had been stolen by the defendant." Those are the words of the prosecutor himself. So, we are supposed to believe that, on the one hand, he was careless, that he lost his instinct for self-preservation, took fright, and ran away, leaving incriminating evidence behind on the floor, but that, barely two minutes later, having struck down yet another person, he was immediately possessed, if you please, of the most callous and calculating instinct for self-preservation. But all right, let us assume that that's how it was: herein lies the subtlety of the psychology—under one set of circumstances I may be as bloodthirsty and sharp-eyed as a Caucasian eagle, and the very next moment as blind and helpless as a wretched mole. But if, having committed murder, I am so bloodthirsty and cruelly calculating as to jump down merely to see whether a witness is alive or not, why on earth should I then spend a full five minutes fussing over this new victim of mine, and perhaps end up with fresh witnesses against me? Why should I wipe the injured man's head and stain my handkerchief with blood, if that handkerchief can be used later as evidence against me? Surely, if I am so calculating and cruel-hearted, would it not be better, having jumped down, simply to strike the injured servant across the head again and again with the same pestle and to finish him off, thereby eliminating a witness and taking a big load off my mind? And lastly, I jump down to check if the man is alive or not, and there on the path I leave behind another piece of evidence, that is the selfsame pestle which I took from the two women, who saw me take it and can always identify it as belonging to them. And it is not that I left it on the path by mistake, that I dropped it absent-mindedly, in a state of confusion. No, I threw away my weapon deliberately, because it was found about fifteen paces from where Grigory was struck down. The question arises: why did I do that? I did it precisely because I felt wretched at having killed a man, an old servant, and it was in a state of remorse, therefore, with a curse, that I flung away the pestle, because it was the instrument of murder—why else, what other reason could I have for throwing it away with such force? If I was able to feel pain and remorse for having killed a man, then it goes without saying that I did not kill my father; had I killed my father, I would not have jumped down to examine the injured man out of pity, I would have been guided by a different feeling, pity would have been the last thing to motivate me—more likely, self-preservation, that's the fact of the matter. I repeat, far from fussing over him for a full five minutes, he would just have smashed his skull in once and for all. There was room for pity and kindness precisely because his conscience was clear to start with. That is an alternative psychological analysis. Gentlemen of the jury, I am deliberately resorting to psychology myself in order to demonstrate that one can make of it anything one wants. It all depends on who is using it. Psychology lures even the most serious people into realms of fantasy, and quite without their realizing it. I am talking about an excess of psychology, gentlemen of the jury, in effect, a kind of abuse of psychology.' Here again, approving laughter at the prosecutor's expense was heard from the audience. I shall not repeat the whole of the defence counsel's speech in detail, I shall merely select a few instances, the most salient points.

11

THERE WAS NO MONEY. THERE WAS NO ROBBERY

THERE was one point in the defence counsel's speech which caused not a little consternation amongst the audience, namely, a complete denial of the existence of the fateful three thousand roubles and, consequently, of the possibility of their having been stolen.

'Gentlemen of the jury,' resumed the counsel for the defence, 'one peculiar feature of this case cannot possibly escape an unbiased outsider, namely, the defendant is charged with robbery, but there is absolutely no proof of anything having actually been stolen. We are told that a specific sum of three thousand roubles was taken—but whether it actually existed, no one knows. Judge for yourselves: first, how did we learn that there was this three thousand roubles; and secondly, who saw the money? The one person who saw it and said that it was in the addressed envelope was the servant Smerdyakov. It was also he who communicated this information to the defendant and his brother Ivan Fyodorovich before the tragedy occurred. The information was also conveyed to Miss Svetlova. However, none of these three persons actually saw the money themselves; again, only Smerdyakov saw it, but then the question arises: if it is true that the money really did exist and that Smerdyakov saw it, when did he last see it? And what if, without telling him, his master had taken the money from under the mattress and had put it back in his safe box? Remember, according to Smerdyakov the money was under the bedding, under the mattress; the defendant would have had to pull it out from under the mattress, and yet the bedding was in no way rumpled, and this point is carefully noted in the report. How could the defendant have failed to rumple the bedding at all, and, what is more, with his blood-stained hands, not to have left any marks on the clean, fine bedlinen with which the bed had been specially made up that evening? You may ask: what about the envelope on the floor? It is worth dwelling on this envelope. I was not a little surprised when, just now, talking about this envelope, my learned colleague himself—note this well, gentlemen, the prosecutor himself—to demonstrate the incongruity of the supposition that Smerdyakov could have been the murderer, stated: "Had there not been that envelope, had it not been left behind on the floor as evidence, had the thief taken it away with him, then no one in the whole world would have known that it existed, that there had been money in it, and, consequently, that the accused had stolen the money." And so, according to the prosecutor himself, it is only on the strength of this torn scrap of paper with the inscription on it that the defendant is being accused of theft: otherwise, he tells us, no one would have known that a theft had been committed, or perhaps that there had even been any money. But surely, the fact that a scrap of paper was lying on the floor cannot of itself be sufficient proof that there had been money in it and that this money had been stolen? "But," you may say, "Smerdyakov saw the money in the envelope," but when, when did he last see it? That's what I want to know. I spoke to Smerdyakov and he told me that he saw it two days before the murder! But what is to prevent me from assuming that events took the following course: suppose old Fyodor Pavlovich, having locked himself in his house, had suddenly decided in a fit of hysterically impatient expectation and for want of anything better to do, to take out the envelope and open it. "If I just show her the envelope," he might have argued, "she might not believe me, but if I show her a wad of three thousand roubles, all in hundred-rouble notes, that will have a greater effect and is bound to make her mouth water." And so he tears open the envelope, takes out the money, and, with the careless nonchalance of a rightful owner, throws the empty envelope on the floor, without worrying of course whether it might be used in evidence. Just consider, gentlemen of the jury, can there be a more likely explanation? Indeed not! You see, if something even remotely similar took place, the accusation of theft collapses as a matter of course: if there was no money, it follows that there was no theft. If the fact of the envelope being on the floor could be used as evidence that it had contained money, why could I not use it to prove the opposite, namely that the envelope was lying on the floor precisely because it did not contain any money, the money having been removed previously by the owner himself? Yes; but if it was indeed Fyodor Pavlovich who removed the money from the envelope, where did the money disappear to in that case, for none of it was found in the house during the search? Firstly, some money was found in his safe box, and secondly, he could have removed it that morning or even the night before, disposed of it in some way, given it to someone, posted it—or, indeed, he could have changed his mind and radically revised his whole plan of action, without ever considering it was necessary to inform Smerdyakov about it beforehand. And how, when there is even the remotest possibility of such an interpretation, can one insist with such certainty and persistence that the defendant committed the murder with theft as a motive, or even that any theft took place? That would surely be to enter the realm of fiction. If one is to insist that such-and-such a thing has been stolen, one ought to be able to describe it, or at least prove beyond all shadow of a doubt that it existed. But no one has even seen it. Recently in St Petersburg a young man* of about eighteen, hardly more than a youth, a market delivery boy, entered a *bureau de change* in broad daylight, axe in hand, and, bold as you please, murdered the owner of the *bureau* and fled with fifteen hundred roubles in cash. About five hours later he was arrested; he had the whole of the fifteen hundred on him, with the exception of fifteen roubles which he had managed to spend. Moreover, a clerk who had returned to the *bureau* after the murder informed the police not only that a sum of money had been stolen, but also the denomination of the notes, that is, how many multi-coloured notes, how many blue ones, how many red ones, and the number and value of the missing gold coins, and when the murderer was apprehended precisely those notes and coins were found on him. In addition to everything else, the murderer made a full and frank confession that it was he who had committed the murder and taken the said money. Gentlemen of the jury, that is what I call evidence! In that instance we know, we can see, we are aware of a sum of money, and we cannot say that it never existed. Is that true in the present case? And yet it is a matter of life and death; a man's fate is at stake. All well and good, I hear you say, but wasn't he living it up that same night, wasn't he throwing his money about left, right and centre? He had fifteen hundred roubles to start with—where did they come from? Surely, the very fact that only fifteen hundred was accounted for, while the missing half was nowhere to be found, is ample proof that this was not the same money and that it had not come from that envelope. According to the most accurate time calculation made during the preliminary investigation it was demonstrated beyond all shadow of a doubt that, having left the two maidservants in order to go to Perkhotin, the accused did not stop off at his home—or anywhere else for that matter—but was always in the company of other people, and could not therefore have split up the three thousand and hidden one half somewhere in the town. And yet this is precisely the basis on which the prosecution has built its supposition that the money is hidden in some nook or cranny in Mokroye. But then why not in the vaults of Udolpho Castle,* gentlemen? What an improbable, totally fanciful proposition! And observe, one has only to destroy this particular proposition, namely that the money is hidden in Mokroye, for the whole of the accusation of robbery to fly clean out of the window, otherwise where can the fifteen hundred roubles be, where can it have got to? By what miracle did the money disappear, if it has been proven that the defendant did not stop off anywhere? Are we really prepared to destroy a man's life on the basis of such fiction? It will be said that he still couldn't explain how he came to be in possession of the fifteen hundred roubles which he had to start with, particularly since everyone knew that, before that night, he had no money. Who knew? The defendant has given a clear and confident explanation of where he got the money from and, if you ask me, gentlemen of the jury, if you ask me—nothing could possibly be more plausible than this explanation, nor more in keeping with the defendant's character and inherent tendencies. The prosecutor has demonstrated a particular fondness for the figments of his own imagination: a weak-willed man who had consented to accept three thousand roubles offered to him under such ignominious circumstances would not, we are told, have divided the money and sewn one half into a makeshift purse, and even if he had done so he would have unsewn the purse every other day to help himself to a hundred at a time, and thus would have gone through the lot in a month. All this, remember, was stated in a tone that brooked no opposition. But what if the reality was quite different, what if we have been presented with a piece of fiction featuring a totally imaginary character? That's the whole point, the character is imaginary. I hear an objection: there are witnesses who will testify that in Mokroye, a month before the murder, he spent the whole of the three thousand that he had received from Miss Verkhovtseva, every last kopeck of it, hence he couldn't have divided it. But who are these witnesses? The court has already seen the reliance that can be placed on their credibility. Besides, we're always liable to exaggerate what we see in another person's hand. The point is, none of those witnesses actually counted the money personally, they merely made a guess. After all, the witness Maksimov testified that the defendant had twenty thousand in his hand. You see, gentlemen of the jury, since psychology is a two-edged sword, let me actually apply the other side of the blade and see whether I get the same results.

'A month before the murder, Miss Verkhovtseva entrusted the defendant with three thousand roubles to post, but the question arises: were the conditions under which she entrusted the money to him in fact as shameful and demeaning as we have been led to believe? In Miss Verkhovtseva's original testimony concerning this matter she suggested quite otherwise; in her later testimony, however, all we heard were cries of hatred, of revenge, of long-suppressed animosity. But the very fact that the witness perjured herself in her original testimony gives us every right to conclude that her later testimony could be untruthful too. The prosecutor "does not want, he does not dare to" (his words) delve into that love affair. So be it, I too shall desist; however, I shall merely permit myself to observe that if a pure and highly moral young lady—such as Miss Verkhovtseva undoubtedly is—can allow herself suddenly, without warning, to change her original testimony with the clear intention of discrediting the defendant, then it goes without saying that her testimony was not delivered dispassionately, with cold detachment. Are we then going to be denied the right to conclude that, to a large extent, the scorned woman could have been exaggerating? Yes, that's right, exaggerating the shame and ignominy implied in her offer of the money. In fact, it was offered in such a way that it could easily have been accepted, especially by such a frivolous person as the defendant. The main thing is that at the time he was shortly expecting to receive from his father the three thousand which, according to his calculation, was due to him. It was naïve of him, but it was precisely his naïvety which led him to believe that his father would pay up, that the money was coming to him, and that consequently he would later be able to post the sum that Miss Verkhovtseva had entrusted to him and thus settle his debt. But the prosecutor refuses outright to accept that he could have divided the money and sewn it in a purse that very day: "He's not the type, it would be quite unlike him to have done that sort of thing." But did he not himself proclaim that the Karamazovs were larger than life; did he not draw our attention to the two extremes that a Karamazov can encompass? Precisely, a Karamazov is a man of opposites, of extremes, a man who can call a halt in the midst of the most reckless abandon the moment he feels himself subject to another force. And that other force was love, none other than the love which had flared up in him like a tinder-box, and, to feed that love he needed money, far, far more than he needed it to go on a spree with that same lady-love of his. Were she to say to him: "I'm yours, I don't want Fyodor

Pavlovich," he'd have taken her and run away with her—but he'd have needed the means with which to do it. That would have been even more important than going on a spree with her. Karamazov, of all people, would have understood that. That was the one thing that was worrying him, that was preying on his mind—so what could have been more natural than for him to have taken some of the money and hidden it, just in case he needed it later? Meanwhile, time was passing, and Fyodor Pavlovich had not come up with the three thousand; on the contrary, it became evident that he had set it aside for the express purpose of luring away the defendant's sweetheart. "If Fyodor Pavlovich doesn't pay up," he thinks, "I'll be a thief in Katerina Ivanovna's eyes." And so he has an idea: he'll give Miss Verkhovtseva the fifteen hundred roubles that he's still carrying about with him in that purse of his, and say to her: "I'm a scoundrel, but not a thief." So now there's a twofold reason for him to guard the fifteen hundred roubles as if his life depended on it, and certainly every reason not to undo the purse and help himself to the money a hundred roubles at a time. Why should the defendant be denied a sense of honour? Yes, he has a sense of honour—granted, a distorted one, granted, very frequently a mistaken one—but the fact remains that he has one, he has this honour to the point of obsession, and he has demonstrated it. Now, however, the picture becomes more complicated, the defendant's agony of jealousy reaches its climax, and his disturbed faculties of reasoning conflict painfully again and again with the original dilemma: "If I return the money to Katerina Ivanovna, where will I get the money to run away with Grushenka?" All his excesses, his drinking bouts, his acts of violence in drinking-dens throughout that month were perhaps the result of his bitterness, his inability to come to terms with his situation. Finally this dilemma became so acute that he grew desperate. He sent his younger brother to ask his father for the last time to let him have the three thousand, and, without waiting for a reply, he burst into the house himself and ended up by violently assaulting his father in front of witnesses. That was the end of that; his father, having received a beating, was unlikely to give him anything now. And that same day, beating his breast—note that that was just where the purse was hanging round his neck—

he swears to his brother that he has the means to cease being a scoundrel, but that he will remain a scoundrel all the same, because he knows he will use this money to his own ends, he hasn't the will-power, the strength of character to resist. Why, oh, why does the prosecution refuse to believe Aleksei Karamazov's evidence, given so openly, so sincerely, in such an uncontrived and truthful manner? Why, on the contrary, am I supposed to believe that there is money hidden in some cranny in the vaults of Udolpho Castle? That same evening, after the conversation with his brother, the defendant wrote that fateful letter, and it is this very letter which is now the principal, the most incriminating piece of evidence that he took the money! "I'll ask everybody I can for money, and if no one gives me any, I'll kill my father and take the money out of the envelope tied with the pink ribbon under his mattress, provided Ivan has left"—a full statement of intent to murder, so who else could have done it? "Everything happened just as he'd written it down!" says the prosecution. But, firstly, the letter was written when he was drunk and in a state of extreme agitation; secondly, in referring to the envelope he merely repeated what Smerdyakov had said, for he himself had not seen the envelope; and thirdly, written it may have been, but did everything in fact happen as written? That is what has to be proved. Did the defendant in fact pull out the envelope from under the pillow, did he find the money, did it even exist? And was the defendant really after money when he went to his father's house; think about it, just think about it! He ran there hell for leather, not in order to commit a robbery but to find out where she was, this woman who had broken his heart—consequently, he wasn't following any plan, any written statement of intent—that is to say, he ran there not to commit a premeditated robbery, but on impulse, on the spur of the moment, in a state of frenzied jealousy! But, you will say, on arrival he nevertheless committed the murder and helped himself to the money. But did he in fact commit the murder? I reject the accusation of theft outright: an accusation of theft cannot be made if it is not possible to indicate precisely what has been stolen, that is axiomatic! But whether he did actually commit the murder without stealing the money remains to be seen. Or is that just more fiction?

12

NEITHER WAS THERE A MURDER

'REMEMBER, gentlemen of the jury, we are dealing here with a man's life, and therefore we cannot be too careful. We have heard the prosecution solemnly declare that, up to the very last moment—in fact up to today, the day of the trial—it hesitated to accuse the defendant outright of actual premeditated murder; indeed, the prosecution hesitated right up to the moment that that fateful, "drunken" letter was presented to the court today. "It all happened as written!" But I keep coming back to the same point: he was running to her, running to look for her, to find out where she was. Surely that is a fact that is beyond dispute. Had she happened to be at home, he would not have run off anywhere; instead, he would have stayed with her and would not have done what he said in the letter. He set off on an impulse, on the spur of the moment; as for the letter, perhaps he had forgotten all about it at the time. "He grabbed the pestle," we are told—and remember that, from this one pestle, a whole psychological edifice has been fabricated for our benefit as to why he must have regarded the pestle as a weapon, grabbed it to use as a weapon, and so on and so forth. A very simple idea occurs to me here: what would have happened if the pestle had been lying not in full view, not on the shelf from which the defendant grabbed it, but in a sideboard? It would definitely not have caught his eye then, and he would have run off empty-handed, without a weapon, and perhaps would not have killed anyone at all. How therefore can the pestle be considered an offensive weapon and as evidence of premeditation? Yes, but he had been shouting his head off in all the taverns about killing his father, and two days before the murder, the evening he got drunk and wrote the letter, he was quiet and only quarrelled with a merchant's clerk in the tavern because, it is said, "a Karamazov can't help picking a quarrel". To which I shall reply that if he had decided to commit such a murder, if he had planned it, committed it to paper, he definitely would not have picked a quarrel with the clerk—come to that, he would not even have gone to the tavern, perhaps, because someone who is planning such a deed wants to lie low, to become inconspicuous, and wishes to be neither seen nor heard: "Pretend I don't exist," he thinks—instinctively rather than purely rationally. Gentlemen of the jury, psychology cuts both ways, and we too know a thing or two about psychology. As for that month of shouting his mouth off in the taverns, it's no different from what children shout, or from drunken revellers quarrelling as they emerge from their drinking-dens. "I'll kill you!" they shout, but they don't, do they? And even that fateful letter—couldn't that also have been just drunken intemperance, like the shouts of the departing drinkers: "I'll kill you, I'll kill you all!" Why could it not have happened like that, why not? Why is this letter significant, why could it not on the contrary be simply ridiculous? Well, because his father's corpse was found, because a witness saw the defendant escaping from the garden with a weapon and was himself struck down by him, so everything happened as he had written it down, hence the letter is not ridiculous, it is significant. Thank God, we have come to the point at last: "He was in the garden, therefore he must have committed the murder." Two words: he *was*, and *therefore*, it goes without saying, he must have... this covers everything, those two words are the sum total of the accusation—"He was, therefore he must have..." But what if there is no *therefore*, even though he *was*? Oh, I agree the totality, the combination of facts is really quite remarkable. But consider all these facts in isolation, however, and do not be swayed by their overall effect: why, for instance, will the prosecution not under any circumstances accept the veracity of the defendant's testimony that he ran away from his father's window? Remember even the sarcastic way in which the prosecution referred to the respect and filial piety that suddenly overcame the accused. But what if there really was something of the kind, if not respect, then at least filial piety? "My mother must have prayed for me at that moment," the defendant subsequently testified at the inquiry, and so, as soon as he had ascertained that Miss Svetlova was not in his father's house, he ran off. "But he could not have ascertained that simply by looking through the window," objects the prosecution. And why couldn't he? Surely the window had been opened in response to the signal given by the defendant. At that point Fyodor Pavlovich could have uttered some word or other, or called out something that would have told the defendant immediately that Miss Svetlova was not there. Why do we have to jump to such conclusions? A thousand things may occur in real life and escape the attention of the most imaginative writer of fiction. "Ah, but Grigory saw that the door was open, therefore the defendant must have been in the house, and, it follows, he must have committed the murder." About this door, gentlemen of the jury... You see, only one person testified that the door was open, and that person was in such a state at the time that... But granted, granted that the door was open, granted that the defendant had opened it and lied about it in an instinctive act of self-preservation—understandable enough in the circumstances, you'll agree—granted that he gained access to the house, that he was in the house—so what? Even if he was in the house, why does that necessarily mean that he committed the murder? He may have burst in, run through the rooms, pushed his father aside, he may even have hit his father, but then, finding that Miss Svetlova was not there, he ran away, relieved that she was not there and that he had not killed his father. Perhaps that was precisely why, a minute later, having injured Grigory in the heat of the moment, he jumped down from the fence to tend him—because he was capable of genuine feelings of pity and compassion; because he had resisted the temptation to kill his father; because, not having killed his father, he felt his heart was pure and suffused with joy. The prosecutor has described with graphic eloquence the defendant's dreadful state of mind in Mokroye, when the prospect of love had revealed itself to him again, beckoning him to a new life, just when he was no longer capable of love, because behind him lay the bloodstained corpse of his father, and ahead of him—retribution. And yet, nevertheless, the prosecutor did allow for the possibility of love, which he explained according to his own brand of psychology: "His drunken condition... a prisoner being taken to his place of execution... the long wait ahead... etcetera, etcetera." But I ask my learned friend, has he not invented a quite different person? Is the defendant really so callous, so heartless, that he could have thought about love and about dissembling before the court at that moment if he really had the blood of his father on his hands? No, no, I repeat, no! As soon as it became evident that she loved him, that she was beckoning him, promising him new happiness—I swear, he would have felt a double, a treble compulsion to kill himself, and had he really left his father's corpse in that room, he certainly would have done so! Oh no, he would not have forgotten where his pistols were! I know the defendant: the cruel, stony heartlessness attributed to him by the prosecution is out of keeping with his character. He would have killed himself, that is certain; he did not kill himself, precisely because his mother was praying for him and his heart was innocent of his father's blood. That night in Mokroye he agonized, he grieved only over the old man Grigory, whom he had struck down, and he prayed to God that the old man would regain consciousness, that the blow would not prove fatal, and that he would not be punished for it. Why shouldn't such an interpretation of events be admissible? What firm evidence is there that the defendant is lying? But, you will say again, what about his father's corpse? If he ran out without killing the old man, then who did kill him?

'I repeat, the whole basis of the prosecution's case is this: if he didn't commit the murder, who did? We are told that there is no one else. Gentlemen of the jury, is that really so? Is it really and truly the case that there is no one else? We have heard the prosecution enumerate everyone who was in the house that night. There were five people in all. Three of them, I agree, can definitely be discounted: the murdered man himself, the old man Grigory, and his wife. That obviously leaves the defendant and Smerdyakov, and the prosecutor solemnly declares that the only reason the defendant points the finger at Smerdyakov is because there is no one else for him to accuse, and that if there were some sixth person, even the faintest hint of a sixth person, the defendant, overcome with shame, would immediately cease accusing Smerdyakov and would instead point to that sixth person. But, gentlemen of the jury, why should I not draw precisely the opposite conclusion? There are two people—the defendant and Smerdyakov—what is to prevent me from saying that you are accusing my client solely because you cannot find anyone else to accuse? And the reason you have no one else to accuse is because, from the very beginning, you quite arbitrarily excluded Smerdyakov from the list of suspects. Yes, true, it is only the defendant, his two brothers, and Miss Svetlova who have pointed the finger at Smerdyakov. But there are other dissenting voices: the public at large is preoccupied, albeit only vaguely, with a certain question; a certain suspicion is growing, a vague rumour is circulating, one senses a certain expectation. Finally, there is the evidence of a certain combination of facts— very striking, although I must admit rather inconclusive. First, we have on the very day of the murder that epileptic fit, the authenticity of which the prosecution was at such pains to defend and substantiate. Then followed Smerdyakov's unexpected suicide on the very eve of the trial. And then, in court today, the no less unexpected testimony of the defendant's younger brother, who up till now, had believed his brother guilty but who suddenly produced the money and named Smerdyakov as the murderer into the bargain! I am fully convinced, together with the bench and the prosecution, that Ivan Karamazov was sick, that he was delirious, that his testimony could really have been a desperate attempt, conceived in delirium, to save his brother by putting the blame on the dead man. And so the name of Smerdyakov has cropped up yet again, and one cannot but detect a touch of mystery here. It is, gentlemen of the jury, as though something has been left unsaid, left hanging in the air. Perhaps it will all become clear in due course. But for the time being let that be, we shall return to it later. Meanwhile I shall make a few comments on the analysis of the late Smerdyakov's character, for example, which was presented so subtly and skilfully by the prosecutor. But while I marvel at his skill, I cannot, however, accept his analysis. I met Smerdyakov, I saw him and spoke to him; I formed a very different impression of him. Physically he was weak, that is true, but in character, in spirit—oh no, he was not the weakling that the prosecution has described. In particular, I failed to find any signs of timidity in him, that timidity which the prosecutor was at pains to describe to us. As for ingenuousness, he was devoid of it; on the contrary, I discovered a façade of naïvety concealing an immense sense of mistrust, and a mind capable of great deliberation. The prosecution was too gullible in assuming that he was simple-minded. The impression he created on me was absolutely unequivocal: I was convinced that here was a thoroughly malicious creature, exceedingly ambitious, spiteful, and consumed with jealousy. I gathered a certain amount of information: he hated his name and was ashamed of his birth, grinding his teeth as he recalled "I'm Smerdyashchaya's bastard." He had no respect for his childhood benefactors, Grigory and his wife. He cursed and ridiculed Russia. His ambition was to go to France, to become a Frenchman. He had for a long time frequently bemoaned his impecuniousness. I do not think he had ever loved anyone except himself, and his self-esteem was astonishingly high. Fine clothes, a clean shirt, and a pair of polished boots was his idea of culture. Regarding himself as Fyodor Pavlovich's illegitimate son (there is evidence to support this), he must have hated his status compared to that of his master's legitimate children: they had everything and he had nothing, they had all the privileges, would receive all the inheritance, while he was just a cook. He informed me that he and Fyodor Pavlovich put the money in the envelope together. The purpose for which this money was designated— money which could have gone to improve his circumstances— was, of course, abhorrent to him. On top of that, the three thousand roubles were all in unused, hundred-rouble notes—I made a point of asking him about this. One should never show a large amount of money all at once to a greedy, self-indulgent person who has never set eyes on such a sum. A wad of large-denomination notes could have had a harmful effect on his imagination, with consequences which might not be apparent at first. My learned colleague has outlined for us, with extraordinary subtlety, all the arguments for and against the possibility that Smerdyakov committed the murder, and he asks specifically why the latter should have feigned an epileptic fit. Ah, well, he could simply not have been faking the fit at all, it could have been a real fit, and the patient could have recovered naturally. Perhaps not recovered altogether, but come to, regained consciousness, as happens with epileptic fits. The prosecution asks: "Just when could Smerdyakov have committed the murder?" But it's very easy to say when. He could have regained consciousness and woken from his deep sleep (because he was only asleep—an epileptic attack is always followed by a deep sleep) just as old Grigory grabbed the defendant's foot as he climbed over the fence, and yelled out for all the neighbourhood to hear: "You

killed your father!" This sudden, unexpected cry in the silence
and the darkness could in fact have woken Smerdyakov, who
was perhaps sleeping less soundly by this time; he could have
started to wake up quite naturally an hour or so before. Getting
out of bed, he sets off—almost unconsciously and completely
aimlessly—in the direction of the shouting, to see what's going
on. He is still in a daze, still half-asleep, but he finds his way
into the garden, approaches the lighted windows and hears the
dreadful news from his master, who is of course overjoyed to see
him. His mind immediately springs into action. His frightened
master tells him in detail what has happened. And gradually, in
his deranged and sickly brain, an idea takes shape—terrible and
yet enticing and ruthlessly logical: to kill the old man, take the
three thousand roubles, and then blame it all on the young
master; who else but the young man would be suspected, who
else but he would be blamed? He had been there, all the
evidence pointed to that. He could have been overwhelmed by a
powerful compulsion to lay his hands on the money, together
with the conviction that he could act with impunity. I can assure
you, these sudden and irresistible impulses are often opportun-
istic, and, most importantly, they take such murderers quite
unawares, when only a minute before, perhaps, it would not even
have entered their heads to commit a murder! And so Smerdyakov could have entered his master's room and carried out the
deed. With what, with what weapon? Well, with the first stone
that came to hand in the garden. But what for, to what end?
Well, the three thousand roubles could have set him up for life.
Oh no, I am not contradicting myself here: the money could
really have existed. And perhaps Smerdyakov was the only one
in fact who knew where to find it, where precisely his master had
hidden it. What about the wrapping that the money was in, the
torn envelope on the floor? Earlier, when the prosecutor, talking
of this envelope, put forward his extremely subtle theory that
only an inexperienced thief, just such a one as Karamazov, would
have left it on the floor, whereas Smerdyakov would never have
done so, would never have left behind such evidence against
himself—at that moment, gentlemen of the jury, as I listened, I
suddenly realized that I was hearing something extraordinarily
familiar. And you know, I had already heard that same theory,

that conjecture about what Karamazov might have done with the envelope, just two days previously from Smerdyakov himself, and that's not all; what astonished me most was that he seemed to be feigning naïvety, anticipating, putting an idea into my head so that I myself would draw the conclusion that he intended. Might he not have done the same thing to the investigators? And perhaps to my learned colleague too? You may say: what about the old woman, Grigory's wife? Surely she must have heard the sick man groaning nearby the whole night. Granted, she did hear him. But we are on extremely shaky ground here. I know of a certain lady who complained bitterly that she was being kept awake all night by a pug-dog in the yard. And yet, as it turned out subsequently, the poor dog had only barked once or twice throughout the whole night. And this is very natural—a person is asleep and then she suddenly hears a groan, she wakes up annoyed that she has been disturbed, but falls asleep again at once. About two hours later there is another groan, she wakes up again, and again falls asleep; finally, a couple of hours later, there is yet another groan—in all, three or four in the night. The sleeper awakes the next morning, complaining that someone has been groaning all night and constantly waking her up. But that is just how it seems to her; the two-hour periods of sleep have passed unnoticed and she does not remember them, she remembers only the few minutes of wakefulness, and that is why it seems to her that she has been kept awake all night. "But why, why", exclaims the prosecution, "didn't Smerdyakov admit his guilt in his suicide note? He had no qualms of conscience about doing the one but not the other." But just a moment: conscience leads to repentance, and he may not have felt repentance, but only despair. Repentance and despair are totally dissimilar. Despair can be malicious and irreconcilable, and at the moment of committing suicide a person might hate those he was jealous of all his life twice as intensely. Gentlemen of the jury, beware of a miscarriage of justice! Why should the picture that I have painted, everything I have suggested to you, be so improbable? I challenge you to find a flaw in my argument, a discrepancy, an incongruity! But should there be even the remotest possibility that I am right, the least suggestion of verisimilitude in my conjectures—you must refrain from convicting the defendant.

And surely there is more than a remote possibility. I swear by all that is holy that I fully believe my interpretation of the circumstances surrounding the murder. But what perturbs and frightens me above all is the thought that, out of the whole list of allegations hurled at the defendant by the prosecution, there is not a single one which is even remotely accurate and which will withstand scrutiny, and that it is merely the totality of these allegations which is being used to destroy the unfortunate man. Yes, the sum total is terrifying; that blood, blood dripping from the defendant's fingers, his bloodstained clothes, the dark night, its silence rent by the cry of "murderer!", the victim screaming as he falls with a smashed skull, and then all that multitude of declarations, of evidence, of gestures, of shouts—all this exerts such a powerful, such a subversive influence upon the ability to reach a verdict, but, gentlemen of the jury, surely not upon your judgment! Remember, you have been invested with boundless authority, the authority "to bind and to loose".* But the greater the authority, the more awesome its application! I do not retract one iota of what I said just now, but be that as it may, suppose I were to agree with the prosecution for a moment that my hapless client stained his hands with his father's blood. This is purely hypothetical; I repeat, I do not doubt his innocence for a moment, but for the sake of argument I shall presume that the defendant is guilty of patricide. However, bear with me a little in my hypothesis. I feel conscience-bound to tell you something else, because I perceive a great struggle raging in your hearts and minds... Forgive me, gentlemen of the jury, for referring to your hearts and minds. But I want to be sincere and honest to the end. Let us all be sincere!...'

At this point the defence counsel was interrupted by a fairly loud burst of applause. True enough, he had spoken these last words with such a note of sincerity that everyone felt he really did perhaps have something to say, and that whatever he was about to say just then would be of the utmost importance. But at the sound of the applause the judge threatened sternly to clear the courtroom if this sort of thing were repeated. Everyone fell silent, and Fetyukovich resumed in quite a new, emotionally charged tone, completely different from the one in which he had spoken hitherto.

13

TRUTH PERVERTED

'IT is not the totality of the evidence which threatens to convict
my client, gentlemen of the jury,' he went on, 'no, in reality, my
client is in danger of being convicted by one single fact: his aged
father's corpse! If it were a simple murder you would surely, in
view of the paucity of the evidence, the lack of proof, and the
ridiculousness of the allegations (if taken individually rather than
in their totality), dismiss the accusation—or, at least, think twice
before condemning a man purely on account of his reputation,
for which, alas, he has only himself to blame! But we are not
dealing with simple murder here, we are dealing with patricide!
This raises the stakes to the extent that even the most insignificant and unsubstantiated of the prosecution's allegations suddenly
acquire significance and veracity, even in the most unprejudiced
of minds. So how can one acquit a man accused of such a crime?
Surely one cannot commit murder and walk free? That is what
every man feels almost intuitively in his heart. Yes, it is a terrible
thing to shed the blood of one's father—who begat me, who
loved me, who for my sake did not spare himself, who felt for
me when I suffered all my childhood illnesses, who struggled for
my happiness all his life, and who lived his life only through my
joys and triumphs! Oh, to kill such a father—it does not even
bear thinking about! Gentlemen of the jury, what is a father, a
true father? What an august title, what an awesome concept is
contained in the very word itself! I have indicated something of
the nature of a true father and what he should be. In the present
case with which we are so preoccupied and which is causing us
so much heartache—in the present case, the father, the late
Fyodor Pavlovich Karamazov, bore no resemblance whatsoever
to that idealization of a father that we have been picturing in our
minds. That is the trouble. Yes, there are some fathers who are
indeed a problem. Let us examine this problem a little closer
then; in view of the gravity of the decision which we are called
upon to take, gentlemen of the jury, we must not balk at anything.
Now, above all, we must not be afraid, must not, as it were,
shrink from certain things, as children or timorous women do,

to borrow the felicitous expression used by my learned colleague. In his impassioned speech my learned adversary (and he was my adversary, even before I had spoken a word), my adversary declared several times: "No, I shall not permit anyone to defend the accused, I shall not concede his defence to the defence counsel who has come from St Petersburg—I am both pro-secutor and counsel for the defence!" He said that several times, forgetting to mention, however, that if this unfortunate man in the dock could still, after twenty-three years, retain a sense of gratitude for the gift of just a pound of nuts from the one man who had befriended him in his parental home, then surely such a person would also have remembered, for all those twenty-three years, the times that he ran around barefoot in his father's place, "in the backyard, with no shoes on, his trousers hanging on by just one button", as the warm-hearted Doctor Herzenstube has described. Gentlemen of the jury, what need is there for us to delve deeper into this tragedy, to repeat what is already common knowledge! What did my client find when he came back to his father's house? Why should my client be represented as an unfeeling egoist, as a monster? He is foolhardy, he is wild and hotheaded, and we are passing judgement on him here for that, but who is to blame for his fate, who is to blame for the fact that, along with his innate goodness, along with his noble and sensitive heart, he had such an abominable upbringing? Did anyone ever teach him what life was all about, attend to his education, love him—even just a little—in his childhood? My client was left to God's tender care, like an animal in the wild. Perhaps he yearned to see his father after so many years of separation, perhaps he had recalled his childhood thousands of times, as in a dream, exorcizing the disturbing ghosts of his childhood, and perhaps he longed with all his heart to vindicate his father and embrace him. And what happened? He was met with nothing but cynical taunts, mistrust, and deceit as regards the disputed money; daily, "over a glass of brandy", he heard nothing but conversations and attitudes to life that were enough to turn the stomach, and, finally, he beheld his father planning to snatch his paramour from him, from his own son, using that selfsame money— gentlemen of the jury, that was disgusting and cruel! And that same old man then proceeded to complain to all and sundry of

his son's cruelty and disrespect, to malign him in public, to
slander him, to buy up his promissory notes in order to have him
sent to prison! Gentlemen of the jury, I put it to you that people
such as my client—to all appearances cruel-hearted, reckless,
unruly characters—are, more often than not, extraordinarily
tender-hearted, only they do not show it. Don't laugh, don't
laugh at my proposition! My learned colleague was mocking my
client cruelly just now, portraying him as an admirer of Schiller,
a lover of "the fine and the exalted". I would not have ridiculed
that had I been in his place, had I been prosecuting! Yes, such
souls—I want to defend such souls as these, so seldom understood, so often maligned—such souls very often yearn for what
is tender, beautiful, and just, yearn, without being aware of it
themselves, for all that is in contradiction to their own natures,
their recklessness, their cruelty. Seemingly passionate and cruel,
they are capable of loving to distraction with an essentially
spiritual, exalted love. Again, do not laugh at me: more often
than not this is precisely the case with such natures! It is merely
that they are unable to conceal their—sometimes very coarse—
passions—and it is this which causes consternation, it is this
which draws attention, and no one sees the man within. All these
passions, however, are quickly satisfied, and when he meets a
noble, sublime being, this apparently coarse and cruel man seeks
spiritual regeneration, an opportunity to mend his ways, to
become better, to become noble and honest—"noble and fine",
that hackneyed phrase. I said just now that I shall not permit
myself to touch upon my client's romance with Miss Verkhovtseva. However, a word or two would not be out of order: what
we heard earlier was not a testimony, but an outburst by a
frenzied and vengeful woman, and it ill behoves one who has
betrayed people herself to accuse others of betrayal! Had she
only stopped to think, even for a moment, she would not have
testified as she did! Do not believe her; no, my client is not the
"monster" she said he was! He who loved mankind said, before
He was crucified: "I am the good shepherd: the good shepherd
giveth his life for the sheep, that not one should perish..."* Let
us not, therefore, condemn a man's soul to perdition! I asked
just now: what is a father? And I replied that it was an exalted
title. But a word, gentlemen of the jury, must not be abused, and

I shall take the liberty of being perfectly frank: a father such as the late Karamazov cannot be—is not worthy to be—called a father. Filial love, if the father is not deserving of it, is an absurdity, an impossibility. Love cannot be born of nothing, God alone can create something out of nothing. "Fathers, provoke not your children,"* wrote the apostle, his heart consumed by love. It is not for my client's sake that I am citing these sacred words now, I am repeating them for the benefit of all fathers. Who gave me the authority to teach those among you who are fathers? No one. But, as a human being and a citizen, I call upon you—*vivos voco!** We are not here on this earth for long, we commit many bad deeds, and we say much that we should not. Therefore, let us all take advantage of any opportunity of social interaction to say a kind word to one another. That's what I'm doing while I'm here, I am taking advantage of the opportunity. Not for nothing has this forum been entrusted to us by a higher authority—all Russia is listening to us. It is not just to those fathers present that I speak, I appeal to all fathers: "Fathers, provoke not your children!" Before we make any demands upon our children, let us first fulfil Christ's will ourselves. Otherwise we are not fathers, but enemies to our children; nor are they our children, but rather our enemies, and it is we ourselves who have made enemies of them! "For with the same measure that ye mete withal it shall be measured to you again."* These are not my words, it is prescribed in the Scriptures: do unto others as they do unto you. How then can we blame our children if they do unto us as we do unto them? Recently in Finland a servant girl was suspected of having secretly given birth to a child. They began to investigate and, in the attic of the house, in a corner behind some bricks, they found a trunk that no one had known about, forced it open, and found the corpse of the newly born infant whom she had killed. In the same trunk they found the skeletons of two other infants whom she confessed she had killed at birth. Gentlemen of the jury, was she a mother to her children? True, she gave birth to them, but was she a mother to them? Could any one of us bring ourselves to call her by the sacred title of mother? Let us be bold, gentlemen of the jury, let us even be brazen—truly it is even incumbent upon us to be so in this instance—and let us not be afraid of using certain words and notions, like those Moscow merchants' wives who were afraid of "brass" and "brimstone".* No, let us show on the contrary that our development has not been unaffected by the progress of recent years, and let me say openly: to father a child does not make one a father, a father is one who, having fathered a child, proves himself worthy of fatherhood. There is another point of view of course, another definition of the word "father", which incorporates the idea that a father, even though he may be a monster, even though he may be a fiend to his children, nevertheless remains a father simply because he has sired a child. But this definition is, so to speak, mystical; I cannot accept it intellectually, I can only believe in it—or, to be more precise, as with much else that cannot be understood but which religion commands us nevertheless to believe—accept it as a *matter of faith*. In that case, let it stay beyond the confines of the real world. In the real world, which not only bestows rights but itself imposes enormous obligations—in this world, if we want to behave like civilized human beings—come to that, if we want to behave like Christians—we should, indeed we must, put into practice only those ideas which have been tested against reason and experience, which have been tempered in the crucible of empirical analysis; in a word, we must act rationally, not mindlessly as in a dream or in delirium, so as not to harm our fellow man, not to stifle him or destroy him. That, then, will be a truly Christian approach, not merely something metaphysical, but a sensible and a truly philanthropic approach...'

At this juncture there were loud bursts of applause from all over the hall, but Fetyukovich began to wave his hands impatiently, as though begging not to be interrupted and to be allowed to finish what he had to say. Silence fell. The defence counsel continued.

'Do you think, gentlemen of the jury, that our children—or rather our youth—can be spared such issues as they begin to think for themselves? No, they cannot, and let us not expect of them a forbearance of which they are not capable! The sight of an unworthy father perforce raises awkward questions in the mind of a youth, especially when he compares him to the worthy fathers of other children, his peers. He is fobbed off with answers to these questions. "He fathered you, you are his flesh and blood, and so you should love him." The youth cannot help disputing this. "Surely he didn't love me when he sired me," he reflects, with mounting surprise, "surely he didn't beget me for my own sake: he didn't know me, he didn't even know my sex at that moment, at that moment of passion, when he was flushed with wine, perhaps; his liking for drink is probably all I've inherited from him—that's all the good he's done me... So why should I love him merely for begetting me and then for the rest of my life failing to love me?" Perhaps you will consider these questions impertinent and cruel, but don't expect too much forbearance from a young mind. "Drive nature out through the door, and she will make her way back through the window."* But the main thing is not to be afraid of "brass and brimstone", and to resolve the question according to the precepts of common sense and philanthropy, rather than according to metaphysical reasoning. So how should it be resolved? I suggest thus: let the son stand before the father and let him ask straight out: "Father, tell me, why should I love you? Father, prove to me that I should love you!" And if the father is willing and able to answer him and give him proof, there you have a truly proper family, based not merely on mystical prejudice, but on sensible, self-regulating, and strictly humane principles. On the other hand, if the father fails to prove that he is worthy of love, that's the end of that family: he is not a father to him, and from then on the son is free and within his rights to regard his father as a stranger, and even as his enemy. This forum of ours, gentlemen of the jury, should serve as a school of truth and common sense!'

Here the defence counsel was interrupted by wild, almost frenzied applause. Of course, not everybody in the hall applauded, but a good half of them did. It was fathers and mothers who applauded. From the balcony, where the ladies were sitting, came shrieks and hoots. They were waving their handkerchiefs. The president began to ring the bell vigorously. He was visibly annoyed by the behaviour in the hall, but he simply did not dare to 'clear' it, as he had previously threatened—even the distinguished old men wearing decorations of honour on their tailcoats, sitting on the reserved seats behind him, were applauding and waving their handkerchiefs—so that when the noise abated, the judge contented himself merely with reiterating his previous threat to 'clear' the hall, while the triumphant and excited Fetyukovich continued his speech.

'Gentlemen of the jury, you remember that frightful night, about which so much has been said today, when the son, having scaled the fence and gained access to his father's house, found himself face to face at last with his enemy, the swindler who begat him. I maintain with all certitude that it was not money that he was after at that moment: as I have already pointed out, the accusation of theft is an absurdity. Nor did he enter the house to commit murder; oh no, if that had been his intention, he would at least have provided himself with a weapon in advance, but he grabbed the brass pestle on the spur of the moment, without thinking, without knowing why. Let us assume that he did trick his father with the signal, let us assume he did enter—as I have already said, I don't believe that story for one moment—but let us, for argument's sake, assume that it's true! Gentlemen of the jury, I swear by all that is holy, that had it not been his father, but an unrelated rival, he would have dashed through the rooms and convinced himself that the woman was not there, and then run off at full pelt without harming his rival; he might have hit him, perhaps pushed him, but that's all, because his mind would have been on other things, he would not have had time, he would have wanted to find out where she was. But his father! It was the sight of his father that did it, the sight of his enemy, of the man who had detested him from childhood, had wronged him, and was now his monstrous rival! An irresistible feeling of hatred overwhelmed him, banishing all rationality: everything welled up at once! It was diminished responsibility on grounds of insanity—and also nature avenging herself, blindly and inexorably as is her way, by upholding her eternal laws. But I maintain, I insist—it was not murder—no, he merely swung the pestle in disgust and indignation, not intending to kill, not realizing that the blow would kill him. Had he not had the fateful pestle in his hand he would have given his father a beating, perhaps, but he would not have killed him. When he ran off, having knocked the old man down, he did not know whether he was dead or not. To kill without malice aforethought is not murder. Neither is it patricide. No, the murder of such a father does not deserve to be called patricide. Only someone prejudiced in favour of fathers could consider such a murder patricide! But was it, was it in fact murder? From the depths of my heart I appeal to you! Let us suppose we convict him, gentlemen of the jury, and he says to himself: "These people did nothing to alleviate my fate, nothing to guide me, to educate me, nothing to reform me, to make me into a human being. Ye gave me no meat, and ye gave me no drink, and naked as I was in prison, ye did not visit me,* and now you have condemned me to penal servitude. I am quits with them, I owe no one anything now, till the end of time. They have been vicious, and I shall be vicious. They have been cruel, and I shall be cruel." That is what he will say, gentlemen of the jury! And I solemnly assure you that by convicting him, you will only make it easier for him, you will ease his conscience, he will curse rather than rue the blood he has shed. At the same time, you will destroy all vestiges of a human being in him, for he will remain vicious and blind for the rest of his life. But if you wish to punish him dreadfully, terribly, to inflict the most frightful punishment imaginable upon him, and yet save his soul for all eternity, then suffocate him with your mercy! You will see, you will hear what a shudder of terror will pass through his soul. "Am I to endure such mercy, am I to be accorded so much love, am I worthy of it?" he will cry. Oh, I know that heart of his, that wild yet noble heart of his, gentlemen of the jury. He will prostrate himself before your act of mercy, he yearns for a great act of love, he will be seared by it and be resurrected for ever. There are souls which, in their misery, bear a grudge against the whole world. But overwhelm such a soul with mercy, offer it love, and it will become so full of benign aspirations that it will curse its deed. The soul will respond and see how merciful God is, and how marvellous and just people are. He will be terrified, he will be overwhelmed by repentance and by a sense of the immeasurable indebtedness stretching ahead of him. And he will not say then, "I am quits." He will say, "I am guilty before all men and I am the unworthiest of men." And he will exclaim with tears of repentance and over-powering, agonizing gratitude: "Others are better than I, because they have decided not to destroy, but to save me!" Oh, it would be so easy for you to perform this act of mercy because, in the absence of any evidence bearing the least resemblance to truth, it would be inconceivable for you to pronounce him guilty. Better to acquit ten guilty men than to punish one innocent one*—do you hear that majestic voice from our glorious past? In all humility I must remind you that the law in Russia is intended not just for the punishment but also for the salvation of the wrongdoer! Let other nations follow the letter of the law and punish; we shall follow the spirit of the law and we shall save and resurrect the sinners. And if that is so, if that is really what Russia and her laws are all about—then, forward Russia! Let us not be intimidated by those mad troikas from which other nations turn away in disgust! It will not be the mad troika, but the triumphal Russian coach which will inexorably and majestically reach its destination. My client's fate is in your hands, our Russian truth is also in your hands. You will rescue it, you will stand up for it, you will prove that there is someone to look after it, that it is in good hands!'

14

TRUST THE PEASANTS!

THAT is how Fetyukovich ended his speech; this time, the delight of the audience knew no bounds and there was a tumultuous burst of applause. To contain it would have been unthinkable: women were crying, many of the men were crying too, even a couple of the dignitaries shed a tear or two. The president relented and even waited before ringing his bell. 'To try to restrain such enthusiasm would have been a sacrilege,' the ladies of our town subsequently insisted. The defence counsel himself was genuinely moved. Such were the conditions in the hall when our Ippolit Kyrillovich rose to his feet once more to raise a few objections. He was greeted with hostility. 'What? What's all this? Who does he think he is, to object?' muttered the ladies. But even if all the women of the world, led by the prosecutor's lady-wife Mrs Ippolit Kyrillovich herself had been protesting—even then it would have been impossible to restrain him at that moment. He turned pale, he shook with agitation; his

opening words were quite unintelligible; he was spluttering,
mispronouncing, and stumbling over words. He soon recovered,
however. But I shall quote only a few sentences from this speech.

   'I am reproached for inventing a great deal of fiction. But what
about counsel for the defence, hasn't he piled fiction upon
fiction? It's a marvel he didn't turn it all into a poem for good
measure. While waiting for his mistress, Fyodor Pavlovich tears
up the envelope and flings it on the floor. We are even told what
he said on that particular occasion. Isn't that straight out of a
novel? And where's the proof that he took the money out of the
envelope, and who heard what he said? A dim-wit of an idiot,
Smerdyakov, presented as some kind of Byronic hero wreaking
revenge on society for his bastardy—is that not a poetic fantasy
in the manner of Byron? And the son, breaking into his father's
house and killing him, but at the same time not killing him, that
you wouldn't even find in a poem, let alone a novel; it's a riddle
set by the sphinx, which it itself cannot solve, of course. If he
killed him, he killed him. But he killed him and yet he didn't kill
him—what is one to make of that? Further, we are solemnly
informed that this is a forum for truth and common sense, and
lo and behold, from this "forum of common sense" we hear
counsel for the defence declaring—nay, swearing—that to call
the murder of a father "patricide" is mere prejudice! But if
patricide were prejudice and if every child were to ask his father,
"Father, why should I love you?" then what would become of us,
what would become of the foundations of society, what would
become of the family? Patricide, you see, is merely the Moscow
merchant's wife's "brimstone"! All the most precious, the most
sacred canons in the warp and woof of Russian jurisprudence
have been distorted and trivialized merely for the sake of
securing an acquittal for what is unpardonable. "Oh, overwhelm
him with mercy," exclaims counsel for the defence, but that is
just what the criminal wants, and everyone will reap the harvest
tomorrow. And then again, is counsel for the defence surely not
being unduly modest in calling merely for the acquittal of the
accused? Why not ask to set up a patricide trust, to commemorate
his achievement for posterity and for the younger generation?
The Scriptures and religion itself have been amended: all that,
we are told, is just metaphysics, and we alone are the keepers of

true Christianity, tried and tested by intellectual analysis and sound common sense. And behold, we are presented with a false likeness of Christ! *"For with the same measure that ye mete withal it shall be measured to you again,"* proclaims counsel for the defence and, at the same instant, deduces that Christ preached "do as you have been done by"—and this from the forum of truth and common sense! We dipped into Holy Scriptures the night before our address, in order to show that, after all, we too are familiar with a work of some originality which could always be quoted to good effect, should the need arise, you understand! But, "do as you have been done by" is just what Christ told us to abhor, He bade us shun such practice, because that is the way of the evil world; we, however, must forgive and turn the other cheek, rather than do unto others as they do unto us. That is what Our Lord taught us, and not that it is just a matter of convention to forbid children to murder their fathers. And let us not seek, from the pulpit of truth and common sense, to amend the word of Our Lord, whom counsel for the defence deigns to refer to merely as the "crucified philanthropist", in opposition to the whole of Orthodox Russia, which lifts up its voice unto Him "Thou Who art our God...!"'*

The president intervened here, cutting short the overenthusiastic orator and asking him not to exaggerate, to keep within reasonable bounds, and so on and so forth, as is usual for chairmen in such instances. There was unrest in the hall, too. The public were restive, some even letting out cries of indignation. Fetyukovich did not bother to reply directly, he merely came forward, placed his hand on his heart and, in offended tones, said a few dignified words. He touched lightly and derisively upon 'fiction' and 'psychology' and at one point let slip the apt quotation: 'Jupiter, you are angry, that means you are in the wrong',* which caused a ripple of appreciative laughter in the audience, seeing that Ippolit Kyrillovich bore not the slightest resemblance to Jupiter. Then, as regards the allegation that he was condoning patricide by the younger generation, Fetyukovich retorted full of dignity that he was not even going to argue the point. As to the 'false likeness of Christ' and his reference to Christ not as God, but merely as the 'crucified philanthropist', which is contrary to the tenets of the Orthodox faith and quite

inappropriate for a 'forum of truth and common sense', Fetyukovich hinted that this was in the nature of 'character assassination', and that when he had set out to come here he had hoped
that in taking on this case he would at least be spared allegations
that could 'slander me personally as a citizen and a loyal
subject...' But the president ruled him out of order too on this
point, and Fetyukovich, to the accompaniment of a universally
approbatory murmur from the hall, bowed to all sides and
concluded his response. As for Ippolit Kyrillovich, he was, in the
opinion of the ladies, 'really done for'.

After that, the defendant himself was asked if he wished to say
anything. Mitya rose to his feet, but said very little. He was
exhausted both physically and mentally. The air of strength and
defiance with which he had entered the courtroom in the
morning had all but vanished. He seemed to have undergone an
experience that would remain with him all his life and which had
taught him, made him understand, something very important
which he had not comprehended hitherto. His voice had grown
weak, and he no longer shouted as he had before. There was a
new element present in his words, something cowed, vanquished,
and humbled.

'What am I to say, gentlemen of the jury? My hour of
reckoning has come; I feel the hand of God upon me. A fitting
end to a profligate life! But I swear to you before God that I am
not guilty of my father's blood! I repeat for the last time: I did
not kill him. I have been reckless, but I have loved virtue. I have
striven to mend my ways every moment of my life, and yet I have
lived like a wild beast. My thanks to the prosecutor; he has told
me a lot about myself that I didn't know, but it is not true that I
killed my father, that's where he's wrong! My thanks also to my
defence counsel; I wept as I listened to him, but it is not true
that I killed my father, and he ought not to have even suspected
me of that! And don't believe what the doctors say; I am quite
sane, it's just that my heart is so heavy. If you show mercy, if you
acquit me, I'll pray for you. I'll strive to become better, you have
my word on it, as God is my witness. But if you convict me, I'll
break my sword over my own head and, having done so, I'll kiss
the fragments! Spare me, though, don't deprive me of my God,

I know what I'm like: I shall rebel! My heart is heavy, gentle-men... have mercy!'

He slumped down on his seat, his voice broke; it was all he could do to finish the sentence. Then the bench summarized the issues, and both the defence and prosecution were invited to make their final submissions. I shall not, however, relate this in detail. Finally, the jury rose to leave the courtroom and to commence their deliberations. The president was exhausted, and his voice was weak as he delivered his final words of guidance. 'Be impartial, do not be influenced by the eloquent speech of the defence, but deliberate carefully, remember that a huge responsibility rests on your shoulders...', and so on and so forth. The jury withdrew and the proceedings were adjourned. This was the chance to leave one's seat, to take a stroll, to exchange opinions with other people, to have a bite to eat at the buffet. It was very late, about one o'clock in the morning, but no one was in a hurry to leave. Everyone was so tense and wound-up that they could not relax. They were all waiting with bated breath—though, come to think of it, not all of them. The ladies outwardly were in a state of hysterical impatience, but at heart they were calm: 'He's bound to be acquitted.' They were enthusiastically anticipating a not guilty verdict. It has to be admitted that, among the men too, there were a great many who were convinced that an acquittal was inevitable. Some were glad, some frowned, and yet others looked dejected: they did not want an acquittal. Fetyukovich himself was firmly convinced that he would win. He was surrounded on all sides by people offering congratulations and trying to ingra-tiate themselves with him.

He was later said to have told one group: 'There are invisible bonds uniting the defence counsel with the members of the jury. They exist and manifested themselves even in the course of my address. I was aware of them, they really do exist. You can rest assured, the case is as good as won.'

'So what are our peasants going to say?' said a fat, freckled, fierce-looking gentleman, approaching one group of men engrossed in a discussion; he was a landowner whose estate was on the outskirts of the town.

'They're not all peasants, you know. There are four clerks amongst them.'

'Yes, clerks,' said a member of the rural council, also coming to join the group.

'I say, do you happen to know Prokhor Ivanovich Nazaryev, that merchant chap with the medal, who's on the jury?'

'What about him?'

'Awfully clever.'

'But he hasn't said a word.'

'Neither has he, so much the better. He could run rings round the fellow from St Petersburg, or anybody else from there, for that matter. He's got twelve children, would you believe it!'

'Look here, is he really not going to get off?' trumpeted one of our young clerks in another group.

'Of course he is,' came a decisive voice.

'It would be a crying shame, a disgrace, not to acquit him!' the clerk persisted. 'So he murdered him, but there are fathers and fathers! And after all, he was in such a frenzy... Perhaps he just brandished the pestle, but didn't mean to fell the old fellow. Pity they had to drag the lackey into all this, though. It's all turned out to be a bit of a farce. If I'd been counsel for the defence, I'd have told them straight out: he committed the murder, but he isn't guilty, and to hell with you!'

'But that's exactly what he did; the only thing he didn't say was "to hell with you".'

'But he very nearly said it, Mikhail Semyonych,' chirped a third voice.

'Have a heart, gentlemen, didn't they acquit that actress last Passiontide, the one who slit her lover's wife's throat?'

'Yes, but she didn't make a good job of it.'

'So what, she made a start!'

'What about that bit of his about the children? That was splendid, wasn't it?'

'Absolutely.'

'And all that stuff about mysticism, how about that, eh?'

'Look, never mind mysticism,' exclaimed someone else, 'you'd do better to worry about what's going to happen to Ippolit after today! Come tomorrow, his missis is going to scratch his eyes out for what he said about Mitenka.'

'Is she here?'

'Of course not! If she'd been here, she'd have scratched them out on the spot. She's at home with toothache. He-he-he!'

'He-he-he!'

In a third group:

'If you ask me, Mitenka will probably get off scot-free.'

'I wouldn't be surprised if he had a real knees-up in the *Stolichny Gorod* tomorrow, and spent the next ten days blind drunk.'

'He's the very devil!'

'You may well say that—the devil must have had a hand in this. Where else would he be, if not here?'

'Gentlemen, you must admit he was eloquent. Only thing is, people can't go around smashing their fathers' skulls. Otherwise where'll it all end?'

'And that coach, remember the coach?'

'Yes, he turned a peasant's cart into a coach.'

'And tomorrow he'll turn the coach back into a cart, "if the need arises, if the need arises," as the man said.'

'No flies on some people these days. Is there truth in Russia, gentlemen, or have we lost it altogether?'

Just then the bell sounded. The jury had been conferring for exactly one hour; no more, no less. An audible silence descended as soon as the public had taken their seats. I well remember the jury returning to the hall. At last! I shall not quote the counts one by one—I have forgotten them, in any case. I only remember the answer to the president's first and principal question, that is, 'Did he kill with the premeditated intention of stealing the money?' (I do not recall the exact wording.) There was a deathly hush. The foreman of the jury, a clerk and the youngest member, proclaimed in a loud and clear voice in the deathly silence:

'Yes, guilty!'

And then it was the same story on all the other charges: guilty again and again, and with no mitigating circumstances! This was something that no one had expected; nearly everyone had been convinced that there were mitigating circumstances. The deathly hush in the hall remained unbroken, it was as if everyone—those eager for a guilty verdict, and those eager for an acquittal—had been turned to stone. But that was only the initial response.

Then a terrible chaos ensued. Amongst the menfolk were many who were delighted. Some were even rubbing their hands with glee. Those who were disappointed seemed downcast, they shrugged their shoulders, whispered, and seemed not quite to have taken it in. But, my God, how the ladies carried on! I thought there would be a riot. At first they seemed not to believe their ears. And then suddenly there was an outcry in the hall: 'What's all this? What do they think they're up to?' They all leapt to their feet. They probably imagined that the verdict could be quashed and changed. At that instant Mitya got up suddenly and, stretching forth his arms, cried out in a heart-rending voice:

'I swear by God and His dread judgement that I am not guilty of my father's blood! Katya, I forgive you! My brothers, my friends, have pity on the other one!'

He broke down and burst into loud sobs, wailing unintelligibly in a terrible, unrecognizable, inhuman voice. From the back row of the gallery came a piercing shriek: it was Grushenka. Before the start of the judicial pleadings, she had persuaded someone to let her back into the courtroom. Mitya was led away. Sentencing was postponed until the next day. The whole court-room rose in confusion, but I did not stay to listen. I remember only a few comments overheard on the steps at the exit.

'Twenty years down the mines.'*

'At least.'

'Trust the peasants!'

'They really did for poor old Mitenka!'

The end of the fourth and last part.

EPILOGUE

1

PLANS FOR MITYA'S ESCAPE

FIVE days after the trial, very early in the morning, shortly after eight o'clock, Alyosha went to Katerina Ivanovna's to finalize some details concerning a matter of considerable importance to them both, and also to enlist her help. She sat and talked to him in that same room where she had once received Grushenka; Ivan Fyodorovich lay feverish and unconscious in the next room. Straight after that scene in the courtroom, ignoring the inevitable gossip and condemnation of society, Katerina Ivanovna had asked them to transfer the sick and unconscious Ivan Fyodorovich to her house. One of the two relatives with whom she lived had left for Moscow directly after the scene in court; the other was still there. But even if they had both gone away, Katerina Ivanovna would not have decided otherwise, and would have continued to care for the invalid and to sit with him day and night. Varvinsky and Herzenstube were treating him; the doctor from Moscow had returned, having refused to give a prognosis of Ivan's illness. The two remaining doctors had done their best to reassure Katerina Ivanovna and Alyosha, but it was obvious that they could not hold out any firm hope. Alyosha visited his sick brother twice a day. But this time he was on a particularly delicate mission, and he anticipated that it would be very difficult to broach the subject. Meanwhile, he was in a hurry; he had another urgent matter to deal with elsewhere that same morning, and speed was essential. They had already been talking for a quarter of an hour. Katerina Ivanovna was pale, exhausted, and at the same time desperately agitated; she already sensed why Alyosha had come.

'Don't worry about his reservations,' she told Alyosha firmly. 'One way or another, he'll realize it's the only solution; he must escape! That unhappy, heroic man, that man of honour and conscience—not him, no, not Dmitry Fyodorovich, but the one in the next room who's sacrificed himself for his brother,' added Katya, her eyes sparkling, 'he told me all about the escape plan long ago. You know, he was already making arrangements... I've told you something about it... You see, it'll probably happen during the third stage of the march* when the exiles are being taken to Siberia. But that's a long way off yet. Ivan Fyodorovich went to see the commandant who'll be in charge of the third stage. The only thing we don't know is who'll be in overall charge of the march; it's impossible to find out in advance. Tomorrow, perhaps, I'll tell you in detail the whole plan that Ivan Fyodorovich described to me the night before the trial, in case anything... That was the time, you'll recall, when you found us quarrelling; he was already going down the stairs, and when I saw you I made him come back—do you remember? Do you know what we'd been quarrelling about?'

'No, I don't,' said Alyosha.

'Of course, he didn't let on to you, but it was in fact about the escape plan. He had already explained the main part to me three days before—that's when we started quarrelling, and we quarrelled for the whole three days. The reason was that when he told me that in the event of his being convicted Dmitry Fyodorovich would flee abroad with that slut, I lost my temper—I'm not going to tell you why, I don't know why myself... Oh, of course, I was angry about that slut, and especially about her fleeing abroad with Dmitry!' Katerina Ivanovna burst out, her lips trembling with fury. 'As soon as Ivan Fyodorovich saw that I was angry about that creature he immediately thought I was jealous of her because of Dmitry, and that I probably still loved Dmitry. That's when the first row started. I didn't want to explain, nor could I bring myself to apologize; it was hard for me to accept that such a man could suspect me of having loved that... And all this, you realize, after I had told him myself outright long before that I didn't love Dmitry, that I loved only him! I only lost my temper with him because I was so angry about that creature! Three days later, that same evening you arrived, he brought me a sealed envelope that I was to open in case anything happened to him. Somehow he knew he was going to fall ill! He told me that the detailed arrangements for the escape were in the envelope, and that if he died or became seriously ill I should rescue Mitya myself. He left some money with me at the same time, almost ten thousand—the same money that the prosecutor, who heard from someone or other that he had cashed it, mentioned in his speech. I was quite overwhelmed by the fact that Ivan Fyodorovich had not abandoned the idea of rescuing his brother, and that although he still suspected me of loving Dmitry, I was the very one in whom he had confided his plans for the escape! That was a sacrifice! You won't really understand just what a sacrifice it was, Aleksei Fyodorovich! I wanted to fall at his feet in admiration, but it suddenly occurred to me that he would think I was simply overjoyed to know that Mitya was going to be rescued (and he certainly would have thought that), and the very possibility of such an unjustified idea infuriated me so much that, instead of kissing his feet, I made another scene! Oh, I'm so miserable! That's what I'm like—I have such a dreadful, perverse character! Oh, you'll see: I shall continue to be like that until he deserts me for someone else who's easier to live with, like Dmitry did, but then... no, I shan't be able to bear it, I shall kill myself! And when you came that time and I invited you in and called him back, and he came, I was seized with such anger at the look of hatred he gave me, as if he despised me, that I shouted out—remember?—that it was *he, he alone* that told me that his brother Dmitry was the murderer! I deliberately slandered him so as to hurt him once more; he had never, never told me that his brother was the murderer—on the contrary, it was I who told him! Oh, my rage is the cause of all this! And it was I who caused that damned scene at the trial. He wanted to show me his nobility of spirit, and that even if I did love his brother, he wouldn't destroy him out of revenge and jealousy. So that's why he came and spoke out at the trial... It was me, I'm the cause of everything, I alone am guilty!'

Katya had never made such an admission to Alyosha before, and he felt that she had reached that unbearable degree of suffering when the proudest of hearts, racked by pain, abandons its pride and is overcome by sorrow. Alyosha knew of another dreadful reason for her present misery, however hard she had tried to conceal it from him since Mitya's conviction; but for some reason he would have found it too painful if she were to humble herself to such an extent as to discuss it with him now. She was suffering for her 'betrayal' at the trial, and Alyosha felt that her conscience was driving her to confess to him—especially to him, Alyosha—with tears, with weeping, with hysterics, and beating her breast. But he feared that moment, and wanted to spare the sufferer. It was becoming all the more difficult to raise the matter of what he had come to ask of her. He began to speak of Mitya again.

'It's all right, it's all right, don't worry about him!' Katya interrupted sharply and firmly. 'This is just a passing phase, I know him, I know him only too well. You can be sure he'll agree to escape. The main thing is he doesn't need to do anything immediately; he's still got plenty of time to make up his mind. By then, Ivan Fyodorovich will be better and will arrange everything, so it'll be off my shoulders. Don't you worry, he'll agree to escape. Well, he's agreed already; you don't think he'd leave his woman behind, do you? And they won't let her go to the penal colony with him, so he'll have to make a break for it, won't he? The main problem is that he's afraid of you, he's afraid you won't approve of his escaping—from a moral point of view, that is—but you must be magnanimous and say it's all right, since your approval is absolutely vital,' she added venomously. She stopped for a moment, and her lips twisted into a smile.

'He's been talking about some sort of hymns in there', she resumed, 'about the cross he has to carry, about some sort of duty; I remember Ivan Fyodorovich talking a lot about that— and if you could have heard how he talked,' Katya exclaimed suddenly, with unrestrained emotion, 'if you could have seen how much he loved the poor man at that moment, as he was telling me about him, how much, at the same time as he hated him perhaps! And I, oh, at that time I listened to his story and observed his tears with a disdainful smile! Talk of being rotten! It's I who's been the snake in the grass, I! It was I who caused his fever! And the other one, the one who's been sentenced, can you see him as a martyr?' Katya concluded angrily. 'He doesn't know the meaning of the word. His kind don't martyr themselves!'

A kind of hatred and scornful revulsion had crept into these words. And yet it was she who had betrayed him. 'Well, perhaps it's because she feels so guilty about him that she hates him at times,' Alyosha thought to himself. He wanted it to be only 'at times'. He had recognized a challenge in Katya's words, but he did not rise to it.

'That's why I asked you to come today, to get you to promise me that you'd persuade him. Or do you think running away would be wrong, not heroic enough, or, as they say... not the Christian thing?' she added even more challengingly.

'No, it's all right. I'll tell him everything,' Alyosha muttered. 'He wants you to go and see him today,' he added suddenly, looking her straight in the eyes. She shook all over, and recoiled slightly from him as they sat on the sofa.

'Me... is it really possible?'

'It is possible and you must!' Alyosha began determinedly, enthusiastically. 'He needs you very much, especially now. I wouldn't have brought this up and caused you premature suffering, if it weren't unavoidable. He's ill, he's like a madman, and he keeps asking for you. He's not asking you to come for a reconciliation, just to come and appear at the door. He's changed a lot since the trial. He understands how grievously he's wronged you. He doesn't ask your forgiveness. He says himself, "I can't be forgiven," but he just wants you to come to the door...'

'Suddenly you...', stammered Katya, 'I've had a feeling for days you'd come and ask me that... I knew he'd send for me!.. It's impossible!'

'It may be impossible, but go. Remember, he has just realized for the first time how deeply he has offended you; he never fully understood it before! He says that if you refuse to come, he'll be unhappy for the rest of his life. You hear that; a man condemned to twenty years' hard labour still dreams of being happy—doesn't that make you pity him? Remember,' Alyosha burst out, challenging her, 'you'll be visiting a convicted man who is innocent. His hands are clean, there is no blood on them! Think of the endless suffering he will have to endure, and go and visit him now! Go to him, give him the strength to face the dark... stand in the doorway and just... Really, you have to do this, you *must*!' Alyosha concluded, putting particular stress on the word 'must'.

'I must, but... I can't,' Katya almost groaned, 'he'll look at me... I can't do it.'

'You have to look him in the eyes. How are you going to live the rest of your life if you don't make up your mind to do this now?'

'I'd rather suffer all my life.'

'You have to go, you *must*,' Alyosha insisted again, implacably.

'But why today, why now?.. I can't leave my patient...'

'You can for a minute. It won't take long. If you don't go, he'll work himself up into such a state by tonight. I'm not lying to you. Have pity!'

'You should have pity on me,' Katya reproached him bitterly, and burst into tears.

'So you'll go!' said Alyosha, unmoved by her tears. 'I'll go and tell him you're coming.'

'No, whatever you do, don't tell him!' Katya cried, horrified. 'I'll go, but don't tell him I'm coming; I'll definitely go, but perhaps I won't go in... I just don't know...'

Her voice broke. She was breathing heavily. Alyosha got up to leave.

'But what if someone's there?' she said quietly, suddenly going very pale again.

'That's why you must go at once, so that you won't meet anyone there. No one will be there, I assure you. We'll be expecting you,' he concluded emphatically, and left the room.

2

FOR A MOMENT A LIE BECOMES THE TRUTH

ALYOSHA hurried to the hospital where Mitya had been admitted. Two days after the end of the trial he had fallen ill with nervous exhaustion and had been admitted to the prison ward in our town hospital. But in response to a request from Alyosha and many others, including Mrs Khokhlakova and Lise, Dr Varvinsky had not put him with the other prisoners, but in the same side ward where Smerdyakov had lain. A guard stood at the end of the corridor and the window was barred, so Varvinsky did not lose any sleep over breaking the prison rules. He was a kind and sympathetic young man, and he understood how hard it would be for someone like Mitya to be thrust into the company of murderers and criminals, and that he would need time to adjust. Both doctors and guards—and even the chief of police—turned a blind eye to visits from relatives and friends. But during these days only Alyosha and Grushenka had visited Mitya. Rakitin had tried to see him twice, but Mitya had asked Dr Varvinsky not to admit him.

Alyosha found him sitting on his bed in a hospital dressing-gown, with a slight fever and with a towel soaked in vinegar and water wrapped round his head. He looked at Alyosha vaguely, but somehow there was a brief hint of fear in his glance.

Since the trial he had generally become very morose. He would sometimes remain silent for up to half an hour, apparently turning some weighty and distressing matter over in his mind, and quite oblivious of his surroundings. If he did emerge from his stupor and begin to speak, he talked disjointedly and with absolutely no reference to things that were really important. Sometimes he looked miserably at his brother. He seemed to find it easier to be in Grushenka's company than with Alyosha. It is true that he never talked to her, but as soon as she came in his whole face was suffused with joy. Alyosha sat down next to him on the bed and said nothing. He had been waiting anxiously for Alyosha this time, but he did not dare to ask anything. He could not imagine that Katya would agree to visit him, and yet he felt that if she did not come life would be quite unbearable. Alyosha understood how he felt.

'They say', Mitya began, playing for time, 'that Trifon Borisych has totally demolished his inn; he's taken up the floorboards, ripped the panels off the walls, they say he's taken the whole gallery apart—he keeps looking for the treasure, that money, the one thousand five hundred that the prosecutor said I'd hidden there. Ever since he got back he's been behaving like a madman. Serves the crook right! The guard here told me about it; he comes from there.'

'Listen,' said Alyosha, 'she's coming, but I don't know when, maybe today, maybe in a day or two, I don't know, but she's coming, that's for sure.'

Mitya shuddered, started to say something, but then fell silent. The news had a terrible effect upon him. He obviously desperately wanted to find out in detail about the conversation, but he was afraid to ask now; anything cruel and scornful from Katya would have been like a knife in his heart at that moment.

'By the way, she told me to be sure to put your mind at rest about escaping. If Ivan isn't better in time, she'll see to it herself.'

'You've already told me that,' said Mitya thoughtfully.

'And you've already told Grusha,' commented Alyosha.

'Yes,' Mitya admitted. 'She isn't coming this morning,' he looked nervously at his brother. 'She isn't coming till this evening. When I told her yesterday that Katya was arranging things she didn't say anything, but simply made a face. She just whispered, "Not her again!" She understood that it was important. I didn't dare pursue it any further. Anyway, she seems to understand now that Katya loves Ivan, not me, doesn't she?'

'Is that true?' Alyosha burst out.

'Perhaps not. Anyway, she isn't coming this morning,' Mitya repeated quickly. 'I've asked her to do something... Listen, Ivan's going to come out of this better than us. He's the one who'll survive, not us. He'll recover.'

'You know, Katya has been terribly worried about him, but she too is almost certain he's going to recover,' said Alyosha.

'That means she's convinced he's going to die. It's just fear that makes her think he's getting better.'

'Ivan's got a strong constitution. I too hope he'll get better,' Alyosha remarked in troubled tones.

'Yes, he'll get better, but that one is convinced he's going to die. She's really unhappy...'

Silence fell. Something very important was gnawing away at Mitya.

'Alyosha, I love Grushenka terribly,' he said suddenly, in a voice that shook with sobs.

'They won't let her be with you *there*,' Alyosha interjected.

'And there's something else I wanted to say to you,' Mitya went on in a voice that was suddenly vibrant, 'if anyone tries to assault me on the way or when I'm out *there*, I shan't let him, I'll kill him, and they'll shoot me. And I'll get twenty years, you know! Even here they don't show me any respect. The guards never address me properly. All last night I lay there taking stock; I'm not ready for it! I can't accept it! I was ready to sing my "hymn", and besides, I can't stand the guards' familiarity! For

Grusha I'd have put up with anything, anything... except, perhaps, a beating... but they won't let her go *there*.'

Alyosha smiled gently.

'Listen, Mitya,' he said, 'I'll tell you what I think about this once and for all. And you know I wouldn't lie to you. Just listen: you're not ready to carry such a cross. And, what's more, there's no need for you, unprepared as you are, to carry such a heavy cross. If you had killed father, I should regret your refusal to take up your cross. But you're innocent, and such a cross is far too heavy for you. You wanted through your suffering to resurrect another man within yourself; just think of that other man all your life, wherever you may have to go—and in my view that'll be enough. The fact that you refused to carry that heavy cross will serve simply to arouse an even greater feeling of responsibility in you, and from then on, all your life, that feeling will help to resurrect your soul even more—more, perhaps, than if you had actually gone *there*. Because you wouldn't last out there, you'd rail against it, and in the end perhaps you'd say "I give up." The lawyer was quite right. It's not given to everyone to bear the heaviest burden; for some it's impossible... That's my opinion for what it's worth. If others—officers, soldiers—had to answer for your escape, I should not "give you permission" to escape,' said Alyosha with a smile. 'But they assure me (the route commander himself told Ivan) that if we go about it the right way it won't cause too much fuss and those involved will get off lightly. Of course, bribery is dishonourable, even in these circumstances, but I'm in no position to judge on this point because, to tell the truth, if Ivan and Katya were to ask me for example to fix it for you, I know that I would go and bribe whoever I had to; I must be honest. And that's why I shan't judge you, ever. Remember, I shall never condemn you. And anyway, that's inconceivable; how could I be your judge in this matter? Well, I think I've covered everything.'

'But I will be my own judge!' exclaimed Mitya. 'I shall make a break for it—that was already decided, without you; they can't keep Mitka Karamazov down, can they? But I shall condemn myself nevertheless, and I shall spend the rest of my life atoning for my sins! Isn't that the way the Jesuits talk—the way we're talking now?'

'Yes,' Alyosha smiled gently.

'I love you because you always tell the whole truth and never hide anything!' exclaimed Mitya, laughing joyfully. 'So there is a Jesuit lurking in my Alyosha after all! I should give you a kiss for that! Well now, listen to the rest, I'll reveal the other half of my soul to you. I've thought it out and this is what I've decided: if I escape, even with money and a passport, even if I get to America, I shall be reassured by the thought that I'm escaping not to find joy or happiness, but in truth to another kind of punishment, just as harsh as here! Just as harsh, I tell you honestly, Aleksei, just as harsh! I know America, to hell with it, and I hate it before I've even been there. Grusha can come with me, but look at her: could she be American? She's Russian, Russian to the core, she'll pine for her homeland, and every hour of the day I'll have to watch and know that it's because of me she's unhappy, because of me she's taken up such a cross—what has she done to deserve it? And I'm afraid that those cowboys over there will prove to be too much for me, even though every last one of them is perhaps better than me! I hate America already! They may have the most incredible engineers, but to hell with them, they're not my sort of people, not kindred spirits! It's Russia I love, Aleksei, I love the Russian God, although I'm a scoundrel! Yes, I shall give up the ghost there!' he exclaimed, his eyes suddenly flashing. His voice shook with emotions.

'So, this is what I've decided, Alyosha, listen!' he resumed, having overcome his emotion. 'Grusha and I will go there—and we'll plough the land, we'll work by ourselves among the wild bears, in some distant part. There must be some deserted corner over there! They say there are still some redskins somewhere, in the back of beyond—that's where we'll go, to the land of the last of the Mohicans. And we'll start learning the language straight away, Grusha and I. Nothing but work and grammar for at least three years. In three years we'll have learnt to speak English like real English people. And as soon as we've learnt it—that'll be the end of America for us! We'll come back here to Russia, as American citizens. Don't worry, we won't show our faces here. We'll go into hiding somewhere in the far north or down south. I'll have changed by that time, and so will she; I'll get a doctor over there in America to fix me up with a wart—they're full of tricks over there. Or else I'll poke out one of my eyes and grow a grey beard down to my waist (I'll go grey from homesickness), and hope no one will recognize me. And if I'm recognized, they can send me to the salt-mines—so what, it doesn't matter! Here too we'll plough the land somewhere in the back of beyond, and I'll pass myself off as an American for the rest of my life. At least we'll die in our native land. That's my plan and I won't change it. Do you approve?'

'Yes,' said Alyosha, not wanting to contradict him. Mitya was silent for a moment, and then he said suddenly:

'They really had it in for me at the trial, didn't they? They really did the dirty on me!'

'Even if they hadn't rigged it, you'd have been found guilty,' sighed Alyosha.

'Yes, the people here have had enough of me! Anyway, who cares about them, but it's hard all the same!' Mitya groaned miserably.

They fell silent again for a while.

'Alyosha, put me out of my misery here and now!' Mitya burst out. 'Tell me, is she coming today or not? What did she say? And how did she sound?'

'She said she'd come, but I don't know if it'll be today. It's not easy for her, you know,' Alyosha looked apprehensively at his brother.

'Of course it isn't, how could it be easy. Alyosha, this will drive me mad. Grusha keeps looking at me. She understands. Oh, Lord God, make me humble; what am I asking for? I'm asking for Katya! Do I know what I'm asking? This wretched Karamazov impetuosity! No, I'm incapable of accepting suffering! I'm a scoundrel, and there's nothing more to be said!'

'Here she is!' said Alyosha.

At that instant Katya appeared in the doorway. She stood there gazing at Mitya for a moment in a kind of bewilderment. He leapt to his feet in a flash, his face paled and he looked terrified, but at once a timid, pleading smile flitted across his lips and, suddenly, impetuously, he stretched both hands out to Katya. When she saw that, she rushed to him. She seized his hands, pushed him almost forcibly on to the bed, and sat down next to him, still holding his hands and squeezing them convulsively. They both attempted to speak several times, but stopped and went on gazing silently at each other, smiling strangely, as though transfixed; about two minutes passed.

'Have you forgiven me or not?' Mitya muttered at last, and the very next moment, turning to Alyosha, his face contorted with joy, he cried out:

'You heard what I asked, you heard!'

'That's why I loved you, because you always had a generous heart!' Katya burst out suddenly. 'And you don't need my forgiveness, it is I who need yours; but it doesn't matter whether you forgive me or not, you will be a festering sore in my soul all my life, and I in yours—that's how it has to be,' she stopped for breath.

'Why did I come?' she began again, frantically and hurriedly. 'To kiss your feet, to squeeze your hands, like this, till it hurts; do you remember how I used to squeeze them in Moscow, telling you again that you were a god to me, that you were my joy, that I loved you hopelessly?' she groaned miserably, and suddenly pressed her lips to Mitya's hand hungrily. Tears flooded from her eyes.

Alyosha stood silent and embarrassed; in no way had he expected what he was now witnessing.

'Love has passed, Mitya,' Katya began again, 'but that which has been is still so dear it hurts me. Remember that for ever. But now, for one brief moment, let's pretend what might have been,' she murmured with a crooked smile, gazing joyfully into his eyes once more. 'You love another now, and so do I, but I shall always love you all the same, and you me; did you know that? Listen, you must love me, love me all your life!' she cried, her voice trembling almost threateningly.

'I will, and... you know, Katya,' Mitya too began to speak, drawing breath between each word, 'you know, I loved you five days ago, that evening... when you fainted and they carried you out... Yes, all my life. That's how it will be, that's how it will be for ever...'

They went on like that, babbling ecstatically, mouthing meaningless phrases which were not even true, perhaps, and yet at that moment everything was true, they themselves believed that unreservedly.

'Katya,' Mitya exclaimed suddenly, 'do you believe I killed him? I know you don't believe it now, but then... when you were testifying... Surely you didn't believe it!'

'I didn't believe it then either! I never believed it! I hated you, and suddenly I convinced myself... just for that moment... While I was testifying, I convinced myself and I believed what I was saying... but as soon as I finished my testimony I stopped believing. You must know everything. I forgot I'd come to mortify myself!' she said in an altogether different tone from her murmured endearments of the previous moment.

'You're making things difficult for yourself, lady!' Mitya burst out involuntarily.

'Let me go,' she whispered, 'I'll come back again, it's too much for me now!...'

She stood up, but suddenly gave a loud cry and stumbled backwards. Suddenly but quite silently Grushenka had entered the room. No one was expecting her. Katya strode quickly to the door and, as she drew level with Grushenka, stopped abruptly, white as a sheet, and softly, almost in a whisper, groaned:

'Forgive me!'

Grushenka stared at her for a moment and then, her voice poisoned with anger, replied venomously:

'We're wicked, my girl, both of us! We're both wicked! Why should we forgive each other? But save him, and I'll pray for you for the rest of my life.'

'You won't forgive her!' Mitya cried out to Grushenka, full of reproach.

'Don't worry, I'll see they release him for you!' Katya said quickly, and ran from the room.

'Couldn't you have forgiven her when she'd begged your forgiveness?' Mitya exclaimed bitterly.

'Mitya, don't you dare reproach her, you have no right!' Alyosha shouted angrily.

'That was her proud lips talking, not her heart,' said Grushenka with a kind of revulsion. 'Let her get you out of here—then I'll forgive her...'

She fell silent, as though stifling something in herself. She was still unable to regain her composure. She had come quite on the spur of the moment, it turned out later, suspecting nothing, and not expecting to find what she did.

'Run after her, Alyosha!' Mitya implored his brother. 'Tell her... I don't know what... but don't let her go like that!'

'I'll be back before the evening!' shouted Alyosha, and ran after Katya. He caught up with her when she was already outside the hospital grounds. She was walking fast, hurrying, but as soon as Alyosha caught up with her, she said:

'No, I can't humiliate myself in front of that woman! I asked her to forgive me, because I wanted the ultimate humiliation. She didn't forgive me... I love her for that!' she added, her voice distorted and with a glint of wild anger in her eyes.

'My brother really wasn't expecting her,' muttered Alyosha. 'He was sure she wouldn't come...'

'No doubt. Let's forget it,' she cut him short. 'Listen, I can't come to the funeral with you now. I've sent some flowers for the grave. I think they've still got some money. Tell them that if they're ever in need, I'll see that they're all right... Now, leave me, let me go, please. You're already late, there's the bell for the service... Leave me, please!'

3

ILYUSHECHKA'S FUNERAL.
THE SPEECH AT THE STONE

HE really was late. They were waiting for him, and had almost decided to carry the beautiful little coffin, decorated with flowers, to the church without him. It was the coffin of Ilyushechka, the poor child. He had died two days after the trial. Ilyusha's schoolfriends greeted Alyosha at the gate outside the house with shouts of welcome. They had been waiting impatiently for him, and were delighted that he had arrived at last. In all there were about twelve of them gathered there, each with his satchel or bag over his shoulder. 'Papa will cry, stay with papa,' had been Ilyusha's dying request, and the boys had remembered this. At their head was Kolya Krasotkin.

'I'm so glad you've come, Karamazov!' he exclaimed, extending his hand to Alyosha. 'The atmosphere here's unbearable. Honestly, I can hardly stand it. Snegiryov isn't drunk—we know for a fact that he hasn't touched a drop today—but you could've fooled me... I can usually take anything, but this is awful. Karamazov, if you can spare a moment, could I ask you one more question before you go in?'

'What is it, Kolya?' Alyosha stopped for a moment.

'Is your brother guilty or innocent? Did he kill him, or was it the servant? Whatever you say I'll believe you. I haven't slept for four nights thinking about it.'

'It was the servant; my brother's innocent,' Alyosha answered.

'That's what I think too!' cried the boy Smurov suddenly.

'So he's going to end up an innocent victim on the altar of truth!' exclaimed Kolya. 'Even though it's the end for him, still he's happy! I could envy him!'

'How can you say that, how can you envy him, and what for?' protested Alyosha, astonished.

'Oh, if only I too could sacrifice myself one day for truth,' enthused Kolya.

'But not for something like that, not in such disgrace, such horrific circumstances!' said Alyosha.

'Of course... I would like to die for the whole of humanity, and if that means disgrace, so what; let our names perish!* I respect your brother!'

'Me too!' came a sudden and unexpected cry from among the group; it was that same boy who, as I have mentioned elsewhere, knew who founded Troy, and as on that occasion, having shouted out he blushed scarlet to the tips of his ears.

Alyosha went into the room. Ilyusha lay in the pale-blue, white-lined coffin, his hands folded on his breast, and his eyes closed. The features of his emaciated face had hardly changed at all, and, strangely, almost no smell emanated from the corpse. The expression on his face was serious and somewhat thoughtful. His crossed hands were particularly beautiful, as if carved out of marble. Some flowers had been placed in his hands and the whole coffin, inside and out, was already covered in flowers which had been sent by Lise Khokhlakova first thing that morning. But more flowers had arrived from Katerina Ivanovna, and when Alyosha opened the door the Staff Captain, a bunch of flowers in his trembling hands, was strewing them around his darling boy. He hardly glanced at Alyosha as he entered—in fact, he would not look at anyone, not even at his simpleton, weeping wife, his 'mummikins', who kept trying to stand up on her painful legs and look closer at her dead son. The children had picked Ninochka up in her chair and placed her right by the coffin. She sat, her head pressed against it, and seemed to be crying quietly. Snegiryov's expression was at once animated and distraught, but at the same time quarrelsome. There was a kind of madness in his gestures and in his occasional utterances. 'Old chap, my dear old chap!' he exclaimed from time to time, looking at Ilyusha. He had had a habit, even when Ilyusha was alive, of calling him 'old chap, my dear old chap', by way of affection.

'Papa, give me some flowers too, take some from his little hands, give me that white one!' begged his feeble-minded 'mummikins' tearfully. Either because she liked the little white rose in Ilyusha's hands so much, or because she wanted to have it to remind herself of him, she had become very agitated and was reaching out for the flower.

'I shall not give it to anyone; I shall not give anything to anyone!' snapped the Staff Captain cruelly. 'They're his flowers, not yours. Everything's his, nothing's yours!'

'Papa, give mama the flower!' Ninochka suddenly lifted her tear-soaked face.

'I shan't give anything to anyone, least of all to her! She didn't love him. She took the little cannon away from him that time, and he g-g-ave it to her,' the Staff Captain suddenly began to sob out loud at the memory of how Ilyusha had handed over his little cannon to his mother. The poor deranged woman promptly burst into tears, weeping quietly, with her hands covering her face. The boys, seeing at last that the father did not want to release the coffin, although it was time to leave, suddenly formed a solid ring around the coffin and began to lift it.

'I don't want to bury him in the graveyard!' wailed Snegiryov suddenly. 'I'll bury him by the stone, by our stone. That's what Ilyusha wanted. I won't let you take him away!'

He had been saying before, for the whole of the last three days, that he would bury him by the stone, but Alyosha,

Krasotkin, his landlady and her sister, and all the boys had protested.

'What an idea, burying him by an unconsecrated stone, like a suicide!' said the old landlady severely. At least it's consecrated ground in the graveyard. They'll pray for him there. He'll be able to hear the singing from the church, and the deacon reads so well and so clearly that he'll hear every word, just as if they were spoken over his grave.'

At last the Staff Captain made a gesture of resignation. 'Take him wherever you like.' The boys lifted the coffin, but as they passed the mother they stopped for a moment and lowered it so that she could say goodbye to Ilyusha. But seeing that dear little face close up, which for three whole days she had seen only from a distance, she suddenly began to tremble all over and to rock her grey head hysterically backwards and forwards against the coffin.

'Mama, make the sign of the cross, bless him, kiss him,' Ninochka called to her. But she kept rocking her head like an automaton, and suddenly, without speaking, her face contorted and riven by grief, she began to beat her breast. They carried the coffin further. When they carried it past Ninochka, she pressed her lips to those of the dead boy for the last time. Alyosha had intended, as he went out, to ask the landlady to keep an eye on those remaining behind, but she fore-stalled him.

'It goes without saying, I'll stay with them, we're Christians too.' Thus saying, the old woman began to cry.

They did not have far to carry it to the church, about three hundred paces, not more. It was a clear, windless day; a bit frosty, but not excessively so. The church bells were still ringing. Snegiryov, in his old coat, short, more of a summer coat, his head bare and his old, wide-brimmed felt hat in his hands, hurried frantic and distraught behind the coffin. He was consumed by some overriding anxiety, and kept on putting out his hand suddenly to support the head of the coffin, only getting in the way of the bearers, or he would run alongside, trying to find somewhere to join the procession. A flower fell on to the snow and he rushed to pick it up, as if heaven knows what might result from the loss of that one little flower.

'The crust, we've forgotten the crust,' he cried suddenly in a panic. But the boys immediately reminded him that he had already picked up the bread, and that it was now in his pocket. He took it out of his pocket for a moment and, having reassured himself, became calmer.

'Ilyushechka told me to do it, Ilyushechka,' he explained to Alyosha. 'I was sitting by his bed during the night, and suddenly he said, "Papa, when they've buried my coffin, crumble a crust of bread on to my grave so that the sparrows will come there; I shall hear them, and I'll be happy that I'm not lying there alone."'

'That's a very good idea,' said Alyosha. 'It should be done more often.'

'Every day, every day,' murmured the Staff Captain, seeming to cheer up.

At last they reached the church, and on entering and placed the coffin in the centre of the nave. All the boys gathered round it and remained standing respectfully throughout the service. The church was an ancient one and was quite poor, many of the icons had no frames, but they say that one prays better in such churches. Snegiryov seemed a little calmer during the liturgy for the dead, although from time to time he showed signs of that same compulsive and somewhat confused anxiety; he kept going up to the coffin to straighten the shroud or Ilyusha's headband;* when a candle fell from the candlestick he rushed to replace it, and stayed fussing over it interminably. He grew calmer after that, and stood meekly at the head of the coffin, stupefied, his expression preoccupied and uncomprehending. After the Epistle he suddenly whispered to Alyosha, who was standing next to him, that they had not read it *properly*, but he did not elaborate further. He started to join in when they sang the Song of the Cherubim, but then he stopped, bent down on his knees, pressed his forehead against the cold, stone floor of the church, and remained thus for some time. At last the funeral service proper began, and candles were distributed. The distraught father began to fuss again, but the moving, emotional funeral-chanting shook and reawakened his soul. He suddenly seemed to shrivel up, and began to sob spasmodically, restraining his sobbing at first, but then crying aloud. But when the moment came to bid farewell to

Ilyushechka and close the coffin, he threw his arms around the coffin, as though to prevent them from closing it, and began to cover the lips of his dead son with long, hungry kisses. At last they persuaded him to desist, and they had already led him down the steps when suddenly he stretched out his hand and snatched several flowers from the coffin. He looked at them as if a new idea had occurred to him, causing him to forget momentarily why he was there. He seemed to be slipping little by little into a reverie, and now offered no resistance when they lifted the coffin and carried it towards the grave. It was not far; the plot was an expensive one in that part of the churchyard which abutted the church—Katerina Ivanovna had paid for it. After the usual rites, the gravediggers lowered the coffin into the earth. Snegiryov, with his flowers in his hand, leaned so low over the open coffin that the boys feared for him, and grabbed him by his coat and began to pull him back. But he seemed to have lost track already of what was going on. When they began to fill in the grave, he started pointing to the earth they were throwing in, but no one could make out what he wanted, and he suddenly fell silent. At this point someone reminded him that he should crumble the bread, and he became terribly agitated, pulled out the crust, and began to break off pieces and scatter them on the grave. 'There you are little birds, there you are sparrows, fly on to the grave!' he murmured anxiously. One of the boys pointed out to him that it was awkward for him to break the bread with the flowers in his hand, and that he should give them to someone to hold for a while. But he would not part with them, he even panicked suddenly about his flowers, as if they wanted to take them away from him, but having surveyed the grave and apparently assured himself that everything had been completed, that the bread had been crumbled, he suddenly to their surprise turned and set off quite calmly homewards. His pace, however, became quicker and more headlong; he was hurrying, almost running. The boys and Alyosha kept up with him.

'Flowers for mummikins, flowers for mummikins! Mummikins was hurt,' he babbled. Someone called out to him to put on his hat, or he would catch cold, but he threw the hat down on the snow as if in anger, saying repeatedly, 'I don't need a hat, I don't want a hat!' Smurov picked it up and fell into step behind him.

All the boys, without exception, were crying—Kolya and the boy who knew who discovered Troy more than any of them. Smurov, although weeping uncontrollably and still holding the hat, managed nevertheless, practically without pausing, to pick up a piece of brick that appeared as a red object on the snowy path and threw it at a flock of sparrows that was flying past quickly. He missed, of course, and ran on crying. Halfway home Snegiryov suddenly stopped, stood for a moment as though struck by a thought, and then, turning back abruptly towards the church, ran towards the grave they had just left. But the boys caught up with him at once, and grabbed him from all sides. Whereupon, as if his strength had failed him, as if struck down, he collapsed on to the snow and, beating his breast, howling and sobbing, began to scream out: 'My boy, Ilyushechka, my dear old chap!' Alyosha and Kolya went to help him up, exhorting and encouraging him.

'Come on now, Captain, a brave man has to pull himself together,' Kolya muttered.

'You're spoiling the flowers,' said Alyosha, 'and "mummikins" is waiting for them, she's sitting there crying because you wouldn't give her some of Ilyushechka's flowers before. Ilyusha's little bed is still there...'

'Yes, yes, I must take them to mama!' Snegiryov remembered suddenly. 'They'll take the bed away, they'll take it away!' he added, and, apparently suddenly panic-stricken at the thought that they really would take the bed away, he leapt to his feet and ran home. But it was not far, and they all arrived together. Snegiryov threw open the door and shouted to his wife, whom he had treated so cruelly shortly before:

'Mama, my dear, Ilyushechka has sent you some flowers, your poor legs are bad!' he cried, proffering the bunch of flowers, which had become frozen and dishevelled from his struggle in the snow. But at that very moment he noticed by Ilyusha's bed in the corner Ilyusha's little boots, standing side by side where the landlady had just placed them, old boots, faded, scruffy, and repaired. Seeing them, he threw up his arms, rushed to them, and fell on his knees; he seized one boot and, pressing his lips to it, started kissing it frantically, crying, 'Ilyushechka, my dear old chap, where are your little feet?'

'Where have you taken him? Where have you taken him?'

howled the mad woman in harrowing tones. Ninochka too now began to sob. Kolya rushed from the room, and the boys began to follow him. Alyosha was the last to leave. 'Let them have a good cry,' he said to Kolya. 'It's no use trying to comfort them now. Let's wait a bit and then go back.'

'Yes, there's nothing we can do, it's awful,' Kolya agreed. 'You know, Karamazov,' he lowered his voice suddenly, so that no one would hear, 'I'm so sad, and I'd give anything in the world if it would only bring him back to life!'

'Oh! So would I!' said Alyosha.

'What do you think, Karamazov, should we come back this evening? He'll get drunk, you know.'

'Perhaps he will. You and I will come back, just the two of us, no need for any of the others, just to sit with them for an hour, with his mother and Ninochka; if the whole lot of us come it'll only remind them of everything,' Alyosha suggested.

'The landlady's laying the table now—there'll be the wake or whatever, the priest will be there; should we go back now, Karamazov, or not?'

'Certainly,' said Alyosha.

'It's strange, isn't it, Karamazov, such grief, and then suddenly some sort of pancakes; our religion is so strange!'

'They're going to have salmon too,' remarked the boy who knew who founded Troy, loudly.

'I wish you'd shut up, Kartashov, and not make any more of your stupid remarks, especially when no one's speaking to you and no one even cares whether you exist,' Kolya snapped at him irritably. The boy flushed with anger, but did not dare to answer back. Meanwhile, they were all ambling slowly along the path, and suddenly Smurov exclaimed:

'There's Ilyusha's stone! That's where they wanted to bury him.'

They all stopped in silence by the big stone. Alyosha looked at it, and the whole scene that Snegiryov had described to him flashed before his eyes—Ilyushechka clinging to his father and crying, 'Papa, papa, how they humiliated you!' Something shuddered in his soul. With a serious and solemn expression he gazed around at all the dear, shining faces of those schoolboys, Ilyusha's friends, and suddenly he addressed them:

'Boys, I want to say a word to you here, on this particular spot.'

The boys gathered round him at once, and their attentive, expectant gaze was fixed upon him.

'Boys, we shall soon be parting. I must spend some time with my two brothers now, one of them's been sent to the penal colony and the other's on his deathbed. But I shall leave this town soon, perhaps for a very long time. So we have to part, my friends. Let us agree here by Ilyusha's stone never to forget, first, Ilyushechka, and secondly, one another. And whatever may happen to us in this life, even if we don't meet again for twenty years, we'll still remember how we buried that poor child at whom we'd previously thrown stones—by the little bridge, you remember?—and then how we all grew to love him. He was a wonderful boy, kind and brave, with a sense of honour and an understanding of the insult to his father's pride, which he fought to avenge. So, firstly, we shall remember him, boys, all our lives. And whether we're occupied with matters of the greatest importance, whether we're showered with honours or overcome by some devastating calamity—never forget, my friends, how good it was to be together here, united by that feeling of kindness and generosity which now, while we are conscious of our love for that poor boy, has perhaps made us better than we really are. My little doves—let me call you that, doves, because you are all very like them, those gentle little grey birds, at this moment, as I look on your dear beloved faces, my beloved children—perhaps you will not understand what I'm going to say to you, because I often speak quite incomprehensibly, but nevertheless take note of my words, and one day you will come to understand them. Remember that nothing is nobler, stronger, more vital, or more useful in future life than some happy memory, especially one from your very childhood, from your family home. A lot is said about upbringing, but the very best upbringing, perhaps, is some lovely, holy memory preserved from one's childhood. If a man carries many such memories with him, they will keep him safe throughout his life. And even if only one such memory stays in our hearts, it may prove to be our salvation one day. Perhaps we shall grow wicked, we may not be able to refrain from some evil action, we may mock the tears of others and of those who say, as

Kolya exclaimed just now, "I want to suffer for all people"—perhaps these too we shall taunt cruelly. But still, no matter how wicked we become—which, God grant, we may never be—when we recall how we buried Ilyusha, how we loved him in these last days, and how we talked together by this stone with such closeness and affection, then even the cruellest and most cynical amongst us—if such there be—will not dare to mock the kindness and goodness of this moment! Moreover, that memory alone, perhaps, will restrain that person from some great wickedness, and he will think about it and will say, "Yes, I was good then, I was brave and honourable." He may still ridicule it inwardly—that doesn't matter, people often make fun of what is kind and good; that's only frivolity—but I assure you, boys, that even as he mocks he will immediately say in his heart, "No, I was wrong to mock, because one should not make fun of that!"'

'I understand what you're saying, Karamazov, it will certainly be like that,' exclaimed Kolya, his eyes sparkling. The boys were beginning to get excited and they also wanted to respond, but they restrained themselves, gazing approvingly at the speaker.

'I say this in case we should become bad,' went on Alyosha, 'but there's no reason why we should become bad, is there, boys? In the first place, and above all, if we're kind and honourable, then we'll never forget one another. I repeat that once more. I give you my word, boys, that I shall never forget a single one of you; I shall remember every face that is turned to me now, even in thirty years' time. A few moments ago, Kolya told Kartashov that he wouldn't care whether he existed or not. But how could I forget that Kartashov exists, and that he no longer blushes as he did when he discovered who founded Troy, but now looks at me with his kind, cheerful countenance. Boys, my dear boys, let us all be generous and brave like Ilyushechka; clever, brave, and generous like Kolya (who, however, will be much cleverer when he grows up); and let us be like Kartashov, shy, but intelligent and gentle. Oh, why am I talking about those two? All of you, boys, are dear to me from now on, I take you all to my heart, and I ask you all to take me to yours. Well now, who was it that united us in this good and noble feeling of emotion, whom we shall remember henceforth always, all our lives, whom we shall choose to remember—none other than Ilyushechka, that dear, kind boy, that boy who will be dear to us for ever and ever! We shall never forget him, we shall cherish his memory eternally in our hearts from now on, for ever and ever!'

'Yes, yes, eternally, for ever and ever,' shouted all the boys, their voices ringing and their faces radiant.

'We shall remember his face, his clothes, even his little boots, and his little coffin, and his unhappy, wretched father, and how he stood up for him so bravely, against the whole class!'

'We'll remember, we will!' shouted the boys again. 'He was brave, he was good.'

'Oh, how I loved him!' exclaimed Kolya.

'Ah, my children, my dear friends, don't be afraid of life! How good life is when one does something noble and true!'

'Yes, yes,' repeated the boys ecstatically.

'Karamazov, we all love you,' erupted one voice, apparently that of Kartashov.

'We love you, we do,' they all joined in. Many of them had tears glistening in their eyes.

'Hurrah for Karamazov!' called Kolya, carried away.

'And eternal remembrance for the dead boy!' said Alyosha emotionally.

'Eternal remembrance!' the boys joined in again.

'Karamazov,' cried Kolya, 'is it true what religion teaches, that we shall all rise from the dead, that we shall live again and see one another again, and Ilyushechka?'

'Certainly, we shall be resurrected, certainly, we shall see one another again and we shall tell one another happily, joyfully, everything that has happened,' replied Alyosha, half laughing and half overcome with emotion.

'How marvellous that'll be,' burst out Kolya.

'Well now, let's have done with talking and go to his wake. Don't let eating pancakes worry you. After all, it's an old custom, it's always been done from time immemorial, and besides it's a good custom,' laughed Alyosha. 'Come on, let's go! Now we'll all walk hand in hand.'

'And always, all our lives, we'll walk hand in hand! Hurrah for Karamazov!' Kolya shouted again ecstatically, and, once more, all the boys echoed his cry.

EXPLANATORY NOTES

Principal Sources Consulted and Abbreviations Used

AV	The Bible, King James' Authorized Version.
BDPF	*Dictionary of Phrase and Fable*, E. Cobham Brewer (New York, 1978).
BDS	*A Biographical Dictionary of the Saints*, F. G. Holweck (B. Hurder Book Co, 1924).
BL	*Butler's Lives of the Saints* (Burns and Oates, 1956).
BS	*The Book of Saints*, 6th edition (A. & C. Black, London, 1989).
CBQ	*Cassell's Book of Quotations*, W. Guerney Benham (London, 1907).
CD	*Classical Dictionary*, J. Lempriere (London, 1824).
CNDF	*Character Names in Dostoevsky's Fiction*, Charles E. Passage (Ann Arbor, Mich., 1982).
CW	*Collected Works* of Dostoevsky, in 30 vols., *Polnoye Sobraniye Sochineniy v tridtsati tomakh* (Nauka, Leningrad, 1976).
DD	*A Dostoevsky Dictionary*, Richard Chapple (Ann Arbor, Mich., 1983).
DW	F. M. Dostoevsky, *Diary of a Writer*, in *CW*.
Enc., FP	*Encyclopaedic Dictionary*, F. Pavlenkov (Trud, St Petersburg, 1913).
KC	*A Karamazov Companion*, Victor Terras (Madison, Wis., 1981).
ODS	*The Oxford Dictionary of Saints*, David Hugh Farmer (Oxford, 1987).

Symbols

' after a consonant in transliteration of Russian words indicates softening of the preceding consonant.

3 *Anna Grigoryevna*: Anna Grigoryevna Dostoevskaya, née Snitkina (1846–1918), Dostoevsky's second wife.

6 *The second novel*: sequel to *The Karamazov Brothers*, which was never written. Dostoevsky planned to begin work on it in 1882 (*CW*, 15. 485–6).

9 *Fyodor*: Russian variant of 'Theodore' ('gift of God'). Apart from the psychological significance of the author's own name being the

same, there are any number of Theodores in church history; but the one that Dostoevsky probably had in mind when naming his enigmatic and contradictory hero is Theodore of Sykeon (AD 613). Theodore of Sykeon was the son of a harlot who kept an inn and a father who was a circus artist, specializing in acrobatic camel-riding; he seems to have had nothing to do with his son later, leaving the upbringing of the child to the mother.

Theodore was ordained a priest when very young, and went on a pilgrimage to Jerusalem. He was always driven by a desire to escape the world and lead a life of penitence. At his own request, a wooden cage was made in which he passed the time from Christmas to Palm Sunday. He then moved into an iron cage, suspended on the face of a rock in mid-air, above the cave where he dwelt; he ordered an iron breastplate to be made for him, with iron rings for his hands and feet, and an iron collar and belt. The outfit was completed by an iron staff with a cross on it. His fasts were spectacular; bears and wolves were his friends; and he enjoyed powers of healing and clairvoyance, which once included his deep suspicion of a finely wrought silver chalice which turned out to be made from a prostitute's chamber-pot. Feast-day, 22 April (*ODS, BL*).

9 *Aleksei*: see note to p. 63.

roubles: at this period a rouble was roughly worth £2 ($3 approx.).

Dmitry: the name comes from the ancient Greek military hero Demetrius, surnamed Poliorcetes (destroyer of towns), who lived in the third century BC and attained the status of a god amongst the Athenians. For a period of about seven years, he was King of Macedonia and was continually at war with the neighbouring states. Demetrius rendered himself famous for his fondness for dissipation when among the dissolute, and for his love of virtue and military glory in the field of battle. He has been commended as a great warrior, a claim which he amply justifies by his ingenious inventions, his warlike engines, and stupendous machines in his war with the Rhodians. He has been blamed for his voluptuous indulgences; and his biographer observes that no Grecian prince had more wives and concubines than Poliorcetes. His obedience and reverence to his father Antigonus have been justly admired (*CD*).

Ivan: Russian variant of 'John', the commonest of all given names in Christian countries (see *CNDF* 95).

12 *Lord, now lettest thou thy servant*: Luke 2: 29. Also the opening line of a Russian Orthodox prayer read at vespers (*CW* 15).

13 *Proudhon*: Pierre Joseph Proudhon (1809–65), French socialist philosopher and savant: *La propriété, c'est le vol* ('Property is theft': *Principle of Right* (1840), ch. 1). Cf. *La propriété exclusive est un vol dans la nature* ('Exclusive property is a theft against nature': Brissot de Warville, 1780) (*CBQ*).

Bakunin: Mikhail Aleksandrovich Bakunin (1814–76), Russian populist revolutionary, founder of the anarchist movement in Europe, and an ardent revolutionary activist throughout his life.

Paris revolution of February 1848: the three-day revolution which brought down Louis-Philippe and ushered in the *Deuxième République*. See *Histoire de la révolution de 1848* by A. de Lamartine (Brussels, 1849), a book which Dostoevsky had in his library.

a thousand serfs: until the emancipation of the serfs in 1861, the value of an estate was assessed by the number of male serfs (referred to as 'souls') registered on it. Miusov's estate of a thousand serfs would rank amongst the bigger in the land. The General's estate, mentioned in 'Rebellion', Bk. 5, Ch. 4, held twice as many (see note to p. 304). By far the greatest number of serfs was owned by the Tsar himself on his private estates around the country.

See Daniel Field, *The End of Serfdom* (Cambridge, Mass., 1976). The population of hereditary nobles who could hold serfs numbered *c.*300,000 (men) in 1858 (p. 11); the population of serfs in the Empire in 1858 was 11,338,047 male serfs and about 12,000,000 female serfs, i.e. only slightly less than 40 per cent of the population of the Empire (p. 13); 80 per cent of the serfs lived on estates comprising more than 100 'souls', held by less than 25 per cent of the serf-owning population (p. 13).

17 *klikushi*: plural (fem. sing., *klikusha*), noun formed from the verb *klikat'*, to call, hence, by extension, to yelp, shriek.

19 *district Marshal of Nobility*: the highest elective post in a district, immediately below the district governor, the latter being appointed directly by the Tsar.

21 *ecclesiastical courts*: the powers of the ecclesiastical courts were severely curtailed after the legal reforms of 1864, in which Dostoevsky evinced a great deal of personal interest.

23 *starets*: from the Russian *stary*, old. *Starets* (pl. *startsy*)—a monk,

usually one extremely rigorous in self-denial, an ascetic, a guru, a man of particularly high spiritual authority. A starets was not always a monk; he could well have been a layman who had travelled to the holy places—especially Mount Athos in Greece, or Jerusalem—and then returned to Russia to lead a mendicant life, teach, etc. Rasputin called himself a starets.

26　*holy fool*: the 'holy fool', *yurodivy*, is a common figure in Russian literature and folklore, embracing any religious zealot, ranging from the mildly eccentric to the village idiot, who is often thought to be the bearer of the word of God ('Jesters do oft prove prophets': Shakespeare, *King Lear*, v. iii. 71).

28　*social status*: the population of Tsarist Russia was divided into four principal categories: nobility, clergy, urban residents, and rural residents (*Enc.*, FP).

31　*Lutheran-like*: Fyodor Pavlovich purports to share the general opinion in Russia that Lutheranism is the religion of progress and enlightenment.

　　Il faudrait les inventer: 'it would be necessary to invent them' (see note to p. 294).

　　J'ai vu l'ombre d'un cocher: 'I saw the shadow of a coachman scrubbing the shadow of a carriage with the shadow of a brush': *Mémoires, contes et autres œuvres de Charles Perrault* ('Memoirs, stories and other works by Charles Perrault') (Paris, 1842).

32　*My Lord and my God*: John 20: 24–9.

33　*fourth estate*: the 'three estates of the realm' are the Lords Spiritual, the Lords Temporal, and the Commons. *Ane pleasant satyre of the Three Estatis* is a play by Sir David Lindsay, produced in 1535. The press, owing to its greatly enhanced influence and power, became known as 'The fourth estate' about the end of the eighteenth century. Edmund Burke is credited with having invented the term, but it does not appear in his published works. In Rabelais's *Pantagruel*, when Pantagruel visits the island of the Papimanes, he is met by four persons, a monk, a falconer, a lawyer, and a husbandman, and is told that they are *les quatre estatz de l'isle* ('the four estates of the island') (bk. 4, ch. 48) (see also *BDPF*).

　　Tower of Babel: Genesis 11: 1–9.

　　If thou wilt be perfect: Matthew 19: 21; Mark 10: 21; Luke 18: 22.

34　*in Sinai and on Mount Athos*: monastery of St Catherine in Sinai, and the complex of monasteries on Mount Athos in Greece.

the Tatar yoke: 1243–1480. The Tatar or Mongol yoke left an indelible mark on the Russian nation. *Grattez le Russe—trouverez le tartare*: 'Scratch a Russian and you'll find a Tatar' (Sketches for *The Karamazov Brothers*, *CW*, 15. 203).

the Troubles: The Time of Troubles (1601–13), in Russian *Smutnoye vremya*, is usually reckoned to have begun with the accession to the throne of Boris Godunov, regent during the reign of Ivan the Terrible's heir Fyodor (1584–98). Boris was suspected of the murder of Fyodor's younger brother and heir, Dmitry. 'False Dmitry', who ruled for the next eleven months, was overthrown by Prince Shuysky, who in turn was challenged by False Dmitry II (the Thief of Tushinsk). Prince Shuysky was forced to renounce the throne in 1610, having been defeated by King Sigismund of Poland. Sigismund was driven from Moscow by two legendary heroes of Russian history, Kuzma Minin, who was a butcher by trade, and Prince Pozharsky; a statue dedicated to them stands in Red Square. In 1613 Mikhail Romanov was elected tsar.

the fall of Constantinople: Constantinople, capital of the Eastern Roman Empire, Tsargrad in old Russian, was captured by the Turks in 1453. In the eyes of Russian Orthodoxy, Moscow was to be the future bastion of the Christian faith, Rome having long been pronounced the capital of the kingdom of the Antichrist, as exemplified by the Pope.

Païsy Velichkovsky: 1722–94, the most renowned of the Russian startsy.

Optina Pustyn of Kozelsk: one of two monasteries founded in the fourteenth century by a band of *razboyniki*, outlaws (Robin Hood figures), who ruled the local countryside.

self-abnegation: abnegation of self before a spiritual mentor is found in religions of both East and West. For example, in esoteric Hinduism the chela submits totally to the guru. The concept is also encountered in the Western monastic orders, Jesuit training, and in medieval Rosicrucianism. Abnegation of the ego was practised in the pre-Christian West of antiquity, in the Hibernian mysteries, the school of Pythagoras, and elsewhere. Increasing independence of the soul in the West and moral suspicion of others have made such binding, non-voluntary compacts largely anachronistic today. (Cf. the comments of Rudolf Steiner in, e.g., *Knowledge of the Higher Worlds: How Is It Achieved?*).

35 *Catechumens depart!*: Greek κατηχούμενος, Latin *catechumenus*,

one who is being instructed. In the Orthodox Church, a catechumen is a person who is being prepared for baptism. The exclamation, pronounced during the liturgy, bids those who are not yet baptized to leave the church.

40 *Who made me a judge over you?*: 'who made me a judge or a divider over you?' Luke 12: 14.

45 *Un chevalier parfait!*: see note to p. 111.

46 *von Sohn*: see note to p. 110.

48 *hieromonks*: a hieromonk is a monk who is also an ordained priest.

49 *in statu pupillari*: student status.

50 *the Schism*: the *raskol*, schism, took place in the Russian Orthodox Church in the seventeenth century, when the reforms of Patriarch Nikon (1605–81) were opposed (ineffectually) by a section of the Church who came to be known as Old Believers (*raskolniki*). The settlement of vast tracts of the Russian hinterland is owed to the Old Believers who fled the severe state persecution; others went to China, as well as all over Eastern Europe—up to 10 million people were affected (*Enc.*, FP).

rizas: a riza is a saint's robe, depicted in gold leaf on an icon.

punctuality is the politeness of kings: *l'exactitude est la politesse des rois*, a motto attributed to Louis XVIII, King of France, 1814–24.

51 *ispravnik*: district chief of police.

Napravnik: E. Napravnik (1839–1916), Russian composer, appointed first musical director of the Mariinsky Theatre in 1869 (renamed Kirov Theatre during the Soviet period, now restored to its original name).

52 *an out-and-out clown ... quite likely I've got the devil in me*: in medieval Russia, jesting and buffoonery were regarded as being diabolically inspired, and were strongly disapproved of by the Church.

Diderot: the French philosopher Denis Diderot (1713–84) visited Russia at the invitation of Catherine the Great.

Platon: Pyotr Levshin (1737–1812), Archbishop of Moscow, religious tutor to the heir to the throne, Paul, subsequently Paul I.

The fool hath said: Psalms 14: 1; 53: 1.

'I believe,' he cried out, 'and let me be baptized': parody on popular religious texts in which pagans accept baptism with extraordinary readiness when confronted by the proselytizers of the faith.

Princess Dashkova: Yekaterina Romanovna Dashkova (1743–1810), Catherine the Great's confidante, who helped Catherine in the palace coup of 1762 which brought her to the throne.

Potemkin: Grigory Aleksandrovich Potemkin (1739–91), Russian military leader, statesman, and Catherine the Great's lover.

55 *the paps which gave thee suck*: 'the paps which thou hast sucked': Luke 11: 27.

Master . . . what shall I do: Matthew 19: 16; Mark 10: 17; Luke 10: 25; 18: 18.

56 *the father of lies*: cf. 'for he is a liar, and the father of it': John 8: 44.

Chety-Miney: Russian Orthodox Saints' Calendar, first printed in Kiev, 1689–1705.

holy miracle-worker: St Denis of Paris (original name St Dionysius), popularly regarded as the patron saint of France. Born in Italy, he was sent to convert Gaul (*c*.250 AD). He was beheaded by the Parisii. Previous attempts to put him to death by fire, crucifixion, and savaging by wild dogs had proved unsuccessful. After his beheading, he is said to have picked up his head and, led by an angel, walked the two miles from Montmartre to where the abbey church of St Denis now stands. He is venerated as the patron saint of headaches and rabies. In artistic depictions, he is shown as a beheaded bishop, carrying his own mitred head.

61 *Nastasyushka*: diminutive form of Nastya (Anastasia), also Nastenka.

My little boy: 'An echo of Fyodor Mikhailovich's own grief after the death in 1878 of our son Alyosha. He was three months short of three years. That same year [my husband] started on *The Karamazov Brothers*' (*CW* 15. 532).

Nikitushka: diminutive form of Nikita.

63 *Rachel weeping for her children*: Matthew 2: 18 (Jeremiah 31: 15).

but in the end it will turn to quiet joy: cf. Jeremiah 31: 13; John 16: 20.

Aleksei the man of God: (see *CW* 15. 474–6). St Alexis, the son of a Roman nobleman, left his parental home on his wedding day to lead the life of a recluse, returned after seventeen years, lived in his parents' home without being recognized, and suffered many privations and humiliations; one of the most popular figures in

Russian hagiography. According to David Hugh Farmer, Alexis of Rome probably never existed: see *ODS*.

65 *over ten righteous ones*: cf. Luke 15: 7.

70 *author*: Ivan Turgenev, see *Fathers and Sons* (1862).

77 *kingdom not of this world*: John 18: 36.

    for so it has been promised: Daniel 2: 44.

78 *the pagan Roman state chose to embrace Christianity*: Christianity became the established religion of Rome at the beginning of the fourth century. At the Council of Nicea in 325, the Emperor Constantine was proclaimed head of the Church, thus sealing the union between Church and state.

79 *according to the Russian way of thinking*: Dostoevsky believed ardently in socialism based on a Christian ethos: 'Russian socialism is not to be found in temporal covenants such as communism; ultimate salvation for Russia will come from the resplendent communion in Christ' (*DW*, Jan. 1881, ch. 1, para. 4).

82 *As for Rome, it was pronounced a state*: along with other Slavophile thinkers, Dostoevsky held that Roman Catholicism is based not on the morality of love, but on a regimented, hierarchical bureaucratic state mechanism: 'there the Church, having confounded its Ideal, has long ago been transformed into a State' (*DW*, Apr. 1880, ch. 3).

    society . . . rests merely on seven righteous men: this may refer to the idea, common in esoteric doctrines, that a human community, city, nation, or people will be preserved from destruction so long as it contains a tiny number of right-thinking or right-living men. Thus in Genesis (18: 20–33) God says to Abraham that, although Sodom is morally sick, 'I will not destroy it for ten's sake', i.e. if ten righteous men were to be found there. Only Lot, his wife, and two daughters being found, Sodom had to be destroyed. The Jewish Hasidim have a similar myth, namely, that if ten (sometimes said to be seven) righteous men exist on earth, the evolution of the earth will continue and the earth will not be destroyed.

    The number 'seven' is a potent number in certain pagan, Christian, and non-Christian rituals and modes of thought, as in the seven Bodhisattvas who become Buddhas, or the 'Seven Rishis of the Great Bear'. See Revelation 3: 1: 'Unto the angel of the church in Sardis write; These things saieth he that hath the seven Spirits of God, and the seven stars . . .'

83 . *It is not for you to know the times or the seasons*: Acts 1: 7; I Thessalonians 5: 1.

even at the doors: Matthew 24: 33; Mark 13: 29.

Pope Gregory VII: pope 1073–85, who strove to establish the temporal authority of the Church.

Satan's third temptation: Matthew 4: 8–10.

The star will shine forth from the East: This undoubtedly refers to the prediction given to King Herod of the birth of the Messiah. In Matthew 2: 2 the wise men from the East came to Jerusalem, saying 'Where is he that is born King of the Jews? for we have seen his star in the east, and are come to worship him.' And in Revelations 22: 16 Christ says: 'I am the root and the offspring of David, *and* the bright and morning star.'

It has been said that the current of culture arises in the East and moves West, eventually dying in the Americas. Thus Rudolf Steiner claimed that, on the death of the Atlantean age and civilization, the Aryans, under the leadership of Manu, migrated to India, forming the pre-Vedic Indian culture. When that culture itself became decadent, a new culture was founded in Persia by Zoroaster or Zarathustra (the name means 'Morning Star'). That culture was, in its turn, succeeded by the cultures of the Middle East, particularly those of Egypt and Babylonia. Following the decline of those cultures, the cultures of Greece and then Rome arose. Since the fifteenth century AD the Northern European or Germanic/Anglo-Saxon culture has emerged, the culture that is still dominant today.

In the manner of those adhering to a blind faith, Russians of the nineteenth century and even of today seem to feel some inchoate instinct for their national future; the 'Messianic' aspect of Russia and Russian Orthodoxy (perverted in Soviet Marxism) is due to this feeling of preparation for a glorious future. (See Rudolf Steiner, *Occult Science* and *Lectures upon the Apocalypse*; the several works of Valentin Tomberg (privately printed in Riga, 1936–9, repr. by Candeur Manuscripts, Spring Valley, New York, 1977–9); Maria Schindler, *Europe: a Cosmic Picture* (New Knowledge Books, Horsham, Sussex, 1975–6); cf. various predictions by the American psychic Edgar Cayce: 'Upon Russia's religious development rests the future of the world': *The Sleeping Prophet* (Jess Stearn/Bantam Books, 1965), 85.)

December Revolution: brought about the end of the Second Republic in France following the coup d'état of 1851 by Louis Napoléon Bonaparte.

87 *who confuse socialism and Christianity*: in 1870 Dostoevsky was planning a series of articles on the theme of socialism and Christianity: see letter to M. Pogodin, 26 Feb. 1873: 'In my opinion Socialism and Christianity are antithetic' (*CW* 15. 536, n. to p. 64.)

   who does not believe in God or his own immortality: cf. 'It is beyond doubt that all morality depends on whether a soul is immortal or not' (Blaise Pascal, *Pensées*).

88 *set your affections*: a conflation of Colossians 3: 2 and Philippians 3: 20.

89 *Schiller's 'Robbers'*: Friedrich Schiller (1759–1805) is frequently invoked and quoted in *The Karamazov Brothers*. The drama *The Robbers* was written in 1781.

90 *the order of St Anne with crossed swords*: the order of St Anne was one of the eight orders of decoration of Imperial Russia, crossed swords indicating the military nature of the honour.

92 *across a pocket handkerchief*: true to the farcical nature of the scene, Fyodor Pavlovich, in his mock fighting mode, chooses one of the most bizarre forms of duelling on record, enacted in Schiller's *Cabal and Love*, Act 4, Sc. 3. In an 1884 translation of the play into English by T. C. Wilkinson, the relevant scene reads as follows: FERDINAND: . . . enough to send a scoundrel like you into the next world [*pressing a pistol on him, while pulling out his pocket handkerchief*]. Take it! Catch hold of this handkerchief! I had it from the jade herself. MARSHALL: Across the handkerchief? Are you raving? What are you thinking of? FERDINAND: Take hold of this end, I tell you! Else you'll be missing your aim, coward! How he trembles, the coward! (Sonnenschein & Co., London, 1884). In an earlier (1795) anonymous translation, the same scene goes as follows: FERDINAND: I have sense enough left to settle matters with you—here sir, take one of these pistols immediately. BARON: One of those pistols? Are you mad, Major? FERDINAND: Directly take one of them or I'll break your bones for you this instant!— See how the coward trembles! (Published by T. Boosey, London, 1795).

93 *loved much*: Luke 7: 47.

100 *Pushkin, the bard of women's feet*: or 'legs' (the Russian word *nozhka* can mean either). For this so-called 'pedal digression' Pushkin

was censured by the prudes of the day, notably the poet D. Minayev (1835–69). See the note to p. 741. Rakitin's poem is, of course, Dostoevsky's way of getting his own back on Pushkin's detractors.

107 *pirozhki*: sing. *pirozhok*. Small, individual yeast-pastry pies made with a variety of fillings.

110 *von Sohn*: an actual murder case heard in the St Petersburg District Court on 28–29 Mar. 1870. In the main, Fyodor Pavlovich's description fits the details of the case.

111 *plus de noblesse que de sincérité*: 'more nobility of spirit than sincerity'.

"veray parfit gentil knight": Chaucer, *The Canterbury Tales*. Cf. *Parfait knight sans peur et sans reproche*.

auricular confession: auricular confession was introduced into church practice by Pope Innocent III (Giovanni Lotario, Count of Segni) at the fourth Lateran Council in 1215.

112 *self-flagellation*: Fyodor Pavlovich refers to practices dating from the seventeenth century, associated with a cult which held that spiritual cleansing from the 'powers of evil' was to be achieved by scourging the body. This extremist and highly nonconformist sect had elements which went even further: to be cleansed and redeemed, one must be sullied first, therefore sinning (more often than not in the form of orgiastic excess) was actively encouraged. Rasputin was reputedly a *khlyst*, follower of the *khlysty*, flagellants.

It was said of old: probably from a source similar to that below; see note to p. 114.

113 *Yeliseyev Bros*: famous vintners in old St Petersburg.

seven Councils: the Orthodox Church recognizes only the first seven Ecumenical Councils which were held before the Great Schism in 1054. The first Council, at which Arianism was declared a heresy, and nearly all subsequent Councils, condemned someone.

114 *And again it is written*: cf: 'It is a great joy to accept patiently whatever comes and as the Lord enjoins to love a neighbour that hates you' (St Mark the Ascetic, text 47, *Philocalia*, 120 (Faber edn., vol. I). *Philocalia* (Russian *Dobrotolyubie*) is a collection of religious texts translated into Russian from the Greek, to which Dostoevsky had access (the English edition is a translation from the Russian).

122 *Isaac the Syrian*: a sixth-century Father of the Church, ascetic and writer.

123 *Lizaveta Smerdyashchaya*: 'Smelly Lizaveta'. *Smerdyashchaya* is the participial form of the verb *smerdet'*, to stink.

   two 'arshins': arshin (old Russian linear measure) = 0.71m = 2.33 ft.

127 *Smerdyakov*: the text indicates the original invented nature of the surname. Substituting the letter *l* for the *r*, for the benefit of English readers, one gets (Mr) Smeldyakov, leading to Smel(l)dyakov, Smel(l)yakov, Smel(l)of, Smelly, or plain Mr Smell.

131 *Glory on earth to the Highest*: cf. Luke 2: 14: 'Glory to God in the highest . . .'.

   desyatina: (old Russian) = 2.7 acres.

   pood: (old Russian) = 16.38 kg. = 36lbs.

   Do not believe the false and shallow crowd: taken from Nekrasov's (Russian poet, 1821–77) *When from the darkness . . .*, a poem already quoted by Dostoevsky in *The Village of Stepanchikovo* (1859) and *Notes from Underground* (1864). Dostoevsky also gave a public reading of this poem at a charity event on 21 Nov. 1880, as recorded by A. Dostoevskaya in her *Reminiscences*.

133 *the fairy tale*: Pushkin's tale in verse. *Tale of the Fisherman and the Little Golden Fish* (not to be confused with goldfish!).

   Be noble, O Man!: from Goethe's *Das Göttliche* (1783).

134 *An die Freude*: Schiller's (1785) famous expression of optimism and faith in humanity on which the last, choral movement of Beethoven's Ninth Symphony is based.

   And ruddy-faced Silenus: the closing lines of the poem *Bas-Relief* (1842) by the Russian poet A. Maikov. Silenus was a primitive deity in the legends of Asia Minor. He is said to have prompted the god Dionysus to invent viticulture and bee-keeping. He is described as a little old man, pot-bellied, with a bald head and snub nose, his whole body very hairy; never without his skin of wine, always drunk, and riding on an ass (O. Seyffert, *A Dictionary of Classical Antiquities*, William Glaisher, 1891).

   'Timidly in rocks concealed': Dmitry, in his usual erratic manner, proceeds to quote from quite a different poem; he does get the poet right, however, it is Schiller, *Eleusinian Festival*, stanzas 2–4. Dostoevsky uses V. Zhukovsky's free Romantic translation. The

extracts quoted here are an adaptation (to reflect Zhukovsky's changes) of a translation by E. P. Arnold-Foster (1901). There is another very fine translation of this poem into English by Sir Edward Bulwer-Lytton (1875).

135 *Would man rise from degradation*: *Eleusinian Festival*, stanza 7.

Ceres: the goddess of corn and harvests in Greek mythology. She had a daughter by Jupiter, whom she called Proserpine, 'fruit-bearing'. This daughter was carried away by Pluto as she was gathering flowers in the plains near Enna. The rape of Proserpine was grievous to Ceres, who sought her all over Sicily, and, when night came, she lit two torches in the flames of Mount Etna to continue her search by night the world over. During Ceres' search for her daughter the cultivation of the earth was neglected and the ground became barren. A festival in honour of Ceres is depicted, for example, in part II of Berlioz's *The Trojans*.

136 *Joy in Nature's wide dominion*: *Hymn to Joy*, F. Schiller. The translation used here is by Edgar Alfred Bowring (1883).

begin with the ideal of the Madonna and finish with that of Sodom: Mitya's soul is torn between these two ideals, the strife between them being the very source of his life's energy. Cf. *L'homme est ni ange ni bête, et le malheur est que qui veut faire l'ange fait la bête*: 'Man is neither angel nor beast, and the misfortune is that he who wishes to be an angel becomes a beast' (Blaise Pascal).

138 *Paul de Kock*: Paul de Kock (1793–1871), a French writer, very popular in nineteenth-century Russia, considered *risqué* and low-brow.

149 *There were tender words*: the source of this quotation is unknown. The assumption must be that the couplet is an original composition.

Staff Captain: in the Russian Imperial Army an officer's rank in infantry, artillery, and engineering regiments between Lieutenant and Captain. The rank was abolished in the former Soviet Army, the order of seniority below Captain being Senior Lieutenant, Lieutenant, Junior Lieutenant, Warrant Officer, etc. In the British and US armies the order is Captain, Lieutenant, Warrant Officer, etc. (*CW* 15. 543).

156 *Our Balaam's ass*: Numbers 22: 21–31.

157 *God created light*: Genesis 1: 3–5, 14–19.

Evenings on a Farm near Dikanka: Nikolai Gogol's first collection of stories, published 1831–2.

158 *Universal History*: A history textbook by S. Smaragdov (St Petersburg, 1845).

160 *the painter Kramskoy*: Ivan Kramskoy (1837–87), leader of the anti-academic association of Russian painters known as the Wanderers. His picture *The Contemplative* was first exhibited in St Petersburg on 9 Mar. 1878.

a Russian soldier: Warrant-Officer Foma Danilov of the 2nd Turkestan battalion, captured by the Kipchaks and put to death in Margelan on 21 Nov. 1875 (*DW*, Jan. 1877, ch. 1, para. 3.)

164 *it is written in the Scriptures*: Matthew 17: 20: 'If ye have faith as a grain of mustard seed, ye shall say unto this mountain, Remove hence to yonder place; and it shall remove . . .'; 21: 21: 'if ye shall say unto this mountain, Be thou removed, and be thou cast into the sea; it shall be done'; see also Mark 11: 23; Luke 17: 6.

167 *koulibiaca*: a type of fish pie; a Russian gastronomic delicacy.

With what measure ye mete, it shall yourself be measured: Matthew 7: 1; Luke 6: 38; Mark 4: 24.

168 *Tout cela c'est de la cochonnerie*: 'it's a complete pigsty'.

Marquis de Sade: Marquis de Sade (1740–1814), French writer notorious for depicting perverse pleasure derived from the exercise of cruelty (*sadism*).

170 *il y a du Piron làdedans*: 'there's a touch of Piron in him': Alexis Piron (1689–1773), French poet and playwright with a penchant for licentiousness.

Credo: 'I believe'.

A Hero of Our Time . . . Arbenin: *A Hero of Our Time*, the novel by the Russian poet Yury Lermontov (1815–41). Arbenin, however, is the protagonist in Lermontov's drama *Masquerade*. The brandy has gone to Fyodor Pavlovich's head.

173 *feastdays of the Holy Virgin*: the principal feasts of the Holy Virgin are the Nativity (8 Sept.), Presentation of the Blessed Virgin (21 Nov.), Annunciation (25 Mar.), Intercession of the Holy Virgin (1 Sept.), and Assumption (15 Aug.).

176 *Aesop*: Aesopus, Phrygian mythologist and philosopher who, originally a slave, procured his liberty by the sallies of his genius. He is best known for his fables. His acerbic wit proved to be his undoing. While consulting the oracle at Delphi, he had made some disparaging remarks about the Delphians, who were so incensed by his witticisms that they cast him from a rock to his

death in 561 BC. His biographer, Maximus Planudes, represents him as a clownish figure, short of stature and deformed. Dmitry's spontaneous association (subsequently reiterated by Ivan) of his father with the man of wisdom and genius is highly significant, indicating the subconscious regard in which he and others hold the old reprobate (see *CD*).

205 *Therapon*: Greek Θεράπων, meaning 'ministrant'. After the 1917 Revolution, the Russian orthography was updated; one of the changes was to dispense with the letter Θ, the reason being that it was merely an orthographic relic from the Greek, without the phonal *th* characteristic. Θ was pronounced either as *f* (*mifologiya*, mythology) or as *t* (*teatr*, theatre). 'Thomas' in modern Russian is 'Foma'; similarly 'Theodore', 'Fyodor'. By analogy, the Soviet editors of Dostoevsky have transcribed Θεράπωντ as 'Ferapont', which, from an English point of view, is a further corruption of the original and suppresses the underlying meaning of the word.
The fact that modern Russian for 'therapy' is *'terapiya'* is an added justification for using *Th* (rather than *F*) in transcribing the name of Dostoevsky's hero into English.

211 *he strongly accented the letter 'o'*: a feature of a northern Russian dialect.

212 *Laodicean Council*: Laodicea (present-day Latakia, Syria), venue of an important Church Council held in AD 360 or 370.

214 *in the spirit and glory of Elias*: cf. Luke 1: 17: 'And he shall go before him in the spirit and power of Elias, to turn the hearts of the fathers to the children . . .'.

215 *and the gates of hell shall not prevail*: Matthew 16: 18.

220 *like chaff in the wind*: Psalm 1: 4: 'The ungodly *are* not so: but *are* like the chaff which the wind driveth away.'

227 *C'est tragique*: 'It's tragic'.

232 *Goulard's extract*: or Goulard's water. A solution of subacetate of lead, used as a lotion to treat inflammation. Introduced in 1806 by the French surgeon Thomas Goulard (*OED*).

242 *Den Dank, Dame*: 'Madame, I can do without your gratitude' (from Schiller's ballad 'Der Handschuh' ('The Glove')).

252 *Stolichny Gorod*: the Capital City, an inn.

253 *And nothing in the whole of Nature*: from the poem *Demon* by Aleksander Pushkin.

Mr Chernomazov: an intentional, pre-Freudian slip on the author's part: *chërny* (pronounced *chorny*) is Russian for 'black'; *kara* means 'black' in Turkish; *maz* comes from the Russian *mazat'*, to smear, to stain; conflating these concepts, one may interpret 'Karamazov' as 'Blackstain', 'Blackman'. 'Karamazov' is not an established Russian surname; it was made up by Dostoevsky along the lines indicated above.

256 *a student*: universities ran special courses for women only (hence *kursistka*, a female member of a course). Full-time student status was not available to women at the time.

to seek justice for Russian women on the banks of the Neva: women's rights were among the top priorities of the Russian radical movement (*KC* 206, n. 174). 'The banks of the Neva' is a poetic reference to St Petersburg.

264 *In the province of K*: traditional Russian literary device for referring to a place that the author wishes to remain nameless. Any letter, or even two, may be used. Cf. the title of Chekhov's short story *In the Town of S*; also, 'Through the hotel gates of the provincial town NN, rolled a handsome, well-sprung *brichka*, such as gentlemen bachelors, retired Lieutenant-Colonels, Staff Captains, landowners with about a hundred peasant serfs to their name, in a word, all those who are known as gentlemen of independent means, are wont to ride in', the opening lines of Gogol's *Dead Souls*.

278 *like Famusov in his last scene ... Chatsky ... Sofia*: characters in Griboyedov's play, variously translated from the Russian as *Woe from Wit; Wit Works Woe; The Misfortune of Being Clever; Clever by Half*, and, in the 1993 version by Anthony Burgess, *Chatsky: The Importance of Being Stupid*, none of which quite captures the simplicity and directness of the Russian original, *Gore ot yma*.

281 *tore her guts out*: commentators trace the origin of this phrase to Exodus 13: 2, 12 (see *CW*, 15. 549).

282 *the father of the present one*: Smerdyakov gets it wrong. The 'present one'—Napoleon III—was Napoleon I's nephew, i.e. the son of Napoleon I's brother, Louis Bonaparte, the first King of Holland.

Petrovka: name of a street in central Moscow.

289 *professions de foi*: 'declarations of faith'.

292 *"Do you believe or don't you believe at all?"*: standard question from the ritual of the consecration of a bishop, in response to which the bishop-elect recites the Creed.

294 *s'il n'existait pas Dieu il faudrait l'inventer*: 'if God did not exist, it would be necessary to invent Him': Voltaire, *Epistles: A l'auteur du livre des trois imposteurs* ('To the Author of a Book on the Three Impostors') in Ivan's own rendering (see note to p. 31).

meet somewhere at infinity: the Russian mathematician Nikolai Lobachevsky (1793–1856) was the founder of non-Euclidean, Lobachevskian geometry. Lobachevskian geometry accepts all of Euclid's axioms, except the fifth, which deals with parallel lines. At its simplest, parallel lines in Euclid never meet, but, from the time he first formulated his postulates in the fourth century BC, the best mathematical brains have tried, for over 2,000 years, to supply the requisite analytical proof: from Ptolemy (second century AD) to Proclus (fifth century AD), from Ibn-al-Khaitam of Iraq (end of tenth, beginning of eleventh century), and Giovanni Saccheri (1733)—the latter attempting to prove Euclid's fifth axiom by disproving its converse—to the German mathematician J. H. Lambert (*c.*1766, published 1786). We read the following in the *Encyclopaedia Britannica*: 'In 1763 the German mathematician Georg Simon Klügel listed nearly 30 attempts to prove axiom 5 and concluded that the alleged proofs were all unsound. Fifty years later a new generation of geometers, still working on the same problem, were becoming more and more frustrated. One of them, a Hungarian named Farkas Bolyai, wrote in a letter to his son János: "I entreat you, leave the science of parallels alone . . . I have travelled past all reefs of this infernal Dead Sea and have always come back with a broken mast and torn sail." The son, refusing to heed this warning, continued to think about parallels until, in 1823, he saw the whole truth and declared, in his youthful enthusiasm, "I have created a new universe from nothing."' Bolyai Junior published (1832) his observations in a 24-page appendix to his father's textbook. But the honour of publishing the first book on non-Euclidean geometry, and pioneering its study, goes to Lobachevsky (1829–30); it would be fair to say that he did to Euclidean geometry what Einstein did to Newtonian physics. So important was the breakthrough in the field of geometry that it led the American mathematician George Bruce Halsted, who was unfamiliar with Lobachevsky's work at the time, to hail Bolyai's publication as 'the most extraordinary two dozen pages in the whole history of thought'. Lobachevsky, in spite of a general indifference to his ideas in the West, maintained a steady stream of publications in Russian as well as in French and German. In 1837 his *Géometrie imaginaire* ('Imaginary Geometry') was published, and it was not until much later that his work appeared in English, under the title *Geometrical Researches on the Theory of Parallels* (1891; 2nd edn., 1914), translated from the German by Halsted. This study of Lobachevskian geometry was further extended by Bernhard Riemann, amongst others (1826–66), who concluded that the non-Euclidean approach to the principle of parallelism must imply ultimate curvature of space, or, to put it graphically, an astronomer looking out into space through an infinitely powerful telescope would see the back of his head. Hence space—the universe, in fact—is unbounded rather than being infinite. Taking this as the point of departure, it was but a small step for Einstein to take before making his giant leap into his Theory of Relativity. Ivan, who represents the ordinary 'thinking' man, the ordinary intellectual, the interested observer, rather than an authoritative man of science in his own right, could only stand and marvel in awe at the astonishing progress in the evolution of human knowledge, and, ever humourless, he reflects on his anxieties and bewilderment in a horror-laden atmosphere. Cf. the far healthier attitude of the benign Colonel Rostanev in *The Village of Stepanchikovo*, who is also far from indifferent to astronomy as well as to man's progress in technology, railway engineering, and the like.

Hyperbolic geometry (Riemannian geometry) has found an important application in space flight navigation.

295 *the Word*: 'in the beginning was the Word, and the Word was with God, and the Word was God': John 1: 1.

296 *John the Merciful*: John the Merciful, Patriarch of Alexandria (sixth–seventh centuries). See Flaubert's *La Légende de Saint Julien l'Hospitalier* (1876). Julian was guilty of patricide.

298 *as gods*: 'For God doth know that in the day ye eat thereof, then your eyes shall be opened, and ye shall be as gods, knowing good and evil': Genesis 3: 5.

the Turks and the Circassians: in his *Diary of a Writer*, Dostoevsky often wrote about the atrocities committed in the Balkans.

299 *six inches from its face*: 10 a.m., 21 Apr. 1993, BBC Radio 4, news bulletin: 'babes held in mothers' arms and shot dead'. Mayhem in the Balkans continues unabated.

to crack the wind of the poor phrase: Shakespeare, *Hamlet*, I. iii.

300 *with us it's more likely to be birching, flogging, and whipping*: although the death penalty in Russia was abolished by Empress Yelizaveta

Petrovna, corporal punishment of the most barbaric kind continued to be practised unabated late into the nineteenth century.

302 *Nekrasov*: the Russian poet Nikolai Nekrasov (1821–77). The
poem referred to is *Before Twilight.*

a little girl of seven: this is based on an actual court case, the V.
Kronenberg trial. See Dostoevsky's *Diary of a Writer*, Feb. 1876,
ch. 2. The defence counsel was V. Spasovich, a possible model
for Fetyukovich, Dmitry's defence counsel.

303 *A little girl of five*: also based on a court case, the Eugene and
Aleksandra Brunst trial, as recorded in the daily *Voice*, 79, 80, 82
(1879).

304 *our Tsar Liberator*: Alexander II (1818–81) came to the throne in
1855 and introduced a series of major reforms: emancipation of
the serfs (1861), legal reforms (1862), abolition of corporal
punishment and branding of convicts (1863); he was assassinated
in 1881.

a fabulously rich landowner: the story appeared in the *Russian
Herald*, 9 (1877), 'Reminiscences of a Serf'.

309 *Le Bon Jugement de la très sainte et gracieuse Vierge Marie*: 'the wise
judgement of the Blessed and Holy Virgin Mary'.

310 *Behold, I come quickly*: 'Behold, I come quickly: hold that fast
which thou hast, that no man take thy crown': Revelation 3: 11;
also 22: 7, 12, 20.

But of that day and hour: Matthew 24: 36; also Mark 13: 32.

Heaven makes no pledges: Schiller, *Sehnsucht* ('Longing'), 1801.

311 *a terrible new heresy*: the Reformation.

A great star: 'there fell a great star from heaven, burning as it were
a lamp, and it fell upon the third part of the rivers, and upon the
fountains of waters; And the name of the star is called Wormwood:
and the third part of the waters became wormwood; and many
men died of the waters, because they were made bitter' Revelation
8: 10–11.

Lord appear unto us: to suit his argument, Ivan is probably drawing
on, and, in the process, distorting, Psalm 118: 27: 'God is the
Lord, which hath shewed us light . . .'.

And blessed you as he passed: closing lines of his poem 'These
Forsaken Villages . . .', by F. Tyutchev (1803–73).

They burned the evil heretics: from the poem 'Coriolanus' by A.
Polezhayev (1805–38).

311 *as the lightning cometh out of the east*: Matthew 24: 27: 'For as the lightning cometh out of the east, and shineth even unto the west; so shall also the coming of the Son of man be.' See also Luke 17: 24.

312 *ad majorem gloriam Dei*: the motto of the Jesuit Order is *Ad majorem Dei gloriam*, 'To the greater glory of God'.

Talitha cumi: 'And he took the damsel by the hand, and said unto her, Talitha cumi; which is, being interpreted, Damsel, I say unto thee, arise. And straightway the damsel arose, and walked...': Mark 5: 40–2.

314 *Idea*: in the original Russian text this word is not capitalized, and its use is rather obscure. Cf. 'This new created world ... how good, how faire, Answering his great Idea': Milton, *Paradise Lost*, vii. 557. 'Idea' is capitalized in Richard Bentley's (London) edition of 1732, and in the *OED*. All the editions of *Paradise Lost* after 1735 that I consulted print 'idea' without an initial capital.

315 *I want to make you free*: 'And ye shall know the truth, and the truth shall make you free': John 8: 32; 'If the Son therefore shall make you free, ye shall be free indeed': John 8: 37.

to bind and to loose: 'And I will give unto thee the keys of the kingdom of heaven: and whatsoever thou shalt bind on earth shall be bound in heaven: and whatsoever thou shalt loose on earth shall be loosed in heaven': Matthew 16: 19.

tempted You: 'Then was Jesus led up of the Spirit into the wilderness to be tempted of the devil': Matthew 4: 1–11; see also Luke 4: 1–13.

317 *He maketh fire come down from heaven*: 'And they worshipped the dragon which gave power unto the beast: and they worshipped the beast, saying, Who is like unto the beast?': Revelation 13: 4.

320 *your Father*: Matthew 4: 6. Ivan paraphrases the Biblical text.

for man seeks not so much God as miracles: cf. Pascal's thoughts on miracles: 'Miracles are more important than you imagine...' (*Pensées*).

321 *and we shall believe that it is you*: 'If he be the King of Israel, let him now come down from the cross, and we will believe him': Matthew 27: 42.

from each of the twelve tribes of Israel: see Revelation 7: 4–8.

322 *living on locusts and roots*: 'And the same John had his raiment of

camel's hair, and a leathern girdle about his loins; and his meat was locusts and wild honey': Matthew 3: 4; see also Mark 1: 6.

already eight centuries ago: in 756 Pepin the Short, King of the Franks, had laid the foundations for secularizing papal power by increasing the territorial dominions of Pope Stephen II, and given credence to the view that the Church of Rome had effectively begun to turn its back on Christ.

323   *and on it will be written 'Mystery'*: see Revelation 13; 17: 3–17.

325   *It is said and prophesied*: Matthew 24: 30; Revelation 12: 7–11; 17: 14; 19: 19–21; 20: 1–3.

326   *It is said that the whore*: 'The waters which thou sawest, where the whore sitteth, are peoples, and multitudes, and nations, and tongues. And the ten horns which thou sawest upon the beast, these shall hate the whore, and shall make her desolate and naked, and shall eat her flesh, and burn her with fire': Revelation 17: 15–16.

Dixi: 'I have spoken'.

331   *your Pater Seraphicus*: an explicit echo from Act V of Goethe's *Faust*, pt. II, where Pater Seraphicus leads a chorus of blessed boys to even higher awareness of God's presence and eternal love; also a name by which St Francis of Assisi was known (*KC* 239, n. 331).

337   *servant Lichard*: Lichard (corruption of 'Richard') is King Gvidon's faithful servant in *The Tale of Prince Bova*, a Russian rendering of a medieval French romance (see note to p. 782).

358   *Schemahieromonk*: a monk under a stricter order of monastic discipline than a hieromonk.

363   *There was a man in the land of Uz*: Job 1: 1. 'I am reading the Book of Job and it is driving me out of my mind: sometimes I have to stop and will spend up to an hour at a time pacing up and down in my room, almost in tears . . . This book, Anya—it may sound strange—has been one of the first in my life to make an impression upon me . . .' (Dostoevsky, letter to his wife, 10 June 1875).

364   *Thy servant will cry out and curse Thy name*: here and in subsequent passages from the Book of Job, Zosima quotes from memory. Cf. 'put forth thine hand now, and touch all that he hath, and he will curse thee to thy face': Job 1: 11.

Blessed be the name of the Lord now and forever: cf. 'Naked came I out of my mother's womb, and naked shall I return thither: the

Lord gave and the Lord hath taken away; blessed be the name of the Lord': Job 1: 21.

366   *of Abraham and Sarah*: Genesis 11: 29–31; 12–18, 20–23.

of Isaac and Rebecca: Genesis 24–7.

of how Jacob: Genesis 28–32.

and in his sleep wrestled with the Lord: Genesis 32: 24–32.

How dreadful is this place: Genesis 28: 17.

Joseph: Genesis 37–50.

367   *Esther and the haughty Vashti*: Book of Esther.

Jonah in the belly of the whale: Jonah.

'Chety-Miney'. . . Aleksei the man of God: (see notes to pp. 55 and 63).

Mary of Egypt: a fifth-century saint.

370   *for the month and the year*: Revelations 9: 15.

371   *a prominent event at the time*: most likely the Decembrist uprising, 14 Dec. 1825.

380   *he trembles at the thought of losing his money*: cf. *Quas dederis, solas semper habebis opes* ('The wealth you give away is the only wealth you will ever truly possess'): Martial (*CBQ*).

the sign of the Son of man will appear in heaven: Matthew 24: 30 ('And then shall appear the sign of the Son of man in heaven: and then shall all the tribes of the earth mourn, and they shall see the Son of man coming in the clouds of heaven with power and great glory').

387   *the Russian version*: the Bible was translated into Russian from Old Church Slavonic *c.*1860.

395   *cursed be their anger, for it was fierce*: 'Cursed be their anger, for it was fierce; and their wrath, for it was cruel . . .': Genesis 49: 7.

two centuries of slavery: Tatar yoke. See note to p. 34.

398   *as is laid down in the Gospels*: 'And whosoever will be chief among you, let him be your servant . . .': Matthew 20: 27; see also 23: 11; 'If any man desire to be first, *the same* shall be last of all, and servant of all': Mark 9: 35; 'And whosoever of you will be the chiefest, shall be servant of all': Mark 10: 44.

the head of the corner: Psalm 118: 22; see also Matthew 21: 42.

shall perish by the sword: 'for all they that take the sword shall perish with the sword': Matthew 26: 52.

399 *come to pass*: cf. 'And except those days should be shortened, there should no flesh be saved: but for the elect's sake those days shall be shortened': Matthew 24: 22.

400 *Love children in particular*: 'Verily I say unto you, Except ye be converted, and become as little children, ye shall not enter into the kingdom of heaven': Matthew 18: 1–10; see also 19: 13–15.

402 *sit in judgement over anyone*: 'Judge not, that ye be not judged . . .': Matthew 7: 1–5.

404 *What is hell?*: argument drawn from the writings of Isaac the Syrian (see note to p. 122) (*CW* 15. 569–70).

the rich man and Lazarus: Luke 16: 19–31.

406 *to suck blood from his own body*: image derived from Isaac the Syrian (*CW* 15. 570).

418 *it is his finger*: cf. 'And the magicians did so with their enchantments to bring forth lice, but they could not: so there were lice upon man, and upon beast. Then the magicians said unto Pharaoh, This is the finger of God . . .': Exodus 8: 18–19.

443 *It's only a fable*: in a letter to his publisher N. Lyubimov (16 Sept. 1879), Dostoevsky wrote: 'please make sure you edit the legend of *the spring onion* properly. It's a gem; I wrote it down from the words of a peasant woman, surely *for the first time ever*. I at least have never heard it before until now.' Evidently Dostoevsky was not familiar with *Russian National Folk Legends*, a collection in Russian compiled by A. Afanasyev (Moscow, 1859; London, 1859), which contains a similar story, 'Christ's Friend' (pp. 30–2), though the difference is worth noting. The initial elements are the same: a wicked woman is burning in a lake of pitch, but the person who throws her a lifeline is her own son, and it is him she upbraids for not being careful enough in pulling her out. She shouts at him: 'You clumsy oaf, you nearly killed me!' Whereupon the rope snaps, and she falls back into the burning pitch.

451 *cast seven devils out of her*: 'Now when Jesus was risen early the first day of the week, he appeared first to Mary Magdalene, out of whom he had cast seven devils': Mark 16: 9; see also Luke 8: 1–2.

452 *Cana of Galilee*: 'And the third day there was a marriage in Cana of Galilee; and the mother of Jesus was there . . .': John 2: 1–11.

454 *Historians*: Dostoevsky probably had Renan's *Life of Jesus* in mind, in which there are numerous references to the poverty of the population amongst which Jesus preached (*CW* 15. 572).

486 *Turgenev*: Dostoevsky parodies *Enough: From the Notes of a Deceased Writer*, one of Turgenev's short stories.

488 *the holy martyr Varvara*: St Barbara (the Roman *b* becomes Russian *v*). According to the legend, she was shut up in a tower by her father, who killed her for having converted to Christianity, whereupon he was struck dead by lightning. She was, until the cult was suppressed in 1969, the patron saint of pyrotechnicians, artillerymen, architects, founders, stonemasons, gravediggers, fortifications, and magazines, and a protectress against lightning, fire, sudden death, and impenitence, i.e. those who have died before having made a confession. In artistic depictions, she is normally represented holding a tower, with a palm of martyrdom, or a chalice or feather, and trampling on a Saracen (BS). (During the First World War, there was a tendency amongst gunners to put themselves under the patronage of St Joan of Arc, since it was believed that the latter excelled in the tactical disposition of artillery.)

489 *the author Shchedrin*: Dostoevsky engaged in literary polemics with Mikhail Saltykov, pen-name Schedrin (1826–89).

The Modernist: generally known in English as *the Contemporary*, of which Saltykov was a co-editor, it was banned by the authorities in 1866 for its progressive views.

493 *And just the hushed breath of silence*: an aptly chosen line from Pushkin's fairy tale in verse, *Ruslan and Ludmila*. Russians are familiar with Pushkin from childhood, and if, earlier on, Mitya could quote Schiller at length, which is a little far-fetched, he could certainly be expected to know his Pushkin. Mitya alters the wording slightly to fit the context, a point which cannot be successfully demonstrated in translation, of course.

506 *the eternally youthful Phoebus, praising and glorifying God*: Mitya lumps together paganism and Christianity. Phoebus, a name given to Apollo, personifies the sun and its brightness; the phrase 'glorifying and praising God' occurs in Luke 2: 20 and in the Acts 3: 8.

Mastryuk: a character in a folk ballad who was stripped of his clothes and all he had while he lay asleep.

Unreliable, deceitful: a quotation from Tyutchev's translation of Schiller's *Das Siegesfest* ('Victory Banquet'), referring to the unfaithful Clytemnestra.

510 *poddyovka*: a kind of sleeveless coat, worn by peasants and tradesmen.

armyak: a peasant's overcoat of coarse, heavy fabric.

513 *Thou wouldst not think how ill all's here about my heart*: Shakespeare, *Hamlet*, v. ii.

Alas! poor Yorick: *Hamlet*, v. i.

514 *One last tale I'll tell*: from Pushkin's *Boris Godunov*, the opening line of Pimen's monologue.

520 *and went straight to hell*: derived from the folk legend 'The Dream of the Most Holy Mother of God', of which there are several published versions (*CW* 15. 575).

526 *Panie*: this chapter is peppered with Polish words and phrases. Because of the relative similarity between Polish and Russian, much of what was said would have been immediately comprehensible to Russian ears. This is certainly true of the forms of address. *Panie*, sir, is the vocative case of *pan*, meaning 'Mr', the plural of *panie* is *panowie*, gentlemen. Strictly speaking, *pani* means 'Mrs', but, colloquially, it also stands for 'Miss' and also for 'madam', i.e. the vocative of address. Dostoevsky subjects the rest of the Polish dialogue to quite a lot of mutilation, and it may be of interest to the English-speaking reader to see the tricks he has got up to, as the effect cannot be reflected in translation. Quite apart from presenting the Poles as a couple of stuck-up idiots, he transliterates their Polish into Cyrillic—a provocative gesture, to say the least, seeing that the Polish people, along with other Catholic Slavs, use the Roman alphabet—Cyrillic being tantamount to anathema for them. It should be noted that Dostoevsky makes no attempt to transliterate the French or German text into Cyrillic. Furthermore, the Polish that the Poles use is frequently distorted and Russified, and, as if to rub salt into the wound, Dostoevsky provides the Russian translation in brackets in the text, even where the meaning of the Polish would be readily comprehensible to any Russian.

531 *Agrippina*: Polish for 'Agrafena'.

533 *that Gogol wrote his Dead Souls with him in mind*: Nikolai Gogol's novel *Dead Souls* (1842) features a landowner by the name of Maksimov.

534 *Fenardi*: a famous juggler of the period.

Piron: see note to p. 170.

534   *Is that you Boileau? What a ridiculous attire!*: the Russian fabulist
       Krylov's parody on an inept translation of Boileau's *Art poétique*
       (1674).

535   *You're as clueless as the rest*: from an epigram by Konstantin
       Batyushkov (1787–1855). Sapho or Sappho (630–570 BC),
       renowned poetess of antiquity, is said to have conceived such a
       passion for a youth named Phaon that, upon his refusal to gratify
       her desires, she threw herself into the sea. Batyushkov parodies a
       failed woman poet who would have been well advised to follow
       Sapho's example.

535   *Pas même académicien*: 'Here lies Piron who was nothing, / Not
       even a member of the *Académie*'; Piron's sarcastic epigraph on not
       being elected to the *Académie française*.

536   *To Russia inside her pre–1772 borders!*: the Bar Confederation of
       1768, a union of Polish patriots to promote the independence of
       Poland, led, in 1772, to the First Partition of Poland between
       Russia, Prussia, and Austria, and was much hated by the Poles.

543   *szlachcic*: member of the Polish nobility.

550   *la sabotière*: a country clog-dance (*sabot*, French for 'clog').

552   *Let this terrible cup pass from me!*: cf. 'O my Father, if it be possible,
       let this cup pass from me . . .': see also Mark 14: 36 and Luke
       22: 42.

561   *Judicial investigation*: three persons are involved in the initial
       investigation of Dmitry: the chief of police, investigative magis-
       trate, and prosecutor. In the English system, only the police would
       question the suspect; in the French system, the police would carry
       out an initial investigation. After the suspect is charged, the *juge
       d'instruction* (examining magistrate) semi-formally interrogates the
       accused, and then decides if there is sufficient evidence for the
       case to go to trial. From a modern, Western viewpoint, it seems
       very odd that the chief of police is accompanied not only by the
       investigative magistrate, but also by the person who will prosecute
       at the trial.

       The confusion of investigative, prosecuting, and judicial func-
       tions increases as one moves from West to East. In the Soviet
       system, which took matters further, the *Prokuror*'s office worked
       parallel to the militia (police) in the investigative process. The
       office also decided whether there was sufficient evidence for a full
       trial, and also prosecuted at the trial. The difference between the
       tsarist system and the Soviet was that, under the tsarist system, (i)

the judges and defence counsel were usually independent of the prosecution process, and (ii) there was a jury (post-1840 reforms). Under the Soviet system, the judge sat with two nominal 'assessors', and acquittal was a rarity.

570 *yeralash*: a card game of the whist variety.

574 *independent observers*: members of the public co-opted by the police to act as independent witnesses during all police inquiries and investigations following a crime.

576 *A soul's journey through torments*: according to Russian Orthodox eschatology, souls of the departed are subjected to torments (twenty in all) by evil spirits, in preparation for the Day of Judgement. Souls of saints are left unmolested.

582 *Diogenes with his lantern*: Diogenes of Sinope (420–c.324 BC). The ancient Greek Cynic philosopher was observed to be walking in the street at noon with a lighted lantern in his hands, and in reply to questions, said: 'I am looking for a true human being.' Another of his appurtenances was his famous tub, which he was wont to carry about on his head and which served him as a house and a place of repose. His fame spread far and wide and even reached Alexander the Great's ears, who condescended to visit the philosopher in his tub. He asked Diogenes if there was anything in which he could gratify or oblige him. 'Yes, get out of my sunshine,' was the only answer which the philosopher gave. Such an independence of mind so pleased the monarch that he turned to his courtiers, and said: 'Were I not Alexander, I would wish to be Diogenes' (*CD*). Dostoevsky introduces the incident with the lantern into his earlier novel, *The Village of Stepanchikovo*.

591 *Surrender, suffer and be still*: see F. Tyutchev's poem 'Silentium!'

593 *passons*: 'let's move on'.

605 *c'est fini*: 'that's enough'.

632 *civil servant of the twelfth grade*: in 1722 Peter the Great introduced his Table of Ranks, assigning to each civil servant and member of the armed forces a grade in a table of fourteen grades, fourteen being the lowest. Most of the grades remained in force until 1917.

638 *zipun*: a peasant coat of coarse fabric, usually having no collar.

641 *But the thunder has crashed*: the Russian proverb goes: Not until he hears the clap of thunder, will the muzhik cross himself. In a letter of 16 Nov. 1879 to his publisher Lyubimov, Dostoevsky was at pains to explain that the trait fits Mitya's character rather accurately.

647 *a wind 'dry and sharp'*: Dostoevsky quotes a phrase from Nekra-
     sov's poem 'Before the Rain' (1846).

651 *Smaragdov*: in *A Short Outline of General History for Schools* by S.
     Smaragdov (St Petersburg, 1845) (several editions), the founders
     of Troy are not mentioned. In another textbook by the same
     author, *A Guide to Ancient History for High Schools* (St Petersburg,
     1840), which also went through several editions, two names, Tros
     and his son Ilus, are given.

657 *how perilous your years!*: from Ivan Dmitriev's fable, *The Cat, the
     Cockerel, and the Mouse* (1802).

685 *or Curative Foolery*: a translation from the French, published in
     Russia in 1785. It recounts the amorous adventures of a French-
     man in Constantinople.

688 *sine qua non*: *condicio sine qua non*, an indispensable condition.

691 *an instrument of police repression*: Count Dmitry Tolstoy (1823–89),
     who was Minister of Education, 1865–80, was responsible for a
     whole series of reactionary enactments, which included general
     maintenance of a rigorous disciplinary regime in schools and an
     intensive concentration on the classics, with a particular emphasis
     on the study of language and the rules of grammar, to the
     detriment of other subjects and wider educational aims. It must
     be remembered that Dostoevsky, who had himself received a
     technical education, was a fervent advocate of mathematics and
     classical education in schools (see *CW* 15. 582–3; *KC* 348, n.
     108).

694 *it would be necessary to invent him*: see note to p. 294.

     Candide: satirical-philosophical novel by Voltaire (1759).

695 *old Belinsky*: Vissarion Belinsky (1810–48), founder of the socio-
     logical school of Russian literary criticism.

     Tatiana . . . Onegin: principal characters in Pushkin's novel in
     verse, *Evgeny Onegin*.

     Les femmes tricottent: 'women knit'.

696 *Section Three . . . Chain Bridge*: Section Three was the Imperial
     Secret Police, which, from 1838 onwards, was based by the Chain
     Bridge in St Petersburg.

     The Bell: Russian subversive émigré magazine, published in
     London by Aleksander Herzen (1812–1870), for illegal distribu-
     tion in Russia. The couplet quoted by Kolya did not appear in the
     Bell, but in another émigré magazine, the *Northern Star*.

704 *If I forget thee, Jerusalem, let my tongue cleave*: cf. 'If I do not remember thee, let my tongue cleave to the roof of my mouth; if I prefer not Jerusalem above my chief joy': Psalms 137: 6.

707 *pickthank*: one who curries favour with another.

Fenya and her mother, Grushenka's cook: elsewhere we are told that Grushenka's cook was Fenya's grandmother, one of Dostoevsky's extremely rare lapses; see Book 8, Ch. 3, 'Prospecting for gold', p. 491.

718 *cette charmante personne*: 'this charming person'.

719 *Skotoprigonyevsk*: a composite name from the Russian words for 'cattle' and 'to drive'. Vladimir Nabokov renders it into English as 'Oxtown' (see Vladimir Nabokov, *Lectures on Russian Literature* (Weidenfeld & Nicolson, London, 1981), 132). Dostoevsky must have modelled the name on some such Western original as Cattleville, or Oxenford, or even Oxford, but, because there is no tradition in Russia of naming towns in association with droving, the end result is comical in the extreme, suggesting a 'dump' of a town in the back of beyond, and, of course, totally fictitious.

721 *Dainty little foot in pain*: see note to p. 100.

722 *They want to erect a monument to your Pushkin for his 'women's feet'*: the proposal to erect a Pushkin monument was first put forward in 1862. An appeal for funds was launched in 1871, as a result of which a number of articles appeared in newspapers and magazines. The monument was unveiled on 6 June 1880. Two days later, on 8 June, Dostoevsky made his famous Pushkin speech at a public meeting of the Society for the Appreciation of Russian Literature.

723 *the new courts*: very far-reaching legal reforms were instituted in Russia in the middle of the nineteenth century. On 20 Nov. 1864 four separate and independent legal codes were introduced. Court proceedings were made public, the judiciary was separated from the administrative authorities, the appointment of judges was made permanent, the jury system was established, universal equality of rights of all subjects in the eyes of the law was recognized, certain categories of mental derangement—to wit, diminished responsibility—were accepted as valid defence pleas. Although Dostoevsky the publicist looked upon these reforms with a measure of scepticism, particularly in view of the numerous instances of abuse that they engendered, he himself argued in favour of diminished responsibility while supporting a defence

case, which proved to be successful, of one Kornilova, a young woman who was tried for the murder of her step-daughter (*CW* 15. 587).

726   *vous comprenez, cette affaire et la mort terrible de votre papa*: 'you know, this business and the terrible death of your father'.

738   *Claude Bernard*: Claude Bernard (1813–78) was an eminent French physiologist. Amongst other things, he demonstrated the role of the pancreas in the human digestive system, and the existence of nerve centres independent of the central spino-cerebellar system. His *Introduction to the Study of Experimental Medicine* (1865) laid the foundations of experimental physiology. His works were translated into Russian, and were widely read in scientific circles. To Mitya, however, he was just a trumped-up confidence trickster, no doubt reflecting Dostoevsky's own healthy disrespect for all men of science and so-called experts.

738   *De opinibus non est disputandum*: Mitya's own version of *de gustibus non disputandum*, 'there is no disputing about tastes'.

741   *Dainty little foot a little bent*: Rakitin's poem is in the style of Dmitry Minayev (1835–99), a Russian satirical poet who sniggered at Pushkin's fascination for women's feet or legs (in everyday Russian usage, the same word stands for both). Putting the poem into Rakitin's mouth was, of course, Dostoevsky's own way of getting back at Minayev and poets of his ilk.

745   *to the uttermost farthing*: cf. 'Therefore if thou bring thy gift to the altar, and there rememberest that thy brother hath ought against thee; Leave there thy gift before the altar, and go thy way; first be reconciled to thy brother, and then come and offer thy gift. Agree with thine adversary quickly, while thou art in the way with him; lest at any time the adversary deliver thee to the judge, and the judge deliver thee to the officer, and thou be cast into prison. Verily I say unto thee, Thou shalt by no means come out thence, till thou hast paid the uttermost farthing': Matthew 5: 23–6.

772   *he'd lose all his hereditary rights*: even in present-day Britain, persons who are convicted of a crime suffer a considerable loss of civil rights, i.e. their right to vote, freedom of association, and, of course, freedom of movement.

782   *your faithful servant Lichard*: Smerdyakov had already referred to himself as the faithful Lichard, but that was with regard to Mitya (see note to p. 337). The irony is that Smerdyakov's literary progenitor, Lichard, was as faithful to King Gvidon as he was to his evil wife, when she decided to murder her husband.

784 *The Sermons of St Isaac the Syrian*: Isaac the Syrian, known as
Isaacus Ninivita in the West, an anchorite and bishop towards the
end of the sixth century, was popular in Muscovite Russia. See
also p. 122 (*KC* n. 257).

797 *qui frisait la cinquantaine*: 'who was touching fifty'.

799 *c'est charmant*: 'that's charming'.

800 *c'est noble, c'est charmant*: 'that's noble, that's charming.

c'est chevaleresque: 'that's gallant'.

801 *I donated ten roubles towards our Slav brethren!*: the reference is to
the protracted Russo-Turkish conflict, which resulted in six
officially declared wars in the period 1768–1878 (reverberations
still wreaking mayhem two centuries later, in the Balkans). The
rallying cry for the Russians was liberation from the yoke of Islam.
The devil coming down on the side of the Orthodox Christians to
the tune of ten imperial roubles (approx. £20) reveals Dostoevsky
at his most ironic.

Satanas sum et nihil humani a me alienum puto: a 'diabolically'
clever inversion of a line from Terence's (Publius Terentius Afer,
*c.*190–159 BC) *Heauton timorumenos* ('The Self-Tormentor'), I. 1,
25, *Homo sum, humani nihil a me alienum puto*, ('I am a man and
think nothing appertaining to mankind foreign to me'). Cf. 'For
nothing human foreign was to him', James Thomson (1700–48),
To the Memory of the Lord Talbot. It is significant that the devil
should pick on Terence, a great wit and profound psychologist of
the ancient world, another of his famous sayings being, *Ego
meorum solus sum meus* ('Of my friends, I am the only one I have
left'), *Phormio*, IV. i. 21.

802 *C'est du nouveau, n'est-ce pas?*: 'that's a new one, isn't it?'

Leo Tolstoy: people will always be divided as to who is the greater
novelist, Dostoevsky or Tolstoy. There is, in fact, a fascinating
book drawing a parallel between the two authors: Dmitry Merezhkovsky's *Tolstoy and Dostoevsky* (a far more penetrating analysis
than George Steiner's *Tolstoy or Dostoevsky*). What makes Dostoevsky stand out is his riotous sense of humour. The fun that
Dostoevsky must have had in writing the above reference to
Tolstoy could only have been exceeded by Tolstoy's pleasure in
reading it.

803 *waters above the firmament*: cf. 'And God made the firmament, and
divided the waters which *were* under the firmament from the
waters which *were* above the firmament ...': Genesis 1: 7.

803 *Quelle idée!*: 'what an idea!'

    Gatsouk: in Moscow in the 1870s and 1880s, A. Gatsouk (1832–91) published *Gatsouk's Politico-Literary, Artistic and Trade Gazette*, as well as a *Baptismal Calendar* with an illustrated weekly supplement.

804 *Count Mattei*: Count Cesare Mattei (1809–96), famous Italian homeopath, began his career as a politician, but, after suffering a serious financial set-back, he took up homeopathy. To him belongs the invention of some pills, very much sought-after at the time, which he called white, blue, and green electricity. Count Mattei spent great sums of money exporting them as contraband to neighbouring countries. On his death, he left a fortune of about 20 m. francs, most of which he donated to charity (see *Encyclopaedia*, Brockhaus & Efron, 1896).

    le diable n'existe point: 'the devil does not exist'.

805 *to vaudeville and that sort of thing*: excerpt from Khlestakov's (see note below) speech in Act 3, Sc. 6 of Gogol's *The Inspector-General* (1836): 'Yes, I'm already known all over. I'm friends with some pretty actresses. I've also turned my hand to vaudeville and that sort of thing . . . I get to see various writers a lot, and I'm on first name terms with Pushkin.'

    Khlestakov: the charlatan hero of Gogol's comedy, *The Inspector-General*, see note above.

806 *Je pense donc je suis*: 'I think, therefore I am': René Descartes (1596–1650), *Discours de la méthode*, 1673.

809 *anchorite fathers and the women without sin*: a quotation from Pushkin's poetic rendering of a prayer by the fourth-century saint Ephraim the Syrian.

810 *the actor Gorbunov*: Ivan Gorbunov (1831–96), talented actor, writer, and storyteller, whom Dostoevsky knew personally and admired.

811 *Ah, mon père*: 'Oh, father'.

    et à moi si peu de peine!: *Tendre Gaussain, quoi! si jeune et si belle,* | *Et votre cœur cède au premier aveu!* | *Que voulez-vous, cela leur fait, dit-elle,* | *Tant de plaisir et me coûte si peu.*

    ('What was that, sweet Gaussain? So young and so pretty, | Yielding your heart at the first supplication! | Well, what can I do, I know 'tis a pity, | But it costs me so little to relieve his frustration'). An epigram on the French actress Jeanne-Catherine Gaussain (1711–67).

Belinsky: see note to p. 695.

812 *Star of the Lion and the Sun ... the Pole Star or Sirius*: one must not forget that this is a nightmare; the devil's (Ivan's) reasoning powers are somewhat disjointed and *non-sequiturs* are to be expected. The Star of the Lion and the Sun was a Persian order sometimes awarded to Russian officials who had served in the Caucasus. The Pole Star was a Swedish order, as well as the name of the Decembrists' almanac, published 1823–5; and a separate cultural and political periodical, 'The Polar Star', was published abroad in 1855–62 and in 1869.

Faust:

> FAUST: ... *wer bist du denn?*
> (... 'so what are you then?')
> MEPHISTOPHELES: *Ein Teil von jener Kraft,*
> *Die stets das Böse will und stes das Gute shaft.*
> ('A part of that eternal force
> Which, wreaking evil, fosters only good')

> (Goethe (1749–1832), *Faust*, ll. 1335–7)

813 *à la Heine*: Heinrich Heine (1797–1856), German poet.

savant: man of learning.

"The Geological Cataclysm": the devil has, on the whole, been pretty discreet in not showing off his erudition, but this may have been an instance where he could not refrain from giving an oblique reference to his familiarity with the writings of Ernest Renan (1823–92), who had a wide readership in the Europe of the day. His *Histoire des origines du christianisme*, of which *La Vie de Jésus* is the first volume, is the work most likely to have aroused the devil's interest. There Renan comments, in the light of positive science, on the geological cataclysms spoken of by Jesus. See also note on *The star will shine forth from the East* (p. 83) for yet another indication of the source of 'The Geological Cataclysm'.

815 *Ah, mais c'est bête enfin!*: 'enough's enough!'

Luther's ink-well!: Luther believed in the existence of the devil. He claimed that he had seen the devil in the shape of a pig or flickering lights, and that, at Wartburg, the devil was cracking nuts and throwing the shells into his bed. The apocryphal story of Luther and his ink-well is the most famous of all. Luther was translating the Bible in the Wartburg Castle in Thuringia, and when the devil came to tempt him, he threw an ink-well at the devil. A dark stain on Luther's wall was, for a long time, held to be where the ink-well had shattered, presumably missing the devil. Luther's followers and sightseers who subsequently visited the cell, scraped and chipped away the plaster until there was nothing left of the stain. Ivan's nightmare is very reminiscent of Luther's hallucinations, *dialogus cum diabolo* (*CW* 15. 595–6).

815 *un chien dehors*: there is the following entry in Dostoevsky's notebook for 1876–77: *Baptiste, tout de suite ce mot à son adresse. Tout de suite? Madame ignore peut-être le temps qu'il fait, c'est à ne pas mettre un chien dehors. Mais Baptiste, vous n'êtes pas un chien.* ('Baptiste, go and deliver this message immediately! Immediately? Madam perhaps is not aware of what the weather is like outside! It's not fit to put a dog out. But, Baptiste, you're not a dog') (*CW* 15. 596).

817 *"a cherub pure"*: a quotation putatively either from Lermontov's *Demon*, or from Schiller's *Ode to Joy*, in a Russian translation by A. Strugovshchikov (*CW* 15. 596).

820 *Le mot de l'énigme*: 'the clue to the riddle'.

827 *the exhibits*: as exhibits in judicial trials of the 1870s, anything that came to hand was made use of, and that fact was often commented on in the Russian press of the day. In one affair of arson in 1878, it was said that: 'Among the exhibits was a counter from a haberdasher's shop, under which counter the fire had been started, and which had burnt. The proportions of the counter were such that it proved impossible to convey the said counter into the courtroom.'

court usher: 'bailiff' in America.

828 *titular councillor*: a civilian rank of the ninth grade in the Table of Ranks (see note to p. 632).

842 *The last two also appeared as ordinary witnesses for the prosecution*: it has been suggested that this is the procedural error constituting the 'judicial mistake'. Experts who are asked to pronounce upon the fitness, or otherwise, of the accused to stand trial must not act as witnesses for either side (*KC*, 405, n. 59). V. Rak has drawn attention to the fact that it was against the law for a person to function in this dual capacity in a criminal trial, and that Dostoevsky knew it. In 1877, the case of Ekaterina Kornilova, in which Dostoevsky took a deep interest, had been reopened on account of an analogous technicality. Conceivably, Dostoevsky was creating an opening for a successful appeal by Dmitry in the sequel to the novel. Even today, in Anglo-American procedural praxis, it

would be considered highly improper for an expert who has pronounced upon the fitness, or otherwise, of the accused to plead to appear as a non-expert witness in the substantive trial.

Herrnhuter of some kind or a Moravian Brother: the Herrnhutters were a community of Moravian brethren, founded in 1727 by Count von Zinzendorf (1700–60), a German Protestant leader. The Moravian, or Bohemian, Brotherhood was an evangelical sect originating with the Hussites, followers of the Bohemian martyrs, Jan Huss (1371–1415) and Jerome of Prague (1370–1416). There are still communities of such Protestant sects in a number of countries, particularly Pennsylvania, USA; Saskatchewan, Canada; and Paraguay, where they were also (see note to p. 911) guaranteed exemption from military service by General Stroessner.

847 *Gott der Vater, Gott der Sohn und Gott der Heilige Geist!*: 'God the Father, God the Son, and God the Holy Ghost!'

848 *without having to take the oath*: members of the clergy were exempt from swearing an oath, see Matthew 5: 33–6: 'Thou shalt not forswear thyself . . .'. The other reason Alyosha did not have to swear an oath was because of his kinship with the accused, as in the case of Ivan, too, of course (see note to p. 859). (In Russian law, witnesses testifying when members of their own family were on trial were exempt from taking an oath.)

859 *as an unsworn witness*: see note to p. 848.

860 *sarafan*: a Russian national dress for women.

panyova: a linen skirt worn by Russian peasant women.

861 *Bread and circuses!*: *Duas tantum res anxius optat,* | *Panem et Circences* ('Two things only the people anxiously desire: bread and the circus games'): Juvenal, *Satires* x. 80.

872 *"he lived amongst us"*: 'He lived amongst us, | A people that to him were alien . . .' (Pushkin's tribute (1834) to the Polish poet Adam Mickiewicz (1798–1855)).

a jaunty troika rushing headlong towards an unknown destination: an image from Gogol's *Dead Souls*.

the Sobakeviches, the Nozdryovs, or the Chichikovs: grotesque characters in Gogol's novel *Dead Souls*.

873 *"as the sun in a droplet of water"*: a line from G. Derzhavin's ode *God*.

après moi le déluge: 'when I'm gone, to hell with everyone!'

911   *in the British parliament*: a slight anachronism, as the political situation referred to is that of 1876, rather than that of a decade earlier, when the action of the novel is meant to take place. Relations between Britain and Russia were strained in 1876; the British were wary of Russian efforts to liberate the Balkan Slavs from Turkish rule, seeing this as a pretext to move to Constantinople and the Mediterranean. In a political article of September 1876, Dostoevsky had written: 'And so Viscount Beaconsfield— an Israelite by birth (né Disraeli)—in an address at some banquet, suddenly divulges to Europe an extraordinary secret, to the effect that all those Russians, headed by Cherniaev, who rushed into Turkey to save the Slavs, are simply socialists, communists, and communards ... [who] ... constitute a threat to Europe, and menace the British farmers with future socialism in Russia and in the East!' (*KC*, 424–5, n. 230; *DW*, Sept. 1876, ch. 1, para. 1; *CW*, 15. 600).

   and cut off their supply of grain: this refers to Russian, specifically Ukrainian, exports of grain, especially wheat, to Western and Central Europe. Throughout the nineteenth century (after the retreat of Napoleon), the Russian Empire was a large exporter of wheat. This process was intensified by the presence, in the Volga region and the Ukraine, of many large communities of Germans; their ancestors had mostly been invited to settle by Catherine the Great. They included those who had moved East to escape religious persecution and governmental obligations (particularly military service, from which they were exempted in Russia). The best known of these German sects were the Mennonites, Hutterites, and Moravian Brothers. The German communities were far more productive than the Russian estates, because they introduced agricultural machinery and new farming methods. Besides, they did not drink. When the American and Canadian wheat-growing regions opened up (from *c.*1850), wheat from the Russian Empire became less competitive, until the 1914 war. Domestic unrest, revolution, and then collectivization, plus a growing Soviet population, made Russia a large importer of grain. The main exporting ports from the Russian Empire in the nineteenth century were Kronstadt (St Petersburg) and Odessa.

   'strike the hearts with unsuspected power': from Pushkin's poem *Reply to Anonymous* (1830).

918   *in St Petersburg, a young man*: an actual trial which came before the St Petersburg District Court on 15 January 1879 (*CW* 15. 600).

919   *Udolpho Castle*: the reference is to Ann Radcliffe's *The Mysteries of Udolpho* (1794). Ann Radcliffe's novels were Dostoevsky's favourite reading in childhood.

932   *to bind and to loose*: cf. 'And I will give unto thee the keys of the kingdom of heaven: and whatsoever thou shalt bind on earth shall be bound in heaven: and whatsoever thou shalt loose on earth shall be loosed in heaven': Matthew 16: 19; see also 18: 18.

935   *that not one should perish*: cf. John 10: 11 and 10: 14–15.

936   *Fathers, provoke not your children*: 'Fathers, provoke not your children to anger ...': Colossians 3: 21; see also Ephesians 6: 1–4.

    vivos voco!: the opening words of Schiller's *Song of the Bell*: *Vivos voco. Mortuos plango* ('I call the living. I mourn the dead').

    measured to you again: see note to p. 167.

937   *"brass" and "brimstone"*: the reference is to a character in Ostrovsky's play *Hard Times*, a merchant's wife who is terrified at the sound of these biblical references.

938   *make her way back through the window*: cf. *Naturam expellas furca, tamen usque recurret* ('You may drive out nature with a fork, but she will ever return again'). Horace, *Epistles*, book I. 10, 24; *Chassez le naturel, il revient au galop* ('Drive out nature and it comes back at a gallop'); *Natur zieht stärker dänn sieben Ochsen* ('Nature draws stronger than seven oxen'). The line that Dostoevsky uses is borrowed from an essay by Nikolai Karamzin (1766–1826), historian and novelist, who probably translated the observation from the French, as it appears in La Fontaine's fable *La Chatte metamorphosée en femme* ('Cat turned into a woman').

940   *ye did not visit me*: cf. 'For I was an hungred, and ye gave me meat: I was thirsty, and ye gave me drink: I was a stranger and ye took me in: Naked, and ye clothed me: I was sick, and ye visited me: I was in prison, and ye came unto me': Matthew 25: 35–6.

941   *than to punish one innocent one*: the 'majestic voice' belongs to Peter the Great, and the citation is from his *Military Statute* of 1716.

943   *Thou who art Our God ...!*: a refrain occurring in Orthodox *acathisti*.

    Jupiter, you are angry, that means you are in the wrong: the exact source has not been traced, but there are numerous references to an angry Jupiter in literature, *Jupiter tonans* ('thundering Jupiter').

948 *Twenty years down the mines*: Mitya is sentenced to twenty years' hard labour. In the opinion of B. Reizov, Dostoevsky chose this period because that was the length of sentence given to Mitya's prototype, Ensign Ilyinsky, who, like Mitya, had been falsely accused of patricide. Dostoevsky used this sentence in his novel without investigating the point any further. In fact, Mitya, who was accused of murdering his father and found guilty on all counts, should have been sentenced to lifelong penal servitude, according to the laws of Imperial Russia. The law of 1845 states: Whosoever is found guilty of premeditated murder of one's father or mother will be subject to the loss of all legal rights and exile to hard labour in the Siberia mines for life. On arrival at their destination in the mines, the convicts in question are not to be considered for remission under any circumstances; only in cases of complete infirmity through old age are they to be relieved of their workload, and even then without permission to be freed from the precincts of the penal settlement (B. Reizov, *The Story behind the 'Karamazov Brothers'*). (*CW* 15. 604)

952 *march*: exiles to Siberia were usually marched there, unless given special permission to go by guarded carriage. The march would be in numerous stages: firstly to some provincial mustering centre, then on the 'Sibirsky trakt' across the Urals, and, in some cases, on to Sakhalin, an island north of Japan, eleven time-zones away. Traditionally, the column would halt by the stone monument in the Urals which says 'Europe-Asia', and prayers would be said by those who would probably never see European Russia again. Obviously, the more remote the location, the better the chance of a successful escape. On the march, the convicts would be roped or shackled together in a line, and, on arrival at the penal settlement, their heads would be clean-shaven, *boule à zéro*, but on one side only. Special, distinctive, prison clothes were not provided.

965 *let our names perish!*: Kolya is quoting Pierre Vergniaud (1753–93), politician and famous orator, member of the Gironde, from one of his speeches at the *Convention nationale* (1792): *Périssent nos noms, pourvu que la chose publique soit sauvée.* He was guillotined along with his fellow Girondists.

968 *headband*: a ribbon, bearing an image of Our Saviour, Mother of God, or St John the Divine, tied round the head of a deceased at Orthodox funerals.

American Literature

British and Irish Literature

Children's Literature

Classics and Ancient Literature

Colonial Literature

Eastern Literature

European Literature

Gothic Literature

History

Medieval Literature

Oxford English Drama

Poetry

Philosophy

Politics

Religion

The Oxford Shakespeare

A complete list of Oxford World's Classics, including Authors in Context, Oxford English Drama, and the Oxford Shakespeare, is available in the UK from the Marketing Services Department, Oxford University Press, Great Clarendon Street, Oxford OX2 6DP, or visit the website at www.oup.com/uk/worldsclassics.

In the USA, visit www.oup.com/us/owc for a complete title list.

Oxford World's Classics are available from all good bookshops. In case of difficulty, customers in the UK should contact Oxford University Press Bookshop, 116 High Street, Oxford OX1 4BR.